Popular American Literature
of the 19th Century

Popular American Literature of the 19th Century

EDITED BY

Paul C. Gutjahr

Indiana University, Bloomington

New York   Oxford
OXFORD UNIVERSITY PRESS
2001

Oxford University Press

Oxford   New York
Athens   Auckland   Bangkok   Bogotá   Buenos Aires   Calcutta
Cape Town   Chennai   Dar es Salaam   Delhi   Florence   Hong Kong   Istanbul
Karachi   Kuala Lumpur   Madrid   Melbourne   Mexico City   Mumbai
Nairobi   Paris   São Paulo   Shanghai   Singapore   Taipei   Tokyo   Toronto   Warsaw

and associated companies in
Berlin   Ibadan

Copyright © 2001 by Oxford University Press, Inc.

Published by Oxford University Press, Inc.
198 Madison Avenue, New York, New York 10016
http://www.oup-usa.org

Oxford is a registered trademark of Oxford University Press

Library of Congress Cataloging-in-Publication Data

Popular American literature of the 19th century/edited by Paul C. Gutjahr.
    p. cm.
   ISBN 0-19-514140-7 (alk. paper)
    1. American literature—19th century. 2. United States—Civilization—19th
century—Literary collections. 3. Popular literature—United States. I. Gutjahr, Paul C.
PS535 .P66 2001
813′.308—dc21   00-041647

Printing number: 9 8 7 6 5 4 3 2 1
Printed in the United States of America
on acid-free paper

For Karen

Outside of a dog, a book is man's best friend.
Inside of a dog, it's too dark to read.
—GROUCHO MARX

Contents

---

*Works presented in their entirety.

Figures

Preface

One of the wonders of printed material is its persuasive power. It can threaten, promise, cajole, and insinuate ideas of lasting influence. Such influence manifests itself in a number of ways, but perhaps one of the most obvious is found in the development of national mythologies. For example, consider the story of George Washington cutting down a cherry tree, a deed he then nobly confesses with the now immortal words, "I can't tell a lie." It is a story that has become synonymous with George Washington, yet it was a fable created by Parson Weems in his tremendously popular biography of the first president.

True or not, such stories reveal a great deal about a culture's thought and life. This volume gathers popular stories that tap into a wide range of nineteenth-century American self-perceptions, fears, dreams, and longings. The nineteenth century is particularly important for such stories because it was a period when these tales increasingly reached their audience in printed forms. The highly oral culture of the eighteenth century was giving way to a more print-bound culture in the nineteenth century. This change meant that ever wider audiences could gain access to, and be influenced by, the same information. In the nineteenth century, the world of American citizens was increasingly formed, framed, and fractured by the power of print.

Behind the growing print culture found in the nineteenth-century United States stands the fact that American publishing came of age in this century. Whereas printed material had been relatively scarce at the close of the eighteenth century, with most families owning perhaps a Bible and an almanac, by the time of the Civil War thousands of tracts, novels, self-help books, tour guides, magazines, and newspapers were littering American parlors. Publishers at the turn of the nineteenth century rarely produced print runs over two thousand copies. By midcentury, American publishing had so radically changed that editions of 30,000, 75,000, even 100,000, copies were common. The forty newspapers published during the American Revolution gave way by the 1860s to more than two thousand daily and weekly papers. By the end of the century, books and other forms of published material were reaching the remotest parts of the country as an ever more advanced transportation network, an increasingly efficient mail system, and an army of some fifty thousand door-to-door book salesmen offered an unprecedented range of printed goods to American readers.

The amazing growth of America's publishing enterprises did not happen in a vacuum. It grew in a reciprocal relationship with rising American literacy rates and multiplying motivations for the consumption of printed matter. As the century wore on, a number of factors propelled American reading habits, including desires for economic gain, social distinction, political involvement, and entertainment.

Reading offered people an opportunity for greater social mobility. Those able to read were better able to adapt to the changing employment market of the nineteenth century, in which literacy skills were increasingly prized for the better paying, more prestigious jobs. The massive quantities of self-help books and reform literature that circulated among Americans in the nineteenth century also helped people know how to think and act in ways that distinguished them as socially refined. Such social distinction could also be attained by studying the Greek and Roman classics, an oft-used marker of gentility and good social breeding.

Americans also read so that they might gain the information they needed to participate in their local and national governments. From an early age, Americans were taught that democracy demanded participation, and meaningful participation demanded accurate information. Thus, the political interests of nineteenth-century readers helped fuel a tremendous rise in newspaper circulation and the appearance of a host of printed matter such as political biographies and verbatim reproductions of countless legislative speeches and debates.

And Americans read because it was fun. There was great pleasure to be found in learning new things and entering new worlds. The genres of history, travel, and adventure enjoyed enormous popularity. The astounding popularity of Ik Marvel's *Reveries of a Bachelor* can be attributed, at least in part, to the way in which this work incorporated all three of these genres. Reading also changed from a largely oral activity where a father might read aloud the Bible or Bunyan's *Pilgrim's Progress* to his family to a much more individualized practice. This change opened the door for readers to enjoy a wider, often more illicit, range of material. Once shunned as corrupting, novel reading became a central avenue toward entertainment before the end of the century.

This collection was conceived with the desire to capture some of the excitement and diversity of the print culture that was so influential in nineteenth-century American thought and culture. It makes available material, relatively inaccessible today, that was vital to the cultural and intellectual conversations found in this period. The authorship of the selections is primarily American, simply because space limitations forbade including a sampling of the huge array of foreign printed material avidly consumed by Americans. The popularity of the following selections lay not so much in the number of copies printed or sold—although publication data certainly constitute one measure of public interest—as in the prominence of these works in the cultural conversations of the day. Hence, the selection of texts was based on a desire to obtain the best mixture of material that circulated in notable numbers, but also captured some of the most commonly accepted, and thus influential, cultural and intellectual currents of their day.

Two other factors influenced the choice of texts: a preference for depth over breadth, and an interest in presenting works standing in dialogue with one another. The rationale here is simple. Reading entire works and longer excerpts gives one a fuller appreciation of an author's intellectual design, and enables one to examine narrative arcs and developed lines of argument. Reading works speaking to—and against—other works recreates something of the dynamic of the vital cultural conversations taking place in this period. (The list on pages xxi–xxiii identifies some of the essential thematic intersections among the texts in this collection.)

This collection makes no claim to cover all, or even most, of the important facets of nineteenth-century popular literature. But it does open a modest window into the vast array of literature avidly produced and just as avidly consumed in this period. Through this window, it is hoped that readers will catch informative glimpses that will entice them into further explorations of the splendidly diverse and always amazing print culture that influenced every aspect of American life.

One other detail of which the reader should be aware concerns footnotes. There are two kinds in this anthology. First, there are numbered footnotes, which contain material I have added as commentary on the texts. Second, there are footnotes denominated by symbols, which are original footnotes found in the actual nineteenth-century texts.

Acknowledgments

Many people helped bring this book to completion, and to all of them I owe a great debt of gratitude. The inspiration for this collection originally came from Jay Fliegelman, who first introduced me to nineteenth-century American popular literature. His intellectual influence and personal kindness has exercised a profound influence on my own academic career. I am also deeply grateful to Tony English, the sponsoring editor of this collection. Tony personifies all that is good about academic publishing.

Two sources of funding have allowed me to take time to frame this project: The Center for the Study of Religion at Princeton University under the directorship of Robert Wuthnow and Marie Griffith, and the Christian Scholars Foundation under the directorship of Bernard Draper.

A host of people have generously given of their time and expertise. I have had wonderful friends and mentors at Indiana University. David Nordloh has helped me at almost every stage of this work. Jim Adams, Jonathan Elmer, Peter Lindenbaum, Steve Watt, and Nick Williams also offered insights and encouragement as this project moved along. Both Leon Jackson and Charles Johanningsmeier went above and beyond the call of duty in helping me talk through the conceptualization of the contents of this work. Martin Harris was also a wonderful aid in helping get the book's illustrations in order. Countless others also offered their assistance: Bill Bell, Robert Brown, JoAnn Castagna, Bruce Fort, Elizabeth and Milton Gaither, Ellen Garvey, Robert Gross, Melissa Homestead, Toni Johnson-Woods, Robert Kelly, Lucia Knoles, Robert Lewis, Deborah Long, Janet McCorey, David Morgan, Steve Stein, Avril Torrence, Deb Walberg, and James West III. The kindness of all these individuals should not be imposed upon; any fault to be found in this collection is my responsibility alone.

My family, as always, has been a rich source of encouragement. My mother and father have long supported my career in more ways than I can count. My wife, Cathy, listened to endless dinnertime conversations about the status of this project. My sons, Isaac and Jeremiah, have used the scrap paper generated from various drafts of this work to draw literally thousands of crayon pictures, a fact that in numerous ways reminds me not to take my work so seriously.

Most of all, I would like to thank my sister, Karen, to whom I dedicate this volume. Long ago, she introduced me to the magic of popular literature by reading me countless Nancy Drew and Hardy Boys mysteries, Marx brothers' routines, and ghost stories. I thank her for those reading times, and for a lifetime of caring for, and putting up with, her younger brother.

Thematic Connections

Singleness and Marriage

Hymen's Recruiting Sergeant
Sheppard Lee
Quaker City
"The Wife's Victory"
"The Married Shrew"
Reveries of a Bachelor
"John Jenkins"
"Miggles"
The Silent Partner
Plucky Phil
The Master Workman's Oath
In His Steps

Domesticity and Gender Roles

Hymen's Recruiting Sergeant
The Pearl
Awful Disclosures
Treatise on Domestic Economy
Quaker City
"The Wife's Victory"
"The Married Shrew"
Reveries of a Bachelor
Uncle Tom's Cabin
Ten Nights in a Bar-Room
"John Jenkins"
"The Luck of Roaring Camp"
"Miggles"
The Silent Partner
McGuffey's First Eclectic Reader
Plucky Phil
The Master Workman's Oath

Care and Education of the Young

Life of Washington
"To Mothers"
"Murderers of Fathers"
The Pearl
Awful Disclosures
"The Wife's Victory"
"The Married Shrew"
Ten Nights in a Bar-Room
"The Luck of Roaring Camp"
"Miggles"
The Silent Partner
McGuffey's First Eclectic Reader
The Master Workman's Oath

Masculinity

Life of Washington
Hymen's Recruiting Sergeant
"Murderers of Fathers"
Awful Disclosures
Quaker City
Reveries of a Bachelor
Ten Nights in a Bar-Room
"The Luck of Roaring Camp"
"Miggles"
The Silent Partner
Plucky Phil
The Master Workman's Oath

Proper Conduct

Life of Washington
"Murderers of Fathers"
The Pearl
Awful Disclosures
Treatise on Domestic Economy
"The Wife's Victory"
"The Married Shrew"
Ten Nights in a Bar-Room
"John Jenkins"
"The Luck of Roaring Camp"
The Silent Partner
McGuffey's First Eclectic Reader
The Master Workman's Oath
In His Steps

Temperance

"Murderers of Fathers"
Quaker City
"The Married Shrew"
Ten Nights in a Bar-Room
"John Jenkins"
The Silent Partner
The Master Workman's Oath
In His Steps

Novel Reading

"Beware of Bad Books"
"Novel-Reading"
The Pearl
Sheppard Lee
Quaker City
"The Married Shrew"
Reveries of a Bachelor
In His Steps

Social Reform

"Murderers of Fathers"
Awful Disclosures
Sheppard Lee
Quaker City
"The Married Shrew"
Uncle Tom's Cabin
Ten Nights in a Bar-Room
"John Jenkins"
The Silent Partner
In His Steps

Religion

Life of Washington
"The Forgiving African"
"Poor Sarah"
"To Mothers"
"Beware of Bad Books"
"Murderers of Fathers"
"Novel-Reading"
The Pearl
Awful Disclosures
Treatise on Domestic Economy
Quaker City
"The Wife's Victory"
"The Married Shrew"
Reveries of a Bachelor
Uncle Tom's Cabin
"John Jenkins"
The Silent Partner
In His Steps

Urban

"Murderers of Fathers"
Awful Disclosures
Quaker City
"The Married Shrew"
The Master Workman's Oath

Rural

The Pearl
Sheppard Lee
"The Married Shrew"
Reveries of a Bachelor
Ten Nights in a Bar-Room"
The Silent Partner
McGuffey's First Eclectic Reader

The South

Sheppard Lee
"The Wife's Victory"
Uncle Tom's Cabin
Six Species of Men
The Master Workman's Oath

Slavery

"The Forgiving African"
Sheppard Lee
Uncle Tom's Cabin
Six Species of Men

Science

Sheppard Lee
The Illustrated Self-Instructor
Six Species of Men

The West

"Muck-a-Muck"
"The Luck of Roaring Camp"
"Miggles"
"Plain Language from Truthful James"
"Further Language from Truthful
    James"
"The Latest Chinese Outrage"
Plucky Phil

Race

"The Forgiving African"
"Poor Sarah"
The Illustrated Self-Instructor
Sheppard Lee
Quaker City
Uncle Tom's Cabin
Six Species of Men
"Muck-a-Muck"
"Plain Language from Truthful James"
"Further Language from Truthful
    James"
"The Latest Chinese Outrage"
Plucky Phil

Class

"Poor Sarah"
Sheppard Lee
Quaker City
"The Married Shrew"
The Silent Partner
The Master Workman's Oath
In His Steps

Business

Treatise on Domestic Economy
Quaker City
Uncle Tom's Cabin
Ten Nights in a Bar-Room
"The Latest Chinese Outrage"
The Silent Partner
The Master Workman's Oath
In His Steps

1

Mason Locke Weems
(1759–1825)

MASON LOCKE WEEMS was arguably one of early America's most important traveling book salesmen. He was also an Episcopal priest and spent much of his life moralizing in either spoken or written forms. Ordained in 1784, Weems spent little of his life as a traditional rector. He left his parish in 1792 and began his long affiliation with America's nascent book trade. He began by reprinting books, trying his own hand at writing, and then in 1794 joined forces with the Philadelphia publisher Mathew Carey. For nearly three decades, Weems traveled up and down the East Coast selling books, sometimes Carey's, sometimes the works of other publishers, and sometimes his own.

In 1800, Weems composed the first of the many semifactual biographies he would write, *A History of the Life and Death, Virtues and Exploits of General George Washington*. He wrote it knowing full well that he could capitalize on the outpouring of grief over Washington's recent death on December 14, 1799. Weems's knowledge of the book-buying public proved sound; the slender volume sold extremely well. Weems revised his life of Washington several times, substantially enlarging it in 1808 when he renamed the work *The Life of Washington; with Curious Anecdotes, Equally Honourable to Himself and Exemplary to His Young Countrymen*. As this change in title indicates, his life of Washington was a moral tale. Weems did not only tell his readers Washington's story, but he made that story a kind of sermon, full of information on what made Washington a saint and how others might attain the same sort of moral perfection.

His moralizing did not end with his life of Washington. He continued to write pamphlets on a wide range of issues such as drinking, dueling, murder, gambling, and adultery. Perhaps his most successful treatise in this vein was his *Hymen's Recruiting Sergeant,* thought to have first appeared in 1805. Recommending the joys of marriage, *Hymen's Recruiting Sergeant* would also undergo numerous revisions and reprintings. American publishers were still selling copies of it well into the 1840s.

Weems's moral lessons highlight a tension found throughout nineteenth-century popular literature. While edification was clearly a value, Weems's years of experience as a salesman also told him that for edifying tales to sell, they also needed to entertain. Consequently, lines between fact and fiction, didacticism and diversion blurred.

THE LIFE OF WASHINGTON

With Curious Anecdotes, Equally Honorable to Himself and Exemplary to His Young Countrymen

CHAPTER I

Oh! as along the stream of time thy name
Expanded flies, and gathers all its fame;
May then these lines to future days descend,
And prove thy COUNTRY's good thine *only end!*

"Ah, *gentlemen!*"—exclaimed Bonaparte[1]—'twas just as he was about to embark for Egypt . . . some young Americans happening at Toulon, and anxious to see the mighty Corsican, had obtained the honour of an introduction to him. Scarcely were past the customary salutations, when he eagerly asked, "*how fares your countryman, the great* WASHINGTON?" "He was very well," replied the youths, brightening at the thought that they were the countrymen of Washington; "he was very well, general, when we left America."—"*Ah, gentlemen!*" rejoined he, "*Washington can never be otherwise than well:—The measure of his fame is full—Posterity shall talk of him with reverence as the founder of a great empire, when my name shall be lost in the vortex of Revolutions!*"

Who then that has a spark of virtuous curiosity, but must wish to know the history of him whose name could thus awaken the sigh even of Bonaparte? But is not his history *already* known? Have not a thousand orators spread his fame abroad, bright as his own Potomac, when he reflects the morning sun, and flames like a sea of liquid gold, the wonder and delight of all the neighbouring shores? Yes, they have indeed spread his fame abroad . . . his fame as Generalissimo of the armies, and first President of the councils of his nation. But this is not *half* his fame. . . . True, he is there seen in *greatness,* but it is only the greatness of public character, which is no evidence of *true greatness;* for a public character is often an artificial one. At the head of an army or nation, where gold and glory are at stake, and where a man feels himself the *burning focus* of unnumbered eyes; he must be a paltry fellow indeed, who does not play his part pretty handsomely . . . even the common passions of pride, avarice, or ambition, will put him up to his metal, and call forth his best and bravest doings. But let all this heat and blaze of public situation and incitement be withdrawn; let him be thrust back into the shade of private life, and you shall see how soon, like a forced plant robbed of its hot-bed, he will drop his false foliage and fruit, and stand forth confessed in native stickweed sterility and worthlessness. . . . There

Mason Locke Weems, *The Life of Washington; with Curious Anecdotes, Equally Honorable to Himself and Exemplary to His Young Countrymen,* 9th edition. Philadelphia: Mathew Carey, 1809.
[1]Napoléon Bonaparte (1769–1821) became ruler of France soon after the French Revolution. He kept Europe in an almost constant state of war for more than a decade, and he was a student of the military tactics George Washington used during the American Revolution. In 1798, Napoléon invaded Egypt to threaten England's trade route with India.

was Benedict Arnold[2]—while strutting a BRIGADIER GENERAL on the public stage, he could play you the *great man,* on a handsome scale . . . he out-marched Hannibal,[3] and out-fought Burgoyne[4] . . . he chaced the British like curlews, or cooped them up like chickens! and yet in the *private walks of life,* in Philadelphia, he could swindle rum from the commissary's stores, and, with the aid of loose women, retail it by the gill!! . . . And there was the great duke of Marlborough[5] too—his public character, a thunderbolt in war! Britain's boast, and terror of the French! But his private character, what? Why a *swindler* to whom not *Arnold's self* could hold a candle; a perfect nondescript of baseness; a shaver of farthings from the poor sixpenny pay of his own brave soldiers!!!

It is not then in the glare of *public,* but in the shade of *private life,* that we are to look for the man. Private life is always *real* life. Behind the curtain, where the eyes of the million are not upon him, and where a man can have no motive but *inclination,* no excitement but *honest nature,* there he will always be sure to act *himself;* consequently, if he act greatly, he must be great indeed. Hence it has been justly said, that, "our *private deeds,* if *noble,* are noblest of our lives."

Of these private deeds of Washington very little has been said. In most of the elegant orations pronounced to his praise, you see nothing of Washington below *the clouds*—nothing of Washington the *dutiful son*—the affectionate brother—the cheerful school-boy—the diligent surveyor—the neat draftsman—the laborious farmer—and widow's husband—the orphan's father—the poor man's friend. No! this is not the Washington you see; 'tis only Washington the HERO, and the Demigod. . . . Washington the *sun beam* in council, or the *storm* in war.

And in all the ensigns of character, amidst which he is generally drawn, you see none that represent him what he really was, "*the Jupiter Conservator,*"[6] *the friend and benefactor of men.* Where's his bright ploughshare that he loved—or his wheat-crowned fields, waving in yellow ridges before the wanton breeze—or his hills whitened over with flocks—or his clover-covered pastures spread with innumerous herds—or his neat-clad servants, with songs rolling the heavy harvest before them? Such were the scenes of *peace, plenty,* and *happiness,* in which Washington delighted. But his eulogists have denied him *these,* the only scenes which belong to man the GREAT, and have trick'd him up in the vile drapery of man the *little.* See! there he stands! with the port of Mars "*the destroyer,*" dark frowning over the fields of war . . . the lightning of Potter's blade is by his side—the deep-mouthed cannon is before him, disgorging its flesh-mangling balls—

---

[2]Benedict Arnold (1741–1801) was a brilliant American general who shifted his allegiance to the British in the middle of the American Revolution.

[3]Hannibal (247–183 B.C.) was one of the most successful Carthaginian general during the Punic Wars. One of his many amazing military feats was crossing the Alps with elephants to march on Rome.

[4]A British general, John Burgoyne (1722–1792) became famous when he captured Fort Ticonderoga during the American Revolution.

[5]The duke of Marlborough (1650–1722) was one of Britain's greatest generals who led the British in ten successful campaigns against the French.

[6]Jupiter was the most powerful and highest ranking Roman god. He used thunderbolts as his weapon and was also known as the "Light-Bringer." Jupiter was especially interested in upholding oaths and served as the chief divine protector of the Roman Republic.

his war-horse paws with impatience to bear him, a speedy thunderbolt, against the pale and bleeding ranks of Britain!—These are the drawings usually given of Washington; drawings masterly no doubt, and perhaps justly descriptive of him in some scenes of his life; but scenes they were, which I am sure his soul *abhorred,* and in which at any rate, you see nothing of his *private virtues.* These old fashioned commodities are generally thrown into the back ground of the picture, and treated, as the grandees at the London and Paris routs, treat their good old *aunts* and *grandmothers,* huddling them together into the *back rooms,* there to wheeze and cough by themselves, and not depress the fine laudanum-raised spirits of the *young sparklers.* And yet it was to those *old-fashioned virtues* that our hero owed every thing. For they in fact were the food of the great actions of him, whom men call Washington. It was they that enabled him, first to triumph over *himself,* then over the *British,* and uniformly to set such bright examples of *human perfectibility* and *true greatness,* that compared therewith, the history of his capturing Cornwallis and Tarleton,[7] with their buccaneering legions, sounds almost as *small* as the story of old General Putnam's[8] catching his wolf and her lamb-killing whelps.

Since then it is the private virtues that lay the foundation of all human excellence—since it was these that exalted Washington to be *"Columbia's[9] first* and *greatest Son,"* be it our first care to present these, in all their lustre, before the admiring eyes of our *children.* To *them* his private character is *every thing;* his public, hardly *any thing.* For how glorious soever it may have been in Washington to have undertaken the emancipation of his country; to have stemmed the long tide of adversity; to have baffled every effort of a wealthy and warlike nation; to have obtained for his countrymen the completest victory, and for himself the most unbounded power; and then to have returned that power, accompanied with all the weight of his own great character and advice to establish a government that should immortalize the blessings of liberty . . . however glorious, I say, all this may have been to himself, or instructive to future generals and presidents, yet does it but *little* concern our *children.* For who among us can hope that his son shall ever be called, like Washington, to direct the storm of war, or to ravish the ears of deeply listening Senates? To be constantly placing him then, before our children, in this high character, what is it but like springing in the clouds a golden Phœnix,[10] which no mortal calibre can ever hope to reach? Or like setting pictures of the Mammoth before the *mice* whom "not all the manna of Heaven" can ever raise to equality? Oh no! give us his *private virtues!* In *these,* every youth is interested, because in these every youth may become a Washington—a Washington in piety and patriotism,—in industry and honour—and consequently a Washington, in what alone deserves the name, SELF ESTEEM and UNIVERSAL RESPECT.

---

[7]Charles Cornwallis (1738–1805) and Banastre Tarleton (1754–1833) were both high-ranking British officers who were defeated in the American Revolution. Ironically, Cornwallis was one of the best British generals of the war, yet he suffered a major defeat at Yorktown, Virginia, in 1781, deciding the war in America's favor.

[8]Rufus Putnam (1738–1824) was a general during the American Revolution, who later used his name and resources to help settle the vast frontier regions of Ohio.

[9]Columbia is another name for the United States.

[10]The Phoenix is a legendary bird known for its remarkable beauty and ability to cheat death by rising from the funeral pyre that supposedly consumed it.

CHAPTER II

❦ Birth and Education

Children like tender osiers take the bow;
And as they first are form'd for ever grow.

To this day numbers of good Christians can hardly find faith to believe that Washington was, bona fide, *a Virginian! "What! a buckskin!"* say they with a smile, *"George Washington a buckskin! pshaw! impossible! he was certainly an European: So great a man could never have been born in America."*

So *great a man could never have been born in America!*—Why that's the very *prince of reasons* why he should have been born here! Nature, we know, is fond of *harmonies;* and *paria paribus,* that is, *great things to great,* is the rule she delights to work by. Where, for example, do we look for the *whale* "the biggest born of nature?" not, I trow, in a *millpond,* but in the main ocean; *"there go the great ships,"* and there are the spoutings of whales amidst their boiling foam.

By the same rule, where shall we look for Washington, the greatest among men, but in *America?* That greatest Continent, which, rising from beneath the frozen pole, stretches far and wide to the south, running almost *"whole the length of this vast terrene,"* and sustaining on her ample sides the roaring shock of half the watery globe. And equal to its size, is the furniture of this vast continent, where the Almighty has reared his cloud-capt mountains, and spread his sea-like lakes, and poured his mighty rivers, and hurled down his thundering cataracts in a style of the *sublime,* so far superior to any thing of the kind in the other continents, that we may fairly conclude that great men and great deeds are designed for America.

This seems to be the verdict of honest analogy; and accordingly we find America the honoured cradle of Washington, who was born on Pope's creek, in Westmoreland county, Virginia, the 22d of February, 1732. His father, whose name was Augustin Washington, was also a Virginian, but his grandfather (John) was an Englishman, who came over and settled in Virginia in 1657.

His father fully persuaded that a marriage of virtuous love comes nearest to angelic life, early stepped up to the *altar* with glowing cheeks and joy sparkling eyes, while by his side, with soft warm hand, sweetly trembling in his, stood the angel form of the lovely Miss Dandridge.

After several years of great domestic happiness, Mr. Washington was separated, by death, from this excellent woman, who left him and two children to lament her early fate.

Fully persuaded still, that *"it is not good for man to be alone,"* he renewed, for the second time, the chaste delights of matrimonial love. His consort was Miss Mary Ball, a young lady of fortune, and descended from one of the best families in Virginia.

From his intermarriage with this charming girl, it would appear that our Hero's father must have possessed either a very pleasing person, or highly polished manners, or perhaps *both; for,* from what I can learn, he was at that time at least 40 years old! while she, on the other hand, was universally toasted as the belle of the Northern Neck, and in the full bloom and freshness of love-inspiring sixteen. This I have from one who tells me that he has carried down many a sett dance with her; I mean that amiable and pleasant old gentleman, John Fitzhugh, Esq. of Stafford, *who* was, all his life, a neighbour and intimate of the Washington family. By his first wife, Mr. Washington had two children, both sons—Lawrence and Augustin. By his second wife, he had five children, four sons and a daughter—George, Samuel, John, Charles, and Elizabeth. Those *over delicate* ones, who are ready to faint at thought of a second marriage, might do well to remember, that the greatest man that ever lived was the son of this second marriage!

Little George had scarcely attained his fifth year, when his father left Pope's creek, and came up to a plantation which he had in Stafford, opposite to Fredericksburg. The house in which he lived is still to be seen. It lifts its low and modest front of faded red, over the turbid waters of Rappahannock; whither, to this day, numbers of people repair, and, with emotions unutterable, looking at the weatherbeaten mansion, exclaim, *"Here's the house where the Great Washington was born!"*

But it is all a mistake; for he was born, as I said, at Pope's creek, in Westmoreland county, near the margin of his own roaring Potomac.

The first place of education to which George was ever sent, was a little *"old field school,"* kept by one of his father's tenants, named Hobby; an honest, poor old man, who acted in the double character of sexton and schoolmaster. On his skill as a gravedigger, tradition is silent; but for a teacher of youth, his qualifications were certainly of the humbler sort; making what is generally called an A. B. C. schoolmaster. Such was the preceptor who first taught Washington the knowledge of letters! Hobby lived to see his young pupil in all his glory, and rejoiced exceedingly. In his cups—for, though a *sexton,* he would sometimes drink, particularly on the General's birth-days—he used to boast, that "*'twas he, who, between his knees, had laid the foundation of George Washington's greatness."*

But though George was early sent to a schoolmaster, yet he was not on that account neglected by his father. Deeply sensible of the *loveliness* and *worth* of which human nature is capable, through the *virtues* and *graces* early implanted in the heart, he never for a moment, lost sight of George in those all-important respects.

To assist his son to overcome that selfish spirit which too often leads children to fret and fight about trifles, was a notable care of Mr. Washington. For this purpose, of all the presents, such as cakes, fruit, &c. he received, he was always desired to give a liberal part to his play-mates. To enable him to do this with more alacrity, his father would remind him of the love which he would hereby gain, and the frequent presents which would in return be made *to him;* and also would tell of that great and good God, who delights above all things to see children love one another, and will assuredly reward them for acting so amiable a part.

Some idea of Mr. Washington's plan of education in this respect, may be collected from the following anecdote, related to me twenty years ago by an aged lady, who was a distant relative, and when a girl spent much of her time in the family.

"On a fine morning," said she, *"in the fall of 1737, Mr. Washington, having little George by the hand, came to the door and asked my cousin Washington and myself to walk with him to the orchard, promising he would show us a fine sight. On arriving at the orchard, we were presented with a fine sight indeed. The whole earth, as far as we could see, was strewed with fruit: and yet the trees were bending under the weight of apples, which hung in clusters like grapes, and vainly strove to hide their blushing cheeks*

behind the green leaves. Now, George, said his father, look here, my son! don't you remember when this good cousin of yours brought you that fine large apple last spring, how hardly I could prevail on you to divide with your brothers and sisters; though I promised you that if you would but do it, God Almighty would give you plenty of apples this fall. Poor George could not say a word; but hanging down his head, looked quite confused, while with his little naked toes he scratched in the soft ground. Now look up, my son, continued his father, look up, George! and see there how richly the blessed God has made good my promise to you. Wherever you turn your eyes, you see the trees loaded with fine fruit; many of them indeed breaking down, while the ground is covered with mellow apples more than you could ever eat, my son, in all your life time."

George looked in silence on the wide wilderness of fruit; he marked the busy humming bees, and heard the gay notes of birds, then lifting his eyes filled with shining moisture, to his father, he softly said, *"Well, Pa, only forgive me this time; see if I ever be so stingy any more."*

Some, when they look up to the oak whose giant arms throw a darkening shade over distant acres, or whose single trunk lays the keel of a man of war, cannot bear to hear of the time when this mighty plant was but an acorn, which a pig could have demolished: but others, who know their value, like to learn the soil and situation which best produces such noble trees. Thus, parents that are *wise* will listen well pleased, while I relate how moved the steps of the youthful Washington, whose single worth far outweighs all the oaks of Bashan and the red spicy cedars of Lebanon. Yes, they will listen delighted while I tell of their Washington in the days of his youth, when his little feet were swift towards the nests of birds; or when, wearied in the chace of the butterfly, he laid him down on his grassy couch and slept, while ministering spirits, with their roseate wings, fanned his glowing cheeks, and kissed his lips of innocence with that fervent love which makes *the Heaven!*

Never did the wise Ulysses[11] take more pains with his beloved Telemachus, than did Mr. Washington with George, to inspire him with an *early love of truth.* "Truth, George," (said he) "is the loveliest quality of youth. I would ride fifty miles, my son, to see the little boy whose heart is so *honest,* and his lips so *pure,* that we may depend on every word he says! O how lovely does such a child appear in the eyes of every body! His parents doat on him; his relations glory in him; they are constantly praising him to their children, whom they beg to imitate him. They are often sending for him, to visit them; and receive him, when he comes, with as much joy as if he were a little angel, come to set pretty examples to their children.

"But, Oh! how different, George, is the case with the boy who is so given to lying, that nobody can believe a word he says! He is looked at with aversion wherever he goes, and parents dread to see him come among their children. Oh, George! my son! rather than see you come to this pass, dear as you are to my heart, gladly would I assist to nail you up in your little coffin, and follow you to your grave. Hard, indeed, would it be to me to give up my son, whose little feet are always so ready to run about with me, and whose fondly looking eyes and sweet prattle make so large a part of my happiness: but still I would give him up, rather than see him a common liar.

---

[11]Ulysses is the hero of Homer's epic poem, *The Odyssey,* who had a son named Telemachus.

"Pa, (said George very seriously) do I ever tell lies?"

"No, George, I *thank God* you do not, my son; and I rejoice in the hope you never will. At least, you shall never, from me, have cause to be guilty of so shameful a thing. Many parents, indeed, even compel their children to this vile practice, by barbarously beating them for every little fault; hence, on the next offence, the little terrified creature slips out a *lie!* just to escape the rod. But as to yourself, George, you know I have *always* told you, and now tell you again, that, whenever by accident you do any thing wrong, which must often be the case, as you are but a poor little boy yet, without *experience* or *knowledge,* never tell a falsehood to conceal it; but come *bravely* up, my son, like a *little man,* and tell me of it: and instead of beating you, George, I will but the more honour and love you for it, my dear."

This, you'll say, was sowing good seed!—Yes, it was: and the crop, thank God, was, as I believe it ever will be, where a man acts the true parent, that is, the *Guardian Angel,* by his child.

The following anecdote is a *case in point.* It is too valuable to be lost, and too true to be doubted; for it was communicated to me by the same excellent lady to whom I am indebted for the last.

"When George," said she, "was about six years old, he was made the wealthy master of a *hatchet!* of which, like most little boys, he was immoderately fond, and was constantly going about chopping every thing that came in his way. One day, in the garden, where he often amused himself hacking his mother's pea-sticks, he unluckily tried the edge of his hatchet on the body of a beautiful young English cherry-tree, which he barked so terribly, that I don't believe the tree ever got the better of it. The next morning the old gentleman finding out what had befallen his tree, which, by the by, was a great favourite, came into the house, and with much warmth asked for the mischievous author, declaring at the same time, that he would not have taken five guineas for his tree. Nobody could tell him any thing about it. Presently George and his hatchet made their appearance. *George,* said his father, *do you know who killed that beautiful little cherry-tree yonder in the garden?* This was a *tough question;* and George staggered under it for a moment; but quickly recovered himself: and looking at his father, with the sweet face of youth brightened with the inexpressible charm of all-conquering truth, he bravely cried out, "*I can't tell a lie, Pa; you know I can't tell a lie. I did cut it with my hatchet."—Run to my arms, you dearest boy,* cried his father in transports, *run to my arms; glad am I, George, that you killed my tree; for you have paid me for it a thousand fold. Such an act of heroism in my son, is more worth than a thousand trees, though blossomed with silver, and their fruits of purest gold.*

It was in this way, by interesting at once both his *heart* and *head,* that Mr. Washington conducted George with great ease and pleasure along the happy paths of virtue. But well knowing that his beloved charge, soon to be a man, would be left exposed to numberless temptations, both from himself and from others, his heart throbbed with the tenderest anxiety to make him acquainted with that GREAT BEING, whom to know and love, is to possess the surest defence against vice, and the best of all motives to virtue and happiness. To startle George into a lively sense of his Maker, he fell upon the following very curious but impressive expedient:

One day he went into the garden, and prepared a little bed of finely pulverized earth, on which he wrote George's name at full, in large letters—then strewing in plenty of cabbage seed, he covered them up and smoothed all over nicely with the roller. This bed he purposely prepared close along side of a gooseberry walk, which happening at this time to be well hung with ripe fruit, he knew would be honoured with George's visits pretty regularly every day. Not many mornings had passed away before in came George, with eyes wild rolling, and his little cheeks ready to burst with *great news.*

"O Pa! come here! come here!"

"What's the matter, my son, what's the matter?"

"O come here, I tell you, Pa, come here! and I'll show you such a sight as you never saw in all your life time."

The old gentleman suspecting what George would be at, gave him his hand, which he seized with great eagerness, and tugging him along through the garden, led him up point blank to the bed whereon was inscribed, in large letters, and in all the freshness of newly sprung plants, the full name of

GEORGE WASHINGTON

"There, Pa!" said George, quite in an ecstasy of astonishment, "did you ever see such a sight in all your life time?"

"Why it seems like a curious affair, sure enough, George!"

"But, Pa, who did make it there, who did make it there?"

"It grew there by *chance,* I suppose my son."

"By *chance,* Pa! O no! no! it never did grow there by *chance,* Pa; indeed that it never did!"

"High! why not, my son?"

"Why, Pa, did you ever see any body's name in a plant bed before?"

"Well, but George, such a thing might happen, though you never saw it before!"

"Yes, Pa, but I did never see the little plants grow up so as to make *one single* letter of my name before. Now, how could they grow up so as to make *all* the letters of my name! and then standing one after another, to spell *my name so exactly!*—and all so neat and even too, at top and bottom!! O Pa, you must not say *chance* did all this. Indeed *somebody* did it; and I dare say now, Pa, *you* did do it just to scare *me,* because I am your little boy."

His father smiled, and said, "Well George, you have guessed right—I indeed *did* it; but not to *scare* you, my son; but to learn you a great thing which I wish you to understand. I want, my son, to introduce you to your *true* Father."

"High, Pa, an't *you* my *true* father, that has loved me, and been so good to me always?"

"Yes, George, I am your father as the world calls it: and I love you very dearly too. But yet with all my love for you, George, I am but a poor good-for-nothing sort of a father in comparison of one you have."

"Aye! I know, well enough whom you mean, Pa. You mean God Almighty, don't you?"

"Yes, my son, I mean him indeed. *He is* your *true* Father, George."

"But, Pa, where is God Almighty? I did never *see* him yet."

"True, my son; but though you never *saw* him, yet he is always with you. You did not see me when ten days ago I made this little plant bed, where you see your name in such beautiful green letters; but though you did not *see* me here, yet you know I was here!!"

"Yes, Pa, that I do—I know you was here."

"Well then, and as my son could not believe that *chance* had made and put together so exactly the *letters* of his name, (though only sixteen) then how can he believe that *chance* could have made and put together all those millions and millions of things that are now so exactly fitted to his good? That my son may look at every thing around him, see! what fine eyes he has got! and a little pug nose to smell the sweet flowers! and pretty ears to hear sweet sound! and a lovely mouth for his bread and butter! and O, the little ivory teeth to cut it for him! and the dear little tongue to prattle with his father! and precious little hands and fingers to hold his playthings! and beautiful little feet for him to run about upon! and when my little rogue of a son is tired with running about, then the still night comes for him to lie down, and his mother sings, and the little crickets chirp him to sleep! and as soon as he has slept enough, and jumps up fresh and strong as a little buck, there the sweet golden light is ready for him! When he looks down into the water, there he sees the beautiful silver fishes for him! and up in the *trees* there are the apples, and peaches, and *thousands* of sweet fruits for him! and *all, all around* him, wherever my dear boy looks, he sees every thing just to his *wants and wishes;*—the bubbling springs with cool sweet water for him to drink! and the wood to make him sparkling fires when he is cold! and beautiful horses for him to ride! and strong oxen to work for him! and the *good* cows to give him milk! and bees to make sweet honey for his sweeter mouth! and the little lambs, with snowy wool, for beautiful clothes for him! Now, these and all the *ten thousand thousand other good things* more than my son can ever think of, and all so exactly fitted to his use and *delight*. . . . Now how could chance ever have done all this for my little son? Oh George! . . ."

He would have gone on, but George, who had hung upon his father's words with looks and eyes of all-devouring attention, here broke out—

"Oh Pa, that's enough! that's enough! It can't be chance, indeed, it can't be chance, that made and gave me all these things."

"What was it then, do you think, my son?"

"Indeed, Pa, I don't know, unless it was *God Almighty!*"

"Yes, George, he it was, my son, and nobody else."

"Well, but Pa, (continued George) does God Almighty give me *every thing?* Don't you give me *some things,* Pa?"

"I give *you* something, indeed! Oh! how can I give you any thing, George! I, who have nothing on earth that I can call my own, no, not even the breath I draw!"

"High, Pa! isn't that great big house your house, and this garden, and the horses yonder, and oxen, and sheep, and trees, and every thing, isn't all yours, Pa?"

"Oh no! my son! no! Why you make me shrink into nothing, George, when you talk of all these belonging to *me,* who can't even make *a grain of sand!* Oh, how could I, my son, have given life to those great oxen and horses, when I can't give life even to a fly?— no! for if the poorest fly were killed, it is not your father, George, nor all the men in the world, that could ever make him alive again!"

At this, George fell into a profound silence, while his pensive looks showed that his youthful soul was labouring with some idea never felt before. Perhaps it was at that moment, that the good Spirit of God ingrafted on his heart that germ of *piety,* which filled his after life with so many of the precious fruits of *morality.*

CHAPTER III

George's father dies—his education continued by his mother—
his behaviour under school-master Williams

Thus pleasantly, on wings of down, passed away the few short years of little George's and his father's *earthly* acquaintance. Sweetly ruled by the sceptre of REASON, George almost adored his father; and thus sweetly *obeyed* with all the cheerfulness of Love, his father doated on George. . . . And though very different in their years, yet parental and filial love rendered them so mutually dear, that the old gentleman was often heard to regret, that *the school took his little companion so much from him*—while George, on the other hand, would often quit his playmates to run home and converse with his more beloved father.

But George was not long to enjoy the pleasure or the profit of such a companion; for scarcely had he attained his tenth year, before his father was seized with the gout in the stomach, which carried him off in a few days. George was not at home when his father was taken ill. He was on a visit to some of his cousins in Chotank, about twenty miles off; and his father, unwilling to interrupt his pleasures, for it was but seldom that he visited, would not at first allow him to be sent for. But finding that he was going very fast, he begged that they would send for him in all haste . . . he often asked if he was come, and said how happy he should be, once more to see his little son, and give him his blessing before he died. But alas! he never enjoyed that last mournful pleasure; for George did not reach home until a few hours before his father's death, and then he was speechless! The moment he alighted, he ran into the chamber where he lay. But oh! what were his feelings when he saw the sad change that had passed upon him! when he beheld those eyes, late so *bright* and *fond,* now reft of all their lustre, faintly looking on him from their hollow sockets, and through swelling tears, in mute but melting language, bidding him a LAST, LAST FAREWELL! . . . Rushing with sobs and cries, he fell upon his father's neck . . . he kissed him a thousand and a thousand times, and bathed his clay-cold face with scalding tears.

O happiest youth! Happiest in that love, which thus, to its enamoured soul strained an aged an[d] expiring sire. O! worthiest to be the founder of a JUST and EQUAL GOVERNMENT, lasting as thy own deathless name! And O! happiest old man! thus luxuriously expiring in the arms of such a child! O! well requited for teaching him that LOVE OF HIS GOD (*the only fountain of every virtuous love*) in return for which he gave thee ('twas all he had) *himself*—his *fondest company*—his *sweetest looks and prattle.* He now gives thee his little strong embraces, with artless sighs and tears; faithful to thee still, his feet will follow thee to thy grave: and when thy beloved corse is let down to the stones of the pit, with streaming eyes he will rush to the brink, to take *one more* look, while his bursting heart will give thee its last trembling cry. . . . *O my father! my father!*

But, though he had lost his best of friends, yet he never lost those divine sentiments which that friend had so carefully inculcated. On the contrary, interwoven with the fibres of his heart, they seemed to "grow with his growth, and to strengthen with his strength." The *memory* of his father, often bathed with *a tear*— the memory of his father now sleeping in his grave, was felt to impose a more sacred obligation to do what, 'twas known, would rejoice his departed shade. This was very happily displayed, in every part of his deportment, from the moment of his earliest intercourse with mankind.

Soon after the death of his father, his mother sent him down to Westmoreland, the place of his nativity, where he lived with his half-brother Augustin, and went to school to a Mr. Williams, an excellent teacher in that neighbourhood. He carried with him his virtues, *his zeal for unblemished character, his love of truth, and detestation of whatever was false and base.* A gilt chariot with richest robes and liveried servants, could not half so substantially have befriended him; for in a very short time, so completely had his virtues secured the love and confidence of the boys, his *word* was just as current among them as a *law.* A very aged gentleman, formerly a school-mate of his, has often assured me, (while pleasing recollection brightened his furrowed cheeks,) that nothing was more common, when the boys were in high dispute about a question of fact, than for some little shaver among the mimic heroes, to call out *"well boys! George Washington was there; George Washington was there; he knows all about it; and if he don't say it was so, then we will give it up,"*—*"done,"* said the adverse party. Then away they would trot to hunt for George. Soon as his verdict was heard, the party favoured would begin to crow, and then all hands would return to play again.

About five years after the death of his father, he quitted school for ever, leaving the boys in tears for his departure: for he had ever lived among them, in the spirit of a brother. He was never guilty of so brutish a practice as that of fighting them himself, nor would he, when able to prevent it, allow them to fight one another. If he could not disarm their savage passions by his arguments, he would instantly go to the master, and inform him of their barbarous intentions.

"The boys," said the same good old gentleman, "were often angry with George for this"—But he used to say, "angry or not angry, you shall never, boys, have my consent to a practice so shocking! shocking even in *slaves* and *dogs;* then how utterly scandalous in little boys at school, who ought to look on one another as brothers. And what must be the feelings of our tender parents, when, instead of seeing us come home smiling and lovely, as the JOYS OF THEIR HEARTS! they see us creeping in like young *blackguards,* with our heads *bound up, black eyes,* and *bloody clothes!* And what is all this for? Why, that we *may get praise!!* But the truth is, a quarrelsome boy was never sincerely praised! Big boys, of the *vulgar sort,* indeed may praise him; but it is only as they would a silly game cock, that fights for their *pastime*—and the little boys are sure to praise him, but it is only as they would a bull dog—to keep him from tearing them!!"

Some of his historians have said, and many believe, that Washington was a *Latin scholar!* But 'tis an error. He never learned a syllable of Latin. His second and last teacher, Mr. Williams, was indeed a capital hand—but not at Latin; for of that he understood perhaps as little as Balaam's ass[12]—but at *reading, spelling, English grammar,*

---

[12]Balaam was an Old Testament prophet (Num. 22–24) whose donkey, although it was only a beast of burden, recognized an angel of the Lord.

arithmetic, surveying, book-keeping and geography, he was indeed famous. And in these useful arts, 'tis said, he often boasted that he had made *young George Washington as great a scholar as himself.*

Born to be a soldier, Washington early discovered symptoms of nature's intentions towards him. In his 11th year, while at school under old Mr. Hobby, he used to divide his play-mates into two parties, *or armies.* One of these, for distinction sake, was called *French,* the other *American.* A big boy at the school, named William Bustle, commanded the former, George commanded the latter. And every day, at play-time, with corn-stalks for muskets, and calabashes for drums, the two armies would turn out, and march, and counter-march, and file off or fight their mimic battles, with great fury. This was fine sport for George, whose passion for active exercise was so strong, that at play-time no weather could keep him within doors. His *fair cousins,* who visited at his mother's, used to complain, that *"George was not fond of their company, like other boys; but soon as he had got his task, would run out to play."* But such trifling play as marbles and tops he could never abide. They did not afford him exercise enough. His delight was in that of the manliest sort, which, by stringing the limbs and swelling the muscles, promotes the kindliest flow of blood and spirits. At jumping with a long pole, or heaving heavy weights, for his years he hardly had an equal. And as to running, the swift-footed Achilles could scarcely have matched his speed.

"Egad! he ran wonderfully," said my amiable and aged friend, John Fitzhugh, esq. who knew him well. *"We had nobody here-abouts, that could come near him. There was young Langhorn Dade, of Westmoreland, a confounded clean made, tight young fellow, and a mighty swift runner too . . . but then he was no match for George: Langy, indeed, did not like to give it up; and would brag that he had sometimes brought George to a tie. But I believe he was mistaken: for I have seen them run together many a time; and George always beat him easy enough."*

Col. Lewis Willis, his play-mate and kinsman, has been heard to say, that he has often seen him throw a stone across Rappahannock, at the lower ferry of Fredericksburg. It would be no easy matter to find a man, now-a-days, who could do it.

Indeed, his father before him was a man of extraordinary strength. His gun, which to this day is called *Washington's fowling-piece,* and now the property of Mr. Harry Fitzhugh, of Chotank, is of such enormous weight, that not one man in a hundred can fire it without a rest. And yet throughout that country it is said, that he made nothing of holding it off at arms length, and blazing away at the swans on Potomac; of which he has been known to kill *rank* and *file,* seven or eight at a shot.

But to return to George. . . . It appears that from the start he was a boy of an uncommonly warm and noble heart; insomuch that Lawrence, though but his *half-brother,* took such a liking to him, even above his *own* brother Augustin, that he would always have George with him when he could get him; and often pressed him to come and live with him. But, as if led by some secret impulse, George declined the offer, and went up, as we have seen, to work, in the back-woods, as Lord Fairfax's surveyor! However, when Lawrence was taken with the consumption, and advised by his physicians to make a trip to Bermuda, George could not resist any longer, but hastened down to his brother at Mount Vernon, and went with him to Bermuda. It was at Bermuda that George took the small-pox, which marked him rather agreeably than otherwise. Lawrence never recovered, but returned to Virginia, where he died just after his brother George had fought his hard battle against the French and Indians, at Fort Necessity, as the reader will presently learn.

Lawrence did not live to see George after that; but he lived to hear of his fame; for as the French and Indians were at that time a great public terror, the people could not help being very loud in their praise of a youth, who with so slender a force had dared to meet them in their own country, and had given them such a check.

And when Lawrence heard of his favourite young brother, that he had fought so gallantly for his country, and that the whole land was filled with his praise, he *wept* for joy. And such is the victory of love over nature, that though fast sinking under the fever and cough of a consumption in its extreme stage, he did not seem to mind it, but spent his last moments in fondly talking of his brother George, who, he said, "*he had always believed, would one day or other be a great man!*"

On opening his will, it was found that George had lost nothing by his dutiful and affectionate behaviour to his brother Lawrence. For having now no issue, (his only child, a little daughter, lately dying) he left to George all his rich lands in Berkley, together with his great estate on Potomac, called MOUNT VERNON,[13] in honour of old Admiral Vernon, by whom he had been treated with great politeness, while a volunteer with him at the unfortunate siege of Carthagena, in 1741.

CHAPTER XIII

❧ Character of Washington

Let the poor witling argue all he can,
It is Religion still that makes the man.

When the children of the years to come, hearing his great name re-echoed from every lip, shall say to their fathers, "*what was it that raised Washington to such height of glory?*" let them be told that it was HIS GREAT TALENTS, CONSTANTLY GUIDED AND GUARDED BY RELIGION. For how shall man, *frail man,* prone to inglorious ease and pleasure, ever ascend the arduous steps of virtue, unless animated by the *mighty hopes* of religion? Or what shall stop him in his swift descent to infamy and vice, if unawed by that dread power which proclaims to the guilty that their secret crimes are seen, and shall not go unpunished? Hence the wise, in all ages, have pronounced, that "*there never was a truly great man without religion.*"

There have, indeed, been *courageous generals,* and *cunning statesmen,* without religion, but mere courage or cunning, however paramount, never yet made a man great.

---

[13]George Washington inherited this five-thousand-acre estate (in Virginia) from his elder half brother, Lawrence. It was named for Adm. Edward Vernon, with whom Lawrence had served in the Caribbean. After his father's death, George spent part of his youth at Mount Vernon with Lawrence.

> Admit that this can conquer, that can cheat!
> 'Tis phrase absurd to call a villain *great!*
> Who wickedly is wise, or madly brave,
> Is but the more a fool, the more a knave.

No! To be truly great, a man must have not only great talents, but those talents must be constantly exerted on great, i.e. good actions—*and perseveringly* too—for if he should turn aside to vice—farewell to his heroism. Hence, when Epaminondas was asked which was the greatest man, himself or Pelopidas?[14] he replied, "*wait till we are dead:["]* meaning that the all of heroism depends on *perseverance* in great good actions. But, sensual and grovelling as man is, what can incline and elevate him to those things like religion, that divine power, to whom alone it belongs to present those vast and eternal *goods* and *ills* which best alarm our fears, enrapture our hopes, inflame the worthiest loves, rouse the truest avarice, and in short touch every spring and passion of our souls in favour of virtue and noble actions.

Did SHAME restrain Alcibiades from a base action in the presence of Socrates?[15] *"Behold,"* says religion, *"a greater than Socrates is here!"*

Did LOVE embolden Jacob[16] to brave fourteen years of slavery for an earthly beauty? Religion springs that eternal love, for whose sake good men can even glory in laborious duties.

Did the ambition of a civic crown animate Scipio[17] to heroic deeds? Religion holds a crown, at the sight of which the laurels of a Cæsar[18] droop to weeds.

Did avarice urge Cortez[19] through a thousand toils and dangers for wealth? Religion points to those treasures in heaven, compared to which all diamond beds and mines of massy gold are but trash.

Did good Aurelius[20] study the happiness of his subjects for this world's glory? Religion displays that world of glory, where those who have laboured to make others happy, shall *"shine like stars for ever and ever."*

---

[14]The Theban leaders Epaminondas and Pelopidas worked together to break the military dominance of Sparta and bring Thebes to central power in ancient Greece for a short period (371–362 B.C.).

[15]Alcibiades (450–404 B.C.) was an early student and ally of the great Greek philosopher Socrates (470–399 B.C.), but later abandoned Socrates' teachings for political power and its rewards.

[16]Jacob waited fourteen years to marry Rachel (Gen. 29).

[17]Name of two Roman generals, both renowned for their brilliant strategies in the wars between Rome and Carthage.

[18]Julius Caesar (100–44 B.C.) was a great Roman general and politician who played a pivotal role in turning the Roman Republic into the Roman Empire. His military exploits often were rewarded with the much coveted victory crown of laurel leaves.

[19]Hernán Cortés (1485–1547) was an early explorer of Central America who was driven by a thirst for the riches and fame that accompanied the conquest of new lands for Spain.

[20]Marcus Aurelius (A.D. 121–180) was both a Roman emperor and a distinguished stoic philosopher who wrote extensively on how to best pursue contentment amid life's tribulations.

Does the FEAR of death deter man from horrid crimes? Religion adds infinite horrors to that fear—it warns them of a death both of soul and body in hell.

In short, what motives under heaven can restrain men from vices and crimes, and urge them on, full stretch, after individual and national happiness, like those of religion? For lack of these motives, alas! how many who once dazzled the world with the glare of their exploits, are now eclipsed and set to rise no more!

There was Arnold, who, in courage and military talents, glittered in the same firmament with Washington, and, for a while, his face shone like the star of the morning; but alas! for lack of Washington's religion, he soon fell, like Lucifer, from a heaven of glory, into an abyss of never-ending infamy.

And there was general Charles Lee,[21] too, confessedly a great wit, a great scholar, a great soldier, but, after all, not a great man. For, through lack of that magnanimous benevolence which religion inspires, he fell into the vile state of *envy,* and, on the plains of Monmouth, rather than fight to immortalize Washington, he chose to retreat and disgrace himself.

There was the gallant general Hamilton[22] also—a gigantic genius—*a statesman* fit to rule the mightiest monarchy—a *soldier "fit to stand by Washington, and give command."* But alas! for lack of religion, see how all was lost! preferring the praise of man to that praise *"which cometh from God,"* and pursuing the phantom honour up to the pistol's mouth, he is cut off at once from life and greatness, and leaves his family and country to mourn his hapless fate.

And there was the fascinating colonel Burr.[23] A man born to be *great*—brave as Cæsar, polished as Chesterfield,[24] eloquent as Cicero,[25] and, lifted by the strong arm of his country, he rose fast, and bade fair soon to fill the place where Washington had sat. But, alas! lacking religion, he could not wait the spontaneous fall of the rich honours ripening over his head, but in evil hour stretched forth his hand to the forbidden fruit, and by that fatal act was cast out from the Eden of our republic, and amerced of greatness for ever.

But why should I summon the Arnolds and Lees, the Hamiltons and Burrs of the earth to give sad evidence, that no valour, no genius alone can make men great? do we not daily meet with instances, of youth amiable and promising as their fond parents' wishes, who yet, merely for lack of religion, soon make shipwreck of every precious

---

[21]At the revolutionary war battle of Monmouth in 1778, Charles Lee ordered a retreat that cost General Washington a victory. He was later court-martialed for this act.

[22]Not known for his commitment to religion, Alexander Hamilton (1755–1804) was an immensely pragmatic and gifted leader both during and after the Revolution. His career was cut short when he was killed in a duel by Aaron Burr.

[23]Aaron Burr (1756–1836) attained such important posts as vice president under Thomas Jefferson, but is remembered chiefly for the duel in which he killed Alexander Hamilton. His reputation and career never fully recovered after Hamilton's death.

[24]Philip Dromer Stanhope (1694–1773), the fourth earl of Chesterfield, was a famous British statesman and diplomat. His famous *Letters to His Son* and *Letters to His Godson* became tremendously popular guides on manners.

[25]Along with the Athenian Demosthenes (384–322 B.C.), the Roman Marcus Tullius Cicero (106–43 B.C.) was widely considered one of the two greatest orators of the ancient Western world.

hope, sacrificing their gold to gamblers, their health to harlots, and their glory to grog—making conscience their curse, this life a purgatory, and the next a hell!! In fact, a young man, though of the finest talents and education, without religion, is but like a gorgeous ship without ballast. Highly painted and with flowing canvas, she launches out on the deep; and, during a smooth sea and gentle breeze, she moves along stately as the pride of ocean; but, as soon as the stormy winds descend, and the blackening billows begin to roll, suddenly she is overset, and disappears for ever. But who is this coming, thus gloriously along, with masts towering to heaven, and his sails white, looming like the mountain of snows? Who is it but *"Columbia's first and greatest son!"* whose talents, like the sails of a mighty ship spread far and wide, catching the gales of heaven, while his capacious soul, stored with the rich ballast of religion, remains firm and unshaken as the ponderous rock. The warm zephyrs of prosperity breathe meltingly upon him—the rough storms of adversity descend—the big billows of affliction dash, but nothing can move him; his eye is fixed on God! the *present joys* of an approving conscience, and the hope of that glory which fadeth not away; these comfort and support him.

"There exists," says Washington, *"in the economy of nature, an inseparable connexion between duty and advantage."*—The whole life of this great man bears glorious witness to the truth of this his favourite aphorism. At the giddy age of fourteen, when the spirits of youth are all on tiptoe for freedom and adventures, he felt a strong desire to go to sea; but, very opposite to his wishes, his mother declared that she could not bear to part with him. His trial must have been very severe; for I have been told that a midshipman's commission was actually in his pocket—his trunk of clothes on board the ship—his honour in some sort pledged—his young companions importunate with him to go—and his whole soul panting for the promised pleasures of the voyage; but religion whispered *"honour thy mother, and grieve not the spirit of her who bore thee."*

Instantly the glorious boy sacrificed inclination to duty—dropt all thoughts of the voyage, and gave tears of joy to his widowed mother, in clasping to her bosom a dear child who could deny himself to make her happy.

'Tis said, that, when he saw the last boat going on board, with several of his youthful friends in it—when he saw the flash and heard the report of the signal gun for sailing, and the ship in all her pride of canvas rounding off for sea, he could not bear it, but turned away, and, half choked with grief, went into the room where his mother sat. *"George, my dear!"* said she, *"have you already repented that you made your mother so happy just now?"* Upon this, falling on her bosom, with his arms round her neck, and a gush of tears, he said, *"my dear mother, I must not deny that I am sorry; but, indeed, I feel that I should be much more sorry, were I on board the ship, and knew that you were unhappy."*

"Well," replied she embracing him tenderly, *"God, I hope, will reward my dear boy for this, some day or other."* Now see here, young reader, and learn that HE who prescribes our duty, is able to reward it. Had George left his fond mother to a broken heart, and gone off to sea, 'tis next to certain that he would never have taken that active part in the French and Indian war, which, by securing to him the hearts of his countrymen, paved the way for all his future greatness.

Now for another instance of the wonderful effect of religion on Washington's fortune. Shortly after returning from the war of Cuba, Lawrence (his *half* brother) was taken with the consumption, which made him so excessively fretful, that his *own* brother, Augustin, would seldom come near him. But George, whose heart was early under the softening and sweetening influences of religion, felt such a tenderness for his poor sick brother, that he not only put up with his peevishness, but seemed, from what I have been told, never so happy as when he was with him. He accompanied him to the island of Bermuda, in quest of health—and, after their return to Mount Vernon, often as his duty to lord Fairfax permitted, he would come down from the back woods to see him. And while with him he was always contriving or doing something to cheer and comfort his brother. Sometimes with his gun he would go out in quest of partridges and snipes, and other fine flavoured game, to tempt his brother's sickly appetite, and gain him strength. At other times he would sit for hours and read to him some entertaining book— and, when his cough came on, he would support his drooping head, and wipe the cold dew from his forehead, or the phlegm from his lips, and give him his medicine, or smooth his pillow; and all with such alacrity and artless tenderness as proved the sweet- est cordial to his brother's spirits. For he was often heard to say to the Fairfax family, into which he married, that "*he should think nothing of his sickness, if he could but always have his brother George with him.*" Well, what was the consequence? Why, when Lawrence came to die, he left almost the whole of his large estate to George, which served as another noble step to his future greatness.

For further proof of "*the inseparable connexion between duty and advantage,*" let us look at Washington's conduct through the French and Indian war.[26] To a man of his uncommon military mind, and skill in the arts of Indian warfare, the pride and precipi- tance of general Braddock[27] must have been excessively disgusting and disheartening. But we hear nothing of his *threatening* either to leave or supplant Braddock. On the con- trary, he nobly brooked his rude manners, gallantly obeyed his rash orders, and, as far as in him lay, endeavoured to correct their fatal tendencies.

And, after the death of Braddock, and the desertion of Dunbar,[28] that weak old man, governor Dinwiddie,[29] added infinitely to his hardships and hazards, by appointing him to the defence of the frontiers, and yet withholding the necessary forces and supplies. But though by that means, the western country was continually overrun by the enemy, and cruelly deluged in blood—though much wearied in body by marchings and watch- ings, and worse tortured in soul, by the murders and desolations of the inhabitants, he shrinks not from *duty*—still seeking the smiles of conscience as his greatest good; and as the sorest evil, dreading its frowns, he bravely maintained his ground, and, after three years of unequalled dangers and difficulties, succeeded.

---

[26]The French and Indian War was a nine-year war (1754–1763) in which the British and French fought for control of North America.

[27]Edward Braddock (1695–1755) was best known as an unsuccessful British commander in the French and Indian War who died of wounds sustained in battle.

[28]Thomas Dunbar (?–1767) served alongside Washington under Braddock during the French and Indian War. After Braddock was killed along with many of his troops, Dunbar withdrew with his command to the safety of Philadelphia, leaving much of Virginia unprotected from the French and Indians.

[29]Robert Dinwiddie (1690?–1770) was governor of Virginia during the French and Indian War. After Braddock's death, he made Washington responsible for defending the Virginia frontier. Washington constantly sought more supplies and troops from Dinwiddie, who was slow to provide them.

Well, what was the consequence? why it drew upon him, from his admiring countrymen, such an unbounded confidence in his principles and patriotism, as secured to
him the command of the *American armies,* in the revolutionary war!

And there again the connexion between *"duty and advantage"* was as gloriously
displayed. For though congress was, in legal and political knowledge an enlightened
body, and for patriotism equal to the senators of Republican Rome, yet certainly in military matters they were no more to be compared to him, than those others were to Hannibal. But still, though they were constantly thwarting his counsels, and in place of good
soldiers sending him raw militia, thus compelling inactivity, or ensuring defeat—dragging out the war—dispiriting the nation—and disgracing him, yet we hear from him no
gusts of passion; no dark intrigues to supplant congress, and, with the help of an idoliz-
ing nation and army, to snatch the power from their hands, and make himself king. On
the contrary, he continues to treat congress as a virtuous son his respected parents. He
points out wiser measures, but in defect of their adoption, makes the best use of those
they give him, and at length, through the mighty blessing of God, established the independence of his country, and then went back to his plough.

Well, what was the consequence? why, these noble acts so completely filled up the
measure of his country's love for him, as to give him that first of all felicities, the felicity to be the guardian angel of his country, and able by the magic of his name, to scatter
every cloud of danger that gathered over her head.

For example, at the close of the war, when the army, about to be disbanded without
their wages, was wrought up to such a pitch of discontent and rage, as seriously to
threaten *civil war,* see the wonderful influence which their love for him gave him over
themselves! In the height of their passion, and that a very natural passion too, he but
makes a short speech to them, and the storm is laid! the tumult subsides! and the soldiers,
after all their hardships, consent to ground their arms, and return home without a penny
in their pockets!!!

Also, in that very alarming dispute between Vermont and Pennsylvania, where the
furious parties, in spite of all the efforts of congress and their governors, had actually
shouldered their guns, and were dragging on their cannon for a bloody fight—Washington only dropt them a few lines of his advice, and instantly they faced about for their
homes, and laying by their weapons, seized their ploughs again, like dutiful children, on
whose kindling passions a beloved father had shaken his hoary locks!!

And, in the western counties of Pennsylvania, where certain blind patriots, affecting
to strain at the gnat of a small excise, but ready enough to swallow the hellish camel of
rebellion, had kindled the flames of civil war,[30] and thrown the whole nation into a
tremor, Washington had just to send around a circular to the people of the union, stating
the infinite importance of maintaining the SACRED REIGN OF THE LAWS, and instantly twenty
thousand well-armed volunteers dashed out among the insurgents, and without shedding
a drop of blood, extinguished the insurrection!

In short, it were endless to enumerate the many horrid insurrections and bloody

---

[30]In the years immediately following the American Revolution, the United States was threatened
by civil war. Everything from state borders to taxation was in dispute with no central power to
adjudicate matters. Washington attempted to diffuse these problems by working to establish a
strong, centralized federal government.

wars which were saved to this country by Washington, and all through the divine force of *early religion!* for it was this that enabled him inflexibly to do his duty, by imitating God in his glorious works of wisdom and benevolence; and all the rest followed as naturally as light follows the sun.

We have seen at page 15 of this little work,[31] with what pleasure the youthful Washington hung upon his father's lips, while descanting on the adorable wisdom and benevolent designs of God in all parts of this beautiful and harmonious creation. By such lessons in the book of nature, this virtuous youth was easily prepared for the far higher and surer lectures of revelation, I mean that blessed gospel which contains the MORAL philosophy of heaven. There he learnt, that *"God is love"*—and that all that he desires, with respect to men, is to glorify himself in their happiness—and since VIRTUE is indispensable to that happiness, the infinite and eternal weight of God's attributes must be for virtue, and against vice; and consequently that God will sooner or later gloriously reward the one and punish the other. This was the creed of Washington. And looking on it as the only basis of human virtue and happiness, he very cordially embraced it himself, and wished for nothing so much as to see all others embrace it.

I have often been told by colonel Ben Temple, (of King William county, Virginia), who was one of his aids in the French and Indian war, that he has frequently known Washington, on the sabbath, read the scriptures and pray with his regiment, in the absence of the chaplain; and also that, on sudden and unexpected visits into his marquee, he has, more than once, found him on his knees at his devotions.

The Reverend Mr. Lee Massey, long a rector of Washington's parish, and from early life his intimate, has assured me a thousand times, that "he never knew so constant a churchman as Washington. And his behaviour in the house of God," added my reverend friend, "was so deeply reverential, that it produced the happiest effects on my congregation, and greatly assisted me in my moralizing labours. No company ever kept him from church. I have been many a time at Mount Vernon on the sabbath morning, when his breakfast table was filled with guests. But to him they furnished no pretext for neglecting his God, and losing the satisfaction of setting a good example. For instead of staying at home out of a false complaisance to them, he used constantly to invite them to accompany him."

His secretary, judge Harrison, has frequently been heard to say, that, "whenever the general would be spared from camp on the sabbath, he never failed riding out to some neighbouring church, to join those who were publicly worshipping the Great Creator."

And while he resided at Philadelphia, as president of the United States, his constant and cheerful attendance on divine service was such as to convince every reflecting mind that he deemed no levee so honourable as that of his Almighty Maker; no pleasures equal to those of devotion; and no business a sufficient excuse for neglecting his supreme benefactor.

In the winter of '77, while Washington, with the American army lay encamped at Valley Forge, a certain good old FRIEND, of the respectable family and name of Potts, if I mistake not, had occasion to pass through the woods near head-quarters. Treading his way along the venerable grove, suddenly he heard the sound of a human voice, which as he ad-

---

[31]See p. 10 of this anthology.

vanced increased on his ear, and at length became like the voice of one speaking much in earnest. As he approached the spot with a cautious step, whom should he behold, in a dark natural bower of ancient oaks, but the commander in chief of the American armies on his knees at prayer! Motionless with surprise, friend Potts continued on the place till the general, having ended his devotions, arose, and, with a countenance of angel serenity, retired to headquarters: friend Potts then went home, and on entering his parlour called out to his wife, "Sarah, my dear! Sarah! All's well! all's well! George Washington will yet prevail!"

"What's the matter, Isaac?" replied she; "thee seems moved."

"Well, if I seem moved, 'tis no more than what I am. I have this day seen what I never expected. Thee knows that I always thought the sword and the gospel utterly inconsistent; and that no man could be a soldier and a christian at the same time. But George Washington has this day convinced me of my mistake."

He then related what he had seen, and concluded with this prophetical remark—"If George Washington be not a man of God, I am greatly deceived—and still more shall I be deceived if God do not, through him, work out a great salvation for America."

When he was told that the British troops at Lexington, on the memorable 19th of April, 1775, had fired on and killed several of the Americans, he replied, "*I grieve for the death of my countrymen, but rejoice that the British are still so determined to keep God on our side,*" alluding to that noble sentiment which he has since so happily expressed; viz. "*The smiles of Heaven can never be expected on a nation that disregards the eternal rules of order and right, which Heaven itself has ordained.*"

When called by his country in 1775, to lead her free-born sons against the arms of Britain, what charming modesty, what noble self-distrust, what pious confidence in Heaven, appeared in all his answers. "*My diffidence in my own abilities, says he, was superseded by a confidence in the rectitude of our cause and the patronage of Heaven.*"

And when called to the presidency by the unanimous voice of the nation, thanking him for his great services past, with anticipations of equally great to come, his answer deserves approbation.

"*When I contemplate the interposition of providence, as it was visibly manifested in guiding us through the revolution, in preparing us for the reception of a general government, and in conciliating the good will of the people of America towards one another after its adoption; I feel myself oppressed and almost overwhelmed with a sense of the divine munificence. I feel that nothing is due to my personal agency in all those complicated and wonderful events, except what can simply be attributed to the exertions of an honest zeal for the good of my country.*"

And when he presented himself for the first time before that august body, the congress of the U. States, April 30th, 1789—when he saw before him the pride of Columbia in her chosen sons, assembled to consult how best to strengthen the chain of love between the states—to preserve friendship and harmony with foreign powers—to secure the blessings of civil and religious liberty—and to build up our young republic a great and happy people among the nations of the earth—never patriot entered on such important business with fairer hopes, whether we consider the unanimity and confidence of the citizens, or his own and the abilities and virtues of his fellow-counsellors.

But all this would not do; nothing short of the *divine friendship* could satisfy Washington. Feeling the magnitude, difficulty, and danger of managing such an assemblage of communities and interests; dreading the machinations of bad men, and well knowing the insufficiency of all second causes, even the *best;* he piously reminds congress of the wisdom of imploring the benediction of the *great first Cause,* without which he knew that his beloved country could never prosper.

"It would," says he, "be peculiarly improper to omit, in this first official act, my fervent supplications to that Almighty Being who rules over the universe; who presides in the councils of nations; and whose providential aids can supply every human defect, that his benediction may consecrate to the liberties and happiness of the people of the United States, a government instituted by themselves for these essential purposes, and may enable every instrument employed in its administration to execute with success the functions allotted to his charge. In tendering this homage to the great Author of every public and private good, I assure myself that it expresses your sentiments not less than my own; nor those of my fellow-citizens at large less than either. No people can be bound to acknowledge and adore the invisible hand which conducts the affairs of men, more than the people of the United States. Every step, by which they have advanced to the character of an independent nation, seems to have been distinguished by some token of providential agency. These reflections, arising out of the present crisis, have forced themselves too strongly on my mind to be suppressed. You will join with me, I trust, in thinking, that there are none, under the influence of which the proceedings of a new and free government can more auspiciously commence."

And after having come near to the close of this the most sensible and virtuous speech ever made to a sensible and virtuous representation of a free people, he adds—"I shall take my present leave: but not without resorting *once more* to the benign Parent of the human race in humble supplication, that, since he has been pleased to favour the American people with opportunities for deliberating with perfect tranquillity, and dispositions for deciding with unparalleled unanimity, on a form of government for the security of their union, and the advancement of their happiness; so his divine blessings may be equally conspicuous in the enlarged views, the temperate consultations, and the wise measures, on which the success of this government must depend."

In this constant disposition to look for national happiness only in national morals, flowing from the *sublime* affections and blessed hopes of religion, Washington agreed with those great legislators of nations, Moses, Lycurgus, and Numa.[32] "*I ask not gold for Spartans,*" said Lycurgus. "*Virtue is better than all gold.*" The event showed his wisdom. The Spartans were invincible all the days of their own virtue, even 500 years.

"I ask not wealth for Israel," cried Moses.—"But O that they were wise!—that they did but fear God and keep his commandments! the Lord himself would be their sun and shield." The event proved Moses a true prophet. For while they were religious they were unconquerable. "United as brothers, swift as eagles, stronger than lions, one could chase a thousand, and two put ten thousand to flight."

"Of all the dispositions and habits which lead to the prosperity of a nation," says Washington, "religion is the indispensable support. Volumes could not trace all its connexions with private and public happiness. Let it simply be asked, where is the security

---

[32]All famous lawmakers of the ancient world: Moses for the Israelites, Lycurgus for the Spartans, and Numa for the Romans.

for property, for reputation, for life itself, if there be no fear of God on the minds of those who give their oaths in courts of justice!"

But some will tell us, that *human laws* are sufficient for the purpose!

Human laws!—Human nonsense! For how often, even where the cries and screams of the wretched called aloud for lightning-speeded vengeance, have we not seen the sword of human law loiter in its coward scabbard, afraid of angry royalty? Did not that vile queen Jezebel,[33] having a mind to compliment her husband with a vineyard belonging to poor Naboth, suborn a couple of villains to take a false oath against him, and then cause him to be dragged out with his little motherless, crying babes, and barbarously stoned to death?

Great God! what bloody tragedies have been acted on the poor ones of the earth, by kings and great men, who were *above* the laws, and had no sense of religion to keep them in awe! And if men be not above the laws, yet what horrid crimes! what ruinous robberies! what wide-wasting flames! what cruel murders may they not commit in *secret,* if they be not withheld by the sacred arm of religion! "In vain, therefore," says WASHINGTON, "would that man claim the tribute of patriotism, who should do any thing to discountenance religion and morality, those great pillars of human happiness, those firmest props of the duties of men and citizens. The mere politician, equally with the pious man, ought to respect and cherish them."

But others have said, and with a serious face too, that a *sense of honour,* is sufficient to preserve men from base actions! O blasphemy to sense! Do we not daily hear of *men of honour,* by dice and cards, draining their fellow-citizens of the last cent, reducing them to a dung-hill, or driving them to a pistol? Do we not daily hear of *men of honour* corrupting their neighbours' wives and daughters, and then murdering their husbands and brothers in duels? Bind such selfish, such inhuman beings, by a sense of honour!! Why not bind roaring lions with cobwebs? "No," exclaims Washington, "whatever a sense of honour may do on men of refined education, and on minds of a peculiar structure, reason and experience both forbid us to expect that national morality can prevail, in exclusion of religious principles."

And truly Washington had abundant reason, from his own *happy experience,* to recommend religion so heartily to others.

For besides all those inestimable favours which he received from her at the hands of her celestial daughters, the *Virtues;* she threw over him her own magic mantle of *Character.* And it was this that immortalized Washington. By inspiring his countrymen with the profoundest veneration for him as the *best of men,* it naturally smoothed his way to supreme command; so that when War, that monster of hell, came on roaring against America, with all his death's heads and garments rolled in blood, the nation unanimously placed Washington at the head of their armies, from a natural persuasion that so good a man must be the peculiar favourite of Heaven, and the fastest friend of his country. How far this precious instinct in favour of goodness was corrected, or how far Washington's conduct was honourable to religion and glorious to himself and country, bright ages to come, and happy millions yet unborn, will, we hope, declare.

---

[33]Jezebel was King Ahab's queen in the Old Testament (1 Kings 17–21). She has become synonymous with the wicked, treacherous woman who stops at nothing to get her way.

———

HYMEN'S[1] RECRUITING SERGEANT

*Or the New Matrimonial Tat-too,[2] for the Old Bachelors
With Some Elegant Songs*

Inviting all, both big and small,
    A lovely wife to take;
No longer lead—Oh! Shameful deed!
    The life of worthless rake.

❧

'Tis madess sure, you must agree,
    To lodge alone at thirty-three!
For writings, penn'd by heav'n, have shewn,
    That man can ne'er be blest alone.

FRENEAU

❧

God prosper long, Columbia[3] dear,
    In plenty, love and peace;
And grant henceforth, that bach'lors old,
    'Mongst pretty maids may cease!!

❧ To All the Singles Whether Masculines or Feminines, throughout the United States

Dear Gentles,

I am very clear that our *Buckskin heroes* are made of, at least, as *good* stuff as any the *best* of the *beef* or *frog-eating* gentry on t'other side the water. But neither this, nor all our fine speeches to our president, nor all his fine speeches to us again, will ever save us from the British gripe, or Carmagnole[4] hug, while they can out-number us, *ten to one!* No, my friends, 'tis population, 'tis *population alone,* that can save our Bacon.

This text follows the following edition: Mason L. Weems, *Hymen's Recruiting Sergeant, Or the New Matrimonial Tat-too, for the Old Bachelors. With Some Elegant Songs.* Greenfield, Mass.: Printed for the Public, 1817.

[1]In Greek mythology, Hymen is the God of marriage, but there is also a play on words here, as a hymen is an anatomical term for the virginal membrane.

[2]A tat-too was a military drum or bugle signal that called soldiers in the evening to go to their quarters.

[3]Another name for the United States.

[4]Carmagnole was a style of popular dress during the French Revolution that came to symbolize French political radicalness and violence.

List, then, ye Bach'lors, and ye Maidens fair,
If truly you do love your country dear;
O list with rapture to the great decree,
Which *thus* in Genesis, you all may see:
"*Marry and raise up soldiers might and main,*"
Then laugh you may, at England, France, and Spain.

Wishing you all, the *hearing ear*—the *believing heart*—and a saving antipathy to *apes,*
I remain your's, dear Gentles[5]

> *In the bonds of Love and Matrimony,*
> *M. L. Weems.*

❧ Hymen's Recruiting Sergeant

And the Lord said, "It is not good for man to be alone."
GENESIS, CHAP. II. VERSE 18

No, verily, nor for the woman neither. But, what says the preacher? Why, "*I will,*" says Paul,[6] (and Paul, you know, was a sound divine) "*that the young women marry, and love their husbands; and raise up children.*" Well said, most noble, patriotic Paul! May the children of Columbia hearken to thy counsel! that there be no more old Bachelors in our land, like scrubby oaks standing selfishly alone, while our maidens, like tender vines lacking support, sink to the ground; but that, united in wedlock's *blest embraces,* they may grow up together as the trees of the Lord, whose summits reach the skies, and their branches overspread the nations, making their country the pride and glory of the earth!

"*I will that the young people marry,*" says Paul.

> Aye, that's the point; there let us fix our eyes;
> There all the *honour,* all the *blessing* lies.

For,

1. If you are for *pleasure*—Marry!
2. If you prize *rosy health*—Marry!
3. And even if *money* be your *object*—Marry.

Now, let's to the point, and prove these precious truths. Draw near, ye bachelors of the willing ear, while, with the grey quill of experience I write,

I. THE PLEASURES OF THE MARRIED STATE

---

[5]Gentles, as opposed to commoners, were people who composed the higher, more refined strata of society.

[6]Saint Paul of the New Testament. Here, Weems summarizes and reformulates Paul's teachings on marriage for his own purposes.

Believe me, Citizen Bachelor, never man yet received his full *allowance head'd up and running over,* of this life's joys, until it was measured out to him by the generous hand of a loving wife.

A man, with half an eye, may see that I am not talking here of those droll matches which, now and then, throw a whole neighbourhood into a *wonderation;* where scores of good people are call'd together to eat minch-pies, and to hear a blooming nymph of *fourteen* promise to take—*"for better and for worse"*—an old icicle of fourscore! Or to see the *sturdy glowing youth,* lavishing amorous kisses on the shrivelled lips of his *great-grand-mother bride!* Oh cursed lust of pelf![7] From such matches, good Lord, deliver all true hearted republicans! For *such matches* have gone a great way to make those *sweetest notes, husband wife,* to sound prodigiously *out-o'-tunish.* The old husband, after all his honey-moon looks, grunts a jealous *bass,* while young Madam, wretched in spite of her coach and lutestrings, squeaks a scolding treble; making, between them, a fine cat-and-dog concert of it for life!!

But I am talking of a match of *true love,* between two persons who, having *virtue* to relish the transports of a tender friendship, and *good sense* to estimate their infinite value, wisely strive to fan the delightful flame by the same endearing attentions which they paid to each other during the sweet days of courtship. O, if there be a heaven on earth, we must (next to the love of God) seek it in such a marriage of innocence and love! On the bright list of their felicities, I would set down, as

THE FIRST BLISS OF MATRIMONY,

the charming society, the tender friendship it affords! Without a friend it is not for man to be happy. Let the old Madeira sparkle in his goblets, and princely dainties smoke upon his table; yet, if he have to sit down with him, no friend of the love-beaming eye, alas! the banquet is insipid, and the cottagers *"dinner of herbs where love is,"* must be envied.

Let the pelf-scraping Bachelor drive on alone towards heaven in his *solitary* sulky;[8] the Lord help the poor man, and send him good speed! But that's not my way of travelling. No! give me a sociable *chaise* with a *dear good angel* by my side, the thrilling touch of whose sweetly-folding arm may flush my spirits into rapture, and inspire a devotion suited to the place, that *best devotion*—gratitude and *love!!*

Yes, the sweetest drop in the cup of life is a friend; but where, on earth, is the friend that deserves to be compar'd with an *affectionate wife?* that *generous creature,* who, for your sake, has left father and mother—looks to you alone for happiness—wishes in your society to spend her cheerful days—in your beloved arms to draw her latest breath—and fondly thinks the slumbers of the grave will be sweeter when lying by your side! The marriage of two such fond hearts, *in one united,* forms a state of friendship, of all others, the most perfect and delightful. 'Tis marriage of *souls,* of persons, of wishes, and of *interest.*

Are you poor? Like another *self,* she *toils* and *slaves* to better your fortune. Are you sick? She is the tenderest of all nurses; she never leaves your bedside; she sustains your fainting head, and strains your feverish cheeks to her dear anxious bosom. How luxurious is sickness with such a companion!

---

[7]money

[8]A single-seat vehicle with wheels.

Are you prosperous? It multiplies your blessings, *ten thousand fold,* to share them with one so beloved. Are you in her *company?* Her very *presence* has the effect of the *sweetest conversation,* and her looks, though *silent,* convey a *something* to the heart, of which none but happy husbands, have any idea. Are you going abroad? She accompanies you to the door—the tender embrace—the *fond lengthen'd* kiss—the last soul-melting look—precious evidence of love! these go along with you; they steal across your delighted memory, soothing your journey; while dear conjugal love gives transport to every glance *at home,* and sweetens every nimble step of your glad return. There, soon as your beloved form is seen, she flies to meet you. Her voice is music—the pressure of her arms is rapture, while her *eyes,* heaven's sweetest messengers of love! declare the tumultuous joy that heaves her generous bosom. Arm in arm she hurries you into the smiling habitation, where, the *fire fair blazing,* and the vestment warm, the neat apartment and delicious repast, prepared by her eager love, fill your bosom with a joy *too big for utterance.*

Compared with a life like this, merciful God! how disconsolate is the condition of the old Bachelor! how barren of all joy! Solitary and comfortless at home he strolls abroad into company. Meeting with no tenderness, nor affection, to sweeten company, he soon tires, and, with a sigh, gets up to *go home again.*—Poor man! his eyes are upon the ground, and his steps are slow; for, alas! home has no attractions. He sees nothing there but gloomy walls and lonesome chambers. Alone he swallows his silent supper— he crawls to his bed, and, trembling, coils himself up in cold sheets, sadly remembering, that with tomorrow's joyless sun, the same dull round begins again!!

SONG I

In the world's crooked path, where I've been,
> There to share in life's gloom my poor heart,
The sunshine that soften'd the scene
> Was—*a smile from the wife of my heart!*

Not a swain when the lark quits her nest,
> But to labour, with glee, will depart,
If, at eve, he expects to be blest
> With—*a smile from the wife of his heart.*

Come, then, crosses and cares as they may,
> Let my mind still this maxim impart,
That the comfort of man's fleeting day
> Is—*a smile from the wife of his heart.*

SONG II

When fortune frowns, and friends forsake,
> A loving wife still cheers us;
Our grief or raptures she'll partake;
> Distresses but endear us.

While man's professions all will fly,
> Nor dying will abet you;

> But meet your corpse as passing by,
>   And, with a sigh, forget you.

> While round your bed the *mourning fair*
>   Hangs, like a drooping willow,
> Each pang or sigh still anxious share,
>   Nor leave your woe-worn pillow.

> Then charge your glasses to the fair;
>   May beauty ne'er be slighted—
> That source of bliss, by whom we are
>   *Conceived, brought forth, delighted.*

> Then, O! protect the lovely fair;
>   Be mindful of your duty!
> May vengeance ne'er the villain spare,
>   A foe to love and beauty.

SECOND BLISS OF MATRIMONY

It gives us lovely children, to perpetuate our names; to enjoy the fruits of our honest industry, and to derive to us a sort of new existence, which we fondly hope will be more prudent and happy than the first.

Ye tender parents! say, what music in nature is equal to that which thrills through your delighted nerves when your little prattlers, with infant voice, attempt to lisp your names!

See Florio and Delia! happy pair! Surrounded by their young ones, blooming as spring—sweet as smiling innocence—and laughing like the *Graces!*[9]—pulling at their knees to catch the envied kiss—while the fond parents, with eyes swimming with delight, gaze on them and on each other, filled with gratitude to Heaven for such precious treasures, and daily and gloriously employed in training them up to virtue and happiness. Delightful task! pleasure more than mortal! A pleasure which, according to Moses, the Almighty himself enjoyed when he beheld the works of his hands, and saw that all was good.

Compared with *pleasures* so *exquisite,* with pursuits so dignified and important as those of the married lady, the amusements of the *single* are, sometimes at least, rather diminutive and girlish.

Delia was lately visited by a wealthy old maid, a cousin of her's, who entertained her with a world of chat about her diamond necklaces, gold ear-rings, and so forth, which she displayed with great satisfaction. She was scarcely done, before Delia's children, returning from school, ran into the room with blooming cheeks and joy-sparkling eyes, to kiss their mother.—Delia, then, with all the transports of a happy parent, exclaimed, *"these, my dear cousin, are my jewels, and the only ones I admire."* Glorious speech! Worthy of an American lady! For those living ornaments which give to our country plenty in peace, and security in war, add a brighter lustre to the fair, than all the sparkling jewels of the East.

---

[9]In Greek mythology, the Graces were a group of goddesses characterized by fertility, charm, and beauty.

Item—The pleasures which a fond parent finds in the circle of his children are the purest and most exquisite in nature; kings and conquerors have gladly left their crowded levees to caress and play with these, their little cherubs: Nay, he who was greater than all earthly kings and conquerors, used to delight in the company of the *little innocents,* and said, "*Suffer little children to come unto me, and forbid them not; for of such is the kingdom of God," and he took them up in his arms, and kissed them, and blessed them.*[10]

The *prime minister* of Agesilaus,[11] coming into the palace, found that great prince in high romp with his children. Just as the old Ahitophel[12] (a *Bachelor,* of course) was beginning to relax his stern features into a grin, the king pleasantly observed, "My friend, don't say a word in this matter, until *you become a parent.*" A fond parent finds likewise something *wonderfully improving* in the society of his children. Even a stranger cannot look on their sweet countenances, without feeling the charm of innocence, and catching something of their amiable spirit; how, then can a parent otherwise than catch from them the finest sentiments of tenderness and humanity? gazing on their beloved faces till his heart aches within him; straining them to his bosom till the tear starts into his eye, how can he be cruel even to the children of the stranger.

That French Hannibal,[13] Bonaparte, (who is a married man) at the head of an inferior force fell in with the Austrians. Just as they were advancing to action, Bonaparte seeing two poor little children in the fields, crying at the sight of so many dreadful faces, commanded the troops to halt, till, with the assistance of a corporal, he had removed them out of danger.—The eyes of the Frenchmen sparkled on their gallant chief. They raised the song of war—(the Marseilles' hymn)—the song of heroes fighting for their *hoary sires,* their weeping wives and helpless babes. The Austrians fell before them, as the fields of ripe corn fall before the flames that are driven on by the storms of Heaven.

SONG I

FLORIO TO DELIA

Though fools spurn Hymen's gentle pow'rs,
We, who improve his golden hours,
   By sweet experience know
That marriage, rightly understood,
Gives, to the tender and the good,
   A *Paradise* below.

Our babes shall richest comforts bring;
If tutor'd right, they'll prove a spring
   Whence pleasures ever rise;

---

[10]A quote from Jesus found in Matt. 19:14, Mark 10:14, and Luke 18:16.

[11]Agesilaus was a Spartan king who came to personify the aggressive Spartan military spirit.

[12]Ahitophel was a trusted, and later traitorous, advisor to King David in the Old Testament (2 Sam. 15–23).

[13]Hannibal (247–183 B.C.) was perhaps the greatest general ancient Carthage ever produced. He invaded Italy and won astounding victories against the armies of the Roman Republic.

We'll form their minds, with studious care,
To all that's manly, good and fair,
   And train them for the skies.

While they our wisest hours engage,
They'll glad our youth, support our age,
   And crown our hoary hairs;
They'll grow in virtue every day;
And thus our fondest loves repay,
   And recompense our cares.

SONG II

How blest has my time been! what days have I known
Since wedlock's soft bondage made Delia my own!
So joyful my heart is, so easy my chain,
That freedom is tasteless and roving a pain.

Through walks grown with woodbines as often we stray,
Around us our boys and girls frolic and play;
How pleasing their sport is, the wanton ones see,
And borrow their looks from my Delia and me.

What though, on her cheeks, the rose lose its hue,
Her ease and good humour bloom all the year thro':
Time still, as he flies, adds increase to her truth,
And gives to her *mind,* what he takes from her *youth.*

Ye shepherds so gay, who make love to ensnare,
And cheat with false vows the *too-credulous fair,*
   In search of true pleasures how vainly you roam!
   To hold it for life you must find it at home.

SONG III

Tho' grandeur flies my humble roof,
   Tho' wealth is not my share,
Tho' lowly is my little cot,
   Yet happiness is there.

A tender wife with *mild controul,*
   By sympathy refin'd,
When tumults rage within my breast,
   Becalms my troubled mind.

Three pledges of our mutual love,
   Kind Providence has giv'n,
And competence to nurse their hopes,
   Is all we ask of heaven.

With arm entwin'd in arm we sit,
   And join their bands to pray:

And teach the accents of their tongue,
  To hail the God of day.

Accept, great Father of us all,
  Accept their little pray'rs;
And grant the nurslings of our youth
  May bless our silver hairs!

THE THIRD BLISS OF MATRIMONY

It increases the pleasure of defraying family expenses. "Where love is," said the great
William Penn, "*there is no task; or, if there be, the task is pleasant.*" To part with money
is oft'-times a hard task—*a bitter pill!* nothing but love can gild it completely. For want
of this charming *gold-leaf,* the pill is apt to stick by the way, and to cause wry faces. I
was lately an eye-witness to something of this sort. An old Bachelor, who, from the vulgar error that a wife is an expensive piece of furniture, kept house for himself, had cheapened a parcel of *tea* and *sugar;* nicely avoirdupoised,[14] and neatly wrapped up, they were
presented to him; alas! the painful moment is come, and he must bid adieu to his gold! I
saw the sigh of his bosom arise! while the colour fled from his pallid cheek!!—when he
smote his hand upon his pocket, his heart fail'd him, and he exclaim'd, not without a
*groan, "Ah! 'tis a sad thing to be obliged to lay out so much money on these nick-nacks!
But, yet what a plague can one do without a cup of tea for one's friends?"* With that, he
dragged up his purse into open day-light; but full as reluctantly as ever poor rogue haul'd
off his doublet to receive Moses's law from the twining cow-hide.[15]

    But, *O! wonder-working love!* to *thee* the fond husband *owes,* and gratefully will
own, that the purchase of conveniences, for his family, is one of the sweetest luxuries of
life. The happy Florio has often assured me, that the appropriation of these *good things*
to *himself* could never afford him a thousandth-part the pleasure which he derives from
purchasing them for his beloved *wife* and *children.*—"*How charmingly,*" says he, "*will
Delia appear in this, and what a look will she give me when I present it to her! and, at
sight of these, what transports will our dear little ones be thrown into! what frantic joys!
what sparking eyes! what rapturous kisses.*"—Ye poor, leafless Bachelors! Ye withered
stems of the barren fig! O! think of these things, and yet be happy. Verily, you know not
yourselves so well as he that made you; therefore, believe him when he assures, that "*It
is not good for man to be alone.*"[16]

FOURTH BLISS OF MATRIMONY

'Tis the only money-making state! At this I see a smile bright'ning on the face of the
old Bachelor.—"*Egad,*" quoth he, "*prove but that, and* I'm *your man. Many a good
day ago should I have been married, but was afraid I was not able to maintain a
wife.*"

---

[14]measured

[15]As reluctant as a criminal is to remove his jacket so that he can be whipped.

[16]God reflecting upon his creation in the Garden of Eden (Gen. 2:18).

Maintain a wife! Citizen Bachelor, you mistake the matter quite. The Creator did not send the ladies here to be your *pensioners,* but your *help-mates.* And many a family do I know, now in *easy circumstances,* that would, long ere this, have been on the parish, had it not been for the virtues of the *petticoats.*

SONG

The Husband's Fire-Side

The hearth was clean, the fire clear,
    The kettle on for tea:
And Florio, in his elbow chair,
    As blest as man could be.

Bright Delia, who his heart possessed,
    And was his new-made bride,
With head reclin'd upon his breast,
    Sat toying by his side.

Stretch'd at his feet, in happy state,
    A fav'rite dog was laid;
By whom a little sportive cat,
    In wanton humour play'd.

His Delia's hand he gently press'd;
    She stole an amorous kiss;
And blushing, modestly confess'd
    The fulness of her bliss.

Young Florio, with a heart elate,
    Thus pray'd Almighty Jove—
"O Source of Good! be this my fate,
"Just so to live and love."

And as for you, young sparks, who are pleased to think of a wife as of an *elegant play-thing,* intended only to *dress* and *dance, visit* and *spend money,* please to look at the following picture of a *good wife,* drawn by the pencil of Solomon, (with a touch or two of an American brush.) Prov. xxxi.[17]

Verse 10. Behold a virtuous woman, for her price is above rubies.

12. She riseth with the day, and prepareth breakfast for her household; yea before the sun is risen she hath her maidens at work.

13. She seeketh wool and flax, and layeth her hand willingly to the spindle, while her right hand merrily turneth the wheel.

14. She looketh well to the way of her family, and eateth not the bread of idleness.

15. She regardeth not the snow; for her household are clothed in *fearnought.*

16. By her much industry her cheeks are made ruddy like the rose of Sharon; yea,

[17]Weems substantially changes Proverbs, chapter 31 here.

her nerves are strengthened, so that when she heareth talk of the hysterics, she marvelleth thereat.

17. Her house is the habitation of neatness, so that the heart of her husband is refreshed when he entereth into her chamber.

18. She maketh fine linen and selleth it, and delivereth much cloth to the merchants.

19. Her husband is known in the gates by the fineness of his apparel, for she maketh him cloathing of silk and purple.

20. Her turkey cometh in plenteously in his season, and the fat duck, yea, also the green goose is oft-times seen self-basted at her spit.

21. Her poultry multiplyeth exceedingly in the land, even as the black-birds in the corn field for multitude; so that she feedeth her household daintily on chicken pies.

22. Her kine[18] are fat, and well favoured. They know not of the hollow horn; for while the winter is yet afar off, she provideth them an house; their rack is filled with hay; and their manger lacketh no food; hence her dairy is stored with milk, and her firkins with choice butter.

23. Her children rise up, and call her blessed; her husband also, and he praiseth her.

24. She will do him good and not evil all the days of her life.

Now, Citizen Bachelor, will you any longer talk about *maintaining* such a wife as this! And such a wife every *good girl* in America will make, if married to the *lad* of her heart.

Yes, she will do him good—What will not a generous woman do for the husband of her love! Did not queen Eleanor, when her husband (king Edward) was pierced with a poisoned arrow, instantly apply her sweet lips to the ghastly wound, and extract the venom at the loss of her own precious life? Blest saint! thy shining is now in heaven, and thy place *far above all nuns.*

Did not Mrs. Ackland (the wife of a British major, last war) leave her dearest relations, to cross the stormy seas, following her husband to America, the scene of war and blood, that she might see his face, and share his dangers? Dear unhappy woman! what were your agonies, when, arriving near Saratogo, you saw your husband's regiment holding unequal fight with Morgan, sinking fast under the dreadful fire of his riflemen! The sad remains of his slaughtered troops returned: but he returned not.

She flew to the fatal field. She found him low, weltering in blood; with a feeble cry she sunk on his face; his eyes swam in tears; but his voice was not heard. The warriors of Columbia wept around. The rifles fell from their hands. Enmity was no more: and nature, dear common mother, smiling through tears, enjoyed the generous sorrows of her sons. They bore the bleeding hero to their own hospital. There she attended him day and night, till she could convey him to New-York, where she sunk under a consumption, brought on by so much anxiety and fatigue.

O what will not generous woman do for the husband of her love! she will enrich him, not only by her own *industry* and *management,* the natural fruits of her love, but also by those excellent habits of Industry and Frugality which she forms in him.

He will be far more industrious, because he is working for the dear woman he loves; and love, we know makes light work.

---

[18]cows

Who has not heard of Mr. Goodridge, (Portsmouth, Virginia) or what sea has not been ploughed by his numerous keels? and yet Mr. Goodridge owed it all, (under heaven) to a *good wife.* While a bachelor, he worked hard and made money; but it was all soon squandered on frolicking and grog. At twenty-two he married a girl, poor in wealth, but rich in *love, industry* and *health.* For the sake of her he instantly quitted his old tipling companions and prodigality.—He possessed in the world but one negro man and a flat (a large open boat) in which he coasted it along up James river to the mouth of Nansemond, 14 miles, for oyster-shells to Portsmouth and Norfolk. Happy as a prince, when he was returning with his load, to see his dear girl. In a couple of years he picked up money enough to buy just such another boat and a slave for his wife. See them now in their two little boats (dearer far in the sight of God, than any two first rate men of war) holding their loving course up the river for their humble freight. After carrying on their oyster-shell trade for some years with great success, they purchased a *little shop,* afterwards a *store,* and in about thirty years, they had as many as fifteen sail of vessels at sea!

And as to that great fortune-making virtue, *frugality,* the good Lord have mercy on the Bachelors! for there is not one in ten of them who has so good a notion of it as a *monkey;* for thrifty Jacko will put away the balance of any good *nugs* that he happens to fall in with; but, among young Bachelors, the eternal cry is, *Who will show us any fun? Hurra,* for the *horse-race,* the *cock-fight,* the *billiard-table,* or the *bagmo.* Dash go the dollars! the hard scrapings, and tight savings of a poor old father's life.

> Glorious youth! the sharper cries,
> Glorious youth! the w——e replies.

But, (Lord, what is man without a wife!) this *glorious* youth is soon seen sneeking along with the sheriff; his creditors fasten upon him, and pick him to the bone. Choused[19] out of his estate, and ashamed to lift up his booby face, he stalks among his *rich relations,* on whom he has the honour to be billetted for life. This is the end of many *a green-horn,* who runs into bad company and ruin, for want of a beloved wife, to make his home and plough a pleasure to him.

But see Florio, married to the charming woman he loves, is under no temptation to go abroad into expensive and dangerous amusements. His home is his *Paradise;* he never leaves it but with *regret,* he returns to it with joy. His Delia, and his sweet little prattlers constitute his circle of happiness. For their sakes, he applies, with double pleasure, to business; shuns all unnecessary expense; studies every decent art of economy, and is getting rich very fast.

SONG

> The man who, for life, is blest with a wife,
>   Is, sure, in a happy condition;
> Go things as they will, she's fond of him still;
>   She's *comforter, friend and physician.*
>
> Pray where is the joy, to trifle and toy?
>   Yet dread *some disaster* from beauty!

---

[19]cheated

But sweet is the bliss of a conjugal kiss,
   Where love mingles pleasure with duty.

One extravagant Miss, won't cost a man less
   Than twenty good wives that are saving:
For, wives they will spare, that their children may share,
   But Misses forever are craving.

A good old gentleman, a *Friend,* driving along one morning through a certain street in Philadelphia, saw his son sneaking out of a *brothel!* Young Hopeful, having a quick eye, caught the venerable form of his father, and instantly slunk back, confused. The old gentleman order'd his coachman to stop at the door, and call'd out, "*Isaac! My son! My son! Never, while thee lives, be asham'd to come out of a bawdy-house; but, forever be asham'd to go into one.*"

Ah! my friend, an ounce of *prevention* is better than a pound of *cure.* Had thee, like Abraham of old, but sought out for thy son some lovely *Rebekah,*[20] some *sweet loving wife,* to comfort the young man, there would have been no need to chase him out of a *bawdy-house.* But, alas! "*The love of money is the root of all evil; which, while some covet for their children, they suffer them to err from the path of innocence, and to pierce them through with many sorrows.*" Paul.[21]

HINT TO PARENTS

"*Neighbour Franklin,*" said a gentleman of Philadelphia to the old Doctor, "*I have made, to-day, a run of excellent small beer; can thee tell me how to preserve it; for my poor neighbours, some of them are rather too fond of my small-beer?*" "*Why,*" replied the Doctor, "*I believe there's nothing like clapping a pipe of good wine along side of it.*"

That youth can hardly be one of the *elect,* who can leave the *pure nectar* of a dear wife's embraces, for the accursed cup of a harlot's arms.

FIFTH BLISS OF MATRIMONY

It excites the noblest virtues. The man who truly loves his wife, desires, above all things, to be beloved by her. This tender sentiment has contributed wonderfully to polish and exalt human nature. What charming manners! what amiable dispositions! what heroic virtues! what divine characters have not generous husbands assumed and cultivated, to make themselves more worthy of their beloved consorts, and to give them the pleasure to hear their praises!

SONG

Love Likes to Imitate

I have found out a gift for my fair,
   I have found where the wood-pigeons breed;

---

[20]Abraham's son, Isaac, married the lovely virgin Rebekah (Gen. 24).

[21]Another biblical paraphrase by Weems (1 Tim. 6:10).

But let me that plunder forbear,
　　She will say— "'*twas a barbarous deed!*

"*For he ne'er could be true,*" she averr'd,
　　'*Who could rob a poor bird of its young;*"
And I lov'd her the more, when I hear'd
　　Such *tenderness* fall from her tongue.

I have heard her with sweetness unfold,
　　How that pity was due to a dove;
That it ever attended the bold,
　　And she call'd it the sister of love.

But her voice such a pleasure conveys,
　　So much I her accents adore,
That whatever of *goodness* she says,
　　Methinks I still *love her the more.*

When that great man, Epaminondas,[22] was asked which had been the happiest days of his life, he replied, "the day on which I obtained that victory over the enemies of my country, and remembered that my *wife* was *alive* to *hear the news.*"

Yes, a fond husband has an infinite advantage over the old Bachelor, a tenfold animation to every thing great and good. He anticipates the raptures of his beloved family on hearing of his noble actions, and the high respect which a grateful public will pay them for his sake. And, on the other hand, the very thought of a base action startles him; its dreadful effects on his wife and children! He sees them *drowned in tears,* hanging their heads, and ashamed to go into company forever after. Accurst idea! No; if it be the will of all-wise Heaven, that my children be poor, let them inherit an *honest* poverty, and let their little cottage be cheered with the sweet beams of innocence.

SIXTH BLISS OF MATRIMONY

It preserves youth from the harlot's clutches. 'Tis heaven's decree that the race of man shall be kept alive by the union of the two sexes. To render that union certain, he cropt a twig of *love* from the tree of life, and planted it in the human bosom. This sweet passion, wisely directed, (to wedlock) is a source of the purest satisfaction; but degenerating into brutish lust, it hurries poor deluded youth into dangers, and evils, the very thought of which is enough to make a parent tremble. Alas! poor Eugenio! Eugenio was the handsomest young bachelor, Carolina ever boasted; his fortune a clear 10,000*l.* and his education liberal. In the full-bloom of twenty-three, he went out to London to complete his studies of the law. At the play-house he was ensnared by the fatal charms of a beautiful harlot, in whose distempered arms he met destruction. Bitter were his lamentations, when he found that no medicines could cure, and that all his own, and the fond hopes of his friends were blasted forever. He returned a mere skeleton to Carolina, and there died

---

[22]Epaminondas (410–362 B.C.) was a leader who tirelessly worked to position Thebes above Sparta as the dominant power in ancient Greece.

in the arms of his broken-hearted parents. Thus short was the life, thus miserable the end of one who was entitled to match with any of the finest women in all America.

> Once, from my window as I cast mine eye
> On those that pass, in giddy numbers by,
> A youth among the foolish youths I spy'd,
> Who took not sacred wisdom for his guide:
> Just as the sun withdrew his radiant light,
> And evening soft led on the shades of night,
> He stole, in covert twilight, to his fate
> And pass'd the corner near the harlot's gate;
> When lo! she comes! and in such glaring dress,
> As fitly did the harlot's mind express.
> The youths he seiz'd, and laying quite aside,
> Blest Modesty, the female's justest pride,
> *"I come this moment just to meet my dear,*
> *"And lo! in happy hour, I meet thee here."*
> Upon her tongue did such smooth mischief dwell,
> And from her lips such welcome flattery fell,
> Th' unguarded youth, in silken fetters ty'd,
> Resign'd his sense, and *swift to ruin hied!*
> Not so the man to whom indulgent heaven,
> That tender bosom friend, a wife has given.
> Him, blest in her chaste arms, no fears dismay,
> No secret checks of guilt his joys allay;
> No sad disease, nor false embrace is here,
> His joys are safe, his raptures all sincere.
> Then O! my sons, attend! attend may they,
> Whom youthful vigour would to sin betray!
> Dare to be wise! haste—wed the blooming bride,
> In sense and truth her lovely sex's pride.
> Her tender love can best thy soul secure,
> And turn thy footsteps from the harlot's door;
> Who, with curs'd charms, lures the unwary in,
> And soothes, with flattery, their souls to sin;
> Lest you, too late, of her fell pow'r complain,
> And fall where thousands mightier have been slain.

SEVENTH BLISS OF MATRIMONY

It preserves youth from black eyes and broken heads. If lust has slain its thousands of inconsiderate bachelors, anger has slain its tens of thousands. Against this too, an amiable wife is one of the best of antidotes. *Our sex* is hard and unloving, too fond of quarrelling and throat-cutting. Lovely woman was given to soothe and to soften; and, verily, the young man who walks without one of these charming guards, *walks in jeopardy every hour.* Draco is a young Bachelor. For amusement-sake he often strolls to a tavern, whither he carries with him the ill-temper he got from nature, increased by long habits of tyrannizing over little negro slaves. He soon falls in with young men as self-will'd and passionate as himself. Contradictions lead the van! contentions follow! abuse succeeds contention! and blows, black eyes, and broken heads bring up the rear.

> Great God! on what a slender thread
>> Hangs man without a wife!
> Untimely oft by *lust or hate.*
>> He ends his wretched life!

> Dangers stand thick through all the ground,
>> To raise the Bach'lor's tomb;
> And fiercest passions wait around,
>> To drive the sinner home.

It was once hoped that the religion of *love* founded by Christ, would have preserved our young Bachelors from these hateful passions; but that religion has rather lost ground among people of *weak heads.* Such, however, still have hearts; and all hearts are within reach of the *ladies.* Their sweet looks and gentle manners may yet recover them to humanity. How often have we seen, that when a company of wrangling Bachelor-politicians had worked themselves up into redness and rage, threatening battle royal, the sudden entrance of a fine girl has instantly called them to order, and made the old heroes look as sweet and smiling as so many bride-grooms. Now, gracious heaven! if a single glance from lovely woman can thus turn *passion* into *peace, fury,* into *friendship,* what may not be expected from the happy man who is married to one of these all-refining charmers? This is Florio's case. Married to Delia, the gentlest of her sex, his temper sweetened and his manners polished, by his passion for her, he gradually, as is the *nature* of love, falls into an imitation of those gentle virtues he so highly admires in her. These graces, thus naturally learned from her, he carries with him into the circle of his acquaintance, where they make him dear to every body. Hence, when he takes leave of Delia in the morning to go into company, her tender bosom is not alarmed with fears that he may come home at night with a black eye or broken head, or be brought in a corpse, murdered in some bloody fray. No, No; thank God, she knows that he is safe; she knows that he loves and is beloved by every body. 'Tis to this amiable wife that Florio is indebted for much of his engaging manners. *She* taught him

> "To feel the generous passion rise,
> "Grow *good by loving, mild by sighs.*"

EIGHTH BLISS OF MATRIMONY

It preserves a young man from that worse than hellish practice, duelling.
  "The single state," says Dr. Johnson,[23] "has no joys." *No wonder* then so many young

---

[23]Dr. Samuel Johnson (1709–1784) was a biographer, essayist, poet, and lexicographer. He is commonly considered one of the great literary figures of eighteenth-century England.

fools with hot livers and fiery bloods, are in such a passion to be quit of it. But the case is very different with him whose *life* is *happy,* and who has such strong ties (a dear wife and children) to attach him to it. "I have often wondered," said Florio, "how a married man can ever be tempted to fight a duel. When I am sitting with Delia, surrounded by my *romping laughing* little ones, those precious parts and members of myself, who hang on me not only for the tenderest joys of life, but for bread and protection, I feel my life so inestimably valuable, that to sport with it and risk it in a duel, appears to me to be the most horrid crime that I could possibly commit. If I am but slightly indisposed, Delia is wretched; were I in a duel to get shot through the head, and to be left on the field weltering in blood, is there a tongue on earth, that could tell her the tidings! And what would become of my poor deserted orphans? Who, like their *parent,* would press them to his bosom, dry up their tears, bear with their infirmities, supply their wants, and thus lead them through the paths of virtue here, to endless happiness hereafter."

O blessed matrimony, of *Prudence* and *Love!* What tongue can tell thy benefits to *Man?* Instituted of God in Paradise, honoured of Christ by his first miracle; you still convert the desert into an Eden, the commonest water into the richest wine. Reuniting man to his other *half,* you restore him to his *natural,* his *dearest* friend. Calling him from the deadly haunts of harlots, gamblers and duelists, you lead him into the peaceful circle of his beloved wife and children; there you harmonize his passions, sweeten his temper, and, by inspiring him with the love of innocence and of virtue, you give him to taste the purest felicities of this life, and prepare him to drink of those rivers of love and joy which flow at God's right hand for ever more.

O generous parents! natural guardians of your children! Encourage them to marry; to marry early. 'Tis the voice of *all wisdom, human* and *divine.*

What says God himself? "*'Tis not good for man to be alone.*" Then least of all for a *young* man.

What says Solomon? "*My son, rejoice with the wife of thy youth, and let her be as the loving fawn and pleasant roe; let her breasts satisfy thee at all times, and be always ravished with her love; for why, my son, wilt thou embrace the bosom of a harlot, whose way is the way of hell, going down by the chambers of death.*"[24]

And what says the American Solomon? "*Early marriages are the best; they settle young men and keep them out of bad company and connections, which too often prove their ruin, both in mind, body and estate.*"

And if after *Solomon* and *Franklin,* we dare mention Common Sense, what says *Common Sense?* Why, *Early Marriages are best.* They *fix,* on youth, the *virgin passions,* which if suffered to wander from *beauty* to *beauty,* contract at length such a *taste* for *variety,* that though married at last to the most elegant woman on earth, she would find her arms deserted for those of a cook-wench!!!

With this great view then, (early marriage) for sweet heaven's sake let us cease to educate our children as *fine Ladies* and *Gentleman,* when we have *nothing to give them!* This most unfortunate practice has strangled more matches, and propagated more vice and misery than any other. By bringing up your son to be ashamed of work—to scorn it as fit for none but negroes—to affect the *airs,* company and pleasures of the great, when

---

[24]Another biblical paraphrase by Weems (Prov. 5:18f).

you can't perhaps give him 500*l.* on earth, you are doing him the *greatest* of all possible injuries. You cut him off from the happiness of marrying the woman he loves, though bright and good as an angel, if *she have not money.* And you set him upon all the crimes and curses of courting, cringing and lying to the woman *he loves not,* just for the sake of her land and negroes; and after trotting him up and down the country with a negro-fellow and portmanteau[25] at his tail, courting every rich old body he can hear of—knocking about like a shuttle-cock, backwards and forwards from widow to maid and from maid to widow—Now, by a smile vaulted up to the highest ceiling of hope; then, by a frown, tumbled on the hard floor of despondence: to-day, blest as an angel, in full prospect of marrying a *fine fortune*—to-morrow, curst as a demon, at seeing his girl and guineas borne off by a hated rival. Thus after running the gauntlet, between *sour-looking fathers, bridling mothers,* and *haughty jilting daughters,* for ten or fifteen years perhaps, the poor wretch is further from a fortune than he was at first. Nay, grey, wrinkled, and ugly—over head and ears in debt—dunned by creditors—depressed in spirits—hail fellow well met with gamblers, pick-pockets, highwaymen, horse thieves and duellists, he takes refuge in hard drinking, turns desperate, and from extremity of wretchedness, blow out his brains, or compels justice to hang him up like a dead dog despised!!

O for God's sake, and as you prize your son's happiness, train him up by times to habits of industry, and give him a *good profession,* or *trade.* This will soon put him in the way to maintain a family. By the time he is twenty-one, his Creator kindly prepares for him a help-mate, and invites him to the happy union by the sweet whispers of love. He sees the charming maid—"Grace in all her steps, heaven in her eye, in every gesture dignity and charm." He feels a joy unfelt before. Eagerly inquiring after the lovely stranger, every tongue celebrates her virtues—her *industry,* her *modesty,* her *sweetness of temper,* her *prudence,* her *admirable attention* to her *parents,* her *brothers* and *sisters!* He is in raptures. She also has heard him extolled as a dutiful son, a tender brother, and an industrious, honourable young man. Trembling he tells her his passion—In her enchanting blushes he reads his happy destiny—She consents to make him blest. In the full bloom of *twenty-one,* with a mind pure as unsun'd snow, chaste and delicate as an angel, he clasps the yielding maid. Love and conscious innocence exalt their joys to raptures! And while the fortune-hunter is anxiously trotting up and down, to and fro in the earth, like another poor d—l seeking what wealthy maid or widow he may devour, our Florio and his Delia, like Milton's happy pair, *"emparadis'd in each other's arms, enjoy their fill of bliss on bliss."* They too, by *waiting,* might have married some good rich old bodies, with negroes, land and chariots, to make a noise in the world; but what's the world to them, its pomps, its vanities, and its nonsense all, who in each other clasp every virtue that can ensure competence and bliss? They feel the generous wish to surround each other's *dearer self,* with all this life's comforts; to *these, love* gives the flavour of *dainties.* They *feel, "that better is a dinner of herbs where love is, than stall-fed beef, and hatred there-with."*[26]

---

[25]porter
[26]Prov. 15:17.

FLORIO'S SONG

When first this humble roof I knew,
    With various cares I strove,
My grain was scarce, my sheep were few,
    My all of life was love.

By mutual toil our board was dress'd,
    The spring our drink bestow'd,
But when her lip the brim had press'd,
    The *cup with nectar flow'd!*

Sweet love and peace this dwelling shar'd,
    No other guest came nigh;
In *them* was given, tho' gold was spar'd,
    What gold could *never buy.*

No value has the splendid lot,
    But as the mean to prove,
That from the palace to the set,
    The all of life is love.

But, says the fortune-hunting Bachelor, "Is not a full cradle and an empty cup-board a great evil?" True; but none but a great sluggard and drunkard need ever have that evil to complain of. "Well, but (quoth he again) is not the education of children confoundedly expensive and heavy on a poor fellow? yes, if that poor fellow chooses to play the *fool* and *miseducate* them. If he choose his daughter to spend her time in reading novels, lying a-bed, mimicking the fashions, trailing her silks, and playing the *fine lady,* he'll find her expensive enough, aye, and *long* enough too, I'll warrant. And if he is for bringing up his son for a *fine gentleman,* dressing like a jay, cantering away to horse-races, betting on odd tricks, drinking and blustering at taverns, he'll find him abundantly expensive; and after all his toil and trouble to maintain this fine young gentleman of a son, he must be constantly getting between him and the sheriff, giving bail of some sort or other. Children thus educated are the heaviest cross, cost, and curse of a man's life. But, "my children," says Florio, "are my *wealth.* My love for them and their dear mother, called forth that industry and economy which first gave me property, and now they improve it. My daughters scorn to be gaping after the vain fashions and finery of the ambitious rich, but find their happiness in their gratitude to heaven, their industry, innocence, and mutual love. They affect not the trifling part of *fine ladies,* but the high character of *useful women.* Their dear fingers milk our cows, make our butter, spin and weave our apparel, prepare our food, beautify our house with flowers, and render us a thousand important services: while our *sons,* one of them manages our farm, another superintends our mill, and the third keeps our *store. Love* sweetens their service—*parental affection* enhances its value, and their tenderness and fidelity afford us perpetual delight." Happy parents who have such *dear children* to *govern!* Happy children who have *such parents to obey!* "*Good children are a treasure from the Lord—blessed is the man whose quiver is full of them.*"[27]

Dear Bachelors, as it fared with the ingenious general Hamilton,[28] who found after writing *volumes* on the *blessings of government,* that, the more he wrote, the more he might, even so, (if I may compare little men with great) it fares with *me* writing on the *felicities* of the *married state.* I have written already, I think, a full *quantum sufficit*[29] to satisfy any reasonable Bachelor among you, that the married life is, of *all lives,* the most happy; and a good wife, of all *goods,* the most precious. I have shown, that "*her price is far above rubies,*" insomuch that, *without* her, Adam, though in Paradise, could not be happy. I have shown that she is so *truly* a part of man (*bone* of his *bone,* and flesh of *his* flesh) that separated from her, man is but like "*an odd volume of a set of books,*" a mere thing of *vexation;* or, "*like the half of an old pair of shears,*" hardly worth laying by "*to scrape a trencher.*" In fact, I have shown that a good wife is "Heaven's *last best* gift *to man*"—his *angel and minister of graces* innumerable—his *Sal Polycrestum* or *gem* of many virtues—his *Pandora,* or casket of celestial jewels—that her *presence* forms his best company—her *voice,* his sweetest music—her *smiles,* his brightest day—her *kiss,* the guardian of his innocence—her *arms,* the pale of his safety, the balm of his health, the balsam of his life—her *industry,* his surest wealth—her *economy,* his safest steward—her *lips,* his faithfullest counsellors—her *bosom,* the softest pillow of his cares—and her *prayers,* the able advocates of heaven's blessings on his head. My willing pen has, for an hour past, been pouring these delightful truths over the preceding pages; and yet, on looking back upon the subject, I feel pretty nearly, I suppose, as the benevolent Latrobe feels, when, on looking over blue winding Schuylkill, he rejoices that he has yet in store such a fair Jordan of purifying waters for the yellow fever. Such, dear gentlemen, and greater also, is my joy, when after all the effusions of my pen on the subject, I look back and see what a noble tide of arguments in favour of *conjugal bliss,* I have yet to pour down upon you, to wash out the leprous stains of old Bachelorism; and extinguish, if *possible,* the pestilence of celibacy. Yes, I have yet to run out upon you, (I mean only the *stiff-necked* and *unbelieving*) another and a *heavier* tier of *obligations* to marry—Obligations founded on the mighty base of *goods, national, universal,* and *eternal.* I have yet to show you, that if you love the *Creator,* you ought to *marry,* to make his creatures *happy*—that if you love *mankind,* you ought to *marry,* to perpetuate the glorious *race*—that if you love your *country,* you ought to *marry,* to raise up soldiers to defend it—in fine, that if you wish well to *earth* or to *heaven,* you ought to marry, to give good citizens to the one, and glorious angels to the other.

Now, citizen Bachelor, if to render such *important services,* "*the prophet had bid thee to do some great thing, oughtest thou not cheerfully to have done it? how much more then when he saith unto thee—marry!*" *Marry* that *dear creature* whom God took out thy side, the *warm region* of the heart, to be thy heart's comfort, and thy life's companion—

---

[27]Another biblical paraphrase by Weems (Ps. 127:5).

[28]Alexander Hamilton (1755–1804) was both a soldier during the American Revolution and a noted political theorist after it. He was a champion of a strong, centralized government.

[29]A sufficient amount.

Marry *friendship, love, youth, beauty, tenderness, truth, health, wealth, innocence* and *happiness, individual* and *national; temporal* and *eternal.*

To these *sweet persuasives* to wedlock, dear Bachelors, I could add many others of a rougher aspect; I could tell you what the great legislators of all nations have thought of *old Bachelors,* and how cheap they have held them; I could tell you what *broad hints* of disapprobation were shown them by those mighty republicans, the *Greeks* and *Romans;* how they were jeered and jested, taxed and tormented; how (degraded to *wood-cutters* and *water-pumpers,* to *scavengers* and *watchmen,*) they were obliged to cleanse the streets, and bawl the time of night! while the justly *privileged* and happy *married men,* fondly clasp'd in beauty's arms, were spending the downy hours in sweet connubial bliss; but I *spare* you! May the words which you have at this time read with your *outward* eyes, make such an impression on your *inmost* feelings, that you may, soon as convenient, renounce the sorrows and insignificance of celibacy, and assume the *dignity,* the *usefulness,* and *joy* of the married state! *Then,* and not till then, shall you find the true relish of your *fatted calf;* your water shall be turned into wine; the throbbings of your bosoms shall be quieted; and, happier than the penitents of old, you shall have rejoicings over you, not in *Heaven* only, but also on the *earth.*

SONG

I am marry'd, and happy. With wonder hear this,
   Ye rovers and rakes of the age;
Who laugh at the mention of conjugal bliss,
   And whom only loose pleasures engage.

You may laugh; but believe me you're all in the wrong
   When you merrily marriage deride;
For to marriage the permanent pleasures belong,
   And to them we can only confide.

The joys which from lawless connections arise,
   Are fugitive—never sincere—
Oft stolen with haste—or snatch'd by surprise—
   Interrupted by doubt and by fear.

But those which in legal attachments we find,
   When the heart is with *innocence pure,*
Are from ev'ry embitt'ring reflection refin'd
   And to life's latest hour will endure.

The love which ye boast of, deserves not that name:
   True love is with sentiment join'd;
But yours is a *passion*—a feverish flame—
   Rais'd without the consent of the mind.

When, chastity shamming, *ye mistresses* hire,
   With this and with that ye are cloy'd;
Ye are led, and misled, by a flatt'ring false fire;
   And are oft, by that fire destroy'd.

If you ask me, from whence my felicity flows?
    My answer is short—*from a wife;*
Whom for *cheerfulness, sense,* and *good nature* I chose,
    Which are beauties that charm us for life.

To make home the seat of *perpetual delight,*
    Ev'ry hour *each* studies to seize,
And we find ourselves happy from morning to night,
    By—*our mutual endeavours to please!*

SONG (BY DR. DODDRIDGE)[30]

When on thy bosom I recline,
Enraptur'd still to call thee mine,
    To call thee mine for life,
I glory in those sacred ties,
Which *modern* rakes and fools despise,
    Of husband and of wife.

One mutual flame inspires our bliss:
The melting look, th' extatic kiss,
    E'en years have not destroy'd:
Some sweet sensation, ever new,
Springs up, and proves the maxim true,
    That love can ne'er be cloy'd.

Have I a wish—'tis all for thee;
Hast thou a wish—'tis all for me;
    So sweet our moments move,
That angels look with ardent gaze,
Well pleas'd to see our happy days,
    And bid us live and love.

If cares arise—and cares will come—
Thy bosom is my softest home,
    I lull me there to rest;
And is there aught disturbs my fair,
I bid her sigh out all her care,
    And lose it in my breast.

Wishing you every felicity that *lovely* wives and beauteous babes can afford to gentlemen of *sensibility* and *patriotism,* I remain, dear Bachelors,
                                                    Your very sincere *friend,*
                                                    M. L. Weems.

---

[30]Philip Doddrige (1701–1751) was a famous American Christian hymn writer.

2

American Tract Society
(1825–Present)

WITH THE DISESTABLISHMENT of religion in the early nineteenth century, American Protestants began to turn to a number of benevolent societies in order to help ensure the virtue and Christian character of the nation. Many of these societies were involved in publishing. Organizations such as the American Bible Society (1816), the American Sunday School Union (1824), and American Tract Society (1825) spearheaded a print revolution in the United States as they used the latest publishing technology to flood the nation with Christian literature.

By the late 1820s, the American Tract Society was distributing five million pages of printed material annually, making its material among the most widely circulated and familiar literature of the antebellum period. The majority of tracts from the Society were four to sixteen pages in length, but the Society also printed longer works such as editions of the New Testament, Richard Baxter's *Call to the Unconverted,* and annual releases of its immensely popular *Christian Almanac.* The Society used a vast system of volunteers and colporteurs—paid traveling agents—to distribute its literature.

The first article of the American Tract Society's Constitution stated that the society's goal was "to diffuse a knowledge of our Lord Jesus Christ as the redeemer of sinners, and to promote the interests of vital godliness and sound morality, by the circulation of Religious Tracts, calculated to receive the approbation of all Evangelical Christians." In order to obtain this Evangelical approbation, the Society attempted to avoid all sectarianism, whether it be theological or political. For example, before the Civil War the Society took pains to avoid publishing inflammatory literature on slavery. The Society constantly worked to produce material that would encourage the participation of the broadest possible Protestant coalition. Thus, while much of its material came from British authors, the literature of the American Tract Society offers a revealing look into the mainstream intellectual currents of nineteenth-century American Protestantism. And although in its early years it stood against the novel, the millions of moral tales it distributed in tract form helped set the stage for the popularity of religious fiction in the United States.

TRACT NO. 92
THE FORGIVING AFRICAN
An Authentic Narrative

Journeying on business through the western part of the state of New-York, in the summer of 1816, I stopped at an inn on Saturday evening, in a thinly settled part of the country, and put up for the Sabbath. Upon inquiry, I was informed that there was no place of public worship within a number of miles. The thought of spending the Lord's day in such a situation spread a gloom over my mind. But how often is God better to us than our fears! Being weary with my journey, and having committed myself to the Keeper of Israel, I retired to rest, under an affecting sense of the goodness of God. The morning dawned upon me in a composed frame of spirit; and every thing seemed to conspire to produce in me wonder, adoration, and love. As I cast my eyes over the rich scenery of nature's works, I could not but exclaim, raising my thoughts to the Maker of them all, These "thus wondrous fair, Thyself how wondrous then!" The day did not pass without some lively tokens of the divine presence. The pages of the written word were open before me, and I was enabled to see the beauty of its doctrines, and to taste the sweetness of its promises.

Towards the close of the day, being disturbed by the noisy and profane conversation of some persons who had called at the inn, I "went out in the field to meditate at eventide." I directed my steps towards the wood, in a path which led through beautiful fields richly laden with the bounties of Providence. I had but just penetrated the border of the forest, when the sound of a voice fell upon my ear. I paused; the tone seemed to be that of supplication. Approaching the place whence it proceeded, I perceived, beside a large oak, a negro woman, apparently advanced in life, upon her knees, with her hands clasped together, and her eyes steadfastly fixed upon heaven. I listened, and was struck with astonishment, to hear one of the sable daughters of Ethiopia, in the most importunate manner, raising her prayer to God. Never before did I witness such simplicity, such fervor, such engagedness. Like a true daughter of Jacob, she seemed to have power with the Angel of God. That part of her prayer which I distinctly heard, was confined to herself and her master.

"O Lord, bless my master. When he calls upon thee to damn his soul, do not hear him, do not hear him, but hear me—save him—make him know he is wicked, and he will pray to thee. I am afraid, O Lord, I have wished him bad wishes in my heart—keep me from wishing him bad—though he whips me and beats me sore, tell me of my sins, and make me pray more to thee—make me more glad for what thou hast done for me, a poor negro."

As she arose from her kneeling posture, her eye glanced upon me. Ingenuous confusion overspread her countenance on being thus discovered. She was preparing hastily to retreat, when I called to her in a mild tone, bade her not to be alarmed, and told her I was pleased to find her so well employed. Encouraged by the mildness of my address, she came towards me. I inquired into her situation and circumstances, and she seemed very happy of the opportunity of making them known. I asked her why she came to this place to pray? She answered that her master was a very wicked man, and would not, if he knew it, allow her to pray at all. The reason of her coming there at this time to pray, was, that her master had been beating her that day, and she was afraid she had not felt right towards him, and that she had done wrong also by not submitting with more resignation to her unhappy lot. I asked her how she came to think it was her duty to pray? She said she had once heard a woman pray in a barn—that the woman prayed for the whole world—said they were all sinners, and going the road to hell—and that after she heard this woman's prayer, she thought it was her duty to pray too. But for a long time she felt that she was so bad that she could not pray. After a while she found that she could pray, and that she loved to pray. It seemed to do her good, she said, after her master had been beating her, to go away into the fields or woods and pray to the Lord. I found she had never enjoyed the means of any kind of instruction—she could not read—had never heard a sermon, nor been to a place of worship. Nor had she ever communicated her feelings to any person before. She was once surprised and detected by her mistress at prayer, who coming to call her in haste one morning, found her on her knees, and withdrew.

I inquired of her whether there were no religious people in the place. She mentioned as the only one, the woman before spoken of, whom she had heard pray a number of times; but she had never conversed with her. I then told her that there were many people in the world who had similar sentiments with her's respecting God and prayer. Her eyes sparkled on hearing this intelligence; she listened with eagerness while I entered into some particulars respecting the new birth and the way of salvation through a crucified Redeemer. The truths of the Gospel were to her as cold water to a thirsty soul. Her countenance, now glowing with wonder, now suffused with tears, now lighted up with joy, is still present to my imagination. She appeared very anxious to be instructed herself: but this was not all: she entreated me to go and converse and pray with her master; and to pray for him when alone. When I was about leaving her, never expecting to see her again in this world, I exhorted her to continue in the exercise of a submissive and forgiving spirit towards her master, and to commit herself into the hands of Him who judgeth righteously; encouraging her with the prospect of a speedy release from all her sufferings, and that, in due season, if she persevered in well doing, she would, through grace, reap a rich reward in the kingdom of glory.

Never was I so fully convinced that the religion of Christ consists very much in *the spirit of love and forgiveness.* The native pride of the human heart is quick-sighted in discerning ill treatment: violent and unrelenting in its resentments. Too many, alas! even of those who bear the Christian name, and profess an assured hope of pardon from their final Judge, know not how to forget or forgive an offence of a fellow worm. Such a professor may appear to be planted in the vineyard of the Lord; but his fruits are the grapes of Sodom and the clusters of Gomorrah.

This poor woman, often cruelly treated by the hands of an unkind and unfeeling master, showed nothing like anger or revenge. While smarting under the wounds inflicted by his cruelty, she would retire beyond the sight and hearing of mortals, to pray for his welfare. When speaking of the conduct of her master, she did not dwell upon his faults with seeming pleasure and delight. The ingenuousness of her love and compassion manifested itself in a very different manner. Her love to God showed itself in secret, persevering, and importunate prayer for her master; in earnestly requesting me to go and converse and pray with him; and in entreating me, with a countenance visibly marked with sincerity and love, to pray for him when I was alone. Nothing did she appear to desire more than her master's eternal welfare. Such a spirit as this must be religion; it is the very spirit of Christ; and if so, nothing short of such a temper can be religion. It is an easy thing to talk and pray—words are light and airy things—but to love our enemy, to do all in our power to promote his present and future wellbeing—this requires grace indeed.

Reader, have you from the heart forgiven all who have injured you? If not, can you hope God will forgive you? Think of your offences against him, in thought, in word, and conduct. Think of the love of Christ in dying for his enemies, that all who believe in him may be saved. Go to him, confessing your sins and trusting in his mercy. Henceforward let love to God and love to man reign in your heart, that, when weighted in the balance of eternal truth, you may not be found wanting the meek and holy temper of this poor slave.

TRACK NO. 128
POOR SARAH
Or, The Indian Woman

It was a comfortless morning in the month of March, 1814, when I first became acquainted with Poor Sarah. She called to solicit a few crusts, saying that she "desired nothing but crums—they were enough for her poor old body, just ready to crumble into dust." I had heard of *Sarah*, a pious Indian woman, and was therefore prepared to receive her with kindness. Remembering the words of my Lord, "Inasmuch as ye have done it unto one of the *least* of these my brethren, ye have done it unto me,"[1] I was ready to impart to her a portion of the little which I had, and regretted that I had no more to give. "And how," I said to her, "have you managed, this long cold winter?" "O Misse," she replied, "God better to Sarah than she fear. When winter come on Sarah was in great doubt: no husband, no child here but——, she wicked, gone a great deal. What if great snow come? what if fire go out? my neighbor great way off: what if sick all alone? what if die? nobody know it. While I think so in my heart, then I cry: while crying, something speak in my mind, and say, Trust in God, Sarah; he love his people, he never leave them, he never forsake them; he never forsake Sarah: he is friend indeed; go tell Jesus, Sarah, he love to hear prayer, he often hear Sarah when she pray. So I wipe my eyes, don't cry any more; go out in the bushes where nobody see, fall down on my old knees and pray. God give me great many words; I pray a great while. God make all my mind peace. When I get up I go in the house, but can't stop praying in my mind. All my heart burn

---

[1] Matt. 25:40.

with love to God; willing to live cold, go hungry, be sick, die all alone, if God be there. He know best; Sarah don't know. So I feel happy, and great many days go singing the good hymn:

> 'Now I can trust the Lord for ever;
> 'He can clothe, and he can feed;
> 'He my rock, and he my Savior,
> 'Jesus is a friend indeed.' "

"Well, Sarah, have you been comfortably supplied?" "O yes," she replied, "I never out corn meal once all winter." "But how do you cook it, Sarah, so as to make it comfortable food?" "Oh, I make porridge, Misse; sometimes I get out, like to-day, and I go get some crusts of bread and some salt to put into it; then it is so nourishing to this poor old body; but when I can get none, then I make it good as I can, and kneel down, pray God to bless it to me; and I feel as if God feed me, and be so happy here"—(laying her hand on her heart.) Oh, what a lesson, thought I, for my repining heart. "But do you have no meat, or other necessaries, Sarah?" "Not often, Misse: sometimes I get so hungry for it I begin to feel wicked, then think how Jesus hungry in the desert. But when Satan tempt him to sin to get food, he would not. So I say, Sarah won't sin to get victuals. I no steal, no eat stolen food, though I be hungry ever so long. Then God gives me a small look of himself, his *Son,* and his glory. And I think in my heart, they all be mine soon; then I no suffer hunger any more—my Father's house have many mansions." "Sarah," said I, "you seem to have some knowledge of the Scriptures; can you read?" "I can spell out a little, I can't read like you white folks; oh if I could!" Here she burst into tears: but after regaining her composure, she added, "This, Misse, what I want above all things, more than victuals or drink. O how often I beg God to teach me to read, and he do teach me some. When I take Bible, kneel down and pray, he shows me great many words, and they be so sweet, I want to know a great deal more. O when I get home to heaven, then I know all, then I no want to read any more."

In this strain of simple piety she told me her first interesting story. And when she departed I felt a stronger evidence of her being a true child of God than I have acquired of some professors by a long acquaintance. In one of her many visits she afterward made me, she gave me in substance the following account of her conversion. She lived until she became a wife and a mother, without hope and without God in the world; having been brought up in extreme ignorance. Her husband treated her with great severity, and she became dejected and sorrowful: to use her own simple language, "I go sorrow, sorrow, all day long. When night come, husband come home angry; then I think, oh if Sarah had one friend! but Sarah no friend. I no want to tell neighbor I got trouble, that only make it worse. So I be quiet, tell nobody, only cry night and day for one good friend. One Sunday, good neighbor come and say, Come, Sarah, go to meeting. So I call my children, tell them stay in the house while I go. When I got there minister tell all about Jesus; how he was born in a stable, go suffer all his life, die on the great cross, was buried, rise again, and go up into heaven, so always be sinner's friend. He say too, if you got trouble, go tell Jesus; he best friend in sorrow, he bring you out of trouble, he support you, make you willing to suffer. So when I go home, I think great deal what minister say, think this the friend I want, this the friend I cry for so long. Poor ignorant Sarah never hear so much about Jesus before. Then I try to tell Jesus how I want such a friend. But, oh, my heart so hard, can't feel, can't pray, can't love Jesus, though he so good. This make me sorrow more and more. When Sunday come, want to go again. Husband say, No, I beat you if you go. So I wait till he be gone off hunting, then shut up children safe, and run to meeting, sit down in the door, hear minister tell how bad my heart is—no love to God, no love to Jesus, no love to pray. So then, I see why I can't have Jesus for my friend, because I got so bad heart: then I go praying all the way home, 'Jesus, make my heart better.' When get home, find children safe, feel glad husband no come; only sorrow because my wicked heart. But don't know how to make it better. When I go sleep, then dream I can read good book: dream I read there, Sarah must be born again: in morning keep thinking what that word mean. When husband go to work, run over to my good neighbor, ask her if the Bible say so. Then she read me where that great man go to see Jesus by night, because he afraid to go in the daytime.[2] Think he just like Sarah. She must go in secret, to hear about Jesus, else husband be angry. Then I feel encouraged in mind, determined to have Jesus for my friend. So ask neighbor how to get a good heart. She tell me, Give your heart to Jesus, he will give the Holy Spirit to make it better. Sarah don't know what she mean—never hear about the Holy Spirit. She say I must go to meeting next Sunday, she will tell minister about me—he tell me what to do. So Sarah go to hear how she must be born again. Minister say, You must go and fall down before God; tell him you are grieved because you sin—tell him you want a better heart—tell him, for Christ Jesus' sake, give the Holy Spirit, to make your heart new. Then Sarah go home light, because she know the way. When I get home my husband angry because I go to meeting and don't stay at home and work. I say, Sarah can't work any more on Sunday, because it is sin against God. I rather work nights when moon shine. So he drive me hoe corn that night, he so angry. I want to pray great deal, so go out hoe corn, pray all the time. When come in the house, husband sleep. Then I kneel down, and tell Jesus take my bad heart— can't bear my bad heart, pray give me the Holy Spirit, make my heart soft, make it all new. So, a great many days, Sarah go begging for a new heart. Go meeting all Sundays; if husband beat me, never mind it; go hear good neighbor read Bible every day. So after a great while God make all my mind peace. I love Jesus; love pray to him, love tell him all my sorrows: He take away my sorrow, make all my soul joy; only sorrow because can't read the Bible and learn how to be like Jesus; want to be like his dear people the Bible tell of. So I make a great many brooms, and go get a Bible for them. When I come home husband call me a fool for it; say he burn it up. Then I go hide it; when he is gone then I get it, kiss it many times, because it Jesus' good word. Then I go ask neighbor if she learn me to read? she say, Yes. Then I go many days to learn my letters, pray God all the while to help me to read his holy word. So, Misse, I learn to read good hymn; learn to spell out many good words in the Bible. So every day I take my Bible, tell my children that be God's word, tell them how Jesus die on cross for sinners: then make them all kneel down, I pray God give them new hearts; pray for husband too, he so wicked. O how I sorrow for him, fear his soul must go in the burning flame." "Sarah," said I, "how long

---

[2]The story of Nicodemus in John 3:1–21.

did your husband live?" "O he live great many year." "Did he repent and become a good man?" "No, no, Misse, I afraid not; he sin more and more. O me, when he got sick, my soul in great trouble for him; talk every day to him, but he no hear Sarah. I say, how can you bear to go in the burning fire where the worm never die, where the fire never go out. At last he get angry, bid me hold my tongue. So I don't say any more, only mourn over him every day before God. Afterward, when he was drowned, my heart say, Father, thy will be done—Jesus do all things well. Sarah can't help him now, he be in God's hands; all is well. So then I give my heart all away to Jesus, tell him I be all his; serve him all my life; beg the Holy Spirit to come and fill all my heart, make it all clean and white like Jesus. Pray God to help me learn more of his sweet word. And now, Sarah live a poor Indian widow great many long years, and always find Jesus friend, husband, brother, all. He make me willing to suffer; willing to live great while in this bad world if he see best; but above all, he gives me a great good hope of glory when I die. So now I wait patient till my change come."

She used to bring bags of sand into the village, and sell it for food. Sometimes she brought grapes and other kinds of fruit. But as she walked by the way she took little notice of any thing except children, to whom she sometimes gave an affectionate word of exhortation to be good, say their prayers, learn to read God's good word, & c., accompanied with a bunch of grapes or an apple. Thus she engaged the affection of many a little heart. She seemed absorbed in meditation as she walked, and was sometimes seen with her hands uplifted in the attitude of prayer. One day I asked her how she could bring such heavy loads, old as she was, and feeble. "Oh," said she, "when I get a great load, then I go and pray God to give me strength to carry it. So I go on, thinking all the way how good God is, to give his only Son to die for poor sinner; think how good Jesus is, to suffer so much for such poor creature; how good the Holy Spirit was, come into my bad heart, and make it all new: so these sweet thoughts make my mind so full of joy I never think how heavy sand be on my old back." Here, said I to myself, learn how to bear the trials and afflictions of life.

One day she passed with a bag of sand: on her return she called on me. I inquired how much Mrs.—— gave her for the sand. She was unwilling to tell, and I feared she was unwilling lest I should withhold my accustomed mite, on account of what she had already received: I therefore insisted she should let me see. She at length consented; and I drew from the bag a bone, not having on it meat enough for half a meal. "Is this all? Did that rich woman turn you off so? How cruel, how hard-hearted!" I exclaimed. "Misse," she replied, "this made me afraid to let you see it; I was afraid you would be angry; I hope she will have a bigger heart next time; only she forget now that Jesus promise to pay her all she give Sarah. Don't be angry; I pray God to give her a great deal bigger heart." The conviction, that she possessed in an eminent degree the Spirit of Him who said, "Bless them that curse you,"[3] and prayed for his murderers, rushed upon my mind. I think I never felt deeper self-abhorrence and abasement. I left her for a moment, and, from the few comforts I possessed, gave her a portion. She received them with the most visible marks of gratitude, arose to depart, went to the door, and then turned, looking me in the face with evident con-

---

[3]Matt. 5:44; Luke 6:28.

cern. "Sarah," said I, "what would you have?" (supposing she wanted something I had not thought of and feared to ask.) "O my good Misse," said she, "nothing, only I am afraid your big heart feel some proud, because you give me more for nothing than Misse——— for sand." This faithfulness, added to her piety and gratitude, completed the swell of feeling already rising in my soul; and bursting into tears, I said, "O Sarah! when you pray that Mrs.——— may have a bigger heart, don't forget to pray that I may have an humble one." "I will, Misse, I will," she exclaimed with joy, and hastened on her way.

Another excellence in her character was, that she loved the house of God; and often appeared there when, from bad weather or other causes, the seats of others were empty. She was early, clean, and whole in her apparel, though it was sometimes almost as much diversified with patches as the coat of the Shepherd of Salisbury plain. She was very old and quite feeble, yet she generally stood, during public service, with eyes riveted on the preacher. I have sometimes overtaken her on the steps, after service, and said to her, "Have you had a good day, Sarah?" "All good, sweeter than honey," she would reply.

In the spring of 1817 it was observed by her friends that she did not appear at meeting, as usual, and one of her particular female benefactors asked her the reason; when she with streaming eyes told her, that her clothes had become so old and ragged that she could not come with comfort or decency; but said she had been praying God to provide for her in this respect, a great while, and telling Jesus how much she wanted to go to his house of prayer, and expressed a strong desire to be resigned and submissive to his will. This was soon communicated to a few friends, who promptly obeyed the call of Providence, and soon furnished this suffering member of Christ with a very decent suit of apparel. This present almost overpowered her grateful heart. She received it as from the hand of her heavenly Father and kind Redeemer, in answer to her prayer, and she said she would go and tell Jesus how good his dear people were to his poor old creature, and pray her good Father to give them a great reward.

Two of the garments given her she received with every mark of joy. On being asked why she set so high a value on these, she replied: "O these just what I pray for so long, so to lay out my poor old body clean and decent, like God's dear white people, when I die." These she requested a friend to keep for her, fearing to carry them home, lest they should be taken from her. She was, however, persuaded to wear one of them to meeting, upon condition that if she injured that another should be provided; the other was preserved by her friend, and made use of at her death. An aged female who gave her one of these garments, says, she never saw any body so grateful: "Sarah said she could not pay me. She wondered why people were so kind to such a poor old creature She hoped God would reward me, and all of them."

I doubt not but that her prayer was heard, and will be answered in their abundant reward. The last visit I had from her was in the summer of 1817. She had attended a funeral, and called on me as she returned. She complained of great weariness, and pain in her

---

Note. The subject of this narrative lived in the eastern part of Connecticut; her hut was in a retired spot near a pond; a beautiful sheet of water, which it overlooked from the North-west; and was at about an equal distance from the meeting houses of Tolland and Ellington. It was impossible to put down her words exactly as spoken, but the sense is always retained, and generally the exact expressions.

limbs, and showed me her feet, which were much swollen. I inquired the cause: "Oh," said she, with a serene smile, "death comes creeping on; I think in the grave-yard today, Sarah must lie here soon." "Well, are you willing to die? Do you feel ready?" "I think, if my bad heart tells true, I am willing to do just as Jesus bids me; if he say, You must die, then I glad to go and be with him; if he say, Live, and suffer a great deal more, I willing. I think Jesus know best. Sometimes I get such look of heaven, I long to go and see Jesus; see the happy angels, see the holy saints; to throw away my bad heart, lay down my old body, and go where no sin be. Then I tell Jesus: he say, Sarah, I prepare a place for you,[4] then come take you to myself. Then I be quiet like a child, don't want to go till he call me." Much more she said upon this interesting subject, which indicated a soul ripe for heavenly glories. When we parted I thought it very doubtful whether we ever met again below. In the course of three weeks from this time I heard that Sarah was removed to a better world.

———

TRACT NO. 175
TO MOTHERS

In the vicinity of P—— there was a pious mother, who had the happiness of seeing her children, in very early life, brought to the knowledge of the truth, walking in the fear of the Lord, and ornaments in the Christian Church. A clergyman, who was travelling, heard this circumstance respecting this mother, and wished very much to see her, thinking that there might be *something* peculiar in her mode of giving religious instruction, which rendered it so effectual. He accordingly visited her, and inquired respecting the manner in which she discharged the duties of a mother, in educating her children.

The woman replied, that she did not know as she had been more faithful than any Christian mother would be, in the religious instruction of her children. After a little conversation, however, she said:

"While my children were infants on my lap, as I washed them, I raised my heart to God, that he would wash them in that blood which cleanseth from sin. As I clothed them in the morning, I asked my Heavenly Father to clothe them with the robe of Christ's righteousness. As I provided them food, I prayed that God would feed their souls with the bread of heaven, and give them to drink the water of life. When I have prepared them for the house of God, I have plead that their bodies might be fit temples for the Holy Ghost to dwell in. When they left me for the week-day school, I followed their infant footsteps with a prayer, that their path through life might be like that of the just, which shineth more and more unto the perfect day. And as I committed them to the rest of the night, the silent breathing of my soul has been, that their Heavenly Father would take them to his embrace, and fold them in his paternal arms."

Here is the influence of the *silent, unseen* exertions of a mother: an influence which will be felt, when those external accomplishments, and fleeting enjoyments which many

———

[4]Echoing John 14:2–3.

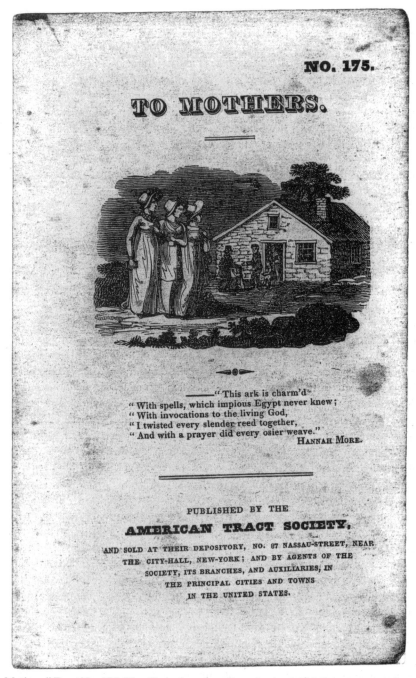

"To Mothers," Tract No. 175 (New York: American Tract Society). This is a representative cover of the shorter tracts distributed from this society. (Courtesy, The American Tract Society, Garland, Texas)

labour to give their children, shall be forgotten, or remembered only as the means of facilitating a rapid descent to the world of sorrow. In this little story two things strike our attention: these efforts were made *early,* and with a *reliance on the divine blessing.* This mother *felt* that she received her children from God, and was accountable to him for the manner in which she trained them up. She knew that her labours would be vain, unless God should in mercy grant her the aid of his Spirit, to sanctify and save the soul; therefore, through *all* the duties of the day, and all the interesting periods of childhood, she looked up to a God who is ever near to those who will call upon him, and who will listen to their cries. How happy must be that household whose God is the Lord; what heavenly joy beams from every countenance, and with what glorious hopes do they look beyond the grave to that mansion provided for them in their Father's house; and thrice happy must be that *mother,* who, in the fear of God, and in reference to eternity, has thus performed her duty.

There are feelings in a *mother's* bosom, which are known only by a mother: the tie which binds her to her children, is one compared with which all other ties are feeble. It is to these feelings that the fact just stated will speak a language which must be understood; and it must strike a note on this chord that will vibrate through every fibre of the soul. While appeals are often made to him who has lived long in sin, that fall like the sound of the empty wind upon his ear; and the voice of warning thunders in its truths to hearts of adamant; the appeal now made, is to an ear which is not deaf, to a heart which can feel.

The noise and tumult of the active world often drown the "still small voice"[1] of the Gospel, which sounds in the ears of the man of business; and worldly wisdom and strict calculation sometimes lead men to neglect the question, "What will it profit a man, if he gain the whole world, and lose his soul?"[2] But this Tract is designed for a different situation in life; for those who do not mingle in the bustle and hurry of the world; who are retired to a more quiet, though not to an unimportant sphere. In some hour of silent meditation this may fall into the hands of a *mother;* and the duties it recommends can be performed even while engaged in the common business of the family.

It is no fiction of poetry that,

"Just as the twig is bent, the tree's inclined."

"When the mind begins to open, and the attention is first arrested by the objects that surround us, much depends upon her, who, in that tender period, shall make the *first* impressions upon that mind, and first direct its attention.

It is *then* that the mother has an access and an influence which cannot be attained at any other period. The first inquiries of the little infant must be answered by her who gave it birth. As he gazes upon those twinkling stars that glitter in the evening sky, and asks, "Who made those shining things?" it is a mother's duty to tell the little prattler of that great and good being who dwells in the heavens, and who is the Father of all our mercies.

And as the mind enlarges, the mother tells the little listener of that Jesus who lay in a manger, and died on the cross. And when she softens its pillow for its nightly slumbers, and watches its closing eyes, it is her privilege to hear it lisp, *"Our Father,"* and direct it

---

[1]Kings 19:12.

[2]Matt. 16:26; Mark 8:36.

to love that Father whose name it so early speaks. Let this golden opportunity pass, these days of childhood roll away, and the mind be filled only with fabled stories, or sportive songs, and the precious immortal is trained for some other state than the paradise above. Do you say that you are *ignorant,* and are not capable of giving instruction? As your child clings to your bosom and directs his inquiring countenance to you for some interesting story, you know enough to tell him of some hero or king; and can you not tell him of the King of Zion, the Prince of Peace? And what more could the learned philosopher tell this infant mind?

You are *unknown* and *obscure,* did you say? But you are known to your child, and your influence with your child is greater than that of a Legislator or General. "Say not, I, who am obscure, may act without restraint, especially when secluded from the world, in the retirement of my family. *Obscure! You* are *immortal.* You must go to the *judgment;* and every whisper of your life will be exhibited, before an assembled universe! *Secluded!*—What if the eye of the world does not follow you into the domestic circle? Is it not restraint enough that your *child* is there? That child has a *soul,* worth more than a million globes of gold. That child, too, may become a legislator, or a judge, or a pastor in a church. Take care, you who are a mother! You act under a dreadful responsibility. You cannot *stir,* without touching some string that will vibrate after your head is laid in the dust. One word of pious counsel, or one word of sinful levity or passion, uttered in the hearing of your child, may produce an effect on your children's children. Nay, its influence may be felt on the other side of the globe, and may extend into eternity." Your words are received with confidence, and *"My mother told me so,"* is an argument of sufficient weight to convince the child of the most important truths.

Here you have an influence which no other creature can have, and can exert it in circumstances the most favourable. It is not to open to a son the stores of science, that may qualify him to rank among the learned and the wise of the world: it is not to adorn a daughter with those accomplishments which shall attract the attention of those who crowd the hall of pleasure, or move in the circle of refinement and fashion.

But the object is far more *noble,* more worthy the undivided attention of those who live for immortality. That child who now prattles on your knee, or sports around your dwelling, may yet tell some perishing heathen of Jesus of Nazareth; may yet be an able soldier in the army of Immanuel, and may plant the standard of the cross on the shores of Greenland, or under the burning sun of Africa. *Look at facts.* What first led the pious and eminently useful John Newton[3] to the knowledge of the truth? The instructions of his mother, given at the early period of *four years,* fastened upon his conscience, and led him to a Saviour.

Can you estimate the effect of his labours? Not till you can compute the usefulness of Buchanan and Scott, who were converted by his instrumentality—till you can see the full blaze of that light which the former carried into the heart of heathen India; and witness the domestic comfort and brightening hopes occasioned by the labours of the latter. Who taught young Timothy, an early labourer in the vineyard of Jesus Christ, the first

---

[3]John Newton (1725–1807) was an English slave trader who converted to Christianity. He then enjoyed an active ministry that included writing the hymn "Amazing Grace."

lessons of religious truth? Who led Samuel, a prophet and a judge in Israel, while he was yet *young,* to the house of the Lord, and dedicated him to the service of the God of heaven?[4] *A praying mother.*

Though the seed thus sown in childhood may not spring up and bring forth fruit while under the maternal eye, yet we must not conclude that it is lost. A clergyman recently met a seaman in the street of a neighbouring city, and pressed upon him the duty of attending to the concerns of his soul. The hardy mariner burst into tears, and exclaimed, "*Stop, stop,* don't talk to me so; it is just as my mother talked to me when I was a boy." A mother's counsel had followed him through all his wanderings, and still the words of her who prayed for him retained their hold on his conscience. The time has come when it is esteemed a greater honour to be the mother of a Brainerd or a Martyn,[5] than of a Cæsar or Napoleon. And suppose the mothers of these men, whose characters, though so widely different, are so universally known, should, from their unchanging state, look upon those sons whom they have nourished; what would be the view presented to them? Who would not choose to have given birth to the Christian heroes? It is not for this short state of existence only that you are to train your children. The little group that now cluster around you are destined for immortality. When the world on which they stand shall have passed away, and its pleasures and its honours shall be forgotten, then they whom you have introduced to this state of being will but begin to live. Their characters are now forming for *eternity,* and you are aiding to form them.

Though you may not design it, though you may quiet yourself, that if you can do them no good, you will not do them injury; yet you exert an influence which *is* felt, and will be felt when your head is laid in the dust. Let, then, this appeal to a mother's feelings be heard, let it come to your own bosom, and ponder it in your heart.

Do you know the way to a throne of mercy; and can you kneel before it, and forget the children of your love? Can you watch their closing eyes, and not commit them to your God? Can you labour that they may enjoy the good things of this fleeting world, and not *pray* that God would prepare them for that upon which they will soon enter? You see them growing up around you without hope and without God in the world: though you may be unable to do more, can you refuse to *pray,* that he who in a peculiar manner extends the arms of mercy to those in the morning of life, would take them to his embrace, and prepare them for his kingdom?

You have seen the hand of disease fasten upon them, and have passed days of anxious toil and nights of sleepless solicitude to arrest their malady; and have cried from a bursting heart, "Oh, spare my child!" You have seen the object of your tenderest affection sinking in the arms of death, and with a heart rent with anguish have said with the nobleman, "Come down ere my child die." And when the last duties of parental affection were performed, and the grave had closed over the child of your bosom, you have perhaps looked back to the time when it was under your care, and mourned that you thought no more of its immortal part, that you prayed no more for its precious soul.

---

[4]1 Sam. 1–2.

[5]David Brainerd (1718–1747) and Henry Martyn (1781–1812) were both Protestant missionaries who spent their lives winning souls, not wars.

If you have passed through scenes like these; if you have thus felt; then remember those now in life and health, and improve the opportunity now given you.

The time for your exertion is very *short*. Soon your children will arrive at that period of life when a mother's influence will be very feebly felt, unless it has been *early* exerted. Would you find in them a rich source of consolation when your head shall become white with years, and your body be bending to the grave; then you will *now* commit them to him who can sanctify and save the soul. Should you go down to the grave and leave these objects of your love in a cold, unfeeling world, what better can you do for them than to secure the friendship of one who sticketh closer than a brother, and whose love is stronger than death.

The tender tie which now binds you to them will soon be dissolved; you cannot resist the stroke which shall tear them from your bosom. You may have felt the pang— your heart may have been filled with sorrow. O then, if you ever pray, if your soul ever went out to *your* Father and *your* God, in humble petitions; tell him of your children who know him not: when you know what it is to wrestle in secret with the God of Jacob, give him back in faith your *children*.[6] Then you may hope, through grace, to say, in that other world to which you are going, "Lord, here am I, and the children thou hast given me."

Should this paper fall into the hands of a mother who never *prayed* even for herself; she *must,* she *cannot but* pray for those to whom she has given life. *Prayerless mother! spare,* oh, *spare* your child; stop where you now are, on the threshold of eternity, and remember, as you gaze on that countenance which smiles in your bosom, that you have *never prayed* for its soul, which will live for ever. Have you a mother's feelings, and can you still neglect it?

Oh! give me poverty, give me pain; leave me friendless and forsaken by the world— but leave me not to the embrace of a *prayerless mother*—leave not my soul to the care of one who never raised her weeping eyes to heaven, to implore its blessings on my head.

Are you a *mother,* and can you close your eyes upon the scenes of earth, and remember that you never raised, even in your silent breathings, the desires of your heart to heaven for a child, perhaps your only darling?

In some lonely hour, when the labours of the day are ended, and you have performed the last act of kindness for your sleeping babes; kneel, if you never have before, kneel before Him who seeth your heart in that silent hour, and utter one short prayer, one broken petition of penitence, faith, and love to the Saviour of sinners, for your dear children.

---

[6]Gen. 32:24–32.

TRACT NO. 493
BEWARE OF BAD BOOKS

Why, what harm will *books* do me? The same harm that personal intercourse would with the bad men who wrote them. That "A man is known by the company he keeps," is an old proverb; but it is no more true than that a man's character may be determined by knowing what books he reads. If a good book can be read without making one better, a bad book cannot be read without making one worse.

Lord Bacon[1] makes the pithy remark, that "In the body there are three degrees of that we receive into it, aliment, medicine, and poison; whereof aliment is that which the nature of man can perfectly alter and overcome; medicine is that which is partly converted by nature and partly converteth nature; and poison is that which worketh wholly upon nature, without nature being able to work at all upon it: *so in the mind, whatsoever knowledge reason cannot at all work upon and convert, is a mere* INTOXICATION, *and endangereth a dissolution of the mind and understanding.*"

Bad books are like ardent spirits; they furnish neither "aliment" nor "medicine"— they are "*poison*." Both *intoxicate*—one the mind, the other the body; the thirst for each increases by being fed, and is never satisfied; both ruin—one the intellect, the other the health, and together, the soul. The makers and venders of each are equally guilty and equally corrupters of the community; and the safeguard against each is the same—*total abstinence from all that intoxicates mind or body.*

Here we have a definition of what we mean by "*bad books:*" whatever books neither feed the mind nor purify the heart, but *intoxicate the mind and corrupt the heart.* Works of science, art, history, theology, etc., furnish "aliment" or "medicine:" books of fiction, romance, infidelity, war, piracy, and murder, are "*poison,*" more or less diluted, and are as much to be shunned as the drunkard's cup. They will "bite like a serpent, and sting like an adder."

Books of mere fiction and fancy are generally bad in their character and influence. Their authors are commonly bad men, and wicked men do not often write good books. A stream does not rise higher than its fountain. Their principles are often corrupt, encouraging notions of chivalry, worldly honor, and pleasure, at war with the only true code of morals. They insult the understanding of the reader, by assuming that the great object of reading is amusement. The *effects* are such as might be expected. Familiarity with popular fiction gives a disrelish for simple truth: engenders a habit of reading merely for amusement, which destroys the love of sober investigation, and blasts the hope of mental improvement; renders scientific and historical reading tedious; gives false views of the perfectibility of human nature, thus leading to disappointments in the relations of life; and dwarfs the intellectual and moral powers, except the imagination, which is rendered morbid and unhealthy by constant excitement. The Bible becomes a

---

[1]Lord Francis Bacon (1561–1626) was an English statesman, lawyer, and philosopher. He was particularly interested in how one acquires knowledge.

wearisome book; spiritual classics, like those of Baxter, Bunyan, Flavel, and Dod-dridge,[2] though glowing with celestial fire, become insipid and uninteresting; and the influence of the pulpit is undermined, by diverting the attention from serious things, and lessening the probability that truth will take effect upon the conscience; or if it does for a time, the bewitching novel furnishes a ready means of stifling conviction and grieving away the Spirit of God. A merchant in H. was under conviction for sin, during a revival of religion. A pious friend called, and, to his surprise, found him engaged in reading a worthless novel. To his remonstrance against such trifling, he replied. "I'm so interested in this book, I must finish it: and *then* I will attend to the affairs of my soul." He finished the book. He attended to the concerns of his soul—never! Thousands have perished by similar seductive influences.

Beware of the foul and exciting romance. All that is said above will apply with ten-fold intensity to this class of reading, for which it paves the way. The writer of modern romance chooses his scenes from the places of debauchery and crime, and familiarizes the reader with characters, sentiments, and events, that should be known only to the police. Licentious scenes and obscene imagery are unblushingly introduced, and the imagination polluted by suggestions and descriptions revolting to the pure in heart. "*Public poisoners*" was the title long since justly given to writers of this class. It was lately testified in open court, by the father of one whose guilty course has brought ruin upon herself, disgrace upon her family, and death upon her lover, that all was occasioned by his daughter's "reading the impure works of Eugene Sue and Bulwer."[3] To yield to such a hellish charm, is like the voluntary sacrifice of one's body and soul on the drunk-ard's altar. *Mental delirium tremens* is as sure a consequence of habitual intoxication from such reading, as is that awful disease the certain end of the inebriate. Beware of it!

Beware of infidel books, and of all writings which ridicule the Bible. You will meet them, with a more or less guarded avowal of their object, in the newspaper, the tract, and the volume. Infidelity is a system of *negations;* it is nothing—believes nothing—does nothing good. Beware of it, in whatever form it approaches you, as you value temporal happiness and prosperity, the peace of society, and eternal well-being. No man enters eternity an infidel.

Beware of books of war, piracy, and murder. The first thought of crime has been sug-gested by such books. The murderer of Lord William Russell confessed on the scaffold, that the reading of one such book led him to the commission of his crime. Another, who was executed for piracy, was instigated to his course by a book of piratical tales. The state-prisons are filled with criminals who were incited to crime by similar means. They stimulate the love of adventurous daring, cultivate the baser passions, and prompt to deeds of infamy. Away with them!

Do you still need to be persuaded to beware of the poison that would paralyze your

---

[2]The Puritan ministers Richard Baxter (1615–1691), John Bunyan (1628–1688), and John Flavel (1627–1691), as well as the hymn writer Philip Doddridge (1702–1751), were all influential Protestant writers.

[3]Eugene Sue (1804–1857) was a French author of sensational novels, and Edward George Bulwer-Lytton (1803–1873) was a prolific English romance and historical novelist.

conscience, enervate your intellect, pervert your judgment, deprave your life, and perhaps ruin your soul?

Beware of bad books, because if *you,* and others like you, *will let them alone, they will soon cease to be published.* Every such book you buy encourages the guilty publisher to make another. Thus you not only endanger your own morals, but pay a premium on the means of ruining others.

Beware, because *your example is contagious.* Your child, your servant, your neighbor, may be led to read what will be injurious for time and eternity; or not to "touch the unclean thing," as your example may prompt.

Beware, because *good books are plenty and cheap,* and it is folly to feed on chaff or poison, when substantial, healthful food may as well be obtained.

Beware of bad books, because *they waste your time.* "Time is money;" it is more— it is *eternity!* You live in a sober, redeemed world, and it is worse than folly to fritter away the period of probation in mere amusement. God did not bring us into being, and sustain that being—the Redeemer did not shed his blood a ransom for our sins—the Holy Spirit has not bestowed upon us the book divine, that we might flit from flower to flower like the butterfly, neglecting all the ends of rational and immortal being, and go to the judgment mere triflers.

Beware of bad books, because principles imbibed and images gathered from them *will abide in the memory and imagination for ever.* The mind once polluted is never freed from its corruption—*never,* unless by an act of boundless grace, through the power of the Spirit of God.

Beware of them, because *they are one of the most fruitful sources of eternal destruction.* They are read in solitude. Their ravages are internal. Foundations of morality are undermined. The fatal arrow is fixed in the soul, while the victim only sees the gilded feather that guides its certain aim. He is lost, and descends to a hell the more intolerable, from a contrast with the scenes of fancied bliss with which the heart was filled by the vile, though gifted destroyer. The precious book of life was given to show you how you might secure the enrolment of your name among the saints in light; but you chose the book of death, with present fascinations of a corrupt press, and the surest means of securing a dreadful doom. If your epitaph were truly written, the passerby in —— graveyard would read,

"M——ACQUIRED A TASTE FOR READING BAD BOOKS, DIED WITHOUT HOPE, AND 'WENT TO HIS OWN PLACE.' "

Shall this be your epitaph, dear reader? If not, make this pledge before God: "*Henceforth I will beware of bad books, and never read what can intoxicate, pollute, or deprave the mind and heart.*"

TRACT NO. 512
MURDERERS OF FATHERS, AND
MURDERERS OF MOTHERS*

BY REV. EDWARD HITCHCOCK, D.D.
PRESIDENT OF AMHERST COLLEGE

In the Scriptures, as well as in common language, murder does not always mean the destruction of natural life by an act of violence. "Whosoever hateth his brother," says John, "is a murderer;" that is, he has the essential spirit of a murderer. We say, also, that he is a murderer who unnecessarily pursues a course of conduct by which the reputation or happiness of another is destroyed, and his life shortened. In this sense, then, murder is a common crime, committed by multitudes who never imagine that they are guilty— committed sometimes upon those who are truly beloved by the murderer, and are his best friends. And strange as it may seem, this crime is more common among the young than any other class, and their parents are the victims. I shall not charge any of my youthful readers with being murderers of fathers, and murderers of mothers; but as I point out some of the principal modes in which they may become such, let them honestly inquire, whether they have not already commenced the fearful work.[1]

1. The young man may become the murderer of his father and his mother *by making the idle and the immoral, the unprincipled or the irreligious, his chosen companions.*

The principles on which the remarks I am about to make are founded, apply equally to youth of either sex. But for the sake of brevity, I shall speak only of young men. From his earliest days, it is the strong desire and effort of Christian parents to preserve the mind of their son free from the impurities and fascinations of vice; and until they find him associating with the idle, the unprincipled, and the immoral, they imagine their efforts to be successful. But his choice of companions reveals the plague-spot on his heart. He would not associate with the wicked, if he did not relish their society; and he would not relish it, if the contagion of vice had not invaded his purity of principle and feeling. With the love of sin in his heart, what now shall prevent the inexperienced youth from the lawless indulgence of his passions, with reckless companions to lead the way? How feeble will be the warning voice of parental affection to resist the strong current of sinful inclination. As yet he knows not from experience the bitter consequences of a sinful course. But parents know that *"the wages of sin is death"*[2]—death to all true peace of mind—death to all hopes of usefulness and reputation—death temporal, and death eternal. The son, however, imagines no danger from his associates. He sees in them honor-

---

*1 Timothy, 1:9.
[1] 1 John 3:15.
[2] Rom. 6:23.

able feelings and noble purposes, and only occasionally do they show their aversion to what they call bigotry and intolerance in religion, and unreasonable strictness of morality. And what danger in such society to him, who has so much respect for religion, and who knows how to take care of himself? Alas, his parents realize that his danger is more imminent than if he consorted with the openly profligate, because he feels in no danger, and drinks in the poison without knowing it. The dreadful anticipation of having their child ruined for this world and another, fills their hearts with such anguish as a parent only can know. It brings upon them early gray hairs, ploughs deep furrows upon their foreheads, and urges them prematurely towards the grave. It is in fact slow, but in many cases, certain murder. Yet how easy for you, O young man, by abandoning those companions, to save your parents, and to save yourself!

2. The young man may murder his father and his mother *by immoral and ungrateful conduct.*

Fearful as parents are, when their son shows a fondness for idle or immoral companions, that he will soon become like them in practice, they cannot give up the fond hope that God's restraining grace and parental admonition may save him from actual dissipation and profligacy. But when they find that the fear of God and the warnings of conscience are so overcome that habitual wickedness is committed, it is as if a deep murderer's stab had been aimed at their hearts. Can it be, that their darling boy, whom they had successfully taught to be industrious and economical, has become a reckless, idle spendthrift; not merely of money, but of time and opportunities far more valuable than money? Can it be, that one lately so obedient to parental authority, and so tenderly alive to his parents' happiness, now tramples on their authority, and is indifferent to their feelings? Can it be, that one instructed so carefully to regard the Sabbath as holy time, now devotes that day to the perusal of secular newspapers or novels, to wandering about the streets, to rides of pleasure, and to the society of irreligious companions? Once he rarely ventured far, by day or by night, without parental advice and permission; and he failed not to kneel, at an early hour of the evening, at the family altar of devotion, as a delightful preparation for early and sweet repose. But he has learnt to trust his own feelings when and where to go, and what company to keep; and often is he, when the hour of evening prayer arrives, at the convivial board, joining in the lascivious song and the Bacchanalian[3] shout, instead of supplication and praise to Jehovah. Parental admonition and entreaty awaken only disgust and insolence, and his father and mother perceive that they have lost their hold upon the conscience of their son. Such a transformation of a frank, open-hearted child, into a reckless, unfeeling profligate, changes parental anxiety into agony. And yet their feelings must be in a great measure concealed from him who causes their anguish, lest his hard heart should lead him to add to his other crimes, mockery and insult towards those who gave him birth. Therefore must they bear the trial in silence, and let it prey upon their spirits, until they sigh for a release from a world that is to them only a scene of hopelessness and suffering.

It is in the way pointed out under this head, that is, by immoral and ungrateful con-

---

[3]Sharing the characteristics of the orgylike Roman festival of Bacchus, the deity of wine.

duct, that very many become murderers of fathers, and murderers of mothers. Therefore let me dwell longer upon this point, and refer to some specific examples.

The time has come when the youth must quit the paternal roof, to become, it may be, an apprentice in some handicraft, or to engage in mercantile or agricultural pursuits. Going to some country town reputed as moral and religious, his parents feel less solicitude for his safety. But when hints reach them of his prodigal habits, irregular hours, profane language, and neglect of business, their hearts begin to writhe with torturing anticipations. By letter and personal address, they lift loud the note of warning. But in his haggard countenance and reckless conduct, they read the broad marks of dissipation. Out of the reach of watchful and controlling parents, evil companionship has led to evil actions; and now it will require little short of a miracle to save him from ruin. Instead of rising to respectability and distinction, as his fond parents had hoped, he will grovel along through the years of manhood, useless and known only for his vices, seeking only low pleasures and low society, with a broken constitution, and a mind ignorant and degraded, until an early grave opens to receive him. But often he will drag down his broken-hearted parents to the same narrow house; and there will they lie, the murderer and the murdered, side by side, till they go up together to the final judgment.

It may be, that the youth, on leaving home, is sent to the city, and for a time is aware that dangers of almost every name will meet him there. But vice soon becomes familiar to his observation: fascinating companions, graceful in manners, and generous in professions, introduce him to the social circle, where a magic influence comes over him to dispel every fear of danger. The same companions lead him to the theatre, a place where he finds much to amuse and delight, and little apparently to injure; and hence he infers that its dangers have been exaggerated by his parents, and he ventures again and again to the brilliant and enchanting spot. The snare is well laid and baited, and the bird falls into it and is taken. But this is only the gilded entrance to the dark labyrinth of iniquity. With his passions excited by the scenes of the theatre, the youth is easily lured by cunning companions into the gaming-house, and the place of the midnight carousal. Maddened there by the alcoholic bowl, he soon becomes as bold and reckless as his most unprincipled companions. The next step is to enter her house whose "steps take hold on hell." There the last trace of moral and religious principle in his bosom is blotted out; the voice of conscience is effectually smothered; and when his purse becomes empty by his dissipation, he is prepared to replenish it from the coffers of his employer. Deeper and deeper does he dip his hand into the forbidden treasure, until detection follows, and the brand of infamy is publicly stamped upon his character. If he escapes the penitentiary, it is only to be looked upon with scorn by the world, and with pity by the Christian; and after herding for a time with the dregs of society, to be thrown into the drunkard's and the felon's grave, unnoticed and unlamented. But what a terrible termination of a parent's fond hopes! What a dreadful metamorphosis of a beloved son, whom they sent forth untarnished, and with lofty expectations, from their Christian home! How much worse to bear than the assassin's dagger, was each successive development of his depravity; and how terribly must the final result have completed a father's and a mother's immolation!

Perhaps the youth leaves home for the college, or the academy; and for one, it may be, where there are many influences and strong, in favor of religion and morality. But the purest of them has its dangers; and some of these dangers are peculiar, and assail the young man unawares, and he falls an easy prey to the wiles of the wicked. At home he had been taught, that a man could not be placed in any circumstances where he could be released from obligations to obey the laws of religion and morality, or might connive at wickedness in others, and omit to bear testimony against it. But in the literary institution to which he attaches himself, he finds that he must modify these so-called puritanical notions. *Certain rules of honor,* instead of strict moral and religious principle, must regulate all his conduct towards his companions. He cannot find any one who can tell him exactly what these rules are; but he is distinctly informed, that they require him to close his eyes and ears as much as possible against the wickedness of his fellow-students, and to wink at immoral conduct in them, which he would feel bound to expose in any other member of the community. At any rate, he must suffer undeserved punishment himself, rather than expose the evil deeds of a classmate; and always be ready to vindicate the honor and reputation of his fellows. At first, his rigid views of duty are shocked by such requisitions; but finding that compliance or persecution awaits him, many a young man has not moral courage enough to take his firm stand on the platform of the Bible. He submits to the trammels imposed upon him, and thus sacrifices his independence; for this is only the beginning of his degradation.

Those who have driven him to abandon one important point, well know that he can be made to yield others. The next step is to draw him into the society of the idle and the reckless: and alas, what literary institution does not contain some such? There for a time he meets with little to shock his moral sensibilities, except perhaps an occasional joke upon religion, an inuendo against bigotry and intolerance, and possibly a little profaneness. His companions are indeed jovial, but they are amiable and gentlemanly; and their society occasionally seems almost essential to relieve the monotony and cheerlessness of college life. Ere long, however, the oath becomes more frequent, the mirth more boisterous, and the card-table and the wine-cup are introduced. To escape detection, these convivial entertainments must be deferred till the midnight hour, and of course the subsequent day be devoted to recovery from the debauch. The youth's literary standing soon sinks; he loses his habits of study, and falls under censure; but instead of reforming, he is irritated by expostulation and warning. Detection serves only to lead him to adopt more effectual measures to avoid it in future.

In short, he has become almost irreclaimably dissipated before his parents are aware that he has turned aside at all from the right path. They had supposed him possessed of superior talents; and with virtuous principles, that he would be proof against temptation. The intimation of his deviations, therefore, comes upon them with the suddenness and severity of the assassin's stab. With the earnestness of parental affection, they immediately appeal to every principle in their son which they suppose capable of being called into action. They cannot believe that he has so soon abandoned his bright hopes of future distinction, nor lost his respect for parental authority, or his filial attachments, nor become insensible to the sanctions of religion. They, therefore, press upon him all these considerations; and that is usually the crisis in the young man's history. If parental authority and affection triumph, and he relents, and breaks off his bad habits, and abandons his evil companions, he will be saved from utter ruin. But if his proud heart spurns a parent's counsel and exhortation, the last hold upon him is gone, and it will be but a short time before he reaches the bottom of the gulf of infamy. If he should be smuggled through college, it will be only to tantalize a little longer his parents' hopes, and to throw himself upon the community as a useless weight. Those parents must see him still grovelling with the idle and the dissipated; and thankful should they be, if his broken constitution should carry him prematurely to the grave by natural disease, before his depravity has outraged society so that he must expiate his crimes in the dungeon for life, or upon the scaffold. But how much easier for his wretched parents to fall by the literal murderer's assault, than thus to be suspended on the rack of uncertainty year after year, and at last to feel life and hope expire together. Alas, how many parents are at this moment stretched upon that rack, and destined to the same extinction of life and hope.

In all the examples that I have now given, and indeed as a general fact, the beginning and chief agent of ruin to the inexperienced youth, is the secret convivial frolic with jovial and unprincipled companions. And in fact, in no other place will his religious principles sooner yield, or parental lessons be forgotten, or the fear of God and man be cast off, and his low appetites and passions triumph over reason and conscience. For there the lewd and ribald song soon salutes his ears; low, vulgar wit takes the place of reason; the sober and the religious are made the butt of ridicule; and there, sometimes at least, the cup of intoxication goes round, and the youth, perhaps almost for the first time, "looks upon the wine when it is red, when it giveth its color in the cup, when it moveth itself aright," until his firmest temperance principles are overcome, and the fatal cup is lifted to his mouth; and with that first draught he swallows scorpions and daggers. True, he may have no suspicion of the dangers that await him there; nay, he may suppose that by entering that circle he is only preparing himself for the circles of gentility and fashion, and that unless he does there learn to sip the alcoholic bowl with politeness, he can never be admitted to the society of the wealthy and influential. But his father and mother know, every experienced man knows, because again and again have they seen the fatal process carried through, that the young man, however firm he may suppose his principles and yet uncorrupt his practice, who enters these convivial circles, has placed one foot within the purlieus of hell. He has entered a moral Maelstrom, and begun those fatal gyrations, which, without miraculous deliverance, will become swifter and swifter, narrower and narrower, until he goes down like lightning into the central vortex, and disappears for ever. O terrible delusion! To what multitudes of talented and amiable, yet inexperienced young men, has the convivial frolic proved fatal for this world and another. "Can a man take fire in his bosom, and his clothes not be burnt? Can one go upon hot coals, and his feet not be burnt?"

But parents are not thus deceived; and as one development after another comes out, as wicked actions succeed to wicked companionship, they see and know the fatal end to which he is hastening. Though his path be crooked, they know how slippery and downward it is, and how difficult for one who has entered upon it to thread his way back to virtue and to heaven. For one who has thus returned, they have seen a thousand buried beneath the waves of everlasting infamy and despair. Each successive act of wickedness, therefore, of which their son is guilty, makes a deeper and a deeper murderer's stab into their hearts. They know that idleness and duplicity, intemperance, profaneness, and licentiousness, are sins that not only paralyze the conscience, but rot out the heart and the intellect, and leave the miserable victim to sink down early, a loathsome mass of corruption, into hell.

One other mode of murdering fathers and mothers I ought to describe under this head, because it approaches nearer to literal murder than any which has been named. As the father approaches the dotage of old age, he is apt to repose an overweening confidence in a favorite son, and in an unguarded hour, *transfers to him his property.* And it would indeed seem that a father might be sure of an ample support and kind treatment from an own son, whom he had treated thus generously; for to that father he was indebted for existence, for support in infancy, for an education, and now for an estate earned by a life of labor. But alas, melancholy facts show that there are some so devoid of natural affection, as well as of all honorable feeling and religious principle, as to feel their parents to be a burden, so soon as they have obtained their property; and who will treat them unkindly for the very purpose of shortening their days. It is base enough for a child to refuse to sustain his aged and feeble parents because they have been unable to bequeath him any property. But when they have actually done this, it becomes barbarous and detestable in the extreme; and if there be any sin which will provoke God to punish it in a special manner, it is this. But why do I enlarge? For he who has become so dead to every sentiment of nature and religion as to abuse an aged parent, has a conscience too deeply enveloped by the callous folds of selfishness and meanness to be reached by any words of mine.

3. The young man may murder his father and his mother *by embracing dangerous religious error.*

Men embrace errors in religion, either because they lead unholy lives, or cherish a self-righteous, unsubmissive spirit. The more wicked a man's life, the more reckless must he be in his opinions, in order to quiet his conscience. Self-righteousness and pride require a system of error more refined, and more capable of literary embellishment; and the nearer it approaches in appearance to the true Gospel, the more acceptable will it be, because conscience, that stern advocate for evangelical piety in the heart, will be thus more easily satisfied. But it is essential, that such a system be wanting in all that is vital in the Gospel, or it will not quiet the fears of one who expects to enter heaven without a new heart. The particular form of error embraced is of little consequence in the view of the parent, provided it leave his son to rest easy without a new heart. He may fancy that he differs so little from his father that it is of small importance; while yet it is as mysterious to him as it was to Nicodemus, how a man can be born again. Ignorant of this doctrine, his parents know that he differs enough from them to shut him out of heaven as certainly as if with the fool he had said, "There is no God;" for, "*Except a man be born again, he cannot see the kingdom of God.*"[4]

It is the loss of his soul, not a bigoted attachment to a particular creed, that makes these parents so anxious. They well know how easy it is for the advocates of almost any error, even of Atheism itself, to array a list of names distinguished in literature and sci-

---

[4]John 3:3.

ence as its supporters; and they know, too, how fascinating to the youthful mind, is a reputation for talents and learning. Whatever religious opinions such men embrace, the young are ready to suppose safe and true; although, in fact, such men are probably of all others most apt to embrace error, because they usually give less serious attention to the subject, have more pride of opinion, and are usually more stubborn in their prejudices. Besides, when a man has once adopted some plausible and popular system of error, and thrown around it the drapery of literature and philosophy, he is the most unlikely of all men to see his lost condition, and flee to that only name under heaven whereby he can be saved. Therefore it is that these parents are so distressed when they find their son reposing quietly upon the gilded and downy couch of error, where he is most likely to be "given up to strong delusions to believe a lie, that he might be damned."

4. The young man may murder his father and his mother *by neglecting personal religion.*

The grand object of all their toils and prayers for their child, is his conversion. Until this great change pass over him, they feel as if the grand business of life, for which chiefly he was created, had been neglected. For, without a new heart, they know he must be lost; and yet he, like others, is liable at any moment to be summoned into eternity. Hence, though he be moral and amiable, a respecter of religion, and even distinguished among men, they look with comparative indifference and dissatisfaction upon all his acquisitions which leave him destitute of a new heart. Can it be, that they have brought up a child only to endure everlasting misery? From his earliest days they consecrated him in prayer and faith to God; and as he grew up, every opportunity was seized upon to store his mind with the truths of religion, and to impress his conscience with his guilt and danger. Sometimes his heart seemed to relent, and the tear of anxiety was seen in his eye. But these signs proved only the morning cloud and early dew; and though the years of his minority are almost or quite gone, he still remains unconverted; and every year the work is delayed, only deepens parental anxiety, because the hope of his salvation so rapidly diminishes.

During the childhood and youth of most persons, there are certain memorable events, each of which forms a sort of crisis in their history. One of these is sickness. At such a time, when the youth needs the supports of religion, he finds that he has none on which he dare rest. His morality, his kind feelings towards others, his upright and honorable conduct, and even his attention to the outward forms of religion, he finds will not form a resting-place for his soul, in that dark valley he seems about to enter. Oh, had he listened to parental instruction and entreaty while in health, he might now have had a rock to stand upon, amid the surging billows. If he should recover, surely he cannot longer neglect the great salvation. So feels the youth, and so feel his parents. He does recover; but his former stupor creeps over him again, and his agonized parents have every reason to expect that his next sickness will find him, like the last, entirely unprepared to die.

It may be that the youth is called to severe affliction, in the sudden departure of a brother, a sister, or chosen companion. A dying friend sounds in his ears a piercing note of warning. It falls upon him like a sudden peal of thunder, and awakens him from his deep spiritual slumbers. Strong hope that the hour of his conversion has come, springs up in the bosom of his affectionate parents. But the cup of happiness, which with a trembling hand they are lifting to their lips, is destined to be dashed upon the ground, leaving only the dregs of disappointment for them to taste. Their son's religious impressions gradually wear away, and he sinks into a deeper sleep than ever, while they awake to keener suffering.

Another season of deep solicitude and strong hope to Christian parents, is a revival of religion. If their son be not awakened and converted then, they know how faint is the probability that he will turn to God during the season of general indifference that too often follows a time of special religious interest. Nay, they fear, that having resisted the special influences of such a season, his heart will be so hardened that no future means will avail to subdue it. Intense, therefore, is the anxiety which Christian parents feel for their unconverted and unawakened son, during such a work. They have long beheld him twisted and crushed in the folds of the hydra-headed monster sin, and now they see approaching a more than Herculean Deliverer,[5] ready to set the dying captive free. Alas, must they see their child spurn the only power that can deliver him, and permit the monster to wind another coil around his heart? He does not, indeed, see how bitter is the anguish of disappointment in their souls, when the special work of God draws to a close, and he remains unconverted. But their closets, the midnight hour, the stars of heaven, and the God of heaven witness their deep distress, when, from a bleeding heart, the parent exclaims, "Is Ephraim my dear son? Is he a pleasant child?" "How can I give thee up, Ephraim? How can I deliver thee, Israel?" Ah, they must give him up; but it will break their hearts. They will go down to an early grave, murdered by a beloved son.

In view of this subject, thus presented, let the young man who reads these pages honestly inquire, whether he is not really, though perhaps unconsciously, among the murderers of fathers, and the murderers of mothers. Is he not the child of pious parents, and yet wedded to a companionship with those whom he knows to be idle, or unprincipled, or immoral, or irreligious? Nay, is he not conscious of indulging in some immoral practices? Has he not fortified himself in the belief of principles which effectually shield him from conviction of sin, and keep the slumbers of spiritual death unbroken? At least, does he not, from year to year, neglect personal religion, even under the loudest calls and the most urgent appeals, and the rebukes of conscience, and the strivings of the Spirit? If such be your character, in any of these respects, little do you know what a bitter cup you are compelling your father and mother to drink. It is known, that certain poisons may be administered in so small doses as to be unnoticed at the time, but great enough, by repetition, to insure the death of the victim. That fatal act you are practising upon your dearest earthly friends, who would gladly endure suffering and death, could they ward them off from you.

This charge you may think extravagant and untrue. The smile of affection meets you under the paternal roof, and the tenderest solicitude is manifested for your welfare. Ah, natural affection will glow in those parents' hearts till they are cold in the grave; nor will the hope of your conversion entirely abandon them, while you live and they

---

[5]The Hydra was a nine-headed gigantic monster. As one head was cut off, two grew back in its place. Hercules eventually found a way to kill the monster.

can pray. But knowing as they do, how dangerous are the companions with whom you associate, or the evil habits you indulge, or the religious errors you have embraced, or your long-continued indifference and stupidity respecting your own salvation, their hearts sink with discouragement; they tremble lest you are given over to blindness of mind and hardness of heart, and their faith falters when they pray for your conversion. Though concealed from your eye, a secret anguish on your account is preying upon their life. The mother who bore you—she whose tears fell often upon your infant cheek, as over your cradle she agonized in prayer for your early conversion—she who has often grown pale with midnight watchings by your sick-bed—she who first taught your infant lips the language of prayer—she who has followed you with her prayers, and tears, and counsels, in all your wanderings—that mother's heart you are now filling with deep distress, if indeed that distress and her toils for you have not already carried her down to an early grave. That father, too, who has cheerfully foregone a thousand pleasures, and made a thousand sacrifices, and submitted to multiplied cares and toils, for your support and education—whose hopes have been centred in you, and who has long felt as if death would be welcome, could it secure your conversion—O, what desolation reigns in that father's heart, as he sees you, after all his prayers and labors, still moving unconcernedly on the road to death. Or it may be, that his early grey hairs ere now have been brought down with sorrow to the grave. Oh, you are the murderer of those parents, whether you realize it or not, as really as if you had stolen to their bed at midnight, and buried the fatal steel in their bosoms; and for that deed you must answer at the final day of trial, when the wounds you have inflicted will be exposed to the view of the universe.

But after all, though there is a solemn reality in these representations, I am fully aware that most of those who are thus the murderers of fathers, and the murderers of mothers, are totally unconscious of the influence they are exerting upon their parents' happiness. Nay, though they must know that every wrong course they take, and even their continued neglect of religion, cannot but thwart the strongest desires of those parents' hearts, still they cling to them with strong attachment. For filial affection is a chord in the human heart that retains its sensibility when sin has paralyzed every thing besides; and even the desperate criminal, who has set heaven and earth at defiance, melts and weeps at the name of father or mother. Would to God I could make that chord vibrate, till it should rouse you, O ye unconverted young men, from the stupor of sin, and convert you, from the murderers, into the temporal saviors of your parents. Should you see that father and mother in the hands of the literal assassin, and their blood were streaming, and their death-cry came into your ears for help, how would you rush to their rescue, though a hundred swords were drawn to oppose you. Ah, they *are* in the assassin's hands—but *thou*, unconverted youth, art the man. They *are* covered with wounds, and their lifeblood is flowing out like water. But your sins, your unbelief and stupidity, are the sword that has cloven their hearts asunder. They *are* crying for help: but it is to God for your conversion. The language of Christ for his murderers is theirs: "Father, forgive them, for they know not what they do."[6] But can you be forgiven, if you persist in destroying the

------

[6]Luke 23:34.

peace and happiness of those who gave you being, and commit suicide, also, upon your own most precious soul? Never! Yet if you will be persuaded to yield your heart to the claims of the Lord Jesus Christ, forgiveness, free, and full, and everlasting, will be lavished upon you. The wounds you have inflicted upon your earthly parents will be healed as if by miraculous touch; and your father on earth, and your Father in heaven, will joyfully exclaim, "Bring forth the best robe, and put it on him; and put a ring on his hand, and shoes on his feet. For this my son was dead, and is alive again, he was lost, and is found."[7]

TRACT NO. 515
NOVEL-READING

Few persons suspect how many novels are written, and printed, and sold. There are about five thousand five hundred offered for sale in this country. If a man were to read one a week for seventy-five years, he would not be through the list. There are, of course, many novel-readers. Something on a great scale will be the result. What will it be; good or evil? Let us see.

It is natural to inquire, Who write novels? A few pious persons have written works which are sometimes called novels. But they are too serious for the gay, and too gay for the serious. So they are seldom read. Others are written by moral persons, who really seem anxious to teach some truth in an easy way. But nearly or quite all such are thought dull; and so they lie, covered with dust, on the shelves of the bookseller, are sent to auction, and used as waste paper. The popular novels of our day are, to a great extent, written by men who are known to be lax in principle, and loose in life. England and France contain no men who are more free from the restraints of sound morality, than their leading novelists. They are literal and "literary debauchees."

But do not novels contain many good things, which cannot be learned elsewhere? I answer, they do not. It is confessed that they never teach science. It is no less true, that they pervert history, or supplant it by fiction. This is throughout true of Walter Scott,[1] who has excelled all modern novelists in the charms of style. The literature of novels is commonly poor, and that of the best cannot compare with the standard English and French classics. Even Scott's best tales are intended to ridicule the best men, and to excuse or extol the worst men of their age. Like Hume,[2] he was an apologist of tyrants, whose crimes ought to have taken away both their crowns and their lives. I beseech you not to read novels. I will give my reasons.

---

[7]Reference to Jesus' story of the return of the prodigal son, Luke 15:11–32.

[1]Sir Walter Scott (1771–1832) was an immensely popular Scottish novelist, who is considered by many to be the greatest English writer of historical novels.

[2]David Hume (1711–1776) was a Scottish philosopher who wrote important works on epistemology and religious skepticism.

1. Their *general tendency* is to evil. They present vice and virtue in false colors. They dress up vice in gayety, mirth, and long success. They put virtue and piety in some odious or ridiculous posture. Suspicion, jealousy, pride, revenge, vanity, rivalries, resistance of the laws, rebellion against parents, theft, murder, suicide, and even piracy are so represented in novels as to diminish, if not to take away the horror which all the virtuous feel against these sins and crimes. Almost all that is shocking in vice is combined with some noble quality, so as to make the hero on the whole an attractive character. The thief, the pirate, and especially the rake, are often presented as successful, elegant, and happy. Novels abound in immodest and profane allusions or expressions. Wantonness, pride, anger, and unholy love, are the elements of most of them. They are full of exaggerations of men and things. They fill the mind with false estimates of human life. In them the romantic prevails over the real. A book of this sort is very dangerous to the young, for in them the imagination is already too powerful for the judgment.

2. Novels beget *a vain turn of mind.* So true is this, that not one in a hundred of novel-readers is suspected, or is willing to be suspected of being devout. Who by reading a novel of the present day was ever inclined to prayer or praise? Novel-reading is most unhappy in its effects on the female mind. It so unfits it for devotion, that even in the house of God levity or tedium commonly rules it. Thus practical atheism is engendered. The duties of life are serious and weighty. They whose trade it is to trifle and to nourish vanity, cannot be expected to be-well-informed, or well-disposed respecting serious things. However much novel-readers may weep over fictitious misery, it is found that they generally have little or no sympathy with real suffering. Did you never know a mother to send away a sick child, or a daughter to neglect a sick mother, for the purpose of finishing a novel? If irreligion and impiety do not flourish under such influences, effects cannot be traced to causes.

3. The price of these books is often low, yet the *cost* of them in a lifetime is very great. Miss W. borrowed some books, yet she paid seventy dollars in one year for novels alone. Doing this for fifteen years, she would spend one thousand and fifty dollars. Yet her nephews and nieces were growing up without an education. Mrs. L. stinted her family in groceries, that she might have a new novel every month. Mr. C. pleaded want of means to aid to orphan asylum, yet he paid more than sixty dollars a year for novels for his daughters. Novels have, in the last five years, cost the people of the United States from twelve to fifteen millions of dollars. For one, they have paid thirty thousand dollars. This waste is wanton. No good is received in return.

4. Novel-reading is a great *waste of time*—time,

> That stuff that life is made of,
> And which, when lost, is never lost alone,
> Because it carries souls upon its wings.

Nothing is so valuable as that which is of great use, yet cannot be bought with any thing else. We must have time to think calmly and maturely of a thousand things, to improve our minds, to acquire the knowledge of God, and to perform many pressing duties. The business of life is to act well our part here, and prepare for that solemn exchange of worlds which awaits us. He whose time is spent without economy and wasted on trifles, will awake and find himself undone, and will "mourn at the last, when his flesh and his body are consumed, and say, How have I hated instruction, and my heart despised reproof!"

5. The effects of novel-reading on *morals* are disastrous. Many young offenders are made so by the wretched tales which now abound. In one city, in less than three months, three youths were convicted of crimes committed in imitation of the hero of a novel. Here is a court of justice in session. Blood has been shed. Men are on trial for their lives. All the parties involved are intelligent and wealthy. The community is excited. Crowds throng the court-room from day to day. The papers are filled with the letters which led to the tragical end of one, and the misery of many. The whole scene is painful in the highest degree. Among the witnesses is one of manly form, polished manners, and hoary locks. Even the stranger does him reverence. His country has honored him. He must testify, and so sure as he does, he will tell the truth; for he has honor, and blood is concerned. He says, The husband of my daughter was "kind, honorable, and affectionate," and "if my daughter has been in an unhappy state of mind, I attribute it to the impure works of Eugene Sue and Bulwer."[3] All these cases have been judicially investigated and published to the world. They have filled many a virtuous mind with horror, and every judicious parent with concern.

Nor is novel-reading a wholesome recreation. It is not a recreation at all. It is an ensnaring and engrossing occupation. Once begin a novel, and husband, children, prayer, filial duties, are esteemed trifles until it is finished. The end of the story is the charm. Who reads a novel a second time?

Some say, Others do it, and so may we. But others are no law to us. The prevalence of an evil renders it the more binding on us to resist the current.

Novel-reading makes none wiser, or better, or happier. In life it helps none. In death it soothes none, but fills many with poignant regrets. At the bar of God, no man will doubt that madness was in his heart, when he could thus kill time and vitiate his principles. I add,

1. Parents, know what books your children read. If there were not a novel on earth, you still should select their reading. Leave not such a matter to chance, to giddiness, or vice. Give your children good books. A bad book is poison. If you love misery, furnish novels to your children.

2. Young people, be warned in time. Many, as unsuspecting as you, have been ruined. Be not rebellious, to your own undoing. Listen to the voice of kindness, which says, Beware, beware of novels.

3. Pastors, see that you do all in your power to break up a practice which will ruin your young people, and render your ministry fruitless. I was shocked when I heard of one of you recommending a novel which exposed the arts of the Jesuits. The Jesuits are indeed bad, but not worse than Sue.

---

[3]Both Eugene Sue (1804–1857) and Edward George Earle Bulwer-Lytton (1803–1873) were prolific novelists who wrote sensational, entertaining stories.

4. Booksellers, let me say a word. A young man, with a hurried manner, entered a druggist's shop and asked for an ounce of laudanum. It was refused. He went to another and got it, and next morning was a corpse. Which of these druggists acted right? You sell poison when you sell novels. They kill souls. You sell for gain. "Woe to him that coveteth an evil covetousness to his house, that he may set his nest on high, that he may be delivered from the power of evil! Thou hast consulted shame to thy house by cutting off many people, and hast sinned against thy soul. For the stone shall cry out of the wall, and the beam out of the timber shall answer it."[4] You may make money by depraving the public morals, but for all these things God will bring you into judgment.

---

[4]Hab. 2:11.

3

Gift Books

As THE QUANTITY of American published material grew exponentially in the years leading up to the Civil War, books increasingly were sold for reasons besides being simply read. A new genre appeared known as "gift books" or "annuals." Almost exclusively pitched toward female readers, in the early 1830s these books tended to be small, include a few illustrations, and hold a host of varied stories and poems. Throughout the rest of the century, these books grew in physical size, number of illustrations, ornateness of bindings, and amount of content. They were most often designed as gifts to be given by a girl or woman (and sometimes men) to a friend or loved one, and they were often geared to particular seasons such as Christmas, New Year, or Easter.

As the century progressed, the number and locations of gift book publishers grew. By the 1850s, scores of gift book editions were circulating, as both northern and southern publishers produced thousands of volumes each year. Various titles would often be recycled under different names by different publishers, so that tracking editions of gift books in all their guises is often a hopelessly complex task. Such complexity, however, stands as yet one more testimony to the voracious appetite Americans had for these volumes. Stories of quite well-known American authors such as Catharine Maria Sedgwick, Nathaniel Hawthorne, and Sarah Hale were often found in these books, and they became an important way for authors to establish their reputation among the American reading public.

The Pearl; or Affection's Gift is a representative of an early American gift book. It includes an array of short pieces that could be enjoyed by the individual or by a group as they were read aloud. It is but a single example of a genre of books that celebrated both the varied content and the form of books in America's growing print marketplace.

Representative of early antebellum gift book covers, *The Pearl; or Affection's Gift* was bound in a leather cover with a gold border (Philadelphia: Thomas T. Ash, 1833; 4″ × 6″).

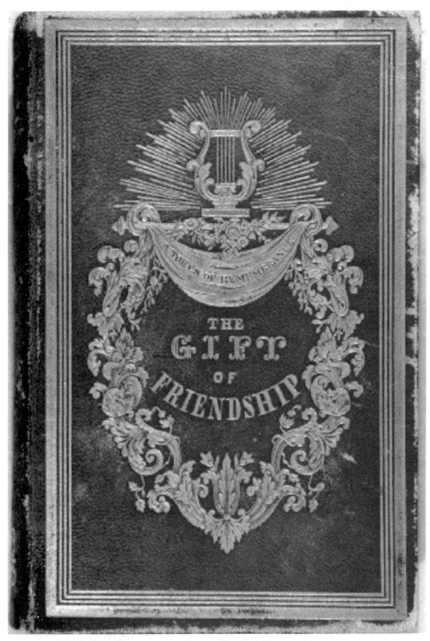

As the century progressed, gift books increasingly appeared in different sizes. Their covers also became more elaborate. The same gift book could also appear in a range of cover designs and colors. This is the cover of *The Gift of Friendship* (Philadelphia: Henry F. Anners, 1848; 4.5″ × 7″). Clearly, there was an importance to reading the exterior, as well as the interior, of these books.

———

THE PEARL

Or Affection's Gift
A Christmas and New Year's Present

❧ Preface

Every exertion has been made by the publisher to make this fifth volume of THE PEARL every way equal if not superior to its predecessors. The writers are more numerous, and some of their articles certainly surpass any former ones from the same pens.

The embellishments are all appropriate, and most of them are entirely new. "At Rest," painted by Mr. THOMAS SULLY; and "Innocence," mezzotintoed by J. SARTAIN, are both very beautiful, and obtained at much cost. "Who's There" and "The Culprit Detected" possess strength of character but seldom met with in small prints.

The style of binding is changed this season to that of embossed morocco.

A copy of the work, handsomely bound, will be presented to those contributors who may decline pecuniary acknowledgements.

The PEARL will be continued for 1834, and contributions are solicited, either in prose or poetry. The writers must always bear in mind that our work is for youth, and therefore articles to be appropriate must be instructive as well as amusing.

❧ The Colloquy

Scene—Chestnut street. Christmas Eve.

HAL AND JAMES

'Come, Hal, just tell me now,' said James,
　'What shall I buy for Kate?
I wish to please her—take great pains—
　Tell quick, for it is late.
Just hark! the clock is striking six,
　While the bells are chiming gay
For Christmas Eve. My mind I'll fix—
　Come, have you nought to say?'

'Why, yes,' said Hal, 'there's things enough;
　A scrap-box you can buy,
With scissors, needles, and *such stuff;*
　They are for sale near by.'

The Pearl; or Affection's Gift. A Christmas and New Year's Present. Philadelphia: Thomas T. Ash, 1833.

"Innocence," frontispiece illustration for *The Pearl; or Affection's Gift,* 1833.

'No,' answer'd James, 'she has a score
    Of boxes and such things;
But can't we think of something more—
    Chains, ribbons, bracelets, rings,

'And books?' 'No, no,' said Hal, 'don't think
    Of books until next week;
For one, of fabled stream I'll drink—
    Oblivion's draught I'll seek.
But, James, is Kate so hard to please?
    Come, boy, make up your mind;
We'd better not stand here and freeze,
    A Christmas gift to find.'

'One thing I know, we could not fail,'
    Said Hal, 'to please this girl,

Had we the gifts of fairy tale,
   Its magic lamp, or pearl.'
'Its *Pearl!* why, Hal, we both forgot
   "The PEARL for thirty-three,"
The very thing, now, is it not?—
   "Affection's Gift" so free.'

A. D. W.
Stockbridge.

Innocence

BY MRS. L. H. SIGOURNEY

My lamb, where hast thou been
   Sporting about all day,
Cropping thy food in pastures green,
   Where the bright waters play?
But of the sunny vale
   Thou 'rt weary now, I see;
Come to these shades, and tell thy tale,
   And rest thy head on me.

I have been sporting too,
   Where grow thy favourite flowers,
Among the lilies fresh with dew,
   Among the vine-clad bowers;—
And by yon chrystal stream,
   Where droops the willow tree,
I sweetly slept, and had a dream,
   A pleasant dream of thee.

And music all around
   Seem'd breathing when I woke,
From nest, and brook, and rose-deck'd bound,
   And from my heart it broke.
Why does thy bosom beat?
   Hath aught disturb'd thy peace?
Dear lamb, did brambles wound thy feet,
   Or rend thy snowy fleece?

Come, I will soothe thy pain,
   If thou wilt tell me free,
And lull thee with that cooing strain
   The young dove taught to me:
Thou by my side shalt run,

Friend and companion dear,
For since thou hast no evil done,
    What evil need'st thou fear?

Hartford, Ct.

❧ Annette

BY MRS. CHILDS

'Whither art going, pretty Annette?
Your little feet you'll surely wet;
Your cloak is twisted out of place—
The sun is shining on your face—
And do you know the fresh warm air
Is tossing back your silky hair?'

'Lady, my feet I often wet,
But it has never harmed me yet.
I love to have the sun and air
Playing about my face and hair;
It makes me lively, bright, and strong,
And clears the voice for my morning song;
If tanned, my mother does not care—
She'd rather I'd be good than fair.'

'But do you venture all alone,
So far away from your own dear home?—
Not even a dog to frisk and play,
And guide you on your lonely way.'

'My mother could not spare the maid;
And I am not at all afraid,
The wind, that tangles smoothest curls,
Is all that harms good little girls.
There cannot be a lonely way
On such a pleasant summer day.
I talk aloud to the pretty birds:
The echoing hills give back my words.
In the running brook the speckled trout
At sight of my shadow glides about—
The miller on the soft green grass
Flies away when my feet would pass—
The hum-bird stops his restless wing,
As if he loved to hear me sing—
And busy bees through shining hours

"Annette" from *The Pearl,* 1833.

Play hide and seek in op'ning flowers.
All things, I see, are very gay;
Lady, the world is full of play.
The clear sky looks so blue and mild—
How *can* there be a lonesome child?'

'Sweet wand'rer in the cool green wood,
I'm sure your heart is very good—
And that is why the fair earth seems
Just waking up from heavenly dreams.
There's something in thy loving voice,
That makes my inmost heart rejoice.
Pray tell me, have I asked you yet,
What's in your basket, dear Annette?'

'Lady, the nurse who watched my slumber,
And sung me stories without number,
Is now too ill to work for pay,
And she grows poorer every day.
Custards, and broth, and jellies good,
My mother sends to her for food.
I bring the water from her well,
And all my pretty stories tell.
Sometimes she loves to hear me read;
Her little garden I can weed;
And all the money in my purse
I gladly spend for my old nurse—
But if I stay to talk so free,
She'll wonder what's become of me.'

'Farewell, sweet wand'rer of the wood!
I knew your little heart was good—
And that is why the fair earth seems
Just waking up from heavenly dreams.'

❧ The Fashionable Boarding School

It is a common remark, that density of population is unfavourable to the virtue of any community; and it is for this reason, perhaps, that there is so much more wickedness in large cities than in villages. If the principle be correct, it will apply in different degrees to every modification of society; and of course schools, in which large numbers meet together, will not be exempt from its operation. There is no doubt that this tendency of numbers may be in some measure counteracted by vigilance and skill on the part of teachers and superintendents; but, alas! these are often wanting.

These thoughts have been suggested by some facts which have recently come to my knowledge in regard to two young ladies—Mary Lewis and her cousin Sarah Lewis—who were sent to a fashionable school in one of our large cities under the following circumstances.

Mary's parents resided in New England; Sarah's had removed from New England during her early childhood to Cincinnati, where her mother died not long after. The brothers had often regretted the almost total suspension of intercourse between their families, occasioned by the distance which separated them; and when Sarah's father, after having given her all the advantages which the schools of Cincinnati afforded, determined to send her away to *complete her education*—this was the term he used—he begged that Mary might be permitted to join her. 'The widow of our lamented friend, Kirkland,' he said, in his letter on the subject, "has consented to receive the girls into her family, and thus they will have an opportunity of finishing their education, and of cultivating that reciprocal acquaintance and friendship, which I am sure we both earnestly desire for them, under the happiest auspices.'

This letter was received by Mary's father, when the family were all sitting, just after dinner, in the sick room of her mother—who, being an invalid, was often confined to it many months at a time, though her complaints were not of a nature that involved present danger. The groupe embraced but one person not hitherto mentioned, Mary's 'sister Louisa,' the child of a former marriage, and many years older than Mary—who had been as a mother to her in consequence of the ill health of Mrs. Lewis.

'Well, Molly,' said Mr. Lewis, after reading the letter aloud, 'what do you say of your uncle's proposition?'

'I should like to accept it, of all things,' replied Mary. 'I am sure from Sarah's letters that I shall find her a pleasant companion, and then, you know, I have been saying for this year past, that it was high time for me to see a little of the world, and get away from sister Louisa's leading strings.'

'Sister Louisa's leading strings, indeed,' retorted Louisa, as she patted Mary's ears in mock resentment, 'it is true that you have been in leading strings all your life, but you have been the leader, and *I* the led—*n'est-ce pas?*'[1]

'Never mind examining that matter too closely,' said Mary. 'At any rate, either from your indulgence, or my extreme docility, it seldom happens that we pull opposite ways; but I think it is time I should learn to act alone for myself, which I am sure I shall never be apt to do, while I have you close at hand to advise with and consult upon all occasions—don't you think so, papa?'

'Yes, dear, I think you are quite right, but then—'

'O, papa,' interrupted Mary, 'pray let us dispense with buts and ifs on this occasion—they have been the torment of my life—thwarting at least half my projects, and constituting an immense subtrahend[2] to be deducted from the sum of my pleasures. There, sister Louisa,' she added, 'you see I have for once used that puzzling awkward term in its proper sense.'

'Well,' said Mr. Lewis, 'I decide at once, my daughter, that you may go, if you please, that is, with your mother's acquiescence; and if you choose, you shall be permitted to enter upon your new scene of life, unforewarned of its dangers or difficulties, and unincumbered with that, to you, most disagreeable of all burdens—advice.'

'Thank you, papa—and another thing I beg to be excused from, viz: from having it supposed that I go to complete my education. I have been sister Louisa's pupil too long not to know that it is but just commenced, and should go on, progressing, to the end of life. It seems to me a very strange notion, common among girls, that at a certain age their education is to be completed.'

'They think so,' said Mr. Lewis, 'because they have no idea of any other education than that which is acquired at school. Hence it happens that there are comparatively so few intelligent, cultivated women to be met with in society. So soon as they forget what they have learned at school, and it is soon forgotten, all trace of the education which has been acquired at a great expense, both of time and money, disappears. They should remember that that education is good for nothing which does not elevate the stan-

---

[1] Isn't it so?

[2] The number to be subtracted.

dard of one's pursuits, and conduce to a permanent habit of intellectual cultivation and improvement.'

'It appears to me,' said Louisa, 'that young ladies cannot be too early, or too much impressed with the truth of the modern doctrine, upon which improved systems of teaching are founded, viz:—that many studies which are pursued in school are to be regarded not as ends, but as means, whose use is to invigorate the powers of the mind, for future exercise; whereas, they are too apt to think, when they leave school, that they have done all that is necessary with and for their minds, and are at liberty to turn their whole attention to dress and amusement.'

'I hear, Louisa,' said Mary jokingly, 'I hear every word, but I don't think I could remember any more at once. And what do you say, mother, about my leaving you?'—she continued, as she stood by her mother's rocking chair, put her arms around her neck, and leaned her cheek upon hers—'you have not uttered one word during this interesting discussion; are you willing, quite willing, that I should leave you?'

'Yes, dear, if your father thinks it best.'

'It will be easier to say good b'ye to all the rest of the house, than to your sick room, mother. How shall I do without it?'

'Rather ask how it will do without you, sweet.'

'You *will* miss my bustling ways and prating tongue a little, then?'

'My winter, Mary, will be as much of an experiment as yours. I have never done without you before.'

'I am sure you have never done with me much—that is, I have never done much for you. Sister Louisa does every thing. If it were not for her I could not think of leaving you.'

'Well, darling, I hope you will have a pleasant and profitable winter. It will wear away at last in my sick room, as elsewhere, for time never stays his wheels, although sometimes their motion seems hardly perceptible.'

'And I shall come back in pleasant company, mother—with the birds and the flowers—so we shall all have a happy meeting together.'

'God grant it, my love; but let us talk no more of this now. Get the new book you were speaking of, and read aloud.'

Mr. Lewis knew to what he was trusting when he told Mary she should be left to her own guidance in the new sphere upon which she was about to enter. She was thoroughly well principled, strong minded, and sagacious, and had many more what may be termed *common sense notions* than are often met with in one of her age. She loved her friends, too, with an ardent affection, through the medium of which her father knew she would still be subject to home influences, though beyond the reach of their immediate operation.

Something of the difference which existed in the character of the two cousins might have been inferred from the different manner in which they were affected at parting. Sarah left home without a single emotion to repress the buoyancy of a youthful spirit, exulting in its favourite, kindred element—variety, novelty; but Mary, although she had boasted her determination not to shed a single tear on the occasion, found herself entirely overcome at last; nor, although her father was with her, did she open her lips until they had got on several miles.

Mary had been in the habit, all summer, of dressing a little flower table that stood in her mother's room; containing a box of sand, which being moistened, kept the flowers that were put in it very fresh. Though it was now quite late in the season, she still continued to gather enough for her purpose, and it was the last thing which she did on the morning of her departure. When she had completed her work, she threw herself on the bed beside her mother, who seldom rose until a late hour, and said, 'Mother, by and by when you get up and have had your breakfast, if you feel able you must walk to the flower table, which I have just filled with fresh flowers, and think of me—it looks prettier than ever this morning.'

Mrs. Lewis felt her heart so heavy when Mary had actually gone, that she protracted her rising to a later hour than usual. She remembered Mary's request, however, and going to the flower table, as soon as she had taken her coffee, discovered a little note tucked in among the flowers, which upon examination she found addressed, 'To my dear Mother.' It was as follows:— 'When you look at my flowers, dear mother, you will miss me, I know. When Pashmataha, the Indian chief, died at Washington, he said his people would hear the tidings, "like the sound of the fall of the mighty oak in the stillness of the wood." I do not suppose that my departure will produce quite so sublime or powerful an emotion as that, but when you find that I am actually gone, I believe you will feel as if something lay heavily at your heart. So, to lighten that feeling, I leave this little note lurking among the flowers, that it may seem as if I still lingered behind, or as if I had come back to take one kiss more. It will be a long, long time before I smooth your pillow, or moisten your hands with cologne water again, but I shall think of you by day and by night. So once more good b'ye, dearest mother.

'Your affectionate daughter,
M. L.'

'P. S. I wonder if ever I shall be patient as you are if I have to be sick as much.'

Mrs. Lewis, after reading this note, showed it to Louisa; then, with a trembling hand and tearful eye she placed it in her bosom, and kept it there day after day, until her husband returned with fresh remembrances.

'Dear child,' said Louisa, 'so pure minded, ardent, and sensitive, how will she ever bear the trials of a school! She unites the feelings of a child with the maturity of mind that belongs to riper years.'

The two brothers and the two cousins arrived safely at the place of destination. It was a happy meeting, and Mary's first impressions of her cousin confirmed those which had been made by her letters. She was good natured and full of vivacity. A week was devoted by the whole party to seeing sights, and what was still more important and interesting to the parties concerned, seeing each other. At the end of that time the brothers returned to their respective homes, and the girls commenced attending school.

Mary's first letter after this period was addressed to Louisa, and as it gives her first impressions of the school, I will transcribe a portion of it.

'Dear sister Louisa—You bade me tell you every thing, and that is just what I wish you to do; for cousin Sarah and I do not think as much alike as I hoped we should; and except her, there is no one here to whom I can open my heart. Mrs. Kirkland is kind enough; but her manner does not invite or encourage confidence. Perhaps it is my fault, but I have not made a single acquaintance yet that I like very much, though Sarah has already half a dozen intimate friends. The girls in the school seem to me different from any I have known before; perhaps it is the difference between town and country, or between fashionable and unfashionable. Education seems to be regarded by them as a ceremony—a sort of process that must be gone through previous to their "*coming out,*" and important only in that view. They tell over their studies as a catholic does his beads, all as a matter of form. Out of school their conversation is chiefly of beaux and dress, and as I do not know a beau in the world, and have no inordinate passion for dress, we seem to have nothing in common. Now and then I laugh at them a little, or sometimes about them, with Sarah; but she is quite disposed to take their part.

'We have many disputes as to what constitutes a lady. I insist upon it, that there are hardly any young *ladies* in the school, they are so very hoydenish[3] in their manners. For instance, they call each other by their sirnames. If one of them wanted my pencil, she would be very apt to say, "Here, Lewis, lend me your pencil."'

In Mary's next letter the following passages occurred:—'I spoke to you, in my last, of the almost total absence of refinement in our school; but I have a still heavier charge to prefer against it. If you will believe me, sister Louisa, there is also a lamentable want of truth and honesty. If it is so in all schools, I am glad that I have been taught at home. There are a few girls very smart and ambitious. These will not scruple to use unfair means, when others fail, for outstripping each other. The mass is composed of those, who, with little ambition, and no fondness for study, feel nevertheless the necessity of maintaining a decent rank in the classes; and this they will endeavour to do with the least possible trouble, adopting all the aids, whether honest or not, in their power. Some hold a book in their lap while reciting—some write their phrases upon a slate, and contrive to hold it in a convenient position for facilitating correct recitation—and it is not at all uncommon to copy French exercises from another's book. As for compositions, I have heard one of the girls boast of her adroitness in "manufacturing over," as she called it, something that she had picked up in a review.

'Sarah is shocked because I say there is so much lying in the school. But are not all false pretences lies? and if made for unworthy purposes, base lies? If I give in, as my own composition, something which I have taken from a book, is it not as much a falsehood, as if I were to say, in so many words, "this is all from my own head?"'

Mary was naturally upright and single-hearted, and all her associations had been with those who were like her in this respect. Of course many things which she now saw, were not only revolting to her sense of right, but affected her with the emotion produced by a disagreeable discovery. It is, I fear, too true, that, in almost every school, there are to be found some whose ambition leads to jealousy, ill will, and injustice, towards their rivals—and others, whose laziness or incapacity, or both, seek some false covering.

It must not be supposed, that Mary indulged this freedom of remark upon what she daily witnessed, to any besides those friends at home, with whom she had been accustomed to the most entire intercommunion of thought and feeling. Her lady-like ways,—her perfect good nature and evident sense,—and more than all, perhaps, on account of its novelty, that entire independence of mind, which prevented her from being af-

---

[3]A hoyden is a female of boisterous or carefree behavior.

fected by the general tone of feeling and sentiment which prevailed in the school, made her generally liked, though she manifested no particular preferences towards any of her companions.

Probably another reason for her being on such good terms with them all, was this— that her scholarship was not so distinguished as to excite any rivalry. It was always respectable; for she had a clear intelligent mind, habits of industry founded upon principle, and a genuine love of improvement; but she had not the faculty of committing regular school lessons with the facility which characterised the acquisitions of many whose powers were in other respects inferior to her own. In one department, however, she soon attained the head, viz. in composition, for here she was aided by that general improvement of mind which she had derived from a general course of reading—such as is usually incompatible with the multifarious pursuits of a regular school, and furnishes a strong argument for home education. Her resources in this respect were beyond those of most young ladies not only at her age, but even after.

With Sarah, the effect of these new associations was far different. No tender mother had watched over her youth, and taught her how to 'keep diligently' her own 'heart.' Without the aid of fixed principle, and without half Mary's native sense, she very soon fell in with the general habits of the school. Mary, who loved her cousin, perceived this with pain, and sometimes ventured a gentle remonstrance; but Sarah's invariable reply was, that she knew no other way but to do at Rome as the Romans do. Frivolous and indolent, she had but too much need of adopting unlawful expedients in order to maintain appearances.

One morning Mary said to her, 'We had better not go out shopping, as you proposed, before school, for you have not yet written your French exercises, and that lesson comes first to-day.'

'O never mind,' said Sarah, 'I can *manage,* and I am afraid that pretty handkerchief that I want, will be gone.'

When they reached the school about ten minutes before the time, Sarah seized Mary's book, ran off to the desk, and copied her exercises. She finished just as the class was summoned.

The teacher found them so unusually correct, that he did not hesitate to say, 'Miss Sarah Lewis, these exercises have been copied.'

'Oh no, sir,' she replied, 'I wrote them last evening.'

He brushed his hand over them by way of reply, and the whole page was blotted. Mary's face was instantly suffused with a deep blush of shame for her cousin, but Sarah's embarrassment was slight and momentary. She smiled, and a titter went through the class. The fraud contradicted no rule in their code of honour.

There was one young lady in the school, Harriett Mildmay, who maintained a decided pre-eminence above the rest in scholarship, and had long been, in that respect, the acknowledged head of the school. No king on his throne was ever more jealous of an usurper, than was she of any one whose claims to this honour threatened to supersede hers. It was a thought not to be endured, that she should find herself excelled in any department; and though Mary Lewis gave her no uneasiness in other respects, she was evidently very much troubled by her success in composition. Week after week Mary's compositions were marked No. 1. At length the tables were turned. Harriett was again pronounced first;

and though Mary knew it was in her power to prefer and prove a charge of plagiarism, she would not do it, but contented herself with simply pointing out the source whence the chief material of Harriett's composition had been derived, to Sarah—not supposing that Sarah, who numbered Harriett among her 'intimate' friends, would ever mention the circumstance.

Sarah, however, had a habit of universal communicativeness, which no consideration of delicacy or prudence was sufficient to repress, and Harriett became aware that she was detected. As often happens in similar instances, she was as much provoked, as indignant, as if the charge had been a false one; and the dislike towards Mary, which had been long gathering in her breast, but which she had been ashamed to betray, because she knew there was no sufficient reason for it, was now manifested without reserve.

It was among the regulations of the school that there should be a public review of all the studies, in the middle and at the expiration of every term. On each occasion of this kind twelve young ladies were selected to write compositions, which, after being read aloud, were referred to a committee, chosen for the purpose, by whose decision the scale of their comparative merits was adjusted.

Two prizes constituted the honours of the evening; one for general scholarship, and the other for the best composition. Harriett Mildmay was almost sure of obtaining the first, but was very much afraid that the other would be adjudged to Mary Lewis. Mary, too, had her hopes; for though so unpretending, she was not insensible to the pleasure of acknowledged superiority. There were two reasons why she particularly wished to succeed; first, because it would gratify her friends at home—and secondly, because she attached a very high value to intellectual cultivation, and was glad of an opportunity to show that, though less apt at set lessons than many of her school-mates, she could more than compete with them in a higher department of education.

Harriett and Sarah had many conferences upon the subject, weighing probabilities, and discussing their mutual hopes. Sarah preferred that Harriett should succeed, for she had become somewhat alienated from Mary by their total dissimilarity of taste and feeling. She thought, too, that Mary was comparatively indifferent upon the subject; or at least, that she would be much less affected by defeat than Harriett.

As the day approached, Harriett became more and more uneasy, and at length she said, 'Sarah, we must contrive some plan or other to prevent Mary's triumph. I cannot endure the thought of being eclipsed for the first time at one of our public reviews, and by Mary too.'

'But cannot you contrive to get something for a composition which you are sure will be better than hers?'

'No, I should not dare write any thing, for this occasion, that was not entirely my own, for fear of being detected by some of the company. But I have thought of a plan that I can adopt, if you approve of it. You know that Mrs. Mayo (the mistress of the establishment) does not see the compositions beforehand; and nobody will think of counting them as they are read, so as to know whether there are really twelve. So if I can contrive to abstract Mary's from the parcel, which you know is tied up with a ribbon, and laid upon the centre table, nobody will miss it; and I am sure she will never speak out about it, at least until it is all over. Do you think she would care much about it?'

'No,' said Sarah, 'I have no idea she would, for she is not at all ambitious.'

'And beside,' rejoined Harriett, 'it is not at all certain, you know, but that the decision would be in my favour, even if I chose to run the risk.'

'But how will you contrive your plan?'

'You know I am one of the committee of arrangements to prepare the room. Mary always uses white paper, and I will use white too, but I will take care to present all the other girls with some that is pink, and too elegant to be resisted. When the parcel is laid upon the table, I will pretend to the girls that I have suddenly recollected a word or two in my composition, wrongly spelt, and must take it in order to alter them. There being no mark to distinguish one from another in the parcel, and Mary's and mine being both on white paper, I must of course look at both to see which is which. Meanwhile you must be at hand, taking a survey of the room, and just at that moment you must contrive to divert the attention of the rest of the girls, which you can easily do by offering them candy or something of the sort. Then, instead of replacing both the compositions, I will tuck Mary's under the table-cloth. When the evening is over, I can find some excuse for remaining last in the room, and I will give the cloth a pull, by which means the paper, concealed beneath, will fall to the floor. The servant who puts up the room in the morning, will find it, and the whole will pass off as an accident. Is not that a capital plot?'

'Most excellent,' replied Sarah, who, though she had nothing malicious in her disposition, and would never have originated such a plan, was too thoughtless to weigh seriously its motives or its consequences, and too frivolous and weak minded not to adopt it, when proposed, without scruple.

The important evening arrived. The assembly of spectators was more numerous and brilliant than usual, and the review passed off very creditably to the different classes; the young ladies, by some magic or other, reciting almost equally well. Those who have been familiar with the private apparatus of a public examination; such, I mean, as is often, though not always resorted to, may perhaps account for this circumstance, without difficulty. The prize of scholarship was then adjudged by Mrs. Mayo to Harriett Mildmay; who, according to the prescribed ceremony, advanced to receive it, kiss the hand which bestowed it, and returned to her seat, followed by the admiring gaze of the assembly.

The compositions were reserved for the conclusion of the scene, and came next in order. 'Now,' thought Mary, 'is perhaps my turn; but how can I ever go through such a disagreeable ceremony; so conspicuous! I had almost rather not have a prize.'

She listened as one after another of the compositions was read, in breathless anxiety to recognise her own. The last that remained was at length unfolded. She coloured and looked down; but that colour was succeeded by paleness when she found herself still disappointed.

'What can this mean!' she was ready to exclaim; 'I am sure I gave in my composition with my own hand, and saw Mrs. Mayo tie it up with the rest!'

An almost breathless silence prevailed while the committee withdrew into a little adjoining library to consult together upon the merits of the compositions. In a few moments they returned; and the senior member announced their decision in favour of Miss Mildmay. She had already advanced to receive the prize, when he requested a few moments' delay. He happened to be an extremely precise old gentleman, and in replacing the compositions upon the table, he took it into his head to count them, and ascertain if the number was right. Perceiving there were but eleven, he returned to the library to find the missing one, and being unsuccessful in his search, asked if there were not some mistake—if twelve were not the appointed number.

Mrs. Mayo replied in the affirmative, and went up to examine the eleven, and see whose was missing. Perceiving none that had the signature of Mary Lewis, she addressed her by name, saying, 'I am sure, Miss Lewis, that I took one from you, and tied it up with the rest.'

Mary could only assent in silence.

Mrs. Mayo looked anxious and somewhat agitated. 'There is certainly some mistake,' said she; 'it may possibly have fallen when the parcel was untied.' After looking under the table she shook the cloth, and the lost paper dropt upon the floor.

Mary looked surprised, and Harriett was observed to crimson. Mrs. Mayo made no comments, but requested that it might be read, which was no sooner done, than the committee reversed their former decision, and gave another, as juries sometimes give their verdict, without retiring, in favour of Miss Lewis, at the same time politely expressing the hope that Miss Mildmay, having already received one of the prizes, would willingly relinquish the other.

It was some time before Mary moved from her seat, after it was evident that Mrs. Mayo awaited her. At length she passed very hastily to receive the prize; and, instead of returning to her seat, left the room by an adjoining door, until she could recover herself a little. Refreshments were now ordered, and soon after the company took their leave.

What impression had been made upon their minds by the incident which I have related, it was impossible to say; but Mrs. Mayo was perfectly aware that the lost composition could not have been *under* the table-cloth by accident. She requested the young ladies to wait a few moments before separating, declared her conviction that there had been intentional wrong committed against Miss Lewis, and her determination to investigate the affair in the morning.

The feelings of Harriett Mildmay that night were little to be envied. Though she had considerable hope of escaping detection, yet she did not feel quite easy on that score; and then her mortification had been greatly aggravated by the circumstances which attended the defeat of her hopes. To have been once preferred to the honour she so eagerly sought, and then to have been obliged to relinquish it the moment Mary's claim came in competition with hers, was worse than if she had only shared defeat with the other competitors.

It had been previously arranged that Mary and Sarah Lewis should remain that night and share a bed with some of Mrs. Mayo's boarders. It happened that Mary slept with one of them who had been on the committee of arrangements, and related to her the circumstance of Harriett Mildmay's taking her composition from the parcel, and replacing it again; and added, 'I was standing at a looking-glass opposite to the table at the time, and saw her slip another paper under the cloth, but I did not think any thing about it then. Mrs. Mayo says she shall examine us all in the morning, and you may depend upon it I shall give in my testimony.'

'O no!' said Mary, 'I wish you would not mention it to any body. It would be terrible to have Harriett disgraced before the whole school, and her chance of reformation would be much less after that.'

'But, then, happening to sit near Mrs. Mayo, as she moved from her seat to the table, I whispered in her ear, "look under the cloth," for the solution of the mystery flashed into my mind all of a sudden, and now I must explain in order to exculpate myself.'

'Well, let me take the affair into my own hands,' said Mary, 'I will take care to save you from all blame or suspicion, and you must promise not to reveal what you know, without my leave.'

This promise obtained, Mary was glad to close her eyes to rest, for even the attainment of the prize was not sufficient to counteract the disagreeable effect which the incidents of the evening produced upon her mind; and she was glad to forget them in the oblivion of sleep.

Immediately after breakfast on the following morning, she sought an interview with Mrs. Mayo, telling her that she believed she had discovered a solution of the mystery, and would communicate it upon condition that Mrs. Mayo would keep it a secret, and forego her designed investigation of the affair.

Mrs. Mayo replied that she thought the culprit, whoever it might be, deserved to be publicly disgraced; but nevertheless she would yield to Mary's generous intercession, reserving the right of private remonstrance and admonition.

When Mrs. Mayo had an explanation with Miss Mildmay, after commenting upon the extreme impropriety of her conduct, and the infamy as well as wickedness of attempting to gain her ends by fraud and injustice, she did not fail to inform her that she owed to Mary's magnaminous interference her exemption from public disgrace.

Harriett's heart was not yet so 'hardened' as to be unaffected by Mary's magnanimity. Though too proud to manifest a change of manner towards her at once, by degrees all trace of her former aversion disappeared, and a friendly intercourse was established between them.

It was fortunate for Harriett that such a crisis arrived. It opened her eyes to the great inconvenience as well as disgrace and wickedness of falsehood in all its forms, and produced a marked change in her character, which had considerable influence in improving that of the school.

When the time approached for the public examination, which was to take place at the close of the term, Mary proposed to Mrs. Mayo to resign her privilege of competing for the prize composition, in favour of a young lady who she knew was extremely anxious to obtain it, in order to gratify a beloved brother by whom she was supported at the school; and Harriett followed Mary's example.

We have not time to follow our favourite home, whither she returned with inexpressible delight, and was welcomed with a joy corresponding to her own.

'Well, sister Louisa,' she said, a few hours after her arrival, 'I have taken a peep into the world, and love my own little corner here better than ever; and I have, perhaps, learned to act for myself; but nevertheless I have no doubt I shall still be very glad to be saved that trouble occasionally.'

What she had seen, felt, heard and experienced, during her absence, constituted materials for many an entertaining conversation; these she called her *school fund.*

The two cousins exhibited the same diversity of character in after life. Sarah became a mere woman of the world, in the inferior sense of that term, who acted from caprice and whim, rather than from principle, and proposed to herself amusement and display, as the chief objects of life. Mary, on the contrary, adopted for her motto, '*l'utile est la belle.*'[4] Her refinement, her sweet manners, her intelligent and agreeable conversation, rendered her the charm of every circle where she was known; and when called upon to fulfil the higher relations of life, she took rank in that honourable class of devoted wives and devoted mothers, who find their highest gratification in a diligent and thorough performance of their appropriate duties. As a wife, she sympathised in all her husband's pursuits, and participated in all his interests; as a mother, she regarded the mind as the noblest part of the beings committed to her care, and moral loveliness as more attractive than personal beauty or accomplishment.

Mary was often heard to express the opinion, that although Sarah would never have been much distinguished for superior excellence, she might have been a much more rational woman, but for the unfortunate bias which her pliant character received at the genteel boarding school.

❧ My Sister Mary

BY MRS. CHILD

UNCLE: Louise! Mary must live with me,
And I'll give you, for company,
A pretty bird with glossy wings,
That hops about and sweetly sings.
Her garden, filled with lovely flowers,
Shall have two honey-suckle bowers,
And golden fish, in sparkling water,
If she will come and be my daughter.

LOUISA: But she's *my* sister, Uncle Carey—
My own sweet loving sister Mary.
I cannot spare her for a day,
She helps me at my work and play;
How I should cry if she were gone!
I could not dress my doll alone;
Therefore, dear uncle, I do pray
You will not make her go away.
Good cousin Jane may live with you,
She has no little sister Loo.
You may give her the bright Canary,

---

[4]That which is useful is pretty.

"My Sister Mary" from *The Pearl,* 1833.

And let me keep dear sister Mary.
I'm very sure she will not go
From little Loo, who loves her so.
UNCLE: Now blessings on your gentle heart!
I should be loth to see ye part;
E'en angels might rejoice like me,
In the pure love of infancy.
You need not cling to her in fear—
You shall not lose your playmate, dear;
My words were merely meant to prove
The strength and fervour of your love;
I will give her the bright Canary,
And she shall be *your* sister Mary.

❧ The Cadet's Sister

A DRAMATIC DIALOGUE FOUNDED ON FACT

BY MISS LESLIE

The scene is at Mrs. Lesmore's house in one of the towns on the banks of the Hudson—the time is the latter part of a summer afternoon—Mrs. Lesmore sewing at a table in her front parlour—Laura seated opposite to her, with her drawing materials.

LAURA: Dear mother, I believe I must put up my drawing for this day. I cannot draw as well even as usual, my mind being so much engrossed with the expectation of seeing my brother this afternoon. I feel too happy to think of any thing else. See, I have made the squaw's face quite too dark even for an Indian, and her child's hair looks as stiff as bristles. If I touch the warrior again, I shall certainly spoil him.

MRS. LESMORE: Your sketch is not so bad, my dear, as you describe it; but I think you had better give up drawing for the present. To-morrow you will feel more composed.

LAURA: I am sorry, for I had set my mind on finishing this group of Indians before Marcus came home; particularly as it is from an original design by a young officer that he is intimately acquainted with. Marcus, you know, is extremely desirous that I should improve in my drawing, and I hope in time to able to sketch from nature and from my own imagination, almost as beautifully as he does.

MRS. LESMORE: Well, my dear, it gives me pleasure to tell you that you *do* improve rapidly. Mr. Mitford considers you one of his best pupils.

LAURA: And Marcus will be glad to find that I am head of the first class at French school. Now if I could only have taken lessons in music, what pleasure it would give me to play to Marcus after he comes home. However, as he is accustomed every morning and evening to hear the fine band at West Point, perhaps mere piano-playing might seem to him very insipid.

MRS. LESMORE: My dear, you must not regret that you cannot be instructed in music. I do not think you have any decided talent for that charming science, and your voice is not such as to authorize the hope that you would ever sing well.

LAURA: Still, dear mother, I might make up in application for what is wanting in natural genius. If I could be enabled to take lessons on the piano, you have no idea how attentive and assiduous my instructor would find me. I would willingly practise five or six hours every day, and I would take such pains, and be so unremitting in my endeavours, that I think I should at length acquire as much proficiency as the generality of young girls.

MRS. LESMORE: There is no accomplishment more expensive than that of music. There is none that requires more time and closer attention, and there is none that is sooner forgotten. To play even tolerably, is frequently the work of years; and to play *well,* you must have constant instruction from an excellent and consequently an expensive teacher, and you must practise regularly and carefully for several hours every day. Then, after all, it is impossible to be a good musician without an excellent ear, considerable taste, and a large share of native genius. Also, a fine voice is indispensable, for ladies that play are generally expected to sing. There are many other considerations. Music is the most costly of all accomplishments. In the first place, a high price must be given for a good instrument; a good teacher, as I before remarked, always commands a large compensation; and a great deal of money must necessarily be expended in buying songs and pieces. I have always been of opinion that persons in moderate circumstances should not allow their children to be instructed in music unless they evince an extraordinary talent for it, or expect eventually to pursue it as a profession. Think yourself fortunate, my dear Laura, in having it in your power to learn drawing, dancing, and French; beside all the usual branches of a good English education.

LAURA: Well, mother, I have now put away all my drawing apparatus. Will you give me some sewing to pass away the time till Marcus arrives?

MRS. LESMORE: Yes, you may hem this frill.

LAURA: Some one rings at the front door. Perhaps it is dear Marcus, (*running to the window.*) Oh! no. It is that tiresome Mrs. Clapperton, come back already from New York. And she is as teasing and disagreeable as she is tiresome. She never visits us but to say something that is mortifying or painful, or to ask impertinent questions.

MRS. LESMORE: My dear Laura, you must not allow yourself to speak so freely of any acquaintance of the family.

LAURA: I am glad to hear you call her *an acquaintance* only. But I might have been sure you never classed her among your *friends.* Oh! how different she is from dear Mrs. Elwood, whose visits always make us cheerful and happy.

[MRS. CLAPPERTON enters—very expensively drest.]

MRS. CLAPPERTON: My dear Mrs. Lesmore, I hope you are well. It seems an age since I last saw you. And my sweet Laura too—as industrious as ever, I suppose. Well, you are certainly right. There is no knowing what may happen, and your accomplishments may one day be turned to profitable account. It is a fine thing for girls to be able to get their own living.

[She sits down on a chair that LAURA has placed for her.]

MRS. LESMORE: When did you return from New York, Mrs. Clapperton?

MRS. CLAPPERTON: I got home last evening about sunset.

MRS. LESMORE: I suppose you found the city as gay as usual.

MRS. CLAPPERTON: Oh! quite as much so—dear, delightful Broadway was always so crowded that we found it difficult to get along. That is, on the west side, for it is not the fashion to walk on the other. And the Battery is thronged every evening.

MRS. LESMORE: Was the steam-boat very full yesterday when you came up?

MRS. CLAPPERTON: Yes, very—and I was glad that we were not to pass the night on board. Oh! I must not forget to tell you, Mrs. Lesmore, that on the day we went down to the city we heard a great deal about your son Marcus, from a cadet named Wansley, that we took on board at West Point, and whom Mr. Clapperton suspected had been dismissed for some misdemeanor, because he talked so unfavourably of the academy and the professors and officers. You know that successful cadets generally speak highly of the institution and of all who are connected with it.

MRS. LESMORE: Was this cadet acquainted with my dear Marcus?

MRS. CLAPPERTON: Yes, I asked him; and he said that he knew Marcus Lesmore perfectly well. I must confess that he told me some strange things about him.

LAURA: I am sure he could tell you nothing to his disadvantage.

MRS. LESMORE: My son, I know, stands very high in his class.

MRS. CLAPPERTON: I made no inquiries on that subject; but I asked young Wansley if Marcus Lesmore was liked in the corps; that is, if he was popular with the other cadets.

MRS. LESMORE: I hope the answer was in the affirmative.

MRS. CLAPPERTON: Why—not exactly—in short, my dear Mrs. Lesmore, I am sorry to tell you that your son does not seem to be a favourite with his companions.

LAURA: How is that possible?

MRS. LESMORE: I am indeed amazed. With his kind feelings and good temper, I see not how he can be otherwise than in favour with them.

MRS. CLAPPERTON: Why, you know that boys seldom set much value on money, and that they usually spend it freely even when they have but little. It seems, however, that your son is so close an economist, that, to speak the plain truth, he has lost the regard of all his companions. None are now on terms of intimacy with him, and he has got the nickname of 'young Elwees.'

MRS. LESMORE: You astonish and distress me—if this is indeed true, how much my son must have changed!

MRS. CLAPPERTON: Every body is liable to change.

MRS. LESMORE: It cannot be true—it is incredible.

MRS. CLAPPERTON: Few mothers will believe any thing against their children.

LAURA: (*With tears in her eyes.*) My dear brother to be nicknamed Elwees, after that wretched old miser. Why does not Marcus knock down every boy that calls him so?

MRS. CLAPPERTON: Oh! of course they take care not give him that appellation to his face. And even if they did, people are not very apt to resent indignities when they are conscious of deserving them.

MRS. LESMORE: Mrs. Clapperton, you both offend and afflict me. I doubt if your informant was able to support his allegation by any thing like proof.

MRS. CLAPPERTON: Oh! yes, indeed—he went into particulars. For instance, Mr. Wansley told me that Marcus Lesmore is as saving as possible, even in his most trifling expenses, and that he acts as if every cent was to him an object of consequence. He is particularly careful of his clothes, and tries his utmost to make them last as long as possible. He never sends down to the city for new novels, or any other books of amusement. He has discontinued his newspaper, and does not take a single magazine. He never goes to the shop where they sell fruit and soda water. He has with his own hands made various little things for his room, rather than go to the expense of buying them. When the cadets have a ball he stays away because he will not be one of the subscribers to it; and for the same reason he is never seen at a concert or other entertainment. In short, he declines subscribing to any thing, and seems resolutely bent on saving as much money as possible. He has been going on in this penurious way for the last two years, therefore it is strange you should not have heard something of it before this time. Oh! there is another thing I must not forget. During the summer recess he never, like the other cadets, asks permission to visit the city, but he remains in camp all the time.

MRS. LESMORE: Oh! no, not quite all the time—he always comes up to pass a few days with his mother and sister.

MRS. CLAPPERTON: But he goes no where else.

MRS. LESMORE: It is true that his anxiety to make the most of his time, while his education is yet unfinished, and his desire to improve in tactics (the branch which is particularly practised during encampment), has hitherto prevented him from paying us long visits. But this being his last year, he is now exempt from military duty, and he can remain with us several weeks, and next summer he will be commissioned. Still, I am surprised and shocked at what you tell me. My son's disposition was always generous and liberal; exactly like his father's.

MRS. CLAPPERTON: Excuse me, my dear Mrs. Lesmore, but as Marcus knows that his father's liberality injured the circumstances of the family, perhaps he thinks it better to keep on the safe side, and accustom himself thus early to habits of strict economy. I admire his prudence, but I am sorry he should go such lengths as to be accounted *mean*.

LAURA: Oh! but indeed, a mean boy is such an unnatural character. I am certain my dear Marcus cannot deserve it.

MRS. CLAPPERTON: Well, I can assure you that from what Mr. Wansley said, Marcus Lesmore has actually obtained that character, and is believed by the whole corps of cadets to deserve it. I am very sorry, for in the opinion of boys there is nothing more contemptible than a young miser. And I must own that I have never heard of his sending any little presents to his mother and sister.

MRS. LESMORE: Mrs. Clapperton, say nothing on that subject. He undoubtedly finds his pay little enough for his unavoidable expenses.

MRS. CLAPPERTON: How is it, then, that as young Wansley assured me the cadets can generally defray all their 'unavoidable expenses,' with their allowance of twenty-eight dollars a month, and have still something left for other purposes? So close as he is, I really think Marcus must by this time have saved a little fortune. He must have money in the bank, or perhaps he intends buying a house. Well, it is very prudent, though certainly not very common, for a boy of eighteen to think of providing for his old age.

MRS. LESMORE: You must excuse me, Mrs. Clapperton, but I cannot bear any jesting at the expense of my son.

MRS. CLAPPERTON: Well, do not be angry, but I have not told you the half that I heard about him. Wansley related some of the most curious anecdotes.

MRS. LESMORE: What you have already told has given me so much pain, that I would rather hear no more.

MRS. CLAPPERTON: Your Marcus is certainly very different from my William, whose money flies as if it was dust. He is never satisfied except when he is down at New York; and when there, he goes every night to the theatre, and frequently to a ball after the play is over. He is continually hiring horses and gigs, and going on water-parties. And he never spends less than a dollar a day at the confectioner's or oyster houses. Then, since his trip to Philadelphia, he will not wear even a light summer jacket, unless it is made at Watson's. But I like to see a boy of spirit, and I make his father indulge him in every thing he wants. However, I must now take my leave, for I expect in the next boat five new dresses, which were not quite finished before I left the city; and I must despatch John to the wharf to be ready to get the boxes. If you call to-morrow morning I will show them to you. They are all in the very first style. So good b'ye.

MRS. LESMORE: Good afternoon, Mrs. Clapperton.

[LAURA accompanies MRS. CLAPPERTON to the door, and then returns.]

LAURA: (*Bursting into tears*). Oh! my dear mother!

MRS. LESMORE: My beloved girl, I am as much grieved and mortified as you can be, at what Mrs. Clapperton has been telling us.

LAURA: I am sure it cannot be true.

MRS. LESMORE: There is undoubtedly some exaggeration, both on the part of Mrs. Clapperton and that of the cadet who was her informant. But the charge is of so unusual a nature that I fear it must have some foundation, otherwise no one would dare to advance it.

LAURA: I believe it to be mere slander. But Marcus is so sensible and so amiable, that it is surprising he should have a single enemy.

MRS. LESMORE: Whatever may be the good qualities of a young man, he will never be popular with his associates if they have reason to suspect him of any thing that borders on parsimony. In the eyes of youth meanness is an unpardonable fault.

LAURA: But how he must have changed! When he was a boy at home, his money was always laid out in some way or other as soon as it was given to him. And he was so generous to his friends and to me, and so willing to share whatever he had.

MRS. LESMORE: It is true, as Mrs. Clapperton rudely and ill-naturedly reminded us, that Marcus has never sent even the most trifling present to you or to me.

LAURA: Oh! dearest mother, never allude to that again. I dare say he finds his pay quite little enough.

MRS. LESMORE: But if other cadets can live on their pay, and still allow themselves many indulgences—Oh! Laura, Laura, I fear indeed, that all is not right.

LAURA: Oh! that Marcus would arrive, and then we might immediately ascertain the truth.

MRS. LESMORE: It is torture to think ill of him even for a few moments.

LAURA: I hear a wheelbarrow stop at the door; it must be Marcus's baggage—(*she runs to the window*) ah! here he is!

MRS. LESMORE: My dear Marcus!

[They hasten to the front door, and then return to the parlour with MARCUS, *who throws his cap on the table, and seats himself on the sofa between his mother and sister.]*

MARCUS: Well, my dear mother, here I am once more. We had every thing to make our passage from West Point delightful; but still it seemed to me a very long one— I was so impatient to arrive at my beloved home.

MRS. LESMORE: How much you have grown! You look half a head taller than when we last saw you.

LAURA: And how much handsomer you are now, than before you went to West Point.

MARCUS: (*smiling*) You must allow something for my uniform—(*a pause*) But, my dear mother, you look disturbed and uneasy, and Laura has certainly been in tears. What has happened?—tell me at once.

LAURA: Did you never hear of any one crying with joy?

MARCUS: But joy is not the cause of the tears that are *now* filling your eyes. I have more penetration than to believe that the only emotion you feel at this moment is pleasure on seeing me again, after a long separation. There is something else—something has happened—some recent cause of affliction—some new misfortune.

MRS. LESMORE: Oh! no—no—

MARCUS: Dearest mother, tell me the whole—neither you nor Laura receive me as you did when I came home last summer. Something, I am sure, is wrong.

MRS. LESMORE: Marcus—I *will* tell you.

LAURA: (*in a low voice to Mrs. Lesmore*) Dear mother, do not say any thing about the cadets calling him 'young Elwees.'

MRS. LESMORE: Mrs. Clapperton has just been here, having recently returned from New York.

MARCUS: I am glad her visit to you was over before my arrival. I think her a very foolish, impertinent woman.

MRS. LESMORE: When she was going down the river, a cadet (probably one that had just been dismissed) came on board at West Point. Mrs. Clapperton got into conversation with him, and asked some questions concerning you.

MARCUS: May I know what he said of me?

MRS. LESMORE: He said that—how can I tell you—I know not in what manner to begin.

LAURA: Oh! dear mother, tell it not at all—at least not till to-morrow. Let us try to be as happy as we can this first evening of Marcus's return.

MARCUS: My curiosity is now so highly excited that I must entreat, and, were I not addressing my mother, I would say, I must *insist* on knowing.

MRS. LESMORE: Well, then, Marcus, I have been surprised and mortified to hear that you are accused by your companions of an extraordinary disposition to—to—what shall I call it?

LAURA: To economize rather strictly. Dear mother, you know that economy is a virtue.

[MARCUS rises, and traverses the room in much emotion.]

MRS. LESMORE: In plain terms—that you are more saving of your money than is usual, or indeed becoming in a youth of your age. That you carefully avoid every expense that is not absolutely necessary. That you join in no amusement which is likely to cost you any thing and that you take the utmost pains to live on as little as possible.

MARCUS: It is all true.

LAURA: True!—Oh Marcus!

MRS. LESMORE: Can it indeed be true, that you have carried your economy so far that it is remarked and commented upon by all the cadets, and that some of them look coldly on you, while others ridicule you?

MARCUS: I know they do—and they have nicknamed me 'young Elwees.'

LAURA: Oh! Marcus! Why is all this?

MARCUS: Have you not always told me, dear mother, that every one should endeavour to live within his income—is it then right that I should expend the whole of mine?

MRS. LESMORE: I have always supposed that your pay is no more than sufficient for the expenses incident to your situation.

MARCUS: Excuse me, dear mother, it *is* more than sufficient.

MRS. LESMORE: But not if you live like other cadets. I am extremely sorry that this singular and strict economy should have made you unpopular with your comrades; but a young man that is suspected of meanness never has many friends.

MARCUS: Have you heard any thing else against me? Has any one, told you that I have neglected my studies, or infringed on the rules of the institution; that I have on any occasion evinced a refractory or insubordinate spirit; or that I have ever been guilty of any thing dishonourable or immoral?

MRS. LESMORE: Oh! no, no—all that we have heard, all that we know, convinces us of the contrary.

MARCUS: Then, as, according to the old aphorism, 'every one has his fault,' let me beg a little indulgence for mine.

MRS. LESMORE: But, Marcus, parsimony, or meanness, if I must speak plainly, is a fault so unusual, so extraordinary in a very young person, that I own it both surprises and grieves me to hear it attributed to you.

LAURA: Dear brother, only just tell us why you are so saving of your clothes, and why you avoid partaking of the few amusements that are within your reach; and above all, why you have discontinued your newspaper?

MARCUS: As to my clothes, no one can say that I ever make a shabby or slovenly appearance.

LAURA: You certainly look very nicely now.

MARCUS: As to amusements, they are always matters of taste. My companions amuse themselves in their way, and I in mine.

LAURA: But we have heard that you never buy any books—you that were always so fond of reading!

MARCUS: I have not yet read all the books in the public library belonging to the academy.

LAURA: But books of amusement, dear Marcus.

MARCUS: I shall have time enough after I am commissioned to read books of that description. At present it is my duty to restrict myself to such works as will be useful to me in my profession, and with these I can amply supply myself from the library.

LAURA: All this is very right and proper, Marcus, but still it is not like a boy.

MRS. LESMORE: Marcus, there is some mystery connected with this subject. I know that your natural disposition is generous and liberal, and that your perseverance in this system of rigid economy must have cost you many painful sacrifices. There must be some powerful motive, and your family ought to know it. Tell us, then, dear Marcus.

[He remains silent.]

LAURA: Oh! Marcus, will you not speak when your sister, your only sister, entreats you?

MRS. LESMORE: Or must you be told that your mother *commands* you?

[MARCUS bows to his mother, casts down his eyes, and then throws his arms round LAURA's neck.]

LAURA: Dear Marcus, why have you so long been acting unlike yourself? What is the cause?

MARCUS: (*deeply affected*)—*You,* Laura, you are the cause.

LAURA: I—Oh! explain yourself.

MARCUS: (*taking a hand of each*)—Mother—sister—what shall I say?—You know that my father left you in circumstances far from affluent. Fortunately he had yielded to my earnest desire, and permitted me to prepare myself at West Point for a military life. I had often, after you became a widow, heard you regret your inability to afford my sister such an education as she would have had if my father still lived. I, in the mean time, was enjoying the benefit of an excellent course of instruction at the expense of my country; and when I thought of my dear Laura, I often wished that she was a boy, and could participate in the same advantages. But then again, I consoled myself by reflecting on her happiness in being always with her mother, and on the mutual comfort and pleasure you both derived from being always together. Knowing that the narrowness of your income would not permit either of you to mix much in society, and that you live in comparative retirement, I anticipated the satisfaction it would give you both if Laura could be enabled to cultivate the talents that Heaven has bestowed on her. And when impressed with this idea, after the thought had once struck me—how shall I go on?—in short, I determined to live as economically as possible myself, in the hope of being able, at the end of the year, to save enough to meet the expenses of my sister's education.

LAURA: (*in tears*)—Dear, dear Marcus.

MARCUS: I tried the experiment, and I found it practicable; but I did not wish my mother and sister to know it, lest they should refuse to accept the fruits of my savings. Therefore, I always contrived to send the money down to New York, that the letter which enclosed it might not have the West Point post mark. I wrote in a disguised hand a few lines implying that this money was the gift of an unknown friend of the late Colonel Lesmore, and that it was designed to assist in the education of his daughter. All is now explained.

MRS. LESMORE: (*embracing him*)—My beloved son!

LAURA: (*Pressing his hand to her heart*)—My darling brother.

MRS. LESMORE: How could I for a moment suppose that my dear Marcus might be unable to justify himself, however appearances and reports were against him. And now, my child, I have some excellent news for you, which I heard but yesterday, and which I have not yet disclosed to Laura, as I wished to reserve it as an addition to our happiness on the evening of your arrival at home. Mr. Adamson, by whose bankruptcy your father was ruined, has just returned from the West Indies, where he has made a fortune by some lucky speculations. He is now able to pay all his creditors, and, being a very conscientious man, he is determined to do it immediately. The sum that will fall to our share is large enough to enable us in future to dispense with any further assistance from the kindness of dear Marcus. We shall now have an income that will be amply sufficient.

LAURA: Delightful news!

MRS. LESMORE: And now, my dear Marcus, you must promise me that on your return to West Point you will be again yourself, and cease to practise that rigid economy which, while it was so advantageous to your sister, must have subjected you to perpetual inconveniences and annoyances.

MARCUS: Dear mother, I will do as you wish me; and now that I have no longer the same motive for self-denial, I confess that I shall resume my former, and let me add, my natural habits, with pleasure. My comrades shall again see me in my own character. But I can assure you that my satisfaction in the thought of being able to benefit my dear Laura, amply compensated for any pain or inconvenience that I endured in consequence.

LAURA: How could you persevere so long when the cadets ridiculed you, and called you a young miser?

MARCUS: I bore the opprobrium patiently, because I knew it to be unmerited. It is much easier to suffer under an erroneous imputation, than to endure the shame and self-reproach of a real fault.

MRS. LESMORE: You have chosen, my dear Marcus, the profession of arms, and should the peace of our country be again invaded, you must, in the hour of danger, take your chance for life or death; and as personal intrepidity is one of the attributes of your sex, I trust that when the hour comes you will not swerve from your duty. But how highly to be prized is that moral courage which, in a good cause, can submit without shrinking to daily and hourly privations, and endure with patience the painful suspicion of a fault most opposite to the truth.

There are many who, with unshaken firmness, can 'see the front of battle lour,' but the energy of mind is far more rare that can steadily submit to a long course of self-denial, to unjust animadversions, and to unmerited ridicule, and find sufficient consolation in the silent and secret exercise of the best feelings of generosity and affection.

The Pebble and the Acorn

BY H. F. GOULD

'I am a pebble, and yield to none,'
Were the swelling words of a tiny stone.
'Nor change nor season can alter me,
I am abiding while ages flee.
The pelting hail and the drizzling rain
Have tried to soften me long, in vain;
And the tender dew has sought to melt,
Or to touch my heart, but it was not felt.
None can tell of the pebble's birth,
For I am as old as the solid earth.
The children of man arise, and pass
Out of the world, like blades of grass.
And many a foot on me has trod
That's gone from sight, and under the sod!
I am a pebble! but who art thou,
Rattling along from the restless bough?'

The acorn was shocked at this rude salute,
And lay for a moment, abashed and mute.
She never before had been so near
This gravelly ball, the mundane sphere,
And she felt for a while perplexed to know
How to answer a thing so low.
But to give reproof of a nobler sort
Than the angry look, or the keen retort,

At length, she said, in a gentle tone,
'Since it has happened that I am thrown
From the lighter element where I grew,
Down to another so hard and new,
And beside a personage so august,
Abased, I will cover my head with dust,
And quickly retire from the sight of one
Whom time, nor season, nor storm, nor sun,
Nor the gentle dew, nor the grinding wheel,
Has ever subdued, or made to feel.'
And soon, in the earth, she sunk away
From the comfortless spot where the pebble lay.

But it was not long ere the soil was broke
By the peering head of an infant oak;
And, as it arose, and its branches spread,
The pebble looked up, and wondering said,
'A modest acorn! never to tell
What was enclosed in her simple shell—
That the pride of the forest was then shut up
Within the space of her little cup!
And meekly to sink in the darksome earth,
To prove that nothing could hide her worth.
And, oh! how many will tread on me,
To come and admire the beautiful tree,
Whose head is towering towards the sky,
Above such a worthless thing as I.
Useless and vain, a cumberer here,
I have been idling from year to year;
But never from this shall a vaunting word
From the humbled pebble again be heard,
Till something without me, or within,
Can show the purpose for which I've been!'
The pebble could not its vow forget,
And it lies there, wrapped in silence, yet.

❧ The Juvenile Ball

BY THE AUTHOR OF 'LIGHTS OF EDUCATION'

'Well,' cried Charles Moreton, on his return from a youthful assembly, with his sister Anna, 'if I were to see a brother of mine behave as those little urchins did, at Mrs. Austin's, I should take him out pretty quickly, I know. Anna, did you see the Ogdens?'

'Yes,' answered Anna, 'one of them took the last cake from a waiter as the servant handed it to me, and then said, that the young ladies could get no refreshments, but many of the other boys were just as bad.'

'I dare say they were,' said Charles, 'and *many* of the *girls* behaved shamefully too; I think they eat enough to make themselves sick for a week.'

'I know they did, Charles, and I was so afraid Mrs. Austin and the other ladies would believe me as bad as the rest, that I did not eat a thing the whole night, so I intend to have a little bread and butter now, and may be you would like to have some, Charles, for I suppose you were too scornful to eat in such a society of ill behaved children, and you almost *sixteen.*'

'Oh no, Miss Anna, I was not too *scornful* by any means, if I had had a chance; but I suppose I know more of the manners of a *gentleman* than to run about after the servants, as these little monkeys did.'

'Well, children,' said Mrs. Moreton, 'it appears from this that you have both returned from a feast unsatisfied, and I am glad to find that you were more attentive to preserve your good manners than to destroy your good appetites, which shall now be more healthfully exercised.'

While the young people were enjoying their excellent supper of bread and butter and milk, Mrs. Moreton expressed her surprise that such impoliteness as they described should be suffered to appear at any party where grown people presided.

'Oh, mother!' exclaimed Charles, with all the consequence of sixteen, 'what can two or three grown people do among such a mob of children—boys no bigger than George, and girls that can hardly walk, the little fat things: they are all Misters and Misses, to be sure—Miss *Dumpling* and Mr. *Lumpkin.* But you can have no idea what babies they are. I suppose George is not going to Mrs. Calvert's, is he, mother?'

George, who was very diligently studying his lessons, lifted up his head for the second time, as his name was mentioned, and now looked appealingly to his mother and his sister Sophia, who was a year or two older than Charles.

'I hope George has learned to conduct himself properly,' said Mrs. Moreton, 'and for that reason he shall go.'

'Well, I guess it is the last *children's* party that I shall ever go to, even if I am *invited;* and since I must take care how George minds his lessons in good manners, I'm sure I will not have much pleasure in this.'

'Why, Charles,' said Sophia, 'I think you give yourself more uneasiness than is necessary about George's behaviour, for, in general, he is a very polite little boy; I never saw *him* keep his seat, while his sisters were standing; and I believe, brother, when papa and mama are both away, he always offers the choice of the arm-chairs to you.'

'Oh yes! it is easy enough for him to be civil, when he is by himself; but wait till he gets with boys of his own size; and then, Sophia, *you* would not like to be a whole evening watching him, and have no pleasure yourself.'

'No; and for that reason, I would not watch him so much, as to let him have no pleasure either.'

'But I intend to watch him, Sophia, and take care that he does not disgrace his family; I've seen too much of it with other boys.'

'Well, Charles,' said Mrs. Moreton, now interposing, 'if you please, we will put a stop to this disagreeable discussion. I hope I could trust George to take care of his sister and himself, were you to decline Mrs. Calvert's invitation.'

'But, mama,' said George, for the first time discomposing his philosophy so far, as to join in this debate, 'if Charles thinks he would like to go to the party, only for me, I could stay at home; I don't much care about it.'

'No; George,' said his mother, 'though, I dare say, there will be many young gentlemen and ladies at this entertainment, who fancy themselves men and women; yet, as the eldest of Mrs. Calvert's children is scarcely eleven, her invitation is really more adapted to you; and therefore, I intend, if your father has no objection, that you shall go.'

Mr. Moreton now came in from another room, where he had been writing; and soon after George retired to rest. When he was gone, Mrs. Moreton spoke to Charles very reasonably, on his treatment of this little brother.

'You ought to remember, Charles, that he is not ten years old, and, therefore, his faults are excusable; especially, when a word or two judiciously said is often sufficient to correct them; and I must say, that of all my children, he appears to possess in the greatest degree, the *untaught principle* of civility. I am sure you observe every day, the extremely polite temper with which he receives your reprimands.'

Mrs. Moreton uttered these last words with a pleasant smile, which Charles could not avoid returning.

'Well, I think any person may be good tempered, if he is either a boy or a man; but it does put a *fellow out so much* to be neither one thing nor another.'

'Then, Charles,' said his father, laughing, 'let me advise you to cultivate a little of George's philosophy, that you may go more smoothly along this tiresome stage of our journey through life.'

'And do you think, father, that George is always so easy as he seems at home, and nothing ever puts him in a passion? I know I saw him knock a boy over yesterday, about his own size; and he never told me what it was for.'

'Did you ask him?'

'No, I did not, sir; I told him to go in the house though, and let the boy alone.'

'And was the boy more communicative?'

'No, sir, for while I was talking to George, he sneaked off.'

'No great sign of his being in the right. But, my dear, (speaking to Mrs. Moreton,) ask George about the affair; and if *he* was in the *wrong*, I will not let him go to this party.'

'Oh! I am sure, sir, George must have had provocation,' cried Charles, in a moment, sensible that his petulance rendered him unkind.

'We will soon know, however,' said his father. 'I do not suppose, my love, that George is yet undressed; will you go to him?'

Mrs. Moreton instantly complied. When she entered George's room, she found him seated on a low chair at the foot of his bed, slowly pulling off his stockings, very slowly indeed, while his eyes were fixed admiringly on a splendid red bird, of South America, beautifully preserved, and given to him by a Spanish gentleman, for saying '*Como esta usted, señor;*'[5] and he had hung it up opposite to his bed, that he might contemplate the bright colours as soon as he opened his eyes every morning; when may be his reflections took a *fabulous* range over the countries the bird had passed through; but as he never made a confession of this, we have no right to take it for granted.

---

[5]How are you, mister?

'George,' said Mrs. Moreton, 'I am come to ask you something.'

'Then will you sit down, mama? may be you want my little chair;' and he slided off on the floor, quietly continuing his employment, but turning his eyes from the object of their admiration, to his mother. She smiled as she took the seat.

'What was the cause of your quarrel with that boy yesterday? Your father wishes to know, George.'

'The boy that I hit, mother—did Charles tell father about it?'

'Yes, but then he said you must have had some provocation.'

'No, I had not, mother; the boy never did any thing to me; but he had no business to want to come into our yard, after that poor kitten, and go to kill it.'

'What kitten, George?'

'Why, a poor little cat he was flinging stones at ever so often; it did not belong to him; but when I told him to quit, he struck me, and so I gave it back. He was not much bigger than I, though may be he considered himself "a *touch* above *hypocrisy,*" as Charles says.'

Mrs. Moreton laughed at this version of her son's favourite phrase. Whenever he meant to express an *assumption* of superiority in any respect, he would say 'it was a touch above *mediocrity;*' but this word, translating to suit his own capacity, George now rendered *hypocrisy,* which, being rather better suited to the undisguised pretensions of vanity and pride, the phrase was afterwards laughingly adopted with that amendment.

'Well, George, I see nothing to blame in your conduct, as you state it. But what became of the cat?'

'Why, the cook said it might stay here to catch mice; so we feed it.'

'Very well, my dear. Now, good night, and do not let your bird make you forget your prayers.'

'Oh, it could not do that, mother, even if it was to talk. Indeed, may be then it would tell me, I must pray a great deal more to One who made such a nice bird, and me.'

'My dear little fellow,' cried Mrs. Moreton, 'if every person cherished such holy thoughts of the divine Creator, we should not see Him so often apparently forsaking the work of his own hands. Continue, my child, thus gratefully to love him, and he never will forsake you.'

She then returned to the parlour, and related her conversation with George; to which his father and sister listened with unmixed pleasure; but Charles, whose feeling heart was now forcibly struck with the harshness of his judgment, heard it with a countenance at one time softened by tears, and another brightened by smiles, while he internally resolved to guard vigilantly over the sallies of a temper, that was less apt to remark with wisdom than with anger the faults of those who were entered on the period of existence which he had just left, for one more difficult still, where presumption is no greater security from temptation, and error is so much more dangerous. But to return to the story.

The evening of the party at length arrived; and while Charles, who had been detained rather late in his father's office, was attiring himself, with particular neatness, Miss Moreton gave a few words of advice to George and her little sister, who were already dressed, and in the parlour.

'But I wish, Sophia,' said Anna, 'that you would tell brother to let George have a little pleasure by himself. Charles has forgot all about the other night.'

'Oh! then I shall speak to him. I am sure George will behave politely. You know, my dear (addressing him) that you are very easily made ill, and so for this reason too you must only eat a little of the nice things that are handed to you, and never take any that are not.'

'Charles says *he* will help *me*,' said George, while he drew out his little cambric handkerchief, and quietly wiped a tear from each eye.

'Never mind, George,' said his sister, soothingly. 'I will speak to Charles, and tell him to let you alone, if you do not behave *badly*—here he comes,'—and Charles entered the room.

His slight and uncommonly graceful person was set off with becoming attire, and his accommodating locks, easily yielding to the prevailing mode, waved lightly over a brow, where honour and talent appeared seated. Perhaps his sister may be pardoned for regarding him with some admiration, if not for telling him, while she did so; that she thought *this evening* he was *rather* a *good looking* youth.

'Indeed, I think so myself, Sophia,' said Charles, while, smiling at this partly real, partly assumed vanity, he strode forward, with a considerable display of his small feet, toward a large mirror, that reflected his entire person, where he contemplated his figure with much affected complacency.

Mr. and Mrs. Moreton were not in the room, and Sophia thought she had a good opportunity, while he seemed so well pleased with himself, to say something to Charles in favour of his brother.

'Oh! Sophia, do not make yourself uneasy about the *children;* they will enjoy themselves at all events—they have a better chance than I; George looks quite handsome to-night, so I dare say the Miss Calverts will patronize him; and Anna must feel quite happy, when *Tommy* and *Sammy* are both invited.'

Anna, who was only thirteen, laughed heartily at this jest of her brother; for though it had been repeated every time they were invited to spend an evening out, during the whole season, it had not yet lost its zest; for all she had by no means invited the attentions of the little gentlemen in question.

Mr. and Mrs. Moreton here entered the room, and when they saw their children in such perfect good humour, for even George was then smiling at his brother's lively sallies, (of which he was a great admirer,) they thought, I dare say, and with reason, that three more interesting young persons would not appear among the number assembling that night.

When they arrived at Mr. Calvert's, they were immediately conducted into the room where Mrs. Calvert was conversing with a few ladies, who had come to witness this juvenile rout. The young people to the great number of two hundred, nearly covering the area of two lofty apartments, looked like a fresh blow of spring flowers. Mrs. Calvert received the Moretons with peculiar pleasure, and introduced them to the other ladies. She had often remarked the pleasing and gentlemanly behaviour of Charles in company, while she knew Anna was a general favourite with persons of all ages, being at once sensible and innocent; pretty and not vain. George was as yet a young stranger; and when Mrs. Calvert requested his brother to attend particularly to the ladies who were nearest his own age, and who might require in some degree the presence of such a master of ceremonies, George wandered through the rooms, little noticed as he thought, and free to reap his own harvest of enjoyment. All Mrs. Calvert's children were pretty, and the two oldest, being about his own size, attracted his particular attention. He presented them with several choice effusions from the poets who write upon sugar plumbs; and he would have danced with them all night, had he been instructed in this accomplishment. However, whenever he saw they were in want of partners, he would endeavour to prevail on the little gentlemen who attended practising balls to hand them out, though his polite attention was not always crowned with the success it deserved. Some fancied themselves too awkward, others preferred the company of the dark waiters, a few suffered themselves to be led within a short distance, when, finding they were not assisted in their advances by the encouragement of these inexperienced belles, they drew back with rude modesty, and returned to join again in the pursuits of their uncouth companions, who now began to fill the apartments with noise and confusion, to the dismay of the lady of the house. She never having before given way to the popular tide in favour of children's balls, was now utterly at a loss how to act, without offending the parents of the young persons, whose rudeness she observed; some of whom, strange as it may appear, were themselves of the best educated and politest class, and who would, no doubt, have been shocked, had they witnessed the ill-bred conduct of so many of their sons, and I am sorry that truth compels me to add, too many of their daughters. But the scene perhaps will be best described in the language of some of the older ladies and gentlemen, who now maintained the position of observers, though formerly they might not have been very different from the characters they were criticising.

'Did you ever see such rude children?' said one of those to Anna Moreton. 'Look at all the boys round that waiter, the servants can't get near the girls, to give them any thing.'

'Oh, yes, they can,' cried another young lady, 'for I saw a little one just now throw the lemonade out of her glass, into a boy's face, and she, at least, got too much.'

'Oh! how shockingly rude!'

'Yes, but indeed the boy provoked her; he kept throwing papers on her head all the evening.'

'I wonder what boy it was,' said Anna innocently.

'It was that one with fair hair standing near Amelia Calvert.'

'Are you sure?' asked Anna.

'Oh yes! I know it was that very one; I've seen him running about all the evening.'

Anna said no more, though she felt deeply mortified—it was her brother George.

Just as this occurred, another young lady joined them, laughing at first immoderately, and then exclaiming, 'Well, I never did see any thing so ridiculous as these little girls. I do believe some of them had their heads dressed by Daix—and to hear how they talk of fashion and the beaux! I declare it is quite a farce. Just come over, and listen to them; they will not observe us, if we keep from laughing.'

They were going, when, at the moment, a young gentleman came up to ask Anna's hand for the next dance,—so her companions left her and crossed the room to the little group of chatterers, assembled in a corner, to talk over the important matters we have mentioned. No one, of course, could have expected a rational conversation from such a confusion of voices, but any one might have been astonished at the full-grown absurdity of the sentences that occasionally extended beyond the ears of the infant listeners, in the shrillness of the infant tongue.

'Elizabeth, he must be in love with you.'

'Oh! miss, an't you ashamed?'

'Why, doesn't he walk with you from school every day?

'No, miss, he does not.'

'Elizabeth, how can you say so? Don't I see him? And I know *this much,* that you're in love with him.'

'It's no such thing, miss, I hate him worse than a rattlesnake. Don't *you* think he's *horrid ugly?*'

'No—I think he's *beautiful.*'

'Isn't that a pretty frock of Maria Wilson's?' exclaimed another voice from the crowd.

'No—I saw a heap of that stuff at Selcheap's—Ma never buys any thing there; she says they keep such mean goods, she would not have them for a gift. Ma always buys my frocks at Costmore's, if they're ever so much dearer. But look, I declare all the boys are coming over here. Did you ever see such behaviour?'

'What shall we do?'

'Let us go and sit down.'

'Oh! they're not coming here after all—they are going over to sit on the sofa, and eat all the things they have in their pockets.'

'Yes, so they are; and they'll just throw those two little babies down, that are play-ing there. An't *they* a great deal *too small* to be here?'

'Oh! they are Mrs. Calvert's own babies; and I suppose the nurses will take them out again presently. I *do think* they are the sweetest little things—let us go over and see them,'—and with this convenient excuse, they all moved toward the young gentlemen. When they were gone, their fair critics laughed heartily at the folly of such premature disciples of fashion; notwithstanding they exposed themselves to an equal share of ridicule from those who were older than they.

'It is a pity there are so few large boys here this evening; they are so much better behaved,' said one.

'Indeed I never observed it,' said the other, 'I know some of them, last night at Mrs. Albright's, drank such a quantity of Champagne, that they couldn't behave *at all.*'

'Oh! that was only John Mackintosh and his set—but did you ever see such a gen-teel, handsome boy as Charles Moreton? I declare he is quite elegant. He wanted me to take his arm, and walk about the rooms with him just now; but I didn't like—I thought it would look so conspicuous at a private party.'

'Oh! indeed I think so *too—I* wouldn't have done it for any thing;' but the young lady said this in a tone which seemed to betray some latent mortification that the offer had not been made to her.

'Is that Charles Morton's brother?' asked her companion, 'the little boy with white hair just before you—some one said it was.'

'Indeed I hope it is not, for he's one of the worst boys here; and I told Anna Morton so, a minute before you came up to us; and she will certainly be angry if he is her brother.'

The dancing now commenced again, and at its close, the last refreshments were handed round, and the servants in the usual manner incommoded by the young gentle-men. Mrs. Calvert, completely tired, no longer exerted herself to restore order through-out this chaos; and the ladies who were with her had scarcely succeeded in their best endeavours to correct any of the abuses of the evening.

A man with a heavy salver now entered a door, near which had been placed, rather injudiciously, a beautiful lamp; and just as he reached the stand on which it shone, he stumbled, and in trying to recover his footing, the lamp was overturned, and its contents spilled upon a splendid carpet; the only one which had not been removed for the dancers. The apartment seemed for a moment obscured; and immediately a crowd of inquirers rushed in to know how the accident happened.

'Why, madam,' said the servant to Mrs. Calvert, 'it was just on account of that young gentleman, who has been following me all about the passages, and every where, to take the things away; so, as I came by the lamp, he was behind, and tripped me up; and that's the way it got knocked over.'

All eyes were now turned on the delinquent, who looked perfectly aghast—it was George Moreton. Anna's distress could scarcely be concealed.

'Charles, I think you forgot to watch your brother to-night,' said one young gentleman.

'That's worse than *mine ever* did,' said another.

'I am glad to find that *my* brothers are not the worst boys in Baltimore,' cried a third.

'Charles Moreton said they *were*,' added a fourth; while Charles, whose anger was more strongly excited by these remarks, seized the child by the arm, and, shaking him not very gently, asked him how he came to break the lamp.

'If I did break it, I didn't mean to do it,' cried George, bursting into tears.

'Then what were you doing by the stand?'

'I was looking at the picture behind the door.'

'Yes, the picture of *cakes* and *comfits* on the waiter, I suppose. Come, sir, you and I had better go home. Anna, will you please to get your cloak and bonnet?'

'Charles,' said Anna, weeping at the sight of her little brother's tears, 'perhaps George did not do it.'

'Mrs. Calvert,' continued Charles, paying no attention to his sister, 'we are very sorry—Anna and I—that George has behaved so badly; I am sure my father will punish him; and I think he must see now himself, that he *is too small* to go to parties.'

At this, George's tears redoubled, and he was taken home, a most unhappy little boy. The rest of the company separated soon after; none perfectly satisfied with *all* the events of the evening; and Mrs. Calvert dismissed her daughters to their late rest, with these memorable words,—'Now, children, I will never hear you express a wish for such a party again; I would be glad if your indulgent uncle had not persuaded me to give you this; but remember it is the first and the last that you shall have seen, before your education is completed.'

She then bid them good night, with her usual affection; and I am happy to state, that the little girls' sleep was not in the least retarded by what she had said.

When George reached home, with his indignant brother, and his pitying sister, he found his parents sitting up for them in the parlour; and with pain they listened to Charles's account of his conduct, to which Anna could not add one extenuating word.

'Why,' said his father, 'did you behave in this manner, George? Were all those nice things only tempting my son to forget he was ever to be a gentleman?'

'I did not think I was eating too much, when they handed the cakes to me, father,' sobbed out the child.

'Oh! I am sorry you conducted yourself so disgracefully, George—but go to bed.'

Poor George retired with a breaking heart, and eyes too full of tears to see his beautiful red-bird. He wept himself to sleep, and dreamed he was a *guinea-pig*.

The next day was the last of the week; and Mrs. Calvert's house could scarcely be arranged, before the young ladies and gentlemen, now disengaged from school, came to pay their respects to the *Misses Calvert,* after their party. But those little girls not being permitted by their mother a circle of morning visitors, even on a Saturday, they showed a fashionable attention by leaving their cards.

The last ring of the bell, however, announced a visitor to Mrs. Calvert, and the lady was admitted. She held a little boy by the hand, who seemed very anxious to escape, casting many looks back upon the door; but the lady urged him forward, and introduced him as her son.

'Mrs. Calvert, he has come to make an apology for his conduct last night. What did you do, my son? Tell this lady.'

'I broke a lamp,' said he, with sturdy resolution.

'Oh, no, my dear, I understand it was a son of Mr. Moreton that caused one of the servants to overturn it.'

'No, it was not he, it was I; but I never said so till mother saw oil on my clothes, and then I would not tell a lie.'

'And you never thought another little boy might be blamed for your fault?'

'No, for I ran away as fast as I could; but I saw one standing just before the lamp, looking at a picture, when the door opened; and so, when I was gone, I dare say they thought it was he that broke it.'

'And are you the same boy that offended a little girl so much, that she threw a glass of lemonade at you?'

'Yes, but she had no business to do that.'

'Certainly—I am not excusing her, I am only concerned for your offences at present. Were you particularly troublesome to the servants, following them through the house?'

The child was silent; he seemed growing sullen.

'I merely ask, my dear, because for all the rudeness of another this little Moreton has been blamed.'

'Well, they had no business to blame him, if he did not do it.'

'That was rightly said, sir, and proves that you have correct principles at least, if you are not always the politest little boy; and so I think you will come with me to Mr. Moreton's.'

The boy looked at his mother.

'You must go with Mrs. Calvert, my son.'

'But you will come with us, mother?'

'No, Edward, I have not the least acquaintance with Mrs. Moreton, and Mrs. Calvert must have the trouble of introducing you. And remember, my son, to tell every circumstance that can vindicate the boy, who has no doubt suffered a great deal on your account.'

Mrs. Calvert was soon attired for her walk, and the ladies left the house together, but parted before they reached Church street, where Mr. Moreton resided. When Mrs. Calvert entered the house, the family had all assembled, for it was near the dinner hour; and she was very politely received by every one except George, who, confined to one corner, and kept hard at study, did not consider himself as one of the company. Mrs. Calvert called him over to her.

'Father will not let me,' said the poor little fellow.

'But I have something particular to say to you. Mr. Moreton, will you permit your son to leave his seat?'

'Certainly, madam, if you desire it;' and he led George forward. Mrs. Calvert then called out, 'Come in, Edward Eccleston.'

The young gentleman obeyed; and, to the astonishment of every one, when the two boys met, they exhibited such an extraordinary resemblance, though unconnected by any degree of relationship, that you might easily have taken them together for twins, and apart for each other.

'Now, Master Eccleston,' continued Mrs. Colvert, 'will you tell who was really guilty of all the rude actions for which this boy was condemned last night? You know the offender.'

'Yes, ma'am, it was I.'

'Then I did *not* throw down the lamp?' cried George. 'I thought perhaps I did when they said so, because my back was against it.'

'Yes, but you never touched it at all, I know; for I tripped the man myself.'

Here Charles Moreton left the room for a few moments. On returning, he found George engaged in a very friendly parting with Edward Eccleston, who now left them, pleased with his own conduct, gratified at the praises he received, and promising great endeavours in future to make his manners adorn his principles. After he was gone, Charles took hold of his brother's hand, and pressed it affectionately, while he closed it upon a beautiful pocket-book, such as had been long the secret desire of George's heart, with pencil and penknife, and every thing complete.

'Oh! Charles,' cried he, looking in his brother's face with grateful pleasure, 'but don't you want it yourself?'

'No, George, I want to give it to you—keep it; and whenever I am angry without a just cause, then let me see it.'

While this scene was passing between the two brothers, Mrs. Calvert obtained a promise from Mr. and Mrs. Moreton, to let George and Anna spend a more quiet evening with her and her children the next week.

'My little girls will be so happy if they can show them all the curiosities that their father has collected for us in different countries—with these, I suppose, they will imagine themselves quite companionable; and they must have this one gratification before they leave town.'

'Why, you are not going to send your dear little daughters away from you, Mrs. Calvert?' said Mrs. Moreton.

'Yes, ma'am—I am disgusted with the present style of the children in Baltimore; and a particular friend of mine, a lady of the best education and most refined manners, residing in the country, proposes to teach a few girls; Caroline and Amelia, I intend, shall be the first of her scholars.'

'Then you do not approve of educating them in town?'

'According to the prevailing mode, I certainly do not; for what progress can young people possibly make in useful knowledge, when their minds are filled with the love of dress, or distracted with solicitude for admiration, in the continued found of company they are permitted to see! But you must certainly have avoided all this, Mrs. Moreton, your children are so different from most of those I see.'

'I hope they deserve your compliment, Mrs. Calvert, though I have endeavoured, rather to render their minds above the influence of ridiculous fashions, than to keep them entirely out of their view; your daughters, as yet, are infants; and, perhaps, every silly example should be carefully avoided with them; but Charles and Anna, at least, are old enough to make a good use even of the follies they are sometimes exposed to observe. One hundred or more children collected together, out of the limits of restraint, exceed my ideas of temperance, in every respect; but a moderate enjoyment of the pleasures of society, does not, I think, as a consequence, interfere with the proper course of education; if it did, it would certainly be better to confine young people to the circle of their own families; for, when the mind becomes possessed with worthless and trifling thoughts, to the exclusion of every thing useful, or necessary, or truly ornamental, the purpose of education is totally defeated, and the parents and the teachers labour in vain.'

After expressing perfect accordance with these sentiments, Mrs. Calvert rose to take leave. The day which George and Anna spent at her house, will perhaps form the subject of a future story.

❧ Dialogue

ELIZA: I wish I was a small bird,
   Among the leaves to dwell,
To scale the sky in gladness,
   Or seek the lonely dell.
My matin[6] song should celebrate
   The glory of the earth,
And my vesper hymn ring gladly
   With the thrill of careless mirth.

CAROLINE: I wish I was a flow'ret,
   To blossom in the grove;
I'd spread my opening leaflets
   Among the plants I love.
No hand should roughly cull me,
   And bid my odours fly;
I silently would ope to life,
   And quietly would die.

LOUISA: I wish I was a gold fish,
   To seek the sunny wave,

---

[6]Early morning.

To part the gentle ripple,
    And amid its coolness lave.
I would glide through day delighted,
    Beneath the azure sky,
And when night came on in softness,
    Seek the star-light's milder eye.

MOTHER: Hush, hush, romantic prattlers!
    You know not what you say,
When *soul,* the crown of mortals,
    You would lightly throw away.
What is the songster's warble,
    And the rose's blush refin'd,
To the noble thought of *Deity*
    Within your opening mind?

C. G.
Charleston, S. C.

❧ The Playthings*

BY H. F. GOULD

'Oh! mother, here's the very top
    That brother used to spin;
The vase with seeds I've seen him drop
    To call our robin in;
The line that held his pretty kite,
    His bow, his cup, and ball,
The slate on which he learned to write,
    His feather, cap, and all!'

'My dear, I'd put the things away,
    Just where they were before:
Go, Anna, take him out to play,
    And shut the closet-door.
Sweet innocent! he little thinks
    The slightest thought expressed
Of him that's lost, how deep it sinks
    Within a mother's breast!'

---

*The 'Playthings' was first published in a periodical about six months ago, but was thought too good to be rejected on that account—*Ed.*

"Who's There?" from *The Pearl*, 1833.

❧ Who's There?

John Wheeler was an honest boy, but he was very ignorant, and, unfortunately, he lived with a farmer, whose wife told him a great many frightful stories. He was naturally strong and bold, but he had heard so many monstrous accounts, in which there was not one word of truth, that he was literally afraid of his own shadow. John's elder brother had gone to sea; and at home he had two sisters, Peggy and Sally.

The farm where he lived was at some distance from his father's house, and was separated from it by a small forest. John had promised his sisters that he would spend a certain evening with them, while his parents had gone to a wedding in a neighbouring town. It was late before he completed his day's work, and the moon was shining bright when he entered the wood. It was beautiful to see the old trees all clothed in a robe of moonbeams; and to watch the light and shadow glancing over the ground, as if they pursued each other in sport. If John had not been rendered timid by the stories he had heard, he would have enjoyed his quiet evening walk, in a place where no sound disturbed the pleasant silence, but the occasional chirp or hum of some happy insect. The innocent are always calm, unless evil thoughts have been put into their minds by the influence of others who are not as good as themselves. Poor John! the clear tranquillity of the night was a terror to him. The distant bushes looked like gipsies pointing their guns at him; and the trees rustling in the wind sounded like giants whispering to each other. As he pursued his way, his heart beat faster and faster. He heard a noise, an awful noise—he quickened his steps—still the noise continued, and grew louder. He ventured to look behind him, and he saw—a tall black figure following him! Then the poor boy ran and ran, as if twenty wild tigers were chasing him. He did not even stop to take breath, although it seemed as if he must drop down with fatigue.

As he approached his father's door, he once more ventured to look around—the tall black figure was still behind him! With one violent effort, he bounced into the door, and bolted it after him. And there he stood, holding his hand upon his throbbing heart, and breathing as if he were taking a shower-bath. His sister Peggy, hearing the door shut violently, came to inquire into the cause. 'Why, John,' she exclaimed, 'what *is* the matter? How pale you look! and how you shake!'

'Oh! Peggy,' he replied, in a most distressed tone of voice, 'Oh! I have seen the awfulest sight! A great giant dressed in black ran after me all the way through the woods!'

Then Peggy opened her eyes wide, and looked round cautiously, as she whispered, 'And have you bolted the door, John?'

Her brother told her that he had drawn the lower bolt; and she proposed to stand upon the wash-bench and bolt the other. The door was then locked, and the key conveyed up stairs. Then John recounted minutely all the particulars of what he had seen, or thought he had seen, as he walked through the woods; and Peggy told of an old man her grandmother had known, who was chased by a horseman that carried his own head in his hand, and threw it at every body he could reach. Even little Sally told about gipsies that hid away in closets to steal children; and of a giant who built his house on the top of a bean, and ate up the little boys who came there. The more the foolish children talked in this way, the more they were frightened. They huddled close up to each other, and as they listened their eyes opened wider and wider. John, after looking fearfully all round the room, began, 'I will tell you a story about a haunted house. Once there was a man'—

'Oh! John, did you hear that?' exclaimed Peggy.

'What? what?' said John, turning pale.

'Oh! John, you will take care of us—won't you?' said little Sally, who was clinging to his knees.

'Hush! hush!'

A loud knock was heard.

'How I do wish father was at home,' said Sally.

Again the knock was repeated.

'Give me the candle,' said John, assuming a sudden bravery, 'perhaps it is somebody come to see father on business.'

'Don't leave me alone—don't leave me alone,' sobbed little Sally, keeping hold of his frock with her trembling hands, 'I am afraid it is that naughty black giant that chased you through the woods.'

At these words, John's courage quite forsook him; and he stood the very image of terror, looking first upon one sister, and then upon the other. At last, Peggy said, 'John, I'll get grandfather's great sword, and we will go and ask who is there; and if it be the giant, and he should break the door down, you can chop off his head with the sword.'

'But how can I reach him?' asked John.

Little Sally whispered, 'You can stand upon the stairs, you know.'

So John took the great sword; and Peggy, with the light in one hand, grasped his frock with the other; and Sally, keeping fast hold of Peggy's gown, came behind.

'Who's there?' said John; and his voice was so dry and husky, you would have thought he had not tasted water for a fortnight.

'A friend!' was answered, in a deep, hollow tone.

John trembled so, he could hardly stand.

'What an awful voice!' exclaimed Peggy.

'Do you think it is the giant?' whispered Sally.

'How strangely the dog acts, barking and scratching so!' said Peggy.

'Let us put out the light and hide ourselves,' said John.

'But, John,' replied the elder sister, 'there is a window in the kitchen unfastened. What *shall* we do?'

John hesitated; but feeling as if he ought to be the protector, he finally stammered out, 'If you will set the light under the stairs, and come with me, I will fasten the window.'

Still keeping hold of each other, they went into the kitchen. But scarcely had they entered, when the two foremost screamed aloud, and ran away.

'Did you see that man making up faces outside the window?' said one.

'And did you see that great long tail?' said another.

Away they all scrambled to their mother's chamber, and hid themselves under the bed.

When they had become a little more tranquil, they began to talk in an under tone.

'How I wish brother Mark would live at home,' said Peggy, 'he never used to be afraid of any thing.'

'And how droll he was,' added Sally, 'how many pretty stories he told us; and how he mimicked the sailors calling to one another.'

The words had hardly passed her lips, when a loud and prolonged 'Hil-loa!' was heard beneath the window.

'He hears what we are talking about,' whispered Sally.

'Don't speak again,' said John, 'I am afraid he knows where we are.'

A short quick bark from the dog made them start again. These silly children actually remained more than an hour crouched under the bed. At last chaise-wheels were heard, and presently the pleasant sound of their father's voice. Still keeping fast hold of each other, they descended to open the door for their parents. The dog seemed very impatient—now scratching against the door, and now putting his nose to the threshold. Carlo was wiser than the children; for, when the door opened, who should come in, shaking hands with father and mother, but their own brother Mark? After the first congratulations were over, 'You rogues!' he exclaimed, 'why didn't you open the door? I have been try-ing a whole hour to get into the house.'

John blushed, and turned away his head as he answered, 'we were afraid to open the door.'

'Afraid of what?' asked the good-natured sailor, sharing his caresses between his sisters and the dog.

Little Sally, nodding her head in a very mysterious manner, whispered in his ear, 'A giant! a great black giant!'

At this, Mark laughed very loud; and when Peggy remembered how droll John looked, holding the great sword in his trembling hands, she could not help laughing too. John coloured very red, and had half a mind to be angry, because he knew he was very ridiculous.

'I don't care,' muttered he, in a sulky tone, 'Peggy saw him making up faces at the window, as well as I did; and she saw a great tail too.'

This made the sailor laugh still louder and longer, until father and mother knew not what to make of his conduct. He told them they should soon see what he was laughing about; and he went out to the barn, and brought a monkey to the window.

'Here is my present for Sally,' said he, as he entered, 'I have brought a fine parrot for Peggy. When I come home again, I will bring another black giant to make up faces at John.'

Peggy joined in the laugh, but she acknowledged that Mark's voice did sound fright-fully when he said, 'a friend.'

'I spoke so, because I didn't want you to guess who was at the door,' replied her brother.

Poor John was sadly mortified; he wanted to hide away under his mother's bed again. He tried to excuse himself by saying, that he should not have behaved so foolishly, if something black had not followed him through the woods, and made a noise behind him all the way.

Mark laughed at him a good deal for being such a stout protector to his sisters, and told him that if ever he saw or heard any thing worse than himself, he would bring him home an elephant; but when he saw the tears come to his brother's eyes, the merry sailor changed the discourse, and began to talk about his adventures.

When it was time for John to depart, he could not conceal his reluctance to go through the dreaded woods.

'I *did* see a black figure behind me; and the faster I ran, the louder noise it made; nobody can beat me out of that, for I saw it for certain with my own eyes.'

Mark smiled, and very good-naturedly offered to go through the woods with him.

John at first talked very fast; but, as they proceeded, he became silent, and walked much quicker. At last, he looked timidly back, and then he fairly ran for it. His brother ran after him, and caught him by the shoulder, saying, 'Don't behave like a fool, John. Do be more of a man. What are you frightened at now?'

'I saw *two* black things,' replied the boy, breathing very hard.

'Well, John, so do I see two black things,' said Mark, 'look at them well, and see what they are. Now don't you feel ashamed? You have been running away from your own shadow!'

More mortified than ever, John still insisted, though he could not speak in a very confident tone, that he certainly had heard a noise.

'Run again,' said his brother, 'and tell me whether you hear it now.'

The coward did as he was requested, and blushed as he said he did hear it. Mark suspected by his looks that he was no longer afraid of the noise; and he said, 'Come, Jack, be honest, now, and tell me what you think the noise is.'

John rubbed his head with his hand, and looked down with his face, and looked up with his eyes, after the manner which people call *sheepish,* and stammered out, 'I guess it was the creaking of my new shoes.'

Mark could not refrain from a hearty laugh. When they came in sight of the farmhouse, he bade his brother good night, and added, 'you have been frightened almost to death to-night with your own shadow, and the creaking of your new shoes; I tell you again that when you hear or see any thing worse than yourself, I will bring you home an elephant.'

❧ On the Death of a Beautiful Boy

BY MRS. L. H. SIGOURNEY

I saw thee at thy mother's side, ere she in dust was laid,
And half believ'd some cherub form had from its mansion stray'd;
But when I traced the wondering woe that seized thy infant thought,
And 'mid the radiance of thine eye a liquid chrystal wrought,
I felt how strong that faith must be to vanquish nature's tie,
And bid from one so beautiful to turn away *and die.*

I saw thee in thy graceful sports, beside thy father's bower—
Amid his broad and bright parterre,[7] thyself the fairest flower;
And heard thy tuneful voice ring out upon the summer air,
As though a bird of Eden poured its joyous carol there:
And linger'd with delighted gaze, to the dark future blind,
While with thy lovely sister's hand thine own was fondly twin'd.

I saw thee bending o'er thy book, and mark'd the glad surprise,
With which the sun of science met thy sparkling eaglet eyes;
But when thy deep and brilliant mind awoke to bold pursuit,
And from the tree of knowledge pluck'd its richest, rarest fruit—
I shrank from such precocious power, with strange, portentous fear,
A shuddering presage that thy race must soon be finish'd here.

I saw thee in the house of God, and lov'd the reverent air,
With which thy beauteous head was bow'd low in thy guileless prayer,
Yet little deem'd how soon thy place would be with that blessed band,

---

[7]Garden beds divided and arranged in an ornamental pattern.

Who ever near the Eternal Throne in sinless worship stand;—
Ah! little deem'd how soon the grave must lock thy glorious charms,
And leave thy spirit free to find a sainted mother's arms.

❧ Story of an Orphan

BY MRS. CHARLES SEDGWICK

'Who did father say was coming here to tea this evening, mother?'

'A Mr. Malcolm from Ohio.'

'A farmer then, I suppose.'

'Why a farmer? Do you think that all the people that live in Ohio are farmers?'

'Yes, I supposed that every body who went there, went to clear up land.'

'That used to be the case; but now Ohio contains many flourishing towns and villages; and people of all trades and professions are found there. Mr. Malcolm, however, *is* a farmer. He once lived with your grandfather as a labourer; he has been industrious and prosperous; and is a man of very respectable character.'

'Did father know him formerly.'

'Yes; I have no doubt Mr. Malcolm has given him many a good ride on his shoulders, when he was a little boy.'

This conversation passed between Alice Grey and her mother. Just at that moment, Mr. Grey entered with his guest. Mr. Malcolm seemed about fifty, had a pleasant, intelligent countenance, and the air of a substantial yeoman. Mrs. Grey rose to shake hands with him, and Alice gave her hand too.

'Thank you, my little lady, for this welcome,' said he. 'I suspect you are as warm-hearted as your father used to be. I never made him a whistle, cut him a good long stick for a horse, or brought him berries, after my day's work, that he did not put both his arms around my neck, and give me a good hug.'

'Those were pleasant times,' said Mr. Grey, 'I have never forgotten them. You have had a houseful of children of your own to wait upon since then, I believe?'

'Yes, a houseful indeed; and now grandchildren are taking their places. But where are the rest of yours?'

'I have only two besides this girl, and here they come. Master Robert, and Henry, let me introduce you to Mr. Malcolm, an old friend of mine.'

Mr. Malcolm gave each of the boys a hearty shake of the hand; and it was not long before Henry, the youngest, was upon his knee.

'This is the way I sit when father tells me a story,' said he. 'If you live in Ohio, cannot you tell me about some bears?'

'Don't trouble Mr. Malcolm,' said his father, 'I claim his visit to myself;' and they proceeded to talk upon that inexhaustible theme, 'the western country.'

After tea, Henry again assumed his place on Mr. Malcolm's knee, who said to him, 'you asked me for a story, little boy, and I will tell you one.'

Henry started up and said eagerly, 'about Ohio?'

'Not exactly about Ohio, but about a man who lives in Ohio. I had it from himself.

'When he was a little boy, his mother died, leaving four children. It was principally by her efforts that the family had been kept together, for the father was what is called shiftless; boys, do you know what shiftless means? A shiftless man is a man who cannot make shift to live. Not long after his wife's death, the father, finding himself very much in debt, and getting discouraged, ran off, leaving his children as helpless as a brood of young birds, when the old ones have been brought down by the gun of the fowler before their brood is half fledged.

'None of them was old enough to take care of the rest. At first they were all put in the poor house, where they were dull and miserable enough; but soon they were removed, one after another, by persons who took them for service, with the intention of bringing them up. George, the subject of my story, fell to the lot of a man who had himself had a pretty hard life in his younger days, under a very severe father; and who seemed to think the treatment he had received was good enough for others. His chief design in regard to George seemed to be, to get as much work out of him as possible, and with as little expense of food or clothing. George did not mind the work much, for he was not a lazy boy; nor did he feel disposed to complain about his food, for he had never been accustomed to dainty fare, and could live any how.

'But there was one thing he did miss. His mother had been a good, kind mother, and he remembered her; he remembered how she praised him when he did right, and how softly she chid him if he did wrong; and the tears sometimes came into his eyes, as he thought that when he tried his utmost to please his master, he only saved himself a scolding—and that was all. If he did wrong, his master's words cut him as sharp as razors. His mistress was a good deal the same—a hard sort of woman.

'But George had good health—enough to eat, such as it was—and was kept pretty busy, so that he had not time to be very unhappy. His chief trouble was that he could not go to school more, for he liked his books. He sometimes was allowed to go a month or two in the middle of winter, but that was all. One summer, when he was about twelve years old, his master told him that if he would do so much, making his day's work equal to what boys of fifteen or sixteen usually perform, he should go to school all winter. George exerted himself very much, worked so well that the neighbours thought him a wonder, and looked forward to the winter as the time when he should get fully paid.

'His master kept his word pretty well; he did not generally keep him home more than a day or a half a day in the week. But he neglected to get him a new suit of winter clothes according to his custom, saying that as he was going to give up George's time so long, he could not afford them. So the old ones had to answer for week days and Sundays too, and before spring were covered with patches.

'Thoughtless boys—for I don't suppose they meant to do any harm—teazed him, and called him Joseph, because he had a coat of many colours. "The neighbours," who are always knowing and meddling, said it was a shame he was not better dressed after all his hard work, and added, with a wise shake of the head, "that he ought to get it out of his master some how or other."

'There lived near the school house a poor widow: George, being a good natured boy, often did chores and drew water for her in play-time, and sometimes when he staid at noon. Observing him very shabbily dressed, she told him she had a new suit of clothes in the house which would just fit him. A son of hers, who had worked for them in the summer, and got them made up in the fall, died before he ever had a chance to wear them. She said George should have them for just what the cloth cost; she would give in the making and trimmings, because he had been so kind to her. George asked his master's permission to accept the offer; but he refused, saying the warm weather would come before a great while; and his old clothes would do till then.

'Poor George remembered what the neighbours had said—that he ought to get some new clothes out of his master some way or other. He pondered upon these words a good deal.

'One day he went to mill; there he met a man who said to him, "I believe you are a trusty boy—here are five dollars I was just going to pay Mr. Dodge (George's master), for apples and potatoes that I bought last fall—but I am called off another way—so I wish you would take the money, and ask your master to send the receipt the next time you come to mill. You may leave it with the miller."

"'Now is my chance," thought George, "it is clear that my master ought to have given me some clothes. I earned them twice over last summer. The neighbours said so— and if he won't give me my due, why should not I take it?"

He knew the woman was about moving away; he thought he would buy the clothes, and keep them concealed until she had actually gone. He trusted that it would be a good while before the man would call for his receipt, and that by that time he should have got money some how or other to pay back—if not, he would run away. So foolishly will boys reason, when they are likely to get into mischief and trouble by their own folly or wickedness.

'George accomplished his plan, and, as soon as the woman was fairly off, produced the clothes, saying that when the woman found he would not buy them, she said she would give them to him, as they were of no use to her. Mr. Dodge thought this rather strange; but it passed away and he thought no more about it.

'In the mean while George did not much enjoy his new clothes, and wished many times that he had never taken them. It was not long before the same man who had given him the money, called on Mr. Dodge on some other business, and asked whether he had ever sent a receipt for that money. This led to an explanation, as Mr. Dodge had never received it.

'George was at the barn, and heard his name called pretty loud and earnest. Ever since parting with that money, he had felt startled whenever he was told that his master wanted him. This was a new feeling, and very uncomfortable.

'He went to the house with slow and reluctant steps.

'"George," said his master, "where are those five dollars you were to pay to me the other day?"

'George had never told a lie in his life; but he dared not now confess the truth.

'"I lost it, sir," said he, "and was afraid to tell you."

'"You lost it! you rascal—I know better—you bought those clothes with it."

'George fell on his knees—begged his master's pardon—and told the whole story. He said he was very sorry—that he had never done such a thing before, and would never do such a thing again—that he would go without any new clothes the next fall, &c. &c.; but his master was very angry, declaring that he did not want a thief and a liar in his house—that the jail was the only proper place for him; and to the jail he should go.

'Poor George felt most dreadfully—felt as if he had not a friend in the world. He knew that the jail was in a town twelve miles off, where nobody knew him, and he knew nobody. He was examined before a justice, committed, and sent off.

'He arrived at the jail just at night, one cold gloomy day in the month of February. The jailor and his wife seemed to feel sorry for him, and gave him a good supper at their own table, before he was taken into jail; but when he got to his solitary room, and heard the lock turned upon him, he felt as if he were buried alive. He immediately went to bed, and cried himself to sleep; and he cried all the next day. Except the man who brought his food, nobody looked in upon his solitude, but some people who came to the little wicket in the door, to stare at the young thief.

'Among others were two boys, one of whom called George names; asked him if he was not ashamed to be a thief; and said every thing that he could to teaze him. The other boy said nothing, but gave George a couple of apples, and tried to silence his companion.

'That evening, just as George had gone to bed, about twilight, the door was unlocked, and the jailor entered, accompanied by a lady. George had been vexed by having so many people to stare at him; and immediately covered up his head.

'"I have not come to see you out of curiosity, George," said she, "but because I wish to be a friend to you, and try to comfort you. My son was here this afternoon—the same boy that gave you the apples—and he begged me to come and see you, because you were a poor motherless boy. Are you glad to have me come and see you, George?"

'"Yes, ma'am," said he, for her voice fell as soft upon his heart, as moonlight upon stormy water; but still he did not uncover his head.

'"I have children, George," continued the lady, "and if they were to be left orphans, I should wish kind-hearted people to befriend them. For the same reason I am ready to befriend you. If you had had a kind mother to watch over you, I dare say you would not have done this wicked thing."

'Still George made no reply, although he had a comfortable feeling at his heart, to which it had been long a stranger.

'"Do you like to read, George?" she asked.

'"Yes, ma'am."

'"Then I will leave some books to entertain you, and will come again soon. The next time I come, I hope you will speak to me; my name is Mrs. Somers."

'George slept well that night, and did not cry when he waked in the morning, for the thought of that kind lady comforted him.

'The next time she came, that good boy, Charles Somers, her son, came with her. She talked to George a great deal, and read to him, and instructed him from the Bible. Either she or Charles came almost every day to see him.

'The trial came on not long after: poor George was convicted and sentenced to be imprisoned in the common jail three months. It seemed to him an awful doom to be shut up there just as the spring was coming on, when every living thing would be moving to and fro on the earth, and all *nature* would be free. Charles Somers was so sorry for him, that he went over and staid with him all that evening.

The next day Mrs. Somers visited him again. She told him that he must be patient, that he had done wrong, and it was right he should be punished—that it was best for him, and he must make the best of it.

'You love to learn, George,' said she; 'and you can learn a great deal in these three months that you are to be here. I will furnish you with books, and sometimes will hear you lessons; when I can't, Charles will. In this way you will be improving yourself; and the time will pass off more rapidly."

'The lady was as good as her word. George studied well, and learned more in those three months, than he had learned from books in all his life before. This was not all—Mrs. Somers got an Indian woman, who lived with the jailor, to show him how to make baskets, that he might be earning a little money; and she furnished materials and candles, so that he could work in the evening. He soon became quite handy at it, and made a good many. As fast as he made them, Charles Somers sold them for him; and people were very good about buying, out of pity.

'By and by Charles brought him the money that he had laid up; they counted it over, and it was just three dollars and a half.

'"Now, George," said Charles, "you can buy you some clothes;" for George's master had taken away all his clothes, except those old ones that he had on; and if Mrs. Somers had not given him a couple of shirts, he could not have been decent.

'"No," said George, "if I can earn enough more, I had rather pay back that five dollars to Mr. Dodge."

'"But he has got the clothes that you bought with the five dollars."

'"Never mind that; he may keep them if he chooses; but I had rather pay the money."

'Mrs. Somers was very much pleased when she heard this plan of George's. The first time she saw him, she praised him for it; said it was right; and that he need not be anxious about the clothes, for as soon as he was out of jail, Mr. Somers would try to find a good place for him, where he would soon earn some.

'George dared not ask her if he might live with her; but the bare possibility of such a thing made him do his very best to please her.

'It was not long before George had a fresh lot of baskets ready for sale. Charles took them to the next town and disposed of the whole. His whole funds now amounted to a little more than five dollars; and that sum was sent off at once to Mr. Dodge.

'At last the time came for George to be released; and to his great joy he found he was to live with Mr. and Mrs. Somers. You may be sure he did his best to serve them well and faithfully. As soon as Mr. Dodge received the money, he came to get George to live with him for he knew his labour was very profitable to him; but George would not go. Mr. Dodge tried to tempt him with the clothes, saying he should have them right back again; but George replied that he could work and earn some. When Mr. Dodge was going away, Mr. Somers told him that he thought as George had paid the money, he was entitled to the clothes; and, after some hesitation, he concluded to send them.

'To cut a long story short, George gave such good satisfaction, that he remained with his kind friends until he was twenty-one; and then Mr. Somers gave him a hundred dollars in money, and a hundred acres of his Ohio land, to begin life with.

'In Ohio he prospered so well, that when Mr. Somers went out to see his property there, four years after, he found him with a good comfortable log house, and a nice wife and baby. His farm was pretty much cleared up, so as to yield him a considerable crop, and he had some live stock.

'"I am delighted to find you so thriving, George," said Mr. Somers.

'"I owe it all to you and your lady, sir," said he. "If it had not been for her kindness, I might have been a vagabond to this day—for who would have employed the little friendless thief?"''

When Mr. Malcolm had finished—'Do you know that man?' said Henry, who had been intently listening to the story.

'Yes, I know him very well; and he is now what they call a pretty rich farmer. He has one daughter married to a doctor, another to a lawyer; and two of his sons are commanders of boats on the Mississippi.'

'I should like to see that man,' said Henry.

'When your father comes to Ohio, ask him to bring you to my house, and you shall see him. I am that very George, boys, and I have told you this story, that you may learn from it to practise kindness towards those whom all the world are ready to forsake.'

The boys looked in astonishment. 'Grandfather's name was not Somers,' said Robert.

'No, it was Grey; but I could not keep my secret till the end of my story, without taking another name for him.'

'And was that Charles my uncle Charles?'

'Yes, and I have been thirty miles out of my way on this very journey on purpose to see him. He is a good deal older than your father, and one of the best men that ever lived.'

'And did not father know that you was George?'

'No, I suppose not, for he was born about the time that I went to live there.'

'No,' said Mr. Grey, 'the story is new to me; but, without novelty, would have been very interesting. O, how I wish my father and mother were alive, to see their grandchildren listening to it!'

'They are dead and gone, but not forgotten,' said Mr. Malcolm, as he brushed away a tear with his brawny hand,—'I wish all the world were like them.'

The children were all sorry when Mr. Malcolm took his leave; and the boys said they should certainly go and see him in Ohio.

Mater

❧ Charade

My first a simile supplies,
When the enraptur'd lover sighs,
Which aids him fondly to declare
That the fond nymph is passing fair.
When belles in birth-night suit appear,
My second decks Augusta's ear;
Or, let the voice of sorrow speak,
It trembles on Camilla's cheek:
A heav'n-sent gem, which mercy lends,
Thus to adorn her fav'rite friends.
My whole we joyfully prefer,
Because 'tis spring's sweet harbinger;
Though (as by chance we elsewhere find)
Its charms are to our sight confin'd;
And, like full many a reigning toast,
To please the eye its utmost boast.

"At Rest" from *The Pearl,* 1833.

❧ The Child and Dog

Oh! breathing picture of Childhood bright.
With its blossoming visions of pure delight!
A dream of the Past, in this scene I see—
A landscape which beameth no more for me.
How many blessings were gather'd there—
How glad was the day-beam,—how clear the air!
At every step there were roses strown;
Where have their leaves and their fragrance gone?

Beautiful Child! as I look on thee,
With thy parted lips, and thy features free;
With the silken curls on thy cheek that lie,—
With the laughing light in that tameless eye—
As I look on these, I am lost in thought
Of what young existence to me hath brought;
And as thus this picture those scenes recall,
I look around—they are vanished all!

They are vanished all!—and alone I stand
On the bark that hath borne me from Boyhood's land;

Yet, as breezes from Araby roam o'er the sea,
So those earliest raptures return to me.
Thrice happy the heart that remembers them long;
They freshen the soul with a fountain of song;
They point to that land of enjoyment above,
Where Hope lies at rest on the bosom of Love.

Willis Gaylord Clark
Philadelphia, August, 1832.

Soliloquy in a School-Room, at the Close of a Winter's Day

'From grave to gay.'

The last is gone, and I am left alone,
Weary, and worn with care. Day after day
Floats down the stream of time, and in its wake
The waters close, and not a trace is left
That it has ever been. And is it thus?
Have I done nought to-day that will remain
Though time flew onward? Is there not one heart
On which I've traced, perchance with trembling hand,
The words of truth eternal? Have I kept
No feet from error's path?—upon no eye
Shed the fair rays of intellectual light?
Or, better still, have I not touch'd the chords
Of love and sympathy in guileless hearts?
Yes, I would hope—but, hush! what means that noise?
    'Tis the voice of those at play,
    Who have been confin'd all day;
    Now they laugh and now they shout;
    That they're happy there's no doubt.
    With their sleds away they go,
    O'er the pure, the sparkling snow;
    Now again, by yonder tree,
    Hear them shout, 'draw me,' 'draw me.'
    Now they form a team of boys,
    I should know that by the noise,
    'Tis to draw home little Sue,
    And Mary dear is going too.
    That is right; I'm glad to see
    Boys have learn'd polite to be;
    That is right, for 'tis the hour
    When *eatables* exert their power

On hungry children just from school,
Where to eat is ''gainst the rule.'
No wonder, then, they haste to see
The ready table spread for tea.
Now the sun is sinking fast,
And his light not long will last;
See how earth, in the bright ray,
Smiles as on a summer's day!
I'll go forth, ere yet his light
Vanishes at touch of night;
And no longer waste my time
Or my thoughts on useless rhyme.

                                                    A. D. W.
                                                    Stockbridge.

❧ Reverses

BY THE AUTHOR OF 'LIGHTS OF EDUCATION'

On the coldest day in one of the most severe winters that ever visited our uncertain climate, a lovely and delicate woman, wrapped in a rich cloak lined with fur, and whose
thin slippers had been covered over with protecting moccasons, was seen to take her slippery path through a very unfashionable district of Baltimore; yet frequently, shrinking
from the keenness of the air, or uncertain of her way, she would hesitate, and turn round
to question a servant lad who attended her steps. When answered, she appeared still
more perplexed, till, arriving at the entrance of a miserable street, she made a pause, and
looked through the dark perspective as if she were afraid, when a circumstance that
might have weakened another's resolution, appeared all at once to strengthen hers.

The wind, which had been increasing in power every moment, as it swept over the
wastes of snow accumulating round our city for weeks, at length came up this dismal
avenue with fresh vigour, darkening the air, and whitening the earth. While the pulsations of her heart were quickened to painfulness, as the freezing blood retired from her
cheeks, she faced the tempest, and went on. Fortunately she was not exposed to all the
sickening sensations that usually assail us near the habitations of the irredeemable
poor—I mean the vicious and the idle; for the snow already covered over the last deposit
of those wretched cabins, and there was not a rag, nor a fish-bone, nor a potatoe-skin, to
be seen; but every broken door and shattered window seemed yielding to the blast, and
about to disclose to her view scenes of sorrow, that even the most charitable lady would
recoil from attempting to relieve. Our *incognita*[8] had nearly reached the centre of the
street, when the servant began to remonstrate; but just at this time the wind subsided a

---

[8]A female with her identity concealed.

little, and two children appeared emerging out of an intersecting alley, and approaching the elegant stranger.

'Oh Goody! what a pretty lady!' cried one.

'Take care, ma'am, you don't get your feet wet in that deep gutter; Kitty just fell in,' said the other—'It's right there,' pointing to the crossing place.

The lady could not help smiling at the looks of admiration with which the child regarded her, as these cautions were given, and in return asked, 'My dear, do you know any poor woman in this street, very much distressed, with two small children, twins, and nothing to give them to eat or wear?'

The girl turned to her companion—'Kitty, do you know any poor woman about here, with *two twins,* and nothing to give them to eat?'

'No, I don't, but perhaps mother does; and if the lady would come in and warm herself till the wind stops, she could ask her. Will you, ma'am?'

The stranger hesitated till she had examined the exterior of the dwelling she was invited to enter, when, finding it much superior to the surrounding buildings in decency of appearance, she willingly followed Kitty, who now bid adieu to her school companion, the other little girl, and led the way into a narrow passage, which had just been scrubbed, and covered at intervals with pieces of rag carpet, to preserve it from the soiling of such feet as her own, just extricated from a mud-puddle. At the door of a small apartment, which, during this inclement season, was used as a kitchen and parlour, the child stopt, and while opening it she exclaimed, 'Mother, here's a lady.'

The good woman, whose name was Wilson, started with some surprise at the stranger's appearance, but immediately very civilly invited her in, where she witnessed a scene of comfort, as gratifying as unexpected. The furniture of the room was common, to be sure, but it had been kept in excellent order, and was very neatly arranged. The table placed for dinner in the middle of the floor, stood ready to receive a roast loin of pork, and a dish of hommony, both smoking on the top of the stove, where they had just been cooked; and the bread that was already on the table, looked not many degrees less white or less light than the snow out of doors. Mrs. Wilson had that minute finished ironing a quantity of clothes, and they were now hanging on a line at the back of the stove, to air; an elderly woman sat near a cradle, rocking it, and mending a boy's jacket.

The visitor approached the cradle, and looked at the sleeping babe. The grandmother drew down the nice covering, that her little darling might be seen to advantage, when the lady, smiling with tender benevolence, said a few sincere words in the baby's praise; but as dinner was ready, she reflected that she might be encroaching on the good people's time, and so she turned to Mrs. Wilson, and asked her the same question that had puzzled her daughter.

'No, madam, there is not any woman in this street that has twins.'

'Then I have been greatly deceived; but it was a very decent woman directed me here, and it appeared a case of such instant distress, that I gave her several things at the time.'

'Was she a young woman, madam?'

'Yes, a very pretty young woman, with black eyes; she wore a straw bonnet trimmed with yellow ribbons, and a red merino shawl.'

'Mother,' said Mrs Wilson, 'that must be Polly Sharp. Why, madam, she is no better than an impostor; she goes about constantly, telling the ladies similar stories; sometimes people have twins, and sometimes they are dying of consumption; sometimes they are dead, and not a bit of clothes to bury them in; but there is not a word of truth in all she says.'

'And is there then no real distress in such a neighbourhood as this?'

'I wish I could say so, madam; but it is distress that no one can relieve for more than a day at a time, because if you give them ever so much now, it will be all the same to-morrow. They are creatures, madam, that would not carry a stick of wood across the street in summer, to save them from perishing with cold in winter. Indeed it is a great drawback on the industrious people about, as we cannot see them starve while we have any thing to eat. For all we know, they might be just as well off, if they would only quit their bad habits, and work.'

'But you must consider there is sickness, to which the poor are especially exposed.'

'That is true, madam, and then any of us might want help; but even this oftener comes from bad living than any other cause. There is a woman, now, just across the street, that we have been tending as well as we could for better than a week, and she not only brought poverty and disgrace on her husband, but sickness and death on herself, by idleness and drink. He is as bad as she is now, but they were once quite above the common order, and might have risen wonderfully in the world, only they got into this evil way; and now he is gone off, and left his wife for the neighbours to take care of.'

While Mrs. Wilson was speaking, her husband came in, with his little son, from the glass-house, where he had constant and profitable employment, being the most faithful and active workman there. He was a fine looking person, upon whom temperance and industry had wrought their usual good effects, producing health, strength, and cheerfulness. The stranger immediately rose, and apologised to Mrs. Wilson for so long intruding on their time—'But,' said she, 'if there is any thing necessary for the comfort of the woman you mention, or if any other case of distress should occur within your knowledge, your little daughter could come to me at any time,' and she gave a card with her address,—*Mrs. Horace Hume, North Charles Street.*

'Thank you, madam,' said Mrs. Wilson, reading the card, 'but Mrs. Lambert will not want much more while she lives, I believe; and that we can easily give her. It is the child that she won't part from, and which she would rather take to the grave with her, that troubles me.'

'But when she cares so little about herself, is it not a wonder that she regards her child so much?'

'Oh! madam, if it was her own, she would not, I dare say; for the life she has led lately must keep her from feeling like a natural mother. But she will not allow that she is dying, and so she is afraid to let the child go, for fear its father won't give her the money for keeping it so long.'

'And who is the father of this unhappy child?'

'It was one Captain Graham, madam, who brought a large vessel here from foreign parts. His lady was on board, but he had to bring her ashore, where she died soon after their baby was born, which was christened Louisa after her. My mother went out nursing sick people then, and she was with Mrs. Graham at the time. The captain had to go on a long voyage again, so mother recommended Mrs. Lambert to him as a nurse for the baby till he came back. A nice decent young woman she was then; but that is more than two years ago, and we have never heard a word of him since, so I suppose he died abroad.'

Mrs. Hume listened to this story with great interest, and she thought it offered the best chance for realizing a wish she had often formed, of obtaining a companion for her own little daughter, who might be educated with her, and divide the indulgence and consideration which parents are so apt to render injurious when they lavish them on one child. Mrs. Hume's principal motive, however, had been to make this *one* child happy by the society of another; and, charmed with the idea of effecting so much good in pursuing her pleasure, she was determined to see Mrs. Lambert, and Kitty seemed to read her thoughts.

'I wish, mother, the lady could see Captain Graham's little child; and perhaps Mrs. Lambert would let her take it.'

'I would like to try, at least,' said Mrs. Hume, 'and if you can wait a little longer for your dinner, my dear, perhaps you will show me where she lives.'

Kitty was quite pleased at her proposal, and, for the first time in her life, that lady entered the abode of profligate poverty. The snow, which had now ceased to fall, was drifted by the door, and prevented its closing, or opening wider than barely to admit Mrs. Hume and her guide, one by one, into a filthy passage, divided from two small rooms. The first of these was totally uninhabitable, the windows being quite broken to pieces, and the chimney an open receptacle for every element except fire. The second disclosed a scene at which the heart of the lady sickened.

It was the last struggle of one of the many victims of depravity to retain a wretched life. A very decent woman, of the working class, at length closed those uneasy eyes, that so long had looked on nothing but ruin. It seems almost unnecessary to say any thing about the apartment. Imagine it with scarcely a spark of fire in its narrow hearth, and no more furniture than the miserable bed, with its tattered covering, that hardly supported the sinking head—cold, dark, and dirty, and you will see it yourself. But where is the child? In that obscure corner, drawn up into the smallest space, with its head covered over, to keep itself warm—there it lies fast asleep.

Kitty, not knowing at first what it was, stirred it with her foot, and the child, awakened too suddenly, ran screaming to the bed, and threw itself on the cold bosom of its nurse, only to suffer the first sensations of death. Vainly did she cry, and press her little hands on that icy heart. No feeling answered hers; and when Mrs. Hume approached to soothe such bitter grief, the babe, at once alarmed and angry, ran away from the bed, and never stopped till she reached the back ground of the dwelling, which extended a few paces beyond the house, to the remains of a pigsty, that, with its accumulated heap of rubbish, formed one of the enclosures of this dismal court. There she remained, trembling and screeching, between two frozen puddles, till, by degrees, Kitty allured her with a piece of gingerbread (when she was half perished) back into the house, whence the corpse had just been removed, to be laid out in that of the good neighbour. To her Mrs. Hume gave money for defraying the funeral expenses. Bitterly did the infant lament the loss of one guardian, and with difficulty could she be made to understand the promises of another; but at length she suffered them to put her in the carriage which Mrs. Hume had sent for; and after this lady had taken leave of her kind little guide, and told her that the family must apply to her, in any case of distress, she drove home.

It would not be possible to ascertain with certainty, all the sensations excited in the mind of a child who could hardly speak, by such a sudden reverse of her prospects in life; though one might infer, from the look of painful amazement which her features wore, that the change was but little to her taste. Mr. Hume's house was large, and richly furnished, and finely situated near the Park, which in summer afforded pleasant and shady walks for his little daughter, who now came into the parlour, dressed in a beautiful yellow poplin frock and worked apron, to see the young stranger her mama had brought home.

'Come to me, Agnes,' said Mrs. Hume, 'here is a pretty little sister for you. I know you will love her.'

'No, I will not,' cried the child. 'Go away, ugly, ugly baby,' giving it a push, which caused the ready tears to flow again; and not without the exercise of much patient tenderness on the part of Mrs. Hume, was the little creature soothed once more, and rendered sufficiently neat to be presented to Mr. Hume when he came home to dine. He was pleased at seeing the amiable wish of his lady so far gratified, and suffered her, without a dissenting word, to place the children opposite to each other at the table, with a servant to wait upon them, and their mutual discontent very visible in their faces. Agnes asked for a great variety of things, and was indulged rather too much by her fond parents. Louisa, who was about a year younger, persisted in eating nothing but potatoes, the only article of food on the table with which she appeared in the least acquainted. After dinner, Mrs. Hume, with great satisfaction, cut out another yellow poplin frock, and commenced her design of having the children dressed exactly alike. But it seemed remarkable, that, while she was exerting herself to obtain this personal resemblance, the traits of the children's tempers should spontaneously appear in such decided contrast, as if determined to mark the difference in their early fate. Agnes, the daughter of wealthy and indulgent parents, displayed an infant's pride and tyranny, from the moment she saw an object on which they could be exercised; while Louisa, the child of sorrow, nursed in poverty, and inured to neglect, exhibited, in an equal degree, the weaker errors that so naturally spring from this estate,—shrinking abasement and timid subjection.

I have described the effect of their first meeting. As the children associated together, these traits disappeared, or were only visible for a short time when the purchase of some new playthings called out the dark spirit again. Upon these occasions Agnes would throw away her own toys if she liked Louisa's better, and say it was her mama who bought them; and then Louisa would let Agnes have all, while she went into a corner to nurse her silent discontent, without any. This, however, did not often happen in Mrs. Hume's presence—when it did, she would gently contrive to pacify both the children; and had they been directed by her alone, though, it must be owned, her judgment was not always so acute as her feelings were tender, they might have contrived to live together, with no greater cause for mutual aversion than those momentary and trifling disagreements.

But unfortunately there was a servant in the house, who had nursed Agnes from her birth, and she, jealous of the first appearance of another favourite, assiduously cultivated the faults of her youthful charge, and opposed them with all her art against the growth of an influence superior to her own. And it must be confessed also, that as the children grew up, some slight difference might be seen, even in Mrs. Hume, between the tender benevolence with which she cherished an unfortunate orphan, and the feelings of maternal fondness, to which some pride was naturally, though unhappily added; for Agnes was exceedingly handsome, and exhibited to every eye that peculiar look of distinction, which, as if in mockery of the very mutable nature of fortune and rank, in our country, is sometimes bestowed on 'the children of men.'

Beside this, she evinced great quickness of perception, learning easily, if not thoroughly, every thing she was taught; and being quite as anxious to display, as to acquire knowledge, it will not be thought surprising that her parents over-rated her talents, and her teachers were perfectly satisfied with them.

The full character of Louisa's mind was not yet developed in her unformed features; but since she never learned any thing that she was not made to understand, and this required more time and patience than could be often devoted to one in a school of a hundred, she easily acquired the reputation of dulness, and suffered for a time all the disgrace of being a dunce, when every perception was alive to render it painful.

And could not even the sweet voice of her patroness call these perceptions into useful exercise? It appears not, except in the branches of sewing and embroidery, which the little girls learned from her. There are minds upon which dependence, when *felt,* acts like a blight; and, with the increasing pride of Agnes, and the constant persecution of the nurse, of which she dreaded to complain, there came a vague remembrance of her infant days over Louisa's mind, to darken the thoughts of her present state, and at length induce her to shun the society of those she had most reason to love. Mrs. Hume had given each of the children a small room, that their studies might not interfere, when she found they so unequally studied together; and here upon every vacancy in school, where she certainly did not improve so much as to encourage the attention of her teachers, for which reason she was altogether neglected, Louisa had lately retired to muse over her own plans in solitude. What these were, remaining an impenetrable secret to Agnes and her nurse, they informed Mrs. Hume of it, who then spoke to the little girl herself.

'What do you now lock your door for every day, my dear Louisa, so that Agnes can never get in to see what you are doing? Nurse says from this she is sure it must be something wrong.'

'But it is not, mama, and Agnes and the nurse might both come in, only they would laugh at me if they did.'

'And why, my dear? What are you employed about?'

'I am trying to learn, ma'am,' answered Louisa, with an agitated voice, and blushing very much.

'But you do not succeed, my poor Louisa,' said Mr. Hume, laughing, and playfully putting his hand over her head, before he left the room.

Mrs. Hume's curiosity was now satisfied, or her scruples removed, and she told Agnes that in future Louisa should not be disturbed, when she chose to be alone in her study, whatever her occupations might be.

This incident occurred when Louisa was nearly thirteen; and before the next midsummer recess, Mrs. Hume received a letter from a particular friend, requesting that Agnes might be permitted to spend the few weeks of vacation with her in the country; and to secure a compliance with her wishes, she included the nurse in her invitation, as an additional guard on the young lady's safety. No letter could have arrived more happily for Louisa, since Mr. and Mrs. Hume agreed to the request contained in it; and when Agnes and her evil counsellor were gone, those deep affections, so long closed in by their restraining power, flowed from the orphan's heart with a double tide, astonishing her protectors; and Mrs. Hume could not avoid observing, now she was left alone to enliven their domestic hours, that there was a self-renouncing principle in Louisa's love which Agnes had never shown in hers; while sentiments of admiration were soon added to those of affection, as the traits of genius and virtue daily unfolded their beauty in the light air of freedom.

One morning Mrs. Hume was expressing a wish for her husband's miniature, that she might have it set as an ornament; but she feared that he never would consent to give the time required for painting it. Louisa made no remarks; and a few days after, she retired from the dining room before the dessert appeared, which was remarked by Mr. and Mrs. Hume, as not according with her usual good *taste,* I should say, but that the word in this case might convey a doubtful sense, and I mean good *manners.* She, however, returned almost immediately, with two small plates of ivory, upon which were traced miniature busts of her protectors, very handsomely executed, and exhibiting the most perfect resemblance. There were a few complimentary verses at the back of each picture, evidently dictated by the truest feeling, and perhaps promising better poetry in future. She presented each of her patrons the other's portrait. At first they appeared more surprised than pleased, for, thinking only of one person who might have painted them, and knowing she was an expensive artist, they supposed Louisa had incurred a debt, the first appearance of a habit which they had ever condemned.

'Who painted these miniatures, Louisa?' asked Mrs. Hume.

'I did, mama.'

'You did—with no teacher, my love? How can that be?'

'Miss Mason told me how to prepare the colours, when she saw me take so much interest in drawing. I bought the paints with my own money last Christmas; the ivory plates Miss Mason gave me herself.'

'But how did you see her painting?'

'Oh! I have gone to her room many a time, because she asked me, after I had been there once with some of the girls, who wanted to have their pictures taken; and she promised never to tell you till I chose.'

'But the likeness is so perfect; who taught you that, Louisa?' said Mr. Hume, looking at her with pleasure.

'Oh! I learned that by *heart,* sir, long ago'—and the blush and the smile that brightened her face showed the exquisite loveliness of the awakened mind within.

The patroness embraced her with a mother's pride, while she said, 'Then, Louisa, this was the wicked employment that kept you so much away from us?'

'Yes, mama; but I had to do other things beside. Come with me, and I will let you see them.'

Mrs. Hume went, and on entering Louisa's 'prison-house,' she discovered, with astonishment, that this child had actually acquired, by patient and quiet study, not assisted by any one, the principles of all the knowledge that many teachers had failed to convey, remarkable application assisting natural talents so much, though the last with her were so lately developed, and the other very long ill directed. Beside some small pieces translated from the French and Spanish, observations on the lives of celebrated men, and notes on historical events, written in a neat hand, with correct outlines of maps, and several pretty drawings, which Louisa arranged on the table, she had in a small basket an entire set of infant's clothes, cut out by an old pattern of her own, and a lady's morning cap, very neatly worked. This she now took out, and tied on Mrs. Hume's head with white ribbon, while she gazed delighted on the fair countenance, surrounded by that simple border.

'And now, mama,' said she, presenting her with the basket, 'will you take these clothes, and give them to some little child, as poor as I was when you took me home?'

'Louisa, my own dearest girl, who told you this? I spoke to every one that knew it to conceal it from you, and Mr. Hume said he would discharge any servant who spoke of the circumstance.'

'Ah! but I remembered it, mama, and that made me try so much, that you might have some return for all your goodness to me.'

'And you were occupied in this manner, Louisa, when your preceptors thought you were a dunce?'

'Well, perhaps I am a dunce, mama,' said she, smiling with a very contrary expression in her features, 'but I have patience with myself, and there is only one more that has.'

Here she threw her arms round Mrs. Hume, and as that lady bent her head to the grateful orphan's, their precious tears were mingled.

When they returned to the dining room, Mr. Hume was informed of Louisa's progress, upon which he drew the little girl towards him, and, smoothing the hair from her brow, he looked on her countenance attentively, and then, turning to the lady, he said with a smile, 'I am now more convinced than ever of the truth of Mr. Wormwood's opinion, my love. So far from thinking that one person can teach another person every thing, I believe that no person can teach another person any thing.'

'Then how are they to learn? I suppose I must ask,' said Mrs. Hume, laughing.

'Teach themselves, my dear,—behold the example.'

When Agnes returned from her long visit, she found all opinions changed in regard to Louisa, who had now attained an height above any servile power. But though the nurse could no longer grieve her, with Agnes she felt even more unhappy than before, since her despotic pride, now aggravated by jealousy, was fast producing hatred in her heart; so nearly are all sinful thoughts allied. Was it not a pity that two lovely children should be rendered wretched by the mere cultivation of an infant's faults? At the renewed unkindness of her companion, Louisa's mind darkened again. She would not complain—regard for her protectors prevented this; but they observed how her temper was changing, though the cause still continued unknown; and perhaps they might have seen her speaking countenance more sadly shaded, as the light of genius and the trace of knowledge departed, but for another reverse.

One day Mr. Hume brought home a newspaper, in which there was an advertisement from Boston, offering a reward of two thousand dollars for the discovery of a child called Louisa Graham, left several years before under the care of a woman in Baltimore of the name of Lambert. Ample testimony was required, as the child would be the heiress of a large fortune. The first feelings of Louisa on hearing this were certainly delightful—but

I hasten to vindicate her from the charge of avarice—she thought only of the great debt of gratitude she owed her benefactors, and the poor that *she* would relieve now. She would overload Agnes with presents, and even the nurse was to be made ashamed of herself by gifts. In this, however, I am afraid there was some pride mingling with her Christian feelings, and that she anticipated a triumph; but it was soon corrected when she thought of leaving her dearest friends to go to New England, where she must be acknowledged as the daughter of Captain Graham, before she could inherit his fortune. Mr. Wilson gladly accepted Mr. Hume's offer to accompany him and Louisa to Boston, with such proofs of her birth as must obtain the reward.

Louisa's great likeness to her parents, who had been well known and much esteemed in their native place, established the truth of other evidence, and she was immediately acknowledged as the heiress of an immense property, which had accumulated in the hands of an uncle, from a small fortune which Captain Graham consigned to his care for the use of his daughter, when he felt the approach of death on his return passage from Brazil, about a year after he had been in Baltimore. This uncle, instead of restoring his niece to her family, made no inquiries respecting her, and dishonourably appropriated the money to his own use during his life, which must have rendered his death particularly unwelcome, if he really believed in no other atonement than fifty times multiplying her original wealth, and having it settled so securely on her as to be altogether out of the power of any one who might have no more principle than he had shown.

With the reward offered in the advertisement, Mr. Wilson returned to Baltimore, and bought a small neat house and garden, removed from all disgraceful neighbours, yet quite as convenient to his work as where I first noticed him; and here he continued with his family, always industrious and respectable.

Louisa Graham would now have been perfectly happy, were she permitted to enjoy her advantages with her dear friends in her native place, but this was contrary to her uncle's will. Until she completed her eighteenth year, she was to remain in Boston, under the immediate direction of her guardians. After this, she would be of age, when the interest of her fortune, accumulating during four years, was to be given to her on her birthday, that she might make an establishment suited to her taste. This was a great error, since so large a sum placed at once into such unpractised hands, might have done Louisa more injury than first retaining her father's bequest; but an alarmed conscience will sometimes counsel us to correct with a bad judgment the faults of a guilty principle.

Happily the result was directed by a wiser Being. Miss Graham had never ceased writing to her friends in Baltimore by every opportunity, and for two or three years they answered her letters punctually, but after this they wrote very seldom, and their communications were short and mournful. Perhaps no previous anxiety equalled what Louisa felt from her seventeenth to her eighteenth year, though surrounded by all the enjoyments that new wealth could procure, or new friends could bestow; and no sooner did she reach that age of freedom, than she set off, with a respectable escort, for Baltimore.

On arriving there she made immediate inquiries for Mr. Hume, and was directed to a small cheap house in the suburbs, where she now alighted from her carriage with a beating heart, and a footman knocked at the door. It was opened by an ignorant looking servant girl, who stared in stupid wonder at the interesting stranger, and twice heard her ask for Mrs. Hume, before she invited her in; then, gazing back all the time, she led the way to a small parlour, where that sweet lady, in the pale shadow of her former loveliness, was reclining on an easy chair. Just before her, from a lower seat, Agnes was looking on her mother; and what sorrow did those eyes bespeak, while her lips were uttering the tenderest persuasions to induce her to eat of some delicacy, prepared by her own hands from directions in a cookery book, which was the only literary work, except one, that she had studied for a long time past. Mrs. Hume gazed with a mother's entrancing love, on her graceful and now really beautiful daughter, as she extended her hand to take what she offered; but at this moment the door opened, a sudden exclamation alarmed the invalid, and she let the bowl fall. The next moment she was in the arms of Louisa Graham. Agnes rose immediately, overjoyed yet embarrassed; her self-reproach chastening the delight she felt at her friend's unaltered feeling. But when she was clasped to that heart, which affliction and prosperity had equally tried, the best feelings of her nature overcame the last struggles of her pride, and while she rejoiced, she wept bitterly.

When the first violent effects of this meeting were over, Louisa inquired anxiously of Mrs. Hume the cause of these changes she saw.

'You know, my dear Louisa,' said that lady, 'Mr. Hume was the chief proprietor of a large manufacturing establishment, which he unfortunately suffered to be under the direction of another person, who has so involved the concern, that it must now be sold for the debts; and we will have little or nothing left. My health could not endure Mr. Hume's distress, and, but for the efforts of our darling child, who has come out like some pure metal from the furnace, I think I should have died. Agnes studied every thing that could render us comfortable in poverty. Our meals are prepared under her direction, and all the other domestic arrangements she overlooks. We have an ignorant servant, and therefore it is necessary; but the manner in which she does these things proves to us that the Almighty has blessed her by adversity. If her father then could forget the imprudence to which he attributes his failure, even as we are now, we might be happy.'

'And I am sure he will forget it the moment he sees me,' cried Louisa, with great vivacity. 'But what has become of your nurse, mama?'

'Why, on the mere rumour of our misfortune, she married, and went to New York. This was the first proof we had of her heartless selfishness, but we have never heard from her since, nor do we ever wish to hear again. Her behaviour at the time almost broke this poor girl's heart, who thought all her unkindness to you, of which I have been since informed, proceeded from the woman's affection to herself. This circumstance a little influenced our conduct towards you, my dear Louisa, and prevented our writing very frequently. We feared the effect of your fortune on your own heart or ours.'

'Oh! my beloved—my only mother! when can mere wealth repay all the benefits I received from you? Then use my fortune as if it were your own at any other time, but *now* I must dispose of it myself.'

Louisa then sent away the carriage, and quietly seated herself, to wait for Mr. Hume. When he came, she saw the most affecting of all those reverses in him. His once handsome, stately person, had grown thin and stopping; his dark hair was changing into grey; his fine features were withered, and his pleasant countenance disturbed and overcast. But it brightened the instant he saw Louisa,—and it remained bright, for, with all the energy of grateful affection, she insisted on his purchasing in the establishment, which was to be sold the next morning, and commencing the business again on his own account. To this he at length consented, on condition that Louisa should receive the annual interest of the money advanced, which was, however, reduced to a mere nominal income, since she only accumulated from it a fortune for Agnes, with whom she ever after lived in the most delightful friendship. Mrs. Hume, restored to her former situation in life, soon recovered her health and cheerfulness, as Mr. Hume did his portliness and good temper; while he continued to prosper in his affairs, from the time he commenced to regulate them himself.

❧ Rebus

A hero by Achilles slain;
A Grecian general next attain;
An emperor that govern'd Rome;
A Tuscan prince soon met his doom;
A sign the zodiac will produce;
A metal that's of general use;
The daughter of a Trojan king;
A mount that poets often sing;
Those games the ancients did celebrate;
A flower for sweets none adequate;
A Carthage queen to consummate;
These initials conceiv'd and conjoin'd, you'll declare
'Tis the name of an instrument us'd by the fair.

❧ The Child's Winter Thoughts

BY MRS. L. H. SIGOURNEY

Winter hath hid my flowers.—I cannot find
A single violet where so many grew;
And all my garden-beds, so nicely fring'd
With verdant box, are cover'd thick with snow.
He has not left one lingering pink to please
My little sister. Why, 'tis very hard
For Winter so to come, and take away
What was my own, and I had toil'd to keep
Healthful, and free from weeds.
                    They say he rocks
The wearied flowers to sleep, as some good nurse
Compels the infant to resign its sports,
And take its needful slumbers. Well, I thought

My roses all looked sleepy,—and I know
When one is tir'd, how very sweet it is
To shut the eyelids close, and know no more
Until the wakening of a mother's kiss.
      Winter seems stern, and hath an angry voice;—
I hope he will not harm my tender buds,
That just had put their tender leaflets forth,
And look'd so frighten'd.
             But I know who rules
Harsh Winter, and spreads out the spotless show,
Like a soft curtain, over every herb
And shrinking plant, that it may rest secure
And undisturbed. He shields the loneliest shrub
That strikes its rough root at the mountain's base,
With the same gentle and protecting love
As the moss rose. Yea, *He doth care for all;*—
The lily, and the aspen, and the moss
That clothes the ancient wall, and hath no friend
To watch it, and no fragrance to repay.
      Father in Heaven! I thank thee for the rest
Thou giv'st my weary flowers. Grant them to wake
At Spring's first call, and rear their beauteous heads
Rejoicing,—as my baby-brother springs
From his sweet cradle sleep, with tiny arms
Outstretch'd, and eyes like my own violets bright.
Hartford, Ct.

❧ The History of a Day

Some have written histories of countries, of battles and sieges, the storming of cities, the intrigues of courts, the progress of civilization, the rise and fall of empires, embracing the condition of man from the first dawn of the regular efforts of his mind, until he has attained his present astonishing perfection; and these histories have no doubt contributed to help forward the human intellect in its onward course. But so may the history of much less important matters. The history of a fly or a beetle, of a flower or a bird, may both improve and delight very cultivated minds; and I hope the subject which I have chosen, the history of my adventures in a single day, when a lad of only ten years of age, may not be found entirely without interest or utility.

    I will premise that my father lived, at the time of my history, in the Carse of Gowrie in Scotland, a very beautiful and fertile district, deriving its name from the Earls of Gowrie, very renowned in the history of that romantic country, for their daring and adventurous spirit, and for the tragic fate of the last of their race. My father had a brother who had gone to India in early life, and married there; his wife, however, died a few years after their union, leaving him one child, a daughter. This event determined him to

"The Culprit Detected" from *The Pearl,* 1833.

come to his native land, and to give up the remainder of his life to the education of his darling Emily. But his constitution had been shattered by the heats of a torrid climate, and he died on his passage home. My father became the guardian of Emily, and I her chosen and almost only companion.

Emily Wedderburn was a very lovely child, and about a year younger than myself; she was small and delicate for her age; I was remarkably robust and stout for mine, and it naturally fell to my share to provide her every thing which her own strength was unequal to procure. She was very fond of flowers, and minerals, and fossils, and indeed of every natural production, and had displayed considerable taste in arranging them. In her little garden she had almost every species of moss and wild flower to be found within ten miles round; and I was never so happy as when, accompanied by her, we wandered over the hills and vallies, and into the deep dells, in quest of their wild treasures. But, gentle reader, you can easily imagine that poetical kind of employment would be apt to seduce an imaginative lad from more dull, but certainly equally indispensable duties;

and that it is not surprising that the flowing Livy,[9] the sweet Virgil,[10] to say nothing of the crabbed niceties of the grammarians, should be neglected in spite of all the frowns of the pedagogue, and the terrors of the birch, for companionship so sweet, and for pursuits at once so romantic and so congenial to a youthful mind.

My father too was a good, easy man, who allowed us to take our own way. He left Emily to the care of her governess, and me to the village schoolmaster; and believing them both to be competent, he gave himself no trouble about the technical part of our education. He probably went to an extreme in his system of non-interference with teachers or children, but the opposite course of constant, invariable interference with both is doubly injurious. I have known parents who locked up the minds of their children, and guarded them as carefully as they did their plate; the misspelling of a word threw them into a fever, and produced a long letter to the unfortunate teacher. If they discovered that a lesson had not been completely studied, the culprit was doomed to suffer the pains of solitary confinement, and taste the luxuries of bread and water, instead of roast beef and plum pudding. The children of such parents must pare their nails by rule, study by rule, run by rule, and choose their companions by rule. The effect of such a system, however, invariably is to deprive the boys of all natural character and buoyancy of spirit, which are so essential to success in every stage of life, and in every pursuit, and to give them instead, cramped faculties and cold hearts. The unfortunate subjects of such a system are kept in a kind of treadmill, and never know the pleasure of free and uncontrolled motion. But to my story.

The memorable day in the calendar of my youth was as fine as the sun ever shone upon. But as I bent my steps towards school, I felt a heaviness of spirit which was little in accordance with the beauty of the morning, and which was as prophetic of some coming calamity as the lightning is of rain. To the schoolboy, 'coming events cast their shadows before,' and he can see distinctly how the fact takes place, the uplifted arm of the pedant, and its quick and heavy descent, and feel his fingers smart with the anticipated blow. All this I saw as I plodded my weary way to school; I felt my spirit flag, and I heartily wished that the schoolmaster and school were twenty miles off. The fact was that I was even worse prepared than usual, or, to speak more correctly, was not prepared at all, for saying a single lesson.

My sweet cousin had spread so many allurements for me the day before, that it was impossible for me to resist, and 'the sentinel stars' had long 'set their watch in the sky,' before I thought of opening a book. I then concluded that it was too late to redeem the errors of a day, and, at the request of Emily, I read for her fairy tales until bed-time. But I put my faith in an early rise tomorrow. To-morrow, the greatest promiser and the worst performer in the world, what hopes has it not blasted!—what schemes has it not defeated! Still upon this notorious cheat I put my trust, and, like the rest of the fools, I was disappointed.

The bright beams of the morning sun awoke me, and I had scarcely huddled on my clothes before the breakfast bell rang. I was now reduced to my last alternative, that of

---

[9]Livy (59 B.C.–A.D. 17) was one of ancient Rome's greatest historians.

[10]Virgil (70–19 B.C.) is widely considered to be the greatest Roman poet.

running over some of my lessons on the way to school; but the apprehensions which I have already described so muddled my brain, that the elegant strains of my favourite Virgil appeared to my bewildered mind wholly incomprehensible; and in that woful plight I entered the drear dominions of Peter Black, whose business it had been for many a long year to whip Latin and Geometry into the boys of the parish.

Peter was a teacher of the old school, stern, inflexible, peremptory, and despotic as the Grand Turk. He would listen to no excuse, receive no apology; and, like the ancient Grecian lawgiver, he had but one punishment for all offences, whether against grammar or good order, namely, a severe whipping. I do not say that Peter had no kindly corner in his heart, but I can say that I never discovered it; and if he did not take pleasure in beating the boys, their cries and tears were at least wholly indifferent to him. His outer man corresponded perfectly with the inner; his features were small and sharp; his eyes grey, deeply sunk, and overshadowed by huge eyebrows, which gave a singularly fierce expression to his whole physiognomy. Never had literature a more unamiable professor; but, notwithstanding, he had a great reputation as a scholar and a teacher.

As I entered, his eyes met mine, and his glance seemed to penetrate into the secret recesses of my mind, and to expose all my weakness. My troubles very soon began. I broke down on the celebrated ass's bridge, made false quantities, and committed all sorts of blunders. The concentrated range of the pedant burst upon me like a torrent; he beat me unmercifully, but instead of the castigations clearing my ideas, it only added to their confusion; my brain seemed to whirl round like a top, and I committed the most egregious mistakes in the most familiar things. To ask for mercy would have been as wise as to ask the winds not to blow, the water not to run, or the fire not to burn; and all that now remained for me was to endure in sullen silence the punishments which my own inconsiderate folly had produced.

The hour of dismissal approached, an hour as dear to the school-boy as honey to the bee, or the sight of home to the weary traveller; but that hour, so rich in fun and frolic, brought to me only disappointment and sorrow: for when Peter gave the well known signal which set every little urchin a-packing up his books, and opened the door to their impatience, I alone was ordered to remain, and I had the mortification to hear the key turn in the lock, and cut off my last hope of retreat, leaving me to silence and my own reflections.

Travellers have described the awful solitariness of the desert, its profound silence, and the melancholy effect which that silence has upon the mind; but I am persuaded that it falls far short of the painful stillness of the deserted school-room to the unhappy culprit, who is doomed to be its only inhabitant during the hours which are given to play and good living to his more fortunate or deserving companions; the sharp stings of hunger, which, like an uneasy creditor, demanding to be satisfied, add to the effect of his forlorn situation. Oh, how I sighed when I recollected what the proper employment of two hours would have saved me from! I thought the time would never pass away, and I longed, with an intensity which I yet well remember, for the freedom of open fields and a good dinner. Time certainly had laid aside his wings, and swelled the amount of a few hours into as many days. I would have given any thing even to see the face of my grim instructor, and I felt a thrill of delight dart through my frame, when I heard the old rusty lock creak as it obeyed the key, and saw Peter, followed by the boys, enter the room.

The remainder of school hours passed away without any remarkable occurrence;

Peter was rather in a better humour than usual, or, more correctly, somewhat less grum;[11] and the happy time came when the doors were thrown open, and I was enabled to rush out into the long wished for open air. Away I went whistling with my satchel over my shoulder, as joyous as a bird just escaped from the cage. I had already passed Gowrie's common, famous for a battle, and for one of those mysterious cairns, or mounds of stone, no doubt set up as a memorial of some great event, the memory of which is now extinct; the village and church were past, and I was fast approaching the house of John Cameron, an old man who had for many years mended the shoes for half the clowns in the neighbourhood.

John, or Jock, as he was called, had never aspired to the glory of making a new pair of shoes all his life, but he was unrivalled in the art of patching. John too had cultivated with great care a few apple-trees of the very best sort known in Scotland, and the sign of 'Choice Fruit sold here,' showed that John added to the profits of his mending, those of his orchard. But, being close to the road side, and right on the highway to school, it threw great temptations in the way of pennyless boys, who made frequent inroads upon John's property, and not unfrequently succeeded in depriving the worthy old man of a large quantity of his choice fruit, and, consequently, of no small part of his revenue. But the good man was vigilant as an Argus,[12] and it was firmly believed by the boys that he would go to sleep with one eye, and keep the other open as a watchful sentinel upon his much prized fruit. The effect too of these depredations had made John particularly crusty during the fruit season; and woe to unlawful intruders within the precincts of the orchard, if once fairly within his clutches!

When I came within sight of the golden fruit, which was rich, ruddy, ripe, I seemed to feel the pains of hunger redoubled, and I plunged my hand into the deepest recesses of my pocket, in the hope of fishing up some fugitive pence, but my search was as vain as that of the astronomers for the lost Pleiad.[13] I found nothing but emptiness, but my desire for possessing myself of the fruit, lawfully or unlawfully, became stronger and stronger every moment. I looked around and observed no one in sight. I peeped through the fence to see whether the watchful protector of the grove of Pomona[14] was on guard. It was almost a miracle, but such was the fact, that he was not to be seen, and I immediately concluded that he had been called from home, or was engaged with some favoured crony over a glass of ale. Having taken all these precautions, I then mounted the fence, and laid hold of an overhanging branch, and began to put the rich burden that it bore into my hat, when I heard the door creak, and beheld the enraged John sally forth from his fortress, armed with a leathern strap. The purpose to which he meant to apply it was no secret to me, but I might have escaped if my presence of mind had not deserted me. As it was, like the unfortunate bird under the fabled charm of the snake, I fell into the jaws of the enemy. The sequel need not be told, for the artist to whom I told the adventure many years afterwards, has so admirably bodied forth the whole scene of the Culprit Detected, that words can add nothing to the effect.

---

[11]gloomy

[12]Mythical person who reportedly had one hundred eyes.

[13]A group of seven stars in the constellation Taurus, only six of which can be seen by the naked eye.

[14]The Roman goddess of fruits and fruit trees.

I went home hungry, weary, and in pain, like some disconsolate knight after a series of defeats and a harassing flight; but the remembrance of the misfortunes of *the day* feelingly demonstrated to me the folly of putting off till to-morrow what should be done to-day; for to playing till the last hour with my dear Emily, I traced all my sufferings and disgraces.

The future was brighter. I worked until I extorted praise even from the pedant, a thing unheard of in the history of his life. I conciliated John by sending him many a good job, and buying instead of pilfering his choice fruit; and Emily herself found all her wants fully supplied.

❧ Enigma

Design'd by fate to guard the crown,
　　Aloft in air I reign,
Above the monarch's haughty frown,
　　Or statesman's plotting brain:
In hostile fields, when danger's near,
　　I'm found amidst alarms;
In crowds, where peaceful beaux appear,
　　I instant fly to arms.

❧ A New England Ballad

An incident as early in the settlement of New England as 1630, has been faithfully followed in the subjoined verses, which are written with the hope of drawing the attention of juvenile readers to that interesting era in our national history.

A boat was bound from Shawmut* Bay
　　To Plymouth's stormy shore,
And on her rough and fragile hull
　　Five daring men she bore.

With them would Mary Guerard go,
　　In cold December's time,
Though delicate and gently bred,
　　For such a rugged clime.

'Dear father, do not part from me,'
　　Entreatingly she cried,
'But when you seek the troubled sea,
　　Retain me by your side.

---

*Boston.

'My youthful spirits mount in joy
　　Upon my bosom's throne,
And I can brave the storms with *you,*
　　But I shall weep *alone.*'

They launch their shallop[15] on the bay,
　　And give her to the breeze,
While Mary cheers her father's heart
　　Upon the sparkling seas.

How sweetly on that savage coast
　　Her maiden laughter rung!
How doatingly on that fair face
　　The busy oars-men hung!

But tempests rose, and 'mid the rocks
　　Their leaky boat was thrown;
A bed of ice form'd under them—
　　Their ocean path unknown.

Those five stout hearts with chasten'd looks
　　Await their mournful doom,
And Mary, Shawmut's gentle flower,
　　Expects a frozen tomb.

And now that group of pilgrim souls
　　'Dispose thomselves to die;'*
How bless'd were they in that dread hour
　　To put their trust on high.

But near a lone and surgy cape,[†]
　　Land! land! an oarsman spied—
With effort strong they clear the skiff,
　　And catch the favouring tide,

And hoisting up their stiffen'd sail,
　　The dangerous way explore,
Till chill, and faint, with sinking hearts,
　　They reach the houseless shore.

Along the glaz'd and crackling ice
　　They move in agony,
When, starting forward on their track,
　　The group two red men see,

---

[15]A large, heavy boat with one or more masts.

*Massachusetts Colony Records.

[†]Cape Cod.

Who, with the warmth of untaught hearts,
   Their generous helps prepare,
Cover, and feed, and nourish them,
   With hospitable care.

But cold had struck the chill of death
   On Guerard's manly frame;
Fainter and fainter grew the breath
   Which sigh'd his Mary's name.

And she, that lone and lovely one,
   Sank like a shooting star,
That, springing out from all its kin,
   Falls scatter'd from afar:

Yet gather'd strength o'er that rough bed
   On which her father lay,
And on her fair breast laid his head,
   And bent her own to pray;

And not until his failing sigh
   Had bless'd her to the last,
Down by his side in anguish lay,
   And clasp'd his body fast,

And shriek'd, in tones of piercing woe,
   'Return, return to me,
Leave, leave me not in sorrow here,
   Or let me die with thee!'

Solemn and stern the Indians stood,
   While death was passing by,
But when his parting wing was flown,
   Loud rose their funeral cry.

They laid the body carefully,
   Like a brother whom they lov'd;
The sandy soil, a frozen mass,
   A scanty covering prov'd.

The wolves came howling for their dead,
   And then those Indians wild,
As if by tender instinct led
   For his deserted child,

Rais'd o'er the grave a noble pile
   Of trees securely bound,
Which kept the hungry fiends away
   Mid solitude profound.

All died but one of that strong band
   Who steer'd from Shawmut Bay,
And her, the young and gentle maid,
   The blossom on their way.

The Indians bore her to her home,
   Where, like a stricken flower
When winter winds have passed away,
   She grac'd her native bower.

But often in her after years,
   She thought of that lone grave,
Where ocean's breezes moan'd and sigh'd,
   And dash'd the gather'd wave;

And bless'd the red men of the soil,
   Who gave her succour there,
And sought for them with deeds of love,
   And ask'd for them in prayer.

C. G.
Charleston, S. C.

❧ Greece

BY T. H.

Greece is a country situated in the south of Europe. It occupies only a small space, as may be seen on the map; but the importance of nations is not always in proportion to their extent of territory, but rather to the influence they exert on the condition of mankind. The history of this celebrated country illustrates this statement very strikingly, for it had and still has a more powerful influence on mankind than that of any other nation, no matter how large. The Greeks were early distinguished for their love of the fine arts, such as painting, sculpture, and architecture, and their excellence in these arts has never been equalled. Their literature too was of the noblest kind, and their poets, orators, and historians, have become the models of all who aspire to excellence in any department of human knowledge.

The Greeks were ardent lovers of liberty; which was shown in the noble resistance they made upon many occasions both to foreign and domestic tyranny. The free institutions, which they cherished as their most valuable possessions, next to the altars of their gods, had a fine effect upon the character of this people, making them the most intelligent, industrious, and enterprising of all the nations of antiquity. They formed colonies in all the countries of the then known world, and carried wherever they went their fine taste for the arts and for literature, and thus were the means of civilising mankind.

When Greece fell before the Roman power, and lost her national independence for ever, then it was that their haughty conquerors became subject to the intellectual superiority of the Greeks. The Romans were at that time a barbarous people, but it was impossible for them to remain insensible to the great beauties of Grecian art, and, as many fine specimens of it were taken to Rome, it soon became the fashion to admire, and afterwards to imitate them. Grecian philosophy and literature were likewise cultivated. The most eminent men in Rome went to Greece to study under the best masters, and those who were able sent their sons there to be educated, or hired Greek tutors to reside in their families. Greek schools of philosophy, and eloquence, and the arts, were instituted in the capital, and, in a short time, throughout the empire. The very superstitions of the Greeks were adopted by their servile imitators, for temples were erected to the Greek divinities, which, it is said, received more homage than those that were exclusively Roman.

Thus we see in the history of this people, a beautiful instance of the effect of mind, in making greater and more lasting conquests than can be achieved by the sword.

The modern Greeks are a lively and intelligent people, possessing many points of resemblance to their ancestors; but they are much debased by superstition and a long course of the worst government that ever was instituted. They have lately made a noble effort to obtain their freedom, and every friend of mankind fervently wishes that they may not be disappointed.

❧ Crossing the Brook

Shrink not, thou little trembler; place thy foot
Firmly upon the rock, and let thy heart
Still its swift pulses.—Thou hast nought to fear,
For is *she* not beside thee, with her eye
Solicitous to find thee out the trace,
And guard thee from all danger?—she to whom
Thou art the jewel, given in gracious hour
By the benevolent Providence. Now
One little step, and on the velvet bank,
Thick with its yielding grass and mazy flowers,
Wooing all senses open to delight,
Thou art in safety.
                Thou hast travell'd far,
With much misgiving, though with little need,
For I that loved thee would have rather been
Rack'd with stern pains myself, than, risk'd by me,
Beheld thee made the prey of any hurt
Of frame or spirit, howsoever light.
Look back upon thy journey. See yon tree,—
Its root thrust out, and swelling with the stream,
Gave the first foothold when thou leftst the bank.
Then came the trickling waters to thy knees,
Climbing, until in terror thou didst cry,
'Save me, Oh mother!' and thy shrinking limbs
Task'd all my strength to bear thee to yon rock,
On which thou tookst so very long a rest,

"Crossing the Brook" from *The Pearl*, 1833.

And left at last with such unwillingness.
And so thy perils, with a few strides more,
Are ended, and thou now begin'st to smile
At thy own terrors.
                    Henceforth thou wilt learn—
And when I teach thee there is nought to fear,
Step firmly, with a heart all confidence—
That the great God, and she whose love to thee,
Though with no power like his, is not less great,
Will keep thee from all danger and alarm,
If thou wilt heed their language.
                              Now look up

And kiss me—kiss thy mother, my sweet boy,
'Tis all that, in return, thou now canst give;
But every mother, looking on her child,
As I on thee this moment, will have said,
'How much, how very much to her it is!'

K.

Philadelphia, July, 1832.

❧ Susanna Meredith

OR, THE VILLAGE SCHOOL
A TALE

BY MISS LESLIE

Susanna Meredith was the orphan niece of Mrs. Weatherwax, an elderly lady who was 'preceptress' of a school at a large and flourishing village in one of the middle sections of the Union. The aunt of our young heroine was educating her with a view to her becoming an assistant in the seminary; and, indeed, poor Susanna had already been inducted into the most laborious duties of that office, though her age was not yet fourteen.

It must not be supposed that Mrs. Weatherwax's establishment bore any resemblance to that English village school, whose sign has been so facetiously described as containing these words, 'Children taught reading, writing, and grammar, for sixpence a week. Them as learns manners pays eightpence.' On the contrary, hers was a lyceum[16] of high pretence, and very select; none being admitted whose parents were not likely to pay their quarter bills.

Mrs. Weatherwax was not one of those teachers who strew the path of learning with flowers. With her, as with most hard, dull, heavy-minded people, the letter was always paramount to the spirit. Provided that her pupils could repeat the exact words of their lessons, it was to her a matter of indifference whether they understood a single one of those words or not; and, in fact, as her own comprehension was not very extensive, it was by no means surprising that the governess should carefully avoid the dangerous ground of explanation.

Their chief class-book was Murray's English Reader, where the little girls were expected to be interested and edified by dialogues between Locke and Bayle,[17] orations of Cicero,[18] and parliamentary speeches of Lord Mansfield.[19] And twice a week, by way of variety, they were indulged with a few pages of Young's Night Thoughts. Every Sat-

---

[16]A place of study or instruction.

[17]John Locke (1632–1704) and Pierre Bayle (1647–1706) were English and French philosophers, respectively, who differed in their views of religion.

[18]Marcus Tullius Cicero (106–43 B.C.) was a renowned Roman statesman and orator.

[19]William Murray Mansfield (1705–1793) was chief justice of the King's Bench of Great Britain and made his mark in his contributions to commercial law.

urday they were required to manufacture certain articles called composition, which were moral and sentimental letters on Beneficence, Gratitude. Modesty, Friendship, &c. Mrs. Weatherwax also gave them lessons in something she denominated French, in which most of the words were pronounced in English, or rather as if the letters that composed them retained the English pronunciation, calling for instance, the three summer months, *Jewin, Juliet,* and *Aught.**

They wrote, or rather scratched their copies with metallic pens, to save the trouble of mending, and they learned geography 'with the use of the globes,' though all that was ever done with the globes was to twirl them. And now and then a young lady of peculiar genius accomplished, in the course of three months, a stool-cover or urn-stand, worked on canvass, and representing in caricature a cat, a dog, or a flower-basket.

Susanna Meredith had much native talent, united with the most indefatigable application, and, considering how little real benefit she derived from the tutorage of her aunt, her progress in every thing she attempted was surprising. Her unpretending good sense, and her mild and obliging manners, tinctured with a touch of melancholy, the consequence of feeling deeply the loss of her parents, (both of whom had died about the same time,) excited the esteem and affection of her young companions, whose indignation was often roused by the manner in which poor Susanna was treated by her aunt. She swept and dusted the school-room, washed the desks, took care of the books, fixed the sewing, inspected the sums, and taught the little ones to read; and she never, in any one instance, succeeded in pleasing Mrs. Weatherwax.

Her services were compensated by being allowed to wear her aunt's left-off clothes, (after she had altered them between school hours so as to fit herself,) and by having permission to sit at table with Mrs. Weatherwax, and drink the grounds of the coffee in the morning, or the drainings of the well-watered tea-pot in the evening; and to eat at dinner the skinny, bony, or gristly parts of the meat, or the necks and backs of the poultry. Not that Mrs. Weatherwax did not provide amply for herself, but, though she said it was indispensably necessary for *her* to sustain her strength by plenty of good food, yet the same necessity did not exist with a young girl like Susanna, whom eating heartily would incapacitate for study. The old lady's studies being over, she saw no motive for abstemiousness on her own part.

It was on a warm afternoon in the early part of July, that Mrs. Weatherwax, having dined even more plentifully than usual, felt herself much inclined to drowsiness, and resorted to her ordinary mode of keeping herself awake by exercising a strict watch on her pupils, and scolding and punishing them accordingly. Like a peevish child, Mrs. Weatherwax was always cross when she was sleepy. The girls, in whispers, expressed more than ever their longings for the summer vacation; after which, it was understood that Mrs. Weatherwax was to retire on her fortune; she having made enough to enable her to give up her school to a lady from New England, who had engaged to retain Susanna Meredith as an assistant, and to pay her a small salary, which her aunt was to receive till she was of age.

About a dozen of her pupils were standing up in a row before Mrs. Weatherwax, reading aloud and loudly from the Night Thoughts, and in that monotonous tone which

---

*Juin, Juillet, and Août.

children always fall into when they have no comprehension of the subject. Each read a paragraph, and there was much miscalling of words, much false emphasis, and much neglect of the proper stops. But of these errors the governess was only at any time capable of distinguishing the first, and as she grew more sleepy, her corrections of pronunciation became less frequent, and at last they ceased altogether. In vain did Maria Wilson call 'the opaque of nature,' the *O. P. Q. of nature,* and in vain were 'futurities' denominated *fruiterers,* and 'hostilities' termed *hostlers.*[20] No word of reproof was now heard.

The girls looked from their books at Mrs. Weatherwax, and then at each other, biting their lips to suppress their laughter, for her eye-lids, though drooping, were not yet quite closed. Gradually, her neck seemed to lose something of its usual stiffness, and to incline towards her shoulder; her head slowly went to one side; and in a few minutes, her tightly shut eyes, her audible breathing, and her book dropping from her hand and falling on the floor without waking her, gave positive assurance that the governess had really and truly fallen fast asleep in her arm-chair.

As this fact became apparent, the faces of her pupils brightened, and two of the most courageous were deputed by the others to approach close to her, and to examine if she absolutely *was* in a profound slumber. Their report was favorable; and in a moment all restraint was thrown aside, and a scene of joyous tumult ensued, in which great risks were run of wakening the sleeper. At first they moved on tiptoe, spoke in whispers, and smothered their laughter; but, grown bolder by practice, they at length ventured on such daring exploits, that the continuation of their governess's nap seemed almost miraculous.

*Some of them immediately fell to rummaging the desk that always sat on Mrs. Weatherwax's table, and from it they joyfully re-possessed themselves of some of their forfeited playthings.

Lucy Philips took a snuff box from the old lady's pocket, and threw snuff into the faces of two other girls, who sneezed so loudly in consequence, that Mrs. Weatherwax was observed to start in her sleep.

Ellen Welbrook hastened to the release of her younger sister Mary, who had been sentenced to stand for an hour on a high stool, with a fool's cap on her head, as a punishment for saying 'Pallas' instead of 'Minerva,' as she recited her lesson of mythology; and who, now that she could do so with impunity, scowled awfully at the slumbering governess, and shook her little fist in defiance.

Fanny Mills, the *beauty* of the school, pinned up a small silk shawl into a turban, and placing in it a peacock's feather, taken from behind the top of the looking glass, she practised attitudes, and surveyed herself in the mirror with much complacency.

Catherine Ramsay diverted herself and her companions by spreading out her frock as wide as it would extend, and making ridiculous mock curtsies to her sleeping governess.

Lydia Linnel, a little girl whose chief delight was in cutting paper, tore out several blank leaves from her copy-book, seized a pair of scissors, and strewed the floor with mimic dolls and houses.

---

[20]Servants who attend horses.

*This scene was suggested by Richter's celebrated picture of 'The Girl's School.'

And Isabel Smithson and Margaret Wells boldly walked out at the front door to go and buy cakes.

There was also much unmeaning scampering, prancing, scrambling, and giggling, without any definite object; and work-boxes, baskets, chairs, and stools, were overturned in the confusion.

And what did Susanna Meredith during this saturnalia?[21] Concerned at the disrespect so unanimously evinced towards her aunt, and still more concerned at knowing that the old lady's unpopularity was too well deserved, Susanna remained steadily at her desk, engaged at her writing piece, and unwilling to raise her eyes, or to see what was going on; but still not surprised that the children should thus testify their joy at this short and unexpected relief from the iron rule of Mrs. Weatherwax.

Two of the elder girls approached her—'Come, Susanna,' said Anne Clarkson, 'lay aside your pen, and join us in our fun while we have an opportunity. I know in your heart you would like to do so.'

'Excuse me,' replied Susanna, 'I am unwilling to do any thing while my aunt is asleep, that I would not attempt if she were awake.'

'Now you are quite too good,' said Martha Stevens, 'do not try to make us believe that you feel any great respect for such an aunt as this.'

'I rather think,' said Catherine Ramsay, coming up at the moment, 'that prudence keeps Susanna out of the scrape, lest Dame Weatherwax should waken suddenly and catch her. But only look at what I have found in the old damsel's desk. You know my mother is going to have a tea party to-morrow evening for those western people that arrived yesterday, and among the rest she has invited Waxy. And so our accomplished preceptress has made in this little book, memorandums of the subjects on which she intends talking. She is preparing for a grand show-off by way of astonishing the natives, as brother Jack would say. Here is the book—I just now found it hidden away in the very back part of the desk. Only read these memorandums, and see how they will make you laugh.'

SUSANNA: Oh! no, indeed—nothing could induce me to meddle with that memorandum book. I beg of you to return it to its place in my aunt's desk. It is highly dishonourable to read any writing that you know is not intended to be seen.

CATHERINE: Well, then, I'll be dishonourable for once, and so, I'll answer for it, will every girl in the school but yourself. But see, the little ones have taken flight into the garden. Suppose we all adjourn thither. We can have better fun there, and without so much risk of waking old Waxy.

SUSANNA: Let me entreat you to put back that memorandum book.

CATHERINE: Not I, indeed—it shall be read in a committee of the whole. You had better come and hear it. I am sure it will divert you.

SUSANNA: I really cannot join in such unwarrantable proceedings. I would much rather stay here. Do, pray, give me the book, and let me put it back.

---

[21]Saturnalia was the Roman festival of Saturn, known for its unrestrained merrymaking that extended even to slaves.

CATHERINE: No, no,—not, at least, till we have taken the cream of it. Come, then, girls, let us all be off into the garden.

In an instant they were out of the school-room, but Catherine Ramsay, turning back, and putting her head in at the door, said, 'Now, Susanna, do not carry your honour so far as to wake your aunt, and betray us all as soon as our backs are turned. She is sleeping away now as if she was not to awaken for a hundred years, like the princess in the fairy tale; though no one, I am sure, will ever call her the Sleeping Beauty. There is one good thing in fat people—they always sleep soundly.'

SUSANNA: Catherine, what have you seen in me to authorise the suspicion that I could act so meanly as to betray you to my aunt?

CATHERINE: Oh! nothing—but I thought that with *you,* duty would be always above honour. Now mind that you do not deceive us. Of all things in the world, I despise an informer.

So saying, she turned from the door, and ran out to the group that were romping through the garden in the very hey-day of frolic, galloping mischievously over the flower-beds, committing the most reckless depredations on the currant bushes, climbing the old cherry tree, and riding each other on the gate; while Dido, Mrs. Weatherwax's only servant, a black girl about sixteen, stood in the kitchen door, and held by its sides to avoid falling down with laughter.

Catherine waved above her head the memorandum book, and assembling the elder girls round her, they threw themselves on the grass plat, while with a loud voice she read as follows.

MEMORANDUMS FOR MRS. RAMSAY'S PARTY.

To stir my tea a long time, that I may say, 'I like all the composite parts of the beverage to be both saturated and coagulated.'

To fan myself, that I may say, 'how sweetly the zephyrs of Boreas[22] temper the heat of Phoebus.'[23]

To talk of the late eclipse, and to explain that it was caused by the sun going behind the equator.

To speak highly of the writings of Miss Hannah More,[24] and to say that she is known throughout the civil world, and has spread over Maine and Georgia.

To speak French at times; for instance, if there is any cheese among the relishes at tea, to say that I am particularly fond of frommage.* Also, if there are raspberries, to express my liking for framboys.† If the servant should stumble in carrying round the waiter, to say that he has made a fox pass.‡

---

[22]Strong, sweeping winds of Boreas, the Greek god of the north wind.

[23]Another name for Apollo, Greek and Roman god of sunlight.

[24]Hannah More (1745–1833) was an English writer particularly well known for her religious, moral tracts.

*Fromage, cheese.

†Framboises, raspberries.

‡Faux pas, false step.

Catherine had proceeded thus far, when Susanna appeared at the door, and made a sign that her aunt showed symptoms of waking. Hastily, and as quietly as possible, all the girls returned to the school-room, which Susanna, during their absence, had restored to its usual order. They took their seats on the benches, and found much difficulty in checking their mirth. The breathing of Mrs. Weatherwax was now less loud; she twisted her head, threw out her arms, and was evidently about to awaken.

Catherine hastily slipped the memorandum book into Susanna's hand, whispering, 'Oh! pray, pray, put it back into the desk immediately.' And the little heroine of the fool's cap hurried that ornament again on her head, and jumped on the stool of disgrace; but in so doing she stumbled, the stool tipped over, and fell with so much noise as effectually to waken Mrs. Weatherwax, who started upright in her chair, rubbed her eyes, and exclaimed, 'What is all this? I really think I was almost beginning to lose myself—I do believe I must have been nodding, or something very near it.'

The girls held down their heads, put their books before their mouths, and made great efforts to smother their laughter, and Catherine Ramsay rose up, and said very saucily, 'I hope, madam, you feel the better for your nap.'

'Nap!' exclaimed the governess, 'who will dare to say that I have been taking a nap?' And, according to the custom of persons who have been overtaken with sleep in company, she declared she had heard every thing that had passed.

'So much the worse for us, then,' said Catherine, in a half whisper to the girl that sat next to her.

'Come, go on,' said the governess, rubbing her eyes, 'go on with your reading. You have been a long time getting through that last page.'

The girls tried to compose themselves to read; and, in a few minutes, to their great relief, the clock struck five, and Mrs. Weatherwax, who was hardly more than half awake, gladly dismissed the school. They could scarcely wait till they had got out of doors, before they simultaneously burst into a loud laugh at the idea of the old lady's perfect unconsciousness of all that had gone on during her sleep.

The memorandum book was very small, and on receiving it from Catherine, Susanna slipt it into one of her pockets; she saw that while school continued, she would have no opportunity of replacing it in the desk; but she determined to do so after her aunt had sat down to tea. That repast Susanna prepared as usual in the little back parlour, and when it was ready she announced it to Mrs. Weatherwax; but what was her confusion on seeing her aunt, as soon as she rose from her chair, turn the key which was sticking in the desk, and deposit it in her pocket! In what manner now was Susanna to restore the memorandum book to the desk, before her aunt should discover that it had been removed?

After tea, Mrs. Weatherwax told Susanna to make haste in washing up the cups, and then bring her sewing into the school-room. She did so, and found her aunt most ominously employed in searching for hard words in Entick's Dictionary, evidently with a view of obtaining further materials for her memorandum book. Susanna, who had often seen Mrs. Weatherwax thus occupied, when she had a visit in prospect, raised her eyes frequently from the pillow-case she was hemming, and stole uneasy glances at her aunt.

At last she saw her unlock the desk—'My stars!' exclaimed Mrs. Weatherwax, 'who has dared to meddle in my desk? Somebody, I see, has been here.' She searched into its farthest recesses, and then called out, 'I can't find my private memorandum book—has any one dared to take it away?'—fixing her large eyes full on poor Susanna, who, unused to any thing that resembled deception, buried her face in her work.

Mrs. Weatherwax, however, seized her niece by the arm, and dragging her forward, pulled away her hands, exclaiming, 'Now look me full in the face, and say you did not take that memorandum book out of my desk. Speak out—speak loud.'

'I did not,' replied Susanna, trying to look at her aunt's inflamed visage, 'I did not, indeed.'

'I do not believe you,' vociferated Mrs. Weatherwax, shaking her, 'so I shall make bold to search.'

She thrust her hand into Susanna's pocket, and drew out the memorandum book, which she held up triumphantly.

'Indeed, indeed, I did not take it from the desk,' sobbed poor Susanna.

'Then you know who did,' cried Mrs. Weatherwax, 'so tell me this instant.'

Susanna was silent.

'I know you took it yourself,' continued Mrs. Weatherwax, 'it's exactly like you.'

'Oh! aunt,' cried Susanna, 'it is not like me to do such a thing.'

'Not another word,' pursued the enraged governess,—'I shall believe that you did it, till you can prove your innocence by telling me the real culprit. But I am certain it was yourself, and I shall punish you accordingly. I suppose you took care to read every word of it?'

Susanna, much hurt at so unjust a suspicion, would have persisted in asseverating her innocence, but she feared being compelled to a disclosure of the real offender, and she kept silent, replying only by her tears.

Mrs. Weatherwax, highly incensed, bestowed on her a torrent of opprobrious and strangely sounding epithets, (none of which were to be found in Entick's Dictionary,) and ordered her immediately to bed, though it was still day-light. Poor Susanna could not sleep, and passed a very uncomfortable night.

In the morning her aunt came to inform her that she should be locked up for a week in her chamber—'Not, however, in idleness,' she continued, 'for I have plenty of sewing for you. You shall begin immediately to make up my new linen. But you shan't show your face in the school-room, for I will allow you no chance of whispering to all the girls the contents of that memorandum book.'

'I really did not read one line of it,' said Susanna.

'You did not read it,' said Mrs. Weatherwax, 'that's a likely story indeed. Then what did you steal it for? Yes—you shall be shut up in this room, and you shall sew at my linen from morning till night, and you shall live on short allowance too, I promise you.'

Poor Susanna cried, but submitted.

When the girls assembled at school, they were surprised to see nothing of Susanna, but Mrs. Weatherwax told them she was sick. When school was over for the morning, Catherine Ramsay and several of the other girls asked permission to go to Susanna's room to see her. This request was promptly refused by Mrs. Weatherwax, on the plea that company always made sick people worse.

'Poor Susanna!' murmured Catherine, 'all I wonder at is that she should ever be well.'

In the evening Mrs. Weatherwax put herself into full dress, and went to Mrs. Ramsay's tea party, where Catherine and her cousin Lucy Philips could scarcely keep their countenances when they heard the old lady take occasion to bring out, one after another, all the set speeches that she had noted in her memorandum book. When the tea waiter was brought in, (on which Catherine had taken care that there should be a plate of sliced cheese,)—'Now,' whispered the mischievous girl, 'she is going to say frommage.' And when the raspberries were handed round—'Now she is going to talk of framboys'—and so she did. But as no servant happened to stumble, there was unluckily no opportunity for the fox-pass.

Susanna had been invited to this party, but Mrs. Weatherwax alleged her illness as an excuse for not bringing her.

Mrs. Ramsay's house was only on the opposite side of the road, and about nine o'clock, Catherine put some of the best cakes into a little basket, with two oranges, and slipped over to Mrs. Weatherwax's.

The door was opened by Dido, the black girl, with the kitchen lamp in her hand. When Catherine told her that she wished to see Susanna, as Mrs. Weatherwax had said she was very sick, the girl grinned widely and said, 'La! bless you, Miss Caterine, han't you got no more sense than to b'lieve old Missus? Miss Susannar an't no more sick than I am—she's only shot up for a punishing. I wanted to walk her about as soon as the old woman's back was turned, (for all she gave me the key, and charged and overcharged me to keep her fast); but Miss Susannar would not agree to be let out. She's too paticlar about doing what's 'xactly right, and old Missus won't even let nobody in to see her. She's 'hibited her from all 'munication with the known world.'

'But I must and will see her,' said Catherine, giving the black girl a cake and an orange.

'To be sure you shall, bless your heart,' replied Dido, 'so folly on after me, and I'll 'duct you up stairs to her sorrowful dungeon prison.'

As they proceeded up the staircase, Dido, who went before with the light, turned her head and said, 'I say, Miss Caterine, don't you hate old Missus?'

'To be sure I do,' replied Catherine.

'That's me 'xactly,' exclaimed the girl—'Me and you are birds of a feather. I hate her like pison. When people's mean, and pinching, and cross, and hard-hearted beside, they can't expect folks to love them.'

'Mean people are always cross,' remarked Catherine.

'If I didn't visit about among the neighbours,' continued the girl, 'I couldn't make out at all—old Missus keeps us so short of victuals.'

They now arrived at the door of Susanna's room, which Dido threw open, saying, 'There sets the poor creature. Here, Miss Susannar, raise up your head from the window bench, and look at Miss Caterine axing to see you.'

She then withdrew into a corner to suck her orange, while Catherine threw her arms round Susanna's neck, and eagerly inquired what was the matter, and on what pretext Mrs. Weatherwax had shut her up.

Susanna wept, but said nothing.

'I'll tell you what, Miss Caterine,' cried Dido, 'it's all about something that old Missus calls her random book, that she says Miss Susannar stole out of her desk. I just put my ear to the keyhole a minute (as I always do,) and I heard her last night proper loud and high. She couldn't have scolded worse if she'd stole a pocket-book full of bank notes. Now I don't b'lieve Miss Susannar ever steals any thing.'

'Oh! Susanna,' exclaimed Catherine, 'I fear you are indeed suffering for that vile memorandum book which I took out of the desk myself, and thoughtlessly put into your hands to replace. And have you really allowed yourself to be unjustly blamed and punished, rather than betray so worthless a person as I am?'

An explanation now ensued, and Catherine declared she would go home that moment, and proclaim the truth to Mrs. Weatherwax. Susanna, unwilling that any thing should be said or done which might lead to an exposure of her aunt, besought Catherine to wait at least till next morning, when she could see Mrs. Weatherwax before the school assembled. They were still arguing the point, when a heavy step was heard ascending the stairs, and Mrs. Weatherwax, in all her terrors, stood before them.

The tea party was over, and, attracted by the light in Susanna's room, the old lady hastened thither immediately, to ascertain the cause. Catherine instantly ran up to her, and made a frank declaration of her own delinquency and Susanna's innocence, but which Mrs. Weatherwax pertinaciously insisted on disbelieving. The fact was, the old lady had that strange delight which is felt by some people, in trampling on the oppressed, and in oppressing every one that is unfortunately in their power. Being very much incensed, and determined to punish somebody, she preferred venting her anger on poor Susanna in a way that she was accustomed to, rather than to devise a mode of correction for such a spirit as that of Catherine Ramsay. Also, she prudently remembered that Catherine was the child of wealthy parents.

'Why, Mrs. Weatherwax,' said Catherine, 'do you persist in pretending to believe that the memorandum book was taken out of your desk by Susanna, and not by me?'

'Yes, I do,' answered the governess, 'notwithstanding this fit of generosity, (as I suppose you call it,) in laying the blame on yourself. I know she took it. All her ways are low and grovelling.'

'They are no such thing,' interrupted Catherine.

'A young lady like you,' pursued Mrs. Weatherwax, 'the only daughter of Mr. and Mrs. Ramsay, with her father in the Assembly, could not be guilty of any thing so dishonourable.'

'I stand corrected,' said Catherine, colouring, 'I own it was dishonourable. Nevertheless I actually did it. I felt so full of mischief at the moment, that I was capable of any thing, and I had no thought of the consequences. Do you say that Susanna is still to be kept a prisoner in her room?'

Mrs. Weatherwax thought to herself, 'I will keep her there till she has finished making my linen, which will be more advantageous to me just now than what she does in the school; and I will make Dido sweep and dust, and put the school-room in order.' Then raising her voice, the old lady exclaimed loudly, 'I say that Susanna Meredith *shall* go through the whole of the punishment.'

'Well, madam,' said Catherine, 'I repeat once more that I alone am guilty. If I do not see Susanna in her place again to-morrow morning, I shall explain the whole to my father and mother, and then I am well persuaded they will at once take me away from your school.'

So saying, Catherine immediately walked out of the room with an air of resolute defiance, and returned to her own home.

Mrs. Weatherwax, much enraged, scolded a while longer, blamed poor Susanna for having put 'all this impudence,' as she called it, into Catherine's head, and again locking up her unfortunate niece, she retired for the night.

Next morning about breakfast time, a letter was brought to Mrs. Weatherwax, which she read with much surprise and emotion, and then carefully secured it in her desk. She sat a while and pondered, and afterwards repaired to Susanna's apartment, with a face drest in smiles, and a voice subdued to unusual softness.

'Good morning, my love,' said she, kissing her cheek, 'you may now come down stairs. Lay aside your sewing—breakfast is ready.'

Susanna, much surprised at these unprecedented indications of kindness, gladly obeyed, and Mrs. Weatherwax actually herself placed a chair for her at table. On this happy morning, her aunt gave her a cup of good coffee, before the pot was filled up with water, and put into it plenty of cream and sugar. She also helped her to some ham and eggs, (though she had often told her that relishes were unfit for children,) and she repeatedly handed her the plate of warm cakes, exhorting her to eat heartily.

Susanna was thoroughly amazed, and began to fear that all this was only a dream.

When the children assembled, Mrs. Weatherwax had not yet appeared in the schoolroom, and Catherine Ramsay, flying up to Susanna, congratulated her on her evident release, saying, 'I am glad I threatened Mrs. Weatherwax with quitting her school, and I know if I *had* explained all, my father and mother would have taken me away at once. They would have done so long before this time, only that the old woman is so soon to give up.'

'Oh! Catherine,' exclaimed Susanna, 'do not speak so disrespectfully of my aunt. You know not how kind she has been to me this morning.'

Mrs. Weatherwax now came in, and said to her niece in the mildest manner possible, 'Susanna, you need not trouble yourself to-day to hear the little girls their lessons. You may go to the store and choose yourself a couple of frocks, and then take them to Becky Walker the mantuamaker,[25] and get yourself fitted for them. Tell her you must have them made at once.'

The children all opened their eyes wide with amazement, and poor Susanna stood motionless, affected almost to tears at her aunt's unaccountable kindness. 'If you please, aunt,' said she, in a faltering voice, 'I would rather you should choose the frocks for me. I am so unaccustomed to getting things for myself.'

'Well, then, my dear,' answered Mrs. Weatherwax, 'I will go with you after school; but I thought it would gratify you to leave the choice to yourself. There are, beside the frocks, some other things that I think you would like to have.'

In the course of the morning, the grateful Susanna had an opportunity of saying to Catherine, 'Well, what do you think now? Is not my aunt kind?'

'Think!' answered Catherine, 'why, I am thinking of a farce that I saw at the theatre when I was last in the city. A farce in which a termagant lady and a good-humoured cobbler's wife are transformed by a conjuror into each other's likenesses, and placed in each other's houses. We are all as much astonished as were the servants of lady Loverule, when they found themselves treated with kindness by Nell Jobson, whom they supposed

---

[25]A person who sews loose-fitting gowns.

to be their mistress. I am inclined to believe that some such conjuror has been at work last night. This cannot be the real old Waxy.'

'Oh! do not talk so,' said Susanna.

'Well,' replied Catherine, 'I only hope the illusion may last as long as you wish it.'

But Mrs. Weatherwax (as one of the little girls remarked in a whisper) 'could not get good all at once;' and as, from some unknown motive, she now thought it expedient to be all mildness towards Susanna, so she vented a proportionate quantity of ill-humour on the other girls—always excepting Catherine Ramsay, and three or four more who had rich parents.

At dinner Mrs. Weatherwax helped Susanna to an excellent slice of roast lamb, and gave her a large piece of currant pie, not telling her as usual that pastry was unwholesome for children, and that she had better finish with a crust of bread. To be brief, her kindness continued so to increase, that Susanna could scarcely, indeed, believe in her identity. And the mystery of this inexplicable goodness in all that regarded her neice, and which abated not during two weeks, caused much speculation among the school girls.

Not only two new frocks were procured for Susanna, but also a new bonnet, and many other articles of dress, so that she now made a very good appearance. She was no longer kept all day in the school-room, but she was allowed the afternoon to herself, and desired to sew, or read, or walk, or do whatever she pleased. But so much timidity had been ground into her by seven years of oppression and hard usage, that poor Susanna was afraid to avail herself freely of the indulgences that were now offered to her option.

Things had gone on in this manner for about a fortnight, when Mrs. Weatherwax, after receiving a second letter, announced to her pupils that she would give them a holiday the next day. This holiday, she told them, was on account of the expected arrival of Mr. Manderson from South Carolina, the grandfather of Susanna Meredith. This gentleman was going to remove to Boston, his native place, and, on his way thither, intended stopping at the village to see Susanna. Mrs. Weatherwax also announced that Mr. Manderson was a man of great wealth, and that death having deprived him of all his four children, he had determined to take Susanna home with him, and make her his heiress. The girls were all delighted with this news, of which Susanna herself had only been apprised that morning, and which, of course, made her very happy. Catherine Ramsay was now furnished with a key to all Mrs. Weatherwax's extraordinary kindness towards Susanna for the last two weeks.

The truth was that Mr. Manderson's first letter informed Mrs. Weatherwax, that he had deeply repented having discarded his eldest daughter in consequence of her marriage with Mr. Meredith during a visit to the north, and to whom he had objected as being a man of no property, and of obscure family. But that having recently lost the last of his children, he had determined on claiming his long-neglected granddaughter, the orphan of his favourite Louisa.

Mrs. Weatherwax was the step-sister of Susanna's father, and had been set up in her school by money with which he had furnished her in his most prosperous days. She had taken charge of Susanna on the death of the child's parents, pretending to do so out of pure benevolence, but in reality with a view of availing herself of her niece's services.

Mr. Manderson's second letter notified the precise day on which he expected to reach the village; and Mrs. Weatherwax had an apartment prepared for him, determined to insist on his staying at her house.

The holiday was given. A dinner extraordinary was in the progress of preparation, and the hour of his expected arrival approached. Susanna was drest in the handsomest of her new frocks, and seated beside her aunt, engaged, by her order, in working a bobbinet collar. Mrs. Weatherwax, also in her best, was arranged, in her arm-chair, with a French book in her hand: and Dido, every few minutes, deserted her cookery to look out at the gate.

At length a carriage stopped before the house, and, at the moment that the over-delighted Dido ushered Mr. Manderson into the parlour, the arm of Mrs. Weatherwax was fondly encircling the waist of Susanna.

'Is that my grand-daughter?' exclaimed Mr. Manderson, as Susanna rose timidly to meet his embrace.

'Yes, sir,' said Mrs. Weatherwax, who on this occasion thought it expedient to display some French—'Here she is, looking like a button de rose,* as she always does, and with nothing to trouble her gaiety de cure† but the thought of leaving her poor fond aunt, whose greatest bonehewer‡ is loving and petting her. Is it not so, Susanna?'

To conclude, Mr. Manderson was much affected by Susanna's resemblance to her deceased mother, and he felt that the only atonement he could make for his undue severity to the unfortunate Mrs. Meredith, was to take her child to his heart, and cherish her with the warmest tenderness.

He stayed till next morning; and in the mean time, Mrs. Weatherwax so entirely over-acted her part, as to convince Mr. Manderson that her excessive fondness for Susanna was any thing but real. The old lady also gave frequent hints of a wish to be invited to pay him and Susanna a visit when he should be settled at his own house, taking care to inform him, that on the first of August she was going to resign her school, and should after that be quite at leisure. But none of these hints made any impression on Mr. Manderson. As he could not for a moment think of allowing his grand-daughter to be under the slightest obligation to such a woman, he required of Mrs. Weatherwax an estimate of Susanna's expenses, during the whole time she had been in her charge. Mrs. Weatherwax, fearing that nothing else was to be obtained from the old gentleman, made out a bill of enormous length, amounting to five times as much as her actual expenditure on Susanna. Mr. Manderson looked only at the total, and without any comment, gave her a check for that sum; but he did not present Mrs. Weatherwax with a handsome watch that he had brought with him as a gift for her.

Dido, the black girl, took an opportunity of begging Susanna 'to speak a good word for her' to her grandfather, that she might be allowed to go and live with them. 'For you know, Miss Susannar,' said she, 'old Missus is going to board out when she breaks up, and she would be glad enough to get rid of me, as she don't want me no more; and she has been trying to get some of the neighbours to take me off her hands, only none of them won't have me.'

---

*Bouton de rose, rose-bud.
†Gaieté de cœur, literally, gaiety of heart.
‡Bonheur, happiness.

This business was soon arranged. Dido's indentures were duly transferred to Mr. Manderson, and from that moment she called herself Miss Susanna's waiting-woman.

Susanna took an affectionate leave of her young companions, particularly of Catherine Ramsay, who parted from her with many tears, and was invited by Mr. Manderson to spend the ensuing winter with his grand-daughter.

Susanna was soon established in an elegant mansion with her grandfather, who engaged an amiable and accomplished woman as governess, to complete her education, assisted by the best masters. And Catherine Ramsay improved greatly during the long visit which she paid next winter to her excellent young friend.

❧ Vale of Wyoming

Some years ago, about the middle of the month of June, business, aided by inclination, induced me to visit the beautiful vale of Wyoming.[26] This classic spot, rendered so by Campbell's exquisite poetical tale of Gertrude, I had frequently seen before; but every time that the magnificent yet tranquil scene is exhibited, fresh subjects of admiration are elicited. On approaching it from the south, as you reach the summit of the mountain which bounds it in that direction, the whole panoramic exhibition bursts at once on the sight. How paltry and puerile appear the finest scenic representations when compared with such touches of nature's pencilling!

It was the most attractive period of the season, and the season one of the most delightful. The superb foliage of the trees on the surrounding hills assumed its freshest tints, the grain-covered plains waved in graceful motion under the influence of a balmy wind; which, with the crystal Susquehanna meandering smoothly over its pebbly bed, formed a *tout ensemble*[27] of enchanting loveliness. Scarcely a sound was audible, save the soothing echo of a distant waterfall, or the gentle murmuring of the placid stream.

While slowly passing to the upper part of the valley, my mind readily cast a retrospect over the vista of time that had elapsed since the dreadful affair, well known as the *massacre of Wyoming*. Musing on the great change that had taken place—where a handsome town had supplanted the wigwams, and highly cultivated fields the tangle and the brake—of the lowing of cattle and the bleating of flocks in the former haunts of the panther and the bear—how the original occupants of the soil are extinguished, or driven far from the graves of their sires, and the firm establishment of their pale successors—painful emotions were felt amidst the conviction of improvement. No wonder that the aborigines made a desperate struggle to retain this delectable spot—combining at once all the advantages of planting, hunting, and fishing within view of their humble homes.

My feelings were becoming wound up to an unpleasant sense of excitement, when I was interrupted by the appearance of an Indian—a survivor of the once numerous race

---

[26]A valley in Northeastern Pennsylvania along the Susquehanna.

[27]The general effect.

who inhabited the banks of the Susquehanna. At first his scowl was fierce—but probably, from meeting in my countenance no corresponding expression, his features relaxed,
and we entered into conversation. The aged warrior was about to revisit the graves of his
fathers—take a final farewell, and return to the scattered tribe to which he belonged. The
impulse was natural, yet I remonstrated—knowing the hostility that still rankled in the
bosoms of many of the inhabitants of the valley. But it was in vain. We separated—
the same day I departed for home—but I never heard of his having left the valley of
Wyoming.

Y.

❧ Enigmas

1

Something—nothing—as you use me;
Small, or bulky, as you choose me;
Eternity I bring to view,
The sun and all the planets too;
The morn and I may disagree,
But all the world resembles me.

2

'Tis known that I destroy'd the world,
And all things in confusion hurl'd;
And yet I do preserve all in it,
Through each revolving hour and minute:
I tremble with each breath of air,
And yet can heaviest burdens bear;
I many kill, I many cure;
Some prize me much, some can't endure;
Around the earth's huge ball I roam;
To myriads I prove a home;
And if you're pos'd, and cannot guess me yet,
Look, and your puzzled face I'll counterfeit.

3

What is the longest and shortest thing in the world, the swiftest and the slowest, the
most divisible and the most extended, the least valued and the most regretted; without
which nothing can be done; which devours all that is small, yet gives life to all that is
great?

🐦 Charades

1

My first is to engage the mind;
The warrior to my next retires;
If you're to be my whole inclin'd,
   'Twill serve to mod'rate your desires.

2

My first's a being or the human race;
   My second is a hill in scripture nam'd;
My total shows the splendid dwelling place
   Of those for opulence and titles fam'd.

3

My first in lonely grots[28] and cells,
In velvet softness often dwells;
And round my second loves to cling,
Like any fond endearing thing.
My whole is own'd the royal flower,
The pride of every garden bower;
Its fragrance fills the gales around,
With richer sweets than else are found;
All other flowers their homage show—
'Tis rivall'd but by beauty's glow.

4

My first is capable of sense and sound;
My second, though not globular, is round;
'Tis endless, though it be not everlasting:
My whole's an ornament my first's made fast in.

5

My first or sumptuous is or simply plain;
   My second oft is in the village yard;
Till next year, ladies, should we meet again,
   Accept my whole in token of regard.

---

[28]A grot is a grotto, or cave.

4

Maria Monk

(1816–1849?)

AMERICAN PROTESTANTISM HAS long had a virulent anti-Catholic strain, which manifested itself with particular ferocity in the years leading up to the Civil War. Believing that Catholics disdained the Holy Bible, gave divine status to the Virgin Mary, and traded precious democracy for a monarchy led by the pope, nineteenth-century Protestants put immense amounts of time and energy into attempting to convert Catholics to Protestantism.

As German and Irish Catholics immigrated to the United States in ever increasing numbers in the 1820s and 1830s, Protestants unleashed a massive array of anti-Catholic propaganda with the hopes of mobilizing ever greater resources against the insidious Catholic menace. No piece of antebellum anti-Catholic literature enjoyed greater popularity than *Awful Disclosures, by Maria Monk, of the Hotel Dieu Nunnery of Montreal,* a convent-captivity narrative supposedly written by Maria Monk. A treatise that purportedly chronicled the lascivious and murderous nature of Catholic convent life, Maria Monk told a tale of her life as a former nun and how she eventually escaped convent life, giving birth to a son in 1835.

In the first twenty-five years of publication, *Awful Disclosures* would sell more than three hundred thousand copies, an absolutely staggering figure in the period. It would also prove to be the catalyst behind the appearance of a host of other Catholic and anti-Catholic material. Almost upon its release in book form, questions were raised about the authenticity of Maria Monk's background as a nun and the contents of the book. Sides were taken energetically, and a massive amount of material appeared proving and disproving Monk's claims. The truth of the issue initially remained obscure, but later it became increasingly clear that Maria Monk was mentally unstable and that her tale was a fantastic fabrication. Such revelations, however, did not stop thousands of Americans from continuing to view *Awful Disclosures* as a completely trustworthy exposé of Catholicism.

The book itself is a fascinating window into early nineteenth-century religious tensions, as well as a commentary on the role of motherhood in the young republic. In *Awful Disclosures,* the malevolent influence of Catholicism threatens the very ideals and form of American motherhood, as mothers (whether they be mother superiors, mothers who give up their daughters to the convent, or pregnant nuns) all come to misdirect their energies to destroy that which they have been entrusted to nurture.

AWFUL DISCLOSURES, BY MARIA MONK, OF THE HOTEL DIEU NUNNERY OF MONTREAL

❧ Preface

This volume embraces the contents of the first editions of my "Awful Disclosures," together with the Sequel of my Narrative, giving an account of events after my escape from the Nunnery, and of my return to Montreal to procure a legal investigation of my charges. It also furnishes all the testimony that has been published against me, of every description, as well as that which has been given in confirmation of my story. At the close, will be found a Review of the whole Subject, furnished by a gentleman well qualified for the purpose; and, finally, a short Supplement, giving further particulars interesting to the public.

I present this volume to the reader, with feelings which, I trust, will be in some degree appreciated when it has been read and reflected upon. A hasty perusal, and an imperfect apprehension of its contents, can never produce such impressions as it has been my design to make by the statements I have laid before the world. I know that misapprehensions exist in the minds of some virtuous people. I am not disposed to condemn their motives, for it does not seem wonderful, that in a pure state of society, and in the midst of Christian families, there should be persons who regard the crimes I have mentioned as too monstrous to be believed. It certainly is creditable to American manners and character, that the people are inclined, at the first sight, to turn from my story with horror.

There is also an excuse for those, who, having received only a general impression concerning the nature of my Disclosures, question the propriety of publishing such immorality to the world. They fear that the minds of the young at least may be polluted. To such I have to say, that this objection was examined, and set aside, long before they had an opportunity to make it. I solemnly believe it is necessary to inform parents at least, that the ruin from which I have barely escaped, lies in the way of their children, even if delicacy must be in some degree wounded by revealing the fact. I understand the case, alas! from too bitter experience. Many an innocent girl may this year be exposed to the dangers of which I was ignorant. I am resolved, that so far as depends on me, not one more victim shall fall into the hands of those enemies in whose power I so lately have been. I know what it is to be under the domination of Nuns and Priests; and I maintain, that it is a far greater offence against virtue and decency to conceal, than to proclaim their crimes. Ah! had a single warning voice even whispered to me a word of caution, had even a gentle note of alarm been sounded to me, it might have turned back my foot from the Convent when it was upon the threshold! If, therefore, there is any one now bending a step that way, whom I have not yet alarmed, I will cry *beware!*

But the virtuous reader need not fear, in the following pages, to meet with vice presented in any dress but her own deformity. No one can accuse me of giving a single

These selections follow an edition that appeared in the first year of the work's release: *Awful Disclosures, by Maria Monk, of the Hotel Dieu Nunnery of Montreal.* New York: Published by Maria Monk, 1836.

Eng.ᵈ by W.L.Ormsby

Bring me before a court
Maria Monk

Maria Monk, dressed as a nun and holding her baby, demands of her readers that they test the truth of her tale by bringing the issue before a court (*Awful Disclosures, by Maria Monk, of the Hotel Dieu Nunnery of Montreal,* 1836).

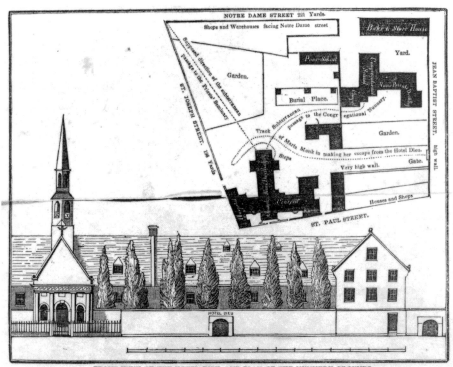

FRONT VIEW OF THE HOTEL DIEU, AND PLAN OF THE NUNNERY GROUNDS.

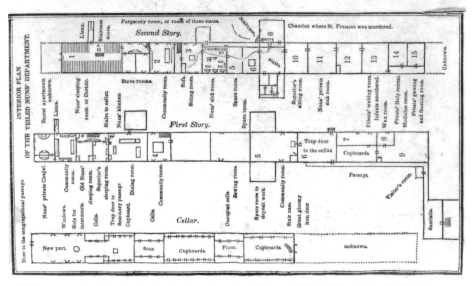

Foldout maps included at the beginning of early editions of Maria Monk's *Awful Disclosures.*
One map shows the nunnery's interior rooms, while the other map offers an exterior
picture of the nunnery along with the route Maria Monk took in her escape
(*Awful Disclosures, by Maria Monk, of the Hotel Dieu Nunnery of Montreal,* 1836).
(Courtesy, Special Collections, Princeton University Library)

attraction to crime. On the contrary, I intend my book shall be a warning to those who may hereafter be tempted by vice; and with the confidence that such it will prove to be, I commend it to the careful examination of virtuous parents, and am willing to abide by their unbiased opinion, with regard both to my truth, my motives, and the interest which the public have in the developments it contains.

I would now appeal to the world, and ask, whether I have not done all that could have been expected of me, and all that lay in my power, to bring to an investigation the charges I have brought against the priests and nuns of Canada. Although it was necessary to the cause of truth, that I should, in some degree, implicate myself, I have not hesitated to appear as a voluntary self-accuser before the world. While there was a hope that the authorities in Canada might be prevailed upon to bring the subject to a legal investigation, I travelled to Montreal, in a feeble state of health, and with an infant in my arms only three weeks old. In the face of many threats and dangers, I spent nearly a month in that city, in vain attempts to bring my cause to a trial. When all prospect of success in this undertaking had disappeared, and not till then, I determined to make my accusations through the press; and, although misrepresentations and scandals, flattery and fear, have been resorted to, to nullify or to suppress my testimony, I have persevered, although, as many of my friends have thought, at the risk of abduction or death.

I have, I think, afforded every opportunity that could be reasonably expected, to judge of my credibility. I have appealed to the existence of things in the Hotel Dieu Nunnery, as the great criterion of the truth of my story. I have described the apartments, and now, in this volume, have added many further particulars, with such a draft of them as my memory has enabled me to make. I have offered, in case I should be proved an impostor, to submit to any punishment which may be proposed—even to a redelivery into the hands of my bitterest enemies, to suffer what they may please to inflict.

Now, in these circumstances, I would ask the people of the United States, whether my duty has not been discharged? Have I not done what I ought, to inform and to alarm them? I would also solemnly appeal to the Government of Great Britain, under whose guardianship is the province oppressed by the gloomy institution from which I have escaped, and ask, whether such atrocities ought to be tolerated, and even protected, by an enlightened and Christian power? I trust the hour is near, when the dens of the Hotel Dieu will be laid open, when the tyrants who have polluted it will be brought out, with the wretched victims of their oppression and crimes.

CHAPTER I

❧ Early Recollections

Early Life—Religious Education neglected—First Schools—Entrance into the School of the Congregational Nunnery—Brief Account of the Nunneries in Montreal— The Congregational Nunnery—The Black Nunnery—The Grey Nunnery—Public Respect for these Institutions—Instruction Received—The Catechism—The Bible.

My parents were both from Scotland, but had been resident in Lower Canada some time before their marriage, which took place in Montreal; and in that city I have spent most of my life. I was born at St. John's, where they lived for a short time. My father was an officer under the British government, and my mother has enjoyed a pension on that account ever since his death.

According to my earliest recollections, he was attentive to his family; and a particular passage from the Bible, which often occurred to my mind in after life, I may very probably have been taught by him, as after his death I do not recollect to have received any religious instruction at home; and was not even brought up to read the scriptures: my mother, although nominally a Protestant, not being accustomed to pay attention to her children in this respect. She was rather inclined to think well of the Catholics, and often attended their churches. To my want of religious instruction at home, and the ignorance of my Creator, and my duty, which was its natural effect, I think I can trace my introduction to Convents, and the scenes which I am to describe in this narrative.

When about six or seven years of age, I went to school to a Mr. Workman, a Protestant, who taught in Sacrament-street, and remained several months. There I learned to read and write, and arithmetic as far as division. All the progress I ever made in those branches was gained in that school, as I have never improved in any of them since.

A number of girls of my acquaintance went to school to the nuns of the Congregational Nunnery, or Sisters of Charity, as they are sometimes called. The schools taught by them are perhaps more numerous than some of my readers may imagine. Nuns are sent out from that Convent to many of the towns and villages of Canada to teach small schools; and some of them are established as instructresses in different parts of the United States. When I was about ten years old, my mother asked me one day if I should not like to learn to read and write French; and I then began to think seriously of attending the school in the Congregational Nunnery. I had already some acquaintance with that language, sufficient to speak it a little, as I heard it every day, and my mother knew something of it.

I have a distinct recollection of my first entrance into the Nunnery; and the day was an important one in my life, as on it commenced my acquaintance with a Convent. I was conducted by some of my young friends along Nôtre Dame–street, till we reached the gate. Entering that, we walked some distance along the side of a building towards the chapel, until we reached a door, stopped, and rung a bell. This was soon opened, and entering, we proceeded through a long covered passage till we took a short turn to the left, soon after which we reached the door of the school-room. On my entrance, the Superior met me, and told me first of all, that I must always dip my fingers into the holy water at her door, cross myself, and say a short prayer; and this she told me was always required of Protestant as well as Catholic children.

There were about fifty girls in the school, and the nuns professed to teach something of reading, writing, arithmetic, and geography. The methods however were very imperfect, and little attention was devoted to them, the time being in a great degree engrossed with lessons in needle-work, which was performed with much skill. The nuns had no very regular parts assigned them in the management of the schools. They were rather rough and unpolished in their manners, often exclaiming, "c'est un menti," (that's a lie,) and "mon Dieu," (my God,) on the most trivial occasions. Their writing was quite poor, and it was not uncommon for them to put a capital letter in the middle of a word. The only book on geography which we studied, was a catechism of geography, from which we learnt by heart a few questions and answers. We were sometimes referred to a map, but it was only to point out Montreal or Quebec, or some other prominent name, while we had no instruction beyond.

It may be necessary for the information of some of my readers, to mention that there are three distinct Convents in Montreal, all of different kinds; that is, founded on different plans, and governed by different rules. Their names are as follows:—

1st. The Congregational Nunnery.

2d. The Black Nunnery, or Convent of Sister Bourgeoise.

3d. The Grey Nunnery.

The first of these professes to be devoted entirely to the education of girls. It would require however only a proper examination to prove that, with the exception of needle-work, hardly any thing is taught excepting prayers and the catechism; the instruction in reading, writing, &c., in fact, amounting to very little, and often to nothing. This Convent is adjacent to that next to be spoken of, being separated from it only by a wall. The second professes to be a charitable institution for the care of the sick, and the supply of bread and medicines for the poor; and something is done in these departments of charity, although but an insignificant amount, compared with the size of the buildings, and the number of the inmates.

The Grey Nunnery, which is situated in a distant part of the city, is also a large edifice, containing departments for the care of insane persons and foundlings. With this, however, I have less personal acquaintance than with either of the others. I have often seen two of the Grey nuns, and know that their rules, as well as those of the Congregational Nunnery, do not confine them always within their walls, like those of the Black Nunnery. These two Convents have their common names (Black and Grey) from the colours of the dresses worn by their inmates.

In all these three Convents, there are certain apartments into which strangers can gain admittance, but others from which they are always excluded. In all, large quantities of various ornaments are made by the nuns, which are exposed for sale in the *Ornament* Rooms, and afford large pecuniary receipts every year, which contribute much to their incomes. In these rooms visiters often purchase such things as please them from some of the old* and confidential nuns who have the charge of them.

From all that appears to the public eye, the nuns of these Convents are devoted to the charitable objects appropriate to each, the labour of making different articles, known to be manufactured by them, and the religious observances, which occupy a large portion of their time. They are regarded with much respect by the people at large; and now and then when a novice takes the veil,[1] she is supposed to retire from the temptations and

---

*The term "old nun," does not always indicate superior age.

[1] A novice is a candidate for admission to a religious order. A novice becomes an official member of the convent upon taking certain vows and going through a ceremony known as taking the veil, which symbolically represents marriage to Christ.

troubles of this world into a state of holy seclusion, where, by prayer, self-mortification, and good deeds, she prepares herself for heaven. Sometimes the Superior of a Convent obtains the character of working miracles; and when such a one dies, it is published through the country, and crowds throng the Convent, who think indulgences are to be derived from bits of her clothes or other things she has possessed; and many have sent articles to be touched to her bed or chair, in which a degree of virtue is thought to remain. I used to participate in such ideas and feelings, and began by degrees to look upon a nun as the happiest of women, and a Convent as the most peaceful, holy, and delightful place of abode. It is true, some pains were taken to impress such views upon me. Some of the priests of the Seminary often visited the Congregational Nunnery, and both catechised and talked with us on religion. The Superior of the Black Nunnery adjoining, also, occasionally came into the School, enlarged on the advantages we enjoyed in having such teachers, and dropped something now and then relating to her own Convent, calculated to make us entertain the highest ideas of it, and to make us sometimes think of the possibility of getting into it.

Among the instructions given us by the priests, some of the most pointed were those directed against the Protestant Bible. They often enlarged upon the evil tendency of that book, and told us that but for it many a soul now condemned to hell, and suffering eternal punishment, might have been in happiness. They could not say any thing in its favour: for that would be speaking against religion and against God. They warned us against it, and represented it as a thing very dangerous to our souls. In confirmation of this, they would repeat some of the answers taught us at catechism, a few of which I will here give. We had little catechisms ("Le Petit Catechism") put into our hands to study; but the priests soon began to teach us a new set of answers, which were not to be found in our books, from some of which I received new ideas, and got, as I thought, important light on religious subjects, which confirmed me more and more in my belief in the Roman Catholic doctrines. These questions and answers I can still recall with tolerable accuracy, and some of them I will add here. I never have read them, as we were taught them only by word of mouth.

Question. "Pourquoi le bon Dieu n'a pas fait tous les commandemens?

Réponse. "Parce que l'homme n'est pas si fort qu'il peut garder tous ses commandemens.

Q. "Why did not God make all the commandments?

A. "Because man is not strong enough to keep them.

And another. *Q.* "Pourquoi l'homme ne lit pas l'Evangile?

R. "Parce que l'esprit de l'homme est trop borné et trop faîble pour comprendre qu'est ce que Dieu a écrit.

Q. "Why are men not to read the New Testament?"

A. "Because the mind of man is too limited and weak to understand what God has written."

These questions and answers are not to be found in the common catechisms in use in Montreal and other places where I have been, but all the children in the Congregational Nunnery were taught them, and many more not found in these books.

CHAPTER II

◆ Congregational Nunnery

Story told by a fellow Pupil against a Priest—Other Stories—Pretty Mary—Confess to Father Richards—My subsequent Confessions—Left the Congregational Nunnery.

There was a girl thirteen years old whom I knew in the School, who resided in the neighbourhood of my mother, and with whom I had been familiar. She told me one day at school of the conduct of a priest with her at confession, at which I was astonished. It was of so criminal and shameful a nature, I could hardly believe it, and yet I had so much confidence that she spoke the truth, that I could not discredit it.

She was partly persuaded by the priest to believe he could not sin, because he was a priest, and that any thing he did to her would sanctify her; and yet she seemed somewhat doubtful how she should act. A priest, she had been told by him, is a holy man, and appointed to a holy office, and therefore what would be wicked in other men, could not be so in him. She told me that she had informed her mother of it, who expressed no anger nor disapprobation, but only enjoined it upon her not to speak of it; and remarked to her, that as priests were not like other men, but holy, and sent to instruct and save us, whatever they did was right.

I afterward confessed to the priest that I had heard the story, and had a penance to perform for indulging a sinful curiosity in making inquiries; and the girl had another for communicating it. I afterward learned that other children had been treated in the same manner, and also of similar proceedings in other places.

Indeed, it was not long before such language was used to me, and I well remember how my views of right and wrong were shaken by it. Another girl at the School, from a place above Montreal, called the Lac, told me the following story of what had occurred recently in that vicinity. A young squaw, called la Belle Marie, (pretty Mary,) had been seen going to confession at the house of the priest, who lived a little out of the village. La Belle Marie was afterward missed, and her murdered body was found in the river. A knife was also found covered with blood, bearing the priest's name. Great indignation was excited among the Indians, and the priest immediately absconded, and was never heard from again. A note was found on his table addressed to him, telling him to fly if he was guilty.

It was supposed that the priest was fearful that his conduct might be betrayed by this young female; and he undertook to clear himself by killing her.

These stories struck me with surprise at first, but I gradually began to feel differently, even supposing them true, and to look upon the priests as men incapable of sin; besides, when I first went to confession, which I did to Father Richards, in the old French church, (since taken down,) I heard nothing improper; and it was not until I had been several times, that the priests became more and more bold, and were at length indecent in their questions and even in their conduct when I confessed to them in the Sacristie.[2]

---

[2]A room where sacred vessels and vestments are kept, and where clergy dress in preparation for services.

This subject I believe is not understood nor suspected among Protestants; and it is not my intention to speak of it very particularly, because it is impossible to do so without saying things both shameful and demoralizing.

I will only say here, that when quite a child, I had from the mouths of the priests at confession what I cannot repeat, with treatment corresponding; and several females in Canada have recently assured me, that they have repeatedly, and indeed regularly, been required to answer the same and other like questions, many of which present to the mind deeds which the most iniquitous and corrupt heart could hardly invent.

There was a frequent change of teachers in the School of the Nunnery; and no regular system was pursued in our instruction. There were many nuns who came and went while I was there, being frequently called in and out without any perceptible reason. They supply school teachers to many of the country towns, usually two for each of the towns with which I was acquainted, besides sending Sisters of Charity to different parts of the United States. Among those whom I saw most, was Saint Patrick, an old woman for a nun, (that is, about forty,) very ignorant, and gross in her manners, with quite a beard on her face, and very cross and disagreeable. She was sometimes our teacher in sewing, and was appointed to keep order among us. We were allowed to enter only a few of the rooms in the Congregational Nunnery, although it was not considered one of the secluded Convents.

In the Black Nunnery, which is very near the Congregational, is an hospital for sick people from the city; and sometimes some of our boarders, such as were indisposed, were sent there to be cured. I was once taken ill myself and sent there, where I remained a few days.

There were beds enough for a considerable number more. A physician attended it daily; and there are a number of the veiled nuns of that Convent who spend most of their time there.

These would also sometimes read lectures and repeat prayers to us.

After I had been in the Congregational Nunnery about two years, I left it, and attended several different schools for a short time; but I soon became dissatisfied, having many and severe trials to endure at home, which my feelings will not allow me to describe; and as my Catholic acquaintances had often spoken to me in favour of their faith, I was inclined to believe it true, although, as I before said, I knew little of any religion. While out of the nunnery, I saw nothing of religion. If I had, I believe I should never have thought of becoming a nun.

CHAPTER VI

Taking the Veil

Taking the Veil—Interview afterward with the Superior—Surprise and horror at her Disclosures—Resolution to Submit.

I was introduced into the Superior's room on the evening preceding the day on which I was to take the veil, to have an interview with the Bishop. The Superior was present, and the interview lasted about half an hour. The Bishop on this as on other occasions appeared to me habitually rough in his manners. His address was by no means prepossessing.

Before I took the veil, I was ornamented for the ceremony, and was clothed in a rich dress belonging to the Convent, which was used on such occasions; and placed not far from the altar in the chapel, in the view of a number of spectators who had assembled, perhaps about forty. Taking the veil is an affair which occurs so frequently in Montreal, that it has long ceased to be regarded as a novelty; and, although notice had been given in the French parish church as usual, only a small audience had assembled, as I have mentioned.

Being well prepared with a long training, and frequent rehearsals, for what I was to perform, I stood waiting in my large flowing dress for the appearance of the Bishop. He soon presented himself, entering by the door behind the altar; I then threw myself at his feet, and asked him to confer upon me the veil. He expressed his consent, and threw it over my head, saying, "Receive the veil, O thou spouse of Jesus Christ;" and then turning to the Superior, I threw myself prostrate at her feet, according to my instructions, repeating what I had before done at rehearsals, and made a movement as if to kiss her feet. This she prevented, or appeared to prevent, catching me by a sudden motion of her hand, and granted my request. I then kneeled before the Holy Sacrament, that is, a very large round wafer held by the Bishop between his fore-finger and thumb, and made my vows.

This wafer I had been taught to regard with the utmost veneration, as the real body of Jesus Christ, the presence of which made the vows uttered before it binding in the most solemn manner.

After taking the vows, I proceeded to a small apartment behind the altar, accompanied by four nuns, where was a coffin prepared, with my nun name engraven upon it:

"SAINT EUSTACE."[3]

My companions lifted it by four handles attached to it, while I threw off my dress, and put on that of a nun of Sœur Bourgeoise; and then we all returned to the chapel. I proceeded first, and was followed by the four nuns; the Bishop naming a number of worldly pleasures in rapid succession, in reply to which I as rapidly repeated—Je renonce, je renonce, je renonce"—[I renounce, I renounce, I renounce.]

The coffin was then placed in front of the altar, and I advanced to lay myself in it. This coffin was to be deposited, after the ceremony, in an outhouse, to be preserved until my death, when it was to receive my corpse. There were reflections which I naturally made at that time, but I stepped in, extended myself, and lay still. A pillow had been placed at the head of the coffin, to support my head in a comfortable position. A large, thick black cloth was then spread over me, and the chanting of Latin hymns immediately commenced. My thoughts were not the most pleasing during the time I lay in that situation. The pall, or Drap Mortel, as the cloth is called, had a strong smell of incense, which was always disagreeable to me, and then proved almost suffocating. I recollected also a

---

[3]Saint Eustace (second century) was the most famous of the early Christian martyrs. Refusing to sacrifice to the Roman gods, he was roasted to death inside a brass bull.

story I had heard of a novice, who, in taking the veil, lay down in her coffin like me, and was covered in the same manner, but on the removal of the covering was found dead.

When I was uncovered, I rose, stepped out of my coffin, and kneeled. The Bishop then addressed these words to the Superior, "Take care and keep pure and spotless this young virgin, whom Christ has consecrated to himself this day." After which the music commenced, and here the whole was finished. I then proceeded from the chapel, and returned to the Superior's room, followed by the other nuns, who walked two by two, in their customary manner, with their hands folded on their breasts, and their eyes cast down upon the floor. The nun who was to be my companion in future, then walked at the end of the procession. On reaching the Superior's door, they all left me, and I entered alone, and found her with the Bishop and two priests.

The Superior now informed me, that having taken the black veil, it only remained that I should swear the three oaths customary on becoming a nun; and that some explanations would be necessary from her. I was now, she told me, to have access to every part of the edifice, even to the cellar, where two of the sisters were imprisoned for causes which she did not mention. I must be informed, that one of my great duties was, to obey the priests in all things; and this I soon learnt, to my utter astonishment and horror, was to live in the practice of criminal intercourse with them. I expressed some of the feelings which this announcement excited in me, which came upon me like a flash of lightning but the only effect was to set her arguing with me, in favour of the crime, representing it as a virtue acceptable to God, and honourable to me. The priests, she said, were not situated like other men, being forbidden to marry; while they lived secluded, laborious, and self-denying lives for our salvation. They might, indeed, be considered our saviours, as without their services we could not obtain the pardon of sin, and must go to hell. Now, it was our solemn duty, on withdrawing from the world, to consecrate our lives to religion, to practise every species of self-denial. We could not become too humble, nor mortify our feelings too far; this was to be done by opposing them, and acting contrary to them; and what she proposed was, therefore, pleasing in the sight of God. I now felt how foolish I had been to place myself in the power of such persons as were around me.

From what she said I could draw no other conclusion, but that I was required to act like the most abandoned of beings, and that all my future associates were habitually guilty of the most heinous and detestable crimes. When I repeated my expressions of surprise and horror, she told me that such feelings were very common at first, and that many other nuns had expressed themselves as I did, who had long since changed their minds. She even said, that on her entrance into the nunnery, she had felt like me.

Doubts, she declared, were among our greatest enemies. They would lead us to question every point of duty, and induce us to waver at every step. They arose only from remaining imperfection, and were always evidence of sin. Our only way was to dismiss them immediately, repent, and confess them. They were deadly sins, and would condemn us to hell, if we should die without confessing them. Priests, she insisted, could not sin. It was a thing impossible. Every thing that they did, and wished, was of course right. She hoped I would see the reasonableness and duty of the oaths I was to take, and be faithful to them.

She gave me another piece of information which excited other feelings in me, scarcely less dreadful. Infants were sometimes born in the convent: but they were always baptized and immediately strangled! This secured their everlasting happiness; for the baptism purified them from all sinfulness, and being sent out of the world before they had time to do any thing wrong, they were at once admitted into heaven. How happy, she exclaimed, are those who secure immortal happiness to such little beings! Their little souls would thank those who kill their bodies, if they had it in their power!

Into what a place and among what society had I been admitted! How differently did a Convent now appear from what I had supposed it to be! The holy women I had always fancied the nuns to be, the venerable Lady Superior, what were they? And the priests of the Seminary adjoining, some of whom indeed I had had reason to think were base and profligate men, what were they all? I now learnt they were often admitted into the nunnery, and allowed to indulge in the greatest crimes, which they and others called virtues.

After having listened for some time to the Superior alone, a number of the nuns were admitted, and took a free part in the conversation. They concurred in every thing which she had told me, and repeated, without any signs of shame or compunction, things which criminated themselves. I must acknowledge the truth, and declare that all this had an effect upon my mind. I questioned whether I might not be in the wrong, and felt as if their reasoning might have some just foundation. I had been several years under the tuition of Catholics, and was ignorant of the Scriptures, and unaccustomed to the society, example, and conversation of Protestants; had not heard any appeal to the Bible as authority, but had been taught, both by precept and example, to receive as truth every thing said by the priests. I had not heard their authority questioned, nor any thing said of any other standard of faith but their declarations. I had long been familiar with the corrupt and licentious expressions which some of them use at confessions, and believed that other women were also. I had no standard of duty to refer to, and no judgment of my own which I knew how to use, or thought of using.

All around me insisted that my doubts proved only my own ignorance and sinfulness; that they knew by experience they would soon give place to true knowledge, and an advance in religion; and I felt something like indecision.

Still, there was so much that disgusted me in the discovery I had now made, of the debased characters around me, that I would most gladly have escaped from the nunnery, and never returned. But that was a thing not to be thought of. I was in their power, and this I deeply felt, while I thought there was not one among the whole number of nuns to whom I could look for kindness. There was one, however, who began to speak to me at length in a tone that gained something of my confidence,—the nun whom I have mentioned before as distinguished by her oddity, Jane Ray,[4] who made us so much amusement when I was a novice. Although, as I have remarked, there was nothing in her face, form, or manners, to give me any pleasure, she addressed me with apparent friendliness; and while she seemed to concur with some things spoken by them, took an opportunity

---

[4]Introduced earlier, Jane Ray is an older nun (some thirty years of age) who is of an independent and ungovernable nature. Upon receiving the veil, she did not take a new name, but kept her own. Monk tells the reader that "her irregularities were found to be numerous, and penances were of so little use in governing her, that she was pitied by some, who thought her partially insane. She was therefore commonly spoken of as mad Jane Ray. . . ."

to whisper a few words in my ear, unheard by them, intimating that I had better comply with every thing the Superior desired, if I would save my life. I was somewhat alarmed before, but I now became much more so, and determined to make no further resistance. The Superior then made me repeat the three oaths; and when I had sworn them, I was shown into one of the community rooms, and remained some time with the nuns, who were released from their usual employments, and enjoying a recreation day, on account of the admission of a new sister. My feelings during the remainder of that day, I shall not attempt to describe; but pass on to mention the ceremonies which took place at dinner. This description may give an idea of the manner in which we always took our meals, although there were some points in which the breakfast and supper were different.

At 11 o'clock the bell rung for dinner, and the nuns all took their places in a double row, in the same order as that in which they left the chapel in the morning, except that my companion and myself were stationed at the end of the line. Standing thus for a moment with our hands placed one on the other over the breast, and hidden in our large cuffs, with our heads bent forward, and eyes fixed on the floor; an old nun who stood at the door, clapped her hands as a signal for us to proceed, and the procession moved on, while we all commenced the repetition of litanies. We walked on in this order, repeating all the way, until we reached the door of the dining-room, where we were divided into two lines; those on the right passing down one side of the long table, and those on the left the other, till all were in, and each stopped in her place. The plates were all ranged, each with a knife, fork, and spoon, rolled up in a napkin, and tied round with a linen band marked with the owner's name. My own plate, knife, fork, &c., were prepared like the rest, and on the band around them I found my new name written:—"Saint Eustace."

There we stood till all had concluded the litany; when the old nun who had taken her place at the head of the table next to the door, said the prayer before meat, beginning "Benedicite,"[5] and we sat down. I do not remember of what our dinner consisted, but we usually had soup and some plain dish of meat, the remains of which were occasionally served up at supper as a fricassee. One of the nuns who had been appointed to read that day, rose and began a lecture from a book put into her hands by the Superior, while the rest of us ate in perfect silence. The nun who reads during dinner, stays afterward to dine. As fast as we finished our meals, each rolled up her knife, fork, and spoon in her napkin, and bound them together with the band, and set with hands folded. The old nun then said a short prayer, rose, stepped a little aside, clapped her hands, and we marched towards the door, bowing as we passed before a little chapel or glass box, containing a wax image of the infant Jesus.

Nothing important occurred until late in the afternoon, when as I was sitting in the community room, Father Dufrèsne called me out, saying he washed to speak with me. I feared what was his intention; but I dared not disobey. In a private apartment he treated me in a brutal manner; and from two other priests, I afterward received similar usage that evening. Father Dufrèsne afterward appeared again; and I was compelled to remain in company with him until morning.

I am assured that the conduct of priests in our Convent has never been exposed, and is not imagined by the people of the United States. This induces me to say what I do,

---

[5]"Bless you"; a blessing asked at meals.

notwithstanding the strong reasons I have to let it remain unknown. Still, I cannot force myself to speak on such subjects except in the most brief manner.

CHAPTER VIII

❧ Description of Apartments

Description of Apartments in the Black Nunnery, in order.—1st Floor—2d Floor— The Founder—Superior's Management with the Friends of Novices— Religious Lies—Criminality of concealing Sins at Confession.

I will now give from memory, a general description of the interior of the Convent of Black nuns, except the few apartments which I never saw. I may be inaccurate in some things, as the apartments and passages of that spacious building are numerous and various; but I am willing to risk my credit for truth and sincerity on the general correspondence, between my description and things as they are. And this would, perhaps, be as good a case as any by which to test the truth of my statements, were it possible to obtain access to the interior. It is well known, that none but veiled nuns, the bishop, and priests, are ever admitted; and, of course, that I cannot have seen what I profess to describe, if I have not been a Black nun.* The priests who read this book, will acknowledge to themselves the truth of my description; but will, of course, deny it to the world, and probably exert themselves to destroy my credit. I offer to every reader the following description, knowing that time may possibly throw open those secret recesses, and allow the entrance of those who can satisfy themselves, with their own eyes, of its truth. Some of my declarations may be thought deficient in evidence; and this they must of necessity be in the present state of things. But here is a kind of evidence on which I rely, as I see how unquestionable and satisfactory it must prove, whenever it shall be obtained.

If the interior of the Black Nunnery, whenever it shall be examined, is materially different from the following description, then I can claim no confidence of my readers. If it resembles it, they will, I presume, place confidence in some of those declarations, on which I may never be corroborated by true and living witnesses.

I am sensible that great changes may be made in the furniture of apartments; that new walls may be constructed or old ones removed; and I have been credibly informed, that masons have been employed in the nunnery since I left it. I well know, however, that entire changes cannot be made; and that enough must remain as it was to substantiate my description, whenever the truth shall be known.

THE FIRST STORY

Beginning at the extremity of the right wing of the Convent, towards Notre Dame-street, on the first story, there is—

---

*I ought to have made an exception here, which I may enlarge upon in future. Certain other persons are sometimes admitted.

1st. The nuns' private chapel, adjoining which is a passage to a small projection of the building, extending from the upper story to the ground, with very small windows. Into the passage we were sometimes required to bring wood from the yard, and pile it up for use.

2d. A large community-room, with plain benches fixed against the wall to sit, and lower ones in front to place our feet upon. There is a fountain in the passage near the chimney at the farther end, for washing the hands and face, with a green curtain sliding on a rod before it. This passage leads to the old nuns' sleeping-room on the right, and the Superior's sleeping-room, just beyond it, as well as to a staircase which conducts to the nuns' sleeping-room, or dortoir, above. At the end of the passage is a door opening into—

3d. The dining-room; this is larger than the community-room, and has three long tables for eating, and a chapelle, or collection of little pictures, a crucifix, and a small image of the infant Saviour in a glass case. This apartment has four doors, by the first of which we are supposed to have entered, while one opens to a pantry, and the third and fourth to the two next apartments.

4th. A large community-room, with tables for sewing, and a staircase on the opposite left-hand corner.

5th. A community-room for prayer, used by both nuns and novices. In the farther right-hand corner is a small room partitioned off, called the room for the examination of conscience, which I had visited while a novice by permission of the Superior, and where nuns and novices occasionally resorted to reflect on their character, usually in preparation for the sacrament, or when they had transgressed some of the rules. This little room was hardly large enough to contain half a dozen persons at a time.

6th. Next beyond is a large community-room for Sundays. A door leads to the yard, and thence to a gate in the wall on the cross street.

7th. Adjoining this is a sitting room, fronting on the cross street, with two windows, and a storeroom on the side opposite them. There is but little furniture, and that very plain.

8th. From this room a door leads into what I may call the wax-room, as it contains many figures in wax, not intended for sale. There we sometimes used to pray, or meditate on the Saviour's passion. This room projects from the main building; leaving it, you enter a long passage, with cupboards on the right, in which are stored crockery-ware, knives and forks, and other articles of table furniture, to replace those worn out or broken—all of the plainest description; also, shovels, tongs, &c. This passage leads to—

9th. A corner room, with a few benches, &c. and a door leading to a gate on the street. Here some of the medicines were kept, and persons were often admitted on business, or to obtain medicines with tickets from the priests; and waited till the Superior or an old nun could be sent for. Beyond this room we were never allowed to go; and I cannot speak from personal knowledge of what came next.

THE SECOND STORY

Beginning, as before, at the western extremity of the same wing, but on the second story, the farthest apartment in that direction which I ever entered was—

1st. The nuns' sleeping-room, or dormitory, which I have already described. Here is an access to the projection mentioned in speaking of the first story. The stairs by which we came up to bed are at the farther end of the room; and near them a crucifix and font of holy water. A door at the end of the room opens into a passage, with two small rooms, and closets between them, containing bedclothes. Next you enter—

2d. A small community-room, beyond which is a passage with a narrow staircase, seldom used, which leads into the fourth community-room, in the first story. Following the passage just mentioned, you enter by a door—

3d. A little sitting-room, furnished in the following manner: with chairs, a sofa, on the north side, covered with a red-figured cover and fringe, a table in the middle, commonly bearing one or two books, an inkstand, pens, &c. At one corner is a little projection into the room, caused by a staircase leading from above to the floor below, without any communication with the second story. This room has a door opening upon a staircase leading down to the yard, on the opposite side of which is a gate opening into the cross street. By this way the physician is admitted, except when he comes later than usual. When he comes in, he usually sits a little while, until a nun goes into the adjoining nuns' sick-room, to see if all is ready, and returns to admit him. After prescribing for the patients he goes no farther, but returns by the way he enters; and these two are the only rooms into which he is ever admitted, except the public hospital.

4th. The nuns' sick-room adjoins the little sitting-room on the east, and has, I think, four windows towards the north, with beds ranged in two rows from end to end, and a few more between them, near the opposite extremity. The door from the sitting-room swings to the left, and behind it is a table, while a glass case, to the right, contains a wax figure of the infant Saviour, with several sheep. Near the northeastern corner of this room are two doors, one of which opens into a long and narrow passage leading to the head of the great staircase that conducts to the cross street. By this passage the physician sometimes finds his way to the sick-room, when he comes later than usual. He rings the bell at the gate, which I was told had a concealed pull, known only to him and the priests, proceeds up-stairs and through the passage, rapping three times at the door of the sick-room, which is opened by a nun in attendance, after she has given one rap in reply. When he has visited his patients, and prescribed for them, he returns by the same way.

5th. Next beyond this sick-room, is a large unoccupied apartment, half divided by two partial partitions, which leave an open space in the middle. Here some of the old nuns commonly sit in the daytime.

6th. A door from this apartment opens into another, not appropriated to any particular use, but containing a table, where medicines are sometimes prepared by an old nun, who is usually found there. Passing through this room, you enter a passage, with doors on its four sides: that on the left, which is kept fastened on the inside, leads to the staircase and gate; that in front, to private sick-rooms, soon to be described.

7th. That on the right leads to another, appropriated to nuns suffering with the most loathsome disease. There were usually a number of straw mattresses in that room, as I well knew, having helped to carry them in after the yard-man had filled them. A door beyond enters into a storeroom, which extends also beyond this apartment. On the right, another door opens into another passage, crossing which, you enter by a door—

8th. A room with a bed and screen in one corner, on which nuns were laid to be examined before their introduction into the sick-room last mentioned. Another door, opposite the former, opens into a passage, in which is a staircase leading down.

9th. Beyond this is a spare-room, sometimes used to store apples, boxes of different things, &c.

10th. Returning now to the passage which opens on one side upon the stairs to the gate, we enter the only remaining door, which leads into an apartment usually occupied by some of the old nuns, and frequently by the Superior.

11th, and 12th. Beyond this are two more sick-rooms, in one of which those nuns stay who are waiting their accouchement, and in the other, those who have passed it.

13th. The next is a small sitting-room, where a priest waits to baptize the infants previous to their murder. A passage leads from this room, on the left, by the doors of two succeeding apartments, neither of which have I ever entered.

14th. The first of them is the "holy retreat," or room occupied by the priests, while suffering the penalty of their licentiousness.

15th. The other is a sitting-room, to which they have access. Beyond these the passage leads to two rooms, containing closets for the storage of various articles, and two others where persons are received who come on business.

The public hospitals succeed, and extend a considerable distance, I believe, to the extremity of the building. By a public entrance in that part, priests often come into the nunnery; and I have often seen some of them thereabouts, who must have entered by that way. Indeed, priests often get into the "holy retreat" without exposing themselves to the view of persons in other parts of the Convent, and have been first known to be there, by the yard-man being sent to the Seminary for their clothes.

The Congregational Nunnery was founded by a nun called Sister Bourgeoise. She taught a school in Montreal, and left property for the foundation of a Convent. Her body is buried, and her heart is kept, under the nunnery, in an iron chest, which has been shown to me, with the assurance that it continues in perfect preservation, although she has been dead more than one hundred and fifty years. In the chapel is the following inscription: "Sœur Bourgeoise, Fondatrice du Convent"—Sister Bourgeoise, Founder of the Convent.

Nothing was more common than for the Superior to step hastily into our community-rooms, while numbers of us were assembled there, and hastily communicate her wishes in words like these:—

"Here are the parents of such a novice: come with me, and bear me out in this story." She would then mention the outlines of a tissue of falsehoods, she had just invented, that we might be prepared to fabricate circumstances, and throw in whatever else might favour the deception. This was justified, and indeed most highly commended, by the system of faith in which we were instructed.

It was a common remark made at the initiation of a new nun into the Black nun department, that is, to receive the black veil, that the introduction of another novice into the Convent as a veiled nun, caused the introduction of a veiled nun into heaven as a saint, which was on account of the singular disappearance of some of the older nuns at the entrance of new ones!

To witness the scenes which often occurred between us and strangers, would have struck a person very powerfully, if he had known how truth was set at naught. The Superior, with a serious and dignified air, and a pleasant voice and aspect, would commence a recital of things most favourable to the character of the absent novice, and representing her as equally fond of her situation, and beloved by the other inmates. The tale told by the Superior, whatever it was, however unheard before might have been any of her statements, was then attested by us, who, in every way we could think of, endeavoured to confirm her declarations, beyond the reach of doubt.

Sometimes the Superior would intrust the management of such a case to some of the nuns, whether to habituate us to the practice in which she was so highly accomplished, or to relieve herself of what would have been a serious burden to most other persons, or to ascertain whether she could depend upon us, or all together, I cannot tell. Often, however, have I seen her throw open a door, and, say, in a hurried manner, "Who can tell the best story?"

One point, on which we received frequent and particular instructions was, the nature of falsehoods. On this subject I have heard many a speech, I had almost said many a sermon; and I was led to believe that it was one of great importance, one on which it was a duty to be well informed, as well as to act. "What!" exclaimed a priest one day—"what, a nun of your age, and not know the difference between a wicked and a religious lie!"

He then went on, as had been done many times previously in my hearing, to show the essential difference between the two different kinds of falsehoods. A lie told merely for the injury of another, for our own interest alone, or for no object at all, he painted as a sin worthy of penance. But a lie told for the good of the church or Convent, was meritorious, and of course the telling of it a duty. And of this class of lies there were many varieties and shades. This doctrine has been inculcated on me and my companions in the nunnery, more times than I can enumerate; and to say that it was generally received, would be to tell a part of the truth. We often saw the practice of it, and were frequently made to take part in it. Whenever any thing which the Superior thought important, could be most conveniently accomplished by falsehood, she resorted to it without scruple.

There was a class of cases in which she more frequently relied on deception than any other.

The friends of novices frequently applied at the Convent to see them, or at least to inquire after their welfare. It was common for them to be politely refused an interview, on some account or other, generally a mere pretext; and then the Superior usually sought to make as favourable an impression as possible on the visitors. Sometimes she would make up a story on the spot, and tell the strangers; requiring some of us to confirm it, in the most convincing way we could.

At other times she would prefer to make over to us the task of deceiving, and we were commended in proportion to our ingenuity and success.

Some nun usually showed her submission, by immediately stepping forward. She would then add, perhaps, that the parents of such a novice, whom she named, were in waiting, and it was necessary that they should be told such, and such, and such things. To perform so difficult a task well, was considered a difficult duty, and it was one of the most certain ways to gain the favour of the Superior. Whoever volunteered to make a story on the spot, was sent immediately to tell it, and the other nuns present were hurried off with her under strict injunctions to uphold her in every thing she might state. The Superior, as there was every reason to believe, on all such occasions, when she did not herself appear, hastened to the apartment adjoining that in which the nuns were going, there to listen through the thin partition, to hear whether all performed their parts aright. It was not uncommon for her to go rather further, when she wanted time to give such explanations as she could have desired. She would then enter abruptly, ask, "Who can tell a good story this morning?" and hurry us off without a moment's delay, to do our best at a venture, without waiting for instructions. It would be curious, could a stranger from "the wicked world" outside the Convent witness such a scene. One of the nuns, who felt in a favourable humour to undertake the proposed task, would step promptly forward, and signify her readiness in the usual way: by a knowing wink of one eye, and a slight toss of the head.

"Well, go and do the best you can," the Superior would say; "and all the rest of you must mind and swear to it." The latter part of the order, at least, was always performed; for in every such case, all the nuns present appeared as unanimous witnesses of every thing that was uttered by the spokesman of the day.

We were constantly hearing it repeated, that we must never again look upon ourselves as our own; but must remember, that we were solemnly and irrevocably devoted to God. Whatever was required of us, we were called upon to yield under the most solemn considerations. I cannot speak on every particular with equal freedom; but I wish my readers clearly to understand the condition in which we were placed, and the means used to reduce us to what we had to submit to. Not only were we required to perform the several tasks imposed upon us at work, prayers, and penances, under the idea that we were performing solemn duties to our Maker, but every thing else which was required of us, we were constantly told, was something indispensable in his sight. The priests, we admitted, were the servants of God, specially appointed by his authority, to teach us our duty, to absolve us from sin, and to lead us to heaven. Without their assistance, we had allowed we could never enjoy the favour of God: unless they administered the sacraments to us, we could not enjoy everlasting happiness. Having consented to acknowledge all this, we had no objection to urge against admitting any other demand that might be made for or by them. If we thought an act ever so criminal, the Superior would tell us that the priests acted under the direct sanction of God, and *could not sin.* Of course, then, it could not be wrong to comply with any of their requests, because they could not demand any thing but what was right. On the contrary, to refuse to do any thing they asked, would necessarily be sinful. Such doctrines admitted, and such practices performed, it will not seem wonderful when I mention that we often felt something of their preposterous character.

Sometimes we took pleasure in ridiculing some of the favourite themes of our teachers; and I recollect one subject particularly, which at one period afforded us repeated merriment. It may seem irreverent in me to give the account, but I do it to show how things of a solemn nature were sometimes treated in the Convent, by women bearing the title of saints. A Canadian Novice, who spoke very broken English, one day remarked that she was performing some duty "for the God." This peculiar expression had something ridiculous to the ears of some of us; and it was soon repeated again and again, in application to various ceremonies which we had to perform. Mad Jane Ray seized upon it with avidity, and with her aid it soon took the place of a by-word in conversation, so that we were constantly reminding each other, that we were doing this and that thing, how trifling and unmeaning soever, "for the God." Nor did we stop here: when the Superior called upon us to bear witness to one of her religious lies, or to fabricate the most spurious one the time would admit; to save her the trouble, we were sure to be reminded, on our way to the stranger's room, that we were doing it "for the God." And so it was when other things were mentioned—every thing which belonged to our condition, was spoken of in similar terms

I have hardly detained the reader long enough on the subject, to give him a just impression of the stress laid on confession. It is one of the great points to which our attention was constantly directed. We were directed to keep a strict and constant watch over our thoughts; to have continually before our minds the rules of the Convent, to compare the one with the other, remember every devotion, and tell all, even the smallest, at confession, either to the Superior, or to the priest. My mind was thus kept in a continual state of activity, which proved very wearisome; and it required the constant exertion of our teachers, to keep us up to the practice they inculcated.

Another tale recurs to me, of those which were frequently told us to make us feel the importance of unreserved confession.

A nun of our Convent, who had hidden some sin from her confessor, died suddenly, and without any one to confess her. Her sisters assembled to pray for the peace of her soul, when she appeared, and informed them, that it would be of no use, but rather troublesome to her, as her pardon was impossible.* The doctrine is, that prayers made for souls guilty of unconfessed sin, do but sink them deeper in hell; and this is the reason I have heard given for not praying for Protestants.

The authority of the priests in every thing, and the enormity of every act which opposes it, were also impressed upon our minds, in various ways, by our teachers. A "Father" told us the following story one day at catechism.

A man once died who had failed to pay some money which the priest had asked of him; he was condemned to be burnt in purgatory until he should pay it, but had permission to come back to this world, and take a human body to work in. He made his appearance therefore again on earth, and hired himself to a rich man as a labourer. He worked all day with the fire burning in him, unseen by other people; but while he was in bed that night, a girl in an adjoining room, perceiving the smell of brimstone, looked through a crack in the wall, and saw him covered with flames. She informed his master, who questioned him the next morning, and found that his hired man was secretly suffering the pains of purgatory, for neglecting to pay a certain sum of money to the priest. He, therefore, furnished him the amount due; it was paid, and the servant went off immediately to heaven. The priest cannot forgive any debt due unto him, because it is the Lord's estate.

While at confession, I was urged to hide nothing from the priest, and have been told by them, that they already knew what was in my heart, but would not tell, because it was necessary for me to confess it. I really believed that the priests were acquainted with my thoughts; and often stood in great awe of them. They often told me they had power to strike me dead at any moment.

---

*Since the first edition, I have found this tale related in a Romish book, as one of very ancient date. It was told to us as having taken place in our Convent.

CHAPTER XVII

❧ Treatment of Young Infants

Treatment of young Infants in the Convent—Talking in Sleep—Amusements—
Ceremonies at the public interment of deceased Nuns—Sudden disappearance of the
Old Superior—Introduction of the new one—Superstition—Alarm of a Nun—
Difficulty of Communication with other Nuns.

It will be recollected, that I was informed immediately after receiving the veil, that infants were occasionally murdered in the Convent. I was one day in the nuns' private sick-room, when I had an opportunity, unsought for, of witnessing deeds of such a nature. It was, perhaps, a month after the death of Saint Francis. Two little twin babes, the children of Sainte Catharine, were brought to a priest, who was in the room, for baptism. I was present while the ceremony was performed, with the Superior and several of the old nuns, whose names I never knew, they being called Ma tante, Aunt.

The priests took turns in attending to confession and catechism in the Convent, usually three months at a time, though sometimes longer periods. The priest then on duty was Father Larkin. He is a good-looking European, and has a brother who is a professor in the college. He baptized and then put oil upon the heads of the infants, as is the custom after baptism. They were then taken, one after another, by one of the old nuns, in the presence of us all. She pressed her hand upon the mouth and nose of the first, so tight that it could not breathe, and in a few minutes, when the hand was removed, it was dead. She then took the other, and treated it in the same way. No sound was heard, and both the children were corpses. The greatest indifference was shown by all present during this operation; for all, as I well knew, were long accustomed to such scenes. The little bodies were then taken into the cellar, thrown into the pit[6] I have mentioned, and covered with a quantity of lime.

I afterward saw another new-born infant treated in the same manner, in the same place: but the actors in the scene I choose not to name, nor the circumstances, as every thing connected with it is of a peculiarly trying and painful nature to my own feelings.

These were the only instances of infanticide I witnessed; and it seemed to be merely owing to accident that I was then present. So far as I know, there were no pains taken to preserve secrecy on this subject; that is, I saw no attempt made to keep any of the inmates of the Convent in ignorance of the murder of children. On the contrary, others were told, as well as myself, on their first admission as veiled nuns, that all infants born in the place were baptized and killed, without loss of time; and I had been called to witness the murder of the three just mentioned, only because I happened to be in the room at the time.

---

[6]Earlier in her account, Maria Monk is sent to the convent's cellar for coal, where she discovers several cells holding nuns held prisoner and "a hole dug so deep into the earth that I could perceive no bottom . . . and unprotected by any kind of curb, so that one might easily have walked into it, in the dark."

That others were killed in the same manner during my stay in the nunnery, I am well assured.

How many there were I cannot tell, and having taken no account of those I heard of, I cannot speak with precision; I believe, however, that I learnt through nuns, that at least eighteen or twenty infants were smothered, and secretly buried in the cellar, while I was a nun.

One of the effects of the weariness of our bodies and minds, was our proneness to talk in our sleep. It was both ludicrous and painful to hear the nuns repeat their prayers in the course of the night, as they frequently did in their dreams. Required to keep our minds continually on the stretch, both in watching our conduct, in remembering the rules and our prayers, under the fear of the consequences of any neglect, when we closed our eyes in sleep, we often went over again the scenes of the day; and it was no uncommon thing for me to hear a nun repeat one or two of our long exercises in the dead of night. Sometimes, by the time she had finished, another, in a different part of the room, would happen to take a similar turn, and commence a similar recitation; and I have known cases in which several such unconscious exercises were performed, all within an hour or two.

We had now and then a recreation-day, when we were relieved from our customary labour, and from all prayers except those for morning and evening, and the short ones said at every striking of the clock. The greater part of our time was then occupied with different games, particularly backgammon and drafts, and in such conversation as did not relate to our past lives, and the outside of the Convent. Sometimes, however, our sports would be interrupted on such days by the entrance of one of the priests, who would come in and propose that his fête, the birthday of his patron saint, should be kept by "the saints." We saints!

Several nuns died at different times while I was in the Convent; how many I cannot say, but there was a considerable number: I might rather say, many in proportion to the number in the nunnery. The proportion of deaths I am sure was very large. There were always some in the nuns' sick-rooms, and several interments took place in the chapel.

When a Black nun is dead, the corpse is dressed as if living, and placed in the chapel in a sitting posture, within the railing round the altar, with a book in the hand, as if reading. Persons are then freely admitted from the street, and some of them kneel and pray before it. No particular notoriety is given, I believe, to this exhibition out of the Convent; but such a case usually excites some attention.

The living nuns are required to say prayers for the delivery of their deceased sister from purgatory, being informed, as in all other such cases that if she is not there, and has no need of our intercession, our prayers are in no danger of being thrown away, as they will be set down to the account of some of our departed friends, or at least to that of the souls which have no acquaintances to pray for them.

It was customary for us occasionally to kneel before a dead nun thus seated in the chapel, and I have often performed that task. It was always painful, for the ghastly countenance being seen whenever I raised my eyes, and the feeling that the position and dress were entirely opposed to every idea of propriety in such a case, always made me melancholy.

The Superior sometimes left the Convent, and was absent for an hour, or several hours, at a time, but we never knew of it until she had returned, and were not informed where she had been. I one day had reason to presume that she had recently paid a visit to the priests' farm, though I had not direct evidence that such was the fact. The priests' farm is a fine tract of land belonging to the Seminary, a little distance from the city, near the Lachine road with a large old-fashioned edifice upon it. I happened to be in the Superior's room on the day alluded to, when she made some remark on the plainness and poverty of her furniture. I replied, that she was not proud, and could not be dissatisfied on that account; she answered—

"No; but if I was, how much superior is the furniture at the priests' farm! the poorest room there is furnished better than the best of mine."

I was one day mending the fire in the Superior's room, when a priest was conversing with her on the scarcity of money; and I heard him say, that very little money was received by the priests for prayers, but that the principal part came with penances and absolutions.

One of the most remarkable and unaccountable things that happened in the Convent, was the disappearance of the old Superior. She had performed her customary part during the day, and had acted and appeared just as usual. She had shown no symptoms of ill health, met with no particular difficulty in conducting business, and no agitation, anxiety, or gloom, had been noticed in her conduct. We had no reason to suppose that during that day she had expected any thing particular to occur, any more than the rest of us. After the close of our customary labours and evening lecture, she dismissed us to retire to bed, exactly in her usual manner. The next morning the bell rang, we sprang from our bed, hurried on our clothes as usual, and proceeded to the community-room in double line, to commence the morning exercises. There, to our surprise, we found Bishop Lartigue; but the Superior was nowhere to be seen. The Bishop soon addressed us, instead of her, and informed us, that a lady near him, whom he presented to us, was now the Superior of the Convent, and enjoined upon us the same respect and obedience which we had paid to her predecessor.

The lady he introduced to us was one of our oldest nuns, Saint Du ****, a very large, fleshy woman, with swelled limbs, which rendered her very slow in walking, and often gave her great distress. Not a word was dropped from which we could conjecture the cause of this change, nor of the fate of the old Superior. I took the first opportunity to inquire of one of the nuns, whom I dared talk to, what had become of her; but I found them as ignorant as myself, though suspicious that she had been murdered by the orders of the Bishop. Never did I obtain any light on her mysterious disappearance. I am confident, however, that if the Bishop wished to get rid of her privately and by foul means, he had ample opportunities and power at his command. Jane Ray, as usual, could not allow such an occurrence to pass by without intimating her own suspicions more plainly than any other of the nuns would have dared to do. She spoke out one day, in the community-room, and said, "I'm going to have a hunt in the cellar for my old Superior."

"Hush, Jane Ray!" exclaimed some of the nuns, "you'll be punished."

"My mother used to tell me," replied Jane, "never to be afraid of the face of man."

It cannot be thought strange that we were superstitious. Some were more easily terrified than others, by unaccountable sights and sounds: but all of us believed in the power and occasional appearance of spirits, and were ready to look for them at almost any time. I have seen several instances of alarm caused by such superstition, and have experienced it myself more than once. I was one day sitting mending aprons, beside one of the old nuns, in a community-room, while the litanies were repeating; as I was very easy to laugh, Saint Ignace, or Agnes, came in, walked up to her with much agitation, and began to whisper in her ear. She usually talked but little, and that made me more curious to know what was the matter with her. I overheard her say to the old nun, in much alarm, that in the cellar, from which she had just returned, she had heard the most dreadful groans that ever came from any being. This was enough to give me uneasiness. I could not account for the appearance of an evil spirit in any part of the Convent, for I had been assured that the only one ever known there, was that of the nun who had died with an unconfessed sin, and that others were kept at a distance by the holy water that was rather profusely used in different parts of the nunnery. Still, I presumed that the sounds heard by Saint Ignace must have proceeded from some devil, and I felt great dread at the thought of visiting the cellar again. I determined to seek further information of the terrified nun; but when I addressed her on the subject, at recreation-time, the first opportunity I could find, she replied, that I was always trying to make her break silence, and walked off to another group in the room, so that I could obtain no satisfaction.

It is remarkable that in our nunnery, we were almost entirely cut off from the means of knowing any thing, even of each other. There were many nuns whom I know nothing of to this day, after having been in the same rooms with them every day and night for many months. There was a nun, whom I supposed to be in the Convent, and whom I was anxious to learn something about from the time of my entrance as a novice; but I never was able to learn any thing concerning her, not even whether she was in the nunnery or not, whether alive or dead. She was the daughter of a rich family, residing at Point aux Trembles, of whom I had heard my mother speak before I entered the Convent. The name of her family I think was Lafayette, and she was thought to be from Europe. She was known to have taken the black veil; but as I was not acquainted with the name of the Saint she had assumed, and I could not describe her in "the world," all my inquiries and observations proved entirely in vain.

I had heard before my entrance into the Convent, that one of the nuns had made her escape from it during the last war, and once inquired about her of the Superior. She admitted that such was the fact; but I was never able to learn any particulars concerning her name, origin, or manner of escape.

CHAPTER XIX

❧ The Priests of the District

The Priests of the District of Montreal have free access to the Black Nunnery—Crimes committed and required by them—The Pope's Command to commit indecent Crimes— Characters of the Old and New Superiors—The timidity of the latter—I began to be employed in the Hospitals—Some account of them—Warning given me by a sick Nun—Penance by Hanging.

I have mentioned before, that the country, as far down as Three Rivers, is furnished with priests by the Seminary of Montreal; and that these hundred and fifty men are liable to be occasionally transferred from one station to another. Numbers of them are often to be seen in the streets of Montreal, as they may find a home in the Seminary.

They are considered as having an equal right to enter the Black Nunnery whenever they please; and then, according to our oaths, they have complete control over the nuns. To name all the works of shame of which they are guilty in that retreat, would require much time and space, neither would it be necessary to the accomplishment of my object, which is, the publication of but some of their criminality to the world, and the development, in general terms, of scenes thus far carried on in secret within the walls of that Convent, where I was so long an inmate.

Secure against detection by the world, they never believed that an eyewitness would ever escape to tell of their crimes, and declare some of their names before the world; but the time has come, and some of their deeds of darkness must come to the day. I have seen in the nunnery, the priests from more, I presume, than a hundred country places, admitted for shameful and criminal purposes: from St. Charles, St. Denis, St. Mark's, St. Antoine, Chambly, Bertier, St. John's, &c. &c.

How unexpected to them will be the disclosures I make! Shut up in a place from which there has been thought to be but one way of egress, and that the passage to the grave, they considered themselves safe in perpetrating crimes in our presence, and in making us share in their criminality as often as they chose, and conducted more shamelessly than even the brutes. These debauchees would come in without ceremony, concealing their names, both by night and by day, where the cries and pains of the injured innocence of their victims could never reach the world, for relief or redress for their wrongs; without remorse or shame, they would glory in torturing, in the most barbarous manner, the feelings of those under their power; telling us, at the same time, that this mortifying the flesh was religion, and pleasing to God.

We were sometimes invited to put ourselves to voluntary sufferings in a variety of ways, not for a penance, but to show our devotion to God. A priest would sometimes say to us—

"Now, which of you have love enough for Jesus Christ to stick a pin through your checks?"

Some of us would signify our readiness, and immediately thrust one through up to the head. Sometimes he would propose that we should repeat the operation several times on the spot; and the cheeks of a number of nuns would be bloody.

There were other acts occasionally proposed and consented to, which I cannot name in a book. Such the Superior would sometimes command us to perform; many of them things not only useless and unheard of, but loathsome and indecent in the highest possible degree. How they could ever have been invented I never could conceive. Things were done worse than the entire exposure of the person, though this was occasionally required of several at once, in the presence of priests.

The Superior of the Seminary would sometimes come and inform us, that he had received orders from the Pope, to request that those nuns who possessed the greatest devotion and faith, should be requested to perform some particular deeds, which he named or described in our presence, but of which no decent or moral person could ever endure to speak. I cannot repeat what would injure any ear, not debased to the lowest possible degree. I am bound by a regard to truth, however, to confess, that deluded women were found among us, who would comply with those requests.

There was a great difference between the characters of our old and new Superior, which soon became obvious. The former used to say she liked to walk, because it would prevent her from becoming corpulent. She was, therefore, very active, and constantly going about from one part of the nunnery to another, overseeing us at our various employments. I never saw in her any appearance of timidity: she seemed, on the contrary, bold and masculine, and sometimes much more than that, cruel and cold-blooded, in scenes calculated to overcome any common person. Such a character she had particularly exhibited at the murder of Saint Francis.[7]

The new Superior, on the other hand, was so heavy and lame, that she walked with much difficulty, and consequently exercised a less vigilant oversight of the nuns. She was also of a timid disposition, or else had been overcome by some great fright in her past life; for she was apt to become alarmed in the night, and never liked to be alone in the dark. She had long performed the part of an old nun, which is that of a spy upon the younger ones, and was well known to us in that character, under the name of Ste. Margarite. Soon after her promotion to the station of Superior, she appointed me to sleep in her apartment, and assigned me a sofa to lie upon. One night, while I was asleep, she suddenly threw herself upon me, and exclaimed in great alarm, "Oh! mon Dieu! mon Dieu! Qu'est que ça?" Oh, my God! my God! What is that? I jumped up and looked about the room, but saw nothing, and endeavoured to convince her that there was nothing extraordinary there. But she insisted that a ghost had come and held her bed-curtain, so that she could not draw it. I examined it, and found that the curtain had been caught by a pin in the valance, which had held it back; but it was impossible to tranquillize her for some time. She insisted on my sleeping with her the rest of the night, and I stretched myself across the foot of her bed, and slept there till morning.

During the last part of my stay in the Convent, I was often employed in attending in the hospitals. There are, as I have before mentioned, several apartments devoted to the sick, and there is a physician of Montreal, who attends as physician to the Convent. It must not be supposed, however, that he knows any thing concerning the private hospitals. It is a fact of great importance to be distinctly understood, and constantly borne in mind, that he is never, under any circumstances, admitted into the private hospital-rooms. Of those he sees nothing more than any stranger whatever. He is limited to the care of those patients who are admitted from the city into the public hospital, and one of the nuns' hospitals, and these he visits every day. Sick poor are received for charity by the institution, attended by some of the nuns, and often go away with the highest ideas of their charitable characters and holy lives. The physician himself might perhaps in some cases share in the delusion.

I frequently followed Dr. Nelson through the public hospital, at the direction of the Superior, with pen, ink, and paper in my hands, and wrote down the prescriptions which he ordered for the different patients. These were afterward prepared and administered by the attendants. About a year before I left the Convent, I was first appointed to attend the private sick-rooms, and was frequently employed in that duty up to the day of my depar-

---

[7]Earlier in the narrative, Maria tells of the convent trial of Saint Francis, in which the bishop and four other priests condemn her to death because she would not kill infants, obey orders from superiors to do immoral acts, and wished to escape the convent.

ture. Of course, I had opportunities to observe the number and classes of patients treated there; and in what I am to say on the subject, I appeal with perfect confidence to any true and competent witness to confirm my words, whenever such a witness may appear.

It would be vain for anybody who has merely visited the Convent from curiosity, or resided in it as a novice, to question my declarations. Such a person must necessarily be ignorant of even the existence of the private rooms, unless informed by some one else. Such rooms, however, there are, and I could relate many things which have passed there during the hours I was employed in them, as I have stated.

One night I was called to sit up with an old nun, named Saint Clare, who, in going down-stairs, had dislocated a limb, and lay in a sick-room adjoining an hospital. She seemed to be a little out of her head a part of the time, but appeared to be quite in possession of her reason most of the night. It was easy to pretend that she was delirious, but I considered her as speaking the truth, though I felt reluctant to repeat what I heard her say, and excused myself from mentioning it even at confession, on the ground that the Superior thought her deranged.

What led her to some of the most remarkable parts of her conversation, was a motion I made, in the course of the night, to take the light out of her little room into the adjoining apartment, to look once more at the sick persons there. She begged me not to leave her a moment in the dark, for she could not bear it. "I have witnessed so many horrid scenes," said she, "in this Convent, that I want somebody near me constantly, and must always have a light burning in my room. I cannot tell you," she added, "what things I remember, for they would frighten you too much. What you have seen are nothing to them. Many a murder have I witnessed; many a nice young creature has been killed in this nunnery. I advise you to be very cautious—keep every thing to yourself—there are many here ready to betray you."

What it was that induced the old nun to express so much kindness to me I could not tell, unless she was frightened at the recollection of her own crimes, and those of others, and felt grateful for the care I took of her. She had been one of the night-watches, and never before showed me any particular kindness. She did not indeed go into detail concerning the transactions to which she alluded, but told me that some nuns had been murdered under great aggravations of cruelty, by being gagged, and left to starve in the cells, or having their flesh burnt off their bones with red-hot irons.

It was uncommon to find compunction expressed by any of the nuns. Habit renders us insensible to the sufferings of others, and careless about our own sins. I had become so hardened myself, that I find it difficult to rid myself of many of my former false principles and views of right and wrong.

I was one day set to wash some of the empty bottles from the cellar, which had contained the liquid that was poured into the cemetery there. A number of these had been brought from the corner where so many of them were always to be seen, and placed at the head of the cellar stairs, and there we were required to take them and wash them out. We poured in water and rinsed them; a few drops, which got upon our clothes, soon made holes in them. I think the liquid was called vitriol, or some such name; and I heard some persons say, that it would soon destroy the flesh, and even the bones of the dead. At another time, we were furnished with a little of the liquid, which was mixed with a quantity of water, and used in dying some cloth black, which was wanted at funerals in the chapels. Our hands were turned very black by being dipped in it, but a few drops of some other liquid were mixed with fresh water and given us to wash in, which left our skin of a bright red.

The bottles of which I spoke were made of very thick, dark coloured glass, large at the bottom, and from recollection, I should say held something less than a gallon.

I was once much shocked, on entering the room for the examination of conscience, at seeing a nun hanging by a cord from a ring in the ceiling, with her head downward. Her clothes had been tied round with a leathern strap, to keep them in their place, and then she had been fastened in that situation, with her head some distance from the floor. Her face had a very unpleasant appearance, being dark-coloured and swollen by the rushing in of the blood; her hands were tied, and her mouth stopped with a large gag. This nun proved to be no other than Jane Ray, who for some fault had been condemned to this punishment.

This was not, however, a solitary case; I heard of numbers who were "hung," as it was called, at different times; and I saw Saint Hypolite and Saint Luke undergoing it. This was considered a most distressing punishment; and it was the only one which Jane Ray could not endure, of all she had tried.

Some of the nuns would allude to it in her presence, but it usually made her angry. It was probably practised in the same place while I was a novice; but I never heard or thought of such a thing in those days. Whenever we wished to enter the room for the examination of conscience, we had to ask leave; and after some delay were permitted to go, but always under a strict charge to bend the head forward, and keep the eyes fixed upon the floor.

CHAPTER XX

❧ More Visits

More visits to the imprisoned Nuns—Their fears—Others temporarily put into the Cells—Reliques—The Agnus Dei—The Priests' private Hospital, or Holy Retreat—Secret Rooms in the Eastern Wing—Reports of Murders in the Convent—The Superior's private Records—Number of Nuns in the Convent—Desire of Escape—Urgent reason for it—Plan—Deliberation—Attempt—Success.

I often seized an opportunity, when I safely could, to speak a cheering or friendly word to one of the poor prisoners, in passing their cells, on my errands in the cellars. For a time I supposed them to be sisters; but I afterward discovered that this was not the case. I found that they were always under the fear of suffering some punishment, in case they should be found talking with a person not commissioned to attend them. They would often ask, "Is not somebody coming?"

I could easily believe what I heard affirmed by others, that fear was the severest of their sufferings. Confined in the dark, in so gloomy a place, with the long and spacious arched cellar stretching off this way and that, visited only now and then by a solitary nun, with whom they were afraid to speak their feelings, and with only the miserable society of each other; how gloomy thus to spend day after day, months, and even years, without any prospect of liberation, and liable every moment to any other fate to which the Bishop or Superior might condemn them! But these poor creatures must have known something of the horrors perpetrated in other parts of the building, and could not have been ignorant of the hole in the cellar, which was not far from their cells, and the use to which it was devoted. One of them told me, in confidence, she wished they could get out. They must also have been often disturbed in their sleep, if they ever did sleep, by the numerous priests who passed through the trapdoor at no great distance. To be subject to such trials for a single day would be dreadful; but these nuns had them to endure for years.

I often felt much compassion for them, and wished to see them released; but at other times, yielding to the doctrine perpetually taught us in the Convent, that our future happiness would be proportioned to the sufferings we had to undergo in this world, I would rest satisfied that their imprisonment was a real blessing to them. Others, I presume, participated with me in such feelings. One Sunday afternoon, after we had performed all our ceremonies, and were engaged as usual, at that time, with backgammon and other amusements, one of the young nuns exclaimed, "Oh, how headstrong are those wretches in the cells—they are as bad as the day they were first put in!"

This exclamation was made, as I supposed, in consequence of some recent conversation with them, as I knew her to be particularly acquainted with the older one.

Some of the vacant cells were occasionally used for temporary imprisonment. Three nuns were confined in them, to my knowledge, for disobedience to the Superior, as she called it. They did not join the rest in singing in the evening, being exhausted by the various exertions of the day. The Superior ordered them to sing, and as they did not comply, after her command had been twice repeated, she ordered them away to the cells.

They were immediately taken down into the cellar, placed in separate dungeons, and the doors shut and barred upon them. There they remained through that night, the following day, and second night, but were released in time to attend mass on the second morning.

The Superior used occasionally to show something in a glass box, which we were required to regard with the highest degree of reverence. It was made of wax, and called an Agnus Dei.[8] She used to exhibit it to us when we were in a state of grace: that is, after confession and before sacrament. She said it had been blessed *in the very dish in which our Saviour had eaten.* It was brought from Rome. Every time we kissed it, or even looked at it, we were told it gave a hundred days release from purgatory to ourselves, or if we did not need it, to our next of kin in purgatory, if not a Protestant. If we had no such kinsman, the benefit was to go to the souls in purgatory not prayed for.

Jane Ray would sometimes say to me, "Let's kiss it—some of our friends will thank us for it."

I have been repeatedly employed in carrying dainties of different kinds to the little private room I have mentioned, next beyond the Superior's sitting-room, in the second story, which the priests made their *"Holy Retreat."* That room I never was allowed to enter. I could only go to the door with a waiter of refreshments, set it down upon a little

---

[8] A cake of wax, blessed by the pope, stamped with a figure of a lamb bearing a cross and flag.

stand near it, give three raps on the door, and then retire to a distance to await orders. When any thing was to be taken away, it was placed on the stand by the Superior, who then gave three raps for me, and closed the door.

The Bishop I saw at least once when he appeared worse for wine, or something of the kind. After partaking of refreshments in the Convent, he sent for all the nuns, and, on our appearance, gave us his blessing, and put a piece of poundcake on the shoulder of each of us, in a manner which appeared singular and foolish.

There are three rooms in the Black Nunnery which I never entered. I had enjoyed much liberty, and had seen, as I supposed, all parts of the building, when one day I observed an old nun go to a corner of an apartment near the northern end of the western wing, push the end of her scissors into a crack in the panelled wall, and pull out a door. I was much surprised, because I never had conjectured that any door was there; and it appeared, when I afterward examined the place, that no indication of it could be discovered on the closest scrutiny. I stepped forward to see what was within, and saw three rooms opening into each other; but the nun refused to admit me within the door, which she said led to rooms kept as depositories.

She herself entered and closed the door, so that I could not satisfy my curiosity; and no occasion presented itself. I always had a strong desire to know the use of these apartments: for I am sure they must have been designed for some purpose of which I was intentionally kept ignorant, otherwise they would never have remained unknown to me so long. Besides, the old nun evidently had some strong reasons for denying me admission, though she endeavoured to quiet my curiosity.

The Superior, after my admission into the Convent, had told me that I had access to every room in the building; and I had seen places which bore witness to the cruelties and the crimes committed under her commands or sanction; but here was a succession of rooms which had been concealed from me, and so constructed as if designed to be unknown to all but a few. I am sure that any person, who might be able to examine the wall in that place, would pronounce that secret door a surprising piece of work. I never saw any thing of the kind which appeared to me so ingenious and skilfully made. I told Jane Ray what I had seen, and she said, at once, "We will get in and see what is there," But I suppose she never found an opportunity.

I naturally felt a good deal of curiosity to learn whether such scenes, as I had witnessed in the death of Saint Francis, were common or rare, and took an opportunity to inquire of Jane Ray. Her reply was—

"Oh, yes; and there were many murdered while you was a novice, whom you heard nothing about."

This was all I ever learnt on the subject; but although I was told nothing of the manner in which they were killed, I supposed it to be the same which I had seen practised, viz. by smothering.

I went into the Superior's parlour one day for something, and found Jane Ray there alone, looking into a book with an appearance of interest. I asked her what it was, but she made some trifling answer, and laid it by, as if unwilling to let me take it. There are two bookcases in the room; one on the right as you enter the door, and the other opposite, near the window and the sofa. The former contains the lecture-books and other printed volumes, the latter seemed to be filled with note and account books. I have often seen the keys in the bookcases while I have been dusting the furniture, and sometimes observed letters stuck up in the room; although I never looked into one, or thought of doing so, as we were under strict orders not to touch any of them, and the idea of sins and penances was always present with me.

Some time after the occasion mentioned, I was sent into the Superior's room, with Jane, to arrange it; and as the same book was lying out of the case, she said, "Come, let us look into it." I immediately consented, and we opened it, and turned over several leaves. It was about a foot and a half long, as nearly as I can remember, a foot wide, and about two inches thick, though I cannot speak with particular precision, as Jane frightened me almost as soon as I touched it, by exclaiming. "There, you have looked into it, and if you tell of me, I will of you."

The thought of being subjected to a severe penance, which I had reason to apprehend, fluttered me very much; and although I tried to overcome my fears, I did not succeed very well. I reflected, however, that the sin was already committed, and that it would not be increased if I examined the book. I, therefore, looked a little at several pages, though I still felt a good deal of agitation. I saw, at once, that the volume was a record of the entrance of nuns and novices into the Convent, and of the births that had taken place in the Convent. Entries of the last description were made in a brief manner, on the following plan: I do not give the names or dates as real, but only to show the form of entering them.

Saint Mary delivered of a son, March 16, 1834.

Saint Clarice delivered of a daughter, April 2, 1834.

Saint Matilda delivered of a daughter, April 30, 1834.

No mention was made in the book of the death of the children, though I well knew not one of them could be living at that time.

Now I presume that the period the book embraced, was about two years, as several names near the beginning I knew, but I can form only a rough conjecture of the number of infants born, and murdered of course, records of which it contained. I suppose the book contained at least one hundred pages, that one fourth were written upon, and that each page contained fifteen distinct records. Several pages were devoted to the list of births. On this supposition there must have been a large number, which I can easily believe to have been born there in the course of two years.

What were the contents of the other books belonging to the same case with that which I looked into, I have no idea having never dared to touch one of them; I believe, however, that Jane Ray was well acquainted with them, knowing, as I do, her intelligence and prying disposition. If she could be brought to give her testimony, she would doubtless unfold many curious particulars now unknown.

I am able, in consequence of a circumstances which appeared accidental, to state with confidence the exact number of persons in the Convent one day of the week in which I left it. This may be a point of some interest, as several secret deaths had occurred since my taking the veil, and many burials had been openly made in the chapel.

I was appointed, at the time mentioned, to lay out the covers for all the inmates of the Convent, including the nuns in the cells. These covers, as I have said before, were linen bands, to be bound around the knives, forks, spoons, and napkins, for eating. These were for all the nuns and novices, and amounted to two hundred and ten. As the number of novices was then about thirty, I know that there must have been at that time about one hundred and eighty veiled nuns.

I was occasionally troubled with a desire of escaping from the nunnery, and was much distressed whenever I felt so evil an imagination rise in my mind. I believed that it was a sin, a great sin, and did not fail to confess at every opportunity, that I felt discontent. My confessors informed me that I was beset by an evil spirit, and urged me to pray against it. Still, however, every now and then, I would think, "Oh, if I could get out!"

At length one of the priests, to whom I had confessed this sin, informed me, for my comfort, that he had begun to pray to Saint Anthony, and hoped his intercession would, by-and-by, drive away the evil spirit. My desire of escape was partly excited by the fear of bringing an infant to the murderous hands of my companions, or of taking a potion whose violent effects I too well knew.

One evening, however, I found myself more filled with the desire of escape than ever; and what exertions I made to dismiss the thought, proved entirely unavailing. During evening prayers, I became quite occupied with it; and when the time for meditation arrived, instead of falling into a doze as I often did, although I was a good deal fatigued, I found no difficulty in keeping awake. When this exercise was over, and the other nuns were about to retire to the sleeping room, my station being in the private sick-room for the night, I withdrew to my post, which was the little sitting-room adjoining it.

Here, then, I threw myself upon the sofa, and, being alone, reflected a few moments on the manner of escaping which had occurred to me. The physician had arrived a little before, at half-past eight; and I had now to accompany him, as usual, from bed to bed, with pen, ink, and paper, to write down his prescriptions for the direction of the old nun, who was to see them administered. What I wrote that evening, I cannot now recollect, as my mind was uncommonly agitated; but my customary way was to note down briefly his orders in this manner:

1 d salts, St. Matilde.

1 blister, St. Genevieve, &c. &c.

I remember that I wrote three such orders that evening, and then, having finished the rounds, I returned for a few minutes to the sitting-room.

There were two ways of access to the street from those rooms: first, the more direct, from the passage adjoining the sick-room, down-stairs, through a door, into the nunnery-yard, and through a wicket-gate; that is the way by which the physician usually enters at night, and he is provided with a key for that purpose.

It would have been unsafe, however, for me to pass out that way, because a man is kept continually in the yard, near the gate, who sleeps at night in a small hut near the door, to escape whose observation would be impossible. My only hope, therefore, was, that I might gain my passage through the other way, to do which I must pass through the sick-room, then through a passage, or small room, usually occupied by an old nun; another passage and staircase leading down to the yard, and a large gate opening into the cross street. I had no liberty ever to go beyond the sick-room, and knew that several of the doors might be fastened. Still, I determined to try; although I have often since been astonished at my boldness in undertaking what would expose me to so many hazards of failure, and to severe punishment if found out.

It seemed as if I acted under some extraordinary impulse, which encouraged me to do what I should hardly at any other moment have thought of undertaking. I had set but a short time upon the sofa, however, before I rose, with a desperate determination to make the experiment. I therefore walked hastily across the sick-room, passed into the nun's room, walked by her in a great hurry, and almost without giving her time to speak or think, said,—"A message!" and in an instant was through the door, and in the next passage. I think there was another nun with her at the moment; and it is probable that my hurried manner, and prompt intimation that I was sent on a pressing mission to the Superior, prevented them from entertaining any suspicion of my intention. Besides, I had the written orders of the physician in my hand, which may have tended to mislead them; and it was well known to some of the nuns, that I had twice left the Convent and returned from choice; so that I was probably more likely to be trusted to remain than many of the others.

The passage which I had now reached had several doors, with all which I was acquainted; that on the opposite side opened into a community-room, where I should probably have found some of the old nuns at that hour, and they would certainly have stopped me. On the left, however, was a large door, both locked and barred; but I gave the door a sudden swing, that it might creak as little as possible, being of iron. Down the stairs I hurried, and making my way through the door into the yard, stepped across it, unbarred the great gate, and was at liberty!

5

Robert Montgomery Bird

(1806–1854)

ROBERT MONTGOMERY BIRD'S early training was in medicine, having received a degree from the University of Pennsylvania in 1827. After a single year, he gave up his medical practice and began an incredibly prolific writing career, which spanned the genres of poetry, drama, novel writing, essays, and short stories. His plays met with great success, but by the 1830s he was principally writing novels, the most famous of which was the frontier tale *Nick of the Woods* (1837).

In 1833, Bird accompanied the famous actor Edwin Forrest throughout the South. During their trip, he kept a diary of the economic and social features of the region, reflections that would appear in his later writings. One such writing was *Sheppard Lee,* perhaps his most exotic and complex novel. Supposedly an autobiography of a man named *Sheppard Lee,* the book was published anonymously by Harper and Brothers in 1836. In the story, Sheppard Lee apparently dies and goes on to inhabit the bodies of five other men. In the end, we find out that he has simply been hallucinating, but the various transmigrations of his soul allow Bird to write a revealing, often comically satiric, commentary on a wide variety of American antebellum beliefs and behaviors, from the Puritan work ethic to politics to slavery.

In *Sheppard Lee,* Bird offers his most extended psychological treatment of human motivation. It is centered on the power and persistence of the individual will and how tangible facets of nature such as the physical body influence the more intangible facets such as emotion and character. Here Bird distinguishes himself in a class with Charles Brockden Brown, Edgar Allan Poe, and Nathaniel Hawthorne as his own literary effort joins theirs in attempting to explore the complexities of individual responsibility in a world where natural and supernatural influences commingle to help direct human behavior.

SHEPPARD LEE

WRITTEN BY HIMSELF

"Let those shine now that never shone before,
And those that always shone now shine the more."
ADVERTISEMENT TO HUNT'S BLACKING

BOOK I

CONTAINING INSTRUCTIONS HOW TO SPEND
AND HOW TO RETRIEVE A FORTUNE

CHAPTER I

*The Author's Preface,—which the reader, if in a great hurry,
or if it be his practice to read against time, can skip.*

I have often debated in my mind whether I should give to the world, or for ever lock up
within the secrecy of my own breast, the history of the adventures which it has been my
lot in life to experience. The importance of any single individual in society, especially
one so isolated as myself, is so little, that it can scarcely be supposed that the community
at large can be affected by his fortunes, either good or evil, or interested in any way in
his fate. Yet it sometimes happens that circumstances conspire to elevate the humblest
person from obscurity, and to give the whole world an interest in his affairs; and that man
may safely consider himself of some value in his generation, whose history is of a character to instruct the ignorant and inexperienced. Such a man I consider myself to be; and
the more I reflect upon my past life, the more I am convinced it contains a lesson which
may be studied with profit; while, at the same time, if I am not greatly mistaken, the lesson will be found neither dry nor repulsive, but here and there, on the contrary, quite
diverting. The psychologist (I hate big words, but one cannot do without them) and the
metaphysician will discover in my relation some new subjects for reflection; and so perhaps will the doctor of medicine and the physiologist: but while I leave these learned
gentlemen to discuss what may appear most wonderful in my revealments, I am most
anxious that the common reader may weigh the value of what is, at least in appearance,
more natural, simple, and comprehensible.

It will be perceived that many of the following adventures are of a truly extraordinary character. There are some men—and to such my story will seem incredible
enough—who pride themselves on believing nothing that they do not know, and who
endeavour, very absurdly, to restrict the objects of belief to those that admit of personal

Robert Montgomery Bird, *Sheppard Lee*. New York: Harper & Brothers, 1836.

cognizance. There are others again who boast the same maxim, but have a more liberal understanding of the subjects of knowledge, and permit themselves to believe many things which are susceptible of satisfactory proof, but not of direct cognition. Now I must declare beforehand, in order to avoid all trouble, that, from the very nature of the life I have led, consisting of the strangest transitions and vicissitudes, it is impossible I should have laid up proofs to satisfy any one of the truth of my relation who is disposed to be incredulous. If any one should say, "I doubt," all the answer I could make would be, "Doubt, and be hanged,"—not, however, meaning any offence to anybody; though it is natural one should be displeased at having his veracity questioned. I write for the world at large, which is neither philosophic nor skeptical; and the world will believe me: otherwise it is a less sensible world than I have all along supposed it to be.

CHAPTER II

The birth and family of Sheppard Lee, with some account
of his temper and complexion of mind.

I was born somewhere towards the close of the last century,—but, the register-leaf having been torn from the family Bible, and no one remaining who can give me information on the point, I am not certain as to the exact year,—in the State of New-Jersey, in one of the oldest counties that border upon the Delaware river. My father was a farmer in very good circumstances, respectable in his degree, but perhaps more famous for the excellent sausages he used to manufacture for the Philadelphia market, than for any quality of mind or body that can distinguish one man from his fellows. Taking the hint from his success in this article of produce, he gradually converted his whole estate into a market-farm, raising fine fruits and vegetables, and such other articles as are most in demand in a city; in which enterprise he succeeded beyond his highest expectations, and bade fair to be, as in the end he became, a rich man. The only obstacle to a speedy accumulation of riches was a disproportionate increase in the agents of consumption,—his children multiplying on his hands almost as fast as his acres, until he could count eleven in all; a number that filled him at one time with consternation. He used to declare no apple could be expected to ripen on a farm where there were eleven children; and as for watermelons and sugar-corn, it was folly to think of raising them longer. But fate sent my father relief sooner and more effectually than he either expected or desired: nine of the eleven being removed by death in a space of time short of six years. Three (two of whom were twin sisters) were translated in the natural way, falling victims to an epidemic, and were buried in the same grave. A fourth was soon after killed by falling out of an apple-tree. My eldest brother, then a boy of fourteen years old, upon some freak, ran away from home (for he was of a wild, madcap turn), and, getting into an oyster-boat, made a voyage into the bay, where he was lost; for, having fallen overboard, and not being able to swim, a clumsy fellow, who thought to save him in that way, clutched him round the neck with a pair of oyster-tongs, and thereby strangled him. Two others were drowned in a millpond, where they were scraping for snapping-turtles. Another, who was the wag of the family, was killed by attempting to ride a pig, which, running in great alarm through a broken fence into the orchard, dashed his brains out against a white-oak rail; and the ninth died of a sort of hysterical affection, caused by this unlucky exploit of his brother; for he could not cease laughing at it, notwithstanding its melancholy termination, and he died of the fit within twenty-four hours.

Thus, in a few years, there remained but two of all the eleven children,—to wit, my oldest sister Prudence and myself. My mother (from whom I had my Christian name Sheppard, that being her maiden name) died several years before this last catastrophe, her mind having been affected, and indeed distracted, by so many mournful losses occurring in such rapid succession. She fell into a deep melancholy, and died insane.

Being one of the youngest children, I grieved but little for the loss of my brothers and sisters; nor was I able to appreciate the advantage which, in a worldly point of view, their death must prove to me. My father, however, perceived the difference; for, having now so few to look after and be chargeable to him, he could with great propriety consider himself a rich man. He immediately resolved, as I was now his only son, that I should have a good education; and it was not his fault if, in this particular, I fell short of his expectations. I was sent to good schools, and, in course of time, was removed to the college at Nassau Hall, in Princeton, where I remained during three years; that is, until my father's decease; when I yielded to the natural indolence of my temper, and left the college, or rather (for I had formed no resolution on the subject) procrastinated my return from day to day, until it was too late to return.

My natural disposition was placid and easy,—I believe I may say sluggish. I was not wanting in parts, but had as little energy or activity of mind as ever fell to the share of a Jerseyman; and how my father ever came to believe I should make a figure in the world, I cannot conceive, unless it was because he knew he had a fortune to leave me, and saw me safely lodged in a college. It is very certain he encouraged a strong belief that I should one day be a great man; and, I fancy, it was for this reason he showed himself so favourable to me in his will. He left me the bulk of his property, bestowing upon my sister, who had recently married, little beyond a farm which he had purchased in a neighbouring county, but which was a valuable one, and quite satisfied her husband.

But my father was a better judge of sausages than of human character. Besides being deficient, as I humbly confess, in all those qualities that are necessary to the formation of a great man, I had not the slightest desire to be one. Ambition was a passion that never afflicted my mind; and I was so indifferent to the game of greatness which was playing around me, that, I seriously declare, there was a President of the United States elected to office, and turned out again, after having served his regular term, without my knowing any thing about it. I had not even the desire, so common to young men who find themselves in possession of a fortune, to launch out into elegant expenses, to dash about the country with fine horses, servants, and clothes, and to play the spendthrift in cities. On the contrary, I no sooner found myself arrived at my majority, which was a few months after my father's death, than I sat down very quietly on the farm, resolved to take the world easily; which I supposed I might easily do. I had some idea of continuing to conduct the estate, as my father had done before me; but it was a very vague one; and having made one or two efforts to bear myself like a man of business, I soon found the effort was too tiresome for one of my disposition; and I accordingly hired an overseer to manage the property for me.

CHAPTER III

The pleasures of having nothing to do.—Some thoughts on Matrimony.

Having thus shuffled the cares of business from my shoulders to another's, my time began to weigh a little heavily on my hands, and I cast about for some amusement that might enable me to get rid of it. As there was great abundance of small game, such as quails, partridges, and rabbits, in the neighbourhood, I resolved to turn sportsman; and, in consequence, I bought me a dog and gun, and began to harry the country with some spirit. But having the misfortune to shoot my dog the first day, and, soon after, a very valuable imported cow, belonging to a neighbour, for which I was obliged to pay him enormous damages, and meeting besides with but little luck, I grew disgusted with the diversion. My last shot was soon fired; for, having forgotten the provisions of our game-laws, I killed a woodcock too early in the summer, for which, on the information of a fellow who owed me a grudge, I was prosecuted, although it was the only bird I ever killed in all my life, and soundly fined; and this incensed me so much, that I resolved to have nothing more to do with an amusement that cost so much money, and threw me into so many difficulties.

I was then at a loss how to pass my time, until a neighbour, who bred fine horses, persuaded me to buy a pair of blooded colts, and try my luck on the turf; and this employment, though rather too full of cares and troubles to suit me exactly, I followed with no little spirit, and became more proud of my horses than I can well express, until I came to try them on the race-course, where it was my luck, what with stakes and betting together, to lose more money in a single day, than my father had ever made in two years together. I then saw very clearly that horse-racing was nothing better than gambling, and therefore both disreputable and demoralizing; for which reason I instantly gave it up, heartily sick of the losses it had occasioned me.

My overseer, or steward,—for such he may be considered,—whom I always esteemed a very sensible fellow, for he was shrewd and energetic, and at least ten years my senior, then advised me, as I was a young man, with money enough, to travel a little, and see the world: and accordingly I went to New-York, where I was robbed of my luggage and money by a villain whose acquaintance I made in the steamboat, and whom I thought a highly intelligent, gentlemanly personage; though, as it afterward appeared, he was a professor from Sing-Sing,[1] where he had been sawing stone for two years, the governor of New-York having forgiven him, as is the custom, the five other years for which he was committed for, I believe, a fraud committed on his own father.

This loss drove me home again; but being reencouraged by my overseer, I filled my purse and set out a second time, passing up the Hudson river, with which I was prodigiously pleased, though not with the Overslaugh, where we stuck fast during six hours. I then proceeded to Saratoga, where I remained for two weeks, on account of its being fashionable; but, I declare to Heaven, I was never so tired of any place in my life. I then went to Niagara, which, in spite of the great noise it made, I thought the finest place in the world; and there, I think, I should have continued all summer, had it not been for the

---

[1] A famous New York prison.

crowds of tiresome people that were eternally coming and going, and the great labour of climbing up and down the stairs. However, I was so greatly pleased with what I saw, both at Niagara and along the way, that I should have repeated my travels in after years, as the most agreeable way of passing time, had it not been for the dangers and miseries of such enterprises; for, first, the coaches were perpetually falling over, or sticking in the mud, or jolting over stones, so that one had no security of life or limb; and, secondly, the accommodations at the inns along the road were not to my liking, the food being cooked after the primitive systems of Shem, Ham, and Japheth,[2] and the beds stuck together in the rooms as if for boys at a boarding-school. It is possible that these things are better ordered now; but, from what I have since seen and heard, I am of opinion there is a fine field for cooks, carpenters, and chamber-maids, in the agricultural regions of America. In those days I loved ease and comfort too well to submit to such evils as could be avoided; and, accordingly, after a little experience in the matter, I ceased travelling altogether, the pleasures bearing no sort of proportion to the discomforts.

My time still weighing upon my hands, I was possessed with a sudden idea (which my steward, however, endeavoured to combat), namely, that the tedium of my existence might be dispelled by matrimony; and I resolved to look around me for a wife. After much casting about, I fixed my eyes upon a young lady of the village (for I must inform the reader that my farm was on the skirts of a village, and a very respectable one too, although there were many lazy people in it), who, I thought, was well filled to make me comfortable; and as she did not seem averse to my first advances, I began to be quite particular, until all the old women in the country declared it was a match, and all the young fellows of my own age, as well as all the girls I knew, became extremely witty at my expense. These things, however, rather encouraged me than otherwise; I believed I was advancing my happiness by the change I contemplated in my condition; and I was just on the point of making formal proposals to the young lady, when an accident set me to considering the enterprise entirely in a new light.

My charmer lived in the house of a married sister, who had a large family of children,—a pack of the most ill-bred imps, I verily believe, that were ever gathered together in any one man's house; but, for politeness' sake, during the first weeks of my courtship, the young sinners were kept out of my way, and, what with cuffing and feeding with sugarplums, were preserved in some sort of order, so that I was not annoyed by them. After a while, however, and when matters had proceeded some length, it was thought unnecessary to treat me longer as a stranger; the children were suffered to take care of themselves; and the consequence was, that, in a short time, I found myself in a kind of Pandemonium[3] whenever I entered the house, with such a whining, and squeaking, and tumbling, and bawling, and fighting among the young ones, as greatly discomposed my nerves; and, to make the matter worse, the mother made no difficulty at times, when the squabbling grew to a height, of taking a switch to one, and boxing the ears of another, and scolding roundly at a third, to reduce them to order; and all this in my presence, and under the nose of my charmer.

---

[2]Noah's sons (Gen. 5–10).

[3]In Milton's *Paradise Lost,* Pandemonium is the name of Satan's palace in Hell.

I began to fancy the married life could not be altogether so agreeable as I had pictured it to my imagination; and in this belief I was confirmed by a visit to my sister, who had three children of her own, all of whom, as I now perceived (for I had not noticed it before, having no particular inducement to make me observant), were given to squabbling and bawling, just like other children, while my sister did her share of boxing and scolding. I thought to myself, "What should *I* do with a dozen children squeaking all day and night in my house, and a scolding wife dragooning them into submission?"

The thought disconcerted me, and the fear of such a consummation greatly chilled the ardour of my affection; so that the young lady, observing my backwardness, and taking offence at it, cast her eyes upon another wooer who had made her an offer, and, to my great satisfaction, married him on the spot.

I was never more relieved in my life, and I resolved to reflect longer upon the subject before making advances of that nature a second time. My overseer, who had from the first (for I made him my confidant) been opposed to the match, on the ground that I ought to enjoy my liberty, at least until I was thirty, was greatly rejoiced at the rupture, and swore that I had made a lucky escape; for he had always thought, in his own mind, that the lady was at bottom, though she concealed it from me, a Tartar[4] and fire-eater. In this, however, he was mistaken; for, from all I have heard of her since, she has proved a most amiable and sweet-tempered woman, and her husband is said to be very happy with her.

CHAPTER IV

How to conduct a farm to the best advantage, and steer clear of the lawyers.

It is not my intention to dwell longer upon the history of this period of my life, nor to recount in detail how my easy and indolent temper at last proved the ruin of me. I gave myself up to laziness, neglecting my affairs to such a degree that they soon became seriously entangled; and, to make a long story short, I found myself, before I had completed my twenty-eighth year, reduced from independence, and almost affluence, to a condition bordering upon actual poverty. My farm, under the management of Mr. Aikin Jones (for that was my steward's name), went gradually to ruin; my orchards rotted away, without being replanted; my meadows were converted into swamps; my corn-fields filled with gullies; my improvements fell into decay; and my receipts began to run short of my expenses. Then came borrowing and mortgaging, and, by-and-by, the sale of *this* piece of land to remove the encumbrance upon *that;* until I suddenly found myself in the condition of my father when he began the world; that is to say, the master of a little farm of forty acres,—the centre and nucleus of the fifteen hundred which he had got possession of and bequeathed to me, but which had so soon slipped through my fingers. There was this difference, however, between us; the land, when my father obtained it, was in good condition; it was now (so well had it prospered under Jones's hands) entirely worn out and empoverished, and not worth a fourth part of its original value.

---

[4]A person of violent temper.

To add to my chagrin, I discovered that Mr. Aikin Jones, whom I had treated rather as a friend than servant, had abused my confidence; in other words, that he was a rogue and villain, who had taken advantage of my disinclination to business, and my ignorance, as I believe I must call it, to swindle me out of my property, which he had the best opportunities to do. Whether he effected his purpose by employing my own funds or not, I cannot say; but, it is very certain, all the different mortgages in which I was entangled came, some how or other, by hook and by crook, into his hands and he took care to make the best use of them. In a word, Mr. Jones became a rich man, and I a poor one; and I had the satisfaction, every day when I took a walk over my forty-acre farm, as the place was familiarly called, though the true name was Watermelon Hill, to find myself stopped, which way soever I directed my steps, by the possessions of Mr. Aikin Jones, my old friend and overseer, whom I often saw roll by in his carriage, while I was trudging along through the mud.

At the same time that I met with this heavy misfortune, I had to endure others that were vexations enough. My brother-in-law and sister had their suspicions of Mr. Jones, and often cautioned me against him, though in vain,—not that I had any very superstitious reliance on the gentleman's integrity, but because I could not endure the trouble of examining into his proceedings and accounts, and chose therefore to believe him honest. This, and my general indolence and indifference to my affairs, incensed them both to that degree, that my sister did not scruple to tell me to my face that I had lost all the little sense I ever possessed; while my brother-in-law took the freedom of saying of me in public, "that I was wrong in the upper story,"—in other words, that I was mad; and he had the insolence to hint "that it ran in my blood,—that I had inherited it from my mother," she, as I mentioned before, having lost her mind before her decease. I was so much irritated by these insults on their part, that I quarrelled with them both, though by no means of a testy or choleric disposition; and it was many years before we were reconciled. Having therefore neither friends nor family, I was left to bear my misfortunes alone; which was a great aggravation of them all.

CHAPTER V

The Author finds himself in trouble.—Some account of his Servant, honest James Jumble.

I have always described myself as of an easy, contented disposition; and such I was born. But misfortune produces sad changes in our tempers, as it was soon my lot to experience. Before, however, I describe the change that took place in mine, it is fit I should let the reader understand to what condition I was reduced by the perfidy of Jones,—or, as I should rather say, by my own culpable neglect of my affairs.

My whole landed possessions consisted of a farm of forty acres, which I had, after the fashion of some of my richer neighbours in other states suffered to fall into the most wretched condition imaginable. My meadow-lands, being broken in upon by the river, and neglected, were converted into quagmires, reed-brakes, and cat-tail patches, the only use of which was to shelter wild-fowl and mire cattle. However, my live-stock was scanty enough, and the only sufferers were my neighbours, whose cows easily made their way through my fences, and stuck fast in the mud at their pleasure. My fields were overgrown here with mullein and St. John's-wort, and there with sand-burs and poke-berries. My orchards were in an equally miserable condition,—the trees being old, rotten, or worm-eaten, half of them torn down by the winds, and the remainder fit for nothing but firewood. My barn was almost roofless; and as for a stable, I had so little occasion for one, that my old negro-man Jim, of whom I shall have more to say hereafter, or his wife Dinah, or both together, thinking they could do nothing better with it, helped the winds to tear it to pieces, especially in the winter, when it formed a very convenient woodpile. My dwelling-house was also suffering from decay. It was originally a small frame building; but my father had added to it one portion after another, until it became spacious; and the large porches in front and on the rear, gave it quite a genteel, janty air. But this it could not long keep; the sun and rain gradually drove the white paint from the exterior, and the damps getting inside, the fine paper-hangings, pied and spotted, peeled from the walls. The window-frames rotted, and the glasses left them one after another; and one day in a storm one half the front porch tumbled down, and the remainder, which I propped up as well as I could, had a mighty mean and poverty-stricken appearance. The same high wind carried away one of my chimneys, which, falling on a corner of the roof, crushed that into the garret, and left one whole gable-end in ruins.

It must not be supposed that my property presented altogether this wretched appearance at the moment of my losses. It was in truth bad enough then; but I am now describing it as it appeared some few years after, when my miseries were accumulated in the greatest number, and I was just as poor as I could be.

In all this period of trouble and vexation I had but one friend, if I dare call him such; though I should have been glad half the time to be rid of him. This was my negro-man Jim, or Jim Jumble, as he was called, of whom I spoke before,—an old fellow that had been a slave of my father, and was left to me in his will. He was a crabbed, self-willed old fellow, whom I could never manage, but who would have all things his own way, in spite of me. As I had some scruples of conscience about holding a slave, and thought him of no value whatever, but, on the contrary, a great trouble, I resolved to set him free, and accordingly mentioned my design to him; when, to my surprise, he burst into a passion, swore he would *not* be free, and told me flatly I was his master, and I should take care of him; and the absurd old fool ended by declaring, if I made him a free man he would have the law of me, "he would, by ge-hosh!"

I never could well understand the cause of his extreme aversion to being made free; but I suppose, having got the upper hand of me, and being wise enough to perceive the difference between living, on the one hand, a lazy life, without any care whatever, as my slave, and, on the other, labouring hard to obtain a precarious subsistence as a free man, he was determined to stick by me to the last, whether I would or not. Some little affection for me, as I had grown up from a boy, as it were, under his own eye, was perhaps at the bottom of his resolution; but if there were, it was of a strange quality, as he did nothing but scold and grumble at me all day long. I remember, in particular, that, when the match I spoke of before was broken off, and he had heard of it, he came to me in a great passion, and insolently asked "what I meant by courting a wife, who would be a good mistress to him, and not marrying her?" and, on my condescending to explain the reasons of my change of mind, he told me plumply, "I had no more sense than a nigger; for women was women, and children children; and he was tired living so long in a house with none but me and Massa Jones for company."

I suppose it was old Jim's despair of my ever marrying, that put him upon taking a wife himself; for one day, not long after I was reduced to the forty-acre farm, he brought home a great ugly free negro-woman, named Dinah, whom he installed into the kitchen without the least ceremony, and without so much as even informing me of his intention. Having observed her two or three times, and seeing her at last come bouncing into the dinner-room to wait on me, I asked her who she was, and what she wanted; to which she answered, "she was Jim's wife, and Jim had sent her in to take care of me."

It was in this way the old rascal used me. It was in vain to complain; he gave me to understand in his own language, "He knew what was what, and there was no possuming an old nigger like him; and if I had made *him* overseer, instead of Massa Jones, it would have been all the better for me."

And, in truth, I believe it would; for Jim would never have cheated me, except on a small scale; and if he had done no work himself, it is very certain he would have made everybody else work; for he was a hard master when he had anybody under him.

I may here observe, and I will do the old fellow the justice to confess, that I found him exceedingly useful during all my difficulties. What labour was bestowed upon the farm, was bestowed almost altogether by him and his wife Dinah. It is true he did just what he liked, and without consulting me,—planting and harvesting, and even selling what he raised, as if he were the master and owner of all things, and laying out what money he obtained by the sales, just as his own wisdom prompted; and finding I could do nothing better, I even let him have his own way; and it was perhaps to my advantage that I did.

But I grew poorer and poorer, notwithstanding; and at that period, which I shall ever be inclined to consider as the true beginning of my eventful life, I was reduced almost to the point of despair; for my necessities had compelled me to mortgage the few miserable acres I had left, and I saw nothing but utter ruin staring me in the face.

CHAPTER VI

Sheppard Lee experiences his share of the respect that is accorded to "honest poverty."—His ingenious and highly original devices to amend his fortune.

It may be asked, why I made no efforts to retrieve my fortunes? I answer to that, that I made many, but was so infatuated that I never once thought of resorting to the most obvious, rational, and only means; that is to say, of cultivating with industry my forty acres, as my father had done before me. This idea, so sluggish was my mind, or so confused by its distresses, never once occurred to me; or if it did, it presented so many dreary images, and so long a prospect of dull and disagreeable labour, that I had not the spirit to pursue it. The little toil I was forced to endure—for my necessities now compelled me at times to work with my own hands—appeared to me intolerably irksome; and I was glad to attempt any thing else that seemed to promise me good luck, and did not require positive labour.

The first plan of bettering my fortune that I conceived, was to buy some chances in a lottery, which I thought an easy way of making money; as indeed it is, when a man can make any. I had my trouble for my pains, with just as many blanks as I had bought tickets; upon which I began to see clearly that adventuring in a lottery was nothing short of gambling, as it really is; and so I quitted it.

I then resolved to imitate the example of a neighbour, who had made a great sum of money by buying and selling to advantage stock in a southern gold-mining company; and being very sanguine of success, I devoted all the money I could scrape together to the purpose, and that so wisely, that a second instalment being suddenly demanded, I had nothing left to discharge it with, and no means of raising any; the consequence of which was, that I was forced to sell at the worst time in the world, and retired from the concern with just one fifth the sum I had invested in it. I saw then that I had no talent for speculating, and I began to have my doubts whether stock-jobbing was not just as clear gambling as horse-racing and lottery speculation.

I tried some ten or a dozen other projects with a view to better my condition, but as I came off with the same luck from all, I do not think it necessary to mention them. I will, however, state, as a proof how much my difficulties had changed my mind on that subject, that one of them was of a matrimonial character. My horror of squabbling children and scolding wives melted away before the prospect of sheriffs and executions; and there being a rich widow in the neighbourhood, I bought me a new coat, and made her a declaration. But it was too late in the day for me, as I soon discovered; for besides giving me a flat refusal, she made a point of revealing the matter to all her acquaintance, who did nothing but hold me up to ridicule.

I found that my affairs were falling into a desperate condition; and not knowing what else to do, I resolved to turn politician, with the hope of getting some office or other that might afford me a comfortable subsistence.

This was the maddest project that ever possessed my brain; but it was some time before I came to that conclusion. But, in truth, from having been the easiest and calmest tempered man in the world, I was now become the most restless and discontented, and incapable of judging what was wise and what foolish. I reflected one day, that of my old school and college mates who were still alive, there was not one who had not made some advance in the world, while I had done nothing but slip backwards. It was the same thing with dozens of people whom I remembered as poor farmers' boys, with none of the advantages I had possessed, but who had outstripped me in the road to fortune, some being now rich cultivators, some wealthy manufacturers and merchants, while two or three had got into the legislature, and were made much of in the newspapers. One of my old companions had emigrated to the Mississippi, where he was now a cotton-planter, with a yearly revenue of twenty or thirty thousand dollars; another had become a great lawyer in an adjacent state; and a third, whom I always thought a very shallow, ignorant fellow, and who was as poor as a rat to boot, had turned doctor, settled down in the village, and, besides getting a great practice, had married the richest and finest girl in all the county. There was no end to the number of my old acquaintances who had grown wealthy and distinguished; and the more I thought of them, the more discontented I became.

My dissatisfaction was increased by discovering with what little respect I was held among these happy people. The doctor used to treat me with a jocular sort of familiarity, which I felt to be insulting; the lawyer, who had eaten many a dinner at my table, when I was able to invite him, began to make me low bows, instead of shaking hands with me; and the cotton-planter, who had been my intimate friend at college, coming to the village on a visit to his relations, stared me fiercely in the face when I approached him, and with a lordly "hum—ha!" asked me "Who the devil I might be?" As for the others, they treated me with as little consideration; and I began to perceive very plainly that I had got into the criminal stage of poverty, for all men were resolved to punish me. It is no wonder that poverty is the father of crime, since the poor man sees himself treated on all hands as a culprit.

I had never before envied a man for enjoying more consideration in the world than myself: but the discovery that I was looked upon with contempt filled me with a new subject for discontent. I envied my richer neighbours not only for being rich, but for being what they considered themselves, my superiors in standing. I may truly say, I scarce ever saw, in those days, a man with a good coat on his back, without having a great desire to beat him. But as I was a peaceable man, my anger never betrayed me into violence.

CHAPTER VII

The Author becomes a Politician, and seeks for an office.—The result of that project.

My essay in politics was soon made. I spent a whole week in finding out who were the principal office-holders, candidates, and busybodies, both in the state and the general governments; and which were the principal parties; there being so many, that an honest man might easily make a mistake among them. Being satisfied on these points, I chose the strongest party, on the principle that the majority must always be right, and attended the first public meeting that was held, where I clapped my hands and applauded the speeches with so much spirit, that I was taken notice of and highly commended by several of the principal leaders. In truth, I pleased them so well, that they visited me at my house, and encouraged me to take a more prominent part in the business of politics; and this I did, for at the next meeting, I got up and made a speech; but what it was about I know no more than the man in the moon, otherwise I would inform the reader. My only recollection of it is, that there was great slashing at the banks and aristocrats that ground the faces of the poor; for I was on what our opponents called the hurrah side, and these were the things we talked about. I received uncommon applause; and, in fact, there was such a shouting and clapping of hands, that I was obliged to put an end to my discourse sooner than I intended.

But I found myself in great favour with the party, and being advised by the leaders, who considered I had a talent that way, to set about converting all I knew in the county who were not of our party, and they hinting that I should certainly, in case the county was gained (for our county happened to be a little doubtful at that time), be appointed to the postoffice in the village, I mounted my old horse Julius Cesar, and set out with greater zeal than I had ever shown in my life before. I visited everybody that I knew, and a great many that I did not know; and, wherever I went, I held arguments, and made speeches, with a degree of industry that surprised myself, for certainly I was never industrious before. It is certain, also, that there was never a labourer in the field of politics that better deserved his reward,—never a soldier of the party ranks that had won a better right to a share in the spoils of victory. I do not pretend to say, indeed, that I converted anybody to our belief; for all seemed to have made up their minds beforehand; and I never yet knew or heard of a man that could be argued out of his politics, who had once made up his mind on the subject. I laboured, however, and that with astonishing zeal; and as I paid my own expenses, and treated all thirsty souls that seemed approachable in that way to good liquor, I paid a good round sum, that I could ill spare, for the privilege of electioneering; and was therefore satisfied that my claim to office would hold good.

And so it did, as was universally allowed by all the party; but the conviction of its justice was all I ever gained in reward of my exertions. The battle was fought and won, the party was triumphant, and I was just rejoicing in the successful termination of my hopes, when they were blasted by the sudden appointment of another to the very office which I considered my own. That other was one of the aforesaid leaders, who had been foremost in commending my zeal and talents, and in assuring me that the office should be mine.

I was confounded, petrified, enraged; the duplicity and perfidy of my new friends filled me with indignation. It was evident they must all have joined in recommending my rival to the office; for he was a man of bad character, who must, without such recommendations, have missed his aim. All therefore had recommended him, and all had promised their suffrages to me! "The scoundrels!" said I to myself. I perceived that I had fallen among thieves; it was clear that no party could be in the right, which was led by such unprincipled men; there was corruption at the heart of the whole body; the party consisted of rogues who were gaping after the loaves and fishes; their honesty was a song—their patriotism a farce. In a word, I found I had joined the wrong party, and I resolved to go over to the other, sincerely repenting the delusion that had made me so long the advocate of wrong and deception.

But fortune willed otherwise. I had arrived at the crisis of my fate; and before I could put my purpose into execution, I was suddenly involved in that tissue of adventure, which, I have no doubt, will be considered the most remarkable that ever befell a human being.

CHAPTER VIII

A description of the Owl-roost, with Mr. Jumble's ideas in relation to Captain Kid's money.

For five mortal days I remained at home, chewing the bone of reflection; and a hard bone it was. On the sixth there came a villanous constable with a—the reader may suppose what. I struck a bargain with him, and he took his leave, and Julius Cesar also, saddle, bridle, and all; whereby I escaped an introduction to the nearest justice of the peace. The next visit, I had good reason to apprehend, would be from the sheriff; for, having failed to pay up the interest on the mortgage, the mortgagee had discoursed, and that in no very mysterious strain, on the virtues of a writ of *Venditioni Exponas,*[5] or some other absurd and scoundrelly invention of the lawyers. I was at my wits' end, and I wished that I was a dog; in which case I should have gone mad, and bitten the new postmaster and all his friends.

"Very well," said I to myself, "the forty-acre is no longer mine." I clapped on my hat, and walked into the open air, resolved to take a look at it before the sheriff came to convince me it belonged to some other person. As I passed from the door, I looked up to the broken porch: "May it fall on the head of my successor," I said.

It was a summer eve,—a day in July; but a raw wind blew from the northeast, and the air was as chill as in November. I buttoned my coat, and as I did so, took a peep at my elbows: I required no second look to convince me that I was a poor man.

The ruined meadows of which I have spoken, lie on a little creek that makes in from the Delaware. Their shape is the worst in the world, being that of a triangle, the longest leg of which lies on the water. Hence the expense of embanking them is formidable,—a circumstance for which the muskrats have no consideration. The apex of the angle is a bog, lying betwixt two low hillocks, or swells of ground, between which crawls a brook, scarce deep enough to swim a tadpole, though an ox may hide in the mud at the bottom. It oozes from a turfy ledge or bar, a few feet higher than the general level of the hollow, which terminates above it in a circular basin of two acres in area. This circular basin is verdant enough to the eye, the whole surface being covered by a thick growth of alders, arrow-wood, water-laurels, and other shrubs that flourish in a swamp, as well as a bountiful sprinkling of cat-tails on the edges. The soil is a vegetable jelly; and how any plant of a pound in weight could ever sustain itself on it, I never was able to comprehend. It is thought to be the nearest road to the heart of the Chinese empire; to find which, all that is necessary to do is, to take a plunge into it head foremost, and keep on until you arrive at daylight among the antipodes.

The whole place has a solitary and mournful appearance, which is to many made still more dreary and even sepulchral by the appearance of a little old church, built by the Swedes many a year ago, but now in ruins, and the graveyard around it, these being but a short distance off, and on the east side of the hollow. The spot is remote from my dwelling, and apparently from all others; nevertheless there is a small farmhouse—it was once mine—on a by-road, not many rods from the old church. A path, not often trodden, leads from my house to the by-road, and crosses the hollow by the grassy ledge spoken of before. It is the shortest path to the village, and I sometimes pursued it when walking thither.

This lonesome spot had a very bad name in our neighbourhood, and was considered to be haunted. Its common name was the Owl-roost, given it in consequence of the vast numbers of these birds that perched, and I believe nested in the centre of the swamp, where was a place comparatively dry, or supposed to be so, for I believe no one ever visited it, and a clump of trees larger than those in other places. Some called the place Captain Kid's

---

[5]A rarely cited legal term, the translation of the Latin is, "You expose to sale." It was a court order, which required a sheriff to order the sale of goods that a debtor or creditor had been unable to sell to settle a debt.

Hole,[6] after that famous pirate who was supposed to have buried his money there, as he is supposed to have buried it in a hundred thousand other dismal spots along the different rivers of America. Old Jim Jumble was a devout believer in the story, and often tried his luck in digging for the money, but without success; which he attributed to the circumstance of his digging in the daytime, whereas midnight was, in his opinion, the only true time to delve for charmed treasure. But midnight was the period when the ghosts came down from the old graveyard to squeak about the swamp; and I never heard of Jim being found in that neighbourhood after nightfall. The truth is, the owls never hear any one go by after dark without saluting him with a horrible chorus of hooting and screeching, that will make a man's hair rise on his head; and I have been sometimes daunted by them myself.

To this place I directed my steps; and being very melancholy, I sat down at the foot of a beech-tree that grew near the path. I thought of the owls, and the ghosts, and of Captain Kid into the bargain, and I marvelled to myself whether there could be any foundation for the belief that converted such nooks into hiding-places for his ill-gotten gold. While I thought over the matter, I began to wish the thing could be true, and that some good spirit might direct me to the spot where the money lay hid; for, sure enough, no one in the world had greater necessity for it than I. I conned over the many stories that old Jim had told me about the matter, as well as all the nonsensical ceremonies that were to be performed, and the divers ridiculous dangers to be encountered by those who sought the treasure; all which were mere notions that had entered his absurd head, but which he had pondered over so often and long, that he believed they had been told him by others.

The great difficulty, according to his belief, and a necessary preliminary to all successful operations, was first to discover exactly the spot where the treasure lay buried; and, indeed, this seemed to be a very needful preliminary. The discovery was to be made only by dreaming of the spot three nights in succession. As to dreaming twice, that was nothing: Jim had twenty times dreamed two nights together that he had fallen upon the spot; but upon digging it discovered nothing. Having been so lucky as to dream of a place three successive nights, then the proper way to secure the treasure, as he told me, would be, to select a night when the moon was at the full, and begin digging precisely at twelve o'clock, saying the Lord's prayer backwards all the time, till the money was found. And here lay the danger; a single blunder in the prayer, and wo betide the devotee! for the devil, who would be standing by all the time, would that moment pounce upon his soul, and carry it away in a flame of brimstone.

CHAPTER IX

Sheppard Lee stumbles upon a happy man, and quarrels with him.

While I sat pondering over these matters, and wondering whether *I* could say the prayer backwards, and doubting (for, to my shame be it spoken, I had not often, of late years,

---

[6]William Kidd (1645–1701) was a legendary pirate whose buried treasure inspired a legion of storytellers and treasure hunters.

said it *forward*), I heard a gun go off in the meadow; and rising, and walking that way, I discovered a sportsman who had just shot a woodcock, which his dog carried to him in his mouth. I knew the gunner at first sight to be a gentleman of Philadelphia, by the name of Higginson, a brewer, who was reputed to be very wealthy, and who had several times before visited our neighbourhood, for the purpose of shooting. I knew little of him except his name, having never spoken to him. The neighbours usually addressed him as squire, though I knew not for what reason. He was a man of forty or forty-five years old, somewhat fat and portly, but with a rosy, hearty complexion, looking the very personification of health and content; and, indeed, as I gazed at him, strolling up and down with his dog and gun, I thought I had never before seen such a picture of happiness.

But the sight only filled me with gloom and anger. "Here," said I to myself, "is a man rich and prosperous, who passes his whole life in an amusement that delights him, goes whither he likes, does what he will, eats, drinks, and is merry, and the people call him squire wherever he goes. I wish I were he; for, surely, he is the happiest man in the world!"

While I pondered thus, regarding him with admiration and hatred together, a bird rose at his feet, and he shot it; and the next moment another, which he served in the same way.

I noted the exultation expressed in his countenance, and I was filled with a sudden fury. I strode up to him while he was recharging his piece, and as I approached him, he looked up and gave me a nod of so much complacency and condescension together, that it rendered me ten times madder than ever.

"Sir," said I, looking him full in the face, "before you shoot any more birds here, answer me a question. Who do you go for—the Administration, or the Opposition?"

This was a very absurd way of beginning a conversation with a stranger; but I was in such a fury I scarce knew what I said. He gave me a stare, and then a smile, and nodding his head good-humouredly, replied,

"Oh! for the Administration, to be sure!"

"You do, sir!" I rejoined, shaking my fist at him. "Then, sir, let me tell you, sir, you belong to a scoundrelly party, and are a scoundrel yourself, sir: and so, sir, walk off my place, or I'll prosecute you for a trespass."

"You insolent ragamuffin!" said he.

Ragamuffin! Was I sunk so low that a man trespassing on my own property could call me ragamuffin?

"You poor, miserable shote!"[7]—

So degraded that I could be called a pig?

"You half-starved old sand-field Jersey kill-deer!"—

A Jersey kill-deer!

"You vagabond! You beggar! You Dicky Dout!"—

I was struck dumb by the multitude and intensity of his epithets; and before I could recover speech, he shouldered his gun, snapped his fingers in my face, and whistling to his dog, walked off the ground. Before he had gone six steps, however, he turned round,

---

[7]A young weaned pig.

gave me a hard look, and bursting into a laugh, exclaimed, tapping his forehead as he spoke,—

"Poor fellow! you're wrong in your upper story!"

With that he resumed the path, and crossed over to the old church, where I lost sight of him.

"Wrong in my upper story!" It was the very phrase which Tom Alderwood, my brother-in-law, had applied to me, and which had given me such mortal offence that I had never forgiven him, and had refused to be reconciled, even when, as my difficulties began to thicken about me, he came to offer me his assistance. "Wrong in my upper story!" I was so much confounded by the man's insolence, that I remained rooted to the spot until he had got out of sight; and then, not knowing what else to do, I returned home; when I had a visit from old Jim, who entered the apartment, and not knowing I had sold my horse, cried out, "Massa Sheppard, want money to shoe Julius Cesar 'morrow morning. Blacksmith swear no trust no more."

"Go to the devil, you old rascal!" said I, in a rage.

"Guess I will," said Jim, shaking his head; "follow hard after massa."

That insinuation, which struck me as being highly appropriate, was all I got for supper; for it was Jim's way, when I offended him of an afternoon, to sneak off, taking Dinah with him, and thus leave me to shift for myself during the whole night as I could. There was never a more tyrannical old rascal than Jim Jumble.

CHAPTER X

Sheppard Lee has an extraordinary dream, which promises to be more advantageous than any of his previous ones.

I went therefore supperless to bed; but I dreamed of Captain Kid's money, and the character of my dream was quite surprising. I thought that my house had fallen down in a high wind, as, indeed, it was like enough to do, and that I was sitting on a broken chair before the ruins, when Squire Higginson made his appearance, looking, however, like a dead man; for his face was pale, and he was swathed about with a winding-sheet. Instead of a gun he carried a spade in his hand; and a great black pig followed at his heels in place of his dog. He came directly towards me, and looking me full in the face, said, "Sheppard Lee, what are you doing here?" but I was struck with fear, and could make no reply. With that, he spoke again, saying, "The sheriff is coming to levy on your property; get up, therefore, and follow me." So saying, he began to walk away, whistling to the pig, which ran at his heels like a dog; and I found myself impelled to follow him. He took the path to the Owl-roost, and, arriving there, came to a pause, saying, "Sheppard Lee, you are a poor man, and eaten up with discontent; but I am your friend, and you shall have all your wishes." He then turned to the pig, which was rooting under a gum-tree, and blowing his whistle, said, "Black Pig, show me some game, or I'll trounce you;" and immediately the pig began to run about snuffing, and snorting, and coursing like a dog, so that it was wonderful to behold him. At last the squire, growing impatient, and finding fault with the animal's ill success, for he discovered nothing, took a whip from under his shroud, and fell to beat-
```
```

ing him; after which the pig hunted more to his liking; and, having coursed about us for a while, ran up to the beech-tree, under which I had sat the day before, and began with snout and hoof to tear up the earth at its roots. "Oho!" said Squire Higginson, "I never knew Black Pig to deceive me. We shall have fine sport now." Then, putting the spade into my hands, he bade me dig, exhorting me to be of good heart, for I was now to live a new life altogether. But before I struck the spade into the earth he drew a mark on the ground, to guide me, and the figure was precisely that of a human grave. Not daunted by this circumstance, for in my dream it appeared natural enough, I began to dig; and after throwing out the earth to a depth just equal to the length of the spade, I discovered an iron coffin, the lid of which was in three pieces, and, not being fastened in any way, was therefore easily removed. Judge of my transports when, having lifted up the piece in the middle, I found the whole coffin full of gold and silver, some in the form of ancient coins, but the most of it in bars and ingots, I would have lifted up the whole coffin, and carried it away at once, but that was impossible; I therefore began to fill my pockets, my hat, my handkerchief, and even my bosom; until the squire bade me cease, telling me I should visit the treasure at the same hour on the following night. I then replaced the iron cover, and threw the earth again into the grave, as the squire commanded; and then leaving him, and running home as hard as I could, in fear lest some one should see me, I fell into a miry place, where I was weighed down by the mass of gold I had about me, and smothered. In the midst of my dying agonies I awoke, and found that all was a dream.

Ah! how much torment a poor man has dreaming of riches! The dream made me very melancholy; and I went moping about all that day, wishing myself anybody or any thing but that I was, and hiding in the woods at the sight of any one who chanced to pass by, for I thought everybody was the sheriff. I went to bed the following night in great disorder of spirit, and had no sooner closed my eyes than I dreamed the same dream over again. The squire made his appearance as before, led me to the Owl-roost, and set the black pig hunting until the grave was found. In a word, the dream did not vary in a single particular from that I had had the night before; and when I woke up the next day, the surprise of such an occurrence filled me with new and superstitious ideas, and I awaited the next night with anxious expectations, resolved, if the dream should be repeated again, to go dig at the place, and see what should come of it.

Remembering what old Jim had said in regard to the full of the moon, I went to a neighbour's to look at his almanack (for I had none of my own), and discovered, to my unspeakable surprise and agitation, though I had half known it before, that the moon we then had would be at her full between ten and eleven o'clock on the following morning.

Such a coincidence betwixt the time of my dreams and the proper period for hunting the treasure (since at the full moon was the proper time), was enough of itself to excite my expectations; and the identity between the two visions was so extraordinary, that I began to believe that the treasure did really exist in the Owl-roost, which, being very solitary, and yet conveniently accessible from the river through the medium of the creek, was one of the best hiding-places in the world, and that I was the happy man destined to obtain it.

I went to bed accordingly the third night with a strong persuasion that the vision would be repeated: I was not disappointed. I found myself again digging at the beech-roots, and scraping up great wedges of gold and silver from the iron coffin. What was remarkable in this dream, however, was, that when I had picked up as much as I could carry, the squire nodded to me, and said, "Now, Sheppard Lee, you know the way to Captain Kid's treasure, and you can come to-morrow night by yourself." And what was further observable, I did not dream of falling into a miry place on this occasion, but arrived safely home, and beheld with surprise and delight that my house, which I had left in ruins, was standing up more beautiful than ever it had been, newly painted from top to bottom, and the pillars of the porch were gilded over, and shining like gold.

While enjoying this agreeable prospect I awoke, and such was the influence of the vision on my mind, and the certain belief I now cherished that the vast treasure was mine,—a whole coffinful of gold and silver,—that I fell to shouting and dancing; so that old Jim Jumble, who ran up into my chamber to see what was the matter, was persuaded I had gone mad, and began to blubber and scold, and take on in the most diverting way in the world.

I pacified him as well as I could, but resolved to keep my secret until I could surprise him with the sight of my treasure, all collected together in the house; and I proceeded without delay to make such preparations as were proper for the coming occasion. I took a spade and mattock, and carried them to the hollow, where I hid them among the bushes. But this I found difficult to do as secretly as I wished; for old Jim, either from suspecting what I was after, or believing I had lost my mind, kept dogging me about; so that it was near midday before I succeeded in giving him the slip, and carrying my tools to the hollow.

CHAPTER XI

In which the reader is introduced to a personage who may claim his acquaintance hereafter.

In this place, to my dismay, I stumbled upon a man, who, from the character he had in the neighbourhood, I was afraid was hunting the treasure, as well as myself. He was an old German doctor, called Feuerteufel, which extraordinary name, as I had been told, signified, in German, *Fire-devil.* He had come to our village about two weeks before, and nobody knew for what reason. All day long he wandered about among the woods, swamps, and marshes, collecting plants and weeds, stones, animals, and snakes, which he seemed to value very highly. Some thought he was a counterfeiter in disguise, and others called him a conjurer. Many were of opinion he was hunting for gold-mines, or precious stones; while others had their thoughts, and said he was the devil, his appearance being somewhat grim and forbidding. As for myself, having lighted upon him once or twice in the woods, I did not know what to think of him; but I did not like his looks. He was very tall and rawboned, with long arms, and immense big hands; his skin was extremely dark and pock-marked, and he had a mouth that ran from ear to ear, and long, bushy, black hair. His eyes were like saucers, and deep sunk in their sockets, with tremendous big black eyebrows ever frowning above them; and what made him look remarkable was, that although he was ever frowning with his eyes, his mouth was as continually grinning in a sort of laugh, such as you see in a man struck with a palsy in the head. He was the terror of all the children, and it was said the dogs never barked at him.

I found him in the hollow, hard by the beech-tree, and had scarce time to fling my implements among the bushes before he saw me. He was standing looking over towards the old church, where there was a funeral procession; for that morning the neighbours were burying a young man that had taken laudanum for love two days before, but had only expired the previous evening.

As soon as the German beheld me, he started like a guilty man, and made as if he would have run away; but suddenly changing his mind, he stepped towards me, and just as we met he stooped down and pulled a flower that struck his eye. Then rising up, he grinned at me, and nodding, said, "Gooten morrow, mine prudder; it ish gooten dag!"— though what he meant by "*gooten dag*" I know no more than the man in the moon, having never studied German. I did not at all like his appearance in this spot at such a time; but I reflected at last that he was only culling samples, and had paused near the beech-tree to look at the funeral, as would have been extremely natural in any man. But I liked the appearance of the funeral still less at such a particular time, and I thought there was something ominous in it.

But my mind was fixed upon the treasure I was soon to enjoy too firmly to be long drawn off by any such doleful spectacle; and accordingly, having waited impatiently until the attendants on the funeral had all stalked away, as well as the German doctor, I stole towards the beech-tree, and surveyed the ground at its roots. There were some stones lying among them, which I removed, as well as the long grass that waved over their tops; and looking closely, I thought I could see among some of the smaller roots of the tree, that were pleached together on the surface of the earth, a sort of arrangement very much in shape of a grave. This was a new proof to me that the treasure lay below, and I considered that my good angel had platted these roots together, in order to direct me in what spot to dig.

I could scarce avoid beginning on the instant; but, I remembered, that was not the hour. I therefore concealed my spade and mattock, and went home; when the first thing I did was to hunt me up a book that had the Lord's prayer in it (for I feared to trust to my memory alone), and write this out backwards with the greatest care; and I then spent the remainder of the day in committing the words to memory in that order; but I found it a difficult task.

As the evening drew nigh, I found myself growing into such a pitch of excitement, that, fearing I should betray the secret to Jim Jumble, who was constantly prying in upon me, I resolved to walk to the village, and there remain until the hour for seeking the treasure should draw nigh. I had another reason for this step; for my watch having gone, some month or two before Julius Cesar, to satisfy a hungry fellow to whom I owed money, I knew not how to be certain of the hour, unless by learning it of some one in the village; and to the village I accordingly went soon after sunset.

CHAPTER XII

Sheppard Lee visits the village, makes a patriotic speech, and leaves the fence.

Having arrived at the village, I proceeded to a tavern, which was the chief place of resort, especially after nightfall, for all the idlers and topers of the town, of whom there were great numbers, the village at that time being a place of but little business.

I found some ten or a dozen already assembled in the bar-room, drinking brandy, smoking, chewing, talking politics, and swearing. I had no sooner entered than some of them, who were discoursing loudly concerning the purity and economy of the government, and the honesty of those who supported it, appealed to me (my electioneering pilgrimage through the country having caused me to be looked upon as quite a knowing politician) to assist them in the argument they were holding.

Remembering the scurvy way in which I had been treated by the party, I felt strongly tempted to give them a piece of my mind on the other side of the question; but I thought of my buried treasure, and conceiving it unwise to begin the quarrel at that time, I made them no answer, but sat down in a corner, where I hoped to escape observation. Here I employed myself conning over the prayer backwards, until I was assured I was perfect in the exercise.

I then—still keeping aloof from the company—gave my mind up to a consideration of what I should do when I had transferred Captain Kid's hoards of gold from the coffin to my house.

The first thing I resolved to do was to pay my debts, which, how greatly soever they oppressed me, were not actually very fearful in amount; after which I was determined to rebuild my house, restore my fields to their original condition, and go to law with Mr. Aikin Jones, who I had no doubt had cheated me out of my property. It did not occur to me that, by such a step, I should get rid of my second fortune as expeditiously as I had the first; all that I thought on was the satisfaction of having my revenge on the villain, whom I should have punished in perhaps a more summary way, had it not been for my respect for the laws, and my being naturally a peaceable man. But I did not think long of Mr. Jones; the idea of the great wealth I was soon to possess filled my mind, and I gave myself up to the most transporting reveries.

From these I was roused by hearing some one near me pronounce the words "*Captain Kid's money*"—the idea that was uppermost in my own mind; and looking round in a kind of perturbation, I saw a knot of people surrounding Feuerteufel, the German doctor, one of whom was discoursing on the subject of the treasure in the Owl-roost, and avowing his belief that he—that is, the German doctor—was conjuring after it; an imputation that gained great credit with the company, there being no other way to account for his visit to our village, and his constant perambulations through the woods and marshes in the neighbourhood of the Owl-roost.

The German doctor, to my great relief, replied to this charge by expanding his jaws as if he would have swallowed the speaker, though he was guilty of nothing beyond a laugh, which was in depth and quality of tone as if an empty hogshead had indulged in the same diversion. His voice was indeed prodigiously deep and hollow, and even his laugh had something in it solemn and lugubrious. "Mine friends," said he, in very bad English, "I fos can do men' creat t'ings; put I can no find no Captain Kitt's money not at all. I toes neffer looks for coldt, except in places fare Gott puts it; t'at iss, in t'a coldt-mines!" With that, he laughed again, and looking upon the people about him with great contempt, he walked up stairs to his chamber—for he lodged in the inn.

Soon after this occurrence, and just when I had sunk again into a revery, a man stepped up to me, and saluted me in a way well suited to startle me.

"Sir," said he, "friend Kill-deer, before you scratch your head any more on this bench, answer me a question. What do you go for,—brandy-toddy or gin-sling?"

It was Squire Higginson, and he looked very good-humoured and waggish; but as I had dreamed of him so often, and always as being in his grave-clothes, I was rather petrified at his appearance, as if it were that of a spectre, rather than a mortal man. As for our quarrel in the meadow, it had slipped my mind altogether, until, having recovered my composure a little, it was recalled to my recollection by the associations arising out of his words.

But I remembered the circumstance at last, and being moreover offended by his present freedom, which was nothing less than sheer impertinence, I told him I desired to have nothing to say to him; on which he fell into a passion, and told me "I might go to the devil for a ragamuffin and a turncoat politician." But, mad as he was, he ended his speech by bursting into a laugh, and then, tapping his forehead as before, and nodding his head and winking, he left the bar-room to seek his chamber—for *he* put up at the tavern, as well as the German doctor.

These insults threw me into some ferment, and being irritated still farther by the remarks of the company, especially when some one asked what the squire meant by calling me "a turncoat politician," I allowed myself to be thrown into a passion; in the course of which I gave such of my old friends as were present to know that I had forsworn their party, and considered it to be composed of a pack of the corruptest scoundrels in the country.

This unexpected denunciation produced a great explosion; my old friends fell upon me tooth and nail, as the saying is, reviling me as a traitor and apostate. But, on the other hand, those of the opposition who happened to be present ranged themselves on my side, applauding my honesty, judgment, and spirit to such a degree, that I was more than ever convinced I had been on the wrong side. I met reproaches with contempt, and threats with defiance; opposed words to words, and assertions to assertions (for, in politics, we do not make use of arguments); and finding myself triumphantly victorious, I mounted into a chair, and made a speech that was received by my new friends with roars of applause. Intoxicated with these marks of approbation, I launched at once into a sea of declamation, in which I might have tossed about during the whole night, had I not by chance, while balking for a word, rolled my eyes upon the clock that stood opposite to me in the bar, and perceived that it wanted just a quarter of an hour to twelve o'clock. In a moment I forgot every thing but the treasure that awaited me in the Owl-roost; I stopped short in the middle of a sentence, took one more look at the clock, and then, leaping down from the chair, rushed from the tavern without saying a word, and, to the amazement of friend and foe, ran at full speed out of the village; and this gait I continued until I had reached the old Swedes' Church; for I had taken the footpath that led in that direction.

CHAPTER XIII

What befell the author on his way to the Owl-roost.

As it was now the full of the moon, there was of course light enough for my purpose; but the sky was dappled with clouds very dense and heavy, some of which crossing the moon every minute or two, there was a constant alternation of light and darkness, so that the trees and all other objects were constantly changing their appearance, now starting up in bold relief, white and silvery from the darkness, and now vanishing again into gloom.

A cloud passed over the moon just as I reached the old church; and the wall of the burial-ground having fallen down at a certain place, where the rubbish obstructed the path, it was my ill luck to break my shin against a fragment; the pain of which caused me to utter a loud groan. To my amazement and horror, this interjection of suffering was echoed from the grave-yard hard by, a voice screaming out in awful tones, "O Lord! O Lord!" and casting my eyes round, I beheld, as I thought, three or four shapes, that I deemed nothing less than devils incarnate, dancing about among the tomb-stones.

I was seized with such terror at this sight, that, forgetting my hurt and the treasure together, I took to my heels, and did not cease running until I had left the church some quarter of a mile behind me; and I am not certain I should have come to a halt then, had it not been my fate to tumble over a cow that lay ruminating on the path; whereby, besides half breaking my neck, and cruelly scratching my nose, I stunned myself to that degree, that it was some two or three minutes before I was able to rise.

I had thus time to recollect myself, and reflect that I was running away from Captain Kid's money, the idea of losing which was not to be tolerated a moment.

But how to get to the Owl-roost without falling into the hands of the devils or spectres at the old church, was what gave me infinite concern. The midnight hour—the only one for attempting the treasure with success—was now close at hand; so that there was no time left me to reach the place by a roundabout course through the woods to the right, or over the meadows to the left. I must pass the old church, or I must perhaps give up the treasure.

There was no time to deliberate; the figures I had seen, and the cries I had heard, might have been coinages of my own brain; nay, the latter were perhaps, after all, only the echoes of my own voice, distorted into something terrible by my fears. I was not naturally superstitious, and had never before believed in ghosts. But I cannot recollect what precise arguments occurred to me at that moment, to cause me to banish my fears. The hope of making my fortune was doubtless the strongest of all; and the moon suddenly shining out with the effulgence almost of day, I became greatly imboldened, and, in a word, set forward again, resolved, if met by a second apparition, and driven to flight, to fly, not backwards, but *forwards,*—that is, in the direction of the Owl-roost.

On this occasion, it was my fortune to be saluted by an owl that sat on the old wall among some bushes, and hooted at me as I went by; and notwithstanding that the sound was extremely familiar to my ears, I was thrown into a panic, and took to my heels as before; though, as I had resolved, I ran onward, pursuing the path to the swamp. It is quite possible there may have been a crew of imps and disimbodied spirits jumping among the graves as before; but, as I had the good fortune to be frightened before I caught sight of them, I did not stop to look for them; and, for the same reason, I heard no more awful voices shrieking in my ears. I reached the Owl-roost and the memorable beech-tree, where the necessity of acting with all speed helped me to get rid of my terror. I knew that I had not a moment to spare, and running to the bushes where I had hidden my mattock and spade, I fetched them to the tree, and instantly began to dig, not forgetting to pray backwards all the while, as hard as I could.

CHAPTER XIV

*Sheppard Lee digs for the buried treasure, but makes
a blow with the mattock in the wrong place.*

I was but an ill hand at labour, and of the use of the spade and mattock I knew nothing. The nature of the ground in which I was digging made the task especially difficult and disagreeable. There were many big stones scattered about in the earth, which jarred my arms horribly whenever I struck them; so that (all my efforts to the contrary notwith-standing) I was, every minute or two, interrupting my prayer with expressions which were neither wise nor religious, but highly expressive of my torture of body and mind. And then I was digging among the toughest and vilest roots in the world, some of which I thought I should never get through; for I had not remembered to provide myself with an axe, and I was afraid to go home for one, lest some evil accident or discovery might rob me of the expected treasure.

Accordingly, I had to do with a tougher piece of labour than I had ever undertaken before in my whole life; and I reckon I worked a full hour and a half, before I had got the hole I was excavating as deep as I supposed would be necessary. I succeeded at last, however, in throwing out so much earth, that when I measured the depth of the pit with my spade, I found the handle just on a level with the surface of the ground.

But I was not so near the treasure as I supposed; I struck my mattock into the clay, scarce doubting that I should hear the ring of the iron coffin. Instead of reaching that, however, I struck a great stone, and with a force that made the mattock-helve fly out of my hands to my chin, which it saluted with a vigour that set all my teeth to rattling, knocking me down into the bargain.

Having recovered from the effects of this blow, I fell to work again, thumping and delving until I had excavated to the depth of at least five feet. My heart began to fail me, as well as my strength, as I got so deep into the earth without finding the gold, for I began to fear lest my dreams had, after all, deceived me. In my agitation of mind, I handled my tools so blindly, that I succeeded in lodging my mattock, which was aimed furiously at a root, among the toes of my right foot; and the pain was so horribly acute, that I leaped howling out of the pit, and sinking down upon the grass, fell straightway into a trance.

CHAPTER XV

*In which Sheppard Lee finds himself in a quandary which the reader will allow
to be the most wonderful and lamentable ever known to a human being.*

When I awoke from this trance, it was almost daybreak.

I recovered in some confusion of mind, and did not for a moment notice that I was moving away from the place of my disaster; but I perceived there was something strange in my feelings and sensations. I felt exceedingly light and buoyant, as if a load had been taken, not merely from my mind, but from my body; it seemed to me as if I had the power of moving whither I would without exertion, and I fancied that I swept along without putting my feet to the ground. Nay, I had a notion that I was passing among shrubs and bushes, without experiencing from them any hinderance to my progress whatever. I felt no pain in my foot, which I had hit such a violent blow, and none in my hands, that had been wofully blistered by my work; nor had I the slightest feeling of weariness or fatigue. On the whole, my sensations were highly novel and agreeable; but before I had time to analyze them, or to wonder at the change, I remembered that I was wandering away from the buried treasure.

I returned to the spot, but only to be riveted to the earth in astonishment. I saw, stretched on the grass, just on the verge of the pit, the dead body of a man; but what was my horror, when, perusing the ashy features in the light of the moon, I perceived my own countenance! It was no illusion; it was *my* face, *my* figure, and dressed in *my* clothes; and the whole presented the appearance of perfect death.

The sight was as bewildering as it was shocking; and the whole state of things was not more terrifying than inexplicable. *There* I lay on the ground, stiff and lifeless; and *here* I stood on my feet, alive, and surveying my own corpse, stretched before me. But I forgot my extraordinary duality in my concern for myself—that is to say, for that part of me, that *eidolon*,[8] or representative, or duplicate of me, that was stretched on the grass. I stooped down to raise the figure from earth, in an instinctive desire to give myself aid, but in vain I could not lift the body; it did not seem to me that I could even *touch it,*—my fingers, strive as I might, I could not bring into contact with it.

My condition, or *conditions* (for I was no longer of the singular number) at this time, can be understood only by comparing my confusion of senses and sensations to that which occurs in a dream, when one beholds himself dead, surveys his body, and philosophizes or laments, and is, all the time, to all intents and purposes, without being surprised at it, *two persons,* one of which lives and observes, while the other is wholly defunct. Thus I was, or appeared to be, without bestowing any reflection upon such an extraordinary circumstance, or being even conscious of it, two persons; in one of which I lived, but forgot my existence, while trembling at the death that had overcome me in the other. My true situation I did not yet comprehend, nor even dream of; though it soon turned out to be natural enough, and I understood it.

I was entirely overcome with horror at my unfortunate condition; and seeing that I was myself unable to render myself any assistance, I ran, upon an impulse of instinct, to the nearest quarter where it was to be obtained. This was at the cottage, or little farmhouse, which I spoke of before as standing on the by-road, a little beyond the old church. It was occupied by a man named Turnbuckle, whom I knew very well, and who was a very industrious, honest man, although a tenant of Mr. Aikin Jones.

I arrived at his house in an amazingly short space of time, rather flying, as it seemed to me, through the air, than running over the marsh and up the rugged hill. It was the gray of the morning when I reached his house, and the family was just stirring within. As I ran towards the door, his dogs, of which he had a goodly number, as is common with poor men, set up a dismal howling, clapped their tails between their legs, and sneaked off among the bushes; a thing that surprised me much, for they were usually very savage of temper. I called to Turnbuckle by name, and that in a voice so piteous that, in half a minute, he and his eldest son came tumbling out of the house in the greatest haste and

---

[8]phantom

wonder. No sooner, however, had they cast eyes on me, than they uttered fearful cries; the old man fell flat on his face, as if in a fit, and the son ran back into the house, as if frightened out of his senses.

"Help me, Thomas Turnbuckle," said I; "I am lying dead under the beech-tree in the hollow: come along and give me help."

But the old man only answered by groaning and crying; and at that moment the door opened, and his eldest son appeared with a gun, which he fired at me, to my inexpressible terror.

But if I was frightened at this, how much more was I horrified when the old man, leaping up at the discharge, roared out, "O Lord! a ghost! a ghost!" and ran into the house.

I perceived it all in a moment: the howling of the dogs, which they still kept up from among the bushes,—the fear of Turnbuckle and his family, all of whom, old and young, male and female, were now squeaking in the house, as if Old Nick had got among them,—my being in two places together, and a thousand other circumstances that now occurred to me, apprized me of the dreadful fact, which I had not before suspected: I was a dead man!—my body lay in the marsh under the beech-tree, and it was my spirit that was wandering about in search of assistance!

As this terrible idea flashed across my mind, and I saw that I was a ghost, I was as much frightened as the Turnbuckles had been, and I took to my heels to fly from myself, until I recollected myself a little, and thought of the absurdity of such a proceeding. But even this fatal conception did not remove my anxiety in relation to my poor body,—or *myself,* as I could not help regarding my body; and I ran back to the beech-tree in a kind of distraction, hoping I might have been revived and resuscitated in my absence.

I reached the pit, and stared wildly about me—my body was gone,—vanished! I looked into the hole I had excavated; there was nothing in it but the spade and mattock, and my hat, which had fallen from my head when I leaped out of it, after hurting my foot. I stared round me again; the print of my body in the grass, where it had lain, was quite perceptible (for it was now almost broad day), but there was no body there, and no other vestige excepting one of my shoes, which was torn and bloody, being the identical one I had worn on the foot hurt by the mattock.

CHAPTER XVI

Sheppard Lee finds comfort when he least expects it.
The extraordinary close of the catastrophe.

What had become of me? that is, what had become of my body? Its disappearance threw me into a phrensy; and I was about to run home, and summon old Jim Jumble to help me look for it, when I heard a dog yelping and whining in a peculiarly doleful manner, at some little distance down in the meadow; and I instantly ran in that direction, thinking that perhaps the bloodthirsty beast might be at that very moment dragging it away to devour it,— or hoping, at the least, to light upon some one who could give me an account of it.

I ran to a place in the edge of the marsh where were some willow-trees, and an old worm fence, the latter overgrown with briers and elder-bushes; and there, to my exceeding surprise, I discovered the body of Squire Higginson (for he was stone dead), lying against the fence, which was broken, his head down, and his heels resting against the rails, and looking as if, while climbing it, he had fallen down and broken his neck. His gun was lying at his side, undischarged, and his dog, whose yelping had brought me to the spot, was standing by; but I must add, that, as soon as I approached him, the animal betrayed as much terror as Turnbuckle's dogs had done, and ran howling away in the same manner.

Greatly incensed as I had been with Squire Higginson, I felt some concern to see him lying in this lamentable condition, his face blackened with blood, as if he had perished from suffocation; and stooping down, I endeavoured to take off his neckcloth and raise his head, in the hope that he might yet recover. But I reckoned without my host,— I had forgotten that I was a mere phantom or spirit, possessing no muscular power whatever, because no muscles; for, even in walking and running, as I was now aware, I was impelled by some unknown power within me, and not at all carried by my legs. I could not bring my hand into contact either with his cravat or head, and for a good reason, seeing there was no substance in me whatever, but all spirit.

I therefore ceased my endeavours, and began to moralize, in a mournful mood, upon his condition and mine. He was dead, and so was I; but there seemed to be this difference between us, namely, that I had lost my body, and he his soul,—for after looking hard about me, I could see nothing of it. His body, as it lay there in the bushes, was perfectly useless to him, and to all the world beside; and my spirit, as was clear enough, was in a similar predicament. Why might I not, that is to say, my spirit,—deprived by an unhappy accident of its natural dwelling,—take possession of a tenement which there remained no spirit to claim, and thus, uniting interests together, as two feeble factions unite together in the political world, become a body possessing life, strength, and usefulness?

As soon as this idea entered my mind (or *me,* for I was all mind), I was seized with the envy that possessed me when I first met the squire shooting over my marshes. "How much better it would be," I thought, "to inhabit his body than my own! In my own fleshly casing, I should revive only to poverty and trouble;" (I had forgot all about Captain Kid's money) "whereas, if once in the body of Squire Higginson, I should step out into the world to possess riches, respect, content, and all that man covets. Oh that I might be Squire Higginson!" I cried.

The words were scarce out of my mouth, before I felt myself vanishing, as it were, into the dead man's nostrils, into which I—that is to say, my spirit—rushed like a breeze of air; and the very next moment I found myself kicking the fence to pieces in a lusty effort to rise to my feet, and feeling as if I had just tumbled over it.

"The devil take the fence, and that Jersey kill-deer that keeps it in such bad order!" I cried, as I rose up, snatching at my gun, and whistling for my dog Ponto. *My* dog Ponto! It was even the truth; I was no more Sheppard Lee, the poor and discontented,—no longer a disimbodied spirit, wandering about only to frighten dogs out of their senses; but John Hazlewood Higginson, Esq., solid and substantial in purse and flesh, with a rosy face, and a heart as cheerful as the morning, which was now reddening over the whole east. If I had wanted any proof of the transformation beyond that furnished by my own senses and sensations, it would have been provided by my dog Ponto, who now came running up, leaping on and about me with the most extravagant joy.

"God be thanked!" I cried, dancing about as joyously as the dog; "I am now a respectable man, with my pockets full of money. Farewell, then, you poor miserable Sheppard Lee! you ragamuffin! you poor wretched shote! you half-starved old sand-field Jersey kill-deer! you vagabond! you beggar! you Dicky Dout, with the wrong place in your upper story! you are now a gentleman and a man of substance, and a happy dog into the bargain. Ha, ha, ha!" and here I fell a laughing out of pure joy; and giving my dog Ponto a buss, as if that were the most natural act in the world, and a customary way of showing my satisfaction, I began to stalk towards my old ruined house, without exactly knowing for what purpose, but having some vague idea about me, that I would set old Jim Jumble and his wife Dinah to shouting and dancing; an amusement I would willingly have seen the whole world engaged in at that moment.

CHAPTER XVII

A natural mistake, which, although it procures the Author a rough reception at his own house, has yet the good effect to teach him the propriety of adapting his manners to his condition.

I had not walked twenty yards, before a woodcock that was feeding on the edge of the marsh started up from under my nose, when, clapping my gun to my shoulder, I let fly at him, and down he came.

"Aha, Ponto!" said I, "when did I ever fail to bring down a woodcock? Bring it along, Ponto, you rascal.—Rum-te, ti, ti! rum-te, ti, ti!" and I went on my way singing for pure joy, without pausing to recharge, or to bag my game. I reached my old house, and began to roar out, without reflecting that I was now something more than Sheppard Lee, "Hillo! Jim Jumble, you old rascal get up and let me in."

"What you want, hah?" said old Jim, poking his head from the garret-window of the kitchen, and looking as sour as a persimmon before frost. "Guess Massa Squire Higginson drunk, hah? What you want? S'pose I'm gwyin to git up afo' sunrise for not'in', and for anybody but my Massa Sheppard?"

"Why, you old dog," said I, in a passion, "I am your master Sheppard; that is, your master John Hazlewood, Higginson, Esquire; for as for Sheppard Lee, the Jersey kill-deer, I've finished him, you rascal; you'll never see him more. So get down, and let me into the house, or I'll—"

"You will, hah?" said Jim; "you will *what?*"

"I'll shoot you, you insolent scoundrel!" I exclaimed, in a rage,—as if it were the most natural thing in the world for me to be in one; and as I spoke, I raised my piece; when "Bow—wow—wough!" went my old dog Bull, who had not bitten a man for two years, but who now rushed from his kennel under the porch, and seized me by the leg.

"Get out, Bull, you rascal!" said I, but he only bit the harder; which threw me into such a fury that I clapped the muzzle of my gun to his side, and, having one charge remaining, blew him to pieces.

"Golla-matty!" said old Jim, from the window, whence he had surveyed the combat; "golla-matty! shoot old Bull!"

And with that the black villain snatched up the half of a brick, which I suppose he kept to daunt unwelcome visitors, and taking aim at me, he cast it so well as to bring it right against my left ear, and so tumbled me to the ground. I would have blown the rascal's brains out, in requital of this assault, had there been a charge left in my piece, or had he given me time to reload; but as soon as he had cast the brick, he ran from the window, and then reappeared, holding out an old musket that, I remembered, he kept to shoot wild ducks and muskrats in the neighbouring marsh with. Seeing this formidable weapon, and not knowing but that the desperado would fire upon me, I was forced to beat a retreat, which I did in double quick time, being soon joined by my dog Ponto, who had fled, like a coward, at the first bow-wough of the bulldog, and saluted in my flight by the amiable tones of Dinah, who now thrust her head from the window, beside Jim's, and abused me as long as I could hear.

BOOK VI[9]

Containing a History and a Moral

CHAPTER I

In which Sheppard Lee finds every thing black about him.

When I opened my eyes I found that I was lying in a hovel, very mean of appearance, yet with a certain neatness and cleanliness about it that prevented it from looking squalid. It is true that the floor, which was of planks, was somewhat awry and dilapidated; that the little window, which, with the door, furnished, or was meant to furnish, its only light, was rather bountifully bedecked with old hats and scraps of brown paper; and that the walls of ill-plastered logs displayed divers gleaming chinks, and vistas through them of the sunny prospects without. Nevertheless, the place did not look amiss for a poor man, and, in my experience as a philanthropist, I had seen hundreds much more miserable.

An old woman sat at the fireplace, nodding over a stew, the fumes of which were both savoury and agreeable. The old woman was, however, as black as the outside of her stew-pan—in other words, a negress; and this circumstance striking upon the chords of association, I began to remember what had lately befallen me. A terrible suspicion flashed into my mind. Had I not—but before I could ask myself the question, my hand, which I had raised to scratch my head, came into contact with a mop of elastic wool, such as never grew upon the scalp of a white man. I started up in bed and looked at my hands and arms; they were of the hue of ebony—or, to speak more strictly, of smoked mahogany. I saw a fragment of looking-glass hanging on the wall within my reach. I snatched it down, and took a survey of my physiognomy. Miserable me! my *face* was as black as my arms—and, indeed, somewhat more so—presenting a sable globe, broken only by two red lips of immense magnitude, and a brace of eyes as white and as wide as plain China saucers, or peeled turnips.

---

[9]After inhabiting Squire Higginson's body for a time, Sheppard Lee has adventures that move him into the following, successive bodies: a dandy who had just committed suicide (I. Dulwar Dawkins), an old miser (Abram Skinner), and a recently murdered Quaker philanthropist (Zechariah Longstraw). We join the story here as Sheppard Lee enters the body of a southern slave.

"Whaw dah!" cried the old woman, roused by the noise I made; "whaw dat, you nigga Tom? what you doin' dah? Lorra bless us! if a nigga break a neck, can't a nigga hold-a still?"

Alas! and had my fate brought me to this grievous pass? Was there no other situation in life sufficiently wretched, but that I must take up my lot in the body of a miserable negro slave? How idle had been all my past discontent! how foolish the persuasion I had indulged five different times, that I was, on each occasion, the most unhappy of men! I had forgotten the state of the bondman, the condition of the expatriated African. *Now* I was at last to learn in reality what it was to be the victim of fortune, what to be the exemplar of wretchedness, the true repository of all the griefs that can afflict a human being. Already I felt, in imagination, the blow of the task-master on my back, the fetter on my limb, the iron in my soul; and when the old woman made a step towards me, perhaps to discover why I made no reply to her questions, I was so prepossessed with the idea of whips and lashes, that I made a dodge under the bedclothes, as if to escape a thwack.

"Golly matty! is de nigga mad?" cried the Jezebel.[10] "I say, you nigga Tom, what you doin'? How you neck feel now?"

"My neck?" thought I, recollecting that it had been broken, and wondering in what way it had been mended. I clapped my hands to it; it was very stiff and sore: while I felt at it, the old woman told me some great doctor had twisted a great "kink" out of it; but I bestowed little notice on what she said. My mind ran upon other matters; I could think of nothing but cowhides and cat-o'-nine-tails, that were to welcome me to bondage.

"Aunty," said I—*why* I addressed the old lady thus I know not; but I have observed that negroes always address their seniors by the titles of uncle and aunt, and I suppose the instinct was on me—"am I a slave?"

"What a fool nigga to ax a question!" said she. "What you gwying to be, den, but old Massa Jodge's nigga-boy Tom? What you git up faw, ha?"—(I was making an attempt to rise)—"Massa docta say you stay a-bed. What you git up faw, ha?"

"I intend to run away," said I; and truly that was the notion then uppermost in my mind; and it is very likely I should have made a bolt for the door that moment, had I not discovered an uncommon weakness in my lower limbs, which prevented my getting out of bed.

"Whaw! what a fool!" cried the beldam,[11] regarding me with surprise and contempt; "what you do when you run away, ha? Who'll hab you? who'll feed you? who'll take care of you? who'll own a good-fo'-nothin' runaway nigga I say, ha? Kick him 'bout h'yah, kick him 'bout dah, poor despise nigga, wid no massa, jist as despise as any free nigga! You run away, ha? what den?" continued my sable monitress, warming into eloquence as she spoke: "take up constable, clap him in jail, salt him down cowskin. Dat all? No! sell him low price, send Mississippi—what den? Work in de cotton-field, pull at de cane. Dat all? No! cussed overseer wid a long whip—cut h'yah, cut dah, cut high, cut low—whip all day, cuff all night—take all de skin off—oh! dey do whip to de debbil in

---

[10]Jezebel was the treacherous wife of King Ahab (1 Kings 17–21).

[11]Old woman.

de Mississippi!" And as the old lady concluded, to give more effect to her expressions, she fell to rubbing her back and dodging her head from side to side, until I had the liveliest idea in the world of that very castigation of which I stood in such horror.

CHAPTER II

In which Sheppard Lee is introduced to his master.

Just at this moment, to make my anguish more complete, in stepped a tall and dignified person, bearing a huge walking-stick; with which I was so certain he would proceed to maul me, that I made a second dive under the bedclothes, loudly beseeching him for mercy.

To my surprise, however, instead of beating me, he spoke to the old woman, whom he called aunt Phœbe (and who, in return, entitled him Massa Jodge), asked "if I was not light-headed?" said that "it was a great pity I had so hard a time of it," that "I was very much hurt," that "he would be sorry to lose me," and so on; and, in fine, expressed what he said in accents so humane and gentle that I was encouraged to steal a peep at him; seeing which he sat down on a stool, felt my pulse, and giving me quite a good-natured look, asked me "if I felt in much pain?"

I was astonished that he should treat me thus, if my master. But, surveying him more intently, I perceived there was little in his appearance to justify any fears of cruelty. He was an aged man, with a head of silver that gave him an uncommonly venerable air; and, though his visage was grave, it expressed a native good-humour and amiableness.

My terrors fled before his soothing accents and benevolent looks; but being still confused, I was unable to reply in proper terms to his questions; so that when he asked me, as he soon did, what I meant by crying for mercy, I made answer, "Oh Lord, sir, I was afraid you was going to beat me!" at which he laughed, and said "my conscience was growing tenderer than common;" adding, that "there was no doubt I deserved a trouncing, as did every other boy on his estate; for a set of greater scoundrels than his was not to be found in all Virginia; and if they had their deserts, they would get a round dozen apiece every day."

He then began to ask me particularly about my ailments; and I judged from his questions and certain occasional remarks which he let fall, that I had been lying insensible for several days, that my neck had been put out of place, or dislocated, and reduced again by some practitioner of uncommon skill. And here, lest the reader should think such a circumstance improbable, I beg leave to say that I have lately seen an account of a similar operation performed by an English surgeon on the neck of a fox-hunting squire; and as the story appeared in the newspapers, there can be no doubt of its truth.

While the gentleman—my master—was thus asking me of my pains, and betraying an interest in my welfare that softened my heart towards him, there came into the hovel a young lady of a very sweet countenance, followed by two or three younger girls and a little boy, all of whom seemed glad to see me, the little boy in particular, shaking me by the hand, while his youthful sisters (for all were my master's children) began to drag from a basket and display before my eyes the legs of a roasted chicken, a little tart, a jelly, and divers other dainty viands, which they had brought with them, as they said, "for poor sick Tom," and insisted upon seeing him eat on the spot. As for the young lady, the eldest sister, she smiled on them and on me (for I was not backward to accept and dispose of the savoury gifts), but told me I must not be imprudent, nor eat too much, and I would soon be well. "What!" thought I, "does a slave ever eat too much?"

It is astonishing what a revolution was effected in my feelings by the gentle deportment of my master, and the kindly act of his children. I looked upon them and myself with entirely new dyes, I felt a sort of affection for them steal through my spirit, and I wondered why I had ever thought of them with fear. I took a particular liking to the little boy, who, by-the-by, was a namesake of mine, he being Massa Tommy, and I plain Tom, and I had an unaccountable longing come over me to take him on my back and go galloping on all-fours over the grass at the door. I had no more thoughts of running away to avoid the dreadful lash, and the shame of bonds; and, my master and his children presently leaving the hovel, having first charged me to keep myself quiet and easy, I fell sound asleep, and dreamed I lay a whole day on my back on a clay-bank, eating johnny-cake and fried bacon.

CHAPTER III

An old woman's cure for a disease extremely prevalent
both in the coloured and uncoloured creation.

The next day I was visited again by my master, and by other members of his family whom I had not seen before, and of whom I shall say nothing now, having occasion to mention them hereafter. The children brought me "goodies" as before, and little Tommy told me to "make haste and get well, for there were none of the other 'boys' "—meaning negroes—"who knew how to gallop the cock-horse half so well as I." In short, I was treated like a human being, and fed like a king, and began to grow wondrous content with my situation. The doctor also came, and having fingered about my neck for a while, declared my case to be the most marvellous one ever known, and concluded by telling me I was well enough to get up, and that I might do so whenever I chose.

Now this was a matter of which I was as well satisfied as he could be, being quite certain I never was better in my life; but I felt amazing delight in lolling a-bed, doing nothing except feeding on the good things with which my master's children so liberally supplied me; and, I believe, had they left the matter to be decided by my own will, I should have been lying on that bed, luxuriating in happy laziness, to this day. It is certain I fabricated falsehoods without number, for the mere purpose of keeping my bed; for whenever my master, who came to inquire about me at least once a day, ventured to hint I was well enough to get up if I would but choose to think so, I felt myself unaccountably impelled to declare, with sighs and groans, that I could scarce move a limb, and that I suffered endless pangs; all which was false, for I was strong as a horse, and without any pain whatever.

"Well, well," my venerable master used to say, "I know you are cheating me, you rascal. But that's the way with you all. A negro will be a negro; and, sure, I have the laziest set of scoundrels on my estate that ever ate up a good-natured master."

Unhappily, for so I then thought it, old aunt Phœbe, who had been appointed to nurse me, and who was very conscientious about her master's interest in all cases where her own was not involved, was by no means so easily imposed upon as the old gentleman; and on the seventh day after I opened my eyes, she dispelled a pleasing revery in which I was indulging, by bidding me arise and begone. I began to plead my pains: "Can't play 'possum with me!" said she; "good-for-nothin' nigga, not worth you cawn!" and, not deigning to employ any other argument, she took a broomstick to me, and fairly beat me out of the hovel. I thought it was very odd I should get my first beating of a fellow-slave, and I was somewhat incensed at the old woman for her cruelty; but by-and-by, when I had taken a seat in the sunshine, snuffed the fresh autumn air, and looked about me a little, I fell into a better humour with her, and—if that were possible—with myself.

CHAPTER IV

Some account of Ridgewood Hill, and the Author's occupations.

My master's lands lay on and near the Potomac, and his house was built on a hill, which bore his own name, and gave name also to the estate—that is, Ridgewood Hill. It overlooked that wide and beautiful river, being separated from it only by a lawn, which in the centre was hollow, and ran down to the river in a ravine, while its flanks or extremities, sloping but gently in their whole course, suddenly fell down to the shore in wooded bluffs, that looked very bold and romantic from the water. In the hollow of the lawn was a little brook, that rose from a spring further up the hill, and found its way to the river through the ravine, where it made many pretty little pools and cascades among the bushes; while a creek, that was wide but shallow, swept in from the river above, and went winding away among the hills behind.

My master's house was ancient, and, I must say, not in so good repair as it might have been; but there were so many beautiful trees about it that one would not think of its defects, the more especially as it appeared only the more venerable for them. It looked handsome enough from the river; and even from the negro-huts, which were nearer the creek, it had an agreeable appearance; particularly when the children were playing together on the lawn, which they did, and sometimes white and black together, nearly all day long. They were thus engaged in their sports when aunt Pbœbe drove me from the hovel; and I remember how soon my indignation at the unceremonious ejection was pacified by looking on the happy creatures, thus enjoying themselves on the grass, while my master and his eldest daughter sat on the porch, regarding them with smiles.

How greatly I had changed within a few short days! Instead of being moved by the sight of juvenile independence and happiness to think of my own bitter state of servitude, I was filled with a foolish glee; and little Tommy running up to me with shouts of joy, down I dropped on my hands and knees, and taking him on my back, began to trot, and gallop, and rear, and curvet over the lawn, to the infinite gratification of himself, his little sisters, and the children of my own colour, all of whom rewarded my efforts of horseship with screams of approbation. Now the reader will be surprised to hear it, but I, Tom the slave (I never remember to have heard myself called any thing but Tom), enjoyed this foolish sport just as much as Tommy the rider, to whom I felt, I think, some such feelings of affection—I know not how I got them, but feel them I did—as a father experiences while playing the courser to his own child. Nay, I was thrown into such good-humour, and felt so content with myself, that when my master came to me, and bade me "take care lest I should hurt myself by my exertions," I told him, in the fervour of my heart, I was doing very well, and that I was as strong as ever I had been; which caused him to laugh, and say I was growing marvellous honest of a sudden.

About this time the field-hands returned from their daily labour, and, having despatched their evening meal, they came, the women and children with them, under the trees before the door, with banjoes, fiddles, and clacking-bones (that is, a sort of castanets made of the ribs of an ox), and began to sing and dance, as was their custom always every fair evening; for my master greatly delighted, as he said, to see the poor devils enjoy them-selves; in which the poor devils were ever ready to oblige him. They had no sooner begun the diversion, than I was seized with an unaccountable desire to join them, which I did, dancing with all my might, and singing and clapping my hands, the merriest and happiest of them all. And this sort of amusement, I may as well now inform the reader, we were in the habit of repeating so long as the mildness of the weather permitted.

CHAPTER V

In which the Author further describes his situation, and philosophizes on the state of slavery.

Having thus shown myself to be perfectly cured of my broken neck, it followed that, as a slave, I was now compelled to go into the fields and labour. This I did, at first, very reluc-tantly; but by-and-by I discovered there was but little toil expected of me, or indeed of any other bondman; for the overseer was a good-natured man like his employer, and lazy like ourselves. I do not know how it may be with the slaves on other estates; but I must confess that, so far as mere labour went, there was less done by, and less looked for from, my mas-ter's hands, than I have ever known to be the case with the white labourers of New-Jersey. My master owned extensive tracts of land, from which, although now greatly impover-ished and almost exhausted, he might have drawn a princely revenue, had he exacted of his slaves the degree of labour always demanded of able bodied hirelings in a free state. But such was not the custom of Virginia, or such, at least, was not the custom of my mas-ter. He was of a happy, easy temper, neglectful of his interest, and though often—nay, I may say incessantly—grumbling at the flagrant laziness of all who called him master, and at the yearly depreciation of his lands, he was content enough if the gains of the year coun-terbalanced the expenses; and as but a slight degree of toil was required to effect this happy object, it was commonly rendered, and without repugnance, on the part of his slaves. His great consolation, and he was always pronouncing it to himself and to us, was, "that his hands were the greatest set of scoundrels in the world,"—which, if unutterable laziness be scoundrelism, was true. He was pretty generally beloved by them; which, I suppose, was because he was so good-natured; though many used to tell me they loved him because he was their "right-born master,"—that is, put over them by birth, and not by purchase; for he lived upon the land occupied by his fathers before him, and his slaves were the descendants of those who had served them.

The reader, who has seen with what horror and fear I began the life of a slave, may ask if, after I found myself restored to health and strength, I sought no opportunity to give my master the slip, and make a bold push for freedom. I did not; a change had come over the spirit of my dream: I found myself, for the first time in my life, content, or very nearly so, with my condition, free from cares, far removed from disquiet, and, if not actually in love with my lot, so far from being dissatisfied, that I had not the least desire to exchange it for another.

Methinks I see the reader throw up his hands at this, crying, "What! content with slavery!" I assure him, now I ponder the matter over, that I am as much surprised as himself, and that I consider my being content with a state of bondage a very singular and unaccountable circumstance. Nevertheless, such was the fact. I was no longer Sheppard Lee, Zachariah Longstraw, nor anybody else, except simply Tom, Thomas, or Tommy, the slave. I forgot that I once had been a freeman, or, to speak more strictly, I did not remember it, the act of remembering involving an effort of mind which it did not comport with my new habits of laziness and indifference to make, though perhaps I *might* have done so, had I chosen. I had ceased to remember all my previous states of existence. I could not have been an African had I troubled myself with thoughts of any thing but the present.

Perhaps this defect of memory will account for my being satisfied with my new condition. I had no recollection of the sweets of liberty to compare and contrast with the disgusts of servitude. Perhaps my mind was stupified—sunk beneath the ordinary level of the human understanding, and therefore incapable of realizing the evils of my condition. Or, perhaps, after all, considering the circumstances of my lot with reference to those of my mind and nature, such evils did not in reality exist.

The reader may settle the difficulty for himself, which he can do when he has read a little more of my history. In the meanwhile, the fact is true: I was satisfied with my lot—I was satisfied even with *myself.* The first time I looked at my new face I was shocked at what I considered its ugliness. But having peeped at it a dozen times or more, my ideas began to alter, and, by-and-by, I thought it quite beautiful. I used to look at myself in aunt Phœbe's glass by the hour, and I well remember the satisfaction with which I listened to the following rebuke of my vanity from her, namely, "All you pritty young niggurs with handsome faces is good for nothin, not wuth so much as you cawn!" In short, I was something of a coxcomb; and nothing could equal the pride and happiness of my heart, when, of a Sabbath morning, dressed in one of my master's old coats well brushed up, a bran-new rabbit-fur hat, the gift of little Tommy, a ruffled shirt, and a white neckcloth, with a pair of leather gloves swinging in one hand, and a peeled beechen wand by way of cane in the other, I went stalking over the fields to church in the little village, near to which my master resided.

I say again, I cannot account for my being so contented with bondage. It may be, however, that there is nothing necessarily adverse to happiness in slavery itself, unaccompanied by other evils; and that when the slave is ground by no oppression and goaded by no cruelty, he is not apt to repine or moralize upon his condition, nor to seek for those torments of sentiment which imagination associates with the idea of slavery in the abstract.

Of one thing, at least, I can be very certain. I never had so easy and idle a time of it in my whole life. My little master Tommy had grown very fond of me. It is strange anybody should be fond of a slave; but it is true. It appears I was what they call a mere field-hand, that is, a labourer, and quite unfit for domestic service. Nevertheless, to please

Tommy, I was taken from the tobacco-fields, and, without being appointed to any peculiar duty about the house, was allowed to do what I pleased, provided I made myself sufficiently agreeable to young master. So I made him tops, kites, windmills, corn-stalk fiddles, and little shingle ships with paper sails, gave him a trot every now and then on my book, and had, in return a due share of his oranges and gingerbead.

In this way my time passed along more agreeably than I can describe. My little master, it is true, used to fall into a passion and thump me now and then; but that I held to be prime fun; particularly as,—provided I chose to blubber a little, and pretend to be hurt,—the little rogue would relent, and give me all the goodies he could beg, borrow, or steal, to "make up with me," as he called it.

Little Tommy and his sisters, four in number, were the children of my master by a second wife, who had died two years before. The oldest was the young lady of whom I have already spoken, and she was, I believe, not above seventeen. Her name was Isabella, and she was uncommonly handsome. A young gentleman of the neighbourhood, named Andrews, was paying court to her. Indeed, she had a great many admirers, and there was much company came to see her.

My master's oldest son, the only child left by his first wife, lived on a plantation beyond the creek, being already married, and having children. His name was George, like his father, and the slaves used to distinguish them as "Massa Cunnel Jodge," and "Massa Maja Jodge;" for all the gentlemen in those parts were either colonels or majors. The major's seat being at so short a distance, and the plantation he cultivated a part of the colonel's great estate of Ridgewood Hill, we used to regard him as belonging still to our master's family, and the slaves on both plantations considered themselves as forming but a single community. Nevertheless, we of the south side had a sort of contempt for those of the north; for "Massa Maja," though a good master, was by no means so easy as his father. He exacted more work; and when he rode into the fields on our side, as he often did, he used to swear at us for lazy loons, and declare he would, some day or other turn over a new leaf with us.

CHAPTER VI

Recollections of slavery.

I must again repeat what I have said, namely, that I was contented with my servile condition, and that I was so far from looking back with regret to my past life of freedom, that I ceased at last to remember it altogether. I was troubled with no sense of degradation, afflicted with no consciousness of oppression; and instead of looking upon my master as a tyrant who had robbed me of my rights, I regarded him as a great and powerful friend, whose protection and kindness I was bound to requite with a loyal affection, and with so much of the labour of my hands as was necessary to my own subsistence. What would have been my feelings had my master been really a cruel and tyrannical man, I will not pretend to say; but doubtless they would have been the opposite of those I have confessed.

The above remarks apply equally to my fellow-bondmen, of whom there were, young and old, and men and women together, more than a hundred on the two estates. The exact number I never knew; but I remember there were above twenty able-bodied men, or "full hands," as they were called, when all were mustered together. There were many, especially among the women, who were great grumblers; but that was their nature: such a thing as serious discontent was, I am persuaded, entirely unknown. The labours of the plantation were light, the indulgences granted frequent and many. There was scarce a slave on the estate who, if he laboured at all, did not labour more for himself than his master; for all had their little lots or gardens, the produce of which was entirely their own, and which they were free to sell to whomsoever they listed. And hard merchants they were sometimes, even to my master, when he would buy of them, as he often did. I remember one day seeing old aunt Phœbe, to whom he had sent to buy some chickens, fall into a passion and refuse to let the messenger have any, because her master had forgotten to send the money. "Go tell old Massa Jodge," said she, with great ire, "I no old fool to be cheated out of my money; and I don't vally his promise to pay not *dat!*"—snapping her fingers—"he owe me two ninepence already!" And the old gentleman was compelled to send her the cash before she complied with his wishes.

The truth is, my master was, in some respects, a greater slave than his bondmen; and all the tyranny I ever witnessed on the estate was exercised by *them,* and at his expense; for there was a general conspiracy on the part of all to cheat him, as far as was practicable, out of their services, while they were, all the time, great sticklers for their own rights and privileges. He was, as I have said before, universally beloved; but his good-nature was abused a thousand times a day.

There existed no substantial causes for dissatisfaction; and there was therefore the best reason for content. Singing and dancing were more practised than hard work. In a word, my master's slaves were an idle, worthless set, but as happy as the day was long. I may say the same of myself; I certainly was a very merry and joyous personage, and my companions, who envied me for being the favourite of young master, used to call me Giggling Tom.

But there is an end to the mirth of the slave, as well as the joy of the master. A cloud at last came betwixt me and the sun; a new thought awoke in my bosom, bringing with it a revolution of feeling, which extended to the breasts of all my companions. It was but a small cause to produce such great effects; but an ounce of gunpowder may be made to blow up an army, and a drop of venom from the lip of a dog may cause the destruction of a whole herd.

CHAPTER VII

A scene on the banks of the Potomac, with the
humours of an African improvisatore.[12]

Beneath the bluff, and at the mouth of the creek which divided the two plantations, was a wharf or landing, where our fishing-boats (for we had a good fishery hard by) used to discharge their cargoes, and where, also, small shallops, coming with supplies to the

---

[12]One who improvises (usually extemporaneously).

plantation, put out their freight. Here, one day, some seven or eight of the hands were engaged removing a cargo of timber, which had just been discharged by a small vessel; my master having bought it for the express purpose of repairing the negro-houses, and building a new one for a fellow that was to be married; for it seems, his crops of corn and tobacco had turned out unusually well, and when that happened the slaves were the first who received the benefit.

Hither I strolled, having nothing better to do, to take a position on the side of the bluff, where I could both bask in the sunshine, which was very agreeable (for it was now the end of October, though fine weather), and overlook the hands working—which was still more agreeable; for I had uncommon satisfaction to look at others labouring while I myself was doing nothing.

Having selected a place to my liking, I lay down on the warm clay, enjoying myself, while the others intermitted their labour to abuse me, crying, "Cuss' lazy nigga, gigglin' Tom dah! why you no come down work?" having employed themselves at which for a time, they resumed their labours; and I, turning over on my back and taking a twig that grew nigh betwixt my teeth, began to think to myself what an agreeable thing it was to be a slave and have nothing to do.

By-and-by, hearing a great chattering and laughing among the men below, I looked down and beheld one of them diverting himself with a ludicrous sport, frequently practised by slaves to whom the lash is unknown. He was frisking and dodging about pretty much as aunt Phœbe had done when endeavouring to show me how the whip was handled in Mississippi; and, like her, he rubbed his back, now here, now there, now with the right, now with the left hand; now ducking to the earth, now jumping into the air, as though some lusty overseer were plying him, whip in hand, with all his might. The wonder of the thing was, however, that Governor (for that was the fellow's name) had in his hand a pamphlet, or sheet of printed paper, the contents of which he was endeavouring both to convey to his companions and to illustrate by those ridiculous antics. The contents of the paper were varied, for varied also was the representation.

"Dah you go, nigga!" he cried, leaping as if from a blow; "slap on 'e leg, hit right on 'e shin! yah, yah, yah—chah, chah, ch-ch-ch-ch-ah! chah, chah, massa!—oh de dam overseeah! dat de way he whip a nigga!" Then pausing a moment and turning a leaf of the book, he fell to leaping again, crying—"What *dat?* dat *you,* Rose? what you been doin? stealin' sugah?

> "Jump! you nigga gal!
>   Hab a hard massa!
> So much you git for stealin' sugah!
>   So much for lickin' lassa!

"Dem hard massa, licky de gals!"

> "Ole Vaginnee, nebber ti-ah!
> What 'e debbil's de use ob floggin' like fia-ah!"

Then came another scene. "Yah, yah, yah!—what dat? Massa Maja kickin' de pawson! I say, whaw Pawson Jim? you Jim pawson, he-ah you git 'em!" And then another—Lorra-gorry, what he-ah? He-ah a nigga tied up in a gum—

    "Oh! de possum up de gum-tree,
      'Coony in de hollow:
    Two white men whip a nigga,
      How de nigga holla!

"Jump, nigga, jump! yah, yah, yah! did you ebber see de debbil? jump, nigga, jump! two white men whip a nigga? gib a nigga fay-ah play!

    "When de white man comes to sticky, sticky,
    Lorra-gorr! he licky, licky!

"Gib a nigga fay-ah play!"

And so he went on, describing and acting what he affected to read, to the infinite delight of his companions, who, ceasing their work, crowded round him, to snatch a peep at the paper, which, I observed, no one got a good look at without jumping back immediately, rubbing his sides, and launching into other antics, in rivalry with Governor.

CHAPTER VIII

*The Author descends among the slaves, and suddenly
becomes a man of figure, and an interpreter of new doctrines.*

I was moved with curiosity to know what they had laid their hands on, and I descended the bank to solve the mystery. The paper had passed from the hands of Governor to those of a fellow named Jim, or Parson Jim, as we usually called him; for he was fond of praying and preaching, which he had been allowed to do until detected in a piece of roguery a few weeks before by Master Major, who, besides putting a check on his clerical propensities for the future, saluted him with two or three kicks well laid on, on the spot. It was to this personage and his punishment that Governor alluded, when he cried, "What he-ah? Massa Maja kickin' de pawson!" as mentioned above. Although a great rogue, he was a prime favourite among the negroes, who had a great respect for his learning; for he could read print, and was even thought to have some idea of writing. This fellow was employed, on the present occasion, at the ox-cart; and, as it is no part of a slave's system to do the work of others, he had been sitting apart singing a psalm, while the others were loading his cart; and apart he had remained, until a call was made upon him to explain so much of the paper, being the printed portion, as Governor could not. The paper, it is here proper to observe, had been found by Governor among the boards and scantling; though how it got there no one knew, nor was it ever discovered. It was a pamphlet, or magazine, I know not which (and the name I have unfortunately forgotten), containing, besides a deal of strange matter about slavery, some half a dozen or more wood-cuts, representing negroes in chains, under the lash, exposed in the market for sale, and I know not what other situations; and it was these which had afforded the delighted Governor so much matter for mimicry and merriment. There was one cut on the first page, serving as a frontispiece; it represented a negro kneeling in chains, and raising his fettered hands in beseeching to a white man, who was lashing him with a whip. Beneath it was a legend, which being, or being deemed, explanatory of the picture, and at the same time the initial sentence of the book, Parson Jim was essaying to read: and thus it was he proceeded:—

"T-h-e, *the*—dat's *de;* f-a-t-e, *fat*—*de fat;* o-f, *ob*—*de fat ob;* t-h-e, *de*—*de fat ob de;* s-l-a-v-e, *slave*—*de fat ob de slave.* My gorry, what's dat? Brederen, I can't say as how I misprehends dat."

"Yah, yah, yah!" roared Governor; "plain as de nose on you face. *De fat ob de slave*—what he mean, heh? Why, gorry, you dumb, nigga, he mean—massa, dah, is whippin de fat out ob de nigger! Dem hard massa dat-ah, heh? Whip de fat out!

"Lorra-gorry, massa, don't like you whippy:
Don't sell Gubbe'nor down a Mississippi!"

"Let me read it," said I.

"*You* read, you nigga! whar you larn to read?" cried my friends. It was a question I could not well answer; for, as I said before, the memory of my past existence had quite faded from my mind: nevertheless, I had a feeling in me as if I *could* read; and taking the book from the parson, I succeeded in deciphering the legend—"THE FATE OF THE SLAVE."

"Whaw dat?" said Governor; "de chain and de cowhide? Does de book say *dat's* de luck for nigga? Don't b'leeb'm; dem lie; Massa Cunnel nebber lick a nigga in 'm life!"

The reading of that little sentence seemed, I know not why, to have cast a sudden damper on the spirits of all present. Until that moment, there had been much shouting, laughing, and mimicking of the pains of men undergoing flagellation. Every picture had been examined, commented on, and illustrated with glee; it associated only the idea of some idle vagabond or other winning his deserts. A new face, a new interpretation was given to the matter by the words I had read. The chain and scourge appeared no longer as the punishment of an individual; they were to be regarded as the doom of the race. The laughing and mimicry ceased, and I beheld around me nothing but blank faces. It was manifest, however, that the feeling was rather indignation than anxiety; and that my friends looked upon the ominous words as a libel upon their masters and themselves.

"What for book say dat?" cried Governor, who, from being the merriest, had now become the angriest of all; "who ebber hear of chain a nigga, except nigga runaway or nigga gwyin' down gin' will to Mississippi? Who ebber hear of lash a nigga, except nigga sassbox, nigga thief, nigga drunk, nigga break hoss' lea?"

"Brudders," said Parson Jim, "this here is a thing what is 'portant to hear on; for, blessed be Gorra-matty, there is white men what writes books what is friends of the Vaginnee niggar."

"All cuss' bobbolitionist!" said Governor, with sovereign contempt—"don't b'leeb in 'm. Who says chain nigga in Vaginnee? who says cowhide nigga in Vaginnee? *De fate ob de slave!* Cuss' lie! An't *I* slave, hah? Who chains Gubbe'nor? who licks Gubbe'nor? Little book big lie!"

And "little book big lie!" echoed all, in extreme wrath. The parson took things more coolly. He rolled his eyes, hitched up his collar, stroked his chin, and suggesting the propriety of reading a little farther, proposed that "brudder Tom, who had an uncommon good hidear of that ar sort of print, should hunt out the root of the matter;" and lamented that "it was a sort of print *he* could not well get along with without his spectacles."

CHAPTER IX

What it was the negroes had discovered among the scantling.

Thus called upon, I made a second essay, and succeeded, though not without pain, in deciphering enough of the text to give me a notion of the object for which the tract had been written. It was entitled "An Address to the Owners of Slaves," and could not, therefore, be classed among those "incendiary publications" which certain over-zealous philanthropists are accused of sending among slaves themselves, to inflame them into insurrection and murder. No such imputation could be cast upon the writer. His object was of a more humane and Christian character; it was to convince the master he was a robber and villain, and, by this pleasing mode of argument, induce him to liberate his bondmen. The only ill consequence that might be produced was, that the book might, provided it fell into their hands, convince the bondmen of the same thing; but that was a result for which the writer was not responsible—he addressed himself only to the master. It began with the following pithy questions and answers—or something very like them—for I cannot pretend to recollect them to the letter.

"Why scourgest thou this man? and why dost thou hold him in bonds? Is he a murderer? a house-burner? a ravisher? a blasphemer? a thief? No. What then is the crime for which thou art punishing him so bitterly? He is a negro, and my slave."

Then followed a demand "how he became, and by what right the master claimed him as a slave;" to which the master replied, "By right of purchase," exhibiting, at the same time, a bill of sale. At this the querist expressed great indignation, and calling the master a robber, cheat, and usurper, bade him show, as the only title a Christian would sanction, "a bill of sale signed by the negro's Maker!" who alone had the right to dispose of man's liberty; and he concluded the paragraph by averring, "that the claim was fraudulent; that the slave was unjustly, treacherously, unrighteously held in bonds; and that he was, or of right should be, as free as the master himself."

Here I paused for breath; my companions looked at me with eyes staring out of their heads. Astonishment, suspicion, and fear were depicted in their countenances. A new idea had entered their brains. All opened their mouths, but Governor was the only one who could speak, and he stuttered and stammered in his eagerness so much that I could scarcely understand him.

"Wh-wh-wh-wh-what dat!" he cried; "hab a right to fr-fr-fr-freedom, 'case Gorramatty no s-s-s-sell me? Why den, wh-wh-wh-*who's* slave? Gorra-matty no trade in niggurs! I say, you Pawson Jim, wh-wh-wh-what *you* say dat doctrine?"

The parson was dumb-founded. The difficulty was solved by an old negro, who rolled his quid of tobacco and his eyes together, and said,

"Whaw de debbil's de difference? Massa Cunnel no *buy* us; we *born* him slave, ebbery nigga he-ah!"

Unluckily, the very next paragraph was opened by the quotation from the Declaration of Independence, that "all men were born free and equal," which was asserted to be true of all men, negroes as well as others; from which it followed that the master's claim to the slave born in thraldom was as fraudulent as in the case of one obtained by purchase.

"Whaw dat?" said Governor; "Decoration of Independence say *dat?* Gen'ral Jodge Washington, him make dat; and Gen'ral Tommie Jefferson, him put hand to it! 'All men born free equal.' A nigga is a man! who says *no* to dat? How come Massa Cunnel to be massa den?"

That question had never before been asked on Ridgewood Hill. But all now asked it, and all, for the first time in their lives, began to think of their master as a foe and usurper. The strangely-expressed idea in the pamphlet, namely—that none but their Maker could rightfully sell them to bondage, and that other in relation to natural freedom and equality, had captivated their imaginations, and made an impression on their minds not readily to be forgotten. Black looks passed from one to another, and angry expressions were uttered; and I know not where the excitement that was fast awaking would have ended, had not our master himself suddenly made his appearance descending the bluff.

For the first time in their lives, the slaves beheld his approach with terror; and all, darting upon the timber, began to labour with a zeal and bustling eagerness which they had never shown before. But, first, the pamphlet was snatched out of my hands, and concealed in a hollow of the bank. Our uncommon industry (for even Parson Jim and myself were seized with a fit of zeal, and gave our labour with the rest) somewhat surprised the venerable old man. But as the timber was destined to contribute to our own comforts, he attributed it to a selfish motive, and chiding us good-humouredly and with a laugh, said, "That's the way with you, you rogues; you can work well enough when it is for yourselves."

"Dat's all de tanks we gits!" muttered Governor, hard by. "Wonder if we ha'n't a better right to work than Massa Jodge to make us?"

CHAPTER X

The effect of the pamphlet on its reader and hearers.

We had seen the last day of content on Ridgewood Hill. That little scrap of paper, thrown among us perhaps by accident, or, as I have sometimes thought, dropped by the fiend of darkness himself, had conjured up a thousand of his imps, who, one after another, took up their dwelling in our breasts, until their name was Legion. My fellow-slaves cared little now for singing and dancing. Their only desire, in the intervals of labour, was to assemble together below the bluff, and dive deeper into the mysteries of the pamphlet; and as I was the only one who could explain them, and was ready enough to do so, I often neglected my little friend Tommy to preside over their convocations.

Nor were these meetings confined to the original finders of the precious document. The news had been whispered from man to man, and the sensation spread over the whole estate, so that those who lived with the major were as eager to escape from their labours and listen to the new revelation as ourselves. Nay, so great was the curiosity among them, that many who could not come when I was present to expound the secrets of the book, would betake themselves to the bluff, to indulge a look at it, and guess out its contents as they could from the pictures. And by-and-by, the news having spread to a distance, we had visiters also from the gangs of other plantations.

It was perhaps a week or more before the composition was read through and understood by us all; and in that time it had wrought a revolution in our feelings as surprising as it was fearful. And now, lest the reader should doubt that the great effects I am about to record should have really arisen from so slight a cause as a little book, I think it proper to tell him more fully than I have done what that little book contained.

It was, as I have said, an address to the owners of slaves, and its object purported to be to awaken their minds to the cruelty, injustice, and wickedness of slavery. This was sought to be effected, in the first place, by numerous cuts, representing all the cruelties and indignities that negro slaves had suffered, or could suffer, either in reality, or in the imaginations of the philanthropists. Some of these were horrible, many shocking, and all disgusting; and some of them, I think, were copied out of Fox's Book of Martyrs, though of that I am not certain. The moral turpitude and illegality of the institution were shown, or attempted to be shown, now by arguments that were handled like daggers and broad-axes, and now by savage denunciations of the enslaver and oppressor, who were proved to be murderers, blasphemers, tyrants, devils, and I know not what beside. The vengeance of Heaven was invoked upon their heads, coupled with predictions of the retribution that would sooner or later fall upon them, these being borne out by monitory allusions to the servile wars of Rome, Syria, Egypt, Sicily, St. Domingo, &c. &c. It was threatened that Heaven would repeat the plagues of Egypt in America, to punish the task-masters of the Ethiopian, as it had punished those of the Israelite, and that, in addition, the horrors of Hayti[13] would be enacted a second time, and within our own borders. It was contended that the negro was, in organic and mental structure, the white man's equal, if not his superior, and that there was a peculiar injustice in subjecting to bondage *his* race, which had been (or so the writer averred), in the earlier days of the world, the sole possessors of knowledge and civilization; and there were many triumphant references to Hannibal, Queen Sheba, Cleopatra, and the Pharaohs, all of whom were proved to have been woolly-headed, and as bright in spirit as they were black in visage. In short, the book was full of strange things, and, among others, of insurrection and murder; though it is but charitable to suppose that the writer did not know it.

There was scarce a word in it that did not contribute to increase the evil spirit which its first paragraph had excited among my companions. It taught them to look on themselves as the victims of avarice, the play-things of cruelty, the foot-balls of oppression, the most injured people in the world: and the original greatness of their race, which was an idea they received with uncommon pleasure, and its reviving grandeur in the liberated Hayti, convinced them they possessed the power to redress their wrongs, and raise themselves into a mighty nation.

With the sense of injury came a thirst for revenge. My companions began to talk of violence and dream of blood. A week before there was not one of them who would not have risked his life to save his master's; the scene was now changed—my master walked daily, though without knowing it, among volcanoes; all looked upon him askant, and muttered curses as he passed. A kinder-hearted man and easier master never lived; and it

[13]Beginning in 1791, Haiti experienced a series of bloody slave revolts that would briefly result in a black-governed French protectorate.

may seem incredible that he should be hated without any real cause. Imaginary causes are, however, always the most efficacious in exciting jealousy and hatred. In affairs of the affections, slaves and the members of political factions are equally unreasonable. The only difference in the effect is, that the one cannot, while the other can, and *does,* change his masters when his whim changes.

That fatal book infected my own spirit as deeply as it did those of the others, and made me as sour and discontented as they. I began to have sentimental notions about liberty and equality, the dignity of man, the nobleness of freedom, and so forth; and a stupid ambition, a vague notion that I was born to be a king or president, or some such great personage, filled my imagination, and made me a willing listener to, and sharer in, the schemes of violence and desperation which my fellow-slaves soon began to frame. It is wonderful, that among the many thoughts that now crowded my brain, no memory of my original condition arose to teach me the folly of my desires. But, and I repeat it again, the past was dead with me; I lived only for the present.

A little incident that soon befell me will show the reader how completely my feelings were identified with my condition, and how deeply the lessons of that unlucky pamphlet had sunk into my spirit. My little playmate, master Tommy, who was not above six years old, being of an irascible temper, sometimes quarrelled with me; on which occasions, as I mentioned before, he used to beat me; a liberty I rather encouraged than otherwise, since I gained by it—though my master strictly forbade the youth to take it. Now, as soon as my head began to fill with the direful and magnificent conceptions of a malecontent and conspirator, I waxed weary of child's play and master Tommy, who, falling into a passion with me for that reason, proceeded, on a certain occasion, to pommel my ribs with a fist about equal in weight to the paw of a gadfly. I was incensed, I may say enraged, at the poor child, and repaid the violence by shaking him almost to death. Indeed, I felt for a while as if I could have killed him; and I know not whether I might not have done it (for the devil had on the sudden got into my spirit), had not his father discovered what I was doing, and run to his assistance. I then pretended that I had shaken him in sport, and thus escaped a drubbing, of which I was at first in danger. The threat of this, however, sank deeply into my mind, and I ever after felt a deep hatred of both father and son. This may well be called a blind malice, for neither had given me any real cause for it.

CHAPTER XI

The hatching of a conspiracy.

In the meanwhile the devil was doing his work among the others, and disaffection grew into wrath and fury, that were not so perfectly concealed but that my master, or rather his eldest son, who was of a more observant disposition, began to suspect that mischief was brewing; and in a short time it was reported among us that our master had marked some of us as being dangerous, and was resolved to sell us to a Mississippi trader who was then in the county. This was reported by a spy, a house-servant, who professed to have overheard the conversation, and who reported, besides, that our master and his son were furbishing up their fire-arms, and laying in a terrible supply of balls and powder.

Now whether this account was true or not I never knew, and I suppose I never shall until I am in my grave. It was enough, however, to drive us to a phrensy, those in partic- ular who had been indicated as the intended victims of the Mississippi trader; and the more especially, as those men had wives and children, from whom they were told they were to be parted. One of these was the blacksmith of the estate, who, being a resolute and fierce-tempered fellow, instantly began to convert all the old horseshoes and iron hoops about his shop into a kind of blades or spear-heads, which we fastened upon poles, and hid away in secret places. There were among us three or four men who had muskets, with which they used to shoot wild fowl on the river, there being great abundance at this season. These weapons were also put into requisition; besides which we stored away butcher-knives and bludgeons, old scythe-blades and sickles beaten straight, until we could boast quite an armory. And here I may observe, that the faster these weapons increased upon our hands, the more deadly became our resolutions, the more fierce and malignant our desires; until, having at last what we thought a sufficiency for our purpose, we gave a loose to our passions, and determined upon a plan of proceedings that may well be called infernal.

I believe that when we began to collect these offensive weapons we had but vague ideas of mischief, thinking rather of defending ourselves from some meditated outrage on the part of our master, than of beginning an assault, upon him ourselves. But now, the armory being complete, and several cunning fellows, who had been spying out among the surrounding plantations, bringing us word that the gangs (so they sometimes call the whole number of hands on a farm) of most of them were ready to strike with us for free- dom; another having brought us word that a great outbreaking had already taken place south of James river, which, however, was not true; a third reminding us that we were more numerous than our masters; and a fourth bidding us remember that the negroes had once, as the little book told us, been the masters of all the white men in the world, and might be again; I say, these things being represented to us, as we were handling our arms and thinking what execution we could do with them, we shook hands together, and kiss- ing the little pamphlet (for which we had conceived a high regard), as we had seen white men kiss the book in courts of law, we swore we would exterminate all the white men in Virginia, beginning with our master and his family.

CHAPTER XII

How the spoils of victory were intended to be divided.

The chief men in the conspiracy were, by all consent, the fellow called Governor, of whom I have said so much before; Parson Jim, who, although a little in the background at first, had soon taken a foremost stand, and was, indeed, the first to propose murder; myself,—not that I was really very active or fiery in the matter, but because I had become prominent as the reader of the little book; Cesar, the blacksmith; and a fellow named Zip, or Scipio, who was the chief fiddler and banjo-player, and had been therefore in great favour with the family, until he lost it by some misconduct.

The parson having uttered the diabolical proposal I mentioned before, and seeing it well received, got up to make a speech to inflame our courage. There was in his oration a good deal of preaching, with a considerable sprinkling of scraps from the Bible, such as he had picked up in the course of his clerical career. What he chiefly harped on was that greatness of the negro nation spoken of before, and he discoursed so energetically of the great kings and generals, "the great Faroes and Cannibals," as he called them, who had distinguished the race in olden time, that all became ambitious to figure with similar dignity in story.

"What *you* speak raw, pawson?" said Governor, interrupting him, and looking round with the air of a lord; "I be king, hah? and hab my sarvants to wait on me!"

"What you say dah, Gub'nor?" cried Zip the fiddler, with equal spirit: "You be king, I be president."

"I be emp'ror, like dat ah nigga in High-ty!" said another.

"I be constable!" cried a fourth.

"You be cuss'! you no go for de best man!" cried Governor, in a heat: "I be constable myself, and I lick any nigga I like! Who say me *no,* hah? I smash him brain out—dem nigga!" Governor was a tyrant already, and all began to be more or less afraid of him. "I'll be de great man, and I shall hab my choice ob de women: what you say *dat?* I sall hab Missa Isabella faw my wife! Who say me *no* dah?"

"Berry well!" cried Scipio: "I hab Missa Edie"—that is, Miss Edith, the next in age, who was, however, not yet thirteen, and therefore but a poor little child.

"Brudder Zip," said Jim the parson, "I speak fust dah! The labourer is wordy ob his hiah—I shall put my hand to de plough, and I shall hab Missa Edie for *my* wife. After me, if you please, brudder Zip!"

"Hold you jaw, Zip," said King Governor to the fiddler, who was ready to knock the parson down. "You shall hab Massa Maja's wife, and you shall cut his head off fust. As faw de oder niggas he-ah, what faw use ob quar'lin? We shall have wifes enough when we kills white massas; gorry! we shall hab pick!"

And thus my companions apportioned among themselves, in prospective, the wives and daughters of their intended victims; and thus, doubtless, they would have apportioned them in reality, had the bloody enterprise been allowed the success its projectors anticipated. I remember that my blood suddenly froze within my veins when the conspiracy had reached this point; and the idea of seeing those innocent, helpless maidens made the prey of brutal murderers, was so shocking to my spirit that I lost speech, and could scarce support myself on my feet.

While I stood thus confused among them, the conspirators determined upon a plan of action by which, as far as I understood it, the houses of my master and his son, the two being previously murdered, were to be set on fire at the same moment, on the following night, and at the sight of the flames the slaves on several neighbouring plantations were to fall upon their masters in like manner: after which, the gangs from all the burnt estates were to meet at a common rendezvous, and march in a body against the neighbouring village, the sacking of which they joyously looked forward to as the first step in a career of conquest and triumph—in other words, of murder and rapine.

Who would have thought that a little book, framed by a philanthropist, for the humane purpose of turning his neighbour from the error of his way, should have lighted a torch in his dwelling only to be quenched by blood! I am myself a witness that the pamphlet was not one of those incendiary publications of which so much is said, as being designed for the eyes of slaves themselves, to exasperate them to revolt. By no means; it was addressed to the master, and of course was only designed for him. Why the pictures were put in it, however, I cannot imagine, since it may be supposed the master could understand the argument and exhortation of the writer well enough without them. Perhaps they were intended to divert his children.

The book, however, whatever may have been the object for which it was written, had the effect to make a hundred men, who were previously contented with their lot in life, and perhaps as happy as any other men ordained to a life of labour, the victims of dissatisfaction and rage, the enemies of those they had once loved, and, in fine, the contrivers and authors of their own destruction.

CHAPTER XIII

The attack of the insurgents upon the mansion at Ridgewood Hill.

I said, that when the conspiracy reached the crisis mentioned before, I was suddenly seized with terror. I began to think with what kindness I had been treated by those I had leagued to destroy; and the baseness and ingratitude of the whole design struck me with such force, that I was two or three times on the point of going to my master, and revealing it to him while he had yet the power to escape. But my fears of him and of my fellow-ruffians deterred me. I thought he looked fierce and stern; and as for my companions, I conceited that they were watching me, dogging my every step, prepared to kill me the moment I attempted to play them false. It was unfortunate that my rudeness to Master Tommy had caused me to be banished the house; for although my master did not beat me, he was persuaded my violence in that case was not altogether jocose, and therefore punished me by sending me to the fields. Hence I had no opportunity to see him in private, unless I had sought it, which would have exposed me to observation.

The night came, and it came to me bringing such gloom and horror, that my agitation was observed by Governor and others, who railed at me for a coward, and threatened to take my life if I did not behave more like a man. This only increased my alarm; and, truly, my disorder of mind became so great, that I was in a species of stupid distraction when the moment for action arrived; for which reason I retain but a confused recollection of the first events, and cannot therefore give a clear relation of them.

I remember that there was some confusion produced by an unexpected act on the part of our master, who, it was generally supposed, designed crossing the creek to visit the major, having ordered his carriage and the ferry-boat to be got ready, and it was resolved to kill him while crossing the creek on his return; after which we were to fire a volley of guns, as a signal to the major's gang, and then assault and burn our master's dwelling. Instead of departing, however, when the night came, he remained at home, shut up with the overseer and young Mr. Andrews, his daughter's lover; and it was reported that they had barred up the doors and windows, and were sitting at a table covered with loaded pistols; thus making it manifest that they suspected our intentions, and were resolved to defend themselves to the last.

For my part, I have never believed that our master suspected his danger at all; he perceived, indeed, that an ill spirit had got among his people, but neither he nor any of his family really believed that mischief was intended. Had they done so, he would undoubtedly have procured assistance, or at least removed his children. The windows were barred indeed, and perhaps earlier than usual, which may have been accidental; and as for the fire-arms on the table, I believe they were only fowling-pieces, which my master, Mr. Andrews, and the overseer, who was a great fowler, and therefore much favoured by my master, who was a veteran sportsman, were getting ready to shoot wild ducks with in the morning.

My companions, however, were persuaded that our victims were on their guard; and the hour drawing nigh at which they had appointed to strike the first blow, and give the signal to the neighbouring gangs, they were at a loss, not knowing what to do; for they were afraid to attack the house while three resolute men, armed with pistols, stood ready to receive them. In this conjuncture it was proposed by Governor, who, from having been a fellow notorious for nothing save monkey tricks and waggery, was now become a devil incarnate, he was so bold, cunning, and eager for blood, to fire the pile of timber where it stood near the quarters, or negro-huts; the burning of which would serve the double purpose of drawing our intended victims from the house, and giving the signal to the neighbouring estates.

The proposal was instantly adopted, and in a few moments the pile of dry resinous wood was in a flame, burning with prodigious violence, and casting a bright light over the whole mansion, the lawn, and even the neighbouring river. At the same moment, and just as we were about to raise the treacherous alarm, we heard a sudden firing of guns and shouting beyond the creek at the major's house, which made us suppose the negroes there had anticipated us in the rising.

Emulous[14] not to be outdone, our own party now set up a horrid alarm of "Fire!" accompanied with screams and yells that might have roused the dead, and ran to the mansion door, as if to demand assistance of their master.

Never shall I forget the scene that ensued. I stood rooted to the ground, not twenty steps from the house, when the door was thrown open, and my master rushed out, followed by Andrews and the overseer. They had scarce put foot on the porch before six or seven guns, being all that the conspirators could muster, and which the owners held in readiness, were discharged at them, and then they were set upon by others with the spears. The light of the fire illuminated the porch, so that objects were plainly distinguishable; yet so violent was the rush of assailants, so wild the tumult, so brief the contest, that I can scarce say I really witnessed the particulars of the tragedy. I beheld, indeed, my master's gray hairs, for he was of towering stature, floating an instant over the heads of the assailants; but the next moment they had vanished; and I saw but a single white man struggling in the hall against a mass of foes, and crying out to Miss Isabella by name, "to escape with the children." Vain counsel, vain sacrifice of safety to humanity; the faithful overseer (for it was he who made this heroic effort to save his master's children, his master and young Andrews lying dead or mortally wounded on the

---

[14]jealous

porch) was cut down on the spot, and the shrieks of the children as they fled, some into the open air by a back door, and others to the upper chambers, and the savage yells of triumph with which they were pursued, told how vainly he had devoted himself to save them.

CHAPTER XIV

The tragical occurrences that followed.

While I stood thus observing the horrors I had been instrumental in provoking, as incapable of putting a stop to as of assisting in them, I saw two of the children, little Tommy and his youngest sister, Lucy, a girl of seven or eight years, running wildly over the lawn, several of my ruffian companions pursuing them. The girl was snatched up by old aunt Phœbe, who, with other women, had come among us, wringing her hands, and beseeching us not to kill their young misses, and was thus saved. As for the boy, he caught sight of me, and sprang into my arms, entreating me "not to let them kill him, and he would never hurt me again in all his life, and would give me all his money."

Poor child! I would have defended him at that moment with my life, for my heart bled for what had already been done; but he was snatched out of my hands, and I saw no more of him. I heard afterward, however, that he was not hurt, having been saved by the women, who had protected in like manner his two little sisters, Jane and Lucy. As for the others, that is, Isabella and Edith, I witnessed their fate with my own eyes; and it was the suddenness and horror of it that, by unmanning me entirely, prevented my giving aid to the boy when he was torn from my arms.

The fire had by this time spread from the timber to an adjacent cabin, and a light equal to that of noon, though red as blood itself, was shed over the whole mansion, on the roof of which was a little cupola, or observatory, open to the weather, where was room for five or six persons to sit together, and enjoy the prospect of the river and surrounding hills; and on either side of this cupola was a platform, though without a balustrade, on which was space for as many more.

The observatory being strongly illuminated by the flames, and my eyes being turned thitherward by a furious yell which was suddenly set up around me, I beheld my master's daughter Isabella rush into it,—that is, into the observatory,—from the staircase below, hotly pursued, as was evident from what followed. She bore in her arms, or rather dragged after her, for the child was in a swoon, her sister Edith, who was but small of stature and light; and as she reached this forlorn place of refuge, she threw down the trapdoor that covered its entrance, and endeavoured to keep it down with her foot. There was something inexpressibly fearful in her appearance, independent of the dreadfulness of her situation, separated only by a narrow plank from ruffians maddened by rage and carnage, from whom death itself was a boon too merciful to be expected, and from whom she was to guard not only herself, but the feeble, unconscious being hanging on her neck. Her hair was all dishevelled, her dress torn and disordered, and her face as white as snow; yet there was a wild energy and fierceness breathing from every feature, and she looked like a lioness defending to the last her young from the hunters, from whom she yet knows there is no escape.

The trapdoor shook under her foot, and was at last thrown violently up; and up, with screams of triumph, darted the infuriated Governor, followed by Jim and others, to grasp their prey. Their prey had fled: without uttering a word or scream, she sprang from the cupola to the platform at its side, and then, with a fearlessness only derived from desperation, and still bearing her insensible sister, she stepped upon the roof, which was high and steep, and ran along it to its extremity.

Even the ferocious Governor was for a moment daunted at the boldness of the act, and afraid to follow; until the parson—well worthy he of the name!—set him the example by leaping on the shingles, and pursuing the unhappy girl to her last refuge. He approached—he stretched forth his arm to seize her; but he was not destined to lay an impure touch on the devoted and heroic creature. I saw her lay her lips once on those of the poor Edith—the next instant the frail figure of the little sister was hurled from her arms, to be dashed to pieces on the stones below. In another, the hapless Isabella herself had followed her having thrown herself headlong from the height, to escape by death a fate otherwise inevitable.

Of what followed I have but a faint and disordered recollection. I remember that the fall of the two maidens caused loud cries of horror from the men, and of lamentation from the women; and I remember, also, that these were renewed almost immediately after, but mingled with the sound of fire-arms discharged by a party of foes, and the voices of white men (among which I distinguished that of my master's son, the major) calling upon one another to "give no quarter to the miscreants." A party of armed horsemen had in fact ridden among us, and were now dealing death on all hands from pistols and sabres. From one of the latter weapons I myself received a severe cut, and was at the same time struck down by the hoofs of a horse, and left insensible.

CHAPTER XV

*The results of the insurrection, with a truly strange
and fatal catastrophe that befell the Author.*

When I recovered my senses I found myself a prisoner, bound hand and foot, and lying, with six or seven of my late companions, in a cart, in which, groaning with pain, for most of us were wounded, and anticipating a direful end to our dreams of conquest and revenge, we were trundled to the village, and there deposited in the county jail, to repent at leisure the rashness and enormity of our enterprise.

The power of that little pamphlet, of which I have said so much, to produce an effect for which we must charitably suppose it was not intended, was shown in the numbers of wretches by whom the prison was crowded; for it had been used to inflame the passions of the negroes on several different estates, all of whom had agreed to rise in insurrection, although, as it providentially happened the revolt extended to the length of murder only on Ridgewood Hill. The conspiracy was detected—I believe confessed by a slave—on a plantation adjacent to that of my master's son; who, being informed of it, and assisted by a party that brought the news, proceeded to seize the ringleaders in his own gang, some of whom, attempting to make their escape, were fired on; and this was the cause of the volley which we had heard, and supposed was fired by our fellow-conspirators beyond the creek. The major then crossed over to his father's estate, but too late to avert the tragedy which I have related. His father, his eldest sister, and her lover were already dead; as for the younger, Edith, she was taken up alive, but cruelly mangled, and she expired in a few hours. The faithful and devoted overseer, I have the happiness to believe, ultimately escaped with his life; for, although covered with wounds, and at first reported dead, he revived sufficiently to make deposition to the facts of the assault and murder, as far as he was cognizant of them, and I heard he was expected to recover.

Of those who perished, the father, the children, and the gallant friend, there was not one who was not, a fortnight before, respected and beloved by those who slew them; and at their death-hour they were as guiltless of wrong, and as deserving of affection and gratitude, as they ever had been. How, therefore, they came to be hated, and why they were killed, I am unable to divine. All that I know is, that we who loved them read a book which fell in our way, and from that moment knew them only as enemies—objects on whom we had a right to glut our fiercest passions.

As for ourselves—my deluded companions, at least—their fate can be easily imagined. Some were killed at the scene of murder; among others the chief leader, Governor, who was shot on the roof of the house. Parson Jim was wounded on the same place, and, rolling from the roof, was horribly crushed by the fall, but lingered in unspeakable agonies for several days, and then died. Scipio, the fiddler, was taken alive, tried, condemned, and executed, with many others whose participation in the crime left them no hope of mercy.

With these, I was myself put upon trial and adjudged to death; for although it was made apparent that I had not lifted my hand against any one, it was proved that I was more than privy to the plot—that I had been instrumental in fomenting it; and the known favour with which I had been treated, added the double die of ingratitude to my offence. I was therefore condemned, and bade to expect no mercy; nor did I expect it; for the fatal day appointed for the execution having arrived, a rope was put round my neck, and I was led to the gibbet.

And now I am about to relate what will greatly surprise the reader—I was not only found guilty and condemned—I was hanged! Escape was impossible, and I perceived it. The anguish of my mind—for in anguish it may be supposed I looked forward to my fate—was increased by the consciousness—so long slumbering—that flashed on it, as I was driven to the fatal tree, that I was, in reality, *not* Tom the slave, but Sheppard Lee the freeman, and that I possessed a power of evading the halter, or any other inconvenience, provided I were allowed but one opportunity to exercise it. But where was I now to look for a dead body? It is true, there were bodies enough by-and-by, when my accomplices were tucked up around me; but what advantage could I derive from entering any one of them, since my fate must be equally certain to be hanged?

My distress, I repeat, was uncommonly great, and in the midst of it I was executed; which put an end to the quandary.

CHAPTER XVI

In which it is related what became of the Author after being hanged.

Here, it would seem, that my history should find its natural close; but I hope to convince the world that a man may live to record his own death and burial. I say *burial;* for, from all I have heard, I judge that I was buried as well as hanged, and that I lay in the earth in a coarse lead coffin, from two o'clock in the afternoon of a November day, until nine at night; when certain young doctors of the village, who were desirous to show their skill in anatomy, came to the place of execution, and dug up the three best bodies, of which, as my good luck would have it, my own was one—Zip the fiddler's being another, while the third was that of a young fellow named Sam, notorious for nothing so much as a great passion he had for butting with his head against brick walls, or even stone ones, provided they were smooth enough.

The young anatomists, previous to hacking us, resolved to try some galvanic[15] experiments on us, having procured a battery for that purpose; and they invited a dozen or more respectable gentlemen to be present, and witness the effects of that extraordinary fluid, galvanism, on our lifeless bodies.

The first essayed was that of the unfortunate Scipio, who, being well charged, began, to the admiration of all present, to raise first one arm, and then the other, then to twist the fingers of his left hand in a peculiar way, as if turning a screw, inclining his head the while towards his left shoulder, and then to saw the air, sweeping his right hand to and fro across his breast, with great briskness and energy, the fingers of his left titillating at the air all the while, so as to present the lively spectacle of a man playing the fiddle; and, indeed, it was judged, so natural was every motion, that had the party been provided with a fiddle and bow to put into his hands, they would have played such a jig as would have set all present dancing.

The next experiment tried was upon the body of Sam, whose muscles were speedily excited to exercise themselves in the way to which they had been most accustomed, though not in one so agreeable to the chief operator; for, in this case, the lifeless corpse suddenly lifting up its head, bestowed it, with a jerk of propulsion equal in force to the but of a battering-ram, full against the stomach of the operator, whereby he was tumbled head over heels, and all the breath beaten out of his body.

The reader may suppose, as it was proved to be the virtue of galvanism to set the dead muscles doing those acts to which the living ones had been longest habituated, that I, upon being charged, could do nothing less than throw myself upon my hands and knees, and go galloping about the table, as I had been used to do over the lawn, when master Tommy was mounted upon my back.

Such, however, was not the fact. The first thing I did upon feeling the magical fluid penetrate my nerves, was to open my eyes and snap them twice or thrice; the second to utter a horrible groan, which greatly disconcerted the spectators; and the third to start bolt upright on my feet, and ask them "what the devil they were after?" In a word, I was

---

[15]Involving electric current.

suddenly resuscitated, and to the great horror of all present, doctors and lookers-on, who, fetching a yell, that caused me to think I had got among condemned spirits in purgatory, fled from the room, exclaiming that I "was the devil, and no niggur!" What was particularly lamentable, though I was far from so esteeming it, one of them, a young gentleman who had come to the exhibition out of curiosity, being invited by one of the doctors, was so overcome with terror, that before he reached the door of the room he fell down in a fit, and being neglected by the others, none of whom stopped to give him help, expired on the spot.

As for me, the cause of all the alarm, I believe I was ten times more frightened than any of the spectators, especially when I came to recollect that I had just been hanged, and that I would, in all probability, be hanged again, unless I now succeeded in making my escape. As for the cause of my resuscitation, and the events that accompanied it, I was then entirely ignorant of them; and, indeed, I must confess I learned them afterward out of the newspapers. I knew, however, that I had been hanged, and that I had been, by some extraordinary means or other, brought to life again; and I perceived that if I did not make my escape without delay, I should certainly be recaptured by the returning doctors.

I ran towards the door, and then, for the first time, beheld that unfortunate spectator who had fallen dead, as I mentioned before, and lay upon the floor with his face turned up. I recollected him on the instant, as being a young gentleman whom I had once or twice seen at my late master's house. All that I knew of him was, that his name was Megrim, that he was reputed to be very wealthy, and a great genius, or, as some said, eccentric, and that he was admired by the ladies, and, doubtless, because he *was* a genius.

As I looked him in the face, I heard in the distance the uproar of voices, which had succeeded the flight of the doctors, suddenly burst out afresh, with the sound of returning footsteps; and a loud bully-like voice, which I thought very much like that of the under-turnkey at the prison—a man whom I had learned to fear—cried out, "Let *me* see your devil; for may I be cussed up hill and down hill if I ever seed a bigger one than myself."

Horrible as was the voice, I was not dismayed. I saw at my feet a city of refuge, into which my enemies could not pursue me. My escape was within my own power.

"Master," said I, touching my head (for I had no hat) to the corpse, "if it is all the same to you, I beg you'll let me take possession of your body."

As I pronounced the words the translation was effected, and that so rapidly, that just as I drew my first breath in the body of Mr. Megrim, it was knocked out of me by the fall of my old one, which—I not having taken the precaution to stand a little to one side—fell down like a thunderbolt upon me, bruising me very considerably about the precordia.

In this state, being half suffocated, and somewhat frightened, I was picked up and carried away by my new friends, and put to bed, where, having swallowed an anodyne, I fell directly sound asleep.

And here, before proceeding farther, I will say, that the doctors and their friends were greatly surprised to discover my late body lying dead, having expected to find it as animated as when they left it. But by-and-by, having reflected that the galvanism, or artificial life, infused into its nerves had been naturally exhausted at last, whereupon it as naturally followed that the body should return to its lifeless condition, they began to aver that the most surprising part of the business was, that it had kept me alive so long, and enabled me, after groaning and speaking as I had actually done, to walk so far from the table on which I had been lying.

On the whole, the phenomenon was considered curious and wonderful; and an account of it having been drawn up by the doctors, and headed "Extraordinary Case of the Effects of Galvanism on a Dead Body," it was printed for the benefit of scientific men throughout the world, in a medical journal, where, I doubt not, it may be found at this day.

6

Catharine Esther Beecher

(1800–1878)

CATHARINE BEECHER WAS the eldest daughter of Lyman Beecher, making her part of one of the most famous and distinguished families in nineteenth-century America. She had as siblings the noted author Harriet Beecher Stowe and preacher Henry Ward Beecher. Losing her fiancé in a shipwreck early in her life, she never married. Instead, she dedicated herself to helping her extended family and tirelessly working for the cause of women's education.

In 1823 she established the first of several rigorous academies she founded for women. Her educational philosophy was driven by the conviction that women played a key role in the development and well-being of the country as a whole, and thus they needed to be educated in earnest, not simply taught to paint, sew, and play the piano.

Although she wrote constantly on the cause of women's education, her most famous and enduring work was *A Treatise on Domestic Economy,* which first appeared in 1841. It proved so popular and influential that it was reprinted annually for the next fifteen years. In it, Beecher combined her views on women's role in society with the immensely popular literary genres of self-help and etiquette books. Beecher instructed women on everything from the unique social status of American women to how to wash feathers and trim wicks.

A Treatise on Domestic Economy would become most famous for how it clearly articulated a view of two spheres of influence: the male sphere outside the home and the female sphere within the home. Within this twin sphere ideology, Beecher championed what would later become known as "domestic feminism," a view that held that while women were still responsible for the domestic world of the home, their every action influenced the world at large. Whether educating their children to be good citizens or creating a safe place for a weary husband to rejuvenate himself, women were pivotal agents of influence entrusted with duties essential to cultivating the virtuous character necessary for the survival of democracy in the United States.

A TREATISE ON DOMESTIC ECONOMY FOR THE USE OF YOUNG LADIES AT HOME AND AT SCHOOL

CHAPTER I

❧ The Peculiar Responsibilities of American Women

American Women should feel a peculiar interest in Democratic Institutions. The maxim of our Civil Institutions. Its identity with the main principle of Christianity. Relations involving subordination; why they are needful. Examples. How these relations are decided in a Democracy. What decides the Equity of any Law or Institution. The principle of Aristocracy. The tendency of Democracy in respect to the interests of Women. Illustrated in the United States. Testimony of De Tocqueville. In what respects are Women subordinate? and why? Wherein are they equal or superior in influence? and how are they placed by courtesy? How can American Women rectify any real disadvantages involved in our Civil Institutions? Opinion of De Tocqueville as to the influence and example of American Democracy. Responsibilities involved in this view, especially those of American Women.

There are some reasons why American women should feel an interest in the support of the democratic institutions of their Country, which it is important that they should consider. The great maxim, which is the basis of all our civil and political institutions, is, that "all men are created equal," and that they are equally entitled to "life, liberty, and the pursuit of happiness."[1]

But it can readily be seen, that this is only another mode of expressing the fundamental principle which the Great Ruler of the Universe has established, as the law of His eternal government. "Thou shalt love thy neighbor as thyself;"[2] and "Whatsoever ye would that men should do to you, do ye even so to them."[3] These are the Scripture forms, by which the Supreme Lawgiver requires that each individual of our race shall regard the happiness of others, as of the same value as his own; and which forbids any institution, in private or civil life, which secures advantages to one class, by sacrificing the interests of another.

The principles of democracy, then, are identical with the principles of Christianity.

But, in order that each individual may pursue and secure the highest degree of happiness within his reach, unimpeded by the selfish interests of others, a system of laws must be established, which sustain certain relations and dependencies in social and civil

---

Catharine E. Beecher, *A Treatise on Domestic Economy for the Use of Young Ladies at Home and at School*. Boston: Marsh, Capen, Lyon, and Webb, 1841.

[1] Both of these quotations are from the Declaration of Independence.

[2] Matt. 19:19.

[3] Matt. 7:12.

life. What these relations and their attending obligations shall be, are to be determined, not with reference to the wishes and interests of a few, but solely with reference to the general good of all; so that each individual shall have his own interest, as much as the public benefit, secured by them.

For this purpose, it is needful that certain relations be sustained, that involve the duties of subordination. There must be the magistrate and the subject, one of whom is the superior, and the other the inferior. There must be the relations of husband and wife, parent and child, teacher and pupil, employer and employed, each involving the relative duties of subordination. The superior in certain particulars is to direct, and the inferior is to yield obedience. Society could never go forward, harmoniously, nor could any craft or profession be successfully pursued, unless these superior and subordinate relations be instituted and sustained.

But who shall take the higher, and who the subordinate, stations in social and civil life? This matter, in the case of parents and children, is decided by the Creator. He has given children to the control of parents, as their superiors, and to them they remain subordinate, to a certain age, or so long as they are members of their household. And parents can delegate such a portion of their authority to teachers and employers, as the interests of their children require.

In most other cases, in a truly democratic state, each individual is allowed to choose for himself, who shall take the position of his superior. No woman is forced to obey any husband but the one she chooses for herself; nor is she obliged to take a husband, if she prefers to remain single. So every domestic, and every artisan or laborer, after passing from parental control, can choose the employer to whom he is to accord obedience, or, if he prefers to relinquish certain advantages, he can remain without taking a subordinate place to any employer.

Each subject, also, has equal power with every other, to decide who shall be his superior as a ruler. The weakest, the poorest, the most illiterate, has the same opportunity to determine this question, as the richest, the most learned, and the most exalted.

And the various privileges that wealth secures, are equally open to all classes. Every man may aim at riches, unimpeded by any law or institution that secures peculiar privileges to a favored class at the expense of another. Every law, and every institution, is tested by examining whether it secures equal advantages to all; and if the people become convinced that any regulation sacrifices the good of the majority to the interests of the smaller number, they have power to abolish it.

The institutions of monarchical and aristocratic nations are based on precisely opposite principles. They secure, to certain small and favored classes, advantages which can be maintained, only by sacrificing the interests of the great mass of the people. Thus, the throne and aristocracy of England are supported by laws and customs, that burden the lower classes with taxes, so enormous, as to deprive them of all the luxuries, and of most of the comforts, of life. Poor dwellings, scanty food, unhealthy employments, excessive labor, and entire destitution of the means and time for education, are appointed for the lower classes, that a few may live in palaces, and riot in every indulgence.

The tendencies of democratic institutions, in reference to the rights and interests of the female sex, have been fully developed in the United States; and it is in this aspect, that the subject is one of peculiar interest to American women. In this Country, it is established, both by opinion and by practice, that women have an equal interest in all social and civil concerns; and that no domestic, civil, or political, institution, is right, that sacrifices her interest to promote that of the other sex. But in order to secure her the more firmly in all these privileges, it is decided, that, in the domestic relation, she take a sub-ordinate station, and that, in civil and political concerns, her interests be intrusted to the other sex, without her taking any part in voting, or in making and administering laws. The result of this order of things has been fairly tested, and is thus portrayed by M. De Tocqueville,[4] a writer, who, for intelligence, fidelity, and ability, ranks second to none.*

The following extracts present his views.

"There are people in Europe, who, confounding together the different characteris-tics of the sexes, would make of man and woman, beings not only equal, but alike. They would give to both the same functions, impose on both the same duties, and grant to both the same rights. They would mix them in all things,—their business, their occupations, their pleasures. It may readily be conceived, that, by *thus* attempting to make one sex equal to the other, both are degraded; and from so preposterous a medley of the works of Nature, nothing could ever result, but weak men and disorderly women.

"It is not thus that the Americans understand the species of democratic equality, which may be established between the sexes. They admit, that, as Nature has appointed such wide differences between the physical and moral constitutions of man and woman, her manifest design was, to give a distinct employment to their various faculties; and they hold, that im-provement does not consist in making beings so dissimilar do pretty nearly the same things, but in getting each of them to fulfil their respective tasks, in the best possible man-ner. The Americans have applied to the sexes the great principle of political economy, which governs the manufactories of our age, by carefully dividing the duties of man from those of woman, in order that the great work of society may be the better carried on.

"In no country has such constant care been taken, as in America, to trace two clearly distinct lines of action for the two sexes, and to make them keep pace one with the other, but in two pathways which are always different. American women never manage the out-ward concerns of the family, or conduct a business, or take a part in political life; nor are they, on the other hand, ever compelled to perform the rough labor of the fields, or to make any of those laborious exertions, which demand the exertion of physical strength. No families are so poor, as to form an exception to this rule.

---

[4]Alexis de Tocqueville (1805–1859) was a French political scientist and historian who visited the United States and wrote *Democracy in America* (1835–1840), an insightful commentary on the country's social and political system.

*The work of this author, entitled 'Democracy in America,' secured for him a prize from the National Academy, at Paris. The following extract expresses an opinion, in which most of the best qualified judges would coincide.

"The manner of conducting the inquiry which the Author has instituted; the intimate acquain-tance with all our institutions and relations, every where evinced; the careful and profound thought; and, above all, the spirit of truth, which animates and pervades the whole work, will not only commend it to the present generation, but render it a monument of the age in which it is pro-duced." "In Europe, it has already taken its stand with Montesquieu, Bacon, Milton, and Locke. In America, it will be regarded, not only as a classic philosophical treatise of the highest order, but as indispensable in the education of every statesman, and of every citizen who desires thoroughly to comprehend the institutions of his Country."

"If, on the one hand, an American woman cannot escape from the quiet circle of domestic employments, on the other hand, she is never forced to go beyond it. Hence it is, that the women of America, who often exhibit a masculine strength of understanding, and a manly energy, generally preserve great delicacy of personal appearance, and always retain the manners of women, although they sometimes show that they have the hearts and minds of men.

"Nor have the Americans ever supposed, that one consequence of democratic principles, is, the subversion of marital power, or the confusion of the natural authorities in families. They hold, that every association must have a head, in order to accomplish its object; and that the natural head of the conjugal association is man. They do not, therefore, deny him the right of directing his partner; and they maintain, that, in the smaller association of husband and wife, as well as in the great social community, the object of democracy is, to regulate and legalize the powers which are necessary, not to subvert all power.

"This opinion is not peculiar to one sex, and contested by the other. I never observed, that the women of America considered conjugal authority as a fortunate usurpation of their rights, nor that they thought themselves degraded by submitting to it. It appears to me, on the contrary, that they attach a sort of pride to the voluntary surrender of their own will, and make it their boast to bend themselves to the yoke, not to shake it off. Such, at least, is the feeling expressed by the most virtuous of their sex; the others are silent; and in the United States, it is not the practice for a guilty wife to clamor for the rights of woman, while she is trampling on her holiest duties.

"Although the travellers, who have visited North America, differ on a great number of points, they agree in remarking, that morals are far more strict, there, than elsewhere. It is evident that, on this point, the Americans are very superior to their progenitors, the English." "In England, as in all other countries of Europe, public malice is constantly attacking the frailties of women. Philosophers and statesmen are heard to deplore, that morals are not sufficiently strict; and the literary productions of the country constantly lead one to suppose so. In America, all books, novels not excepted, suppose women to be chaste; and no one thinks of relating affairs of gallantry.

"It has often been remarked, that, in Europe, a certain degree of contempt lurks, even in the flattery which men lavish upon women. Although a European frequently affects to be the slave of woman, it may be seen, that he never sincerely thinks her his equal. In the United States, men seldom compliment women, but they daily show how much they esteem them. They constantly display an entire confidence in the understanding of a wife, and a profound respect for her freedom. They have decided that her mind is just as fitted as that of a man to discover the plain truth, and her heart as firm to embrace it, and they have never sought to place her virtue, any more than his, under the shelter of prejudice, ignorance, and fear.

"It would seem, that in Europe, where man so easily submits to the despotic sway of woman, they are nevertheless curtailed of some of the greatest qualities of the human species, and considered as seductive, but imperfect beings, and (what may well provoke astonishment) women ultimately look upon themselves in the same light, and almost consider it as a privilege that they are entitled to show themselves futile, feeble, and timid. The women of America claim no such privileges.

"It is true, that the Americans rarely lavish upon women those eager attentions which are commonly paid them in Europe. But their conduct to women always implies, that they suppose them to be virtuous and refined; and such is the respect entertained for the moral freedom of the sex, that, in the presence of a woman, the most guarded language is used, lest her ear should be offended by an expression. In America, a young unmarried woman may, alone, and without fear, undertake a long journey.

"Thus the Americans do not think that man and woman have either the duty, or the right, to perform the same offices, but they show an equal regard for both their respective parts; and, though their lot is different, they consider both of them, as beings of equal value. They do not give to the courage of woman the same form, or the same direction, as to that of man; but they never doubt her courage: and if they hold that man and his partner ought not always to exercise their intellect and understanding in the same manner, they at least believe the understanding of the one to be as sound as that of the other, and her intellect to be as clear. Thus, then, while they have allowed the social inferiority of woman to subsist, they have done all they could to raise her, morally and intellectually, to the level of man; and, in this respect, they appear to me to have excellently understood the true principle of democratic improvement.

"As for myself, I do not hesitate to avow, that, although the women of the United States are confined within the narrow circle of domestic life, and their situation is, in some respects, one of extreme dependence, I have nowhere seen women occupying a loftier position; and if I were asked, now that I am drawing to the close of this work, in which I have spoken of so many important things done by the Americans, to what the singular prosperity and growing strength of that people ought mainly to be attributed, I should reply,—*to the superiority of their women.*"

This testimony of a foreigner, who has had abundant opportunities of making a comparison, is sanctioned by the assent of all candid and intelligent men, who have enjoyed similar opportunities.

It appears, then, that it is in America, alone, that women are raised to an equality with the other sex; and that, both in theory and practice, their interests are regarded as of equal value. They are made subordinate in station, only where a regard to their best interests demands it, while, as if in compensation for this, by custom and courtesy, they are always treated as superiors. Universally, in this Country, through every class of society, precedence is given to woman, in all the comforts, conveniences, and courtesies, of life.

In civil and political affairs, American women take no interest or concern, except so far as they sympathize with their family and personal friends; but in all cases, in which they do feel a concern, their opinions and feelings have a consideration, equal, or even superior, to that of the other sex.

In matters pertaining to the education of their children, in the selection and support of a clergyman, in all benevolent enterprises, and in all questions relating to morals or manners, they have a superior influence. In all such concerns, it would be impossible to carry a point, contrary to their judgement and feelings; while an enterprise, sustained by them, will seldom fail of success.

If those who are bewailing themselves over the fancied wrongs and injuries of women in this Nation, could only see things as they are, they would know, that, whatever remnants of a barbarous or aristocratic age may remain in our civil institutions, in reference to the interests of women, it is only because they are ignorant of it, or do not use their influence to have them rectified; for it is very certain that there is nothing reasonable which American women would unite in asking, that would not readily be bestowed.

The preceding remarks, then, illustrate the position, that the democratic institutions of this Country are in reality no other than the principles of Christianity carried into operation, and that they tend to place woman in her true position in society, as having equal rights with the other sex; and that, in fact, they have secured to American women a lofty and fortunate position, which, as yet, has been attained by the women of no other nation.

There is another topic, presented in the work of the above author, which demands the profound attention of American women.

The following is taken from that part of the Introduction to the work, illustrating the position, that, for ages, there has been a constant progress, in all civilized nations, towards the democratic equality attained in this country.

"The various occurrences of national existence have every where turned to the advantage of democracy; all men have aided it by their exertions; those who have intentionally labored in its cause, and those who have served it unwittingly; those who have fought for it, and those who have declared themselves its opponents, have all been driven along in the same track, have all labored to one end;" "all have been blind instruments in the hands of God."

"The gradual developement of the equality of conditions, is, therefore, a Providential fact; and it possesses all the characteristics of a Divine decree: it is universal, it is durable, it constantly eludes all human interference, and all events, as well as all men, contribute to its progress."

"The whole book, which is here offered to the public, has been written under the impression of a kind of religious dread, produced in the Author's mind, by the contemplation of so irresistible a revolution, which has advanced for centuries, in spite of such amazing obstacles, and which is still proceeding in the midst of the ruins it has made."

"It is not necessary that God Himself should speak, in order to disclose to us the unquestionable signs of His will. We can discern them in the habitual course of Nature, and in the invariable tendency of events."

"If the men of our time were led, by attentive observation, and by sincere reflection, to acknowledge that the gradual and progressive developement of social equality is at once the past and future of their history, this solitary truth would confer the sacred character of a Divine decree upon the change. To attempt to check democracy, would be, in that case, to resist the will of God; and the nations would then be constrained to make the best of the social lot awarded to them by Providence."

"It is not, then, merely to satisfy a legitimate curiosity, that I have examined America; my wish has been to find instruction by which we may ourselves profit." "I have not even affected to discuss whether the social revolution, which I believe to be irresistible, is advantageous or prejudicial to mankind. I have acknowledged this revolution, as a fact already accomplished, or on the eve of its accomplishment; and I have selected the nation, from among those which have undergone it, in which its developement has been the most peaceful and the most complete, in order to discern its natural consequences, and, if it be possible, to distinguish the means by which it may be rendered profitable. I confess, that in America I saw more than America; I sought the image of democracy itself, with its inclinations, its character, its prejudices, and its passions, in order to learn what we have to fear, or to hope, from its progress."

It thus appears, that the sublime and elevating anticipations which have filled the mind and heart of the religious world, have become so far developed, that philosophers and statesmen perceive the signs of its approach and are predicting the same grand consummation. There is a day advancing, "by seers predicted, and by poets sung," when the curse of selfishness shall be removed; when "scenes surpassing fable, and yet true," shall be realized; when all nations shall rejoice and be made blessed, under those benevolent influences which the Messiah came to establish on earth.

And this is the nation, which the Disposer of events designs shall go forth as the cynosure[5] of nations, to guide them to the light and blessedness of that day. To us is committed the grand, the responsible privilege, of exhibiting to the world, the beneficent influences of Christianity, when carried into every social, civil, and political institution, and though we have, as yet, made such imperfect advances, already the light is streaming into the dark prison-house of despotic lands, while startled kings and sages, philosophers and statesmen, are watching us with that interest which a career so illustrious, and so involving their own destiny, is calculated to excite. They are studying our institutions, scrutinizing our experience, and watching for our mistakes, that they may learn whether "a social revolution, so irresistible, be advantageous or prejudicial to mankind."

There are persons, who regard these interesting truths merely as food for national vanity; but every reflecting and Christian mind, must consider it as an occasion for solemn and anxious reflection. Are we, then, a spectacle to the world? Has the Eternal Lawgiver appointed us to work out a problem involving the destiny of the whole earth? Are such momentous interests to be advanced or retarded, just in proportion as we are faithful to our high trust? "What manner of persons, then, ought we to be," in attempting to sustain so solemn, so glorious a responsibility?

But the part to be enacted by American women, in this great moral enterprise, is the point to which special attention should here be directed.

The success of democratic institutions, as is conceded by all, depends upon the intellectual and moral character of the mass of the people. If they are intelligent and virtuous, democracy is a blessing; but if they are ignorant and wicked, it is only a curse, and as much more dreadful than any other form of civil government, as a thousand tyrants are more to be dreaded than one. It is equally conceded, that the formation of the moral and intellectual character of the young is committed mainly to the female hand. The mother writes the character of the future man; the sister bends the fibres that hereafter are the forest tree; the wife sways the heart, whose energies may turn for good or for evil the destinies of a nation. Let the women of a country be made virtuous and intelligent, and the men will certainly be the same. The proper education of a man decides the welfare of an individual; but educate a woman, and the interests of a whole family are secured.

If this be so, as none will deny, then to American women, more than to any others on earth, is committed the exalted privilege of extending over the world those blessed influences, that are to renovate degraded man, and "clothe all climes with beauty."

No American woman, then, has any occasion for feeling that hers is an humble or insignificant lot. The value of what an individual accomplishes, is to be estimated by the importance of the enterprise achieved, and not by the particular position of the laborer.

---

[5]director

The drops of heaven that freshen the earth are each of equal value, whether they fall in the lowland meadow, or the princely parterre.[6] The builders of a temple are of equal importance, whether they labor on the foundations, or toil upon the dome.

Thus, also, with those labors that are to be made effectual in the regeneration of the Earth. The woman who is rearing a family of children; the woman who labors in the schoolroom; the woman who, in her retired chamber, earns, with her needle, the mite to contribute for the intellectual and moral elevation of her country; even the humble domestic, whose example and influence may be moulding and forming young minds, while her faithful services sustain a prosperous domestic state;—each and all may be cheered by the consciousness, that they are agents in accomplishing the greatest work that ever was committed to human responsibility. It is the building of a glorious temple, whose base shall be coextensive with the bounds of the earth, whose summit shall pierce the skies, whose splendor shall beam on all lands, and those who hew the lowliest stone, as much as those who carve the highest capital, will be equally honored when its top-stone shall be laid, with new rejoicings of the morning stars, and shoutings of the sons of God.

CHAPTER XII

❧ On Domestic Manners

What are Good-manners. Defect in American Manners. Coldness and Reserve of the Descendants of the Puritans accounted for. Cause of the Want of Courtesy in American Manners. Want of Discrimination. Difference of Principles regulating Aristocratic and Democratic Manners. Rules for regulating the Courtesies founded on Precedence of Age, Office, and Station, in a Democracy. Manners appropriate to Superiors and Subordinates. Peculiar Defect of Americans in this Respect. This to be remedied in the Domestic Circle, alone. Rules of Precedence to be enforced in the Family. Manners and tones towards Superiors to be regulated in the Family. Treatment of grown Brothers and Sisters by Young Children. Acknowledgement of Favors by Children to be required. Children to ask leave or apologize in certain cases. Rules for avoiding Remarks that would the Feelings of Others. Rules of Hospitality. Conventional Rules. Rules for Table Manners. Caution as to teaching these Rules to Children. Caution as to Allowances to be made for those deficient in Good-manners. Comparison of English and American Manners. America may hope to excel all Nations in Refinement, Taste, and Good-breeding; and why. Effects of Wealth and Equalisation of Labor. Allusion to the Manners of Courts in the past Century.

Good-manners are the expressions of benevolence in personal intercourse, by which we endeavor to promote the comfort and enjoyment of others, and to avoid all that gives needless pain. It is the exterior exhibition of the Divine precept which requires us to do to others as we would that they should do to us. It is saying, by our deportment, to all around, that we consider their feelings, tastes, and convenience, as equal in value to our own.

---

[6]An ornamental garden bed.

Good-manners lead us to avoid all practices that offend the taste of others; all violations of the conventional rules of propriety; all rude and disrespectful language and deportment; and all remarks that would tend to wound the feelings of another.

There is a defect in the manners of the American people, especially in the free States, which is a serious one, and which can never be efficiently remedied, except in the domestic circle, and in early life. It is a deficiency in the free expression of kindly feelings and sympathetic emotions, and a want of courtesy in deportment. The causes, which have led to this result, may easily be traced.

The forefathers of this Nation, to a wide extent, were men who were driven from their native land, by laws and customs which they believed to be opposed both to civil and religious freedom. The sufferings they were called to endure, the subduing of those gentler feelings which bind us to country, kindred, and home, and the constant subordination of the passions to stern principle, induced characters of great firmness and self-control. They gave up the comforts and refinements of a civilized country, and came as pilgrims to a hard soil, a cold clime, and a heathen shore. They were constantly called to encounter danger, privations, sickness, loneliness, and death; and all these, their religion taught them to meet with calmness, fortitude, and submission. And thus it became the custom and habit of the whole mass, to repress, rather than to encourage, the expression of feeling.

Persons who are called to constant and protracted suffering and privation, are forced to subdue and conceal emotion; for the free expression of it would double their own suffering, and increase the sufferings of others. Those, only, who are free from care and anxiety, and whose minds are mainly occupied by cheerful emotions, are at full liberty to unveil their feelings.

It was under such stern and rigorous discipline, that the first children in New England were reared; and the manners and habits of parents are usually, to a great extent, transmitted to children. Thus it comes about, that the descendants of the Puritans, now scattered over every part of the Nation, are predisposed to conceal the gentler emotions, while their manners are calm, decided, and cold, rather than free and impulsive. Of course, there are very many exceptions to these predominating results.

The causes, to which we may attribute a general want of courtesy in manners, are certain incidental results of our democratic institutions. Our ancestors, and their descendants, have constantly been combating the aristocratic principle, which would exalt one class of men at the expense of another. They have had to contend with this principle, not only in civil, but in social, life. Almost every American, in his own person, as well as in behalf of his class, has had to assume and defend the main principle of democracy,—that every man's feelings and interests are equal in value to those of every other man. But, in doing this, there has been some want of clear discrimination. Because claims founded on distinctions of mere birth and position were found to be injurious, many have gone to the extreme of inferring that all distinctions, involving subordination, are useless. Such would regard children as equals to parents, pupils to teachers, domestics to their employers, and subjects to magistrates; and that, too, in all respects.

The fact, that certain grades of superiority and subordination are needful, both for individual and for public benefit, has not been clearly discerned; and there has been a gradual tendency to an extreme, which has sensibly affected our manners. All the proprieties and courtesies which depend on the recognition of the relative duties of superior and subordinate, have been warred upon, and thus we see, to an increasing extent, disrespectful treatment of parents from children, of teachers from pupils, of employers from domestics, and of the aged from the young. Children too often address their parents in the same style and manner as they do their companions. Domestics address their employers, and the visiters of the family, as they do their associates; while, in all classes and circles, there is a gradual decay in courtesy of address.

In cases, too, where kindness is rendered, it is often accompanied with a cold unsympathizing manner, which greatly lessens its value, while kindness or politeness is received in a similar style of *nonchalance,* as if it were but the payment of a just due.

It is owing to these causes, that the American people, especially the inhabitants of New England, do not do themselves justice. For, while those, who are near enough to learn their real character and feelings, can discern the most generous impulses, and the most kindly sympathies, they are so veiled, in a composed and indifferent demeanor, as to be almost entirely concealed from strangers.

These defects in our national manners, it especially falls to the care of mothers, and all who have charge of the young, to rectify; and if they seriously undertake the matter, and wisely adapt means to ends, these defects will be remedied. With reference to this object, the following ideas are suggested.

The law of Christianity and of democracy, which teaches that all men are born equal, and that their interests and feelings should be regarded as of equal value, seems to be adopted in aristocratic circles, with exclusive reference to the class in which the individual moves. The courtly gentleman addresses all of his own class with politeness and respect, and in all his actions seems to allow that the feelings and convenience of others are to be regarded the same as his own. But his demeanor to those of inferior station is not based on the same rule.

Among those who make up aristocratic circles, such as are above them, are deemed of superior, and such as are below, of inferior, value. Thus, if a young, ignorant, and vicious coxcomb, happens to be born a lord, the aged, the virtuous, the learned, and the well-bred of another class must give his convenience the precedence, and must address him in terms of respect. So when a man of noble birth is thrown among the lower classes, he demeans himself in a style, which, to persons of his own class, would be deemed the height of assumption and rudeness.

Now the principles of democracy require, that the same courtesy, which we accord to our own circle, shall be extended to every class and condition; and that distinctions of superiority and subordination shall depend, not on accidents of birth, fortune, or occupation, but solely on those relations, which the good of all classes equally require. The distinctions demanded in a democratic state, are simply those, which result from relations that are common to every class, and which are for the benefit of all.

It is for the benefit of all, that children be subordinate to parents, pupils to teachers, the employed to their employers, and subjects to magistrates. In addition to this, it is for the general wellbeing, that the comfort and convenience of the delicate and feeble should be preferred to that of the strong and healthy, who would suffer less by any deprivation.

It is on these principles, that the rules of good-breeding, in a democratic state, must be founded. It is, indeed, assumed, that the value of the happiness of each individual is the same as that of every other; but as there always must be occasions, where there are advantages which all cannot enjoy, there must be general rules for regulating a selection. Otherwise, there would be constant scrambling among those of equal claims, and brute force must be the final resort, in which case the strongest would have the best of every thing. The democratic rule, then, is, that superiors in age, station, or office, have precedence of subordinates; and that age and feebleness have precedence of youth and strength.

It is on this principle, that the feebler sex has precedence of more vigorous man, while the young and healthy give precedence to age or feebleness.

There is, also, a style of deportment and address, which is appropriate to these different relations. It is suitable for a superior to secure compliance with his wishes from those subordinate to him, by commands; but a subordinate must secure compliance with his wishes, from a superior, by requests. It is suitable for a parent, teacher, or employer, to admonish for neglect of duty; it is not suitable for an inferior to take such a course to a superior. It is suitable for a superior to take precedence of a subordinate, without any remark; but in such cases, an inferior should ask leave, or offer an apology. It is proper for a superior to use the language and manners of freedom and familiarity which would be improper from a subordinate to a superior.

It is a want of proper regard to these proprieties, which occasions the chief defect in American manners. It is very common to see children talking to their parents in a style proper only between equals; so, also, the young address their elders, and those employed their employers, in a style which is inappropriate to their relative positions. It is not merely towards superiors that a respectful address is required; every person likes to be treated with courtesy and respect, and therefore the law of benevolence demands such demeanor towards all whom we meet in the social intercourse of life. "Be ye courteous," is the direction of the Apostle, in reference to our treatment of *all.*

It is in early life, and in the domestic circle, alone, that good-manners can be successfully cultivated. There is nothing that so much depends on *habit,* as the constantly recurring proprieties of good-breeding; and if a child grows up without forming such habits, it is very rarely the case that they can be formed at a later period. The feeling that it is of little consequence how we behave at home, if we conduct properly abroad, is a very fallacious one. Persons who are careless and illbred at home, may imagine that they can assume good-manners abroad; but they mistake. Fixed habits of tone, manner, language, and movements, cannot be suddenly altered; and those who are illbred at home, even when they try to hide their bad habits, are sure to violate many of the obvious rules of propriety, and yet be unconscious of it.

And there is nothing which would so effectually remove prejudice against our democratic institutions, as the general cultivation of good-breeding in the domestic circle. Good-manners are the exterior of benevolence, the minute and often recurring exhibitions of "peace and good-will;" and the nation, as well as the individual, which most excels in the exterior, as well as the internal principle, will be most respected and beloved.

The following are the leading points, which claim attention from those who have the care of the young.

In the first place, in the family, there should be required a strict attention to the rules of precedence, and those modes of address appropriate to the various relations to be sustained. Children should always be required to offer their superiors, in age or station, the precedence in all comforts and conveniences, and always address them in a respectful tone and manner. The custom of adding "Sir," or "Ma'am," to "Yes," or "No," is a valuable practice, as a perpetual indication of a respectful recognition of superiority. It is now going out of fashion, even among the most wellbred people; probably from want of consideration of its importance. Every remnant of courtesy in address, in our customs, should be carefully cherished, by all who feel a value for the proprieties of good-breeding.

If parents allow their children to talk to them, and to the grown persons in the family, in the same style in which they address each other, it will be vain to hope for the courtesy of manner and tone, which good-breeding demands in the general intercourse of society. In a large family, where the elder children are grown up and the younger are small, it is important to require the latter to treat the elder as superiors. There are none so ready as young children to assume airs of equality; and if they are allowed to treat one class of superiors in age and character disrespectfully, they will soon use the privilege universally. This is the reason why the youngest children of a family are most apt to be pert, forward, and unmannerly.

Another point to be aimed at, is, to require children always to acknowledge every act of kindness and attention, either by words or manner. If they are trained always to make grateful acknowledgements, when receiving favors, one of the objectionable features in American manners will be avoided.

Again, children should be required to ask leave, whenever they wish to gratify curiosity, or use an article which belongs to another. And if cases occur, when they cannot comply with the rules of good-breeding, as, for instance, when they must step between a person and the fire, or take the chair of an older person, they should be required either to ask leave, or offer an apology.

There is another point of good-breeding, which cannot, in all cases, be applied by children, in its widest extent. It is that which requires us to avoid all remarks which tend to embarrass, vex, mortify, or in any way wound the feelings, of another. To notice personal defects; to allude to others' faults, or the faults of their friends; to speak disparagingly of the sect or party to which a person belongs; to be inattentive, when addressed in conversation; to contradict flatly; to speak in contemptuous tones of opinions expressed by another;—all these are violations of the rules of good-breeding, which children should be taught to regard. Under this head, comes the practice of whispering, and staring about, when a teacher, or lecturer, or clergyman, is addressing a class or audience. Such inattention is practically saying that what the person is uttering is not worth attending to, and persons of real good-breeding always avoid it. Loud talking and laughing, in a large assembly, even when no exercises are going on; yawning and gaping in company; and not looking in the face a person who is addressing you, are deemed marks of ill-breeding.

Another branch of good-manners, relates to the duties of hospitality. Politeness requires us to welcome visiters with cordiality; to offer them the best accommodations; to address conversation to them; and to express, by tone and manner, kindness and respect. Offering the hand to all visiters, at one's own house, is a courteous and hospitable custom; and a cordial shake of the hand, when friends meet, would abate much of the coldness of manner ascribed to Americans.

The last point of good-breeding to be noticed, refers to the conventional rules of propriety and good taste. Of these, the first class relates to the avoidance of all disgusting or offensive personal habits, such as fingering the hair; cleaning the teeth or nails; picking the nose; spitting on carpets; snuffing, instead of using a handkerchief, or using the article in an offensive manner; lifting up the boots or shoes, as some men do, to tend them on the knee, or to finger them;—all these tricks, either at table or in society, children should be taught to avoid.

Another branch under this head, may be called *table manners.* To persons of good-breeding, nothing is more annoying, than violating the conventional proprieties of the table. Reaching over another person's plate; standing up to reach distant articles, instead of asking to have them passed; using one's own knife, and spoon, for butter, salt, or sugar, when it is the custom of the family to provide separate utensils for the purpose; setting cups, with tea dripping from them, on the table-cloth, instead of the mats or small plates provided for the purpose; using the table-cloth instead of the napkins provided; eating fast and in a noisy manner; putting large pieces in the mouth; looking and eating as if very hungry, or as if anxious to get at certain dishes; sitting at too great a distance from the table, and dropping food; laying the knife and fork on the table-cloth, instead of on the bread, or the edge of the plate;—all these particulars children should be taught to avoid. It is always desirable, too, to require children, when at table with grown persons, to be silent, except when addressed by others; or else their chattering will interrupt the conversation and comfort of their elders. They should always be required, too, to wait *in silence,* till all the older persons are helped.

All these things should be taught to children, gradually, and with great patience and gentleness. Some parents, who make good-manners a great object, are in danger of making their children perpetually uncomfortable, by suddenly surrounding them with so many rules, that they must inevitably violate some one or other a great part of the time. It is much better to begin with a few rules, and be steady and persevering with these till a habit is formed, and then take a few more, thus making the process easy and gradual. Otherwise, the temper of children will be injured; or, hopeless of fulfilling so many requisitions, they will become reckless and indifferent to all.

But in reference to those who have enjoyed advantages for the cultivation of good-manners, and who duly estimate its importance, one caution is important. Those who never have had such habits formed in youth, are under disadvantages, which no benevolence of temper can remedy. They may often violate the taste and feelings of others, not from a want of proper regard for them, but from ignorance of custom, or want of habit, or abstraction of mind, or from other causes, which demand forbearance and sympathy, rather than displeasure. An ability to bear patiently with defects in manners, and to make candid and considerate allowance for a want of advantages, or for peculiarities in mental habits, is one mark of the benevolence of real good-breeding.

The advocates of monarchical and aristocratic institutions have always had great plausibility given to their views, by the seeming tendencies of our institutions to insubordination and bad-manners. And it has been too indiscriminately conceded, by the defenders of our institutions, that such are these tendencies, and that the offensive points in American manners, are the necessary result of democratic principles.

But it is believed that both facts and reasonings are in opposition to this opinion. The following extract from the work of De Tocqueville exhibits the opinion of an impartial observer, when comparing American manners with those of the English, who are confessedly the most aristocratic of all people.

He previously remarks on the tendency of aristocracy to make men more sympathizing with persons of their own peculiar class, and less so towards those of lower degree; which he illustrates by the deportment of nobles to their boors,[7] and slaveholders towards slaves. And he claims that the progress in equality of conditions has always been attended with a corresponding refinement of manners and humanity of feeling. "While the English," says he, "retain the bloody traces of the dark ages in their penal legislation, the Americans have almost expunged capital punishments from their codes. North America is, I think, the only country upon earth, in which the life of no one citizen has been taken for political offence in the course of the last fifty years."

He then contrasts American manners with the English, claiming that the Americans are much the most affable, mild, and social. "In America, where the privileges of birth never existed, and where riches confer no peculiar rights on their possessors, men acquainted with each other are very ready to frequent the same places, and find neither peril nor advantage in the free interchange of their thoughts. If they meet by accident, they neither seek nor avoid intercourse; their manner is therefore natural, frank, and open." "If their demeanor is often cold and serious, it is never haughty or constrained." But an "aristocratic pride is still extremely great among the English; and as the limits of aristocracy are ill-defined, every body lives in constant dread, lest advantage should be taken of his familiarity. Unable to judge at once of the social position of those he meets, an Englishman prudently avoids all contact with them. Men are afraid lest some slight service rendered should draw them into an unsuitable acquaintance; they dread civilities, and they avoid the obtrusive gratitude of a stranger as much as his hatred."

Thus *facts* seem to show that when the most aristocratic nation in the world is compared, as to manners, with the most democratic, the judgement of strangers is in favor of the latter.

And if good-manners are the outward exhibition of the democratic fundamental principle of impartial benevolence and equal rights, surely the nation that adopts this rule, both in social and civil life, is the most likely to secure the desirable exterior. The aristocrat, by his principles, extends the exterior of impartial benevolence to his own class only; the democratic principle requires it to be extended *to all.*

There is reason, therefore, to hope and expect more refined and polished manners in America, than in any other land; while all the developments of taste and refinement, such as poetry, music, painting, sculpture, and architecture, it may be expected, will come to a higher state of perfection, here, than in any other nation.

If this Country increases in virtue and intelligence, as it may, there is no end to the wealth that will pour in as the result of our resources of climate, soil, and navigation, and the skill, industry, energy, and enterprise, of our countrymen. This wealth, if used as intelligence and virtue will dictate, will furnish the means for a superior education to all classes, and all the facilities for the refinement of taste, intellect, and feeling.

Moreover, in this Country, labor is ceasing to be the badge of a lower class; so that already it is disreputable for a man to be "a lazy gentleman." And this feeling will

---

[7]peasants

increase, till there will be such an equalisation of labor, as will afford all the time need-ful for every class to improve the many advantages offered to them. Already, in Boston, through the munificence of some of her citizens, there are literary and scientific advan-tages offered to all classes of the citizens, rarely enjoyed elsewhere. In Cincinnati, too, the advantages of education, now offered to the poorest classes, without charge, surpass what, a few years ago, most wealthy men could purchase, for any price. And it is believed, that a time will come, when the poorest boy in America can secure advantages, which will equal what the heir of the proudest peerage can now command.

The records of the courts of France and Germany, (as detailed by the Duchess of Orleans,[8]) in and succeeding the brilliant reign of Louis the Fourteenth,—a period which was deemed the acme of elegance and refinement,—exhibit a grossness, a vulgarity, and a coarseness, not to be found among the lowest of our respectable poor. And the biogra-phy of Beau Nash,[9] who attempted to reform the manners of the gentry in the times of Queen Anne,[10] exhibits violations of the rules of decency, which the commonest yeoman of this Land would feel disgraced in perpetrating.

This shows that our lowest classes, at this period, are more refined than were the highest in aristocratic lands, a hundred years ago; and another century may show the lowest classes, in wealth, in this Country, attaining as high a polish, as adorns those who now are leaders of good-manners in the courts of kings.

CHAPTER XIV

☙ On Habits of System and Order

Question of the Equality of the Sexes, frivolous and useless. Relative Importance and Diffi-culty of the Duties a Woman is called to perform. Her Duties not trivial. More difficult than those of the Queen of a great Nation. A Habit of System and Order necessary. Right Appor-tionment of Time. General Principles. Christianity to be the Foundation. Intellectual and Social Interests to be preferred to Gratification of Taste or Appetite. The Latter to be last in our Estimation. No Sacrifice of Health allowable. Neglect of Health a Sin in the Sight of God. Regular Season of Rest appointed by the Creator. Divisions of Time. Systematic Arrangement of House Articles, and other Conveniences. Regular Employment for each Member of a Fam-ily. Children can be of great Service. Boys should be taught Family Work. Advantage to them in afterlife. Older Children to take care of Infants of a Family.

The discussion of the question of the equality of the sexes, in intellectual capacity, seems both frivolous and useless, not only because it can never be decided, but because there

---

[8]Anne-Marie-Louie Motpensier (1627–1693), duchess of Orleans, was a princess of the royal house of France and writer of short novels and literary portraits.

[9]Englishman Richard "Beau" Nash (1674–1762) made himself into an important judge and stan-dard of proper etiquette and fashion in the eighteenth century.

[10]Anne (1675–1714) was an English queen who reigned from 1702 to 1714.

would be no possible advantage in the decision. But one topic, which is often drawn into this discussion, is of far more consequence; and that is, the relative importance and difficulty of the duties a woman is called to perform.

It is generally assumed, and almost as generally conceded, that women's business and cares are contracted and trivial; and that the proper discharge of her duties demands far less expansion of mind and vigor of intellect, than the pursuits of the other sex. This idea has prevailed, because women, as a mass, have never been educated with reference to their most important duties; while that portion of their employments which are of least value, have been regarded as the chief, if not the sole concern of a woman. The covering of the body, the conveniences of residences, and the gratification of the appetite, have been too much regarded as the sole objects on which her intellectual powers are to be exercised.

But as society gradually shakes off the remnants of barbarism, and the intellectual and moral interests of man rise in estimation above the merely sensual, a truer estimate is formed of woman's duties, and of the measure of intellect requisite for the proper discharge of them. Let any man of sense and discernment become the member of a large household, in which a well-educated and pious woman is endeavoring systematically to discharge her multiform duties; let him fully comprehend all her cares, difficulties, and perplexities; and it is probable he would coincide in the opinion, that no statesman, at the head of a nation's affairs, had more frequent calls for wisdom, firmness, tact, discrimination, prudence, and versatility of talent, than such a woman.

She has a husband, whose peculiar tastes and habits she must accommodate; she has children, whose health she must guard, whose physical constitution she must study and develope, whose temper and habits she must regulate, whose principles she must form, whose pursuits she must direct. She has constantly changing domestics, with all varieties of temper and habits, whom she must govern, instruct, and direct; she is required to regulate the finances of the domestic state, and constantly to adapt expenditures to the means and to the relative claims of each department. She has the direction of the kitchen, where ignorance, forgetfulness, and awkwardness are to be so regulated, that the various operations shall each start at the right time, and all be in completeness at the same given hour. She has the claims of society to meet, calls to receive and return, and the duties of hospitality to sustain. She has the poor to relieve; benevolent societies to aid; the schools of her children to inquire and decide about; the care of the sick; the nursing of infancy; and the endless miscellany of odd items constantly recurring in a large family.

Surely it is a pernicious and mistaken idea, that the duties which tax a woman's mind are petty, trivial, or unworthy of the highest grade of intellect and moral worth. Instead of allowing this feeling, every woman should imbibe, from early youth, the impression, that she is training for the discharge of the most important, the most difficult, and the most sacred and interesting duties that can possibly employ the highest intellect. She ought to feel that her station and responsibilities, in the great drama of life, are second to none, either as viewed by her Maker, or in the estimation of all minds whose judgement is most worthy of respect.

She, who is the mother and housekeeper in a large family, is the sovereign of an empire demanding as varied cares, and involving more difficult duties, than are really exacted of her, who, while she wears the crown, and professedly regulates the interests of the greatest nation on earth, finds abundant leisure for theatres, balls, horseraces, and every gay pursuit.

There is no one thing, more necessary to a housekeeper, in performing her varied duties, than *a habit of system and order;* and yet the peculiarly desultory nature of women's pursuits, and the embarrassments resulting from the state of domestic service in this Country, render it very difficult to form such a habit. But it is sometimes the case, that women, who could and would carry forward a systematic plan of domestic economy, do not attempt it, simply from a want of knowledge of the various modes of introducing it. It is with reference to such, that various modes of securing system and order, which the Writer has seen adopted, will be pointed out.

A wise economy is nowhere more conspicuous, than in the right *apportionment of time* to different pursuits. There are duties of a religious, intellectual, social, and domestic, nature, each having different relative claims on attention. Unless a person has some general plan of apportioning these claims, some will intrench on others, and some, it is probable, will be entirely excluded. Thus, some find religious, social, and domestic, duties, so numerous, that no time is given to intellectual improvement. Others, find either social, or benevolent, or religious, interests, excluded by the extent and variety of other engagements.

It is wise, therefore, for all persons to devise a general plan, which they will at least keep in view, and aim to accomplish, and by which, a proper proportion of time shall be secured for all the duties of life.

In forming such a plan, every woman must accommodate herself to the peculiarities of her situation. If she has a large family, and a small income, she must devote far more time to the simple duty of providing food and raiment, than would be right were she in affluence and with a small family. It is impossible, therefore, to draw out any general plan, which all can adopt. But there are some *general principles,* which ought to be the guiding rules, when a woman arranges her domestic employments. These general principles are to be based on Christianity, which teaches us to "seek first the kingdom of God," and to place food, raiment, and the conveniences of life, as of secondary account. Every woman, then, ought to start with the assumption, that religion is of more consequence than any worldly concern, and that whatever else may be sacrificed, this shall be the leading object in all her arrangements, in respect to time, money, and attention. It is also one of the plainest requisitions of Christianity, that we devote some of our time and efforts to the comfort and improvement of others. There is no duty so constantly enforced, both in the Old and New Testament, as the duty of charity, in dispensing to those who are destitute of the blessings we enjoy. In selecting objects of charity, the same rule applies to others, as well as to ourselves; that their moral and religious interests are of the first concern, and that for them, as well as ourselves, we are to "seek first the kingdom of God."

Another general principle, is, that our intellectual and social interests are to be preferred to the mere gratification of taste or appetite. A portion of time, therefore, must be devoted to the cultivation of the intellect and the social affections.

Another general principle, is, that the mere gratification of appetite is to be placed *last* in our estimate, so that, when a question arises as to which shall be sacrificed, some intellectual, moral, or social, advantage, or some gratification of sense, we should invariably sacrifice the last.

Another general principle, is, that, as health is indispensable to the discharge of every duty, nothing that sacrifices that blessing is to be allowed, in order to gain any other advantage or enjoyment. There are emergencies, when it is right to risk health and life, to save ourselves and others from greater evils; but these are exceptions, which do not vacate the general rule. Many persons imagine, that, if they violate the laws of health in performing religious or domestic duties, they are guiltless before God. But such greatly mistake. We as directly violate the law "thou shalt not kill," when we do what tends to risk or shorten our own life, as if we should intentionally run a dagger into a neighbor. True, we may escape any fatal or permanently injurious effects, and so may a dagger or bullet miss the mark, or do only transient injury. But this, in either case, makes the sin none the less. The life and happiness of all His creatures are dear to our Creator; and He is as much displeased, when we injure our own interests, as when we injure others. So that the idea that we are excusable if we harm no one but ourselves, is most false and pernicious. These, then, are the general principles, to guide a woman in systematizing her duties and pursuits.

The Creator of all things is a Being of perfect system and order; and to aid us in our duty, in this respect, he has divided our time, by a regularly returning day of rest from worldly business. In following this example, the intervening six days may be subdivided to secure similar benefits. In doing this, a certain portion of time must be given to procure the means of livelihood, and for preparing food, raiment, and dwellings. To these objects, some must devote more, and others less, attention. The remainder of time not necessarily thus employed, might be divided somewhat in this manner: The leisure of two afternoons and evenings could be devoted to religious and benevolent objects, such as religious meetings, charitable associations, Sunday school visiting, and attention to the sick and poor. The leisure of two other days might be devoted to intellectual improvement, and the pursuits of taste. The leisure of another day might be devoted to social enjoyments, in making or receiving visits; and that of another to miscellaneous domestic pursuits, not included in the other particulars.

It is probable that few persons could carry out such an arrangement, very strictly; but every one can make out a systematic arrangement of time, and at least *aim* at accomplishing it; and they can also compare the time which they actually devote to these different objects, with such a general outline, for the purpose of modifying any mistaken proportions.

Instead of attempting some such systematic employment of time, and carrying it out so far as they can control circumstances, most women are rather driven along by the daily occurrences of life, so that, instead of being the intelligent regulators of their own time, they are the mere sport of circumstances. There is nothing which so distinctly marks the difference between weak and strong minds, as the fact, whether they control circumstances, or circumstances control them.

It is very much to be feared, that the apportionment of time, actually made by a great portion of women, exactly inverts the order required by reason and Christianity. Thus the furnishing a needless variety of food, the conveniences of dwellings, and the adornments of dress, often take a larger portion of time, than is given to any other object. Next after this, comes intellectual improvement; and last of all, benevolence and religion.

It may be urged, that it is indispensable for most persons to give more time to earn a livelihood, and to prepare food, raiment, and dwellings, than to any other object. But it may be asked, how much time devoted to these objects is employed in preparing varieties of food, not necessary, but rather injurious, and how much is spent for those parts of dress and furniture not indispensable, and merely ornamental? Let a woman subtract from her domestic employments, all the time given to pursuits which are of no use, except as they gratify a taste for ornament, or minister increased varieties to tempt appetite, and she will find, that much, which she calls "domestic duties," and which prevent her attention to intellectual, benevolent, and religious, objects, should be called by a very different name. No woman has a right to give up attention to the higher interests of herself and others, for the ornaments of taste or the gratification of the palate. To a certain extent, these lower objects are lawful and desirable; but, when they intrude on nobler interests, they become selfish and degrading.

Some persons endeavor to systematize their pursuits, by apportioning them to particular hours of each day. For example, a certain period before breakfast, is given to devotional duties; after breakfast, certain hours are devoted to exercise and domestic employments; other hours to sewing, or reading, or visiting; and others to benevolent duties. But, in most cases, it is more difficult to systematize the hours of each day, than it is to sustain some regular division of the week.

In regard to the minutiæ of domestic arrangements, the Writer has known the following methods adopted. *Monday,* with some of the best housekeepers, is devoted to preparing for the labors of the week. Any extra cooking, the purchasing of articles to be used during the week, and the assorting of clothes for the wash, and mending such as would be injured without;—these and similar items belong to this day. *Tuesday* is devoted to washing, and *Wednesday* to ironing. On *Thursday,* the ironing is finished off, the clothes folded and put away, and all articles which need mending put in the mending basket, and attended to. *Friday* is devoted to sweeping and housecleaning. On *Saturday,* and especially the last Saturday of every month, every department is put in order; the castors and table furniture are regulated, the pantry and cellar inspected, the trunks, drawers, and closets arranged, and every thing about the house put in order for *Sunday.* All the cooking needed for Sunday is also prepared. By this regular recurrence of a particular time for inspecting every thing, nothing is forgotten till ruined by neglect.

Another mode of systematizing, relates to providing proper supplies of conveniences, and proper places in which to keep them. Thus, some ladies keep a large closet, in which are placed the tubs, pails, dippers, soap-dishes, starch, bluing, clothes-line, clothes-pins, and every other article used in washing; and in the same or another place are kept every convenience for ironing. In the sewing department, a trunk, with suitable partitions, is provided, in which are placed, each in its proper place, white thread of all sizes, colored thread, yarns for mending, colored and black sewing-silks and twist, tapes and bobbins of all sizes, white and colored welting-cords, silk braids and cords, needles of all sizes, papers of pins, remnants of linen and colored cambric, a supply of all kinds of buttons used in the family, black and white hooks and eyes, a yard measure, and all the patterns used in cutting and fitting. These are done up in separate parcels and labelled. In another trunk, are kept all pieces used in mending, arranged in order, so that any article can be found without loss of time. A trunk like the first mentioned, will save many steps, and often much time and perplexity; while purchasing thus by the quantity makes them come much cheaper than if bought in little portions as they are wanted. Such a trunk should be kept locked, and a smaller supply, for current use, be kept in a work-basket.

The full supply of all conveniences in the kitchen and cellar, and a place appointed for each article, very much facilitates domestic labor. For want of this, much vexation and loss of time is occasioned, while seeking vessels in use, or in cleansing those used by different persons for various purposes. It would be far better for a lady to give up some expensive article in the parlor, and apply the money, thus saved, for kitchen conveniences, than to have a stinted supply where the most labor is to be performed. If our Countrywomen would devote more to comfort and convenience, and less to show, it would be a great improvement. Mirrors and piertables in the parlor, and an unpainted, gloomy, ill-furnished kitchen, not unfrequently are found under the same roof.

Another important item, in systematic economy, is the apportioning of *regular* employment to the various members of a family. If a housekeeper can secure the cooperation of *all* her family, she will find that "many hands make light work." There is no greater mistake, than in bringing up children to feel that they must be taken care of, and waited on, by others, without any corresponding obligations on their part. The extent to which young children can be made useful in a family, would seem surprising to those who have never seen a *systematic* and *regular* plan for securing their services. The Writer has been in a family, where a little girl of eight or nine washed and dressed herself and little brother, and made their little beds before breakfast, set and cleared all the tables at meals, with a little help from a grown person in moving tables and spreading cloths, while all the dusting of parlors and chambers was also neatly performed by her. A little brother of ten, brought in and piled all the wood used in the kitchen and parlor, brushed the boots and shoes neatly, went on errands, and took all the care of the poultry. They were children whose parents could afford to hire this service, but who chose to have their children grow up healthy and industrious, while proper instructions, system, and encouragement, made these services rather a pleasure than otherwise to the children.

Some parents pay their children for such services; but this is hazardous, as tending to make them feel that they are not bound to be helpful without pay, and also as tending to produce a hoarding, money-making spirit. But where children have no hoarding propensities, and need to acquire a sense of the value of property, it may be well to let them earn money for some extra services, rather as a favor. When this is done, they should be taught to spend it for others, as well as for themselves; and in this way, a generous and liberal spirit will be cultivated.

There are some mothers, who take pains to teach their boys most of the domestic arts which their sisters learn. The Writer has seen boys mending their own garments, and aiding their mother or sisters in the kitchen, with great skill and adroitness; and at an early age they usually very much relish joining in such occupations. The sons of such mothers, in their college life, or in roaming about the world, or in nursing a sick wife or infant, find occasion to bless the forethought and kindness which prepared them for such emergencies. Few things are in worse taste, than for a man needlessly to busy himself in women's work; and yet a man never appears in a more interesting attitude, than when, by skill in such matters, he can save a mother or wife from care and suffering. The more a boy is taught to use his hands in every variety of domestic employment, the more his faculties, both of mind and body, are developed; for mechanical pursuits exercise the intellect, as well as the hands. The early training of New England boys, in which they turn their hand to almost every thing, is one great reason of the quick perceptions, versatility of mind, and mechanical skill, for which that portion of our Countrymen are distinguished.

The Writer has known one mode of systematizing the aid of the older children in a family, which, in some cases of very large families, it may be well to imitate. In the case referred to, when the oldest daughter was eight or nine years old, an infant sister was given to her as her special charge. She tended it, made and mended its clothes, taught it to read, and was its nurse and guardian through all its childhood. Another infant was given to the next daughter, and thus the children were all paired in this interesting relation. In addition to the relief thus afforded to the mother, the elder children were thus qualified for their future domestic relations, and both older and younger bound to each other by peculiar ties of tenderness and gratitude.

In offering these examples of various modes of systematizing, one suggestion may be worthy of attention. It is not infrequently the case, that ladies, who find themselves cumbered with oppressive cares, after reading remarks on the benefits of system, immediately commence the task of arranging their pursuits, with great vigor and hope. They divide the day into regular periods, and give each hour its duty; they systematize their work, and endeavor to bring every thing into a regular routine. But in a short time, they find themselves baffled, discouraged, and disheartened, and finally relapse into their former desultory ways, with a sort of resigned despair. The difficulty, in such cases, is, that they attempt too much at a time. There is nothing which so much depends upon *habit,* as a systematic mode of performing duty; and where no such habit has been formed, it is impossible for a novice to start at once into a universal mode of systematizing, which none but an adept could carry through. The only way for such persons, is, to begin with a little at a time. Let them select some three or four things, and resolutely attempt to conquer at these points. In time, a habit will be formed of doing a few things at regular periods, and in a systematic way. Then it will be easy to add a few more; and thus, by a gradual process, the object can be secured, which it would be vain to attempt by a more summary course. Early rising is almost a *sine qua non*[11] to success, in such an effort; but where a woman lacks either the health or the energy to secure a period for devotional duties before breakfast, let her select that hour of the day in which she will be least liable to interruption, and let her then seek strength and wisdom from the only true Source. At this time, let her take a pen and make a list of all the things which she considers as duties. Then let a calculation be made, whether there is time enough in the day or the week for all these duties. If there is not, let the least important be stricken from the list, as what are not duties and must be omitted. In doing this, let a woman remember, that, though "what we shall eat, and what we shall drink, and wherewithal we shall be clothed," are matters requiring due attention, they are very apt to take a wrong relative importance, while social, intellectual, and moral, interests, receive too little regard.

In this Country, eating, dressing, and household furniture and ornaments, take far too large a place in the estimate of relative importance; and it is probable that most

---

[11]Something absolutely essential.

women could modify their views and practice, so as to come nearer to the Saviour's requirements. No woman has a right to put a stitch of ornament on any article of dress or furniture, or to provide one superfluity in food, until she is sure she can secure time for all her social, intellectual, benevolent, and religious, duties. If a woman will take the trouble to make such a calculation as this, she will usually find that she has time enough to perform all her duties easily and well.

It is impossible for a conscientious woman to secure that peaceful mind, and cheerful enjoyment of life, which all should seek, who is constantly finding her duties jarring with each other, and much remaining undone, which she feels that she ought to do. In consequence of this, there will be a secret uneasiness, which will throw a shade over the whole current of life, never to be removed, till she so efficiently defines and regulates her duties, that she can fulfil them all.

And here the Writer would urge upon young ladies the importance of forming habits of system, while unembarrassed with multiplied cares which will make the task so much more difficult and hopeless. Every young lady can systematize her pursuits, to a certain extent. She can have a particular day for mending her wardrobe, and for arranging her trunks, closets, and drawers. She can keep her workbasket, her desk at school, and all her conveniences in proper places, and in regular order. She can have regular periods for reading, walking, visiting, study, and domestic pursuits. And by following this method, in youth, she will form a taste for regularity, and a habit of system, which will prove a blessing to her through life.

CHAPTER XVI

❧ On Economy of Time and Expenses

Economy of Time. Value of Time. Right Apportionment of Time. Laws appointed by God for the Jews. Proportions of Property and Time the Jews were required to devote to Intellectual, Benevolent, and Religious Purposes. The Levites. The weekly Sabbath. The Sabbatical Year. Three sevenths of the Time of the Jews devoted to God's Service. Christianity removes the Restrictions laid on the Jews, but demands all our Time to be devoted to our own best Interests and the Good of our Fellow-men. Some Practical Good to be the Ultimate End of all our Pursuits. Enjoyment connected with the Performance of every Duty. Great Mistake of Mankind. A Final Account to be given of the Apportionment of our Time. Various Modes of economizing Time. System and Order. Uniting several Objects in one Employment. Employment of Odd Intervals of Time. We are bound to aid Others in economizing Time. ECONOMY OF EXPENSES. Necessity of Information on this Point. Contradictory Notions. General Principles in which all agree. Knowledge of Income and Expenses. Every One bound to do as much as she can to secure System and Order. Examples. Evils of Want of System and Forethought. Young Ladies should early learn to be systematic and economical. Articles of Dress and Furniture should be in keeping with each other, and with the Circumstances of the Family. Mistaken Economy. Education of Daughters away from Home injudicious. Nice Sewing should be done at Home. Cheap Articles not always most economical. Buying by wholesale economical only in special cases. Penurious Savings made

*by getting the Poor to work cheap. Relative Obligations of the Poor and the Rich
in regard to Economy. Economy of Providence in the Unequal Distribution of
Property. Carelessness of Expense not a Mark of Gentility.
Beating down Prices improper in Wealthy People. Inconsistency in
American would-be Fashionables.*

ON ECONOMY OF TIME

The value of time, and our obligation to spend every hour for some useful end, are what few minds properly realize. And those, who have the highest sense of their obligations in this respect, sometimes greatly misjudge in their estimate of what are useful and proper modes of employing time. This arises from limited views of the importance of some pursuits, which they would deem frivolous and useless, but which are, in reality, necessary to preserve the health of body and mind, and those social affections, which it is very important to cherish. Christianity teaches, that, for all the time afforded us, we must give account to God; and that we have no right to waste a single hour. But time which is spent in rest or amusement, is often as usefully employed, as if it were devoted to labor or devotion. In employing our time, we are to make suitable allowance for sleep, for preparing and taking food, for securing the means of a livelihood, for intellectual improvement, for exercise and amusement, for social enjoyments, and for benevolent and religious duties. And it is the *right apportionment* of time to these various duties, which constitutes its true economy.

In making this apportionment, we are bound by the same rules as relate to the use of property. We are to employ whatever portion is necessary to sustain life and health, as the first duty; and the remainder we are so to apportion, that our highest interests shall receive the greatest allotment, and our physical gratifications the least.

The laws of the Supreme Ruler, when He became the civil as well as the religious Head of the Jewish theocracy, is an example which it would be well for all attentively to consider, when forming plans for the apportionment of time and property. To estimate this properly, it must be borne in mind, that the main object of God was to preserve His religion among the Jewish nation, and that they were not required to take any means to propagate it among other nations, as is now required by Christianity. So low were they in the scale of civilization and mental development, that a system, which confined them to one spot, as an agricultural people, and prevented their growing very rich, or having extensive commerce with other nations, was indispensable to prevent their relapsing into the low idolatries and vices of the nations around them.

The proportion of time and property, which every Jew was required to devote to intellectual, benevolent, and religious purposes, were as follows.

In regard to property, they were required to give one tenth of all their yearly income, to support the Levites[12] and the priests and religious service. Next, they were required to give the first fruits of all their corn, wine, oil, and fruits, and the first-born of all their cat-

---

[12]Of the twelve tribes of Israel, the tribe of Levi was set aside to carry out the nation's religious duties (Num. 3).

tle, for the Lord's treasury, to be employed for the priests, the widow, the fatherless, and the stranger. The first-born, also, of their children, were the Lord's, and were to be redeemed by a specified sum, paid into the sacred treasury. Besides this, they were required to bring a freewill offering to God, every time they went up to the three great yearly festivals. In addition to this, regular yearly sacrifices, of cattle and fowls, were required of each family, and occasional sacrifices for certain sins or ceremonial impurities. In reaping their fields, they were required to leave the corners for the poor, unreaped, and not to glean their fields, or olive and vineyards; and if a sheaf was left, by mistake, they were not to return for it, but leave it for the poor. When a man sent away a servant, he was thus charged: "Furnish him liberally out of thy flock, and out of thy floor, and out of thy winepress."[13] When a poor man came to borrow money, they were forbidden to deny him, or to take any interest; and if, at the sabbatical, or seventh, year, he could not pay, the debt was to be cancelled. And to this command, is added the significant caution, "Beware that there be not a thought in thy wicked heart, saying, the seventh year, the year of release, is at hand; and thine eye be evil against thy poor brother, and thou givest him nought; and he cry unto the Lord against thee, and it be sin unto thee. Thou shalt surely give him," "because that for this thing the Lord thy God shall bless thee in all thy works, and in all that thou puttest thine hand unto."[14] Besides this, the Levites were distributed through the land, with the intention that they should be instructers and priests in every part of the nation. Thus, one twelfth of the people were set apart, having no landed property, to be priests and teachers; and the other tribes were required to support them liberally.

In regard to the time taken from secular pursuits, for the support of religion, an equally liberal amount was demanded. In the first place, one seventh part of their time was taken for the weekly sabbath, when no kind of work was to be done. Then the whole nation were required to meet at the appointed place, three times a year, which, including their journeys, and stay there, occupied eight weeks, which was another seventh of their time. Then the sabbatical year, when no agricultural labor was to be done, took another seventh of their time from their regular pursuits, as they were an agricultural people. This was the amount of time and property demanded by God, simply to sustain religion and morality within the bounds of that nation. Christianity demands the spread of its blessings to all mankind, and so the restrictions laid on the Jews are withheld, and all our wealth and time, not needful for our own best interest, is to be employed in improving the condition of our fellow-men.

In deciding respecting the rectitude of our pursuits, we are bound to aim at some practical good, as the ultimate object. With every duty of this life, our benevolent Creator has connected some species of enjoyment, to draw us to perform it. Thus the palate is gratified, by performing the duty of nourishing our bodies; the principle of curiosity is gratified, in pursuing useful knowledge; the desire of approbation is gratified, when we perform benevolent and social duties; and every other duty has an alluring enjoyment connected with it. But the great mistake of mankind has consisted in seeking the pleasures, connected with these duties, as the sole aim, without reference to the main end that

---

[13]Deut. 15:14.
[14]Deut. 15:9–10.

should be held in view, and to which the enjoyment should be made subservient. Thus, men seek to gratify the palate, without reference to the question whether the body is properly nourished; and follow after knowledge, without inquiring whether it ministers to good or evil.

But, in gratifying the implanted desires of our nature, we are bound so to restrain ourselves, by reason and conscience, as always to seek the main objects of existence,—the highest good of ourselves and others; and never to sacrifice this, for the mere gratification of our sensual desires. We are to gratify appetite, just so far as is consistent with health and usefulness, and no further. We are to gratify the desire for knowledge, just so far as will enable us to do most good by our influence and efforts; and no further. We are to seek social intercourse, to that extent, which will best promote domestic enjoyment and kindly feelings among neighbors and friends. And we are to pursue exercise and amusement, only so far as will best sustain the vigor of body and mind. And for the right apportionment of time, to these and various other duties, we are to give an account at the final day.

Instead of attempting to give any very specific rules on this subject, some modes of economizing time will be suggested. The most powerful of all agencies, in this matter, is, that habit of system and order, in all our pursuits, which has been already pointed out. It is probable, that a person, who is regular and systematic in employing time, will accomplish thrice the amount, that could otherwise be secured.

Another mode of economizing time, is, by uniting several objects in one employment. Thus, exercise, or charitable efforts, can be united with social enjoyments, as is done in associations for sewing or visiting the poor. Instruction and amusement can also be combined. Pursuits like music, gardening, drawing, botany, and the like, unite intellectual improvement with amusement, social enjoyment, and exercise.

With housekeepers, and others whose employments are various and desultory, much time can be saved by preparing employments for little odd intervals. Thus, some ladies prepare, and keep in the parlor, light work, to take up when detained there; some keep a book at hand, in the nursery, to read while holding or sitting by a sleeping infant. One of the most popular poetesses of our Country very often shows her friends, at their calls, that the thread of the knitting never need interfere with the thread of agreeable discourse.

It would be astonishing, to one who had never tried the experiment, how much can be accomplished, by a little planning and forethought, in thus finding employment for odd intervals of time.

But besides economizing our own time, we are bound to use our influence and example to promote the discharge of the same duty by others. A woman is under obligations so to arrange the hours and pursuits of her family, as to promote systematic and habitual industry; and if, by late breakfasts, irregular hours for meals, and other hinderances of this kind, she interferes with, or refrains from promoting regular industry in, others, she is accountable to God for all the waste of time consequent on her negligence. The mere example of a systematic and industrious housekeeper, has a wonderful influence in promoting the same virtuous habit in others.

ON ECONOMY IN EXPENSES

It is impossible for a woman to practise a wise economy in expenditures, unless she is taught how to do it, either by a course of experiments, or by the instruction of those who have had experience. It is amusing to notice the various, and oftentimes contradictory, notions of economy, among judicious and experienced housekeepers; for there is probably no economist, who would not be deemed lavish or wasteful, in some respects, by another equally experienced and judicious person, who, in some other points, would herself be equally condemned by the other. These diversities are occasioned by different early habits, and by the different relative value given by each to the different modes of enjoyment, for which money is expended.*

But, though there may be much disagreement in minor matters, there are certain general principles, which all unite in sanctioning. The first, is, that care be taken to know the amount of income and of current expenses, so that the proper relative proportion be preserved, and the expenditures never exceed the means. Few women can do this, thoroughly, without keeping regular accounts. The habits of this Nation, especially among business-men, are so desultory, and the current expenses of a family, in many points, are so much more under the control of the man than of the woman, that many women, who are disposed to be systematic in this matter, cannot follow their wishes. But there are often cases, when much is left undone in this particular, simply because no effort is made. Yet every woman is bound to do as much as is in her power, to accomplish a systematic mode of expenditure, and the regulation of it by Christian principles.

The following are examples of different methods which have been adopted, for securing a proper adjustment of expenses to the means.

The first, is that of a lady, who kept a large boarding-house, in one of our cities. Every evening, before retiring, she made an account of the expenses of the day; and this usually occupied her not more than fifteen minutes, at a time. On each Saturday, she took an inventory of the stores on hand, and of the daily expenses, and also of what was due to her; and then made an exact estimate of her expenditures and profits. This, after the first two or three weeks, never took more than an hour, at the close of the week. Thus, by a very little time, regularly devoted to this object, she knew, accurately, her income, expenditures, and profits.

Another friend of the Writer lives on a regular salary. The method adopted, in this case, is to calculate to what the salary amounts, each week. Then an account is kept of what is paid out, each week, for rent, fuel, wages, and food. This amount of each week is deducted from the weekly income. The remainders of each week are added, at the close of a month, as the stock from which is to be taken, the dress, furniture, books, travelling expenses, charities, and all other expenditures.

Another lady, whose husband is a lawyer, divides the year into four quarters, and the

---

*The Writer, not long since, met an amusing illustration of this. "Anna," said a wealthy lady, to her daughter, who had returned from an expensive boarding-school, and was playing on the piano, "where is *the* fine needle?" "I have broken it," was the reply. "Where is the coarse one, then?" "Ellen is using it." "Then just step over, and ask Mrs. C. to lend me her fine needle." The daughter went, and returned, saying, "Mrs. C. says she has lost hers, and has not had time to get another." A visiter, present, sent off for her wellstocked workbasket; and the remarks afterwards made, by the lady, in regard to its supplies, showed that she deemed her visiter lavish and extravagant in this matter. The wealthy lady hired out most of her plain sewing; and all her tailoring and mantua-making. The visiter cut and made all the garments for her family, and each thought the other uneconomical.

income into four equal parts. She then makes her plans, so that the expenses of one quarter shall never infringe on the income of another. So resolute is she, in carrying out this determination, that if, by any mischance, she is in want of articles before the close of a quarter, for which she has not the means, she will subject herself to temporary inconvenience, by waiting, rather than violate her rule.

Another lady, whose husband is in a business, which he thinks makes it impossible for him to know what his yearly income will be, took this method. She kept an account of all her disbursements, for one year. This she submitted to her husband, and obtained his consent that the same sum should be under her control, the coming year, for similar purposes, with the understanding that she might modify future apportionments, in any way her judgement and conscience might approve.

A great deal of uneasiness and discomfort is caused to both husband and wife, in many cases, by an entire want of system and forethought, in arranging expenses. Both keep buying what they think they need, without any calculation as to how matters are coming out, and with a sort of dread of running in debt, all the time harassing them. Such never know the comfort of independence. But, if a man or woman will only calculate what the income is, and then plan so as to know that all the time they live within it, they secure one of the greatest comforts, which wealth ever bestows, and what many of the rich, who live in a loose and careless way, never enjoy. It is not so much the amount of income, as the regular and correct apportionment of expenses, that makes a family truly comfortable. A man, with ten thousand a year, is often more harassed, for want of money, than the systematic economist, who supports a family on only six hundred a year.

As it is very important that young ladies should learn systematic economy in expenses, it will be a great benefit for every young girl to begin, at twelve or thirteen, to make her own purchases, under the guidance of her mother or some other friend. And if parents would ascertain the actual expense of a daughter's clothing, for a year, and give the sum to her, in quarterly payments, requiring a regular account, it would be of great benefit in preparing her for future duties. How else are young ladies to learn properly to make purchases, and to be systematic and economical? The art of system and economy can no more come by intuition, than the art of watchmaking or bookkeeping; and how strange it appears, that so many young ladies take charge of a husband's establishment, without having had either instruction or experience in the leading duty of their station!

The second general principle of economy, is, that, in apportioning an income, among various objects, the most important should receive the largest supply, and that all retrenchments be made in matters of less importance. In a previous chapter, some general principles have been presented, to guide in this duty. Some additional hints will here be added, on the same topic.

In regard to dress and furniture, much want of judgement and good taste is often seen, in purchasing some expensive article, which is not at all in keeping with the other articles connected with it. Thus, a large sideboard, or elegant mirror, or sofa, which would be suitable only for a large establishment, with other rich furniture, is crowded into too small a room, with coarse and cheap articles around it. So, also, sometimes a parlor, and company-chamber, will be furnished in a style suitable only for the wealthy, while the table will be supplied with shabby linen, and imperfect crockery, and every other part of the house will look, in comparison with these fine rooms, mean and niggardly. It is not at all uncommon, to find very showy and expensive articles in the part of the house visible to strangers, when the children's rooms, kitchen, and other back portions, are on an entirely different scale.

So in regard to dress, a lady will sometimes purchase an elegant and expensive article, which, instead of attracting admiration from the eye of taste, will merely serve as a decoy to the painful contrast of all other parts of the dress. A woman of real good taste and discretion, will strive to maintain a relative consistency between all departments, and not, in one quarter, live on a scale fitted only to the rich, and in another, on one appropriate only to the poor.

Another mistake in economy is often made, by some of the best-educated and most intelligent of mothers. Such will often be found spending day after day at the needle, when, with a comparatively small sum, this labor could be obtained of those who need such earnings. Meantime, the daughters of the family, whom the mother is qualified to educate, or so nearly, that she could readily keep ahead of her children, are sent to expensive boarding-schools, where their delicate frames, their plastic minds, and their moral and religious interests, are relinquished to the hands of strangers. And the expense, thus incurred, would serve to pay the hire of every thing the mother can do in sewing, four or five times over. The same want of economy is shown in communities, where, instead of establishing a good female school in their vicinity, the men of wealth send their daughters abroad, at double the expense, to be either educated or spoiled, as the case may be.

Another species of poor economy, is manifested in neglecting to acquire and apply mechanical skill, which, in consequence, has to be hired from others. Thus, all the plain sewing will be done by the mother and daughters, while all that requires skill will be hired. Instead of this, others take pains to have their daughters instructed in mantua-making,[15] and the simpler parts of millinery,[16] so that the plain work is given to the poor, who need it, and the more expensive and tasteful operations are performed in the family. The Writer knows ladies, who not only make their own dresses, but also their caps, bonnets, and artificial flowers.

Some persons make miscalculations in economy, by habitually looking up cheap articles, while others go to the opposite extreme, and always buy the best of every thing. Those ladies, who are considered the best economists, do not adopt either method. In regard to cheap goods, the fading colors, the damages discovered in use, the poorness of material, and the extra sewing demanded to replace articles lost by such causes, usually render such bargains very dear, in the end. On the other hand, though some articles, of the most expensive kind, wear longest and best, yet, as a general rule, articles at medium prices do the best service. This is true of table and bed linens, broadcloths, shirtings, and the like; though, in these cases, it is often found that the coarsest and cheapest last the longest.

Buying by wholesale, and keeping a large supply on hand, is economical only in large families, where the mistress is careful; but in other cases, the hazards of accident, and the temptation to a lavish use, will make the loss outrun the profits.

---

[15]Making loose-fitting gowns or mantles.

[16]Apparel for a woman's head.

There is one mode of economizing, which, it is hoped, will every year grow more rare; and that is, making penurious savings by getting the poor to work as cheap as possible. Many amiable and benevolent women have done this, on principle, without reflecting on the want of Christian charity thus displayed. Let every woman, in making bargains with the poor, conceive herself placed in the same circumstances, toiling hour after hour, and day after day, for a small sum, and then deal with others as she would be dealt by in such a situation. *Liberal prices,* and *prompt payment,* should be an unfailing maxim in dealing with the poor.

The third general principle of economy, is, that all articles should be so used, and taken care of, as to secure the longest service with the least waste. Under this head, come many particulars in regard to the use and preservation of articles, which will be found more in detail in succeeding chapters. It may be proper, however, here to refer to one very common impression, as to the relative obligation of the poor and the rich in regard to economy. Many seem to suppose, that those who are wealthy, have a right to be lavish and negligent in the care of expenses. But this surely is a great mistake. Property is a talent, given by God, to spend for the welfare of mankind; and the needless waste of it, is as wrong in the rich, as it is in the poor. The rich are under obligations to apportion their income, to the various objects demanding attention, by the same rule as all others; and if this will allow them to spend more for superfluities than those of smaller means, it never makes it right to misuse or waste any of the bounties of Providence. Whatever is no longer wanted for their own enjoyment, should be carefully saved, to add to the enjoyment of others.

It is not always that men understand the economy of Providence, in that unequal distribution of property, which, even under the most perfect form of government, will always exist. Many, looking at the present state of things, imagine that the rich, if they acted in strict conformity to the law of benevolence, would share all their property with their suffering fellow-men. But such do not take into account the inspired declaration, that a man's life consisteth not in the abundance of that which he possesseth, or, in other words, life is made valuable, not by great possessions, but by such a character as prepares a man to enjoy what he holds. God perceives that human character can be most improved by that kind of discipline which exists, when there is something valuable to be gained by industrious efforts. This stimulus to industry, never could exist in a community where all are just alike, as it does in a state of society where every man sees enjoyments possessed by others, which he desires and may secure by effort and industry. So in a community where all are alike as to property, there would be no chance to gain that noblest of all attainments, a habit of self-denying benevolence, which toils for the good of others, and takes from one's own store to increase the enjoyments of another.

Instead, then, of the stagnation both of industry and of benevolence, which would follow the universal and equable distribution of property, one class of men, by superior advantages of birth, or intellect, or patronage, come into possession of a great amount of capital. With these means, they are enabled, by study, reading, and travel, to secure expansion of mind, and just views of the relative advantages of moral, intellectual, and physical enjoyments. At the same time, Christianity imposes obligations corresponding with the increase of advantages and means. The rich are not at liberty to spend their treasures for themselves, alone. Their wealth is given, by God, to be employed for the best good of mankind; and their intellectual advantages are designed, primarily, to enable them to judge correctly, in employing their means most wisely for the general good.

Now, suppose a man of wealth inherits ten thousand acres of real estate: it is not his duty to divide it among his poor neighbors and tenants. It is probable, that, if he took this course, most of them would spend all in thriftless waste and indolence, or in mere physical enjoyments. Instead of thus putting his capital out of his hands, he is bound to retain it, and so employ it, as to raise his neighbors and tenants to such a state of virtue and intelligence, that they could secure far more, by their own efforts and industry, than he could bestow by dividing his capital.

In this view of the subject, it is manifest, that the unequal distribution of property is no evil. The great difficulty is, that so large a portion of those who hold great capital, instead of using their various advantages for the common good, employ the chief of them for mere selfish indulgences; thus inflicting as much mischief on their own souls, as results to others from their culpable neglect. A great portion of the rich seem to be acting on the principle, that the more God bestows on them, the less are their obligations to practise any self-denial, in fulfilling his benevolent plan of raising our race to intelligence and holiness.

There are not a few, who seem to imagine that it is a mark of gentility to be careless of expenses. But this notion is owing to a want of knowledge of the world. As a general fact, it will be found, that persons of rank, and wealth, abroad, are much more likely to be systematic and economical, than persons of inferior standing in these respects. Even the most frivolous, among the rich and great, are often found practising a rigid economy, in certain respects, in order to secure gratifications in another direction. And it will be found so common, among persons of vulgar minds and little education and less sense, to make a display of profusion and indifference to expense, as a mark of their claims to gentility, that the really genteel look upon it rather as a mark of low breeding. So that the sort of feeling which some persons cherish, as if it were mean to be careful of small sums, and to be attentive to relative prices, in making purchases, is founded on mistaken notions of gentility and propriety.

But one caution is needful, in regard to another extreme. When a lady of wealth is seen roaming about in search of cheaper articles, or trying to beat down a shopkeeper, or making a close bargain with those she employs, the impropriety is glaring to all minds. A person of wealth has no occasion to spend time in looking for extra cheap articles; her time could be more profitably employed in distributing to the wants of others. And the practice of beating down tradespeople, is vulgar and degrading, in any one. A woman, after a little inquiry, can ascertain what is the fair and common price of things; and if she is charged an exorbitant sum, she can decline taking the article. If the price be a fair one, it is inappropriate to search for another article which is below the regular charge. If a woman finds that she is in a store where they charge high prices, expecting to be beat down, she can simply mention, that she wishes to know the lowest price, as it is contrary to her principles to beat down charges.

There is one inconsistency, found among that class who are ambitious of being ranked among the aristocracy of society, which is worthy of notice. It has been remarked, that, in the real aristocracy of other lands, it is much more common than with us, to practice systematic economy. And such do not hesitate to say so, when they cannot afford certain indulgences. This practice descends to subordinate grades; so that foreign ladies, when they come to reside in this Country, seldom hesitate in assigning the true reason, when they cannot afford any gratification.

But in this Country, it will be found, that many, most fond of copying aristocratic examples, are on this point rather with the vulgar. Not a few of those young persons, beginning life with parlors and dresses in a style fitting only to established wealth, go into expenses which they can ill afford, and are ashamed even to allow that they are restrained from any expense by motives of economy. Such a confession is never extorted, except by some call of benevolence, and then they are very ready to declare that they cannot afford to bestow even a pittance. In such cases, it would seem as if the direct opposite of Christianity had gained possession of their tastes and opinions. They are ashamed to appear to deny themselves; but very far from any shame in denying the calls of benevolence.

7

George Lippard
(1822–1854)

AFTER STUDYING FIRST to become a Methodist minister and then a lawyer, George Lippard turned to writing as a career. He began with satirical newspaper pieces in the early 1840s, but in 1844 he began to serialize what would become one of the best-selling novels in antebellum America, *The Quaker City; or, The Monks of Monk-Hall*. Representative of a popular nineteenth-century literary genre scholars have come to call city-mysteries novels, *The Quaker City* flew off booksellers' shelves, selling sixty thousand copies in its first year and then ten thousand copies annually for the next decade.

Lippard based *The Quaker City* on a much-publicized 1843 Philadelphia murder case that resulted from the abduction and seduction of a respectable woman on the false promise of marriage. Lippard added countless elements to this story, which created tremendous interest in Philadelphia as local readers attempted to separate fact from fiction. The book itself is an odd mixture of elements, including: anti-Catholicism, anti-Protestantism, secret societies, domesticity gone awry, the gothic, popular science, seduction and rape, economic injustice, necrophilia, prostitution, temperance work, and adultery.

Lippard was a dedicated social reformer who used his writing to disseminate his views on American social evils and how they might be cured. His own philosophy was on the radical end of the spectrum for its day, concentrating on equality in terms of both class and gender. At the core of *The Quaker City* stands Lippard's belief in humanity's boundless capacity for evil and hypocrisy, and an equally strong conviction that it is only in confronting the darkest elements of the human heart that a better society might be created.

THE QUAKER CITY

Or, The Monks of Monk Hall
A Romance of Philadelphia Life, Mystery, and Crime

❧ Preface to This Edition

My Publishers ask me to write a Preface for this new Edition of the Quaker City. What shall I say? Shall I at this time enter into a full explanation of the motives which induced me to write this Work? Shall I tell how it has been praised—how abused—how it has on the one hand been cited as a Work of great merit, and on the other, how it has been denounced as the most immoral work of the age?

The reader will spare me the task. The Quaker City has passed through many Editions in America, as well as in London. It has also been translated and numerous editions of it have been published in Germany, and a beautiful edition in four volumes, is now before me, bearing the imprint of Otto Wigand, Leipsic, as Publisher, and the name of Frederick Gerstaker, as the Author.

Taking all these facts into consideration, it seems but just that I should say a word for myself on this occasion.

The motive which impelled me to write this Work may be stated in a few words.

I was the only Protector of an Orphan Sister. I was fearful that I might be taken away by death, leaving her alone in the world. I knew too well that law of society which makes a virtue of the dishonor of a poor girl, while it justly holds the seduction of a rich man's child as an infamous crime. These thoughts impressed me deeply. I determined to write a book, founded upon the following idea:

That the seduction of a poor and innocent girl, is a deed altogether as criminal as deliberate murder. It is worse than the murder of the body, for it is the assassination of the soul. If the murderer deserves death by the gallows, then the assassin of chastity and maidenhood is worthy of death by the hands of any man, and in any place.

This was the first idea of the Work. It embodies a sophism, but it is a sophism that errs on the right side. But as I progressed in my task, other ideas were added to the original thought. Secluded in my room, having no familiarity with the vices of a large city, save from my studentship in the office of an Attorney-General—the Confessional of our Protestant communities—I determined to write a book which should describe all the phases of a corrupt social system, as manifested in the city of Philadelphia. The results of my labors was this book, which has been more attacked, and more read, than any work of American fiction ever published.

And now, I can say with truth, that whatever faults may be discovered in this Work, that my motive in its composition was honest, was pure, was as destitute of any idea of

George Lippard, *The Quaker City; or, The Monks of Monk Hall, a Romance of Philadelphia Life, Mystery, and Crime.* Philadelphia: Leary, Stuart, 1876.

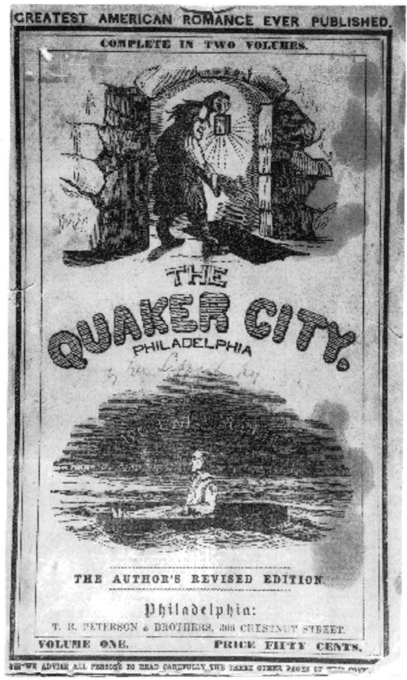

Bastard title page from George Lippard's *The Quaker City*, 1845.
(Courtesy, the American Antiquarian Society)

sensualism, as certain of the persons who have attacked it without reading a single page, are of candor, of a moral life, or a heart capable of generous emotions.

To the young man and young woman who may read this book when I am dead, I have a word to say:

Would to God that the evils recorded in these pages, were not based upon facts. Would to God that the experience of my life had not impressed me so vividly with the colossal vices and the terrible deformities, presented in the social system of this Large City, in the Nineteenth Century. You will read this work when the hand which pens this line is dust. If you discover one word in its pages, that has a tendency to develop one impure thought, I beseech you reject that word. If you discover a chapter, a page, or a line, that conflicts with the great idea of Human Brotherhood, promulgated by the Redeemer, I ask you with all my soul, reject that chapter, that passage, that line. At the same time remember the idea which impelled me to produce the book. Remember that my life from the age of sixteen up to twenty-five was one perpetual battle with hardship and difficulty, such as do not often fall to the lot of a young man—such as rarely is recorded in the experience of childhood or manhood. Take the book with all its faults and all its virtues. Judge it as you yourself would wish to be judged. Do not wrest a line from these pages, for the encouragement of a bad thought or a bad deed.

George Lippard.
[1849 Edition]

INSCRIBED TO THE MEMORY OF CHARLES BROCKDEN BROWN

❧ The Origin and Object of This Book

One winter night I was called to the bedside of a dying friend. I found him sitting up in his death-couch, pale and trembling yet unawed by the gathering shadows of the tomb. His white hairs fell over his clammy brow, his dark grey eye, glared with the unnatural light, which, heralds the approach of death. Old K——had been a singular man. He had been a profound lawyer, without fame or judgeship. In quiet he pursued his dreamy way, deriving sufficient from his profession, to support him in decency and honor. In a city, where no man has a friend, that has not money to back him, the good old lawyer had been my friend. He was one of those old-fashioned lawyers who delight to bury themselves among their books, who love the law for its theory, and not for its trick and craft and despicable chicanery. Old K——had been my friend, and now I sat by his bedside in his last hour.

"Death is coming," he said with a calm smile, "but I dread him not. My accounts with God are settled; my face is clammy with the death-sweat, but I have no fear. When I am gone, you will find in yonder desk, a large pacquet, inscribed with your name. This pacquet, contains the records of my experience as a private councillor and a lawyer, for the last thirty years. You are young and friendless, but you have a pen, which will prove your best friend. I bequeath these Papers to you; they may be made serviceable to yourself and to the world——"

In a faint voice, I asked the good old lawyer, concerning the nature of these records.

"They contain a full and terrible developement of the Secret Life of Philadelphia. In that pacquet, you will find, records of crimes, that never came to trial, murders that have never been divulged; there you will discover the results of secret examinations, held by official personages, in relation to atrocities almost too horrible for belief——"

"Then," said I, "Philadelphia is not so pure as it looks?"

"Alas, alas, that I should have to say it," said the old man with an expression of deep sorrow, "But whenever I behold its regular streets and formal look, I think of The Whited Sepulchre,[1] without all purity, within, all rottenness and dead men's bones. Have you courage, to write a book from those papers?"

"Courage?"

"Aye, courage, for the day has come, when a man dare not speak a plain truth, without all the pitiful things of this world, rising up against him, with adder's tongues and treacherous hands. Write a book, with all your heart bent on some good object, and for every word you write, you will find a low-bred calumniator, eager to befoul you with his slanders. Have you courage, to write a book from the materials, which I leave you, which shall be devoted to these objects. To defend the sanctity of female honor; to show how miserable and corrupt is that Pseudo-Christianity which tramples on every principle ever preached or practised by the Saviour Jesus; to lay bare vice in high places, and strip gilded crimes of their tinsel. Have you courage for this?"

I could only take the old man's hand, within my own, and murmur faintly, "I'll try!"

"Have you courage, to lift the cover from the Whited Sepulchre, and while the world is crying honor to its outward purity, to show the festering corruption that rankles in its depths? Then those records are yours!"

I sat beside the deathbed of the old man all night long. His last hours were past in calm converse, full of hope and trust in God. Near the break of day, he died. God bless him! He was my friend, when I had nothing but an orphan's gratitude, to tender in return for his friendship. He was a lawyer, and *honest;* a Christian and yet no bigot; a philosopher and yet no sceptic.

After his funeral, I received the pacquet of papers, inscribed with my name, and endorsed, REVELATIONS OF THE SECRET LIFE OF PHILADELPHIA, *being the records of thirty years practice as a councillor,* by * * * K——.

The present book is founded upon those portions of the Revelations, more intimately connected with the present day.

With the same sincerity with which I have written this Book of the Quaker City, I now give it to my countrymen, as an illustration of the life, mystery and crime of Philadelphia.

---

[1]Matt. 23:77.

BOOK THE FIRST
THE FIRST NIGHT

Mary, the Merchant's Daughter

CHAPTER FIRST

❧ The Wager in the Oyster-Cellar

"I say, gentlemen, shall we make a night of it? That's the question gents. Shall we elevate the—the devil along Chesnut street, or shall we subside quietly to our homes? Let's
toss up for it—which shall have the night—brandy and oysters, or quilts and feather-
beds?" And as he spoke, the little man broke loose from the grasp of his friends, and
retiring to the shelter of an awning-post, flung his cloak over his shoulder with a vast deal
of drunken dignity, while his vacant eyes were fixed upon the convivial group scattered
along the pavement.

"Brandy"—cried a gentleman distinguished by a very pursy figure, enveloped in a
snow-white overcoat, and a very round face, illuminated by a pear-shaped nose—
"Brandy is a gentleman—a per—perfect gentleman. He leaves no head-ache next morning by way of a card. Champagne's a sucker—a hypocritical scoundrel, who first goes
down your throat, smooth as oil, and then—a—a—very much so—how d——d irregular these bricks are—puts a powder-mill in your head and blows it up—dam 'im!—
Mem:—Byrnewood—d'ye hear? write to the corporation to-morrow, about these curst
mountainous pavements—" And having thus said, the pursy gentleman retreated to the
shelter of another awning-post, leaving the two remaining members of the convival
party, in full possession of the pavement, which they laid out in any given number of gar-
den-plots without delay.

"Byrnewood—d'ye hear?" exclaimed the tallest gentleman of the twain, gathering
his frogged overcoat closer around him, while his mustachioed lip was wreathed in
a drunken smile—"Look yonder at the statehouse—sing—singular phenomenon!
There's the original steeple and a duplicate. Two steeples, by Jupiter! Remarkable effect
of moonlight! Very—Doesn't it strike you, Byrnewood, that yonder watch-box is
walking across the street, to black the lamp-post's eyes—for—for—making a face at
him?"

The gentleman thus addressed, instead of replying to the sagacious query of his
friend, occupied a small portion of his leisure time in performing an irregular Spanish
dance along the pavement, terminating in a pleasant combination of the cachuca, with a
genuine New Jersey double-shuffle. This accomplished, he drew his well proportioned
figure to its full height, cast back his cloak from his shoulders, and turned his face to the
moonlit sky. As he gazed upon the heavens, clear, cold, and serene as death, the moonlight falling over his features, disclosed a handsome tho' pallid face, relieved by long
curling locks of jet black hair. For a moment he seemed intensely absorbed amid the
intricacies of a philosophical reverie, for he frequently put his thumb to his nose, and

described circles in the air with his outspread fingers. At last tottering to a seat on a fire-plug, he delivered himself of this remarkable expression of opinion—

"Miller[2] the Prophet's right! Right I say! The world—d——n the plug, how it shakes—the world is coming to an end for certain—for, d'ye see boys—there's *two* moons shining up yonder this blessed night sure as fate—"

The scene would have furnished a tolerable good subject for an effective convivial picture.

There, seated on the door-way step of a four storied dwelling, his arms crossed over his muscular chest, his right hand grasping a massive gold-headed cane, Mr. Gustavus Lorrimer, commonly styled the handsome Gus Lorrimer, in especial reference to his well-known favor among the ladies, presented to the full glare of the moonbeams, a fine manly countenance, marked by a brilliant dark eye, a nose slightly aquiline, a firm lip clothed with a mustache, while his hat tossed slightly to one side, disclosed a bold and prominent forehead, relieved by thick clusters of rich brown hair. His dark eye at all times full of fire, shone with a glance of unmistakeable humor, as he regarded his friend seated on the fire-plug directly opposite the doorway steps.

This friend—Mr. Byrnewood, as he had been introduced to Lorrimer—was engaged in performing an extemporaneous musical entertainment on the top of the fire-plug with his fingers, while his legs were entwined around it, as though the gentleman was urging a first-rate courser at the top of his speed.

His cloak thrown back from his shoulders, his slight though well-proportioned and muscular form, was revealed to the eye, enveloped in a closely fitting black frock-coat. His face was very pale, and his long hair, which swept in thick ringlets to his shoulders, was dark as a raven's wing, yet his forehead was high and massive, his features regular, and his jet-black eye, bright as a flame-coal. His lips, now wreathing in the very silly smile peculiar to all worshippers of the bottle-god, were, it is true, somewhat slight and thin, and when in repose inclining to severity in expression; yet the general effect of his countenance was highly interesting, and his figure manly and graceful in its outlines, although not so tall by half-a-head as the magnificent Gus Lorrimer.

While he is beating a tattoo on the fire-plug, let us not forget our other friends, Col. Mutchins, in his snow-white overcoat and shiny hat; and Mr. Sylvester J. Petriken, in his glazed cap and long cloak, as leaning against opposite awning posts, they gaze in each others faces and afford a beautiful contrast for the pencil of our friend Darley.

Col. Mutchins' face, you will observe, is very much like a picture of a dissipated full-moon, with a large red pear stuck in the centre for a nose, while two small black beads, placed in corresponding circles of crimson tape, supply the place of eyes. The Colonel's figure is short, thick-set, and corpulent; he is very broad across the shoulders, broader across the waist, and very well developed in the region of the hands and boots. The gentleman, clinging nervously to the opposite awning post, is remarkable for three

---

[2]William Miller (1782–1849) founded an American religious movement known as Millerism. Miller prophesied that Christ would return in 1843 (later adjusted to October 22, 1844). At one point, Miller estimated that between fifty thousand and one hundred thousand Americans believed in his views.

things—smallness of stature, slightness of figure, and slimness of legs. His head is very large, his face remarkable for its pallor, is long and square—looking as though it had been laid out with a rule and compass—with a straight formal nose, placed some distance above a wide mouth marked by two parallel lines, in the way of lips. His protuberant brow, faintly relieved by irregular locks of mole-skin colored hair, surmounted by a high glazed cap, overarches two large, oyster-like eyes, that roll about in their orbits with the regularity of machinery. These eyes remind you of nothing more, than those glassy things which, in obedience to a wire, give animation to the expressive face of a Dresden wax-doll.

And over this scene of quadruple convivialism, shone the midnight moon, her full glory beaming from a serene winter sky, upon the roofs and steeples of the Quaker City. The long shadows of the houses on the opposite side of the way, fell darkly along the street, while in the distance, terminating the dim perspective, arose the State-House buildings, with the steeple shooting upward into the clear blue sky.

"That champagne—" hiccuped Mr. Petriken, clinging to the awning-post, under a painful impression that it was endeavoring to throw him down—"That champagne was very strong—and the oysters—Oh my——"

"As mortal beings we are subject to sud—sudden sickness—"observed the sententious Mutchins, gathering his awning-post in a fonder embrace.

"I say, Byrnewood—how shall we terminate the night? Did I understand you that the d——l was to be raised? If so, let's start. Think how many bells are to be pulled, how many watch-boxes to be attacked, how many—curse the thing, I believe I'm toddied—watchmen to be licked. Come on boys?"

"Hist! Gus! You'll scare the fire-plug. He's trying to run off with me—the scoundrel. Wait till I put the spurs to him, I say!"

"Come on boys. Let's go round to Smokey Chiffin's oyster cellar and have a cozy supper. Come on I say. Take my arm, Byrnewood—there, steady—here Petriken, never mind the awning-post, take this other arm—now Mutchins hook Silly's arm and let's travel——"

But Mutchins—who, by the way, had been out in a buffaloe hunt the year before—was now engaged in an imaginary, though desperate fight with a Sioux warrior, whom he belabored with terrific shrieks and yells.

"D——n the fool—he'll have us all in the watch house—" exclaimed Lorrimer, who appeared to be the soberest of the party by several bottles—"Fun is fun, but this thing of cutting up shines in Chesnut street, after twelve, when it—keep steady Silly—amounts to yelling like a devil in harness is—un-un-der-stand me, no fun. Come along, Mutchy my boy!"

And arm in arm, linked four abreast, like horses very tastelessly matched, the boon companions tottered along Chesnut street, toward Smokey Chiffin's oyster cellar, where they arrived, with but a single interruption.

"Hao-pao-twel-o-glor-a-a-damuley-mor!"

This mysterious combination of sounds emanated from a stout gentleman in a slouching hat, and four or five overcoats, who, with a small piece of cord-wood in his hand met our party breast to breast, as they were speeding onward in full career.

"I say stranger—do that over again—will yo'?" shrieked Petriken, turning his square face over his shoulder and gazing at the retreating figure with the cord-stick and the overcoats—"Jist do that again if you please. Let me go I tell you, Gus. Don't you see, this is some—dis-distinguished vocal-ist from London? What a pathos there is in his voice—so deep—so full—why Brough is nothing to him! Knock Wood, and Seg-Seguin—and Shrival—and a dozen more into a musical cocked-hat, and they can't equal our mys-mysterious friend—"

"I say you'd better tortle on my coveys—" cried he of the great coats and cord stick, in a subterranean voice—"Or p'r'aps, my fellers, ye'd like to tend Mayor Scott's tea-party—would ye?"

"Thank you kindly—" exclaimed Gus Lorrimer in an insinuating tone, "otherwise engaged. But my friend—if you will allow me to ask—what *do* you mean by that infernal noise you produced just now? Let us into the lark?"

The gentleman of the cord stick and overcoats, was however beyond hearing by this time, and our friends moved on their way. Byrnewood observing in an under tone, somewhat roughened by hiccups, that on his soul, he believed that queer old cove, in the slouched hat, meant by his mysterious noise to impart the important truth that *it was half-past twelve o'clock and a moonlight morning.*

Descending into Smokey Chiffin's subterranean retreat, our friends were waited upon by a very small man, with a sharp face and a white apron, and a figure so lank and slender, that the idea involuntarily arose to the spectators mind, of whole days and nights of severe training, having been bestowed upon a human frame, in order to reduce it to a degree of thinness quite visionary.

"Come my 'Virginia abstraction'—" exclaimed Lorrimer—"Show us into a private room, and tell us what you've got for supper—"

"This way sir—this way gents—" cried Smokey Chiffin, as the thin gentleman was rather familiarly styled—"What got for supper? Woodcock sir? excellent sir. Venison sir; excellent sir. Oysters sir, stewed, sir, fried sir, roasted sir, or in the shell sir. Excellent sir. Some right fresh, fed on corn-meal sir. What have sir? Excellent sir. This way gents—"

And as he thus delivered his bill of fare, the host, attended by his customers, disappeared from the refrectory proper, through an obscure door into the private room.

There may be some of our readers who have never been within the confines of one of those oyster-caverns which abound in the Quaker City. For their especial benefit, we will endeavor to pencil forth a few of the most prominent characteristics of the "Oyster Saloon by Mr. Samuel Chiffin."

Lighted by flaring gas-pipes, it was divided into two sections by a blazing hot coal stove. The section beyond the stove, wrapt in comparative obscurity, was occupied by two opposing rows of 'boxes,' looking very much like conventual stalls, ranged side by side, for the accommodation of the brothers of some old-time monastery. The other section, all light, and glitter, and show, was ornamented at its extreme end, by a tremendous mirror, in which a toper might look, time after time, in order to note the various degrees of drunkenness through which he passed. An oyster-box, embellished by a glorious display of tin signs with gilt letters, holding out inviting manifestations of "oysters stewed fried or in the shell," occupied one entire side of this section, gazing directly in the face of the liquor bar placed opposite, garnished with an imposing array of decanters, paint gilding, and glasses.

And the company gathered here? Not very select you may be sure. Four or five gentlemen with seedy coats and effloresent noses were warming themselves around the stove, and discussing the leading questions of the day; two individuals whose visits to the bar had been rather frequent, were kneeling in one corner, swearing at a very ragged dog, whom they could'nt persuade to try a glass of 'Imperial Elevator,' and seated astride of a chair, silent and alone, a young man whose rakish look and ruffled attire betrayed the medical student on his first 'spree' was endeavouring to hold himself steady, and look uncommonly sober; which endeavour always produces, as every body knows, the most riduculous phase of drunkenness.

These Oyster Cellers are queer things. Like the caverns of old story, in which the Giants,[3] those ante-diluvian rowdies, used to sit all day long, and use the most disreputable arts to inveigle lonely travellers into their clutches, so these modern dens, are occupied by a jolly old Giant of a decanter, who too often lures the unsuspecting into his embrace. A strange tale might be told, could the stairway leading down into the Oyster Celler be gifted with the power of speech. Here Youth has gone down laughing merrily, and here Youth has come up, his ruddy cheek wrinkled and his voice quavering with premature age. Here Wealth has gone down, and kept going down until at last he came up with his empty pocket, turned inside out, and the gripe of grim starvation on his shoulder. Here Hope, so young, so gay, so light-hearted has gone down, and came up transformed into a very devil with sunken cheeks, bleared eyes, and a cankered heart. Oh merry cavern of the Oyster Celler, nestling under the ground so close to Independence Hall, how great the wonders, how mighty the doings, how surprising the changes accomplished in your pleasant den, by your jolly old Giant of a Decanter!

It is here in this Oyster Celler, that we open the fearful tragedy which it is the painful object of our narrative, to tell. Here amid paint, and glitter and gilding, amid the clink of glasses and the roar of drinking songs, occurred a scene, which trifling and insipid as it may appear to the casual observer, was but the initial letter to a long and dreary alphabet of crime, mystery and bloodshed.

In a room, small and comfortable, lighted by gas and warmed by a cheerful coal-fire, around a table furnished with various luxuries, and garnished with an array of long necked bottles, we find our friends of the convivial party. Their revel had swelled to the highest, glass clinked against glass, bottle after bottle had been exhausted, voices began to mingle together, the drinking song and the prurient story began to pass from lip to lip, while our sedate friend, Smokey Chiffin, sate silently on the sofa, regarding the drunken bout with a glance of quiet satisfaction.

"Let me see—let me see"—he murmured quietly to himself—"Four bottles o'Cham. at two dollars a bottle—four times two is eight. Hum—hum. They'll drink six more. Let's call it twelve altogether. Say twenty-four shiners for supper and all. Hum—hum—Gus pays for all. That fellow Petriken's a sponge. Wonder when Col. Mutchins

---

[3]In Greek mythology, the Giants lost a titanic struggle with the Olympians. After most of them were slain, they were buried or retreated under mountains, where they still cause problems by doing such things as luring people into caves or causing volcanic explosions.

will call for the cards? Don't know who this fellow Byrnewood is? New face—may be he's a *roper** too? We'll see—we'll see."

"Give us your hand, Gus"—cried Byrnewood, rising from his seat and flinging his hand unsteadily across the table—"Damme, I like you old fellow. Never—never—knew until to-night—met you at Mutchin's room—wish I'd known you all my life—Give us your hand, my boy!"

Calm and magnificent, Gustavus extended his hand, and exclaimed, in a voice, which champagne could not deprive of its sweetness, that it gave him pleasure to know such a regular bird as Mister Byrnewood; great pleasure; extraordinary pleasure.

"You see, fellows, I believe I'll take a spree for three days—wont go home, or to the store in Front street. Mean to keep it up until after Christmas. Wants three days o'Christmas—mean to jolly—ha—ha—how the room reels."

"Gentle-men—I don't know what is the matter with me—" observed Petriken, who rested his elbows helplessly on the table, as he looked around with his square face, lengthened into a vacant stare—"There's somethin' queer a-goin' on with my eyes. I seem to see spiders—lots o' 'em—playin' corner-ball with roaches. See anything o' the kind, Mutchins?"

"Why—why—" replied that sententious gentleman as his red round face was over-spread by a commiserating smile—"Why the fact is—Silly—you've been drinkin'. By the bye does'nt it strike you that there's something queer going on with that gas light. I say, Smokey, is'nt there a beetle tryin' to mash his brains out against that gas-pipe?"

"Gentlemen—I will give you a toast!" exclaimed Lorrimer, as he stood erect, the bold outline of his manly form, his handsome face, the high forehead relieved by thick masses of brown hair, the aquiline nose, the rounded chin, and the curving lip darkened by a mustache, all shown to advantage in the glowing light—"Gentlemen fill your glasses—no heeltaps! Woman!"

"Woman!" shrieked the other three, springing unsteadily to their feet, and raising their glasses on high—"Woman! Three times three—hip-hip-hurrah!"

"Women!" muttered Sylvester Petriken—"Women for ever! when we're babies she nusses us, when we're boys she lathers us, when we're men she bedevils and bewitches us!"

"Woman—" muttered Colonel Mutchins—"without her what 'ud life be? A dickey without a 'plete,' a collar without starch!"

"We can't help it if we fascinate 'em?" exclaimed Byrnewood—"Can we Gus?"

"All fate, my boy—all fate. By the bye—set down boys. I've got a nice little adventure of my own to tell. Smokey—bring us some soda to sober off with—"

"Gentlemen—" cried Petriken, sinking heavily in his chair—"Did any of you see the last number of my magazine? 'The Ladies' Western Hemisphere and Continental Organ.' Offers the following inducements to sub—subscribers—one fashion-plate and

---

*This genteel term is applied to a well dressed edition of the vulgar stool-pigeon, used by gam-blers, to decoy the unwary into their dens. The stool-pigeon is the loafer decoy, the roper is very aristocratic, prevails in the large hotel and is called a—gentleman.

two steel engravings per number—48 pages, octavo—Sylvester J. Petriken, Editor and Proprietor, office 209 Drayman's alley, up stairs. Damme, Mutchins, what's your idea of fleas?"

There was not, it is true, the most visible connexion between the Ladies Continental Organ and the peculiar insect, so troublesome to young puppies and very small kittens, yet as Mr. Petriken was not exactly sober, and Col. Mutchins very far from the temperance pledge, the idea seemed to tickle them both immensely and they joined in a hearty laugh, which terminated in another glass from a fresh bottle of champagne.

"Let's have your story, Gus!" shouted Byrnewood—"Let's have your story! Damme—life's but a porcelain cup—to-day we have it, tomorrow we hav'nt—why not fill it with sweetness?"

As he said this, in tones indistinct with liquor he flung his long curling hair back from his brow, and tossed his glass unsteadily on high.

Life a porcelain cup, why not fill it with sweetness? Great God of Mercy! Could the terrible future, which was to break, in a few brief hours, with all its horrors, on the head of this young man, who now sat unconsciously at the drinking board, have at that moment assumed a tangible form, it would have stood like an incarnate devil at his shoulder, its outstretched hand, pouring the very gall of despair into the cup of his life, crowding it to the brim with the wormwood of death.

"Well boys for my story. It's a story of a sweet girl, my boys—a sweet girl about sixteen, with a large blue eye, a cheek like a ripe peach, and a lip like a rose-bud cleft in two—"

"Honor bright Gus. Damme, that's a quotation from my last Ladies' Western Hem. Damme Gus——"

"Byrnewood do hold poor Silly down. There's this material difference, boys, between a ripe peach or a cleft rose-bud, and a dear little woman's lips or cheek. A ripe peach won't throb and grow warm if you lay your cheek against it, and I never yet heard of a rose-bud that kissed back again. She's as lovely a girl as ever trod the streets of the Quaker City. Noble bust—slender waist—small feet and delicate hands. Her hair? damme, Byrnewood, you'd give your eyes for the privilege of twining your hands through the rich locks of her dark brown hair——"

"Well, well, go on. Who is this girl; uncover the mystery!"

"Patience, my boy, patience. A little of that soda if you please. Now, gentlemen, I want you to listen attentively, for let me tell you, you don't hear a story like mine every day in the year."

Half sobered by the combined influences of the soda water and the interest of Lorrimer's story, Byrnewood leaned forward, fixing his full dark eyes intently upon the face of Gus, who was seated opposite; while Col. Mutchins straightened himself in his chair, and even Petriken's vacant face glowed with a momentary aspect of sobriety.

"I see, boys, that you expect something nice. (Smokey put some more coal on the fire.) Well Byrnewood, you must know I'm a devil of a fellow among the girls—and—and—d——n the thing, I don't know how to get at it. Well, here goes. About two weeks ago I was strolling along Chesnut street towards evening, with Boney (that's my big wolf dog, you know?) at my heels. I was just wondering where I should spend the evening;

whether I should go to see Forrest at the Walnut,[4] or take a turn round town; when who should I see walking ahead of me, but one of the prettiest figures in the world, in a black silk mantilla, with one of these saucy kiss-me-if-you-dare bonnets on her head. The walk of the creature, and a little glimpse of her ankle excited my curiosity, and I pushed ahead to get a view of her face. By Jupiter, you never saw such a face! so soft, so melting, and— damme—so innocent. She looked positively bewitching in that saucy bonnet, with her hair parted over her forehead, and resting each cheek in a mass of the richest curls, that ever hung from the brow of mortal woman——"

"Well, Gus, we'll imagine all this. She was beautiful as a houri,[5] and priceless as the philosopher's stone[6]——"

"Byrnewood you are too impatient. A pretty woman in a black silk mantilla, with a lovely face peeping from a provoking bonnet, may seem nothing to you, but the strangest part of the adventure is yet to come. As I looked in the face of this lovely girl, she, to my utter astonishment addressed me in the softest voice in the world, and——"

"Called you by name?"

"No. Not precisely. It seems she mistook me for some gentleman whom she had seen at a country boarding-school. I took advantage of her mistake, walked by her side for some squares along Chesnut street, and——"

"Became thoroughly acquainted with her, I suppose?" suggested Byrnewood.

"Well, you may judge so, when I mention one trifling fact for your consideration. This night, at three o'clock, this innocent girl, the flower of one of the first families in the city, forsaking home and friends, and all that these sweet girls are wont to hold dear, will seek repose in my arms—"

"She can't be *much*—" exclaimed Byrnewood, over whose face a look of scornful incredulity had been gathering for some few moments past—"Pass that champagne, Petriken my boy. Gus, I don't mean to offend you, but I rather think you've been humbugged by some 'slewer?' "*

A frown darkened over Lorrimer's brow, and even as he sate, you might see his chest heave and his form dilate.

"Do you mean to doubt my word—*Sir?*"

"Not at all, not at all. But you must confess, the thing looks rather improbable. (Will you smoke, Col.?) May I ask whether there was any one in company with the lady when first you met her?"

"A Miss something or other—I forget her name. A very passable beauty of twenty and upwards, and I may add, a very convenient one, for she carried my letters, and otherwise favored my cause with the sweet girl."

"And this 'sweet girl' is the flower of one of the first families in the city?" asked Byrnewood with a half formed sneer on his upper lip.

---

[4]Edwin Forrest (1806–1872) was one of the nineteenth century's most famous and controversial actors. He often performed at the Walnut Street Theatre in Philadelphia.

[5]In Muslim belief, a houri is one of the beautiful maidens that live in paradise with the blessed.

[6]Stone capable of turning base metals into gold.

*A cant term used by profligates for female servants of indifferent character.

"She is—" answered Lorrimer, lighting a cigar.

"And this girl, to-night, leaves home and friends for you, and three hours hence will repose in your arms?"

"She will—" and Lorrimer vacantly eyed a column of smoke winding upward to the ceiling.

"You will not marry her?"

"Ha-ha-ha! You're ahead of me now. Only a pretended marriage, my boy. As for this 'life interest' in a woman, it don't suite my taste. A nice little sham marriage, my boy, is better than ten real ones——"

"You would be a d——d fool to marry a woman who flung herself in your power in this manner. How do you know she is respectable? Did you ever visit her at her father's house? What is her name? Do enlighten us a little——"

"You're 'cute, my boy, mighty 'cute, as the Yankees says, but not so 'cute as you think. Her name? D'ye think I'm so particularly verdant as to tell it? I know her name, could tell you the figure of her father's wealth, but have never been inside of the threshold of her home. Secret meetings, secret walks and even an assumed name, are oftentimes wonderfully convenient."

"Gus, here is a hundred dollar bill on the Bank of North America. I am, as you see, somewhat interested in your story. I will stake this hundred dollars that the girl who seeks your arms to-night, is not respectable, is not connected with one of the first families in the city, and more than all has never been any better than a common lady of the sidewalk—"

"Book that bet, Mutchins. You heard it, Silly. And now, Byrnewood, here is another hundred, which I will deposit with yours in Mutchins' hands until the bet is decided. Come with me and I'll prove to you that you've lost. You shall witness the wedding—ha, ha—and to your own sense of honor will I confide the secret of the lady's name and position—"

"The bet is booked and the money is safe"—murmured the sententious Mutchins, enclosing the notes in the leaves of his pocket-book—"I've heard of many rum go's but *this is* the rummest go of all."

"If I may be allowed to use the expression, this question involves a mystery. A decided mystery. For instance, what's the ladys name? There is a point from which Hypothesis may derive some labor. 'What's in a name'—as Shakespeare says. I say, gents, let's pick out a dozen names, and toss up which shall have it?"

This rather profound remark of Mr. Petriken's was received with unanimous neglect.

It was observable that during this conversation, both Lorrimer and Byrnewood had been gradually recovering from the effects of their debauch. Lorrimer seemed somewhat offended at the distrust manifested by Byrnewood; who, in his turn, appeared to believe the adventure just related with very many doubts and modifications.

Lorrimer leaned over the table and whispered in Sylvester's ear.

"Damme—damme my fellow"—murmured Sylvester, apparently in reply to the whispered remark of his friend—"It cannot be done. Why man its a penitentiary offence."

Lorrimer again hissed a meaning whisper in the ear of the little man.

"Well, well, as it is your wish I'll do it. A cool fifty, did you say? You think a devlish sight of the girl—do you then? I must provide myself with a gown and prayer book? I flatter myself I'll rather become them—three o'clock, did you say?"

"Aye—aye—" answered Lorrimer, turning to the rubicund face of Col. Mutchins and whispering hurriedly in his ear.

A pleasant smile overspread the face of the benevolent man, and his pear-shaped nose seemed to grow expressive for a single moment.

"D——d good idea? I'll be your too-confiding uncle? Eh? Stern but relenting? I'll bless the union with my benediction—*I'll give the bride away?*"

"Come along Byrnewood. Here Smokey is the money for our supper. Mark you gentlemen, Mr. Petriken and Col. Mutchins—the hour is three o'clock. Don't fail me, if the d——l himself stands in the way. Take my arm Byrnewood and let's travel—"

"Then 'hey for the wedding.' Daylight will tell who wins!"

And as they left the room arm in arm, bound on the adventure so suddenly undertaken, and so full of interest and romance, Petriken looked vacantly in Mutchin's face, and Mutchins returned the look with a steady gaze that seemed to say—'How much did he give you, old boy?'

Whether Sylvester translated the look in this manner, it is difficult to tell, but certain it is, that as he poured a bumper from a fresh bottle of champagne, he motioned the Colonel to do the same, and murmured in an absent manner, or perhaps by way of a sentiment, the remarkable words—

"Fify dollars! Egad that 'ill buy two steel engravings and three fashion plates for the next number of the Ladies' Western Hemisphere. 'Economy is wealth,' and the best way to learn to fly is to creep—creep very low, remarkably low, d——d low—*always creep!*"

CHAPTER SECOND

❧ Mary, the Merchant's Daughter

Leaning gently forward, her shawl falling carelessly from her shoulders, and her bonnet thrown back from her brow, the fair girl impressed a kiss on the cheek of her father, while the glossy ringlets of her hair mingled their luxuriant brown with the white locks of the kind old man.

The father seated on the sofa, his hands clasping her slight and delicate fingers, looked up into her beaming face with a look of unspeakable affection, while a warm glow of feeling flushed over the pale face of the mother, a fine matronly dame of some forty-five, who stood gazing on her daughter, with one hand resting on the husband's shoulder.

The mild beams of an astral lamp diffused a softened and pleasing light through the parlor. The large mirror glittering over the mantle, the curtains of crimson silk depending along the windows, the sofa on which the old man was seated, the carpet of the finest texture, the costly chairs, the paintings that hung along the walls, and in fine all the appointments of the parlor, designated the abode of luxury and affluence.

The father, who sate on the sofa gazing in the face of his child, was a man of some sixty years, with a fine venerable countenance, wrinkled by care and time, with thin locks of snow-white hair falling along his high pale forehead. In his calm blue eye, look-ing forth from the shadow of a thick grey eyebrow, and in the general contour of his face, you might trace as forcible a resemblance to his daughter, as ever was witnessed between an old man just passing away from life, and a fair young girl, blooming and blushing on the very threshold of womanhood. The old man was clad in glossy black, and his entire appearance, marked the respectable merchant, who, retiring from active business, sought in the quietude of his own home, all the joys, that life, wealth or affection united and linked in blessings, have in their power to bestow.

The mother, who stood resting her hand on her husband's shoulder, was, we have said, a fine matronly dame of forty-five. A mild pale face, a deep black eye, and masses of raven hair, slightly sprinkled with the silver threads of age, parted over a calm fore-head, and tastefully disposed beneath a plain cap of lace, gave the mother an appearance of sweetness and dignity combined, that was eminently effective in winning the respect and love of all who looked upon her.

"Mary—my child—how lovely you have grown!" exclaimed the Merchant, in a deep quiet tone, as he pressed her fair hands within his own, and looked up in her face.

"Nonsense! You will make the child vain—" whispered the wife playfully, yet her face flushed with affection, and her eyes shone an answer to her husband's praise.

The girl was indeed beautiful.

As she stood there, in that quiet parlor, gazing in her father's face, she looked like a breathing picture of youth, girlhood and innocence, painted by the finger of God. Her face was very beautiful. The small bonnet thrown back from her forehead, suffered the rich curls of her brown hair to escape, and they fell twining and glossy along each swelling cheek, as though they loved to rest upon the velvet skin. The features were reg-ular, her lips were full red and ripe, her round chin varied by a bewitching dimple, and her eyes were large, blue and eloquent, with long and trembling lashes. You looked in those eyes, and felt that all the sunlight of a woman's soul was shining on you. The face was lovely, most lovely, the skin, soft, velvety, blooming and transparent, the eyes full of soul, the lips sweet with the ripeness of maidenhood, and the brow calm and white as alabaster, yet was there no remarkable manifestation of thought, or mind, or intellect vis-ible in the lines of that fair countenance. It was the face of a woman formed to lean, to cling, to love, and never to lean on but one arm, never to cling but to one bosom, never to love but once, and that till death and forever.

The fair round neck, and well-developed bust, shown to advantage in the close fit-ting dress of black silk, the slender waist, and the ripening proportions of her figure, ter-minated by slight ankles and delicate feet, all gave you the idea of a bud breaking into bloom, a blossom ripening into fruit, or what is higher and holier, a pure and happy soul manifesting itself to the world, through the rounded outlines of a woman's form.

"Come, come father, you must not detain me any longer—" exclaimed the daughter in a sweet and low-toned voice—"You know aunt Emily has been teasing me these two weeks, ever since I returned from boarding-school, to come and stay with her all night. You know I was always a favorite with the dear old soul. She wants to contrive some agreeable surprise for my birth-day, I believe. I'm sixteen next Christmas, and that is three days off. Do let me go, that's a good father——"

"Had'nt you better put on your cloak, my love?" interrupted the Mother, regarding the daughter with a look of fond affection—"The night is very cold, and you may suffer from exposure to the winter air—"

"Oh no, no, no mother—" replied the fair girl, laughingly—"I *do* so hate these cloaks—they're so bungling and so heavy! I'll just fling my shawl across my shoulders, and run all the way to Aunt Emily's. You know it's only two squares distant in Third Street—"

"And then old Lewey will see you safe to the door?" exclaimed the Mother—"Well, well, go along my dear child, take good care of yourself, and give my love to your Aunt—"

"These old maids are queer things"—said the Merchant with a smile—"Take care Mary or Aunt Emily will find out all your secrets—"

And the old man smiled pleasantly to himself, for the idea of a girl, so young, so innocent, having any secrets to be found out, was too amusing to be entertained without a smile.

A shade fell over the daughters face so sudden and melancholy that her parents started with surprise.

"Why do you look so sad, my child!" exclaimed the Father, looking up in his daughter's face. "What is there in the world to sadden *you*, my Mary?"

"Nothing, father, nothing—" murmured Mary, flinging her form on her fathers bosom and twining her arms round his neck as she kissed him again and again—"Only I was thinking—just thinking of Christmas, and——"

The fair girl rose suddenly from her fathers bosom, and flung her arms hurriedly around her mother's neck, imprinting kiss after kiss on her lips.

"Good bye mother—I'll be back—I'll be back—to-morrow."

And in an instant she glided hastily to the door and left the room.

"Lewey is'nt it very cold to night!" she asked as she observed the white-haired negro-servant waiting in the hall, wrapped up in an enormous overcoat, with a comforter around his neck and a close fur cap surmounting his grey wool and chubby round face—"I'm sorry to take you out in the cold, Lewey."

"Bress de baby's soul—" murmured the old negro opening the door—"Habbent I nuss you in dese arms when you warnt so high? Lewey take cold? Debbil a cold dis nigger take for no price when a-waitin' on missa Mary—"

Mary stood upon the threshold of her home looking out into the cold starlit night. Her face was for a moment overshadowed by an expression of the deepest melancholy, and her small foot trembled as it stepped over the threshold. She looked hurriedly along the gloomy street, then cast her glance backwards into the entry, and then with a wild bound she retraced her steps, and stood beside her father and her mother.

Again she kissed them, again flung her arms round their necks, and again bounded along the entry crying laughingly to her parents—"Good night—good night—I'll be back to-morrow."

Again she stood upon the threshold, but all traces of laughter had vanished from her face. She was sad and silent, and there were tears in her eyes. At least the old negro said so afterwards, and also that her tiny foot, when resting on the door-sill, trembled like any leaf.

Why should her eye grow dim with tears and her foot tremble? Would not that tiny foot, when next it crossed the threshold, bound forward with a gladsome movement, as the bride sprung to meet her father and her mother once again? Would not that calm blue eye, now filled with tears, grow bright with a joy before unknown, when it glanced over the husband's form, as for the first time he stood in the father's presence? Would not Christmas Eve be a merry night for the bride and all her friends as they went shouting merrily through the luxuriantly furnished chambers of her father's mansion? Why should *she* fear to cross the threshold of her home, when her coming back was to be heralded with blessings and crowned with love?

How will the future answer these trembling questions of that stainless heart?

She crossed the threshold, and not daring to look back, hurried along the gloomy street. It was clear, cold, starlight, and the pathways were comparatively deserted. The keen winter wind nipped her cheek, and chilled her form, but above her, the stars seemed smiling her 'onward,' and she fancied the good angels, that ever watch over woman's first and world-trusting love, looking kindly upon her from the skies.

After traversing Third street for some two squares, she stood before an ancient three-storied dwelling, at the corner of Third and——streets, with the name of 'Miss. E. Graham,' on the door plate.

"Lewey you need'nt wait—" she said kindly—yet not without a deeper motive than kindness—to the aged Negro who had attended her thus far—"I'll ring the bell myself. You had better hurry home and warm yourself—and remember, Lewey, tell father and mother that they need not expect me home before to-morrow at noon. Good night, Lewey."

"Good night, Missa Mary, Lor' Moses lub your soul—" muttered the honest old Negro, as, pulling his fur cap over his eyes, he strode homeward—"Dat ar babby's a angel, dat is widout de wings. De Lor grant when dis here ole nigger gets to yander firmey-ment—dat is if niggers gets dar at all—he may be 'pinted to one ob de benches near Missa Mary, so he can wait on her, handy as nuffin—dats all. She's a angel, and dis here night, is a leetle colder dan any night in de memory ob dat genel'man de Fine Col'ector nebber finds—de berry oldest inhabitant."

Thus murmuring, Lewey trudged on his way, leaving Mary standing in front of Aunt Emily's door. Did she pull the bell? I trow not, for no sooner was the negro out of sight, than the tall figure of a woman, dressed in black, with a long veil drooping over her face, glided round the corner and stood by her side.

"Oh—Bessie—is that you?" cried Mary, in a trembling voice—"I'm so frightened I don't know what to do—Oh Bessie—Bessie don't you think I had better turn back—"

"*He* waits for you—" said the strange woman, in a husky voice.

Mary hurriedly laid her hand on the stranger's arm. Her face was overspread with a sudden expression of feeling, like a gleam of sunshine, seen through a broken cloud on a stormy day, and in a moment, they were speeding down Third street toward the southern districts of the Quaker City. Another moment, and the eye might look for them in vain.

And as they disappeared the State House clock rung out the hour of nine. This, as the reader will perceive, was just four hours previous to the time when Byrnewood and Lorrimer closed their wager in the subterranean establishment along Chesnut street. To the wager and its result we now turn our attention and the readers interest.

CHAPTER THIRD

✒ Byrnewood and Lorrimer

The harsh sound of their footsteps, resounding along the frozen pavement, awoke the echoes of the State House buildings, as linked arm in arm, Byrnewood and Lorrimer hurried along Chesnut street, their figures thrown in lengthened shadow by the beams of the setting moon.

The tall, manly and muscular figure of Lorrimer, attired in a close-fitting black overcoat, presented a fine contrast to the slight yet well-proportioned form of Byrnewood, which now and then became visible as the wind flung his voluminous cloak back from his shoulders. The firm and measured stride of Lorrimer, the light and agile footsteps of Byrnewood, the glowing countenance of the magnificent Gus, the pale solemn face of the young Merchant, the rich brown hair which hung in clustering masses around the brow of the first, and the long dark hair which fell sweeping to the very shoulders of his companion, all furnished the details of a vivid contrast, worthy the effective portraiture of a master in our sister-art.

"Almost as cold as charity, Byrnewood my boy—" exclaimed Lorrimer, as he gathered Byrnewood's arm more closely within his own—"Do you know, my fellow, that I believe vastly in faces?"

"How so?"

"I can tell a man's character from his face, the moment I clap my eye on him. I like or dislike at first sight. Now there's Silly Petriken's face—how do you translate it?"

"The fact is, Lorrimer, I know very little about him. I was introduced to him, for the first time, at a party, where he was enrapturing some sentimental old maids, with a few quires of sonnets on every thing in general. Since that occasion I have never met him, until tonight, when he hailed me in Chesnut street, and forced me into Mutchin's room at the United States Hotel. You know the rest—"

"Well, well, with regard to Petriken, a single word. Clever fellow, clever, but like Mutchins, he sells for a reasonable price. I buy them both. By Jupiter! the town swarms with such fellows, who will sell themselves to any master for a trifle. Petriken—poor fellow—his face indicates his character—a solemn pimp, a sententious parasite. Mutchins is just the other way—an agreeable jolly old-dog of a pander. They hire themselves to me for the season—I use and, of course, despise them—"

"You're remarks are truly flattering to these worthy gentlemen!" said Byrnewood, drily.

"And now my fellow, you may think me insincere, but I tell you frankly, that the moment I first saw your face, I liked you, and resolved you should be my friend. For your sake I am about to do a thing which I would do for no living man, and possibly no dead one——"

"And that is—" interrupted Byrnewood.

"Just listen my fellow. Did you ever hear any rumors of a queer old house down town, kept by a reputable old lady, and supported by the purses of goodly citizens, whose names you never hear without the addition of 'respectable,' 'celebrated,' or—ha—ha—'pious'—*most* 'pious?' A queer old house my good fellow, where, during the long hours of the winter nights, your husband, so kind and good, forgets his wife, your merchant his ledger, your lawyer his quibbles, your parson his prayers? A queer old house, my good fellow, where wine and women mingle their attractions, where at once you sip the honey from a red-lip, and a sparkling bubble from the champagne? Where luxuriantly-furnished chambers resound all night long with the rustling of cards, or the clink of glasses, or—it may be—the gentle ripple of voices, murmuring in a kiss? A queer old house, my dear fellow, in short, where the very devil is played under a cloak, and sin grows fat within the shelter of quiet rooms and impenetrable walls—"

"Ha—ha—Lorrimer you are eloquent! Faith, I've heard some rumors of such a queer old house, but always deemed them fabulous—"

"The old house is a fact, my boy, a fact. Within its walls this night I will wed my pretty bride, and within its walls, my fellow, despite the pains and penalties of our Club, you shall enter—"

"I should like it of all things in the world. How is your club styled?"

"All in good time, my friend. Each member, you see, once a week, has the privilege of introducing a friend. The same friend must never enter the Club House twice. Now I have rather overstepped the rules of the Club in other respects—it will require all my tact to pass you in to-night. It shall be done, however—and mark me—you will obtain a few fresh ideas of the nature of the *secret life* of this good Quaker City—"

"Why Lorrimer—" exclaimed Byrnewood, as they approached the corner of Eighth and Chesnut—"You seem to have a pretty good idea of life in general—"

"Life?" echoed the magnificent Gus, in that tone of enthusiasm peculiar to the convivialist when recovering from the first excitement of the bottle—"Life? What is it? As brilliant and as brief as a champagne bubble! To day a jolly carouse in an oyster cellar, to-morrow a nice little pic nic party in a grave-yard. One moment you gather the apple, the next it is ashes. Every thing fleeting and nothing stable, every thing shifting and changing, and nothing substantial! A bundle of hopes and fears, deceits and confidences, joys and miseries, strapped to a fellow's back like Pedlar's wares—"

"Huzza! Bravo—the *Reverend* Gus Lorrimer preaches. And what moral does your reverence deduce from all this!"

"One word, my fellow—ENJOY! Enjoy till the last nerve loses its delicacy of sense; enjoy till the last sinew is unstrung; enjoy till the eye flings out its last glance, till the voice cracks and the blood stagnates; *enjoy,* always *enjoy,* and at last——"

"Aye, aye—that terrible *at last*——"

"At last, when you can enjoy no longer, creep into a nice cozy house, some eight feet deep, by six long and two wide, wrap yourself up in a comfortable quilt of white, and tell the worms—those jolly gleaners of the scraps of the feast of life—that they may fall to and be d——d to 'em—"

"Ha—ha—Lorrimer! Who would have thought this of you?"

"Tell me, my fellow, what business do you follow?"

"Rather an abrupt question. However, I'm the junior partner in the importing house of Livingston, Harvey, & Co., along Front street—"

"And I—" replied Gustavus slowly and with deliberation—"And I am junior and senior partner in a snug little wholesale business of my own. The firm is Lorrimer, & Co.—the place of business is everywhere about town—and the business itself is enjoyment, nothing but enjoyment; wine and woman forever! And as for the capital—I've an unassuming sum of one hundred thousand dollars, am independent of all relations, and bid fair to live at least a score of years longer. Now my fellow, you know me—come, spice us up a few of your own secrets. Have you no interesting little *amour* for my private ear?"

"By Heaven, I'd forgotten all about it!" cried Byrnewood starting aside from his companion as they stood in the full glare of the gas-lamp at the corner of Eighth and Chesnut street—"I'd forgotten all about the letter!"

"The letter? What letter?"

"Why just before Petriken hailed me in Chesnut street this evening—or rather *last* evening—a letter was placed in my hands, which I neglected to read. I know the handwriting on the direction, however. It's from a dear little love of a girl, who, some six months ago, was a servant in my father's house. A sweet girl, Lorrimer—and—you know how these things work—she was lovely, innocent and too confiding, and I was but a—man—"

"And she a 'slewer.' Rather a low walk of business for *you,* my boy. However, let's read the letter by lamplight—"

"Here it is—'Dear Byrnewood—I would like very much to see you to-night. I am in great distress. Meet me at the corner of Fourth and Chesnut streets at nine o'clock or you will regret it to the day of your death. Oh for God's sake do meet me—Annie.' What a pretty hand she writes—Eh! Lorrimer! That 'for God's sake' is rather cramped—and—egad! there's the stain of a tear—"

"These things are quite customary. These letters and these tears. The dear little women can only use these arguments when they yield too much to our persuasions—"

"And yet—d——n the thing—how unfortunate for the girl my acquaintance has proved! She had to leave my father's house on account of—of—the *circumstance* becoming too apparent, and her parents are very poor. I should have liked to have seen her to-night. However, it will do in the morning. And now, Lorrimer, which way?"

"To the 'queer old house' down town. By the bye, there goes the State House—one o'clock, by Jupiter! We've two good hours yet to decide the wager. Let's spend half an hour in a visit to a certain friend of mine. Here, Byrnewood, let me instruct you in the mysteries of the 'lark'—"

And, leaning aside, the magnificent Gus whispered in the ear of his friend, with as great an appearance of mystery as the most profound secret might be supposed to demand.

"Do you take, my fellow?"

"Capital, capital—" replied Byrnewood, crushing the letter into his pocket—"We shall crowd this night with adventures—that's certain!"

The dawn of daylight—it is true—closed the accounts of a night somewhat crowded with incidents. Did these merry gentlemen who stood laughing so cheerily at the corner of Eighth and Chesnut streets, at the hour of one, their faces glowing in the light of the midnight moon, did they guess the nature of the incidents which five o'clock in the morning could disclose? God of Heaven—might no angel of mercy drop from the skies and warn them back in their career?

No warning came, no omen scared them back. Passing down Eighth street, they turned up Walnut, which they left at Thirteenth. Turning down Thirteenth they presently stood before a small old fashioned two storied building, with a green door and a bull window, that occupied nearly the entire width of the front, protruding in the light. A tin sign, placed between the door and window, bore the inscription, "*. *****, ASTROLOGER."

"Wonder if the old cove's in bed—" exclaimed Lorrimer, and as he spoke the green door opened, as if in answer to his question, and the figure of a man, muffled up in the thick folds of a cloak with his hat drawn over his eyes, glided out of the Astrologer's house, and hurried down Thirteenth street.

"Ha—ha—devilish cunning, but not so cunning as he thinks!" laughed Byrnewood—"I saw his face—it's old Grab-and-Snatch, the President of the——Bank, which every body says is on the eve of a grand blow-up!"

"The respectable old gentleman has been consulting the stars with regard to the prospects of his bank—ha—ha! However, my boy, the door is open—let's enter! Let's consult this familiar of the fates, this intimate acquaintance of the Future!"

CHAPTER FOURTH

❧ The Astrologer

In a small room, remarkable for the air of comfort imparted by the combined effects of the neatly white-washed walls, the floor, plainly carpeted, and the snug little wood-stove roaring in front of the hearth, sat a man of some forty-five winters, bending over the table in the corner, covered with strange-looking books and loose manuscripts.

The light of the iron lamp which stood in the centre of the table, resting on a copy of Cornelius Agrippa, fell full and strongly over the face and form of the Astrologer, disclosing every line of his countenance, and illumining the corner where he sat, while the more distant parts of the room were comparatively dim and shadowy.

As he sat in the large old-fashioned arm-chair, bending down earnestly over a massive manuscript, covered with strange characters and crossed by intricate lines, the lamp-beams disclosed a face, which somewhat plain and unmeaning in repose, was now agitated by an expression of the deepest interest. The brow, neither very high nor very low, shaded by tangled locks of thin brown hair, was corrugated with deep furrows, the eyebrows were firmly set together, the nostrils dilated, and the lips tightly compressed, while the full grey eyes, staring vacantly on the manuscript, indicated by the glassy film spread over each pupil, that the mind of the Astrologer, instead of being occupied with outward objects, was buried within itself, in the contemplation of some intricate subject of thought.

There was nothing in the dress of the man, or in the appearance of his room, that might realize the ideas commonly attached to the Astrologer and his den. Here were no melodramatic curtains swinging solemnly to and fro, brilliant and terrible with the emblazoned death's-head and cross-bones. Here were no blue lights imparting a lurid radiance to a row of grinning skeletons, here were no ghostly forms standing pale and erect, their glassy eyes freezing the spectator's blood with horror, here was neither goblin, devil, or mischievous ape, which, as every romance reader knows, have been the companions of the Astrologer from time immemorial; here was nothing but a plain man, seated in an old-fashioned arm chair, within the walls of a comfortable room, warmed by a roaring little stove.

No cap of sable relieved the Astrologer's brow, no gown of black velvet, tricked out with mysterious emblems in gold and precious stones, fell in sweeping folds around the outlines of his spare figure. A plain white overcoat, much worn and out at the elbows, a striped vest not remarkable for its shape or fashion, a cross-barred neckerchief, and a simple linen shirt collar completed the attire of the astrologer who sat reading at the table.

The walls of the room were hung with the Horoscopes of illustrious men, Washington, Byron, and Napoleon, delineated on large sheets of paper, and surrounded by plain frames of black wood; the table was piled with the works of Sibly, Lilly, Cornelius Agrippa and other masters in the mystic art; while at the feet of the Astrologer nestled a fine black cat, whose large whiskers and glossy fur, would seem to afford no arguments in favor of the supposition entertained by the neighbors, that she was a devil in disguise, a sort of familiar spirit on leave of absence from the infernal regions.

"I'm but a poor man—" said the Astrologer, turning one of the leaves of the massive volume in manuscript which he held in his hand—"I'm but a poor man, and the lawyer, and the doctor, and the parson all despise me, and yet—" his lip wreathed with a sneering smile—"this little room has seen them all within its walls, begging from the humble man some knowledge of the future! Here they come—one and all—the fools, pretending to despise my science, and yet willing to place themselves in my power, while they affect to doubt. Ha-ha—here are their Nativities one and all—That" he continued, turning over a leaf—"is the Horoscope of a clergyman—Holy man of God!—He wanted to know whether he could ruin an innocent girl in his congregation without discovery. And that is the Horoscope of a lawyer, who takes fees from both sides. His desire is to know, whether he can perjure himself in a case now in court without detection. Noble counsellor! This Doctor—" and he turned over another leaf—"told me that he had a delicate case in hand. A pretty girl had been ruined and so on—the seducer wants to destroy the fruit of his crime and desires the doctor to undertake the job. Doctor wants to know what moment will be auspicious—ha-ha!"

And thus turning from page to page, he disclosed the remarkable fact, that the great, the good, and the wise of the Quaker City, who met the mere name of astrology, when uttered in public, with a most withering sneer, still under the cover of night, were happy to steal to the astrologer's room, and obtain some glimpses of their future destiny through the oracle of the stars.

"A black-eyed woman—lusty and amorous—wants to know whether she can present her husband with a pair of horns on a certain night? I warned her not to proceed in her course of guilt. She does proceed—and will be exposed to her husband's hate and public scorn—" And thus murmuring, the Astrologer turned to another leaf.

"The Horoscope of a puppy-faced editor! A spaniel, a snake, and an ape—he is a combination of the three. Wants to know when he can run off with a lady of the *ballet* at the theatre, without being caught by his creditors? Also, whether next Thursday is an auspicious day for a little piece of roguery he has in view? The penitentiary looms darkly in the distance—let the editor of the 'DAILY BLACK MAIL' beware—"

Another leaf inscribed with a distinguished name, arrested the Astrologer's attention.

"Ha—ha! This fellow is a man of fashion, a buck of Chesnut street, and—and a Colonel! He lives—*I* know *how*—the fashionables who follow in his wake don't *dream* of his means of livelihood. He has committed a crime—an astounding crime—wants to know whether his associate will betray him! I told him *he* would. The Colonel laughed at me, although he paid for the knowledge. In a week the fine, sweet, perfumed gentleman will be lodged at public expense—"

The Astrologer laid down the volume, and in a moment seemed to have fallen into the same train of thought, marked by the corrugated brow and glassy eye, that occupied his mind at the commencement of this scene. His lips moved tremulously, and his hands ever and anon were pressed against his wrinkled brow. Every moment his eye grew more glassy, and his mouth more fixedly compressed, and at last, leaning his elbows on the table with his hands nervously clasped, his gaze was fixed on the blank wall opposite, in a wild and vacant stare that betrayed the painful abstraction of his mind from all visible objects.

And as he sat there enwrapt in thought, a footstep, inaudible to his ear, creaked on the stairway that ascended into the Astrologer's chamber from the room below, and in a moment, silent and unperceived, Gus Lorrimer stood behind his chair, looking over his head, his very breath hushed and his hands upraised.

"In all my history I remember nothing half so strange. All is full of light except one point of the future, and that is dark as death!" Thus ran the murmured soliloquy of the Astrologer—"And yet they will be here to-night—here—here both of them, or there's no truth in the stars. Lorrimer must beware——"

"Ha—ha—ha—" laughed a bold and manly voice—"An old stage trick, that. You didn't hear my footsteps on the stairs—did you? Oh no—oh no. Of course you didn't. Come—come, my old boy, that claptrap mention of my name, is rather too stale, even for a three-fipenny-bit melo-drama—"

The sudden start which the Astrologer gave, the unaffected look of surprise which flashed over his features at the sight of the gentleman of pleasure, convinced Lorrimer that he had done him rank injustice.

"Sit down, sir—I have much to say to you—" said the Astrologer, in a voice strikingly contrasted with his usual tone, it was so deep, so full and so calmly deliberate— "Last Thursday morning at this hour you gave me the day and hour of your birth. You wished me to cast your horoscope. You wished to know whether you would be successful in an enterprise which you mediated. Am I correct in this?"

"You are, my old humbug[7]—that is my *friend*—" replied Lorrimer, flinging himself into a seat.

"Humbug?" cried the other with a quiet sneer—"You may alter your opinion after a-while, my young friend. Since last Thursday morning I have given the most careful attention to your horoscope. It is one of the most startling that ever I beheld. You were born under one of the most favorable aspects of the heavens, born, it would seem, but to succeed in all your wishes; and yet your future fate is wrapt in some terrible mystery—"

---

[7]An imposter, deceiver.

"Like a kitten in a wet blanket, for instance?" said Lorrimer, in the vain endeavor, to shake off a strange feeling of awe, produced by the manner of the Astrologer.

"This night I was occupied with your horoscope when a strange circumstance attracted my attention. Even while I was examining book after book, in the effort to see more clearly into your future, I discovered that you were making a new acquaintance at some festival, some wine-drinking or other affair of the kind. This new acquaintance is a man with a pale face, long dark hair and dark eyes. So the stars tell me. Your fate and the fate of this young man are linked together till death. So the heavens tell me, and the heavens never lie."

"Yes—yes—my friend, very good—" replied Gustavus with a smile—"Very good, my dear sir. Your conclusions are perfect—your prophetic gift without reproach. But you forget one slight circumstance:—I have made no new acquaintance to-night! I have been at no wine-drinking! I have seen no interesting young man with a pale face and long dark hair—"

"Then my science is a lie!" exclaimed the Astrologer, with a puzzled look—"The stars declare that this very night, you first came in contact with the man, whose fate henceforth is linked with your own. The future has a doom in store for one of ye. The stars do not tell me which shall feel the terror of the doom, but that it will be inflicted by one of ye upon the other, is certain—"

"Well, let us suppose, for the sake of argument, that I did meet this mysterious young man with long black hair. What follows?"

"Three days ago, a young man, whose appearance corresponds with the indication given by the stars of the new acquaintance you were to make this very night, came to me and desired me to cast his horoscope. The future of this young man, is as like yours as night is to-night. He too is threatened with a doom—either to be suffered or inflicted. This doom will lower over his head within three days. At the hour of sunset on next Saturday—Christmas Eve—a terrible calamity will overtake him. At the same hour, and in the same manner, a terrible calamity will blacken your life forever. The same doubt prevails in both cases—whether you will endure this calamity in your own person, or be the means of inflicting its horrors on some other man, doomed and fated by the stars—"

"What connection has this young man with the 'new acquaintance' which you say I have formed to-night?"

"I suspect that this young man and your new acquaintance are *one*. If so, I warn you, by your soul, beware of him—this stranger to you!"

"And why *beware of me?*" said a calm and quiet voice at the shoulder of the Astrologer.

As though a shell had burst in the centre of that quiet room, he started, he trembled, and arose to his feet. Byrnewood, the young merchant, calm and silent, stood beside him.

"I warn ye." He shrieked in a tone of wild excitement, with his grey eyes dilating and flashing beneath the woven eyebrows—"I warn ye both—beware of each other! Let this meeting at my house be your last on earth, and ye are saved! Meet again, or pursue any adventure together, and ye are lost and lost forever! I tell ye, scornful men that ye are, that ask my science to aid you, and then mock its lessons, I tell ye, by the Living God who writes his will, in letters of fire on the wide scroll of the firmament, that in the hand of the dim Future is a Goblet steeped in the bitterness of death, and that goblet one or the other must drink, within three little days!"

And striding wildly along the room, while Byrnewood stood awed, and even the cheek of Lorrimer grew pale, he gave free impulse to one of those wild deliriums of excitement peculiar to his long habits of abstraction and thought. The full truth, the terrible truth, seemed crowding on his brain, arrayed in various images of horror, and he shrieked forth his interpretation of the future, in wild and broken sentences.

"Young man, three days ago you sought to know the future. You had never spoken to the man who sits in yonder chair. I cast your horoscope—I found your destiny like the destiny of this man who affects to sneer at my science. My art availed me no further. I could not identify you with the man who first met Lorrimer this night, amid revelry and wine. Now I can supply the broken chain. You and his new-formed acquaintance are *one*. And now the light of the stars breaks more plainly on me—*within three days, one of you will die by the other's hand——*"

Lorrimer slowly arose to his feet, as though the effort gave him pain. His cheek was pale, and beaded drops of sweat stood on his brow. His parted lips, his upraised hands and flashing eyes attested his interest in the astrologer's words. Meanwhile, starting suddenly aside, Byrnewood veiled his face in his hands, as his breast swelled and quivered with sudden emotion.

Stern and erect, in his plain white overcoat, untricked with gold or gems, stood the Astrologer, his tangled brown hair flung back from his brow, while, with his outstretched hand and flashing eye, he spoke forth the fierce images of his brain.

"Three days from this, as the sun goes down, on Christmas eve, one of you will die by the other's hand. As sure as there is a God in Heaven, his stars have spoken, and it will be so!"

"What will be the manner of *the death?*" exclaimed Lorrimer, in a low-tuned voice, as he endeavored to subdue the sudden agitation inspired by the Astrologer's words, while Byrnewood raised his head and awaited the answer with evident interest.

"There is the cloud and the mystery—" exclaimed the Astrologer, fixing his eye on vacancy, while his outstretched hand trembled like a leaf in the wind—"The death will overtake the doomed man on a river, and yet it will not be by water; it will kill him by means of fire and yet he will not perish in the midst of flames—"

There was a dead pause for a single instant. There stood the Astrologer, his features working as with a convulsive spasm, the light falling boldly over his slight figure and homely attire, and there at his side, gazing in his face, stood Byrnewood, the young merchant, silent as if a spell had fallen on him, while on the other side, Gustavus Lorrimer, half recoiling, his brow woven in a frown, and his dark eyes flashing with a strange glance, seemed making a fearful effort to command his emotion, and dispel the gloom which the wierd prophecy had flung over his soul.

"Pah! What fools we are! To stand here listening to the ravings of a madman or a knave—" cried Byrnewood, with a forced laugh, as he shook off the spell that seemed to bind him—"What does he know of the future—more than we? Eh? Lorrimer? Perhaps, sir, since you are so familiar with fate, destiny and all that, you can tell us the nature of the adventure on which Lorrimer is bound to-night?"

The Astrologer turned and looked upon him. There was something so calmly scornful in his glance, that Byrnewood averted his eyes.

"The adventure is connected with the honor of an innocent woman—" said the

Astrologer—"More than this I know not, save that a foul outrage will be done this very night. And—hark ye sir—either the heavens are false, or your future destiny hangs upon this adventure. Give up the adventure at once, go back in your course, part from one another, part this moment never to meet again, and you will be saved. Advance and you are lost!"

Lorrimer stood silent, thoughtful and pale as death. It becomes me not to look beyond the veil that hangs between the Visible and the Invisible, but it may be, that in the silent pause of thought which the libertine's face manifested, his soul received some indications of the future from the very throne of God. Men call these sudden shadows, presentiments; to the eyes of angels they may be, but messages of warning spoken to the soul, in the spirit-tongues of those awful beings whose habitation is beyond the threshold of time. What did Lorrimer behold that he stood so silent, so pale, so thoughtful? Did Christmas Eve, and the River, and the Death, come terrible and shadow-like to his soul?

"Pshaw! Lorrimer you are not frightened by the preachings of this fortune-teller?" cried Byrnewood with a laugh and a sneer—"You will not give up the girl? Ha—ha—scared by an owl! Ha—ha—What would Petriken say? Imagine the rich laugh of Mutchins—ha—ha—Gus Lorrimer scared by an owl!"

"Give up the girl?" cried Lorrimer, with a blasphemous oath, that profaned the name of the Saviour—"Give up the girl? Never! She shall repose in my arms before daylight! Heaven nor hell shall scare me back! There's your money Mister Fortune Teller—your croaking deserves the silver, the d——l knows! Come on Byrnewood—let us away."

"Wait till I pay the gentleman for our coffins—" laughed Byrnewood, flinging some silver on the table—"See that they're ready by Saturday night, old boy? D'ye mind? You are hand-in-glove with some respectable undertaker—no doubt—and can give him our measure. Good bye—old fellow—good bye! Now, Lorrimer, away—"

"Away, away to Monk-hall!"

And in a moment they had disappeared down the stairway, and were passing through the lower room toward the street.

"On Christmas Eve, at the hour of sunset—" shrieked the Astrologer, his features convulsed with anger, and his voice wild and piercing in its tones—"One of you will die by the other's hand! The winding sheet[8] is woven, and the coffin made—you are rushing madly on your doom!"

CHAPTER FIFTH

❧ Dora Livingstone

It was a nice cozy place, that old counting-house room, with its smoky walls, its cheerful coal-fire burning in the rusty grate, and its stained and blackened floor. A snug little room, illuminated by a gaslight, subdued to a shadowy and sleepy brilliancy, with the Merchant's Almanac and four or five old pictures scattered along the walls, an old oaken

---

[8]A sheet used to encircle a corpse before burial.

desk with immense legs, all carved and curled into a thousand shapes, standing in one corner, and a massive door, whose glass window opened a mysterious view into the regions of the warehouse, where casks of old cogniac lay, side by side, in lengthened rows, like jolly old fellows at a party, as they whisper quietly to one another on the leading questions of the day.

Seated in front of the coal fire, his legs elevated above his head, resting on the mantel-piece, a gentleman, of some twenty-five years, with his arms crossed and a pipe in his mouth, seemed engaged in an earnest endeavour to wrap himself up in a cloak of tobacco smoke, in order to prepare for a journey into the land of Nod, while the tumbler of punch standing on the small table at his elbow, showed that he was by no means opposed to that orthodox principle which recognizes the triple marriage of brandy, lemon and sugar, as a highly necessary addition to the creature comforts of the human being, in no way to be despised or neglected by thinking men.

You would not have called this gentleman well-proportioned, and yet his figure was long and slender, you could not have styled his dress eminently fashionable, and yet his frock coat was shaped of the finest black cloth, you would not have looked upon his face as the most handsome in the world, and yet it was a finely-marked countenance, with a decided, if not highly intellectual, expression. If the truth must be told, his coat, though fashioned of the finest cloth, was made a little too full in one place, a little too scant in another, and buttoned up somewhat too high in the throat, for a gentleman whose ambition it was to flourish on the southern side of Chesnut street, amid the animated cloths and silks of a fashionable promenade. And then the large black stock, encircling his neck, with the crumpled, though snow-white, shirt collar, gave a harsh relief to his countenance, while the carelessly-disposed wristbands, crushed back over the upturned cuffs of his coat, designated the man who went in for comfort, and flung fashion to the haberdashers and dry goods clerks.

As for his face, whenever the curtain of tobacco smoke rolled aside, you beheld, as I have said, a finely-marked countenance, with rather lank cheeks, a sharp aquiline nose, thin lips, biting and sarcastic in expression, a full square chin, and eyes of the peculiar class, intensely dark and piercing in their glance, that remind you of a flame without heat, cold, glittering and snake-like. His forehead was high and bold, with long and lanky black hair falling back from its outlines, and resting, without love-lock or curl, in straight masses behind each ear.

"Queer world this!" began our comfortable friend, falling into one of those broken soliloquies, generated by the pipe and the bowl, in which the stops are supplied by puffs of smoke, and the paragraph terminated by a sip of the punch—"Don't know much about other worlds, but it strikes me that if a prize were offered somewhere by somebody, for the queerest world a-going, this world of ours might be rigged up nice, and sent in like a bit of show beef, as the premium queer world. No man smokes a cigar that ever tried a pipe, but an ass. I was a small boy once—ragged little devil *that* Luke Harvey, who used to run about old Livingstone's importing warehouse. Indelicate little fellow: wore his ruffles out behind. Kicked and cuffed because he was poor—served him right— dammim. Old Liv. died—young Albert took the store—capital, cool one hundred thousand. Luke Harvey rose to a clerkship. Began to be a fine fellow—well-dressed, and of course virtuous. D——d queer fellow, Luke. Last year taken into partnership along with a young fellow whose daddy's worth at least one hun. thousand. Firm now—Living-stone, Harvey, & Co. Clever punch, that. Little too much lemon—d——d it, the sugar's out.

"Queer thing, that! Some weeks ago respectable old gentleman in white cravat and hump-back, came to counting house. Old fellow hailed from Charleston. Had rather a Jewish twang on his tongue. Presented Livingstone a letter of credit drawn by a Charleston house on our firm. Letter from Grayson, Ballenger, & Co., for a cool hundred thousand. Old white cravat got it. D——n that rat in the partition—why can't he eat his victuals in quiet? Two weeks since, news came that G. B. & Co. never gave such letter—a forgery, a complete swindle. Comfortable, that. Hot coals on one's bare skull, quite pleasant in comparison. Livingstone in New York—been trying for a week to track up the villain. Must get new pipe to-morrow. Mem. get one with Judas Iscariot[9] painted on the bowl. Honest rogue, that. Went and hanged himself after he sold his master. Wonder how full the town would be if all who have sold their God for gold would hang them-selves? Hooks in market house would rise. Bear queer fruit—eh? D——d good tobacco. By the bye—must go home. Another sip of the punch and I'm off. Ha—ha—good idea that of the handsome Colonel! Great buck, man of fashion and long-haired Apollo.[10] Called here this evening to see me—smelt like a civet cat.[11] Must flourish his pocket-book before my eyes by way of a genteel brag. Dropped a letter from a bundle of notes. Valuable letter that. Wouldn't part with it for a cool thousand—rather think it will raise the devil—let me see—"

And laying down his pipe, Mr. Luke Harvey drew a neatly-folded billetdoux[12] from an inside pocket of his coat, and holding it in the glare of the light perused its direction, which was written in a fair and delicate woman's hand.

"'Col. Fitz-Cowles—United States Hotel'"—he murmured—"good idea, Colonel, to drop *such* a letter out of your pocket-book. Won't trouble you none? 'Spose not—ha, ha, ha—d——d good idea!"

The idea appeared to tickle him immensely, for he chuckled in a deep, self-satisfied tone as he drew on his bearskin overcoat, and even while he extinguished the gas-light, and covered up the fire, his chuckle grew into a laugh, which deepened into a hearty guf-faw, as striding through the dark warehouse, he gained the front door, and looked out into the deserted street.

"Ha-ha-ha—to drop such a dear creature's letter!"—he laughed, locking the door of the warehouse—"Wonder if it won't raise h——l? I loved a woman once. Luke, you were a d——d fool *that* time. Jilted—yes jilted. That's the word I believe? Maybe I won't have my revenge? Perhaps not—very likely not—"

With this momentous letter, so carelessly dropped by the insinuating millionaire, Colonel Fitz-Cowles resting on his mind, and stirring his features with frequent spas-modic attacks of laughter, our friend, Mr. Harvey, pursued his way along Front street,

---

[9]The disciple who betrayed Jesus.

[10]The Greek and Roman god of sunlight, prophecy, and music.

[11]skunk

[12]A love letter.

and turning up Chesnut street, arrived at the corner of Third, where he halted for a few moments in order to ascertain the difference in time, between his gold-repeater and the State House clock, which had just struck one.

While thus engaged, intently perusing the face of his watch by the light of the moon, a stout middle-aged gentleman, wrapped up in a thick overcoat, with a carpet bag in his hand, came striding rapidly across the street, and for a moment stood silent and unperceived at his shoulder.

"Well Luke—is the repeater right and the State House wrong?" said a hearty cheerful voice, and the middle-aged gentleman laid his hand on Mr. Harvey's shoulder.

"Ah-ha! Mr. Livingstone! Is that you?" cried Luke, suddenly wheeling round, and gazing into the frank and manly countenance of the new-comer—"When did you get back from New York?"

"Just this moment arrived. I did not expect to return within a week from this time, and therefore come upon you by a little surprise. I wrote to Mrs. L. yesterday, telling her I would not be in town until the Christmas holidays were over. She'll be rather surprised to see me, I suppose?"

"Rather!" echoed Luke, drily.

"Come Luke, take my arm, and let's walk up toward my house. I have much to say to you. In the first place have you any thing new?"

While Mr. Harvey is imparting his budget of news to the senior partner of the firm of Livingstone, Harvey & Co., as they stroll slowly along Chesnut street, we will make some few notes of his present appearance.

Stout, muscular, and large-boned, with a figure slightly inclining towards corpulence, Mr. Livingstone strode along the pavement with a firm and measured step, that attested all the matured strength and vigor peculiar to robust middle age. He was six feet high, with broad shoulders and muscular chest. His face was full, bold, and massive, rather bronzed in hue, and bearing some slight traces of the ravages of small-pox. Once or twice as he walked along, he lifted his hat from his face, and his forehead, rendered more conspicuous by some slight baldness, was exposed to view. It was high, and wide, and massive, bulging outward prominently in the region of the reflective organs, and faintly relieved by his short brown hair. His eyes, bold and large, of a calm clear blue, were rendered strangely expressive by the contrast of the jet-black eyebrows. His nose was firm and Roman in contour, his mouth marked by full and determined lips, his chin square and prominent, while the lengthened outline of the lower jaw, from the chin to the ear, gave his countenance an expression of inflexible resolution. In short, it was the face of a man, whose mind, great in resources, had only found room for the display of its tamest powers, in enlarged mercantile operations, while its dark and desperate elements, from the want of adversity, revenge or hate to rouse them into action, had lain still and dormant for some twenty long years of active life. He never dreamed himself that he carried a hidden hell within his soul.

Had this man been born poor, it is probable that in his attempt to rise, the grim hand of want would have dragged from their lurking-places, these dark and fearful elements of his being. But wealth had lapped him at his birth, smiled on him in his youth, walked by him through life, and the moment for the trial of all his powers had never happened. He was a fine man, a noble merchant, and a good citizen—we but repeat the stereotyped phrases of the town—and yet, quiet and close, near the heart of this cheerful-faced man, lay a sleeping devil, who had been dozing away there all his life, and only waiting the call of destiny to spring into terrible action, and rend that manly bosom with his fangs.

"Have you heard any news of the—forger?" asked Luke Harvey, when he had delivered his budget of news—"Any intelligence of the respectable gentleman in the white cravat and hump-back?"

"He played the same game in New York that he played in our city. Wherever I went, I heard nothing but 'Mr. Ellis Mortimer, of Charleston, bought goods to a large amount here, on the strength of a letter of credit, drawn on your house by Grayson, Ballenger, & Co.,' or that 'Mr. Mortimer bought goods to a large amount in such-and-such a-store, backed by the same letter of credit—' No less than twelve wholesale houses gave him credit to an almost unlimited extent. In all cases the goods were despatched to the various auctions and sold at half-cost, while Mr. Ellis Mortimer pocketed the cash—"

"And you have no traces of this prince of swindlers?"

"None! all the police in New York have been raising heaven-and-earth to catch him for this week past, but without success. At last I have come to the conclusion that he is lurking about this city, with the respectable sum of two hundred thousand dollars in his possession. I am half-inclined to believe that he is not alone in this business—there may be a combination of scoundrels concerned in the affair. To-morrow the police shall ransack every hiding-hole and cranny in the city. My friend, Col. Fitz-Cowles gave me some valuable suggestions before I left for New York—I will ask his advice, in regard to the matter, the first thing in the morning—"

"Very fine man, that Col. Fitz-Cowles—" observed Luke, as they turned down Fourth street—"Splendid fellow. Dresses well—gives capital terrapin suppers at the United States—inoculates all the bucks about town with his style of hat. Capital fellow—Son of an English Earl—ain't he, Mr. Livingstone?"

"So I have understood—" replied Mr. Livingstone, not exactly liking the quiet sneer which lurked under the innocent manner of his partner—"at least so it is rumored—"

"Got lots of money—a millionaire—no end to his wealth. By the bye, where the d——l did he come from? isn't he a Southern planter with acres of niggers and prairies of cotton?"

"Luke, that's a very strange question to ask me. You just now asked me, whether he was the son of an English Earl—did'nt you?"

"Believe I did. To tell the truth, I've heard both stories about him, and some dozen more. An heir-apparent to an English Earldom, a rich planter from the South, the son of a Boston *magnifique*,[13] the only child of a rich Mexican—these things you will see, don't mix well. Who the devil is our long-haired friend, anyhow?"

"Tut-tut—Luke this is all folly. You know that Col. Fitz-Cowles is received in the best society, mingles with the *ton*[14] of the Quaker City, is 'squired about by our judges and lawyers, and can always find scores of friends to help him spend his fortune—"

"Fine man, that Col. Fitz-Cowles. Very," said the other in his dry and biting tone.

---

[13] An admirable person.

[14] Fashionable element.

"Do you know, Luke, that I think the married men the happiest in the world?" said Livingstone, drawing the arm of his partner closely within his own—"Now look at my case for instance. A year ago I was a miserable bachelor. The loss of one hundred thousand dollars then, would have driven me frantic. Now I have a sweet young wife to cheer me, her smile welcomes me home; the first tone of her voice, and my loss is forgotten!"

The Merchant paused. His eye glistened with a tear, and he felt his heart grow warm in his bosom, as the vision of his sweet young wife, now so calmly sleeping on her solitary bed rose before him. He imagined her smile of welcome as she beheld him suddenly appear by her bedside; he felt her arms so full and round twining fondly round his neck, and he tried to fancy—but the attempt was vain—the luxury of a kiss from her red ripe lips.

"You may think me uxorious, Luke—" he resumed in his deep manly voice—"But I do think that God never made a nobler woman than my Dora! Look at the sacrifice she made for my sake? Young, blooming, and but twenty summers old, she forgot the disparity of my years, and consented to share my bachelor's-home—"

"She *is* a noble woman—" observed Luke, and then he looked at the moon and whistled an air from the very select operatic spectacle of 'Bone Squash.'

"Noble in heart and soul!" exclaimed Livingstone—"confess, Luke that we married men live more in an hour than you dull bachelors in a year—"

"Oh—yes—certainly! You may well talk when you have such a handsome wife! Egad—if I was'nt afraid it would make you jealous—I would say that Mrs. Livingstone has the most splendid form I ever beheld—"

There was a slight contortion of Mr. Harvey's upper lip as he spoke, which looked very much like a sneer.

"And then her heart, Luke, her heart! So noble, so good, so affectionate! I wish you could have seen her, where first I beheld her—in a small and meanly furnished apartment, at the bed-side of a dying mother! They were in reduced circumstances, for her father had died insolvent. He had been my father's friend, and I thought it my duty to visit the widowed mother and the orphan daughter. By-the-bye, Luke, I now remember that I saw you at their house in Wood street once—did you know the family?"

"Miss Dora's father had been kind to me—" said Luke in a quiet tone. There was a strange light in his dark eye as he spoke, and a remarkable tremor on his lip.

"Well, well, Luke—here's my house—exclaimed Mr. Livingstone, as they arrived in front of a lofty four storied mansion, situated in the aristocratic square, as it is called, along south Fourth street. "It is lucky I have my dead-latch key. I can enter without disturbing the servants. Come up stairs, into the front parlor with me, Luke; I want to have a few more words with you about the forgery—"

They entered the door of the mansion, passed along a wide and roomy entry, ascended a richly carpeted staircase, and, traversing the entry in the second story, in a moment stood in the centre of the spacious parlor, fronting the street on the second floor. In another moment, Mr. Livingstone, by the aid of some Lucifer matches which he found on the mantle, lighted a small bed-lamp, standing amid the glittering volumes that were piled on the centre table. The dim light of the lamp flickering around the room, revealed the various characteristics of an apartment furnished in a style of lavish magnificence. Above the mantle flashed an enormous mirror, on one side of the parlor was an inviting sofa, on the other, a piano; two splendid ottomans stood in front of the fireless hearth, and, curtains of splendid silk hung drooping heavily along the three lofty windows that looked into the street. In fine, the parlor was all that the upholsterer and cabinet maker combined could make it, a depository of luxurious appointments and costly furniture.

"Draw your seat near the centre table, Luke—" cried Mr. Livingstone, as he flung himself into a comfortable rocking chair, and gazed around the room with an expression of quiet satisfaction—"Don't speak too loud, Luke, for Dora is sleeping in the next room. You know I want to take her by a little surprise—eh, Luke? She doesn't expect me from New York for a week yet—I am the last person in the world she thinks to see to-night. Clearly so—ha—ha!"

And the merchant chuckled gaily, rubbed his hands together, glanced at the folding doors that opened into the bed-chamber, where slept his blooming wife, and then turning round, looked in the face of Luke Harvey with a smile, that seemed to say—'I can't help it if you bachelors are miserable—pity you, but can't help it.'

"It *would* be a pity to awaken Mrs. Livingstone—" said Luke fixing his brilliant dark eye on the face of the senior partner, with a look so meaning and yet mysterious, that Mr. Livingstone involuntarily averted his gaze—"A very great pity. By the bye, with regard to the forgery—"

"Let me recapitulate the facts. Some weeks ago we received a letter from the respectable house of Grayson, Ballenger, & Co., Charleston, stating that they had made a large purchase in cotton from a rich planter—Mr. Ellis Mortimer, who, in a week or so, would visit Philadelphia, with a letter of credit on our house for one hundred thousand dollars. They gave us this intimation in order that we might be prepared to cash the letter of credit at right. Well, in a week a gentleman of respectable exterior appeared, stated that he was Mr. Ellis Mortimer, presented his letter of credit; it was cashed and we wrote to Grayson, Ballenger, & Co., announcing the fact—"

"They returned the agreeable answer that Mr. Ellis Mortimer had not yet left Charleston for Philadelphia, but had altered his intention and was about to sail for London. That the gentleman in the white cravat and hump-back was an imposter, and the letter of credit a—forgery. There was considerable mystery in the affair; for instance, how did the imposter gain all the necessary information with regard to Mr. Mortimer's visit, how did he acquire a knowledge of the signature of the Charleston house?"

"Listen and I will tell you. Last week, in New York, I received a letter from the Charleston house announcing these additional facts. It appears that in the beginning of fall they received a letter from a Mr. Albert Hazelton Munroe, representing himself as a rich planter in Wainbridge, South Carolina. He had a large amount of cotton to sell, and would like to procure advances on it from the Charleston house. They wrote him an answer to his letter, asking the quality of the cotton, and so forth, and soliciting an interview with Mr. Munroe when he visited Charleston. In the beginning of November Mr. Munroe, a dark-complexioned man, dressed like a careless country squire, entered their store for the first time, and commenced a series of negotiations about his cotton, which had resulted in nothing, when another planter, Mr. Ellis Mortimer, appeared in the scene, sold his cotton, and requested the letter of credit on our house. Mr. Munroe was in the store every day—was a jolly unpretending fellow—familiar with all the clerks—and on intimate terms with Messrs. Grayson, Ballenger, & Co. The letter written to our house, intimating the intended visit of Mr. Mortimer to this city, had been very carelessly left open for a few moments on the counting house desk, and Mr. Munroe was observed glancing over its contents by one of the clerks. The day after that letter had been despatched to Philadelphia, Mr. Albert H. Munroe suddenly disappeared, and had not been heard of since. The Charleston house suspect him of the whole forgery in all its details—"

"Very likely. He saw the letter on the counter—forged the letter of credit—and despatched his accomplice to Philadelphia without delay—"

"Now for the consequences of this forgery. On Monday morning next we have an engagement of one hundred thousand dollars to meet, which, under present circumstances, may plunge our house into the vortex of bankruptcy. Unless this imposter is discovered, unless his connection with this Munroe is clearly ascertained before next Monday, I must look forward to that day as one of the greatest danger to our house. You see our position, Luke?"

"Yes, yes—" answered Luke, as he arose, and, advancing, gazed fixedly into the face of Mr. Livingstone—"I see *our* position, and I see *your* position in more respects than one—"

"Confound the thing, man, how you stare in my face. Do you see anything peculiar about my countenance, that you peruse it so attentively?"

"Ha—ha—" cried Luke, with a hysterical laugh—"Ha—ha! Nothing but—horns. Horns, sir, I say—horns. A fine branching pair! Ha—ha—Why damn it, Livingstone, you won't be able to enter the church door, next Sunday, without stooping—*those* horns are so d——d large!"

Livingstone looked at him with a face of blank wonder. He evidently supposed that Luke had been seized with sudden madness. To see a man who is your familiar friend and partner, abruptly break off a conversation on matters of the most importance, and stare vacantly in your face as he compliments you on some fancied resemblance which you bear to a full-grown stag, is, it must be confessed, a spectacle somewhat unfrequent in this world of ours, and rather adapted to excite a feeling of astonishment whenever it happens.

"Mr. Harvey—are—you—mad?" asked Livingstone, in a calm deliberate tone.

Harvey slowly leaned forward and brought his face so near Livingstone's that the latter could feel his breath on his cheek. He applied his mouth to the ear of the senior partner, and whispered a single word.

When a soldier, in battle, receives a bullet directly in the heart, he springs in the air with one convulsive spasm, flings his arms aloft and utters a groan that thrills the man who hears it with a horror never to be forgotten. With that same convulsive movement, with that same deep groan of horror and anguish Livingstone, the merchant, sprang to his feet, and confronted the utterer of that single word.

"Harvey—" he said, in a low tone, and with white and trembling lips, while his calm blue eye flashed with that deep glance of excitement, most terrible when visible in a calm blue eye—"Harvey, you had better never been born, than utter that word again. To trifle with a thing of this kind is worse than death. Harvey, I advise you to leave me—I am losing all command of myself—there is a voice within me tempting me to murder you—for God's sake quit my sight—"

Harvey looked in his face, fearless and undaunted, though his snake-like eye blazed like a coal of fire, and his thin lips quivered as with the death spasm.

"*Cuckold!*"[15] he shrieked in a hissing voice, with a wild hysterical laugh.

Livingstone started back aghast. The purple veins stood out like cords on his bronzed forehead, and his right hand trembled like a leaf as it was thrust within the breast of his coat. His blue eye—great God! how glassy it had grown—was fixed upon the form of Luke Harvey as if meditating where to strike.

"To the bedchamber—" shrieked Luke. "If *she* is there, I am a liar and a dog, and deserve to die. *Cuckold,* I say, and will prove it—to the bedchamber!"

And to the bedchamber with an even stride, though his massive form quivered like an oak shaken by the hurricane, strode the merchant. The folding door slid back—he had disappeared into the bedchamber.

There was silence for a single instant, like the silence in the graveyard, between the last word of the prayer, and the first rattling sound of the clods upon the coffin.

In a moment Livingstone again strode into the parlor. His face was the hue of ashes. You could see that the struggle at work within his heart was like the agony of the strong man wrestling with death. *This* struggle was tenfold more terrible than death—death in its vilest form. It forced the big beaded drops of sweat out from the corded veins on his brow, it drove the blood from his face, leaving a black and discolored streak beneath each eye.

"She is not there—" he said, taking Luke by the hand, which he wrung with an iron grasp, and murmured again—"She is not there—"

"False to her husband's bed and honor—" exclaimed Luke, the agitation which had convulsed his face, subsiding into a look of heart-wrung compassion, as he looked upon the terrible results of his disclosure—"False as hell, and vile as false!"

An object on the centre table, half concealed by the bed-lamp arrested the husband's attention. He thrust aside the lamp and beheld a note, addressed to himself, in Mrs. Livingstone's hand.

With a trembling hand the merchant tore the note open, and while Luke stood fixedly regarding him, perused its contents.

And as he read, the blood came back to his cheeks, the glance to his eyes, and his brow reddened over with one burning flush of indignation.

"Liar and dog!" he shouted, in tones hoarse with rage, as he grasped Luke Harvey by the throat with a sudden movement—"Your lie was well coined, but look here! Ha—ha—" and he shook Luke to and fro like a broken reed—"Here is my wife's letter. Here, sir, look at it, and I'll force you to eat your own foul words. Here, expecting that I might suddenly return from New York, my wife has written down that she would be absent from home to-night. A sick friend, a school-day companion, now reduced to widowhood and penury, solicited her company by her dying bed, and my wife could not refuse. Read, sir—oh read!"

"Take your hand from my throat or I'll do you a mischief—" murmured Luke, in a choaking voice as he grew black in the face. "I will, by God—"

---

[15]The husband of an unfaithful wife.

"Read—sir—oh read!" shouted Livingstone, as he force Luke into a chair and thrust the letter into his hands—"Read, sir, and then crawl from this room like a vile dog as you are. To-morrow I will settle with you—"

Luke sank in the chair, took the letter, and with a pale face, varied by a crimson spot on each cheek, he began to read, while Livingstone, towering and erect, stood regarding him with a look of incarnate scorn.

It was observable that while Luke perused the letter, his head dropped slowly down as though in the endeavor to see more clearly, and his unoccupied hand was suddenly thrust within the breast of his overcoat.

"That is a very good letter. Well written, and she minds her stops—" exclaimed Luke calmly, as he handed the letter back to Mr. Livingstone—"Quite an effort of composition. I didn't think Dora had so much tact—"

The merchant was thunderstruck with the composure exhibited by the slanderer and the liar. He glanced over Luke's features with a quick nervous glance, and then looked at the letter which he held in his hand.

"Ha! This is not the same letter!" he shouted, in tones of mingled rage and wonder—"This letter is addressed to Col. 'Fitz-Cowles'—"

"It was dropped in the counting house by the Colonel this evening—" said Luke, with the air of a man who was prepared for any hazard—"The Colonel is a very fine man. A favorite with the fair sex. Read it—*Oh* read—"

With a look of wonder Mr. Livingstone opened the letter. There was a quivering start in his whole frame, when he first observed the handwriting.

But as he went on, drinking in word after word, his countenance, so full of meaning and expression, was like a mirror, in which different faces are seen, one after another, by sudden transition. At first his face grew crimson, then it was pale as death in an instant. Then his lips dropped apart, and his eyes were covered with a glassy film. Then a deep wrinkle shot upward between his brows, and then, black and ghastly, the circles of discolored flesh were visible beneath each eye. The quivering nostrils—the trembling hands—the heaving chest—did man ever die with a struggle terrible as this?

He sank heavily into a chair, and crushing the letter between his fingers, buried his face in his hands.

"Oh my God—" he groaned—"Oh my God—and I loved her so!"

And then between the very fingers convulsively clutching the fatal letter, there fell large and scalding tears, drop by drop, pouring heavily, like the first tokens of a coming thunderbolt, on a summer day.

Luke Harvey arose, and strode hurriedly along the floor. The sight was too much for him to bear. And yet as he turned away he heard the groans of the strong man in his agony, and the heart-wrung words came, like the voice of the dying, to his ear—

"Oh my God, oh my God, and I loved her so!"

When Luke again turned and gazed upon the betrayed husband, he beheld a sight that filled him with unutterable horror.

There, as he sat, his face buried in his hands, his head bowed on his breast, his brow was partly exposed to the glare of the lamp-beams, and all around that brow, amid the locks of his dark brown hair, were streaks of hoary white. The hair of the merchant had withered at the root. The blow was so sudden, so blighting, and so terrible, that even his strong mind reeled, his brain tottered, and in the effort to command his reason, his hair grew white with agony.*

"Would to God I had not told him—" murmured Luke—"I knew not that he loved her so—I knew not—and yet—ha, ha, *I* loved her once—"

"Luke—my friend—" said Livingstone in a tremulous voice as he raised his face—"Know you anything of *the place*—named in—the letter?"

"I do—and will lead you there—" answered Luke, his face resuming its original expression of agitation—"Come!" he cried, in a husky voice, as olden-time memories seemed striving at his heart—"Come!"

"Can you gain me access to the house—to *the—the* room?"

"Did I not track them thither last night? *Come!*"

The merchant slowly rose and took a pair of pistols from his carpet bag. They were small and convenient travelling pistols, mounted in silver, with those noiseless 'patent' triggers that emit no clicking sound by way of warning. He inspected the percussion caps, and sounded each pistol barrel.

"Silent and sure—" muttered Luke—"They are each loaded with a single ball."

"Which way do you lead? To the southern part of the city?"

"To Southwark—" answered Luke, leading the way from the parlor—"To the rookery, to the den, to the pest-house—"

In a moment they stood upon the door step of the merchant's princely mansion, the vivid light of the December moon, imparting a ghastly hue to Livingstone's face, with the glassy eyes, rendered more fearful by the discolored circles of flesh beneath, the furrowed brow, and the white lips, all fixed in an expression stern and resolute as death.

Luke flung his hand to the south, and his dark impenetrable eyes shone with meaning. The merchant placed his partner's arm within his own, and they hurried down Fourth street with a single word from Luke—

"To Monk-hall!"

CHAPTER SIXTH

❧ Monk-Hall[†]

Strange traditions have come down to our time, in relation to a massive edifice, which, long before the Revolution, stood in the centre of an extensive garden, surrounded by a brick wall, and encircled by a deep grove of horse-chesnut and beechen trees. This edifice was located on the out-skirts of the southern part of the city, and the garden overspread some acres, occupying a space full as large as a modern square.

This mansion, but rarely seen by intrusive eyes, had been originally erected by a wealthy foreigner, sometime previous to the Revolution. Who this foreigner was, his name or his history, has not been recorded by tradition; but his mansion, in its general

---

*This is a fact, established by the evidence of a medical gentleman of the first reputation.

[†]No reader who wishes to understand this story in all its details will fail to peruse this chapter.

construction and details, indicate a mind rendered whimsical and capricious by excessive wealth.

The front of the mansion, one plain mass of black and red brick, disposed like the alternate colors of a chessboard, looked towards the south. A massive hall-door, defended by heavy pillars, and surmounted by an intricate cornice, all carved and sculptured into hideous satyr-faces; three ranges of deep square windows, with cumbrous sash frames and small panes of glass; a deep and sloping roof, elaborate with ornaments of painted wood along the eaves, and rising into a gabled peak directly over the hall-door, while its outlines were varied by rows of substantial chimneys, fashioned into strange and uncouth shapes,—all combined, produced a general impression of ease and grandeur that was highly effective in awing the spirits of any of the simple citizens who might obtain a casual glance of the house through the long avenue of trees extending from the garden gate.

This impression of awe was somewhat deepened by various rumors that obtained through the southern part of the Quaker City. It was said that the wealthy proprietor, not satisfied with building a fine house with three stories above ground, had also constructed three stories of spacious chambers below the level of the earth. This was calculated to stir the curiosity and perhaps the scandal of the town, and as a matter of course strange rumors began to prevail about midnight orgies held by the godless proprietor in his subterranean apartments, where wine was drunken without stint, and beauty ruined without remorse. Veiled figures had been seen passing through the garden gate after night, and men were not wanting to swear that these figures, in dark robes and sweeping veils, were pretty damsels with neat ankles and soft eyes.

As time passed on, the rumors grew and the mystery deepened. The neatly-constructed stable at the end of the garden was said to be connected with the house, some hundred yards distant, by a subterranean passage. The two wings, branching out at either extremity of the rear of the mansion, looked down upon a courtyard, separated by a light wicket fence from the garden walks. The court-yard, overarched by an awning in summer time, was said to be the scene of splendid festivals to which the grandees of the city were invited. From the western wing of the mansion arose a square lantern-like structure, which the gossips called a tower, and hinted sagely of witchcraft and devildom whenever it was named. They called the proprietor, a libertine, a gourmand, an astrologer and a wizard. He feasted in the day and he consulted his friend, the Devil, at night. He drank wine at all times, and betrayed innocence on every occasion. In short the seclusion of the mansion, its singular structure, its wall of brick and its grove of impenetrable trees, gave rise to all sorts of stories, and the proprietor has come down to our time with a decidedly bad character, although it is more than likely that he was nothing but a wealthy Englishman, whimsical and eccentric, the boon-companion and friend of Governor Evans, the rollicking Chief Magistrate of the Province.

Although tradition has not preserved the name of the mysterious individual yet the title of his singular mansion, is still on record.

It was called—Monk-hall.

There are conflicting traditions which assert that this title owed its origin to other sources. A Catholic Priest occupied the mansion after the original proprietor went home to his native land, or slid into his grave; it was occupied as a Nunnery, as a Monastery, or as a resort for the Sisters of Charity; the mass had been said within its walls, its subterranean chambers converted into cells, its tower transformed into an oratory of prayer—such are the dim legends which were rife some forty years ago, concerning Monk-hall, long after the city, in its southern march, had cut down the trees, overturned the wall, levelled the garden into building lots and divided it by streets and alleys into a dozen triangles and squares.

Some of these legends, so vague and so conflicting, are still preserved in the memories of aged men and white-haired matrons, who will sit by the hour and describe the gradual change which time and improvement, those twin desolators of the beautiful, had accomplished with Monk-hall.

Soon after the Revolution, fine brick buildings began to spring up along the streets which surrounded the garden, while the alleys traversing its area, grew lively with long lines of frame houses, variously fashioned and painted, whose denizens awoke the echoes of the place with the sound of the hammer and the grating of the saw. Time passed on, and the distinctive features of the old mansion and garden were utterly changed. Could the old proprietor have risen from his grave, and desired to pay another visit to his friend, the Devil, in the subterranean chambers of his former home, he would have had, to say the least of it, a devil of a time in finding the way. Where the old brick wall had stood he would have found long rows of dwelling houses, some four storied, some three or one, some brick, some frame, a few pebble-dashed, and all alive with inhabitants.

In his attempt to find the Hall, he would have had to wind up a narrow alley, turn down a court, strike up an avenue, which it would take some knowledge of municipal geography to navigate. At last, emerging into a narrow street where four alleys crossed, he would behold his magnificent mansion of Monk-hall with a printing office on one side and a stereotype foundry on the other, while on the opposite side of the way, a mass of miserable frame houses seemed about to commit suicide and fling themselves madly into the gutter, and in the distance a long line of dwellings, offices, and factories, looming in broken perspective, looked as if they wanted to shake hands across the narrow street. The southern front of the house—alas, how changed—alone is visible. The shutters on one side of the hall-door are nailed up and hermetically closed, while, on the other, shutters within the glasses bar out the light of day. The semi-circular window in the centre of the gabled-peak has been built up with brick, yet our good friend would find the tower on the western wing in tolerable good preservation. The stable one hundred yards distant from Monk-hall—what has become of it? Perhaps it is pulled down, or it may be that a splendid dwelling towers in its place? It is still in existence, standing amid the edifices of a busy street, its walls old and tottering, its ancient stable-floor turned into a bulk window, surmounted by the golden balls of a Pawnbroker, while within its precincts, rooms furnished for household use supply the place of the stalls of the olden-time. Does the subterranean passage still exist? Future pages of our story may possibly answer that question.

Could our ancient and ghostly proprietor, glide into the tenements adjoining Monk-hall, and ask the mechanic or his wife, the printer or the factory man to tell him the story of the strange old building, he would find that the most remarkable ignorance prevailed in regard to the structure, its origin and history. One man might tell him that it had been a factory, or a convent, or the Lord knows what, another might intimate that it had been a church, a third (and he belonged to the most numerous class) would reply in a surly tone that he knew nothing about the old brick nuisance, while in the breasts of one or two aged men and matrons, yet living in Southwark, would be discovered the only chronicles of the ancient structure now extant, the only records of its history or name. Did our spirit-friend glide over the threshold and enter the chambers of his home, his eye would, perhaps, behold scenes that rivalled, in vice and magnificence, anything that legend chronicled of the olden-time of Monk-hall, although its exterior was so desolate, and its outside-door of green blinds varied by a big brass plate, bore the respectable and saintly name of "Abijah K. Jones," in immense letters, half indistinct with dirt and rust.

Who this Abijah K. Jones was, no one knew, although the owner of the house, a good christian, who had a pew in ——church, where he took the sacrament at least once a month, might have been able to tell with very little research. Yet what of that? Abijah K. Jones might have nightly entertained the infernal regions in his house, and not a word been said about it; because, as the pious landlord would observe, when cramming Abijah's rent-money into the same pocket-book that contained some tract-society receipts,—"Good tenant that!—pays his rent with the regularity of clockwork!"

CHAPTER SEVENTH

❧ The Monks of Monk Hall

The moon was shining brightly over the face of the old mansion, while the opposite side of the alley lay in dim and heavy shadow. The light brown hue of the closed shutters afforded a vivid contrast to the surface of the front, which had the strikingly gloomy effect always produced by the intermixture of black and red brick, disposed like the colors of a chessboard, in the structure of a mansion. The massive cornice above the hall-door, the heavy eaves of the roof, the gabled peak rising in the centre, and the cumbrous frames of the many windows,—all stood out boldly in the moonlight, from the dismal relief of the building's front.

The numerous chimneys with their fantastic shapes rose grimly in the moonlight, like a strange band of goblin sentinels, perched of the roof to watch the mansion. The general effect was that of an ancient structure falling to decay, deserted by all inhabitants save the rats that gnawed the wainscot along the thick old walls. The door-plate that glittered on the faded door, half covered as it was with rust and verdigris, with its saintly name afforded the only signs of the actual occupation of Monk-hall by human beings: in all other respects it looked so desolate, so time-worn, so like a mausoleum for old furniture, and crumbling tapestry, for high-backed mahogany chairs, gigantic bedsteads, and strange looking mirrors, veiled in the thick folds of the spider's web.

Dim and indistinct, like the booming of a distant cannon, the sound of the State-House bell, thrilled along the intricate maze of streets and alleys. It struck the hour of two. The murmur of the last stroke of the bell, so dim and indistinct, was mingled with the echo of approaching footsteps, and in a moment two figures turned the corner of an alley that wound among the tangled labyrinth of avenues, and came hastening on toward the lonely mansion; lonely even amid tenements and houses, gathered as thickly together as the cells in a bee-hive.

"I say, Gus, what a devil of a way you've led me!" cried one of the strangers, with a thick cloak wrapped round his limbs—"up one alley and down another, around one street and through another, backwards and forwards, round this way and round that— damme if I can tell which is north or south except by the moon!"

"Hist! my fellow—don't mention names—cardinal doctrine that on an affair of this kind—" answered the tall figure, whose towering form was enveloped in a frogged over-coat—"Remember, you pass in as *my friend*. Wait a moment—we'll see whether old Devil-Bug is awake."

Ascending the granite steps of the mansion, he gave three distinct raps with his gold-headed cane, on the surface of the brass-plate. In a moment the rattling of a heavy chain, and the sound of a bolt, slowly withdrawn, was heard within, and the door of the mansion, beyond the outside door of green blinds, receded about the width of an inch.

"Who's there, a disturbin' honest folks this hour o' the night—" said a voice, that came grumbling through the blinds of the green door, like the sound of a grindstone that hasn't been oiled for some years—"What the devil you want? Go about your business— or I'll call the watch—"

"I say, Devil-Bug, what hour o' th' night is it?" exclaimed Lorrimer in a whispered tone.

"'Dinner time'—" replied the grindstone voice slightly oiled—"Come in sir. Did'nt know 'twas you. How the devil should I? Come in—"

As the voice grunted this invitation, Lorrimer seized Byrnewood by the arm, and glided through the opened door.

Byrnewood looked around in wonder, as he discovered that the front door opened into a small closet or room, some ten feet square, the floor bare and uncarpeted, the ceil-ing darkened by smoke, while a large coal fire, burning in a rusty grate, afforded both light and heat to the apartment.

The heat was close and stifling, while the light, but dim and flickering, disclosed the form of the door-keeper of Monk-hall, as he stood directly in front of the grate, sur-rounded by the details of his den.

"This is *my friend*—" said Lorrimer in a meaning tone—"You understand, Devil-Bug?"

"Yes—" grunted the grindstone voice—"I understand. O'course. But my name is 'Bijah K. Jones, *if* you please, my pertikler friend. I never know'd sich a individooal as Devil-Bug—"

It requires no great stretch of fancy to imagine that his Satanic majesty, once on a time, in a merry mood, created a huge insect, in order to test his inventive powers. Cer-tainly that insect—which it was quite natural to designate by the name of Devil-Bug— stood in the full light of the grate, gazing steadfastly in Byrnewood's face. It was a strange thickset specimen of flesh and blood, with a short body, marked by immensely broad shoulders, long arms and thin destorted legs. The head of the creature was ludi-crously large in proportion to the body. Long masses of siff black hair fell tangled and matted over a forehead, protuberent to deformity. A flat nose with wide nostrils shooting out into each cheek like the smaller wings of an insect, an immense mouth whose heavy lips disclosed two long rows of bristling teeth, a pointed chin, blackened by a heavy beard, and massive eyebrows meeting over the nose, all furnished the details of a countenance, not exactly calculated to inspire the most pleasant feelings in the world. One eye, small black and shapen like a bead, stared steadily in Byrnewood's face, while the other socket was empty, shrivelled and orbless. The eyelids of the vacant socket were joined together like the opposing edges of a curtain, while the other eye gained additional brilliancy and effect from the loss of its fellow member.

The shoulders of the Devil-Bug, protruding in unsightly knobs, the wide chest, and the long arms with talon-like fingers, so vividly contrasted with the thin and distorted legs, all attested that the remarkable strength of the man was located in the upper part of his body.

"Well, Abijah, are you satisfied?" asked Lorrimer, as he perceived Byrnewood shrink back with disgust from the door-keeper's gaze—"*This* gentleman, I say, is *my* friend?"

"So I s'pose," grunted Abijah—"Here, Musquito, mark this man—here, Glow-worm, mark him, I say. This is Monk Gusty's friend. Can't you move quicker, you ugly devils?"

From either side of the fire-place, as he spoke, emerged a tall Herculean negro, with a form of strength and sinews of iron. Moving slowly along the floor, from the darkness which had enshrouded their massive outlines, they stood silent and motionless gazing with look of stolid indifference upon the face of the new-comer. Byrnewood had started aside in disgust from the Devil-Bug, as he was styled in the slang of Monk-hall, but certainly these additional insects, nestling in the den of the other, were rather singular specimens of the glow-worm and musquito. Their attire was plain and simple. Each negro was dressed in coarse corduroy trowsers, and a flaring red flannel shirt. The face of Glow-worm was marked by a hideous flat nose, a receding forehead, and a wide mouth with immense lips that buried all traces of a chin and disclosed two rows of teeth protruding like the tusks of a wild boar. Musquito had the same flat nose, the same receding forehead, but his thick lips, tightly compressed, were drawn down on either side towards his jaw, presenting an outline something like the two sides of a triangle, while his sharp and pointed chin was in direct contrast to the long chinless jaw of the other. Their eyes, large, rolling and vacant, stared from bulging eyelids, that protruded beyond the outline of the brows. Altogether, each negro presented as hideous a picture of mere brute strength, linked with a form scarcely human, as the imagination of man might well conceive.

"This is Monk Gusty's friend—" muttered Abijah, or Devil-Bug, as the reader likes—"Mark him, Musquito—Mark him, Glow-worm, I say. Mind ye now—this man don't leave the house except with Gusty? D'ye hear, ye black devils?"

Each negro growled assent.

"Queer specimens of a Musquito and a Glow-worm, I say—" laughed Byrnewood in the effort to smother his disgust—"Eh? Lorrimer?"

"This way, my fellow—" answered the magnificent Gus, gently leading his friend through a small door, which led from the doorkeeper's closet—"This way. Now for the club—and then for the wager!"

Looking around in wonder, Byrnewood discovered that they had passed into the hall of an old-time mansion, with the beams of the moon, falling from a skylight in the roof far above, down over the windings of a massive staircase.

"This is rather a strange place—eh? Gus?" whispered Byrnewood, as he gazed around the hall, and marked the ancient look of the place—"why the d——I don't *they* have a light—those *insects*—ha-ha—whom we have just left?"

"Secrecy—my fellow—secrecy! Those are the 'police' of Monk-Hall, certain to be at hand in case of a row. You see, the entire arrangements of this place may be explained in one word—it is easy enough for a stranger—that's you, my boy—to find his way *in,* but it would puzzle him like the devil to find his way *out.* That is, without assistance. Take my arm Byrnewood—we must descend to the club room——"

"*Descend?*"

"Yes my fellow. *Descend,* for we hold our meetings one story under ground. Its likely all the fellows—or Monks, to speak in the slang of the club—are now most royally drunk, so I can slide you in among them, without much notice. You can remain there while I go and prepare the bride—ha—ha—ha! the *bride* for your visit—"

Meanwhile, grasping Byrnewood by the arm, he had led the way along the hall, beyond the staircase, into the thick darkness, which rested upon this part of the place, unillumined by a ray of light.

"Hold my arm, as tight as you can—" he whispered—"There is a staircase somewhere here. Softly—softly—now I have it. Tread with care, Byrnewood—In a moment we will be in the midst of the Monks of Monk-Hall—"

And as they descended the subterranean stairway, surrounded by the darkness of midnight, Byrnewood found it difficult to subdue a feeling of awe which began to spread like a shadow over his soul. This feeling it was not easy to analyze. It may have been a combination of feelings; the consideration of the darkness and loneliness of the place, his almost entire ignorance of the handsome libertine who was now leading him—he knew not where; or perhaps the earnest words of the Astrologer, fraught with doom and death, came home to his soul like a vivid presentiment, in that moment of uncertainty and gloom.

"Don't you hear their shouts, my boy—" whispered Lorrimer—"Faith, they must be *drunk* as judges, every man of them! Why Byrnewood, you're as still as death—"

"To tell you the truth, Lorrimer, this place looks like the den of some old wizard— it's so d——d gloomy—"

"Here we are at the door: Now mark me, Byrnewood—you must walk in the clubroom, or Monk's room as they call it, directly at my back. While I salute the Monks of Monk-hall, you will slide into a vacant seat at the table, and mingle in the revelry of the place until I return—"

Stooping through a narrow door, whose receding panels flung a blaze of light along the darkness of the passage, Lorrimer, with Byrnewood at his back, descended three wooden steps, that led from the door-sill to the floor, and in a moment, stood amid the revellers of Monk-hall.

In a long, narrow room, lighted by the blaze of a large chandelier, with a low ceiling and a wide floor, covered with a double-range of carpets, around a table spread with the relics of their feast, were grouped the Monks of Monk-hall.

They hailed Lorrimer with a shout, and as they rose to greet him, Byrnewood glided into a vacant arm-chair near the head of the table, and in a moment his companion had disappeared.

"I'll be with you in a moment, Monks of Monk-hall—" he shouted as he glided through the narrow door—"A little affair to settle up stairs—you know me—nice little girl—ha-ha-ha—"

"Ha-ha-ha—" echoed the band of revellers, raising their glasses merrily on high.

Byrnewood glanced hurriedly around. The room, long and spacious as it was, the floor covered with the most gorgeous carpeting, and the low ceiling, embellished with a faded painting in fresco, still wore an antiquated, not to say, dark and gloomy appearance. The walls were concealed by huge panels of wainscot, intricate with uncouth sculpturings of fawns and satyrs,[16] and other hideous creations of classic mythology. At one end of the room, reaching from floor to ceiling, glared an immense mirror, framed in massive walnut, its glittering surface, reflecting the long festal board, with its encircling band of revellers. Inserted in the corresponding panels of the wainscot, on either side of the small door, at the opposite end of the room, two large pictures, evidently the work of a master hand, indicated the mingled worship of the devotees of Monk-hall. In the picture on the right of the door, Bacchus, the jolly god of mirth and wine, was represented rising from a festal-board, his brow wreathed in clustering grapes, while his hand swung aloft, a goblet filled with the purple blood of the grape. In the other painting, along a couch as dark as night, with a softened radiance falling over her uncovered form, lay a sleeping Venus, her full arms, twining above her head, while her lips were dropped apart, as though she murmured in her slumber. Straight and erect, behind the chair of the President or Abbot of the board, arose the effigy of a monk, whose long black robes fell drooping to the floor, while his cowl hung heavily over his brow, and his right hand raised on high a goblet of gold. From beneath the shadow of the falling cowl, glared a fleshless skeleton head, with the orbless eye-sockets, the cavity of the nose, and the long rows of grinning teeth, turned to a faint and ghastly crimson by the lampbeams. The hand that held the goblet on high, was a grisly skeleton hand; the long and thin fingers of bone, twining firmly around the glittering bowl.

And over this scene, over the paintings and the mirror, over the gloomy wainscot along the walls, and over the faces of the revellers with the Skeleton-Monk, grinning derision at their scene of bestial enjoyment, shone the red beams of the massive chandelier, the body and limbs of which were fashioned into the form of a grim Satyr, with a light flaring from his skull, a flame emerging from each eye, while his extended hands flung streams of fire on either side, and his knees were huddled up against his breast. The design was like a nightmare dream, so grotesque and terrible, and it completed the strange and ghostly appearance of the room.

Around the long and narrow board, strown with the relics of the feast, which had evidently been some hours in progress, sate the Monks of Monk-hall, some thirty in number, flinging their glasses on high, while the room echoed with their oaths and drunken shouts. Some lay with their heads thrown helplessly on the table, others were

---

[16]Fawns are young deer, while satyrs in Greek mythology were forest deities often associated with lechery.

gazing round in sleepy drunkenness, others had fallen to the floor in a state of unconscious intoxication, while a few there were who still kept up the spirit of the feast,
although their incoherent words and heavy eyes proclaimed that they too were fast
advancing to that state of brutal inebriety, when strange-looking stars shine in the place
of the lamps, when the bottles dance and even tables perform the cracovienne, while all
sorts of beehives create a buzzing murmur in the air.

And the Monks of Monk-hall—who are they?

Grim-faced personages in long black robes and drooping cowls? Stern old men with
beads around their necks and crucifix in hand? Blood-thirsty characters, perhaps, or
black-browed ruffians, or wanfaced outcasts of society?

Ah no, ah no! From the eloquent, the learned, and—don't you laugh—from the
pious of the Quaker City, the old Skeleton-Monk had selected the members of his band.
Here were lawyers from the court, doctors from the school, and judges* from the bench.
Here too, ruddy and round faced, sate a demure parson, whose white hands and soft
words, had made him the idol of his wealthy congregation. Here was a puffy-faced Editor side by side with a Magazine Proprietor; here were sleek-visaged tradesmen, with
round faces and gouty hands, whose voices, now shouting the drinking song had re-
echoed the prayer and the psalm in the aristocratic church, not longer than a Sunday ago;
here were solemn-faced merchants, whose names were wont to figure largely in the
records of 'Bible Societies,' 'Tract Societies' and 'Send Flannel-to-the-South-Sea-
Islanders Societies;' here were reputable married men, with grown up children at college, and trustful wives sleeping quietly in their dreamless beds at home; here were
hopeful sons, clerks in wholesale stores, who raised the wine-glass on high with hands
which, not three hours since, had been busy with the cash-book of the employer, here in
fine were men of all classes,—poets, authors, lawyers, judges, doctors, merchants, gamblers, and—this is no libel I hope—*one* parson, a fine red-faced parson, whose glowing
face would have warmed a poor man on a cold day. Moderately drunk, or deeply drunk,
or vilely drunk, all the members of the board who still maintained their arm-chairs, kept
up a running fire of oaths, disjointed remarks, mingled with small talk very much
broken, and snatches of bacchanalian songs, slightly improved by a peculiar chorus of
hiccups.

While Byrnewood, with a sleeping man on either side of him, gazed around in sober
wonder, this was the fashion of the conversation among the Monks of Monk-hall.

"Judge—I say, judge—that last Charge o' yours was capital—" hiccupped a round-
faced lawyer, leaning over the table—"Touched on the vices of the day—ha—ha! 'Dens
of iniquity and holes of wickedness'—its very words!—'exist in city, which want the
strong arm of the law to uproot and ex-ex—d——n the hard words—exterminate
them!' "

"Good—my—very—words—" replied the Judge, who sat gazing around with a
smile of imbecile fatuity—"Yet, Bellamy, not quite so good as your words, when your
wife—how this d——d room swims—found out your *liason* with the Actress! Ha—ha,
gents—too d——d good that—"

---

*This *of course* alludes to Judges of distant country courts.

"Ha—ha—ha—" laughed some dozen of the company—"let's hear it—let's hear it—"

"Why—you—see—" replied the Judge—"Bellamy is *so* d——d fat, (just keep them bottles from dancing about the table!) so *very* fat, that the i-i-idea of his writing a love-letter is rath-rather improbable. Nevertheless—he did—to a pretty actress, Madame De Flum—and left it on his office table. His wife found it—oh Lord—what a scene! ranted—raved—tore her hair. 'My dear—' said our fat friend, 'do be calm—this is the copy of a letter in a breach of promise case, on which I am about to bring suit for a—lady—client. The mistake of the names is the fault of my clerk. Do—oh—*do* be calm.' His wife swallowed the story—clever story for a fat man—very!"

"Friends and Brethren, what shall ye do to be saved?" shouted the beefy-faced parson, in the long-drawn nasal tones peculiar to his pulpit or lecture-room—"When we con-consider the wickedness of the age, when we reflect tha-that there are thousands da-i-ly and hou-r-ly going down to per-per-dition, should we not cry from the depths of our souls, like Jonah from the depths of the sea—I say, give us the brandy, Mutchins!"

"Gentlemen, allow me to read you a poem—" muttered a personage, whose cheeks blushed from habitual kisses of the bottle, as he staggered from his chair, and endeavoured to stand erect—"It's a—poem—on (what an unsteady floor this is—hold it, Petriken, I say)—on the Ten Commandments. I've dedicated it to our Rev-Reverend friend yonder. There's a touch in it, gentlemen—if I may use the expression—above ordinary butter-milk. A sweetness, a path-pathos, a mildness, a-a-vein, gentlemen, of the strictest mo-ral-i-ty. I will read sonnet one—'Thou shalt not take the co-eternal name'— eh? Dammit! This is *a bill!*—I've left the sonnet at home—"

"Curse it—how I'll cut this fellow up in my next Black-Mail!" murmured the puffy-faced editor, in a tone which he deemed inaudible to the poet—"Unless he comes down handsome—I'll give him a stinger, a real scorcher—"

"Will you, though?" shouted the poet, turning round with a drunken stare, and aiming a blow at the half-stupid face of the editor—"Take that you fungus—you abortion— you d——d gleaner of a common sewer—you——"

"Gentlemen, I con-consider myself grossly insulted—" muttered the editor, as the poet's blow took effect on his wig and sent it spinning to the other end of the table—"Is the *Daily Black Mail* come to this?"

Here he made a lunge at the author of the 'Ten Commandments, a Series of Sonnets,' and, joined in a fond embrace, they fell insensible to the floor.

"Take that wig out of my plate—" shouted a deep voice from the head of the table— "Wigs, as a general thing, are not very nice with oysters, but that fellow's wig—ugh! Faugh!"

Attracted by the sound of the voice, Byrnewood glanced towards the head of the table. There, straight and erect, sate the Abbot of the night, a gentleman elected by the fraternity to preside over their feasts. He was a man of some thirty odd years, dressed in a suit of glossy black, with a form remarkable for its combination of strength with symmetry. His face, long and dusky, lighted by the gleam of a dark eye, indicating the man whose whole life had been one series of plot, scheme, and intrigue, was relieved by heavy masses of long black hair—resembling, in its texture, the mane of a horse—which fell in curling locks to his shoulders. It needed not a second glance to inform Byrnewood that he beheld the hero of Chesnut street, the distinguished millionaire, Col. Fitz-Cowles. The elegant cut of his dark vest, which gathered over his prominent chest and around his slender waist, with the nicety of a glove, the plain black scarf, fastened by a breast-pin of solid gold, the glossy black of his dress-coat, shapen of the best French cloth, all disclosed the idol of the tailors, the dream of the fashionable belles, the envy of the dry goods clerks, Algernon Fitz-Cowles. He seemed, by far, the most sober man in the company. Every now and then Byrnewood beheld him glance anxiously toward the door as though he wished to escape from the room. And after every glance, as he beheld one Monk after another kissing the carpet, bottle in hand, the interesting Colonel would join heartily in the drunken bout, raising his voice with the loudest, and emptying his glass with the most drunken. Yet, to the eye of Byrnewood, this looked more like a mere counterfeit of a drunkard's manner than the thing itself. It was evident that the handsome millionaire emptied his glass under the table.

The revel now grew wild and furious. As bottle after bottle was consumed, so the actors in the scene began to appear, more and more, in their true characters. At last all disguise seemed thrown aside, and each voice, joining in the chorus of disjointed remarks, indicated that its owner imagined himself amid the scenes of his daily life.

"Gentlemen—allow—me—to read you a tale—a tale from the German on *Transcendental Essences*—" cried Petriken, rising, for he too was there, forgetful, like Mutchins, of his promise to Lorrimer—"This, gents, is a tale for my next Western Hem.:" here his oyster-like eyes rolled ghastily—"The Ladies Western Hem., forty-eight pages—monthly—offers following inducements—two dollars—" at this point of his handbill the gentleman staggered wofully—"Office No. 209 Drayman's Alley—hurrah Mutchins what's your idea of soft crabs?"

Here the literary gentleman fell heavily to the floor, mingled in the same heap that contained the poet and the wigless editor. In a moment he rose heavily to his feet, and staggered slowly to Mutchin's side.

"Gentlemen of the jury, I charge you—" began the Judge.

"Your honor, I beg leave to open this case—" interrupted the lawyer.

"My friends and brethren," cried the parson—"what shall ye do to be saved—oh—"

"Hand us the brandy—" shouted Mutchins.

"Mutchy—Mutchy—I say—" hiccupped Petriken—"Rem-Rem-em-ber the gown and the prayer book—"

"Silly—we must take a wash-off—" cried Mutchins, starting suddenly from his seat—"The thing—had slipped my memory—this way, my parson—ha, ha, ha—"

And taking Silly by the arm, he staggered from the room in company with the tow-haired gentleman.

"Lord look down upon these thy children, and—" continued the parson, who, like the others, appeared unconscious of the retreat of Petriken and his comrade.

"Hand the oysters this way—" remarked a mercantile gentleman, with a nose decorated by yellowish streaks from a mustard bottle.

"Boys I tell you the fire's up this alley—" cried another merchant—rather an amateur in fires when sober—"Here's the plug—now then—"

"Gentlemen of the Grand Jury, I beg leave to tell you that the amount of sin committed in this place in your very eyesight, cannot be tolerated by the court any longer. Dens of iniquity must be uprooted—who the h——ll flung that celery stalk in my eye?"

"Who soaked my cigar in champagne?"

"Somebody's lit another chandelier—"

"Hand us the brandy—"

"Did you say I didn't put down my name for 'one hundred,' to the Tract Society?"

"No I didn't, but I do now—"

"Say it again, and I'll tie you up in a meal bag—"

"My friends—" said the reverend gentleman, staggering to his feet—"What is this I see—confusion and drunkenness? Is this a scene for the house of God?" He glanced around with a look of sober reproof, and then suddenly exclaimed—"No heeltaps but show your bottoms—ha-ha-ha!"

There was another person who regarded this scene of bestial mirth with the same cool glance as Byrnewood. He was a young man with a massive face, and a deep piercing brown eye. His figure was somewhat stout, his attire careless, and his entire appearance disclosed the young Philadelphia lawyer. Changing his seat to Byrnewood's vicinity, he entered into conversation with the young merchant, and after making some pointed remarks in regard to the various members of the company, he stated that he had been lured thither by Mutchins, who had fancied he might cheat him out of a snug sum at the roulette table, or the farobank in the course of the night.

"Roulette-table—faro-bank?" muttered Byrnewood, incredulously.

"Why, my friend—" cried the young lawyer, who gave his name as Boyd Merivale—"Don't you know that this is one of the vilest rookeries in the world? It unites in all its details the house-of-ill-fame, the clubhouse, and the gambling hell. Egad! I well remember the first time I set my foot within its doors! What I beheld then, I can never forget—"

"You have been here before, then?"

"Yes have I! As I perceive you are unacquainted with the place, I will tell you my experience of

A NIGHT IN MONK-HALL*

Six years ago, in 1836, on a foggy night in spring, at the hour of one o'clock, I found myself reposing in one of the chambers of this mansion, on an old-fashioned bed, side by side with a girl, who, before her seduction, had resided in my native village. It was one o'clock when I was aroused by a hushed sound, like the noise of a distant struggle. I awoke, started up in bed, and looked round. The room was entirely without light, save from the fire-place, where a few pieces of half-burned wood, emitted a dim and uncertain flame. Now it flashed up brightly, giving a strange lustre to the old furniture of the

---

*The reader will remember, that Merivale entered Monk-Hall *for no licentious object, but with the distinct purpose of discovering the retreat of Western.* This story, told in Merivale's own words, is strictly true.

room, the high-backed mahogany chairs, the antiquated bureau, and the low ceiling, with heavy cornices around the walls. Again the flame died away and all was darkness. I listened intently. I could hear no sound, save the breathing of the girl who slept by my side. And as I listened, a sudden awe came over me. True, I heard no noise, but that my sleep had been broken by a most appaling sound, I could not doubt. And the stories I had heard of Monk-hall came over me. Years before, in my native village, a wild rollicking fellow, Paul Western, Cashier of the County Bank, had indulged my fancy with strange stories of a brothel, situated in the outskirts of Philadelphia. Paul was a wild fellow, rather good looking, and went often to the city on business. He spoke of Monk-hall as a place hard to find, abounding in mysteries, and darkened by hideous crimes committed within its walls. It had three stories of chambers beneath the earth, as well as above. Each of these chambers was supplied with trapdoors, through the which the unsuspecting man might be flung by his murderer, without a moment's warning. There was but one range of rooms above the ground, where these trap-doors existed. From the garret to the first story, all in the same line, like the hatchways in a storehouse, sank this range of trap-doors, all carefully concealed by the manner in which the carpets were fixed. A secret spring in the wall of any one of these chambers, communicated with the spring hidden beneath the carpet. The spring in the wall might be so arranged, that a single footstep pressed on the spring, under the carpet, would open the trap-door, and plunge the victim headlong through the aperture. In such cases no man could stride across the floor without peril of his life. Beneath the ground another range of trap-doors were placed in the same manner, in the floors of three stories of the subterranean chambers. They plunged the victim—God knows where! With such arrangements for murder above and beneath the earth, might there not exist hideous pits or deep wells, far below the third story under ground, where the body of the victim would rot in darkness forever? As I remembered these details, the connection between Paul Western, the cheerful bachelor, and Emily Walraven, the woman who was sleeping at my side, flashed over my mind. The child of one of the first men of B——, educated without regard to expense by the doating father, with a mind singularly masculine, and a tall queenly form, a face distinguished for its beauty and a manner remarkable for its ladylike elegance, poor Emily had been seduced, some three years before, and soon after disappeared from the town. Her seducer no one knew, though from some hints dropped casually by my friend Paul, I judged that he at least could tell. Rumors came to the place, from time to time in relation to the beautiful but fallen girl. One rumor stated that she was now living as the mistress of a wealthy planter, who made his residence at times in Philadelphia. Another declared that she had become a common creature of the town, and this—great God, how terrible!—killed her poor father. The rumor flew round the village to-day—next Sunday old Walraven was dead and buried. They say that in his dying hour he charged Paul Western with his daughter's shame, and shrieked a father's curse upon his head. He left no property, for his troubles had preyed on his mind until he neglected his affairs, and he died insolvent.

Well two years passed on, and no one heard a word more of poor Emily. Suddenly in the spring of 1836, when this town as well as the whole Union was convulsed with the fever of speculation, Paul Western, after a visit to Philadelphia, with some funds of the Bank, amounting to near thirty thousand dollars, in his possession, suddenly disappeared, no one knew whither. My father was largely interested in the bank. He despatched me to town, in order that I might make a desperate effort to track up the foot-steps of Western. Some items in the papers stated that the Cashier had fled to Texas, others that he had been drowned by accident, others that he had been spirited away. I alone possessed a clue to the place of his concealment—thus ran my thoughts at all events—and that clue was locked in the bosom of Emily Walraven, the betrayed and deeply-injured girl. Sometime before his disappearance, and after the death of old Walraven, Paul disclosed to me, under a solemn pledge of secresy, the fact that Emily was living in Philadelphia, under his protection, supported by his money. He stated that he had furnished rooms at the brothel called Monk-hall. With this fact resting on my mind, I had hurried to Philadelphia. For days my search for Emily Walraven was in vain. One night, when about giving up the chase as hopeless, I strolled to the Chesnut Street Theatre. Forrest was playing Richelieu—there was a row in the third tier—a bully had offered violence to one of the ladies of the town. Attracted by the noise, I joined the throng rushing up stairs, and beheld the girl who had been stricken, standing pale and erect, a small poignard in her upraised hand, while her eyes flashed with rage as she dared the drunken 'buffer' to strike her again. I stood thunderstruck as I recognized Emily Walraven in the degraded yet beautiful woman who stood before me. Springing forward, with one blow I felled the bully to the floor, and in another moment, seizing Emily by the arm, I hurried down stairs, evaded the constables, who were about to arrest her, and gained the street. It was yet early in the evening—there were no cabs in the street—so I had to walk home with her.

All this I remembered well, as I sat listening in the lonely room.

I remembered the big tears that started from her eyes when she recognized me, her wild exclamations when I spoke of her course of life. "Don't talk to me—" she had almost shrieked as we hurried along the street—"it's too late for me to change now. For God's sake let me be happy in my degradation."

I remembered the warm flush of indignation that reddened over her face, as pointing carelessly to a figure which I observed through the fog, some distance ahead, I exclaimed—"Is not that Paul Western yonder?" Her voice was very deep and not at all natural in its tone as she replied, with assumed unconcern—"I know nothing about the man." At last, after threading a labyrinth of streets, compared to which the puzzling-garden was a mere frolic, we had gained Monk-hall, the place celebrated by the wonderful stories of my friend Western. Egad! As we neared the door I could have sworn that I beheld Western himself disappear in the door but this doubtless, I reasoned, had been a mere fancy.

Silence still prevailed in the room, still I heard but the sound of Emily breathing in her sleep, and yet my mind grew more and more heavy, with some unknown feeling of awe. I remembered with painful distinctness the hang-dog aspect of the door-keeper who had let us in, and the cut-throat visages of his two attendants seemed staring me visibly in the face. I grew quite nervous. Dark ideas of murder and the devil knows what, began to chill my very soul. I bitterly remembered that I had no arms. The only thing I carried with me was a slight cane, which had been lent me by the Landlord of the——Hotel. It was a mere switch of a thing.

As these things came stealing over me, the strange connexion between the fate of Western and that of the beautiful woman who lay beside me, the sudden disappearance of the former, the mysterious character of Monk-hall, the startling sounds which had aroused me, the lonely appearance of the room, fitfully lighted by the glare on the hearth, all combined, deepened the impression of awe, which had gradually gained possession of my faculties. I feared to stir. You may have felt this feeling—this strange and incomprehensible feeling—but if you have not, just imagine a man seized with the night-mare when wide awake.

I was sitting upright in bed, chilled to the very heart, afraid to move an inch, almost afraid to breathe, when, far, far down through the chambers of the old mansion, I heard a faint hushed sound, like a man endeavouring to cry out when attacked by night-mare, and then—great God how distinct!—I heard the cry of 'Murder, murder, murder!' far, far, far below me.

The cry aroused Emily from her sleep. She started up in bed and whispered, in a voice without tremor—"What is the matter Boyd—"

"Listen—" I cried with chattering teeth, and again, up from the depths of the mansion welled that awful sound, *Murder!* Murder! Murder! growing louder every time. Then far, far, far down I could hear a gurgling sound. It grew fainter every moment. Fainter, fainter, fainter. All was still as death.

"What does this mean?" I whispered almost fiercely, turning to Emily by my side— "What does this mean?" And a dark suspicion flashed over my mind.

The flame shot upward in the fireplace, and revealed every line of her intellectual countenance.

Her dark eyes looked firmly in my face as she answered, "In God's name I know not!"

The manner of the answer satisfied me as to her firmness, if it did not convince me of her innocence. I sat silent and sullen, conjuring over the incidents of the night.

"Come, Boyd—" she cried, as she arose from the bed—"You must leave the house. I never entertain visitors after this hour. It is my custom. I thank you for your protection at the theatre, but you must go home—"

Her manner was calm and self-possessed. I turned to her in perfect amazement.

"I will not leave the house—" I said, as a dim vision of being attacked by assassins on the stairway, arose to my mind.

"There is Devil-Bug and his cut-throat negroes—" thought I—"nothing so easy as to give me a 'cliff' with a knife from some dark corner; nothing so secret as my burial-place in some dark hole in the cellar—"

"I won't go home—" said I, aloud.

Emily looked at me in perfect wonder. It may have been affected, and it may have been real.

"Well then, I must go down stairs to get something to eat—" she said, in the most natural manner in the world—"I usually eat something about this hour—"

"You may eat old Devil-Bug and his niggers, if you like—" I replied laughing— "But out of this house my father's son don't stir till broad daylight."

With a careless laugh, she wound her night gown around her, opened the door, and disappeared in the dark. Down, down, down, I could hear her go, her footsteps echoing along the stairway of the old mansion, down, down, down. In a few moments all was still.

Here I was, in a pretty 'fix.' In a lonely room at midnight, ignorant of the passages of the wizard's den, without arms, and with the pleasant prospect of the young lady coming back with Devil-Bug and his niggers to despatch me. I had heard the cry of 'Murder'— so ran my reasoning—they, that is the murderers—would suspect that I was a witness to their guilt, and, of course, would send me down some d———d trap-door on an especial message to the devil.

This was decidedly a bad case. I began to look around the room for some chance of escape, some arms to defend myself, or, perhaps from a motive of laudible curiosity, to know something more about the place where my death was to happen.

One moment, regular as the ticking of a clock, the room would be illuminated by a flash of red light from the fire-place, the next it would be dark as a grave. Seizing the opportunity afforded by the flash, I observed some of the details of the room. On the right side of the fireplace there was a closet: the door fastened to the post by a very singular button, shaped like a diamond; about as long as your little finger and twice as thick. On the other side of the fire-place, near the ceiling, was a small oblong window, about as large as two half sheets of writing paper, pasted together at the ends. Here let me explain the use of this window. The back part of Monk-hall is utterly destitute of windows. Light, faint and dim you may be sure, is admitted from the front by small windows, placed in the wall of each room. How many rooms there are on a floor, I know not, but, be they five or ten, or twenty, they are all lighted in this way.

Well, as I looked at this window, I perceived one corner of the curtain on the other side was turned up. This gave me very unpleasant ideas. I almost fancied I beheld a human face pressed against the glass, looking at me. Then the flash on the hearth died away, and all was dark. I heard a faint creaking noise—the light from the hearth again lighted the place—could I believe my eyes—the button on the closet-door turned slowly round!

Slowly—slowly—slowly it turned, making a slight grating noise. This circumstance, slight as it may appear to you, filled me with horror. What could turn the button, but a human hand? Slowly, slowly it turned, and the door sprung open with a whizzing sound. All was dark again. The cold sweat stood out on my forehead. Was my armed murderer waiting to spring at my throat? I passed a moment of intense horror. At last, springing hastily forward, I swung the door shut, and fastened the button. I can swear that I fastened it as tight as ever button was fastened. Regaining the bed I silently awaited the result. Another flash of light—Great God!—I could swear there was a face pressed against the oblong window! Another moment and it is darkness—creak, creak, creak— is that the sound of the button again? It was light again, and there, before my very eyes, the button moved slowly round! Slowly, slowly, slowly!

The door flew open again. I sat still as a statue. I felt it difficult to breathe. Was my enemy playing with me, like the cat ere she destroys her game!

I absently extended my hand. It touched the small black stick given me by the Landlord of the———Hotel in the beginning of the evening. I drew it to me, like a friend. Grasping it with both hands, I calculated the amount of service it might do me. And as I grasped it, the top seemed parting from the lower portion of the cane. Great God! It was a sword cane! Ha-ha! I could at least strike *one* blow! My murderers should not despatch me without an effort of resistance. You see my arm is none of the puniest in the world; I may say that there are worse men than Boyd Merivale for a fight.

Clutching the sword-cane, I rushed forward, and standing on the threshold of the opened door, I made a lunge with all my strength through the darkness of the recess. Though I extended my arm to its full length, and the sword was not less than eighteen inches long, yet to my utter astonishment, I struck but the empty air! Another lunge and the same result!

Things began to grow rather queer. I was decidedly beat out as they say. I shut the closet door again, retreated to the bed, sword in hand, and awaited the result. I heard a sound, but it was the footstep of poor Emily, who that moment returned with a bed-lamp in one hand, and a small waiter, supplied with a boiled chicken and a bottle of wine in the other. There was nothing remarkable in her look, her face was calm, and her boiled chicken and bottle of wine, decidedly common place.

"Great God—" she cried as she gazed in my countenance—"What is the matter with you? Your face is quite livid—and your eyes are fairly starting from their sockets—"

"Good reason—" said I, as I *felt* that my lips were clammy and white—"That d——d button has been going round ever since you left, and that d——d door has been springing open every time it was shut—"

"Ha-ha-ha—" she laughed—"Would it have sprung open if you had not shut it?"

This was a very clear question and easy to answer; but—

"Mark you, my lady—" said I—"Here am I in a lonely house, under peculiar circumstances. I am waked up by the cry of 'Murder'—a door springs open without a hand being visible—a face peers at me through a window. As a matter of course I suspect there has been foul work done here to-night. And through every room of this house, Emily you must lead the way, while I follow, this good sword in hand. If the light goes out, or if you blow it out, you are to be pitied, for in either case, I swear by Living God, I will run you through with this sword—"

"Ha-ha-ha—" she fairly screamed with laughter as she sprung to the closet-door—"Behold the mystery—"

And with her fair fingers she pointed to the socket of the button, and to the centre of the door. The door has been 'sprung,' as it is termed, by the weather. That is, the centre bulged inward, leaving the edge toward the door-post to press the contrary direction. The socket of the button, by continual wear, had been increased to twice its original size. Whenever the door was first buttoned, the head of the screw pressed against one of the edges of the socket. In a moment the pressure of the edge of the door, which you will remember was directed outward, dislodged the head of the screw and it sank, well-nigh half an inch into the worn socket of the button. Then the button, removed *farther* from the door than at first, would slowly turn, and the door spring open. All this was plain enough, and I smiled at my recent fright.

"Very good, Emily—" I laughed—"But the mystery of this sword—what of that? I made a lunge in the closet and it touched nothing—"

"You are suspicious, Boyd—" she answered with a laugh—"But the fact is, the closet is rather a deep one—"

"Rather—"said I—"and so are you, my dear—"

There may have been something very meaning in my manner, but certainly, although her full black eyes looked fixedly on me, yet I thought her face grew a shade paler as I spoke.

"And my dear—" I continued—"What do you make of the face peeping through the window:—"

"All fancy—all fancy—" she replied, but as she spoke I saw her eye glance hurriedly toward the very window. Did she *too* fear that she might behold a face?

"We will search the closet—" I remarked, throwing open the door—"What have we here? Nothing but an old cloak hanging to a hook—let's try it with my sword!"

Again I made a lunge with my sword: again I thrust at the empty air.

"Emily, there is a room beyond this cloak—you will enter first if you please. Remember my warning about the light if you please—"

"Oh now that I remember, this closet *does* open into the next room—" she said gaily, although her cheek—so it struck me—grew a little paler and her lip trembled slightly—"I had quite forgotten the circumstance—"

"Enter Emily, and don't forget the light—"

She flung the door aside and passed on with the light in her hand. I followed her. We stood in a small room, lighted like the other by an oblong window. There was no other window, no door, no outlet of any sort. Even a chimney-place was wanting. In one corner stood a massive bed—the quilt was unruffled. Two or three old fashioned chairs were scattered round the room, and from the spot where I stood looking over the foot of the bed, I could see the top of another chair, and nothing more, between the bed and the wall.

A trifling fact in Emily's behaviour may be remarked. The moment the light of the lamp which she held in her hand flashed round the room, she turned to me with a smile, and leading the way round the corner of the foot of the bed, asked me in a pleasant voice "Did I see any thing remarkable there?"

She shaded her eyes from the lamp as she spoke, and toyed me playfully under the chin. You will bear in mind that at this moment, I had turned my face toward the closet by which we had entered. My back was therefore toward the part of the room most remote from the closet. It was a trifling fact, but I may as well tell you, that the manner in which Emily held the light, threw that portion of the room, between the foot of the bed and the wall in complete shadow, while the rest of the chamber was bright as day.

Smilingly Emily toyed me under the chin, and at that moment I thought she looked extremely beautiful.

By Jove! I wish you could have seen her eyes shine, and her cheek—Lord bless you—a full blown rose wasn't a circumstance to it. She looked so beautiful, in fact, as she came sideling up to me, that I stepped backward in order to have a full view of her before I pressed a kiss on her pouting lips. I did step back, and did kiss her. It wasn't singular, perhaps, but her lips were hot as a coal. Again she advanced to me, again chucked me under the chin. Again I stepped back to look at her, again I wished to taste her lips so pouting, but rather warm, when—

To tell you the truth, stranger, even at this late day the remembrance makes my blood run cold!

——When I heard a sound like the sweeping of a tree-limb against a closed shutter, it was so faint and distant, and a stream of cold air came rushing up my back.

I turned around carelessly to ascertain the cause. I took but a single glance, and then—by G——d—I sprung at least ten feet from the place. There, at my very back, between the bed and the wall, opposite its foot, I beheld a carpeted space some three feet square, sinking slowly down, and separating itself from the floor. I had stepped my foot upon the spring—made ready for me, to be sure—and the trap-door sank below me.

You may suppose my feelings were somewhat excited. In truth, my heart, for a moment, felt as though it was turning to a ball of ice. First I looked at the trap-door and then at Emily. Her face was pale as ashes, and she leaned, trembling, against the bedpost. Advancing, sword in hand, I gazed down the trap-door. Great God! how dark and gloomy the pit looked! From room to room, from floor to floor, a succession of traps had fallen—far below—it looked like a mile, although that was but an exaggeration natural to a highly excited mind—far, far below gleamed a light, and a buzzing murmur came up this hatchway of death.

Stooping slowly down, sword in hand, my eye on the alert for Miss Emily, I disengaged a piece of linen, from a nail, near the edge of the trap-door. Where the linen—it was a shirt wristband—had been fastened, the carpet was slightly torn, as though a man in falling had grasped it with his finger ends.

The wristband was, in more correct language, a ruffle for the wrist. It came to my mind, in this moment, that I had often ridiculed Paul Western for his queer old bachelor ways. Among other odd notions, he had worn ruffles at his wrist. As I gathered this little piece of linen in my grasp, the trap-door slowly rose. I turned to look for Miss Emily, she had changed her position, and stood pressing her hand against the opposite wall.

"Now, Miss Emily, my dear—" I cried, advancing toward her—"Give me a plain answer to a plain question—and tell me—what in the devil do you think of yourself?"

Perfectly white in the face, she glided across the room and stood at the foot of the bed, in her former position leaning against the post for support. You will observe that her form concealed the chair, whose top I had only seen across the bed.

"Step aside, Miss Emily, my dear—" I said, in as quiet a tone as I could command—"Or you see, my lady, I'll have to use a little necessary force—"

Instead of stepping aside, as a peaceable woman would have done, she sits right down in the chair, fixing those full black eyes of her's on my face, with a glance that looked very much like madness.

Extending my hand, I raised her from the seat. She rested like a dead weight in my arms. She had fainted. Wrapped in her night-gown, I laid her on the bed, and then examined the chair in the corner. Something about this chair attracted my attention. A coat hung over the round—a blue coat with metal buttons. A buff vest hung under this coat; and a high stock, with a shirt collar.

I knew these things at once. They belonged to my friend, Paul Western.

"And so, my lady—" I cried, forgetting that she had fainted; "Mr. Western came home, from the theatre, to his rooms, arrived just before us, took off his coat and vest, and stock and collar—maybe was just about to take off his boots—when he stepped on the spring and in a moment was in—in h——ll—"

Taking the light in one hand, I dragged or carried her, into the other room and laid her on the bed. After half an hour or so, she came to her senses.

"You see—you see—" were her first words uttered, with her eyes flashing like live-coals, and her lips white as marble—"You see, I could not help it, for my father's curse was upon him!"

She laughed wildly, and lay in my arms a maniac.

Stranger, I'll make a short story of the thing now. How I watched her all night till broad day, how I escaped from the house—for Mr. Devil-Bug, it seems, didn't suspect I knew anything—how I returned home without any news of Paul Western, are matters as easy to conceive as tell.

Why didn't I institute a search? Fiddle-faddle! Blazon my name to the world as a visiter to a Bagnio?[17] Sensible thing, that! And then, although I was sure in my own soul, that the clothes which I had discovered belonged to Paul Western, it would have been most difficult to establish this fact in Court. One word more and I have done.

Never since that night has Paul Western been heard of by living man. Never since that night has Emily Walraven been seen in this breathing world. You start. Let me whisper a word in your ear. Suppose Emily joined in Western's murder from motives of revenge, what then were Devil-Bug's? (*He* of course was the real murderer.) Why the money to be sure. Why he troubled with Emily as a witness of his guilt, or a sharer of his money? This is rather a—a *dark house,* and it's my opinion, stranger, that *he murdered her too!*

Ha-ha—why here's all the room to ourselves! All the club have either disappeared, or lie drunk on the floor! I saw Fitz-Cowles—I know him—sneak off a few moments since—I could tell by his eye that he is after some devils-trick! The parson has gone, and the judge has gone, the lawyer has fallen among the slain, and so, wishing you good night, stranger, I'll vanish! Beware of the Monks of Monk-hall!"

Byrnewood was alone.

His head was depressed, his arms were folded, and his eye, gazing vacantly on the table, shone and glistened with the internal agitation of his brain. He sate there, silent, motionless, awed to the very soul. The story of the stranger had thrilled him to the heart, had aroused a strange train of thought, and now rested like an oppressive weight upon his brain.

Byrnewood gazed around. With a sudden effort he shook off the spell of absence which mingled with an incomprehensible feeling of awe, had enchained his faculties. He looked around the room. He was, indeed, alone. Above him, the hideous Satyr chandelier, still flared its red light over the table, over the mirror, and along the gloomy wainscot of the walls. Around the table, grouped in various attitudes of unconscious drunkenness, lay the members of the drinking party, the merry Monks of Monk-hall. There lay the poet, with his sanguine face shining redly in the light, while his hand rested on the bare scalp of the wigless editor, there snored some dozen merchants, all doubled up together, like the slain in battle, and there, a solitary doctor, who had fallen asleep on his knees, was dozing away with one eye wide open, while his right hand brushed away a solitary fly from his pimpled nose.

The scene was not calculated to produce the most serious feelings in the world. There was inebriety—as the refined phrase it—in every shape, inebriety on its face, inebriety with its mouth wide open, inebriety on its knees brushing a fly from its nose, inebriety groaning, grunting, or snoring, inebriety doubled up—mingled in a mass of limbs, heads and bodies, woven together—or flat inebriety simply straightened out on its back

---

[17]A brothel.

with its nose performing a select overture of snores. To be brief, there, scattered over the floor, lay drunkenness—as the vulgar will style it—in every shape, moddled after various patterns, and taken by that ingenious artist, the Bottle, fresh from real life.

Raising his eyes from the prostrate members of the club, Byrnewood started with involuntary surprise as he beheld, standing at the tables-head, the black-robed figure of the Skeleton-Monk, with his hand of bone flinging aloft the goblet, while his fleshless brow glared in the light, from the shadow of the falling cowl. As the light flickered to and fro, it gave the grinning teeth of the Skeleton the appearance of life and animation for a single moment. Byrnewood thought he beheld the teeth move in a ghastly smile; he even fancied that the orbless sockets, gleaming beneath the white brow, flashed with the glance of life, and gazed sneeringly in his face.

He started with involuntary horror, and then sate silent as before. And as you can feel cold or heat steal over you by slow degrees, so he felt that same strange feeling of awe, which he had known that night for the first time in his life, come slowly over him moving like a shadow over his soul, and stealing like a paralysis through his every limb. He sate like a man suddenly frozen.

"My God!" he murmured—and the sound of his voice frightened him—"How strange I feel! Can this be the first attack of some terrible disease—or—is it, but the effect of the horrible story related by the stranger? I have read in books that a feeling like this steals over a man, just before some terrible calamity breaks over his head—this is fearful as death itself!"

He was silent again, and then the exclamation broke from his lips—

"Lorrimer—why does he not return? He has been absent full an hour—what does it mean? Can the words of that—pshaw! that fortune teller have any truth in them? How can Lorrimer injure me—how can I injure him? Three days hence—Christmas—ha, ha—I believe I'm going mad—there's cold sweat on my forehead—"

As he spoke he raised his left hand to his brow, and in the action, the gleam of a plain ring on his finger met his eye. He kissed it suddenly, and kissed it again and again? Was it the gift of his ladye-love?

"God bless her—God bless her! Wo to the man who shall do *her* wrong—and yet poor Annie—"

He rose suddenly from his seat and strode towards the door.

"I know not why it is, but I feel as though an invisible hand, was urging me onward through the rooms of this house! And onward I will go, until I discover Lorrimer or solve the mystery of this den. God knows, I feel—pshaw! I'm only nervous—as though I was walking to my death."

Passing through the narrow door-way, he cautiously ascended the dark staircase, and in a moment stood on the first floor. The moon was still shining through the distant skylight, down over the windings of the massive stairway. All was silent as death within the mansion. Not a sound, not even the murmur of a voice or the hushed tread of a foot-step could be heard. Winding his cloak tightly around his limbs, Byrnewood rushed up the staircase, traversing two steps at a time, and treading softly, for fear of discovery. He reached the second floor. Still the place was silent and dismal, still the column of moonlight pouring through the skylight, over the windings of the staircase only rendered the surrounding darkness more gloomy and indistinct. Up the winding staircase he again resumed his way, and in a moment stood upon the landing or hall of the third floor. This was an oblong space, with the doors of many rooms fashioned in its walls. Another stairway led upward from the floor, but the attention of Byrnewood was arrested by a single ray of light, that for a moment flickered along the thick darkness of the southern end of the hall. Stepping forward hastily, Byrnewood found all progress arrested by the opposing front of a solid wall. He gazed toward his left—it was so dark, that he could not see his hand before his eyes. Turning his glance to the right, as his vision became more accustomed to the darkness, he beheld the dim walls of a long corridor, at whose entrance he stood, and whose farther extreme was illumined by a light, that to all appearance, flashed from an open door. Without a moment's thought he strode along the thickly carpeted passage of the corridor; he stood in the full glow of the light flashing from the open door.

Looking through the doorway, he beheld a large chamber furnished in a style of lavish magnificence, and lighted by a splendid chandelier. It was silent and deserted. From the ceiling to the floor, along the wall opposite the doorway, hung a curtain of damask silk, trailing in heavy folds, along the gorgeous carpet. Impelled by the strange impulse, that had urged him thus far, Byrnewood entered the chamber, and without pausing to admire its gorgeous appointments, strode forward to the damask curtain.

He swung one of its hangings aside, expecting to behold the extreme wall of the chamber. To his entire wonder, another chamber, as spacious as the one in which he stood, lay open to his gaze. The walls were all one gorgeous picture, evidently painted by a master-hand. Blue skies, deep green forests, dashing waterfalls and a cool calm lake, in which fair women were laving their limbs, broke on the eyes of the intruder, as he turned his gaze from wall to wall. A curtain of azure, sprinkled with a border of golden leaves, hung along the farther extremity of the room. In one corner stood a massive bed, whose snow-white counterpane, fell smoothly and unruffled to the very floor, mingling with the long curtains, which pure and stainless as the counterpane, hung around the couch in graceful festoons, like the wings of a bird guarding its resting place.

"The bridal-bed!" murmured Byrnewood, as he flung the curtains of gold and azure, hurriedly aside.

A murmur of surprise, mingled with admiration, escaped from his lips, as he beheld the small closet, for it could scarcely be called a room, which the undrawn curtaining threw open to his gaze.

It was indeed a small and elegant room, lined along its four sides with drooping curtains of faint-hued crimson silk. The ceiling itself was but a continuation of these curtains, or hangings, for they were gathered in the centre, by a single star of gold. The carpet on the floor was of the same faint-crimson color, and the large sofa, placed along one side of the apartment, was covered with velvet, that harmonized in hue, with both carpet and hangings. On the snow-white cloth, of a small table placed in the centre of the room, stood a large wax candle, burning in a candlestick of silver, and flinging a subdued and mellow light around the plate. There was a neat little couch, standing in the corner, with a *toilette* at its foot. The quilt on the couch was ruffled, as though some one had lately risen from it, and the equipage of the *toilette* looked as though it had been recently used.

The faint light falling over the hangings, whose hue resembled the first flush of day, the luxurious sofa, the neat though diminutive couch, the small table in the centre, the carpet whose colors were in elegant harmony with the hue of the curtains, all combined, gave the place an air of splendid comfort—if we may join these incongruous words—that indicated the sleeping chamber of a lovely woman.

"This has been the resting place of the *bride*—" murmured Byrnewood, gazing in admiration around the room—"It looks elegant it is true, but if she is the innocent thing Lorrimer would have me believe, then better for her, to have slept in the foulest gutter of the streets, than to have lain for an instant in this woman-trap—"

There was a woman's dress—a frock of plain black silk—flung over one of the rounds of the sofa. Anxious to gather some idea of the form of the bride—oh foul prostitution of the name!—from the shape of the dress, Byrnewood raised the frock and examined its details. As he did this, the sound of voices came hushed and murmuring to his ear from a room, opposite the chamber which he had but a moment left. Half occupied in listening to these voices, Byrnewood glanced at the dress which he held in his hand, and as he took in its various details of style and shape, the pupil of his full black eye dilated, and his cheek became colorless as death.

Then the room seemed to swim around him, and he pressed his hand forcibly against his brow, as if to assure himself, that he was not entangled in the mazes of some hideous dream.

Then, letting his own cloak and the black silk dress fall on the floor at once, he walked with a measured step toward that side of the room opposite the Painted Chamber.

The voices grew louder in the next room. Byrnewood listened in silence. His face was even paler than before, and you could see how desperate was the effort which he made to suppress an involuntary cry of horror, that came rising to his lips. Extending his hand, he pushed the curtain slightly aside, and looked into the next room.

The extended hand fell like a dead weight to his side.

Over his entire countenance flashed a mingled expression of surprise, and horror, and woe, that convulsed every feature with a spasmodic movement, and forced his large black eyes from their very sockets. For a moment he looked as if about to fall lifeless on the floor, and then it was evident that he exerted all his energies to control this most fearful agitation. He pressed both hands nervously against his forehead, as though his brain was tortured by internal flame. Then he reared his form proudly erect, and stood apparently firm and self possessed, although his countenance looked more like the face of a corpse than the face of a living man.

And as he stood there, silent and firm, although his very reason tottered to its ruin, there glided to his back, like an omen of death, pursuing the footsteps of life, the distorted form of the Door-keeper of Monk-hall, his huge bony arms upraised, his hideous face convulsed in a loathsome grin, while his solitary eye glared out from its sunken socket, like a flame lighted in a skull, grotesque yet terrible.

In vain was the momentary firmness which Byrnewood had aroused to his aid! In vain was the effort that suppressed his breath, that clenched his hands, that forced the clammy sweat from his brow! He felt the awful agony that convulsed his soul rising to his lips—he would have given the world to stifle it—but in vain, in vain were all his superhuman efforts!

One terrific howl, like the yell of a man flung suddenly over a cataract, broke from his lips. He thrust aside the curtain, and strode madly through its folds into the next room.

CHAPTER EIGHTH

☙ Mother Nancy and Long-Haired Bess

'So ye have lured the pretty dove into the cage, at last—" said the old lady, with a pleasant smile, as she poised a nice morsel of buttered toast between her fingers—"This tea is most too weak—a little more out of the caddy, Bessie, dear. Lord! who'd a-thought you'd a-caught the baby-face so easy! Does the kettle boil, my dear? I put it on the fire before you left, and you've been away near an hour, so it ought to be hissing hot by this time. Caught her at last! Hah-hah—hey? Bessie? You're a reg'lar keen one, I must say!"

And with the mild words the old lady arranged the tea things on the small table, covered with a neat white cloth, and pouring out a cup of 'Gunpowder,' chuckled pleasantly to herself, as though she and the buttered toast had a quiet little joke together.

"Spankin' cold night, I tell ye, Mother Nancy—" exclaimed the young lady in black, as she flung herself in a chair, and tossed her bonnet on the old sofa—"Precious time I've had with that little chit of a thing! Up one street and down another, I've been racing for this blessed hour! And the regular white and black 'uns I've been forced to tell! Oh crickery—don't mention 'em, I beg—"

"Sit down, Bess—sit down, Bessie, that's a dove—" said the delighted old lady, crunching the toast between her toothless gums—"and tell us all about it from the first! These things are quite refreshin' to us old stagers."

"What a perfect old d——l—" muttered Bessie, as she drew her seat near the supper table—"These oysters are quite delightful—stewed to a turn, I *do* declare—" she continued, aloud—"Got a little drop o' the 'lively'—hey, Mother?"

"Yes, dovey—here's the key of the closet. Get the bottle, my dear. A leetle—jist a *leetle*—don't go ugly with one's tea—"

While the tall and queenly Bessie is engaged in securing a drop of the lively, we will take a passing glance at Mother Perkins, the respectable Lady Abbess of Monk-hall.

As she sate in that formal arm-chair, straight and erect, her portly form clad in sombre black, with a plain white collar around her neck and a bunch of keys at her girdle, Mother Nancy looked, for all the world, like a quiet old body, whose only delight was to scatter blessings around her, give large alms to the poor, and bestow unlimited amounts of tracts among the vicious. A good, dear, old body, was Mother Nancy, although her face was decidedly prepossessing. A low forehead, surmounted by a perfect tower-of-Babel of a cap, a little sharp nose looking out from two cheeks disposed in immense collops of yellowish flesh, two small grey eyes encircled by a wilderness of wrinkles, a deep indentation where a mouth should have been, and a sharp chin, ornamented with a slight 'imperial' of stiff grey beard; such were the details of a countenance, on which seventy years had showered their sins, and cares, and crimes, without making the dear old lady, for a moment, pause in her career.

And such a career! God of Heaven! did womanhood, which in its dawn, or bloom, or full maturity, is so beautiful, which even in its decline is lovely, which in trembling old age is venerable, did womanhood ever sink so low as this? How many of the graves in an hundred churchyards, graves of the fair and beautiful, had been dug by the gouty hands of the vile old hag, who sate chuckling in her quiet arm-chair? How many of the betrayed maidens, found rotting on the rivers waves, dangling from the garret rafter, starving in the streets, or resting, vile and loathsome, in the Greenhouse;* how many of these will, at the last day when the accounts of this lovely earth will be closed forever, rise up and curse the old hag with their ruin, with their shame, with their unwept death?

The details of the old lady's room by no means indicated her disposition, or the course of her life. It was a fine old room with walls neatly papered, all full of nooks and corners, and warmed by a cheerful wood fire blazing on the spacious hearth. One whole side of the room seemed to have been attacked with some strange eruptive disease, and broken out into an erysipelas of cupboards and closets. An old desk that might have told a world of wonders of Noah's Ark from its own personal experience, could it have spoken, stood in one corner, and a large side-board, on whose top a fat fellow of a decanter seemed drilling some raw recruits of bottles and glasses into military order, occupied one entire side of the room, or cell, of the Lady Abbess.

There are few persons in the world who have not a favourite of some kind, either a baby, or a parrot, or a canary, or a cat, or, in desperate cases, a pig. Mother Nancy had her favourite as well as less reputable people. A huge bull dog, with sore eyes and a ragged tail—that seemed to have been purchased at a second-had store during the hard times— lay nestling at the old lady's feet, looking very much like the candidate whom all the old and surly dogs would choose for Alderman, in case the canine race had the privilege of electing an officer of that honorable class, among themselves. This dog, so old bachelor-like and aldermanic in appearance, the old lady was wont to call by the name of 'Dolph,' being the short for 'Dolphin,' of which remarkable fish the animal was supposed to be a decided copy.

"Here's the 'lively,' Mother Nancy—" observed Miss Bessie, as she resumed her seat at the supper table—"It's the real hot stuff and *no* mistake. The oysters, if you please—a little o' that pepper. Any mustard there? Now then, Mother, let's be comfortable—"

"But" observed the old lady pouring a glass of the 'Lively' from a decanter labelled 'Brandy'—"But Bessie my love, I'm a-waitin' to hear all about this little dove whom you trapped to night—"

It may be as well to remark that Bessie, was a tall queenly girl of some twenty-five, with a form that had once been beautiful beyond description, and even now in its ruins, was lovely to look upon, while her faded face, marked by a high brow and raven-black hair, was still enlivened by the glance of two large dark eyes, that were susceptible of any expression, love or hate, revenge or jealousy; anything but fear. Her complexion was a very faint brown with a deep rose-tint on each cheek. She was still beautiful, although a long career of dissipation had given a faded look to the outlines of her face, indenting a slight wrinkle between her arching brows, and slightly discoloring the flesh beneath each eye.

"This here 'Lively' is first rate, after the tramp I've had—" said Bessie as her eyes

---

*The house for the unknown dead.

grew brighter with the 'lively' effects of the bottle—"You know Mother Nancy its three weeks since Gus mentioned the *thing* to me—"

"What thing, my dear?"

"Why that he'd like to have a little dove for himself—something above the common run. Something from the aristocracy of the Quaker City—you know?"

"Yes my dear. Here Dolph—here Dolph-ee—here's a nice bit for Dolph—"

"Gus agreed to give me something handsome if I could manage it for him, so I undertook the thing. The bread if you please, Mother. You know I'm rather expert in such matters?"

"There ain't you beat my dear. Be quiet Dolph—that's a nice Dolph-ee—"

"For a week all my efforts were in vain. I could'nt discover anything that was likely to suit the taste of Gus—At last he put me on the right track himself—"

"He did, did he? Ah deary me, but Gus is a regular lark. You can't perduce his ekle—"

"One day strolling up Third Street, Gus was attracted by the sight of a pretty girl, sitting at the window of a wealthy merchant, who has just retired from business. You've heard of old Arlington? Try the 'Lively' Mother. Gus made some enquiries; found that the young lady had just returned, from the Moravian boarding school at Bethlehem. She was innocent, inexperienced, and all that. Suited Lorrimer's taste. He swore he'd have her."

"So you undertook to catch her, did ye? Butter my dear?"

"That did I. The way I managed it was a caution. Dressing myself in solemn black, I strolled along Third street, one mild winter evening, some two weeks since. Mary— that's her name—was standing at the front door, gazing carelessly down the street. I tripped up the steps and asked in my most winning tone——"

"You can act the lady when you like, Bess. That's a fact.—"

"Whether Mr. Elmwood lived there? Of course she answered 'No.' But in making an apology for my intrusion, I managed to state that Mr. Elmwood was my uncle, that I had just come to the city on a visit, and had left my aunt's in Spruce street, but a few moments ago, thinking to pay a nice little call on my dear old relative—"

"Just like you Bessie! So you scraped acquaintance with her?"

"Fresh from boarding school, as ignorant of the world as the babe unborn, the girl was interested in me, I suppose, and swallowed the white'uns I cold her, without a single suspicion, The next day about noon, I met her as she was hurrying to see an old aunt, who lived two or three Squares below her father's house. She was all in a glow, for she had been hurrying along rather fast, anxious to reach her aunt's house, as soon as possible. I spoke to her—proposed a walk—she assented with a smile of pleasure. I told her a long story of my sorrows; how I had been engaged to be married, how my lover had died of consumption but a month ago; that he was such a nice young man, with curly hair, and hazel eyes, and that I was in black for his death. I put peach fur over her eyes, by whole hand's full I tell you. The girl was interested, and like all young girls, she was delighted to become the *confidante* of an amiable young lady, who had a little love-romance of real life, to disclose. Oysters, Mother Nancy—"

"The long and short of it was, that you wormed yourself into her confidence? That it my dear? Keep still Dolph or Dolph's mommy would drop little bit of hot tea on Dolph's head—"

"We walked out together for three days, just toward dark in the evening. You can fancy Mother, how I wound myself into the heart of this young girl. Closer and closer every day I tightened the cords that bound us, and on the third evening I believe she would have died for me.—"

"Well, well child, when did Gusty first speak to her? A little more of the "Gunpowder" my dear—"

"One evening I persuaded her to take a stroll along Chesnut Street with me. Gus was at our heels you may be sure. He passed on a little-a-head determining to speak to her, at all hazards. She saved him the trouble. Lord love you Mother Nancy, she spoke to him first—"

"Be still Dolph—be still Dolph-ee! Now Bessie that's a leetle too strong! Not the tea, but the story. She so innocent and baby-like speak first to a strange man? Ask me to believe in tea made out of turnip tops will ye?—"

"She mistook him for a Mr. Belmont whom she had seen at Bethlehem. He did not undeceive her, until she was completely in his power. He walked by her side that evening up and down Chesnut Street, for nearly an hour. I saw at once, that her girlish fancy was caught by his smooth tongue, and handsome form. The next night he met us again, and the next, and the next—Lord pity her—the poor child was *now* entirely at his mercy—"

"Ha—ha—Gusty is sich a devil. Put the kettle on the fire my dear. Let's try a little of the 'Lively.' And how did she—this baby-faced doll—keep these walks secret from the eyes of her folks? Eh? Bessie?"

"Easy as *that*—" replied Bessie gracefully snapping her fingers—"Every time she went out, she told father and mother' that she went to see her old Aunt. I hinted at first, that our friendship would be more romantic, if concealed from all intrusive eyes. The girl took the hint. Lorrimer with his smooth tongue, told her a long story about his eccentric uncle who had sworn he should not marry, for years to come; and therefore he was obliged to keep his attentions to her, hidden from both of their families. Gusty was dependent on this old uncle—you know? Once married, the old uncle would relent as he beheld the beauty and innocence of the young—*wife!* So Gusty made her believe. You can imagine the whole trap. We had her in our power. Last night she consented to leave her home for Lorrimer's *family* mansion. He was to marry her, the approval of his uncle—that imaginary old Gentleman—was to be obtained, and on Christmas Eve, Mr. and—ha, ha, ha—*Mistress* Lorrimer, were to rush into old Middleton's house, fall on their knees, invoke the old man's blessing; be forgiven and be happy! Hand us the toast Mother Nancy—"

"And to night the girl *did* leave the old folk's house? Entered the door of Monk-hall, thinking it was Lorrimer's *family* Mansion, and to-morrow morning at three o'clock will be married—eh? Bess?"

"Married, pshaw! *Over the left.* Lorrimer said he would get that fellow Petriken to personate the Parson—Mutchins the gambler, acts the old uncle; you, Mother Nancy must, dress up for the kind and amiable grandma—suit you to a T? Lorrimer pays high for his rooms you know?"

"'Spose it must be done. It's now after ten o'clock. You left the baby-face sleeping, eh? At half-past two you'll have to rouse her, to dress. Be quiet Dolph or I'll scald its head—that's a dear. Now Bessie tell me the truth, did you never regret that you had undertaken the job? The girl you say is so innocent?"

"Regret?" cried Bess with a flashing eye—"Why should I regret? Have I not as good a right to the comforts of a home, to the smile of a father, the love of a mother, as she?

Have I not been robbed of all these? Of all that is most sacred to woman? Is this innocent Mary, a whit better than I *was* when the devil in human shape first dragged me from my home? I feel happy—aye happy—when I can drag another woman, into the same foul pit, where I am doomed to lie and rot—"

"Yet this thing was *so* innocent—" cried the good old lady patting Dolph on the head—"I confess I laugh at all qualms—all petty scruples, but you were so different when first I knew you—you *Emily,* you—"

"*Emily*—" shrieked the other as she sprung suddenly to her feet—"You hag of the devil—call me by that name again, and as God will judge at the last day, I'll throttle you!" She shook her clenched hand across the table, and her eyes were bloodshot with sudden rage—"*Emily!*" Your mother called you by that name when a little child—" She cried with a burst of feeling, most fearful to behold in one so fallen—"Your father blessed you by that name, the night before you fled from his roof!

'Emily!' Aye, *he,* the foul betrayer, whispered that name with a smile as he entered the Chamber, from which he never came forth again—You remember it old hell-cat, do ye?—"

"Not so loud, Good G——d, not so loud—" Cried the astonished Mother Nancy— "Abuse me Bessie dear—but not so loud; down Dolph don't mind the girl, she's mad— not so loud, I say—"

"I can see him now!" cried the fallen girl, as with her tall form raised to its full height, she fixed her flashing eye on vacancy—"He enters the room—that room with the—the trap-door you know? 'Good night, Emily,' he said, and smiled—'*Emily,*' and— my father had cursed him! I laid me down and rested by another man's side. *He* thought I slept. Slept! ha, ha! When, with my entire soul, I listened to the foot-steps in the next room—ha, ha—when I heard the creaking sound of the falling trap, when I drank in the cry of agony, when I heard that name 'Emily, oh Emily,' come shrieking up the pit of death! My father had cursed him, and he died! 'Emily'—oh my God—" and she wrung her hands in very agony—"Roll back the years of my life, blot out the foul record of my sins, let me, oh God—you are all powerful and can do it—let me be a child again, a little child, and though I crawl through life in the rags of a beggar, I will never cease to bless—oh God—to bless your name—"

She fell heavily to her seat, and, covering her face with her hands, wept the scalding tears of guilt and shame.

"'Gal's been a-takin' opium—" said the old lady, calmly—"And the fit's come on her. 'Sarves her right. 'Told her never to mix her brandy with opium—"

"Did I regret having undertaken the ruin of the girl—" said Bess, in a whisper, that made even the old lady start with surprise—"Regret? I tell ye, old hell-dame as you are, that my very heart strings seemed breaking within me to-night, as I led her from her home—"

"What the d——l did you do it for, then? Here's a nice Dolph—eat a piece o' buttered toast—that's a good Dolph-ee—"

"When the seducer first assailed me—" continued Bess, in an absent tone—"He assailed a woman, with a mind stored with knowledge of the world's ways, a soul full as crafty as his own, a wit sharp and keen as ever dropped poison or sweetness from a woman's tongue! But this girl, so child-like, so unsuspecting, so innocent! my God! how it wrung my heart, when I first discovered that she *loved* Lorrimer, loved him without one shade of gross feeling, loved him without a doubt, warmly, devotedly, with all the trustfulness of an angel-soul, fresh from the hands of God! Never a bird fell more helplessly into the yawning jaws of the snake, that had charmed it to ruin, than poor Mary fell into the accursed wiles of Lorrimer! And yet I, *I* aided him—"

"So you did. The more shame for you to harm sich a dove. Go up stairs, my dear, and let her loose. We'll consent, won't we? Ha-ha! Why Bess, I thought you had more sense than to go on this way. What *will* become of you?"

"I suppose that I will die in the same ditch where the souls of so many of my vile sisterhood have crept forth from their leprous bodies? Eh, Mother Nance? Die in a ditch? *'Emily'* die in a ditch? And then in the next world—ha, ha, ha—I see a big lake of fire, on which souls are dancing like moths in a candle—ha, ha, ha!"

"Reely, gal, you must leave off that opium. Gus promised you some five or six hundred if you caught this gal, and you can't go back now—"

"Yes, I know it! I know it! *Forward's* the word if the next stop plunges me in hell—"

And the girl buried her face in her hands, and was silent again. Let not the reader wonder at the mass of contradictions, heaped together in the character of this miserable wreck of a woman. One moment conversing in the slang of a brothel, like a thing lapped from her birth in pollution; the next, whispering forth her ravings in language indicative of the educated woman of her purer days; one instant glorying in her shame, the next recoiling in horror as she viewed the dark path which she had trodden, the darker path which she was yet to tread—these paradoxes are things of every day occurrence, only to be explained, when the mass of good and evil, found in every human heart, is divided into distinct parts, no more to mingle in one, no more to occasion an eternal contest in the self-warring heart of man.

"Well, well, Bessie—go to bed and sleep a little—that's a dear—" said the old lady, with a pleasing smile—"Opium isn't good for you, and you know it. A leetle nap 'ill do you good. Sleep a bit, and then you'll be right fresh for the wedding. Three o'clock you know—Come along, Dolph, mommy must go 'tend to some little things about the house—Come along, Dolph-*ee*—Sleep a leetle, Bessie, that's a dear!"

CHAPTER NINTH

❧ The Bride

A chapter in which every woman may find some leaves of her own heart,
read with the eyes of a high and holy love

"Mary!"

Oh sweetest name of woman! name by which some of us may hail a wife, or a sister in heaven; name so soft, and rippling, and musical; name of the mother of Jesus, made holy by poetry and religion!—how foully were you profaned by the lips that whispered your sound of gentleness in the sleeper's ear!

"Mary!"

The fair girl stirred in her sleep, and her lips dropped gently apart as she whispered a single word—

"Lorraine!"

"The assumed name of Lorrimer—" exclaimed the woman, who stood by the bed-side—"Gus has some taste, even in his vilest loves! But, with this girl—this child—good Heavens: how refined! He shrunk at the very idea of *her* voice whispering the name which had been shouted by his devil mates at a drinking bout! So he told the girl to call him—not Gusty, no, no, but something musical—*Lorraine!*"

And, stooping over the couch, the queenly woman, with her proud form arrayed in a dress of snow white silk, and her raven-black hair gathered in thick tresses along her neck, so full and round, applied her lips to the ear of the sleeper and whispered in a soft-ened tone—

"Mary! Awake—it is your wedding night!"

The room was still as death. Not a sound save the faint breathing of the sleeper; all hushed and still. The light of the wax candle standing on the table in the centre of the Rose Chamber—as it was called—fell mild and softened over the hangings of faint crimson, with the effect of evening twilight.

The maiden—pure and without stain—lay sleeping on the small couch that occupied one corner of the closet. Her fair limbs were enshrouded in the light folds of a night-robe, and she lay in an attitude of perfect repose, one glowing cheek resting upon her uncovered arm, while over the other, waved the loosened curls of her glossy hair. The parting lips dis-closed her teeth, white as ivory, while her youthful bosom came heaving up from the folds of her night-robe, like a billow that trembles for a moment in the moonlight, and then is suddenly lost to view. She lay there in all the ripening beauty of maidenhood, the light falling gently over her young limbs, their outlines marked by the easy folds of her robe, resembling in their roundness and richness of proportion, the swelling fulness of the rose-bud that needs but another beam of light, to open it into its perfect bloom.

The arching eyebrows, the closed lids, with the long lashes resting on the cheek, the parted lips, and the round chin, with its smiling dimple, all these were beautiful, but oh how fair and beautiful the maiden's dreams. Rosier than her cheeks, sweeter than her breath, lovelier than her kiss—lovely as her own stainless soul, on whose leaves was written but one motto of simple meaning—*"Love in life, in death, and for ever."*

And in all her dreams she beheld but one form, heard the whisper of but one voice, shared the sympathies of but one heart! *He* was her dream, her life, her *God*—him had she trusted with her all, in earth or heaven, him did she love with the uncalculating aban-donment of self, that marks the first passion of an innocent woman!

*And was there aught of *earth* in this love? Did the fever of sensual passion throb in the pulses of her virgin blood? Did she love Lorrimer because his eyes was bright, his form magnificent, his countenance full of healthy manliness? No, no, no! Shame on the fools

---

*The reader who desires to understand thoroughly, the pure love of an innocent girl for a corrupt libertine, will not fail to peruse this passage.

of either sex, who read the first love of a stainless woman, with the eyes of Sense. She loved Lorrimer for a something which he did not possess, which vile worldlings of his class never will possess. For the magic with which her fancy had enshrouded his face and form, she loved him, for the wierd fascination which *her own soul* had flung around his very existence, for a dream of which *he* was the idol, for a waking trance in which *he* walked as her good Angel, for imagination, for fancy, for any thing but *sense,* she loved him.

It was her first love.

She knew not that this fluttering fascination, which bound her to his slightest look or tone—like the charmed bird to the lulling music which the snake is said to murmur, as he ensnares his prey—she knew not that this fluttering fascination, was but the blind admiration of the moth, as it floats in the light of the flame, which will at last consume it.

She knew not that in her own organization, were hidden the sympathies of an animal as well as of an intellectual nature, that the blood in her veins only waited an opportunity to betray her, that in the very atmosphere of the holiest love of woman, crouched a sleeping fiend, who at the first whisperings of her Wronger, would arise with hot breath and blood shot eyes, to wreak enternal ruin on her, woman's-honor.

For this is the doctrine we deem it right to hold in regard to woman. Like man she is a combination of an animal, with an intellectual nature. Unlike man her animal nature is a *passive* thing, that must be roused ere it will develope itself in action. Let the intellectual nature of woman, be the only object of man's influence, and woman will love him most holily. But let him play with her animal nature as you would toy with the machinery of a watch, let him rouse the treacherous blood, let him fan the pulse into quick, feverish throbbings, let him warm the heart with convulsive beatings, and the woman becomes like himself, but a mere animal. *Sense* rises like a vapor, and utterly darkens *Soul.*

And shall we heap shame on woman, because man, neglecting her holiest nature, may devote all the energies which God has given him, to rouse her gross and earthy powers into action? On whose head is the shame, or whose the wrong? Oh, would man but learn the solemn truth—that no angel around God's throne is purer than Woman when her intellectual nature alone is stirred into development, that no devil crouching in the flames of hell is fouler than Woman, when her animal nature alone is roused into action—would man but learn and revere this fearful truth, would woman but treasure it in her inmost soul, then would never a shriek arise to heaven, heaping curses on the betrayer's head, then would never a wrong done to maiden virtue, give the suicide's grave its victim, then in truth, would woman walk the earth, the spirit of light that the holiest Lover ever deemed her!

And the maiden lay dreaming of her lover, while the form of the tall and stately woman, stood by the bedside, like her Evil Angel, as with a mingled smile and sneer, she bade the girl arise, for it was her wedding night. *Her wedding night!*

"Mary! Awake—it is your wedding night!"

Mary murmured in her sleep, and then opened her large blue eyes, and arose in the couch.

"Has—*he* come?" were the first words she murmured in her musical tones, that came low and softened to the listeners ear—"Has *he* come?"

"Not yet—not yet—my dear—" said long-haired Bess, assisting the young maiden to rise from the couch, with all imaginable tenderness of manner—"You see Mary love, it's half-past two o'clock and over, and of course, high time for you to dress. Throw back your night-gown my love, and let me arrange your hair. How soft and silky—it needs but little aid from my hands, to render each tress a perfect charm—"

"Is it not very strange Bessie—" said Mary opening her large blue eyes with a bewildered glance as she spoke.

"What is strange? I see nothing strange except the remarkable beauty of these curls—"

"That I should first meet him, in such a singular manner, that he should love me, that for his sake I should fly to his uncle's mansion and that you Bessie—my dear good friend—should consent from mere friendship to leave your home and bear me company. All this is very strange—how like the stories we read in a book! And his stern old uncle you say has relented?"

"Perfectly resigned to the match my dear. That's the way with all these relations— is not that curl perfect?—when they've made all the mischief they can, and find it amounts to nothing, at the last moment they roll up their eyes, and declare with a sigh— that they're *resigned* to the match. And his dear old grand-ma—She lives here you know? There that is right—your curls should fall in a shower over your snow-white neck—The dear old lady is in a perfect fever to see you! She helped me to get everything ready for the wedding—"

"Oh Bessie—Is it not most sad?" said Mary as her blue eyes shone with a glance of deep feeling—"To think that Albert and you should love one another, so fondly, and after all, that he should die, leaving you alone in this cheerless world! How terrible! *If* Lorraine should die—"

A deep shade of feeling passed over Mary's face, and her lip trembled. Bessie held her head down, for a moment, as her fair fingers, ran twining among the tresses of the Bride. Was it to conceal a tear, or a—smile?

"Alas! *He* is in his grave! Yet it is the *memory* of his love, that makes me take such a warm interest in your union with Lorraine. This plain fillet of silver, with its diamond star—how well it becomes your brow! You never yet found a woman, who knew what it was to love, that would not fight for two true-hearted lovers, against the world! Do you think Mary dear, that I could have sanctioned your flight to this house, if my very soul had not been interested in your happiness? Not I—not I. Now slip off your night-gown my dear—Have you seen the wedding dress?"

"It seems to me—" said Mary, whose thoughts dwelt solely on her love for Lorimer—"That there is something deeply touching in a wedding that is held at this hour of the night! Every thing is calm and tranquil; the earth lies sleeping, while Heaven itself watches over the union of two hearts that are all in all to each other—"

The words look plain and simple, but the tone in which she spoke was one of the deepest feeling. Her very soul was in her words. Her blue eyes dilated with a sudden enthusiasm, and the color went and came along her glowing cheek, until it resembled a fair flower, one moment resting in the shade, the next bathing in the sunlight.

"Let me assist you to put on this wedding dress. Is it not beautiful? That boddice of white silk was Lorrimer's taste. To be sure I gave the dress-maker a few hints. Is it not perfect? How gently the folds of the skirt rest on your figure! It is a perfect fit, I do declare! Why Mary you are *too* beautiful! Well, well, handsome as he is, Lorrimer ought to be half crazy with vanity, when such a Bride is hanging on his arm!"

A few moments sufficed to array the maiden for the bridal.—

Mary stood erect on the floor, blush after blush coursing over her cheek, as she surveyed the folds of her gorgeous wedding dress.

It was in truth a dress most worthy of her face and form. From the shoulders to the waist her figure was enveloped in a boddice of snow-white satin, that gathered over her swelling bosom, with such gracefulness of shape that every beauty of her form,—the width of the shoulders, and the gradual falling off, of the outline of the waist,—was clearly perceptible.

Fitting closely around the bust, it gave to view her fair round neck, half-concealed by the drooping curls of glossy hair, and a glimpse of each shoulder, so delicate and white, swelling away into the fullness of the virgin bosom, that rose heaving above the border of lace. From the waist downward, in many a fold, but with perfect adaptation to her form, the gorgeous skirt of satin, fell sweeping to the floor, leaving one small and tiny foot, enclosed in a neat slipper, that clung to it as though it had grown there, exposed to the eye.

The softened light falling over the rose-hued hangings of the room, threw the figure of the maiden out from the dim back-ground, in gentle and effective prominence. Her brown tresses showering down over each cheek, and falling along her neck and shoulders, waved gently to and fro, and caught a glossy richness from the light. Her fair shoulders, her full bosom, her long but not too slender waist, the downward proportions of her figure, swelling with the full outlines of ripening maidenhood; all arrayed in the graceful dress of snow-white satin, stood out in the dim light, relieved most effectively by the rose-hued hangings, in the background.

As yet her arms, unhidden by sleeve or robe, gave their clear, transparent skin, their fullness of outline, their perfect loveliness of shape, all freely to the light.

"Is it not a gorgeous dress?" said long-haired Bess, as she gazed with unfeigned admiration upon the face and form of the beautiful maiden—"As gorgeous, dear Mary, as you are beautiful!"

"Oh it will be such a happy time!" cried Mary, in a tone that scarcely rose above a whisper, while her blue eyes flashed with a glance of deep emotion—"There will sit my father and there my mother, in the cheerful parlor on Christmas Eve! My father's grey hairs and my mother's kindly face, will be lighted up by the same glow of light. And their eyes will be heavy with tears—with weeping for me, Bessie, their 'lost child,' as they will call me. When behold! the door opens, Lorraine enters with me, his wife, yes, yes *his wife* by his side. We fling ourselves at the feet of our father and mother—for they will be *ours,* then! We crave their forgiveness! Lorraine calls me his wife—we beg their forgiveness and their blessing in the same breath! Oh it will be such a happy time! And my brother he will be there too—*he* will like Lorraine, for he has a noble heart! Don't you see the picture, Bessie? I see it as plainly as though it was this moment before me, and—my father—oh how he will weep when again he clasps his daughter in his arms!"

There she stood, her fair hands clasped trembling together, her eyes flashing in ecstacy, while her heart, throbbing and throbbing like some wild bird, endeavoring to burst the bars of its cage, sent her bosom heaving into view.

Bessie made no reply. True she attempted some common-place phrase, but the words died in her throat. She turned her head away, and—thank God, she was not *yet* fallen to the lowest deep of woman's degradation—a tear, big and scalding, came rolling down her cheek.

And while Mary stood with her eyes gazing on the vacant air, with the manner of one entranced, while Bess—poor and fallen woman!—turned away her face to hide the falling tear, the curtains that concealed the entrance to the Painted Chamber were suddenly thrust aside, and the figure of a man came stealing along with a noiseless footstep.

Gus Lorrimer, silent and unperceived, in all the splendor of his manly beauty, stood gazing upon the form of his victim, with a glance of deep and soul-felt admiration.

His tall form was shown to the utmost advantage, by a plain suit of black cloth. A dress coat of the most exquisite shape, black pantaloons that fitted neatly around his well-formed limbs, a vest of plain white Marseilles,[18] gathering easily across the outlines of his massive chest, a snow-white shirt front, and a falling collar, confined by a simple black cravat; such were the brief details of his neat but effective costume. His manly face was all in a glow with health and excitement. Clustering curls of dark brown hair fell carelessly along his open brow. His clear, dark-hazel eye, gave forth a flashing glance, that failed to reveal anything but the frank and manly qualities of a generous heart. You did not read the villain, in his glance. The aquiline nose, the rounded chin, the curving lip, darkened by a graceful moustache, the arching eyebrows, which gave additional effect to the dark eyes; all formed the details of a countenance that ever struck the beholder with its beaming expression of health, soul, and manliness, combined.

And as Gus Lorrimer stood gazing in silent admiration upon his victim, few of his boon companions would have recognized, in his thoughtful countenance, the careless though handsome face of the reveller, who gave life and spirit to their drinking scenes.

The truth is, there were *two* Lorrimers in *one*. There was a careless, dashing, handsome fellow who could kill a basket of champagne with any body, drive the neatest 'turn out' in the way of horse flesh that the town ever saw, carry a 'frolic' so far that the watchman would feel bound to take it up and carry it a little farther—This was the magnificent Gus Lorrimer.

And then there was a tall, handsome man, with a thoughtful countenance, and a deep, dark hazel eye, who would sit down by the side of an innocent woman, and whisper in her ear, in a low-toned voice for hours together, with an earnestness of manner and an intensity of gaze, that failed in its effect, not once in a hundred times. Without any remarkable knowledge derived from education, this man knew every leaf of woman's many-leaved heart, and knew how to apply the revealings, which the fair book opened to his gaze. His gaze, in some cases, in itself was fascination; his low-toned voice, in too many instances, whispered its sentences of passion to ears, that heard it to their eternal sorrow. This man threw his whole soul, in his every passion. He plead with a woman, like a man under sentence of death pleading for his life. Is it a wonder that he was but rarely unsuccessful? This man, so deeply read in woman's heart, was the 'inner man' of the

---

[18]A firm cotton fabric.

handsome fellow, with the dashing exterior. Assuming a name, never spoken to his ear, save in the soft whispers of one of his many victims, he styled himself Lorraine Lorrimer.

"Oh, Bessie, is not this Love—a strange mystery?" exclaimed Mary, as though communing with her own heart—"Before I loved, my soul was calm and quiet. I had no thought beyond my school-books—no deeper mystery than my embroidery-frame. *Now*—the very air is changed. The atmosphere in which I breathe is no longer the same. Wherever I move *his* face is before me. Whatever may be my thoughts, the thought of *him* is never absent for a moment. In my dreams I see him smile. When awake, his eyes, so deep, so burning in their gaze—even when he is absent—seem forever looking into mine. Oh, Bessie—tell me, tell me—is it given to man to adore his God? Is it not also given to woman to adore the *one* she loves? Woman's *religion* is her *love*—"

And as the beautiful enthusiast, *whose mind had been developed in utter seclusion from the world,* gave forth these revelations of her heart, in broken and abrupt sentences, Lorrimer drew a step nearer, and gazed upon her with a look in which passion rose predominant, even above admiration.

"Oh, Bessie, can it be that his love will ever grow cold? Will his voice ever lose its tones of gentleness, will his gaze ever cease to bind me to him, as it enchains me now?"

"Mary!" whispered a strange voice in a low and softened murmur.

She turned hastily round, she beheld the arms outspread to receive her, she saw the manly face of him she loved all a-glow with rapture, her fair blue eyes returned his gaze, "Lorraine," she murmured, in a faint whisper, and then her head rested upon his bosom, while her form trembled in his embrace.

"Oh, Lorraine—" she again murmured, as, with one fair hand resting upon each arm of her lover, she gazed upward in his face, while her blue eyes shone with all the feeling of her inmost soul. "Oh—Lorraine—will you love me ever?"

"Mary—" he answered, gazing down upon her blushing face, as he uttered her name in a prolonged whisper, that gave all its melody of sound to her ear—"Mary can you doubt me?"

And as there he stood gazing upon that youthful face, now flushed over with an expression of all-trusting love, as he drank in the glance of her large blue eyes, and felt her trembling form resting gently in his arms, the foul purpose of his heart was, for a moment, forgotten, for a moment his heart rose swelling within him, and the thought flashed over his soul, that for the fair creature, who hung fascinated on his every look, his life he could willingly lay down.

"Ha-ha—" muttered Bess, who stood regarding the pair with a glance of doubtful meaning—"I really believe that Lorrimer is quite as much in love, as the poor child! Good idea, that! A man, whose heart has been the highway of a thousand loves—a man like this, to fall in love with a mere baby-face! Mary, dear—" she continued aloud, too happy to break the reverie which enchained the seducer and his victim—"Mary, dear, hadn't I better help you to put on your wedding robe?"

Lorrimer turned and looked at her with a sudden scowl of anger. In a moment his face resumed its smile—

"Mary—" he cried, laughingly—"let me be your costumer, for once. My hands must help you on with the wedding robe. Nay, nay, you must not deny me. Hand me the dress, Bessie—"

It was a splendid robe of the same satin, as the other part of her dress. Gathering tightly around her form, it was designed to remain open in front, while the skirt fell trailing along the floor. Falling aside from the bust, where outlines were so gracefully developed by the tight-fitting boddice of white satin, its opposite sides were connected by interlacing threads of silvercord, crossed and recrossed over the heaving bosom. Long and drooping sleeves, edged with silver lace, were designed to give bewitching glimpses of the maiden's full and rounded arms. In fine, the whole dress was in the style of some sixty years since, such as our grand-dames designated by the euphonious name of 'a gown and curricle.'

"How well the dress becomes you Mary!" exclaimed Lorrimer with a smile as he flung the robe over her shoulders—"How elegant the fall of that sleeve! Ha—ha—Mary, you *must* allow me to lace these silver cords in front. I'm afraid I would make but an awkward lady's-maid. What say you Bessie? Mary, your arms seem to love the light embrace of these drooping sleeves. You must forgive me, Mary, but I thought the style of the dress would please you, so I asked our good friend Bessie here to have it made. By my soul, you give additional beauty to the wedding dress. Is she not beautiful Bessie?"

"Most beautiful—" exclaimed Bess, as for the moment, her gaze of unfeigned admiration was fixed upon the Bride, arrayed in the full splendor of her wedding robes— "Most beautiful!"

"Mary, your hand—" whispered Lorrimer to the fair girl, who stood blushing at his side.

With a heaving bosom, and a flashing eye, Mary slowly reached forth her fair and delicate right hand. Lorrimer grasped the trembling fingers within his own, and winding his unoccupied arm around her waist he suffered her head, with all its shower of glossy tresses, to fall gently on his shoulders. A blush, warm and sudden, came over her face. He impressed one long and lingering kiss upon her lips. They returned the pressure, and clung to his lips as though they had grown there.

"Mary, my own sweet love—" he murmured in a low tone, that thrilled to her very heart—"Now I kiss you as the dearest thing to me in the wide world. Another moment, and from those same lips will I snatch the first kiss of my lovely bride! To the Wedding Room my love!"

Fair and blushing as the dawn, stainless as the new-fallen snow, loving as one of God's own cherubim, he led her gently from the place, motioning onward with his hand as again and again he whispered "To the Wedding Room my love, to the Wedding Room!"

"To the Wedding Room—" echoed Bess who followed in her Brides-maid robes— "To the Wedding Room—ha, ha, ha, say rather to h——ll!"

There was something most solemn, not to say thoughtful and melancholy, in the appearance of that lonely room. It was wide and spacious, and warmed by invisible means, with heated air. Huge panels of wainscotting covered the lofty walls, and even the ceiling was concealed by massive slabs of dark walnut. The floor was all one polished surface of mahogany, destitute of carpet or covering of any kind. A few high-backed mahogany chairs, standing along the walls, were the only furniture of the place. The entrance to the Rose Chamber, was concealed by a dark curtain, and in the western, and northern walls, were fashioned two massive doors, formed like the wainscotting, of dark and gloomy walnut.

In the centre of the glittering mahogany floor, arose a small table or altar, covered with a drooping cloth, white and stainless as the driven snow. Two massive wax candles, placed in candlesticks of silver, stood on the white cloth of the altar, imparting a dim and dusky light to the room. In that dim light the sombre panelling of the walls and the ceiling, the burnished floor of mahogany as dark as the walnut-wood that concealed the ceiling and the walls, looked heavy and gloomy, as though the place was a vault of death, instead of a cheerful Wedding Room.

As yet the place was silent and solitary. The light flickered dimly along the walls, and over the mahogany floor, which shone like a rippling lake in the moonlight. As you gazed upon the desolate appearance of that place, with the solitary wax lights burning like two watching souls, in the centre, you would have given the world, to have seen the room tenanted by living beings; in its present stillness and solitude, it looked so much like, one of those chambers in olden story, where the ghosts of a departed family, were wont to assemble once a year, in order to revive the memories of their lives on earth.

It might have been three o'clock, or even half an hour later, when the western door swung slowly open, and the Clergyman, who was to solemnize this marriage, came striding somewhat unsteadily along the floor. Clad in robes of flowing white—he had borrowed them from the Theatre—with a Prayer Book in his hand, Petriken as he glanced uneasily around the room, did not look at all unlike a Minister of a particular class. His long, square, lugubrious face, slightly varied by red streaks around each eye, was tortured into an expression of the deepest solemnity. He took his position in silence, near the Altar.

Then came the relenting Uncle, striding heavily at the parson's heels—He was clad in a light blue coat with metal buttons, a buff vest, striped trowsers, and an enormous scarf, whose mingled colors of blue and gold, gathered closely around his short fat neck. His full-moon face—looking very much like the face of a relenting uncle, who is willing to bestow mercy upon a wild young dog of a nephew, to almost any extent—afforded a pleasing relief to his pear-shaped nose, which stood out in the light, like a piece of carved work from a crimson wall. Silently the relenting Uncle, took his position beside the venerable Clergyman.

Then dressed in solemn black, the respected Grand-ma of the Bridegroom, who was in *such* a fever to see the Bride, came stepping mincingly along the floor, glancing from side to side with an amiable look that ruffled the yellowish flesh of her colloped cheeks.

The 'imperial' on her chin had been softened down, and with the aid of a glossy dress of black silk, and a tower of Babel cap, she looked quite venerable. Had it not been for a certain twinkle in her eyes, you could have fallen in her arms and kissed her; she looked so much like one of those dear old souls, who make mischief in families and distribute tracts and cold victuals to the poor. The Grand-ma took her position on the left of the Clergyman.

And in this position, gathered around the Altar, they stood for some five minutes silently awaiting the appearance of the Bridegroom and the Bride.

CHAPTER TENTH

❧ The Bridal

"I say Mutchy, my boy—" said Petriken, in a tone that indicated some lingering effects of his late debauch—"How *do* I do it? Clever—hey? D'ye like this face? *Good*—is it? If my magazine fails, I think I'll enter the ministry for good. Why not start a Church of my own? When a man's fit for nothin' else, he can always find fools enough to build him a church, and glorify him into a saint—"

"Do you think I *do* the Uncle well?" whispered Mutchins, drawing his shirt collar up from the depths of his scarf, into which it had fallen—"Devilish lucky you gave me the hint in time. 'Been the d——l to pay if we'd a-disappointed Gus. What am I to say, Silly. 'Is *she* not *beautiful!*' in a sort of an *aside* tone, and then fall on her neck and kiss her? Eh, Silly?'

"That'ill be coming it a little *too* strong—" said Petriken, smoothing back his tow-colored hair—"You're merely to take her by the fingertips, and start as if her beauty overcame you, then exclaim 'God bless you my love, God bless you—' as though your feelings were too strong for utterance—"

"'God bless you, my love—'" echoed Mutchins—"'God bless you'—that will do—hey, Silly? I feel quite an interest in her already. Now Aunty, my dear and kindhearted old relative, what in the d——l are *you* to do?"

"Maybe I'll get up a convulsion or two—" said the dear old lady, as her colloped cheeks waggled heavily with a smile—her enemies would have called it a hideous grin—"Maybe I'll do a hysteric or so. Maybe I won't? Dear me, I'm in sich a fever to see my little pet of a grand-daughter! Ain't I?"

"Hist!" whispered Petriken—"There they are in the next room. I think I heard a kiss. Hush! Here they come—d——n it, I can't find the marriage ceremony—"

No sooner had the words passed his lips, than Lorrimer appeared in the small doorway opening into the Rose Chamber, and stepped softly along the floor of the Walnut Room. Mary in all her beauty hung on his arm. Her robe of satin wound round her limbs, and trailed along the floor as she walked. At her side came Long-haired Bess, glancing in the faces of the wedding guests with a meaning smile.

"Nephew, I forgive you. God bless you, my dear—I approve my nephew's choice— God bless you, my dear—"

And, as though his feelings overcame him, Mutchins veiled his face in a large red handkerchief; beneath whose capacious shelter he covertly supplied his mouth with a fresh morsel of tobacco.

"And is *this* 'my grandchild?' Is this the dear pet? How shall I love her? Shan't I, grandson? Oh my precious, how do you *do?*"

The clergyman saluted the bride with a low bow.

A deep blush came mantling over Mary's face as she received these words of affection and tokens of kindness from the Minister and the relatives of her husband, while a slight, yet meaning, expression of disgust flashed over Lorrimer's features, as he observed the manner in which his minions and panders performed their parts.

With a glance of fire, Lorrimer motioned the clergyman to proceed with the ceremony.

This was the manner of the marriage.

Hand joined in hand, Lorrimer and Mary stood before the altar. The bridesmaid stood near the trembling bride, whispering slight sentences of consolation in her ear. On the right hand of the clergyman, stood Mutchins, his red round face, subdued into an expression of the deepest solemnity; on the other side, the vile hag of Monk-hall, with folded arms, and grinning lips, calmly surveyed the face of the fair young bride.

In a deep-toned voice, Petriken began the sublime marriage ceremony of the Protestant Episcopal Church. There was no hope for the bride now. Trapped, decoyed, betrayed, she was about to be offered up, a terrible sacrifice, on that unhallowed altar. Her trembling tones, joined with the deep voice of Lorrimer in every response, and the marriage ceremony, drew near its completion. "There is no hope for her *now*"—muttered Bess, as her face shone with a glance of momentary compassion—"She is sold into the arms of shame!"

And at that moment, as the bride stood in all her beauty before the altar, her eyes downcast, her long hair showering down over her shoulders, her face warming with blush after blush, while her voice in low tones murmured each trembling response of the fatal ceremony, at the very moment when Lorrimer gazing upon her face with a look of the deepest satisfaction, fancied the fulfilment of the maiden's dishonour, there shrieked from the next chamber, a yell of such superhuman agony and horror, that the wedding guests were frozen with a sudden awe, and transfixed like figures of marble to the floor.

The book fell from Petriken's trembling hands; Mutchins turned pale, and the old hag started backward with sudden horror, while Bess stood as though stricken with the touch of death. Mary, poor Mary, grew white as the grave-cloth, in the face; her hand dropped stiffly to her side, and she felt her heart grow icy within her bosom.

Lorrimer alone, fearless and undaunted, turned in the direction from whence that fearful yell had shrieked, and as he turned he started back with evident surprise, mingled with some feelings of horror and alarm.

There, striding along the floor, came the figure of a young man, whose footsteps trembled as he walked, whose face was livid as the face of a corpse, whose long black hair waved wild and tangled, back from his pale forehead. His eye—Great God!—it shone as with a gleam from the flames of hell.

He moved his trembling lips, as he came striding on—for a moment the word, he essayed to speak, struck in his throat.

At last with a wild movement of his arms, he shouted in a voice whose tones of horror, mingled with heart-rendering pathos, no man would like to hear twice in a life time, he shouted a single word—

"Mary!"

The bride turned slowly round. Her face was pale as death, and her blue eyes grew glassy as she turned. She beheld the form of the intruder. One glance was enough.

"My Brother!" she shrieked, and started forward as though about to spring in the strangers arms; but suddenly recoiling she fell heavily upon the breast of Lorrimer.

There was a moment of silence—all was hushed as the grave.

The stranger stood silent and motionless, regarding the awe-stricken bridal party, with one settled and burning gaze. One and all, they shrank back as if blasted by his look. Even Lorrimer turned his head aside and held his breath, for very awe.

The stranger advanced another step, and stood gazing in Lorrimer's face.

"*My Sister!*" he cried in a husky voice, and then as if all further words died in his throat, his face was convulsed by a spasmodic movement, and he shook his clenched hand madly in the seducer's face.

"Your name—" cried Lorrimer, as he laid the fainting form of the Bride in the arms of Long-haired Bess—"Your name is Byrnewood. This lady is named Mary Arlington. There is some mistake here. The lady is no sister of yours—"

"My name—" said the other, with a ghastly smile—"Ask this palefaced craven what is my name! He introduced me to you, this night by my full name. You at once forgot, all but my first name. My name, sir, is *Byrnewood Arlington.* A name, sir, you will have cause to remember in this world and—devil that you are!—in the next if you harm the slightest hair on the head of this innocent girl—"

Lorrimer started back aghast. The full horror of his mistake rushed upon him. And in that moment, while the fainting girl lay insensible in Bessie's arms; while Petriken, and Mutchins, and the haggard old Abbess of the den, stood stricken dumb with astonishment, quailing beneath the glance of the stranger; a long and bony arm was thrust from behind the back of Byrnewood Arlington, the grim face Devil-Bug shone for a moment in the light, and then a massive hand with talon-fingers, fell like a weight upon the wick of each candle, and the room was wrapt in midnight blackness.

Then there was a trampling of feet to and fro, a gleam of light flashed for a moment, through the passage, opening into the Rose Chamber, and then all was dark again.

"They are bearing my sister away!" was the thought that flashed over the mind of the Brother, as he rushed toward the passage of the Rose Chamber—"I will rescue her from their grasp at the peril of my life!"

He rushed along, in the darkness, toward the curtain that concealed the entrance into the Rose Chamber. He attempted to pass beyond the curtain, but he was received in the embrace of two muscular arms, that raised him from his feet as though he had been a mere child, and then dashed him to the floor, with the impulse of a giant's strength.

"Ha-ha-ha!—" laughed a hoarse voice—"You don't pass here, Mister. Not while 'Bijah's about! No you don't, my feller—ha, ha, ha!"

"A light, Devil-Bug—" exclaimed a voice, that sounded from the centre of the darkened room.

In a moment a light, grasped in the talon-fingers of the Doorkeeper of Monk-Hall, flashed around the place. Silent and alone Gus Lorrimer, stood in the centre of the room, his arms folded across his breast, while the dark frown on his brow was the only outward manifestation of the violence of the struggle that had convulsed his very soul, during that solitary moment of utter darkness. Calling all the resources of his mind to his aid, he had resolved upon his course of action.

"*It is a fearful remedy, but a sure one—*" he muttered as he again faced Byrnewood, who had just risen from the floor, where he had been thrown by Mr. Abijah K. Jones— "Begone Devil-Bug—" he continued aloud—"But wait without and see that Glow-worm and Musquito are at hand," He added in a meaning whisper. "Now Sir, I have a word to say to *you*—" And as he spoke he confronted the Brother of the girl, whose ruin he had contrived with the ingenuity of an accomplished libertine, mingled with all the craft of an incarnate fiend.

Aching in every limb from his recent fall, Byrnewood stood pale and silent, regarding the libertine with a settled gaze. In the effort to command his feelings, he pressed his teeth against his lower lip, until a thin line of blood trickled down to his chin.

"You will allow that this, is a most peculiar case—" he exclaimed with a calm gaze, as he confronted Byrnewood—"One in fact, that demands some painful thought. Will you favor me with ten minutes private conversation?"

"You are very polite—" exclaimed Byrnewood with a withering sneer—"Here is a man, who commits a wrong for which h——ll itself has no name, and then—instead of shrinking from the sight of the man he has injured, beyond the power of words to tell— he cooly demands ten minutes private conversation!"

"It is your interest to grant my request—" replied Lorrimer, with a manner as collected as though he had merely said 'Pass the bottle, Byrnewood!'

"I presume I must submit—" replied Byrnewood—"But after the ten minutes are past—remember—that there is not a fiend in hell whom I would not sooner hug to my bosom, than grant one moment's conversation to—a—a—man—ha, ha—a *man* like you. My sister's honor may be in your power. But remember—that as surely as you wrong her, so surely you will pay for that wrong, with your life—"

"You then, grant me ten minutes conversation? You give me your word that during this period, you will keep your seat, and listen patiently to all, that I may have to say? You nod assent. Follow me, then. A footstep or so this way, will lead us to a pleasant room, the last of this range, where we can talk the matter over—"

He flung open the western door of the Walnut room, and led the way along a narrow entry, up a stairway with some five steps, and in a moment stood before a small doorway, closing the passage at the head of the stairs. At every footstep of the way, he held the light extended at arms length, and regarded Byrnewood with the cautious glance of a man who is not certain at what moment, a concealed enemy may strike him in the back.

"My Library Sir—" exclaimed Lorrimer as pushing open the door, he entered a small oblong room, some twenty-feet in length and about half that extent in width. "A quiet little place where I sometimes amuse myself with a book. There is a chair Sir— please be seated—"

Seating himself upon a small stool, that stood near the wall of the room, furthest from the door, Byrnewood with a single glance, took in all the details of the place, It was a small unpretending room, oblong in form, with rows of shelves along its longest walls, facing each other, supplied with books of all classes, and of every description, from the pondrous history to the trashy novel. The other walls at either end, were concealed by plain and neat paper, of a modern pattern, which by no means harmonized with the ancient style of the carpet, whose half-faded colors glowed dimly in the light. Along the wall of the chamber opposite Byrnewood, extended an old-fashioned sofa, wide and roomy as a small sleeping couch; and from the centre of the place, arose a massive table, fashioned like a chest, with substantial sides of carved oak, supplying the place of legs. To all appearance it was fixed and jointed, into the floor of the room.

Altogether the entire room, as its details were dimly revealed by the beams of the flickering lamp, wore a cheerless and desolate look, increased by the absence of windows from the walls, and the ancient and worn-out appearance which characterized the stool, the sofa and the table; the only furniture of the place. There was no visible hearth, and no sign of fire, while the air cold and chilling had a musty and unwholesome taint, as though the room had not been visited or opened for years.

Placing the lamp on the solitary table, Lorrimer flung himself carelessly on the sofa, and motioned Byrnewood, to draw his seat nearer to the light. As Byrnewood seated himself beside the chest-like table, with his cheek resting on his hand, the full details of his countenance, so pale, so colorless, so corpse-like, were disclosed to the keen gaze of Lorrimer. The face of the Brother, was perfectly calm, although the large black eyes, dilated with a glance that revealed the Soul, turning madly on itself and gnawing its own life, in very madness of thought, while from the lips tightly compressed, there still trickled down, the same thin line of blood, rendered even more crimson and distinct, by the extreme pallor of the countenance.

"You will at least admit, that *I have won the wager*—" said Lorrimer, in a meaning tone, as he fixed his gaze upon the death-like countenance of Byrnewood Arlington.

Byrnewood started, raised his hands suddenly, as if about to grasp the libertine by the throat, and then folding his arms tightly over his chest, he exclaimed in a voice marked by unatural calmness—

"For ten minutes, sir, I have promised to listen to all—*all* you may have to say. Go on, sir. But do not, I beseech you, tempt me too far—"

"Exactly half-past three by my repeater—" cooly replied Lorrimer, looking at his watch—"At twenty minutes of four, our conversations ends. Very good. Now, sir, listen to my proposition. Give me your word of honor, and your oath, that when you leave this house, you will preserve the most positive secrecy with regard to—to—*everything*—you may have witnessed within its walls; promise me this, under your word of honor and your solemn oath, and I will give you my word of honor, my oath, that, in one hour from daybreak, your sister shall be taken to her home, pure and stainless, as when first she left her father's threshold. Do you agree to this?"

"Do you see this hand?" answered Byrnewood, with a nervous tremour of his lips, that imparted an almost savage sneer to his countenance—"Do you see this flame? Sooner than agree to leave these walls, without—my—my—without Mary, pure and stainless, mark ye, I would hold this good right hand in the blaze of this lamp, until the flesh fell blackened and festering from the very bone. Are you answered?"

"Excuse me, sir—I was not speaking of any *anatomical experiments;* however interesting such little efforts in the surgical line, may be to you. I wished to make a compromise—"

"*A compromise!*" echoed Byrnewood.

"Yes, a compromise. That melodramatic sneer becomes you well, but it would suit the pantomimist at the Walnut street Theatre much better. What have I done with the girl, that you, or any other young blood about town, would *not do,* under similar circumstances. Who was it, that entered so heartily into the joke of the *sham* marriage, when it was named in the Oyster Cellar? Who was it called the astrologer a knave—a fortune teller—a catch-penny cheat, when he—simple man!—advised me to give up the girl? I perceive, sir, you are touched. I am glad to observe, that you appreciate the graphic truth of my remarks. You will not sneer at the word '*compromise*' again, will you?"

"Oh, Mary! oh, Mary!"—whispered Byrnewood, drawing his arms yet more closely over his breast, as though in the effort to command his agitation—"Mary! Was I placing your honor in the dice-box, when I made the wager with yonder—*man?* Was it your ruin the astrologer foretold, when he urged this *devil*—to turn back in his career? Was it my *voice* that cheered *him* onward in his work of infamy? Oh Mary, was it for *this,* for *this,* that I loved you as brother never loved sister? Was it for this, that I wound you close to my inmost heart, since first I could think or feel? Was it for *this,* that in the holiest of all my memories, all my hopes, your name was enshrined? Was it for this, that I pictured, again and again, every hour in the day, every moment of the night, the unclouded prospects of your future life? Oh Mary, oh Mary, I may be wrong, I may be vile, I may be sunken as low as the *man* before me, yet my love for you, has been without spot, and without limit! And now Mary—oh *now*—"

He paused. There was a husky sound in his throat, and the blood trickled faster from his tortured lip.

Lorrimer looked at him silently for a moment, and then, taking a small pen-knife from his pocket, began to pare his nails, with a quiet and absent air, as though he did'nt exactly know what to do with himself. He wore the careless and easy look of a gentleman, who having just dined, is wondering where in the deuce he shall spend the afternoon.

"I say, Byrnie my boy—" he cried suddenly, with his eyes fixed or the operations of the knife—"Devilish odd, ain't it? That little affair of yours, with *Annie?* Wonder if she has any *brother?* Keen cut *that*—"

Had Mr. Lorrimer intended the allusion, about the keenness of the 'cut,' for Byrnewood instead of his nail-paring knife, the remark would, perhaps, have been equally applicable. Byrnewood shivered at the name of Annie, as though an ague-fit had passed suddenly over him. The 'cut' was rather keen, and somewhat deep. This careless kind of intellectual surgery, sometimes makes ghastly wounds in the soul, which it so pleasantly dissects.

"May I ask what will be your course, in case you leave this place, without the lady? You are silent. I suppose there will be a suit instituted for '*abduction,*' and a thousand legal et ceteras? This place will be ransacked for the girl, and your humble servant will be threatened with the Penitentiary? A pleasant prospect, truly. Why do you look so earnestly at that hand?"

"You have your pleasant prospects—I have mine—" exclaimed Byrnewood with a convulsive smile—"You see that right hand, do you? I was just thinking, how long it might be, ere that hand would be reddened with your heart's blood—"

"Poh! poh! Such talk is d——d boyish. D'ye agree to my proposition? Yes or no?"

"You have had my answer—"

"In case I surrender the girl to you, will you then promise unbroken secrecy, with regard to the events of this night?"

"I will make no terms whatever with a *scoundrel* and a *coward!*" hissed Byrnewood, between his clenched teeth.

"Pshaw! It is high time this mask should be cast aside—" exclaimed Lorrimer, as his eye flashed with an expression of triumph, mingled with anger and scorn—"And do you suppose that on any condition, or for any consideration, I would leave this fair prize slip from my grasp? Why, innocent that you are, you might have piled oath on oath, until your very breath grew husky in the effort, and still—still—despite of all your oaths, the girl would remain mine!

"Know me as I am! Not the mere man-about-town, not the wine-drinking companion, not the fashionable addle-head you think me, but the *Man of Pleasure!* You will please observe, how much lies concealed in that title. You have talents—these talents have been from childhood, devoted to books, or mercantile pursuits. I have some talent—I flatter myself—and that talent, aided and strengthened in all its efforts, by wealth, from very boyhood, has been devoted to Pleasure, which, in plain English, means—Woman.

"Woman—the means of securing her affection, of compassing her ruin, of enjoying her beauty, has been my book, my study, my science, nay my *profession* from boyhood. And am I, to be foiled in one of the most intricate of all my adventures, by such a child—a mere boy like you? Are you to frighten me, to scare me back in the path I have chosen; to wrest this flower, to obtain which I have perilled so much, are *you* to wrest this flower from *my* grasp? You are *so* strong, *so* mighty, you talk of reddening your hand in my heart's blood—and all such silly vaporing, that would be hissed by the pit-boy's, if they but heard it, spouted forth by a fifth-rate hero of the green-room—and yet with all this—*you are my prisoner—*"

"*Your prisoner?*" echoed Byrnewood slowly rising to his feet.

"Keep cool Sir—" cried Lorrimer with a glance of scorn—"Two minutes of the ten, yet remain. I have your word of honor, you will remember. Yes—*my prisoner!* Why do you suppose for a moment, that I would let you go forth from this house, when you have it in your power to raise the whole city on my head? You know that I have placed myself under the ban of the laws by this adventure. You know that the Penitentiary would open its doors to enclose me, in case I was to be tried for this affair. You know that popular indignation, poverty and disgrace, stare me in the very eyes, the moment this adventure is published to the world, and yet—ha, ha, ha—you still think me, the egregious ass, to open the doors of Monk-Hall to you, and pleasantly bid you go forth, and ruin me forever! Sir, you are my prisoner."

"Ha—ha—ha! I will be even with you—" laughed Byrnewood—"You may murder me, in the act but I still have the power to arouse the neighbourhood. I can shriek for help. I can yell out the cry of Murder, from this foul den, until your doors are flung open by the police, and the secrets of your rookery laid bare to the public gaze—"

"Scream, yell, cry out, until your throat cracks! Who will hear you? Do you know how many feet, you are standing, above the level of the earth? Do you know the thickness of these walls? Do you know that you stand in the Tower-Room of Monk-Hall? Try your voice—by all means—I should like to hear you cry Murder or Fire, or even hurra for some political candidate, if the humor takes you—"

Byrnewood sank slowly in his seat, and rested his cheek upon his hand. His face was even paler than before—the consciousness that he was in the power of this libertine, for life or death, or any act of outrage, came stealing round his heart, like the probings of a surgeon's knife.

"Go on Sir—" he muttered biting his nether lip, until the blood once more came trickling down to his chin—"The hour is yours. *Mine will come—*"

"At my bidding; not a moment sooner—" laughed Lorrimer rising his feet—"Why man, death surrounds you in a thousand forms, and you know it not. You may walk on Death, you may breathe it, you may drink it, you may draw it to you with a fingers-touch, and yet be as unconscious of its presence, as a blind man is of a shadow in the night—"

Byrnewood slowly rose from his seat. He clasped his hands nervously together, and his lips muttered an incoherent sound as he endeavoured to speak.

"Do what you will with me—" he cried, in a husky voice—"But oh, for the sake of God, *do not wrong my sister!*"

"She is in *my* power!" whispered Lorrimer, with a smile, as he gazed upon the agitated countenance of the brother—"She is in *my* power!"

"Then by the eternal God, you are in mine!" shrieked Byrnewood, as with one wild bound, he sprung at the tall form of Lorrimer, and fixed both hands around his throat, with a grasp like that of the tigress when she fights for her young—"You are in my power! You cannot unloose my grasp! Ha—ha—you grow black in the face! Struggle!—struggle!—With all your strength you cannot tear my hands from your throat—you shall die like a felon, by the eternal God!"

Lorrimer was taken by complete surprise. The wild bound of Byrnewood had been so sudden, the grasp of his hands, was so much like the terrific clutch with which the drowning man makes a last struggle for life, that for a single moment, the handsome Gus Lorrimer reeled to and fro like a drunken man, while his manly features darkened over with a hue of livid blackness, as ghastly as it was instantaneous. The struggle lasted but a single moment. With the convulsive grasp tightening around his throat, Lorrimer sank suddenly on one knee, dragging his antagonist with him, and as he sank, extending his arm, with an effort as desperate as that which fixed the clinched fingers around his throat, he struck Byrnewood a violent blow with his fist, directly behind the ear. Byrnewood sank senseless to the floor, his fingers unclosing their grasp of Lorrimer's throat, as slowly and stiffly as though they were seized with a sudden cramp.

"Pretty devilish and d——d hasty!" muttered Lorrimer, arranging his cravat and vest—"Left the marks of his fingers on my throat, I'll be bound! Hallo—Musquito! Hallo, Glow-worm—here's work for you!"

The door of the room swung suddenly open, and the herculean negroes stood in the doorway, their sable faces, agitated by the same hideous grin, while the sleeves of the red flannel shirts, which formed their common costume, rolled up to the shoulders disclosed the iron-sinews of their jet-black arms.

"Mark this man, I say—"

"Yes—Massa—I doo-es—" chuckled Musquito, as his loathsome lips, inclining suddenly downward toward the jaw, on either side of his face, were convulsed by a brutal grin—"Dis nigger nebber mark a man yet, but dat *somefin'* cum ob it—"

"Massa Gusty no want de critter to go out ob dis 'ere door?" exclaimed Glow-worm, as the long rows of his teeth, bristling from his thick lips, shone in the light like the fangs of some strange beast—"'Spose he go out ob dat door? 'Spose de nigger no mash him head, *bad?* Ain't Glow-worm got fist? Hah-hah! 'Sketo did you ebber see dis chile (child) knock an ox down? Hah-hah!"

"You are to watch outside the door all night—" exclaimed Lorrimer, as he stood upon the threshold—"Let him not leave the room on the peril of your lives. D'ye mark me, fellows?"

And as he spoke, motioning the negroes from the room, he closed the door and disappeared.

He had not gone a moment when Byrnewood, recovering from the stunning effect of the blow which had saved Lorrimer's life, slowly staggered to his feet, and gazing around with a bewildered glance.

"'*On Christmas Eve*—'" he murmured wildly, as though repeating words whispered to his ear in a dream— "'*On Christmas Eve, at the hour of sundown, one of ye will die by the other's hand—the winding sheet is woven and the coffin made!*'"

CHAPTER ELEVENTH

❧ Devil-Bug

"It don't skeer me, I tell ye! For six long years, day and night, it has laid by my side, with its jaw broke and its tongue stickin' out, and yet I ain't a bit skeered! There it is now— on my left side, ye mind—in the light of the fire. Ain't it an ugly corpse? Hey? A reel nasty christian, I tell ye! Jist look at the knees, drawed up to the chin, jist look at the eyes, hanging out on the cheeks, jist look at the jaw all smashed and broke—look at the big, black tongue, stickin' from between the teeth—say it ain't an ugly corpse, will ye?

"Sometimes I can hear him groan—*only* sometimes! I've always noticed when anything bad is a-goin to come across me, that critter groans and groans! Jist as I struck him down, he lays afore me now. Whiz—wh-i-z he came down the hatchway—three stories, every bit of it! Curse it, why hadn't I the last trap-door open? He fell on the floor, pretty much mashed up, but—but he wasn't dead—

"He riz on his feet. Just as he lays on the floor—in his shirt sleeves, with his jaw broke and his tongue out—he riz on his feet. Didn't he groan? I put him down, I tell ye! Down—down! Ha! What was a sledge hammer to this fist, in that pertikler minnit? Crack, crack went the spring of the last trap-door—and the body fell—the devil knows where—I don't. I put it out o' my sight, and yet it came back to me, and crouched down at my side, the next minnit. It's been there ever since. If I sleep, or if I'm wide awake, it's there—*there*—always on my left side, where I hain't got no eye to see it, and yet I do— I *do* see it. What a cussed fool I was arter all! To kill him, and he not got a cent in his pockets! Bah! Whenever I think of it I grow feverish. And there he is now—With his d——d ugly jaw. How he lolls his tongue out—and his eyes! *Ugh!* But I ain't a bit skeered. No. Not me. I can bear wuss things than that 'are—"

The light from the blazing coal-fire, streamed around the Door-keeper's den. Seated close by the grate, in a crouching attitude, his feet drawn together, his big hands grasping each knee with a convulsive clutch, his head lowered on his breast, and his face, warmed to a crimson red by the glare of the flame, moistened with thick drops of perspiration; Devil-Bug turned the orbless eye-socket to the floor at his left side, as though it was gifted with full powers of sight, while his solitary eye, grew larger and more burning in its fixed gaze, until at last, it seemed to stand out, from his overhanging brow, like a separate flame.

The agitation of the man was at once singular and fearful. Oozing from his swarthy brow, the thick drops of sweat fell trickling over his hideous face, moistening his matted hair, until it hung, damp and heavy over his eyebrows. The lips of his wide mouth receding to his flat nose and pointed chin, disclosed the long rows of bristling teeth, fixed as closely together, as though the man, had been suddenly seized with lock-jaw. His face was all one loathsome grimace, as with his blazing eye, fixed upon the fire, he seemed gazing upon the floor at his left, with the shrunken and eyeless socket, of the other side of his face.

This creature, who sate crouching in the light of the fire, muttering words of strange meaning to himself, presented a fearful study for the Christian and Philanthropist. His Soul was like his body, a mass of hideous and distorted energy.

Born in a brothel, the offspring of foulest sin and pollution, he had grown from very childhood, in full and continual sight of scenes of vice, wretchedness and squalor.

From his very birth, he had breathed an atmosphere of infamy.

To him, there was no such thing as *good* in the world.

His world—his place of birth, his home in infancy, childhood and manhood, his only theatre of action—had been the common house of ill-fame. No mother had ever spoken words of kindness to him; no father had ever held him in his arms. Sister, brother, friends; he had none of these. He had come into the world without a name; his present one, being the standing designation of the successive Doorkeepers of Monk-hall, which he in vain endeavoured to assume, leaving the slang title bestowed on him in childhood, to die in forgetfulness.

Abijah K. Jones he might call himself, but he was Devil-Bug still.

His loathsome look, his distorted form, and hideous soul, all seemed to crowd on his memory, at the same moment, when the word 'Devil-Bug'—rang on his ear. That word uttered, and he stood apart from the human race; that word spoken, and he seemed to feel, that he was something distinct from the mass of men, a wild beast, a snake, a reptile, or a devil incarnate—any thing but a—man.

The same instinctive pleasure that other men, may feel in acts of benevolence, of compassion or love, warmed the breast of Devil-Bug, when enjoyed in any deed, marked by especial *cruelty*. This word will scarcely express the instinctive impulse of his soul, He loved not so much to kill, as to observe the blood of his victim, fall drop by drop, as to note the convulsive look of death, as to hear the last throttling rattle in the throat of the dying.

For years and years, the instinctive impulse, had worked in his own bosom, without vent. The murder which had dyed his hands, with human blood for the first time, some six years ago, opened wide to his soul, the pathway of crime, which it was his doom and his delight to tread. Ever since the night of the Murder, his victim, hideous and repulsive, had lain beside him, crushed and mangled, as he fell through the death-trap. The corpse was never absent from his fancy; which in this instance had assumed the place of eye-sight. Did he sit—it was at his left side. Did he walk—crushed and mangled as it was, it glided with him. Did he sleep—it still was at his side, ever present with him, always staring him in the face, with all its loathsome details of horror and bloodshed.

Since the night of the Murder, a longing desire had grown up, within this creature, to lay another corpse beside his solitary victim. Were there he thought, two corpses, ever at his side, the terrible details of the mangled form and crushed countenance of the first, would lose half their horror, all their distinctness. He longed to surround himself with the Phantoms of new victims. In the *number* of his crimes, he even anticipated pleasure.

It was this man, this deplorable moral monstrosity, who knew no God, who feared no devil, whose existence was one instinctive impulse of cruelty and bloodshed, it was this Outlaw of heaven and earth and hell, who held the life of Byrnewood Arlington in his grasp.

"It's near about mornin' and that ere boy ought to have somethin' to eat. A leetle to drink—per'aps? Now *sup*-pose, I should take him up, a biled chicken and a bottle o' wine. He sits down by the table o' course to eat—I fix his plate on a pertikler side. As he planks down into the cheer, his foot touches a spring. What is the consekence? He git's a fall and hurts hisself. *Sup*-pose he drinks the wine? Three stories down the hatchway—reether an ugly tumble. He git's crazy, and wont know nothin' for days. Very pecooliar wine—got it from the Doctor who used to come here—dint kill a man, only makes him mad-like. The Man with th' Poker is n't nothin' to this stuff—Hallo! Who's there?"

"Only me, Bijah—" cried a woman's voice, and the queenly form of Long Haired Bess with a dark shawl thrown over her bridesmaid's dress advanced toward the light—"I've just left Lorrimer. He's with the girl you know? He sent me down here, to tell you to keep close watch on that young fellow—"

"Jist as if I couldn't do it mesself—" grunted Abijah in his grind-stone voice—"Always a-orderin' a feller about? That's his way. Spose you cant make yourself useful? Kin you? Then take some biled chicken—and a bottle o' wine up to the younk chap. Guess he's most starved—"

"Shall I get the chicken and the wine?" asked Bess gazing steadily in Abijah's face.

"What the thunder you look in my face that way fur? No you shant git 'em. Git 'em mesself. Wait here till I come back. Do'nt let any one in without the pass word—'What hour of the night—' and the answer 'Dinner time—' you know?"

And as Devil-Bug strode heavily from the den, and was heard going down into the cellars of the mansion, Bess stood silent and erect before the fire, her face, shadowed by an expression of painful thought, while her dark eyes, shot a wild glance from beneath her arching brows, suddenly compressed in a frown.

"Some mischief at work I suppose—" she whispered in a hissing voice—"I've sold myself to shame, but not to Murder!"

A low knock resounded from the front door.

Suddenly undrawing the bolt and flinging the chain aside, Bess gazed through a crevice of the opened door, upon the new-comers, who stood beyond the out-side door of green blinds.

"Who's there?" she said in a low voice.

"Ha—ha—" laughed one of the strangers—"It's bonny Bess. 'What hour of the night' is it, my dear?"

"'Dinner time', you fool—" replied the young lady opening the outside door—"Come in Luke! Ha! There is a stranger with you! *Your friend* Luke?"

"Aye, aye, Bessie my love,—" answered Luke as he entered the den, with the stranger at his side—"Did ye hear the Devil-Bug say, whether there was fire in my room? all right—hey? And *cards* you know Bess—*cards?* This gentleman and I, want to amuse ourselves with a little game. Bye-the-bye—where's Fitz-Cowles? I should like him to join us. Seen him to night my dear?"

"Up stairs you know Luke—" answered Bess with a meaning smile—" '*Veiled figure,*' Luke you know? That's a game above your fancy I should suppose?"

And as she said this with an expressive glance of her dark eye, Bess observed that the stranger who accompanied Luke, was a very tall, stout man, wrapped up in a thick overcoat, whose upraised collar, concealed his face to the very eyes. His eyes were visible for a single moment, however as half-hidden by the shadow of Luke's figure, the stranger strode swiftly across the floor of the den. Bess started, with a feeling of terror, akin to the awe one experiences in the presence of a madman, as those eyes, so calm and yet so burning in their fixed gaze, flashed for a moment in the red light.

"Luke, I am—ready—" said the Stranger in a smothered voice—"To *the room* Luke—to *the Room!*"

Without a word Luke led the way from the den, and in a moment Bess heard the half-hushed sound of their footsteps, as they ascended the staircase of the mansion.

"That's a strange eye for a man who's only *a-goin'* to play cards—" muttered Bess as she stood by the fireplace—"Now it's more like the eye of a man, who's been playin' all night, and lost his very soul in a game with the D——l! Lord!—But that's a wicked eye for a dark night!"

"Here's the biled chicken and the wine—" grated the harsh voice of Devil-Bug, who approached the fire, with a large 'waiter' in his arms—"Take it up to the feller, Bess. He's hungry praps? And d'ye mind gal—set his plate on the side of the table, furthest from the door?"

"Any particular reason for that, 'Bijah?"

"Cuss it gal, cant you do it, without axeing questions? It's only a whim o' mine. That bottle is worth its weight in red goold. Don't taste such Madeery every day I tell you. Poor fellow—guess he's a-most starved—"

"Well, well, I'll take him the chicken and the wine—" exclaimed Bess pleasantly as she took possession of the 'waiter' with its cold chicken and luscious wine—"Hang it though, when I come to think o' it, why couldn't you have taken it up yourself? 'Bijah you're growin' lazy—"

"Mind gal—" grunted Devil-Bug as the girl disappeared through the door—"Set his plate on the side of the table furthest from the door. D'ye hear? It's a whim o' mine—furthest from the door—d'ye hear"

"'Furthest from the door'—" echoed Bess, and in a moment her foot-steps resounded with a low pattering noise along the massive staircase.

"The *Spring*— and the *bottle*—" muttered Devil-Bug as he resumed his seat beside the fire—"It seems to me, I should like to creep up stairs, and listen at his door to see how them things work. The niggers is there: but no matter. May be he'll howl—or groan—or do all sorts of ravin's? Gusty did not exactly tell me to do all this—but I guess he'll grin as wide as any body, *when the thing is done.* It seems to me I should like, to see how them things works. It'ud be nice to listen a bit at his door. Wonder if that gal suspicions anything?"

He rubbed his hands earnestly together, as a man is want to do, under the influence of some pleasing idea, and his solitary eye, dilated and sparkled, with a glance of the most remarkable satisfaction. A slight chuckle shook his distorted frame, and his lips performed a succession of vivid spasms which an ignorant observer might have confounded under the general name of laughter.

"Poor feller—guess he's cold without a fire—" said complacent Devil-Bug as he rubbed his hands cheerfully together—"I might build him a little fire. I might—I might—ha! ha! ha!" he arose slowly to his feet, and laughed so loud, that the echoes of his voice resounded from the den, along the hall, and up the staircase of the mansion— "I might try *that*"—he cried with a hideous glow of exultation—"Wonder *how that* would *work?*"

Opening the door of a closet on one side of the fire-place, he drew from its depths, a small furnace of iron; such as housewives use for domestic purposes. He placed the furnace in the full light of the fire, surveyed it closely, rubbed his hands pleasantly together yet once more, while a deep chuckle shook his form, from head to foot. His face wore an expression of extreme good humor—the visage of a drunken loafer, as he flings a penny to a ragged sweep, was nothing in comparison.

"A leetle kindlin' wood—" he muttered, drawing to the fire an old sack that had lain concealed in the darkness—"And a leetle charcoal! Makes a *rougeing* hot fire! Fat pine and charcoal—ha, ha, ha! Rather guess the poor fellow's cold! Now for a light—Cuss it how the fat pin blazes!"

He waited but a single moment for the wood and charcoal to ignite. It flared up at first in a smoky blaze, and then subsided into a clear and brilliant flame. Seizing the iron handle of the furnace Devil-Bug suddenly raised it from the floor, and rushed from the den, and up the staircase of the mansion, as though his very life hung on his speed. And as he ascended the stairway, the light of the furnace gradually increasing to a vivid flame, was thrown upward over his hideous face, turning the beetling brow, the flat nose and the wide mouth with its bristling teeth, to a hue of dusky red. One moment as he swung the furnace from side to side, you beheld his face and form in a glow of blood red light, and the next it was suddenly lost to view, while the vessel of iron, with its burning coals, seemed gliding up the stairway, impelled by a single swarthy hand, with fingers like talons and sinews starting out from the skin like knotted cords.

"Halloo! I didn't know Monk Luke was in his room—" he muttered, as he paused for a moment before a massive door, opening into the hall, which extended along the mansion, above the first stairway—"There's a streak of light from the keyhole of his door! And voices inside the room—but no matter! The charcoal's a-burnin'—and— wonder how *that'ill work?*"

And up the staircase of the mansion he pursued his way, flinging the blazing furnace from side to side, while his face, grew like the visage of a very devil, as again the words rose to his lips—

"The charcoal's a-burnin'—wonder how *that'*ill work?"

The light still flickered through the keyhole of the massive door.

Within the sombre panels, it shone over the rich furniture of an apartment, long and wide, with high ceiling and wainscotted walls. There was a gorgeous carpet on the floor, a thickly curtained bed in one corner, a comfortable fire burning in the grate, and a large table standing near the center of the room, on which a plain lamp, darkened by a heavy shade, was burning. The shade flung the light of the lamp down over the table—it was covered with books, cards, and wine glasses—and around the carpet, for the space of a yard or more, while the other portions of the apartment, were enveloped in faint twilight.

And in that dim light, near the fire, stood two men, steadfastly regarding each other in the face. The snake-like eye of the tall and slender man, was fixed in keen gaze upon the bronzed face of his companion, whose stout and imposing form seemed yet more large and commanding in its proportions, as occasional flashes from the fireplace lighted up the dim twilight. It was a strange thing, to see those large blue eyes, gleaming from the bronzed face, with such a calm and yet burning lustre.

"Luke—to the—the—*room*—" whispered a voice, husky with suppressed agitation.

"He is calm—" muttered Luke to himself—"I led him a d——l of a way in order to give him time to command his feelings. He is calm now—and it's *too late to go back*."

Extending his hand he reached a small dark lanthern from the mantel-piece, and walked softly across the floor. Opening the door of a wide closet, he motioned Livingstone to approach.

"You see, this is rather a spacious closet—" Luke whispered, as silently drawing Livingstone within the recess, he closed the door, leaving them enveloped in thick darkness—"The back wall of the closet, is nothing less than a portion of the wainscotting of the next room. Give me your hand—it is firm, by G——d!—Do you feel that bolt? It's a little one, but once withdrawn, the panelling swings away from the closet like a door, and—egad!—the next room lays before you!"

While Livingstone stood in the thick darkness of the closet, silent as death, Luke slowly drew the bolt. Another touch, and the door would swing open into the next room. Luke could hear the hard breathing of the Merchant, and the hand which he touched suddenly became cold as ice.

As though by mere accident, in that moment of suspense, when their joined fingers touched the bolt, Harvey allowed the door of the dark lanthern, to spring suddenly open. The face of Livingstone, every line and feature, was disclosed in the light, with appaling distinctness. Luke was prepared for a sight of some interest, but no sooner did the light fall on the Merchant's face, than he gave a start of involuntary horror. It was as though the face of a corpse, suddenly recalled to life, had risen before him. White and livid and ghastly, with the discolored circles of flesh deepening beneath each eye, and with the large blue eyes, steadily glaring from the dark eyebrows, it was a countenance to strike the very heart with fear and horror. The firm lips wore a blueish hue, as though the man had been dead for days, and corruption was eating its way through his vitals. Around his high and massive brow, hung his hair, in slight masses; fearful streaks of white resting like scattered ashes, among the locks of dark brown.

"Well, Luke—you see—I am calm—" whispered Livingstone, smiling, with his lips still compressed—"I—am—calm—"

Luke slowly withdrew the bolt, and closed the door of the lanthern. The secret door, of the wainscotting swung open with a faint noise.

"Listen!" he whispered to Livingstone, as the dark room lay before them—"Listen!"

And with his very breath hushed, Livingstone silently listened. A low sound like a woman breathing in her sleep, came faintly to his ear. Luke felt the Merchant start as though he was reeling beneath a sudden blow.

"Give me the dark lanthern—" whispered Livingstone—"*The pistols I have!*" he continued, hissing the words through his clinched teeth—"The room is dark, but I can discern the outlines of the bed—"

He pressed Luke by the hand with a firm grasp, took the lanthern, carefully closing its door, and strode with a noiseless footstep, into the dark room.

Luke remained in the closet, listening with hushed breath.

There was a pause for a moment. It seemed an age to the listener. Not a sound, not a footstep, not even the rustling of the bed-curtains. All was silent as the grave-vault, which has not been disturbed for years.

Luke listened. He leaned from the closet and gazed into the dark room. It was indeed dark. Not the outline of a chair, or a sofa, or the slightest piece of furniture could he discern. True, near the centre of the place, arose a towering object, whose outlines seemed a shade lighter than the rest of the room. This might be the bed, thought Luke, and again, holding his breath, he listened for the slightest sound.

All was dark and still.

Presently Luke heard a low gurgling noise, like the sound produced by a drowning man. Then all was silent as before.

In a moment the gurgling noise was heard again, and a sudden blaze of light streamed around the room.

CHAPTER TWELFTH

❧ The Tower Room

"My sister is in his power, for any act of wrong, for any deed of outrage! And I cannot strike a blow in her defence! A solitary wall may separate us—in one room the sister pleads with the villain for mercy—in the other, trapped and imprisoned, the brother hears her cry of agony, and cannot—cannot raise a finger in her behalf! Ha! The door is fast—I hear the hushed breathing of negroes on the other side. I have read many legends of a place of torment in the other world, but what devil could contrive a hell like this?"

He flung himself on the sofa, and covered his face with his hands. The lamp burning dimly on the solitary table, flung a faint and dusky light around the walls of the Tower Room.

Byrnewood lay in dim shadow, with his limbs thrown carelessly along the sofa, his outspread hands covering his face, while the long curls of his raven-black hair, fell wild and tangled over his forehead. As he lay there, with his dress disordered and his form resting on the sofa, in an attitude which, careless as it was, resembled the crouching position of one who suffers from the cold chill succeeding fever, you might have taken him for an inanimate effigy, instead of a living and breathing man.

No heaving of the chest, no quick and gasping respiration, no convulsive movements of the fingers, indicated the agitation which shook his soul to its centre. He lay quiet and motionless, his white hands, concealing his livid face, while a single glimpse of his forehead was visible between the tangled locks of his raven hair.

The silence of the room was broken by the creaking of the door, as it swung slowly open.

Bess silently entered the room, holding the waiter with the cold chicken and bottle of Madeira in her hands. She hurriedly closed the door and advanced to the solitary table. Her face was very pale, and her long dark hair, hung in disordered tresses around her full voluptuous neck. The dark shawl which she had thrown over her bridesmaid's dress, had fallen from her shoulders and hung loosely from her arms as she walked. Her entire appearance betrayed agitation and haste.

"He sleeps!" she murmured, arranging the refreshments—provided by Devil-Bug—along the surface of the chest-like table—"'Fix his plate on the side of the table furthest from the door'—what could the monster mean? Ha! There may be a secret spring on that side of the table, which the foot of the victim is designed to touch. I'll warn him of his danger—and then, the *bottle*—"

She said she would warn Byrnewood of his danger, and yet she lingered about the small table, her confused and hurried manner betraying her irresolution and changeability of purpose. Byrnewood still lay silent and motionless on the sofa. As far from slumber as the victim writhing on the rack, he was still unconscious of the presence of Long-haired Bess. His mind was utterly absorbed in the harrowing details of the mental struggle, that shook his soul to its foundations.

At first, arranging the knife and plate on one side of the table, and then on the other, now placing the bottle in one position and again in another, it was evident that Long-haired Bess was absent, confused and deeply agitated. The side-long glance, which every other instant, she threw over her shoulder at the reclining form of Byrnewood, was fraught with deep and painful meaning. At last, with a hurried footstep, she approached the sofa, and glancing cautiously at the door, which hung slightly ajar, she laid her hand lightly on Byrnewood's shoulder.

"I come to warn you of your danger—" she whispered in his ear.

Byrnewood looked up in wonder and then an expression of intolerable disgust impressed every line of his countenance.

"Your touch is pollution—" he said, shaking her hand from his shoulder—"You were one of the minions of the villain. You plotted my sister's dishonor—"

"I come to warn you of your danger!" whispered Bess, with a flashing eye—"You behold refreshments spread for you on yonder table. You see the bottle o' wine. On peril of your life don't drink anything—"

"But rale good brandy—" grated a harsh voice at her shoulder—"Liqu-ood hell-fire for ever! That's the stuff, my feller! Ha! ha! ha!"

With the same start of surprise, Byrnewood sprang to his feet, and Bess turned hurriedly around, while their eyes were fixed upon the face of the new-comer.

Devil-Bug, hideous and grinning, with the furnace of burning coals in his hand, stood before them. His solitary eye rested upon the face of Long-haired Bess with a meaning look, and his visage passed through the series of spasmodic contortions peculiar to his expressive features, as he stood swinging the furnace from side to side.

"You can go, Bessie, my duck—" he said, with a pleasant way of speaking, original with himself. "This 'ere party don't want you no more. You see, my feller citizen—" he continued, turning to Byrnewood—"yer humble servant thought you might be hungry, so he sent you suffin' to eat. Thought you might be cold; so he brung you some coals to warm yesself. You can *re*-tire, Bessie—"

He gently led her to the door, fixing his eye upon her face, with a look, as full of venom as a spiders sting.

"You'd a-spilt it all—would yo'?" he hissed the whisper in her ear as he pushed her from the room—"Good night my dear—" he continued aloud—"You better go home.

Your mammy's a waitin' tea for you. Now I'll make you a little bit o' fire, Mister, if you please—"

"Fire?" echoed Byrnewood—"I see no fire-place—"

"That's all you know about it"—answered Devil-Bug swinging the furnace from side to side—"You think them 'are's books do you? Look a little closer, next time. The walls are only painted like books and shelves—false book-cases you see. And then there's glass doors, jist like real book-cases. They did it in the old times—them queer old chaps as used to keep house here, all alone to themselves. Nice fire-place—aint it?"

He opened two folding leaves of the false book-case near the centre of the wall opposite the door, and a small fire-place neatly white-washed and free from ashes or the remains of any former fire, became visible. Stooping on his knees, Devil-Bug proceeded to arrange the furnace in the hearth, while the half-closed folding leaves of the bookcase, well-night concealed him from view.

"A false bookcase on either side of the room! Ha! Books of all classes, painted on the pannels, within the sashes, with inimitable skill! They deceived me, in the dim light of yonder lamp. What can this mean? By my life, I shrewdly suspect, that these book-cases, conceal secret passages, leading from this den—"

Byrnewood flung himself on the sofa, and again covered his face with his hands.

"Blazes up quite comfortable—" muttered Devil-Bug, as half concealed by the folding doors of the central part of the bookcase, he stooped over the furnace of blazing coal, warming his hands in the flame. "A nice fire, and a nice fire-place. But I'll have to discharge my bricklayer for one thing. Got him to fix up this harth not long ago. Scoundrel walled up the chimbley. Did ye ever hear of sich rascality? Konsekence is, this young gentleman will be rather uncomfortable a cause, the charcoal smoke wont find no vent. If I should happen to shut the door right tight he might die. He might so. Things jist as bad have happened afore now. He *might* die. Ha—ha—ha—" he chuckled as he retired from the fire-place, screening the blazing furnace, with the half-closed doors of the book-case—"Wonder how *that* 'ill work!"

He approached the side of Byrnewood, with that same hideous grin distorting his features, but had not advanced two steps, when he started backward with a moment of involuntary horror.

"Look here you sir—" he whispered grasping Byrnewood by the arm—"Jist look here a minnit. You see the floor at my left side—do you? Now tell us the truth, aint there a dead man layin' there? His jaw broke and his tongue out? Not that I'm afeered, but I wants to satisfy my mind. Jist take a good look while I hold still—"

"I see nothing but the carpet—" answered Byrnewood with a look of loathing, as he observed this strange being, standing before him, motionless as a statue, while his left hand pointed to the floor—"I see nothing but the carpet."

"Don't see a dead man, with his knees drawed up to his breast, and his tongue stickin' out? Well that's queer. I'd take my book oath, that the feller was a layin' there, nasty as a snake—Hows'ever *re*-fresh yourself young man. There's plenty to eat and drink and—" he pointed to the hearth as he spoke—"There's a nice comfortable fire. Good charcoal—and—I wonder's how *that*'ill work—"

Closing the door, he stood in the small recess, at the head of the stairs, leading to the Tower-Room. The huge forms of the negroes, Musquito and Glow-worm, were flung along the floor, while their hard breathing indicated that they slumbered on their watch. Listening intently for a single moment, at the door of the Tower-Room, Devil-Bug slowly turned the key in the lock, and then withdrawing it from the keyhole placed it in his pocket. He stepped carefully over the forms of the sleeping negroes, and passed his hands slowly along the panelling of the recess, opposite the door.

"The spring—ha, ha—I've found it—" he muttered in the darkness.—"The book-cases dont conceal no passage between the walls of this 'ere Tower, and the room itself—do they? O'course they do not. Quiet little places where a feller can say his prayers and eat ground-nuts. Ha! Ha! Ha! I must see how *that*'ill work."

The panelling slid back as he touched the spring and Devil-Bug disappeared into the secret recess or passage, between the false bookcases and the massive walls of the Tower; as the solitary chamber, rising from the western wing of Monk-Hall, was termed in the legends of the place.

Meanwhile within the Tower-Room, Byrnewood Arlington paced slowly up and down the floor, his arms folded, and his face, impressed with a fixed expression, that forced his lips tightly together, darkened his brows in a settled frown and drove the blood from his entire visage, until it wore the livid hues of death.

"My sister in his power! Last night she was pure and stainless—to morrow morning dawns and she will be a thing stained with pollution, dishonored by a hideous crime! No lapse of time, no prayers to Heaven, no bitter tears of repentance can ever wash out the foul stains of her dishonor. And I am a prisoner, while she shrieks for help and shrieks in vain—"

As Byrnewood spoke, striding rapidly along the floor, a grateful warmth began to steal around the room, dispelling the chill and damp, which seemed to infect the very air, with an unwholesome taint.

"And we have been children together! I have held her in these arms, when she was but a babe—a smiling babe, with golden hair and laughing cheeks! And then when she left home for school, how it wrung my soul to part with her! So young, so lighthearted, so innocent! Three years pass—she returns grown up into a lovely girl—whose pure soul, a very devil would not dare to tarnish—she return to bless the sight of her father—her mother, with her laughing face and she is—*dishonored!* I never knew the meaning of the word till now—*dishonored* by a villain—"

He flung himself on the sofa, and covered his face with his hands.

"And yet I, I, wronged an innocent girl, because she was my father's servant! Great God! Can she, have a brother to feel for her ruin? My punishment is just, but Mary—Oh! whom did she ever harm, whom *could* she ever wrong?"

He was silent again. And while his brain was tortured by the fierce struggles of thought, while the memories of earlier days came thronging over his soul—the image of his sister, present in every thought, and shining brightest in each old-time memory—he could feel, the grateful heat which pervaded the atmosphere of the room, restoring warmth and comfort to his limbs, while his blood flowed more freely in his veins.

There was a long pause, in which his very soul was absorbed in a delirium of thought. It may have been the effect of internal agitation, or the result of his half-crazed intellect acting on his physical system, but after the lapse of some few minutes, he was aroused from his reverie, by a painful throbbing around his temples, which for a single moment destroyed all consciousness, and just as suddenly restored him to a keen and terrible sense of his appaling situation. Now his brain seemed to swim in a wild delirium, and in a single instant as the throbbing around his temples grew more violent, his mental vision, seemed clearer and more vigorous than ever.

"I can scarcely breathe!" he muttered, as he fell back on the sofa, after a vain attempt to rise—There is a hand grasping me by the throat—I feel the fingers clutching the veins, with the grasp of a demon. My heart—ah!—it is turning to ice—to ice—and now it is fire! My heart is a ball of flame—the blood boils in my veins—"

He sprung to his feet, with a wild bound and his hands clutched madly at his throat, as though he would free the veins from the grasp of the invisible fingers, which were pressing through the very skin.

He staggered to and fro along the floor, with his arms flung overhead as if to ward off the attacks of some invisible foe.

His face was ghastly pale, one moment; the next it flushed with the hues of a crimson flame. His large black eyes dilated in their glance, and stood out from the lids as though they were about to fall from their sockets. His mouth distended with a convulsive grimace, while his teeth were firmly clenched together. One instant his brain would be perfectly conscious in all its operations, the next his senses would swim in a fearful delirium.

"My God—My God!" he shouted in one of those momentary intervals of consciousness, as he staggered wildly along the floor—"I am dying—I am dying! My breath comes thick and gaspingly—my veins are chilled—ha, ha—they are turned to fire again—"

Even in his delirium he was conscious of a singular circumstance. A portion of the panelling of the false bookcase, along the wall opposite the fire, receded suddenly, within the sash of the central glass-door, leaving a space of black and vacant darkness. The aperture was in the top of the bookcase, near the ceiling of the room.

Turning toward the hearth, Byrnewood endeavoured to regain the sofa, but the room seemed swimming around him, and with a wild movement, he again staggered toward the bookcase opposite the fire.

He started backward as a new horror met his gaze.

A hideous face glared upon him, from the aperture of the book-case, like some picture of a fiend's visage, suddenly thrust against the glass-door of the book-case.

A hideous face, with a single burning eye, with a wide mouth distending in a loathsome grin, with long rows of fang-like teeth, and a protuberent brow, overhung by thick masses of matted hair. This face alone was visible, surrounded by the darkness which marked the square outline of the aperture. It was, indeed, like a hideous picture framed in ebony, although you could see the muscles of the face in motion, while the flat nose was pressed againt the glass of the book-case, and the thick lips were now tightly closed, and again distending in hideous grin.

"Ho! ho! ho!" a laugh like the shout of a devil, came echoing through the glass, faint and subdued, yet wild and terrible to hear—"The charcoal—the charcoal! Wonder how *that'ill work!*"

Byrnewood stood silent and erect, while the throbbing of his temples, the gasping of his breath, and the deadening sensation around his heart, subsided for a single moment.

The full horror of his situation rushed upon him. He was dying by the gas escaping from charcoal, in a room, rendered impervious to the air; closed and sealed for the purpose of this horrible death.

A brilliant idea flashed across his brain.

"I will overturn the furnace—" he muttered, rushing toward the hearth—"I will extinguish the flame!"

With a sudden bound he sprang forward, but in the very action, fell to the floor, like a drunken man.

His breath came in thick convulsive gasps, his heart grew like a mass of fire, while his brain was tortured by one intense and agonizing throb of pain, as though some invisible hand had wound a red hot wire round his forehead. He lay on the floor, with his outspread hands grasping the air in the effort to rise.

"It works, it works!" shouted the voice of Devil-Bug, as his loath-some countenance was pressed against the glass-door of the book-case—"Ha! ha! ha! He is on the floor—he cannot rise—he is in the clutch of death. How the poor feller kicks and scuffles!"

A wild, wild shriek echoing from a distant room came faintly to Byrnewood's ear. That sound of a woman's voice, shrieking for help, in an emphasis of despair, aroused the dying man from the spell which began to deaden his senses.

"It is my sister's voice!" he exclaimed, springing to his feet with a last effort of strength—"She is in the hands of the villain! I will save her—I will save her—"

"The sister outraged! The brother murdered!" shouted Devil-Bug, through the glass-door—"I wonder how *that'ill work!*"

Byrnewood rushed towards the door; it was locked and secured. All hope was in vain. He must die. Die, while his sister's shriek for aid rang on his ears, die, with the loathsome face of his murderer pressed against the glass, while his blazing eye feasted on his last convulsive agonies, die, with youth on his brow, with health in his heart! Die, with all purposed vengeance on his sister's wronger unfulfilled; die, by no sudden blow, by no dagger thrust, by no pistol shot, but by the most loathsome of all deaths, by suffocation.

"Ha! ha!" the thought flashed over his brain—"The hangman's rope were a priceless luxury to me in this dread hour!"

Staggering slowly along the floor, with footsteps as heavy as though he had leaden weights attached to his feet, he approached the chest-like table, and with a faint effort to recover his balance, sunk down on the floor, in a crouching position, while his outspread hands clutched faintly at the air.

In a moment he rolled slowly from side to side, and lay on his back with his face to the ceiling, and his arms extended on either side. His eyes were suddenly covered with a glassy film, his lower jaw separated from the upper, leaving his mouth wide open, while the room grew warmer, the air more dense and suffocating.

"Help—help!" murmured Byrnewood, in a smothered voice, like the sound produced by a man throttled by nightmare—"Help! help!"

" 'By-a-baby, go to sleep'—that's a good feller—" the voice of Devil-Bug came like a faint echo through the glass—"A drop from the bottle 'ud do you good, and—jist reach your right hand a leetle bit further! There ain't no spring there, I *sup*-pose? Ain't there? Ho-ho-ho!"

And Byrnewood could feel a delicious languor stealing over his frame, as he lay there on the floor, helpless and motionless, while the voice of Devil-Bug rang in his ears. The throbbing of his temples had subsided, he no more experienced the quick gasping struggle for breath, his heart no more passed through the quick transitions from cold to heat, from ice to fire, his veins no more felt like streams of molten lead. He was sinking quietly in a soft and pleasing slumber. The film grew more glassy in each eye, his jaws hung further apart, and the heaving of his chest subsided, until a faint and tremulous motion, was the only indication that life had not yet fled from his frame. His outspread arms seemed to grow stiffened and dead as he rested on the floor, while the joints of the fingers moved faintly to and fro, with a fluttering motion, that afforded a strange contrast to the complete repose of his body and limbs. His feet were pointed upward, like the feet of a corpse, arrayed for burial.

The dim light burning on the chest-like table, afforded a faint light to the ghastly scene. There were the untouched refreshments, the cold chicken and the bottle of wine, giving the place the air of a quiet supper-room, there were the false book cases, indicating a resort for meditation and study, there was the cheerful furnace, its glowing flame flashing through the half-closed doors, speaking a pleasant tale of fireside joys and comforts, and there, along the carpet, stiffening and ghastly lay the form of Byrnewood Arlington, slowly and quietly yielding to the slumber of death, while a hideous face peered through the glass-door, all distorted by a sickening grimace, and a solitary eye, that gleamed like a live coal, drank in the tremulous agonies of the dying man.

"Reach his hand a leetle bit further—that's a good feller. Won't have no tumble down three stories, nor nothin', if his fingers touch the spring? Ho-ho! Quiet now, I guess. Jist look how his fingers tremble—He! he! he! Hallo! He's on his feet agin!"

With the last involuntary struggle of a strong man wrestling for his life, Byrnewood Arlington sprang to his feet, and reaching forth his hand with the same mechanical impulse that had raised him from the floor, he seized the bottle of wine; he raised it to his lips, and the wine poured gurgling down his throat.

"Hain't got no opium in, I *sup*-pose? Not the least mossel. Cuss it, how he staggers! Believe my soul he's comin' to life again'—"

Byrnewood glanced around with a look of momentary consciousness. The drugged wine, for a single moment, created a violent reaction in his system, and he became fully sensible of the awful death that awaited him. He could feel the hot air, warming his cheek, he could see the visage of Devil-Bug peering at him thro' the glass-door, and the danger which menaced his sister, came home like some horrible phantom to his soul. He felt in his very soul that but a single moment more of consciousness, would be permitted him, for action. That moment past, and the death by charcoal, would be quietly and surely accomplished.

"Keep me, oh Heaven!" he whispered as his mind ran over various expedients for escape—"Aid me, in this, my last effort, that I may live to avenge my sister's dishonor!"

It was his design to make one sudden and desperate spring toward the glass-door, through which the hideous visage of Devil-Bug, glared in his face and as he madly dashed his hands through the glass, the room would be filled with a current of fresh air.

This was his resolve, but it came too late. As he turned, to make this desperate spring, his heel pressed against an object, rising from the floor, near a corner of the chest-like table. It was but a small object, resembling a nail or spike, which has not been driven to the head, in the planking of a floor, but suffered to remain half-exposed and open to the view.

And yet the very moment Byrnewood's heel, pressed againt the trifling object, the floor on which he stood gave way beneath him, with a low rustling sound, half of the Chamber was changed into one black and yawning chasm, and the lamp standing on the table suddenly disappeared, leaving the place wrapt in thick darkness.

Another moment passed, and while Byrnewood reeled in the darkness, on the verge of the sunken trap-door, a hushed and distant sound, echoed far below as from the depths of some deep and dismal well. The lamp had fallen in the chasm, and the faint sound heard far, far below was the only indication that it had reached the bottom of the gloomy void, sinking down like a well into the cellars of Monk-hall.

Byrnewood tottered on the verge of the chasm, while a current of cold air came sweeping upward from its depths. The foul atmosphere of the Tower Room, lost half its deadly qualities, in a single moment, as the cool air, came rushing from the chasm.

Byrnewood felt the effects of the charcoal rapidly passing from his system, and his mind regained its full consciousness as his hot brow, received the freshning blast of winter air, pouring over the parched and heated skin.

But the current of pure air, came too late for his salvation. Tottering in the darkness on the very verge of the sunken trap-door, he made one desperate struggle to preserve his balance, but in vain. For a moment his form swung to and fro, and then his feet slid from under him; and then with a maddening shriek, he fell.

"God save poor Mary!"

How that last cry of the doomed man shrieked around the panelled walls of the Tower Room!

"Wonder how *that*'ill *work!*" the hoarse voice of Devil-Bug, shrieked through the darkness—"Down—down—*down!* Ah-ha! Three stories—down—down—down! I wonders how that 'ill work!"

Separated from the Tower Room by the glass-door, Devil-Bug pressed his ear against the glass, and listened for the death-groans of the doomed man.

A low moaning sound, like the groan of a man, who trembles under the operations of a surgeon's knife, came faintly to his ear. In a moment, Devil-Bug, thought he heard a sound like a door suddenly opened, and then, the murmur of voices, whispering some quick and hurried words, resounded along the Tower Room. Then there was a subdued noise, like a man struggling on the brink of the chasm, and then a hushed sound, that might have been taken for the tread of a footstep mingled with the closing of a door, came faintly through the glass of the book-case.

Gliding silently from the secret recess, behind the panelling of the Tower Room, Devil-Bug stepped over the forms of the slumbering negroes and descended the stairway leading to the Walnut Room. The scene of the wedding was wrapt in midnight darkness. Passing softly along the floor, Devil-Bug, reached the entrance to the Rose Chamber, and flung the hangings aside, with a cautious movement of his talon-like fingers.

"I merely wanted a light—" exclaimed Devil-Bug, as he stood gazing into the Rose Chamber—"But here's a candle, and a purty sight into the bargain!"

He disappeared through the doorway, and after the lapse of a few moments, again emerged into the Walnut Room, holding a lighted candle in his hand.

"Amazin' circumstance, *that*—" he chuckled, as he strode across the glittering floor—"The brother *fell* in that 'are room, and the sister *fell* in *that;* about the same time. They *fell* in different ways though. Strange world, this. Let's see what become of the brother—Charcoal and opium—ho! ho! ho!"

Before another moment had elapsed, he stood before the door of Tower Room. Musquito and Glow-worm still slumbered on their watch, their huge forms and hideous faces, dimly developed in the beams of the light, which the Doorkeeper carried in his hand. Devil-Bug listened intently for a single moment, but not the slightest sound disturbed the silence of the Tower room.

He opened the door, he strode along the carpet, he stood on the verge of the chasm, produced by the falling of the death-trap.

"Down—down! Three stories, and the pit below! Ha! Let me hold the light, a leetle nearer! Every trap-door is open—he is safe enough! Think I see suffin' white a-flutterin' a-way down there! Hollered pretty loud as he fell—devilish ugly tumble! Guess it 'ill work quite nice for Lorrimer!"

Stooping on his knees with the light extended in his right hand, he again gazed down the hatchway, his solitary eye flashing with excitement, as he endeavoured to pierce the gloom of the dark void beneath.

"He's gone to see his friends below! Sartin sure! No sound—no groan—not even a holler!"

Arising from his kneeling position, Devil-Bug approached the recess of the fire-place. On either side, a plain panell of oak, concealed the secret nook behind the false book-case. Placing his hand cautiously along the panell to the right, Devil-Bug examined the details of the carving in each corner, and along its side, with a careful eye.

"Hasn't been opened to-night—" he murmured—"Leads to the Walnut Room, by a round-a-bout way. Convenient little passage, if that fool had only knowed on it!"

In an instant he stood outside of the Tower Room door, holding the key in one hand, and the candlestick in the other.

"Git up you lazy d——l's!" he shouted, bestowing a few pointed kicks upon the carcases of the sleeping negroes—"Git up and mind your eyes, or else I'll pick 'em out o' your head to play marbles with—"

Glow-worm arose slowly from the floor, and Musquito, opening his eyes with a sleepy yawn, stared vacantly in the Doorkeeper's face.

"D'ye hear me? Watch this feller and see that he don't escape? He's a sleepin' now, but there's no knowin'—Watch! I say watch!"

He shuffled slowly along the narrow passage, looking over his shoulder at the grinning negroes, as he passed along, while his face wore its usual pleasant smile, as he again muttered in his hoarse tones—"Watch him ye dogs—I say watch him!"

Another moment, and he stood before the entrance of the Rose Chamber, holding the curtaining aside, while his eye blazed up with an expression of malignant joy. He raised the light on high, and stood gazing silently through the doorway, as though his eyes beheld a spectacle of strange and peculiar interest.

And while he stood there, chuckling pleasantly to himself, with the full light of the candle, flashing over his loathsome face, two figures, stood crouching in the darkness, along the opposite side of the room, and the eastern door hung slightly ajar, as though they had entered the place but a moment before.

Once or twice Devil-Bug turned, as though the sound of suppressed breathing struck his ear, but every time, the shadow of the candle fell along the opposite side of the room, and the crouching figures were concealed from view.

"Quite a pictur'—" chuckled Devil-Bug as he again gazed through the doorway of the Rose Chamber—"A nice little gal and a handsome feller! Ha! Ha! Ha!"

He disappeared through the curtaining, while his pleasant chuckle came echoing through the doorway, with a sound of continued glee, as though the gentleman was highly amused by the spectacle that broke on his gaze.

The silence of the Rose Chamber was broken by the tread of a footstep and the figure of a man, came stealing through the darkness, with the form of a queenly woman by his side.

"Advance—and save your sister's honor—" the deep-toned whisper broke thrillingly on the air.

The man advanced with a hurried step, flung the curtain hastily aside, and gazed within the Rose Chamber.

The horror of that silent gaze, would be ill-repayed by an Eternity of joy.

CHAPTER THIRTEENTH

✎ The Crime without a Name

"My brother consents? Oh joy, Lorraine—he consents!"

"Your brother consents to our wedding, my love—"

"How did he first discover, that the wedding was to take place to night?"

"It seems that for several days, he has noticed you walking out with Bess. You see, Mary, this excited his suspicions. He watched you with all a brother's care, and to night, tracked Bess and you, to the doors of this mansion. He was not certain however, that it was *you,* whom he seen, enter my uncle's house—"

"And so he watched all night around the building? Oh Lorraine, *he* is a noble brother!"

"At last, grown feverish with his suspicions, he rung the bell, aroused the servant, and when the door was opened, rushed madly up stairs, and reached the Wedding Room. You know the rest. After the matter was explained to him, he consented to keep our marriage secret until Christmas Eve. He has left the house, satisfied that you are in the care of those who love you. To morrow, Mary, when you have recovered from the effects of the surprise,—which your brother's sudden entrance occasioned—to-morrow we will be married!"

"And on Christmas Eve, hand linked in hand, we will kneel before *our* father, and ask his blessing—"

"One kiss, Mary love, one kiss, and I will leave you for the night—"

And leaning fondly over the fair girl, who was seated on the sofa, her form enveloped in a flowing night-robe, Lorrimer wound his right arm gently around her neck, bending her head slowly backward in the action, and suffering her rich curls to fall showering on her shoulders, while her upturned face, all radiant with affection lay open to his burning gaze, and her ripe lips, dropped slightly apart, disclosing the ivory teeth, seemed to woo and invite the pressure of his kiss.

One kiss, silent and long, and the Lover and the fair girl, seemed to have grown to each others lips.

The wax-light standing on the small table of the Rose Chamber, fell mild and dimly over this living picture of youth and passion.

The tall form of Lorrimer, clad in solemn black, contrasting forcibly with the snow-white robes of the Maiden, his arm flung gently around her neck, her upturned face half-hidden by the falling locks of his dark brown hair, their lips joined and their eyes mingling in the same deep glance of passion, while her bosom rose heaving against his breast, and her arms half-upraised seemed about to entwine his form in their embrace—it was a moment of pure and hallowed love on the part of the fair girl, and even the libertine, for an instant forgot the vileness of his purpose, in that long and silent kiss of stainless passion.

"Mary!" cried Lorrimer, his handsome face flushing over with transport, as silently gliding from his standing position, he assumed his seat at her side—"Oh! would that you were mine! We would flee together from the heartless world—in some silent and shadowy valley, we would forget all, but the love which made us one."

"We would seek a home, quiet and peaceful, as that which this book describes—" whispered Mary laying her hand on Bulwer's play of Claude Mellnotte[19]—"I found the volume on the table, and was reading it, when you came in. Oh, it is all beauty and feeling. You have read it Lorraine?"

"Again and again and have seen it played a hundred times.—'The home, to which love could fulfil its prayers, this hand would lead thee'—" he murmured repeating the first lines of the celebrated description of the Lake of Como—"And yet Mary this is mere romance. A creation of the poet's brain. A fiction as beautiful as a ray of light; and as fleeting. I might tell you a story of a real valley and a real lake,—which I beheld last summer—where love might dwell forever, and dwell in eternal youth and freshness.—"

"Oh tell me—tell me—" cried Mary, gazing in his face with a look of interest.

"Beyond the fair valley of Wyoming,[20] of which so much has been said and sung, there is a high and extensive range of mountains, covered with thick and gloomy forests. One day last September when the summer was yet in its freshness and bloom, toward the hour of sunset, I found myself wandering through a thick wood, that covered the summit

[19]Claude Mellnotte is the hero of Edward George Bulwer-Lytton's (1803–1873) play *Lady of Lyons*. Claude Mellnotte was a well-known character who became a type for the fiercely romantic, restless, brilliant young man.

[20]A region in northeastern Pennsylvania along the Susquehanna River.

of one of the highest of these mountains. I had been engaged in a deer-hunt all day—had strayed from my comrades—and now as night was coming on, was wandering, along a winding path, that led to the top of the mountain—"

Lorrimer paused for a single instant, and gazed intently in Mary's face. Every feature was animated with sudden interest and a warm flush, hung freshly on each cheek.

And as Lorrimer gazed upon the animated face of the innocent girl, marking its rounded outlines, its hues of youth and loveliness, its large blue eyes beaming so gladly upon his countenance, the settled purpose of his soul, came to him, like a sudden shadow darkening over a landscape, after a single gleam of sunlight.

It was the purpose of this libertine to dishonor the stainless girl, before he left her presence.

Before day break she would be a polluted thing, whose name and virtue and soul, would be blasted forever.

In that silent gaze, which drank in the beauty of the maiden's face, Lorrimer arranged his plan of action. The book which he had left open the table, the story which he was about to tell, were the first intimations of his atrocious design. While enchaining the mind of the Maiden, with a story full of Romance, it was his intention to wake her animal nature into full action. And when her veins were all alive with fiery pulsations, when her heart grew animate with sensual life, when her eyes swam in the humid moisture of passion, then she would sink helplessly into his arms, and—like the bird to the snake,—flutter to her ruin.

"'Force'—'violence!' These are but the tools of grown-up children, who know nothing of the mystery of woman's heart—" the thought flashed over Lorrimer's brain, as his lip, wore a very slight but meaning smile—"I have deeper means, than these! I employ neither force, nor threats, nor fraud, nor violence! My victim is the instrument of her own ruin—without one rude grasp from my hand, without one threatning word, she swims willingly to my arms!"

He took the hand of the fair girl within his own, and looking her steadily in the eye, with a deep gaze which every instant grew more vivid and burning, he went on with his story—and his design.

"The wood grew very dark. Around me, were massive trees with thick branches, and gnarled trunks, bearing witness of the storms of an hundred years. My way led over a path covered with soft forest-moss, and now and then, red gleams of sunlight shot like arrows of gold, between the overhanging leaves. Darker and darker, the twilight sank down upon the forest. At last missing the path, I knew not which way to tread. All was dark and indistinct. Now falling over a crumbling limb, which had been thrown down by a storm long before, now entangled by the wild vines, that overspread portions of the ground, and now missing my foothold in some hidden crevice of the earth, I wandered wearily on. At last climbing up a sudden elevation of the mountain, I stood upon a vast rock, that hung over the depths below, like an immense platform. On all sides, but one, this rock was encircled by a waving wall of forest-leaves. Green shrubs swept circling around, enclosing it like a fairy bower, while the eastern side, lay open to the beams of the moon, which now rose grandly in the vast horizon. Far over wood, far over mountain, far over ravine and dell, this platform-rock, commanded a distant view of the valley of Wyoming.

"The moon was in the sky, Mary: the sky was one vast sheet of blue, undimmed by a single cloud; and beneath the moonbeams lay a sea of forest-leaves, while in the dim distance—like the shore of this leafy ocean—arose the roofs and steeples of a quiet town, with a broad river, rolling along the dark valley, like a banner of silver, flung over a sable-pall—"

"How beautiful!"

And as the murmur escaped Mary's lips, the hand of Lorrimer grew closer in its pressure, while his left arm, wound gently around her waist.

"I stood entranced by the sight. A cool breeze came up the mountain side, imparting a grateful freshness to my cheek. The view was indeed beautiful, but I suddenly remembered that I was without resting-place or shelter. Ignorant of the mountain paths, afar from any farm-house or village, I had still a faint of hope, of discovering the temporary habitation of some hunter, who had encamped in these forest-wilds.

"I turned from the magnificent prospect—I brushed aside the wall of leaves, I looked to the western sky. I shall never forget the view—which like a dream of fairy-land—burst on my sight, as pushing the shrubbery aside, I gazed from the western limits of the platform-rock.

"There, below me, imbedded in the very summit of the mountain, lay a calm lake, whose crystal-waters, gave back the reflection of forest and sky, like an immense mirror. It was but a mile in length, and half that distance in width. On all sides, sudden and steep, arose the encircling wall of forest trees. Like wine in a goblet, that calm sheet of water, lay in the embrace of the surrounding wall of foliage. The waters were clear, so tranquil, that I could see, down, down, far, far beneath, as if another world, was hidden in their depths. And then from the heights, the luxuriant foliage, a yet untouched by autumn, sank in waves of verdure to the very brink of the lake, the trembling leaves, dipping in the clear, cold waters, with a gentle motion. It was very beautiful Mary and—"

"Oh, most beautiful!"

The left hand of Lorrimer, gently stealing round her form, rested with a faint pressure upon the folds of the night-robe, over her bosom, which now came heaving tremulously into light.

"I looked upon this lovely lake with a keen delight. I gazed upon the tranquil waters, upon the steeps crowned with forest-trees—one side in heavy shadow, the other, gleaming in the advancing moonbeams—I seemed to inhale the quietness, the solitude of the place, as a holy influence, mingling with the very air, I breathed, and a wild transport aroused my soul into an outburst of enthusiasm.

"Here—I cried—is the home for Love! Love, pure and stainless, flying from the crowded city, here can repose, beneath the shadow of quiet rocks, beside the gleam of tranquil waters, within the solitudes of endless forests. Yon sky, so clear, so cloudless, has never beheld a sight of human misery or wo. Yon lake, sweeping beneath me, like another sky, has never been crimsoned by human blood. This quiet valley, hidden from the world now, as it has been hidden since the creation, is but another world where two hearts that love, that mingle in one, that throb but for each other's joy, can dwell forever, in the calm silence of unalloyed affection—"

"A home for love such as angels feel—"

Closer and more close, the hand of Lorrimer pressed against the heaving bosom, with but the slight folds of the night-robe between.

"Here, beside this calm lake, whenever the love of a true woman shall be mine, here, afar from the cares and realities of life, will I dwell! Here, with the means which the accident of fortune has bestowed, will I build, not a temple, not a mansion, not a palace! But a cottage, a quiet home, whose roof shall arise—like a dear hope in the wilderness—from amid the green leaves of embowering trees—"

"You spoke thus, Lorraine? Do I not love you as a true woman should love? Is not your love calm and stainless as the waters of the mountain lake? We will dwell there, Lorraine! Oh, how like romance will be the plain reality of our life!"

"Oh! Mary, my own true love, in that moment as I stood gazing upon the world-hidden lake, my heart all throbbing with strange impulses, my very soul steeped in a holy calm, your form seemed to glide between my eyes and the moonlight! The thought rushed like a prophecy over my soul, that one day, amid the barren wilderness of hearts, which crowd the world, I should fine *one, one* heart, whose impulses should be stainless, whose affection should be undying, whose love should be mine! Oh, Mary, in that moment, I felt that my life would, one day, be illumined by your love—"

"And then you knew me not? Oh, Lorraine, is there not a strange mystery in this affection, which makes the heart long for the love, which it shall one day experience, even before the eye has seen the beloved one?"

Brighter grew the glow on her cheek, closer pressed the hand on her bosom, warmer and higher arose that bosom in the light.

"And there, Mary, in that quiet mountain valley, we will seek a home, when we are married. As soon as summer comes, when the trees are green, and the flowers burst from among the moss along the wood-path, we will hasten to the mountain lake, and dwell within the walls of our quiet home. For a home shall be reared for us, Mary, on a green glade that slopes down to the water's brink, with the tall trees sweeping away on either side.

"A quiet little cottage, Mary, with a sloping roof and small windows, all fragrant with wild flowers and forest vines! A garden before the door, Mary, where, in the calm summer morning, you can inhale the sweetness of the flowers, as they breath forth in untamed luxuriance. And then, anchored by the shore, Mary, a light sail-boat will be ready for us ever; to bear us over the clear lake in the early dawn, when the mist winds up in fleecy columns to the sky, or in the twilight, when the red sun flings his last ray over the waters, or in the silent night, when the moon is up, and the stars look kindly on us from the cloudless sky—"

"Alas! Lorraine! Clouds may come and storms, and winter—"

"What care we for winter, when eternal spring is in our hearts! Let winter come with its chill, and its ice and its snows! Beside our cheerful fire, Mary, with our hands clasping some book, whose theme is the trials of two hearts that loved on through difficulty and danger or death, we will sit silently, our hearts throbbing with one delight, while the long hours of the winter evening glide quietly on. Do you see the fire, Mary? How cheerily its beams light our faces as we sit in its kindly light! My arm is round your waist, Mary, my cheek is laid next to yours, our hands are locked together and your heart, Mary, oh how softly its throbbings fall on my ear!"

"Oh, Lorraine! Why is there any care in the world, when two hearts can make such a heaven on earth, with the holy lessons of an all-trusting love—"

"Or it may be, Mary—" and his gaze grew deeper, while his voice sank to a low and thrilling whisper—"Or it may be, Mary, that while we sit beside our winter fire—a fair babe—do not blush, *my wife*—a fair babe will rest smiling on your bosom—"

"Oh, Lorraine—" she murmured, and hid her face upon his breast, her long brown tresses, covering her neck and shoulders like a veil, while Lorraine wound his arms closely round her form, and looked around with a glance full of meaning.

There was triumph in that glance. The libertine felt her heart throbbing against his breast as he held her in his arms, he felt her bosom panting and heaving, and quivering with a quick fluttering pulsation and as he swept the clustering curls aside from her half-hidden face, he saw that her cheek glowed like a new-lighted flame.

"She is mine!" he thought, and a smile of triumph gave a dark aspect to his hand-some face.

In a moment Mary raised her glowing countenance from his breast. She gazed around, with a timid, frightened look. Her breath came thick and gaspingly. Her cheeks were all a-glow, her blue eyes swam in a hazy dimness. She felt as though she was about to fall swooning on the floor. For a moment all consciousness seemed to have failed her, while a delirious langor came stealing over her senses. Lorrimer's form seemed to swim in the air before her, and the dim light of the room gave place to a flood of radiance, which seemed all at once to pour on her eyesight from some invisible source. Soft murmurs, like voices heard in a pleasant dream, fell gently on her ears, the langor came deeper and more mellow over her limbs; her bosom rose no longer quick and gaspingly, but in long pulsations, that urged the full globes in all their virgin beauty, softly and slowly into view. Like billows they rose above the folds of the night robe, while the flush grew warmer on her cheek, and her parted lips deepened into a rich vermillion tint.

"She is mine!" and the same dark smile flushed over Lorraine's face. Silent and motionless he sat, regarding his victim with a steadfast glance.

"Oh, Lorraine—" she cried, in a gasping voice, as she felt a strange unconscious-ness stealing over her senses—"Oh, Lorraine—save me—save me!"

She arose, tottering on her feet, flinging her hands aloft, as though she stood on the brink of some frightful steep, without the power to retreat from its crumbling edge.

"There is no danger for you, my Mary—" whispered Lorrimer, as he received her falling form in his outspread arms—"There is no danger for you, my Mary—"

He played with the glossy curls of her dark brown hair as he spoke, while his arms gathered her half-swooning form full against his heart.

"She is mine! Her blood is a-flame—her senses swim in a delirium of passion! While the story fell from my lips, I aroused her slumbering woman's nature. Talk of force—ha, ha—She rests on my bosom as though she would grow there—"

As these thoughts half escaped from his lips, in a muttered whisper, his face shone with the glow of sensual passion, while his hazel eye dilated, with a glance, whose intense lustre had but one meaning; dark and atrocious.

She lay on his breast, her senses wrapt in a feverish swoon, that laid her powerless in his arms, while it left her mind vividly sensible of the approaching danger.

"Mary, my love—no danger threatens you—" he whispered playing with her glossy curls—"Look up, my love—*I* am with you, and will shield you from harm!"

Gathering her form in his left arm, secure of his victim, he raised her from his breast, and fixing his gaze upon her blue eyes, humid with moisture, he slowly flung back the night robe from her shoulders. Her bosom, in all its richness of outline, heaving and throbbing with that long pulsation, which urged it upward like a billow, lay open to his gaze.

And at the very moment, that her fair breast was thrown open to his sensual gaze, she sprang from his embrace, with a wild shriek, and instinctively gathered her robe over her bosom, with a trembling movement of her fair white hands. The touch of the seducer's hand, polluting her stainless bosom, had restored her to sudden consciousness.

"Lorraine! Lorraine!" she shrieked, retreating to the farthest corner of the room— "Oh, save me—save me—"

"No danger threatens you, my Mary—"

He advanced, as he spoke, towards the trembling girl, who had shrunk into a corner of the room, crouching closely to the rose-hued hangings, while her head turned over her shoulder and her hands clasped across her bosom, she gazed around with a glance full of terror and alarm.

Lorrimer advanced toward the crouching girl. He had been sure of his victim; he did not dream of any sudden outburst of terror from the half swooning maiden as she lay, helpless on his breast. As he advanced, a change came over his appearance. His face grew purple, and the veins of his eyes filled with thick red blood. He trembled as he walked across the floor, and his chest heaved and throbbed beneath his white vest, as though he found it difficult to breathe.

God save poor Mary, now!

Looking over her shoulder, she caught a gleam of his blood-shot eye, and read her ruin there.

"Mary, there is no danger—" he muttered, in a husky voice, as she shrunk back from his touch—"Let me raise you from the floor—"

"Save me, oh Lorraine—Save me!" she cried, in a voice of terror, crouching closer to the hangings along the wall.

"From what shall I save you?" he whispered, in a voice unnaturally soft and gentle, as though he endeavoured to hide the rising anger which began to gleam from his eye, when he found himself foiled in the very moment of triumph—"From what shall I save you—"

"From yourself—" she shrieked, in a frightened tone—"Oh, Lorraine, you love me. You will not harm me. Oh, save me, save me from yourself!"

Playing with the animal nature of the stainless girl, Lorrimer had aroused the sensual volcano of his own base heart. While he pressed her hand, while he gazed in her eyes, while he wound his embrace around her form, he had anticipated a certain and grateful conquest. He had not dreamed that the humid eye, the heaving bosom, the burning cheek of Mary Arlington, were aught but the signs of his coming triumph. Resistance? Prayers? Tears? He had not anticipated these. The fiend was up in his soul. The libertine had gone too far to recede.

He stood before the crouching girl, a fearful picture of incarnate LUST. Sudden as the shadow after the light this change had passed over his soul. His form arose towering and erect, his chest throbbed with sensual excitement, his hands hung, madly clinched, by his side, while his curling hair fell wild and disordered over his brows, darkening in a hideous frown, and his mustachioed lip wore the expression of his fixed and unalterable purpose. His blood-shot eyes, flashed with the unholy light of passion, as he stood sternly surveying the form of his victim. There was something wild and brutal in their savage glare.

"This is all folly—" he said, in that low toned and husky voice—"Rise from the floor, Mary. You don't think I'd harm you?"

He stooped to raise her from the floor, but she shrank from his extended hands as though there was pollution in his slightest touch.

"Mary, I wish you to rise from the floor!"

His clenched hands trembled as he spoke, and the flush of mingled anger and sensual feeling, deepened over his face.

"Oh, Lorraine!" she cried, flinging herself on her knees before him—"Oh, Lorraine—you will not harm *me?* This is not *you,* Lorraine; it cannot be *you.* You would not look darkly on me, your voice would not grow harsh as it whispered my name—It is not Lorraine that I see—it is an evil spirit—"

It was an evil spirit, she said, and yet looked up into his blood-shot eyes for a gleam of mercy as she spoke, and with her trembling fingers, wrung his clinched right hand, and clasped it wildly to her bosom.

Pure, stainless, innocent, her heart a heaven of love, her mind childlike in its knowledge of the World, she knew not what she feared. She did not fear the shame which the good world would heap upon her, she did not fear the Dishonor, because it would be followed by such pollution that, no man in honor might call her—Wife—no child in innocence might whisper her name as—Mother—she did not fear the foul Wrong, as society with its million tongues and eyes, fears it, and holds it in abhorence, ever visiting the guilt of the man upon the head of his trembling victim.

Mary feared the Dishonor, because her soul, with some strange consciousness of approaching evil, deemed it, a foul Spirit, who had arisen, not so much to visit her with wrong as to destroy the Love, she felt for Lorrimer. Not for herself, but for *his* sake, she feared that nameless crime, which already glared upon her from the blood-shot eyes of her Lover. Her *Lover!*

"Oh, Lorraine, you will not harm me! For the sake of God, save me—save me!"

She clasped his hand with a closer grasp and gathered it tremblingly to her bosom, while her eyes dilating with a glance of terror, were fixed upon his face.

"Mary—this is madness—nothing but madness—" he said in that voice, grown hoarse with passion, and rudely tore his hand from her grasp.

Another instant, and stooping suddenly, he caught her form in his arms, and raised her struggling from her very feet.

"Mary—you—are—mine!" he hissed the whisper in her ear, and gathered her quivering form more closely to his heart.

There was a low-toned and hideous laugh, muttering or growling through the air as he spoke, and the form of Devil-Bug, stole with a hushed footstep from the entrance of the Walnut Chamber, and seizing the light in his talon-fingers, glided from the room, with the same hyena laugh which had announced his appearance.

"The trap—the bottle—the fire, for the *brother*—" he muttered as his solitary eye, glanced upon the Libertine and his struggling victim, neither of whom had marked his entrance—"For the *Sister*—ha! ha! ha! The '*handsome*' Devil-Bug—Monk Gusty—'tends to her! 'Bijah did'nt listen for nothin'—ha, ha! this beats the *charcoal,* quite hollow!"

He disappeared, and the Rose Chamber was wrapt in midnight darkness.

Darkness! There was a struggle, and a shriek and a prayer. Darkness! There was an oath and a groan, mingling in chorus. Darkness! A wild cry for mercy, a name madly shrieked, and a fierce execration. Darkness! Another struggle, a low moaning sound, and a stillness like that of the grave. Now darkness and silence mingle together and all is still.

In some old book of mysticism and superstition, I have read this wild legend, which mingling as it does the terrible with the grotesque, has still its meaning and its moral.

In the sky, far, far above the earth—so the legend runs—there hangs an Awful Bell, invisible to mortal eye, which angel hands alone may toll, which is never tolled save when the Unpardonable Sin is committed on earth, and then its judgment peal rings out like the blast of the archangel's trumpet, breaking on the ear of the Criminal, and on his ear alone, with a sound that freezes his blood with horror. The peal of the Bell, hung in the azure depths of space, announces to the Guilty one, that he is an outcast from God's mercy for ever, that his Crime can never be pardoned, while the throne of the Eternal endures; that in the hour of Death, his soul will be darkened by the hopeless prospect of an eternity of wo; wo without limit, despair without hope; the torture of the never-dying worm, and the unquenchable flame, forever and forever.

Reader! Did the sound of the Judgment Bell, pealing with one awful toll, from the invisible air, break over the soul of the Libertine, as in darkness and in silence, he stood shuddering over the victim of his Crime?

If in the books of the Last Day, there shall be found written down, but *One unpardonable* crime, that crime will be known as the foul wrong, accomplished in the gaudy Rose Chamber of Monk-hall, by the wretch, who now stood trembling in the darkness of the place, while his victim lay senseless at his feet.

There was darkness and silence for a few brief moments, and then a stream of light flashed around the Rose Chamber.

Like a fiend, returned to witness some appalling scene of guilt, which he had but a moment left, Devil-Bug stood in the doorway of the Walnut Chamber. He grimly smiled, as he surveyed the scene.

And then with a hurried gesture, a pallid face and blood-shot eyes, as though some Phantom tracked his footsteps, Lorrimer rushed madly by him, and disappeared into the Painted Chamber. At the very moment of his disappearance, Devil Bug raised the light on high, and started backward with a sudden impulse of surprise.

"*Dead—Dead* and come to life!" he shrieked, and then the gaze of his solitary eye was fixed upon the entrance to the Walnut Room. With a mechanical gesture, he placed the light upon the table and fled madly from the chamber, while the curtains opening into the Walnut Room rustled to and fro, for a single instant, and then a ghastly face, with livid cheeks and burning eyes, appeared between the crimson folds, gazing silently around the place, with a glance, that no living man would choose to encounter, for his weight in gold—it was so like the look of one arisen from the dead.

CHAPTER FOURTEENTH

❧ The Guilty Wife

The light of the dark-lanthern streamed around the spot, where the Merchant stood.

Behind him, all was darkness, while the lanthern, held extended in his left hand, flung a ruddy blaze of light, over the outlines of the massive bed. Long silk curtains, of rich azure, fell drooping in voluminous folds, to the very floor, concealing the bed from view, while from within the gorgeous curtaining, that low softened sound, like a woman breathing in her sleep, came faintly to the Merchant's ear.

Livingstone advanced. The manner in which he held the lanthern flung his face in shadow, but you could see that his form quivered with a tremulous motion, and in the attempt to smother a groan which arose to his lips, a thick gurgling sound like the death-rattle, was heard in his throat.

Gazing from the shadow that enveloped his face, Livingstone, with an involuntary glance took in the details of the gorgeous couch—the rich curtaining of light azure satin, closely drawn around the bed; the canopy overhead surmounted by a circle of glittering stars, arranged like a coronet; and the voluptuous shapes, assumed by the folds, as they fell drooping to the floor, all burst like a picture on his eye.

Beside the bed stood a small table—resembling a lady's work stand—covered with a plain white cloth. The silver sheath of a large Bowie knife, resting on the white cloth, shone glittering in the light, and attracted the Merchant's attention.

He laid the pistol which he held at his right side, upon the table and raised the Bowie knife to the light. The sheath was of massive silver, and the blade of the keenest steel. The handle fashioned like the sheath, of massive silver, bore a single name, engraved in large letters near the hilt. *Algernon Fitz-Cowles,* and on the blade of polished steel, amid a wreath of flowers glittered the motto in the expressive slang of southern braggarts— 'Stranger avoid a snag.'

Silently Livingstone examined the blade of the murderous weapon. It was sharp as a razor, with the glittering point inclining from the edge, like a Turkish dagger. The merchant grasped the handle of this knife in his right hand, and holding the lanthern on high, advanced to the bedside.

"His own knife—" muttered Livingstone—"shall find its way to his cankered heart—"

With the point of the knife, he silently parted the hangings of the bed, and the red glare of the lanthern flashed within the azure folds, revealing a small portion of the sleeping couch.

A moment passed, and Livingstone seemed afraid to gaze within the hangings, for he turned his head aside, more than once, and the thick gurgling noise again was heard in his throat. At last, raising the lanthern gently overhead, so that its beams would fall along a small space of the couch, while the rest was left in darkness, and grasping the knife with a firmer hold he gazed upon the spectacle disclosed to his view.

Her head deep sunken in a downy pillow, a beautiful woman, lay wrapt in slumber. By the manner in which the silken folds of the coverlid were disposed, you might see that her form was full, large and voluptuous. Thick masses of jet-black hair fell, glossy and luxuriant, over her round neck and along her uncovered bosom, which swelling with the full ripeness of womanhood, rose gently in the light. She lay on her side, with her head resting easily on one large, round arm, half hidden by the masses of black hair, streaming over the snow white pillow, while the other arm was flung carelessly along her form, the light falling softly over the clear transparent skin, the full roundness of its shape, and the small and delicate hand, resting gently on the coverlid.

Her face, appearing amid the tresses of her jet-black hair, like a fair picture half-hidden in sable drapery, was marked by a perfect regularity of feature, a high forehead, arching eyebrows and long dark lashes, resting on the velvet skin of each glowing cheek. Her mouth was opened slightly as she slept, the ivory whiteness of her teeth, gleaming through the rich vermillion of her parted lips.

She lay on that gorgeous couch, in an attitude of voluptuous ease; a perfect incarnation of the Sensual Woman, who combines the beauty of a mere animal, with an intellect strong and resolute in its every purpose.

And over that full bosom, which rose and fell with the gentle impulse of slumber, over that womanly bosom, which should have been the home of pure thoughts and wifely affections, was laid a small and swarthy hand, whose fingers, heavy with rings, pressed against the ivory skin, all streaked with veins of delicate azure, and clung twiningly among the dark tresses that hung drooping over the breast, as its globes rose heaving into view, like worlds of purity and womanhood.

It was a strange sight for a man to see, whose only joy, in earth or heaven, was locked within that snowy bosom, and yet Livingstone, the husband, stood firm and silent, as he gazed upon that strange hand, half hidden by the drooping curls.

It required but a slight motion of his hand, and the glare of the light flashed over the other side of the couch. The flash of the lanthern, among the shadows of the bed, was but for a moment, and yet Livingstone beheld the face of a dark-hued man, whose long dark hair mingled its heavy curls with the glossy tresses of his wife, while his hand reaching over her shoulder, rested, like a thing of foul pollution upon her bosom.

They slumbered together, slumbered in their guilt, and the Avenger stood gazing upon their faces while their hearts were as unconscious of his glance, as they were of the death which glittered over them in the upraised knife.

"Wife of mine—your slumber shall be deep and long—"

And as the whisper hissed from between the clenched teeth of the husband, he raised the dagger suddenly aloft, and then brought it slowly down until its point quivered within a finger's width of the heaving bosom, while the light of the lanthern held above his head, streamed over his livid face, and over the blooming countenance of his fair young wife.

The dagger glittered over her bosom; lower and lower it sank until a deeper respiration, a single heartdrawn sigh, might have forced the silken skin upon the glittering point, when the guilty woman murmured in her sleep.

"Algernon—a coronet—wealth and power—" were the broken words that escaped from her lips.

Again the husband raised the knife but it was with the hand clenched, and the sinews stiffened for the work of death.

"Seek your Algernon in the grave—" he whispered, with a convulsive smile, as his blue eyes, all alive with a glance, like a madman's gaze, surveyed the guilty wife—"Let the coronet be hung around your fleshless skull—let your wealth be a coffin, and—ha! ha!—your power—corruption and decay—"

It may have been that some feeling of the olden-time, when the image of that fair young wife dwelt in the holiest temple of his heart, came suddenly to the mind of the avenger, in that moment of fearful suspense, for his hand trembled for an instant and he turned his gaze aside, while a single scalding tear rolled down his livid cheek.

"Algernon—" murmured the wife—"We will seek a home—"

"In the grave!"

And the dagger rose, and gleamed like a stream of flame overhead, and then sank down with a whirring sound.

Is the bosom red with the stain of blood?

Has the keen knife severed the veins and pierced the heart?

The blow of a strong arm, stricken over Livingstone's shoulder, dashed his hand suddenly aside, and the knife sank to the very hilt in the pillow, within a hair's breadth of Dora's face. The knife touched the side of her cheek, and a long and glossy curl, severed from her head by the blow, lay resting on the pillow.

Livingstone turned suddenly round, with a deep muttered oath, while his massive form rose towering to its full height. Luke Harvey stood before him, his cold and glittering eye, fixed upon his face, with an expression of the deepest agitation.

"Stand back Sir—" muttered Livingstone with a quivering lip—"This spot is sacred to me! I want no witness to my wrong—nor to my vengeance!"

"Ha—ha!" sneered Luke bending forward until his eyes glared fixedly in the face of the Husband—"Is this a vengeance for a man like you?"

"Luke—again I warn you—leave me to my shame, and its punishment—"

" 'Shame' 'Punishment!' Ha—ha! You have been wronged in secret, slowly and quietly wronged, and yet would punish that wrong, by a blow that brings but a single pang!"

"Luke—you are right—" whispered Livingstone, his agitated manner subsiding into a look of calm and fearful determination—"The wrong has been secret, long in progress, horrible in result. So let the punishment be. She shall see *the* Death—" and his eyes flashed with a maniac wildness—"She shall see the Death as it slowly approaches, she shall feel it as it winds its very fangs into her very heart, she shall know that all hope is in vain, while my voice will whisper in her freezing ear—'Dora, it is by my will that you die! Shriek—Dora—shriek for aid! Death is cold and icy—I can save you! I your—husband! I can save you, but will not! Die—Adultress—die—' "

"Algernon—" murmured Dora half-awakened from her sleep—"There is a cold hand laid against my cheek—"

"She wakes!" whispered Luke—"The dagger—the lanthern—"

It required but a single moment for Livingstone to draw the knife, from the pillow, where it rested against the blooming cheek of the wife, while Luke, with a sudden moment grasped the lanthern, and closed its door, leaving the Chamber wrapt in midnight darkness.

The husband stood motionless as a stone, and Luke held his very breath, as the voice of Dora broke on their ears, in tones of alarm and terror.

"Algernon—" she whispered, as she started from her slumber—"Awake—Do you not hear the sound of voices, by the bedside? Hist! Could it have been *the* dream? Algernon—"

"Deuced uncomfortable to be waked-up this way—" murmured a sleepy voice— "What's the matter Dora? What about a dream?"

"I was awakened just now from my sleep by the sound of voices.—I thought a blaze of light flashed round the room, while my hus—that is, Livingstone stood at the bedstead. And then I felt a cold hand laid against my cheek—"

"Ha—ha! Rather good, *that!* D'ye know Dora that I had a dream too? I dreamt that I was in the front parlor, second story you know, in your house on Fourth street, when the old fellow came in, and read your note on the table. Ha—ha—and then—are you listening?—I thought that the old gentleman while he was reading, turned to a bright peagreen in the face, and—"

"Hist! Do you not hear some one breathing in the room?"

"Pshaw, Dora, you're nervous! Go to sleep my love. Don't loose your rest for all the dreams in the world. Good night, Dora!"

"A little touch of farce with our tragedy—" half-muttered Luke, as a quiet chuckle shook his frame—"Egad! If they talk in this strain much longer, I'll have to guffaw! It's rather too much for my risibles; this is! A husband standing in the dark by the bedside, while his wife and her paramour are telling their pleasant dreams, in which he figures as the hero—"

Whether a smile passed over Livingstone's face, or a frown, Luke could not tell, for the room was dark as a starlit night, yet the quick gasping sound of a man struggling for breath, heard through the darkness, seem to indicate any thing but the pleasant laugh or the jovial chuckle.

"They sleep again!" muttered Luke—"She has sunken into slumber while Death watches at the bedside. Curse it—how that fellow snores!"

There was a long pause of darkness and silence. No word escaped the Husband's lips, no groan convulsed his chest, no half-muttered cry of agony, indicated the struggle which was silently rending his soul, as with a viper's fangs.

"Livingstone—" whispered Luke after a long pause—"Where are you? Confound it man, I can't hear you breathe. I'm afraid to uncover the light—it may awaken them again. I say Livingstone—had n't we better leave these quarters—"

"I could have borne expressions of remorse from her lips—I could have listened to sudden outpourings of horror wrung from her soul by the very blackness of her guilt, but this grovelling familiarity with vice!"

"Matter-of-fact pollution, as you might observe—" whispered Luke.

"Luke, I tell you, the cup is full to overflowing—but I will drain it to the dregs!"

"Now's your time—" whispered Luke, as, swinging the curtain aside, he suffered the light of the lanthern to fall over the bed—"Dora looks quite pretty. Fitz-Cowles decidedly interesting—"

"And on that bosom have I slept!" exclaimed Livingstone, in a voice of agony, as he gazed upon his slumbering wife—"Those arms have clung round my neck—and *now!* Ha! Luke you may think me mad, but I tell ye man, that there is the spirit of a slow and silent revenge creeping through my veins. *She* has *dishonored* me! Do you read anything like *forgiveness* in my face?"

"Not much o' it I assure you. But come, Livingstone—let's be going. This is not the time nor place for your revenge. Let's travel."

Livingstone laid down the bowie knife, and with a smile of bitter mockery, seized a small pair of scissors from the work-basket which stood on the table.

"You smile, Luke?" he whispered, as, leaning over the bedside, he laid his hand upon the jet-black hair of the slumbering Fitz-Cowles;—"Ha-ha! I will leave the place, but d'ye see, Luke, I must take some slight keepsake, to remind me of the gallant Colonel. A lock of his hair, you know, Luke?"

"Egad! Livingstone, I believe you're going mad! A lock of his hair? Pshaw! You'll want a straight jacket soon—"

"And a lock of my Dora's hair—" whispered Livingstone, as his blue eyes flashed from beneath his dark eyebrows, while his lips wore that same mocking smile—"But you see the knife saved me all trouble. Here is a glossy tress severed by the Colonel's dagger. Now let me wind them together, Luke, let me lay them next to my heart, Luke— yes, smile my fellow—Ha! ha! ha!"

"Hist! Your wife stirs in her sleep—you will awaken them again."

"D'ye know, Luke—" cried Livingstone, drawing his partner close to his side, and looking in his face, with a vacant glance, that indicated a temporary derangement of intellect—"D'ye know, Luke, that I didn't do that, o' my own will? Hist! Luke— closer—closer—I'll tell you. The Devil was at the bedside, Luke; he whispered it in my ear, he bade me take these keepsakes—ha, ha, ha—what a jolly set of fellows we are! And then, Luke—" his voice sank to a thrilling whisper—"He pointed with his iron hand to *the last scene,* in which my vengeance shall be complete. She shall beg for mercy, Luke; aye, on her knees, but—ha, ha, ha—*kill—kill—kill!* is written in letters of blood before my eyes, every where, Luke, every where. Don't you see it?"

He pointed vacantly at the air as he spoke, and seized Luke by the shoulder, as though he would command his attention to the blood-red letters.

Luke was conscious that he stood in the presence of a madman.

Inflexible as he was in his own secret purpose of revenge, upon the woman who had trampled on his very heart, Luke still regarded the Merchant with a feeling akin to broth-erhood. As the fearful fact impressed itself on his soul, that Livingstone stood before him, deprived of reason, an expression of the deepest feeling shadowed the countenance of Luke, and his voice was broken in its tones as he endeavoured to persuade the mad-man, to leave the scene of his dishonor and shame.

"Come! Livingstone! let us go—" said Luke, taking his partner by the arm, and leading him gently toward the closet.

"But I've got the keepsakes safe, Luke—" whispered Livingstone, as that wild light flashed from his large blue eyes—"D'ye see the words in the air, Luke? Now they change to her name—Dora, Dora, Dora! All in blood-red letters. I say Luke, let's have a quiet whist party—there's four of us—Dora and I; you and Fitz-Cowles—"

"I'm willing—" exclaimed Luke, as with a quick movement he seized the pistol—left by Livingstone on the table, and concealed it within the breast of his greatcoat—"Suppose we step into the next room, and get every thing ready for the party—"

"You're keen, Luke, keen, but I'm even with you—" whispered Livingstone as his livid face lighted up with a sudden gleam of intelligence—"Here we stand on the threshold of this closet—we are about to leave my wife's bed-room. You think I'm mad. Do I look like a madman? I know there is no whist-party to be held this night, I know that—Hist. Luke. Don't you see it, all pictured forth in the air? The scene of my vengeance? In colors of blood, painted by the Devil's hand? Yonder Luke—yonder! How red it grows—and then in letters of fire, every where, every where, is written—Dora—Dora—Dora—"

It was a fearful spectacle to see that strong man, with his imposing figure, raised to its full stature and his thoughtful brow, lit up with an expression of idiotic wonder, as standing on the verge of the secret door, he pointed wildly at the blood-red picture which his fancy had drawn in the vacant air while his blue eyes dilated with a maniac glance, and his face grew yet more livid and ghastly.

"Come, Livingstone—" cried Luke gently leading him through the closet—"You had better leave this place—"

"And yet Dora, is sleeping here? My young wife? 'The mother of my children?' Do'ye think Luke, that I'd have believed you last Thursday morning, if you had then told me this? 'Livingstone, this day-week, you will leave a chamber in a brothel, and leave your young wife, sleeping in another man's arms.' But never mind Luke—it will all be right. For I tell ye, it is there, there before me in colors of blood! That last scene of my vengeance! And there—there—in letters of flame—Dora!—Dora! Dora!"

And while the fair young wife slept quietly in the bed of guilt and shame, Luke led the Merchant from the room and from the house.

CHAPTER FIFTEENTH

❧ The Dishonor

All was silent within the Rose Chamber. For a single moment that pale visage glared from the crimson hangings, concealing the entrance to the Walnut Room, and then with a measured footstep, Byrnewood Arlington advanced along the floor, his countenance ghastly as the face of Lazarus, at the very instant, when in obedience to the words of the Incarnate, life struggled with corruption and death, over his cheek and brow.

Bring home to your mind the scene, when Lazarus lay prostrate in the grave, a stiffened corse, his face all clammy with corruption, the closed eyes surrounded by loathsome circles of decay, the cheeks sunken, and the lips fallen in: let the words of Jesus ring in your ears, 'Lazarus, come forth!'"[21] And then as the blue eyelids slowly unclose, as the gleam of life shoots forth from the glassy eye, as the flush of health struggles with the yellowish hue of decay along each cheek, as life and death mingling in that face for a single moment, maintain a fearful combat for the mastery; then I pray you, gaze upon the visage of Byrnewood Arlington, and mark how like it is to the face of one arisen from the dead; a ghastly face, on whose fixed outline the finger-traces of corruption are yet visible, from whose eyes the film of the grave is not yet passed away.

The gaze of Byrnewood, as he strode from the entrance of the Walnut Chamber, was riveted to the floor. Had the eyes of the rattlesnake gleamed from the carpet, slowly drawing its victim to his ruin, Byrnewood could not have fixed his gaze upon the object in the centre of the floor, with a more fearful and absorbing intensity.

There, thrown prostrate on the gaudy carpet, insensible and motionless, the form of Mary Arlington lay at the brother's feet.

He sank silently on his knees.

He took her small white hand—now cold as marble—within his own, he swept the unbound tresses back from her palid brow. Her eyes were closed as in death, her lips hung apart, the lower one trembling with a scarcely perceptible movement, her cheek was pale as ashes, with a deep red tint in the centre.

Byrnewood uttered no sound, nor shrieked forth any wild exclamation of revenge, or wo, or despair. He silently drew the folds of the night-robe round her form, and veiled her bosom—but a moment agone warmed into a glow by the heart's fires, now paled by the fingers of the ravisher—he veiled her fair young bosom from the light.

It was a sad sight to look upon. That face, so fair and blooming, but a moment past, now pale as death, with spot of burning red on the centre of each cheek: that bosom, a moment since, heaving with passion, now still and motionless; those delicate hands with tiny fingers, which had bravely fought for honor, for virtue, for purity, an instant ago, now resting cold and stiffened by her side.

Thick tresses of dark brown hair, hung round her neck. With that same careful movement of his hand, Byrnewood swept them aside. Along the smooth surface of that fair neck like some noisome reptile, trailing over a lovely flower, a large vein, black and distorted, shot upward, darkening the glossy skin, while it told the story of the maiden's dishonor and shame.

"My sister!" was the solitary exclamation that broke from Byrnewood's lips as he gazed upon the form of the unconscious girl, and his large dark eye, dilating as he spoke, glanced around with an expression of strange meaning.

He raised her form in his arms, and kissed her cold lips again and again. No tear trickled from his eyelids; no sigh heaved his bosom; no deep muttered execration manifested the agitation of his soul.

"My sister!" he again whispered, and gathered her more close to his heart.

A slight flush deepening over her cheek, even while he spoke, gave signs of returning consciousness.

Mary slowly unclosed her eyes, and gazed with a wandering glance around the room. An instant passed ere she discovered that she lay in Byrnewood's arms.

---

[21]John 11:43.

"Oh, brother—" she exclaimed, not with a wild shriek, but in a low-toned voice, whose slightest accent quivered with an emphasis of despair—"Oh, brother! Leave me—leave me. I am not worthy of your touch. I am vile, brother, oh, most vile! Leave me—Leave me, for I am lost!"

"Mary!" whispered Byrnewood, resisting her attempt to unwind his arms from her form, while the blood, filling the veins of his throat, produced an effect like strangulation—"Mary! Do not—do not speak thus—I—I—"

He could say no more, but his face dropped on her cold bosom, and the tears, which he had silently prayed for, came at last.

He wept, while that low choking noise, sounding in his throat, that involuntary heaving of the chest, that nervous quivering of the lip, all betokened the strong man wrestling with his agony.

"Do not weep for me, brother—" she said, in the same low-toned voice—"I am polluted, brother, and am not worthy of the slightest tear you shed for me. Unwind your arms—brother, do not resist me—for the strength of despair is in these hands—unwind your arms, and let me no longer pollute you by my touch—"

There was something fearful in the expression of her face as she spoke. She was no longer the trembling child whose young face, marked the inexperience of her stainless heart. A new world had broken upon her soul, not a world of green trees, silver streams and pleasant flowers, but a chaos of ashes, and mouldering flame; a lurid sky above, a blasted soil below, and one immense horizon of leaden clouds, hemming in the universe of desolation.

She had sprung from the maiden into the woman, but a blight was on her soul forever. The crime had not only stained her person with dishonor, but, like the sickening warmth of the hot-house, it had forced the flower of her soul, into sudden and unnatural maturity. It was the maturity of precocious experience. In her inmost soul, she felt that she was a dishonored thing, whose very touch was pollution, whose presence, among the pure and stainless, would be a bitter mockery and foul reproach. The guilt was not hers, but the Ruin blasted her purity forever.

"Unwind your arms, my brother—" she exclaimed, tearing herself from his embrace, with all a maniac's strength—"I am polluted. You are pure. Oh do not touch me—do not touch me. Leave me to my shame—oh, leave me—"

She unwound her form from his embrace, and sank crouching into a corner of the Rose Chamber, extending her hands with a frightened gesture, as though she feared his slightest touch.

"Mary" shrieked Byrnewood, flinging his arms on high, with a movement of sudden agitation—"Oh, do not look upon me thus! Come to me—oh, Mary—come to me, for I am your brother."

The words, the look and the trembling movement of his outspread arms, all combined, acted like a spell upon the intellect of the ruined girl. She rose wildly to her feet, as though impelled by some invisible influence, and fell tremblingly into her brother's arms.

While one dark and horrible thought, was working its way through the avenues of his soul, he gathered her to his breast again and again.

And in that moment of silence and unutterable thought, the curtains leading into the

Painted Chamber were slowly thrust aside, and Lorrimer again appeared upon the scene. Stricken with remorse, he had fled with a madman's haste from the scene of his crime, and while his bosom was torn by a thousand opposing thoughts, he had endeavored to drown the voice within him, and crush the memory of the nameless wrong. It was all in vain. Impelled by an irresistible desire, to look again upon the victim of his crime, he re-entered the Rose Chamber. It was a strange sight, to see the Brother kneeling on the floor, as he gathered his sister's form in his arms, and yet the Seducer, gave no sign nor indication of surprise.

A fearful agitation was passing over the Libertine's soul, as unobserved by the brother or sister, he stood gazing upon them with a wandering glance. His face, so lately flushed with passion, in its vilest hues, was now palest and livid. His white lips, trembled with a nervous moment, and his hands, extended on either side, clutched vacantly at the air, as though he wrestled with an unseen foe.

While the thought of horror, was slowly darkening over Byrnewood's soul, a thought as dark and horrible gathered like a Phantom over the mind of Lorrimer.

A single word of explanation, will make the subsequent scene, clear and intelligible to the reader.

From generation to generation, the family of the Lorrimer's, had been subject to an aberration of intellect, as sudden as it was terrible; always resulting from any peculiar agitation of mind, which might convulse the soul, with an emotion remarkable for its power or energy. It was a hallucination, a temporary madness, a sudden derangement of intellect. It always succeeded an uncontrollable outburst of anger, or grief, or joy. From father to son, since the family had first come over to Pennsylvania, with the Proprietor and Peace-Maker William Penn,[22] this temporary derangement of intellect, had descended as a fearful heritage.

Lorrimer had been subject to this madness, but once in his life, when his father's corse lay stiffened before his eyes. And now, as he stood gazing upon the form of the brother and sister, Lorrimer, felt this temporary madness stealing over his soul, in the form of a strange hallucination, while he became conscious, that in a single moment, the horror which shook his frame, would rise to his lips in words of agony and fear.

"Raise your hands with mine, to Heaven, Mary—" exclaimed Byrnewood as the Thought which had been working over his soul, manifested its intensity in words—"Raise your hands with mine, and curse the author of your ruin! Lift your voice with mine, up to the God, who beheld the wrong—who will visit the wronger with a doom meet, for his crime—lift your voice with mine, and curse him—"

"Oh Byrnewood, do not, do not curse *him*. The wrong has been done but do not, I beseech you, visit his head with a curse—"

"Hear me, oh God, before whom, I now raise my hands, in the vow of justice! In life I will be to this wretch, as a Fate, a Doom, a Curse!

"I am vile—oh God—steeped in the same vices, which blacken the heart of this

---

[22]Lorrimer's family is an ancient one in Pennsylvania, having come over with William Penn (1644–1718), the man who oversaw the founding of the American Commonwealth of Pennsylvania in 1682. William Penn helped plan the initial design of the city of Philadelphia.

man, cankered by the same corruption. But the office, which I now take on myself, raising this right hand to thee, in witness of my fixed purpose, would sanctify the darkest fiend in hell! I am the avenger of my sister's wrong! She was innocent, she was pure, she trusted and was betrayed! I will avenge her! Before thee, I swear to visit her wrong, upon the head of her betrayer, with a doom never to be forgotten in the memory of man. This right hand I dedicate to this solemn purpose—come what will, come what may, let danger threaten or death stand in my path, through sickness and health, through riches or poverty, I now swear, to hold my steady pathway onward, my only object in life—the avengement of my sister's wrong! He *shall* die by this hand—oh God—I swear it by thy name—I swear it by my soul—I swear it by the Fiend who impelled the villain to this deed of crime—"

As he whispered forth this oath, in a voice which speaking from the depths of his chest, had a hollow and sepulchral sound, the fair girl flung herself on his breast, and with a wild shriek essayed to delay the utterance of the curse, by gathering his face, to her bosom.

For a moment her efforts were successful. Lorrimer had stood silent and pale, while the deep-toned voice of Byrnewood Arlington, breaking in accents of doom upon his ear, had aided and strengthened the strange hallucination which was slowly gathering over his brain like a mighty spell.

"There is a wide river before me, its broad waves tinged with the last red rays of a winter sunset—" such were the words he murmured, extending his hand, as though pointing to the scene, which dawned upon his soul—"A wide river with its waves surging against the wharves of a mighty city. Afar I behold steeples and roofs and towers, all glowing in the beams of the setting sun. And as I gaze, the waves turn to blood, red and ghastly blood—and now the sky is a-flame, and the clouds sweep slowly past, bathed in the same crimson hue. All is blood—the river rushes before me, and the sky and the city—all pictured in colors of blood.

"An invisible hand is leading me to my doom. There is Death for me, in yonder river, and I know it, yet down, down to the rivers banks, down, down into the red waters, I must go. Ha! ha! 'Tis a merry death! The blood-red waves rise above me—higher, higher, higher! Yonder is the city, yonder the last rays of the setting sun, glitter on the roof and steeple, yonder is the blood-red sky—and ah! I tell ye I will not die—you shall not sink me beneath these gory waves! Devil! Is not your vengeance satisfied—must you feast your eyes with the sight of my closing agonies—must your hand grasp me by the throat, and your foot trample me beneath the waves? I tell you I will not, will not die—"

"Ha—ha—ha! Here's purty going's on—" laughed the hoarse voice of Devil-Bug, as his hideous form appeared in the doorway of the Walnut Chamber, with his attendant negroes at his back—"Seems the gal helped him off. There he sits—the ornery feller, with his sister in his arms—while Gusty, is a-doin' some ravin's on his own indivdooal hook. Come here Glow-worm—here Musquito—come here my pets, and 'tend to this leetle family party—"

In another instant the Rose Chamber became the scene of a strange picture.

Byrnewood had arisen to his feet, while Lorrimer stood spell-bound by the hallucination which possessed his brain. The handsome Libertine stood in the centre of the room, his form dilating to its full stature, his face the hue of ashes, while with his hazel eyes, glaring on vacancy, he clutched wildly at the air, starting backward at the same moment, as though some invisible hand, was silently impelling him to the brink of the blood-red river, which rolled tumultuously at his feet, which slowly gathered around him, which began to heave upward to his very lips.

On one side, in a half-kneeling position, crouched Mary Arlington, her large blue eyes, starting from her pallid face, as with her upraised hands, crossed over her bosom, she gazed upon the agitated countenance of the seducer, with a glance of mingled awe and wonder; while, on the other side, stern and erect, Byrnewood, with his pale visage darkening in a settled frown, with one foot advanced and his hand upraised, seemed about to strike the libertine to the floor.

In the background, rendered yet more hideous by the dimness of the scene, Devil-Bug stood grinning in derisive triumph as he motioned his attendants, the Herculean negroes, to advance and secure their prey.

There was silence for a single moment. Lorrimer still stood clutching at the vacant air, Mary still gazed upon this face in awe, Byrnewood yet paused in his meditated blow, while Devil-Bug, with Musquito and Glow-worm at his back, seemed quietly enjoying the entire scene, as he glanced from side to side with his solitary eye.

"Unhand me—I will not die—" shrieked Lorrimer, as he fancied that phantom hand, gathering tightly round his throat, while the red waters swept surging to his very lips—"I will not die—I defy—ah! ah! You strangle me—"

"The hour of your death has come! You have said it—and it shall be so!" whispered Byrnewood, advancing a single step, as his dark eye was fixed upon the face of Lorrimer—"While your own guilty heart spreads a blood-red river before your eyes, this hand—no phantom hand—shall work your death!"

He sprang forward, while a shriek arose from Mary's lips, he sprang forward with his eyes blazing with excitement, and his outspread hand ready for the work of vengeance, but as he sprang, the laugh of Devil-Bug echoed at his back, and the sinewy arms of the negroes gathered suddenly round his form and flung him as suddenly to the floor.

"Here's fine goin's on—" exclaimed Devil-Bug, as he glanced from face to face— "A feller who's been a leetle too kind to a gal, stands a-makin' speeches at nothin'. The gal kneels on the carpet as though she were a gettin' up a leetle prayer on her own account; and this 'ere onery feller—git a good grip o' him you bull-dogs—sets up a small shop o' cussin' and sells his cusses for nothin'! Here's a tea party for ye—"

"What does all this mean, Devil-Bug—" exclaimed Lorrimer, in his usual voice, as the hallucination passed from him like a dream, leaving him utterly unconscious of the strange vision which had a moment since absorbed his very soul—"What does all this mean? Ha! Byrnewood and Mary—I remember? *You* are *her* brother—are you not?"

"I am her avenger—" said Byrnewood, with a ghastly smile, as he endeavoured to free himself from the grasp of the negroes—"And your executioner! Within three days you shall die by this hand!"

"Ha-ha-ha!" laughed Devil-Bug—"There's more than one genelman as has got a say in that leetle matter! How d'ye feel, young man? Did you ever take opium afore? You won't go to sleep nor nothin'? We can't do what we like with you? Kin we? Ho-ho-ho! *I vonders how that'ill vork!*"

8

Emma Dorothy Eliza Nevitte Southworth
(1819–1899)

E. D. E. N. SOUTHWORTH BEGAN her long writing career in 1845, after her husband had deserted her to seek his fortune in South America. Initially, writing was a way to supplement her salary as a schoolteacher, as she provided for herself and her two children. Her writings so quickly gained wide popularity that she became one of only a select number of American women writers able to make a comfortable living at their craft. Over the course of her half-century career, Southworth wrote some sixty novels and countless short stories.

Two of her earliest stories, "The Wife's Victory," and its sequel, "The Married Shrew," appeared in *The National Era* in 1847. This was the same periodical that would publish Harriet Beecher Stowe's *Uncle Tom's Cabin* four years later. These stories were based on a common, tried-and-true formula of taking a verse of scripture and illustrating its principle with a story. They are tales with heavy moral overtones, preaching a Christian ethic that runs throughout Southworth's writing. She would enhance the moral quality of her work by claiming that almost all of her stories were based on true events, and thus offered real-world wisdom to her readers.

"The Wife's Victory" and "The Married Shrew" are important not only because they attracted readers to her works (including the literary luminary John Greenleaf Whittier), but they also stand as fascinating early treatments of Southworth's most basic interest: the role of women in society. Although her treatment of the woman's role in these tales is pronounced in its Christian conservativism, her later writings would develop into masterful blends of female submission and female empowerment. Southworth seemed to have an unerring ability to tap into the hopes and fears of American women, and over a fifty-year span made herself into arguably the most read American woman prose writer of the nineteenth century.

THE WIFE'S VICTORY

The husband is head of the wife, even as Christ is head of the Church;
Therefore, as the Church is subject to Christ, so let the wives be to
their own husbands in everything.

EPHESIANS, V. 23, 24

Such duty as the subject owes the prince,
Even such a woman oweth to her husband.

SHAKSPEARE

What thou bid'st
Unargued I obey; so God ordains.
God is thy law; thou mine.

MILTON

"I would not have him, though he owned all the mines of Golconda,"[1] said bright Kate Gleason to her sister, Mrs. Lindal.

"And why not, pray?" said gentle Mary Lindal.

"Oh! because he has got such a horrible temper."

"How do you know that?"

"By a great many signs; by the shape of his head and the colour of his hair, the glance of his eye, the curl of his nose, and the set of his mouth——"

"Oh! stop, stop, stop; of whom are you speaking? That incomparable man, in philanthropy a Howard, in wisdom a Newton, in patriotism a Washington,[2] in——"

"Temper a Bluebeard."[3]

"Kate! I will not hear another word of this. You are speaking of—of—" and Mary Lindal blushed.

"Out with it! of Grenville Dormer Leslie, your future husband. But I give you fair warning, Mary, that though you may feel a vocation to become Mrs. Bluebeard, I am not particularly inspired to play 'Anne! sister Anne!' and run the risk of catching my death of cold by standing on a windy tower, to 'see if anybody is coming,' when he is about to slay you for your disobedience."

E. D. E. N. Southworth, *The Wife's Victory; and Other Nouvellettes.* Philadelphia: T. B. Peterson, 1854.

[1] Territory in southern India famous for its diamonds.

[2] John Howard (1726–1790) was a famous English philanthropist dedicated to the fields of prison reform and public health. Isaac Newton (1642–1727) was a brilliant English physicist and mathematician. George Washington (1732–1799) commanded the American forces during the American Revolution.

[3] Wife-murdering husband in the Charles Perrault fairy tale of the same name.

"But perhaps I shall not *be* disobedient," said Mary.

"Perhaps you shall not *be* disobedient," repeated Kate, with a withering sneer. "Well, for my part, when *I* am married, if ever my husband ventures to lay a command on *me,* I shall make a point of breaking it, at whatever cost of convenience, by way of asserting my independence."

"Not if you love, Kate."

"Either way, either way. Now, I like Lem Dunn very well; and if neither of us change our minds, we may be married when he returns from sea; but fancy Lem Dunn playing husband *a la Grand Turque,*[4] and daring to say, 'you shall' and 'you shall not!' really, if I were in a good humour I should laugh in his face, and if in a bad one, I should be apt to box his ears."

"I must believe you are jesting, Catherine."

"Then I will be as serious as His Eminence Archbishop Leslie[5] himself, and say that I really cannot see why we women should be called upon to 'honour and obey' so implicitly, unless we could be first convinced of their superior excellence by whom such honour and obedience are claimed."

"We are not. We *should* be first convinced of men's superiority, before we give them that 'right Divine' to control our actions and destinies, which by all Christian and human law is the just prerogative of a husband, whether or not he be mentally or morally superior to his wife."

"Pooh! nonsense! fiddlestick! with your Divine prerogative and the rest of it. If a woman marries a fool, I suppose she is bound to obey him!"

"When a woman marries a man whom she feels she cannot respect, she places herself in a false position, from which nothing can extricate her; and, however repugnant, however galling they may become, the same duties of submission and obedience are incumbent upon her, in all cases where they do not clash with the laws of God. A woman, in such a case, is an object of deep commiseration, although, having brought the evil upon herself, by a desecration of all her most holy instincts, she suffers but a just and most fitting expiation of her fault. I could not love, and would not give myself away to a man on whose wisdom I could not rely as on God's, to whose will I could not submit as to God's."

"Idolater! Would you set up an earthly God, and fall down and worship him?"

" 'Wives, submit yourselves to your husbands *as to the Lord!'*[6] There is Scripture for the idolatry, if you choose to call it so."

"Pshaw! If you were not talking foolishly, you would be talking wickedly. 'Satan can quote Scripture for his purpose.' "

"So he can. I am now quite convinced of that fact. But do not let us trifle with such holy and beautiful mysteries, dear Kate. There is another text of Scripture to the same purpose——"

---

[4]Like an absolute dictator.

[5]Possibly a reference to John Leslie (1527–1596), who was a Scottish Roman Catholic bishop who advised Mary Queen of Scots in her plots to overthrow the Protestant English government of the period.

[6]Eph. 5:22.

"Oh, yes! There are hundreds; pray don't recite them."

"Just this one, Kate, I love it so much. 'The head of the woman is man; the head of the man is Christ; and the head of Christ is God.'[7] Is it not a lovely chain, a beautiful climax, from weakness to Omnipotence; like Jacob's ladder[8] from earth to heaven?"

"Sweet Providence! You have put my brains in a complete whirl, with heaven and earth, and chains and ladders, and heads and husbands; but out of the chaos one fact and feeling stands very distinctly. If Lem Dunn expects any such subordination from me, he will find himself very much mistaken; but he is not so presuming, poor Lem Dunn."

"I think *you* will find yourself mistaken in your estimate of his character and expectations."

"Well, perhaps so; in that case, I shall only have a little more trouble in breaking him in. But suppose now, only for argument, that you are deceived in Leslie; suppose his temper to be violent?"

"I will take care not to arouse it."

"His will unbending?"

"I shall not waste my strength nor risk my peace by seeking to bend it."

"His nature selfish?"

"Methinks, as I love and esteem him more highly than myself, I should only unite with him in his self-worship."

"His heart and mind unprincipled and depraved?"

"Impossible! impossible!" exclaimed Mary indignantly. "I will not for a single instant suppose such a thing, even for argument's sake. I have seen my error in permitting you to go on so long. Leslie has none of the bad qualities you have named. He is every way worthy of the highest esteem."

"And if he were not so?"

"If I were his wife, my duties would not be less incumbent upon me—would not be less scrupulously performed. But I shall not find myself in the degrading position of a wife who cannot reverence her husband, in giving myself to Leslie. I obey a Divine instinct that will not mislead me; in loving him, I shall offer the best worship, and in obeying him the most acceptable service to the Deity."

Mary and Catherine Gleason had lost their parents during their infancy, and had become the charge of their grandfather, old Captain Gleason, a retired merchant. At the time Captain Gleason received his granddaughters into his house, he was mourning the loss of his younger son, who was supposed to have perished at sea, on his passage home from Europe. The ship in which he was to have taken passage had never been heard of since her setting sail from Liverpool, and was now believed to have been wrecked. Years flew by, and no clue was obtained to the fate of the lost ship or the lost son.

Mary Gleason, at the age of sixteen, had, in obedience to her grandfather, given her hand to Mr. Lindal, a wealthy merchant, some twenty years her senior. In the second year of her marriage, she became the mother of a lovely little girl. Soon after the birth of the little Sylvia, the failure and death of Mr. Lindal left Mary again dependent on the bounty

---

[7]1 Cor. 11:3.

[8]Jacob has a dream about a ladder leading to heaven with angels ascending and descending on it (Gen. 28:12).

of her grandfather, who received her and her child with the deepest sympathy and affection. Little Sylvia soon became the especial pet and plaything of the whole household.

Although Mary Lindal had faithfully discharged her duties as a wife, she had never loved her husband, except as a friend. Her whole affections centered upon her child, the little Sylvia. She was her constant companion, in doors and out doors, in parlour, chamber, and street, by day; and at night she slept encircled in her arms, pressed to her bosom. At the age of four years, Sylvia had been attacked with a violent and contagious fever. No words can describe the anguish of the mother, as she watched, day after day, and night after night, for weeks, beside the bed of the little sufferer; no pen can portray the joy when, at last, her darling was pronounced out of danger.

Mrs. Lindal was very beautiful, graceful, and accomplished, and a co-heiress with her sister Catherine; consequently, she was much followed and flattered. Notwithstanding her numerous admirers, and some very eligible offers, the seventh year of her widowhood had passed away, and she was still unmarried. In the mean time, Catherine Gleason had grown up to womanhood, more radiantly beautiful than her sister had ever been.

At length, in the twenty-fifth year of her age, Mrs. Lindal became acquainted with Mr. Leslie, the subject of the conversation with which this sketch opens. Mr. Leslie was a man of great personal attractions, pure morals, and distinguished talents. Mary Lindal ever listened to his brilliant conversation with delighted attention. Convinced by his clear-sighted views and able exposition of truth, she had insensibly acquired a habit of shaping her opinions by his own. There was one circumstance about their acquaintance that peculiarly attracted Mary. It was this: He *never* flattered her, never by any chance paid her a compliment, excepting this—the most, the only acceptable one, of constantly seeking her society.

I think it was that agreeable giber, Rochefoucault,[9] who somewhere asserted that any woman may be safely flattered on any subject, from the profundity of her understanding to the exquisite taste of her fan. Without venturing to differ from such authority, I will simply assert that Mary Lindal was an exception to this rule.

At the end of a twelvemonth's acquaintance, Grenville Dormer Leslie and Mary Lindal were married, and took possession of a handsome house, in a fashionable quarter of the city.

An event occurred soon after their marriage, that greatly pained the affectionate heart of Mary. This was the death of her grandfather. The old gentleman had made a will, leaving his property equally divided between the sisters, Mary and Catherine. This property, however, as is frequently the case, was not half so large as had been reported, and his granddaughters inherited only about twenty thousand dollars apiece. A few moments before his death, while holding little Sylvia's hand within his own, Captain Gleason turned his dim eyes on Leslie, and said, "I have been thinking of this poor child, Leslie; if time were allowed me, I would alter my will, giving her mother's share of the property to her at her mother's death, or perhaps at her own marriage. You are wealthy, Leslie, and your children, if you shall have any, will be handsomely provided for, while poor Sylvia—"

---

[9]François de la Rochefoucauld (1613–1680) was a French writer and adventurer, well known for his moral and philosophical maxims.

"Shall fare as one of my own," said Leslie.

"I believe you, and I thank you; now call Mary."

Leslie summoned his wife.

"Mary," said the dying man, as she came up to the bedside, "I leave you a certain sum; I wish you and Leslie to consider it as intrusted to your care for the future use of Sylvia. *You* will, of course, have the use of it for—for many years to come." The old man spoke with difficulty. Turning his fast-failing eyes once more on Mr. and Mrs. Leslie, he added, "I have been so strangely thoughtless of this poor child's future—but now promise to do as I ask you." Mary promised, through her tears, while Leslie assured him that his wishes should be scrupulously fulfilled.

The old man soon after breathed his last.

Six months after the death of Captain Gleason, Mrs. Leslie and Catherine Gleason, who was an inmate of her house, were sitting together in the parlour, engaged in needlework, and talking of the expected return of Lieutenant Lemuel Dunn, the affianced husband of Catherine, whose marriage was to take place upon the promotion of the lieutenant to a captaincy. There was a ring at the hall door, and a few minutes after—

"Mr. Gleason" was announced.

Both ladies rose to receive him, looking strangely at each other, and at him.

"I suppose it is impossible, ladies, that you should remember or recognise a relative who left his native country while you were yet in the nursery. I am Henry Willis Gleason, at your service."

Mrs. Leslie and Miss Gleason stood speechless with surprise and incredulity for an instant, but, quickly recovering their self-possession, greeted their new-found relative with the warmest affection.

"But my father! girls, my dear old father. Where is he! How is he?" The ladies wept. At last, Catherine found words to say—

"It is six months since grandfather went to Heaven."

"Oh! that he had lived to see this day!" exclaimed Mary. "Oh! that he could have lived to be blessed in your return."

"He believed me dead?" questioned Gleason.

"Yes," said Mary, "for the last ten years he has believed you dead."

The reason for his protracted absence and apparent death was now demanded and explained. It was a long story, in substance the following: Ten years before, he had left his native shores, to make a voyage to Europe and a tour of the Continent. After having travelled over the greater part of Europe, he visited the city of St. Petersburg and the court of Russia, where, after a residence of some months, he was so unfortunate as to give offence in some unknown manner to the Emperor, for which he was banished to Siberia for a term of ten years; and these ten years had actually been passed among the everlasting snows of Asiatic Russia. Upon his return to St. Petersburg, after receiving his discharge, he met with some travelling countrymen of his own, who furnished him with money and everything requisite for his comfortable return home. Gleason had but just concluded his narrative, when Leslie entered, who, on being introduced to him, expressed the most sincere satisfaction at his unexpected return.

"Mary," said Mr. Leslie, entering his wife's room, on the morning succeeding that of Gleason's arrival, "Mary, I wish to hold a few moments' counsel with you."

Mrs. Leslie, who, with a flushed cheek and kindling eye, was gazing upon an exquisite picture upon the easel before her, while the brush was half raised in her hand to give another touch to the piece, did not immediately hear the entrance or remark of her husband, and she started with surprise and pain, as an impatient voice exclaimed at her side—

"I wish, madam, you would not consume so much time over that paltry daubing, nor become so engrossed in it as to be utterly unconscious of all that is going on around you."

Mary instantly laid down her brush (and it was years before she again resumed it), and turned with a gentle and cheerful smile to listen to what her husband had to say.

"At the time that Captain Gleason made his will, he supposed his son to be deceased, did he not?"

"Yes; from the loss of the ship, and as Uncle Henry did not return or write."

"And, if he had known that his son was living, he would, of course, have left him the bulk of his property?"

"Doubtless."

"Then you must see, as I do, that the property should and must be restored to him, as the rightful heir."

"The whole of it?"

"Of course, the whole of it."

"Catherine will not agree to it."

"Catherine may do as she pleases with that which she may choose to consider is *justly* as well as legally her own, but the portion left to us must be given to the proper inheritor."

"The portion left to *Sylvia,* you mean," amended the mother, gently.

"I mean nothing of the kind," said Leslie, with cold gravity.

"Surely you remember your promise," said Mary.

"Surely, madam, I remember the promise given to a dying father, who little thought when he exacted it that he had a living son, or that the promise ever would be urged as an excuse for keeping that son out of his just inheritance. I am pained to see, madam, that your feelings as a mother somewhat obscure your sense of justice. I shall be glad to obtain your cheerful co-operation in this matter, but if that is impossible I must act without it."

Mary, who saw that she had been wrong, and that a cloud had gathered upon the brow of her irritable lord, hastened to dissipate it by saying, "Yes, my motherly love *has* made me wish to be unjust; forgive me, and do whatever seems to you to be right; my dear husband, I will subscribe to all."

"Thank you, dear Mary; and now I will confess to you that the giving up of that money will be as great a sacrifice on *my* part as it is on *yours* in behalf of your daughter; for just at this time my business is greatly embarrassed, and the use of twenty thousand dollars for a year or so would be of incalculable benefit to me. But the sacrifice must be made, notwithstanding."

"Yes, it must be made. You are right, as you always are." But the child's interest was sacrificed, not so much to the mother's sense of justice as to her wifely duty—to her husband's will.

"Mary Leslie!" said Catherine, bursting into her sister's bedroom, with a heated and angry brow, "I hope you have not really consented to sign away all that property you had in trust for little Sylvia?"

"Yes," said Mary, quietly.

"And why? why? why have you made your child a beggar?"

"My husband thought it right to give up the property, and I obey his wishes."

"Spaniel!" exclaimed Catherine, with a withering sneer, and flung out of the room.

The necessary arrangements were soon made, and Gleason put in possession of one-half the wealth of his deceased father. Mary Leslie saw that her child's only chance of independence was cut off for ever; but she was a loyal Christian and a loving wife, and she reposed trustingly under the shadow of the goodness of God, and in the righteousness of the husband to whom he had given her. And even though it did sometimes painfully cross her mind, that Leslie might have been a little more gentle with her, in a controversy in which her maternal feelings were so deeply involved, she considered that his somewhat overbearing temper was the sole defect in an otherwise excellent character, and she prayed for patience and strength to "overcome evil with good." She remembered with pride and pleasure the purity and strength of principle that had forced him to alienate a sum which, however finally disposed of, would just now have so materially assisted him in his business. With Kate, however, she had much ado to keep her temper; and she looked forward, with secret joy, to the time when "Lem Dunn's" promotion should deliver her from the trial. Kate often indulged in a recreation which she herself denominated "speaking her mind," and which was anything but an amusement to Mrs. Leslie; so that Mary could not always refrain from repaying her in kind; for, in her love for Kate, there was not, of course, that feminine instinct of submission that characterized her love for her husband. With Mary, love was religion; and her love to God and to her husband always acted upon and augmented each other. Mary Leslie could not, therefore, be unhappy; on the contrary, her daily sacrifice of obedience would have been a source of the greatest heart happiness, but that her husband, from real or seeming insensibility, never noticed the offering, by commending the votary.

But the greatest trial and the greatest triumph of the wife were now at hand.

Twelve months succeeding the events recorded above, Mrs. Leslie sat in her parlour. It was eight o'clock in the evening, the snow was falling fast without, within everything wore an air of the greatest possible comfort. A coal fire was glowing in the grate, a snow-white cloth was laid for tea. Mrs. Leslie reclined upon a lounging chair, near the fire; her face was somewhat paler and thinner than when we noticed her last, but scarcely less attractive. Her large, tender eyes wore an expression of holy and meditative love that was very beautiful. Her work (an embroidered slip) had fallen from her hands upon the carpet. Sylvia sat on a low stool at her feet, dressing a doll. Catherine reclined upon a distant sofa, absorbed in a novel (her constant occupation, when not visiting, dressing or disputing).

"Who are you making this for, mamma?" inquired Sylvia, taking up the little dress.

"*For whom.* You should try to speak correctly, darling," said her mother, coaxingly.

"Well, then, *for whom,* mamma, are you working this little frock?" persisted Sylvia.

"First find out what rule of grammar you have just now transgressed, and then perhaps I may tell you, darling."

"Why can't you tell the child? For my part I don't see the use of mystifying children," exclaimed Kate, throwing aside her book, and coming to the fire.

The front door was now heard to open, and in another instant Mr. Leslie entered.

Going up to Mary, with more tenderness than we have ever yet seen him display, he took her hand, and pressing a kiss upon her brow, said—

"How are you, this evening, sweet wife? Nay, sit still. I will ring for tea, or Sylvia, do *you* do so. Why, Sylvia, an affectionate daughter should be ever on the watch to save her mother trouble."

Sylvia sprang to obey. Tea was soon brought in, and they gathered around the table.

"I bring you good tidings, Catherine. Lieutenant Dunn has received his promotion."

"Then I congratulate the lieutenants. There is one fool the less among their number," said Catherine, piqued, perhaps, that "Lem Dunn" had not hastened to her with the news himself.

"Capt. Dunn is now on duty, but will pay his respects to you to-morrow," said Leslie, divining her cause of dissatisfaction.

After the tea service was removed, the conversation became rather constrained. Catherine took up her everlasting novel, Mary resumed her seat and her needlework. Sylvia, bent on following up the hint of her step-father, began to arrange her mother's work-box, while Leslie walked up and down the floor, after the manner of a man who *has done,* or is *about* to do, something disagreeable. At last he took a seat, drew a letter from his pocket, examined the superscription, turned it over, glanced at Catherine, who had closed the book, and was now looking at him with quiet impudence, and finally replaced the letter in his pocket. He evidently had something to say, but was withheld by the presence of Catherine. I am really mortified to be obliged to record such a weakness on the part of the stately Mr. Leslie, but truth must come, and Mr. Leslie really stood in a little awe of Catherine. He had no sort of influence over her. She would do and say just exactly what she pleased, however disagreeable it might be, and he could not prevent her; nor could he decently turn her out of the house, nor would he descend to quarrel with her. Consequently, Mr. Leslie was ever on his guard to avoid any chance of controversy with Miss Gleason.

Fortunately, Mary, with her usual tact, saw the impatience of Leslie to unburden his mind, and, making an excuse to Catherine, retired early to her own room. Leslie followed her almost immediately.

Catherine's beautiful lips were disfigured by a mocking smile, as her glance followed Leslie from the room.

"Come, Sylvia, honey, let us go up stairs to bed. The Bashaw is meditating some new atrocity. I know it by his looks. He is afraid to let *me* know it, though."

"Ma'am?" said Sylvia, raising her large eyes to the face of her aunt.

"Yes; and I should not wonder if it was against *you* again, too. Perhaps he wants to black your face, and crisp your hair, and sell you for a negro."

"Who—no—of whom are you speaking, Aunt Catherine?"

"Of His Infallibility the Grand Seignior,[10] your step-father."

---

[10]Feudal lord.

"Then, please do not speak of him in that way, Aunt Catherine, and call him bad names."

"Why not, miss?"

"Because mamma would not like it."

"Oh! your mamma is as great a——. But what are you staring me in the face in that manner for? Don't you know it is very rude? Come along up stairs, child."

And they left the room.

"Something has disturbed you, Leslie," said Mary, after waiting for a few moments in vain for Leslie to open the conversation. "May I inquire, without indiscretion, what it is?"

"Certainly, Mary. I have not now, nor have I ever had, any concealments from you. I have never, from a false sentiment of tenderness, withheld from you any cause I might have for anxiety. I have several vexing cases just now. In one of them, you have an especial, perhaps you may think, an exclusive interest."

Leslie then drew the letter from his pocket, and added—

"This letter is from Madame D'Arblay, of New Orleans, now in this city, at the Astor House."

"From whom?"

"Madame D'Arblay, the mother of the late Mr. Lindal, and the grandmother of your daughter, Sylvia."

"Oh! yes; I recollect now having heard that the mother of Mr. Lindal married the second time a Frenchman by the name of D'Arblay, and removed to New Orleans; but that was many years ago."

"Yes. And now she writes that she has been left, by the recent death of Mr. D'Arblay, entirely alone, the sole mistress of a large fortune, without a relative on earth, except her grandchild, our daughter, Sylvia."

"Well?" questioned Mary, pale with a presentiment of what was coming.

"Madame D'Arblay makes us the very handsome proposal to make Sylvia her heiress, on condition that we allow her to return with her grandmother to New Orleans, and reside permanently beneath her roof."

"But I cannot part with Sylvia," said Mrs. Leslie.

"Do not decide hastily, Mary; you must consider in this matter your child's interests, not your own feelings," said Leslie, tenderly but gravely.

"I cannot! I cannot part with her. Indeed, indeed, I cannot," cried Mary, trembling.

"But this is childish, Mary."

"It would break Sylvia's heart to leave me."

"Not at all. By no means. Grief is very short-lived with children of her age."

"Yes! yes!" exclaimed Mary, passionately, "and affection, too! and impressions, too! She will soon forget her mother. She will only be consoled for her separation from, by ceasing to love, her mother!"

"You have not a mother's *disinterestedness,* Mary, or you would be willing to make any sacrifice of your own feelings to secure for your child the immense advantages offered by her grandmother."

"You did not seem to consider wealth such an immense advantage twelve months ago," said Mary, bitterly.

"Mrs. Leslie forgets herself, and forgets what is due to me," said Leslie, rising and walking towards the door, adding, as he was about to leave the room, "I will leave you, Mary, by reflection and solitude, to recover your lost recollection."

Mary sprang to his side, and, seizing his hand, exclaimed, as she burst into tears—

"Forgive me! forgive me! It is the first time; it shall be the last. But my heart is *so* wrung, *so* tortured; you do not know—you could not understand, unless you were a parent. But tell me, then, how you have decided; for that you *have* decided I know, and that your decision is immovable I know; therefore, tell me at once; it will save us a world of useless argument, controversy, and vexation. How have you decided?"

"That Sylvia shall return with her grandmother," said Leslie, gently but firmly.

Mary let fall the hand of her husband, and, growing very faint, sunk back on her chair.

"These are the reasons that have influenced my decision," said Leslie, resuming his seat by her side: "We have deprived Sylvia, justly and righteously, it is true, but we *have* deprived her, of the reversion of a sum that would have made her independent. At the period of that transaction, I believed that I should be able to secure for Sylvia every advantage which that money would have given, and, finally, to have given her a portion of equal amount. I will now admit, that the temporary possession of that sum led me into a speculation which failed by the sudden withdrawal of it. I have never recovered that failure, and I am now on the very brink of insolvency. Nothing but the strictest economy and the most careful financial diplomacy will save me. I have therefore great doubts of ever being able to carry out my plans for Sylvia; consequently, it becomes my duty, my painful duty, to determine that our daughter be given up to her grandmother."

"I did intend to say no more," murmured Mary, in a quivering voice, "yet——"

"Well?"

"Madame D'Arblay, is she a proper person, at her advanced age, to bring up a girl?"

"Read her letter," said Leslie, handing it. "You will find no infirmity there; and for the rest, you have doubtless heard enough of her piety and intelligence to feel secure that the moral and intellectual welfare of your daughter will be safe, while her vast wealth will insure her all the more worldly advantages of which she is now deprived."

"But is it not very sickly at New Orleans?"

"You have not yet read Madame D'Arblay's letter through, or you would see that she spends her summers at her villa on the Gulf, which, she says, is remarkably healthy in its location."

"When shall we have an interview with Madame D'Arblay?"

"I was thinking to-morrow, about twelve o'clock, you had better make her a call."

"And do you know—do you know how long she will stay in the city? I mean, how long shall I yet have dear Sylvia with me?" And the mother burst into tears.

"I do not know, of course, as I have not yet seen Madame D'Arblay. But we will talk no more at present, Mary; you *must* compose yourself. I will leave you for that purpose for a few moments. On my return, let me find you quiet." And Leslie descended the stairs.

Mary threw herself on her knees, and prayed long and earnestly, then arose calmly, and retired to rest.

"See here, Mr. Leslie," exclaimed Kate Gleason, as she entered the breakfast parlour the next morning, "What have you been saying to Mary? She is up in her chamber in tears, and Sylvia is sobbing by her side. I can't get anything out of her, but I know *you* are at the bottom of it. Now, what is it all about?"

"I have no explanations to make you, Miss Gleason," replied Leslie, taking his hat, and leaving the room to evade a quarrel.

"I'll make Lem Dunn call you out for that, sir!" cried Kate, as he went out.

Kate looked the very idea of a beautiful scold, as she stood there, her bosom heaving, her cheeks glowing, eyes sparkling, lips curling and quivering, and the tangled masses of jet-black ringlets falling in tear-sprinkled disorder about her face and neck.

"Captain Dunn!" announced a servant, throwing open the door, and Captain Dunn entered.

"Ah! I'm glad you've come! I'm *very* glad you've come. You're come in *excellent* times. Go after that man! Go after him! He's—he's"——Kate was out of breath.

"What man, dear Kate? What is the matter?" inquired Captain Dunn, in surprise.

"That Leslie!"

"Leslie! Why, what has he done?"

"He has abused his wife, and insulted me; that is, he has made her weep, and treated me with contempt."

"Tell me all about it, Kate—tell me all about it; and if he has been wanting in proper respect to my little betrothed—I'll—I'll annihilate him," said Captain Dunn, laughing; for he had known Leslie too long and too well to imagine that there could be any real cause of complaint. Unfortunately, Catherine could tell him but little about it, and that little was not very much to her credit.

"He's a terrible fellow, Kate," laughed Captain Dunn, as she concluded her account, "a very terrible fellow, indeed. Upon second thought, I should rather not fight him. He would shoot at me—he might hit me—in which case, I might be mortally wounded, and the service would lose"——

"A coward! an arrant coward! a poltroon,[11] who will one day bring disgrace upon the flag, if he is not hung before that day comes!" exclaimed Kate, as she flounced out of the room, in a great passion, passing Leslie, who was about to re-enter.

Captain Dunn was laughing heartily.

"You laugh now, my dear Dunn," said Leslie, smiling, "but will you laugh a year hence?"

"Yes! oh, yes! that is, I hope to do so."

"Have you no misgivings concerning your future peace?" asked Leslie, seriously.

"For my *peace?* I don't know; for my *happiness,* not one. Kate's temper amuses me beyond measure."

"Yet, I heard some ugly names called, as I came in."

"Yes! yes! Oh! I've no doubt Kate will have given me twenty beatings before this time next year."

"You will weary of it."

"Well, when the blows grow unpleasant, I have only to catch the little shrew in my arms, and hold her very tight, until she becomes quiet and good," said Dunn, laughing.

---

[11]The worst sort of coward.

"Ah! and then—do you know what she will do?"

"No. What?"

"Try to frighten you to death, by going into a hysteric fit, or worse—falling into a swoon."

"Ha! ha! ha! Is that Mrs. Leslie's method!"

"No! Bless dear Mary! Don't jest with her name, Dunn."

"I'll be hanged if I don't, just as much as I please. What! Haven't you been jesting with Kate's? 'It's a bad rule that won't work both ways.' "

Mrs. Leslie entered at this moment, equipped for a drive, and Leslie excused himself, and attended his wife to her carriage.

Mrs. Leslie drove to the Astor House, and was shown into the private parlour of Madame D'Arblay. Madame D'Arblay was at this time in her sixty-fifth year. Her tall, graceful, and majestic figure and stately carriage would have rather repulsed the gentle Mary, had not her face been so sweetly prepossessing. Her countenance wore an expression of holy calm, of heavenly goodness, very beautiful to look upon. Mary was at once reassured by her countenance and demeanor. They conversed a long time, the subject being a recapitulation of and enlargement upon the plan proposed in her letter. She made many inquiries, however, about Sylvia, and expressed a great desire to see her. At Mary's earnest entreaty, Madame D'Arblay consented to leave her apartments at Astor's, and take up her abode for the period of her visit at Mrs. Leslie's.

The next hour, Madame D'Arblay was comfortably ensconced in Mary's large easy chair, by the parlour fireside. Sylvia who had fallen in love with her at first sight, was nestling at her feet. Mrs. Leslie sat with her back to the light, to shade as much as possible her tear-stained face. Kate was sulking in her own room, and "would not be entreated" to come down and be sociable. There was so much in the pious and intelligent conversation of Madame D'Arblay to set the fears of Mary at rest on the subject of the welfare of her child, that when the dinner hour arrived, and Leslie, Captain Dunn, "Uncle Gleason," and Kate, had joined them, Mary had actually become cheerful.

The month of Madame D'Arblay's visit drew to a close. Mary, after a severe struggle with herself, and much prayer, had grown composed, and tranquilly prepared Sylvia for her journey. Leslie was unusually attentive and tender towards her; Madame D'Arblay mentally condemned the seeming indifference of Mrs. Leslie to the departure of her child, but she quietly ascribed it to the influence of her second marriage. Kate, with whom Sylvia was a great pet, had out-scolded her prototype and namesake, and was now not upon speaking terms with any of the family, and had banished "Lem Dunn" into perpetual exile—until recalled. Sylvia, child-like, was delighted with her new dresses, new books, and new toys, and the prospect of a long journey and new scenes, and had no room in her heart for painful sensations.

The last evening of Madame D'Arblay's stay arrived.

"Oh! Aunt Catherine! Aunt Catherine!" exclaimed Sylvia, bursting into Kate's sanctum, "to-morrow we're going. I'm so glad. Mamma has just laid out my new blue pelisse and velvet hood, and my nice chinchilla muff, all ready for to-morrow at six."

"Yes, miss!" said Kate, severely, "you seem very much delighted to leave your poor, pale, sick mother, who is grieving herself to death at the idea of parting with *you,* who do not care for her."

A thunderbolt fell upon the child's gladness, and destroyed it all at once. She burst into tears.

"Oh! Aunt Catherine, *is* mamma sorry? Doesn't she want me to go? I thought she wanted me to go. I forgot I had to leave mamma; I only thought of the fun. I will run now and tell mamma that I won't go; no, *that* I won't." And Sylvia made for the door.

"Mr. Leslie will compel you, miss," said Catherine. The name that was a spell to all the household arrested the flying steps of Sylvia for an instant, then saying—

"I will speak with mamma," she ran out.

Mary Leslie, who had nerved her gentle heart to go through the impending trial, was in her own room, still engaged in laying out such articles of dress as would be needed by Sylvia for the next morning. Mrs. Leslie's tranquillity was entirely overthrown by the impetuosity of Sylvia, who now burst into her presence, exclaiming, as she threw herself into her mother's arms, "Mamma! mamma! I can't leave you; I don't want to go any longer, now I know you do not wish it. I *love you,* mamma, better than fine clothes, and grandmothers, and journeys; and so, mamma, I *cannot* go, and I *will not* go."

Mrs. Leslie was quite unprepared for this outburst; Sylvia had been so tractable and so cheerful up to this time. She repressed her tears with difficulty, and replied, with an effort—

"*Cannot* and *will not,* Sylvia! why, what manner of words are those, and where learnt you them? You will, of course, do as your parents wish you."

"Aunt Catherine says that if they send me away from you, mamma, it will break your heart, for that you don't want me to go."

"Catherine is mistaken; listen to *me,* my darling Sylvia. I *do* want you to go; and though I may be very sorry to part with my dear little girl, yet I shall soon get over the grief, because I know it will be for her benefit. And now," added the mother, with an effort at cheerfulness, "let us talk about the fine ride in the cars you will have, and look at the pretty things I have put in your nice little travelling basket."

"No, no, mamma! No, no, mamma! I don't care for the ride in the cars, and don't want the travelling basket. I love *you!* I want to *stay* with you," exclaimed Sylvia, bursting into tears. "Oh, mamma, *don't* let me go! don't, *please* don't. I did not think about parting from you before, and I know I can't! *indeed* I can't!"

There was grief, there was agony, on the mother's countenance, as she crushed back the rising emotions of her heart, and choked back her tears. She struggled to speak, but could not do so with the calmness requisite to soothe her child. She could only press her closer to her bosom in silence. Neither spoke for some moments; at length—

"Mamma, do you know the night you were married, when I slept alone in my little bed? Well, mamma, I cried all night; I could not sleep, because I was away from you. I knew that I should see you soon in the morning, but still I wept; yes, and I wept many nights, too, although you did not know it, and although you were not further off than the next room, and I could see you every day. Now, so many days must come and go, and so many nights pass, and—and—no mother to—to—" and Sylvia, breaking from her mother's hold, threw herself, in a fit of hysterical sobbing, upon the carpet.

"Oh! God, have mercy on me, and give me strength," exclaimed the mother, in strong emotion, as she went toward Sylvia, stood for an instant to gain self-control, then took her child in her arms, and, reseating herself, pressed her to her bosom, smoothed back the shining ringlets of her hair, and imprinted kiss after kiss upon her fair brow, as she talked gently and soothingly to her, and, rocking her to and fro, finally succeeded in subduing her emotion. Exhaustion, after so much excitement, soon put Sylvia to sleep; yet still the mother rocked and sung, even as she had done when the little girl in her arms was a babe—thinking, perhaps, that it might be the last time she should ever hold her thus. At last she arose, and, laying Sylvia on the bed, sunk upon her knees, and poured out her whole soul in prayer to her Creator—first, that this trial might yet be spared her, "if possible;" then, that if it were not, she might have strength and resignation to bear it cheerfully. How earnestly, passionately, fervently, she prayed! And when emotion became so great that words failed, the upturned, straining eye, the clasped hands, and heaving sighs, bore up the silent prayer; and at last, when the weary head sunk upon the folded hands, and thought no longer took the form of words, the heart; the untiring heart, still bore up the prayer, in one intense, absorbing yearning after mercy. Unknown to Mary, there was one spectator to this scene. Leslie was standing within the door. He had entered, silently and unobserved, at the moment that Mary had lain the sleeping Sylvia on the bed, and sunk down by her side in prayer. The first words of the prayer arrested his intention of coming forward or speaking. He had seen, and had heard—and never before had the pure and holy heart of his wife been so unveiled as in that prayer; and while it yet ascended, in all its Christian beauty and eloquence, he quietly withdrew from the room, murmuring, "The angel, the angel, how blind I have been! I must save her this trial; there is but one way, for I must save her without sacrificing Sylvia." He passed to the door of Madame D'Arblay's room, and knocked. The pleasant voice of the old lady bade him enter; he did so, and merely saying—"Will you come with me to Mary's chamber, Madame? She seems much distressed at the thought of parting with her daughter to-morrow." He accompanied her thither, and withdrew. Mary's voice was still heard, but in low, interrupted, and quivering tones. Her tears were falling like rain, and her hands wringing and twisting over each other; but the *words* of Mary's prayer, breathed, as she deemed, to the ear of God alone, unfolded the most secret thoughts and feelings of Mary's profoundly pious heart.

"Oh, God!" exclaimed Madame D'Arblay, "I did not dream of this. Mary, Mary, my dear child, arise. Your prayer is heard and answered."

Mary started in surprise to her feet, and was caught to the bosom of the old lady. "Mary, my dear daughter," said she, "your child shall not be taken from you, neither shall she lose anything by remaining with you. Oh! Mary, how little did I know you! How unjustly have I judged you, when I condemned the indifference with which you seemed to regard a separation from your child. But, Mary, how could you suppose that I would have taken my granddaughter away, had I not thought that you were willing, nay, anxious, for her removal to my abode? Forgive me, Mary, but I fancied that your second marriage had unnaturally alienated your heart from your child; I was therefore the more anxious to receive her. But, Mary, why did you not make me acquainted with your feelings on the subject?"

Mary, who during this long speech had had time to collect herself, replied,—"Mr. Leslie, Madame, had determined that Sylvia should go with you. He thought that her residence beneath your roof would be a solace to you, and an advantage to herself. I could not seek to thwart his purpose, by making an appeal to your sympathies, you know, Madame."

"You were right, my daughter, perfectly right. You have won my deepest love, my highest esteem, Mary Leslie! You have won it by your self-control. You have established yourself firmly and permanently in your husband's respect and affection; more than that, you have proved and known the power of faith and prayer. Never forget it, my child! Now, Mary, I must tell you my improvised plan. Though I will not take Sylvia away, neither will I leave her. I am glad this has happened. I like you so much, Mary, I want to live with you. I have been so solitary; and, after all, a little girl is not company enough for an old woman. So, Mary, if you will give me an easy chair by your fireside, and a place at your table, I will even spend the close of my life with you. I will do everything for Sylvia here, that I would have done at home; and when I die, I will leave her all I possess; and if she marries before that event, I will dower her handsomely. What say you, Mary?"

"Oh, Madame!" exclaimed Mary, seizing her aged hands, and pressing them to her bosom and her lips, "if I have been silent, it has been from deep emotion. Words will not convey my thanks. It will take a lifetime to live my gratitude." At this moment the supper-bell rang, and its alarum awoke Sylvia from her deep sleep, who, when informed of the change in her grandmother's project, was delighted beyond measure; and, after bestowing many caresses on her grandmother and her mamma, ran to tell "Aunt Catherine" the good news. What effect the "good news" had upon Kate may be gathered from the following circumstance: Kate took pen and paper from her desk, and wrote a note. Meeting the errand-boy on the stairs as she descended to supper, she gave him the note, telling him to carry it to Captain Dunn, on board the store ship Endymion, promising to give him a half-dollar if he returned with an answer very quickly. Kate's note ran thus—

"Captain Dunn:

"Will you be so kind as to call at Harpers', and get 'Forest Days' for me. It is just out. Bring it to me *this evening*. Yours, &c.

—*C. Gleason*

"FRIDAY EVENING"—

for Kate, with all her impetuosity, exercised a precaution which I would recommend to all young ladies, and would not commit herself, by writing love-letters or billets-doux;[12] for she said, "I might change my mind, or he might change his; and then—there!" Captain Dunn answered the note in person, and took his seat with the happy family at the supper table. Kate's good-humour was entirely restored. She welcomed back her exile with affectionate frankness. Sylvia's bright eyes were glancing and flashing from one face to another, each countenance seeming to reflect its own gladness. Madame D'Arblay regarded the scene with a look of quiet self-complacency, that seemed to say, "I have made them all happy!" Mary's countenance expressed quiet and grateful happiness. Leslie's eyes were occasionally fixed upon the face of his wife, with looks of ineffable and holy tenderness. Leslie never subjected her love to another trial. He was deeply

---

[12]Romantic notes.

moved by the gentle resignation, the tender submission, with which she had yielded up the dearest object of her affections and her most cherished wishes, to be dealt with according to his good pleasure. That submission had given her a place in and an influence over his heart, that no beauty, grace, or accomplishments—no, nor intellectual nor moral excellence *without it*—could have secured.

A month from this time, a gay party was assembled at Mr. Leslie's to honour the nuptials of Captain Lemuel Dunn, U. S. N., and Miss Catherine Gleason.

The married life of Kate Gleason, who entered upon her duties with views and feelings so opposite to those of Mary, which we have endeavoured to illustrate, will form the subject of another chapter.

THE MARRIED SHREW

A Sequel to The Wife's Victory

Oh! when she's angry, she is keen and shrewd;
She was a vixen when she went to school;
And though she is but little, she is fierce.

— SHAKSPEARE

Kate Dunn entered the gay world of fashion first as a married woman, and decided was her success. Kate's life with her grandfather, and afterwards with the Leslies, had been very domestic, and, as she expressed it, very *triste;*[1] she had gone but little into society. Now she was resolved to have compensation, since no greater obstacle than "Lem Dunn" intervened.

Formerly she was prevented from going to balls and parties by want of proper chaperonage; now her state as a married woman rendered her independent of that. Kate was now resolved to combine all the pleasures of the maiden with the privileges of the matron; consequently, in fashionable society, where her resplendent beauty and sparkling wit drew many admirers, she was always surrounded by a circle of young men, who were very well pleased to carry on a flirtation with a pretty woman, without the fear of a suit for breach of promise before their eyes. There was one man, however, who was constantly banished from her circle, and that man was her husband.

"There are hundreds of intelligent men and pretty women here to-night; go and amuse yourself; I shall not be jealous;" was the *kind* address of Kate to her husband, as he lingered by her side.

Captain Dunn walked off, and *took an extra glass of wine.*

E. D. E. N. Southworth, *The Wife's Victory; and Other Nouvellettes.* Philadelphia: T. B. Peterson, 1854.

[1]sad

"Can you not comprehend that, as we are married now, your attendance can be dispensed with; nay, more—that it is *outré*,[2] absurd, to remember that you have a wife in the room?" was the petulant speech with which she received him when he returned after an hour's absence.

"Decidedly, Captain Dunn, you are making yourself and me appear very ridiculous by this Darby and Joan exhibition of conjugal affection. Positively we shall be cited as a 'pattern couple;' and I know nothing that could be more scandalous or alarming," said Mrs. Dunn to the Captain, as they entered the carriage to return from a large party one evening.

"I don't understand *your* opinions and feelings upon this subject, Catherine, but *I* don't like this fashionable manner of waiting upon any other woman but my own wife, and seeing her attended by any other man except her own husband."

"Oh, indeed, Captain Dunn, you make me quite sick, talking so foolishly about 'own wives' and 'own husbands;' the fact of our marriage is incontrovertible; there is no need to emphasize it so often."

"Kate's head is a little turned by her French romances, but I feel sure her principles are really sound. I will not make myself 'ridiculous,' as she would call it, by fretting and fuming, nor will I annoy her by useless remonstrance *now*. Give her folly its full way; it will soon wear itself out, *or*"—Captain Dunn paused in his mental soliloquy, *poured out and swallowed a glass of wine.*

A few weeks from this time, Captain Dunn was ordered to sea, and made preparations, with a reluctant heart, to leave his bride. A few days previous to joining his ship, he seated himself by the side of Catherine, and, passing his hands caressingly through her ringlets, said:

"You will be very lonesome in this large house when I am gone, dear wife."

"Oh! no, I shan't; I shall fill it with company; don't tumble my curls, please, Captain." Captain Dunn folded his hands, and a sigh escaped him.

"I have been thinking, Kate, of inviting my mother to take up her residence here during my absence."

"To watch your wife, I presume, sir, and to look after your interests, of which you think me incapable."

"Kate! how can you——; I had no thought beyond giving you pleasure, by providing you with a desirable companion."

"Then, Captain, I beg you will not trouble your mother to leave her own home, to come to me; it might greatly inconvenience her."

"Not at all. Since my sister's marriage and departure for Europe, my mother is quite alone, and very sad; she would be more cheerful here with you."

"I do not think so—old people are seldom contented out of their own homes."

"Yes, but with my mother it is different; she has an excellent heart and most serene temper, and is prepared to love you as a daughter. *Besides,* her support has hitherto been my most agreeable duty; but I cannot now sustain the expense of two establishments; so you see the propriety, nay, the necessity, that obliges me to offer her a home here."

[2]Violating social convention.

"I thought it was all on *my* account," sneered Kate; "however, you may be sure she would be much better off in a good boarding-house."

"Madam!" exclaimed Captain Dunn, in angry astonishment; but, quickly controlling himself, and looking seriously in his wife's face, he inquired, "Am I to understand, Catherine, that you are opposed to my mother's presence in this house?"

Notwithstanding all her assurance, Kate's eyes fell, and her cheeks glowed under the gaze that was fixed upon her. She was determined to have her own way, however, though it would require some hardihood to tell the frank and noble-hearted man before her that she *was* opposed to having his mother under their roof. She replied with assumed firmness, but without raising her eyes—

"I have a great respect for your mother, Captain, and will show her every attention in my power; but I *do* dislike the idea of a mother-in-law in the same house with me; I cannot conquer my repugnance to your proposed measure; and you know, Captain, with such feelings on my part, your mother and myself could not get along comfortably together."

"I certainly shall not insult her with the proposition," said Captain Dunn haughtily, as he left the room.

"I have conquered again," thought Kate. "Now, I really *did* feel like giving up once, but it won't do—such feelings must not be encouraged—they would soon enslave me. Men are naturally inclined to be tyrannical, particularly over their wives. Oh! yes, decidedly, I was right in the affair of the mother-in-law. Good heavens! I could not brook a prying, fault-finding mother-in-law in the house." Could Kate have followed with her eye her husband's steps that evening, through the various scenes of dissipation to which he resorted to drown thought, she might have exclaimed, with the conqueror of old, "Another such victory would ruin me."

Captain Dunn was absent three years, during which time Kate led a very gay life, despite the affectionate and repeated remonstrances of Mrs. Leslie and Madame D'Arblay. She thought several times of writing to or visiting Mrs. Dunn, senior; but, unhappily, she did not know her address, being ignorant what arrangement Captain Dunn had finally made for her. The subject had never been mentioned between them since the evening it was first broached. Kate's summers were usually spent at some fashionable watering-place, and her winters in a round of visiting and amusement.

The evening of Captain Dunn's expected return home, it chanced that a brilliant ball was given by Madame la Baronne V——, the lady of the French ambassador. "The beautiful Mrs. Dunn" was among the most admired of the guests.

It was after having gone through a waltz with a distinguished foreigner, that Kate sat down, when a note was placed in her hand, that read as follows:

"Dear Catherine:

"Come home; I am waiting for you; I should hasten to you, but I may not intrude.
"L. D."

"Tell Captain Dunn I will be home in an hour or two," said Catherine to the footman who brought the note.

"Very well, Thomas," said Captain Dunn, on receiving this cool reply; "bring me the morning papers, and *a bottle of port.*"

Notwithstanding the provoking coolness of her message, when Catherine returned, a few hours after, the door was opened by Captain Dunn, who received her in his arms, and strained her to his bosom.

"Good Heavens! Captain," exclaimed Kate, releasing herself, "you take my breath away—and just see how you have crushed my dress and dishevelled my hair. Pray, don't be so energetic."

"You are looking in high health and beauty, my peerless Catherine," said Captain Dunn, as he gazed upon her with pride, not noticing her petulance.

"Do reserve your gallant speeches for other women, Captain, and don't waste them upon your wife."

However deeply pained Captain Dunn might have been by his wife's coolness and levity, nothing of mortification or disapproval was apparent in his manner. Captain Dunn liked to leave all his bad weather at sea.

Some twelve months succeeding this event, Mrs. Dunn presented her husband with a son and heir. "And now," thought the happy father, "my wife will love her home for her child's sake." But Captain Lemuel Dunn "reckoned without his host"ess, as a very few days demonstrated.

"Where is the young sailor?" inquired he, as he took his seat by his wife's easy chair, a few days succeeding the birth of his son.

"Mrs. Tenly has got him."

"Mrs. Tenly—who is she?"

"A young woman whom I have engaged as a wet nurse."

"Now, is it possible, Kate, that you mean to let your child be nursed at the bosom of another woman?"

"Yes; it is both possible and positive—now, don't put on that disagreeable look—it is not usual for ladies of my station"——

"*Your* station—a rough sailor's wife"——

"Well, don't tease me! my delicate health forbids"——

"*Your* delicate health! Why, Kate, you have the finest constitution of any woman I know. You enjoy high—I had almost said rude—health."

"Well, then, if you must have it, I don't intend to spoil my figure by nursing a child. And I have no idea of going about the house in a slovenly wrapper, or ill-fitting corsage, for the sentimental nonsense of nursing my own baby."

"Ha! ha! ha! that's the most amusing reason of all—for *you* to give, Kate, who go about the house all the morning in a loose gown, with your hair in papers!"

"Captain Dunn, you're a bore."

"Well! this nurse—has she lost her own child?"

"No; she is raising it by hand."

"Then you are really *cruel,* as well as silly."

"Captain Dunn, please leave the room; this interview has fatigued me," said Kate, affecting languor.

If the reader will forgive the digression, I will describe a small, mean dwelling, not far from Captain Dunn's handsome house. In the basement story of a dilapidated old house—in a miserable room, with broken-down doors, and cracked and fly-stained window-glasses—on a poor straw bed, covered with a thin, faded counterpane, lay a shivering babe. A coloured girl, in tattered garments, was trying to coax a few embers to burn in the mildewed fireplace. At a cry from the awakened child, the girl gave over her hopeless efforts, and, taking the infant up, she sat down upon a low stool, and commenced rocking it backward and forward in her lap, to still its cries.

At this moment the door opened, and Mrs. Tenly, the fine ladies' nurse, entered, drew near her infant, and, while the tears coursed down her cheeks, looked upon it in silence. The little creature was now lying languidly across the girl's lap; its small limbs hung flaccidly, its tiny features were sharpened and attenuated, and its slumbers were interrupted by distressing moans.

"How has she been, Nelly?" she asked of the negro girl.

"Her has been cryin' a dreat deal, ma'am."

"Poor baby! poor little one! Oh, it is wicked, it is cruel, to give your nourishment to another child—your own nourishment, that nature has provided for your own poor little feeble self—to give it to another babe, and let you perish." The mother wept convulsively, as she took the babe from the little negro.

"Clare t' de Lord, I wouldn't do it, mam;" exclaimed the little girl, as she busied herself making the fire, and heating some water.

"Ah, Nelly, I've tried every other way at getting bread!"

Mrs. Tenly, after washing her little one, and dressed her in her night clothes, indulged herself by rocking her a few moments in her lap. "This will not do for me, though," said she; "that other child will wake and cry, and Mrs. Dunn will be displeased." Pressing her child to her bosom once again, she laid her upon the bed, and prepared to go.

"Oh! Nelly, take *good* care of the baby, and I will bring you something pretty—will you, Nelly?"

"I alluz does take care of her, ma'am."

"And keep the panado warm in the corner, and give it to her when she wakes and cries in the night."

"Yes, ma'am."

Mrs. Tenly turned back to kiss the child again, and tucked her warmly up; then stopped the broken pane of the window, and left the house, her eyes streaming with tears.

This is no exaggerated picture. There are many such cases "I speak that I do *know.*" Mrs. Tenly had come over to this country in an emigrant ship, in company with her husband and some hundred others. They had suffered much from sickness and privation, and many of them were provided for as paupers. But Mrs. Tenly and her husband had found a home in this wretched cellar, where, within a week after their arrival, on the same day she thanked God for the birth of her first child and wept the loss of its father. Upon her recovery from her confinement, she tried, but in vain, to procure needle-work or washing. Her efforts to find a place at service were equally unsuccessful. At this time, the opportunity being presented, she put her child from her bosom, and went out as a nurse.

Mrs. Tenly could at least have gone for a while to the almshouse, which, though humiliating to the poorest and lowest, was yet better than the sacrificing of an infant's life, by cruelly and dishonestly depriving it of its natural rights.

There is but one circumstance that can exempt a woman from the duty of nursing her own children—and that is, ill health; and even then she has no right to engage a nurse, if, by so doing, she deprives another babe of its mother.

One morning, soon after Mrs. Dunn got about again, her nurse entered the room and said, weeping,—

"Will you have the goodness to take charge of your little boy, to-day?"

"Why? What is the matter?"

"My child is dying."

"Indeed! I am very sorry to hear it. Yes, certainly you must go; but what ails your child?"

"I do not know, madam; ever since I left her to come here, she has pined away."

"I am very sorry," said Kate; "I will call over and see her; or—no, I could do no good. I will give you a note to my sister, Mrs. Leslie; she will visit and assist you; it's all in her line. But get a physician, and tell him to send his account to me; and—stay, here is your month's wages."

Thanking Mrs. Dunn for her kindness, as she received the note and the money, Mrs. Tenly withdrew.

An hour after this, Mrs. Leslie stood by the bed of the sick child.

"Oh! Mrs. Leslie, *is* she dying?" sobbed the mother.

"Not dying, surely not dying, and not in any immediate danger, I think—I hope."

"Oh! Mrs. Leslie, ma'am, God bless you for saying that. If my baby only lives, I shall never think anything else a trouble in the world. I'd slave for her all my life."

"We must get her into a sweet, clean, airy room, and then, with the doctor's prescription and *her mother's nursing,* she will recover."

"Oh! ma'am, if I only knew how to thank you; but she won't nurse, ma'am."

"You've tried her, then."

"When I first came home I did, but she couldn't; and then I gave her the powder, and she went to sleep."

"She is awake; try her now."

Mrs. Tenly took the child in her arms, and placed it to her breast.

The babe looked up into her mother's face with a sort of sickly inquiring smile, then let her head sink upon her mother's bosom with a sigh of intense satisfaction.

"Poor little thing, she is happy now," said her mother, smiling through her tears.

"Oh! she will soon get well," said Mrs. Leslie, cheerfully. "And now, Mrs. Tenly, as I too have a little family to look after at home, I must leave for the present, but I will send my daughter over this afternoon."

"I have a commission for you, daughter," said Mrs. Leslie to Sylvia, as she laid aside her walking-dress.

"And I have a commission for you, too, dear mamma; but what is yours?"

"You must get up all your little sister's last winter's clothes, and tie them into a bundle; then tell Martha to put on her bonnet and attend me in the pantry, bringing a large basket with her; finally, get on your pelisse and hood, to accompany her to see a sick child."

"Oh! yes, mamma, I understand;" and Sylvia flew to obey, but, dashing back in an instant, she said—

"Oh! I forgot, mamma, to tell you my commission, or, rather, uncle's. Uncle Harry has been here, and says, will you please find him a housekeeper; he wants one directly."

"Ah! I am very glad he does, Sylvia; I think we can find a very good housekeeper for uncle."

The basket of necessaries was packed and sent. The next day Mrs. Tenly and her sick child were removed into comfortable lodging; and a fortnight after, when the latter was recovered, she was put into the cars, and sent twenty miles into the country, to a farm owned and occupied by Mr. Harry Gleason.

A month succeeding these events, the Leslies and Madame D'Arblay were spending a day at Captain Dunn's. The party were assembled at dinner. Suddenly the door was thrown open, and Uncle Harry Gleason stalked into the room, in a great heat, exclaiming—

"*Well,* Mrs. Leslie, my admirable niece! I always took you for a model of propriety. The veriest demirep[3] could not have made a more glaring solecism[4] in morals than you have done!"

The company all glanced in astonishment from Uncle Harry to Mary, who was looking aghast.

"Yes, ma'am," continued Uncle Harry, "a pretty mess you have made of it. I had a good opinion of you, Mary! I send to you, rather than to an intelligence office; I ask you to find me a proper housekeeper. And what do you do? Whom do you send?"

"I earnestly hope," said Mary, recovering her self-possession, "that Jane Tenly has in no particular discredited my recommendation. She was well thought of in her humble sphere. I always thought her a very good soul."

"And am I to have every good soul in the world thrust upon me? I *hate* good souls. No, ma'am! I didn't *want* a good soul, nor a good soul's *baby,* neither. I wanted a *house-keeper*—meaning a staid, serious, settled old body, who could tuck me up at night, and read me to sleep with Congressional speeches and the President's messages, and so on."

"Well, couldn't Jane do that, uncle?"

"Oh! of course *she* could, beau-*ty*-ful-ly," sneered the old man.

"Of what do you complain, then, sir, and how can we further serve or satisfy you?" inquired Leslie.

"Of what do I complain?" exclaimed Uncle Harry. "I complain of a blue-eyed woman, sir, and a baby, sir. I sent to Madame Propriety, there, for a housekeeper; and what does she send me, sir! A rosy-cheeked woman, and—and—a baby, sir! What will the neighbours say? A man of my age! a gentleman of my integrity, sir! A woman with bright brown hair and a baby, sir!——Well," said the old man, suddenly dropping his voice, "there was but one thing to be done, and that I *did.*"

No one replied.

"And that I did."

Still all were silent.

---

[3]Person of doubtful respectability.

[4]Breach of etiquette.

"Why the devil don't some of you ask me *what* I did?" cried Uncle Harry, losing patience.

"Sent her away again?" suggested Mary.

"*No,* ma'am, I didn't. I never sent a woman away again in all my life, and never mean to. No, no; you know what I did well enough, although you affect stupidity, because you think it will be a mortification to me to tell it of myself. But it ain't, though! not a bit. Guess I'm old enough to judge for myself. Should like to know what right *any* body has to find fault with what *I* do. Well! why *in the devil* don't some of you ask me what I did?"

"What did you do, sir?" asked Mary, coaxingly.

"I married Jane Tenly and the baby—that's what I did."

"Oh! uncle, no!" exclaimed Mary, in a tone of vexation and distress.

Kate drew herself up, and regarded her uncle—scorn writhing her lip, and anger flashing from her eyes.

Leslie, after an involuntary expression of surprise and displeasure, was silent.

Captain Dunn broke into a hearty and good-humoured laugh, as he sprang from his seat, and seized and shook Uncle Harry's hands, exclaiming—

"Well done! that's right! wish you joy with all my heart. God bless you!"

"Ah! Dunn, *you've* got some heart. You see, Dunn, the old man *did* want some one to love. Here are my nieces, to be sure; but I am only a fourth or fifth-rate person in their affections; so, Dunn, you know, the old fellow wanted some one to love, who would be always in his sight; and that poor, meek, blue-eyed woman wanted a friend; and so you see, Dunn"——

"I see! I see! It was the best thing you ever did in your life. You have given a worthy young woman a comfortable home, a respectable position, and, above all, an excellent husband; and you have secured for yourself a handsome, good, and *grateful* wife. I shall be always happy to receive you both at my house."

"Captain Dunn has been indulging too freely in wine, sir, else he would have added—in the *basement* story, as visiters of her late friends, the housemaid and cook!"

"Catherine!" exclaimed Captain Dunn, sternly.

Uncle Harry Gleason bowed to the ground with great ceremony, and withdrew.

"I fear that Captain Dunn *does* indulge too freely in the use of wine," whispered Mary Leslie, when she found herself alone with Leslie that evening.

"I *know* he does," was the reply.

"What can be done?" asked Mary, sadly.

"Very little, I fear. Something, however, we must attempt. I will speak to Dunn. I will be in his company more than hitherto. And—you must remonstrate with *Catherine.* I fear she does not make herself or her home agreeable to her husband."

"I *know* she does not," sighed Mary.

The entrance of Madame D'Arblay and Sylvia, attended by a servant with lights, arrested the conversation. The ladies gathered around their work-table with their sewing, and Leslie, opening a book, read aloud while they plied their needles. A far different scene was enacting at Captain Dunn's.

When the departure of their guests had left the Dunns alone—

"I am grieved and astonished, Catherine," said Captain Dunn, "that you should have treated your uncle so disrespectfully and cruelly."

"I am grieved, but *not astonished,* Captain Dunn, that you have so far forgotten what was due to yourself and me, as to have invited that woman here. A man whose faculties are always obscured by the fumes of wine cannot astonish me by *any* act of absurdity or wickedness."

"What do you mean by *that,* madam?"

"I mean, sir, that you are never sober, and therefore cannot be considered a responsible human being."

"Catherine!"

"Don't you understand me *yet?* You are more stupid than I supposed even. In common parlance, then, you are always *drunk*—and generally, by consequence, a *fool.*"

"This is not to be endured!" exclaimed Captain Dunn, rising hastily, and pacing the floor with rapid strides; then pausing before his wife, he said severely—

"You presume, Catherine, upon your sex, and your feebleness. But have a care; where weakness and womanhood do not imply delicacy and gentleness, they lose their claim upon our forbearance."

"Do you threaten me, sir?" whispered Catherine, in a low, smooth, contemptuous tone of irony. "But of course, why need I be surprised? A man who can connive at the marriage of his cast-off mistress with an honoured relative, and then insult his wife by inviting the abandoned creature to his house, is capable of any act of meanness."

Exasperated to frenzy by the false and monstrous charges contained in this speech, delirious with anger, Captain Dunn raised his hand, and a blow rang sharply upon the cheek of Catherine; and seizing his hat, he rushed madly from the room and the house.

A few minutes after, Mrs. Dunn's maid found her in strong hysterics, and in that condition she was conveyed to bed.

"What in Heaven's name *is* all this dreadful business, Captain?" inquired Uncle Harry, as he entered a private parlour in the——Hotel, occupied temporarily by Captain Dunn.

"I have disgraced myself—that is the amount of it," replied Captain Dunn, bitterly.

"Been drinking?"

"No, no; at least, not much."

"Been forging?"

"I have acted the part of a poltroon."

"Not received an insult or a blow, without knocking the dealer of it down—*not that?"*

"Worse, far worse than that; I have struck my wife."

"Hallelujah! glad on't—better late than never. Hope you gave her a good sound drubbing while you were at it. She's wanted it a long time, the huzzy; she'll treat you all the better, now she's got it, 'specially if she has any fear of the discipline being repeated. Never you mind—*I'm* her uncle, and her natural guardian; and *I* approve of it—*I* uphold you in it," quoth Uncle Harry, his thoughts reverting to Kate's treatment of himself the day previous. "Mind, *I* give you leave, and *I'm* her uncle."

"Pray, do not talk so upon this subject, sir. Believe me, I am sunk very low in my own opinion. I have long dreaded this. I would to Heaven my patience had held out a few days longer, until my ship sailed. Then this rupture might have been delayed, or might never have occurred. Great God! that I, that *I,* should have raised my hand against a weak, defenceless woman!"

"Well, what of it? I don't see why weak, defenceless women are not to be punished when they deserve it, as well as weak, defenceless children," exclaimed the old monster. "Would you feel any great compunction for having chastised a weak, defenceless child, if he deserved it?"

"Your opinions are extremely revolting, Mr. Gleason; but I sent for you to request your good offices with Kate. She refuses to see me, and returns unopened all my notes. I wish you to see her, implore her forgiveness for me, and bring me her answers. Will you do this?"

"No, I sha'n't; for that would neutralize the good effect of the drubbing."

"Then I must see Mrs. Leslie immediately. Will you excuse me?"

"Yes, and accompany you."

The two gentlemen then left the house, and took their way to Leslie's together.

The earnest efforts of the Leslies failed, however, to bring about a reconciliation between the parties. Catherine remained in her own room, outraged and indignant; and Captain Dunn at his hotel, busily preparing for his voyage.

The last day of Captain Dunn's stay arrived. His ship was to sail the next morning. He had made a last ineffectual effort to see his wife. She delighted to afflict him to the last *safe* moment, yet designed to have a full reconciliation before his departure. "Yes," said she, "to-morrow morning I will see him, and forgive him. It will not do to let him go away in despair; for during three years' absence, he may cease to love me—and now this evening to shine the most resplendent star in the constellation of beauty to be assembled at Madame Le Normand's ball. It is very fortunate, by the by, that this shocking affair has not got wind yet."

That night, Mrs. Dunn, superbly attired, seemingly in high beauty and spirits, entered the magnificent saloon of Madame Le Normand.

That night, at the same hour, Captain Dunn took his melancholy way towards his now desolated home. Before leaving his native shores, he wished to look again upon the face of his infant son. The whole front of the house looked dark as he approached it. Entering and groping his way through the gloom, along the dark passage and up the stairs, he reached the nursery door, and entered the room. A small lamp was sitting on the hearth; its feeble rays revealed a scene that sent all the blood from the father's cheek. Straight up in the bed sat the infant, in an attitude fixed and immovable as marble—his cheek blanched—his eyes wide open in a frightful stare—his lips apart with horror, while his gaze was fixed in deadly terror upon a dressed-up bugaboo at the foot of the bed. In an instant, seizing the bundle of sticks and rags that composed this figure, Captain Dunn threw it out of the window, and turned to his boy. The removal of the figure seemed to have dissolved the icy chain that bound the boy; for he now fell back in the bed, in violent convulsions. Seizing the bell-rope, Captain Dunn now rang a peal that presently brought every remaining servant in the house to his presence.

"Thomas," said he to the first one that appeared, "run immediately for Doctor Wise. William," said he to the other man, "where is Mrs. Dunn?"

"At Madame Le Normand's ball, sir."

"And her nurse?"

"Gone out to a tea-drinking, sir."

"And the housemaid and cook? Gone, too, I suppose?"

"Yes, sir."

"You may leave the room. Stay, call me a carriage."

"Yes, sir."

Captain Dunn now turned to his son, whose spasms were over, and having placed him in a comfortable position, awaited the arrival of the physician.

At length, the Doctor entered, and, having looked at the child, ordered a warm bath, wrote a prescription and sent it off.

"And now, Doctor, is there any chance of his recovery?" inquired Captain Dunn, after having given the Doctor a full account of the causes that led to the child's seizure.

"For his full recovery, very little—this will be likely to affect him through life."

Dunn groaned.

"Doctor, could he be removed with safety, by a steamboat journey, some ninety or a hundred miles up the river?"

"With perfect safety," said the Doctor.

"Then, sir, I will trouble you, if you please, to write at length your orders for his treatment on the journey, as I shall take him away to-night."

The physician, with a look of surprise, complied, and soon after took his leave.

Captain Dunn, raising the sleeping infant in his arms, threw a cloak around him, descended the stairs, entered the carriage, which had been some time before the door, and was driven towards the steamboat wharf.

At the same moment of time, Catherine Dunn, radiant with beauty and gayety, was led, smiling, to her place at the head of the cotillion forming in Madame Le Normand's saloon.

Day was dawning when Mrs. Captain Dunn drove up to her own door, and, wearied out with the night's dissipation, would have immediately sought her pillow, when her maid placed a note in her hand. She took it listlessly, and ran her eyes over its contents. They were as follows:

"Farewell, Catherine; farewell, infatuated woman, unduteous wife! neglectful mother! I leave you to the retribution that I pray may overtake you—that I pray may overtake you, in the hope that it may bring you to repentance, happily to reformation. I take your child where he may find, what he has never yet possessed, a mother's care and love—our child, whom your neglect has possibly made an idiot for life."

Frightful was the picture of passion presented by the wretched Catherine! Tearing the paper to atoms, she threw the fragments upon the floor, and would have ground them to powder with her heel. Her bosom heaved with fierce convulsions—her eyes scintillated—then pressing her hands suddenly to her mouth, she sank upon a chair, and thence upon the floor, a stream of dark blood trickling from her lips. Her maid in great alarm raised and placed her upon the bed; then, summoning her fellow servants, sent off for Mrs. Leslie and the physician. Both soon appeared. Mrs. Dunn had broken a blood-vessel, and the long-continued hemorrhage left her in a state of utter prostration, with her life in imminent danger.

On the afternoon of that day, as Catherine lay prostrate, placid, snowy, "like a broken lily on its icy bed," her ear, rendered supernaturally acute by her condition, heard the physician's whispered injunction to her attendants—

"She must be kept perfectly quiet; complete rest is absolutely necessary. She must not be permitted to raise a hand, scarcely to lift an eye-lid, or hear a sound. Even with the best precaution, a second hemorrhage will be very apt to ensue. Her life hangs upon a cobweb shred."

"And is Death hovering so near?" thought Catherine; and in an instant, as though invoked by the powerful magicians, Conscience and Fear, the errors of her past life arose before her. Catherine, like most young people in high health, had never contemplated the possibility of death approaching herself, except at the close of a long, long life, at a remote, out of sight distance. Late at night, Mrs. Leslie, who had never left Catherine's side since her attack, was stealing from the room. The quick senses of the invalid detected her.

"Oh! do not leave me, dearest Mary, to die alone here, with the servants."

"Dearest Catherine, I must go home a few moments, to attend to some little family matters. I will return very soon."

"Ah! go, go; I must not detain you from your family. I have no claim upon you, nor upon any human being *now.* There was one upon whose love I had *every* claim. He would have worn out his life in watching by my side—but him I have outraged, him I have alienated——"

"Oh! Catherine! Catherine! *do* be quiet, love; I will stay with you; but you must be perfectly quiet."

The injunction came too late. The hemorrhage broke out again, and the patient was brought immediately to the very verge of the grave.

At early dawn, at the same hour of Catherine's attack, a steamboat stopped for a few moments, to land a passenger, near the beautiful town of C., on the west bank of the Hudson. Captain Dunn, leaving the boat with his boy in his arms, took his way towards a white cottage, nearly hidden amidst the trees, on the bank of the river. Passing quickly through the white painted gate, and up the neat gravel walk bordered with roses, he paused and rang the door bell. Early as was the hour, the inmates of the cottage were astir. He was met by a cleanly maid servant, who showed him into a neat parlour, and went to summon her mistress. An old lady, in the dress of the Friends, entered the room, and embraced the visiter, saying:

"Welcome, welcome, my dear son. How hast thou been these many days?"

"Indifferent, mother; indifferent! but," said he, uncovering the infant, "I have brought you my son; if you love me, dear madam, take charge of him during my absence."

"But thy wife, Lemuel? Where is she? How is she?" inquired the lady, as she received the child, and proceeded to disencumber him of his outer garments.

"I know not! I care not!"

"What meanest thou, my son?"

"Listen to me, dear mother; I have but an hour to spend with you—I must be on shipboard by noon to-day—so I must be brief with my explanations." Captain Dunn here gave a rapid account of the troubles of his married life. When he concluded, breakfast was placed upon the table, and the old lady arose to pour out the coffee, merely saying, by way of comment upon her son's story—

"Oh! these young people! these young people! One would think, with health, and youth, and competence, they would feel happiness to be a duty; but with their pride and their passions, their petulance and haste, they cast away God's richest gifts with ingratitude, as things of nought."

Twenty-four hours from this time, Captain Dunn, bearing an aching heart in his bosom, had left the shores of his native country.

Two months succeeding this event, Catherine Dunn sat up in bed for the first time since her illness. Her thin and snowy face, with the blue tracing of the veins on her temples and forehead, the languid fall of the long eyelashes, the gentle drooping of the whole figure, gave to her beauty a delicate and spiritual air it had never possessed before, while the deprecating softness of her manner silently appealed to the sympathies of all around her.

An elderly woman, who had been her faithful nurse for many weeks past, and to whose skill and unwearied attention, under Providence, she owed her life, now entered the room.

"If you please, Rebecca, I will lie down now; I feel faint."

"Yes, dear," said the old woman, as she tenderly placed her patient in a recumbent posture, inquiring kindly if she "felt comfortable."

"Very comfortable," answered Catherine; then looking affectionately at her nurse, she said:

"How much I owe you, dear Rebecca—not only my life, but the knowledge of that truth that makes life of value!"

"Thy gratitude is due to thy Creator, my child, and not to the feeble instrument he has been pleased to use. Thou wouldst not thank the cup, Catherine, for the coffee thou hast just taken."

"Ah, why will you not let me thank you, my dear friend—friend indeed, as well as well as Friend by profession? Think—when you came to me, I was as a shipwrecked mariner on an ocean rock—all, all lost—my life not worth a moment's purchase—or, if possibly spared, objectless and aimless. Rebecca! Rebecca! though my first, best gratitude is due to God, I must thank you too, I must love you too."

"I had an interest, dear child, in thy recovery, and in thy spiritual health," said the nurse, looking steadily at Catherine.

"Tell me your matron name," gazing earnestly in her face.

"I am thy husband's mother, Catherine."

The dreaded mother-in-law! The hated mother-in-law! Catherine looked in the sweet face of her nurse, and burst into tears.

"There, my child, drink this, and compose thyself," said the old lady, pouring out a glass of water. Then she continued: "Yes, Catherine, thou wilt think it strange that a woman of my sober class and age should be masquerading in this way; but it came to pass after this manner. Nearly two months ago, hearing that thou wert ill, I came down to visit thee. Finding thee in great need of a mother's care, I determined to remain with thee. As thy state was very precarious, and any surprise would have killed thee, I agreed with Mary Leslie not to make myself known, but to attend thee as thy nurse under my given name only. Thou knowest many of my sect are called only by their given names. Thence it came more natural."

"Ah! dearest madam! I will try to repay you with a daughter's love and duty; but the debt is stupendous. And now, dear madam, will you tell me about my boy? I guessed that my husband, that the Captain, had carried him to you."

"Thy infant is restored to health, Catherine; but for the better salubrity[5] of the air, I left him at home, in charge of a careful and trust-worthy woman, who has been my own personal attendant for *many* years."

"And my husband—was he very much embittered against me?"

"He left thee in high displeasure, Catherine."

"Ah! yes! it could not have been otherwise; and yet I loved him, mother. Wild and passionate as I have been, I loved them both—my husband and child. Yet I never dreamed how deeply until now, that they are gone from me."

"Thou shalt see thy boy soon, dear Catherine. When thou art able to travel, I propose to take thee to my country house on the Hudson. There, the pure air, the quiet scene, and the company of thy boy, will effect thy complete restoration to health."

"But will my husband ever forgive me?" sighed Catherine.

"He should not be obdurate, for he has something to forgive in himself. A little more firmness on his part would have saved you much misery, had that firmness been exercised in the first days of your marriage."

"It would have taken a great deal of firmness, though, mother; for in those days, although I loved the Captain, there was a perverse devil always prompting me to *try* him, to see how far I *might* go with impunity—a wish to drive him to extremity—and I never loved him better than when I saw him in a thorough rage. This must have been insanity; was it not, mother?"

"No, my dear; I think, as thou saidst, it was Satan," said the placid Quaker.[6] "And now I cannot allow thee to talk a moment longer; there is a fever spot already on thy cheek; so I shall draw the curtains, and leave thee to repose, my child."

Three years from the time of the commencement of Catherine Dunn's acquaintance with her mother-in-law, on a winter's evening, the white cottage at C. was lit up brightly. In the cosy parlour the cloth was laid for tea. In a large arm-chair, in one corner, sat an old lady, knitting. Upon an opposite lounge sat a young lady, employing herself with her needle, and in trying to keep awake an urchin of some five years old, who was hanging about her. But, ever and anon, she would start up and peer through the window-blinds or out of the door.

At last, going out upon the piazza, she remained some time, gazing down the moon-lit river. Returning to the parlour, shivering with cold, she said:

"Do you not think the boat is very long, dear mother?"

"No, my dear; it is thy impatience."

"But it is after seven, madam."

"Our clock may be fast, dear."

"Mamma, I'm *so* sleepy," said the child.

"Ah, Lem, *do* try to keep awake, that's a dear boy! See here, I'll draw you a horse on the slate. Don't you want to see papa?"

---

[5]Healthful quality.

[6]Religious tradition known for its deep commitments to peace, honesty, equality, and justice.

"I don't believe papa is coming to-night, and I don't want a horse."

"Hark, mother! I hear the steamboat paddle," said Catherine. "Listen!"—and the colour rushed to her cheeks, and the light to her eyes, as she stood breathlessly waiting. Meantime, the steamboat puffed and blew and paddled past the town. There were no passengers for C. that night. Catherine sank down in her chair, the picture of disappointment and dejection.

"Thou must learn to bear these disappointments with more equanimity, Catherine. Thy husband will probably be up in the morning boat. We must rise very early to receive him; and, in order to do so, let us take tea and go to bed."

Catherine went to bed, and tried to sleep, for she wished very much to be in good looks to receive her husband; and Catherine knew that anxious vigils are bad cosmetics. Saying the multiplication table backwards, and counting a thousand slowly, equally failed in their usually soporific effect. At length, ere the dawn had peeped through the windows, the distant sound of the steamboat paddle struck upon her ear. Starting from her bed, and quickly throwing on her dressing-gown, she went into the parlour. Finding old Mrs. Dunn and her waiting-maid already up and dressed, and busy with their preparation for breakfast, Catherine hastened back, and, quickly performing her toilet, soon rejoined them, leading little Lemuel.

"Now, dear, thou wilt not be disappointed—there is the bell—there are passengers for C. this morning," said the old lady.

Catherine flew to the door, and looked out; then, fluttering in again, she said quickly, while her colour went and came—

"Yes, indeed, mother; he is hurrying up the——Oh! After all, how will he receive me?"

"With love, my poor child; with joy; *do*—don't tremble so. Rachel, bring in the coffee." A step was heard upon the threshold—a hand upon the lock—and Mrs. Dunn and Catherine turned to greet—*Mr. Leslie.* The blank expression of disappointment upon the features of each of the ladies, was far from flattering to their visiter. But the anxious and sorrowful expression upon Leslie's countenance soon awoke other feelings.

"What is the matter? How is Mary?" exclaimed both ladies in a breath.

"Mary is well," said he, taking the hand of each anxious questioner; "but, my dear friends, summon all your fortitude, all your piety; I have come on a most painful errand; I am the messenger of the most afflicting news. Mrs. *Dunn,* your son—Catherine, your husband, has ceased to exist."

"Oh, God! support thy handmaid in this trial!" groaned the old mother, sinking into her chair.

A spasm, for an instant, convulsed the frame of Catherine, but left her perfectly still—her face blanched to marble whiteness—her eyes fearfully dilated. Her calmness was frightful.

"Now, tell me all about it," said she, in a voice of super-natural steadiness, "for I have a presentiment, I have a presentiment"——

"Yes, Catherine, I will; for so I have been *charged,* so I have promised to do. You are aware that your husband was in the habit of indulging freely in the use of intoxicating liquors."

"I was the cause of it; I drove him to drink," said Catherine, in the same unaccountable tone.

434 Emma Dorothy Eliza Nevitte Southworth

"This habit increased upon him fearfully after he sailed; and while in port, at one of the West India islands, *he died* in a fever of intoxication."

"And he died without ever guessing how I loved him; he died without knowing my bitter repentance; he died without forgiving me! But who cares? who cares?" said she, as her eyes grew wildly bright, and she broke into a loud maniac laugh, and, springing up, threw herself—into a pair of arms that pressed her fondly, while a pleasant, manly voice exclaimed:

"Why, dearest Kate, you have been dreaming frightful dreams."

And so she had.

Kate raised her head from the bosom that supported it, and looked up in bewilderment at the face of the speaker. It was Captain Lemuel Dunn, in his uniform, whose arms were around her. With a scream of joy, she buried her face once more in his bosom, and twined her arms around him. An impatient rap was now heard at the door, and Uncle Harry Gleason's voice exclaimed, quickly:

"Come! come! come! be quick with your kissing, Dunn; we *all* want to see her. Kate," he shouted, "get up; we are all here, Mary and all."

"Yes, Kate, get through your toilet quickly, dear one, for they are all here, the whole tribe of Manasseh"[7]—meaning all Leslie's folks and Uncle Harry's family—"all come to pass a few days with us, and to take us back, they insist, to spend Christmas with them."

"I will not leave the room until I have obtained your forgiveness," said Catherine, with tears in her eyes; "and if you knew how sorry"——an embarrassed "I know, I know," from "Lem Dunn," cut short her words, as they passed into the parlour. Kate soon embraced her sister and the little ones, shook hands with Mr. Leslie, and offered her cheek to Uncle Harry, who drew himself up primly, and said:

"No, I thank you, ma'am; I've reformed my morals since my marriage; I don't kiss other men's wives now. I have got one of my own."

"Now, children, come to breakfast," said old Mrs. Dunn, taking her place at the head of the table.

There have been merrier reunions, but there never was a happier family party than the one that, in responding to the old lady's summons, sat down at her plentiful and hospitable board.

[7]One of the twelve tribes of Israel in the Old Testament.

9

⋘◈◈⋙

Orson Squire Fowler and Lorenzo Niles Fowler

(1809–1887 and 1811–1896)

PHRENOLOGY, A SCIENCE centered on discovering and exploiting correlations between the shape of a person's head and that person's personality and intellect, enjoyed incredible popularity among Americans throughout the nineteenth century. Franz Joseph Gall (1758–1828), a Viennese physician, created what others would later call this "science of the mind." Gall argued that the brain could be separated into thirty-seven different "organs," all of which corresponded to a different mental faculty such as "spirituality," "self-esteem," "hope," and "destructiveness." He believed that one could identify every person's strong and weak organs by the shape of his head and then move to improve areas that were underdeveloped and take advantage of one's natural gifts. It was a highly optimistic system that promised tremendous self-improvement based on rigorous self-examination and discipline.

By the 1830s, more than forty phrenological societies had been established in the United States, and by the 1850s even the smallest American towns had been touched by a frenzied interest in the possibilities of phrenology. "Bump doctors" traveled the countryside lecturing, selling phrenological books and tracts, and analyzing the heads of all willing to pay their fees. Countless Americans applied phrenology to the most practical matters of their lives from choosing a mate to picking a career.

The most successful popularizers and educators of phrenology in America were members of the Fowler family: Orson, Lorenzo, Charlotte, and Charlotte's husband, Samuel Wells. Among the earliest traveling phrenologists, Orson and Lorenzo crisscrossed the country, promoting phrenology through their writings, lectures, and consultations. Among the more famous heads they analyzed were John Brown's, Horace Greeley's, Walt Whitman's, Mark Twain's, and Clara Barton's. They eventually stopped traveling to establish the American Phrenological Institute in New York City, edit the country's first phrenological magazine, *American Phrenological Journal,* and work on a host of other phrenological projects and writings. One of their most famous works was *The Illustrated Self-Instructor in Phrenology and Physiology.* First published in 1849, it proved to be one of the century's most popular self-instruction manuals, going through more than twenty editions in the next fifty years.

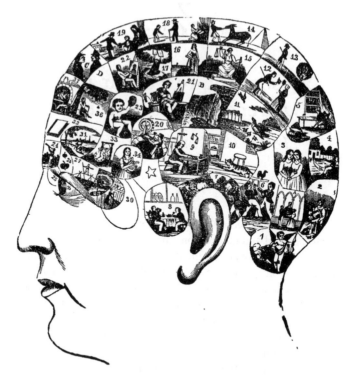

NUMBERING AND DEFINITION OF THE ORGANS.

1 AMATIVENESS, Sexual and connubial love.
2 PHILOPROGENITIVENESS, Parental love.
3. ADHESIVENESS, Friendship—sociability.
4 UNION FOR LIFE, Love of one only.
5 INHABITIVENESS, Love of home.
6 CONTINUITY, One thing at a time.
7 COMBATIVENESS, Resistance—defence.
7 DESTRUCTIVENESS, Executiveness—force.
8 ALIMENTIVENESS, Appetite, hunger.
9 ACQUISITIVENESS, Accumulation.
10 SECRETIVENESS, Policy—management.
11 CAUTIOUSNESS, Prudence, provision.
12 APPROBATIVENESS, Ambition—display.
13 SELF-ESTEEM, Self-respect—dignity.
14 FIRMNESS, Decision—perseverance.
15 CONSCIENTIOUSNESS, Justice—equity
16 HOPE, Expectation—enterprise
17 SPIRITUALITY, Intuition--spiritual revery.
18 VENERATION, Devotion—respect.
19 BENEVOLENCE, Kindness—goodness.
20 CONSTRUCTIVENESS Mechanical ingenuity

21. IDEALITY, Refinement—taste—purity.
B. SUBLIMITY, Love of grandeur.
22. IMITATION, Copying—patterning.
23. MIRTHFULNESS, Jocoseness—wit—fun.
24. INDIVIDUALITY, Observation.
25. FORM, Recollection of shape.
26. SIZE, Measuring by the eye.
27. WEIGHT, Balancing—climbing.
28. COLOR, Judgment of colors.
29. ORDER, Method—system—arrangement
30. CALCULATION, Mental arithmetic.
31. LOCALITY, Recollection of places.
32. EVENTUALITY, Memory of facts.
33. TIME, Cognizance of duration.
34. TUNE, MUSIC—melody by ear.
35. LANGUAGE, Expression of ideas.
36. CAUSALITY, Applying causes to effects.
37. COMPARISON, inductive reasoning.
C. HUMAN NATURE, perception of motives
D. AGREEABLENESS, Pleasantness—suavity

Frontispiece Illustration, "Symbolical Head," from an 1854 edition of Fowlers' *The Illustrated Self-Instructor.*

THE ILLUSTRATED SELF-INSTRUCTOR IN PHRENOLOGY AND PHYSIOLOGY WITH ONE HUNDRED ENGRAVINGS, AND A CHART OF THE CHARACTER

SECTION I

✍ Physiological Conditions as Affecting and Indicating Character

1.—VALUE OF SELF-KNOWLEDGE

"KNOWLEDGE is power"—to accomplish, to enjoy—and these are the only ends for which man was created. ALL knowledge confers this power. Thus, how incalculably, and in how many ways, have recent discoveries in chemistry enhanced human happiness, of which the lucifer match furnishes a *home* example. Increasing knowledge in agriculture is doubling the means of human sustenance. How immeasurably have modern mechanical improvements multiplied, and cheapened all the comforts of life. How greatly have steamboats and railroads added to the former stock of human success and pleasures. Similar remarks apply to all other kinds of knowledge, and as it increases from age to age will it proportionally multiply all forms of human happiness. In fact, its inherent *nature* and legitimate effect is to promote every species of enjoyment and success. Other things being equal, those who know most, by a law of things, can both accomplish and enjoy most; while ignorance instead of being bliss, is the greatest cause of human weakness, wickedness, and woe. Hence, to ENLIGHTEN man, is *the* way to reform and perfect him.

But SELF-knowledge is, of all its other kinds, both the most useful and promotive of personal and universal happiness and success. "Know thyself" was written, in golden capitals, upon the splendid temple of Delphos,[1] as the most important maxim the wise men of Greece could transmit to unborn generations; and the Scriptures wisely command us to "search our own hearts."[2] Since all happiness flows from obeying, and all pain from violating, the LAWS OF OUR BEING, to know our own selves is to know these laws, and becomes the first step in the road of their obedience, which is life. Self-knowledge, by teaching the laws and conditions of life and health, becomes the most efficacious means of prolonging the former and increasing the latter—both of which are *paramount* conditions of enjoying and accomplishing. It also shows us our natural talents, capabili-

---

O. S. and L. N. Fowler, *The Illustrated Self-Instructor in Phrenology and Physiology with One Hundred Engravings, and a Chart of the Character.* New York: Fowler and Wells Publishers, 1854.

[1]Ancient Greek temple dedicated to Apollo. It housed a famous oracle capable of offering an inquirer supernatural knowledge about the past, present, and future.

[2]Scriptural paraphrase, closely resembling Ps. 139:23.

ties, virtues, vices, strong, and weak points, liabilities to err, etc., and thereby points out, unmistakably, those occupations and spheres in which we can and cannot succeed and shine; and develops the laws and conditions of human and personal virtue and moral perfection, as well as of vice, and how to avoid it. It is, therefore, the quintessence of all knowledge; places its possessor upon the very acme of enjoyment and perfection; and bestows the highest powers and richest treasures mortals can possess. In short, to know ourselves perfectly, is to know every law of our being, every condition of happiness, and every cause of suffering; and to *practice* such knowledge, is to render ourselves as perfectly happy, throughout every department of our being, as we can possibly be and live. And since nothing in nature stands alone, but each is reciprocally related to all, and all, collectively, form one magnificent whole—since all stars and worlds mutually act and react upon each other, to cause day and night, summer and winter, sun and rain, blossom and fruit; since every genus, species, and individual throughout nature is second or sixteenth cousin to every other; and since man is the epitome of universal nature, the embodiment of all her functions, the focus of all her light, and representative of all her perfections—of course to understand *him* thoroughly is to know *all* things. Nor can nature be studied advantageously without him for a text-book, nor he without her.

Moreover, since man is composed of mind *and* body, both reciprocally and most intimately related to each other—since his mentality is manifested only by bodily organs, and the latter depends wholly upon the former, of course his mind can be studied only through its ORGANIC relations. If it were manifested independently of his physiology, it might be studied separately, but since all his organic conditions modify his mentality, the two must be studied TOGETHER. Heretofore humanity has been studied by piece-meal. Anatomists have investigated only his organic structure, and there stopped; and mental philosophers have studied him metaphysically, wholly regardless of all his physiological relations; while theologians have theorized upon his moral faculties alone; and hence their utter barrenness, from Aristotle[3] down. As if one should study nothing but the trunk of a tree, another only its roots, a third its leaves, or fruit, without compounding their researches, of what value is such piecemeal study? If the physical man constituted one whole being, and the mental another, their separate study might be useful; but since all we know of mind, and can do with it, is manifested and done wholly by means of physical instruments—especially since every possible condition and change of the physiology correspondingly affects the mentality—of course their MUTUAL relations, and the laws of their RECIPROCAL action, must be investigated *collectively*. Besides, every mental philosopher has deduced his system from his own closet cogitations, and hence their babel-like confusion. But within the last half century, a new star, or rather sun, has arisen upon the horizon of mind—a sun which puts the finger of SCIENTIFIC CERTAINTY upon every mental faculty, and discloses those *physiological* conditions which affect, increase or diminish, purify or corrupt, or in any other way modify, either the mind itself, or its products—thought, feeling, and character—and thereby reduces mental study to that same *tangible* basis of *proportion* in which all science consists; leaving nothing dark or

---

[3]Along with Plato, Aristotle (384–322 B.C.) is considered one of the two greatest intellects produced by ancient Greece. He is best known for his work in philosophy and science.

doubtful, but developing the true SCIENCE OF MIND, and the laws of its action. Of this, the greatest of all discoveries, Gall was the author, and Phrenology and Physiology the instruments which conjointly embrace whatever appertains to mind, and to man, in all his organic relations, show how to perfect the former by improving the latter, and disclose specific SIGNS OF CHARACTER, by which we may know ourselves and our fellow-men with certainty—a species of knowledge most delightful in acquisition, and valuable in application.

2.—STRUCTURE CORRESPONDS WITH CHARACTER

Throughout universal nature, the structure of all things is powerful or weak, hard or soft, coarse or fine, etc., in accordance with its functions; and in this there is a philosophical fitness or adaptation. What immense power of function trees put forth, to rear and sustain aloft, at such great mechanical disadvantage, their ponderous load and vast canvas of leaves, limbs, and fruit or seeds, spread out to all the surgings of tempestuous winds and storms; and the *texture* of wood is as compact and firm as its functional power is prodigious. Hence its value as timber. But tender vegetables, grains, etc., require little power, and accordingly are fragile in structure. Lions, tigers, hyenas, and all powerfully strong beasts, have a correspondingly powerful organic structure. The muscular strength of lions is so extraordinary, that seizing wild cattle by the neck, they dash through thicket, marsh, and ravine, for hours together, as a cat would drag a squirrel, and their roar is most terrific; and so powerful is their structure, that it took Drs. McClintock, Allen, myself, and two experienced "resurrectionists," FOUR HOURS, though we worked with might and main, just to cut off a magnificent Numidian[4] lion's head. So hard and tough were the muscles and tendons of his neck, that cutting them seemed like severing wire, and after slitting all we could, we were finally obliged to employ a powerful purchase to start them. It took over three hard days' work to remove his skin. So compact are the skins of the elephant, rhinoceros, alligator, and some other animals of great muscular might, that rifle-balls, shot against them, flatten and fall at their feet—their structure being as dense as their strength is mighty—while feeble animals have a correspondingly soft structure. In like manner, the flesh of strong persons is dense and most elastic, while those of weakly ones are flabby, and yield to pressure.

Moreover, fineness of texture manifests exquisiteness of sensibility, as seen by contrasting human organism and feelings with brutes, or fine-haired persons with coarse-haired. Of course, a similar relation and adaptation exist between all other organic characteristics and their functions. In short, it is a LAW as philosophical as universal, that the structure of all beings, and of each of their organs, corresponds perfectly with their functions—a law based in the very nature and fitness of things, and governing all shades and diversities of organization and manifestation. Accordingly those who are coarse-skinned are coarse in feeling, and coarse-grained throughout; while those finely organized are fine-minded, and thus of all other textures of hair, skin, etc.

---

[4]Ancient reference to North Africa.

3.—SHAPE CORRESPONDS WITH CHARACTER

Matter, in its primeval state, was "without form, and void,"[5] or gaseous, but slowly condensing, it solidified or CRYSTALLIZED into minerals and rocks—and all rocks and minerals are crystalline—which, decomposed by sun and air, form soil, and finally assume organic, or animal and vegetable forms. All crystals assume *angular* forms, and all vegetables and animals those more or less *spherical,* as seeds, fruits, etc., in proportion as they are lower or higher in the creative scale; though other conditions sometimes modify this result.

Nature also manifests certain types of character in and by corresponding types of form. Thus all trees bear a general resemblance to all other trees in growth and general character, and also in shape; and those most nearly allied in character approximate in shape, as pine, hemlock, firs, etc., while every tree of a given kind is shaped like all others of that kind, in bark, limb, leaf, and fruit. So all grains, grasses, fruits, and every bear, horse, elephant, and human being bear a close resemblance to all others of its kind, both in character and configuration, and on this resemblance all scientific classification is based. And, since this general correspondence exists between all the divisions and subdivisions into classes, genera, and species of nature's works, of course the resemblance is perfect between *all the details* of outward forms and inward mental characteristics; for this law, seen to govern nature in the outline, must of course govern her in all her minutest details; so that every existing outward shape is but the mirrored reflection of its inner likeness. Moreover, since nature always clothes like mentalities in like shapes, as oak, pine, apple, and other trees, and all lions, sheep, fish, etc., in other general types of form, of course the more nearly any two beings approximate to each other in mental disposition, do they resemble each other in shape. Thus, not only do tiger form and character always accompany each other, but leopards, panthers, cats, and all feline species resemble this tiger shape more or less closely, according as their dispositions approach or depart from his; and monkeys approach nearer to the human shape, and also mentality, than any other animal except orang-outangs, which are still more human both in shape and character, and form the connecting link between man and brute. How absolute and universal, therefore, the correspondence, both in general outline and minute detail, between shape and character. Hence the shape of all things becomes a sure index of its mentality.

4.—RESEMBLANCE BETWEEN HUMAN AND
ANIMAL PHYSIOGNOMY AND CHARACTER

Moreover, some men closely resemble one or another of the animal species, in both looks and character; that is, have the eagle, or bull-dog, or lion, or baboon expression of face, and when they do, have the corresponding characteristics. Thus the lion's head and face are broad and stout built, with a heavy beard and mane, and a mouth rendered square by small front and large eye teeth, and its corners slightly turning downward; and that human "Lion of the North"—who takes hold only of some great undertaking, which

---

[5]Gen. 1:2.

The Lion Face

Daniel Webster[6]

he pursues with indomitable energy, rarely pounces on his prey, but when he does, so roars that a nation quakes; demolishes his victim; and is an intellectual king among men—bears no slight physiognomical resemblance in his stout form, square face and mouth, large nose, and open countenance, to the king of beasts.

TRISTAM BURGESS, called in Congress the "Bald Eagle," from his having the aquiline or eagle-bill nose, a projection in the upper lip, falling into an indentation in the lower, his eagle-shaped eyes and eyebrows, as seen in the accompanying engraving, eagle-like in character, was the most sarcastic, tearing, and soaring man of his day, John Randolph[7] excepted. And whoever has a long, hooked, hawk-bill, or common nose, wide mouth, spare form, prominence at the lower and middle part of the forehead, is very fierce when assailed, high tempered, vindictive, efficient, and aspiring, and will fly higher and farther than others.

TIGERS are always spare, muscular, long, full over the eyes, large-mouthed, and have eyes slanting downward from their outer to inner angles; and human beings thus physiognomically characterized, are fierce, domineering, revengeful, most enterprising, not over humane, a terror to enemies, and conspicuous somewhere.

BULL-DOGS, generally fleshy, square-mouthed—because their tusks project and front teeth retire—broad-headed, indolent unless roused, but then terribly fierce, have their

[6]Daniel Webster (1782–1852) was a forceful lawyer and politician, considered to be one of the best orators of his day.

[7]John Randolph (1773–1833) was an American politician best remembered for his aggressive debating style and attachment to the doctrine of states' rights.

The Eagle Face

No. 2. Tristam Burgess

correspondent men and women, whose growling, coarse, heavy voices, full habit, logy yet powerful motions, square face, down-turned corners of mouth, and general physiognomical cast betoken their second-cousin relationship to this growling, biting race, of which the old line-tender at the Newburgh dock[8] is a sample.

SWINE—fat, logy, lazy, good-dispositioned, flat and hollow-nosed—have their cousins in large-abdomened, pud-nosed, double-chinned, talkative, story-enjoying, beer-loving, good-feeling, yes, yes, humans, who love some easy business, and hate HARD work.

Horses, oxen, sheep, owls, doves, snakes, and even frogs, etc., also have their men and women cousins, together with their accompanying characters.

These resemblances are more difficult to describe than to recognize; but the forms of mouth, nose, and chin, and sound of voice, are the best basis of observation.

5.—BEAUTIFUL, HOMELY, AND OTHER FORMS

In accordance with this general law, that shape is as character, well-proportioned persons have harmony of features, and well-balanced minds; whereas those, some of whose features stick right out, and others fall far in, have uneven, ill-balanced characters, so that homely, disjointed exteriors indicate corresponding interiors, while evenly-balanced and exquisitely formed men and women have well-balanced and susceptible mentalities. Hence, women, more beautiful than men, have finer feelings, and greater perfection of character, yet are less powerful—and the more beautifully formed the woman the more exquisite and perfect her mentality. True, some handsome women often make the great-

---

[8]Guard dog commonly found on the docks of Newburgh, a city in southeastern New York on the west bank of the Hudson River.

est scolds, just as the sweetest things, when soured, become correspondingly sour. The finest things, when perverted, become the worst. These two extremes are the worst tempered—those naturally beautiful and fine skinned, become so exquisitely organized, that when perverted they are proportionally bad, and those naturally ugly-formed, become ugly by nature.

Yet ordinary-looking persons are often excellent dispositioned, benevolent, talented, etc., because they have a few POWERFUL traits, and also features—the very thing we are explaining; that is, they have EXTREMES alike of face and character. Thus it is that every diversity of character has its correspondence in both the organic texture and physiognomical form. To elucidate this subject fully we must explain another law, that of

6.—HOMOGENEOUSNESS, OR ONENESS OF STRUCTURE

Every part of every thing bears an exact correspondence to that thing AS A WHOLE. Thus, tall-bodied trees have long branches and leaves, and short-bodied trees, short branches and roots; while creeping vines, as the grape, honey-suckle, etc., have long, slim roots that run under ground as extensively as their tops do above. The Rhode Island greening is a large, well-proportioned apple and its tree is large in trunk, limb, leaf, and root, and symmetrical, while the gillifleur is conical and its tree long limbed and even high to a peak at the top, while flat and broad-topped trees bear wide, flat, sunken-eyed apples. Very thrifty growing trees, as the Baldwin, fall pippin, Bartlet, black Tartarian, etc., generally bear large fruit, while small fruit, as the seckle pear, lady apple, bell de choisa cherry, grow slowly, and have many small twigs and branches. Beautiful trees that bear red fruit, as the Baldwin, etc., have red inner bark; while yellow and green-colored fruits grow on trees the inner kind of whose limbs is yellow or green. Peach-trees, that bear early peaches, have deeply-notched leaves, and the converse of late ones; so that, by these and other physiognomical signs, experienced nurserymen can tell what a given tree is at first sight.

In accordance with this law of unity of structure, long-handed persons have long fingers, toes, arms, legs, bodies, heads, and phrenological organs; while short and broad-shouldered persons are short and broad-handed and fingered, faced, nosed, and limbed, and wide and low bodied. When the bones on the hand are prominent, all the bones, nose included, are generally so, and thus of all other characteristics of the hand and any other part of the body. Hence, let a hand be thrust through a hole, and I will tell the general character of its owner, because if it is large or small, hard or soft, strong or weak, firm or flabby, coarse-grained or fine-textured, even or prominent, rough or smooth, small-boned or large-boned, or whatever else, his whole body is built upon the same principle, with which his brain and mentality also correspond. Hence small-nosed persons have little soul, and large-nosed a great deal of character of some kind; large nostrils indicate powerful lungs and bodies; while narrow nostrils indicate weak ones. Flat noses indicate flat minds, and prominent noses strong points of character; sharp noses, keen, clear intellects and intense feelings; blunt noses, obtuse minds; long noses, long heads; hollow noses, tame characters; finely-formed noses, well-proportioned character, etc.; and thus of every part of the body. And it is meet philosophical, accordant with the principles of adaptation, that this should be thus; and renders observations on character easy and correct. In general, too, tall persons have high heads, and are more aspiring, aim high, and seek conspicuosity, while short ones have flat heads, and seek worldly pleasures. Tall persons are rarely mean, though often grasping; but very penurious persons are often broad built. Small persons generally have exquisite mentalities, yet less power; while great men are rarely dwarfs, though great size often co-exists with sluggishness. To particularize—there are four leading forms which indicate generic characteristics, all existing in every one, yet in different DEGREES. They are these:

7.—THE BROAD, OR VITAL STRUCTURE

Thus, Indian ponies are broad built or thick set, and accordingly very tough, hardy, enduring of labor, and tenacious of life, yet less active and nimble. Bull-dogs, elephants, and all round-favored animals and men, also illustrate this law. Rotundity, with a moderate-sized head, indicates ancestral longevity; and, unless health has been abused, renders it possessor strong constitutioned, slow to ripen, or better as they grow older; full of animal life; self-caring; money-making; fond of animal pleasures; good feeling, yet spirited when roused; impulsive; more given to physical than mental action; better adapted to business than study, and talking than writing; more eloquent than argumentative; wide rather than high or long headed; more glowing than cool in feeling; and more enthusiastic than logical or deep. The preceding likeness represents this class, and his ancestors exceeded 100. He has never been sick; can endure any thing, and can never sit much in doors.

The Vital, or Animal Temperament

No. 3. Hall

Prominent, or Powerful

No. 4. Alexander Campbell

8.—THE MUSCULAR, OR POWERFUL TEMPERAMENT

Gives projecting features, bones, noses, eyebrows, etc., with distinctness of muscle; and renders its possessors strong; tough; thorough going; forcible; easy, yet powerful of motion; perhaps slow, but very stout; strongly marked, if not idiosyncratic; determined; and impressive both physically and mentally, who stamp their character on all they touch, of whom Alexander Campbell[9] is a good example.

9.—THE LONG, OR ACTIVE FORM

Gives ACTIVITY. Thus the gaselle; deer greyhound, weasel, and all long and slim animals, are sprightly, light-motioned, agile, quick, nimble, and full of action; and those persons thus formed are restless, wide awake, always doing, eager, uncommonly quick to think and feel, sprightly in conversation, versatile in talent, flexible, suggestive, abounding in idea, apt at most things; exposed to consumption, because their action exceeds their strength, early ripe, brilliant, and liable to premature exhaustion and disease, because the mentality predominates over the vitality; of which Captain Knight, of the ship. "New World," who has a world-wide reputation for activity, enterprise, daring, impetuousness, promptness, judgment, earnestness of execution, affability, and sprightliness, furnishes a good example.

---

[9]Alexander Campbell (1788–1866) was an important religious leader, helping found the immensely popular Disciples of Christ denomination.

Long, or Active

No. 5. Capt. Knight

10.—THE SHARP AND ANGULAR, OR MENTAL ORGANIZATION

Have ardent desires; intense feelings; keen susceptibilities; enjoy and suffer in the extreme; are whole-souled; sensitive; positive in likes and dislikes; cordial; enthusiastic; impulsive; have their hobbies; abound in good feeling, yet are quick-tempered; excitable; liable to extremes; too much creatures of feeling, and have a great deal of what we call SOUL, or passion, or warmth of feeling. This temperament prevails in BRILLIANT writers or speakers, who are too refined and sensitive for the mass of mankind. They gleam in their career of genius, and are liable to burn out their vital powers on the altar of nervous excitability, and like Pollok, H. K. White, McDonald Clarke, or Leggett, fall victims to premature death. Early attention to the physical training of children, would spare to the world the lives and usefulness of some of the brightest stars in the firmament of science.

11.—COMBINATIONS OF TEMPERAMENT

These shapes, or structures, called temperaments, however, never exist separately; yet since all may be strong, or all weak, or either predominant or deficient, of course their COMBINATIONS with each other and with the Phrenology exert potent influences over character, and put the observer in possession of both the outline and the inner temple of character.

Breadth of organization gives endurance, animal power, and animal feelings; and sharpness gives intensity of action, along with mind as mind and the two united give both that rapidity and clearness of mind and that intense glow of feeling which make the orator. Accordingly, all truly eloquent men will be found to be broad built, round-

Sharp and Angular, or Excitable

No. 6. Voltaire[10]

shouldered, portly, and fleshy, and yet rather sharp-featured. Of these, Sidney Smith[11] furnishes a sample.

His nose indicates the sharpness of the mental temperament, and his fullness of face the breadth of the animal—the blending of which gives that condensation of fervor and intellectuality which make him Sidney Smith. Intensity of feeling is the leading element of good speaking, for this excites feeling, and moves the masses. Wirt had this temperament. It predominates in Preston, and in every man noted for eloquence.

The sharp and broad, combined with smallness of stature, is still more susceptible, yet lacks strength. Such will be extremely happy, or most miserable, or both, and are liable to die young, because their action is too great for their endurance.

The vital mental, or broad and sharp, gives great power of constitution, excellent lungs and stomach, strong enjoying susceptibilities intense love of pleasure, a happy, ease-loving cast of body and mind; powerful passions, most intense feelings, and a story and song-loving disposition; and, with large Tune, superior singing powers. This is, PAR EXCELLENCE, the singing temperament. It also loves poetry and eloquence, and often executes them. Of this organism, its accompanying character, Dempster,[12] furnishes an excellent example.

---

[10]Voltaire (1694–1778) was a famous French writer who had a pronounced influence in the French Enlightenment.

[11]Sidney Smith (1764–1840) was a British admiral who distinguished himself against Napoléon's navy.

[12]Possibly George Dempster (1736?–1818), who was a noted Scottish agriculturalist who also served as a member of British Parliament for twenty-nine years.

The Excitable, Oratorical, or Mental Vital

No. 7. Sidney Smith

THE VITAL MOTIVE APPARATUS, or powerful and animal temperament, is indicated by the broad and prominent in shape, and renders its possessor of good size and height, if not large; well-proportioned; broad-shouldered; muscular, nose and cheek-bones prominent; visage strongly marked; features often coarse and homely; countenance stern and harsh; face red; hair red or sandy, if not coarse; and movements strong, but often awkward, and seldom polished. He will be best adapted to some laborious occupation, and enjoy hard work more than books or literary pursuits; have great power of feeling, and thus require much self-government; possess more talent than he exhibits to others, manifest his mind more in his business, in creating resources and managing matters, than in literary pursuits or mind as such; and improve with age, growing better and more intellectual as he grows older; and manufactures as much animal steam as he can work off, even if he works all the time hard. Such men ACCOMPLISH; are strong-minded; sensible; hard to beat; indomitable; often impulsive; and strong in passion when once aroused; as well as often excellent men. Yet this temperament is capable of being depraved, especially if the subject drinks. Sailors usually have this temperament, because fresh air and hard work induce it.

THE MOTIVE MENTAL TEMPERAMENT, or the prominent and sharp in structure, with the motive predominant, and the vital average or full, is of good size; rather tall and slim; lean and raw-boned, if not homely and awkward; poor in flesh; bones and features prominent, particularly the nose; a firm and distinct muscle, and a good physical organization; a keen piercing, penetrating eye; the front upper teeth rather large and projecting; the hands, fingers, and limbs all long; a long face, and often a high forehead; a firm, rapid, energetic walk; and great ease and efficiency of action, accompanied with little fatigue.

He will have strong desires, and much energy of character; will take hold of projects with both hands, and drive forward in spite of obstacles, and hence is calculated to

Sound Sharp Organization

Vital Motive

No. 8. Dempster

No. 9. Phineas Stevens[13]

accomplish a great deal; is not idle or lazy, but generally prefers to wait upon himself; will move, walk, etc. in a decided, forcible, and straightforward manner; have strong passions; a tough and wiry brain and body; a strong and vigorous mind; good judgment; a clear head, and talents more solid than brilliant; be long-headed; bold; cool; calculating; fond of deep reasoning and philosophizing, of hard thinking, and the graver and more solid branches of learning. This is the thorough-going temperament; imparts business powers; predisposes to hard work, and is indispensable to those who engage in great undertakings, or who would rise to eminence.

One having the mental temperament predominant, the motive full or large, and the vital average to full, will differ in build from the preceding description only in his being smaller, taller in proportion, and more spare. He will have a reflective, thinking, planning, discriminating cast of mind; a great fondness for literature, science, and intellectual pursuits of the deeper graver kind; be inclined to choose a professional or mental occupation; to exercise his body much, but his mind more; will have a high forehead; good moral faculties; and the brain developed more from the root of the nose, over to Philoprogenitiveness,[14] than around the ears. In character, also, the moral and intellectual faculties will predominate. This temperament is seldom connected with depravity, but generally with talent, and a manifestation, not only of superior talents, but of the

---

[13]Phineas Stevens (1706–1756) was a noted hunter, tracker, and soldier. He became a hero during the French and Indian War, in which he successfully defended a fort with only thirty men against more than four-hundred French soldiers.

[14]Character of a loving parent.

Prominent and Sharp

No. 10. Dr. Caldwell

solid, metaphysical, reasoning, investigating intellect; a fondness for natural philosophy, the natural sciences, etc. It is also the temperament for authorship and clear-headed, labored productions. It predominates in Revs. Jonathan Edwards, Wilbur Fiske, N. Taylor, E. A. Parke, Leonard Bacon, Albert Barnes, Oberlin, and Pres. Day; Drs. Parish and Rush; in Hitchcock, Jas. Brown, the grammarian, ex-U.S. Attorney-General Butler, Hugh L. White, Wise, Asher Robbins, Walter Jones, Esq., of Washington, D.C., Franklin, Alex. Hamilton, Chief-Justice Marshall, Calhoun, John Q. Adams, Percival, Noah Webster, Geo. Combe, Lucretia Mott, Catherine Waterman, Mrs. Sigourney, and nearly every distinguished author and scholar.[15] The accompanying engraving of William Cullen Bryant[16] furnishes as excellent an illustration of the shape that accompanies this temperament, as his character does of its accompanying mentality.

THE LONG AND SHARP combine the highest order of action and energy with promptness, clearness, and untiring assiduity and considerable power. Such are best fitted for some light, active business, requiring more brightness and quickness than power, such as merchants.

THE ORGANS THAT ACCOMPANY GIVEN TEMPERAMENTS.—Not only do certain outlines of character and drifts of talent go along with certain kinds of organizations, but certain phrenological developments accompany certain temperaments. As the pepper secretes the smarting, the sugar-cane sweetness, castor-beans and whales, oil, etc., throughout nature, so certain temperaments secrete more brain than others; and some, brain in particular regions of the head; and others, brain in other regions of the head—but all form most of those organs best adapted to carry out those characteristics already shown to accompany the several temperaments. Thus, the vital or animal temperament secretes brain in the neighborhood of the ears, so that along with breadth of body goes that width

---

[15]The Fowlers produce a veritable "who's who" list here of famous eighteenth- and nineteenth-century theologians, writers, politicians, lawyers, and educators to prove their point.

[16]William Cullen Bryant (1794–1878) was a noted early American nature poet and editor of the New York *Evening Post.*

The Mental Motive Temperament

No. 11. William Cullen Bryant

of head which gives that full development of the animal organs which is required by the animal temperament. Thus, breadth of form, width of head, and animality of temperament and character, all go together.

PROMINENCE of organization, or the motive or powerful temperament, gives force of character, and secretes brain in the crown of the head, and over the eyes, along with Combativeness, Destructiveness, Appetite, and Acquisitiveness. These are the very organs required by this temperament; for they complete that force which embodies the leading element of this organization. I never saw this temperament unaccompanied with prodigious Firmness, and great Combativeness and perceptives.

THE MENTAL VITAL.—The finest and most exquisite organization is that which unites the mental in predominance with the animal, the prominent retiring. In this case, the person is rather short, the form light, the face and person full, and the hair brown or auburn, or between the two. It will sometimes be found in men, but much oftener in women. It is the feeling, sentimental, exalted, angelic temperament; and always imparts purity, sweetness, devotion, exquisitensess, susceptibility, loveliness, and great moral worth.

The phrenological organs which accompany this temperament, are smaller Firmness, deficient Self-Esteem, large or very large Approbativeness, smaller Destructiveness, Appetite not large, Adhesiveness and Philoprogenitiveness very large, Amativeness fair; the head wide, not directly round the ears, but at the upper part of the sides, including Ideality, Mirthfulness, Sublimity, and Cautiousness; and a fine top head, rising at Benevolence quite as much as at Firmness, and being wide on the top, whereas the motive temperament gives perhaps a ridge in the middle of the head, but not breadth on the top, and leaves the head much higher at the back part than at Benevolence. Benevo-

Mental Vital

No. 12. Fanny Forrester[17]

lence, however, often accompanies the animal temperament, and especially that quiet goodness which grants favors because the donor is too pliable, or too easy, to refuse them. But for tenderness of sympathy, and whole-souled interest for mankind, no temperament is equal to the vital mental. The motive mental, however, is the one most common in reformers. The reason is this. The mentality imparted by this temperament sees the miseries of mankind, and weeps over them; and the force of character imparted by it pushes vigorously plans for their amelioration. The outer portion of Causality, which plans, often accompanies the animal temperament; the inner, which reasons, the motive mental and mental.

The more perfect these organic conditions, the better. Greater breadth than sharpness, or more vitality than action, causes sluggishness, dullness of feeling, and inertness, while too great action for strength, wears out its possessor prematurely. More prominence than sharpness, leaves talents latent, or undeveloped, while predominant sharpness and breadth, give such exquisite sensibilities, as that many things harrow up all the finer sensibilities of keen-feeling souls. But when all are powerful and EQUALLY BALANCED, they combine all the conditions of power, activity, and susceptibility; allow neither icy coldness, nor passion's burning heat, but unite cool judgment, intense but well-governed feelings, great force of both character and intellect, and perfect consistency and discretion with extraordinary energy; sound common sense, and far-seeing sagacity, with brilliancy; and bestow the highest order of Physiology and Phrenology. Such an organization and character were those of WASHINGTON.

Besides these prominent signs of character, there are many others, among which,

12.—THE LAUGH CORRESPONDS WITH THE CHARACTER

Those who laugh very heartily, have much cordiality and whole-souledness of character, except that those who laugh heartily at trifles, have much feeling, yet little sense. Those whose giggles are rapid, but light, have much intensity of feeling, yet lack power; whereas those who combine rapidity with force in laughing combine them in character.

---

[17]Fanny Forrester was the pen name for Emily Chubbock (1817–1854), a missionary wife and the writer of numerous popular novels for children and young people.

A Well-Balanced Organ

No. 13. Washington

One of the greatest workers I ever employed, I hired just because he laughed heartily, and he worked just as he laughed. But a colored domestic who laughed very rapidly, but LIGHTLY, took a great many steps to do almost nothing, and though she worked fast, accomplished little. Vulgar persons always laugh vulgarly, and refined persons show refinement in their laugh. Those who ha, ha, right out, unreservedly, have no cunning, and are open-hearted in every thing; while those who suppress laughter, and try to control their countenances in it, are more or less secretive. Those who laugh with their mouth closed, are non-committal; while those who throw it wide open, are unguarded and unequivocal in character. Those who, suppressing laughter for a while, burst forth volcano-like, have strong characteristics, but are well governed, yet violent when they give way to their feelings. Then there is the intellectual laugh, the love laugh, the horse laugh, the Philoprogenitive laugh, the friendly laugh, and many other kinds of laugh, each indicative of corresponding mental developments.

13.—THE WALK AS INDICATING CHARACTER

As already shown, texture corresponds to character, and motion to texture, and therefore to character. Those whose motions are awkward, yet easy, possess much efficiency and positiveness of character, yet lack polish; and just in proportion as they become refined in mind, will their mode of carriage be correspondingly improved. A short and quick step, indicates a brisk and active, but rather contracted mind, whereas those who take long steps, generally have long heads; yet if their step be slow, they will make comparatively little progress, while those whose step is LONG AND QUICK, will accomplish proportionately much, and pass most of their competitors on the highway of life. Their heads and plans, too, will partake of the same far-reaching character evinced in their carriage. Those who sluff or drag their heels, drag and drawl in every thing; while those who walk with a springing, bounding step, abound in mental snap and spring. Those whose walk is mincing, affected, and artificial, rarely, if ever, accomplish much; whereas those who walk carelessly, that is naturally, are just what they appear to be, and put on nothing for outside show. Those who, in walking, roll from side to side, lack directness of character, and side every way, according to circumstances; whereas, those who take a bee line—that is, whose body moves neither to the right nor left, but straight forward—have a corresponding directness of purpose, and oneness of character. Those also who tetter up and down when they walk, rising an inch or two every step, will have many corresponding ups and downs in life, because of their irregularity of character and feeling. Those, too, who make a great ado in walking, will make much needless parade in every thing else, and hence spend a great amount of useless steam in all they undertake, yet accomplish little; whereas those who walk easily, or expend little strength in walking, will accomplish great results with a little strength, both mentally and physically. In short, every individual has his own peculiar mode of moving, which exactly accords with his mental character; so that, as far as you can see such modes, you can decipher such outlines of character.

To DANCING, these principles apply equally. Dr. Wieting, the celebrated lecturer on physiology, once asked where he could find something on the temperaments, and was answered, "Nowhere; but if I can ever see you among men, I will give you a PRACTICAL lesson upon it." Accordingly, afterward, chance threw us together in a hotel, in which was a dancing-school that evening. Insisting on the fulfillment of our promise, we accompanied him into the dancing saloon, and pointed out, first, a small, delicately moulded, fine skinned, pocket-Venus, whose motions were light, easy, waving, and rather characterless, who put forth but little strength in dancing. We remarked—"She is very exquisite in feelings, but rather light in the upper story, lacking sense, thought, and strength of mind." Of a large, raw-bonded, bouncing Betty, who threw herself far up, and came down good and solid, when she danced, we remarked—"She is one of your strong, powerful, determined characters, well suited to do up rough work, but utterly destitute of polish, though possessed of great force." Others came in for their share of criticism—some being all dandy, others all business, yet none all intellect.

14.—THE MODE OF SHAKING HANDS

Also expresses character. Thus those who give a tame and loose hand, and shake lightly, have a cold, if not heartless and selfish disposition, rarely sacrificing much for others—probably conservatives, and lack warmth of soul. But those who grasp firmly, and shake heartily, have a corresponding whole-souledness of character, are hospitable, and will sacrifice business to friends; while those who bow low when they shake hands, add deference to friendship, and are easily led, for good or bad, by friends.

15.—THE MOUTH AND EYES PECULIARLY EXPRESSIVE OF CHARACTER

Every mouth differs from every other, and indicates a coincident character. Large mouths express a corresponding quantity of mentality, while small ones indicate a lesser amount of mentality. A coarsely formed mouth indicates power of character, while one finely formed indicates exquisite susceptibilities. Hence small, delicately-formed mouths, indicate only common minds, but very fine feelings, with much perfection of character. Whenever the muscles about the mouth are distinct the character is correspondingly positive, and the reverse. Those who open their mouths wide and frequently, thereby evince an open soul, while closed mouths, unless to hide deformed teeth, are proportionately secretive.

And thus of the eyes. In travelling west, in 1842, we examined a man who made great pretension to religion, but was destitute of Conscience, whom we afterward ascertained to be an impostor. While attending the Farmers' Club, in New York, this scamp came in, and besides keeping his eyes half closed half the time, frequently shut them so as to peep out upon those present, but opened them barely enough to secure vision. Those who keep their eyes half shut, are peekaboos and eaves-droppers, and those who use squinting glasses are no better, unless they merely copy a foolish fashion. The use of quizzing glasses indicates either defective sight or defective mentalities, but are rarely if ever employed except as a fashionable appendage.

Those, too, who keep their coats buttoned up, fancy high-necked and closed dresses, etc., are equally non-communicative, but those who like open, free, flowing garments, are equally open-hearted and communicative.

16.—INTONATIONS AS EXPRESSIVE OF CHARACTER

Whatever makes a noise, from the deafening roar of sea, cataract, and whirlwind's mighty crash, through all forms of animal life, to the sweet and gentle voice of woman, makes a sound which agrees perfectly with its character. Thus the terrific roar of the lion, and the soft cooing of the dove, correspond exactly with their respective dispositions; while the rough and powerful bellow of the bull, the fierce yell of the tiger, the coarse guttural moan of the hyena, and the swinish grunt, the sweet warblings of birds, in contrast with the raven's croak, and owl's hoot, each corresponds perfectly with their respective characteristics. And this law holds equally true of man—that the human intonations are as superior to brutal as human character exceeds animal. Accordingly, the peculiarities of every human being are expressed in his voice, and mode of speaking. Coarse-grained and powerfully animal organizations have a coarse, harsh, and grating voice, while in exact proportion as persons become refined, and elevated mentally, will their tones of voice become correspondingly refined and perfected. We little realize how much of character we infer from this source. Thus, some female friends are visiting me transiently. A male friend, staying with me, enters the room, is seen by my female company, and his walks, dress, manners, etc., closely scrutinized, yet says nothing, and retires, leaving a comparatively indistinct impression as to his character upon my female visitors, whereas, if he simply said yes or no, the mere SOUND of his voice communicates to their minds most of his character, and serves to fix distinctly upon their minds clear and correct general ideas of his mentality.

The barbarous races use the guttural sounds, more than the civilized. Thus Indians talk more down the throat than white men, and thus of those men who are lower or higher in the human scale. Those whose voices are clear and distinct have clear minds, while those who only half form their words, or are heard indistinctly, say by deaf persons, are mentally obtuse. Those who have sharp, shrill intonations have correspondingly intense feelings, and equal sharpness both of anger and kindness, as is exemplified by every scold in the world; whereas those with smooth, or sweet voices have corresponding evenness and goodness of character. Yet contradictory as it may seem, these same persons not unfrequently combine both sharpness and softness of voice, and such always combine them in character. There is also the intellectual, the moral, the animal, the selfish, the benignant, the mirthful, the devout, the love, and many other intonations, each accompanying corresponding peculiarities of characters. In short, every individual is compelled, by every word he utters, to manifest something of his true character—a sign of character as diversified as it is correct.

17.—HAIR, SKIN, ETC., AS INDICATING CHARACTER

Coarseness of texture indicates a coarseness of function; while a fine organization indicates a corresponding fineness of mentality. And since when one part is coarse or fine, all are equally so, so, therefore, coarseness of skin and hair indicate a coarse-grained brain, and coarseness of mind; yet since coarseness indicates power, such persons usually possess a great deal of character of some kind. Hence dark-skinned nations are behind light-haired in all the improvements of the age, and the higher finer manifestations of humanity. So, too, dark-haired persons, like Webster are frequently possessed of great power, yet lack the finer and more delicate shadings of sensibility and purity. Coarse black hair and skin, or coarse red hair and face, indicate powerful animal propensities, together with corresponding strength of character; while fine and light hair indicate quick susceptibilities, together with purity, refinement, and good taste. Fine dark or brown hair, indicates a combination of exquisite susceptibilities with great strength of character; while auburn-colored hair, and a florid countenance, indicate the highest order of exquisiteness and intensity of feeling, yet with corresponding purity of character and love of virtue, together with the highest susceptibilities of enjoyment and suffering. And the intermediate colors and textures indicate intermediate mentalities. Coarse-haired persons should never turn dentists or clerks, but should seek some out-door employment; and would be better contented with rough, hard work than a light or sedentary occupation, although mental and sprightly occupations would serve to refine and improve them; while dark and fine-haired persons may choose purely intellectual occupations, and become lecturers or writers with fair prospects of success. Red-haired persons should seek out-door employment, for they require a great amount of air and exercise; while those who have light, fine hair, should choose occupations involving taste and mental acumen, yet take bodily exercise enough to tone and vigorate their system.

Generally, whenever skin, hair, or features are fine or coarse, the others are equally so. Yet some inherit fineness from one parent, and coarseness from the other, while the color of the eye generally corresponds with that of the skin, and expresses character. Light eyes indicate warmth of feeling, and dark eyes power.

The mere expression of eye conveys precise ideas of the existing and predominant states of the mentality and physiology. As long as the constitution remains unimpaired, the eye is clear and bright, but becomes languid and soulless in proportion as the brain has been enfeebled. Wild, erratic persons, have a half-crazed expression of eye, while calmness, benignancy, intelligence, purity, sweetness, love, lasciviousness, anger, and all the other mental affections, express themselves quite as distinctly in the eye as voice, or any other mode.

18.—PHYSIOGNOMY

Jackson Davis well remarked that, in the spirit land, conversation is carried on mainly, not by words, but by EXPRESSION OF COUNTENANCE—that spirits LOOK their thoughts and motions, rather than talk them. Certain it is that the countenance discloses a greater amount of thought and feeling, together with their nicer shades and phases, than words can possibly communicate. Whether we will or no, we cannot HELP revealing the inner-most recesses of our souls in our faces. By what means is this effected? Clairvoyants say by magnetic centres, called poles; each physical and mental organ has its pole stationed in a given part of the face, so that, when such organ becomes active, it influences such poles, and contracts facial muscles, which express the corresponding emotions. That there exists an intimate relation between the stomach and one part of the face, the lungs and another, etc., is proved by the fact that consumptive patients always have a hectic flush on the cheek, just externally from the lower portion of the nose, while inactive lungs cause paleness, and healthy ones give the rosy cheek; and that dyspeptic patients are always lank and thin opposite the double teeth, while those whose digestion is good, are full between the corners of the mouth and lower portion of the ears. Since, therefore, SOME of the states of some of the internal organs express themselves in the face, of course every organ of the body must do the same—the magnetic pole of the heart beginning in the chin. Those whose circulation is vigorous, have broad and rather prominent chins; while those who are small and narrow-chinned have feeble hearts; and thus all the other internal organs have their magnetic poles in various parts of the face.

In like manner have all the PHRENOLOGICAL organs. In 1841, Dr. Sherwood, La Roy Sunderland, and O. S. Fowler, aided by a magnetic subject, located the poles of most of the phrenological and physiological organs, some of which were as follows: Acquisi-tiveness on each side of the middle portion of the nose, at its junction with the cheek, causing breadth of nose in proportion to the money-grasping instincts, while a narrow nose indicated a want of the speculative turn. Firmness is in the upper lip, midway between its edge and the nose, giving length, prominence, and a compression of the upper lip. Hence, when we would exhort to determined perseverance, we say, "Keep a stiff upper lip." Self-Esteem has its pole externally from that of Firmness, and between the outer portion of the nose and the mouth, causing a fullness, as if a quid of tobacco were under the upper lip. The affections were described as having their poles in the edges of the lips, and hence the philosophy of kissing. The pole of Mirthfulness is located externally, and above the outer corners of the mouth, and hence the drawing up of these corners in laughter. Approbativeness has its pole directly outward from these corners, and hence the approbative laugh does not turn the corners of the mouth upward, but draws them straight back, or outwardly. Like locations were assigned to nearly all the other organs. That physiognomy has its science—that fixed and absolute relations exist between the phrenological organs and given portions of the face is not a matter of question. The natural language of the organs, as seen in the attitudes of the head, indicate not only the presence of large and active organs, but also the signs of their deficiency. Self-Esteem throws the head upward and backward toward the seat of its organ; Approbativeness, back and toward the side; Philoprogenitiveness, directly back, but not upward; Firmness draws the head up, in a stiff, perpendicular position; Individuality thrusts the head forward toward its organ, and gives the man a staring, gazing aspect; small Self-Esteem lets the head droop forward. Man was made both to disclose his own character, and to read that of others. Than this form of knowledge, none is more inviting or useful. Hence God has caused the inherent character of every living being and thing to gush out through every organ of the body, and every avenue of the soul; and also created in both brute and man a character-reading faculty, to take intuitive cognizance of the mental operations. Nor will she let any one lie, any more than lie herself, but compels all to carry the flag of their character at their mast-heads, so that all acquainted with the signs may see and read. If we attempt deception, the very effort convicts us. If all nature's signs of character were fully understood, all could read not only all the main characters of all they see, but even most thoughts and feelings passing in the mind for the time being—a gift worth more than Astor's millions.[18]

19.—REDNESS AND PALENESS OF FACE

Thus far our remarks have appertained to the constant colors of the face, yet those colors are often diversified or changed for the time being.

Thus, at one time, the whole countenance will be pale, at another, very red; each of which indicates the existing states of body and mind. Or thus; when the system is in a perfectly healthy state, the whole face will be suffused with the glow of health and beauty, and have a red, but never an inflamed aspect; yet any permanent injury of health, which prostrates the bodily energies, will change this florid complexion into dullness of countenance indicating that but little blood comes to the surface or flows to the head and a corresponding stagnation of the physical and mental powers. Yet, after a time, this dullness frequently gives way to a fiery redness; not the floridness of health, but the redness of inflammation and false excitement, which indicates a corresponding depreciation of the mental faculties. Very red-faced persons, so far from being the most healthy, are frequently the most diseased, and are correspondingly more animal and sensual in character; because physiological inflammation irritates the propensities more, relatively, than the moral and intellectual faculties, though it may, for the time being, increase the latter also. When the moral and intellectual faculties greatly predominate over the animal, such redness of the face may not cause coarse animality, because while it heightens the animal nature, it also increases the intellectual and moral, which, being the larger, hold them in check, but when the animal about equals the moral and intellectual, this inflammation evinces a greater increase of animality than intellectuality and morality. Gross sensualists, and depraved sinners, generally have a fiery, red countenance. Stand aloof from them, for their passions are all on fire, ready to ignite and

[18]John Jacob Astor (1763–1848) through his involvement in the fur business founded a dynastic business family of immense wealth.

explode on provocations so slight that a healthy physiology would scarcely notice them. This point can hardly be more fully intelligible; but let readers note the difference between a healthy floridness of face, and the fiery redness of drunkards, debauchees, meat-eaters, etc. Nor does an inflamed physiology merely increase the animal nature, but gives a far more *depraved* and sensual cast to it, thus doubly increasing the tendency to depravity.

20.—HEALTH AND DISEASE AS AFFECTING MENTALITY

Health and disease affects the mind as much as body. Virtue, goodness, etc., are only the healthy or normal exercise of our various faculties, while depravity and sin are only the sickly exercise of these same organs. Holiness and moral excellence, as well as badness, depend far less upon the relative SIZE of the phrenological organs, than upon their DIREC-TION or tone and character, and this depends upon the STATE OF THE BODY. Or thus; a healthy physiology tends to produce a healthy action of the phrenological organs, which is virtue and happiness; while an unhealthy physiology produces that sickly exercise of the mental faculties, especially of the animal propensities, which constitutes depravity and produces misery. Hence those phrenologists who look exclusively to the predominant SIZE of the animal organs, for vicious manifestations, and regard their average size as indicative of virtue, have this great lesson to learn, that health of body produces health of mind and purity of feelings, while all forms of bodily disease, in the very nature of things, tend to corrupt the feelings and deprave the soul. While, therefore, phrenologists should scrutinize the size of organs closely, they should observe the STATE OF HEALTH much more minutely, for most of their errors are explainable on this ground: that the organs described produced vicious inclinations, not because they were so large but because they were physically SICK, and hence take on a morally DEFORMED mode of action. Phrenologists, look ye well to these points, more fully explained in our other phrenological works.

SECTION II

✌ Phrenological Conditions as Indicating Character

21.—DEFINITION AND PROOF

PHRENOLOGY points out those relations established by nature between given developments and conditions of BRAIN and corresponding manifestations of MIND. Its simple yet comprehensive definition is this: every faculty of the mind is manifested by means of particular portions of the BRAIN called its organs, the size of which, other things being equal, is proportionate to its power of function. For example: it teaches that parental love is manifested by one organ, or portion of the brain; appetite by another, reason by a third, etc., which are large the stronger these corresponding mental powers.

Are, then, particular portions of the brain larger or smaller in proportion as particular mental characteristics are stronger or weaker? Our short-hand answer is illustrated by the following anecdote. A Mr. Juror was once summoned to attend court, but died before its sitting. It therefore devolved upon Mr. Simple to state to the court the reason of his non-appearance. Accordingly, when Mr. Juror's name was called, Mr. Simple responded, "May it please the court, I have twenty-one reasons why Mr. Juror is not in attendance. The first is, he is DEAD. The second is—" "That ONE will answer," responded the judge. "One such reason is amply sufficient." But few of the many proofs that Phrenology is true will here be stated, yet those few are DECISIVE.

First. THE BRAIN IS THE ORGAN OF THE MIND. This is assumed, because too universally admitted to require proof.

Secondly. Is the brain, then, a SINGLE organ, or is it a bundle of organs? Does the WHOLE brian think, remember, love, hate, etc.; or does one portion reason, another worship, another love money, etc.? This is the determining point. To decide it affirmatively, establishes Phrenology; negatively, overthrows it. It is proved by the following facts.

THE EXERCISE OF DIFFERENT FUNCTIONS SIMULTANEOUSLY.—We can walk, think, talk, remember, love, and many other things all TOGETHER,—the mind being, in this respect, like a stringed instrument, with several strings vibrating at a time, instead of like a flute which stops the preceding sound when it commences succeeding ones; whereas, if it were a single organ, it must stop thinking the instant it began to talk, could not love a friend and express that love at the same time, and could do but one thing at once.

MONOMANIA.—Since mental derangement is caused only by cerebral disorder, if the brain were a single organ, the WHOLE mind must be sane or insane together; whereas most insane persons are deranged only on one or two points, a conclusive proof of the plurality of the brain and mental faculties.

DIVERSITY OF TALENT, or the fact that some are remarkable for sense, but poor in memory, or the reverse; some forgetting names, but remembering faces; some great mechanics, but poor speakers, or the reverse; others splendid natural singers, but no mechanics, etc., etc., conducts us to a similar conclusion.

INJURIES OF THE BRAIN furnish still more demonstrative proof. If Phrenology be true, to wound and inflame Tune, for example, would create a singing disposition; Veneration, a praying desire; Cautiousness, groundless fears; and so of all the other organs. And thus it is. Nor can this class of facts be evaded. They abound in all phrenological works, especially periodicals, and drive and clench the nail of proof.

COMPARATIVE PHRENOLOGY, or the perfect coincidence existing between the developments and characters of animals, constitutes the highest proof of all. Since man and brute are fashioned upon one great model, those same great optical laws governing the vision of both, that same principle of muscular contraction which enables the eagle to soar aloft beyond our vision, and the whale to furrow and foam the vasty deep, and enabling man to walk forth in the conscious pride of his strength, and thus of all their other common functions; of course, if man is created in accordance with phrenological laws, brutes must also be; and the reverse. If, then, this science is true of either, it must be true of both; must pervade all forms of organization. What, then, are the facts?

Phrenology locates the animal propensities at the SIDES of the head, between and around the ears; the social affections in its BACK and lower portion; the aspiring faculties in its CROWN; the moral on its TOP; and the intellectual on the FOREHEAD; the perceptives,

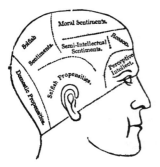

No. 14. Grouping of Organs

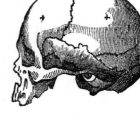

No. 15. Human Skull

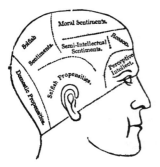

No. 16. Snake

No. 17. Turtle

which, related to matter, OVER THE EYES; and the reflectives in the UPPER part of the fore-head. (See cut No. 14.)

Now since brutes possess at least only weak moral and reflective faculties, they should, if Phrenology were true, have little top head, and thus it is. Not one of all the following drawings of animals, have much brain in either the reflective or moral region. Almost all their mentality consists of the ANIMAL PROPENSITIES, and nearly all their brain is BETWEEN and AROUND THEIR EARS, just where, according to Phrenology, it should be. Yet the skulls of all human beings rise high above the eyes and ears, and are long on top, that is, have intellectual and moral ORGANS, as we know they possess these mental ELE-MENTS. Comparing the accompanying human skull with those of brutes, thus those of snakes, frogs, turtles, alligators, etc., slope straight back from the nose; that is, have al-most no moral or intellectual organs; tigers, dogs, lions, etc., have a little more, yet how insignificant compared with man, while monkeys are between them in these or-gans and their faculties. Here, then, is INDUCTIVE proof of Phrenology as extensive as the whole brute creation on the one hand, contrasted with the entire human family on the other.

Again, Destructiveness is located by Phrenology over the ears, so as to render the head wide in proportion as this organ is developed. Accordingly, all carnivorous animals should be wide-headed at the ears; all herbivorous, narrow. And thus they are, as seen in tigers, hyenas, bears, cats, foxes, ichneumons,[19] etc., compared with rabbits, sheep etc. (Cuts 18, 19, 20, 21, 22, 23, 24, 25, 26, 27, 28, 29, and 30).

To large Destructiveness, in cats, foxes, ichneumons, etc., add large SECRETIVENESS, both in character and head.

Fowls, in like manner, correspond perfectly in head and character. Thus, owls, hawks, eagles, etc., have very wide heads, and ferocious dispositions; while hens, turkeys, etc., have narrow heads, and little Destructiveness in character (cuts 31, 32, and 33).

---

[19]mongooses

Destructive Large

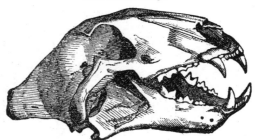

No. 18. Tiger—Side View

No. 19. Hyena—Side View

No. 20. Hyena—Back View

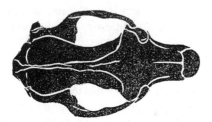

No. 21. Bear—Top View

No. 22. Bear—Back View

Destructive Small

No. 23. Sheep—Top View

No. 24. Rabbit—Side View

The crow (cut 34) has very large Secretiveness and Cautiousness in the head, as he is known to have in character.

Monkeys, too, bear additional testimony to the truth of phrenological science. They possess, in character, strong perceptive powers, but weak reflectives, and powerful propensities, with feeble moral elements. Accordingly they are full over the eyes, but

Secretiveness and Destructiveness Both Large

No. 25.
Fox—Side View

No. 26.
Ichneumon—Side View

No. 27.
Do.—Back View

No. 28.
Cat—Back View

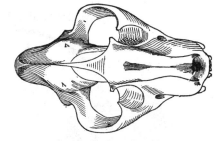

No. 30. Lion—Top View

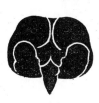

No. 29.
Cat—Side View

Destructiveness Large and Small

No. 31.
Owl—Top View

No. 32.
Hawk—Top View

No. 33.
Hen—Top View

slope straight back at the reasoning and moral faculties, while the propensities engross most of their brain.

The ORANG-OUTANG has more forehead than any other animal, both perceptive and reflective, with some moral sentiments, and accordingly is called the "half-reasoning man," its Phrenology corresponding perfectly with its character.

THE VARIOUS RACES also accord with phrenological science. Thus, Africans generally have full perceptives, and large Tune and Language, but retiring Causality, and accordingly are deficient in reasoning capacity, yet have excellent memories and lingual and musical powers.

Indians possess extraordinary strength of the propensities and perceptives, yet have no great moral or inventive power; and, hence, have very wide, round, conical, and rather low heads.

Secretiveness and Cautiousness Large

No. 35.
Intelligent
Monkey

No. 36.
Do.—Side View

No. 34.
Crow

Some Moral and Reflective Brain

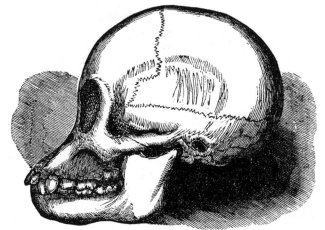

No. 37. The Orang-Outang

Perceptives Larger Than Reflectives

No. 38. African Head

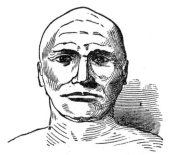

No. 39. Indian Chief

Large and Small Intellects

No. 43. Bacon

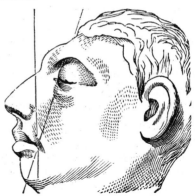

No. 44. Idiot

Indian skulls can always be selected from Caucasian, just by these developments; while the Caucasian race is superior in reasoning power and moral elevation to all the other races, and, accordingly, have higher and bolder foreheads, and more elevated and elongated top heads.

Finally, contrast the massive foreheads of all giant-minded men—Bacons, Franklins, Miltons[20], etc., with idiotic heads.

In short, every human, every brutal head, is constructed throughout strictly on phrenological principles. Ransack air, earth, and water and not one palpable exception ever has been, ever can be adduced. This WHOLE-SOUL view of this science precludes the possibility of mistake. Phrenology is therefore a PART AND PARCEL OF NATURE—A UNIVERSAL FACT.

The Philosophy of Phrenology

All truth bears upon its front unmistakable evidence of its divine origin, in its philosophical consistency, fitness, and beauty, whereas all untruth is grossly and palpably deformed. All truth, also, harmonizes with all other truth, and conflicts with all error, so that to ascertain what is true, and detect what is false, is perfectly easy, Apply this test, intellectual reader, to one after another of the doctrines, as presented in this science. But enough on this point of proofs. Let us proceed to its illustration.

22.—PHRENOLOGICAL SIGNS OF CHARACTER

The brain is not only the organ of the mind, the dome of thought, the palace of the soul, but is equally the organ of the *body,* over which it exerts an all-potent influence for good or ill, to weaken or stimulate, to kill or make alive. In short, the brain is the organ of the

---

[20]Francis Bacon (1561–1626), Benjamin Franklin (1706–1790), and John Milton (1608–1674) were leading intellectuals of their times. Each distinguished himself by contributing to several fields of intellectual inquiry during his lifetime.

body in general, and of all its organs in particular. It sends forth those nerves which keep muscles, liver, bowels, and all the other bodily organs in a high or low state of action; and, more than all other causes, invites or repels disease, prolongs or shortens life, and treats the body as its galley-slave. Hence, healthy cerebral action is indispensable to bodily health. Hence, too, we walk or work so much more easily and efficiently when we take an *interest* in what we do. Therefore those who would be happy or talented must first and mainly keep their BRAIN vigorous and healthy.

The brain is subdivided into two hemispheres, the right and left, by the falciform process of the dura mater, a membrane which dips down one to two inches into the brain, and runs from the root of the nose over to the nape of the neck. This arrangement renders all the phrenological organs DOUBLE. Thus, as there are two eyes, ears, etc., that when one is diseased, the other can carry forward the functions, so there are two lobes to each phrenological organ, one on each side. The brain is divided thus: the feelings occupy that portion commonly covered by the hair, while the forehead is occupied by the intellectual organs. These greater divisions are subdivided into the animal brain, located between and around the ears; the aspiring faculties, which occupy the crown of the head; the moral and religious sentiments, which occupy the top; the physico-perceptives, located over the eyes; and the reflectives, in the upper portion of the forehead. The predominance of these respective groups produces both particular shapes, and corresponding traits of character. Thus, when the head projects far back behind the ears, hanging over and downward in the occipital region, it indicates very strong domestic ties and social affections, a love of home, its relations and endearments, and a corresponding high capacity of being happy in the family, and of making the family happy. Very wide and round heads, on the contrary, indicate strong animal and selfish propensities, while thin, narrow heads, indicate a corresponding want of selfishness and animality. A head projecting far up at the crown, indicates an aspiring, self-elevating disposition, proudness of character, and a desire to be and to do something great; while the flattened crown indicates a want of ambition, energy, and aspiration. A head high, long, and wide upon the top, but narrow between the ears, indicates Causality, moral virtue, much practical goodness, and a corresponding elevation of character; while a low or narrow top head indicates a corresponding deficiency of these humane and religious susceptibilities. A head wide at the upper part of the temples, indicates a corresponding desire for personal perfection, together with a love of the beautiful and refined, while narrowness in this region evinces a want of taste, with much coarseness of feeling. Fullness over the eyes indicates excellent practical judgment of matters and things appertaining to property, science, and nature in general; while narrow, straight eyebrows, indicate poor practical judgment of matter, its quality, relations, and uses. Fullness from the root of the nose upward, indicates great practical talent, love of knowledge, desire to see, and ability to do to advantage, together with sprightliness of mind; while a hollow in the middle of the forehead indicates want of memory and inability to show off to advantage. A bold, high forehead, indicates strong reasoning capabilities, while a retiring forehead indicates less soundness, but more availability of talent.

23.—THE NATURAL LANGUAGE OF THE FACULTIES

Phrenology shows that every faculty, when active, throws head and body in the direction of that faculty. Thus, intellect, in the fore part of the head, throws it directly forward, and

No. 40. Washington Irving

produces a forward hanging motion of the head. Hence intellectual men never carry their heads backward and upward, but always forward; and logical speakers move their heads in a straight line, usually forward, toward their audience; while vain speakers carry their heads backward. Perceptive intellect, when active, throws out the chin and lower portions of the face; while reflective intellect causes the upper portion of the forehead to hang forward, and draws in the chin, as in the engravings of Franklin, Webster, and other great thinkers. Benevolence throws the head and body slightly forward, leaning toward the object which excites its sympathy; while Veneration causes a low bow, which, the world over, is a token of respect; yet, when Veneration is exercised toward the Deity, as in devout prayer, it throws the head UPWARD; and, as we use intellect at the same time, the head is generally directed forward. Ideality throws the head slightly forward, and to one side, as in Washington Irving,[21] a man as gifted in taste and imagination as almost any living writer; and, in his portraits, his finger rests upon this faculty; while in Sterne, the finger rests upon Mirthfulness. Very firm men stand straight up and down, inclining not a hair's breadth forward or backward, or to the right or left; hence the expression, "He is an up-and-down man." And this organ is located exactly on a line with the body. Self-Esteem, located in the back and upper portion of the head, throws the head and body upward and backward. Large feeling, pompous persons, always walk in a very dignified, majestic posture, and always throw their heads in the direction of Self-Esteem; whilst approbative persons throw their heads backward, but to the one side or both. The differ-

---

[21]Washington Irving (1783–1859) was an American author of extreme popularity and international reputation in the early nineteenth century.

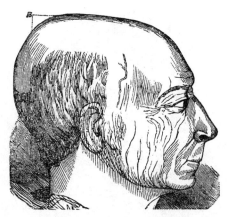

No. 45. A Conceited Simpleton

ence between these two organs being comparatively slight, only the practical Phrenologist's eye can perfectly distinguish them.

There is, moreover, a natural language of money-loving, and that is a leaning forward and turning of the head to one side, as if in ardent pursuit of something, and ready to grasp it with outstretched arms; while Alimentiveness, situated lower down, hugs itself down to the dainty dish with the greediness of an epicure, better seen than described. The shake of the head is the natural language of Combativeness, and means no, or I resist you. Those who are combating earnestly upon politics, or any other subject, shake the head more or less violently, according to the power of the combative feeling, but always shake it slightly inclining *backwards;* while Destructiveness, inclining forward, causes a shaking of the head slightly forward, and turning to one side. When a person who threatens you shakes his head violently, and holds it partially backward, and to one side, never fear—he is only barking; but whenever he inclines his head to one side, and shakes it violently, that dog will bite, whether possessed of two legs or four. The social affections are located in the *back* part of the head; and, accordingly, woman being more loving than man, when not under the influence of the other faculties, usually inclines her head backward toward the neck; and when she kisses children, and those whom she loves, always turns the head directly backward, and rolls it from side to side, on the back of the neck. Thus it is that all the various postures assumed by it individually, are expressive of the present or the permanent activity of their respective faculties.

24.—ORGANIC TONE OR QUALITY OF BRAIN

This condition modifies character more than any other. It is, indeed, the summing up of all. It consists of two kinds, original and acquired. The former, inherited from parents, embraces the pristine vigor and power with which the life principle was started, and gives what we will call SNAP; while the latter embraces the *existing* states of the organism as affected by health or debility, artificial habits—such as dyspeptic and other affections, caused by injurious qualities and quantities of food, by artificial stimulants, as tea, coffee, tobacco, or alcoholic drinks—the deranged or healthy states of the nervous system;

No. 44. Jonathan Edwards[22]

No. 45.
Emerson, an Idiot

too much or too little exercise, abor, sleep, breath, etc., etc.; and whatever other conditions are embraced in health and disease, or in any way affect them. Of course, the parental may be good, but acquired poor, or the reverse, according as the subject is strengthening or enfeebling, building up or breaking down his physical constitution, by correct or erroneous physiological habits. Yet, in most persons, the parental is many hundred per cent better than the acquired.

PARENTAL GOOD, OR VERY GOOD, gives corresponding innate vigor and energy, or that heart and bottom which wears like iron, and bends, willow-like, without breaking, and performs more with a given size, than greater size, and less inherent "snap;" and gives thoroughness and edge to the mentality, just as good steel, well tempered, does to the tool.

PARENTAL FAIR gives a good share of the presiding qualities, yet nothing remarkable; with acquired good, endures and accomplishes much; without it, soon breaks down.

PARENTAL POOR leaves its subject poorly organized, bodily and mentally, and proportionally low in the creative scale.

ACQUIRED GOOD enables whatever of life power there is, to perform all of which it is capable; with parental good, furnishes a full supply of vital power, and that activity which works it all up in mental or physical labor. With parental very good, puts forth a most astonishing amount of effort, and endures wonders without injury; possesses remarkable clearness and wholeness of mind; thinks and feels directly to the purpose; gives point and cogency to every thing; and confers a superior amount of healthy intellectuality, morality, and mentality, in general.

ACQUIRED FAIR, with parental average, gives fair natural talents, and mental and physical vigor, yet nothing remarkable; will lead a common-place life, and possess an everyday charcter, memory, etc.; will not set the world on fire, nor be insignificant, but, with cultivation, will do well.

ACQUIRED POOR will be unable to put forth its inherent power; is weak and inefficient, though desirous of doing something; with parental good, may take hold resolutely, but

---

[22]Jonathan Edwards (1703–1758) was perhaps the premier theologian of the eighteenth-century American Puritanism.

soon tires, and finds it impossible to sustain that powerful action with which it naturally commences.

25.—STATES OF THE NERVOUS SYSTEM

A good nervous condition enables its possessor to put forth sound and healthy mental and physical efforts; gives a calm, quiet, happy, contented frame of mind, and a strong tendency to enjoy every thing—even the bad; makes the most of life's joys, and the least of its sorrows; confers full possession of all its innate powers; and predisposes to a right exercise of all the faculties.

Disordered nerves produce an irritated, craving, dissatisfied state of mind, and a tendency to depravity in some of its forms, with a half paralyzed, lax, inefficient state of mind and body.

26.—SIZE OF HEAD AS INFLUENCING CHARACTER

Size of head and organs, other things being equal, is the great phrenological condition. Though tape measurements, taken around the head, from Individuality to Philoprogenitiveness, give some idea of the size of brain, the fact that some heads are round, others long, some low, and others high, so modifies these measurements that they do not convey any very correct idea of the actual quantity of brain. Yet these measurements range somewhat as follows. Least size of adults compatible with fair talents, $20^1/4$; $20^3/4$ to $21^1/4$, moderate; $21^1/4$ to 22, average; 22 to $22^3/4$, full; $22^3/4$ to $23^3/4$, large; above $23^3/4$, very large. Female heads, $^1/2$ to $^3/4$ below these averages.

Large.—One having a large sized brain, with activity *average,* will *possess* considerable energy of intellect and feeling, yet seldom manifest it, unless it is brought out by some powerful stimulus, and will be rather too indolent to exert, especially his *intellect:* with activity *full,* will be endowed with an uncommon amount of the mental power, and be capable of doing a good deal, yet require considerable to awaken him to that vigorous effort of mind of which he is capable; if his powers are not called out by circumstances, and his organs of practical intellect are only average or full, he may pass through life without attracting notice, or manifesting more than an ordinary share of talent: but if the perceptive faculties are strong, or very strong, and his natural powers put in vigorous requisition, he will manifest a vigor and energy of intellect and feeling quite above mediocrity; be adequate to undertakings which demand originality of mind and force of character, yet, after all, be rather indolent: with activity *great, or very great,* will combine great *power* of mind with great activity; exercise a commanding influence over those minds with which he comes in contact; when he enjoys, will enjoy intensely, and when he suffers, suffer equally so; be susceptible of strong excitement, and, with the organs of the propelling powers, and of practical intellect, large or very large, will possess all the mental capabilities for conducting a large business; for rising to eminence, if not to preeminence; and discover great force of character and power of intellect and feeling: with activity *moderate,* when powerfully excited, will evince considerable energy of intellect and feeling, yet be too indolent and too sluggish to do much; lack clearness and force of idea, and intenseness of feeling; unless literally driven to it, will not be likely to be much or to do much, and yet actually *possess* more vigor of mind, and energy of feeling, than he will manifest; with activity small, or very small, will border upon idiocy.

Very Large.—One having a very large head, with activity *average* or *full,* on great occasions, or when his powers are thoroughly roused, will be truly great; but upon ordinary occasions, will seldom manifest any remarkable amount of mind or feeling, and perhaps pass through life with the credit of being a person of good natural abilities and judgment, yet nothing more; with *great* activity and strength, and large intellectual organs, will be a natural genius, endowed with very superior powers of mind and vigor of intellect; and, even though deprived of the advantages of education, his natural talents will surmount all obstacles, and make him truly talented; with activity *very great,* and the organs of practical intellect and of the propelling powers large, or very large, will possess the first order of natural abilities; manifest a clearness and force of intellect which will astonish the world, and a power of feeling which will carry all before him; and, with proper cultivation, enable him to become a bright star in the firmament of intellectual greatness, upon which coming ages may gaze with delight and astonishment. His mental enjoyment will be most exquisite, and his sufferings equally keen.

Full.—One having a full-sized brain, with activity *great, or very great,* and the organs of practical intellect and of the propelling powers large, or very large, although will not possess *greatness* of intellect, nor a deep, strong mind, will be very clever; have considerable talent, and that so distributed that it will show to be *more* than it really is; is capable of being a good scholar, doing a fine business, and, with advantages and application, of distinguishing himself somewhat; yet he is inadequate to a great undertaking; cannot sway an extensive influence, nor be really great; with activity *full, or average,* will do only tolerably well, and manifest only a common share of talent; with activity *moderate, or small,* will neither be nor do much worthy of notice.

Average, with activity great, manifests a quick, clear, sprightly mind and off-hand talents; and is capable of doing a fair business, especially if the stamina is good; with activity *very great,* and the organs of the propelling powers and of practical intellect large, or very large, is capable of doing a good business, and may pass for a man of fair talent, yet will not be original or profound; will be quick of perception; have a good practical understanding; will do well *in his sphere,* yet never manifest greatness, and out of his sphere, be common-place; with activity only *average,* will discover only an ordinary amount of intellect; be inadequate to any important undertaking; yet, in a small sphere, or one that requires only a mechanical routine of business, may do well; with *moderate or small* activity, will hardly have common sense.

Moderate.—One with a head of only moderate size, combined with *great* or *very great activity,* and the organs of the propelling powers and of practical intellect large, will possess a tolerable share of intellect, yet be more showy than sound; with others to plan for and direct him, will execute to advantage, yet be unable to do much alone; will have a very active mind, and be quick of perception, yet, after all, have a contracted intellect; possess only a small mental calibre, and lack momentum, both of mind and character; with activity only *average, or fair,* will have but a moderate *amount* of intellect, and even this scanty allowance will be too sluggish for action, so that he will neither suffer nor enjoy much; with activity *moderate or small,* will be idiotic.

SMALL OR VERY SMALL.—One with a small or very small head, no matter what may be the activity of his mind, will be incapable of much intellectual effort; of comprehending even easy subjects; or of experiencing much pain or pleasure; in short, will be mentally imbecile.

47.—SIZE OF BRAIN AS AFFECTING MENTALITY

Most great men have great heads. Webster's head measures over 24 inches, and Clay's[23] considerably above 23; and this is about Van Buren's[24] size; Chief Justice Gibson's, the greatest jurist in Pennsylvania, $24^{1}/_{4}$; Napoleon's[25] reached nearly or quite to 24, his hat passing easily over the head of one of his officers, which measured $23^{1}/_{2}$; and Hamilton's[26] hat passed over the head of a man whose head measured $23^{1}/_{2}$. Burke's[27] head was immense, so was Jefferson's,[28] while Franklin's hat passed over the ears of a 24-inch head. Small and average sized heads often astonish us by their brilliancy and learning, and, perhaps, eloquence, yet they fail in that commanding greatness which impresses and sways mind. The phrenological law is, that size, other things being equal, is a measure of power; yet these other conditions, such as activity, power of motive, wealth, physiological habits etc., increase or diminish the mentality, even more than size.

---

[23]Henry Clay (1777–1852) was an American senator of such diplomatic and political skill that he came to be known as "The Great Compromiser."

[24]Martin Van Buren (1782–1862) was the eighth president of the United States.

[25]Napoléon Bonaparte (1769–1821) became ruler of France soon after the French Revolution. He is considered one of the greatest military strategists of the nineteenth century.

[26]Alexander Hamilton (1755?–1804) was one of the premier political theorists of the early United States. He championed a strong central government.

[27]Edmund Burke (1729–1797) was an important eighteenth-century British politician and political philosopher.

[28]Thomas Jefferson (1743–1826) wrote the Declaration of Independence and was the third president of the United States.

10

Donald Grant Mitchell
(1822–1908)

WHILE WOMEN WERE writing what later scholars would term "sentimental fiction" (fiction that encouraged virtue through empathy) by the bucketful throughout the nineteenth century, certain male writers were also writing fiction focused on touching and changing the heart. No male writer had greater success in this vein than Donald Grant Mitchell, who often wrote under the pen name Ik Marvel.

In 1850, Mitchell published *Reveries of a Bachelor,* a tale with the telling subtitle *A Book of the Heart.* Based on a short sketch that originally appeared in the *Southern Literary Messenger, Reveries of a Bachelor* would sell more than a million copies by the end of century. Both men and women readers flocked to the book and its musings on the complicated and conflicted nature of bachelorhood.

Mitchell himself had just crossed the threshold into marital bliss in 1850, almost certainly providing him insights as he wrote his extended rumination on American men and marriage. *Reveries of a Bachelor* presents different angles on the struggle over the choice to marry: either a man will subject himself to the domesticating and wholesome influences of a wife, or he will not.

This simplicity of options, however, belies the complexity of intriguing subtexts found throughout the work. Mitchell's *Reveries* is full of dangers. While the married state poses its own threats to independence and individuality, the harmful influences outside marriage are just as real and imminent. The dangers have both personal and national implications. The bachelor risks far more than simply living a life of regret if he does not marry. To refuse to marry is to hobble the family, the foundational social unit of American life, as well as to open oneself up to the darker sides of sexuality, including everything from masturbation to consorting with prostitutes. Marriage becomes the normative state that will ensure both the health of the bachelor and the health of the nation as sexual drive is harnessed for the positive procreation of a still young nation.

REVERIES OF A BACHELOR

Or, A Book of the Heart

BY IK MARVEL

It is worth the labor—saith Plotinus—to consider well of Love,
whether it be of a God, or a divell, or passion of the minde, or partly
God, partly divell, partly passion.

BURTON'S ANATOMY

❧ Preface

This book is neither more, nor less than it pretends to be; it is a collection of those floating Reveries which have, from time to time, drifted across my brain. I never yet met with
a bachelor who had not his share of just such floating visions; and the only difference
between us lies in the fact, that I have tossed them from me in the shape of a Book.

If they had been worked over with more unity of design, I dare say I might have
made a respectable novel; as it is, I have chosen the honester way of setting them down
as they came seething from my thought, with all their crudities and contrasts, uncovered.

As for the truth that is in them, the world may believe what it likes; for having written to humor the world, it would be hard, if I should curtail any of its privileges of judgment. I should think there was as much truth in them, as in most Reveries.

The first story of the book has already had some publicity; and the criticisms upon it
have amused, and pleased me. One honest journalist avows that it could never have been
written by a bachelor. I thank him for thinking so well of me; and heartily wish that his
thought were as true, as it is kind.

Yet I am inclined to think that bachelors are the only safe, and secure observers of
all the phases of married life. The rest of the world have their hobbies; and by law, as
well as by immemorial custom are reckoned unfair witnesses in everything relating to
their matrimonial affairs.

Perhaps I ought however to make an exception in favor of spinsters, who like us, are
independent spectators, and possess just that kind of indifference to the marital state,
which makes them intrepid in their observations, and very desirable for—authorities.

As for the style of the book, I have nothing to say for it, except to refer to my title.
These are not sermons, nor essays, nor criticisms;—they are only Reveries. And if the
reader should stumble upon occasional magniloquence, or be worried with a little too
much of sentiment, pray, let him remember,—that I am dreaming.

Donald Grant Mitchell, *Reveries of a Bachelor: or, A Book of the Heart.* Ninth Edition. New York: Baker
& Scribner, 1851.

Engraved title page from Donald Grant Mitchell's *Reveries of a Bachelor,* ninth edition (New York: Baker & Scribner, 1851).

But while I say this, in the hope of nicking off the wiry edge of my reader's judg-ment, I shall yet stand up boldly for the general tone, and character of the book. If there is bad feeling in it, or insincerity, or shallow sentiment, or any foolish depth of affection betrayed,—I am responsible; and the critics may expose it to their hearts' content.

I have moreover a kindly feeling for these Reveries, from their very private character; they consist mainly of just such whimseys, and reflections, as a great many brother bach-elors are apt to indulge in, but which they are too cautious, or too prudent to lay before the world. As I have in this matter, shown a frankness, and *naiveté* which are unusual, I shall ask a corresponding frankness in my reader; and I can assure him safely that this is eminently one of those books which were 'never intended for publication.'

In the hope that this plain avowal may quicken the reader's charity, and screen me from cruel judgment,

I remain, with sincere good wishes,
Ik Marvel
New York, Nov., 1850.

◁◦ Over a Wood Fire

I have got a quiet farmhouse in the country, a very humble place to be sure, tenanted by a worthy enough man, of the old New-England stamp, where I sometimes go for a day or two in the winter, to look over the farm-accounts, and to see how the stock is thriving on the winter's keep.

One side the door, as you enter from the porch, is a little parlor, scarce twelve feet by ten, with a cosy looking fire-place—a heavy oak floor—a couple of arm chairs and a brown table with carved lions' feet. Out of this room opens a little cabinet, only big enough for a broad bachelor bedstead, where I sleep upon feathers, and wake in the morning, with my eye upon a saucy colored, lithographic print[1] of some fancy "Bessy."

It happens to be the only house in the world, of which I am *bona-fide*[2] owner; and I take a vast deal of comfort in treating it just as I choose. I manage to break some article of furniture, almost every time I pay it a visit; and if I cannot open the window readily of a morning, to breathe the fresh air, I knock out a pane or two of glass with my boot. I lean against the walls in a very old arm-chair there is on the premises, and scarce ever fail to worry such a hole in the plastering, as would set me down for a round charge for dam-ages in town, or make a prim housewife fret herself into a raging fever. I laugh out loud with myself, in my big arm-chair, when I think that I am neither afraid of one, nor the other.

As for the fire, I keep the little hearth so hot, as to warm half the cellar below, and

---

[1]Popular means of printing in the period capable of making fine, often colored illustrations in both book and poster formats.

[2]genuine

the whole space between the jams, roars for hours together, with white flame. To be sure, the windows are not very tight, between broken panes, and bad joints, so that the fire, large as it is, is by no means an extravagant comfort.

As night approaches, I have a huge pile of oak and hickory placed beside the hearth; I put out the tallow candle on the mantel, (using the family snuffers, with one leg broke,)—then, drawing my chair directly in front of the blazing wood, and setting one foot on each of the old iron fire-dogs, (until they grow too warm,) I dispose myself for an evening of such sober, and thoughtful quietude, as I believe, on my soul, that very few of my fellow-men have the good fortune to enjoy.

My tenant meantime, in the other room, I can hear now and then,—though there is a thick stone chimney, and broad entry between,—multiplying contrivances with his wife, to put two babies to sleep. This occupies them, I should say, usually an hour; though my only measure of time, (for I never carry a watch into the country,) is the blaze of my fire. By ten, or thereabouts, my stock of wood is nearly exhausted; I pile upon the hot coals what remains, and sit watching how it kindles, and blazes, and goes out,—even like our joys!—and then, slip by the light of the embers into my bed, where I luxuriate in such sound, and healthful slumber, as only such rattling window frames, and country air, can supply.

But to return: the other evening—it happened to be on my last visit to my farm-house—when I had exhausted all the ordinary rural topics of thought, had formed all sorts of conjectures as to the income of the year; had planned a new wall around one lot, and the clearing up of another, now covered with patriarchal wood; and wondered if the little rickety house would not be after all a snug enough box, to live and to die in—I fell on a sudden into such an unprecedented line of thought, which took such deep hold of my sympathies—sometimes even starting tears—that I determined, the next day, to set as much of it as I could recal, on paper.

Something—it may have been the home-looking blaze, (I am a bachelor of—say six and twenty,) or possibly a plaintive cry of the baby in my tenant's room, had suggested to me the thought of—Marriage.

I piled upon the heated fire-dogs, the last arm-full of my wood; and now, said I, bracing myself courageously between the arms of my chair,—I'll not flinch;—I'll pursue the thought wherever it leads, though it lead me to the d—(I am apt to be hasty,)—at least—continued I, softening,—until my fire is out.

The wood was green, and at first showed no disposition to blaze. It smoked furiously. Smoke, thought I, always goes before blaze; and so does doubt go before decision: and my Reverie, from that very starting point, slipped into this shape:—

I

❧ Smoke—Signifying Doubt

A wife?—thought I;—yes, a wife!
And why?

And pray, my dear sir, why not—why? Why not doubt; why not hesitate; why not tremble?

Does a man buy a ticket in a lottery—a poor man, whose whole earnings go in to secure the ticket,—without trembling, hesitating, and doubting?

Can a man stake his bachelor respectability, his independence, and comfort, upon the die of absorbing, unchanging, relentless marriage, without trembling at the venture?

Shall a man who has been free to chase his fancies over the wide-world, without lett[3] or hindrance, shut himself up to marriage-ship, within four walls called Home, that are to claim him, his time, his trouble, and his tears, thenceforward forever more, without doubts thick, and thick-coming as Smoke?

Shall he who has been hitherto a mere observer of other men's cares, and business—moving off where they made him sick of heart, approaching whenever and wherever they made him gleeful—shall he now undertake administration of just such cares and business, without qualms? Shall he, whose whole life has been but a nimble succession of escapes from trifling difficulties, now broach without doubtings—that Matrimony, where if difficulty beset him, there is no escape? Shall this brain of mine, careless-working, never tired with idleness, feeding on long vagaries, and high, gigantic castles, dreaming out beatitudes hour by hour—turn itself at length to such dull task-work, as thinking out a livelihood for wife and children?

Where thenceforward will be those sunny dreams, in which I have warmed my fancies, and my heart, and lighted my eye with crystal? This very marriage, which a brilliant working imagination has invested time and again with brightness, and delight, can serve no longer as a mine for teeming fancy: all, alas, will be gone—reduced to the dull standard of the actual! No more room for intrepid forays of imagination—no more gorgeous realm-making—all will be over!

Why not, I thought, go on dreaming?

Can any wife be prettier than an after dinner fancy, idle and yet vivid, can paint for you? Can any children make less noise, than the little rosy-cheeked ones, who have no existence, except in the *omnium gatherum*[4] of your own brain? Can any housewife be more unexceptionable, than she who goes sweeping daintily the cobwebs that gather in your dreams? Can any domestic larder be better stocked, than the private larder of your head dozing on a cushioned chair-back at Delmonico's? Can any family purse be better filled than the exceeding plump one, you dream of, after reading such pleasant books as Munchausen, or Typee?

But if, after all, it must be—duty, or what-not, making provocation—what then? And I clapped my feet hard against the fire-dogs, and leaned back, and turned my face to the ceiling, as much as to say;—And where on earth, then, shall a poor devil look for a wife?

Somebody says, Lyttleton[5] or Shaftesbury[6] I think, that "marriages would be happier if they were all arranged by the Lord Chancellor." Unfortunately, we have no Lord Chancellor to make this commutation of our misery.

---

[3]obstruction

[4]A gathering of all sorts.

[5]Thomas Littleton (1422–1481) wrote the first important English legal text.

[6]Anthony Ashley Cooper Shaftesbury (1671–1713) was a famous English politician and philosopher, who wrote extensively on the moral nature of humanity.

Shall a man then scour the country on a mule's back, like Honest Gil Blas[7] of San-tillane; or shall he make application to some such intervening providence as Madame St. Marc, who, as I see by the Presso, manages these matters to one's hand, for some five per cent. on the fortunes of the parties?

I have trouted, when the brook was so low, and the sky so hot, that I might as well have thrown my fly upon the turnpike; and I have hunted hare at noon, and wood-cock in snow-time,—never despairing, scarce doubting; but for a poor hunter of his kind, with-out traps or snares, or any aid of police or constabulary, to traverse the world, where are swarming, on a moderate computation, some three hundred and odd millions of unmar-ried women, for a single capture—irremediable, unchangeable—and yet a capture which by strange metonymy, not laid down in the books, is very apt to turn captor into captive, and make game of hunter—all this, surely, surely may make a man shrug with doubt!

Then—again,—there are the plaguey wife's-relations. Who knows how many third, fourth, or fifth cousins, will appear at careless complimentary intervals, long after you had settled into the placid belief that all congratulatory visits were at an end? How many twisted headed brothers will be putting in their advice, as a friend to Peggy?

How many maiden aunts will come to spend a month or two with their "dear Peggy," and want to know every tea-time, "if she isn't a dear love of a wife?" Then, dear father-in-law, will beg, (taking dear Peggy's hand in his,) to give a little wholesome counsel; and will be very sure to advise just the contrary of what you had determined to undertake. And dear mamma-in-law, must set her nose into Peggy's cupboard, and insist upon having the key to your own private locker in the wainscot.

Then, perhaps, there is a little bevy of dirty-nosed nephews who come to spend the holydays, and eat up your East India sweetmeats; and who are forever tramping over your head, or raising the Old Harry below, while you are busy with your clients. Last, and worst, is some fidgety old uncle, forever too cold or too hot, who vexes you with his patronizing airs, and impudently kisses his little Peggy!

——That could be borne, however: for perhaps he has promised his fortune to Peggy. Peggy, then, will be rich:—(and the thought made me rub my shins, which were now getting comfortably warm upon the fire-dogs.) Then, she will be forever talking of *her* fortune; and pleasantly reminding you on occasion of a favorite purchase,—how lucky that *she* had the means; and dropping hints about economy; and buying very extravagant Paisleys.[8]

She will annoy you by looking over the stock-list at breakfast time; and mention quite carelessly to your clients, that she is interested in *such* or such a speculation.

She will be provokingly silent when you hint to a tradesman, that you have not the money by you, for his small bill;—in short, she will tear the life out of you, making you pay in righteous retribution of annoyance, grief, vexation, shame, and sickness of heart, for the superlative folly of "marrying rich."

——But if not rich, then poor. Bah! the thought made me stir the coals; but there

---

[7]The roving, adventuresome young hero of a novel by the same name written by the French author Alain-René Lesage (1668–1747).

[8]Shawls with curving designs.

was still no blaze. The paltry earnings you are able to wring out of clients by the sweat of your brow, will now be all *our* income; you will be pestered for pin-money, and pestered with your poor wife's-relations. Ten to one, she will stickle about taste—"Sir Visto's"—and want to make this so pretty, and that so charming, if she *only* had the means; and is sure Paul (a kiss) can't deny his little Peggy such a trifling sum, and all for the common benefit.

Then she, for one, means that *her* children shan't go a begging for clothes,—and another pull at the purse. Trust a poor mother to dress her children in finery!

Perhaps she is ugly;—not noticeable at first; but growing on her, and (what is worse) growing faster on you. You wonder why you did'nt see that vulgar nose long ago: and that lip—it is very strange, you think, that you ever thought it pretty. And then,—to come to breakfast, with her hair looking as it does, and you, not so much as daring to say—"Peggy, *do* brush your hair!" Her foot too—not very bad when decently *chaussée*[9]—but now since she's married, she does wear such infernal slippers! And yet for all this, to be prigging up for an hour, when any of my old chums come to dine with me!

"Bless your kind hearts! my dear fellows," said I, thrusting the tongs into the coals, and speaking out loud, as if my voice could reach from Virginia to Paris—"not married yet!"

Perhaps Peggy is pretty enough—only shrewish.

——No matter for cold coffee;—you should have been up before.

What sad, thin, poorly cooked chops, to eat with your rolls!

——She thinks they are very good, and wonders how you can set such an example to your children.

The butter is nauseating.

——She has no other, and hopes you'll not raise a storm about butter a little turned.—I think I see myself—ruminated I—sitting meekly at table, scarce daring to lift up my eyes, utterly fagged out with some quarrel of yesterday, choking down detestably sour muffins, that my wife thinks are "delicious"—slipping in dried mouthfuls of burnt ham off the side of my fork tines,—slipping off my chair side-ways at the end, and slipping out with my hat between my knees, to business, and never feeling myself a competent, sound-minded man, till the oak door is between me and Peggy!

—"Ha, ha,—not yet!" said I; and in so earnest a tone, that my dog started to his feet—cocked his eye to have a good look into my face—met my smile of triumph with an amiable wag of the tail, and curled up again in the corner.

Again, Peggy is rich enough, well enough, mild enough, only she doesn't care a fig for you. She has married you because father, or grandfather thought the match eligible, and because she didn't wish to disoblige them. Besides, she didn't positively hate you, and thought you were a respectable enough person;—she has told you so repeatedly at dinner. She wonders you like to read poetry; she wishes you would buy her a good cook-book; and insists upon your making your will at the birth of the first baby.

She thinks Captain So-and-So a splendid looking fellow, and wishes you would trim up a little, were it only for appearance' sake.

---

[9]adorned

You need not hurry up from the office so early at night:—she, bless her dear heart!—does not feel lonely. You read to her a love tale; she interrupts the pathetic parts with directions to her seamstress. You read of marriages: she sighs, and asks if Captain So and So has left town? She hates to be mewed up in a cottage, or between brick walls; she does *so* love the Springs!

But, again, Peggy loves you;—at least she swears it, with her hand on the Sorrows of Werter.[10] She has pin-money which she spends for the Literary World, and the Friends in Council. She is not bad looking, save a bit too much of forehead; nor is she sluttish, unless a *negligé* till three o'clock, and an ink stain on the fore finger be sluttish;—but then she is such a sad blue!

You never fancied when you saw her buried in a three volume novel, that it was anything more than a girlish vagary; and when she quoted Latin, you thought innocently, that she had a capital memory for her samplers.

But to be bored eternally about Divine Danté[11] and funny Goldoni,[12] is too bad. Your copy of Tasso,[13] a treasure print of 1680, is all bethumbed and dogs-eared, and spotted with baby gruel. Even your Seneca[14]—an Elzevir[15]—is all sweaty with handling. She adores La Fontaine,[16] reads Balzac[17] with a kind of artist-scowl, and will not let Greek alone.

You hint at broken rest and an aching head at breakfast, and she will fling you a scrap of Anthology—in lieu of the camphor bottle—or chant the αἰαῖ, αἰαῖ, of tragic chorus.[18]

——The nurse is getting dinner; you are holding the baby; Peggy is reading Bruyère.[19]

The fire smoked thick as pitch, and puffed out little clouds over the chimney piece. I gave the fore-stick a kick, at thought of Peggy, baby, and Bruyère.

——Suddenly the flame flickered bluely athwart the smoke—caught at a twig below—rolled round the mossy oak-stick—twined among the crackling tree-limbs—mounted—lit up the whole body of smoke, and blazed out cheerily and bright. Doubt vanished with Smoke, and Hope began with Flame.

---

[10]*The Sorrows of Young Werter* is a novel of unrequited love by Johann von Goethe (1792–1854).

[11]Dante Alighieri (1265–1321) was a renowned Italian poet, writer, and moral philosopher. His most famous work is the *Divine Comedy.*

[12]Carlo Goldoni (1707–1793) was an Italian dramatist famous for his comedies.

[13]Torquato Tasso (1544–1595) was an Italian poet most famous for his epic poem *Jerusalem Liberated,* which dealt with the Christian capture of Jerusalem during the First Crusade.

[14]Lucius Annaeus Seneca (4 B.C.–A.D. 65) was a leading Roman philosopher and statesman.

[15]Famous Dutch publishing family (1587–1681) best known for its editions of Greek and Roman classics.

[16]Jean de La Fountaine (1621–1695) was a master French poet.

[17]Honoré de Balzac (1799–1850) was a French writer considered by many to be one of the greatest writers of all time.

[18]Common phrase of lament in Greek tragedies.

[19]Jean de La Bruyère (1645–1696) was a French writer of satires.

II

❧ Blaze—Signifying Cheer

I pushed my chair back; drew up another stretched out my feet cosily upon it, rested my elbows on the chair arms, leaned my head on one hand and looked straight into the leaping, and dancing flame.

——Love is a flame—ruminated I; and (glancing round the room) how a flame brightens up a man's habitation.

"Carlo," said I, calling up my dog into the light, "good fellow, Carlo!" and I patted him kindly, and he wagged his tail, and laid his nose across my knee, and looked wistfully up in my face; then strode away,—turned to look again, and lay down to sleep.

"Pho, the brute!" said I, "it is not enough after all, to like a dog."

——If now in that chair yonder, not the one your feet lie upon, but the other, beside you—closer yet—were seated a sweet-faced girl, with a pretty little foot lying out upon the hearth—a bit of lace running round the swelling throat—the hair parted to a charm over a forehead fair as any of your dreams;—and if you could reach an arm around that chair back, without fear of giving offence, and suffer your fingers to play idly with those curls that escape down the neck; and if you could clasp with your other hand those little white, taper fingers of hers, which lie so temptingly within reach,—and so, talk softly and low in presence of the blaze, while the hours slip without knowledge, and the winter winds whistle uncared for;—if, in short, you were no bachelor, but the husband of some such sweet image—(dream, call it rather,) would it not be far pleasanter than this cold single night-sitting—counting the sticks—reckoning the length of the blaze, and the height of the falling snow?

And if, some or all of those wild vagaries that grow on your fancy at such an hour, you could whisper into listening, because loving ears—ears not tired with listening, because it is you who whisper—ears ever indulgent because eager to praise;—and if your darkest fancies were lit up, not merely with bright wood fire, but with a ringing laugh of that sweet face turned up in fond rebuke—how far better, than to be waxing black, and sour, over pestilential humors—alone—your very dog asleep!

And if when a glowing thought comes into your brain, quick and sudden, you could tell it over as to a second self, to that sweet creature, who is not away, because she loves to be there; and if you could watch the thought catching that girlish mind, illuming that fair brow, sparkling in those pleasantest of eyes—how far better than to feel it slumbering, and going out, heavy, lifeless, and dead, in your own selfish fancy. And if a generous emotion steals over you—coming, you know not whither, would there not be a richer charm in lavishing it in caress, or endearing word, upon that fondest, and most dear one, than in patting your glossy coated dog, or sinking lonely to smiling slumbers?

How would not benevolence ripen with such monitor to task it! How would not selfishness grow faint and dull, leaning ever to that second self, which is the loved one! How would not guile shiver, and grow weak, before that girl-brow, and eye of innocence. How would not all that boyhood prized of enthusiasm, and quick blood, and life, renew itself in such presence!

The fire was getting hotter, and I moved into the middle of the room. The shadows the flames made, were playing like fairy forms over floor, and wall, and ceiling.

My fancy would surely quicken, thought I, if such being were in attendance. Surely, imagination would be stronger, and purer, if it could have the playful fancies of dawning womanhood to delight it. All toil would be torn from mind-labor, if but another heart grew into this present soul, quickening it, warming it, cheering it, bidding it ever,—God speed!

Her face would make a halo, rich as a rainbow, atop of all such noisome things, as we lonely souls call trouble. Her smile would illumine the blackest of crowding cares; and darkness that now seats you despondent, in your solitary chair for days together, weaving bitter fancies, dreaming bitter dreams, would grow light and thin, and spread, and float away,—chased by that beloved smile.

Your friend—poor fellow!—dies:—never mind, that gentle clasp of *her* fingers, as she steals behind you, telling you not to weep—it is worth ten friends!

Your sister, sweet one, is dead—buried. The worms are busy with all her fairness. How it makes you think earth nothing but a spot to dig graves upon!

——It is more: *she,* she says, will be a sister; and the waving curls as she leans upon your shoulder, touch your cheek, and your wet eye turns to meet those other eyes—— God has sent his angel, surely!

Your mother, alas for it, she is gone! Is there any bitterness to a youth, alone and homeless, like this?

But you are not homeless; you are not alone: *she* is there;—her tears softening yours, her smile lighting yours, her grief killing yours; and you live again, to assuage that kind sorrow of hers.

Then—those children, rosy, fair-haired; no, they do not disturb you with their prattle now—they are yours! Toss away there on the green-sward—never mind the hyacinths, the snowdrops, the violets, if so be any are there; the perfume of their healthful lips is worth all the flowers of the world. No need now to gather wild bouquets to love, and cherish: flower, tree, gun, are all dead things; things livelier hold your soul.

And she, the mother, sweetest and fairest of all, watching, tending, caressing, loving, till your own heart grows pained with tenderest jealousy, and cures itself with loving.

You have no need now of any cold lecture to teach thankfulness: your heart is full of it. No need now, as once, of bursting blossoms, of trees taking leaf, and greenness, to turn thought kindly, and thankfully; for ever, beside you, there is bloom, and ever beside you there is fruit,—for which eye, heart, and soul are full of unknown, and unspoken, because unspeakable, thank-offering.

And if sickness catches you, binds you, lays you down—no lonely moanings, and wicked curses at careless stepping nurses. *The* step is noiseless, and yet distinct beside you. The white curtains are drawn, or withdrawn by the magic of that other presence; and the soft, cool hand is upon your brow.

No cold comfortings of friend-watchers, merely come in to steal a word away from that outer world which is pulling at their skirts; but, ever, the sad, shaded brow of her, whose lightest sorrow for your sake is your greatest grief,—if it were not a greater joy.

The blaze was leaping light and high, and the wood falling under the growing heat.

——So, continued I, this heart would be at length itself;—striving with every thing gross, even now as it clings to grossness. Love would make its strength native and progressive. Earth's cares would fly. Joys would double. Susceptibilities be quickened; Love master self; and having made the mastery, stretch onward, and upward toward Infinitude.

And, if the end came, and sickness brought that follower—Great Follower—which sooner or later is sure to come after, then the heart, and the hand of Love, ever near, are giving to your tired soul, daily and hourly, lessons of that love which consoles, which triumphs, which circleth all, and centereth in all—Love Infinite, and Divine!

Kind hands—none but *hers*—will smooth the hair upon your brow as the chill grows damp, and heavy on it; and her fingers—none but hers—will lie in yours as the wasted flesh stiffens, and hardens for the ground. *Her* tears,—you could feel no others, if oceans fell—will warm your drooping features once more to life; once more your eye lighted in joyous triumph, kindle in her smile, and then——

The fire fell upon the hearth; the blaze gave a last leap—a flicker—then another—caught a little remaining twig—blazed up—wavered—went out.

There was nothing but a bed of glowing embers, over which the white ashes gathered fast. I was alone, with only my dog for company.

III

❧ Ashes—Signifying Desolation

After all, thought I, ashes follow blaze, inevitably as Death follows Life. Misery treads on the heels of Joy; Anguish rides swift after Pleasure.

"Come to me again, Carlo," said I, to my dog; and I patted him fondly once more, but now only by the light of the dying embers.

It is very little pleasure one takes in fondling brute favorites; but it is a pleasure that when it passes, leaves no void. It is only a little alleviating redundance in your solitary heart-life, which if lost, another can be supplied.

But if your heart, not solitary—not quieting its humors with mere love of chase, or dog—not repressing year after year, its earnest yearnings after something better, and more spiritual,—has fairly linked itself by bonds strong as life, to another heart—is the casting off easy, then?

Is it then only a little heart-redundancy cut off, which the next bright sunset will fill up?

And my fancy, as it had painted doubt under the smoke, and cheer under warmth of the blaze, so now it began under the faint light of the smouldering embers, to picture heart-desolation.

——What kind congratulatory letters, hosts of them, coming from old and half-forgotten friends, now that your happiness is a year, or two years old!

"Beautiful."

——Aye, to be sure beautiful!

"Rich."

——Pho, the dawdler! how little he knows of heart-treasure, who speaks of wealth to a man who loves his wife, as a wife should only be loved!

"Young."

——Young indeed; guileless as infancy; charming as the morning.

Ah, these letters bear a sting: they bring to mind, with new, and newer freshness, if it be possible, the value of that, which you tremble lest you lose.

How anxiously you watch that step—if it lose not its buoyancy; How you study the colour on that cheek, if it grow not fainter; How you tremble at the lustre in those eyes, if it be not the lustre of Death; How you totter under the weight of that muslin sleeve—a phantom weight! How you fear to do it, and yet press forward, to note if that breathing be quickened, as you ascend the home-heights, to look off on sunset lighting the plain.

Is your sleep, quiet sleep, after that she has whispered to you her fears, and in the same breath—soft as a sigh, sharp as an arrow—bid you bear it bravely?

Perhaps,—the embers were now glowing fresher, a little kindling, before the ashes—she triumphs over disease.

But, Poverty, the world's almoner, has come to you with ready, spare hand.

Alone, with your dog living on bones, and you, on hope—kindling each morning, dying slowly each night,—this could be borne. Philosophy would bring home its stores to the lone-man. Money is not in his hand, but Knowledge is in his brain! and from that brain he draws out faster, as he draws slower from his pocket. He remembers: and on remembrance he can live for days, and weeks. The garret, if a garret covers him, is rich in fancies. The rain if it pelts, pelts only him used to rain-peltings. And his dog crouches not in dread, but in companionship. His crust he divides with him, and laughs. He crowns himself with glorious memories of Cervantes,[20] though he begs: if he nights it under the stars, he dreams heaven-sent dreams of the prisoned, and homeless Gallileo.[21]

He hums old sonnets, and snatches of poor Jonson's[22] plays. He chants Dryden's[23] odes, and dwells on Otway's rhyme. He reasons with Bolingbroke[24] or Diogenes,[25] as the humor takes him; and laughs at the world: for the world, thank Heaven, has left him alone!

Keep your money, old misers, and your palaces, old princes,—the world is mine!

> I care not, Fortune, what you me deny,—
> You cannot rob me of free nature's grace,

---

[20]Miguel de Cervantes Saavedra (1547–1616) stands as one of Spain's most famous novelists, his crowning work being *Don Quixote.*

[21]Galileo (1564–1642) was an Italian astronomer imprisoned for his scientific challenges to religious orthodoxy.

[22]Ben Jonson (1572–1637) was a famous English dramatist and poet.

[23]John Dryden (1631–1700) was an English poet and playwright who enjoyed immense fame in his day.

[24]Henry St. John Bolingbroke (1678–1751), first viscount, was an English statesman and philosopher.

[25]Diogenes (412?–323 B.C.) was an ancient Greek figure famous for his advocacy of self-sufficiency and rejection of luxury.

    You cannot shut the windows of the sky;
    You cannot bar my constant feet to trace
      The woods and lawns, by living streams, at eve,
    Let health, my nerves and finer fibres brace,
      And I, their toys, to the great children, leave,
    Of Fancy, Reason, Virtue, naught can me bereave!

But—if not alone?

If *she* is clinging to you for support, for consolation, for home, for life—she, reared in luxury perhaps, is faint for bread?

Then, the iron enters the soul; then the nights darken under any sky light. Then the days grow long, even in the solstice of winter.

She may not complain; what then?

Will your heart grow strong, if the strength of her love can dam up the fountains of tears, and the tied tongue not tell of bereavement? Will it solace you to find her parting the poor treasure of food you have stolen for her, with begging, foodless children?

But this ill, strong hands, and Heaven's help, will put down. Wealth again; Flowers again; Patrimonial acres again; Brightness again. But your little Bessy, your favorite child is pining.

Would to God! you say in agony, that wealth could bring fulness again into that blanched cheek, or round those little thin lips once more; but it cannot. Thinner and thinner they grow; plaintive and more plaintive her sweet voice.

"Dear Bessy"—and your tones tremble; you feel that she is on the edge of the grave. Can you pluck her back? Can endearments stay her? Business is heavy, away from the loved child; home, you go, to fondle while yet time is left—but *this* time you are too late. She is gone. She cannot hear you: she cannot thank you for the violets you put within her stiff white hand.

And then—the grassy mound—the cold shadow of head-stone!

The wind, growing with the night, is rattling at the window panes, and whistles dismally. I wipe a tear, and in the interval of my Reverie, thank God, that I am no such mourner.

But gaiety, snail-footed, creeps back to the household. All is bright again;—

    ——the violet bed 's not sweeter
    Than the delicious breath marriage sends forth.

Her lip is rich and full; her cheek delicate as a flower. Her frailty doubles your love.

And the little one she clasps—frail too—too frail; the boy you had set your hopes and heart on. You have watched him growing, ever prettier, ever winning more and more upon your soul. The love you bore to him when he first lisped names—your name and hers—has doubled in strength now that he asks innocently to be taught of this, or that, and promises you by that quick curiosity that flashes in his eye, a mind full of intelligence.

And some hair-breadth escape by sea, or flood, that he perhaps may have had—which unstrung your soul to such tears, as you pray God may be spared you again—has endeared the little fellow to your heart, a thousand fold.

And, now with his pale sister in the grave, all *that* love has come away from the mound, where worms feast, and centers on the boy.

How you watch the storms lest they harm him! How often you steal to his bed late at night, and lay your hand lightly upon the brow, where the curls cluster thick, rising and falling with the throbbing temples, and watch, for minutes together, the little lips half parted, and listen—your ear close to them—if the breathing be regular and sweet!

But the day comes—the night rather—when you can catch no breathing.

Aye, put your hair away,—compose yourself—listen again.

No, there is nothing!

Put your hand now to his brow,—damp indeed—but not with healthful night-sleep; it is not your hand, no, do not deceive yourself—it is your loved boy's forehead that is so cold; and your loved boy will never speak to you again—never play again—he is dead!

Oh, the tears—the tears; what blessed things are tears! Never fear now to let them fall on his forehead, or his lip, lest you waken him!—Clasp him—clasp him harder—you cannot hurt, you cannot waken him! Lay him down, gently or not, it is the same; he is stiff; he is stark and cold.

But courage is elastic; it is our pride. It recovers itself easier, thought I, than these embers will get into blaze again.

But courage, and patience, and faith, and hope have their limit. Blessed be the man who escapes such trial as will determine limit!

To a lone man it comes not near; for how can trial take hold where there is nothing by which to try?

A funeral? You reason with philosophy. A grave yard? You read Hervey[26] and muse upon the wall. A friend dies? You sigh, you pat your dog,—it is over. Losses? You retrench—you light your pipe—it is forgotten. Calumny? You laugh—you sleep.

But with that childless wife clinging to you in love and sorrow—what then?

Can you take down Seneca now, and coolly blow the dust from the leaf-tops? Can you crimp your lip with Voltaire?[27] Can you smoke idly, your feet dangling with the ivies, your thoughts all waving fancies upon a church-yard wall—a wall that borders the grave of your boy?

Can you amuse yourself by turning stinging Martial[28] into rhyme? Can you pat your dog, and seeing him wakeful and kind, say, "it is enough?" Can you sneer at calumny, and sit by your fire dozing?

Blessed, thought I again, is the man who escapes such trial as will measure the limit of patience and the limit of courage!

But the trial comes:—colder and colder were growing the embers.

That wife, over whom your love broods, is fading. Not beauty fading;—that, now that your heart is wrapped in her being, would be nothing.

---

[26]James Hervey (1714–1758) was an Anglican clergyman in England who wrote the popular *Meditations among the Tombs* (1746).

[27]Voltaire (1694–1778) was a French satirist who wrote biting commentaries on a wide range of social and religious issues.

[28]Martial (A.D. 38?–103) was a Roman poet most famous for his Latin epigrams.

She sees with quick eye your dawning apprehension, and she tries hard to make that step of hers elastic.

Your trials and your loves together have centered your affections. They are not now as when you were a lone man, wide spread and superficial. They have caught from domestic attachments a finer tone and touch. They cannot shoot out tendrils into barren world-soil and suck up thence strengthening nutriment. They have grown under the forcing-glass of home-roof, they will not now bear exposure.

You do not now look men in the face as if a heart-bond was linking you—as if a community of feeling lay between. There is a heart-bond that absorbs all others; there is a community that monopolizes your feeling. When the heart lay wide open, before it had grown upon, and closed around particular objects, it could take strength and cheer, from a hundred connections that now seem colder than ice.

And now those particular objects—alas for you!—are failing.

What anxiety pursues you! How you struggle to fancy—there is no danger; how she struggles to persuade you—there is no danger!

How it grates now on your ear—the toil and turmoil of the city! It was music when you were alone; it was pleasant even, when from the din you were elaborating comforts for the cherished objects;—when you had such sweet escape as evening drew on.

Now it maddens you to see the world careless while you are steeped in care. They hustle you in the street; they smile at you across the table; they bow carelessly over the way; they do not know what canker is at your heart.

The undertaker comes with his bill for the dead boy's funeral. He knows your grief; he is respectful. You bless him in your soul. You wish the laughing street-goers were all undertakers.

Your eye follows the physician as he leaves your house: is he wise, you ask yourself; is he prudent? is he the best? Did he never fail—is he never forgetful?

And now the hand that touches yours, is it no thinner—no whiter than yesterday? Sunny days come when she revives; colour comes back; she breathes freer; she picks flowers; she meets you with a smile: hope lives again.

But the next day of storm she is fallen. She cannot talk even; she presses your hand.

You hurry away from business before your time. What matter for clients—who is to reap the rewards? What matter for fame—whose eye will it brighten? What matter for riches—whose is the inheritance?

You find her propped with pillows; she is looking over a little picture-book bethumbed by the dear boy she has lost. She hides it in her chair; she has pity on you.

——Another day of revival, when the spring sun shines, and flowers open out of doors; she leans on your arm, and strolls into the garden where the first birds are singing. Listen to them with her;—what memories are in bird-songs! You need not shudder at her tears—they are tears of Thanksgiving. Press the hand that lies light upon your arm, and you, too, thank God, while yet you may!

You are early home—mid-afternoon. Your step is not light; it is heavy, terrible.

They have sent for you.

She is lying down; her eyes half closed; her breathing long and interrupted.

She hears you; her eye opens; you put your hand in hers; yours trembles;—hers does not. Her lips move; it is your name.

"Be strong", she says, "God will help you."

She presses harder your hand:—"Adieu!"

A long breath—another;—you are alone again. No tears now; poor man! You cannot find them!

——Again home early. There is a smell of varnish in your house. A coffin is there; they have clothed the body in decent grave clothes, and the undertaker is screwing down the lid, slipping round on tip-toe. Does he fear to waken her?

He asks you a simple question about the inscription upon the plate, rubbing it with his coat cuff. You look him straight in the eye; you motion to the door; you dare not speak.

He takes up his hat and glides out stealthful as a cat.

The man has done his work well for all. It is a nice coffin—a very nice coffin! Pass your hand over it—how smooth!

Some sprigs of mignionette are lying carelessly in a little gilt-edged saucer. She loved mignionette.

It is a good staunch table the coffin rests on;—it is your table; you are a housekeeper—a man of family!

Aye, of family!—keep down outcry, or the nurse will be in. Look over at the pinched features; is this all that is left of her? And where is your heart now? No, don't thrust your nails into your hands, nor mangle your lip, nor grate your teeth together. If you could only weep!

——Another day. The coffin is gone out. The stupid mourners have wept—what idle tears! She, with your crushed heart, has gone out!

Will you have pleasant evenings at your home now.

Go into your parlor that your prim housekeeper has made comfortable with clean hearth and blaze of sticks.

Sit down in your chair; there is another velvet-cushioned one, over against yours—empty. You press your fingers on your eye-balls, as if you would press out something that hurt the brain; but you cannot. Your head leans upon your hand; your eyes rest upon the flashing blaze.

Ashes always come after blaze.

Go now into the room where she was sick—softly, lest the prim housekeeper come after.

They have put new dimity upon her chair; they have hung new curtains over the bed. They have removed from the stand its phials, and silver bell; they have put a little vase of flowers in their place; the perfume will not offend the sick sense now. They have half opened the window, that the room so long closed may have air. It will not be too cold.

She is not there.

——Oh, God!—thou who dost temper the wind to the shorn lamb—be kind!

The embers were dark; I stirred them; there was no sign of life. My dog was asleep. The clock in my tenant's chamber had struck one.

I dashed a tear or two from my eyes;—how they came there I know not. I half ejaculated a prayer of thanks, that such desolation had not yet come nigh me; and a prayer of hope—that it might never come.

In a half hour more, I was sleeping soundly. My reverie was ended.

SECOND REVERIE

Sea Coal and Anthracite[29]

❧ By a City Grate

Blessed be letters!—they are the monitors, they are also the comforters, and they are the only true heart-talkers! Your speech and their speeches, are conventional; they are moulded by circumstance; they are suggested by the observation, remark, and influence of the parties to whom the speaking is addressed, or by whom it may be overheard.

Your truest thought is modified half through its utterance by a look, a sign, a smile, or a sneer. It is not individual; it is not integral: it is social and mixed,—half of you, and half of others. It bends, it sways, it multiplies, it retires, and it advances, as the talk of others presses, relaxes, or quickens.

But it is not so of Letters:—there you are, with only the soulless pen, and the snow-white, virgin paper. Your soul is measuring itself by itself, and saying its own sayings: there are no sneers to modify its utterance,—no scowl to scare,—nothing is present, but you, and your thought.

Utter it then freely—write it down—stamp it—burn it in the ink!—There it is, a true soul-print!

Oh, the glory, the freedom, the passion of a letter! It is worth all the lip-talk in the world. Do you say, it is studied, made up, acted, rehearsed, contrived, artistic?

Let me see it then; let me run it over; tell me age, sex, circumstance, and I will tell you if it be studied or real;—if it be the merest lip-slang put into words, or heart-talk blazing on the paper.

I have a little pacquet, not very large, tied up with narrow crimson ribbon, now soiled with frequent handling, which far into some winter's night, I take down from its nook upon my shelf, and untie, and open, and run over, with such sorrow, and such joy,—such tears and such smiles, as I am sure make me for weeks after, a kinder, and holier man.

There are in this little pacquet, letters in the familiar hand of a mother——what gentle admonition;—what tender affection!—God have mercy on him who outlives the tears that such admonitions, and such affection call up to the eye! There are others in the budget, in the delicate, and unformed hand of a loved, and lost sister;—written when she, and you were full of glee, and the best mirth of youthfulness; does it harm you to recall that mirthfulness? or to trace again, for the hundredth time, that scrawling postscript at

---

[29]A hard coal that burns cleanly.

the bottom, with its *i*'s so carefully dotted, and its gigantic *t*'s so carefully crossed, by the childish hand of a little brother?

I have added latterly to that pacquet of letters; I almost need a new and longer ribbon; the old one is getting too short. Not a few of these new, and cherished letters, a former Reverie* has brought to me; not letters of cold praise, saying it was well done, artfully executed, prettily imagined—no such thing: but letters of sympathy—of sympathy which means sympathy—the παθήμι and the συν.[30]

It would be cold, and dastardly work to copy them; I am too selfish for that. It is enough to say that they, the kind writers, have seen a heart in the Reverie—have felt that it was real, true. They know it; a secret influence has told it. What matters it pray, if literally, there was no wife, and no dead child, and no coffin in the house? Is not feeling, feeling; and heart, heart? Are not these fancies thronging on my brain, bringing tears to my eyes, bringing joy to my soul, as living, as anything human can be living? What if they have no material type—no objective form? All that is crude,—a mere reduction of ideality to sense,—a transformation of the spiritual to the earthy,—a levelling of soul to matter.

Are we not creatures of thought and passion? Is any thing about us more earnest than that same thought and passion? Is there any thing more real,—more characteristic of that great and dim destiny to which we are born, and which may be written down in that terrible word—Forever?

Let those who will then, sneer at what in their wisdom they call untruth—at what is false, because it has no material presence: this does not create falsity; would to Heaven that it did!

And yet, if there was actual, material truth superadded to Reverie, would such objectors sympathize the more? No!—a thousand times, no; the heart that has no sympathy with thoughts and feelings that scorch the soul, is dead also—whatever its mocking tears, and gestures may say—to a coffin, or a grave!

Let them pass, and we will come back to those cherished letters.

A mother, who has lost a child, has, she says, shed a tear—not one, but many—over the dead boy's coldness. And another, who has not lost, but who trembles lest she lose, has found the words failing as she read, and a dim, sorrow-borne mist, spreading over the page.

Another, yet rejoicing in all those family ties, that make life a charm, has listened nervously to careful reading, until the husband is called home, and the coffin is in the house.—"Stop!"—she says; and a gush of tears tells the rest.

Yet the cold critic will say—"it was artfully done." A curse on him!—it was not art: it was nature.

Another, a young, fresh, healthful girl-mind, has seen something in the love-picture—albeit so weak—of truth; and has kindly believed that it must be earnest. Aye, indeed is it, fair, and generous one,—earnest as life and hope! Who indeed with a heart at all, that has not yet slipped away irreparably, and forever from the shores of youth—

---

*The first Reverie—Smoke, Flame, and Ashes, was published some months previous to this, in the Southern Literary Messenger.

[30]The "suffering" and the "with."

from that fairy land which young enthusiasm creates, and over which bright dreams hover—but knows it to be real? And so such things will be real, till hopes are dashed, and Death is come.

Another a father, has laid down the book in tears

—God bless them all! How far better this, than the cold praise of newspaper paragraphs, or the critically contrived approval of colder friends!

Let me gather up these letters, carefully,—to be read when the heart is faint, and sick of all that there is unreal, and selfish in the world. Let me tie them together, with a new, and longer bit of ribbon—not by a love knot, that is too hard—but by an easy slipping knot, that so I may get at them the better. And now, they are all together, a snug pacquet, and we will label them, not sentimentally, (I pity the one who thinks it!) but earnestly, and in the best meaning of the term—SOUVENIRS DU CŒUR.[31]

Thanks to my first Reverie, which has added to such a treasure!

—And now to my SECOND REVERIE.

I am no longer in the country. The fields, the trees, the brooks are far away from me, and yet they are very present. A letter from my tenant—how different from those other letters!—lies upon my table, telling me what fields he has broken up for the autumn grain, and how many beeves he is fattening, and how the potatoes are turning out.

But I am in a garret of the city. From my window I look over a mass of crowded house-tops—moralizing often upon the scene, but in a strain too long, and sombre to be set down here. In place of the wide country chimney, with its iron fire-dogs, is a snug grate, where the maid makes me a fire in the morning, and rekindles it in the afternoon.

I am usually fairly seated in my chair—a cozily stuffed office chair—by five or six o'clock of the evening. The fire has been newly made, perhaps an hour before: first, the maid drops a withe of paper in the bottom of the grate, then a stick or two of pine-wood, and after it a hod of Liverpool coal; so that by the time I am seated for the evening, the sea-coal is fairly in a blaze.

When this has sunk to a level with the second bar of the grate, the maid replenishes it with a hod of Anthracite; and I sit musing and reading, while the new coal warms and kindles—not leaving my place, until it has sunk to the third bar of the grate, which marks my bed-time.

I love these accidental measures of the hours, which belong to you, and your life, and not to the world. A watch is no more the measure of your time, than of the time of your neighbors; a church clock is as public, and vulgar as a church-warden. I would as soon think of hiring the parish sexton to make my bed, as to regulate my time by the parish clock.

A shadow that the sun casts upon your carpet, or a streak of light on a slated roof yonder, or the burning of your fire, are pleasant time-keepers,—full of presence, full of companionship, and full of the warning—time is passing!

In the summer season I have even measured my reading, and my night-watch, by the burning of a taper; and I have scratched upon the handle to the little bronze taper-holder, that meaning passage of the New Testament,—Νύξ γαρ ερχεται—the night cometh!

---

[31]Mementoes of the heart.

But I must get upon my Reverie:—it was a drizzly evening; I had worked hard during the day, and had drawn my boots—thrust my feet into slippers—thrown on a Turkish loose dress, and Greek cap—souvenirs to me of other times, and other places—and sat watching the lively, uncertain, yellow play of the bituminous flame.

I

❧ Sea-Coal

It is like a flirt—mused I;—lively, uncertain, bright-colored, waving here and there, melting the coal into black shapeless mass, making foul, sooty smoke, and pasty, trashy residuum! Yet withal,—pleasantly sparkling, dancing, prettily waving, and leaping like a roebuck from point to point.

How like a flirt! And yet is not this tossing caprice of girlhood, to which I liken my sea-coal flame, a native play of life, and belonging by nature to the play-time of life? Is it not a sort of essential fire-kindling to the weightier and truer passions—even as Jenny puts the soft coal first, the better to kindle the anthracite? Is it not a sort of necessary consumption of young vapors, which float in the soul, and which is left thereafter the purer? Is there not a stage somewhere in every man's youth, for just such waving, idle heart-blaze, which means nothing, yet which must be got over?

Lamartine[32] says somewhere, very prettily, that there is more of quick running sap, and floating shade in a young tree; but more of fire in the heart of a sturdy oak:—*Il y a plus de séve folle et d'ombre flottante dans les jeunes plants de la forèt; il y a plus de feu dans le vieux cœur du chêne.*

Is Lamartine playing off his prettiness of expression, dressing up with his poetry,—making a good conscience against the ghost of some accusing Graziella,[33] or is there truth in the matter?

A man who has seen sixty years, whether widower or bachelor, may well put such sentiment into words: it feeds his wasted heart with hope; it renews the exultation of youth by the pleasantest of equivocation, and the most charming of self-confidence. But after all, is it not true? Is not the heart like new blossoming field-plants, whose first flowers are half formed, one-sided perhaps, but by-and-by, in maturity of season, putting out wholesome, well-formed blossoms, that will hold their leaves long and bravely?

Bulwer[34] in his story of the Caxtons, has counted first heart-flights mere fancy-passages—a dalliance with the breezes of love—which pass, and leave healthful heart

---

[32]Alphonse de Lamartine (1790–1869) was a French poet and statesman who played a key role in the French Romantic literary movement.

[33]Graziella is a Lamartine character (in a story by the same name) based on a young working girl with whom Larmartine had fallen in love.

[34]Edward George Bulwer-Lytton (1803–1873) was a popular English novelist best known for his historical works of fiction.

appetite. Half the reading world has read the story of Trevanion and Pisistratus.[35] But Bulwer is—past; his heart-life is used up—*épuisé*.[36] Such a man can very safely rant about the cool judgment of after years.

Where does Shakspeare put the unripe heart-age?—All of it before the ambition, that alone makes the hero-soul. The Shakspeare man 'sighs like a furnace,' before he stretches his arm to achieve the 'bauble, reputation.'

Yet Shakspeare has meted a soul-love, mature and ripe, without any young furnace sighs to Desdemona and Othello. Cordelia, the sweetest of his play creations, loves without any of the mawkish matter, which makes the whining love of a Juliet. And Florizel in the Winter's Tale, says to Perdita,[37] in the true spirit of a most sound heart—

> My desires
> Run not before mine honor, nor my wishes
> Burn hotter than my faith.

How is it with Hector and Andromache?[38]—no sea-coal blaze, but one that is constant, enduring, pervading: a pair of hearts full of esteem, and best love,—good, honest, and sound.

Look now at Adam and Eve, in God's presence, with Milton for showman. Shall we quote by this sparkling blaze, a gem from the Paradise Lost? We will hum it to ourselves—what Raphael sings to Adam—a classic song.

> —Him, serve and fear!
> Of other creatures, as Him pleases best
> Wherever placed, let Him dispose; joy thou
> In what he gives to thee, this Paradise
> And thy fair Eve!

And again.

> —Love refines
> The thoughts, and heart enlarges: hath his seat
> In reason, and is judicious: is the scale
> By which to Heavenly love thou mays't ascend!

None of the playing sparkle in this love, which belongs to the flame of my sea-coal fire, that is now dancing, lively as a cricket. But on looking about my garret chamber, I can see nothing that resembles the archangel Raphael, or 'thy fair Eve.'

There is a degree of moisture about the sea-coal flame, which with the most earnest of my musing, I find it impossible to attach to that idea of a waving, sparkling heart

---

[35]Bulwer-Lytton's historical novels included such figures as Trevanion and Pisistratus. Pisastratus was a famous tyrant in ancient Greece.

[36]exhausted

[37]Desdemona, Othello, Cordelia, Juliet, Florizel, and Perdita are all characters in Shakespeare's plays that represent different facets of familial and romantic love.

[38]Hector is the Trojan hero most celebrated in Homer's *Iliad*. Hector was married to Andromache.

which my fire suggests. A damp heart must be a foul thing to be sure! But whoever heard of one?

Wordsworth[39] somewhere in the Excursion, says:—

> The good die first,
> And they whose hearts are *dry* as summer dust
> Burn to the socket!

What, in the name of Rydal Mount,[40] is a dry heart? A dusty one, I can conceive of: a bachelor's heart must be somewhat dusty, as he nears the sixtieth summer of his pilgrimage;—and hung over with cobwebs, in which sit such watchful gray old spiders as Avarice, and Selfishness, forever on the look out for such bottle-green flies as Lust.

"I will never"—said I—griping at the elbows of my chair,—"live a bachelor till sixty:—never, so surely as there is hope in man, or charity in woman, or faith in both!"

And with that thought, my heart leaped about in playful coruscations,[41] even like the flame of sea-coal;—rising, and wrapping round old and tender memories, and images that were present to me,—trying to cling, and yet no sooner fastened, than off–dancing again, riotous in its exultation—a succession of heart-sparkles, blazing, and going out!

—And is there not—mused I,—a portion of this world, forever blazing in just such lively sparkles, waving here and there as the air-currents fan them?

Take for instance your heart of sentiment, and quick sensibility, a weak, warm-working heart, flying off in tangents of unhappy influence, unguided by prudence, and perhaps virtue. There is a paper by Mackenzie[42] in the Mirror for April, 1780, which sets this untoward sensibility in a strong light.

And the more it is indulged, the more strong and binding, such a habit of sensibility becomes. Poor Mackenzie himself must have suffered thus; you cannot read his books without feeling it; your eye, in spite of you, runs over with his sensitive griefs, while you are half-ashamed of his success at picture-making. It is a terrible inheritance; and one that a strong man or woman will study to subdue: it is a vain sea-coal sparkling, which will count no good. The world is made of much hard, flinty substance, against which your better, and holier thoughts will be striking fire;—see to it, that the sparks do not burn you!

But what a happy, careless life belongs to this Bachelorhood, in which you may strike out boldly right and left! Your heart is not bound to another which may be full of only sickly vapors of feeling; nor is it frozen to a cold, man's heart under a silk boddice—knowing, nothing of tenderness but the name, to prate of; and nothing of soul-confidence, but clumsy confession. And if in your careless out-goings of feeling, you get here, only a little lip vapidity in return; be sure that you will find, elsewhere, a true heart

---

[39]William Wordsworth (1770–1850) was an important English Romantic poet. One of his major volumes of poems, *The Excursion,* appeared in 1814.

[40]Home of the Wordsworth family.

[41]sparkles

[42]Henry Mackenzie (1745–1831) was a Scottish novelist, poet, and playwright, best known for his novel *The Man of Feeling* (1771).

utterance. This last you will cherish in your inner soul—a nucleus for a new group of affections; and the other will pass with a whiff of your cigar.

Or if your feelings are touched, struck, hurt, who is the wiser, or the worse, but you only? And have you not the whole skein of your heart-life in your own fingers to wind, or unwind, in what shape you please? Shake it, or twine it, or tangle it, by the light of your fire, as you fancy best. He is a weak man who cannot twist and weave the threads of his feeling—however fine, however tangled, however strained, or however strong—into the great cable of Purpose, by which he lies moored to his life of Action.

Reading is a great, and happy disentangler of all those knotted snarls—those extravagant vagaries, which belong to a heart sparkling with sensibility; but the reading must be cautiously directed. There is old, placid Burton[43] when your soul is weak, and its digestion of life's humors is bad; there is Cowper[44] when your spirit runs into kindly, half-sad, religious musing; there is Crabbe[45] when you would shake off vagary, by a little handling of sharp actualities. There is Voltaire, a homeopathic doctor, whom you can read when you want to make a play of life, and crack jokes at Nature, and be witty with Destiny; there is Rousseau,[46] when you want to lose yourself in a mental dream-land, and be beguiled by the harmony of soul-music and soul-culture.

And when you would shake off this, and be sturdiest among the battlers for hard, world-success, and be forewarned of rocks against which you must surely smite—read Bolingbroke;—run over the letters of Lyttleton; read, and think of what you read, in the cracking lines of Rochefoucauld.[47] How he sums us up in his stinging words!—how he puts the scalpel between the nerves—yet he never hurts; for he is dissecting dead matter.

If you are in a genial careless mood, who is better than such extemporizers of feeling and nature—good-hearted fellows—as Sterne and Fielding?[48]

And then again, there are Milton and Isaiah,[49] to lift up one's soul until it touches cloud-land, and you wander with their guidance, on swift feet, to the very gates of Heaven.

But this sparkling sensibility to one struggling under infirmity, or with grief or poverty, is very dreadful. The soul is too nicely and keenly hinged to be wrenched with-

---

[43]Robert Burton (1577–1640) was an English writer and Anglican clergyman who wrote *Anatomy of Melancholy* (1621), much praised for its style and wealth of philosophical and psychological information.

[44]William Cowper (1731–1800) was a tremendously popular English nature poet.

[45]George Crabbe (1754–1832) was an English poet who distinguished himself with his commitment to portraying realistic details of everyday life.

[46]Jean-Jacques Rousseau (1712–1778) was an immensely influential French philosopher and political theorist, who wrote extensively on a number of topics ranging from nature to education.

[47]François de la Rochefoucauld (1613–1680) was a French writer and adventurer known for his moral and philosophical maxims.

[48]Laurence Sterne (1713–1768) and Henry Fielding (1707–1754) were both famous and influential early English novelists renowned for their humor and wit.

[49]John Milton (1608–1674) and the Old Testament prophet Isaiah were both recognized for their treatments of the importance of the Messiah in Judeo-Christian thought.

out mischief. How it shrinks, like a hurt child, from all that is vulgar, harsh, and crude! Alas, for such a man!—he will be buffeted, from beginning to end; his life will be a sea of troubles. The poor victim of his own quick spirit he wanders with a great shield of doubt hung before him, so that none, not even friends can see the goodness of such kindly qualities as belong to him. Poverty, if it comes upon him, he wrestles with in secret, with strong, frenzied struggles. He wraps his scant clothes about him to keep him from the cold; and eyes the world, as if every creature in it was breathing chill blasts at him, from every opened mouth. He threads the crowded ways of the city, proud in his griefs, vain in his weakness, not stopping to do good. Bulwer, in the New Timon, has painted in a pair of stinging Pope-like lines, this feeling in a woman:—

> Her vengeful pride, a kind of madness grown,
> She hugged her wrongs, her sorrow was her throne!

Cold picture! yet the heart was sparkling under it, like my sea-coal fire; lifting and blazing, and lighting and falling,—but with no object; and only such little heat as begins and ends within.

Those fine sensibilities ever active, are chasing and observing all; they catch a hue from what the dull and callous pass by unnoticed,—because unknown. They blunder at the great variety of the world's opinions; they see tokens of belief, where others see none. That delicate organization is a curse to a man; and yet poor fool, he does not see where his cure lies; he wonders at his griefs, and has never reckoned with himself their source. He studies others, without studying himself. He eats the leaves that sicken, and never plucks up the root that will cure.

With a woman it is worse; with her, this delicate susceptibility is like a frail flower, that quivers at every rough blast of heaven; her own delicacy wounds her; her highest charm is perverted to a curse.

She listens with fear; she reads with trembling; she looks with dread. Her sympathies give a tone, like the harp of Æolus,[50] to the slightest breath. Her sensibility lights up, and quivers and falls, like the flame of a sea-coal fire.

If she loves—(and may not a Bachelor reason on this daintiest of topics)—her love is a gushing, wavy flame, lit up with hope, that has only a little kindling matter to light it; and this soon burns out. Yet intense sensibility will persuade her that the flame still scorches. She will mistake the annoyance of affection unrequited for the sting of a passion, that she fancies still burns. She does not look deep enough to see that the passion is gone, and the shocked sensitiveness emits only faint, yellowish sparkles in its place; her high-wrought organization makes those sparks seem a veritable flame.

With her, judgment, prudence, and discretion are cold measured terms, which have no meaning, except as they attach to the actions of others. Of her own acts, she never predicates them; feeling is much too high, to allow her to submit to any such obtrusive guides of conduct. She needs disappointment to teach her truth;—to teach that all is not gold that glitters—to teach that all warmth does not blaze. But let her beware how she sinks under any fancied disappointments: she who sinks under real disap-

---

[50]Stringed musical instrument played by the wind.

pointment, lacks philosophy; but she who sinks under a fancied one, lacks purpose. Let her flee as the plague, such brooding thoughts as she will love to cherish; let her spurn dark fancies as the visitants of hell; let the soul rise with the blaze of new-kindled, active, and world-wide emotions, and so brighten into steady and constant flame. Let her abjure such poets as Cowper, or Byron,[51] or even Wordsworth; and if she must poetize, let her lay her mind to such manly verse as Pope's,[52] or to such sound and ringing organry as Comus.[53]

My fire was getting dull, and I thrust in the poker. it started up on the instant into a hundred little angry tongues of flame.

—Just so—thought I—the over-sensitive heart once cruelly disturbed, will fling out a score of flaming passions, darting here, and darting there,—half-smoke, half-flame—love and hate—canker and joy—wild in its madness, not knowing whither its sparks are flying. Once break roughly upon the affections, or even the fancied affections of such a soul, and you breed a tornado of maddened action—a whirlwind of fire that hisses, and sends out jets of wild, impulsive combustion, that make the bystanders,—even those most friendly—stand aloof, until the storm is past.

But this is not all that the dashing flame of my sea-coal suggests.

——How like a flirt!—mused I again, recurring to my first thought—so lively, yet uncertain; so bright, yet so flickering! Your true flirt plays with sparkles; her heart, much as there is of it, spends itself in sparkles; she measures it to sparkle, and habit grows into nature, so that anon, it can only sparkle. How carefully she cramps it, if the flames show too great a heat; how dexterously she flings its blaze here and there; how coyly she subdues it; how winningly she lights it!

All this is the entire reverse of the unpremeditated dartings of the soul at which I have been looking; sensibility scorns heart-curbings, and heart-teachings; sensibility enquires not—how much? but only—where?

Your true flirt has a coarse-grained soul; well modulated and well tutored, but there is no fineness in it. All its native fineness is made coarse, by coarse efforts of the will. True feeling is a rustic vulgarity, the flirt does not tolerate; she counts its healthiest and most honest manifestation, all sentiment. Yet she will play you off a pretty string of sentiment, which she has gathered from the poets; she adjusts it prettily as a Ghobelin[54] weaver adjusts the colors in his *tapis*.[55] She shades it off delightfully; there are no bold contrasts, but a most artistic mellow of *nuances*.[56]

She smiles like a wizzard, and jingles it with a laugh, such as tolled the poor home-

---

[51]George Gordon Byron (1788–1824) was a popular English poet best remembered for his portrayal of the dark, brooding hero in *Don Juan* (1819–1824).

[52]Alexander Pope (1688–1744) was an English poet famous for his satires.

[53]*Comus* (1637) was a masque (play) written by John Milton. It highlights the harmonious bliss of heaven and the distressing conflicts of life on earth.

[54]The Gobelins were a world-famous French family of weavers and clothmakers who specialized in tapestries.

[55]Cloth full of artistic and colorful designs.

[56]Subtle distinctions.

bound Ulysses to the Circean bower.[57] She has a cast of the head, apt and artful as the most dexterous cast of the best trout-killing rod. Her words sparkle, and flow hurriedly, and with the prettiest doubleness of meaning. Naturalness she copies, and she scorns. She accuses herself of a single expression or regard, which nature prompts. She prides herself on her schooling. She measures her wit by the triumphs of her art; she chuckles over her own falsity to herself. And if by chance her soul—such germ as is left of it— betrays her into untoward confidence, she condemns herself, as if she had committed crime.

She is always gay, because she has no depth of feeling to be stirred. The brook that runs shallow over a hard pebbly bottom always rustles. She is light-hearted, because her heart floats in sparkles—like my sea-coal fire. She counts on marriage, not as the great absorbent of a heart's-love, and life, but as a happy, feasible, and orderly conventional-ity, to be played with, and kept at distance, and finally to be accepted as a cover for the faint and tawdry sparkles of an old and cherished heartlessness.

She will not pine under any regrets, because she has no appreciation of any loss: she will not chafe at indifference, because it is her art; she will not be worried with jeal-ousies, because she is ignorant of love. With no conception of the soul in its strength and fulness, she sees no lack of its demands. A thrill, she does not know; a passion, she can-not imagine; joy is a name; grief is another; and Life with its crowding scenes of love, and bitterness, is a play upon the stage.

I think it is Madame Dudevant[58] who says, in something like the same connec-tion:—*Les hiboux ne connaissant pas le chemin par où les aigles vont au soliel.*[59]

——Poor Ned!—mused I, looking at the play of the fire—was a victim and a con-queror. He was a man of a full, strong nature—not a little impulsive—with action too full of earnestness for most of men to see its drift. He had known little of what is called the world; he was fresh in feeling and high of hope; he had been encircled always by friends who loved him, and who, may be, flattered him. Scarce had he entered upon the tangled life of the city, before he met with a sparkling face and an airy step, that stirred some-thing in poor Ned, that he had never felt before. With him, to feel was to act. He was not one to be despised; for notwithstanding he wore a country air, and the awkwardness of a man who has yet the *bien-sèance*[60] of social life before him, he had the soul, the courage, and the talent of a strong man. Little gifted in the knowledge of face-play, he easily mis-took those coy manœuvres of a sparkling heart, for something kindred to his own true emotions.

She was proud of the attentions of a man who carried a mind in his brain; and flat-tered poor Ned almost into servility. Ned had no friends to counsel him; or if he had them, his impulses would have blinded him. Never was dodger more artful at the

---

[57]Ulysses, the hero of Homer's *Odyssey,* must free himself from the enchantress Circe to continue his voyage home.

[58]Amandine Dudevant is the real name of the famous French novelist George Sand (1804–1876).

[59]Owls do not soar as high as eagles.

[60]Wonderful stage.

Olympic Games than the Peggy of Ned's heart-affection. He was charmed, beguiled, entranced.

When Ned spoke of love, she staved it off with the prettiest of sly looks that only bewildered him the more. A charming creature to be sure; coy as a dove!

So he went on, poor fool, until one day—he told me of it with the blood mounting to his temples, and his eye shooting flame—he suffered his feelings to run out in passionate avowal,—entreaty,—everything. She gave a pleasant, noisy laugh, and manifested—such pretty surprise!

He was looking for the intense glow of passion; and lo, there was nothing but the shifting sparkle of a sea-coal flame.

I wrote him a letter of condolence—for I was his senior by a year;—"my dear fellow," said I, "diet yourself; you can find greens at the up-town market; eat a little fish with your dinner; abstain from heating drinks: don't put too much butter to your cauliflower; read one of Jeremy Taylor's[61] sermons, and translate all the quotations at sight; run carefully over that exquisite picture of Geo. Dandin in your Molière,[62] and my word for it, in a week you will be a sound man."

He was too angry to reply; but eighteen months thereafter I got a thick, three-sheeted letter, with a dove upon the seal, telling me that he was as happy as a king: he said he had married a good-hearted, domestic, loving wife, who was as lovely as a June day, and that their baby, not three months old, was as bright as a spot of June day sunshine on the grass.

—What a tender, delicate, loving wife—mused I—such flashing, flaming flirt must in the end make;—the prostitute of fashion; the bauble of fifty hearts idle as hers; the shifting make-piece of a stage scene; the actress, now in peasant, and now in princely petticoats! How it would cheer an honest soul to call her—his! What a culmination of his heart-life; what a rich dream-land to be realized!

——Bah! and I thrust the poker into the clotted mass of fading coal—just such, and so worthless is the used heart of a city flirt; just so the incessant sparkle of her life, and frittering passions, fuses all that is sound and combustible, into black, sooty, shapeless residuum.

When I marry a flirt, I will buy second-hand clothes of the Jews.

—Still—mused I—as the flame danced again—there is a distinction between coquetry and flirtation.

A coquette sparkles, but it is more the sparkle of a harmless and pretty vanity, than of calculation. It is the play of humors in the blood, and not the play of purpose at the heart. It will flicker around a true soul like the blaze around an *omelette au rhum*,[63] leaving the kernel sounder and warmer.

Coquetry, with all its pranks and teasings, makes the spice to your dinner—the

---

[61]Jeremy Taylor (1613–1667) was an Anglican clergyman who distinguished himself as a prolific writer of devotionals.

[62]Enjoy that wonderful illustration in your copy of Molière's (1622–1673) play *George Dandin* (1668).

[63]Rum omelette.

mulled wine to your supper. It will drive you to desperation, only to bring you back hotter to the fray. Who would boast a victory that cost no strategy, and no careful disposition of the forces? Who would bulletin such success as my Uncle Toby's, in a back-garden, with only the Corporal Trim for assailant? But let a man be very sure that the city is worth the siege!

Coquetry whets the appetite; flirtation depraves it. Coquetry is the thorn that guards the rose—easily trimmed off when once plucked. Flirtation is like the slime on water-plants, making them hard to handle, and when caught, only to be cherished in slimy waters.

And so, with my eye clinging to the flickering blaze, I see in my reverie, a bright one dancing before me, with sparkling, coquettish smile, teasing me with the prettiest graces in the world;—and I grow maddened between hope and fear, and still watch with my whole soul in my eyes; and see her features by and by relax to pity, as a gleam of sensibility comes stealing over her spirit;—and then to a kindly, feeling regard: presently she approaches,—a coy and doubtful approach—and throws back the ringlets that lie over her cheek, and lays her hand—a little bit of white hand—timidly upon my strong fingers,—and turns her head daintily to one side,—and looks up in my eyes, as they rest on the playing blaze; and my fingers close fast and passionately over that little hand, like a swift night-cloud shrouding the pale tips of Dian;[64]—and my eyes draw nearer and nearer to those blue, laughing, pitying, teasing eyes, and my arm clasps round that shadowy form,—and my lips feel a warm breath—growing, warmer and warmer——

Just here the maid comes in, and throws upon the fire a pan-ful of Anthracite, and my sparkling sea-coal reverie is ended.

II

❧ Anthracite

It does not burn freely, so I put on the blower. Quaint, and good-natured Xavier de Maistre* would have made, I dare say, a pretty epilogue about a sheet-iron blower; but I cannot.

I try to bring back the image that belonged to the lingering bituminous flame, but with my eyes on that dark blower,—how can I?

It is the black curtain of destiny which drops down before our brightest dreams. How often the phantoms of joy regale us, and dance before us—golden-winged, angel-faced, heart-warming, and make an Elysium[65] in which the dreaming soul bathes, and feels translated to another existence; and then—sudden as night, or a cloud—a word, a step, a thought, a memory will chase them away, like scared deer vanishing over a gray horizon of moor-land!

---

[64]The pale hand of Diana, the elusive Roman goddess of virginity and the hunt.

*Voyage auteur de Ma Chambre.

[65]In Greek mythology, the home of the blessed after their deaths.

I know not justly, if it be a weakness or a sin to create these phantoms that we love, and to group them into a paradise—soul-created. But if it is a sin, it is a sweet and enchanting sin; and if it is a weakness, it is a strong and stirring weakness. If this heart is sick of the falsities that meet it at every hand, and is eager to spend that power which nature has ribbed it with, on some object worthy of its fulness and depth,—shall it not feel a rich relief,—nay more, an exercise in keeping with its end, if it flow out—strong as a tempest, wild as a rushing river, upon those ideal creations, which imagination invents, and which are tempered by our best sense of beauty, purity, and grace?

——Useless, do you say? Aye, it is as useless as the pleasure of looking hour upon hour, over bright landscapes; it is as useless as the rapt enjoyment of listening with heart full and eyes brimming, to such music as the Miserere[66] at Rome; it is as useless as the ecstacy of kindling your soul into fervor and love, and madness, over pages that reek with genius.

There are indeed base-moulded souls who know nothing of this; they laugh; they sneer; they even affect to pity. Just so the Huns under the avenging Attila,[67] who had been used to foul cookery and steaks stewed under their saddles, laughed brutally at the spiced banquets of an Apicius![68]

——No, this phantom-making is no sin; or if it be, it is sinning with a soul so full, so earnest, that it can cry to Heaven cheerily, and sure of a gracious hearing—*peccavi—misericorde!*[69]

But my fire is in a glow, a pleasant glow, throwing a tranquil, steady light to the farthest corner of my garret. How unlike it is, to the flashing play of the sea-coal!—unlike as an unsteady, uncertain-working heart to the true and earnest constancy of one cheerful and right.

After all, thought I, give me such a heart; not bent on vanities, not blazing too sharp with sensibility, not throwing out coquettish jets of flame, not wavering, and meaningless with pretended warmth, but open, glowing and strong. Its dark shades and angles it may have; for what is a soul worth that does not take a slaty tinge from those griefs that chill the blood? Yet still the fire is gleaming; you see it in the crevices; and anon it will give radiance to the whole mass.

——It hurts the eyes, this fire; and I draw up a screen painted over with rough, but graceful figures.

The true heart wears always the veil of modesty—(not of prudery which is a dingy, iron, repulsive screen.) It will not allow itself to be looked on too near—it might scorch; but through the veil you feel the warmth; and through the pretty figures that modesty will robe itself in, you can see all the while the golden outlines, and by that token, you *know* that it is glowing and burning with a pure and steady flame.

---

[66]Catholic mass based on Ps. 51:3 sung the week before Easter.

[67]Attila the Hun (A.D. 406?–453) was one of the most feared leaders of the "barbaric" German tribes who marched against the Roman Empire.

[68]Apicius was a legendary ancient Roman gourmand.

[69]I have sinned—mercy!

With such a heart the mind fuses naturally—a holy and heated fusion; they work together like twins-born. With such a heart, as Raphael says to Adam,

Love hath his seat
In reason, and is judicious.

But let me distinguish this heart from your clay-cold, luke-warm, half-hearted soul;—considerate, because ignorant; judicious, because possessed of no latent fires that need a curb; prudish, because with no warm blood to tempt. This sort of soul may pass scatheless through the fiery furnace of life; strong, only in its weakness; pure, because of its failings; and good, only by negation. It may triumph over love, and sin, and death; but it will be a triumph of the beast, which has neither passions to subdue, or energy to attack, or hope to quench.

Let us come back to the steady and earnest heart, glowing like my anthracite coal.

I fancy I see such a one now:—the eye is deep and reaches back to the spirit; it is not the trading eye, weighing your purse; it is not the worldly eye weighing position; it is not the beastly eye, weighing your appearance; it is the heart's eye, weighing your soul!

It is full of deep, tender, and earnest feeling. It is an eye, which looked on once, you long to look on again; it is an eye which will haunt your dreams,—an eye which will give a colour, in spite of you, to all your reveries. It is an eye which lies before you in your future, like a star in the mariner's heaven; by it, unconsciously, and from force of deep soul-habit, you take all your observations. It is meek and quiet; but it is full, as a spring that gushes in flood; an Aphrodite and a Mercury—a Vauclause and a Clitumnus![70]

The face is an angel face; no matter for curious lines of beauty; no matter for popular talk of prettiness; no matter for its angles, or its proportions; no matter for its colour or its form—the soul is there, illuminating every feature, burnishing every point, hallowing every surface. It tells of honesty, sincerity and worth; it tells of truth and virtue;—and you clasp the image to your heart, as the received ideal of your fondest dreams.

The figure may be this or that, it may be tall or short, it matters nothing,—the heart is there. The talk may be soft or low, serious or piquant—a free and honest soul is warming and softening it all. As you speak, it speaks back again; as you think, it thinks again—(not in conjunction, but in the same sign of the Zodiac;) as you love it loves in return.

——It is the heart for a sister, and happy is the man who can claim such! The warmth that lies in it is not only generous, but religious, genial, devotional, tender, self-sacrificing, and looking heaven-ward.

A man without some sort of religion, is at best a poor reprobate, the foot-ball of destiny, with no tie linking him to infinity, and the wondrous eternity that is begun with him; but a woman without it, is even worse—a flame without heat, a rainbow without colour, a flower without perfume!

A man may in some sort tie his frail hopes and honors, with weak, shifting ground-tackle to business, or to the world; but a woman without that anchor which they call

---

[70]These are famous mythological figures and rivers associated with fertility, abundance, and speed.

Faith, is adrift, and a-wreck! A man may clumsily contrive a kind of moral responsibility, out of his relations to mankind; but a woman in her comparatively isolated sphere, where affection and not purpose is the controlling motive, can find no basis for any system of right action, but that of spiritual faith. A man may craze his thought, and his brain, to trustfulness in such poor harborage as Fame and Reputation may stretch before him; but a woman—where can she put her hope in storms, if not in Heaven?

And that sweet trustfulness—that abiding love—that enduring hope, mellowing every page and scene of life, lighting them with pleasantest radiance, when the world-storms break like an army with smoking cannon—what can bestow it all, but a holy soul-tie to what is above the storms, and to what is stronger than an army with cannon? Who that has enjoyed the counsel and the love of a Christian mother, but will echo the thought with energy, and hallow it with a tear?——*et moi, je pleurs!*[71]

My fire is now a mass of red-hot coal. The whole atmosphere of my room is warm. The heart that with its glow can light up, and warm a garret with loose casements and shattered roof, is capable of the best love—domestic love. I draw farther off, and the images upon the screen change. The warmth, the hour, the quiet, create a home feeling; and that feeling, quick as lightning, has stolen from the world of fancy, (a Promethean theft,)[72] a home object, about which my musings go on to drape themselves in luxurious reverie.

——There she sits, by the corner of the fire, in a neat home dress, of sober, yet most adorning colour. A little bit of lace ruffle is gathered about the neck, by a blue ribbon; and the ends of the ribbon are crossed under the dimpling chin, and are fastened neatly by a simple, unpretending brooch—your gift. The arm, a pretty taper arm, lies over the carved elbow of the oaken chair; the hand, white and delicate, sustains a little home volume that hangs from her fingers. The forefinger is between the leaves, and the others lie in relief upon the dark embossed cover. She repeats in a silver voice, a line that has attracted her fancy; and you listen—or at any rate, you seem to listen—with your eyes now on the lips, now on the forehead, and now on the finger, where glitters like a star, the marriage ring—little gold band, at which she does not chafe, that tells you,—she is yours!

——Weak testimonial, if that were all that told it! The eye, the voice, the look, the heart, tells you stronger and better, that she is yours. And a feeling within, where it lies you know not, and whence it comes you know not, but sweeping over heart and brain, like a fire-flood, tells you too, that you are hers! Irremediably bound as Massinger's[73] Hortensio:

> I am subject to another's will, and can
> Nor speak, nor do, without permission from her!

The fire is warm as ever; what length of heat in this hard burning anthracite! It has scarce sunk yet to the second bar of the grate, though the clock upon the church-tower has tolled eleven.

---

[71]And I cry.

[72]In Greek legend, Prometheus stole fire from the gods in order to give it to humanity.

[73]Philip Massinger (1583–1639?) was an English playwright famous for his comedies and satires.

—Aye,—mused I, gaily—such heart does not grow faint, it does not spend itself in idle puffs of blaze, it does not become chilly with the passing years; but it gains and grows in strength, and heat, until the fire of life, is covered over with the ashes of death. Strong or hot as it may be at the first, it loses nothing. It may not indeed, as time advances, throw out, like the coal-fire, when new-lit, jets of blue sparkling flame; it may not continue to bubble, and gush like a fountain at its source, but it will become a strong river of flowing charities.

Clitumnus[74] breaks from under the Tuscan mountains, almost a flood; on a glorious spring day I leaned down and tasted the water, as it boiled from its sources;—the little temple of white marble,—the mountain sides gray with olive orchards,—the white streak of road,—the tall poplars of the river margin were glistening in the bright Italian sunlight, around me. Later, I saw it when it had become a river,—still clear and strong, flowing serenely between its prairie banks, on which the white cattle of the valley browsed; and still farther down, I welcomed it, where it joins the Arno,—flowing slowly under wooded shores, skirting the fair Florence, and the bounteous fields of the bright Cascino;—gathering strength and volume, till between Pisa and Leghorn,—in sight of the wondrous Leaning Tower, and the ship-masts of the Tuscan port, it gave its waters to its life's grave—the sea.

The recollection blended sweetly now with my musings, over my garret grate, and offered a flowing image, to bear along upon its bosom the affections that were grouping in my Reverie.

It is a strange force of the mind and of the fancy, that can set the objects which are closest to the heart far down the lapse of time. Even now, as the fire fades slightly, and sinks slowly towards the bar, which is the dial of my hours, I seem to see that image of love which has played about the fire-glow of my grate—years hence. It still covers the same warm, trustful, religious heart. Trials have tried it; afflictions have weighed upon it; danger has scared it; and death is coming near to subdue it; but still it is the same.

The fingers are thinner; the face has lines of care, and sorrow, crossing each other in a web-work, that makes the golden tissue of humanity. But the heart is fond, and steady; it is the same dear heart, the same self-sacrificing heart, warming, like a fire, all around it. Affliction has tempered joy; and joy adorned affliction. Life and all its troubles have become distilled into an holy incense, rising ever from your fireside,—an offering to your household gods.

Your dreams of reputation, your swift determination, your impulsive pride, your deep uttered vows to win a name, have all sobered into affection—have all blended into that glow of feeling, which finds its centre, and hope, and joy in HOME. From my soul. I pity him whose soul does not leap at the mere utterance of that name.

A home!—it is the bright, blessed, adorable phantom which sits highest on the sunny horizon that girdeth Life! When shall it be reached? When shall it cease to be a glittering day-dream, and become fully and fairly yours?

It is not the house, though that may have its charms; nor the fields carefully tilled, and streaked with your own foot-paths;—nor the trees, though their shadow be to you

---

[74]River in northern Italy that Mitchell goes on to follow until it empties into the sea.

like that of a great rock in a weary land;—nor yet is it the fireside, with its sweet blaze-play;—nor the pictures which tell of loved ones, nor the cherished books,—but more far than all these—it is the PRESENCE. The Lares[75] of your worship are there; the altar of your confidence there; the end of your worldly faith is there; and adorning it all, and sending your blood in passionate flow, is the ecstasy of the conviction, that, *there* at least you are beloved; that there you are understood; that there your errors will meet ever with gentlest forgiveness; that there your troubles will be smiled away; that there you may unburden your soul, fearless of harsh, unsympathizing ears; and that there you may be entirely and joyfully—yourself!

There may be those of coarse mould—and I have seen such even in the disguise of women—who will reckon these feelings puling sentiment. God pity them!—as they have need of pity.

——That image by the fireside, calm, loving, joyful, is there still: it goes not, how-ever my spirit tosses, because my wish, and every will, keep it there, unerring.

The fire shows through the screen, yellow and warm, as a harvest sun. It is in its best age, and that age is ripeness.

A ripe heart!—now I know what Wordsworth meant, when he said,

> The good die first,
> And they whose hearts are dry as summer dust,
> Burn to the socket!

The town clock is striking midnight. The cold of the night-wind is urging its way in at the door and window-crevice; the fire has sunk almost to the third bar of the grate. Still my dream tires not, but wraps fondly round that image,—now in the far off, chilling mists of age, growing sainted. Love has blended into reverence; passion has subsided into joyous content.

——And what if age comes, said I, in a new flush of excitation,—what else proves the wine? What else gives inner strength, and knowledge, and a steady pilot-hand, to steer your boat out boldly upon that shoreless sea, where the river of life is running? Let the white ashes gather; let the silver hair lie, where lay the auburn; let the eye gleam far-ther back, and dimmer; it is but retreating toward the pure sky-depths, an usher to the land where you wil follow after.

It is quite cold, and I take away the screen altogether; there is a little glow yet, but presently the coal slips down below the third bar, with a rumbling sound,—like that of coarse gravel falling into a new-dug grave.

——She is gone!

Well, the heart has burned fairly, evenly, generously, while there was mortality to kindle it; eternity will surely kindle it better.

——Tears indeed; but they are tears of thanks-giving, of resignation, and of hope!

And the eyes, full of those tears, which ministering angels bestow, climb with quick vision, upon the angelic ladder, and open upon the futurity where she has entered, and upon the country, which she enjoys.

---

[75]Household gods.

It is midnight, and the sounds of life are dead.

You are in the death chamber of life; but you are also in the death chamber of care. The world seems sliding backward; and hope and you are sliding forward. The clouds, the agonies, the vain expectancies, the braggart noise, the fears, now vanish behind the curtain of the Past, and of the Night. They roll from your soul like a load.

In the dimness of what seems the ending Present, you reach out your prayerful hands toward that boundless Future, where God's eye lifts over the horizon, like sunrise on the ocean. Do you recognize it as an earnest of something better? Aye, if the heart has been pure, and steady,—burning like my fire—it has learned it without seeming to learn. Faith has grown upon it, as the blossom grows upon the bud, or the flower upon the slow-lifting, stalk.

Cares cannot come into the dream-land where I live. They sink with the dying street noise, and vanish with the embers of my fire. Even Ambition, with its hot and shifting flame, is all gone out. The heart in the dimness of the fading fire-glow is all itself. The memory of what good things have come over it in the troubled youth-life, bear it up; and hope and faith bear it on. There is no extravagant pulse-flow; there is no mad fever of the brain; but only the soul, forgetting—for once—all, save its destinies, and its capacities for good. And it mounts higher and higher on these wings of thought; and hope burns stronger and stronger out of the ashes of decaying life, until the sharp edge of the grave seems but a foot-scraper at the wicket of Elysium!

But what is paper; and what are words? Vain things! The soul leaves them behind; the pen staggers like a starveling cripple; and your heart is leaving it, a whole length of the life-course behind. The soul's mortal longings,—its poor baffled hopes, are dim now in the light of those infinite longings, which spread over it, soft and holy as day-dawn. Eternity has stretched a corner of its mantle toward you, and the breath of its waving fringe is like a gale of Araby.

A little rumbling, and a last plunge of the cinders within my grate, startled me, and dragged back my fancy from my flower chase, beyond the Phlegethon,[76] to the white ashes, that were now thick all over the darkened coals.

—And this—mused I—is only a bachelor-dream about a pure, and loving heart! And to-morrow comes cankerous life again:——is it wished for? Or if not wished for, is the not wishing, wicked?

Will dreams satisfy, reach high as they can? Are we not after all poor grovelling mortals, tied to earth, and to each other; are there not sympathies, and hopes, and affections which can only find their issue, and blessing, in fellow absorption? Does not the heart, steady, and pure as it may be, and mounting on soul flights often as it dare, want a human sympathy, perfectly indulged, to make it healthful? Is there not a fount of love for this world, as there is a fount of love for the other? Is there not a certain store of tenderness, cooped in this heart, which must, and *will* be lavished, before the end comes? Does it not plead with the judgment, and make issue with prudence, year after year? Does it not dog your steps all through your social pilgrimage, setting up its claims in forms fresh, and odorous as new-blown heath bells, saying,—come away from the heartless,

---

[76]A river of fire in the ancient Greek underworld.

the factitious, the vain, and measure your heart not by its constraints, but by its fulness, and by its depth?—let it run, and be joyous!

Is there no demon that comes to your harsh night-dreams, like a taunting fiend, whispering—be satisfied; keep your heart from running over; bridle those affections; there is nothing worth loving?

Does not some sweet being hover over your spirit of reverie like a beckoning angel, crowned with halo, saying—hope on, hope ever; the heart and I are kindred; our mission will be fulfilled; nature shall accomplish its purpose; the soul shall have its Paradise!

——I threw myself upon my bed: and as my thoughts ran over the definite, sharp business of the morrow, my Reverie, and its glowing images, that made my heart bound, swept away, like those fleecy rain clouds of August, on which the sun paints rainbows—driven Southward, by a cool, rising wind from the North.

——I wonder,—thought I, as I dropped asleep,—if a married man with his sentiment made actual, is, after all, as happy as we poor fellows, in our dreams?

THIRD REVERIE

A Cigar Three Times Lighted

❧ Over His Cigar

I do not believe that there was ever an Aunt Tabithy who could abide cigars. My Aunt Tabithy hated them with a peculiar hatred. She was not only insensible to the rich flavor of a fresh rolling volume of smoke, but she could not so much as tolerate the sight of the rich russet colour of an Havana-labelled box. It put her out of all conceit with Guava jelly, to find it advertised in the same tongue, and with the same Cuban coarseness of design.

She could see no good in a cigar.

"But by your leave, my aunt," said I to her, the other morning,—"there is very much that is good in a cigar."

My aunt who was sweeping, tossed her head, and with it, her curls—done up in paper.

"It is a very excellent matter," continued I, puffing.

"It is dirty," said my aunt.

"It is clean and sweet," said I; "and a most pleasant soother of disturbed feelings; and a capital companion; and a comforter——" and I stopped to puff.

"You know it is a filthy abomination," said my aunt,—"and you ought to be——," and she stopped to put up one of her curls, which with the energy of her gesticulation, had fallen out of its place.

"It suggests quiet thoughts"—continued I,—"and makes a man meditative; and gives a current to his habits of contemplation,—as I can show you," said I, warming with the theme.

My aunt, still fingering her papers,—with the pin in her mouth,—gave a most incredulous shrug.

"Aunt Tabithy"—said I, and gave two or three violent, consecutive puffs,—"Aunt Tabithy, I can make up such a series of reflections out of my cigar, as would do your heart good to listen to!"

"About what, pray?" said my aunt, contemptuously.

"About love," said I, "which is easy enough lighted, but wants constancy to keep it in a glow;—or about matrimony, which has a great deal of fire in the beginning, but it is a fire that consumes all that feeds the blaze;—or about life," continued I earnestly—"which at the first is fresh and odorous, but ends shortly in a withered cinder, that is fit only for the ground."

My aunt who was forty and unmarried, finished her curl with a flip of the fingers,—resumed her hold of the broom, and leaned her chin upon one end of it, with an expression of some wonder, some curiosity, and a great deal of expectation.

I could have wished my aunt had been a little less curious, or that I had been a little less communicative: for though it was all honestly said on my part, yet my contemplations bore that vague, shadowy, and delicious sweetness, that it seemed impossible to put them into words,—least of all, at the bidding of an old lady, leaning on a broom-handle.

"Give me time, Aunt Tabithy,"—said I,—"a good dinner, and after it a good cigar, and I will serve you such a sun-shiny sheet of reverie, all twisted out of the smoke, as will make your kind old heart ache!"

Aunt Tabithy, in utter contempt, either of my mention of the dinner, or of the smoke, or of the old heart, commenced sweeping furiously.

"If I do not"—continued I, anxious to appease her,—"if I do not, Aunt Tabithy, it shall be my last cigar; (Aunt Tabithy stopped sweeping) and all my tobacco money, (Aunt Tabithy drew near me) shall go to buy ribbons for my most respectable, and worthy Aunt Tabithy; and a kinder person could not have them; or one," continued I, with a generous puff, "whom they would more adorn."

My Aunt Tabithy gave me a half-playful,—half-thankful nudge.

It was in this way that our bargain was struck; my part of it is already stated. On her part, Aunt Tabithy was to allow me, in case of my success, an evening, cigar unmolested, upon the front porch, underneath her favorite rose-tree. It was concluded, I say, as I sat; the smoke of my cigar rising gracefully around my Aunt Tabithy's curls;—our right hands joined;—my left was holding my cigar, while in hers, was tightly grasped—her broom-stick.

And this Reverie, to make the matter short, is what came of the contract.

I

❧ Lighted with a Coal

I take up a coal with the tongs, and setting the end of my cigar against it, puff—and puff again; but there is no smoke. There is very little hope of lighting from a dead coal;—no more hope, thought I,—than of kindling one's heart into flame, by contact with a dead heart.

To kindle, there must be warmth and life; and I sat for a moment, thinking,—even before I lit my cigar,—on the vanity and folly of those poor, purblind fellows, who go on puffing for half a lifetime, against dead coals. It is to be hoped that Heaven, in its mercy, has made their senses so obtuse, that they know not when their souls are in a flame, or when they are dead. I can imagine none but the most moderate satisfaction, in continuing to love, what has got no ember of love within it. The Italians have a very sensible sort of proverb,—*amare, e non essere amato, è tempo perduto:*—to love, and not be loved, is time lost.

I take a kind of rude pleasure in flinging down a coal that has no life in it. And it seemed to me,—and may Heaven pardon the ill-nature that belongs to the thought,—that there would be much of the same kind of satisfaction, in dashing from you a lukewarm creature, covered over with the yellow ashes of old combustion, that with ever so much attention, and the nearest approach of the lips, never shows signs of fire. May Heaven forgive me again, but I should long to break away, though the marriage bonds held me, and see what liveliness was to be found elsewhere.

I have seen before now a creeping vine try to grow up against a marble wall; it shoots out its tendrils in all directions, seeking for some crevice by which to fasten and to climb;—looking now above and now below,—twining upon itself,—reaching farther up, but after all, finding no good foothold, and falling away as if in despair. But nature is not unkind; twining things were made to twine. The longing tendrils take new strength in the sunshine, and in the showers, and shoot out toward some hospitable trunk. They fasten easily to the kindly roughness of the bark, and stretch up, dragging after them the vine; which by and by, from the topmost bough, will nod its blossoms over at the marble wall, that refused it succour, as if it said,—stand there in your pride, cold, white wall! we, the tree and I are kindred, it the helper, and I the helped; and bound fast together, we riot in the sunshine, and in gladness.

The thought of this image made me search for a new coal that should have some brightness in it. There may be a white ash over it indeed; as you will find tender feelings covered with the mask of courtesy, or with the veil of fear; but with a breath it all flies off, and exposes the heat, and the glow that you are seeking.

At the first touch, the delicate edges of the cigar crimple, a thin line of smoke rises,—doubtfully for a while, and with a coy delay; but after a hearty respiration or two, it grows strong, and my cigar is fairly lighted.

That first taste of the new smoke, and of the fragrant leaf is very grateful; it has a bloom about it, that you wish might last. It is like your first love,—fresh, genial, and rapturous. Like that, it fills up all the craving of your soul; and the light, blue wreaths of smoke, like the roseate clouds that hang around the morning of your heart life, cut you off from the chill atmosphere of mere worldly companionship, and make a gorgeous firmament for your fancy to riot in.

I do not speak now of those later, and manlier passions, into which judgment must be thrusting its cold tones, and when all the sweet tumult of your heart has mellowed into the sober ripeness of affection. But I mean that boyish burning, which belongs to every poor mortal's lifetime, and which bewilders him with the thought that he has reached the highest point of human joy, before he has tasted any of that bitterness, from which alone our highest human joys have spring. I mean the time, when you cut initials with your jack-knife on the smooth bark of beech trees; and went moping under the long shadows at sunset; and thought Louise the prettiest name in the wide world; and picked flowers to leave at her door; and stole out at night to watch the light in her window; and read such novels as those about Helen Mar, or Charlotte,[77] to give some adequate expression to your agonized feelings.

At such a stage, you are quite certain that you are deeply, and madly in love; you persist in the face of heaven, and earth. You would like to meet the individual who dared to doubt it.

You think she has got the tidiest, and jauntiest little figure that ever was seen. You think back upon some time when in your games of forfeit, you gained a kiss from those lips; and it seems as if the kiss was hanging on you yet, and warming you all over. And then again, it seems so strange that your lips did really touch hers! You half question if it could have been actually so,—and how you could have dared;—and you wonder if you would have courage to do the same thing again?—and upon second thought, are quite sure you would,—and snap your fingers at the thought of it.

What sweet little hats she does wear; and in the school room, when the hat is hung up—what curls—golden curls, worth a hundred Golcondas![78] How bravely you study the top lines of the spelling book—that your eyes may run over the edge of the cover without the schoolmaster's notice, and feast upon her!

You half wish that somebody would run away with her, as they did with Amanda, in the Children of the Abbey;[79]—and then you might ride up on a splendid black horse, and draw a pistol, or blunderbuss, and shoot the villians, and carry her back, all in tears, fainting, and languishing upon your shoulder;—and have her father (who is Judge of the County Court,) take your hand in both of his, and make some eloquent remarks. A great many such re-captures you run over in your mind, and think how delightful it would be to peril your life, either by flood, or fire,—to cut off your arm, or your head, or any such trifle,—for your dear Louise.

You can hardly think of anything more joyous in life, than to live with her in some old castle, very far away from steamboats, and post-offices, and pick wild geraniums for her hair, and read poetry with her, under the shade of very dark ivy vines. And you would have such a charming boudoir in some corner of the old ruin, with a harp in it, and books bound in gilt, with cupids on the cover, and such a fairy couch, with the curtains hung— as you have seen them hung in some illustrated Arabian stories—upon a pair of carved doves!

And when they laugh at you about it, you turn it off perhaps with saying—"it isn't so;" but afterward, in your chamber, or under the tree where you have cut her name, you take Heaven to witness, that it is so; and think—what a cold world it is, to be so careless about such holy emotions! You perfectly hate a certain stout boy in a green jacket, who is forever twitting you, and calling her names; but when some old maiden aunt teases you in her kind, gentle way, you bear it very proudly; and with a feeling as if you could bear a great deal more for *her* sake. And when the minister reads off marriage anonunce-

---

[77]Tragic heroines of novels popular in antebellum America.

[78]Region famous for its diamond mines.

[79]*Children of the Abbey* is a play by Regina Maria Roche (1764–1845).

ments in the church, you think how it will sound one of these days, to have your name, and hers, read from the pulpit;—and how the people will all look at you, and how prettily she will blush; and how poor little Dick, who you know loves her, but is afraid to say so, will squirm upon his bench.

—Heigho!—mused I,—as the blue smoke rolled up around my head,—these first kindlings of the love that is in one, are very pleasant!—but will they last?

You love to listen to the rustle of her dress; as she stirs about the room. It is better music than grown-up ladies will make upon all their harpsichords, in the years that are to come. But this, thank Heaven, you do not know.

You think you can trace her foot-mark, on your way to the school;—and what a dear little foot-mark it is! And from that single point, if she be out of your sight for days, you conjure up the whole image,—the elastic, lithe little figure,—the springy step,—the dotted muslin so light, and flowing,—the silk kerchief, with its most tempting fringe playing upon the clear white of her throat,—how you envy that fringe! And her chin is as round as a peach—and the lips—such lips!—and you sigh, and hang your head; and wonder when you *shall* see her again!

You would like to write her a letter; but then people would talk so coldly about it and beside you are not quite sure you could write such billets as Thaddeus of Warsaw[80] used to write; and anything less warm or elegant, would not do at all. You talk about this one, or that one, whom they call pretty, in the coolest way in the world; you see very little of their prettiness; they are good girls to be sure; and you hope they will get good husbands some day or other; but it is not a matter that concerns you very much. They do not live in your world of romance; they are not the angels of that sky which your heart makes rosy, and to which I have likened the blue waves of this rolling smoke.

You can even joke as you talk of others; you can smile,—as you think—very graciously; you can say laughingly that you are deeply in love with them, and think it a most capital joke; you can touch their hands, or steal a kiss from them in your games, most imperturbably;—they are very dead coals.

But the live one is very lively. When you take the name on your lip, it seems somehow, to be made of different materials from the rest; you cannot half so easily separate it into letters;—write it, indeed you can; for you have had practice,—very much private practice on odd scraps of paper, and on the flyleaves of geographies, and of your natural philosophy. You know perfectly well how it looks; it seems to be written indeed, somewhere behind your eyes; and in such happy position with respect to the optic nerve, that you see it all the time, though you are looking in an opposite direction; and so distinctly, that you have great fears lest people looking into your eyes, should see it too!

For all this, it is a far more delicate name to handle than most that you know of. Though it is very cool, and pleasant on the brain, it is very hot, and difficult to manage on the lip. It is not, as your schoolmaster would say,—a name, so much as it is an idea;— not a noun, but a verb,—an active, and transitive verb; and yet a most irregular verb, wanting the passive voice.

---

[80]Letters from Thaddeus Kosciusko (1746–1817), a Polish army officer and statesman. He gained fame in the American Revolution and then returned to Poland to help lead a nationalist movement against Russian and Prussian control of Poland.

It is something against your schoolmaster's doctrine, to find warmth in the moon-light; but with that soft hand—it is very soft—lying within your arm, there is a great deal of warmth, whatever the philosophers may say, even in pale moonlight. The beams too, breed sympathies, very close-running sympathies,—not talked about in the chapters on optics, and altogether too fine for language. And under their influence, you retain the lit-tle hand, that you had not dared retain so long before; and her struggle to recover it,—if indeed it be a struggle,—is infinitely less than it was;—nay, it is a kind of struggle, not so much against you, as between gladness and modesty. It makes you as bold as a lion; and the feeble hand like a poor lamb in the lion's clutch, is powerless, and very meek;—and failing of escape, it will sue for gentle treatment; and will meet your warm promise, with a kind of grateful pressure, that is but half acknowledged, by the hand that makes it.

My cigar is burning with wondrous freeness; and from the smoke flash forth images bright and quick as lightning—with no thunder, but the thunder of the pulse. But will it all last? Damp will deaden the fire of a cigar; and there are hellish damps—alas, too many,—that will deaden the early blazing of the heart.

She is pretty,—growing prettier to your eye, the more you look upon her, and pret-tier to your ear, the more you listen to her. But you wonder who the tall boy was, who you saw walking with her, two days ago? He was not a bad-looking boy; on the contrary, you think,—(with a grit of your teeth)—that he was infernally handsome! You look at him very shyly, and very closely, when you pass him; and turn to see how he walks, and to measure his shoulders, and are quite disgusted with the very modest, and gentlemanly way, with which he carries himself. You think you would like to have a fisticuff with him, if you were only sure of having the best of it. You sound the neighborhood coyly, to find out who the strange boy is; and are half ashamed of yourself for doing it.

You gather a magnificent bouquet to send her, and tie it with a green ribbon, and a love knot,—and get a little rose-bud in acknowledgment. *That* day, you pass the tall-boy with a very patronizing look; and wonder if he would not like to have a sail in *your* boat?

But by and by, you find the tall boy walking with her again; and she looks sideways at him, and with a kind of grown up air, that makes you feel very boy-like, and humble, and furious. And you look daggers at him when you pass; and touch your cap to her, with quite uncommon dignity;—and wonder if she is not sorry, and does not feel very badly, to have got such a look from you?

On some other day, however, you meet her alone; and the sight of her makes your face wear a genial, sunny air; and you talk a little sadly about your fears and your jeal-ousies; she seems a little sad, and a little glad, together;—and is sorry she has made you feel badly,—and you are sorry too. And with this pleasant twin sorrow, you are knit together again—closer than ever. That one little tear of hers has been worth more to you than a thousand smiles. Now you love her madly; you could swear it—swear it to her, or swear it to the universe. You even say as much to some kind old friend at night-fall; but your mention of her, is tremulous and joyful,—with a kind of bound in your speech, as if the heart worked too quick for the tongue; and as if the lips were ashamed to be pass-ing over such secrets of the soul, to the mere sense of hearing. At this stage, you cannot trust yourself to speak her praises; or if you venture, the expletives fly away with your thought, before you can chain it into language; and your speech, at your best endeavor, is but a succession of broken superlatives, that you are ashamed of. You strain for language that will scald the thought of her; but hot as you can make it, it falls back upon your heated fancy, like a cold shower.

Heat so intense as this consumes very fast; and the matter it feeds fastest on, is—judgment; and with judgment gone, there is room for jealousy to creep in. You grow petulant at another sight of that tall-boy; and the one tear, which cured your first petulance, will not cure it now. You let a little of your fever break out in speech—a speech which you go home to mourn over. But she knows nothing of the mourning, while she knows very much of the anger. Vain tears are very apt to breed pride; and when you go again with your petulance, you will find your rosy-lipped girl taking her first studies in dignity.

You will stay away, you say;—poor fool, you are feeding on what your disease loves best! You wonder if she is not sighing for your return,—and if your name is not running in her thought,—and if tears of regret are not moistening those sweet eyes.

——And wondering thus, you stroll moodily, and hopefully toward her father's home; you pass the door once—twice; you loiter under the shade of an old tree, where you have sometimes bid her adieu; your old fondness is struggling with your pride, and has almost made the mastery; but in the very moment of victory, you see yonder your hated rival, and beside him looking very gleeful, and happy—your perfidious Louise.

How quick you throw off the marks of your struggle, and put on the boldest air of boyhood; and what a dexterous handling to your knife, and a wonderful keenness to the edge, as you cut away from the bark of the beech tree, all trace of her name! Still there is a little silent relenting, and a few tears at night, and a little tremor of the hand, as you tear out—the next day,—every fly leaf that bears her name. But at sight of your rival,—looking so jaunty, and in such capital spirits, you put on the proud man again. You may meet her, but you say nothing of your struggles;—oh no, not one word of that!—but you talk with amazing rapidity about your games, or what not; and you never—never give her another peep into your boyish heart!

For a week, you do not see her,—nor for a month,—nor two months—nor three.

—Puff—puff once more; there is only a little nauseous smoke; and now—my cigar is gone out altogether. I must light again.

II

❧ With a Wisp of Paper

There are those who throw away a cigar, when once gone out; they must needs have plenty more. But nobody that I ever heard of, keeps a cedar box of hearts, labelled at Havanna. Alas, there is but one to light!

But can a heart once lit, be lighted again? Authority on this point is worth something; yet it should be impartial authority. I should be loth to take in evidence, for the fact,—however it might tally with my hope, the affidavit of some rakish old widower, who had cast his weeds, before the grass had started on the mound of his affliction; and I should be as slow to take, in way of rebutting testimony, the oath of any sweet young girl, just becoming conscious of her heart's existence—by its loss.

Very much, it seems to me, depends upon the quality of the fire: and I can easily conceive of one so pure, so constant, so exhausting, that if it were once gone out, whether in the chills of death, or under the blasts of pitiless fortune, there would be no rekindling;—simply because there would be nothing left to kindle. And I can imagine too a fire so earnest, and so true, that whatever malice might urge, or a devilish ingenuity devise, there could no other be found, high or low, far or near, which should not so contrast with the first, as to make it seem cold as ice.

I remember in an old play of Davenport's,[81] the hero is led to doubt his mistress; he is worked upon by slanders, to quit her altogether,—though he has loved, and does still love passionately. She bids him adieu, with large tears dropping from her eyes, (and I lay down my cigar, to recite it aloud, fancying all the while, with a varlet impudence, that some Abstemia is repeating it to me)—

> ——Farewell Lorenzo,
> Whom my soul doth love; if you ever marry,
> May you meet a good wife; so good, that you
> May not suspect her, nor may she be worthy
> Of your suspicion: And if you hear hereafter
> That I am dead, inquire but my last words,
> And you shall know that to the last I loved you.
> And when you walk forth with your second choice,
> Into the pleasant fields, and by chance talk of me,
> Imagine that you see me thin, and pale,
> Strewing your path with flowers!

——Poor Abstemia! Lorenzo never could find such another,—there never could be such another, for such Lorenzo.

To blaze anew, it is essential that the old fire be utterly gone; and can any truly-lighted soul ever grow cold, except the grave cover it? The poets all say no: Othello, had he lived a thousand years would not have loved again;—Desdemona,—nor Andromache,—nor Medea,—nor Ulysses,—nor Hamlet. But in the cool wreaths of the pleasant smoke, let us see what truth is in the poets.

—What is love,—mused I,—at the first, but a mere fancy? There is a prettiness, that your soul cleaves to, as your eye to a pleasant flower, or your ear to a soft melody. Presently, admiration comes in, as a sort of balance-wheel for the eccentric revolutions of your fancy; and your admiration is touched off with such neat quality as respect. Too much of this indeed, they say, deadens the fancy; and so retards the action of the heart machinery. But with a proper modicum to serve as a stock, devotion is grafted in; and then, by an agreeable and confused mingling, all these qualities, and affections of the soul, become transfused into that vital feeling, called Love.

Your heart seems to have gone over to another and better counterpart of your humanity; what is left of you, seems the mere husk of some kernel that has been stolen. It is not an emotion of yours, which is making very easy voyages towards another

---

[81]Edward Davenport (1815–1877) was one of the nineteenth-century America's most skillful and popular actors.

soul,—that may be shortened, or lengthened, at will; but it is a passion, that is only yours, because it is *there;* the more it lodges there, the more keenly you feel it to be yours.

The qualities that feed this passion, may indeed belong to you; but they never gave birth to such an one before, simply because there was no place in which it could grow. Nature is very provident in these matters. The chrysalis does not burst, until there is a wing to help the gauze-fly upward. The shell does not break, until the bird can breathe; nor does the swallow quit its nest, until its wings are tipped with the airy oars.

This passion of love is strong, just in proportion as the atmosphere it finds, is tender of its life. Let that atmosphere change into too great coldness, and the passion becomes a wreck,—not yours, because it is not worth your having;—nor vital, because it has lost the soil where it grew. But is it not laying the reproach in a high quarter, to say that those qualities of the heart which begot this passion, are exhausted, and will not thenceforth germinate through all of your life time?

——Take away the worm-eaten frame from your arbour plant, and the wrenched arms of the despoiled climber will not at the first, touch any new trellis; they cannot in a day, change the habit of a year. But let the new support stand firmly, and the needy tendrils will presently lay hold upon the stranger; and your plant will regain its pride and pomp;—cherishing perhaps in its bent figure, a memento of the Old; but in its more earnest, and abounding life, mindful only of its sweet dependance on the New.

Let the Poets say what they will, these affections of ours are not blind, stupid creatures, to starve under polar snows, when the very breezes of Heaven are the appointed messengers to guide them toward warmth and sunshine!

——And with a little suddenness of manner, I tear off a wisp of paper, and holding it in the blaze of my lamp, relight my cigar: It does not burn so easily perhaps as at first:—it wants warming, before it will catch; but presently, it is in a broad, full glow, that throws light into the corners of my room.

——Just so,—thought I,—the love of youth, which succeeds the crackling blaze of boyhood, makes a broader flame, though it may not be so easily kindled. A mere dainty step, or a curling lock, or a soft blue eye are not enough; but in her, who has quickened the new blaze, there is a blending of all these, with a certain sweetness of soul, that finds expression in whatever feature or motion you look upon. Her charms steal over you gently, and almost imperceptibly. You think that she is a pleasant companion—nothing more: and you find the opinion strongly confirmed day by day;—so well confirmed, indeed, that you begin to wonder—why it is, that she is such a delightful companion? It cannot be her eye, for you have seen eyes almost as pretty as Nelly's; nor can it be her mouth, though Nelly's mouth is certainly very sweet. And you keep studying what on earth it can be that makes you so earnest to be near her, or to listen to her voice. The study is pleasant. You do not know any study that is more so; or which you accomplish with less mental fatigue.

Upon a sudden, some fine day, when the air is balmy, and the recollection of Nelly's voice and manner, more balmy still, you wonder—if you are in love? When a man has such a wonder, he is either very near love, or he is very far away from it; it is a wonder, that is either suggested by his hope, or by that entanglement of feeling which blunts all his perceptions.

But if not in love, you have at least a strong fancy,—so strong, that you tell your friends carelessly, that she is a nice girl,—nay, a beautiful girl; and if your education has been bad, you strengthen the epithet on your own tongue, with a very wicked expletive:—of which the mildest form would be—'deuced fine girl!' Presently, however, you get beyond this; and your companionship, and your wonder, relapse into a constant, quiet habit of unmistakeable love:—not impulsive, quick, and fiery, like the first; but mature and calm. It is as if it were born with your soul, and the recognition of it was rather an old remembrance, than a fresh passion. It does not seek to gratify its exuberance, and force, with such relief as night-serenades, or any Jacques-like[82] meditations in the forest; but it is a quiet, still joy, that floats on your hope, into the years to come,—making the prospect all sunny and joyful.

It is a kind of oil and balm for whatever was stormy, or harmful; it gives a permanence to the smile of existence. It does not make the sea of your life turbulent with high emotions, as if a strong wind were blowing;—but it is as if an Aphrodite had broken on the surface, and the ripples were spreading with a sweet, low sound, and widening far out to the very shores of time.

There is no need now, as with the boy, to bolster up your feelings with extravagant vows: even should you try this in her presence, the words are lacking to put such vows in. So soon as you reach them, they fail you: and the oath only quivers on the lip, or tells its story by a pressure of the fingers. You wear a brusque, pleasant air with your acquaintances, and hint—with a sly look—at possible changes in your circumstances. Of an evening, you are kind to the most unattractive of the wall-flowers,—if only your Nelly is away; and you have a sudden charity for street beggars, with pale children. You catch yourself taking a step in one of the new Polkas, upon a country walk: and wonder immensely at the number of bright days which succeed each other, without leaving a single stormy gap, for your old melancholy moods. Even the chambermaids at your hotel, never did their duty one half so well; and as for your man Tom, he is become a perfect pattern of a fellow.

My cigar is in a fine glow; but it has gone out once, and it may go out again.

—You begin to talk of marriage; but some obstinate Papa, or guardian uncle think that it will never do;—that it is quite too soon, or that Nelly is a mere girl. Or some of your wild oats,—quite forgotten by yourself,—shoot up on the vision of a staid Mamma, and throw a very damp shadow on your character. Or the old lady has an ambition of another sort, which you, a simple, earnest, plodding, bachelor, can never gratify;—being of only passable appearance, and unschooled in the fashions of the world, you will be eternally rubbing the elbows of the old lady's pride.

All this will be strangely afflictive to one who has been living for quite a number of weeks, or months, in a pleasant dream-land, where there were no five per cents, or reputations, but only a very full, and delirious flow of feeling. What care you for any position, except a position near the being that you love? What wealth do you prize, except a wealth of heart, that shall never know diminution;—or for reputation, except that of truth, and of honor? How hard it would break upon these pleasant idealities, to have a weazen-faced old guardian, set his arm in yours, and tell you how tenderly he has at heart

---

[82]private

the happiness of his niece;—and reason with you about your very small, and sparse dividends, and your limited business;—and caution you,—for he has a lively regard for your interests,—about continuing your addresses!

——The kind old curmudgeon!

Your man Tom has grown suddenly a very stupid fellow; and all your charity for withered wall-flowers, is gone. Perhaps in your wrath the suspicion comes over you, that she too wishes you were something higher, or more famous, or richer, or anything but what you are!—a very dangerous suspicion: for no man with any true nobility of soul, can ever make his heart the slave of another's condescension.

But no,—you will not, you cannot believe this of Nelly;—that face of hers is too mild and gracious; and her manner, as she takes your hand, after your heart is made sad, and turns away those rich blue eyes,—shadowed more deeply than ever by the long and moistened fringe;—and the exquisite softness, and meaning of the pressure of those little fingers;—and the low, half sob; and the heaving of that bosom, in its struggles between love, and duty,—all forbid. Nelly, you could swear, is tenderly indulgent, like the fond creature that she is, toward all your short-comings; and would not barter your strong love, and your honest heart, for the greatest magnate in the land.

What a spur to effort is the confiding love of a true-hearted woman! That last fond look of hers, hopeful, and encouraging, has more power within it to nerve your soul to high deeds, than all the admonitions of all your tutors. Your heart, beating large with hope, quickens the flow upon the brain; and you make wild vows to win greatness. But alas, this is a great world—very full, and very rough;

——all up-hill work when we would do;
All down-hill, when we suffer.*

Hard, withering toil only can achieve a name; and long days, and months, and years, must be passed in the chase of that bubble—reputation; which when once grasped, breaks in your eager clutch, into a hundred lesser bubbles, that soar above you still!

A clandestine meeting from time to time, and a note or two tenderly written, keep up the blaze in your heart. But presently, the lynx-eyed old guardian—so tender of your interests, and hers,—forbids even this irregular and unsatisfying correspondence. Now you can feed yourself only on stray glimpses of her figure—as full of sprightliness and grace, as ever; and that beaming face, you are half sorry to see from time to time,—still beautiful. You struggle with your moods of melancholy, and wear bright looks yourself—bright to her, and very bright to the eye of the old curmudgeon, who has snatched your heart away. It will never do to show your weakness to a man.

At length, on some pleasant morning, you learn that she is gone,—too far away to be seen, too closely guarded to be reached. For a while you throw down your books, and abandon your toil in despair,—thinking very bitter thoughts, and making very helpless resolves.

My cigar is still burning; but it will require constant and strong respiration, to keep it in a glow.

------

*Festus.

A letter or two dispatched at random, relieve the excess of your fever; until with practice, these random letters have even less heat in them, than the heat of your study, or of your business. Grief—thank God!—is not so progressive, or so cumulative as joy. For a time, there is a pleasure in the mood with which you recal your broken hopes; and with which you selfishly link hers to the shattered wreck; but absence, and ignorance tame the point of your woe. You call up the image of Nelly, adorning other and distant scenes. You see the tearful smile give place to a blithesome cheer; and the thought of you that shaded her fair face so long, fades under the sunshine of gaiety; or at best, it only seems to cross that white forehead, like a playful shadow, that a fleecy cloud-remnant will fling upon a sunny lawn.

As for you, the world with its whirl and roar, is deafening the sweet, distant notes, that come up through old, choked channels of the affections. Life is calling for earnestness, and not for regrets. So the months, and the years slip by; your bachelor habit grows easy and light with wearing; you have mourned enough, to smile at the violent mourning of others; and you have enjoyed enough, to sigh over their little eddies of delight. Dark shades, and delicious streaks of crimson and gold colour lie upon your life. Your heart with all its weight of ashes, can yet sparkle at the sound of a fairy step; and your face can yet open into a round of joyous smiles,—that are almost hopes,—in the presence of some bright-eyed girl.

But amid this, there will float over you from time to time, a midnight trance, in which you will hear again with a thirsty ear, the witching melody of the days that are gone; and you will wake from it with a shudder into the cold resolves of your lonely, and manly life. But the shudder passes as easy as night from morning. Tearful regrets, and memories that touch to the quick, are dull weapons to break through the panoply of your seared, eager, and ambitious manhood. They only venture out like timid, white-winged flies, when night is come; and at the first glimpse of the dawn, they shrivel up, and lie without a flutter, in some corner of your soul.

And when, years after, you learn that she has returned—a woman, there is a slight glow, but no tumultuous bound of the heart. Life, and time have worried you down like a spent hound. Thy world has given you a habit of easy and unmeaning smiles. You half accuse yourself of ingratitude and forgetfulness; but the accusation does not oppress you. It does not even distract your attention from the morning journal. You cannot work yourself into a respectable degree of indignation against the old gentleman—her guardian.

You sigh—poor thing!—and in a very flashy waistcoat, you venture a morning call.

She meets you kindly,—a comely, matronly dame in gingham, with her curls all gathered under a high-topped comb; and she presents to you two little boys in smart crimson jackets, dressed up with braid. And you dine with Madame—a family party; and the weazen-faced old gentleman meets you with a most pleasant shake of the hand,—hints that you were among his niece's earliest friends, and hopes that you are getting on well?

——Capitally well!

And the boys toddle in at dessert—Dick to get a plum from your own dish; Tom to be kissed by his rosy-faced papa. In short, you are made perfectly at home; and you sit over your wine for an hour, in a cozy smoke with the gentlemanly uncle, and with the very courteous husband of your second flame.

It is all very jovial at the table; for good wine, is I find, a great strengthener of the bachelor heart. But afterward, when night has fairly set in, and the blaze of your fire goes flickering over your lonely quarters, you heave a deep sigh. And as your thought runs back to the perfidious Louise, and calls up the married, and matronly Nelly, you sob over that poor dumb heart within you, which craves so madly a free and joyous utterance! And as you lean over with your forehead in your hands, and your eyes fall upon the old hound slumbering on the rug,—the tears start, and you wish,—that you had married years ago;—and that you too had your pair of prattling boys, to drive away the loneliness of your solitary hearth stone.

——My cigar would not go; it was fairly out. But with true bachelor obstinacy, I vowed that I would light again.

III

❧ Lighted with a Match

I hate a match. I feel sure that brimstone matches were never made in heaven; and it is sad to think, that with few exceptions, matches are all of them tipped with brimstone.

But my taper having burned out, and the coals being all dead upon the hearth, a match is all that is left to me.

All matches will not blaze on the first trial; and there are those, that with the most indefatigable coaxings, never show a spark. They may indeed leave in their trail phosphorescent streaks; but you can no more light your cigar at them, than you can kindle your heart, at the covered wife-trails, which the infernal, gossipping, old match-makers will lay in your path.

Was there ever a bachelor of seven and twenty, I wonder, who has not been haunted by pleasant old ladies, and trim, excellent, good-natured, married friends, who talk to him about nice matches—'very nice matches,'—matches, which never go off? And who, pray, has not had some kind old uncle, to fill two sheets for him, (perhaps in the time of heavy postages) about some most eligible connection,—'of highly respectable parentage!'

What a delightful thing, surely, for a withered bachelor, to bloom forth in the dignity of an ancestral tree! What a precious surprise for him, who has all his life worshipped the wing-heeled Mercury,[83] to find on a sudden, a great stock of preserved, and most respectable Penates![84]

——In God's name,—thought I, puffing vehemently,—what is a man's heart given him for, if not to choose, where his heart's blood, every drop of it is flowing? Who is going to dam these billowy tides of the soul, whose roll is ordered by a planet greater than the moon;—and that planet—Venus? Who is going to shift this vane of my desires, when every breeze that passes in my heaven is keeping it all the more strongly, to its fixed bearings?

---

[83]Roman messenger god, associated with speed and business.

[84]Ancient Roman household gods.

Beside this, there are the money matches, urged upon you by disinterested bachelor friends, who would be very proud to see you at the head of an establishment. And I must confess that this kind of talk has a pleasant jingle about it; and is one of the cleverest aids to a bachelor's day-dreams, that can well be imagined. And let not the pouting lady condemn me, without a hearing.

It is certainly cheerful to think,—for a contemplative bachelor,—that the pretty ermine which so sets off the transparent hue of your imaginary wife, or the lace which lies so bewitchingly upon the superb roundness of her form,—or the graceful boddice, trimmed to a line, which is of such exquisite adaptation to her lithe figure, will be always at her command;—nay, that these are only units among the chameleon hues, under which you shall feed upon her beauty! I want to know if it is not a pretty cabinet picture, for fancy to luxuriate upon—that of a sweet wife, who is cheating hosts of friends into love, sympathy and admiration, by the modest munificence of her wealth? Is it not rather agreeable, to feed your hopeful soul upon that abundance, which, while it supplies her need, will give a range to her loving charities;—which will keep from her brow the shadows of anxiety, and will sublime her gentle nature, by adding to it the grace of an angel of mercy?

Is it not rich, in those days when the pestilent humours of bachelorhood hang heavy on you, to foresee in that shadowy realm, where hope is a native, the quiet of a home, made splendid with attractions; and made real, by the presence of her, who bestows them?—Upon my word—thought I, as I continued puffing,—such a match must make a very grateful lighting of one's inner sympathies; nor am I prepared to say, that such associations would not add force to the most abstract love imaginable.

Think of it for a moment;—what is it, that we poor fellows love? We love, if one may judge for himself, over his cigar,—gentleness, beauty, refinement, generosity, and intelligence,—and far above these, a returning love, made up of all these qualities, and gaining upon your love, day by day, and month by month, like a sunny morning, gaining upon the frosts of night.

But wealth is a great means of refinement; and it is a security for gentleness, since it removes disturbing anxieties; and it is a pretty promoter of intelligence, since it multiplies the avenues for its reception; and it is a good basis for a generous habit of life; it even equips beauty, neither hardening its hand with toil, nor tempting the wrinkles to come early. But whether it provokes greatly that returning passion,—that abnegation of soul,—that sweet trustfulness, and abiding affection, which are to clothe your heart with joy, is far more doubtful. Wealth while it gives so much, asks much in return; and the soul that is grateful to mammon, is not over ready to be grateful for intensity of love. It is hard to gratify those, who have nothing left to gratify.

Heaven help the man who having wearied his soul with delays and doubts, or exhausted the freshness, and exuberance of his youth,—by a hundred little dallyings of love,—consigns himself at length to the issues of what people call a nice match—whether of money, or of family!

Heaven help you—(I brushed the ashes from my cigar) when you begin to regard marriage as only a respectable institution, and under the advices of staid old friends, begin to look about you for some very respectable wife. You may admire her figure, and her family; and bear pleasantly in mind the very casual mention which has been made by some of your penetrating friends,—that she has large expectations. You think that she would make a very capital appearance at the head of your table; nor in the event of your coming to any public honor, would she make you blush for her breeding. She talks well, exceedingly well; and her face has its charms; especially under a little excitement. Her dress is elegant, and tasteful, and she is constantly remarked upon by all your friends, as a 'nice person.' Some good old lady, in whose pew she occasionally sits on a Sunday, or to whom she has sometime sent a papier maché card-case, for the show-box of some Dorcas benevolent society, thinks,—with a sly wink,—that she would make a fine wife for—somebody.

She certainly *has* an elegant figure; and the marriage of some half dozen of your old flames, warn you that time is slipping and your chances failing. And in the pleasant warmth of some after-dinner mood, you resolve—with her image in her prettiest pelisse drifting across your brain—that you will marry. Now comes the pleasant excitement of the chase; and whatever family dignity may surround her, only adds to the pleasurable glow of the pursuit. You give an hour more to your toilette, and a hundred or two more, a year, to your tailor. All is orderly, dignified and gracious. Charlotte is a sensible woman, every body says; and you believe it yourself. You agree in your talk about books, and churches, and flowers. Of course she has good taste—for she accepts you. The acceptance is dignified, elegant, and even courteous.

You receive numerous congratulations; and your old friend Tom writes you—that he hears you are going to marry a splendid woman; and all the old ladies say—what a capital match! And your business partner, who is a married man, and something of a wag—'sympathizes sincerely.' Upon the whole, you feel a little proud of your arrangement. You write to an old friend in the country, that you are to marry presently Miss Charlotte of such a street, whose father was something very fine, in his way; and whose father before him was very distinguished;—you add, in a postscript, that she is easily situated, and has 'expectations.' Your friend, who has a wife that he loves, and that loves him, writes back kindly—'hoping you may be happy;' and hoping so yourself, you light your cigar,—one of your last bachelor cigars,—with the margin of his letter.

The match goes off with a brilliant marriage;—at which you receive a very elegant welcome from your wife's spinster cousins,—and drink a great deal of champagne with her bachelor uncles. And as you take the dainty hand of your bride,—very magnificent under that bridal wreath, and with her face lit up by a brilliant glow,—your eye, and your soul, for the first time, grow full. And as your arm circles that elegant figure, and you draw her toward you, feeling that she is yours,—there is a bound at your heart, that makes you think your soul-life is now whole, and earnest. All your early dreams, and imaginations, come flowing on your thought, like bewildering music; and as you gaze upon her,—the admiration of that crowd,—it seems to you, that all that your heart prizes, is made good by the accident of marriage.

—Ah—thought I, brushing off the ashes again,—bridal pictures are not home pictures; and the hour at the altar, is but a poor type of the waste of years!

Your household is elegantly ordered; Charlotte has secured the best of housekeepers, and she meets the compliments of your old friends who come to dine with you, with a suavity, that is never at fault. And they tell you,—after the cloth is removed, and you sit quietly smoking in memory of the old times,—that she is a splendid woman. Even the old ladies who come for occasional charities, think Madame a pattern of a lady; and so think her old admirers, whom she receives still with an easy grace, that half puzzles you. And as you stand by the ball room door, at two of the morning, with your Charlotte's shawl upon your arm, some little panting fellow will confirm the general opinion, by telling you that Madame is a magnificent dancer; and Monsieur le Comte, will praise extravagantly her French. You are grateful for all this; but you have an uncommonly serious way of expressing your gratitude.

You think you ought to be a very happy fellow; and yet long shadows do steal over your thought; and you wonder that the sight of your Charlotte in the dress you used to admire so much, does not scatter them to the winds; but it does not. You feel coy about putting your arm around that delicately robed figure,—you might derange the plaitings of her dress. She is civil towards you; and tender towards your bachelor friends. She talks with dignity,—adjusts her lace cape,—and hopes you will make a figure in the world, for the sake of the family. Her cheek is never soiled with a tear; and her smiles are frequent, especially when you have some spruce young fellows at your table.

You catch sight of occasional notes perhaps, whose superscription you do not know; and some of her admirers' attentions become so pointed, and constant, that your pride is stirred. It would be silly to show jealousy; but you suggest to your 'dear'—as you sip your tea,—the slight impropriety of her action.

Perhaps you fondly long for some little scene, as a proof of wounded confidence;— but no—nothing of that; she trusts, (calling you 'my dear,') that she knows how to sustain the dignity of her position.

You are too sick at heart, for comment, or for reply.

—And is this the intertwining of soul, of which you had dreamed in the days that are gone? Is this the blending of sympathies that was to steal from life its bitterness; and spread over care and suffering, the sweet, ministering hand of kindness, and of love? Aye, you may well wander back to your bachelor club, and make the hours long at the journals, or at play—killing the flagging lapse of your life! Talk sprightly with your old friends,—and mimic the joy you have not; or you will wear a bad name upon your hearth, and head. Never suffer your Charlotte to catch sight of the tears which in bitter hours, may start from your eye; or to hear the sighs which in your times of solitary musings, may break forth sudden, and heavy. Go on counterfeiting your life, as you have begun. It was a nice match; and you are a nice husband!

But you have a little boy, thank God, toward whom your heart runs out freely; and you love to catch him in his respite from your well-ordered nursery, and the tasks of his teachers—alone;—and to spend upon him a little of that depth of feeling, which through so many years has scarce been stirred. You play with him at his games; you fondle him; you take him to your bosom.

—But papa—he says—see how you have tumbled my collar. What shall I tell mamma?

——Tell her, my boy, that I love you!

Ah, thought I—(my cigar was getting dull, and nauseous,)—is there not a spot in your heart, that the gloved hand of your elegant wife has never reached:—that you wish it might reach?

You go to see a far-away friend: his was not a 'nice match:' he was married years before you: and yet the beaming looks of his wife, and his lively smile, are as fresh and honest as they were years ago; and they make you ashamed of your disconsolate humour. Your stay is lengthened, but the home letters are not urgent for your return: yet they are marvellously proper letters, and rounded with a French *adieu*. You could have wished a little scrawl from your boy at the bottom, in the place of the postscript which gives you the names of a new opera troupe; and you hint as much—a very bold stroke for you.

Ben,—she says,—writes too shamefully.

And at your return, there is no great anticipation of delight; in contrast with the old dreams, that a pleasant summer's journey has called up, your parlour as you enter it—so elegant, so still—so modish—seems the charnel-house of your heart.

By and by, you fall into weary days of sickness; you have capital nurses—nurses highly recommended—nurses who never make mistakes—nurses who have served long in the family. But alas for that heart of sympathy, and for that sweet face, shaded with your pain—like a soft landscape with flying clouds—you have none of them! Your pattern wife may come in from time to time to look after your nurse, or to ask after your sleep, and glide out—her silk dress rustling upon the door—like dead leaves in the cool night breezes of winter. Or perhaps after putting this chair in its place, and adjusting to a more tasteful fold that curtain—she will ask you, with a tone that might mean sympathy, if it were not a stranger to you,—if she can do anything more.

Thank her—as kindly as you can, and close your eyes, and dream:—or rouse up, to lay your hand upon the head of your little boy,—to drink in health, and happiness, from his earnest look, as he gazes strangely upon your pale and shrunken forehead. Your smile even, ghastly with long suffering, disturbs him; there is no interpreter, save the heart, between you.

Your parched lips feel strangely, to his flushed, healthful face; and he steps about on tip-toe, at a motion from the nurse, to look at all those rosy-colored medicines upon the table,—and he takes your cane from the corner, and passes his hand over the smooth ivory head; and he runs his eye along the wall from picture to picture, till it rests on one he knows,—a figure in bridal dress,—beautiful, almost fond;—and he forgets himself, and says aloud—'there's mamma!'

The nurse puts her finger to her lip; you waken from your doze to see where your eager boy is looking; and your eyes too, take in much as they can of that figure—now shadowy to your fainting vision—doubly shadowy to your fainting heart!

From day to day, you sink from life: the physician says the end is not far off; why should it be? There is very little elastic force within you to keep the end away. Madame is called, and your little boy. Your sight is dim, but they whisper that she is beside your bed; and you reach out your hand—both hands. You fancy you hear a sob:—a strange sound! It seems as if it came from distant years—a confused, broken sigh, sweeping over the long stretch of your life: and a sigh from your heart—not audible—answers it.

Your trembling fingers clutch the hand of your little boy, and you drag him toward you, and move your lips, as if you would speak to him; and they place his head near you, so that you feel his fine hair brushing your cheek.—My boy, you must love—your mother!

Your other hand feels a quick, convulsive grasp, and something like a tear drops upon your face. Good God!—Can it be indeed a tear?

You strain your vision, and a feeble smile flits over your features, as you seem to see her figure—the figure of the painting—bending over you; and you feel a bound at your heart—the same bound that you felt on your bridal morning;—the same bound which you used to feel in the spring-time of your life.

——Only one—rich, full bound of the heart;——that is all!

————My cigar was out. I could not have lit it again, if I would. It was wholly burned.

"Aunt Tabithy"—said I, as I finished reading,—"may I smoke now under your rose tree?"

Aunt Tabithy who had laid down her knitting to hear me,—smiled,—brushed a tear from her old eyes,—said,—"Yes—Isaac," and having scratched the back of her head, with the disengaged needle, resumed her knitting.

FOURTH REVERIE

Morning, Noon, and Evening

It is a Spring day under the oaks—the loved oaks of a once cherished home,—now alas, mine no longer!

I had sold the old farm-house, and the groves, and the cool springs, where I had bathed my head in the heats of summer; and with the first warm days of May, they were to pass from me forever. Seventy years they had been in the possession of my mother's family; for seventy years, they had borne the same name of proprietorship; for seventy years, the Lares of our country home, often neglected, almost forgotten,—yet brightened from time to time, by gleams of heart-worship, had held their place in the sweet valley of Elmgrove.

And in this changeful, bustling, American life of ours, seventy years is no child's holiday. The hurry of action, and progress, may pass over it with quick step; but the foot-prints are many and deep. You surely will not wonder that it made me sad and thought-ful, to break the chain of years, that bound to my heart, the oaks, the hills, the springs, the valley——and such a valley!

A wild stream runs through it,—large enough to make a river for English land-scape,—winding between rich banks, where in summer time, the swallows build their nests, and brood by myriads.

Tall elms rise here and there along the margin, and with their uplifted arms, and leafy spray, throw great patches of shade upon the meadow. Old lion-like oaks too, where the meadow-soil hardens into rolling upland, fasten to the ground with their ridgy roots; and with their gray, scraggy limbs, make delicious shelter for the panting workers, or for the herds of August.

Westward of the stream, where I am lying, the banks roll up swiftly into sloping hills, covered with groves of oaks, and green pasture lands, dotted with mossy rocks. And farther on, where some wood has been swept down, some ten years gone, by the axe, the new growth, heavy with the luxuriant foliage of spring, covers wide spots of the slanting land;—while some dead tree in the midst, still stretches out its bare arms to the blast—a solitary mourner, over the wreck of its forest brothers.

Eastward, the ridgy bank passes into wavy meadows, upon whose farther edge, you see the roofs of an old mansion, with tall chimneys and taller elm-trees shading it. Beyond, the hills rise gently, and sweep away into wood-crowned heights, that are blue with distance. At the upper end of the valley, the stream is lost to the eye, in a wide swamp wood, which in the autumn time is covered with a scarlet sheet, blotched here and there by the dark crimson stains of the ash-tops. Farther on, the hills crowd close to the brook, and come down with granite boulders, and scattered birch trees, and beeches,—under which, upon the smoky mornings of May, I have time and again loitered, and thrown my line into the pools, which curl, dark, and still, under their tangled roots.

Below, and looking, southward, through the openings of the oaks that shade me, I see a broad stretch of meadow, with glimpses of the silver surface of the stream, and of the giant solitary elms, and of some old maple that has yielded to the spring tides, and now dips its lower boughs in the insidious current;—and of clumps of alders, and willow tufts,—above which even now, the black-and-white coated Bob-o'-Lincoln, is wheeling his musical flight, while his quieter mate sits swaying on the topmost twigs.

A quiet road passes within a short distance of me, and crosses the brook by a rude timber bridge; beside the bridge, is a broad glassy pool, shaded by old maples, and hickories, where the cattle drink each morning, on their way to the hill pastures. A step or two beyond the stream, a lane branches across the meadows, to the mansion with the tall chimneys. I can just remember now, the stout, broad-shouldered old gentleman, with his white hat, his long white hair, and his white headed cane, who built the house, and who farmed the whole valley around me. He is gone, long since; and lies in a grave-yard looking upon the sea! The elms that he planted shake their weird arms over the mouldering roofs; and his fruit-garden shows only a battered phalanx of mossy limbs, which will scarce tempt the July marauders.

In the other direction, upon this side the brook, the road is lost to view, among the trees; but if I were to follow the windings upon the hill-side, it would bring me shortly upon the old home of my grandfather; there is no pleasure in wandering there now. The woods that sheltered it from the northern winds, are cut down; the tall cherries that made the yard one leafy bower, are dead. The cornice is straggling from the eaves; the porch has fallen; the stone chimney is yawning with wide gaps. Within, it is even worse; the floors sway upon the mouldering beams; the doors all sag from their hinges; the rude frescos upon the parlor-wall are peeling off; all is going to decay.——And my grandfather sleeps in a little grave-yard, by the garden-wall.

A lane branches from the country road, within a few yards of me, and leads back, along the edge of the meadow, to the homely cottage, which has been my special care. Its gray porch, and chimney are thrown into rich relief, by a grove of oaks that skirts the hill behind it; and the doves are flying uneasily about the open doors of the granary, and barns. The morning sun shines pleasantly on the gray group of buildings; and the lowing of the cows, not yet driven afield, adds to the charming homeliness of the scene. But alas, for the poor azalias, and laurels, and vines, that I had put out upon the little knoll before the cottage door—they are all of them trodden down; only one poor creeper hangs its loose tresses to the lattice, all dishevelled, and forlorn!

This bye-lane which opens upon my farm-house, leaves the road in the middle of a grove of oaks; the brown gate swings upon an oak tree,—the brown gate closes upon an oak tree. There is a rustic seat, built between two veteran trees, that rise from a little hillock near by. Half a century ago, there was a rustic seat on the same hillock—between the same veteran trees. I can trace marks of the old blotches upon the bark, and the scars of the nails, upon the scathed trunks. Time, and time again, it has been renewed. This, the last, was built by my own hands,—a cheerful, and a holy duty.

Sixty years ago, they tell me, my grandfather used to loiter here with his gun, while his hounds lay around under the scattered oaks. Now he sleeps, as I said, in the little grave-yard yonder, where I can see one or two white tablets glimmering through the foliage. I never knew him; he died, as the brown stone table says, aged twenty-six. Yesterday I climbed the wall that skirts the yard, and plucked a flower from his tomb. I take out now from my pocket book, that flower—a frail, first-blooming violet,—and write upon the slip of paper, into which I have thrust its delicate stem,—'From my grandfather's tomb:—1850.'

But other feet have trod upon this knoll—far more dear to me. The old neighbors have sometimes told me, how they have seen, forty years ago, two rosy-faced girls, idling on this spot, under the shade, and gathering acorns, and making oak-leaved garlands, for their foreheads.——Alas, alas, the garlands they wear now, are not earthly garlands!

Upon that spot, and upon that rustic seat, I am lying this May morning. I have placed my gun against a tree; my shot-pouch I have hung upon a broken limb. I have thrown my feet upon the bench, and lean against one of the gnarled oaks, between which the seat is built. My hat is off; my book and paper, are beside me; and my pencil trembles in my fingers, as I catch sight of those white marble tablets, gleaming through the trees, from the height above me, like beckoning angel faces.——If they were alive!—two more near, and dear friends, in a world where we count friends, by units!

It is morning,—a bright spring morning under the oaks—these loved oaks of a once cherished home. Last night, I slept in yonder mansion, under the elms. The cattle going to the pasture are drinking in the pool by the bridge; the boy who drives them, is making his shrill halloo echo against the hills. The sun has risen fairly over the eastern heights, and shines brightly upon the meadow land, and brightly upon a bend of the brook below me. The birds,—the blue-birds sweetest and noisiest of all,—are singing over me in the branches. A wood-pecker is hammering at a dry limb aloft; and Carlo pricks up his ears, and listens, and looks at me,—then stretches out his head upon his paws, in a warm bit of the sunshine,—and sleeps.

Morning brings back to me the Past, and the past brings up not only its actualities, not only its events, and memories, but—stranger still,—what might have been. Every little circumstance which dawns on the awakened memory, is traced not only to its actual, but to its possible issues.

What a wide world that makes of the Past!—a great and gorgeous,—a rich and holy world! Your fancy fills it up artist-like; the darkness is mellowed off into soft shades; the bright spots are veiled in the sweet atmosphere of distance; and fancy and memory together, make up a rich dream-land of the past.

And now, as I go on to trace upon paper some of the visions that float across that dream-land of the Morning,—I will not—I cannot say, how much comes fancy-wise, and how much from this vaulting memory. Of this, the kind reader shall himself be judge.

I

❧ The Morning

Isabel and I,—she is my cousin, and is seven years old, and I am ten,—are sitting together on the bank of the stream, under an oak tree that leans half way over to the water. I am much stronger than she, and taller by a head. I hold in my hands a little alder rod, with which I am fishing for the roach and minnows, that play in the pool below us.

She is watching the cork tossing on the water, or playing with the captured fish that lie upon the bank. She has auburn ringlets that fall down upon her shoulders; and her straw hat lies back upon them, held only by the strip of ribbon, that passes under her chin. But the sun does not shine upon her head; for the oak tree above us is full of leaves; and only here and there, a dimple of the sunlight plays upon the pool, where I am fishing.

Her eye is hazel, and bright; and now and then she turns it on me with a look of girl-ish curiosity, as I lift up my rod,—and again in playful menace, as she grasps in her lit-tle fingers one of the dead fish, and threatens to throw it back upon the stream. Her little feet hang over the edge of the bank; and from time to time, she reaches down to dip her toe in the water; and laughs a girlish laugh of defiance, as I scold her for frightening away the fishes.

"Bella," I say, "what if you should tumble in the river?"

"But I won't."

"Yes, but if you should?"

"Why then you would pull me out."

"But if I wouldn't pull you out?"

"But I know you would; wouldn't you, Paul?"

"What makes you think so, Bella?"

"Because you love Bella."

"How do you know I love Bella?"

"Because once you told me so; and because you pick flowers for me that I cannot reach; and because you let me take your rod, when you have a fish upon it."

"But that's no reason, Bella."

"Then what is, Paul?"

"I'm sure I don't know, Bella."

A little fish has been nibbling for a long time at the bait; the cork has been bobbing up and down;—and now he is fairly hooked, and pulls away toward the bank, and you cannot see the cork.

—"Here, Bella, quick!"—and she springs eagerly to clasp her little hands around the rod. But the fish has dragged it away on the other side of me; and as she reaches farther, and farther, she slips, cries—"oh, Paul!"—and falls into the water.

The stream they told us, when we came, was over a man's head;—it is surely over little Isabel's. I fling down the rod, and thrusting one hand into the roots that support the overhanging bank, I grasp at her hat, as she comes up; but the ribbons give way, and I see the terribly earnest look upon her face as she goes down again. Oh, my mother!—thought I,—if you were only here!

But she rises again; this time, I thrust my hand into her dress, and struggling hard, keep her at the top, until I can place my foot down upon a projecting root; and so bracing myself, I drag her to the bank and having climbed up, take hold of her belt firmly with both hands, and drag her out; and poor Isabel, choked, chilled, and wet, is lying upon the grass.

I commence crying aloud. The workmen in the fields hear me, and come down. One takes Isabel in his arms, and I follow on foot to our uncle's home upon the hill.

—"Oh my children!"—says my mother; and she takes Isabel in her arms; and presently with dry clothes, and blazing wood-fire, little Bella smiles again. I am at my mother's knee.

"I told you so, Paul," says Isabel,—"aunty, doesn't Paul love me?"

"I hope so, Bella," said my mother.

"I know so," said I; and kissed her cheek.

And how did I know it? The boy does not ask; the man does. Oh, the freshness, the honesty, the vigor of a boy's heart!—how the memory of it refreshes like the first gush of spring, or the break of an April shower!

But boyhood has its PRIDE, as well as its LOVES.

My uncle is a tall, hard-faced man: I fear him when he calls me—"child"; I love him when he calls me—"Paul." He is almost always busy with his books; and when I steal into the library door, as I sometimes do, with a string of fish, or a heaping basket of nuts to show to him,—he looks for a moment curiously at them, sometimes takes them in his fingers,—gives them back to me, and turns over the leaves of his book. You are afraid to ask him, if you have not worked bravely; yet you want to do so.

You sidle out softly, and go to your mother; she scarce looks at your little stores; but she draws you to her with her arm, and prints a kiss upon your forehead. Now your tongue is unloosed; that kiss, and that action have done it; you will tell what capital luck you have had; and you hold up your tempting trophies;—"are they not great, mother?" But she is looking in your face, and not at your prize.

"Take them, mother," and you lay the basket upon her lap.

"Thank you, Paul, I do not wish them: but you must give some to Bella."

And away you go to find laughing, playful, cousin Isabel. And we sit down together on the grass, and I pour out my stores between us. "You shall take, Bella, what you wish in your apron, and then when study hours are over, we will have such a time down by the big rock in the meadow!"

"But I do not know if papa will let me," says Isabel.

"Bella," I say, "do you love your papa?"

"Yes," says Bella, "why not?"

"Because he is so cold; he does not kiss you Bella, so often as my mother does; and besides, when he forbids your going away, he does not say, as mother does,—my little girl will be tired, she had better not go,—but he says only,—Isabel must not go. I wonder what makes him talk so?"

"Why Paul, he is a man, and doesn't——at any rate, I love him, Paul. Besides, my mother is sick, you know."

"But Isabel, my mother will be your mother too. Come Bella, we will go ask her if we may go."

And there I am, the happiest of boys, pleading with the kindest of mothers. And the young heart leans into that mother's heart;—none of the void now that will overtake it like an opening Koran gulf,[85] in the years that are to come. It is joyous, full, and running over!

"You may go," she says, "if your uncle is willing."

"But mamma, I am afraid to ask him; I do not believe he loves me."

"Don't say so, Paul," and she draws you to her side; as if she would supply by her own love, the lacking love of a universe.

"Go, with your cousin Isabel, and ask him kindly; and if he says no,—make no reply."

And with courage, we go hand in hand, and steal in at the library door. There he sits—I seem to see him now,—in the old wainscotted room, covered over with books and pictures; and he wears his heavy-rimmed spectacles, and is poring over some big volume, full of hard words, that are not in any spelling-book. We step up softly; and Isabel lays her little hand upon his arm; and he turns, and says—"well, my little daughter?"

I ask if we may go down to the big rock in the meadow?

He looks at Isabel, and says he is afraid—"we cannot go."

"But why, uncle? It is only a little way, and we will be very careful."

"I am afraid, my children; do not say any more: you can have the pony, and Tray, and play at home."

"But, uncle——"

"You need say no more, my child."

I pinch the hand of little Isabel, and look in her eye,—my own half filling with tears. I feel that my forehead is flushed, and I hide it behind Bella's tresses,—whispering to her at the same time—"let us go."

"What sir," says my uncle, mistaking my meaning—"do you persuade her to disobey?"

Now, I am angry, and say blindly—"no, sir, I didn't!" And then my rising pride will not let me say, that I wished only Isabel should go out with me.

Bella cries; and I shrink out; and am not easy until I have run to bury my head in my mother's bosom. Alas! pride cannot always find such covert! There will be times when it will harrass you strangely; when it will peril friendships,—will sever old, standing intimacy; and then—no resource, but to feed on its own bitterness. Hateful pride!—to be conquered, as a man would conquer an enemy, or it will make whirlpools in the current

---

[85]Voluminous space.

of your affections—nay, turn the whole tide of the heart into rough, and unaccustomed channels!

But boyhood has its GRIEF too, apart from PRIDE.

You love the old dog Tray; and Bella loves him as well as you. He is a noble old fellow, with shaggy hair, and long ears, and big paws, that he will put up into your hand, if you ask him. And he never gets angry when you play with him, and tumble him over in the long grass, and pull his silken ears. Sometimes, to be sure, he will open his mouth, as if he would bite, but when he gets your hand fairly in his jaws, he will scarce leave the print of his teeth upon it. He will swim, too, bravely, and bring ashore all the sticks you throw upon the water; and when you fling a stone to tease him, he swims round and round, and whines, and looks sorry, that he cannot find it.

He will carry a heaping basket full of nuts too in his mouth, and never spill one of them; and when you come out to your uncle's home in the spring, after staying a whole winter in the town, he knows you—old Tray does! And he leaps upon you, and lays his paws on your shoulder, and licks your face; and is almost as glad to see you, as cousin Bella herself. And when you put Bella on his back for a ride, he only pretends to bite her little feet;—but he wouldn't do it for the world. Aye, Tray is a noble old dog!

But one summer, the farmers say that some of their sheep are killed, and that the dogs have worried them; and one of them comes to talk with my uncle about it.

But Tray never worried sheep; you know he never did; and so does nurse; and so does Bella;—for in the spring, she had a pet lamb, and Tray never worried little Fidele.

And one or two of the dogs that belong to the neighbors are shot; though nobody knows who shot them; and you have great fears about poor Tray; and try to keep him at home, and fondle him more than ever. But Tray will sometimes wander off; till finally, one afternoon, he comes back whining piteously, and with his shoulder all bloody.

Little Bella cries loud; and you almost cry, as nurse dresses the wound; and poor old Tray whines very sadly. You pat his head, and Bella pats him; and you sit down together by him on the floor of the porch, and bring a rug for him to lie upon; and try and tempt him with a little milk, and Bella brings a piece of cake for him,—but he will eat nothing. You sit up till very late, long after Bella has gone to bed, patting his head, and wishing you could do something for poor Tray;—but he only licks your hand, and whines more piteously than ever.

In the morning, you dress early, and hurry down stairs; but Tray is not lying on the rug; and you run through the house to find him, and whistle, and call—Tray!—Tray! At length you see him lying in his old place, out by the cherry tree, and you run to him;—but he does not start; and you lean down to pat him,—but he is cold, and the dew is wet upon him:——poor Tray is dead!

You take his head upon your knees, and pat again those glossy ears, and cry; but you cannot bring him to life. And Bella comes, and cries with you. You can hardly bear to have him put in the ground; but uncle says he must be buried. So one of the workmen digs a grave under the cherry tree, where he died—a deep grave, and they round it over with earth, and smooth the sods upon it—even now I can trace Tray's grave.

You and Bella together, put up a little slab for a tombstone; and she hangs flowers upon it, and ties them there with a bit of ribbon. You can scarce play all that day; and afterward, many weeks later, when you are rambling over the fields, or lingering by the brook, throwing off sticks into the eddies, you think of old Tray's shaggy coat, and of his big paw, and of his honest eye; and the memory of your boyish grief comes upon you; and you say with tears,—"poor Tray!" And Bella too, in her sad, sweet tones, says——"poor old Tray,—he is dead!"

SCHOOL DAYS

The morning was cloudy and threatened rain; besides, it was autumn weather, and the winds were getting harsh, and rustling among the tree-tops that shaded the house, most dismally. I did not dare to listen. If indeed, I were to stay by the bright fires of home, and gather the nuts as they fell, and pile up the falling leaves, to make great bonfires, with Ben, and the rest of the boys, I should have liked to listen, and would have braved the dismal morning with the cheerfullest of them all. For it would have been a capital time to light a fire in the little oven we had built under the wall; it would have been so pleasant to warm our fingers at it, and to roast the great russets on the flat stones that made the top.

But this was not in store for me. I had bid the town boys good bye, the day before; my trunk was all packed; I was to go away—to school. The little oven would go to ruin— I knew it would. I was to leave my home. I was to bid my mother good bye, and Lilly, and Isabel, and all the rest;—and was to go away from them so far, that I should only know what they were all doing—in letters. It *was* sad. And then to have the clouds come over on that morning, and the winds sigh so dismally;—oh, it was too bad, I thought!

It comes back to me as I lie here this bright spring morning, as if it were only yesterday. I remember that the pigeons skulked under the eaves of the carriage house, and did not sit, as they used to do in summer, upon the ridge; and the chickens huddled together about the stable doors, as if they were afraid of the cold autumn. And in the garden, the white hollyhocks stood shivering, and bowed to the wind, as if their time had come. The yellow musk-melons showed plain among the frost bitten vines, and looked cold, and uncomfortable.

——Then they were all so kind, in-doors! The cook made such nice things for my breakfast, because little master was going; Lilly *would* give me her seat by the fire, and would put her lump of sugar in my cup; and my mother looked so smiling, and so tenderly, that I thought I loved her more than I ever did before. Little Ben was so gay too; and wanted me to take his jacknife, if I wished it,—though he knew that I had a bran new one in my trunk. The old nurse slipped a little purse into my hand, tied up with a green ribbon—with money in it,—and told me not to show it to Ben or Lilly.

And cousin Isabel, who was there on a visit, would come to stand by my chair, when my mother was talking to me; and put her hand in mine, and look up into my face; but she did not say a word. I thought it was very odd; and yet it did not seem odd to me, that I could say nothing to her. I daresay we felt alike.

At length Ben came running in, and said the coach had come; and there, sure enough, out of the window, we saw it—a bright yellow coach, with four white horses, and band-boxes all over the top, with a great pile of trunks behind. Ben said it was a grand coach, and that he should like a ride in it; and the old nurse came to the door, and said I should have a capital time; but somehow, I doubted if the nurse was talking honestly. I believe she gave me an honest kiss though,—and such a hug!

But it was nothing to my mother's. Tom told me to be a man, and study like a Tro-jan;[86] but I was not thinking about study then. There was a tall-boy in the coach, and I was ashamed to have him see me cry;—so I didn't, at first. But I remember, as I looked back, and saw little Isabel run out into the middle of the street, to see the coach go off, and the curls floating behind her, as the wind freshened, I felt my heart leaping into my throat, and the water coming into my eyes,—and how just then, I caught sight of the tall boy glancing at me,—and how I tried to turn it off, by looking to see if I could button up my great coat, a great deal lower down than the button holes went.

But it was of no use; I put my head out of the coach window, and looked back, as the little figure of Isabel faded, and then the house, and the trees; and the tears did come; and I smuggled my handkerchief outside without turning; so that I could wipe my eyes, before the tall boy should see me. They say that these shadows of morning fade, as the sun brightens into noon-day; but they are very dark shadows for all that!

Let the father, or the mother think long, before they send away their boy—before they break the home-ties that make a web of infinite fineness and soft silken meshes around his heart, and toss him aloof into the boy-world, where he must struggle up amid bickerings and quarrels, into his age of youth! There are boys indeed with little fineness in the texture of their hearts, and with little delicacy of soul, to whom the school in a dis-tant village, is but a vacation from home; and with whom, a return revives all those grosser affections which alone existed before;—just as there are plants which will bear all exposure without the wilting of a leaf, and will return to the hot-house life, as strong, and as hopeful as ever. But there are others, to whom the severance from the prattle of sisters, the indulgent fondness of a mother, and the unseen influences of the home altar, gives a shock that lasts forever; it is wrenching with cruel hand, what will bear but little roughness; and the sobs with which the adieux are said, are sobs that may come back in the after years, strong, and steady, and terrible.

God have mercy on the boy who learns to sob early! Condemn it as sentiment, if you will; talk as you will of the fearlessness, and strength of the boy's heart,—yet there belong to many, tenderly strung chords of affection which give forth low, and gentle music, that consoles, and ripens the ear for all the harmonies of life. These chords a lit-tle rude, and unnatural tension will break, and break forever. Watch your boy then, if so be he will bear the strain; try his nature, if it be rude or delicate; and if delicate, in God's name, do not, as you value your peace and his, breed a harsh youth spirit in him, that shall take pride in subjugating, and forgetting the delicacy, and richness of his finer affections!

——I see now, looking into the past, the troops of boys who were scattered in the great play-ground, as the coach drove up at night. The school was in a tall, stately build-ing, with a high cupola on the top, where I thought I would like to go up. The school-master, they told me at home, was kind; he said he hoped I would be a good boy, and pat-ted me on the head; but he did not pat me as my mother used to do. Then there was a woman, whom they called the Matron; who had a great many ribbons in her cap, and who shook my hand,—but so stiffly, that I didn't dare to look up in her face.

---

[86]Study with great focus and discipline.

One boy took me down to see the school room, which was in the basement, and the walls were all mouldy, I remember; and when we passed a certain door, he said,—there was the dungeon;—how I felt! I hated that boy; but I believe he is dead now. Then the matron took me up to my room,—a little corner room, with two beds, and two windows, and a red table, and closet; and my chum was about my size, and wore a queer round-about jacket with big bell buttons; and he called the schoolmaster—'Old Crikey'—and kept me awake half the night, telling me how he whipped the scholars, and how they played tricks upon him. I thought my chum was a very uncommon boy.

For a day or two, the lessons were easy, and it was sport to play with so many 'fellows.' But soon I began to feel lonely at night after I had gone to bed. I used to wish I could have my mother come, and kiss me; after school too, I wished I could step in, and tell Isabel how bravely I had got my lessons. When I told my chum this, he laughed at me, and said that was no place for 'homesick, white-livered chaps.' I wondered if my chum had any mother.

We had spending money once a week, with which we used to go down to the village store, and club our funds together, to make great pitchers of lemonade. Some boys would have money besides; though it was against the rules; and one, I recollect, showed us a five dollar bill in his wallet—and we all thought he must be very rich.

We marched in procession to the village church on Sundays. There were two long benches in the galleries, reaching down the side of the meeting-house; and on these we sat. At the first, I was among the smallest boys, and took a place close to the wall, against the pulpit; but afterward, as I grew bigger, I was promoted to the lower end of the first bench. This I never liked;—because it was close by one of the ushers, and because it brought me next to some country women, who wore stiff bonnets, and eat fennel, and sung with the choir. But there was a little black-eyed girl, who sat over behind the choir, that I thought handsome; I used to look at her very often; but was careful she should never catch my eye.

There was another down below, in a corner pew, who was pretty; and who wore a hat in the winter trimmed with fur. Half the boys in the school said they would marry her some day or other. One's name was Jane, and that of the other, Sophia; which we thought pretty names, and cut them on the ice, in skating time. But I didn't think either of them so pretty as Isabel.

Once a teacher whipped me: I bore it bravely in the school: but afterward, at night, when my chum was asleep, I sobbed bitterly, as I thought of Isabel, and Ben, and my mother, and how much they loved me; and laying my face in my hands, I sobbed myself to sleep. In the morning I was calm enough:—it was another of the heart ties broken, though I did not know it then. It lessened the old attachment to home, because that home could neither protect me, nor soothe me with its sympathies. Memory indeed freshened and grew strong; but strong in bitterness, and in regrets. The boy whose love you cannot feed by daily nourishment, will find pride, self-indulgence, and an iron purpose coming in to furnish other supply for the soul that is in him. If he cannot shoot his branches into the sunshine, he will become acclimated to the shadow, and indifferent to such stray gleams of sunshine, as his fortune may vouchsafe.

Hostilities would sometimes threaten between the school and the village boys; but they usually passed off, with such loud, and harmless explosions, as belong to the wars of our small politicians. The village champions were a hatter's apprentice, and a thick set fellow who worked in a tannery. We prided ourselves especially on one stout boy, who wore a sailor's monkey jacket. I cannot but think how jaunty that stout boy looked in that jacket; and what an Ajax[87] cast there was to his countenance! It certainly did occur to me, to compare him with William Wallace (Miss Porter's William Wallace) and I thought how I would have liked to have seen a tussle between them. Of course, we who were small boys, limited ourselves to indignant remark, and thought 'we should like to see them do it'; and prepared clubs from the wood-shed, after a model suggested by a New York boy, who had seen the clubs of the Policemen.

There was one scholar,—poor Leslie, who had friends in some foreign country, and who occasionally received letters bearing a foreign post-mark:—what an extraordinary boy that was;—what astonishing letters;—what extraordinary parents! I wondered if I should ever receive a letter from 'foreign parts?' I wondered if I should ever write one:— but this was too much—too absurd! As if I, Paul, wearing a blue jacket with gilt buttons, and number four boots, should ever visit those countries spoken of in the geographies, and by learned travellers! No, no; this was too extravagant: but I knew what I would do, if I lived to come of age;—and I vowed that I would,—I would go to New York!

Number seven was the hospital, and forbidden ground; we had all of us a sort of hor- ror of number seven. A boy died there once, and oh, how he moaned; and what a time there was when the father came!

A scholar by the name of Tom Belton, who wore linsey gray, made a dam across a little brook by the school, and whittled out a saw-mill, that actually sawed: he had genius. I expected to see him before now at the head of American mechanics; but I learn with pain, that he is keeping a grocery store.

At the close of all the terms we had exhibitions, to which all the towns people came, and among them the black-eyed Jane, and the pretty Sophia with fur around her hat. My great triumph was when I had the part of one of Pizarro's[88] chieftains, the evening before I left the school. How I did look! I had a moustache put on with burnt cork, and whiskers very bushy indeed; and I had the militia coat of an ensign in the town company, with the skirts pinned up, and a short sword very dull, and crooked, which belonged to an old gentleman who was said to have got it from some privateer, who was said to have taken it from some great British Admiral, in the old wars:—and the way I carried that sword upon the platform, and the way I jerked it out, when it came to my turn to say,—'battle! battle!—then death to the armed, and chains for the defenceless!'—was tremendous!

The morning after, in our dramatic hats—black felt, with turkey feathers,—we took our place upon the top of the coach, to leave the school. The headmaster, in green spec- tacles, came out to shake hands with us,—a very awful shaking of hands.—Poor gentle- man!—he is in his grave now.

We gave three loud hurrahs 'for the old school,' as the coach started; and upon the top of the hill that overlooks the village, we gave another round—and still another for the crabbed old fellow, whose apples we had so often stolen.—I wonder if old Bulkeley is living yet?

---

[87]In Homer's *Iliad,* Ajax is one of the fiercest of the Greek warriors.

[88]Francisco Pizarro (1475–1541) was the Spanish conqueror of the Inca empire.

As we got on under the pine trees, I recalled the image of the black-eyed Jane, and of the other little girl in the corner pew,—and thought how I would come back after the college days were over,—a man, with a beaver hat, and a cane, and with a splendid barouche, and how I would take the best chamber at the inn, and astonish the old school-master by giving him a familiar tap on the shoulder; and how I would be the admiration, and the wonder of the pretty girl, in the fur-trimmed hat! Alas, how our thoughts outrun our deeds!

For long—long years, I saw no more of my old school: and when at length the new view came, great changes—crashing like tornadoes,—had swept over my path!—I thought no more of startling the villagers, or astonishing the black-eyed girl. No, no! I was content to slip quietly through the little town, with only a tear or two, as I recalled the dead ones, and mused upon the emptiness of life!

THE SEA

As I look back, boyhood with its griefs and cares vanishes into the proud stateliness of youth. The ambition, and the rivalries of the college life,—its first boastful importance as knowledge begins to dawn on the wakened mind, and the ripe, and enviable compla-cency of its senior dignity,—all scud over my memory, like this morning breeze along the meadows; and like that too, bear upon their wing, a chillness—as of distant ice-banks.

Ben has grown almost to manhood: Lilly is living in a distant home; and Isabel is just blooming into that sweet age, where womanly dignity waits her beauty;—an age that sorely puzzles one who has grown up beside her,—making him slow of tongue, but very quick of heart!

As for the rest——let us pass on.

The sea is around me.—The last headlands have gone down, under the horizon, like the city steeples, as you lose yourself in the calm of the country, or like the great thoughts of genius, as you slip from the pages of poets, into your own quiet reverie.

The waters skirt me right and left: there is nothing but water before, and only water behind. Above me are sailing clouds, or the blue vault, which we call, with childish license—heaven. The sails white and full, like helping friends are pushing me on; and night and day are distent with the winds which come and go—none know whence, and none know whither. A land bird flutters aloft, weary with long flying; and lost in a world where are no forests but the careening masts, and no foliage but the drifts of spray. It cleaves awhile to the smooth spars, till urged by some homeward yearning, it bears off in the face of the wind, and sinks, and rises over the angry waters, until its strength is gone, and the blue waves gather the poor flutterer to their cold, and glassy bosom.

All the morning I see nothing beyond me but the waters, or a tossing company of dolphins; all the noon, unless some white sail—like a ghost, stalks the horizon, there is still nothing but the rolling seas; all the evening, after the sun has grown big and sunk under the water line, and the moon risen, white and cold, to glimmer across the tops of the surging ocean,—there is nothing but the sea, and the sky, to lead off thought, or to crush it with their greatness.

Hour after hour, as I sit in the moonlight upon the taffrail, the great waves gather far back, and break,—and gather nearer, and break louder,—and gather again, and roll down swift and terrible under the creaking ship, and heave it up lightly upon their swelling surge, and drop it gently to their seething, and yeasty cradle,—like an infant in the sway-ing arms of a mother,—or like a shadowy memory, upon the billows of manly thought.

Conscience wakes in the silent nights of ocean; life lies open like a book, and spreads out as level as the sea. Regrets and broken resolutions chase over the soul like swift-winged night-birds, and all the unsteady heights and the wastes of action, lift up distinct, and clear, from the uneasy, but limpid depths of memory.

Yet within this floating world I am upon, sympathies are narrowed down; they can-not range, as upon the land, over a thousand objects. You are strangely attracted toward some frail girl, whose pallor has now given place to the rich bloom of the sea life. You listen eagerly to the chance snatches of a song from below, in the long morning watch. You love to see her small feet tottering on the unsteady deck; and you love greatly to aid her steps, and feel her weight upon your arm, as the ship lurches to a heavy sea.

Hopes and fears knit together pleasantly upon the ocean. Each day seems to revive them; your morning salutation, is like a welcome after absence, upon the shore; and each 'good night' has the depth and fullness of a land 'farewell.' And beauty grows upon the ocean; you cannot certainly say that the face of the fair girl-voyager is prettier than that of Isabel;—oh, no!—but you are certain that you cast innocent, and honest glances upon her, as you steady her walk upon the deck, far oftener than at the first; and ocean life, and sympathy, makes her kind; she does not resent your rudeness, one half so stoutly, as she might upon the shore.

She will even linger of an evening—pleading first with the mother, and standing beside you,—her white hand not very far from yours upon the rail,—look down where the black ship flings off with each plunge, whole garlands of emeralds; or she will look up (thinking perhaps you are looking the same way) into the skies, in search of some stars—which were her neighbors at home. And bits of old tales will come up, as if they rode upon the ocean quietude; and fragments of half forgotten poems, tremulously uttered,—either by reason of the rolling of the ship, or some accidental touch of that white hand.

But ocean has its storms, when fear will make strange, and holy companionship; and even here, my memory shifts swiftly and suddenly.

——It is a dreadful night. The passengers are clustered, trembling, below. Every plank shakes; and the oak ribs groan, as if they suffered with their toil. The hands are all aloft; the captain is forward shouting to the mate in the cross-trees, and I am clinging to one of the stanchions, by the binnacle. The ship is pitching madly, and the waves are top-pling up, sometimes as high as the yard-arm, and then dipping away with a whirl under our keel, that makes every timber in the vessel quiver. The thunder is roaring like a thou-sand cannons; and at the moment, the sky is cleft with a stream of fire, that glares over the tops of the waves, and glistens on the wet decks, and the spars,—lighting up all so plain, that I can see the men's faces in the main-top, and catch glimpses of the reefers on the yard-arm, clinging like death;—then all is horrible darkness.

The spray spits angrily against the canvass; the waves crash against the weather-bow like mountains, the wind howls through the rigging, or, as a gasket gives way, the sail bellying to leeward, splits like the crack of a musket. I hear the captain in the lulls, screaming out orders; and the mate in the rigging, screaming them over, until the lightning comes, and the thunder, deadening their voices, as if they were chirping sparrows.

In one of the flashes, I see a hand upon the yardarm lose his foothold, as the ship gives a plunge; but his arms are clenched around the spar. Before I can see any more, the blackness comes, and the thunder, with a crash that half deafens me. I think I hear a low cry, as the mutterings die away in the distance; and at the next flash of lightning, which comes in an instant, I see upon the top of one of the waves alongside, the poor reefer who has fallen. The lightning glares upon his face.

But he has caught at a loose bit of running rigging, as he fell; and I see it slipping off the coil upon the deck. I shout madly—man overboard!—and catch the rope, when I can see nothing again. The sea is too high, and the man too heavy for me I shout, and shout, and shout, and feel the perspiration starting in great beads from my forehead, as the line slips through my fingers.

Presently the captain feels his way aft, and takes hold with me; and the cook comes, as the coil is nearly spent, and we pull together upon him. It is desperate work for the sailor; for the ship is drifting at a prodigious rate; but he clings like a dying man.

By and by at a flash, we see him on a crest, two oars length away from the vessel.

"Hold on, my man!" shouts the captain.

"For God's sake, be quick!" says the poor fellow; and he goes down in a trough of the sea. We pull the harder, and the captain keeps calling to him to keep up courage, and hold strong. But in the hush, we can hear him say—"I can't hold out much longer;—I'm most gone!"

Presently we have brought the man where we can lay hold of him, and are only waiting for a good lift of the sea to bring him up, when the poor fellow groans out,—"It's no use—I can't—good bye!" And a wave tosses the end of the rope, clean upon the bulwarks.

At the next flash, I see him going down under the water.

I grope my way below, sick and faint at heart; and wedging myself into my narrow birth, I try to sleep. But the thunder and the tossing of the ship, and the face of the drowning man, as he said good bye,—peering at me from every corner, will not let me sleep.

Afterward, come quiet seas, over which we boom along, leaving in our track, at night, a broad path of phosphorescent splendor. The sailors bustle around the decks, as if they had lost no comrade; and the voyagers losing the pallor of fear, look out earnestly for the land.

At length, my eyes rest upon the coveted fields of Britain; and in a day more, the bright face, looking out beside me, sparkles at sight of the sweet cottages, which be along the green Essex shores. Broad sailed yachts, looking strangely, yet beautifully, glide upon the waters of the Thames, like swans; black, square-rigged colliers from the Tyne, lie grouped in sooty cohorts; and heavy, three-decked Indiamen,[89]—of which I had read in story books,—drift slowly down with the tide. Dingy steamers, with white pipes, and with red pipes, whiz past us to the sea; and now, my eye rests on the great palace of Greenwich; I see the wooden-legged pensioners smoking under the palace

---

[89]Large merchant vessels associated with Indian trade.

walls; and above them upon the hill—as Heaven is true—that old, fabulous Greenwich, the great centre of school-boy Longitude.

Presently, from under a cloud of murky smoke heaves up the vast dome of St. Paul's, and the tall Column of the Fire, and the white turrets of London Tower. Our ship glides through the massive dock gates, and is moored, amid that forest of masts, which bears golden fruit for Britons.

That night, I sleep far away from 'the old school,' and far away from the valley of Hillfarm; long, and late, I toss upon my bed, with swift visions in my mind, of London Bridge, and Temple Bar, and Jane Shore, and Falstaff, and Prince Hal, and King Jamie.[90] And when at length I fall asleep, my dreams are very pleasant, but they carry me across the ocean, away from the ship,—away from London,—away even from the fair voyager,—to the old oaks, and to the brooks, and—to thy side—sweet Isabel!

THE FATHER-LAND

There is a great contrast between the easy deshabille of the ocean life, and the prim attire, and conventional spirit of the land. In the first, there are but few to please, and these few are known, and they know us; upon the shore, there is a world to humour, and a world of strangers. In a brilliant drawing-room looking out upon the site of old Charing-Cross, and upon the one-armed Nelson,[91] standing aloft at his coil of rope, I take leave of the fair voyager of the sea. Her white negligé has given place to silks; and the simple careless coiffe of the ocean, is replaced by the rich dressing of a modiste. Yet her face has the same bloom upon it; and her eye sparkles, as it seems to me, with a higher pride;—and her little hand has I think a tremulous quiver in it, (I am sure my own has)—as I bid her adieu, and take up the trail of my wanderings into the heart of England.

Abuse her, as we will,—pity her starving peasantry, as we may,—smile at her court pageantry, as much as we like,—old England, is dear old England still! Her cottage homes, her green fields, her castles, her blazing firesides, her church spires are as old as song; and by song and story, we inherit them in our hearts. This joyous boast, was, I remember, upon my lip, as I first trode upon the rich meadow of Runnymede; and recalled that GREAT CHARTER[92] wrested from the king, which made the first stepping stone toward the bounties of our western freedom.

It is a strange feeling that comes over the Western Saxon, as he strolls first along the green bye-lanes of England, and scents the hawthorn in its April bloom, and lingers at some quaint stile, to watch the rooks wheeling and cawing around some lofty elm tops, and traces the carved gables of some old country mansion that lies in their shadow, and hums some fragment of charming English poesy, that seems made for the scene! This is not sight-seeing, nor travel; it is dreaming sweet dreams, that are fed with the old life of Books.

---

[90]This is a list of famous English locations, as well as historical and literary figures.

[91]Horatio Nelson (1758–1805) is perhaps Britain's most famous and best-loved admiral.

[92]Britain's Magna Carta (document giving away unprecedented royal prerogatives in 1215) was drafted at Runnymede.

I wander on, fearing to break the dream, by a swift step; and winding and rising between the blooming hedgerows, I come presently to the sight of some sweet valley below me, where a thatched hamlet lies sleeping in the April sun, as quietly as the dead lie in history;—no sound reaches me save the occasional clinck of the smith's hammer, or the hedgeman's bill-hook, or the ploughman's 'ho-tup!' from the hills. At evening, listening to the nightingale, I stroll wearily into some close-nestled village, that I had seen long ago from a rolling height. It is far away from the great lines of travel;—and the children stop their play to have a look at me, and rosy-faced girls peep from behind half-opened doors.

Standing apart, and with a bench on either side of the entrance, is the inn of the Eagle and the Falcon,—which guardian birds, some native Dick Tinto[93] has pictured upon the swinging sign-board at the corner. The hostess is half ready to embrace me, and treats me like a prince in disguise. She shows me through the tap-room into a little parlor, with white curtains, and with neatly framed prints of the old patriarchs. Here, alone, beside a brisk fire, kindled with furze, I watch the white flame leaping playfully through the black lumps of coal, and enjoy the best fare of the Eagle and the Falcon. If too late, or too early for her garden stock, the hostess bethinks herself of some small pot of jelly in an out-of-the-way cupboard of the house, and setting it temptingly in her prettiest dish, she coyly slips it upon the white cloth, with a modest regret that it is no better; and a little evident satisfaction—that it is so good.

I muse for an hour before the glowing fire, as quiet as the cat that has come in, to bear me company; and at bed-time, I find sheets, as fresh as the air of the mountains.

At another time, and many months later, I am walking under a wood of Scottish firs. It is near night-fall, and the fir tops are swaying, and sighing hoarsely, in the cool wind of the Northern Highlands. There is none of the smiling landscape of England about me; and the crags of Edinburgh and Castle Stirling, and sweet Perth, in its silver valley, are far to the southward. The larchs[94] of Athol and Bruar Water, and that highland gem— Dunkeld,[95] are passed. I am tired with a morning's tramp over Culloden Moor; and from the edge of the wood, there stretches before me in the cool gray twilight, broad fields of heather. In the middle, there rise against the night-sky, the turrets of a castle; it is Castle Cawdor, where King Duncan was murdered by Macbeth.[96]

The sight of it lends a spur to my weary step; and emerging from the wood, I bound over the springy heather. In an hour, I clamber a broken wall, and come under the frowning shadows of the castle. The ivy clambers up here, and there, and shakes its uncropped branches, and its dried berries over the heavy portal. I cross the moat, and my step makes the chains of the draw-bridge rattle. All is kept in the old state; only in lieu of the warder's horn, I pull at the warder's bell. The echoes ring, and die in the stone courts; but there is no one astir, nor is there a light at any of the castle windows. I ring again, and the

---

[93]Local sign painter.

[94]Pine trees.

[95]Blair Atholl, the Bruar river, and Dunkheld are all located in central Scotland.

[96]In Shakespeare's *Macbeth,* the title character murders his king in order to ascend the royal throne.

echoes come, and blend with the rising night wind that sighs around the turrets, as they sighed that night of murder. I fancy—it must be a fancy,—that I hear an owl scream; I am sure that I hear the crickets cry.

I sit down upon the green bank of the moat; a little dark water lies in the bottom. The walls rise from it gray, and stern in the deepening shadows. I hum chance passages of Macbeth, listening for the echoes—echoes from the wall; and echoes from that far away time when I stole the first reading of the tragic story.

> "Dids't thou not hear a noise?
> I heard the owl scream, and the crickets cry.
> Did not you speak?
> > When?
> > > Now.
> > > > As I descended?
> Ay.
> ——Hark!"——

And the sharp echo comes back——'hark!' And at dead of night, in the thatched cottage under the castle walls, where a dark faced, Gaelic[97] woman, in plaid turban, is my hostess, I wake, startled by the wind, and my trembling lips say involuntarily—'hark!'

Again, three months later, I am in the sweet county of Devon. Its valleys are like emerald; its threads of water stretched over the fields, by their provident husbandry, glisten in the broad glow of summer, like skeins of silk. A bland old farmer, of the true British stamp, is my host. On market days he rides over to the old town of Totness in a trim, black farmer's cart; and he wears glossy topped boots, and a broad-brimmed white hat. I take a vast deal of pleasure in listening to his honest, straight-forward talk about the improvements of the day and the state of the nation. I sometimes get upon one of his nags, and ride off with him over his fields, or visit the homes of the laborers, which show their gray roofs, in every charming nook of the landscape. At the parish church, I doze against the high pew backs, as I listen to the see-saw tones of the drawling curate; and in my half wakeful moments the withered holly sprigs (not removed since Easter) grow upon my vision, into Christmas boughs, and preach sermons to me—of the days of old.

Sometimes, I wander far over the hills into a neighboring park; and spend hours on hours, under the sturdy oaks, watching the sleek fallow deer, gazing at me with their soft, liquid eyes. The squirrels, too, play above me, with their daring leaps, utterly careless of my presence, and the pheasants whir away from my very feet.

On one of these random strolls—I remember it very well—when I was idling along, thinking of the broad reach of water that lay between me, and that old forest home,—and beating off the daisy heads with my cane,—I heard the tramp of horses, coming up one of the forest avenues. The sound was unusual, for the family, I had been told, was still in town, and no right of way lay through the park. There they were, however:—I was sure it must be the family, from the careless way in which they came sauntering up.

---

[97]Scottish

First, there was a noble hound that came bounding toward me,—gazed a moment, and turned to watch the approach of the little cavalcade. Next was an elderly gentleman mounted upon a spirited hunter, attended by a boy of some dozen years, who managed his pony with a grace, that is a part of the English boy's education. Then followed two older lads, and a travelling phæton, in which sat a couple of elderly ladies. But what most drew my attention was a girlish figure, that rode beyond the carriage, upon a sleek-limbed gray. There was something in the easy grace of her attitude, and the rich glow that lit up her face—heightened as it was, by the little black velvet riding cap, relieved with a single flowing plume,—that kept my eye. It was strange, but I thought that I had seen such a figure before, and such a face, and such an eye; and as I made the ordinary salutation of a stranger, and caught her smile, I could have sworn that it was she—my fair companion of the ocean. The truth flashed upon me in a moment. She was to visit, she had told me, a friend in the south of England;—and this was the friend's home;—and one of the ladies of the carriage was her mother; and one of the lads, the school-boy brother, who had teased her on the sea.

I recal now perfectly, her frank manner, as she ungloved her hand to bid me welcome. I strolled beside them to the steps. Old Devon had suddenly renewed its beauties for me. I had much to tell her, of the little out-lying nooks, which my wayward feet had led me to: and she—as much to ask. My stay with the bland old farmer lengthened; and two days hospitalities at the Park ran over into three, and four. There was hard galloping down those avenues; and new strolls, not at all lonely, under the sturdy oaks. The long summer twilight of England used to find a very happy fellow lingering on the garden terrace,—looking, now at the rookery, where the belated birds quarreled for a resting place, and now down the long forest vista, gray with distance, and closed with the white spire of Modbury church.

English country life gains fast upon one—very fast; and it is not so easy, as in the drawing-room of Charing Cross, to say—adieu! But it is said—very sadly said; for God only knows how long it is to last. And as I rode slowly down toward the lodge after my leave-taking, I turned back again, and again, and again. I thought I saw her standing still upon the terrace, though it was almost dark; and I thought—it could hardly have been an illusion—that I saw something white waving from her hand.

Her name—as if I could forget it—was Caroline; her mother called her—Carry. I wondered how it would seem for me to call her—Carry! I tried it;—it sounded well. I tried it—over and over,—until I came too near the lodge. There I threw a half crown to the woman who opened the gate for me. She curtsied low, and said—"God bless you, sir!"

I liked her for it; I would have given a guinea for it: and that night,—whether it was the old woman's benediction, or the waving scarf upon the terrace, I do not know;—but there was a charm upon my thought, and my hope, as if an angel had been near me.

It passed away though in my dreams;—for I dreamed that I saw the sweet face of Bella in an English park, and that she wore a black velvet riding cap, with a plume; and I came up to her and murmured, very sweetly, I thought,—"Carry, dear Carry!" and she started, looked sadly at me, and turned away. I ran after her, to kiss her as I did when she sat upon my mother's lap, on the day when she came near drowning: I longed to tell her, as I did then—I *do* love you. But she turned her tearful face upon me, I dreamed; and then,—I saw no more.

A ROMAN GIRL

—I remember the very words—"*non parlo Francesce, Signore,*—I do not speak French, Signor"—said the stout lady,—"but my daughter, perhaps, will understand you."

And she called—"*Enrica!—Enrica! venite, subito! c'è un forestiere.*"[98]

And the daughter came, her light brown hair falling carelessly over her shoulders, her rich hazel eye twinkling and full of life, the colour coming and going upon her transparent cheek, and her bosom heaving with her quick step. With one hand she put back the scattered locks that had fallen over her forehead, while she laid the other gently, upon the arm of her mother, and asked in that sweet music of the south—"*cosa volete, mamma?*"[99]

It was the prettiest picture I had seen in many a day; and this, notwithstanding I was in Rome, and had come that very morning from the Palace of Borghese.[100]

The stout lady was my hostess, and Enrica—so fair, so young, so unlike in her beauty, to other Italian beauties, was my landlady's daughter. The house was one of those tall houses—very, very old, which stand along the eastern side of the Corso, looking out upon the Piazzo di Colonna. The staircases were very tall, and dirty, and they were narrow and dark. Four flights of stone steps led up to the corridor where they lived. A little trap was in the door; and there was a bell-rope, at the least touch of which, I was almost sure to hear tripping feet run along the stone floor within, and then to see the trap thrown slyly back, and those deep hazle eyes looking out upon me; and then the door would open, and along the corridor, under the daughter's guidance, (until I had learned the way,) I passed to my Roman home. I was a long time learning the way.

My chamber looked out upon the Corso,[101] and I could catch from it a glimpse of the top of the tall column of Antoninus, and of a fragment of the palace of the Governor. My parlor, which was separated from the apartments of the family by a narrow corridor, looked upon a small court, hung around with balconies. From the upper one, a couple of black-eyed girls are occasionally looking out, and they can almost read the title of my book, when I sit by the window. Below are three or four blooming *ragazze*,[102] who are dark-eyed, and have Roman luxuriance of hair. The youngest is a friend of our Enrica, and is of course frequently looking up, with all the innocence in the world, to see if Enrica may be looking out.

Night after night, a bright blaze glows upon my hearth, of the alder faggots which they bring from the Albanian hills. Night after night too, the family come in, to aid my blundering speech, and to enjoy the rich sparkling of my faggot fire. Little Cesare, a dark-faced Italian boy, takes up his position with pencil and slate, and draws by the light of the blaze genii and castles. The old one-eyed teacher of Enrica, lays his snuff box upon the table, and his handkerchief across his lap, and with his spectacles upon his

[98]Come, quickly! Look, there is a foreigner.

[99]What do you want, mother?

[100]The Villa Borghese was built in the early seventeenth century and was known for its stunning gardens and architecture.

[101]Main street in central Rome.

[102]Young girls.

nose, and his big fingers on the lesson, runs through the French tenses of the verb *amare*.[103] The father a sallow-faced, keen-eyed man, with true Italian visage, sits with his arms upon the elbows of his chair, and talks of the Pope, or of the weather. A spruce count from the Marches of Ancona, wears a heavy watch seal, and reads Dante with *furore*.[104] The mother, with arms akimbo, looks proudly upon her daughter, and counts her, as well she may, a gem among the Roman beauties.

The table was round, with the fire blazing on one side; there was scarce room for but three upon the other. Signor *il maestro*[105] was one—then Enrica, and next—how well I remember it—came myself. For I could sometimes help Enrica to a word of French; and far oftener, she could help me to a word of Italian. Her face was rich, and full of feeling; I used greatly to love to watch the puzzled expressions that passed over her forehead, as the sense of some hard phrase escaped her;—and better still, to see the happy smile, as she caught at a glance, the thought of some old scholastic Frenchman, and transferred it into the liquid melody of her speech.

She had seen just sixteen summers, and only that very autumn was escaped from the thraldom of a convent, upon the skirts of Rome. She knew nothing of life, but the life of feeling; and all thoughts of happiness, lay as yet in her childish hopes. It was pleasant to look upon her face; and it was still more pleasant to listen to that sweet Roman voice. What a rich flow of superlatives, and endearing diminutives, from those vermillion lips! Who would not have loved the study, and who would not have loved—without meaning it—the teacher?

In those days, I did not linger long at the tables of lame Pietro in the Via Condotti; but would hurry back to my little Roman parlor——the fire was so pleasant! And it was so pleasant to greet Enrica with her mother, even before the one-eyed *maestro* had come in; and it was pleasant to unfold the book between us, and to lay my hand upon the page—a small page—where hers lay already. And when she pointed wrong, it was pleasant to correct her—over and over;—insisting, that her hand should be here, and not there, and lifting those little fingers from one page, and putting them down upon the other. And sometimes, half provoked with my fault-finding, she would pat my hand smartly with hers;—but when I looked in her face to know what *that* could mean, she would meet my eye with such a kind submission, and half earnest regret, as made me not only pardon the offence,—but tempt me to provoke it again.

Through all the days of Carnival, when I rode pelted with *confetti,* and pelting back, my eyes used to wander up, from a long way off, to that tall house upon the Corso, where I was sure to meet, again and again, those forgiving eyes, and that soft brown hair, all gathered under the little brown sombrero, set off with one pure white plume. And her hand full of bon-bons, she would shake at me threateningly; and laugh—a musical laugh—as I bowed my head to the assault, and recovering from the shower of missiles, would turn to throw my stoutest bouquet at her balcony. At night, I would bear home to the Roman parlor, my best trophy of the day, as a guerdon for Enrica; and Enrica would

---

[103]To love.

[104]passion

[105]teacher

be sure to render in acknowledgment, some carefully hidden flowers, the prettiest that her beauty had won.

Sometimes upon those Carnival nights, she arrays herself in the costume of the Albanian water-carriers; and nothing, one would think could be prettier, than the laced crimson jacket, and the strange head gear with its trinkets, and the short skirts leaving to view as delicate an ankle as could be found in Rome. Upon another night, she glides into my little parlor, as we sit by the blaze, in a close velvet boddice, and with a Swiss hat caught up by a looplet of silver, and adorned with a full blown rose—nothing you think could be prettier than this. Again, in one of her girlish freaks, she robes herself like a nun; and with the heavy black serge, for dress, and the funereal veil,—relieved only by the plain white ruffle of her cap—you wish she were always a nun. But the wish vanishes, when you see her in a pure white muslin, with a wreath of orange blossoms about her forehead, and a single white rose-bud in her bosom.

Upon the little balcony Enrica keeps a pot or two of flowers, which bloom all winter long: and each morning, I find upon my table a fresh rose bud; each night, I bear back for thank-offering, the prettiest bouquet that can be found in the Via Condotti. The quiet fire-side evenings come back;—in which my hand seeks its wonted place upon her book; and my other, *will* creep around upon the back of Enrica's chair, and Enrica *will* look indignant,—and then all forgiveness.

One day I received a large pacquet of letters:—ah, what luxury to lie back in my big arm-chair, there before the crackling faggots, with the pleasant rustle of that silken dress beside me, and run over a second, and a third time, those mute paper missives, which bore to me over so many miles of water, the words of greeting, and of love! It would be worth travelling to the shores of the Ægean, to find one's heart quickened into such life as the ocean letters will make. Enrica threw down her book, and wondered what could be in them?—and snatched one from my hand, and looked with sad, but vain intensity over that strange scrawl.—What can it be?—said she: and she laid her finger upon the little half line—"Dear Paul."

I told her it was—"*Caro mio.*"[106]

Enrica laid it upon her lap, and looked in my face; "It is from your mother?" said she.

"No," said I.

"From your sister?"—said she.

"Alas, no!"

"*Il vostro fratello, dunque?*"[107]

"*Nemmeno*"[108]—said I—"not from a brother either."

She handed me the letter, and took up her book; and presently she laid the book down again; and looked at the letter, and then at me;—and went out.

She did not come in again that evening; in the morning, there was no rose-bud on my table. And when I came at night, with a bouquet from Pietro's at the corner, she asked me—"who had written my letter?"

---

[106]My dear.

[107]Your brother then?

[108]neither

"A very dear friend," said I.

"A lady?" continued she.

"A lady," said I.

"Keep this bouquet for her," said she, and put it in my hands.

"But, Enrica, she has plenty of flowers: she lives among them, and each morning her children gather them by scores to make garlands of."

Enrica put her fingers within my hand to take again the bouquet; and for a moment I held both fingers and flowers.

The flowers slipped out first.

I had a friend at Rome in that time, who afterward died between Ancona and Corinth: we were sitting one day upon a block of tufa in the middle of the Coliseum, looking up at the shadows which the waving shrubs upon the southern wall, cast upon the ruined arcades within, and listening to the chirping sparrows that lived upon the wreck,—when he said to me suddenly—"Paul, you love the Italian girl."

"She is very beautiful," said I.

"I think she is beginning to love you," said he, soberly.

"She has a very warm heart, I believe," said I.

"Aye," said he.

"But her feelings are those of a girl," continued I.

"They are not," said my friend; and he laid his hand upon my knee, and left off drawing diagrams with his cane,—"I have seen, Paul, more than you of this southern nature. The Italian girl of fifteen is a woman;—an impassioned, sensitive, tender creature—yet still a woman: you are loving—if you love—a full-grown heart; she is loving—if she loves—as a ripe heart should."

"But I do not think that either is wholly true," said I.

"Try it," said he, setting his cane down firmly, and looking in my face.

"How?" returned I.

"I have three weeks upon my hands," continued he. "Go with me into the Appenines;[109] leave your home in the Corso, and see if you can forget in the air of the mountains, your blue-eyed Roman girl!"

I was pondering for an answer, when he went on:— "It is better so: love as you might, that southern nature with all its passion, is not the material to build domestic happiness upon; nor is your northern habit—whatever you may think at your time of life, the one to cherish always those passionate sympathies which are bred by this atmosphere, and their scenes."

One moment my thought ran to my little parlor, and to that fairy figure, and to that sweet, angel face: and then, like lightning it traversed oceans, and fed upon the old ideal of home, and brought images to my eye of lost—dead ones, who seemed to be stirring on heavenly wings, in that soft Roman atmosphere, with greeting, and with beckoning.

——"I will go with you," said I.

The father shrugged his shoulders, when I told him I was going to the mountains, and wanted a guide. His wife said it would be cold upon the hills, for the winter was not

[109]Mountain range that extends through much of Italy.

ended. Enrica said it would be warm in the valleys, for the spring was coming. The old man drummed with his fingers on the table, and shrugged his shoulders again, but said nothing.

My landlady said I could not ride. Cesare said it would be hard walking. Enrica asked papa, if there would be any danger? And again the old man shrugged his shoulders. Again I asked him, if he knew a man who would serve us as guide among the Appenines; and finding me determined, he shrugged his shoulders, and said he would find one the next day.

As I passed out at evening, on my way to the Piazzo near the Monte Citorio, where stand the carriages that go out to Tivoli, Enrica glided up to me, and whispered—*"ah, mi dispiace tanto——tanto, Signor!"*[110]

The Appenines

I shook her hand, and in an hour afterward was passing with my friend, by the Trajan forum, toward the deep shadow of San Maggiore, which lay in our way to the mountains. At sunset, we were wandering over the ruin of Adrian's villa, which lies upon the first step of the Appenines. Behind us, the vesper bells of Tivoli were sounding, and their echoes floating sweetly under the broken arches; before us, stretching all the way to the horizon, lay the broad Campagna; while in the middle of its great waves, turned violet-coloured, by the hues of twilight, rose the grouped towers of the Eternal City; and lording it among them all, like a giant, stood the black dome of St. Peter's.

Day after day we stretched on over the mountains, leaving the Campagna far behind us. Rocks and stones, huge and ragged, lie strewed over the surface right and left; deep yawning valleys lie in the shadows of mountains, that loom up thousands of feet, bearing perhaps upon their tops old castellated towns, perched like birds' nests. But mountain and valley are blasted and scarred; the forests even, are not continuous, but struggle for a livelihood; as if the brimstone fire that consumed Nineveh,[111] had withered their energies. Sometimes, our eyes rest on a great white scar of the broken calcareous rock, on which the moss cannot grow, and the lizards dare not creep. Then we see a cliff beetling far aloft, with the shining walls of some monastery of holy men glistening at its base. The wayside brooks do not seem to be the gentle offspring of bountiful hills, but the remnants of something greater, whose greatness has expired;—they are turbid rills, rolling in the bottom of yawning chasms. Even the shrubs have a look, as if the Volscian[112] war-horse had trampled them down to death; and the primroses and the violets by the mountain path, alone look modestly beautiful amid the ruin.

Sometimes, we loiter in a valley, above which the goats are browsing on the cliffs, and listen to the sweet pastoral pipes of the Appenines. We see the shepherds in their rough skin coats, high over our heads. Their herds are feeding, as it seems, on ledges of

---

[110]I don't like this much, sir!

[111]In 612 B.C., the magnificent ancient city of Nineveh was sacked and burned by a combined force of Babylonians, Scythians, and Medes.

[112]Bitter military foes of the Romans known for their cunning.

a hand's breadth. The sweet sound floats and lingers in the soft atmosphere, without a breath of wind to bear it away, or a noise to disturb its melody. The shadows slant more and more as we linger; and the kids begin to group together. And as we wander on, through the stunted vineyards in the bottom of the valley, the sweet sound flows after us, like a river of song,—nor leaves us, till the kids have vanished in the distance, and the cliffs themselves, become one dark wall of shadow.

At night, in some little meagre mountain town, we stroll about in the narrow pass-ways, or wander under the heavy arches of the mountain churches. Shuffling old women grope in and out; dim lamps glimmer faintly at the side altars, shedding horrid light upon painted images of the dying Christ. Or perhaps, to make the old pile more solemn, there stands some bier in the middle, with a figure or two kneeling, at the foot, and ragged boys move stealthily under the shadows of the columns. Presently comes a young priest, in black robes, and lights a taper at the foot, and another at the head—for there is a dead man on the bier; and the parched, thin features look awfully under the yellow light of the tapers, in the gloom of the great building. It is very, very damp in the church, and the body of the dead man seems to make the air heavy, so we go out into the starlight again.

In the morning, the western slopes wear broad shadows, and the frosts crumple, on the herbage, to our tread: across the valley, it is like summer; and the birds—for there are songsters in the Appenines,—make summer music. Their notes blend softly with the faint sounds of some far off convent bell, tolling for morning mass, and strike the frosted and shaded mountain side, with a sweet echo. As we toil on, and the shaded hills begin to glow in the sunshine, we pass a train of mules, loaded with wine. We have seen them an hour before—little black dots twining along the white streak of foot-way upon the mountain above us. We lost them as we began to ascend, until a wild snatch of an Appe-nine song turned our eyes up, and there, straggling through the brush, they appeared again; a foot slip would have brought the mules and wine casks rolling upon us. We keep still, holding by the brushwood, to let them pass. An hour more, and we see them toiling slowly,—mule and muleteer,—big dots, and little dots,—far down where we have been before. The sun is hot and smoking on them in the bare valleys; the sun is hot and smok-ing on the hill-side, where we are toiling over the broken stones. I thought of little Enrica, when she said—the spring was coming!

Time and again, we sit down together—my friend and I—upon some fragment of rock, under the broad-armed chestnuts, that fringe the lower skirts of the mountains, and talk through the hottest of the noon, of the warriors of Scylla,[113] and of the Sabine women,[114]—but oftener—of the pretty peasantry, and of the sweet-faced Roman girl. He too tells me of his life and loves, and of the hopes that lie misty and grand before him:— little did we think that in so few years, his hopes would be gone, and his body lying low in the Adriatic, or tost with the drift upon the Dalmatian shores![115] Little did I think, that here under the ancestral wood,—still a wishful and blundering mortal, I should be gath-

---

[113]In ancient Greek legend, Scylla was a terrible sea monster.

[114]Italian women (located in the Appenine mountains) who were abducted and raped by Romans to populate their growing city.

[115]Eastern coast of the Adriatic Sea.

ering up the shreds, that memory can catch of our Appenine wandering, and be weaving them into my bachelor dreams.

Away again upon the quick wing of thought, I follow our steps, as after weeks of wandering, we gained once more a height that overlooked the Campagna—and saw the sun setting on its edge, throwing into relief the dome of St. Peter's, and blazing in a red stripe upon the waters of the Tiber.

Below us was Palestrina—the Præneste[116] of the poets and philosophers;—the dwelling place of—I know not how many—Emperors. We went straggling through the dirty streets, searching for some tidy-looking osteria. At length, we found an old lady, who could give us a bed, but no dinner. My friend dropped in a chair disheartened. A snub-looking priest came out to condole with us.

And could Palestrina—the *frigidum Præneste* of Horace,[117] which had entertained over and over, the noblest of the Colonna,[118] and the most noble Adrian—could Palestrina not furnish a dinner to a tired traveller?

"*Si, Signore,*"[119] said the snub-looking priest.

"*Si, Signorino,*"[120] said the neat old lady; and away we went upon a new search. And we found bright and happy faces;—especially the little girl of twelve years, who came close by me as I ate, and afterward strung a garland of marigolds, and put it on my head. Then there was a bright-eyed boy of fourteen, who wrote his name, and those of the whole family, upon a fly leaf of my book: and a pretty, saucy-looking girl of sixteen, who peeped a long time from behind the kitchen door, but before the evening was gone, she was in the chair beside me, and had written her name—Carlotta—upon the first leaf of my journal.

When I woke, the sun was up. From my bed I could see over the town, the thin, lazy mists lying on the old camp-ground of Pyrrhus;[121] beyond it, were the mountains, which hide Frascati, and Monte Cavi.[122] There was old Colonna too, that—

> Like an eagle's nest, hangs on the crest
> Of purple Appenine.

As the mist lifted, and the sun brightened the plain, I could see the road, along which Sylla came fuming and maddened after the Mithridaten war.[123] I could see, as I half

---

[116]Palestrina is a name for the ancient Italian city of Praeneste.

[117]The handsome Praeneste written about by Horace, Roman lyric poet (65 B.C.–A.D. 27)

[118]The Colonna family, led by Adrian, was one of fourteenth-century Italy's most influential and wealthy families.

[119]Yes, sir.

[120]More derogatory: yes, little sir.

[121]Pyrrhus (319–272 B.C.) was a Greek king best known for his costly victories against Rome and Macedonia.

[122]Frascati and Monte Cavi were important Roman cities in central Italy, located near Rome.

[123]The Roman general Lucius Sulla marched on Rome (82 B.C.) after defeating the Greek Mithradates. Sulla undertook this march because of differences he had with the ruling patricians of Rome.

dreamed and half slept, the frightened peasantry whooping to their long-horned cattle, as they drove them on tumultuously up through the gateways of the town; and women with babies in their arms, and children scowling with fear and hate,—all trooping fast and madly, to escape the hand of the Avenger;—alas! ineffectually, for Sylla murdered them, and pulled down the walls of their town—the proud Palestrina!

I had a queer fancy of seeing the nobles of Rome, led on by Stefano Colonna,[124] grouping along the plain, their corslets flashing out of the mists,—their pennants dashing above it,—coming up fast, and still as the wind, to make the Mural Præneste, their stronghold against the Last of the Tribunes. And strangely mingling fiction with fact, I saw the brother of Walter de Montreal, with his noisy and bristling army, crowd over the Campagna,[125] and put up his white tents, and hang out his showy banners, on the grassy knolls that lay nearest my eye.

——But the knolls were all quiet; there was not so much as a strolling *contadino*[126] on them, to whistle a mimic fife-note. A little boy from the inn went with me upon the hill; to look out upon the town and the wide sea of land below; and whether it was the soft, warm April sun, or the gray ruins below me, or whether the wonderful silence of the scene, or some wild gush of memory, I do not know, but something, made me sad.

"*Perché cosi penseroso?*—why so sad?" said the quick-eyed boy. "The air is beautiful, the scene is beautiful; Signore is young, why is he sad?"

"And is Giovanni never sad?" said I.

"*Quasi mai,*"[127] said the boy, "and if I could travel as Signore, and see other countries, I would be always gay."

"May you be always that!" said I.

The good wish touched him; he took me by the arms, and said—"Go home with me, Signore; you were happy at the inn last night; go back, and we will make you gay again!"

——If we could be always boys!

I thanked him in a way that saddened him. We passed out shortly after from the city gates, and strode on over the rolling plain. Once or twice we turned back to look at the rocky heights beneath which lay the ruined town of Palestrina;—a city that defied Rome,—that had a king before a ploughshare had touched the Capitoline,[128] or the Janiculan hill! The ivy was covering up richly the Etruscan foundations,[129] and there was a

---

[124]The characters mentioned in this paragraph revolve around narratives based on the life of Cola di Rienzo, a fourteenth-century Roman political figure who futilely attempted to restore the greatness of ancient Rome. Rienzo's story was made famous in Mitchell's time by Bulwer-Lytton's popular historical novel, *Rienzi, the Last of the Tribunes* (1835). The Colonnas and other Italian noble families stood against Rienzo. Rienzo laid siege to these families at Praeneste, where he eventually defeated them. At times, Rienzo was helped by the robber-king Walter de Montreal and his brothers in his military and political exploits.

[125]Low plain surrounding the city of Rome.

[126]peasant

[127]Almost never.

[128]The ancient city of Rome was built on seven hills; the Capitoline was one of them.

[129]The Etruscans were the major power in central Italy until the ascendency of Rome.

quiet over the whole place. The smoke was rising straight into the sky from the chimney tops; a peasant or two, were going along the road with donkeys; beside this, the city was, to all appearance, a dead city. And it seemed to me that an old monk, whom I could see with my glass, near the little chapel above the town, might be going to say mass for the soul of the dead city.

And afterward, when we came near to Rome, and passed under the temple tomb of Metella,[130]—my friend said,—"And will you go back now to your home? or will you set off with me to-morrow for Ancona?"[131]

"At least, I must say adieu," returned I.

"God speed you!" said he, and we parted upon the Piazza di Venezia,—he for his last mass at St. Peter's, and I for the tall house upon the Corso.

ENRICA

I hear her glancing feet, the moment I have tinkled the bell;—and there she is, with her brown hair gathered into braids, and her eyes full of joy, and greeting. And as I walk with the mother to the window to look at some pageant that is passing,—she steals up behind, and passes her arm around me, with a quick electric motion, and a gentle pressure of welcome—that tells more than a thousand words.

It is a pageant of death that is passing below. Far down the street, we see heads thrust out of the windows, and standing in bold relief against the red torch-light of the moving train. Below, dim figures are gathering on the narrow side ways to look at the solemn spectacle. A hoarse chant rises louder, and louder; and half dies in the night air, and breaks out again with new, and deep bitterness.

Now, the first torch-light under us shines plainly on faces in the windows, and on the kneeling women in the street. First, come old retainers of the dead one, bearing long blazing flambeaux.[132] Then comes a company of priests, two by two, bare-headed, and every second one with a lighted torch, and all are chanting.

Next, is a brotherhood of friars in brown cloaks, with sandalled feet;—and the red-light streams full upon their grizzled heads. They add their heavy guttural voices to the chant, and pass slowly on.

Then comes a company of priests, in white muslin capes, and black robes, and black caps,—bearing books in their hands, wide open, and lit up plainly by the torches of churchly servitors, who march beside them; and from the books, the priests chant loud and solemnly. Now, the music is loudest; and the friars take up the dismal notes from the white-capped priests, and the priests before catch them from the brown-robed friars, and mournfully the sound rises up between the tall buildings,—into the blue night-sky, that lies between Heaven and Rome.

---

[130]The large Roman tomb of Caecilia Metella served as a notable landmark on one of the major roads leading to Rome.

[131]Important Roman port city in central Italy.

[132]Flaming torch.

——"*Vede—vede!*"[133]—says Cesare; and in a blaze of the red-torch fire, comes the bier, borne on the necks of stout friars; and on the bier, is the body of a dead man, habited like a priest. Heavy plumes of black wave at each corner.

——"Hist!"—says my landlady.

The body is just under us. Enrica crosses herself; her smile is for the moment gone. Cesare's boy-face is grown suddenly earnest. We could see the pale, youthful features of the dead man. The glaring flambeaux, sent their flaunting streams of unearthly light over the wan visage of the sleeper. A thousand eyes were looking on him; but his face careless of them all, was turned up, straight toward the stars.

Still the chant rises; and companies of priests follow the bier, like those who had gone before. Friars, in brown cloaks, and prelates, and Carmelites[134] come after—all with torches. Two by two—their voices growing hoarse—they tramp, and chant.

For a while the voices cease, and you can hear the rustling of their robes, and their foot-falls, as if your ear was to the earth. Then the chant rises again, as they glide on in a wavy, shining line, and rolls back over the death-train, like the howling of a wind in winter.

As they pass, the faces vanish from the windows. The kneeling women upon the pavement, rise up, mindful of the paroxysm of Life once more. The groups in the doorways scatter. But their low voices do not drown the voices of the host of mourners, and their ghost-like music.

I look long upon the blazing bier, trailing under the deep shadows of the Roman palaces, and at the stream of torches, winding like a glittering, scaled serpent.——It is a priest—say I to my landlady, as she closes the window.

"No, signor,—a young man never married, and so by virtue of his condition, they put on him the priest-robes."

"So I"—says the pretty Enrica—"if I should die, would be robed in white, as you saw me on a carnival night, and be followed by nuns for sisters."

"A long way off may it be, Enrica!"

She took my hand in hers, and pressed it. An Italian girl does not fear to talk of death; and we were talking of it still, as we walked back to my little parlor—my hand all the time in hers—and sat down by the blaze of my fire.

It was holy week—never had Enrica looked more sweetly than in that black dress,—under that long, dark veil of the days of Lent. Upon the broad pavement of St. Peter's,—where the people flocking by thousands, made only side groups about the altars of the vast temple—I have watched her kneeling, beside her mother,—her eyes bent down, her lips moving earnestly, and her whole figure tremulous with deep emotion. Wandering around among the halberdiers of the Pope, and the court coats of Austria, and the bare-footed pilgrims with sandal, shell and staff, I would sidle back again, to look upon that kneeling figure; and leaning against the huge columns of the church, would dream——even as I am dreaming now.

---

[133]Look, look!

[134]The Carmelites are a religious order of the Roman Catholic Church dedicated to education, care for the sick, and other works of charity.

At night-fall, I urge my way into the Sistine Chapel: Enrica is beside me,—looking with me upon the gaunt figures of the Judgment of Angelo.[135] They are chanting the Miserere. The twelve candle-sticks by the altar are put out one by one, as the service continues. The sun has gone down, only the red glow of twilight steals through the dusky windows. There is a pause, and a brief reading from a red-cloaked cardinal, and all kneel down. *She* kneels beside me: and the sweet, mournful flow of the Miserere begins again,—growing in force, and depth, till the whole chapel rings, and the balcony of the choir trembles: then, it subsides again into the low soft wail of a single voice—so prolonged—so tremulous, and so real, that the heart aches, and the tears start——for Christ is dead!

——Lingering yet, the wail dies not wholly, but just as it seemed expiring, it is caught up by another and stronger voice that carries it on, plaintive as ever;—nor does it stop with this—for just as you looked for silence, three voices more begin the lament—sweet, touching, mournful voices,—and bear it up to a full cry, when the whole choir catch its burden, and make the lament change into the wailings of a multitude—wild, shrill, hoarse—with swift chants intervening, as if agony had given force to anguish. Then, sweetly, slowly, voice by voice, note by note, the wailings sink into the low, tender, moan of a single singer—faltering, tremulous, as if tears checked the utterance; and swelling out, as if despair sustained it.

It was dark in the chapel, when we went out; voices were low. Enrica said nothing——I could say nothing.

I was to leave Rome after Easter; I did not love to speak of it—nor to think of it. Rome—that old city, with all its misery, and its fallen state, and its broken palaces of the Empire—grows upon one's heart. The fringing shrubs of the coliseum, flaunting their blossoms at the tall beggar-men in cloaks, who grub below,—the sun glimmering over the mossy pile of the House of Nero,[136]—the sweet sunsets from the Pincian,[137] that make the broad pine-tops of the Janiculan, stand sharp and dark against a sky of gold, cannot easily be left behind. And Enrica with her silver brown hair, and the silken fillet that bound it,—and her deep blue eyes,—and her white, delicate fingers,—and the blue veins chasing over her fair temples——ah, Easter is too near!

But it comes; and passes with the glory of St. Peter's—lighted from top to bottom. With Enrica—I saw it from the Ripetta,[138] as it loomed up in the distance, like a city on fire.

The next day, I bring home my last bunch of flowers, and with it a little richly-chased Roman ring. No fire blazes on the hearth—but they are all there. Warm days have come, and the summer air, even now, hangs heavy with fever, in the hollows of the plain.

I heard them stirring early on the morning on which I was to go away. I do not think I slept very well myself—nor very late. Never did Enrica look more beautiful—never.

---

[135]The famous painter and sculptor Michelangelo (1475–1564) painted a picture of the Last Judgment of Christ, which covered the entire wall behind the altar in the Sistine Chapel.

[136]Ruins of the imperial palace.

[137]Prominent hill located in the city of Rome.

[138]Wonderfully ornate gate sculpted in the Baroque style from which you could see St. Peter's.

All her Carnival robes, and the sad drapery of the Friday of Crucifixion could not so adorn her beauty as that neat morning dress, and that simple rosebud she wore upon her bosom. She gave it to me—the last—with a trembling hand. I did not, for I could not, thank her. She knew it; and her eyes were full.

The old man kissed my cheek—it was the Roman custom, but the custom did not extend to the Roman girls;—at least not often. As I passed down the Corso, I looked back at the balcony, where she stood in the time of Carnival, in the brown Sombrero, with the white plume. I knew she would be there now; and there she was. My eyes dwelt upon the vision, very loth to leave it; and after my eyes had lost it, my heart clung to it,—there, where my memory clings now.

At noon, the carriage stopped upon the hills, toward Soracte, that overlooked Rome. There was a stunted pine tree grew a little way from the road, and I sat down under it,—for I wished no dinner—and I looked back with strange tumult of feeling, upon the sleeping city, with the gray, billowy sea of the Campagna, lying around it.

I seemed to see Enrica—the Roman girl, in that morning dress, with her brown hair in its silken fillet;—but the rose-bud that was in her bosom, was now in mine. Her silvery voice too, seemed to float past me, bearing snatches of Roman songs;—but the songs were sad and broken.

——After all, this is sad vanity!—thought I: and yet if I had espied then some returning carriage going down toward Rome, I will not say—but that I should have hailed it, and taken a place,—and gone back, and to this day perhaps—have lived at Rome.

But the vetturino[139] called me; the coach was ready;—I gave one more look toward the dome that guarded the sleeping city; and then, we galloped down the mountain, on the road that lay towards Perugia, and Lake Thrasimene.

——Sweet Enrica! art thou living yet? Or hast thou passed away to that Silent Land, where the good sleep, and the beautiful?

The visions of the Past fade. The morning breeze has died upon the meadow; the Bob-o'-Lincoln sits swaying on the willow tufts—singing no longer. The trees lean to the brook; but the shadows fall straight and dense upon the silver stream.

Noon has broken into the middle sky; and Morning is gone.

II

❧ Noon

The noon is short; the sun never loiters on the meridian, nor does the shadow on the old dial by the garden, stay long at XII. The Present, like the noon, is only a point; and a point so fine, that it is not measurable by the grossness of action. Thought alone is delicate enough to tell the breadth of the Present.

The Past belongs to God: the Present only is ours. And short as it is, there is more in

---

[139]Carriage driver.

it, and of it, than we can well manage. That man who can grapple it, and measure it, and fill it with his purpose, is doing a man's work: none can do more: but there are thousands who do less.

Short as it is, the Present is great strong;—as much stronger than the Past, as fire than ashes, or as Death than the grave. The noon sun will quicken vegetable life, that in the morning was dead. It is hot and scorching: I feel it now upon my head: but it does not scorch and heat like the bewildering Present. There are no oak leaves to interrupt the rays of the burning NOW. Its shadows do not fall east or west;—like the noon, the shade it makes, falls straight from sky to earth—straight from Heaven to Hell!

Memory presides over the Past; Action presides over the Present. The first lives in a rich temple hung with glorious trophies, and lined with tombs: the other has no shrine but Duty, and it walks the earth like a spirit!

——I called my dog to me, and we shared together the meal that I had brought away at sunrise from the mansion under the elms; and now, Carlo is gnawing at the bone that I have thrown to him, and I stroll dreamily in the quiet noon atmosphere, upon that grassy knoll, under the oaks.

Noon in the country is very still: the birds do not sing: the workmen are not in the field: the sheep lay their noses to the ground; and the herds stand in pools, under shady trees, lashing their sides,—but otherwise, motionless. The mills upon the brook, far above, have ceased for an hour their labor; and the stream softens its rustle, and sinks away from the sedgy banks. The heat plays upon the meadow in noiseless waves, and the beech leaves do not stir.

Thought, I said, was the only measure of the Present: and the stillness of noon breeds thought: and my thought brings up the old companions, and stations them in the domain of NOW. Thought ranges over the world, and brings up hopes, fears, and resolves, to measure the burning NOW. Joy, and grief, and purpose, blending in my thought, give breadth to the Present.

—Where—thought I—is little Isabel now? Where is Lilly—where is Ben? Where is Leslie,—where is my old teacher? Where is my chum, who played such rare tricks—where is the black-eyed Jane?—Where is that sweet-faced girl whom I parted with upon that terrace, looking down upon the old spire of Modbury church? Where are my hopes—where my purposes—where my sorrows?

I care not who you are—but if you bring such thought to measure the Present, the present will seem broad; and it will be sultry as noon—and make a fever of Now.

EARLY FRIENDS

Where are they?

I cannot sit now, as once, upon the edge of the brook, hour after hour, flinging off my line and hook to the nibbling roach, and reckon it great sport. There is no girl with auburn ringlets to sit beside me, and to play upon the bank. The hours are shorter than they were then; and the little joys that furnished boyhood till the heart was full, can fill it no longer. Poor Tray is dead, long ago; and he cannot swim into the pools for the floating sticks; nor can I sport with him hour after hour, and think it happiness. The mound that covers his grave is sunken; and the trees that shaded it, are broken and mossy.

Little Lilly is grown into a woman, and is married; and she has another little Lilly, with flaxen hair, she says,—looking as *she* used to look. I dare say the child is pretty; but it is not my Lilly. She has a little boy too, that she calls Paul;—a chubby rogue—she writes,—and as mischievous as ever I was. God bless the boy!

Ben,—who would have liked a ride in the coach that carried me away to school— has had a great many rides since then—rough rides, and hard ones, over the road of life. He does not rake up the falling leaves for bonfires, as he did once; he is grown a man, and is fighting his way somewhere in our western world, to the short-lived honours of time. He was married not long ago; his wife I remembered as one of my playmates at my first school: she was beautiful, but fragile as a leaf. She died within a year of their marriage. Ben was but four years my senior; but this grief has made him ten years older. He does not say it; but his eye and his figure tell it.

The nurse who put the purse in my hand that dismal morning, is grown a feeble old woman. She was over fifty then; she may well be seventy now. She did not know my voice when I went to see her the other day, nor did she know my face at all. She repeated the name when I told it to her—Paul, Paul,—she did not remember any Paul, except a little boy, a long while ago.

——"To whom you gave a purse when he went away, and told him to say nothing to Lilly or to Ben?"

——"Yes, that Paul"—says the old woman exultingly—"do you know him?"

And when I told her—"she would not have believed it!" But she did; and took hold of my hand again, (for she was blind); and then smoothed down the plaits of her apron, and jogged her cap strings, to look tidy in the presence of 'the gentleman.' And she told me long stories about the old house and how other people came in afterward; and she called me 'sir' sometimes, and sometimes 'Paul.' But I asked her to say only Paul; she seemed glad for this, and talked easier; and went on to tell of my old playmates, and how we used to ride the pony—poor Jacko!—and how we gathered nuts—such heaping piles; and how we used to play at fox and geese through the long winter evenings; and how my poor mother would smile——but here I asked her to stop. She could not have gone on much longer, for I believe she loved our house and people, better than she loved her own.

As for my uncle, the cold, silent man, who lived with his books in the house upon the hill, and who used to frighten me sometimes with his look, he grew very feeble after I had left, and almost crazed. The country people said that he was mad; and Isabel with her sweet heart clung to him, and would lead him out when his step tottered, to the seat in the garden, and read to him out of the books he loved to hear. And sometimes, they told me, she would read to him some letters that I had written to Lilly or to Ben, and ask him if he remembered Paul, who saved her from drowning under the tree in the meadow? But he could only shake his head, and mutter something about how old and feeble he had grown.

They wrote me afterward that he died, and was buried in a far-away place, where his wife once lived, and where he now sleeps beside her. Isabel was sick with grief, and came to live for a time with Lilly; but when they wrote me last, she had gone back to her old home—where Tray was buried,—where we had played together so often, through the long days of summer.

I was glad I should find her there, when I came back. Lilly and Ben were both living nearer to the city, when I landed from my long journey over the seas; but still I went to find Isabel first. Perhaps I had heard so much oftener from the others, that I felt less eager to see them; or perhaps I wanted to save my best visits to the last; or perhaps—(I did think it) perhaps I loved Isabel, better than them all.

So I went into the country, thinking all the way, how she must have changed since I left. She must be now nineteen or twenty; and then her grief must have saddened her face somewhat; but I thought I should like her all the better for that. Then perhaps she would not laugh, and tease me, but would be quieter, and wear a sweet smile—so calm, and beautiful, I thought. Her figure too must have grown more elegant, and she would have more dignity in her air.

I shuddered a little at this; for, I thought,—she will hardly think so much of me then; perhaps she will have seen those whom she likes a great deal better. Perhaps she will not like me at all; yet I knew very well that I should like her.

I had gone up almost to the house; I had passed the stream where we fished on that day, many years before; and I thought that now since she was grown to womanhood, I should never sit with her there again, and surely never drag her as I did out of the water, and never chafe her little hands, and never perhaps kiss her, as I did, when she sat upon my mother's lap—oh, no—no—no!

I saw where we buried Tray, but the old slab was gone; there was no ribbon there now. I thought that at least, Isabel would have replaced the slab;—but it was a wrong thought. I trembled when I went up to the door—for it flashed upon me, that perhaps,— Isabel was married. I could not tell why she should not; but I knew it would make me uncomfortable, to hear that she had.

There was a tall woman who opened the door; she did not know me; but I recognized her as one of the old servants. I asked after the housekeeper first, thinking I would surprise Isabel. My heart fluttered somewhat, thinking that she might step in suddenly herself—or perhaps that she might have seen me coming up the hill. But even then, I thought, she would hardly know me.

Presently the housekeeper came in, looking very grave; she asked if the gentleman wished to see her?

The gentleman did wish it, and she sat down on one side of the fire;—for it was autumn, and the leaves were falling, and the November winds were very chilly.

—Shall I tell her—thought I—who I am, or ask at once for Isabel? I tried to ask; but it was hard for me to call her name; it was very strange, but I could not pronounce it at all.

"Who, sir?"—said the housekeeper, in a tone so earnest, that I rose at once, and crossed over, and took her hand:—"You know me," said I,—"you surely remember Paul?"

She started with surprise, but recovered herself, and resumed the same grave manner. I thought I had committed some mistake, or been in some way cause of offence. I called her—Madame, and asked for—Isabel?

She turned pale, terribly pale—"Bella?" said she.

"Yes, Bella."

"Sir—Bella is dead!"

I dropped into my chair. I said nothing. The housekeeper—bless her kind heart!—

slipped noiselessly out. My hands were over my eyes. The winds were sighing outside, and the clock ticking mournfully within.

I did not sob, nor weep, nor utter any cry.

The clock ticked mournfully, and the winds were sighing; but I did not hear them any longer; there was a tempest raging within me, that would have drowned the voice of thunder.

It broke at length in a long, deep sigh,—"oh God!"—said I. It may have been a prayer;—it was not an imprecation.

Bella—sweet Bella was dead! It seemed as if with her, half the world were dead— every bright face darkened—every sunshine blotted out,—every flower withered,— every hope extinguished!

I walked out into the air, and stood under the trees where we had played together with poor Tray—where Tray lay buried. But it was not Tray I thought of, as I stood there, with the cold wind playing through my hair, and my eyes filling with tears. How could she die? Why *was* she gone? Was it really true? Was Isabel indeed dead—in her coffin— buried? Then why should anybody live? What was there to live for, now that Bella was gone?

Ah, what a gap in the world, is made by the death of those we love! It is no longer whole, but a poor half-world that swings uneasy on its axis, and makes you dizzy with the clatter of its wreck!

The housekeeper told me all—little by little, as I found calmness to listen. She had been dead a month; Lilly was with her through it all; she died sweetly, without pain, and without fear,—what can angels fear? She had spoken often of 'Cousin Paul;' she had left a little pacquet for him, but it was not there; she had given it into Lilly's keeping.

Her grave, the housekeeper told me, was only a little way off from her home— beside the grave of a brother who died long years before. I went there that evening. The mound was high and fresh. The sods had not closed together, and the dry leaves caught in the crevices, and gave a ragged and a terrible look to the grave. The next day, I laid them all smooth—as we had once laid them on the grave of Tray;—I clipped the long grass, and set a tuft of blue violets at the foot, and watered it all with—tears. The home-stead, the trees, the fields, the meadows—in the windy November, looked dismally. I could not like them again;—I liked nothing, but the little mound, that I had dressed over Bella's grave. There she sleeps now,—the sleep of Death!

SCHOOL REVISITED

The old school is there still,—with the high cupola upon it, and the long galleries, with the sleeping rooms opening out on either side, and the corner one, where I slept. But the boys are not there, nor the old teachers. They have ploughed up the play-ground to plant corn, and the apple tree with the low limb, that made our gymnasium, is cut down.

I was there only a little time ago. It was on a Sunday. One of the old houses of the village had been fashioned into a tavern, and it was there I stopped. But I strolled by the old one, and looked into the bar-room, where I used to gaze with wonder upon the enor-mous pictures of wild animals, which heralded some coming menagerie. There was just such a picture hanging still, and two or three advertisements of sheriffs, and a little bill of a 'horse stolen,' and—as I thought—the same brown pitcher on the edge of the bar. I was sure it was the same great wood box that stood by the fire place, and the same whip, and great coat hung in the corner.

I was not in so gay costume, as I once thought I would be wearing, when a man; I had nothing better than a rusty shooting jacket; but even with this, I was determined to have a look about the church, and see if I could trace any of the faces of the old times. They had sadly altered the building; they had cut out its long galleries, and its old fashioned square pews, and filled it with narrow boxes, as they do in the city. The pulpit was not so high, or grand; and it was covered over with the work of the cabinet-makers.

I missed too the old preacher, whom we all feared so much; and in place of him, was a jaunty looking man, whom I thought I would not be at all afraid to speak to, or if need be, to slap on the shoulder. And when I did meet him after church, I looked him in the eye as boldly as a lion—what a change was that, from the school days!

Here and there, I could detect about the church, some old farmer, by the stoop in his shoulders, or by a particular twist in his nose; and one or two young fellows, who used to storm into the gallery in my school days, in very gay jackets, dressed off with ribbons,—which we thought was astonishing heroism, and admired accordingly,—were now settled away into fathers of families; and looked as demure, and peaceable, at the head of their pews, with a white-headed boy or two between them, and their wives, as if they had been married all their days.

There was a stout man too, with a slight limp in his gait, who used to work on harnesses, and strap our skates, and who I always thought would have made a capital Vulcan,—he stalked up the aisle past me, as if I had my skates strapped at his shop, only yesterday.

The bald-pated shoemaker, who never kept his word, and who worked in the brick shop, and who had a son called Theodore,—which we all thought a very pretty name for a shoemaker's son—I could not find. I feared he might be dead. I hoped, if he was, that his broken promises about patching boots would not come up against him.

The old factor of tamarinds and sugar crackers, who used to drive his covered waggon every Saturday evening into the play-ground, I observed, still holding his place in the village choir; and singing—though with a tooth or two gone,—as serenely, and obstreporously as ever.

I looked around the church, to find the black-eyed girl who always sat behind the choir,—the one I loved to look at so much. I knew she must be grown up; but I could fix upon no face positively; once, as a stout woman with a pair of boys, and who wore a big red shawl, turned half around, I thought I recognized her nose. If it was she, it had grown red though; and I felt cured of my old fondness. As for the other, who wore the hat trimmed with fur—she was nowhere to be seen, among either maids, or matrons; and when I asked the tavern-keeper, and described her, and her father, as they were in my school-days, he told me that she had married too, and lived some five miles from the village; and said he,—"I guess she leads her husband a devil of a life!"

I felt cured of her too; but I pitied the husband.

One of my old teachers was in the church; I could have sworn to his face; he was a precise man; and now I thought he looked rather roughly at my old shooting jacket. But

I let him look, and scowled at him a little; for I remembered that he had feruled[140] me once. I thought it was not probable that he would ever do it again.

There was a bustling little lawyer in the village, who lived in a large house, and who was the great man of that town and country,—he had scarce changed at all; and he stepped into the church as briskly, and promptly, as he did ten years ago. But what struck me most, was the change in a couple of pretty, little, white-haired girls, that at the time I left, were of that uncertain age, when the mother lifts them on a Sunday, and pounces them down one after the other upon the seat of the pew;—these were now grown into blooming young ladies. And they swept by me in the vestibule of the church, with a flutter of robes, and a grace of motion, that fairly made my heart twitter in my bosom. I know nothing that brings home upon a man so quick, the consciousness of increasing years, as to find the little prattling girls, that were almost babies in his boyhood—become dashing ladies;—and to find those whom he used to look on patronizingly, and compassionately—thinking they were pretty little girls—grown to such maturity, that the mere rustle of their silk dress will give him a twinge; and their eyes, if he looks at them—make him unaccountably shy.

After service I strolled up by the school buildings; I traced the names that we had cut upon the fence; but the fence had grown brown with age, and was nearly rotted away. Upon the beech tree in the hollow behind the school, the carvings were all overgrown. It must have been vacation, if indeed there was any school at all; for I could see only one old woman about the premises, and she was hanging out a dishcloth, to dry in the sun. I passed on up the hill, beyond the buildings, where in the boy-days, we built stone forts with bastions and turrets; but the farmers had put bastions, and turrets, into their cobble-stone walls. At the orchard fence, I stopped, and looked—from force, I believe, of old habit,—to see if any one were watching;—and then leaped over, and found my way to the early apple tree; but the fruit had gone by. It seemed very daring in me, even then, to walk so boldly in the forbidden ground.

But the old head-master who forbade it, was dead; and Russel and Burgess, and I know not how many others, who in other times, were culprits with me, were dead too. When I passed back by the school, I lingered to look up at the windows of that corner room, where I had slept the sound, healthful sleep of boyhood,—and where too I had passed many—many wakeful hours, thinking of the absent Bella, and of my home.

——How small, seem now, the great griefs of boyhood! Light floating clouds will obscure the sun that is but half risen; but let him be up—mid heaven, and the cloud that then darkens the land, must be thick, and heavy indeed.

——The tears started from my eyes:—was not such a cloud over me now?

COLLEGE

School-mates slip out of sight and knowledge, and are forgotten; or if you meet them, they bear another character; the boy is not there. It is a new acquaintance that you make, with nothing of your fellow upon the benches, but the name. Though the eye and face

[140]beaten

cleave to your memory, and you meet them afterward, and think you have met a friend—the voice or the action will break the charm, and you find only—another man.

But with your classmates, in that later school, where form and character were both nearer ripeness, and where knowledge labored for together, bred the first manly sympathies,—it is different. And as you meet them, or hear of them, the thought of their advance makes a measure of your own—it makes a measure of the NOW.

You judge of your happiness, by theirs,—of your progress, by theirs, and of your prospects, by theirs. If one is happy, you seek to trace out the way by which he has wrought his happiness; you consider how it differs from your own; and you think with sighs, how you might possibly have wrought the same; but *now* it has escaped. If another has won some honorable distinction, you fall to thinking, how the man—your old equal, as you thought, upon the college benches—has outrun you. It pricks to effort, and teaches the difference between now, and then. Life with all its duties, and hopes, gathers upon your Present, like a great weight, or like a storm ready to burst. It is met anew; it pleads more strongly; and action that has been neglected, rises before you—a giant of remorse.

Stop not, loiter not, look not backward, if you would be among the foremost! The great Now, so quick, so broad, so fleeting, is yours;—in an hour it will belong to the Eternity of the Past. The temper of Life is to be made good by big honest blows; stop striking, and you will do nothing: strike feebly, and you will do almost as little. Success rides on every hour: grapple it, and you may win: but without a grapple, it will never go with you. Work is the weapon of honor, and who lacks the weapon, will never triumph.

There were some seventy of us—all scattered now. I meet one here and there at wide distances apart; and we talk together of old days, and of our present work and life,—and separate. Just so ships at sea, in murky weather, will shift their course to come within hailing distance, and compare their longitude, and——part. One I have met wandering in southern Italy, dreaming as I was dreaming—over the tomb of Virgil,[141] by the dark grotto of Pausilippo.[142] It seemed strange to talk of our old readings in Tacitus[143] there upon classic ground; but we did; and ran on to talk of our lives; and sitting down upon the promontory of Baie, looking off upon that blue sea, as clear as the classics, we told each other our respective stories. And two nights after, upon the quay, in sight of Vesuvius, which shed a lurid glow upon the sky, that was reflected from the white walls of the Hotel de Russie, and from the broad lava pavements, we parted—he to wander among the isles of the Ægean, and I to turn northward.

Another time, as I was wandering among those mysterious figures that crowd the foyer of the French opera upon a night of the Masked Ball, I saw a familiar face: I followed it with my eye, until I became convinced. He did not know me until I named his old seat upon the bench of the Division Room, and the hard-faced Tutor G——. Then we talked of the old rivalries, and Christmas jollities, and of this and that one, whom we had

---

[141]Virgil (70–19 B.C.) was a Roman poet best known for his epic, the *Aeneid.*

[142]Part of one of the largest tunnels in the ancient world, built by the Romans between Naples and Pozzuoli in 36 B.C.

[143]Tacitus (A.D. 56–120) was a premier Roman historian and public official.

come upon in our wayward tracks; while the black-robed grisettes stared through their velvet masks;—nor did we tire of comparing the old memories, with the unearthly gaiety of the scene about us, until day-light broke.

In a quiet mountain town of New England, I came not long since upon another: he was hale and hearty, and pushing his lawyer work with just the same nervous energy, with which he used to recite a theorem of Euclid.[144] He was father too of a couple of stout, curly-pated boys; and his good woman, as he called her, appeared a sensible, honest, good-natured lady. I must say that I envied him his wife, much more than I had envied my companion of the opera—his Domino.[145]

I happened only a little while ago to drop into the college chapel of a Sunday. There were the same hard oak benches below, and the lucky fellows who enjoyed a corner seat, were leaning back upon the rail, after the old fashion. The tutors were perched up in their side boxes, looking as prim, and serious, and important, as over. The same stout Doctor read the hymn in the same rhythmical way; and he prayed the same prayer, for (I thought) the same old sort of sinners. As I shut my eyes to listen, it seemed as if the intermediate years had all gone out; and that I was on my own pew bench, and thinking out those little schemes for excuses, or for effort, which were to relieve me, or to advance me, in my college world.

There was a pleasure, like the pleasure of dreaming about forgotten joys—in listening to the Doctor's sermon: he began in the same half embarrassed, half awkward way; and fumbled at his Bible leaves, and the poor pinched cushion, as he did long before. But as he went on with his rusty and polemic vigour, the poetry within him would now and then warm his soul into a burst of fervid eloquence, and his face would glow, and his hand tremble, and the cushion and the Bible leaves be all forgot, in the glow of his thought, until with a half cough, and a pinch at the cushion, he fell back into his strong, but tread-mill argumentation.

In the corner above, was the stately, white-haired professor, wearing the old dignity of carriage, and a smile as bland, as if the years had all been playthings; and had I seen him in his lecture-room, I daresay I should have found the same suavity of address, the same marvellous currency of talk, and the same infinite composure over the exploding retorts.

Near him was the silver-haired old gentleman,—with a very astute expression,—who used to have an odd habit of tightening his cloak about his nether limbs. I could not see that his eye was any the less bright; nor did he seem less eager to catch at the handle of some witticism, or bit of satire,—to the poor student's cost. I remembered my old awe of him, I must say, with something of a grudge; but I had got fairly over it now. There are sharper griefs in life, than professor's talk.

Farther on, I saw the long-faced, dark-haired man, who looked as if he were always near some explosive, electric battery, or upon an insulated stool. He was, I believe, a man of fine feelings; but he had a way of reducing all action to dry, hard, mathematical sys-

---

[144]Euclid (third century B.C.) was a famous ancient mathematician known for his work in geometry.

[145]One who wears a half-mask (sometimes with cloak) at a masquerade ball.

tem, with very little poetry about it. I know there was not much poetry in his problems in physics, and still less in his half-yearly examinations. But I do not dread them now.

Over opposite, I was glad to see still, the aged head of the kind, and generous old man, who in my day presided over the college; and who carried with him the affections of each succeeding class,—added to their respect for his learning. This seems a higher triumph to me now, than it seemed then. A strong mind, or a cultivated mind may challenge respect; but there is needed a noble one, to win affection.

A new man now filled his place in the president's seat; but he was one whom I had known, and been proud to know. His figure was bent, and thin—the very figure that an old Flemish master would have chosen, for a scholar. His eye had a kind of piercing lustre, as if it had long been fixed on books; and his expression—when unrelieved by his affable smile—was that of hard midnight toil. With all his polish of mind, he was a gentleman at heart; and treated us always with a manly courtesy, that is not forgotten.

But of all the faces that used to be ranged below—four hundred men and boys—there was not one, with whom to join hands, and live back again. Their griefs, joys, and toil, were chaining them to their labor of life. Each one in his thought, coursing over a world as wide as my own;—how many thousand worlds of thought, upon this one world of ours.

I stepped dreamily through the corridors of the old Atheneum, thinking of that first, fearful step, when the faces were new, and the stern tutor was strange, and the prolix Livy[146] *so* hard. I went up at night, and skulked around the buildings, when the lights were blazing from all the windows, and they were busy with their tasks—plain tasks, and easy tasks,—because they are certain tasks. Happy fellows—thought I—who have only to do, what is set before you to be done. But the time is coming, and very fast, when you must not only do, but know what to do. The time is coming, when in place of your one master, you will have a thousand masters—masters of duty, of business, of pleasure, and of grief—giving you harder lessons each one of them, than any of your Fluxions.[147]

Morning will pass, and the Noon will come—hot, and scorching.

THE PACQUET OF BELLA

I have not forgotten that pacquet of Bella; I did not once forget it. And when I saw Lilly—now the grown up Lilly, happy in her household, and blithe as when she was a maiden, she gave it to me. She told me too of Bella's illness, and of her suffering, and of her manner, when she put the little pacquet in her hand 'for Cousin Paul.' But this I will not repeat;—I cannot.

I know not why it was, but I shuddered at the mention of her name. There are some who will talk, at table, and in their gossip, of dead friends; I wonder how they do it? For myself, when the grave has closed its gates on the faces of those I love—however busy my mournful thought may be, the tongue is silent, I cannot name their names; it shocks

[146]Livy (59?B.C.–A.D. 17), along with Tacitus, was one of ancient Rome's greatest historians. He had a tremendous influence on the style and philosophy of history writing.

[147]Refers to a difficult, advanced branch of mathematics.

me to hear them named. It seems like tearing open half-healed wounds, and disturbing with harsh worldly noise, the sweet sleep of death.

I loved Bella. I know not how I loved her,—whether as a lover, or as a husband loves a wife; I only know this,—I always loved her. She was so gentle—so beautiful,—so confiding, that I never once thought, but that the whole world loved her, as well as I. There was only one thing I never told to Bella;—I would tell her of all my grief, and of all my joys; I would tell her my hopes, my ambitious dreams, my disappointments, my anger, and my dislikes;—but I never told her how much I loved her.

I do not know why, unless I knew that it was needless. But I should as soon have thought of telling Bella on some winter's day—Bella, it is winter!—or of whispering to her on some balmy day of August—Bella, it is summer!—as of telling her, after she had grown to girlhood.—Bella, I love you!

I had received one letter from her in the old countries; it was a sweet letter, in which she told me all that she had been doing, and how she had thought of me, when she rambled over the woods where we had rambled together. She had written two or three other letters, Lilly told me, but they had never reached me. I had told her too of all that made my happiness; I wrote her about the sweet girl I had seen on shipboard, and how I met her afterward, and what a happy time we passed down in Devon. I even told her of the strange dream I had, in which Isabel seemed to be in England, and to turn away from me sadly, because I called her—Carry.

I also told her of all I saw in that great world of Paris—writing, as I would write to a sister; and I told her too of the sweet Roman girl, Enrica—of her brown hair, and of her rich eyes, and of her pretty Carnival dresses. And when I missed letter after letter, I told her that she must still write her letters, or some little journal, and read it to me when I came back. I thought how pleasant it would be to sit under the trees by her father's house, and listen to her tender voice going through that record of her thoughts, and fears. Alas, how our hopes betray us!

It began almost like a diary, about the time that her father fell sick. "It is"—said she to Lilly, when she gave it to her, "what I would have said to Cousin Paul, if he had been here."

It begins

"——I have come back now to father's house; I could not leave him alone, for they told me he was sick. I found him not well; he was very glad to see me, and kissed me so tenderly that I am sure, Cousin Paul, you would not have said, as you used to say—that he was a cold man! I sometimes read to him, sitting in the deep library window, (you remember it,) where we used to nestle out of his sight, at dusk. He cannot read any more.

"I would give anything to see the little Carry you speak of; but do you know you did not describe her to me at all; will you not tell me if she has dark hair, or light, or if her eyes are blue, or dark, like mine? Is she good; did she not make ugly speeches, or grow peevish, in those long days upon the ocean? How I would have liked to have been with you, on those clear starlit nights, looking off upon the water! But then I think that you would not have wished me there; and that you did not once think of me even. This makes me sad; yet I know not why it should; for I always liked you best, when you were happy; and I am sure you must have been happy then. You say you shall never see her after you have left the ship:—you must not think so, Cousin Paul; if she is so beautiful, and fond, as you tell me, your own heart will lead you in her way, some time again; I feel almost sure of it.

* * * "Father is getting more and more feeble, and wandering in his mind; this is very dreadful; he calls me sometimes by my mother's name; and when I say—it is Isabel,—he says—what Isabel and treats me as if I was a stranger. The physician shakes his head when I ask him of father: oh, Paul, if he should die—what could I do? I should die too—I know I should. Who would there be to care for me? Lilly is married, and Ben is far off, and you Paul, whom I love better than either, are a long way from me. But God is good, and he will spare my father.

* * * "So you have seen again your little Carry! I told you it would be so. You tell me how accidental it was:—ah, Paul, Paul, you rogue, honest as you are, I half doubt you there! I like your description of her too:—dark eyes like mine you say—'almost as pretty;' well, Paul, I will forgive you that; it is only a white lie. You know they must be a great deal prettier than mine, or you would never have stayed a whole fortnight in an old farmer's house, far down in Devon! I wish I could see her: I wish she was here with you now; for it is mid-summer, and the trees and flowers were never prettier. But I am all alone; father is too ill to go out at all. I fear now very much, that he will never go out again. Lilly was here yesterday, but he did not know her. She read me your last letter: it was not so long as mine. You are very—very good to me Paul.

* * * "For a long time I have written nothing: my father has been very ill, and the old housekeeper has been sick too, and father would have no one but me near him. He cannot live long. I feel sadly—miserably; you will not know me when you come home; your "pretty Bella"—as you used to call me, will have lost all her beauty. But perhaps you will not care for that, for you tell me you have found one prettier than ever. I do not know, Cousin Paul, but it is because I am so sad, and selfish—for sorrow is selfish—but I do not like your raptures about the Roman girl. Be careful, Paul: I know your heart: it is quick and sensitive; and I dare say she is pretty, and has beautiful eyes; for they tell me all the Italian girls have soft eyes.

"But Italy is far away, Paul; I can never see Enrica; she will never come here. No—no, remember Devon: I feel as if Carry was a sister now: I cannot feel so of the Roman girl: I do not want to feel so. You will say this is harsh; and I am afraid you will not like me so well for it; but I cannot help saying it. I love you too well, Cousin Paul, not to say it.

* * * "It is all over! Indeed, Paul, I am very desolate! 'The golden bowl is broken'— my poor father has gone to his last home. I was expecting it; but how can we expect that fearful comer—death? He had been for a long time so feeble, that he could scarce speak at all: he sat for hours in his chair, looking upon the fire, or looking out at the window. He would hardly notice me when I came to change his pillows, or to smooth

them for his head. But before he died, he knew me as well as ever. 'Isabel,' he said, 'you have been a good daughter: God will reward you!' and he kissed me so tenderly, and looked after me so anxiously, with such intelligence in his look, that I thought perhaps he would revive again. In the evening he asked me for one of his books, that he loved very much. 'Father,' said I, 'you cannot read; it is almost dark.'

"'Oh, yes,' said he; 'Isabel, I can read now.' And I brought it; he kept my hand a long while; then he opened the book;—it was a book about death.

"I brought a candle, for I knew he could not read without.

"'Isabel, dear,' said he, 'put the candle a little nearer.' But it was close beside him even then.

"'A little nearer, Isabel,'—repeated he, and his voice was very faint; and he grasped my hand hard.

"'——Nearer, Isabel!——nearer!'

"There was no need to do it, for my poor father was dead! Oh! Paul, Paul!—pity me. I do not know but I am crazed. It does not seem the same world it was. And the house, and the trees, oh, they are very dismal!

"I wish you would come home, Cousin Paul: life would not be so very—very blank as it is now. Lilly is kind;—I thank her from my heart. But it is not *her* father who is dead!

* * * "I am calmer now; I am staying with Lilly. The world seems smaller than it did; but Heaven seems a great deal larger: there is a place for us all there, Paul,—if we only seek it! They tell me you are coming home: I am glad. You will not like perhaps to come away from that pretty Enrica, you speak of; but do so, Paul. It seems to me that I see clearer than I did, and I talk bolder. The girlish Isabel you will not find, for I am much older, and my air is more grave; and this suffering has made me feeble—very feeble.

* * * "It is not easy for me to write; but I must tell you that I have just found out who your Carry is. Years ago, when you were away from home, I was at school with her. We were always together. I wonder I could not have found her out from your description; but I did not even suspect it. She is a dear girl, and is worthy of all your love. I have seen her once since you have met her: we talked of you. She spoke kindly—very kindly: more than this, I cannot tell you, for I do not know more. Ah, Paul, may you be happy: I feel as if I had but a little while to live.

* * * "It is even so, my dear Cousin Paul,—I shall write but little more; my hand trembles now. But I am ready. It is a glorious world beyond this—I know it is! And there we shall meet. I did hope to see you once again, and to hear your voice, speaking to me as you used to speak. But I shall not. Life is too frail with me. I seem to live wholly now in the world where I am going:—*there* is my mother, and my father, and my little brother—we shall meet—I know we shall meet!

* * * "The last—Paul. Never again in this world! I am happy—very happy. You will come to me. I can write no more. May good angels guard you, and bring you to Heaven!"

——Shall I go on?

But the toils of life are upon me. Private griefs do not break the force, and the weight of the great—Present. A life—at best the half of it, is before me. It is to be wrought out with nerve and work. And—blessed be God!—there are gleams of sunlight upon it. That sweet Carry, doubly dear to me now, that she is joined with my sorrow for the lost Isabel,——shall be sought for!

And with her sweet image floating before me, the Noon wanes, and the shadows of Evening lengthen upon the land.

III

❧ Evening

The future is a great land:—how the lights, and the shadows throng over it,—bright and dark, slow and swift!

Pride and Ambition build up great castles on its plains,—great monuments on the mountains, that reach heavenward, and dip their tops in the blue of Eternity! Then comes an earthquake—the earthquake of disappointment, of distrust, or of inaction, and lays them low. Gaping desolation widens its breaches everywhere; the eye is full of them, and can see nothing beside. By and by, the sun peeps forth,—as now from behind yonder cloud—and reanimates the soul.

Fame beckons, sitting high in the heavens; and joy lends a halo to the vision. A thousand resolves stir your heart; your hand is hot, and feverish for action; your brain works madly, and you snatch here, and you snatch there, in the convulsive throes of your delirium. Perhaps you see some earnest, careful plodder, once far behind you, now toiling slowly but surely, over the plain of life, until he seems near to grasping those brilliant phantoms which dance along the horizon of the future; and the sight stirs your soul to frenzy, and you bound on after him with the madness of a fever in your veins. But it was by no such action, that the fortunate toiler has won his progress. His hand is steady, his brain is cool; his eye is fixed, and sure.

The Future is a great land; a man cannot go round it in a day; he cannot measure it with a bound; he cannot bind its harvests into a single sheaf. It is wider than the vision, and has no end.

Yet always, day by day, hour by hour, second by second, the hard Present is elbowing us off into that great land of the Future. Our souls indeed, wander to it, as to a homeland; they run beyond time and space, beyond planets and suns, beyond far-off suns and comets, until like blind flies, they are lost in the blaze of immensity, and can only grope their way back to our earth and our time, by the cunning of instinct.

Cut out the Future—even that little Future, which is the Evening of our life, and what a fall into vacuity! Forbid those earnest forays over the borders of Now, and on what spoils would the soul live?

For myself, I delight to wander there, and to weave every day, the passing life, into the coming life,—so closely, that I may be unconscious of the joining. And if so be that I am able, I would make the whole piece bear fair proportions, and just figures,—like those tapestries, on which nuns work by inches, and finish with their lives;—or like those grand frescos, which poet artists have wrought on the vaults of old cathedrals, gaunt, and colossal,—appearing mere daubs of carmine and azure, as they lay upon their backs, working out a hand's breadth at a time,—but when complete, showing—symmetrical, and glorious!

But not alone does the soul wander to those glittering heights where fame sits, with plumes waving in zephyrs of applause; there belong to it, other appetites, which range wide, and constantly over the broad Future-land. We are not merely, working, intellectual machines, but social puzzles, whose solution, is the work of a life. Much as hope may lean toward the intoxicating joy of distinction, there is another leaning in the soul, deeper, and stronger, toward those pleasures which the heart pants for, and in whose atmosphere, the affections bloom and ripen.

The first may indeed be uppermost; it may be noisiest; it may drown with the clamor of mid-day, the nicer sympathies. But all our day is not mid-day; and all our life is not noise. Silence is as strong as the soul; and there is no tempest so wild with blasts, but has a wilder lull. There lies in the depth of every man's soul a mine of affection, which from time to time will burn with the seething heat of a volcano, and heave up lava-like monuments, through all the cold strata of his commoner nature.

One may hide his warmer feelings;—he may paint them dimly;—he may crowd them out of his sailing chart, where he only sets down the harbors for traffic; yet in his secret heart, he will map out upon the great country of the Future, fairy islands of love, and of joy. There, he will be sure to wander, when his soul is lost in those quiet and hallowed hopes, which take hold on Heaven.

Love only, unlocks the door upon that Futurity, where the isles of the blessed, lie like stars. Affection is the stepping stone to God. The heart is our only measure of infinitude. The mind tires with greatness; the heart—never. Thought is worried and weakened in its flight through the immensity of space; but Love soars around the throne of the Highest, with added blessing and strength.

I know not how it may be with others, but with me, the heart is a readier, and quicker builder of those fabrics which strew the great country of the Future, than the mind. They may not indeed rise so high, as the dizzy pinnacles that ambition loves to rear; but they lie like fragrant islands, in a sea, whose ripple is a continuous melody.

And as I muse now, looking toward the EVENING, which is already begun,—tossed as I am, with the toils of the Past, and bewildered with the vexations of the Present, my affections are the architect, that build up the future refuge. And, in fancy at least, I will build it boldly;—saddened it may be, by the chance shadows of evening; but through all, I will hope for a sunset, when the day ends, glorious with crimson, and gold.

CARRY

I said that harsh, and hot as was the Present, there were joyous gleams of light playing over the Future. How else could it be, when that fair being whom I met first upon the wastes of ocean, and whose name even, is hallowed by the dying words of Isabel, is living in the same world with me? Amid all the perplexities that haunt me, as I wander from the present to the future, the thought of her image, of her smile, of her last kind adieu, throws a dash of sunlight upon my path.

And yet why? Is it not very idle? Years have passed since I have seen her: I do not even know where she may be. What is she to me?

My heart whispers—very much!—but I do not listen to that in my prouder moods. She is a woman, a beautiful woman indeed, whom I have known once—pleasantly known: she is living, but she will die, or she will marry;—I shall hear of it by and by, and sigh perhaps—nothing more. Life is earnest around me; there is no time to delve in the past, for bright things to shed radiance on the future.

I will forget the sweet girl, who was with me upon the ocean, and think she is dead. This manly soul is strong, if we would but think so: it can make a puppet of griefs, and take down, and set up at will, the symbols of its hope.

—But no, I cannot: the more I think thus, the less, I really think thus. A single smile of that frail girl, when I recal it,—mocks all my proud purposes; as if, without her, my purposes were nothing.

——Pshaw!—I say—it is idle!—and I bury my thought in books, and in long hours of toil; but as the hours lengthen, and my head sinks with fatigue, and the shadows of evening play around me, there comes again that sweet vision, saying with tender mock-ery—is it idle? And I am helpless, and am led away hopefully and joyfully, toward the golden gates which open on the Future.

But this is only in those silent hours when the man is alone, and away from his working thoughts. At mid-day, or in the rush of the world, he puts hard armor on, that reflects all the light of such joyous fancies. He is cold and careless, and ready for suffer-ing, and for fight.

One day I am travelling: I am absorbed in some present cares—thinking out some plan which is to make easier, or more successful, the voyage of life. I glance upon the passing scenery, and upon new faces, with that careless indifference which grows upon a man with years, and above all, with travel. There is no wife to enlist your sympathies—no children to sport with: my friends are few, and scattered; and are working out fairly, what is before them to do. Lilly is living here, and Ben is living there: their letters are cheerful, contented letters; and they wish me well. Griefs even have grown light with wearing; and I am just in that careless humor—as if I said,—jog on, old world—jog on! And the end will come along soon; and we shall get—poor devils that we are—just what we deserve!

But on a sudden, my eyes rest on a figure that I think I know. Now, the indifference flies like mist; and my heart throbs: and the old visions come up. I watch her, as if there were nothing else to be seen. The form is hers; the grace is hers; the simple dress—so neat, so tasteful,—that is hers too. She half turns her head:—it is the face that I saw under the velvet cap, in the Park of Devon!

I do not rush forward: I sit as if I were in a trance. I watch her every action—the kind attentions to her mother who sits beside her,—her naive exclamations, as we pass some point of surpassing beauty. It seems as if a new world were opening to me; yet I cannot tell why. I keep my place, and think, and gaze. I tear the paper I hold in my hand into shreds. I play with my watch chain, and twist the seal, until it is near breaking. I take out my watch, look at it, and put it back—yet I cannot tell the hour.

——It is she—I murmur—I know it is Carry!

But when they rise to leave, my lethargy is broken; yet it is with a trembling hesita-tion—a faltering as it were, between the present life and the future, that I approach. She knows me on the instant, and greets me kindly;—as Bella wrote—very kindly. Yet she shows a slight embarrassment, a sweet embarrassment that I treasure in my heart, more closely even than the greeting. I change my course, and travel with them;—now we talk of the old scenes, and two hours seem to have made with me the difference of half a life time.

It is five years since I parted with her, never hoping to meet again. She was then a frail girl; she is now just rounding into womanhood. Her eyes are as dark and deep as ever: the lashes that fringe them, seem to me even longer than they were. Her colour is as rich, her forehead as fair, her smile as sweet, as they were before;—only a little tinge of sadness floats upon her eye, like the haze upon a summer landscape. I grow bold to look upon her, and timid with looking. We talk of Bella:—she speaks in a soft, low voice, and the shade of sadness on her face, gathers—as when a summer mist obscures the sun. I talk in monosyllables: I can command no other. And there is a look of sympathy in her eye, when I speak thus, that binds my soul to her, as no smiles could do. What can draw the heart into the fulness of love, so quick as sympathy?

But this passes;—we must part; she for her home, and I for that broad home, that has been mine so long—the world. It seems broader to me than ever, and colder than ever, and less to be wished for than ever. A new book of hope is sprung wide open in my life:——a hope of home!

We are to meet at some time, not far off, in the city where I am living. I look forward to that time, as at school I used to look for vacation: it is a *point d'appui*[148] for hope, for thought, and for countless journeyings into the opening future. Never did I keep the dates better, never count the days more carefully, whether for bonds to be paid, or for dividends to fall due.

I welcome the time, and it passes like a dream. I am near her, often as I dare; the hours are very short with her, and very long away. She receives me kindly—always very kindly; she could not be otherwise than kind. But is it anything more? This is a greedy nature of ours; and when sweet kindness flows upon us, we want more. I know she is kind; and yet in place of being grateful, I am only covetous of an excess of kindness.

She does not mistake my feelings, surely:—ah, no,—trust a woman for that! But what have I, or what am I, to ask a return? She is pure, and gentle as an angel; and I— alas—only a poor soldier in our world-fight against the Devil! Sometimes in moods of vanity, I call up what I fondly reckon my excellencies or deserts—a sorry, pitiful array, that makes me shame-faced when I meet her. And in an instant, I banish them all. And I think, that if I were called upon in some high court of justice, to say why I should claim her indulgence, or her love—I would say nothing of my sturdy effort to beat down the roughnesses of toil—nothing of such manliness as wears a calm front amid the frowns of the world,—nothing of little triumphs, in the every-day fight of life; but only, I would enter the simple plea—this heart is hers!

She leaves; and I have said nothing of what was seething within me;—how I curse my folly! She is gone, and never perhaps will return. I recal in despair her last kind glance. The world seems blank to me. She does not know; perhaps she does not care, if I love her.— Well, I will bear it,—I say. But I cannot bear it. Business is broken; books are blurred; something remains undone, that fate declares must be done. Not a place can I find, but her sweet smile gives to it, either a tinge of gladness, or a black shade of desolation.

---

[148]Focal point.

I sit down at my table with pleasant books; the fire is burning cheerfully; my dog looks up earnestly when I speak to him; but it will never do! Her image sweeps away all these comforts in a flood. I fling down my book; I turn my back upon my dog; the fire hisses and sparkles in mockery of me.

Suddenly a thought flashes on my brain;—I will write to her—I say. And a smile floats over my face,—a smile of hope, ending in doubt. I catch up my pen—my trusty pen; and the clean sheet lies before me. The paper could not be better, nor the pen. I have written hundreds of letters; it is easy to write letters. But now, it is not easy.

I begin, and cross it out. I begin again, and get on a little farther;—then cross it out. I try again, but can write nothing. I fling down my pen in despair, and burn the sheet, and go to my library for some old sour treatise of Shaftesbury, or Lyttleton; and say—talking to myself all the while;—let her go!—She is beautiful, but I am strong; the world is short; we—I and my dog, and my books, and my pen, will battle it through bravely, and leave enough for a tomb-stone.

But even as I say it, the tears start;—it is all false saying! And I throw Shaftesbury across the room, and take up my pen again. It glides on and on, as my hope glows, and I tell her of our first meeting, and of our hours in the ocean twilight, and of our unsteady stepping on the heaving deck, and of that parting in the noise of London, and of my joy at seeing her in the pleasant country, and of my grief afterward. And then I mention Bella,—her friend and mine—and the tears flow; and then I speak of our last meeting, and of my doubts, and of this very evening,—and how I could not write, and abandoned it,—and then felt something within me that made me write, and tell her——all!—— "That my heart was not my own, but was wholly hers;—and that if she would be mine,— —I would cherish her, and love her always!"

Then, I feel a kind of happiness,—a strange, tumultuous happiness, into which doubt is creeping from time to time, bringing with it a cold shudder. I seal the letter, and carry it—a great weight—for the mail. It seems as if there could be no other letter that day; and as if all the coaches and horses, and cars, and boats were specially detailed to bear that single sheet. It is a great letter for me; my destiny lies in it.

I do not sleep well that night;—it is a tossing sleep; one time joy—sweet and holy joy comes to my dreams, and an angel is by me;—another time, the angel fades,—the brightness fades, and I wake, struggling with fear. For many nights it is so, until the day comes, on which I am looking for a reply.

The postman has little suspicion that the letter which he gives me—although it contains no promissory notes, nor moneys, nor deeds, nor articles of trade—is yet to have a greater influence upon my life and upon my future, than all the letters he has ever brought to me before. But I do not show him this; nor do I let him see the clutch with which I grasp it. I bear it, as if it were a great and fearful burden, to my room. I lock the door, and having broken the seal with a quivering hand,—read:—

THE LETTER

"Paul—for I think I may call you so now—I know not how to answer you. Your letter gave me great joy; but it gave me pain too. I cannot—will not doubt what you say: I believe that you love me better than I deserve to be loved; and I know that I am not worthy of all your kind praises. But it is not this that pains me; for I know that you have a generous heart, and would forgive, as you always have forgiven, any weakness of mine. I am proud too, very proud, to have won your love; but it pains me—more perhaps than you will believe—to think that I cannot write back to you, as I would wish to write;—alas, never!"

Here I dash the letter upon the floor, and with my hand upon my forehead, sit gazing upon the glowing coals, and breathing quick and loud.—The dream then is broken!

Presently I read again:

——"You know that my father died, before we had ever met. He had an old friend, who had come from England; and who in early life had done him some great service, which made him seem like a brother. This old gentleman was my god-father, and called me daughter. When my father died, he drew me to his side, and said,— 'Carry, I shall leave you, but my old friend will be your father;' and he put my hand in his, and said—'I give you my daughter.'

"This old gentleman had a son, older than myself; but we were much together, and grew up as brother and sister. I was proud of him; for he was tall and strong, and every one called him handsome. He was as kind too, as a brother could be; and his father was like my own father. Every one said, and believed, that we would one day be married; and my mother, and my new father spoke of it openly. So did Laurence—for that is my friend's name.

"I do not need to tell you any more, Paul; for when I was still a girl, we had promised, that we would one day be man and wife. Laurence has been much in England; and I believe he is there now. The old gentleman treats me still as a daughter, and talks of the time, when I shall come and live with him. The letters of Laurence are very kind; and though he does not talk so much of our marriage as he did, it is only I think, because he regards it as so certain.

"I have wished to tell you all this before; but I have feared to tell you; I am afraid I have been too selfish to tell you. And now what can I say? Laurence seems most to me like a brother;—and you, Paul——but I must not go on. For if I marry Laurence, as fate seems to have decided, I will try and love him, better than all the world.

"But will you not be a brother, and love me, as you once loved Bella;—you say my eyes are like hers, and that my forehead is like hers;—will you not believe that my heart is like hers too?

"Paul, if you shed tears over this letter—I have shed them as well as you. I can write no more now.

"Adieu."

I sit long looking upon the blaze; and when I rouse myself, it is to say wicked things against destiny. Again, all the future seems very blank. I cannot love Carry, as I loved Bella; she cannot be a sister to me; she must be more, or nothing! Again, I seem to float singly on the tide of life, and see all around me in cheerful groups. Everywhere the sun shines, except upon my own cold forehead. There seems no mercy in Heaven, and no goodness for me upon Earth.

I write after some days, an answer to the letter. But it is a bitter answer, in which I forget myself, in the whirl of my misfortunes—to the utterance of reproaches.

Her reply, which comes speedily, is sweet, and gentle. She is hurt by my reproaches, deeply hurt. But with a touching kindness, of which I am not worthy, she credits all my petulance to my wounded feeling; she soothes me; but in soothing, only wounds the more. I try to believe her, when she speaks of her unworthiness;—but I cannot.

Business, and the pursuits of ambition or of interest, pass on like dull, grating machinery. Tasks are met, and performed with strength indeed, but with no cheer. Courage is high, as I meet the shocks, and trials of the world; but it is a brute, careless courage, that glories in opposition. I laugh at any dangers, or any insidious pitfalls;— what are they to me? What do I possess, which it will be hard to lose? My dog keeps by me; my toils are present; my food is ready; my limbs are strong;——what need for more?

The months slip by; and the cloud that floated over my evening sun, passes.

Laurence wandering abroad, and writing to Caroline, as to a sister,—writes more than his father could have wished. He has met new faces, very sweet faces; and one which shows through the ink of his later letters, very gorgeously. The old gentleman does not like to lose thus his little Carry; and he writes back rebuke. But Laurence, with the letters of Caroline before him for data, throws himself upon his sister's kindness, and charity. It astonishes not a little the old gentleman, to find his daughter pleading in such strange way, for the son. "And what will you do then, my Carry?"—the old man says.

——"Wear weeds, if you wish, sir; and love you and Laurence more than ever!"

And he takes her to his bosom, and says—"Carry—Carry, you are too good for that wild fellow Laurence!"

Now, the letters are different! Now they are full of hope—dawning, all over the future sky. Business, and care, and toil, glide, as if a spirit animated them all; it is no longer cold machine work, but intelligent, and hopeful activity. The sky hangs upon you lovingly, and the birds make music, that startles you with its fineness. Men wear cheerful faces; the storms have a kind pity, gleaming through all their wrath.

The days approach, when you can call her yours. For she has said it, and her mother has said it; and the kind old gentleman, who says he will still be her father, has said it too; and they have all welcomed you—won by her story—with a cordiality, that has made your cup full, to running over. Only one thought comes up to obscure your joy;—is it real? or if real, are you worthy to enjoy? Will you cherish and love always, as you have promised, that angel who accepts your word, and rests her happiness on your faith? Are there not harsh qualities in your nature, which you fear may sometime make her regret that she gave herself to your love and charity? And those friends who watch over her, as the apple of their eye, can you always meet their tenderness and approval, for your guardianship of their treasure? Is it not a treasure that makes you fearful, as well as joyful?

But you forget this in her smile: her kindness, her goodness, her modesty, will not let you remember it. She *forbids* such thoughts; and you yield such obedience, as you never yielded even to the commands of a mother. And if your business, and your labor slip by, partially neglected—what matters it? What is interest, or what is reputation, compared with that fullness of your heart, which is now ripe with joy?

The day for your marriage comes; and you live as if you were in a dream. You think well, and hope well for all the world. A flood of charity seems to radiate from all around you. And as you sit beside her in the twilight, on the evening before the day, when you will call her yours, and talk of the coming hopes, and of the soft shadows of the past; and, whisper of Bella's love, and of that sweet sister's death, and of Laurence, a new brother, coming home joyful with his bride,—and lay your cheek to hers—life seems as if it were all day, and as if there could be no night!

The marriage passes; and she is yours,—yours forever.

NEW TRAVEL

Again I am upon the sea; but not alone. She whom I first met upon the wastes of ocean, is there beside me. Again I steady her tottering step upon the deck; once it was a drifting, careless pleasure; now the pleasure is holy.

Once the fear I felt, as the storms gathered, and night came, and the ship tossed madly, and great waves gathering swift, and high, came down like slipping mountains, and spent their force upon the quivering vessel, was a selfish fear. But it is so no longer. Indeed I hardly know fear; for how can the tempests harm *her?* Is she not too good to suffer any of the wrath of heaven?

And in nights of calm,—holy nights, we lean over the ship's side, looking down, as once before, into the dark depths, and murmur again snatches of ocean song, and talk of those we love; and we peer among the stars, which seem neighborly, and as if they were the homes of friends. And as the great ocean-swells come rocking under us, and carry us up and down along the valleys and the hills of water, they seem like deep pulsations of the great heart of nature, heaving us forward toward the goal of life, and to the gates of heaven!

We watch the ships as they come upon the horizon, and sweep toward us, like false friends, with the sun glittering on their sails; and then shift their course, and bear away—with their bright sails, turned to spots of shadow. We watch the long winged birds skimming the waves hour after hour,—like pleasant thoughts—now dashing before our bows, and then sweeping behind, until they are lost in the hollows of the water.

Again life lies open, as it did once before; but the regrets, disappointments, and fruitless resolves do not come to trouble me now. It is the future, which has become as level as the sea; and *she* is beside me,—the sharer in that future—to look out with me, upon the joyous sparkle of water, and to count with me, the dazzling ripples, that lie between us and the shore. A thousand pleasant plans come up, and are abandoned, like the waves we leave behind us; a thousand other joyous plans, dawn upon our fancy, like the waves that glitter before us. We talk of Laurence and his bride, whom we are to meet; we talk of her mother, who is even now watching the winds that waft her child over the ocean; we talk of the kindly old man, her god-father, who gave her a father's blessing; we talk low, and in the twilight hours, of Isabel—who sleeps.

At length, as the sun goes down upon a fair night, over the western waters which we have passed, we see before us, the low blue line of the shores of Cornwall and Devon. In the night, shadowy ships glide past us with gleaming lanterns; and in the morning, we see the yellow cliffs of the Isle of Wight; and standing out from the land, is the dingy sail of our pilot. London with its fog, roar, and crowds, has not the same charms that it once had; that roar and crowd is good to make a man forget his griefs—forget himself, and stupify him with amazement. We are in no need of such forgetfulness.

We roll along the banks of the sylvan river that glides by Hampton Court; and we toil up Richmond Hill, to look together upon that scene of water, and meadow,—of leafy copses, and glistening villas, of brown cottages, and clustered hamlets,—of solitary oaks, and loitering herds—all spread like a veil of beauty, upon the bosom of the Thames. But we cannot linger here, nor even under the glorious old boles of Windsor Forest; but we hurry on to that sweet county of Devon, made green with its white skeins of water.

Again we loiter under the oaks, where we have loitered before; and the sleek deer gaze on us with their liquid eyes, as they gazed before. The squirrels sport among the boughs as fearless as ever; and some wandering puss pricks her long ears at our steps, and bounds off along the hedge rows to her burrow. Again I see Carry in her velvet riding-cap, with the white plume; and I meet her as I met her before, under the princely trees that skirt the northern avenue. I recal the evening when I sauntered out at the park gates, and gained a blessing from the porter's wife, and dreamed that strange dream;——now, the dream seems more real, than my life.—"God bless you!"—said the woman again.

—"Aye, old lady, God has blessed me!"—and I fling her a guinea, not as a gift, but as a debt.

The bland farmer lives yet; he scarce knows me, until I tell him of my bout around his oat-field, at the tail of his long stilted plough. I find the old pew in the parish church. Other holly sprigs are hung now; and I do not doze, for Carry is beside me. The curate drawls the service; but it is pleasant to listen; and I make the responses with an emphasis, that tells more I fear, for my joy, than for my religion. The old groom at the mansion in the Park, has not forgotten the hard-riding of other days; and tells long stories (to which I love to listen) of the old visit of mistress Carry, when she followed the hounds with the best of the English lasses.

—"Yer honor may well be proud; for not a prettier face, or a kinder heart has been in Devon, since mistress Carry left us!"

But pleasant as are the old woods, full of memories, and pleasant as are the twilight evenings upon the terrace—we must pass over to the mountains of Switzerland. There we are to meet Laurence.

Carry has never seen the magnificence of the Juras; and as we journey over the hills between Dole, and the border line, looking upon the rolling heights shrouded with pine trees, and down thousands of feet, at the very road side, upon the cottage roofs, and emerald valleys, where the dun herds are feeding quietly, she is lost in admiration. At length we come to that point above the little town of Gex, from which you see spread out before you, the meadows that skirt Geneva, the placid surface of Lake Leman and the rough, shaggy mountains of Savoy;—and far behind them, breaking the horizon with snowy cap, and with dark pinnacles—Mont Blanc, and the Needles of Chamouni.

I point out to her in the valley below, the little town of Ferney, where stands the deserted chateau of Voltaire; and beyond, upon the shores of the lake, the old home of de Stael;[149] and across, with its white walls reflected upon the bosom of the water, the house where Byron wrote the prisoner of Chillon. Among the grouping roofs of Geneva, we trace the dark cathedral, and the tall hotels shining on the edge of the lake. And I tell of the time, when I tramped down through yonder valley, with my future all visionary, and broken, and drank the splendor of the scene, only as a quick relief to the monotony of my solitary life.

——"And now, Carry, with your hand locked in mine, and your heart mine—yonder lake sleeping in the sun, and the snowy mountains with their rosy hue, seem like the smile of nature, bidding us be glad!"

Laurence is at Geneva; he welcomes Carry, as he would welcome a sister. He is a noble fellow, and tells me much of his sweet Italian wife; and presents me to the smiling, blushing——Enrica! She has learned English now; she has found, she says, a better teacher, than ever I was. Yet she welcomes me warmly, as a sister might; and we talk of those old evenings by the blazing fire, and of the one-eyed *Maestro,* as children long separated, might talk of their school tasks, and of their teachers. She cannot tell me enough of her praises of Laurence, and of his noble heart.—"You were good,"—she says, "but Laurence is better."

Carry admires her soft brown hair, and her deep liquid eye, and wonders how I could ever have left Rome?

—Do you indeed wonder—Carry?

And together we go down into Savoy, to that marvellous valley, which lies under the shoulder of Mont Blanc; and we wandered over the *Mer de Glace,*[150] and picked Alpine roses from the edge of the frowning glacier. We toil at night-fall up to the monastery of the Great St. Bernard,[151] where the new forming ice crackles in the narrow foot-way, and the cold moon glistens over wastes of snow, and upon the windows of the dark Hospice. Again, we are among the granite heights, whose ledges are filled with ice, upon the Grimsel.[152] The pond is dark and cold; the paths are slippery;—the great glacier of the Aar sends down icy breezes, and the echoes ring from rock to rock, as if the ice-God answered. And yet we neither suffer, nor fear.

In the sweet valley of Meyringen, we part from Laurence: he goes northward, by Grindelwald, and Thun,—thence to journey westward, and to make for the Roman girl, a home beyond the ocean. Enrica bids me go on to Rome: she knows that Carry will love its soft warm air, its ruins, its pictures and temples, better than these cold valleys of Switzerland. And she gives me kind messages for her mother, and for Cesare; and should we be in Rome at the Easter season, she bids us remember her, when we listen to the Miserere, and when we see the great *Chiesa*[153] on fire, and when we saunter upon the Pincian hill;——and remember, that it is her home.

---

[149]Madame de Staël (1766–1817) was a prolific French-Swiss writer and novelist.

[150]Sea of Ice.

[151]Living around A.D. 1100, St. Bernard founded hospices on two Alpine passes.

[152]Pass for the Aare River in the south-central part of Switzerland.

[153]church

We follow them with our eyes, as they go up the steep height over which falls the white foam of the clattering Reichenbach;[154] and they wave their hands toward us, and disappear upon the little plateau which stretches toward the crystal Rosenlaui, and the tall, still, Engel-Horner.

May the mountain angels guard them!

As we journey on toward that wonderful pass of Splugen, I recal by the way, upon the heights, and in the valleys, the spots where I lingered years before;—here, I plucked a flower, there, I drank from that cold, yellow glacier water; and here, upon some rock overlooking a stretch of broken mountains, hoary with their eternal frosts, I sat musing upon that very Future, which is with me now. But never, even when the ice-genii were most prodigal of their fancies to the wanderer, did I look for more joy, or a better angel.

Afterward, when all our trembling upon the Alpine paths has gone by, we are rolling along under the chestnuts and lindens that skirt the banks of Como. We recal that sweet story of Manzoni,[155] and I point out, as well as I may, the loitering place of the *bravi*,[156] and the track of poor Don Abbondio.[157] We follow in the path of the discomfited Rienzi,[158] to where the dainty spire, and pinnacles of the Duomo of Milan, glisten against the violet sky.

Carry longs to see Venice; its water-streets, and palaces have long floated in her visions. In the bustling activity of our own country, and in the quiet fields of England, that strange, half-deserted capital, lying in the Adriatic, has taken the strongest hold upon her fancy.

So we leave Padua, and Verona behind us, and find ourselves upon a soft spring noon, upon the end of the iron road which stretches across the lagoon, toward Venice. With the hissing of steam in the ear, it is hard to think of the wonderful city, we are approaching. But as we escape from the carriage, and set our feet down into one of those strange, hearse-like, ancient boats, with its sharp iron prow, and listen to the melodious rolling tongue of the Venetian gondolier:—as we see rising over the watery plain before us, all glittering in the sun, tall, square towers with pyramidal tops, and clustered domes, and minarets; and sparkling roofs lifting from marble walls—all so like the old paintings;— and as we glide nearer and nearer to the floating wonder, under the silent working oar, of our now silent gondolier;—as we ride up swiftly under the deep, broad shadows of palaces, and see plainly the play of the sea-water in the crevices of the masonry,—and turn into narrow rivers shaded darkly by overhanging walls, hearing no sound, but of voices, or the swaying of the water against the houses,—we feel the presence of the place. And the mystic fingers of the Past, grappling our spirits, lead them away—willing and rejoicing captives, through the long vista of the ages, that are gone.

---

[154]Highest waterfalls in the Alps, located in central Switzerland.

[155]Alessandro Manzoni (1785–1873) was a popular Italian romantic poet and novelist.

[156]Men hired as bodyguards or to carry out personal vendettas.

[157]Don Abbondio was a Catholic saint who traveled throughout Italy.

[158]Refers to the fourteenth-century Roman reformer and military leader, Cola di Rienzo. Rienzo dreamed of returning Rome to its former glory, but was killed before he could make his dream a reality.

Carry is in a trance;—rapt by the witchery of the scene, into dream. This is her Venice; nor have all the visions that played upon her fancy, been equal to the enchanting presence of this hour of approach.

Afterward, it becomes a living thing,—stealing upon the affections, and upon the imagination by a thousand coy advances. We wander under the warm Italian sunlight to the steps from which rolled the white head of poor Marino Faliero.[159] The gentle Carry can now thrust her ungloved hand, into the terrible Lion's mouth. We enter the salon of the fearful Ten; and peep through the half opened door, into the cabinet of the more fearful Three. We go through the deep dungeons of Carmagnola and of Carrara; and we instruct the willing gondolier to push his dark, boat under the Bridge of Sighs; and with Rogers'[160] poem in our hand, glide up to the prison door, and read of—

> ——that fearful closet at the foot
> Lurking for prey, which, when a victim came,
> Grew less and less, contracting to a span
> An iron door, urged onward by a screw,
> Forcing out life!

I sail, listening to nothing but the dip of the gondolier's oar, or to *her* gentle words, fast under the palace door, which closed that fearful morning, on the guilt and shame of Bianca Capello.[161] Or, with souls lit up by the scene, into a buoyancy that can scarce distinguish between what is real, and what is merely written,—we chase the anxious step of the forsaken Corinna;[162] or seek among the veteran palaces the casement of the old Brabantio,—the chamber of Desdemona,[163]—the house of Jessica,[164] and trace among the strange Jew money-changers, who yet haunt the Rialto,[165] the likeness of the bearded Shylock.[166] We wander into stately churches, brushing over grass, or tell-tale flowers that grow in the court, and find them damp and cheerless; the incense rises murkily, and rests in a thick cloud over the altars, and over the paintings; the music, if so be that the organ notes are swelling under the roof, is mournfully plaintive.

---

[159]Tragic character in Byron's *Doge of Venice* (1821), which was based on the life of Marin Falier (1274–1355), a prominent citizen of Venice who was executed for leading a plot against the rulers of the city.

[160]Samuel Rogers (1763–1855) was a minor English poet.

[161]Bianca Capello (1548–1587) was a Venetian noblewoman best known for her beauty and scandalous intrigues at court.

[162]Probably refers to the persecuted heroine of Madame de Staël's novel, *Corinna* (1807).

[163]Both Brabantio and Desdemona are characters in Shakespeare's romantic tragedy set in Venice, *Othello*.

[164]Jessica is the daughter of the Jewish Shylock in Shakespeare's *Merchant of Venice*. She marries a Christian and rejects her Jewish heritage.

[165]Central bridge in Venice.

[166]Jewish moneylender in Shakespeare's *Merchant of Venice*.

Of an afternoon we sail over to the Lide, to gladden our eyes with a sight of land and green things, and we pass none upon the way, save silent oarsmen, with barges piled high with the produce of their gardens,—pushing their way down toward the floating city. And upon the narrow island, we find Jewish graves, half covered by drifted sand; and from among them, watch the sunset glimmering over a desolate level of water. As we glide back, lights lift over the Lagoon, and double along the Guideca, and the Grand Canal. The little neighbor isles will have their company of lights dancing in the water; and from among, them, will rise up against the mellow evening sky of Italy, gaunt, unlighted houses.

After the nightfall, which brings no harmful dew with it, I stroll, with her hand within my arm,—as once upon the sea, and in the English Park, and in the home-land— over that great square which lies before the palace of St. Marks. The white moon is riding in the middle heaven, like a globe of silver; the gondoliers stride over the echoing stones; and their long black shadows, stretching over the pavement, or shaking upon the moving water, seem like great funereal plumes, waving over the bier of Venice.

Carrying thence whole treasures of thought and fancy, to feed upon in the after years, we wander to Rome.

I find the old one-eyed *maestro,* and am met with cordial welcome by the mother of the pretty Enrica. The Count has gone to the marches of Ancona. Lame Pietro still shuffles around the boards at the Lepré, and the flower sellers at the corner, bind me a more brilliant bouquet than ever, for a new beauty at Rome. As we ramble under the broken arches of the great aqueduct stretching toward Frascati, I tell Carry, the story of my trip in the Appenines; and we search for the pretty Carlotta. But she is married, they tell us, to a Neapolitan guardsman. In the spring twilight, we wander upon those heights which lie between Frascati and Albano; and looking westward, see that glorious view of the Campagna, which can never be forgotten. But beyond the Campagna, and beyond the huge hulk of St. Peter's, heaving into the sky from the middle waste, we see, or fancy we see, a glimpse of the sea which stretches out and on to the land we love, better than Rome. And in fancy, we build up that home, which shall belong to us, on the return;—a home, that has slumbered long in the future; and which, now that the future has come, lies fairly before me.

HOME

Years seem to have passed. They have mellowed life into ripeness. The start, and change, and hot ambition of youth, seem to have gone by. A calm, and joyful quietude has succeeded. That future which still lies before me, seems like a roseate twilight, sinking into a peaceful, and silent night.

My home is a cottage, near that where Isabel once lived. The same valley is around me; the same brook rustles, and loiters under the gnarled roots of the overhanging trees. The cottage is no mock cottage, but a substantial, wide spreading cottage, with clustering gables, and ample shade;—such a cottage, as they build upon the slopes of Devon. Vines clamber over it, and the stones show mossy through the interlacing climbers. There are low porches, with cozy arm chairs; and generous oriels, fragrant with mignionette, and the blue blossoming violets.

The chimney stacks rise high, and show clear against the heavy pine trees, that ward off the blasts of winter. The dovecote,[167] is a habited dovecote, and the purple-necked pigeons swoop around the roofs, in great companies. The hawthorn is budding into its June fragrance along all the lines of fence; and the paths are trim, and clean. The shrubs,—our neglected azalias and rhododendrons chiefest among them,—stand in picturesque groups upon the close shaven lawn.

The gateway in the thicket below, is between two mossy old posts of stone; and there is a tall hemlock flanked by a sturdy pine, for sentinel. Within the cottage, the library is wainscotted with native oak; and my trusty gun hangs upon a branching pair of antlers. My rod and nets are disposed above the generous book-shelves; and a stout eagle, once a tenant of the native woods, sits perched over the central alcove. An old fashioned mantel is above the brown stone jams of the country fire-place; and along it are distributed records of travel;—little bronze temples from Rome, the *pietro duro*[168] of Florence, the porcelain busts of Dresden, the rich iron of Berlin, and a cup fashioned from a stag's horn, from the Black Forest by the Rhine.

Massive chairs stand here and there, in tempting attitude; strewed over an oaken table in the middle, are the uncut papers, and volumes of the day; and upon a lion's skin stretched before the hearth, is lying another Tray.

But this is not all. There are children in the cottage. There is Jamie—we think him handsome—for he has the dark hair of his mother, and the same black eye, with its long, heavy fringe. There is Carry—little Carry I must call her now—with a face full of glee, and rosy with health; then there is a little rogue some two years old, whom we call Paul—a very bad boy,—as we tell him.

The mother is as beautiful as ever, and far more dear to me; for gratitude has been adding, year by year, to love. There have been times when a harsh word of mine, uttered in the fatigues of business, have touched her; and I have seen that soft eye fill with tears; and I have upbraided myself for causing her one pang. But such things she does not remember; or remembers, only to cover with her gentle forgiveness.

Laurence and Enrica are living near us. And the old gentleman, who was Carry's god-father, sits with me, on sunny days upon the porch, and takes little Paul upon his knee, and wonders if two such daughters as Enrica, and Carry are to be found in the world. At twilight, we ride over to see Laurence; Jamie mounts with the coachman; little Carry puts on her wide-rimmed Leghorn for the evening visit; and the old gentleman's plea for Paul, cannot be denied. The mother too is with us; and old Tray comes whisking along, now frolicking before the horses' heads, and then bounding, off after the flight of some belated bird.

Away from that cottage home, I seem away from life. Within it, that broad, and shadowy future, which lay before me in boyhood and in youth, is garnered,—like a fine mist, gathered into drops of crystal.

And when away—those long letters, dating from the cottage home, are what tie me

---

[167]Pigeon house.

[168]"Hard stone" used in building construction.

to life. That cherished wife, far dearer to me now, than when she wrote that first letter, which seemed a dark veil between me and the future—writes me now, as tenderly as then. She narrates, in her delicate way, all the incidents of the home life; she tells me of their rides, and of their games, and of the new planted trees;—of all their sunny days, and of their frolics on the lawn; she tells me how Jamie is studying, and of little Carry's beauty, growing every day, and of rogueish Paul—so like his father! And she sends me a kiss from each of them; and bids me such adieu, and such 'God's blessing,' that it seems as if an angel guarded me.

But this is not all; for Jamie has written a post script:

——"Dear Father," he says, "mother wishes me to tell you how I am studying. What would you think, father, to have me talk in French to you, when you come back? I wish you would come back though; the hawthorns are coming out, and the apricot under my window is all full of blossoms. If you should bring me a present, as you almost always do,—I would like a fishing rod.

"Your affectionate son,
"Jamie."

And little Carry has her fine, rambling characters running into a second postscript.

"Why don't you come, papa; you stay too long; I have ridden the pony twice; once he most threw me off. This is all from

Carry."

And Paul has taken the pen too, and in his extraordinary effort to make a big P, has made a very big blot. And Jamie writes under it—"This is Paul's work, Pa; but he says it's a love blot, only he loves you ten hundred times more."

And after your return, Jamie will insist that you should go with him to the brook, and sit down with him upon a tuft of the brake, to fling off a line into the eddies, though only the nibbling roach are sporting below. You have instructed the workmen to spare the clumps of bank-willows, that the wood-duck may have a covert in winter, and that the Bob-o-Lincolns may have a quiet nesting place in the spring.

Sometimes your wife,—too kind to deny such favor—will stroll with you along the meadow banks, and you pick meadow daisies in memory of the old time. Little Carry weaves them into rude chaplets, to dress the forehead of Paul, and they dance along the greensward, and switch off the daffodils, and blow away the dandelion seeds, to see if their wishes are to come true. Jamie holds a butter cup under Carry's chin, to find if she loves gold and Paul, the rogue, teases them, by sticking a thistle into sister's curls.

The pony has hard work to do under Carry's swift riding—but he is fed by her own hand, with the cold breakfast rolls. The nuts are gathered in time, and stored for long winter evenings, when the fire is burning bright and cheerily—a true, hickory blaze,—which sends its waving gleams over eager, smiling faces, and over well-stored book shelves, and portraits of dear, lost ones. While from time to time, that wife, who is the soul of the scene, will break upon the children's prattle, with the silver melody of her voice, running softly and sweetly through the couplets of Crabbe's stories, or the witchery of the Flodden Tale.[169]

Then the boys will guess conundrums, and play at fox and geese; and Tray, cherished in his age, and old Milo petted in his dotage, lie side by side, upon the lion's skin, before the blazing hearth. Little Tomtit the goldfinch sits sleeping on his perch, or cocks his eye at a sudden crackling of the fire, for a familiar squint upon our family group.

But there is no future without its straggling clouds. Even now a shadow is trailing along the landscape.

It is a soft and mild day of summer. The leaves are at their fullest. A southern breeze has been blowing up the valley all the morning, and the light, smoky haze hangs in the distant mountain gaps, like a veil on beauty. Jamie has been busy with his lessons, and afterward playing with Milo upon the lawn. Little Carry has come in from a long ride— her face blooming, and her eyes all smiles, and joy. The mother has busied herself with those flowers she loves so well. Little Paul, they say, has been playing in the meadow, and old Tray has gone with him.

But at dinner time, Paul has not come back.

"Paul ought not to ramble off so far," I say.

The mother says nothing; but there is a look of anxiety upon her face, that disturbs me. Jamie wonders where Paul can be, and he saves for him, whatever he knows Paul will like—a heaping platefull. But the dinner hour passes, and Paul does not come. Old Tray lies in the sun-shine by the porch.

Now the mother is indeed anxious. And I, though I conceal this from her, find my fears strangely active. Something like instinct guides me to the meadow: I wander down the brook-side calling—Paul!—Paul! But there is no answer.

All the afternoon we search, and the neighbors search; but it is a fruitless toil. There is no joy that evening: the meal passes in silence; only little Carry with tears in her eyes, asks,—if Paul will soon come back? All the night we search and call:—the mother even braving the night air, and running here and there, until the morning finds us sad, and despairing.

That day—the next—cleared up the mystery; but cleared it up with darkness. Poor little Paul!—he has sunk under the murderous eddies of the brook! His boyish prattle, his rosy smiles, his artless talk, are lost to us forever!

I will not tell how nor when we found him: nor will I tell of our desolate home, and of *her* grief—the first crushing grief of her life.

The cottage is still. The servants glide noiseless, as if they might startle the poor little sleeper. The house seems cold—very cold. Yet it is summer weather; and the south

---

[169]Possibly referring to the alliterative poem "Scottish Fielde," which takes as its subject the Battle of Flodden in 1513.

breeze plays softly along the meadow, and softly over the murderous eddies of the brook.

Then comes the hush of burial. The kind mourners are there:——it is easy for them to mourn! The good clergyman prays by the bier:——'Oh, Thou, who did'st take upon thyself human woe, and drank deep of every pang in life, let thy spirit come and heal this grief, and guide toward that Better Land, where justice and love shall reign, and hearts laden with anguish, shall rest forevermore!'

Weeks roll on; and a smile of resignation lights up the saddened features of the mother. Those dark mourning robes speak to the heart deeper, and more tenderly, than ever the bridal costume. She lightens the weight of your grief by her sweet words of resignation:— "Paul," she says, "God has taken our boy!"

Other weeks roll on. Joys are still left—great and ripe joys. The cottage smiling in the autumn sunshine is there: the birds are in the forest boughs: Jamie and little Carry are there; and she, who is more than them all, is cheerful, and content. Heaven has taught us that the brightest future has its clouds;—that this life is a motley of lights and shadows. And as we look upon the world around us, and upon the thousand forms of human misery, there is a gladness in our deep thanksgiving.

A year goes by; but it leaves no added shadow on our hearth-stone. The vines clamber, and flourish: the oaks are winning age and grandeur: little Carry is blooming into the pretty coyness of girlhood; and Jamie with his dark hair, and flashing eyes, is the pride of his mother.

There is no alloy to pleasure, but the remembrance of poor little Paul. And even that, chastened as it is with years, is rather a grateful memorial that our life is not all here, than a grief that weighs upon our hearts.

Sometimes, leaving little Carry and Jamie to their play, we wander at twilight to the willow tree, beneath which our drowned boy sleeps calmly, for the Great Awaking.[170] It is a Sunday, in the week-day of our life, to linger by the little grave,—to hang flowers upon the head-stone, and to breathe a prayer that our little Paul may sleep well, in the arms of Him who loveth children!

And her heart, and my heart, knit together by sorrow, as they had been knit by joy— a silver thread mingled with the gold—follow the dead one to the Land that is before us; until at last we come to reckon the boy, as living in the new home, which when this is old, shall be ours also. And my spirit, speaking to his spirit, in the evening watches, seems to say joyfully—so joyfully that the tears half choke the utterance—"Paul, my boy, we will be *there!*"

And the mother, turning her face to mine, so that I see the moisture in her eye, and catch its heavenly look, whispers softly—so softly, that an angel might have said it,— "Yes, dear, we will be THERE!"

The night had now come, and my day under the oaks was ended. But a crimson belt yet lingered over the horizon, though the stars were out.

---

[170]Moment in Christian theology that holds that all the faithful who have died will raise again.

A line of shaggy mist lay along the surface of the brook. I took my gun from beside the tree, and my shot-pouch from its limb, and whistling for Carlo—as if it had been Tray—I strolled over the bridge, and down the lane, to the old house under the elms.

I dreamed pleasant dreams that night;——for I dreamed that my Reverie was real.

THE END

11

George Aiken
(1830–1876)

FIRST SERIALIZED IN *The National Era* in 1851, Harriet Beecher Stowe's *Uncle Tom's Cabin: or, Life among the Lowly* was published as a two-volume book on March 20, 1852. Its appearance struck like a lightning bolt on the publishing horizon. Its first day in print, it sold three thousand copies. Within a week, seven thousand more copies had been sold; by the end of the first year, 300,000 copies of *Uncle Tom's Cabin* were in print as the publisher, John P. Jewett, kept eight power presses going around the clock to meet demand. The book proved even more popular in England as no less than six London publishers produced one million copies of the book by the end of 1856. Within a decade of its appearance, *Uncle Tom's Cabin* would be translated into dozens of languages, so that Italians, Hindus, Wallachians, Finns, Armenians, and Javanese could all read the novel in their native tongues.

Such popularity lured a number of playwrights to adapt the novel for the theater. As no effective copyright existed, anyone could try his hand at dramatizing the book in hopes of capitalizing on the story's unprecedented popularity. The most successful version of the play would come out a mere six months after the book had been published. It was reportedly written in a week by George Aiken, an actor and struggling playwright who had little success with staging any of his prior plays. Aiken actually wrote two shorter plays (one ending with the death of Eva, the other ending with the death of Tom), and both became immediately popular. He later combined these plays into one six-act version. Aiken's play, along with various other dramatic adaptations, would play across the country, and those not familiar with Eva and Tom's story through the book were often exposed to the narrative through its numerous dramatic adaptations.

Aiken's play captured many of the tensions found in the book. Stowe herself wanted to write a story that would not so repulse Southerners that they would dismiss it out of hand—although they did anyway. Aiken followed this placating strategy, as he attempted to tread lightly on Southern slavery sensibilities. He added a comic character in Gumption Cute and carefully orchestrated Topsy as a minstrel-show character, playing on minstrelsy's popularity with antebellum audiences. Yet the message of oppression and darkness comes through with strong characters such as George Harris and Eliza, and the while the play remained popular even after the Civil War, it did much to add fuel to the fires of the slavery controversy in the tumultuous 1850s.

UNCLE TOM'S CABIN

Or, Life among the Lowly
A Domestic Drama in Six Acts

CAST OF CHARACTERS

UNCLE TOM

GEORGE HARRIS

GEORGE SHELBY

ST. CLARE

PHINEAS FLETCHER

GUMPTION CUTE

MR. WILSON

DEACON PERRY

SHELBY

HALEY

LEGREE

TOM LOKER

MARKS

SKEGGS

MANN

ADOLF

SAMBO

QUIMBO

DOCTOR

WAITER

HARRY, a child

EVA

ELIZA

CASSY

MARIE

OPHELIA

CHLOE

TOPSY

EMMELINE

George Aiken, *Uncle Tom's Cabin; or, Life among the Lowly. A Domestic Drama in Six Acts.* New York: S. French, 185?.

Broadside advertisement for a performance of George Aiken's play, *Uncle Tom's Cabin,* at the National Theatre in New York, July 18, 1854. Interestingly, the broadside advertises the play as "a veritable Comedy of Tears." (Courtesy, American Antiquarian Society)

❧ Uncle Tom's Cabin

Act I

Scene 1: Plain Chamber

[Enter ELIZA, *meeting* GEORGE.*]*

ELIZA: Ah! George, is it you? Well, I am so glad you've come! [GEORGE *regards her mournfully.*] Why don't you smile, and ask after Harry?

GEORGE: [*Bitterly.*] I wish he'd never been born! I wish I'd never been born myself!

ELIZA: [*Sinking her head upon his breast and weeping.*] Oh, George!

GEROGE: There, now, Eliza; it's too bad for me to make you feel so. Oh! how I wish you had never seen me—you might have been happy!

ELIZA: George! George! how can you talk so? What dreadful thing has happened, or is going to happen? I'm sure we've been very happy till lately.

GEORGE: So we have, dear. But oh! I wish I'd never seen you, nor you me.

ELIZA: Oh, George! how can you?

GEORGE: Yes, Eliza, it's all misery! misery! The very life is burning out of me! I'm a poor, miserable, forlorn drudge! I shall only drag you down with me, that's all! What's the use of our trying to do anything—trying to know anything—trying to be anything? I wish I was dead!

ELIZA: Oh! now, dear George, that is really wicked. I know how you feel about losing your place in the factory, and you have a hard master; but pray be patient—

GEORGE: Patient! Haven't I been patient? Did I say a word when he came and took me away—for no earthly reason—from the place where everybody was kind to me? I'd paid him truly every cent of my earnings, and they all say I worked well.

ELIZA: Well, it *is* dreadful; but, after all, he is your master, you know.

GEORGE: My master! And who made him my master? That's what I think of! What right has he to me? I'm as much of a man as he is! What right has he to make a dray-horse of me?—to take me from things I can do better than he can, and put me to work that any horse can do? He tries to do it; he says he'll bring me down and humble me, and he puts me to just the hardest, meanest and dirtiest work, on purpose.

ELIZA: Oh, George! George! you frighten me. Why, I never heard you talk so. I'm afraid you'll do something dreadful. I don't wonder at your feelings at all; but oh, do be careful—for my sake, for Harry's.

GEORGE: I have been careful, and I have been patient, but it's growing worse and worse—flesh and blood can't bear it any longer. Every chance he can get to insult and torment me he takes. He says that though I don't say anything, he sees that I've got the devil in me, and he means to bring it out; and one of these days it will come out, in a way that he won't like, or I'm mistaken.

ELIZA: Well, I always thought that I must obey my master and mistress, or I couldn't be a Christian.

GEORGE: There is some sense in it in your case. They have brought you up like a child—fed you, clothed you and taught you, so that you have a good education—that is some reason why they should claim you. But I have been kicked and cuffed and sworn at, and what do I owe? I've paid for all my keeping a hundred times over. I won't bear it!—no, I *won't!* Master will find out that I'm one whipping won't tame. My day will come yet, if he don't look out!

ELIZA: What are you doing to do? Oh! George, don't do anything wicked; if you only trust in heaven and try to do right, it will deliver you.

GEORGE: Eliza, my heart's full of bitterness. I can't trust in heaven. Why does it let things be so?

ELIZA: Oh George! we must all have faith. Mistress says that when all things go wrong to us, we must believe that heaven is doing the very best.

GEORGE: That's easy for people to say who are sitting on their sofas and riding in their carriages; but let them be where I am—I guess it would come some harder. I wish I could be good; but my heart burns and can't be reconciled. You couldn't, in my place, you can't now, if I tell you all I've got to say; you don't know the whole yet.

ELIZA: What do you mean?

GEORGE: Well, lately my master has been saying that he was a fool to let me marry off the place—that he hates Mr. Shelby and all his tribe—and he says he won't let me come here any more, and that I shall take a wife and settle down on his place.

ELIZA: But you were married to *me* by the minister, as much as if you had been a white man.

GEORGE: Don't you know I can't hold you for my wife if he chooses to part us? That is why I wish I'd never seen you—it would have been better for us both—it would have been better for our poor child if he had never been born.

ELIZA: Oh! but my master is so kind.

GEORGE: Yes, but who knows?—he may die, and then Harry may be sold to nobody knows who. What pleasure is it that he is handsome and smart and bright? I tell you, Eliza, that a sword will pierce through your soul for every good and pleasant thing your child is or has. It will make him worth too much for you to keep.

ELIZA: Heaven forbid!

GEORGE: So, Eliza, my girl, bear up now, and good-by, for I'm going.

ELIZA: Going, George! Going where?

GEORGE: To Canada; and when I'm there I'll buy you—that's all the hope that's left us. You have a kind master, that won't refuse to sell you. I'll buy you and the boy—heaven helping me, I will!

ELIZA: Oh, dreadful! If you should be taken?

GEORGE: I won't be taken, Eliza—I'll *die* first! I'll be free, or I'll die!

ELIZA: You will not kill yourself?

GEORGE: No need for that; they will kill me, fast enough. I will never go down the river alive.

ELIZA: Oh, George! for my sake, do be careful. Don't lay hands on yourself, or anybody else. You are tempted too much, but don't. Go, if you must, but go carefully, prudently, and pray heaven to help you!

GEORGE: Well, then, Eliza, hear my plan. I'm going home quite resigned, you understand, as if all was over. I've got some preparations made, and there are those that will help me; and in the course of a few days I shall be among the missing. Well, now, good-by.

ELIZA: A moment—our boy.

GEORGE: [*Choked with emotion.*] True, I had forgotten him; one last look, and then farewell!

ELIZA: And heaven grant it be not forever!   [*Exeunt.*]

Scene 2: A dining-room.—Table and chairs.—Dessert, wine, &c., on table.—
SHELBY and HALEY discovered at table.

SHELBY: That is the way I should arrange the matter.

HALEY: I can't make trade that way—I positively can't, Mr. Shelby.

[Drinks.]

SHELBY: Why, the fact is, Haley, Tom is an uncommon fellow! He is certainly worth that sum anywhere—steady, honest, capable, manages my whole farm like a clock!

HALEY: You mean honest, as niggers go. [*Fills glass.*]

SHELBY: No; I mean, really, Tom is a good, steady, sensible, pious fellow. He got religion at a camp-meeting, four years ago, and I believe he really *did* get it. I've trusted him since then, with everything I have—money, house, horses, and let him come and go round the country, and I always found him true and square in everything!

HALEY: Some folks don't believe there is pious niggers, Shelby, but *I do.* I had a fellow, now, in this yer last lot I took to Orleans—'twas as good as a meetin' now, really, to hear that critter pray; and he was quite gentle and quiet like. He fetched me a good sum, too, for I bought him cheap of a man that was 'bliged to sell out, so I realized six hundred on him. Yes, I consider religion a valeyable thing in a nigger, when it's the genuine article and no mistake.

SHELBY: Well, Tom's got the real article, if ever a fellow had. Why, last fall I let him go to Cincinnati[1] alone, to do business for me and bring home five hundred dollars. "Tom," says I to him, "I trust you, because I think you are a Christian—I know you wouldn't cheat." Tom comes back sure enough; I knew he would. Some low fellows, they say, said to him—"Tom, why don't you make tracks for Canada?" "Ah, master

---

[1]Shelby allowed Tom to travel into a free state.

trusted me, and I couldn't," was his answer. They told me all about it. I am sorry to part with Tom, I must say. You ought to let him cover the whole balance of the debt, and you would, Haley, if you had any conscience.

HALEY: Well, I've got just as much conscience as any man in business can afford to keep, just a little, you know, to swear by, as 'twere; and then I'm ready to do anything in reason to 'blige friends, but this yer, you see, is a leetle too hard on a fellow—a leetle too hard! [*Fills glass again.*]

SHELBY: Well, then, Haley, how will you trade?

HALEY: Well, haven't you a boy or a girl that you could throw in with Tom?

SHELBY: Hum! none that I could well spare; to tell the truth, it's only hard necessity makes me willing to sell at all. I don't like parting with any of my hands, that's a fact.

[*HARRY runs in.*]

Hulloa! Jim Crow! [*Throws a bunch of raisins towards him.*] Pick that up now. [HARRY *does so.*]

HALEY: Bravo, little 'un! [*Throws an orange, which* HARRY *catches. He sings and dances around the stage.*] Hurrah! Bravo! What a young 'un! That chap's a case, I'll promise. Tell you what, Shelby, fling in that chap, and I'll settle the business. Come, now, if that ain't doing the thing up about the rightest!

[*ELIZA enters.—Starts on beholding* HALEY, *and gazes fearfully at* HARRY, *who runs and clings to her dress, showing the orange, &c.*]

SHELBY: Well, Eliza?

ELIZA: I was looking for Harry, please, sir.

SHELBY: Well, take him away, then.

[*ELIZA grasps the child eagerly in her arms, and casting another glance of apprehension at* HALEY, *exits hastily.*]

HALEY: By Jupiter! there's an article, now. You might make your fortune on that ar gal in Orleans any day. I've seen over a thousand in my day, paid down for gals not a bit handsomer.

SHELBY: I don't want to make my fortune on her. Another glass of wine. [*Fills the glasses.*]

HALEY: [*Drinks and smacks his lips.*] Capital wine—first chop! Come, how will you trade about the gal? What shall I say for her? What'll you take?

SHELBY: Mr. Haley, she is not to be sold. My wife wouldn't part with her for her weight in gold.

HALEY: Ay, ay! women always say such things, 'cause they hain't no sort of calculation. Just show 'em how many watches, feathers and trinkets one's weight in gold would buy, and that alters the case, I reckon.

SHELBY: I tell you, Haley, this must not be spoken of—I say no, and I mean no.

HALEY: Well, you'll let me have the boy tho'; you must own that I have come down pretty handsomely for him.

SHELBY: What on earth can you want with the child?

HALEY: Why, I've got a friend that's going into this yer branch of the business— wants to buy up handsome boys to raise for the market. Well, what do you say?

SHELBY: I'll think the matter over and talk with my wife.

HALEY: Oh, certainly, by all means; but I'm in a devil of a hurry, and shall want to know as soon as possible, what I may depend on. [*Rises and puts on his overcoat, which hangs on a chair.—Takes hat and whip.*]

SHELBY: Well, call up this evening, between six and seven, and you shall have my answer.

HALEY: All right. Take care of yourself, old boy!   [*Exit.*]

SHELBY: If anybody had ever told me that I should sell Tom to those rascally traders, I should never have believed it. Now it must come for aught I see, and Eliza's child too. So much for being in debt, heigho! The fellow sees his advantage and means to push it.

Scene 3: Snowy landscape.—UNCLE TOM'S Cabin.—Snow on roof.—Praticable door and window.—Dark Stage.—Music.

[Enter ELIZA hastily, with HARRY in her arms.]

ELIZA: My poor boy; they have sold you, but your mother will save you yet!

[Goes to Cabin and taps on window.—AUNT CHLOE appears at window with a large white night-cap on.]

CHLOE: Good Lord! what's that? My sakes alive if it ain't Lizy! Get on your clothes, old man, quick! I'm gwine to open the door.

[The door opens and CHLOE enters, followed by UNCLE TOM in his shirt sleeves, holding a tallow candle.]

TOM: [*Holding the light towards ELIZA.*] Lord bless you! I'm skeered to look at ye, Lizy! Are ye tuck sick, or what's come over ye?

ELIZA: I'm running away, Uncle Tom and Aunt Chloe, carrying off my child! Master sold him!

TOM and CHLOE: Sold him!

ELIZA: Yes, sold him! I crept into the closet by mistress' door to-night, and heard master tell mistress that he had sold my Harry, and you, Uncle Tom, both, to a trader, and that the man was to take possession to-morrow.

CHLOE: The good Lord have pity on us! Oh! it don't seem as if it was true. What has he done that master should sell *him?*

ELIZA: He hasn't done anything—it isn't for that. Master don't want to sell, and mistress—she's always good. I heard her plead and beg for us, but he told her 'twas no use—that he was in this man's debt, and he had got the power over him, and that if he did not pay him off clear, it would end in his having to sell the place and all the people and move off.

CHLOE: Well, old man, why don't you run away, too? Will you wait to be toted down the river, where they kill niggers with hard work and starving? I'd a heap rather die than go there, any day! There's time for ye, be off with Lizy—you've got a pass to come and go any time. Come, bustle up, and I'll get your things together.

TOM: No, no—I ain't going. Let Eliza go—it's her right. I wouldn't be the one to say no—'tain't in natur for her to stay; but you heard what she said? If I must be sold, or all the people on the place, and everything go to rack, why, let me be sold. I s'pose I can bar it as well as any one. Mas'r always found me on the spot—he always will. I never have broken trust, nor used my pass no ways contrary to my word, and I never will. It's better for me to go alone, than to break up the place and sell all. Mas'r ain't to blame, and he'll take care of you and the poor little 'uns! [*Overcome.*]

CHLOE: Now, old man, what is you gwine to cry for? Does you want to break this old woman's heart? [*Crying.*]

ELIZA: I saw my husband only this afternoon, and I little knew then what was to come. He told me he was going to run away. Do try, if you can, to get word to him. Tell him how I went and why I went, and tell him I'm going to try and find Canada. You must give my love to him, and tell him if I never see him again on earth, I trust we shall meet in heaven!

TOM: Dat is right, Lizy, trust in the Lord—he is our best friend—our only comforter.

ELIZA: You won't go with me, Uncle Tom?

TOM: No; time was when I would, but the Lord's given me a work among these yer poor souls, and I'll stay with 'em and bear my cross with 'em till the end. It's different with you—it's more'n you could stand, and you'd better go if you can.

ELIZA: Uncle Tom, I'll try it!

TOM: Amen! The Lord help ye! [*Exit* ELIZA *and* HARRY.]

CHLOE: What is you gwine to do, old man? What's to become of you?

TOM: [*Solemnly.*] Him that saved Daniel in the den of lions—that saved the children in the fiery furnace—Him that walked on the sea and bade the winds to be still—He's alive yet![2] and I've faith to believe He can deliver me!

CHLOE: You is right, old man.

TOM: The Lord is good unto all that trust him, Chloe.

[*Exeunt into Cabin.*]

---

[2]Tom speaks of God's character by referring to three biblical stories: Daniel 6; Daniel 3; Mark 4.

Scene 4: Room in Tavern by the river side.—A large window, through
which the river is seen, filled with floating ice.—Moonlight.—
Table and chairs brought on.

[Enter PHINEAS.*]*

PHINEAS: Chaw me up into tobaccy ends! how in the name of all that's onpossi-
ble am I to get across that yer pesky river? It's a reg'lar blockade of ice! I promised Ruth
to meet her to-night, and she'll be into my har if I don't come. [*Goes to window.*] That's
a conglomerated prospect for a loveyer! What in creation's to be done? That thar river
looks like a permiscuous ice-cream shop come to an awful state of friz. If I war on the
adjacent bank, I wouldn't care a teetotal atom. Rile up, you old varmint, and shake the
ice off your back!

[Enter ELIZA *and* HARRY.*]*

ELIZA: Courage, my boy—we have reached the river. Let it but roll between us
and our pursuers, and we are safe! [*Goes to window.*] Gracious powers! the river is
choked with cakes of ice!

PHINEAS: Holloa, gal!—what's the matter? You look kind of streaked.

ELIZA: Is there any ferry or boat that takes people over now?

PHINEAS: Well, I guess not; the boats have stopped running.

ELIZA: [*In dismay.*] Stopped running?

PHINEAS: Maybe you're wanting to get over—anybody sick? Ye seem mighty
anxious.

ELIZA: I—I—I've got a child that's very dangerous. I never heard of it till last
night, and I've walked quite a distance to-day, in hopes to get to the ferry.

PHINEAS: Well, now, that's onlucky; I'm re'lly consarned for ye. Thar's a man, a
piece down here, that's going over with some truck this evening, if he duss to; he'll be in
here to supper to-night, so you'd better set down and wait. That's a smart little chap. Say,
young 'un, have a chaw tobaccy? [*Takes out a large plug and a bowie-knife.*]

ELIZA: No, no! not any for him.

PHINEAS: Oh! he don't use it, eh? Hain't come to it yet? Well, I have. [*Cuts off a
large piece, and returns the plug and knife to pocket.*] What's the matter with the young
'un? He looks kind of white in the gills!

ELIZA: Poor fellow! he is not used to walking, and I've hurried him on so.

PHINEAS: Tuckered, eh? Well, there's a little room there, with a fire in it. Take the
babby in there, make yourself comfortable till that thar ferryman shows his countenance—I'll stand the damage.

ELIZA: How shall I thank you for such kindness to a stranger?

PHINEAS: Well, if you don't know how, why, don't try; that's the teetotal. Come,
vamoose!   [*Exit* ELIZA *and* HARRY.*]

Chaw me into sassage meat, if that ain't a perpendicular fine gal! she's a reg'lar A

No. 1 sort of female! How'n thunder am I to get across this refrigerated stream of water? I can't wait for that ferryman.

[Enter MARKS.*]*

Halloa! what sort of a critter's this? [*Advances.*] Say, stranger, will you have something to drink?

MARKS: You are excessively kind: I don't care if I do.

PHINEAS: Ah! he's a human. Holloa, thar! bring us a jug of whisky instantaneously, or expect to be teetotally chawed up! Squat yourself, stranger, and go in for enjoyment. [*They sit at table.*] Who are you, and what's your name?

MARKS: I am a lawyer, and my name is Marks.

PHINEAS: A land shark, eh? Well, I don't think no worse on you for that. The law is a kind of necessary evil; and it breeds lawyers just as an old stump does fungus. Ah! here's the whisky.

[Enter WAITER, *with jug and tumblers. Places them on table.]*

Here, you—take that shin-plaster. [*Gives bill.*] I don't want any change—thar's a gal stopping in that room—the balance will pay for her—d'ye hear?—vamoose! [*Exit* WAITER.—*Fills glass.*] Take hold, neighbor Marks—don't shirk the critter. Here's hoping your path of true love may never have an ice-choked river to cross! [*They drink.*]

MARKS: Want to cross the river, eh?

PHINEAS: Well, I do, stranger. Fact is, I'm in love with the teetotalist pretty girl, over on the Ohio side, that ever wore a Quaker[3] bonnet. Take another swig, neighbor. [*Fills glasses, and they drink.*]

MARKS: A Quaker, eh?

PHINEAS: Yes—kind of strange, ain't it? The way of it was this:—I used to own a grist of niggers—had 'em to work on my plantation, just below here. Well, stranger, do you know I fell in with that gal—of course I was considerably smashed—knocked into a pretty conglomerated heap—and I told her so. She said she wouldn't hear a word from me so long as I owned a nigger!

MARKS: You sold them, I suppose?

PHINEAS: You're teetotally wrong, neighbor. I gave them all their freedom, and told 'em to vamoose!

MARKS: Ah! yes—very noble, I dare say; but rather expensive. This act won you your lady-love, eh?

PHINEAS: You're off the track again, neighbor. She felt kind of pleased about it, and smiled, and all that; but she said she could never be mine unless I turned Quaker!

---

[3]The Religious Society of Friends (or Quakers) was founded in 1650 by Englishman George Fox. It is a religious tradition known for its commitment to peace, social justice, and honesty. Quakers were well known for their active opposition to slavery.

Thunder and earth! what do you think of that? You're a lawyer—come, now, what's your opinion? Don't you call it a knotty point?

MARKS: Most decidedly. Of course you refused.

PHINEAS: Teetotally; but she told me to think better of it, and come tonight and give her my final conclusion. Chaw me into mince-meat, if I haven't made up my mind to do it!

MARKS: You astonish me!

PHINEAS: Well, you see, I can't get along without that gal;—she's sort of fixed my flint, and I'm sure to hang fire without her. I know I shall make a queer sort of Quaker, because you see, neighbor, I ain't precisely the kind of material to make a Quaker out of.

MARKS: No, not exactly.

PHINEAS: Well, I can't stop no longer. I must try to get across that candaverous river some way. It's getting late—take care of yourself, neighbor lawyer. I'm a teetotal victim to a pair of black eyes. Chaw me up to feed hogs if I'm not in a ruinatious state!

MARKS: Queer genius, that, very!   [*Exit.*]

[Enter TOM LOKER.*]*

So you've come at last.

LOKER: Yes. [*Looks into jug.*] Empty! Waiter! more whisky!

*[*WAITER *enters with jug, and removes the empty one.—Enter* HALEY.*]*

HALEY: By the land! if this yer ain't the nearest, now, to what I've heard people call Providence! Why, Loker, how are ye?

LOKER: The devil! What brought you here, Haley?

HALEY: [*Sitting at table.*] I say, Tom, this yer's the luckiest thing in the world. I'm in a devil of a hobble, and you must help me out!

LOKER: Ugh! aw! like enough. A body may be pretty sure of that when you're glad to see 'em, or can make something off of 'em. What's the blow now?

HALEY: You've got a friend here—partner, perhaps?

LOKER: Yes, I have. Here, Marks—here's that ar fellow that I was with in Natchez.

MARKS: [*Grasping* HALEY's *hand.*] Shall be pleased with his acquaintance. Mr. Haley, I believe?

HALEY: The same, sir. The fact is, gentlemen, this morning I bought a young 'un of Shelby up above here. His mother got wind of it, and what does she do but cut her lucky with him; and I'm afraid by this time that she has crossed the river, for I tracked her to this very place.

MARKS: So, then, ye're fairly sewed up, ain't ye? He! he! he! it's neatly done, too.

HALEY: This young 'un business makes lots of trouble in the trade.

MARKS: Now, Mr. Haley, what is it? Do you want us to undertake to catch this gal?

HALEY: The gal's no matter of mine—she's Shelby's—it's only the boy. I was a fool for buying the monkey.

LOKER: You're generally a fool!

MARKS: Come now, Loker, none of your huffs; you see, Mr. Haley's a-puttin' us in a way of a good job, I reckon; just hold still—these yer arrangements are my forte. This yer gal, Mr. Haley—how is she?—what is she?

[ELIZA appears, with HARRY, listening.]

HALEY: Well, white and handsome—well brought up. I'd have given Shelby eight hundred or a thousand, and then made well on her.

MARKS: White and handsome—well brought up! Look here, now, Loker, a beautiful opening. We'll do a business here on our own account. We does the catchin'; the boy, of course, goes to Mr. Haley—we takes the gal to Orleans to speculate on. Ain't it beautiful? *[They confer together.]*

ELIZA: Powers of mercy, protect me! How shall I escape these human bloodhounds? Ah! the window—the river of ice! That dark stream lies between me and liberty! Surely the ice will bear my trifling weight. It is my only chance of escape—better sink beneath the cold waters, with my child locked in my arms, than have him torn from me and sold into bondage. He sleeps upon my breast—Heaven, I put my trust in thee! *[Gets out of window.]*

MARKS: Well, Tom Loker, what do you say?

LOKER: It'll do!

[Strikes his hand violently on the table.—ELIZA screams.—They all start to their feet.—ELIZA disappears.—Music, chord.]

HALEY: By the land, there she is now! *[They all rush to the window.]*

MARKS: She's making for the river!

LOKER: Let's after her!

[Music.—They all leap through the window.—Change.]

Scene 5: Snowy Landscape.—Music.

[Enter ELIZA, with HARRY, hurriedly.]

ELIZA: They press upon my footsteps—the river is my only hope! Heaven grant me strength to reach it, ere they overtake me! Courage, my child!—we will be free—or perish!   *[Rushes off.]*

[Enter LOKER, HALEY and MARKS.]

HALEY: We'll catch her yet; the river will stop her!

MARKS: No, it won't, for look! she has jumped upon the ice! She's a brave gal, anyhow!

LOKER: She'll be drowned!

HALEY: Curse that young 'un! I shall lose him, after all.

LOKER: Come on, Marks, to the ferry!

MARKS: Aye, to the ferry!—a hundred dollars for a boat!

[*Music.—They rush off.*]

Scene 6: The entire depth of stage, representing the Ohio River filled with Floating Ice. Bank on right and in front.

[*ELIZA appears, with HARRY, on a cake of ice, and floats slowly across.— HALEY, LOKER and MARKS, on bank, right hand, observing.—PHINEAS on opposite shore.*]

END OF ACT I

Act II

Scene 1: A Handsome Parlor. MARIE *discovered reclining on a sofa.*

MARIE: [*Looking at a note.*] What can possibly detain St. Clare? According to this note, he should have been here a fortnight ago. [*Noise of carriage without.*] I do believe he has come at last.

[*EVA runs in.*]

EVA: Mamma! [*Throws her arms around MARIE'S neck, and kisses her.*]

MARIE: That will do—take care, child—don't you make my head ache! [*Kisses her languidly.*]

[*Enter ST. CLARE, OPHELIA, and TOM, nicely dressed.*]

ST. CLARE: Well, my dear Marie, here we are at last. The wanderers have arrived, you see. Allow me to present my cousin, Miss Ophelia, who is about to undertake the office of our housekeeper.

MARIE: [*Rising to a sitting posture.*] I am delighted to see you. How do you like the appearance of our city?

EVA: [*Running to OPHELIA.*] Oh! is it not beautiful? My own darling home!—is it not beautiful?

OPHELIA: Yes, it is a pretty place, though it looks rather old and heathenish to me.

ST. CLARE: Tom, my boy, this seems to suit you?

TOM: Yes, mas'r, it looks about the right thing.

ST. CLARE: See here, Marie, I've brought you a coachman, at last, to order. I tell you, he's a regular hearse for blackness and sobriety, and will drive you like a funeral, if you wish. Open your eyes, now, and look at him. Now, don't say I never think about you when I'm gone.

MARIE: I know he'll get drunk.

ST. CLARE: Oh! no he won't. He's warranted a pious and sober article.

MARIE: Well, I hope he may turn out well; it's more than I expect, though.

ST. CLARE: Have you no curiosity to learn how and where I picked up Tom?

EVA: *Uncle* Tom, papa; that's his name.

ST. CLARE: Right, my little sunbeam!

TOM: Please, mas'r, that ain't no 'casion to say nothing 'bout me.

ST. CLARE: You are too modest, my modern Hannibal.[4] Do you know, Marie, that our little Eva took a fancy to Uncle Tom—whom we met on board the steamboat—and persuaded me to buy him?

MARIE: Ah! she is so odd!

ST. CLARE: As we approached the landing, a sudden rush of the passengers precipitated Eva into the water—

MARIE: Gracious heavens!

ST. CLARE: A man leaped into the river, and, as she rose to the surface of the water, grasped her in his arms, and held her up until she could be drawn on the boat again. Who was that man, Eva?

EVA: Uncle Tom! [*Runs to him.—He lifts her in his arms.—She kisses him.*]

TOM: The dear soul!

OPHELIA: [*Astonished.*] How shiftless!

ST. CLARE: [*Overhearing her.*] What's the matter now, pray?

OPHELIA: Well, I want to be kind to everybody, and I wouldn't have anything hurt, but as to kissing—

ST. CLARE: Niggers! that you're not up to, hey?

OPHELIA: Yes, that's it—how can she?

ST. CLARE: Oh! bless you, it's nothing when you are used to it!

OPHELIA: I could never be so shiftless!

EVA: Come with me, Uncle Tom, and I will show you about the house. [*Crosses with* TOM.]

TOM: Can I go, mas'r?

ST. CLARE: Yes, Tom; she is your little mistress—your only duty will be to attend to her! [TOM *bows and exits.*]

MARIE: Eva, my dear!

EVA: Well, mamma?

MARIE: Do not exert yourself too much

EVA: No, mamma! [*Runs out.*]

---

[4]Hannibal (247–183 B.C.) was not only one of the ancient world's greatest generals, but he was also an African.

OPHELIA: [*Lifting up her hands.*] How shiftless!

[*ST. CLARE sits next to MARIE on sofa.—OPHELIA next to ST. CLARE.*]

ST. CLARE: Well, what do you think of Uncle Tom, Marie?

MARIE: He is a perfect behemoth!

ST. CLARE: Come, now, Marie, be gracious, and say something pretty to a fellow!

MARIE: You've been gone a fortnight beyond the time!

ST. CLARE: Well, you know I wrote you the reason.

MARIE: Such a short, cold letter!

ST. CLARE: Dear me! the mail was just going, and it had to be that or nothing.

MARIE: That's just the way; always something to make your journeys long and letters short!

ST. CLARE: Look at this. [*Takes an elegant velvet case from his pocket.*] Here's a present I got for you in New York—a daguerreotype[5] of Eva and myself.

MARIE: [*Looks at it with a dissatisfied air.*] What made you sit in such an awkward position?

ST. CLARE: Well, the position may be a matter of opinion, but what do you think of the likeness?

MARIE: [*Closing the case snappishly.*] If you don't think anything of my opinion in one case, I suppose you wouldn't in another.

OPHELIA: [*Sententiously, aside.*] How shiftless!

ST. CLARE: Hang the woman! Come, Marie, what do you think of the likeness? Don't be nonsensical now.

MARIE: It's very inconsiderate of you, St. Clare, to insist on my talking and look-ing at things. You know I've been lying all day with the sick headache, and there's been such a tumult made ever since you came, I'm half dead!

OPHELIA: You're subject to the sick headache, ma'am?

MARIE: Yes, I'm a perfect martyr to it!

OPHELIA: Juniper-berry tea is good for sick headache; at least, Molly, Deacon Abraham Perry's wife, used to say so; and she was a great nurse.

ST. CLARE: I'll have the first juniper-berries that get ripe in our garden by the lake brought in for that especial purpose. Come, cousin, let us take a stroll in the garden. Will you join us, Marie?

MARIE: I wonder how you can ask such a question, when you know how fragile I am. I shall retire to my chamber, and repose till dinner time.   [*Exit.*]

---

[5]Developed in France in the 1830s by Louis Daguerre and Joseph Niepce, daguerreotyping was the first successful form of photography. It was widely popular in antebellum America.

OPHELIA: [*Looking after her.*] How shiftless!

ST. CLARE: Come, cousin! [*As he goes out.*] Look out for the babies! If I step upon anybody, let them mention it.

OPHELIA: Babies under foot! How shiftless!   [*Exeunt.*]

Scene 2: A Garden. TOM *discovered, seated on a bank, with* EVA *on his knee— his button-holes are filled with flowers, and* EVA *is hanging a wreath around his neck.*

[Enter ST. CLARE *and* OPHELIA, *observing.]*

EVA: Oh, Tom; you look so funny.

TOM: [*Sees* ST. CLARE *and puts* EVA *down.*] I begs pardon, mas'r, but the young missis would do it. Look yer, I'm like the ox,[6] mentioned in the good book, dressed for the sacrifice.

ST. CLARE: I say, what do you think, Pussy? Which do you like the best—to live as they do at your uncle's, up in Vermont, or to have a house full of servants, as we do?

EVA: Oh! of course our way is the pleasantest.

ST. CLARE: [*Patting her head.*] Why so?

EVA: Because it makes so many more round you to love, you know.

OPHELIA: Now, that's just like Eva—just one of her odd speeches.

EVA: Is it an odd speech, papa?

ST. CLARE: Rather, as this world goes, Pussy. But where has my little Eva been?

EVA: Oh! I've been up in Tom's room, hearing him sing.

ST. CLARE: Hearing Tom sing, hey?

EVA: Oh, yes! he sings such beautiful things, about the new Jerusalem, and bright angels, and the land of Canaan.

ST. CLARE: I dare say; it's better than the opera, isn't it?

EVA: Yes; and he's going to teach them to me.

ST. CLARE: Singing lessons, hey? You are coming on.

EVA: Yes, he sings for me, and I read to him in my Bible, and he explains what it means. Come, Tom.   [*She takes his hand and they exit.*]

ST. CLARE: [*Aside.*] Oh, Evangeline! Rightly named; hath not heaven made thee an evangel to me?

OPHELIA: How shiftless! How can you let her?

ST. CLARE: Why not?

OPHELIA: Why, I don't know; it seems so dreadful.

ST. CLARE: You would think no harm in a child's caressing a large dog, even if he

---

[6]Animal sacrifice and references building upon such sacrifice are common in the Old Testament (see Numbers 7 and Jer. 11:19).

was black; but a creature that can think, reason and feel, and is immortal, you shudder at. Confess it, cousin. I know the feeling among some of you Northerners well enough. Not that there is a particle of virtue in our not having it, but custom with us does what Christianity ought to do: obliterates the feeling of personal prejudice. You loathe them as you would a snake or a toad, yet you are indignant at their wrongs. You would not have them abused, but you don't want to have anything to do with them yourselves. Isn't that it?

OPHELIA: Well, cousin, there may be some truth in this.

ST. CLARE: What would the poor and lowly do without children? Your little child is your only true democrat. Tom, now, is a hero to Eva; his stories are wonders in her eyes; his songs and Methodist hymns are better than an opera, and the traps[7] and little bits of trash in his pockets a mine of jewels, and he the most wonderful Tom that ever wore a black skin. This is one of the roses of Eden that the Lord has dropped down expressly for the poor and lowly, who get few enough of any other kind.

OPHELIA: It's strange, cousin; one might almost think you was a *professor*, to hear you talk.

ST. CLARE: A professor?

OPHELIA: Yes, a professor of religion.

ST. CLARE: Not at all; not a professor as you town folks have it, and what is worse, I'm afraid, not a *practicer*, either.

OPHELIA: What makes you talk so, then?

ST. CLARE: Nothing is easier than talking. My forte lies in talking, and yours, cousin, lies in doing. And speaking of that puts me in mind that I have made a purchase for your department. There's the article now. Here, Topsy! [*Whistles.*]

[*TOPSY runs on.*]

OPHELIA: Good gracious! what a heathenish, shiftless looking object! St. Clare, what in the world have you brought that thing here for?

ST. CLARE: For you to educate, to be sure, and train in the way she should go. I thought she was rather a funny specimen in the Jim Crow[8] line. Here, Topsy, give us a song, and show us some of your dancing.

[*TOPSY sings a verse and dances a breakdown.*]

OPHELIA: [*Paralyzed.*] Well, of all things! If I ever saw the like!

ST. CLARE: [*Smothering a laugh.*] Topsy, this is your new mistress—I'm going to give you up to her. See now that you behave yourself.

TOPSY: Yes, mas'r.

---

[7]Trappings, personal items.

[8]A popular antebellum minstrel routine, "Jump Jim Crow," served to associate African Americans with the term *Jim Crow*.

ST. CLARE: You're going to be good, Topsy, you understand?

TOPSY: Oh, yes, mas'r.

OPHELIA: Now, St. Clare, what upon earth is this for? Your house is so full of these plagues now, that a body can't set down their foot without treading on 'em. I get up in the morning and find one asleep behind the door, and see one black head poking out from under the table—one lying on the door mat, and they are moping and mowing and grinning between all the railings, and tumbling over the kitchen floor! What on earth did you want to bring this one for?

ST. CLARE: For you to educate—din't I tell you? You're always preaching about educating; I thought I would make you a present of a fresh caught specimen, and let you try your hand on her and bring her up in the way she should go.

OPHELIA: I don't want her, I am sure; I have more to do with 'em now than I want to.

ST. CLARE: That's you Christians, all over. You'll get up a society, and get some poor missionary to spend all his days among just such heathens; but let me see one of you that would take one into your house with you, and take the labor of their conversion upon yourselves.

OPHELIA: Well, I didn't think of it in that light. It might be a real missionary work. Well, I'll do what I can. [*Advances to* TOPSY.] She's dreadful dirty and shiftless! How old are you, Topsy?

TOPSY: Dunno, missis.

OPHELIA: How shiftless! Don't know how old you are? Didn't anybody ever tell you? Who was your mother?

TOPSY: [*Grinning.*] Never had none.

OPHELIA: Never had any mother? What do you mean? Where was you born?

TOPSY: Never was born.

OPHELIA: You mustn't answer me in that way. I'm not playing with you. Tell me where you was born, and who your father and mother were.

TOPSY: Never was born, tell you; never had no father, nor mother, nor nothin'. I war raised by a speculator, with lots of others. Old Aunt Sue used to take car' on us.

ST. CLARE: She speaks the truth, cousin. Speculators buy them up cheap, when they are little, and get them raised for the market.

OPHELIA: How long have you lived with your master and mistress?

TOPSY: Dunno, missis.

OPHELIA: How shiftless! Is it a year, or more, or less?

TOPSY: Dunno, missis.

ST. CLARE: She does not know what a year is; she don't even know her own age.

OPHELIA: Have you ever heard anything about heaven, Topsy? [TOPSY *looks bewildered and grins.*] Do you know who made you?

TOPSY: Nobody, as I knows on, he, he, he! I 'spect I growed. Don't think nobody never made me.

OPHELIA: The shiftless heathen? What can you do? What did you do for your master and mistress?

TOPSY: Fetch water—and wash dishes—and rub knives—and wait on folks—and dance breakdowns.

OPHELIA: I shall break down, I'm afraid, in trying to make anything of you, you shiftless mortal!

ST. CLARE: You find virgin soil, there, cousin; put in your own ideas—you won't find many to pull up.   [*Exit laughing.*]

OPHELIA: [*Takes out her handkerchief.—A pair of gloves falls.—*TOPSY *picks them up slyly and puts them in her sleeve.*] Follow me, you benighted innocent!

TOPSY: Yes, missis.

[As OPHELIA *turns her back to her, she seizes the end of the ribbon she wears around her waist, and twitches it off.—*OPHELIA *turns and sees her as she is putting it in her other sleeve.—*OPHELIA *takes ribbon from her.*]

OPHELIA: What's this? You naughty, wicked girl, you've been stealing this?

TOPSY: Laws! why, that ar's missis' ribbon, an't it? How could it got caught in my sleeve?

OPHELIA: Topsy, you naughty girl, don't you tell me a lie—you stole that ribbon!

TOPSY: Missis, I declare for't, I didn't—never seed it till dis yer blessed minnit.

OPHELIA: Topsy, don't you know it's wicked to tell lies?

TOPSY: I never tells no lies, missis; it's just de truth I've been telling now, and nothin' else.

OPHELIA: Topsy, I shall have to whip you, if you tell lies so.

TOPSY: Laws, missis, if you's to whip all day, couldn't say no other way. I never seed dat ar—it must a got caught in my sleeve. [*Blubbers.*]

OPHELIA: [*Seizes her by the shoulders.*] Don't you tell me that again, you barefaced fibber! [*Shakes her.—The gloves fall on stage.*] There you, my gloves too— you outrageous young heathen! [*Picks them up.*] Will you tell me, now, you didn't steal the ribbon?

TOPSY: No, missis; stole de gloves, but didn't steal de ribbon. It was permiskus.

OPHELIA: Why, you young reprobate!

TOPSY: Yes—I's knows I's wicked.

OPHELIA: Then you know you ought to be punished. [*Boxes her ears.*] What do you think of that?

TOPSY: He, he, he! De Lord, missis; dat wouldn't kill a 'skeeter! [*Runs off laughing.—*OPHELIA *follows indignantly.*]

Scene 3: The Tavern by the River.—Table and chairs.—Jug and glasses on table.—On flat is a printed placard, headed:—"Four Hundred Dollars Reward—Runaway—George Harris!"

[PHINEAS is discovered, seated at table.]

PHINEAS: So yer I am; and a pretty business I've undertook to do. Find the husband of the gal that crossed the river on the ice two or three days ago. Ruth said I must do it, and I'll be teetotally chewed up if I don't do it. I see they've offered a reward for him, dead or alive. How in creation am I to find the varmint? He isn't likely to go round looking natural, with a full description of his hide and figure staring him in the face.

[Enter MR. WILSON.]

I say, stranger, how are ye? [*Rises and comes forward.*]

WILSON: Well, I reckon.

PHINEAS: Any news? [*Takes out plug and knife.*]

WILSON: Not that I know of.

PHINEAS: [*Cutting a piece of tobacco and offering it.*] Chaw?

WILSON: No, thank ye—it don't agree with me.

PHINEAS: Don't, eh? [*Putting it in his own mouth.*] I never felt any the worse for it.

WILSON: [*Sees placard.*] What's that?

PHINEAS: Nigger advertised. [*Advances towards it and spits on it.*] There's my mind upon that.

WILSON: Why, now stranger, what's that for?

PHINEAS: I'd do it all the same to the writer of that ar paper, if he was here. Any man that owns a boy like that, and can't find any better way of treating him than branding him on the hand with the letter H, as that paper states, *deserves* to lose him. Such papers as this ar' a shame to old Kaintuck! that's my mind right out, if anybody wants to know.

WILSON: Well, now, that's a fact.

PHINEAS: I used to have a gang of boys, sir—that was before I fell in love—and I just told 'em:—"Boys," says I, "run now! Dig! put! jest when you want to. I never shall come to look after you!" That's the way I kept mine. Let 'em know they are free to run any time, and it jest stops their wanting to. It stands to reason it should. Treat 'em like men, and you'll have men's work.

WILSON: I think you are altogether right, friend, and this man described here is a fine fellow—no mistake about that. He worked for me some half dozen years in my bagging factory, and he was my best hand, sir. He is an ingenious fellow, too; he invented a machine for the cleaning of hemp—a really valuable affair; it's gone into use in several factories. His master holds the patent of it.

PHINEAS: I'll warrant ye; holds it, and makes money out of it, and then turns round and brands the boy in his right hand! If I had a fair chance, I'd mark him, I reckon, so that he'd carry it *one* while!

[Enter GEORGE HARRIS, disguised.]

GEORGE [*Speaking as he enters.*] Jim, see to the trunks. [*Sees* WILSON.] Ah! Mr. Wilson here?

WILSON: Bless my soul, can it be?

GEORGE: [*Advances and grasps his hand.*] Mr. Wilson, I see you remember me, Mr. Butler, of Oaklands, Shelby county.

WILSON: Ye—yes—yes—sir.

PHINEAS: Holloa! there's a screw loose here somewhere. That old gentleman seems to be struck into a pretty considerable heap of astonishment. May I be teetotally chawed up! if I don't believe that's the identical man I'm arter. [*Crosses to* GEORGE.] How are ye, George Harris?

GEORGE: [*Starting back and thrusting his hands into his breast.*] You know me?

PHINEAS: Ha, ha, ha! I rather conclude I do; but don't get riled, I ain't a bloodhound in disguise.

GEORGE: How did you discover me?

PHINEAS: By a teetotal smart guess. You're the very man I want to see. Do you know I was sent after you?

GEORGE: Ah! by my master?

PHINEAS: No; by your wife.

GEORGE: My wife! Where is she?

PHINEAS: She's stopping with a Quaker family over on the Ohio side.

GEORGE: Then she is safe?

PHINEAS: Teetotally!

GEORGE: Conduct me to her.

PHINEAS: Just wait a brace of shakes[9] and I'll do it. I've got to go and get the boat ready. 'Twon't take me but a minute—make yourself comfortable till I get back. Chaw me up! but this is what I call doing things in short order.   [*Exit.*]

WILSON: George!

GEORGE: Yes, George!

WILSON: I couldn't have thought it!

GEORGE: I am pretty well disguised, I fancy; you see I don't answer to the advertisement at all.

WILSON: George, this is a dangerous game you are playing; I could not have advised you to it.

---

[9]In two shakes, or in a moment.

GEORGE: I can do it on my own responsibility.

WILSON: Well, George, I suppose you're running away—leaving your lawful master, George (I don't wonder at it), at the same time, I'm sorry, George, yes, decidedly. I think I must say that it's my duty to tell you so.

GEORGE: Why are you sorry, sir?

WILSON: Why, to see you, as it were, setting yourself in opposition to the laws of your country.

GEORGE: *My* country! What country have *I,* but the grave? And I would to heaven that I was laid there!

WILSON: George, you've got a hard master, in fact he is—well, he conducts himself reprehensibly—I can't pretend to defend him. I'm sorry for you, now; it's a bad case—very bad; but we must all submit to the indications of Providence, George, don't you see?

GEORGE: I wonder, Mr. Wilson, if the Indians should come and take you a prisoner away from your wife and children, and want to keep you all your life hoeing corn for them, if you'd think it your duty to abide in the condition in which you were called? I rather imagine that you'd think the first stray horse you could find an indication of Providence, shouldn't you?

WILSON: Really, George, putting the case in that somewhat peculiar light—I don't know—under those circumstances—but what I might. But it seems to me you are running an awful risk. You can't hope to carry it out. If you're taken it will be worse with you than ever; they'll only abuse you, and half kill you, and sell you down the river.

GEORGE: Mr. Wilson, I know all this. I *do* run a risk, but—[*Throws open coat and shows pistols and knife in his belt.*] There! I'm ready for them. Down South I never *will* go! no, if it comes to that, I can earn myself at least six feet of free soil—the first and last I shall ever own in Kentucky!

WILSON: Why, George, this state of mind is awful—it's getting really desperate. I'm concerned. Going to break the laws of your country?

GEORGE: My country again! Sir, I haven't any country any more than I have any father. I don't want anything of *your* country, except to be left alone—to go peaceably out of it; but if any man tries to stop me, let him take care, for I am desperate. I'll fight for my liberty, to the last breath I breathe! You say your fathers did it; if it was right for them, it is right for me!

WILSON: [*Walking up and down and fanning his face with a large yellow silk handkerchief.*] Blast 'em all! Haven't I always said so—the infernal old cusses! Bless me! I hope I an't swearing now! Well, go ahead, George, go ahead. But be careful, my boy; don't shoot anybody, unless—well, you'd *better* not shoot—at least I wouldn't *hit* anybody, you know.

GEORGE: Only in self-defense.

WILSON: Well, well. [*Fumbling in his pocket.*] I suppose, perhaps, I an't following my judgment—hang it, I won't follow my judgment. So here, George. [*Takes out a pocket-book and offers* GEORGE *a roll of bills.*]

GEORGE: No, my kind, good sir, you've done a great deal for me, and this might get you into trouble. I have money enough, I hope, to take me as far as I need it.

WILSON: No; but you must, George. Money is a great help everywhere; can't have too much, if you get it honestly. Take it, *do* take it, *now* do, my boy!

GEORGE: [*Taking the money.*] On condition, sir, that I may repay it at some future time, I will.

WILSON: And now, George, how long are you going to travel in this way? Not long or far, I hope? It's well carried on, but too bold.

GEORGE: Mr. Wilson, it is *so bold,* and this tavern is so near, that they will never think of it; they will look for me on ahead, and you yourself wouldn't know me.

WILSON: But the mark on your hand?

GEORGE: [*Draws off his glove and shows scar.*] That is a parting mark of Mr. Harris' regard. Looks interesting, doesn't it? [*Puts on glove again.*]

WILSON: I declare, my very blood runs cold when I think of it—your condition and your risks!

GEORGE: Mine has run cold a good many years; at present, it's about up to the boiling point.

WILSON: George, something has brought you out wonderfully. You hold up your head, and move and speak like another man.

GEORGE: [*Proudly.*] Because I'm a *freeman!* Yes, sir; I've said "master" for the last time to any man: *I'm free!*

WILSON: Take care! You are not sure; you may be taken.

GEORGE: All men are free and equal *in the grave,* if it comes to that, Mr. Wilson.

[Enter PHINEAS.*]*

PHINEAS: Them's my sentiment, to a teetotal atom, and I don't care who knows it! Neighbor, the boat is ready, and the sooner we make tracks the better. I've seen some mysterious strangers lurking about these diggings, so we'd better put.

GEORGE: Farewell, Mr. Wilson, and heaven reward you for the many kindnesses you have shown the poor fugitive!

WILSON: [*Grasping his hand.*] You're a brave fellow, George. I wish in my heart you were safe through, though—that's what I do.

PHINEAS: And ain't I the man of all creation to put him through, stranger? Chaw me up if I don't take him to his dear little wife, in the smallest possible quantity of time. Come, neighbor, let's vamoose.

GEORGE: Farewell, Mr. Wilson. [*Crosses.*]

WILSON: My best wishes go with you, George.   [*Exit.*]

PHINEAS: You're a trump, old Slow-and-Easy.

GEORGE: [*Looking off.*] Look! look!

PHINEAS: Consarn their picters, here they come! We can't get out of the house without their seeing us. We're teetotally treed!

GEORGE: Let us fight our way through them!

PHINEAS: No, that won't do; there are too many of them for a fair fight—we should be chawed up in no time. [*Looks round and sees trap door.*] Holloa! here's a cellar door. Just you step down here a few minutes, while I parley with them. [*Lifts trap.*]

GEORGE: I am resolved to perish sooner than surrender! [*Goes down trap.*]

PHINEAS: That's your sort! [*Closes trap and stands on it.*] Here they are!

[Enter HALEY, MARKS, LOKER and three MEN.]

HALEY: Say, stranger, you haven't seen a runaway darkey about these parts, eh?

PHINEAS: What kind of a darkey?

HALEY: A mulatto chap, almost as light-complexioned as a white man.

PHINEAS: Was he a pretty good-looking chap?

HALEY: Yes.

PHINEAS: Kind of tall?

HALEY: Yes.

PHINEAS: With brown hair?

HALEY: Yes.

PHINEAS: And dark eyes?

HALEY: Yes.

PHINEAS: Pretty well dressed?

HALEY: Yes.

PHINEAS: Scar on his right hand?

HALEY: Yes, yes.

PHINEAS: Well, I ain't seen him.

HALEY: Oh, bother! Come, boys, let's search the house.   [*Exeunt.*]

PHINEAS: [*Raises trap.*] Now, then, neighbor George.

[GEORGE enters, up trap.]

Now's the time to cut your lucky.

GEORGE: Follow me, Phineas.

PHINEAS: In a brace of shakes. [*Is closing trap as HALEY, MARKS, LOKER, &C., re-enter.*]

HALEY: Ah! he's down in the cellar. Follow me boys!

[Thrusts PHINEAS aside, and rushes down trap, followed by the others.
PHINEAS closes trap and stands on it.]

PHINEAS: Chaw me up! but I've got 'em all in a trap. [*Knocking below.*] Be quiet, you pesky varmints! [*Knocking.*] They're getting mighty oneasy. [*Knocking.*] Will you be quiet, you savagerous critters! [*The trap is forced open.* HALEY *and* MARKS *appear.* PHINEAS *seizes a chair and stands over trap—picture.*] Down with you or I'll smash you into apple-fritters! [*Tableau.*][10]

Scene 4: A Plain Chamber.

TOPSY: [*Without.*] You go 'long. No more nigger dan you be! [*Enters—shouts and laughter without—looks off.*] You seem to think yourself white folks. You ain't nerry one—black *nor* white. I'd like to be one or turrer. Law! you niggers, does you know you's all sinners? Well, you is—everybody is. White folks is sinners too—Miss Feely says so—but I 'spects niggers is the biggest ones. But Lor'! ye ain't any on ye up to me. I's so awful wicked there can't nobody do nothin' with me. I used to keep old missis a-swarin' at me half de time. I 'spects I's de wickedest critter in de world. [*Song and dance introduced.*]

[Enter EVA.*]*

EVA: Oh, Topsy! Topsy! you have been very wrong again.

TOPSY: Well, I 'spects I have.

EVA: What makes you do so?

TOPSY: I dunno; I 'spects it's cause I's so wicked.

EVA: Why did you spoil Jane's earrings?

TOPSY: 'Cause she's so proud. She called me a little black imp, and turned up her pretty nose at me 'cause she is whiter than I am. I was gwine by her room, and I seed her coral earrings lying on de table, so I threw dem on de floor, and put my foot on 'em, and scrunched 'em all to little bits—he! he! he! I's so wicked.

EVA: Don't you know that was very wrong?

TOPSY: I don't car'. I despises dem what sets up for fine ladies, when dey ain't nothin' but cream-colored niggers! Dere's Miss Rosa—she gives me lots of 'pertinent remarks. T'other night she was gwine to ball. She put on a beau'ful dress that missis give her—wid her har curled, all nice and pretty. She hab to go down de back stairs—dey am dark—and I puts a pail of hot water on dem, and she put her foot into it, and den she go tumblin' to de bottom of de stairs, and de water go all ober her, and spile her dress, and scald her dreadful bad! He! he! he! I's so wicked!

EVA: Oh! how could you!

TOPSY: Don't dey despise me 'cause I don't know nothing? Don't dey laugh at me 'cause I'm brack, and dey ain't?

EVA: But you shouldn't mind them.

TOPSY: Well, I don't mind dem; but when dey are passing under my winder, I trows dirty water on 'em, and dat spiles der complexions.

---

[10]Actors frozen in the midst of their actions.

EVA: What does make you so bad, Topsy? Why won't you try and be good? Don't you love anybody, Topsy?

TOPSY: Can't recommember.

EVA: But you love your father and mother?

TOPSY: Never had none; ye know, I telled ye that, Miss Eva.

EVA: Oh! I know; but hadn't you any brother, or sister, or aunt, or—

TOPSY: No, none on 'em—never had nothin' nor nobody. I's brack—no one loves me!

EVA: Oh! Topsy, I love you! [*Laying her hand on* TOPSY'S *shoulder.*] I love you because you haven't had any father, or mother, or friends. I love you, and I want you to be good. I wish you would try to be good for my sake.

[TOPSY *looks astonished for a moment, and then bursts into tears.*]

Only think of it, Topsy—*you* can be one of those spirits bright Uncle Tom sings about!

TOPSY: Oh! dear Miss Eva—dear Miss Eva! I will try—I will try! I never did care nothin' about it before.

EVA: If you try, you will succeed. Come with me. [*Crosses and takes* TOPSY'S *hand.*]

TOPSY: I will try; but den, I's so wicked!

[*Exit* EVA, *followed by* TOPSY, *crying.*]

Scene 5: Chamber.

[*Enter* GEORGE, ELIZA *and* HARRY.]

GEORGE: At length, Eliza, after many wanderings, we are again united.

ELIZA: Thanks to these generous Quakers, who have so kindly sheltered us.

GEORGE: Not forgetting our friend Phineas.

ELIZA: I do indeed owe him much. 'Twas he I met upon the icy river's bank, after that fearful, but successful attempt, when I fled from the slave-trader with my child in my arms.

GEORGE: It seems almost incredible that you could have crossed the river on the ice.

ELIZA: Yes, I did. Heaven helping me, I crossed on the ice, for they were behind me—right behind—and there was no other way.

GEORGE: But the ice was all in broken-up blocks, swinging and heaving up and down in the water.

ELIZA: I know it was—I know it; I did not think I should get over, but I did not care—I could but die if I did not! I leaped on the ice, but how I got across I don't know; the first I remember, a man was helping me up the bank—that man was Phineas.

GEORGE: My brave girl! you deserve your freedom—you have richly earned it!

ELIZA: And when we get to Canada I can help you to work, and between us we can find something to live on.

GEORGE: Yes, Eliza, so long as we have each other, and our boy. Oh, Eliza, if these people only knew what a blessing it is for a man to feel that his wife and child belong to *him!* I've often wondered to see men that could call their wives and children *their own,* fretting and worrying about anything else. Why, I feel rich and strong, though we have nothing but our bare hands. If they will only let me alone now, I will be satisfied—thankful!

ELIZA: But we are not quite out of danger; we are not yet in Canada.

GEORGE: True; but it seems as if I smelt the free air, and it makes me strong!

[Enter PHINEAS, dressed as a Quaker.]

PHINEAS: [With a snuffle.] Verily, friends, how is it with thee?—hum!

GEORGE: Why, Phineas, what means this metamorphosis!

PHINEAS: I've become a Quaker! that's the meaning on't.

GEORGE: What—you?

PHINEAS: Teetotally! I was driven to it by a strong argument, composed of a pair of sparkling eyes, rosy cheeks, and pouting lips. Them lips would persuade a man to assassinate his grandmother! [*Assumes the Quaker tone again.*] Verily, George, I have discovered something of importance to the interests of thee and thy party, and it were well for thee to hear it.

GEORGE: Keep us not in suspense!

PHINEAS: Well, after I left you on the road, I stopped at a little, lone tavern, just below here. Well, I was tired with hard driving, and, after my supper, I stretched myself down on a pile of bags in the corner, and pulled a buffalo hide over me—and what does I do but get fast asleep.

GEORGE: With one ear open, Phineas?

PHINEAS: No, I slept ears and all for an hour or two, for I was pretty well tired; but when I came to myself a little, I found that there were some men in the room, sitting round a table, drinking and talking; and I thought, before I made much muster, I'd just see what they were up to, especially as I heard them say something about the Quakers. Then I listened with both ears and found they were talking about you. So I kept quiet, and heard them lay off all their plans. They've got a right notion of the track we are going to-night, and they'll be down after us, six or eight strong. So, now, what's to be done?

ELIZA: What *shall* we do, George?

GEORGE: I know what I shall do! [*Takes out pistols.*]

PHINEAS: Ay—ay, thou seest, Eliza, how it will work—pistols—phitz—poppers!

ELIZA: I see; but I pray it come not to that!

GEORGE: I don't want to involve any one with or for me. If you will lend me your vehicle, and direct me, I will drive alone to the next stand.

PHINEAS: Ah! well, friend, but thee'll need a driver for all that. Thee's quite welcome to do all the fighting thee knows; but I know a thing or two about the road that thee doesn't.

GEORGE: But I don't want to involve you.

PHINEAS: Involve me! Why, chaw me—that is to say—when thee does involve me, please to let me know.

ELIZA: Phineas is a wise and skillful man. You will do well, George, to abide by his judgment. And, oh! George, be not hasty with these—young blood is hot! [*Laying her hand on pistols.*]

GEORGE: I will attack no man. All I ask of this country is to be left alone, and I will go out peaceably. But I'll fight to the last breath before they shall take from me my wife and son! Can you blame me?

PHINEAS: Mortal man cannot blame thee, neighbor George! Flesh and blood could not do otherwise. Woe unto the world because of offenses, but woe unto them through whom the offense cometh! That's gospel, teetotally!

GEORGE: Would not even you, sir, do the same, in my place?

PHINEAS: I pray that I be not tried; the flesh is weak—but I think my flesh would be pretty tolerably strong in such a case; I ain't sure, friend George, that I shouldn't hold a fellow for thee, if thee had any accounts to settle with him.

ELIZA: Heaven grant we be not tempted.

PHINEAS: But if we are tempted too much, why, consarn 'em! let them look out, that's all.

GEORGE: It's quite plain you was not born for a Quaker. The old nature has its way in you pretty strong yet.

PHINEAS: Well, I reckon you are pretty teetotally right.

GEORGE: Had we not better hasten our flight?

PHINEAS: Well, I rather conclude we had; we're full two hours ahead of them, if they start at the time they planned; so let's vamoose.

[*Exeunt.*]

Scene 6: A Rocky Pass in the Hills.—Large set rock and platform.

PHINEAS: [*Without.*] Out with you in a twinkling, every one, and up into these rocks with me! run *now*, if you *ever* did run! [*Music.*]

[PHINEAS *enters, with* HARRY *in his arms.*—GEORGE *supporting* ELIZA.]

Come up here; this is one of our old hunting dens. Come up. [*They ascend the rock.*] Well, here we are. Let 'em get us if they can. Whoever comes here has to walk single file between those two rocks, in fair range of your pistols—d'ye see?

GEORGE: I do see. And now, as this affair is mine, let me take all the risk, and do all the fighting.

PHINEAS: Thee's quite welcome to do the fighting, George; but I may have the fun of looking on, I suppose. But see, these fellows are kind of debating down there, and looking up, like hens when they are going to fly up onto the roost. Hadn't thee better give 'em a word of advice, before they come up, jest to tell 'em handsomely they'll be shot if they do.

[LOKER, MARKS, and three MEN enter.]

MARKS: Well, Tom, your coons are fairly treed.

LOKER: Yes, I see 'em go up right here; and here's a path—I'm for going right up. They can't jump down in a hurry, and it won't take long to ferret 'em out.

MARKS: But, Tom, they might fire at us from behind the rocks. That would be ugly, you know.

LOKER: Ugh! always for saving your skin, Marks. No danger; niggers are too plaguy scared!

MARKS: I don't know why I shouldn't save my skin; it's the best I've got; and niggers do fight like the devil sometimes.

GEORGE: *[Rising on the rock.]* Gentlemen, who are you down there, and what do you want?

LOKER: We want a party of runaway niggers. One George and Eliza Harris, and their son. We've got the officers here, and a warrant to take 'em too. D'ye hear? An't you George Harris, that belonged to Mr. Harris, of Shelby county, Kentucky?

GEORGE: I am George Harris. A Mr. Harris, of Kentucky, did call me his property. But now I'm a freeman, standing on heaven's free soil! My wife and child I claim as mine. We have arms to defend ourselves, and we mean to do it. You can come up if you like, but the first one that comes within range of our bullets is a dead man!

MARKS: Oh, come—come, young man, this an't no kind of talk at all for you. You see we're officers of justice. We've got the law on our side, and the power and so forth; so you'd better give up peaceably, you see—for you'll certainly have to give up at last.

GEORGE: I know very well that you've got the law on your side, and the power; but you haven't got us. We are standing here as free as you are, and by the great power that made us, we'll fight for our liberty till we die!

[During this, MARKS draws a pistol, and when he concludes fires at him.—ELIZA screams.]

GEORGE: It's nothing, Eliza; I am unhurt.

PHINEAS: *[Drawing GEORGE down.]* Thee'd better keep out of sight with thy speechifying; they're teetotal mean scamps.

LOKER: What did you do that for, Marks?

MARKS: You see, you get jist as much for him dead as alive in Kentucky.

GEORGE: Now, Phineas, the first man that advances I fire at; you take the second, and so on. It won't do to waste two shots on one.

PHINEAS: But what if you don't hit?

GEORGE: I'll try my best.

PHINEAS: Creation! Chaw me up if there an't stuff in you!

MARKS: I think I must have hit some on 'em. I heard a squeal.

LOKER: I'm going right up for one. I never was afraid of niggers, and I an't a going to be now. Who goes after me?

[Music.—LOKER dashes up the rock.—GEORGE fires.—He staggers for a moment, then springs to the top.—PHINEAS seizes him.—A struggle.]

PHINEAS: Friend, thee is not wanted here! [*Throws* LOKER *over the rock.*]

MARKS: [*Retreating.*] Lord help us—they're perfect devils!

[Music.—MARKS and Party run off. GEORGE and ELIZA kneel in an attitude of thanksgiving, with the CHILD between them.—PHINEAS stands over them exulting.—Tableau.]

END OF ACT II

Act III

Scene 1: Chamber

[Enter ST. CLARE, *followed by* TOM.*]*

ST. CLARE: [*Giving money and papers to* TOM.] There, Tom, are the bills, and the money to liquidate them.

TOM: Yes, mas'r.

ST. CLARE: Well, Tom, what are you waiting for? Isn't all right there?

TOM: I'm 'fraid not, mas'r.

ST. CLARE: Why, Tom, what's the matter? You look as solemn as a coffin.

TOM: I feel very bad, mas'r. I allays have thought that mas'r would be good to everybody.

ST. CLARE: Well, Tom, haven't I been? Come, now, what do you want? There's something you haven't got, I suppose, and this is the preface.

TOM: Mas'r allays been good to me. I haven't nothing to complain of on that head; but there is one that mas'r isn't good to.

ST. CLARE: Why, Tom, what's got into you? Speak out—what do you mean?

TOM: Last night, between one and two, I thought so. I studied upon the matter then—mas'r isn't good to *himself.*

ST. CLARE: Ah! now I understand; you allude to the state in which I came home last night. Well, to tell the truth, I *was* slightly elevated—a little more champagne on board than I could comfortably carry. That's all, isn't it?

TOM: [*Deeply affected—clasping his hands and weeping.*] All! Oh! my dear young mas'r, I'm 'fraid it will be *loss of all—all,* body and soul. The good book says, "It biteth like a serpent and stingeth like an adder," my dear mas'r.

ST. CLARE: You poor, silly fool! I'm not worth crying over.

TOM: Oh, mas'r! I implore you to think of it before it gets too late.

ST. CLARE: Well, I won't go to any more of their cursed nonsense, Tom—on my honor, I won't. I don't know why I haven't stopped long ago; I've always despised *it,* and myself for it. So now, Tom, wipe up your eyes and go about your errands.

TOM: Bless you, mas'r. I feel much better now. You have taken a load from poor Tom's heart. Bless you!

ST. CLARE: Come, come, no blessing! I'm not so wonderfully good, now. There, I'll pledge my honor to you, Tom, you don't see me so again.

[*Exit* TOM.]

I'll keep my faith with him, too.

OPHELIA: [*Without.*] Come along, you shiftless mortal!

ST. CLARE: What new witchcraft has Topsy been brewing? That commotion is of her raising, I'll be bound.

[Enter OPHELIA, *dragging in* TOPSY.]

OPHELIA: Come here now; I will tell your master.

ST. CLARE: What's the matter now?

OPHELIA: The matter is that I cannot be plagued with this girl any longer. It's past all bearing; flesh and blood cannot endure it. Here I locked her up and gave her a hymn to study; and what does she do but spy out where I put my key, and has gone to my bureau, and got a bonnet-trimming and cut it all to pieces to make dolls' jackets! I never saw anything like it in my life!

ST. CLARE: What have you done to her?

OPHELIA: What have I done? What haven't I done? Your wife says I ought to have her whipped till she couldn't stand.

ST. CLARE: I don't doubt it. Tell me of the lovely rule of woman. I never saw above a dozen women that wouldn't half kill a horse, or a servant, either, if they had their own way with them—let alone a man.

OPHELIA: I am sure, St. Clare, I don't know what to do. I've taught and taught—I've talked till I'm tired; I've whipped her, I've punished her in every way I could think of, and still she's just what she was at first.

ST. CLARE: Come here, Tops, you monkey! [TOPSY *crosses to* ST. CLARE, *grinning.*] What makes you behave so?

TOPSY: 'Spects it's my wicked heart—Miss Feely says so.

ST. CLARE: Don't you see how much Miss Ophelia has done for you? She says she has done everything she can think of.

TOPSY: Lor', yes, mas'r! old missis used to say so, too. She whipped me a heap harder, and used to pull my ha'r, and knock my head again the door; but it didn't do me no good. I 'spects if they's to pull every spear of ha'r out o' my head, it wouldn't do no good neither—I's so wicked! Laws! I's nothin' but a nigger, no ways! [*Goes up.*]

OPHELIA: Well, I shall have to give her up; I can't have that trouble any longer.

ST. CLARE: I'd like to ask you one question.

OPHELIA: What is it?

ST. CLARE: Why, if your doctrine is not strong enough to save one heathen child, that you can have at home here, all to yourself, what's the use of sending one or two poor missionaries off with it among thousands of just such? I suppose this girl is a fair sample of what thousands of your heathen are.

OPHELIA: I'm sure I don't know; I never saw such a girl as this.

ST. CLARE: What makes you so bad, Tops? Why won't you try and be good? Don't you love any one, Topsy?

TOPSY: Dunno nothin' 'bout love; I loves candy and sich, that's all.

OPHELIA: But, Topsy, if you'd only try to be good, you might.

TOPSY: Couldn't never be nothin' but a nigger, if I was ever so good. If I could be skinned and come white, I'd try then.

ST. CLARE: People can love you, if you are black, Topsy. Miss Ophelia would love you, if you were good. [TOPSY *laughs.*] Don't you think so?

TOPSY: No, she can't b'ar me, 'cause I'm a nigger—she'd's soon have a toad touch her. There can't nobody love niggers, and niggers can't do nothin'. I don't car'! [*Whistles.*]

ST. CLARE: Silence, you incorrigible imp, and begone!

TOPSY: He! he! he! didn't get much out of dis chile!   [*Exit.*]

OPHELIA: I've always had a prejudice against negroes, and it's a fact—I never could bear to have that child touch me, but I didn't think she knew it.

ST. CLARE: Trust any child to find that out; there's no keeping it from them. But I believe all the trying in the world to benefit a child, and all the substantial favors you can do them, will never excite one emotion of gratitude, while that feeling of repugnance remains in the heart. It's a queer kind of fact, but so it is.

OPHELIA: I don't know how I can help it—they are disagreeable to me, this girl in particular. How can I help feeling so?

ST. CLARE: Eva does, it seems.

OPHELIA: Well, she's so loving. I wish I was like her. She might teach me a lesson.

ST. CLARE: It would not be the first time a little child had been used to instruct an old disciple, if it were so. Come, let us seek Eva, in her favorite bower by the lake.

OPHELIA: Why, the dew is falling; she mustn't be out there. She is unwell, I know.

ST. CLARE: Don't be croaking, cousin—I hate it.

OPHELIA: But she has that cough.

ST. CLARE: Oh, nonsense, of that cough—it is not anything. She has taken a little cold, perhaps.

OPHELIA: Well, that was just the way Eliza Jane was taken—and Ellen—

ST. CLARE: Oh, stop these hobgoblin, nurse legends. You old hands get so wise, that a child cannot cough or sneeze, but you see desperation and ruin at hand. Only take care of the child, keep her from the night air, and don't let her play too hard, and she'll do well enough.   [*Exeunt.*]

Scene 2: The flat represents the lake. The rays of the setting sun tinge the waters with gold.—A large tree.—Beneath this is a grassy bank, on which EVA *and* TOM *are seated side by side.—*EVA *has a Bible open on her lap.*

TOM: Read dat passage again, please, Miss Eva?

EVA: [*Reading.*] "And I saw a sea of glass, mingled with fire."[11] [*Stopping suddenly and pointing to lake.*] Tom, there it is!

TOM: What, Miss Eva?

EVA: Don't you see there? There's a "sea of glass, mingled with fire."

TOM: True enough, Miss Eva. [*Sings.*]

> Oh, had I the wings of the morning,
> I'd fly away to Canaan's shore;
> Bright angels should convey me home,
> To the New Jerusalem.

EVA: Where do you suppose New Jerusalem[12] is, Uncle Tom?

TOM: Oh, up in the clouds, Miss Eva.

EVA: Then I think I see it. Look in those clouds; they look like great gates of pearl; and you can see beyond them—far, far off—it's all gold! Tom, sing about "spirits bright."

TOM [*Sings.*]

> I see a band of spirits bright,
> That taste the glories there;
> They are all robed in spotless white,
> And conquering palms they bear.

---

[11]Rev. 15:2.

[12]The heavenly city promised as an eternal residence to those who remain faithful to Christ (Rev. 3:21).

EVA: Uncle Tom, I've seen *them.*

TOM: To be sure you have; you are one of them yourself. You are the brightest spirit I ever saw.

EVA: They come to me sometimes in my sleep—those spirits bright—

> They are all robed in spotless white,
> And conquering palms they bear.

Uncle Tom, I'm going there.

TOM: Where, Miss Eva?

EVA: [*Pointing to the sky.*] I'm going *there,* to the spirits bright, Tom; I'm going before long.

TOM: It's jest no use tryin' to keep Miss Eva here; I've allays said so. She's got the Lord's mark in her forehead. She wasn't never like a child that's to live—there was always something deep in her eyes. [*Rises and comes forward.—EVA also comes forward, leaving Bible on bank.*]

[Enter ST. CLARE.]

ST. CLARE: Ah! my little pussy, you look as blooming as a rose! You are better now-a-days, are you not?

EVA: Papa, I've had things I wanted to say to you a great while. I want to say them now, before I get weaker.

ST. CLARE: Nay, this is an idle fear, Eva; you know you grow stronger every day.

EVA: It's all no use, papa, to keep it to myself any longer. The time is coming that I am going to leave you; I am going, and never to come back.

ST. CLARE: Oh, now, my dear little Eva! you've got nerves and low-spirited; you mustn't indulge such gloomy thoughts.

EVA: No, papa, don't deceive yourself, I am *not* any better; I know it perfectly well, and I am going before long. I am not nervous—I am not low-spirited. If it were not for you, papa, and my friends, I should be perfectly happy. I want to go—I long to go!

ST. CLARE: Why, dear child, what has made your poor little heart so sad? You have everything to make you happy that could be given you.

EVA: I had rather be in heaven! There are a great many things here that make me sad—that seem dreadful to me; I had rather there; but I don't want to leave you—it almost breaks my heart!

ST. CLARE: What makes you sad, and what seems dreadful, Eva?

EVA: I feel sad for our poor people, they love me dearly, and they are good and kind to me. I wish, papa, they were all *free!*

ST. CLARE: Why, Eva, child, don't you think they are well enough off, now?

EVA: [*Not heeding the question.*] Papa, isn't there a way to have slaves made free? When I am dead, papa, then you will think of me, and do it for my sake?

ST. CLARE: When you are dead, Eva? Oh, child, don't talk to me so! You are all I have on earth!

EVA: Papa, these poor creatures love their children as much as you do me. Tom loves his children. Oh, do something for them!

ST. CLARE: There, there darling; only don't distress yourself and don't talk of dying, and I will do anything you wish.

EVA: And promise me, dear father, that Tom shall have his freedom as soon as— [*hesitating*]—I am gone!

ST. CLARE: Yes, dear, I will do anything in the world—anything you ask me to. There, Tom, take her to her chamber; this evening air is too chill for her. [*Music.—Kisses her.*]

[TOM takes EVA in his arms, and exits.]

ST. CLARE: [*Gazing mournfully after* EVA.] Has there ever been a child like Eva? Yes, there has been; but their names are always on grave stones, and their sweet smiles, their heavenly eyes, this singular words and ways, are among the buried treasures of yearning hearts. It is as if heaven had an especial band of angels, whose office it is to sojourn for a season here, and endear to them the wayward human heart, that they might bear it upward with them in their homeward flight. When you see that deep, spiritual light in the eye, when the little soul reveals itself in words sweeter and wiser than the ordinary words of children, hope not to retain that child; for the seal of heaven is on it, and the light of immortality looks out from its eyes!   [*Music.—Exit.*]

Scene 3: A corridor

[Enter TOM; he listens at door and then lies down. Enter OPHELIA, with candle.]

OPHELIA: Uncle Tom, what alive have you taken to sleeping anywhere and everywhere, like a dog, for? I thought you were one of the orderly sort, that liked to lie in bed in a Christian way.

TOM: [*Rises.—Mysteriously.*] I do, Miss Feely, I do, but now—

OPHELIA: Well, what now?

TOM: We mustn't speak loud; Mas'r St. Clare won't hear on't; but Miss Feely, you know there must be somebody watchin' for the bridegroom.

OPHELIA: What do you mean, Tom?

TOM: You know it says in Scripture, "At midnight there was a great cry made, behold the bridegroom cometh!"[13] That's what I'm 'spectin' now, every night, Miss Feely, and I couldn't sleep out of hearing, noways.

OPHELIA: Why, Uncle Tom, what makes you think so?

TOM: Miss Eva, she talks to me. The Lord, he sends his messenger in the soul. I

---

[13]Matt. 25:6.

must be thar, Miss Feely; for when that ar blessed child goes into the kingdom, they'll open the door so wide, we'll all get a look in at the glory!

OPHELIA: Uncle Tom, did Miss Eva say she felt more unwell than usual to-night?

TOM: No; but she told me she was coming nearer—thar's them that tells it to the child, Miss Feely. It's the angels—it's the trumpet sound afore the break o' day!

OPHELIA: Heaven grant your fears be vain! Come in, Tom.   [*Exeunt.*]

Scene 4: EVA'S *chamber.* EVA *discovered on a couch.—A table stands near the couch, with a lamp on it. The light shines upon* EVA'S *face, which is very pale.—Scene half dark.—*UNCLE TOM *is kneeling near the foot of the couch.—*OPHELIA *stands at the head.—*ST. CLARE *at back.—Scene opens to plaintive music.*

[After a strain, enter MARIE, *hastily.]*

MARIE: St. Clare! Cousin! Oh! what is the matter now?

ST. CLARE: [*Hoarsely.*] Hush! she is dying!

MARIE: [*Sinking on her knees, beside* TOM.] Dying!

ST. CLARE: Oh! if she would only wake and speak once more. [*Bending over* EVA.] Eva, darling!

EVA: [*Uncloses her eyes, smiles, raises her head and tries to speak.*]

ST. CLARE: Do you know me, Eva?

EVA: [*Throwing her arms feebly about his neck.*] Dear papa! [*Her arms drop and she sinks back.*]

ST. CLARE: Oh, heaven! this is dreadful! Oh! Tom, my boy, it is killing me!

TOM: Look at her, mas'r. [*Points to* EVA.]

ST. CLARE: Eva! [*A pause.*] She does not hear. Oh, Eva! tell us what you see. What is it?

EVA: [*Feebly smiling.*] Oh! love! joy! peace! [*Dies.*]

TOM: Oh! bless the Lord! it's over, dear mas'r, it's over.

ST. CLARE: [*Sinking on his knees.*] Farewell, beloved child! the bright eternal doors have closed after thee. We shall see thy sweet face no more. Oh! woe for them who watched thy entrance into heaven, when they shall wake and find only the cold, gray sky of daily life, and thou gone forever! [*Solemn music, slow curtain.*]

END OF ACT III

Act IV

Scene 1: A Street in New Orleans

[Enter GUMPTION CUTE, *meeting* MARKS.]

CUTE: How do ye dew?

MARKS: How are you?

CUTE: Well, now, squire, it's a fact that I am dead broke and busted up.

MARKS: You have been speculating, I suppose?

CUTE: That's just it and nothing shorter.

MARKS: You have had poor success, you say?

CUTE: Tarnation bad, now I tell you. You see I came to this part of the country to make my fortune.

MARKS: And you did not do it?

CUTE: Scarcely. The first thing I tried my hand at was keeping school. I opened an academy for the instruction of youth in the various branches of orthography, geography, and other graphies.

MARKS: Did you succeed in getting any pupils?

CUTE: Oh, lots on 'em! and a pretty set of dunces they were, too. After the first quarter, I called on the respectable parents of the juveniles, and requested them to fork over. To which they politely answered—don't you wish you may get it?

MARKS: What did you do then?

CUTE: Well, I kind of pulled up stakes and left those diggin's. Well, then I went into Spiritual Rappings[14] for a living. That paid pretty well for a short time, till I met with an accident.

MARKS: An accident?

CUTE: Yes; a tall Yahoo[15] called on me one day, and wanted me to summon the spirit of his mother—which, of course, I did. He asked me about a dozen questions which I answered to his satisfaction. At last he wanted to know what she died of—I said, Cholera. You never did see a critter so riled as he was. "Look yere, stranger," said he, "it's my opinion that you're a pesky humbug![16] for my mother was blown up in a *Steamboat!*" With that he left the premises. The next day the people furnished me with a conveyance, and I rode out of town.

MARKS: Rode out of town?

CUTE: Yes; on a rail!

MARKS: I suppose you gave up the spirits, after that?

CUTE: Well, I reckon I did; it had such an effect on my spirits.

MARKS: It's a wonder they didn't tar and feather you.

CUTE: There was some mention made of that, but when they said *feathers,* I felt as if I had wings, and flew away.

MARKS: You cut and run?

---

[14]Antebellum practice of gathering together, usually under the leadership of a spiritual medium, to listen to the tappings or voices of the dead.

[15]A member of a brutish, vice-ridden race in Jonathan Swift's book *Gulliver's Travels.*

[16]counterfeit

CUTE: Yes; I didn't like their company and I cut it. Well, after that I let myself out as an overseer on a cotton plantation. I made a pretty good thing of that, though it was dreadful trying to my feelings to flog the darkies; but I got used to it after a while, and then I used to lather 'em like Jehu.[17] Well, the proprietor got the fever and ague and shook himself out of town. The place and all the fixings were sold at auction, and I found myself adrift once more.

MARKS: What are you doing at present?

CUTE: I'm in search of a rich relation of mine.

MARKS: A rich relation?

CUTE: Yes, a Miss Ophelia St. Clare. You see, a niece of hers married one of my second cousins—that's how I came to be a relation of hers. She came on here from Vermont to be housekeeper to a cousin of hers, of the same name.

MARKS: I know him well.

CUTE: The deuce you do!—well, that's lucky.

MARKS: Yes, he lives in this city.

CUTE: Say, you just point out the locality, and I'll give him a call.

MARKS: Stop a bit. Suppose you shouldn't be able to raise the wind in that quarter, what have you thought of doing?

CUTE: Well, nothing particular.

MARKS: How should you like to enter into a nice, profitable business—one that pays well?

CUTE: That's just about my measure—it would suit me to a hair. What is it?

MARKS: Nigger catching.

CUTE: Catching niggers! What on airth do you mean?

MARKS: Why, when there's a large reward offered for a runaway darkey, we goes after him, catches him, and gest the reward.

CUTE: Yes, that's all right so far—but s'pose there ain't no reward offered?

MARKS: Why, then we catches the darkey on our own account, sells him, and pockets the proceeds.

CUTE: By chowder, that ain't a bad speculation!

MARKS: What do you say? I want a partner. You see, I lost my partner last year, up in Ohio—he was a powerful fellow.

CUTE: Lost him! How did you lose him!

MARKS: Well, you see, Tom and I—his name was Tom Loker—Tom and I were after a mulatto chap, called George Harris, that run away from Kentucky. We traced him through the greater part of Ohio, and came up with him near the Pennsylvania line. He

---

[17]Old Testament king, who enjoyed great success for a period in striking down his enemies (1 Kings 16, 19 and 2 Kings 9–10).

took refuge among some rocks, and showed fight.

CUTE: Oh! then runaway darkies show fight, do they?

MARKS: Sometimes. Well, Tom—like a headstrong fool as he was—rushed up the rocks, and a Quaker chap, who was helping this George Harris, threw him over the cliff.

CUTE: Was he killed?

MARKS: Well, I didn't stop to find out. Seeing that the darkies were stronger than I thought, I made tracks for a safe place.

CUTE: And what became of this George Harris?

MARKS: Oh! he and his wife and child got away safe into Canada. You see, they will get away sometimes, though it isn't very often. Now what do you say? You are just the figure for a fighting partner. Is it a bargain?

CUTE: Well, I rather calculate our teams won't hitch, no how. By chowder, I haint' no idea of setting myself up, as a target for darkies to fire at—that's a speculation that don't suit my constitution.

MARKS: You're afraid, then?

CUTE: No, I ain't; it's against my principles.

MARKS: Your principles—how so?

CUTE: Because my principles are to keep a sharp lookout for No. 1. I shouldn't feel wholesome if a darkey was to throw me over that cliff to look after Tom Loker.

[Exeunt, arm-in-arm.]

Scene 2: Gothic Chamber. Slow music. ST. CLARE *discovered, seated on sofa.* TOM *to the left.*

ST. CLARE: Oh! Tom, my boy, the whole world is as empty as an egg shell.

TOM: I know it, mas'r, I know it. But oh! if mas'r could look up—up where our dear Miss Eva is—

ST. CLARE: Ah, Tom! I do look up; but the trouble is, I don't see anything when I do. I wish I could. It seems to be given to children and poor, honest fellows like you, to see what we cannot. How comes it?

TOM: "Thou hast hid from the wise and prudent, and revealed unto babes; even so, Father, for so it seemed good in thy sight."[18]

ST. CLARE: Tom, I don't believe—I've got the habit of doubting—I want to believe and I cannot.

TOM: Dear mas'r, pray to the good Lord: "Lord, I believe; help thou my unbelief."[19]

ST. CLARE: Who knows anything about anything? Was all that beautiful love and

---

[18]Matt. 11:25–26.

[19]Mark 9:24.

faith only one of the ever-shifting phases of human feeling, having nothing real to rest on, passing away with the little breath? And is there no more Eva—nothing?

TOM: Oh! dear mas'r, there is. I know it; I'm sure of it. Do, do, dear mas'r, believe it!

ST. CLARE: How do you know there is, Tom? You never saw the Lord.

TOM: Felt Him in my soul, mas'r—feel Him now! Oh! mas'r, when I was sold away from my old woman and the children, I was jest a'most broken up—I felt as if there warn't nothing left—and then the Lord stood by me, and He says, "Fear not, Tom," and He brings light and joy into a poor fellow's soul—makes all peace; and I's so happy, and loves everybody, and feels willin' to be jest where the Lord wants to put me. I know it couldn't come from me, 'cause I's a poor, complaining creature—it comes from above, and I know He's willin' to do for mas'r.

ST. CLARE: [Grasping TOM'S hand.] Tom, you love me!

TOM: I's willin' to lay down my life[20] this blessed day for you.

ST. CLARE: [Sadly.] Poor, foolish fellow! I'm not worth the love of one good, honest heart like yours.

TOM: Oh, mas'r! there's more than me loves you—the blessed Savior loves you.

ST. CLARE: How do you know that, Tom?

TOM: The love of the Savior passeth knowledge.

ST. CLARE: [Turns away.] Singular! that the story of a man who lived and died eighteen hundred years ago, can affect people so yet. But He was no man. [Rises.] No man ever had such long and living power. Oh! that I could believe what my mother taught me, and pray as I did when I was a boy. But, Tom, all this time I have forgotten why I sent for you. I'm going to make a freeman of you; so have your trunk packed, and get ready to set out for Kentuck.

TOM: [Joyfully.] Bless the Lord!

ST. CLARE: [Dryly.] You haven't had such very bad times here, that you need be in such a rapture, Tom.

TOM: No, no, mas'r, 'tain't that; it's being a freeman—that's what I'm joyin' for.

ST. CLARE: Why, Tom, don't you think, for your own part, you've been better off than to be free?

TOM: No, indeed, Mas'r St. Clare—no, indeed!

ST. CLARE: Why, Tom, you couldn't possibly have earned, by your work, such clothes and such living as I have given you.

TOM: I know all that, Mas'r St. Clare—mas'r's been too good; but I'd rather have poor clothes, poor house, poor everything, and have 'em mine, than have the best, if they belonged to somebody else. I had so, mas'r; I think it's natur', mas'r.

---

[20]John 15:13.

ST. CLARE: I suppose so, Tom; and you'll be going off and leaving me in a month or so—though why you shouldn't no mortal knows.

TOM: Not while mas'r is in trouble. I'll stay with mas'r as long as he wants me, so as I can be any use.

ST. CLARE: [*Sadly.*] Not while I'm in trouble, Tom? And when will my trouble be over?

TOM: When you are a believer.

ST. CLARE: And you really mean to stay by me till that day comes? [*Smiling and laying his hand on* TOM's *shoulder.*] Ah, Tom! I won't keep you till that day. Go home to your wife and children, and give my love to all.

TOM: I's faith to think that day will come—the Lord has a work for mas'r.

ST. CLARE: A work, hey? Well, now, Tom, give me your views on what sort of a work it is—let's hear.

TOM: Why, even a poor fellow like me has a work; and Mas'r St. Clare, that has larnin', and riches, and friends, how much he might do for the Lord.

ST. CLARE: Tom, you seem to think the Lord needs a great deal done for him.

TOM: We does for him when we does for his creatures.

ST. CLARE: Good theology, Tom. Thank you, my boy; I like to hear you talk. But go now, Tom, and leave me alone.   [*Exit* TOM.]

That faithful fellow's words have excited a train of thoughts that almost bear me, on the strong tide of faith and feeling, to the gates of that heaven I so vividly conceive. They seem to bring me nearer to Eva.

OPHELIA: [*Outside.*] What are you doing there, you limb of Satan? You've been stealing something, I'll be bound.

[OPHELIA drags in TOPSY.]

TOPSY: You go 'long, Miss Feely, 'tain't none o' your business.

ST. CLARE: Heyday! what is all this commotion?

OPHELIA: She's been stealing.

TOPSY: [*Sobbing.*] I hain't neither.

OPHELIA: What have you got in your bosom?

TOPSY: I've got my hand dar.

OPHELIA: But what have you got in your hand?

TOPSY: Nuffin'.

OPHELIA: That's a fib, Topsy.

TOPSY: Well, I 'spects it is.

OPHELIA: Give it to me, whatever it is.

TOPSY: It's mine—I hope I may die this bressed minute, if it don't b'long to me.

OPHELIA: Topsy, I order you to give me that article; don't let me have to ask you again. [TOPSY *reluctantly takes the foot of an old stocking from her bosom and hands it to* OPHELIA.] Sakes alive! what is all this? [*Takes from it a lock of hair, and a small book, with a bit of crape twisted around it.*]

TOPSY: Dat's a lock of ha'r dat Miss Eva give me—she cut it from her own beau'-ful head herself.

ST. CLARE: [*Takes book.*] Why did you wrap *this* [*pointing to crape*] around the book?

TOPSY: 'Cause—'cause—'cause 'twas Miss Eva's. Oh! don't take 'em away, please! [*Sits down on stage, and putting her apron over her head, begins to sob vehemently.*]

OPHELIA: Come, come, don't cry; you shall have them.

TOPSY: [*Jumps up joyfully and takes them.*] I wants to keep 'em, 'cause dey makes me good; I ain't half so wicked as I used to was.   [*Runs off.*]

ST. CLARE: I really think you can make something of that girl. Any mind that is capable of a *real sorrow* is capable of good. You must try and do something with her.

OPHELIA: The child has improved very much; I have great hopes of her.

ST. CLARE: I believe I'll go down the street, a few moments, and hear the news.

OPHELIA: Shall I call Tom to attend you?

ST. CLARE: No, I shall be back in an hour.   [*Exit.*]

OPHELIA: He's got an excellent heart, but then he's so dreadful shiftless!

[*Exit.*]

Scene 3: Front Chamber

[Enter TOPSY.*]*

TOPSY: Dar's something de matter wid me—I isn't a bit like myself. I haven't done anything wrong since poor Miss Eva went up in de skies and left us. When I's gwine to do anything wicked, I tinks of her, and somehow I can't do it. I's getting to be good, dat's a fact. I 'spects when I's dead I shall be turned into a little brack angel.

[Enter OPHELIA.*]*

OPHELIA: Topsy, I've been looking for you; I've got something very particular to say to you.

TOPSY: Does you want me to say the catechism?

OPHELIA: No, not now.

TOPSY: [*Aside.*] Golly! dat's one comfort.

OPHELIA: Now, Topsy, I want you to try and understand what I am going to say to you.

TOPSY: Yes, missis, I'll open my ears drefful wide.

OPHELIA: Mr. St. Clare has given you to me, Topsy.

TOPSY: Den I b'longs to you, don't I? Golly! I thought I always belonged to you.

OPHELIA: Not till to-day have I received any authority to call you my property.

TOPSY: I's your property, am I? Well, if you say so, I 'spects I am.

OPHELIA: Topsy, I can give you your liberty.

TOPSY: My liberty?

OPHELIA: Yes, Topsy.

TOPSY: Has you got 'um with you?

OPHELIA: I have, Topsy.

TOPSY: Is it clothes or wittles?[21]

OPHELIA: How shiftless! Don't you know what your liberty is, Topsy?

TOPSY: How should I know when I never seed 'um?

OPHELIA: Topsy, I am going to leave this place; I am going many miles away—to my own home in Vermont.

TOPSY: Den what's to become of dis chile?

OPHELIA: If you wish to go, I will take you with me.

TOPSY: Miss Feely, I doesn't want to leave you no how, I loves you, I does.

OPHELIA: Then you shall share my home for the rest of your days. Come, Topsy.

TOPSY: Stop, Miss Feely; does dey hab any oberseers in Varmount?

OPHELIA: No, Topsy.

TOPSY: Nor cotton plantations, nor sugar factories, nor darkies, nor whipping, nor nothin'?

OPHELIA: No, Topsy.

TOPSY: By golly! de quicker you is gwine de better den.

[Enter TOM, *hastily.]*

TOM: Oh, Miss Feely! Miss Feely!

OPHELIA: Gracious me, Tom! what's the matter?

TOM: Oh, Mas'r St. Clare, Mas'r St. Clare!

OPHELIA: Well, Tom, well?

TOM: They've just brought him home and I do believe he's killed.

OPHELIA: Killed?

TOPSY: Oh, dear! what's to become of de poor darkies now?

TOM: He's dreadful weak. It's just as much as he can do to speak. He wanted me to call you.

---

[21]food

OPHELIA: My poor cousin! Who would have thought of it? Don't say a word to his wife, Tom; the danger may not be so great as you think; it would only distress her. Come with me; you may be able to afford some assistance.   [*Exeunt.*]

Scene 4: Handsome Chamber. ST. CLARE *discovered seated on sofa.*
OPHELIA, TOM *and* TOPSY *are clustered around him.* DOCTOR
back of sofa, feeling his pulse. Slow music.

ST. CLARE: [*Raising himself feebly.*] Tom—poor fellow!

TOM: Well, mas'r?

ST. CLARE: I have received my death wound.

TOM: Oh, no, no, mas'r!

ST. CLARE: I feel that I am dying—Tom, pray!

TOM: [*Sinking on his knees.*] I do pray, mas'r! I do pray!

ST. CLARE: [*After a pause.*] Tom, one thing preys upon my mind—I have forgotten to sign your freedom papers. What will become of you when I am gone?

TOM: Don't think of that, mas'r.

ST. CLARE: I was wrong, Tom, very wrong, to neglect it. I may be the cause of much suffering to you hereafter. Marie, my wife—she—oh!—

OPHELIA: His mind is wandering.

ST. CLARE: [*Energetically.*] No! it is coming *home* at last! [*sinks back*] at last! at last! Eva, I come! [*Dies.*] [*Music.—Slow curtain.*]

END OF ACT IV

ACT V

Scene 1: An Auction Mart. UNCLE TOM *and* EMMELINE *at back*—ADOLF,
SKEGGS, MARKS, MANN *and various spectators discovered.*

[MARKS *and* MANN *come forward.*]

MARKS: Hulloa, Alf! What brings you here?

MANN: Well, I was wanting a valet, and I heard that St. Clare's lot was going; I thought I'd just look at them.

MARKS: Catch me ever buying any of St. Clare's people. Spoilt niggers, every one—impudent as the devil.

MANN: Never fear that; if I get 'em, I'll soon have their airs out of them—they'll soon find that they've another kind of master to deal with than St. Clare. 'Pon my word, I'll buy that fellow—I like the shape of him. [*Pointing to* ADOLF.]

MARKS: You'll find it'll take all you've got to keep him—he's deucedly extravagant.

MANN: Yes, but my lord will find that he *can't* be extravagant with *me*. Just let him be sent to the calaboose[22] a few times, and thoroughly dressed down, I'll tell you if it don't bring him to a sense of his ways. Oh! I'll reform him, up hill and down, you'll see. I'll buy him, that's flat.

[Enter LEGREE—he goes up and looks at ADOLF, whose boots are nicely blacked.]

LEGREE: A nigger with his boots blacked—bah! [*Spits on them.*] Holloa, you! [To TOM.] Let's see your teeth. [*Seizes TOM by the jaw and opens his mouth.*] Strip up your sleeve and show your muscle. [TOM *does so.*] Where was you raised?

TOM: In Kentuck, mas'r.

LEGREE: What have you done?

TOM: Had care of mas'r's farm.

LEGREE: That's a likely story. [*Turns to EMMELINE.*] You're a nice looking girl enough. How old are you? [*Grasps her arm.*]

EMMELINE: [*Shrieking.*] Ah! you hurt me.

SKEGGS: Stop that, you minx! No whimpering here. The sale is going to begin. [*Mounts the rostrum.*] Gentlemen, the next article I shall offer you to-day is Adolf, late valet to Mr. St. Clare. How much am I offered? [*Various bids are made. ADOLF is knocked down to MANN for eight hundred dollars.*] Gentlemen, I now offer a prime article—the quadroon girl, Emmeline, only fifteen years of age, warranted in every respect. [*Business as before. EMMELINE is sold to LEGREE for one thousand dollars.*] Now, I shall close to-day's sale by offering you the valuable article known as Uncle Tom, the most useful nigger ever raised. Gentlemen in want of an overseer, now is the time to bid. [*Business as before. TOM is sold to LEGREE for twelve hundred dollars.*]

LEGREE: Now look here, you two belong to me.

[TOM and EMMELINE sink on their knees.]

TOM: Heaven help us, then! [*Music.—LEGREE stands over them exulting. Picture.*]

Scene 2: The Garden of MISS OPHELIA'S House in Vermont

[Enter OPHELIA and DEACON PERRY.]

DEACON: Miss Ophelia, allow me to offer you my congratulations upon your safe arrival in your native place. I hope it is your intention to pass the remainder of your days with us?

OPHELIA: Well, Deacon, I have come here with that express purpose.

DEACON: I presume you were not over-pleased with the South?

OPHELIA: Well, to tell the truth, Deacon, I wasn't; I liked the country very well, but the people there are so dreadful shiftless.

---

[22]Local jail; also a place where slaves were sent to be whipped as punishment.

DEACON: The result, I presume, of living in a warm climate.

OPHELIA: Well, Deacon, what is the news among you all here?

DEACON: Well, we live on in the same even jog-trot pace. Nothing of any consequence has happened.—Oh! I forgot. [*Takes out his handkerchief.*] I've lost my wife; my
Molly has left me. [*Wipes his eyes.*]

OPHELIA: Poor soul! I pity you, Deacon.

DEACON: Thank you. You perceive I bear my loss with resignation.

OPHELIA: How you must miss her tongue!

DEACON: Molly certainly was fond of talking. She always would have the last
word—heigho!

OPHELIA: What was her complaint, Deacon?

DEACON: A very mild and soothing one, Miss Ophelia; she had a severe attack of
the lockjaw.

OPHELIA: Dreadful!

DEACON: Wasn't it? When she found she couldn't use her tongue, she took it so
much to heart that it struck to her stomach and killed her. Poor dear! Excuse my handkerchief; she's been dead only eighteen months.

OPHELIA: Why, Deacon, by this time you ought to be setting your cap for another
wife.

DEACON: Do you think so, Miss Ophelia?

OPHELIA: I don't see why you shouldn't—you are still a good-looking man, Deacon.

DEACON: Ah! well, I think I do wear well—in fact, I may say remarkably well. It
has been observed to me before.

OPHELIA: And you are not much over fifty?

DEACON: Just turned of forty, I assure you.

OPHELIA: Hale and hearty?

DEACON: Health excellent—look at my eye! Strong as a lion—look at my arm! A
No. 1 constitution—look at my leg!!!

OPHELIA: Have you no thoughts of choosing another partner?

DEACON: Well, to tell you the truth, I have.

OPHELIA: Who is she?

DEACON: She is not far distant. [*Looks at* OPHELIA *in a languishing manner.*] I
have her in my eye at this present moment.

OPHELIA: [*Aside.*] Really, I believe he's going to pop. Why, surely, Deacon, you
don't mean to—

DEACON: Yes, Miss Ophelia, I do mean; and believe me, when I say—[*Looking
off.*] The Lord be good to us, but I believe there is the devil coming!

[TOPSY *runs on with bouquet. She is now dressed very neatly.*]

TOPSY: Miss Feely, here is some flowers dat I hab been gathering for you. [*Gives bouquet.*]

OPHELIA: That's a good child.

DEACON: Miss Ophelia, who is this young person?

OPHELIA: She is my daughter.

DEACON: [*Aside.*] Her daughter! Then she must have married a colored man off South. I was not aware that you had been married, Miss Ophelia?

OPHELIA: Married? Sakes alive! What made you think I had been married?

DEACON: Good gracious! I'm getting confused. Didn't I understand you to say that this—somewhat tanned—young lady was your daughter?

OPHELIA: Only by adoption. She is my adopted daughter.

DEACON: O—oh! [*Aside.*] I breathe again.

TOPSY: [*Aside.*] By golly! Dat old man's eyes stick out of 'um head dre'ful. Guess he never seed anything like me afore.

OPHELIA: Deacon, won't you step into the house and refresh yourself after your walk?

DEACON: I accept your polite invitation. [*Offers his arm.*] Allow me.

OPHELIA: As gallant as ever, Deacon. I declare, you grow younger every day.

DEACON: You can never grow old, madam.

OPHELIA: Ah, you flatterer!   [*Exeunt.*]

TOPSY: Dar dey go, like an old goose and gander. Guess dat ole gemblemun feels kind of confectionary—rather sweet on my old missis. By golly! She's been dre'ful kind to me ever since I come away from de South; and I loves her, I does, 'cause she takes such car' on me and gives me dese fine clothes. I tries to be good too, and I's getting 'long 'mazin' fast. I's not so wicked as I used to was. [*Looks out.*] Holloa! dar's some one comin' here. I wonder what he wants now. [*Retires, observing.*]

[*Enter GUMPTION CUTE, very shabby—a small bundle, on a stick, over his shoulder.*]

CUTE: By chowder, here I am again. Phew! it's a pretty considerable tall piece of walking between here and New Orleans, not to mention the wear of shoe-leather. I guess I'm about done up. If this streak of bad luck lasts much longer, I'll borrow sixpence to buy a rope, and hang myself right straight up! When I went to call on Miss Ophelia, I swow if I didn't find out that she had left for Varmount; so I kind of concluded to make tracks in that direction myself, and as I didn't have any money left, why I had to foot it, and here I am in old Varmount once more. They told me Miss Ophelia lived up here. I wonder if she will remember the relationship. [*Sees TOPSY.*] By chowder, there's a darkey. Look here, Charcoal!

TOPSY: [*Comes forward.*] My name isn't Charcoal—it's Topsy.

CUTE: Oh! Your name is Topsy, is it, you juvenile specimen of Day & Martin?[23]

TOPSY: Tell you I don't know nothin' 'bout Day & Martin. I's Topsy and I belong to Miss Feely St. Clare.

CUTE: I'm much obleeged to you, you small extract of Japan,[24] for your information. So Miss Ophelia lives up there in the white house, does she?

TOPSY: Well, she don't do nothin' else.

CUTE: Well, then, just locomote your pins.

TOPSY: What—what's dat?

CUTE: Walk your chalks!

TOPSY: By golly! dere ain't no chalk 'bout me.

CUTE: Move your trotters.

TOPSY: How you does spoke! What you mean by trotters?

CUTE: Why, your feet, Stove Polish.

TOPSY: What does you want me to move my feet for?

CUTE: To tell your mistress, you ebony angel, that a gentleman wishes to see her.

TOPSY: Does you call yourself a gentleman? By golly! you look more like a scar'-crow.

CUTE: Now look here, you Charcoal, don't you be sassy. I'm a gentleman in distress; a done-up speculator; one that has seen better days—long time ago—and better clothes too, by chowder! My creditors are like my boots—they've no soles. I'm a victim to circumstances. I've been through much and survived it. I've taken walking exercise for the benefit of my heath; but as I was trying to live on air at the same time, it was a losing speculation, 'cause it gave me such a dreadful appetite.

TOPSY: Golly! you look as if you could eat an ox, horns and all.

CUTE: Well, I calculate I could, if he was roasted—it's a speculation I should like to engage in. I have returned like the fellow that run away in Scripture; and if anybody's got a fatted calf they want to kill, all they got to do is to fetch him along. Do you know, Charcoal, that your mistress is a relation of mine?

TOPSY: Is she your uncle?

CUTE: No, no, not quite so near as that. My second cousin married her niece.

TOPSY: And does you want to see Miss Feely?

CUTE: I do. I have come to seek a home beneath her roof, and take care of all the spare change she don't want to use.

TOPSY: Den just you follow me, mas'r.

CUTE: Stop! By chowder, I've got a great idee. Say, you Day & Martin, how should you like to enter into a speculation?

---

[23]Well-known blackface minstrel act.

[24]Reference to japanning, which is a process of applying black lacquer to certain types of tableware.

TOPSY: Golly! I doesn't know what a spec—spec—cu—what-do-you-call-'um am.

CUTE: Well, now, I calculate I've hit upon about the right thing. Why should I degrade the manly dignity of the Cutes by becoming a beggar—expose myself to the chance of receiving the cold shoulder as a poor relation? By chowder, my blood biles as I think of it! Topsy, you can make my fortune, and your own, too. I've an idee in my head that is worth a million of dollars.

TOPSY: Golly! is your head worth dat? Guess you wouldn't bring dat out South for de whole of you.

CUTE: Don't you be too severe now, Charcoal; I'm a man of genius. Did you ever hear of Barnum?[25]

TOPSY: Barnum! Barnum! Does he live out South?

CUTE: No, he lives in New York. Do you know how he made his fortune?

TOPSY: What is him fortin, hey? Is it something he wears?

CUTE: Chowder, how green you are!

TOPSY: [*Indignantly.*] Sar, I hab you to know I's not green; I's brack.

CUTE: To be sure you are, Day & Martin. I calculate, when a person says another has a fortune, he means he's got plenty of money, Charcoal.

TOPSY: And did he make the money?

CUTE: Sartin sure, and no mistake.

TOPSY: Golly! now I thought money always growed.

CUTE: Oh, git out! You are too cute—you are cuterer than I am; and I'm Cute by name and cute by nature. Well, as I was saying, Barnum made his money by exhibiting a *woolly* horse; now wouldn't it be an all-fired speculation to show you as the woolly gal?

TOPSY: You want to make a sight of me?

CUTE: I'll give you half the receipts, by chowder!

TOPSY: Should I have to leave Miss Feely?

CUTE: To be sure you would.

TOPSY: Den you hab to get a woolly gal somewhere else, Mas'r Cute. [*Runs off.*]

CUTE: There's another speculation gone to smash, by chowder!   [*Exit.*]

Scene 3: A Rude Chamber. TOM *is discovered, in old clothes, seated on a stool; he holds in his hand a paper containing a curl of* EVA'S *hair. The scene opens to the symphony of "Old Folks at Home."*

TOM: I have come to de dark places; I's going through the vale of shadows. My heart sinks at times and feels just like a big lump of lead. Den it gits up in my throat and

---

[25]Phineas Taylor Barnum (1810–1891) was perhaps the greatest showman of his day, operating a museum of curiosities, a theater, and a traveling circus during his life.

chokes me till de tears roll out of my eyes; den I take out dis curl of little Miss Eva's hair, and the sight of it brings calm to my mind and I feels strong again. [*Kisses the curl and puts it in his breast—takes out a silver dollar, which is suspended around his neck by a string.*] Dere's de bright silver dollar dat Mas'r George Shelby gave me the day I was sold away from old Kentuck, and I've kept it ever since. Mas'r George must have grown to be a man by this time. I wonder if I shall ever see him again.

SONG.—*"Old Folks at Home"*

[*Enter* LEGREE, EMMELINE, SAMBO *and* QUIMBO.]

LEGREE: Shut up, you black cuss! Did you think I wanted any of your infernal howling? [*Turns to* EMMELINE.] We're home. [EMMELINE *shrinks from him. He takes hold of her ear.*] You didn't ever wear earrings?

EMMELINE: [*Trembling.*] No, master.

LEGREE: Well, I'll give you a pair, if you're a good girl. You needn't be so frightened; I don't mean to make you work very hard. You'll have fine times with me and live like a lady; only be a good girl.

EMMELINE: My soul sickens as his eyes gaze upon me. His touch makes my very flesh creep.

LEGREE: [*Turns to* TOM, *and points to* SAMBO *and* QUIMBO.] Ye see what ye'd get if ye'd try to run off. These yer boys have been raised to track niggers, and they'd just as soon chaw one on ye up as eat their suppers; so mind yourself. [*To* EMMELINE.] Come, mistress, you go in here with me. [*Taking* EMMELINE'S *hand, and leading her away.*]

EMMELINE: [*Withdrawing her hand, and shrinking back.*] No, no! let me work in the fields; I don't want to be a lady.

LEGREE: Oh! you're going to be contrary, are you? I'll soon take all that out of you.

EMMELINE: Kill me, if you will.

LEGREE: Oh! you want to be killed, do you? Now, come here, you Tom, you see I told you I didn't buy you jest for the common work; I mean to promote you and make a driver of you, and to-night ye may jest as well be gin to get yer hand in. Now, ye just take this yer gal, and flog her; ye've seen enough on't to know how.

TOM: I beg mas'r's pardon—hopes mas'r won't set me at that. It's what I an't used to—never did, and can't do—no way possible.

LEGREE: Ye'll larn a pretty smart chance of things ye never did know before I've done with ye. [*Strikes* TOM *with whip, three blows.—Music chord each blow.*] There! now will ye tell me ye can't do it?

TOM: Yes, mas'r! I'm willing to work night and day, and work while there's life and breath in me; but this yer thing I can't feel it right to do, and, mas'r I *never* shall do it, *never!*

LEGREE: What! ye black beast! tell *me* ye don't think it right to do what I tell ye!

What have any of you cussed cattle to do with thinking what's right? I'll put a stop to it. Why, what do ye think ye are? Maybe ye think yer a gentleman, master Tom, to be telling your master what's right and what an't! So you pretend it's wrong to flog the gal?

TOM: I think so, mas'r; 'twould be downright cruel, and it's what I never will do, mas'r. If you mean to kill me, kill me; but as to raising my hand agin any one here, I never shall—I'll die first!

LEGREE: Well, here's a pious dog at last, let down among us sinners—powerful holy critter he must be. Here, you rascal! you make believe to be so pious, didn't you never read out of your Bible, "Servants, obey your masters?"[26] An't I your master? Didn't I pay twelve hundred dollars, cash, for all there is inside your cussed old black shell? An't you mine, body and soul?

TOM: No, no! My soul an't yours, mas'r; you haven't bought it—ye can't buy it; it's been bought and paid for by one that is able to keep it, and you can't harm it!

LEGREE: I can't? we'll see, we'll see! Here, Sambo! Quimbo! give this dog such a breaking in as he won't get over this month!

EMMELINE: Oh, no! you will not be so cruel—have some mercy! [*Clings to* TOM.]

LEGREE: Mercy? you won't find any in this shop! Away with the black cuss! Flog him within an inch of his life?

[*Music.*—SAMBO *and* QUIMBO *seize* TOM *and drag him up stage.* LEGREE *seizes* EMMELINE, *and throws her.—She falls on her knees, with her hands lifted in supplication.—*LEGREE *raises his whip, as if to strike* TOM.—*Picture.*]

Scene 4: Plain Chamber

[*Enter* OPHELIA, *followed by* TOPSY.]

OPHELIA: A person inquiring for me, did you say, Topsy?

TOPSY: Yes, missis.

OPHELIA: What kind of a looking man is he?

TOPSY: By golly! he's very queer looking man, anyway; and den he talks to dre'-ful funny. What does you think?—yah! yah! he wanted to 'zibite me as de woolly gal! yah! yah!

OPHELIA: Oh! I understand. Some cute Yankee, who wants to purchase you, to make a show of—the heartless wretch!

TOPSY: Dat's just him, missis; dat's just his name. He tole me dat it was Cute—Mr. Cute Speculashum—dat's him.

OPHELIA: What did you say to him, Topsy?

---

[26]Col. 3:22.

TOPSY: Well, I didn't say much; it was brief and to the point—I tole him I wouldn't leave you, Miss Feely, no how.

OPHELIA: That's right, Topsy; you know you are very comfortable here—you wouldn't fare quite so well if you went away among strangers.

TOPSY: By golly! I know dat; you takes care on me, and makes me good. I don't steal any now, and I don't swar, and I don't dance breakdowns. Oh! I isn't so wicked as I used to was.

OPHELIA: That's right, Topsy; now show the gentleman, or whatever he is, up.

TOPSY: By golly! I guess he won't make much out of Miss Feely. [*Exit.*]

OPHELIA: I wonder who this person can be? Perhaps it is some old acquaintance, who has heard of my arrival, and who comes on a social visit.

[Enter CUTE.*]*

CUTE: Aunt, how do ye do? Well, I swan, the sight of you is good for weak eyes. [*Offers his hand.*]

OPHELIA: [*Coldly drawing back.*] Really, sir, I can't say that I ever had the pleasure of seeing you before.

CUTE: Well, it's a fact that you never did. You see I never happened to be in your neighborhood afore now. Of course you've heard of me? I'm one of the Cutes—Gumption Cute, the first and only son of Josiah and Maria Cute, of Oniontown, on the Onion river, in the north part of this ere State of Varmount.

OPHELIA: Can't say I ever heard the name before.

CUTE: Well, then, I calculate your memory must be a little ricketty. I'm a relation of yours.

OPHELIA: A relation of mine! Why, I never heard of any Cutes in our family.

CUTE: Well, I shouldn't wonder if you never did. Don't you remember your niece, Mary?

OPHELIA: Of course I do. What a shiftless question!

CUTE: Well, you see, my second cousin, Abijah Blake, married her; so you see that makes me a relation of yours.

OPHELIA: Rather a distant one, I should say.

CUTE: By chowder! I'm *near* enough, just at present.

OPHELIA: Well, you certainly are a sort of connection of mine.

CUTE: Yes, kind of sort of.

OPHELIA: And of course you are welcome to my house, as long as you choose to make it your home.

CUTE: By chowder! I'm booked for the next six months—this isn't a bad speculation.

OPHELIA: I hope you left all your folks well at home?

CUTE: Well, yes, they're pretty comfortably disposed of. Father and mother's dead, and Uncle Josh has gone to California. I am the only representative of the Cutes left.

OPHELIA: There doesn't seem to be a great deal of *you* left. I declare, you are positively in rags.

CUTE: Well, you see, the fact is, I've been speculating—trying to get bank-notes—specie-rags, as they say—but I calculate I've turned out rags of another sort.

OPHELIA: I'm sorry for your ill luck, but I am afraid you have been shiftless.

CUTE: By chowder! I've done all that a fellow could do. You see, somehow, everything I take hold of kind of bursts up.

OPHELIA: Well, well, perhaps you'll do better for the future; make yourself at home. I have got to see to some household matters, so excuse me for a short time. [*Aside.*] Impudent and shiftless!   [*Exit.*]

CUTE: By chowder! I rather guess that this speculation will hitch. She's a good-natured old critter; I reckon I'll be a son to her while she lives, and take care of her valuables arter she's a defunct departed. I wonder if they keep the vittles in this ere room? Guess not. I've got extensive accommodations for all sorts of eatables. I'm a regular vacuum, throughout—pockets and all. I'm chuck full of emptiness. [*Looks out.*] Holloa! who's this elderly individual coming upstairs? He looks like a compound essence of starch and dignity. I wonder if he isn't another relation of mine. I should like a rich old fellow now for an uncle.

[*Enter* DEACON PERRY.]

DEACON: Ha! a stranger here!

CUTE: How d'ye do?

DEACON: You are a friend to Miss Ophelia, I presume?

CUTE: Well, I rather calculate that I am a leetle more than a friend.

DEACON: [*Aside.*] Bless me! what can he mean by those mysterious words? Can he be her—no, I don't think he can. She said she wasn't—well, at all events, it's very suspicious.

CUTE: The old fellow seems kind of stuck up.

DEACON: You are a particular friend to Miss Ophelia, you say?

CUTE: Well, I calculate I am.

DEACON: Bound to her by any tender tie?

CUTE: It's something more than a tie—it's a regular double-twisted knot.

DEACON: Ah! just as I suspected. [*Aside.*] Might I inquire the nature of that tie?

CUTE: Well, it's the natural tie of relationship.

DEACON: A relation—what relation!

CUTE: Why, you see, my second cousin, Abijah Blake, married her niece, Mary.

DEACON: Oh! is that all?

CUTE: By chowder, ain't that enough?

DEACON: Then you are not her husband?

CUTE: To be sure I ain't. What put that ere idea into your cranium?

DEACON: [*Shaking him vigorously by the hand.*] My dear sir, I'm delighted to see you.

CUTE: Holloa! you ain't going slightly insane, are you?

DEACON: No, no fear of that; I'm only happy, that's all.

CUTE: I wonder if he's been taking a nipper?

DEACON: As you are a relation of Miss Ophelia's, I think it proper that I should make you my confidant; in fact, let you into a little scheme that I have lately conceived.

CUTE: Is it a speculation?

DEACON: Well, it is, just at present; but I trust before many hours to make it a surety.

CUTE: By chowder! I hope it won't serve you the way my speculations have served me. But fire away, old boy, and give us the prospectus.

DEACON: Well, then, my young friend, I have been thinking, ever since Miss Ophelia returned to Vermont, that she was just the person to fill the place of my lamented Molly.

CUTE: Say, you couldn't tell us who your lamented Molly was, could you?

DEACON: Why, the late Mrs. Perry, to be sure.

CUTE: Oh! then the lamented Polly was your wife?

DEACON: She was.

CUTE: And now you wish to marry Miss Ophelia?

DEACON: Exactly.

CUTE: [*Aside.*] Consarn this old porpoise! if I let him do that he'll Jew me out of my living. By chowder! I'll put a spoke in his wheel.

DEACON: Well, what do you say? will you intercede for me with your aunt?

CUTE: No! bust me up if I do!

DEACON: No?

CUTE: No, I tell you. I forbid the bans.[27] Now, ain't you a purty individual, to talk about getting married, you old superannuated Methuselah[28] specimen of humanity! Why, you've got one foot in etarnity already, and t'other ain't fit to stand on. Go home and go to bed! have your head shaved, and send for a lawyer to make your will, leave your property to your heirs—if you hain't got any, why leave it to me—I'll take care of it, and charge nothing for the trouble.

---

[27]Public announcement of a proposed marriage.

[28]Referring to him as an old man; Methuselah lived to be 969 years old (Gen. 5:26).

DEACON: Really, sir, this language, to one of my standing, is highly indecorous—it's more, sir, than I feel willing to endure, sir. I shall expect an explanation, sir.

CUTE: Now, you see, old gouty toes, you're losing your temper.

DEACON: Sir, I'm a deacon; I never lost my temper in all my life, sir.

CUTE: Now, you see, you're getting excited; you had better go; we can't have a disturbance here!

DEACON: No, sir! I shall not go, sir! I shall not go until I have seen Miss Ophelia. I wish to know if she will countenance this insult.

CUTE: Now keep cool, old stick-in-the-mud! Draw it mild, old timber-toes!

DEACON: Damn it all, sir, what—

CUTE: Oh! Only think, now, what would people say to hear a deacon swearing like a trooper?

DEACON: Sir—I—you—this is too much, sir.

CUTE: Well, now, I calculate that's just about my opinion, so we'll have no more of it. Get out of this! start your boots, or by chowder! I'll pitch you from one end of the stairs to the other.

[Enter OPHELIA.]

OPHELIA: Hoity toity! What's the meaning of all these loud words?

CUTE: ⎱ Well, you see, Aunt—
DEACON: ⎰ Miss Ophelia, I beg—

CUTE: Now, look here, you just hush your yap! How can I fix up matters if you keep jabbering?

OPHELIA: Silence! for shame, Mr. Cute. Is that the way you speak to the deacon?

CUTE: Darn the deacon!

OPHELIA: Deacon Perry, what is all this?

DEACON: Madam, a few words will explain everything. Hearing from this person that he was your nephew, I ventured to tell him that I cherished hopes of making you my wife, whereupon he flew into a violent passion, and ordered me out of the house.

OPHELIA: Does this house belong to you or me, Mr. Cute?

CUTE: Well, to you, I reckon.

OPHELIA: Then how dare you give orders in it?

CUTE: Well, I calculated you wouldn't care about marrying old half-a-century there.

OPHELIA: That's enough; I will marry him; and as for you [*points to the right*], get out.

CUTE: Get out?

OPHELIA: Yes; the sooner the better.

CUTE: Darned if I don't serve him out first though.

[Music.—CUTE makes a dash at DEACON, who gets behind OPHELIA. TOPSY enters with a broom and beats CUTE around stage.—OPHELIA faints in DEACON'S arms.—CUTE falls, and TOPSY butts him, kneeling over him.—Quick drop.]

END OF ACT V

ACT VI

Scene 1: Dark Landscape.—An old, roofless shed. TOM is discovered in shed, lying on some old cotton bagging. CASSY kneels by his side, holding a cup to his lips.

CASSY: Drink all ye want. I knew how it would be. It isn't the first time I've been out in the night, carrying water to such as you.

TOM [*Returning cup*]. Thank you, missis.

CASSY: Don't call me missis. I'm a miserable slave like yourself—a lower one than you can ever be! It's no use, my poor fellow, this you've been trying to do. You were a brave fellow. You had the right on your side; but it's all in vain for you to struggle. You are in the Devil's hands: he is the strongest, and you must give up.

TOM: Oh! how can I give up?

CASSY: You see *you* don't know anything about it; I do. Here you are, on a lone plantation, ten miles from any other, in the swamps; not a white person here who could testify, if you were burned alive. There's no law here that can do you, or any of us, the least good; and this man! there's no earthly thing that he is not bad enough to do. I could make one's hair rise, and their teeth chatter, if I should only tell what I've seen and been knowing to here; and it's no use resisting! Did I *want* to live with him? Wasn't I a woman delicately bred? And he!—Father in Heaven! what was he and is he? And yet I've lived with him these five years, and cursed every moment of my life night and day.

TOM: Oh heaven! have you quite forgot us poor critters?

CASSY: And what are these miserable low dogs you work with, that you should suffer on their account? Every one of them would turn against you the first time they get a chance. They are all of them as low and cruel to each other as they can be; there's no use in your suffering to keep from hurting them!

TOM: What made 'em cruel? If I give out, I shall get used to it, and grow, little by little, just like 'em. No, no, missis, I've lost everything, wife, and children, and home, and a kind master, and he would have set me free if he'd only lived a day longer—I've lost everything in *this* world, and now I can't lose heaven, too; no, I can't get to be wicked besides all.

CASSY: But it can't be that He will lay sin to our account; He won't charge it to us when we are forced to it; He'll charge it to them that drove us to it. Can I do anything more for you? Shall I give you some more water?

TOM: Oh missis! I wish you'd go to Him who can give you living waters![29]

CASSY: Go to him! Where is he? Who is he?

TOM: Our Heavenly Father!

CASSY: I used to see the picture of Him, over the altar, when I was a girl; but *He isn't here!* There's nothing here but sin, and long, long despair! There, there, don't talk any more, my poor fellow. Try to sleep, if you can. I must hasten back, lest my absence be noted. Think of me when I am gone, Uncle Tom, and pray, pray for me.

[*Music.—Exit* CASSY.—TOM *sinks back to sleep.*]

Scene 2: Street in New Orleans

[Enter GEORGE SHELBY.*]*

GEORGE: At length my mission of mercy is nearly finished; I have reached my journey's end. I have now but to find the house of Mr. St. Clare, re-purchase old Uncle Tom, and convey him back to his wife and children, in old Kentucky. Some one approaches; he may, perhaps, be able to give me the information I require. I will accost him.

[Enter MARKS.*]*

Pray, sir, can you tell me where Mr. St. Clare dwells?

MARKS: Where I don't think you'll be in a hurry to seek him.

GEORGE: And where is that?

MARKS: In the grave!

GEORGE: Stay, sir! you may be able to give me some information concerning Mr. St. Clare.

MARKS: I beg pardon, sir. I am a lawyer; I can't afford to *give* anything.

GEORGE: But you would have no objections to selling it?

MARKS: Not the slightest.

GEORGE: What do you value it at?

MARKS: Well, say five dollars, that's reasonable.

GEORGE: There they are. [*Gives money.*] Now answer me to the best of your ability. Has the death of St. Clare caused his slaves to be sold?

MARKS: It has.

GEORGE: How were they sold?

MARKS: At auction—they went dirt cheap.

GEORGE: How were they bought—all in one lot?

MARKS: No, they went to different bidders.

---

[29]Invokes Jesus talking to the Samarian Woman in John 4.

GEORGE: Was you present at the sale?

MARKS: I was.

GEORGE: Do you remember seeing a negro among them called Tom?

MARKS: What, Uncle Tom?

GEORGE: The same—who bought him?

MARKS: A Mr. Legree.

GEORGE: Where is his plantation?

MARKS: Up in Louisiana, on the Red River; but a man never could find it unless he had been there before.

GEORGE: Who could I get to direct me there?

MARKS: Well, stranger, I don't know of any one just at present, 'cept myself, could find it for you; it's such an out-of-the-way sort of hole; and if you are a mind to come down handsomely, why, I'll do it.

GEORGE: The reward shall be ample.

MARKS: Enough said, stranger; let's take the steamboat at once.

[*Exeunt.*]

Scene 3: A Rough Chamber

[Enter LEGREE.—*Sits.]*

LEGREE: Plague on that Sambo, to kick up this yer row between me and the new hands.

*[*CASSY *steals on, and stands behind him.]*

The fellow won't be fit to work for a week now, right in the press of the season.

CASSY: Yes, just like you.

LEGREE: Hah! you she-devil! you've come back, have you? [*Rises.*]

CASSY: Yes, I have; come to have my own way, too.

LEGREE: You lie, you jade! I'll be up to my word. Either you behave yourself, or stay down in the quarters and fare and work with the rest.

CASSY: I'd rather, ten thousand times, live in the dirtiest hole in the quarters, than be under your hoof!

LEGREE: But you are under my hoof, for all that, that's one comfort; so sit down here and listen to reason. [*Grasps her wrist.*]

CASSY: Simon Legree, take care! [LEGREE *lets go his hold.*] You're afraid of me, Simon, and you've reason to be; for I've got the Devil in me!

LEGREE: I believe to my soul you have. After all, Cassy, why can't you be friends with me, as you used to?

CASSY: [*Bitterly.*] Used to!

LEGREE: I wish, Cassy, you'd behave yourself decently.

CASSY: *You* talk about behaving decently! and what have you been doing? You haven't even sense enough to keep from spoiling one of your best hands, right in the most pressing season, just for your devilish temper.

LEGREE: I was a fool, it's a fact, to let any such brangle[30] come up; but when Tom set up his will he had to be broke in.

CASSY: You'll never break *him* in.

LEGREE: Won't I? I'd like to know if I won't! He'll be the first nigger that ever come it round me! I'll break every bone in his body but he shall give up.

[Enter SAMBO, with a paper in his hand, stands bowing.]

LEGREE: What's that, you dog?

SAMBO: It's a witch thing, mas'r.

LEGREE: A what?

SAMBO: Something that niggers gits from witches. Keep 'em from feeling when they's flogged. He had it tied round his neck with a black string.

[LEGREE takes the paper and opens it.—A silver dollar drops on the stage, and a long curl of light hair twines around his finger.]

LEGREE: Damnation. [*Stamping and writhing, as if the hair burned him.*] Where did this come from? Take it off! burn it up! burn it up! [*Throws the curl away.*] What did you bring it to me for?

SAMBO: [*Trembling.*] I beg pardon, mas'r; I thought you would like to see 'um.

LEGREE: Don't you bring me any more of your devilish things. [*Shakes his fist at SAMBO who runs off.—LEGREE kicks the dollar after him.*] Blast it! where did he get that? If it didn't look just like—whoo! I thought I'd forgot that. Curse me if I think there's any such thing as forgetting anything, any how.

CASSY: What is the matter with you, Legree? What is there in a simple curl of fair hair to appall a man like you—you who are familiar with every form of cruelty.

LEGREE: Cassy, to-night the past has been recalled to me—the past that I have so long and vainly striven to forget.

CASSY: Hast aught on this earth power to move a soul like thine?

LEGREE: Yes, for hard and reprobate as I now seem, there has been a time when I have been rocked on the bosom of a mother, cradled with prayers and pious hymns, my now seared brow bedewed with the waters of holy baptism.

CASSY: [*Aside.*] What sweet memories of childhood can thus soften down that heart of iron?

---

[30]Violent disagreement or fight.

LEGREE: In early childhood, a fair-haired woman has led me, at the sound of Sabbath bells, to worship and to pray. Born of a hard-tempered sire, on whom that gentle woman had wasted a world of unvalued love, I followed in the steps of my father. Boisterous, unruly and tyrannical, I despised all her counsel, and would have none of her reproof, and, at an early age, broke from her to seek my fortunes on the sea. I never came home but once after that; and then my mother, with the yearning of a heart that must love something, and had nothing else to love, clung to me, and sought with passionate prayers and entreaties to win me from a life of sin.

CASSY: That was your day of grace, Legree; then good angels called you, and mercy held you by the hand.

LEGREE: My heart inly relented; there was a conflict, but sin got the victory, and I set all the force of my rough nature against the conviction of my conscience. I drank and swore, was wilder and more brutal than ever. And one night, when my mother, in the last agony of her despair, knelt at my feet, I spurned her from me, threw her senseless on the floor, and with brutal curses fled to my ship.

CASSY: Then the fiend took thee for his own.

LEGREE: The next I heard of my mother was one night while I was carousing among drunken companions. A letter was put in my hands. I opened it, and a lock of long, curling hair fell from it, and twined about my fingers, even as that locked twined but now. The letter told me that my mother was dead, and that dying she blest and forgave me! [*Buries his face in his hands.*]

CASSY: Why did you not even then renounce your evil ways?

LEGREE: There is a dread, unhallowed necromancy of evil, that turns things sweetest and holiest to phantoms of horror and affright. That pale, loving mother,—her dying prayers, her forgiving love,—wrought in my demoniac heart of sin only as a damning sentence, bringing with it a fearful looking for of judgment and fiery indignation.

CASSY: And yet you would not strive to avert the doom that threatened you.

LEGREE: I burned the lock of hair and I burned the letter; and when I saw them hissing and crackling in the flame, inly shuddered as I thought of everlasting fires! I tried to drink and revel, and swear away the memory; but often in the deep night, whose solemn stillness arraigns the soul in forced communion with itself, I have seen that pale mother rising by my bed-side, and felt the soft twining of that hair around my fingers, 'till the cold sweat would roll down my face, and I would spring from my bed in horror— horror! [*Falls in chair.—After a pause.*] What the devil ails me? Large drops of sweat stand on my forehead, and my heart beats heavy and thick with fear. I thought I saw something white rising and glimmering in the gloom before me, and it seemed to bear my mother's face! I know one thing; I'll let that fellow Tom alone, after this. What did I want with his cussed paper? I believe I am bewitched sure enough! I've been shivering and sweating ever since! Where did he get that hair? I couldn't have been that! I *burn'd* that up, I know I did! I would be a joke if hair could rise from the dead! I'll have Sambo and Quimbo up here to sing and dance one of their dances, and keep off these horrid notions. Here, Sambo! Quimbo!   [*Exit.*]

CASSY: Yes, Legree, that golden tress was charmed; each hair had in it a spell of terror and remorse for thee, and was used by a mightier power to bind thy cruel hands from inflicting uttermost evil on the helpless!   [*Exit.*]

Scene 4: Street

[*Enter* MARKS, *meeting* CUTE, *who enters, dressed in an old faded uniform.*]

MARKS: By the land, stranger, but it strikes me that I've seen you somewhere before.

CUTE: By chowder! do you know now, that's just what I was a going to say?

MARKS: Isn't your name Cute?

CUTE: You're right, I calculate. Yours is Marks, I reckon.

MARKS: Just so.

CUTE: Well, I swow, I'm glad to see you. [*They shake hands.*] How's your wholesome?

MARKS: Hearty as ever. Well, who would have thought of ever seeing you again. Why, I thought you was in Vermont?

CUTE: Well, so I was. You see I went there after that rich relation of mine—but the speculation didn't turn out well.

MARKS: How so?

CUTE: Why, you see, she took a shine to an old fellow—Deacon Abraham Perry—and married him.

MARKS: Oh, that rather put your nose out of joint in that quarter.

CUTE: Busted me right up, I tell you. The deacon did the handsome thing, though; he said if I would leave the neighborhood and go out South again, he'd stand the damage. I calculate I didn't give him much time to change his mind, and so, you see, here I am again.

MARKS: What are you doing in that soldier rig?

CUTE: Oh, this is my sign.

MARKS: Your sign?

CUTE: Yes; you see, I'm engaged just at present in an all-fired good speculation; I'm a Fillibusterow.[31]

MARKS: A what?

CUTE: A fillibusterow! Don't you know what that is? It's Spanish for Cuban Volunteer; and means a chap that goes the whole porker for glory and all that ere sort of thing.

MARKS: Oh! you've joined the order of the Lone Star!

---

[31]Adventurer; this term and the dialogue that follows refer to an abortive attempt by a small group of Southerners to invade Cuba in 1850 to support a local revolutionary there. The failed attempt resulted in the deaths of more than fifty Americans.

CUTE: You've hit it. You see I bought this uniform at a second-hand clothing store; I puts it on and goes to a benevolent individual and I says to him—appealing to his feelings—I'm one of the fellows that went to Cuba and got massacred by the bloody Spaniards. I'm in a destitute condition—give me a trifle to pay my passage back, so I can whop the tyrannical cusses and avenge my brave fellow sogers what got slewed there.

MARKS: How pathetic!

CUTE: I tell you it works up the feelings of benevolent individuals dreadfully. It draws tears from their eyes and money from their pockets. By chowder! One old chap gave me a hundred dollars to help on the cause.

MARKS: I admire a genius like yours.

CUTE: But I say, what are you up to?

MARKS: I am the travelling companion of a young gentleman by the name of Shelby, who is going to the plantation of a Mr. Legree, on the Red River, to buy an old darkey who used to belong to his father.

CUTE: Legree—Legree? Well, now, I calculate I've heard that ere name afore.

MARKS: Do you remember that man who drew a bowie knife on you in New Orleans?[32]

CUTE: By chowder! I remember the circumstance just as well as if it was yesterday; but I can't say that I recollect much about the man, for you see I was in something of a hurry about that time and didn't stop to take a good look at him.

MARKS: Well, that man was this same Mr. Legree.

CUTE: Do you know, now, I should like to pay that critter off?

MARKS: Then I'll give you an opportunity.

CUTE: Chowder! how will you do that?

MARKS: Do you remember the gentleman that interfered between you and Legree?

CUTE: Yes—well?

MARKS: He received the blow that was intended for you, and died from the effects of it. So, you see, Legree is a murderer, and we are the only witnesses of the deed. His life is in our hands.

CUTE: Let's have him right up and make him dance on nothing to the tune of Yankee Doodle!

MARKS: Stop a bit. Don't you see a chance for a profitable speculation?

CUTE: A speculation! Fire away, don't be bashful; I'm the man for a speculation.

MARKS: I have made a deposition to the Governor of the State of all the particulars of that affair at Orleans.

---

[32]Other versions of the play insert a scene before Act IV, Scene III, where Legree pulls a knife on Marks, but instead fatally wounds St. Clare, who attempts to stop the fight.

CUTE: What did you do that for?

MARKS: To get a warrant for his arrest.

CUTE: Oh! and have you got it?

MARKS: Yes; here it is. [*Takes out paper.*]

CUTE: Well, now, I don't see how you are going to make anything by that bit of paper?

MARKS: But I do. I shall say to Legree, I have got a warrant against you for murder; my friend, Mr. Cute, and myself are the only witnesses who can appear against you. Give us a thousand dollars, and we will tear the warrant and be silent.

CUTE: Then Mr. Legree forks over a thousand dollars, and your friend Cute pockets five hundred of it. Is that the calculation?

MARKS: If you will join me in the undertaking.

CUTE: I'll do it, by chowder!

MARKS: Your hand to bind the bargain.

CUTE: I'll stick by you thro' thick and thin.

MARKS: Enough said.

CUTE: Then shake. [*They shake hands.*]

MARKS: But I say, Cute, he may be contrary and show fight.

CUTE: Never mind, we've got the law on our side, and we're bound to stir him up. If he don't come down handsomely, we'll present him with a neck-tie made of hemp!

MARKS: I declare you're getting spunky.

CUTE: Well, I reckon I am. Let's go and have something to drink. Tell you what, Marks, if we don't get *him,* we'll have his hide, by chowder!   [*Exeunt, arm in arm.*]

Scene 5: Rough Chamber

[Enter LEGREE, followed by SAMBO.]

LEGREE: Go and send Cassy to me.

SAMBO: Yes, mas'r.   [*Exit.*]

LEGREE: Curse the woman! she's got a temper worse than the devil! I shall do her an injury one of these days, if she isn't careful.

[Re-enter SAMBO, frightened.]

What's the matter with you, you black scoundrel?

SAMBO: S'help me, mas'r, she isn't dere.

LEGREE: I suppose she's about the house somewhere?

SAMBO: No, she isn't, mas'r; I's been all over de house and I can't find nothing of her nor Emmeline.

LEGREE: Bolted, by the Lord! Call out the dogs! Saddle my horse! Stop! are you sure they really have gone?

SAMBO: Yes, mas'r; I's been in every room 'cept the haunted garret, and dey wouldn't go dere.

LEGREE: I have it! Now, Sambo, you jest go and walk that Tom up here, right away! [*Exit* SAMBO.]

The old cuss is at the bottom of this yer whole matter; and I'll have it out of his infernal black hide, or I'll know the reason why! I *hate* him— I *hate* him! And isn't he *mine?* Can't I do what I like with him? Who's to hinder, I wonder?

[*TOM is dragged on by* SAMBO *and* QUIMBO.*]

LEGREE: [*Grimly confronting* TOM.] Well, Tom, do you know I've made up my mind to *kill* you?

TOM: It's very likely, Mas'r.

LEGREE: I—*have—done—just—that—thing,* Tom, unless you tell me what do you know about these yer gals? [TOM *is silent.*] D'ye hear? Speak!

TOM: I hain't got anything to tell, mas'r.

LEGREE: Do you dare to tell me, you old black rascal, you don't know? Speak! Do you know anything?

TOM: I know, mas'r; but I can't tell anything. *I can die!*

LEGREE: Hark ye, Tom! ye think, 'cause I have let you off before, I don't mean what I say; but, this time, I have made *up my mind,* and counted the cost. You've always stood it out agin me; now, I'll *conquer ye or kill ye!* one or t'other. I'll count every drop of blood there is in you, and take 'em, one by one, 'till ye give up!

TOM: Mas'r, if you was sick, or in trouble, or dying, and I could save, I'd *give* you my heart's blood; and, if taking every drop of blood in this poor old body would save your precious soul, I'd give 'em freely. Do the worst you can, my troubles will be over soon; but if you don't repent, yours won't never end.

[*LEGREE strikes* TOM *down with the butt of his whip.*]

LEGREE: How do you like that?

SAMBO: He's most gone, mas'r!

TOM: [*Rises feebly on his hands.*] There an't no more you can do! I forgive you with all my soul. [*Sinks back, and is carried off by* SAMBO *and* QUIMBO.]

LEGREE: I believe he's done for finally. Well, his mouth is shut up at last—that's one comfort.

[*Enter* GEORGE SHELBY, MARKS *and* CUTE.]

Strangers! Well, what do you want?

GEORGE: I understand that you bought in New Orleans a negro named Tom?

LEGREE: Yes, I did buy such a fellow, and a devil of a bargain I had of it, too! I believe he's trying to die, but I don't know as he'll make it out.

GEORGE: Where is he? Let me see him!

SAMBO: Dere he is! [*Points to* TOM.]

LEGREE: How dare you speak? [*Drives* SAMBO *and* QUIMBO *off.*]

[GEORGE *exits.*]

CUTE: Now's the time to nab him.

MARKS: How are you, Mr. Legree?

LEGREE: What the devil brought you here?

MARKS: This little bit of paper. I arrest you for the murder of Mr. St. Clare. What do you say to that?

LEGREE: This is my answer! [*Makes a blow at* MARKS, *who dodges, and* CUTE *receives the blow—he cries out and runs off.* MARKS *fires at* LEGREE, *and follows* CUTE.] I am hit!—the game's up! [*Falls dead.* QUIMBO *and* SAMBO *return and carry him off laughing.*]

[GEORGE SHELBY *enters, supporting* TOM.—*Music. They advance and* TOM *falls, center.*]

GEORGE: Oh! dear Uncle Tom! do wake—do speak once more! look up! Here's Master George—your own little Master George. Don't you know me?

TOM: [*Opening his eyes and speaking in a feeble tone.*] Mas'r George! Bless de Lord! it's all I wanted! They hav'n't forgot me! It warms my soul; it does my old heart good! Now I shall die content!

GEORGE: You sha'n't die! you mustn't die, nor think of it. I have come to buy you, and take you home.

TOM: Oh, Mas'r George, you're too late. The Lord has bought me, and is going to take me home.

GEORGE: Oh! don't die. It will kill me—it will break my heart to think what you have suffered, poor, poor fellow!

TOM: Don't call me poor fellow. I *have* been poor fellow; but that's all past and gone now. I'm right in the door, going into glory! Oh, Mas'r George! *Heaven has come!* I've got the victory! the Lord has given it to me! Glory be to His name! [*Dies.*]

[*Solemn music.*—GEORGE *covers* UNCLE TOM *with his cloak, and kneels over him. Clouds work on and conceal them, and then work off.*]

Scene 6: Gorgeous clouds, tinted with sunlight. EVA, *robed in white, is discovered on the back of a milk-white dove, with expanded wings, as if just soaring upward. Her hands are extended in benediction over* ST. CLARE *and* UNCLE TOM, *who are kneeling and gazing up to her. Impressive music.—Slow curtain.*

THE END

12

Timothy Shay Arthur
(1809–1885)

TIMOTHY SHAY ARTHUR's literary reputation today rests almost solely on his 1854 temperance novel, *Ten Nights in a Bar-Room*. Like many of his successful contemporaries, Arthur's literary output showed far more range than this single work would imply. Beginning in the 1840s, he began writing what would eventually become a body of work including 150 novels and collections of short stories. He also edited several influential periodicals, including *Arthur's Home Gazette* (later renamed *The Home Magazine*). Reportedly, more than one million copies of his works were circulating in the United States before the Civil War.

His *Ten Nights in a Bar-Room* was the most popular single piece of temperance literature to appear before the Civil War, no mean feat considering how much temperance material appeared in the opening decades of the nineteenth century. In 1826, the American Society for the Promotion of Temperance was founded, and by 1833 more than four thousand local temperance societies with more than half a million members dotted the American landscape. These societies helped generate and distribute hundreds of thousands of temperance tracts. More than 400,000 copies of *Ten Nights in a Bar-Room* joined these tracts to help reform what one antebellum writer called a "nation of drunkards."

Arthur's *Ten Nights in a Bar-Room* is noteworthy for the way it captures how drinking is far more than simply a private act. It is an activity that blends the personal and communal worlds of the individual. In a larger sense, Arthur was deeply concerned with choices whose consequences spread out like ever-widening concentric circles. Bad decisions could not only destroy an individual, but they could ultimately topple a nation. What was at stake in the temperance cause was but a mirror of what is at stake every time an individual makes a choice that adversely affects his family, his larger community, and his country.

TEN NIGHTS IN A BAR-ROOM
AND WHAT I SAW THERE

❧ Publisher's Preface

[FROM THE 1854 EDITION]

This new temperance volume, by Mr. Arthur, comes in just at the right time, when the subject of restrictive laws[1] is agitating the whole country, and good and true men everywhere are gathering up their strength for a prolonged and unflinching contest. It will prove a powerful auxiliary in the cause.

"Ten Nights in a Bar-Room" gives a series of sharply drawn sketches of scenes, some of them touching in the extreme, and some dark and terrible. Step by step the author traces the downward course of the tempting vender and his infatuated victims, until both are involved in hopeless ruin. The book is marred by no exaggerations, but exhibits the actualities of bar-room life, and the consequences flowing therefrom, with a severe simplicity, and adherence to truth, that gives to every picture a Daguerrean[2] vividness.

❧ Night the First

THE "SICKLE AND SHEAF"

Ten years ago, business required me to pass a day in Cedarville. It was late in the afternoon when the stage set me down at the "Sickle and Sheaf," a new tavern, just opened by a new landlord, in a new house, built with the special end of providing "accommodations for man and beast." As I stepped from the dusty old vehicle in which I had been jolted along a rough road for some thirty miles, feeling tired and hungry, the good-natured face of Simon Slade, the landlord, beaming as it did with a hearty welcome, was really a pleasant sight to see, and the grasp of his hand was like that of a true friend.

I felt, as I entered the new and neatly furnished sitting-room adjoining the bar, that I had indeed found a comfortable resting-place after my wearisome journey.

"All as nice as a new pin," said I, approvingly, as I glanced around the room, up to

---

The following text is taken from an 1856 edition of *Ten Nights in a Bar-Room* with only slight corrections to obvious errors in typesetting and proofreading. Timothy Shay Arthur, *Ten Nights in a Bar-Room and What I Saw There*. Philadelphia: Bradley, 1856.

[1]The state of Maine passed an alcohol prohibition law in 1851, sparking animated discussions at both the state and the federal levels on whether other prohibition laws should be passed.

[2]Daguerrotypes were the first successful form of photography, developed in France in the 1830s. The reference here is to the lifelike or photographic quality of the sketches.

Frontispiece illustration from an 1860 edition of T. S. Arthur's *Ten Nights in a Bar-Room* (Philadelphia: G. G. Evans). Not shown here is the caption to the illustration, which reads "Father Come Home."

the ceiling—white as the driven snow—and over the handsomely carpeted floor. "Haven't seen any thing so inviting as this. How long have you been open?"

"Only a few months," answered the gratified landlord. "But we are not yet in good going order. It takes time, you know, to bring everything into the right shape. Have you dined yet?"

"No. Every thing looked so dirty at the stage-house where we stopped to get dinner, that I couldn't venture upon the experiment of eating. How long before your supper will be ready?"

"In an hour," replied the landlord.

"That will do. Let me have a nice piece of tender steak, and the loss of dinner will soon be forgotten."

"You shall have that, cooked fit for an alderman," said the landlord. "I call my wife the best cook in Cedarville."

As he spoke, a neatly dressed girl, about sixteen years of age, with rather an attractive countenance, passed through the room.

"My daughter," said the landlord, as she vanished through the door. There was a sparkle of pride in the father's eyes, and a certain tenderness in the tones of his voice, as he said—"My daughter," that told me she was very dear to him.

"You are a happy man to have so fair a child," said I, speaking more in compliment than with a careful choice of words.

"I am a happy man," was the landlord's smiling answer; his fair, round face, unwrinkled by a line of care or trouble, beaming with self-satisfaction. "I have always been a happy man, and always expect to be. Simon Slade takes the world as it comes, and takes it easy. My son, sir"—he added, as a boy in his twelfth year, came in. "Speak to the gentleman."

The boy lifted to mine a pair of deep blue eyes, from which innocence beamed, as he offered me his hand, and said, respectfully—"How do you do, sir?" I could not but remark the girl-like beauty of his face, in which the hardier firmness of the boy's character was already visible.

"What is your name?" I asked.

"Frank, sir."

"Frank is his name," said the landlord—"we called him after his uncle. Frank and Flora—the names sound pleasant to our ears. But, you know, parents are apt to be a little partial and over fond."

"Better that extreme than its opposite," I remarked.

"Just what I always say. Frank, my son"—the landlord spoke to the boy, "there's some one in the bar. You can wait on him as well as I can."

The lad glided from the room, in ready obedience.

"A handy boy that, sir; a very handy boy. Almost as good in the bar as a man. He mixes a toddy or a punch just as well as I can."

"But," I suggested, "are you not a little afraid of placing one so young in the way of temptation."

"Temptation!" The open brows of Simon Slade contracted a little. "No, sir!" he replied, emphatically. "The till is safer under his care than it would be in that of one man in ten. The boy comes, sir, of honest parents. Simon Slade never wronged anybody out of a farthing."

"Oh," said I, quickly, "you altogether misapprehend me. I had no reference to the till, but to the bottle."

The landlord's brows were instantly unbent, and a broad smile circled over his good-humoured face.

"Is that all? Nothing to fear, I can assure you. Frank has no taste for liquor, and might pour it out for months without a drop finding its way to his lips. Nothing to apprehend there, sir—nothing."

I saw that further suggestions of danger would be useless, and so remained silent. The arrival of a traveller called away the landlord, and I was left alone for observation and reflection. The bar adjoined the neat sitting-room, and I could see, through the open door, the customer upon whom the lad was attending. He was a well-dressed young man—or rather boy, for he did not appear to be over nineteen years of age—with a fine, intelligent face, that was already slightly marred by sensual indulgence. He raised the glass to his lips, with a quick, almost eager motion, and drained it at a single draught.

"Just right," said he, tossing a sixpence to the young bar-tender. "You are first-rate at a brandy-toddy. Never drank a better in my life."

The lad's smiling face told that he was gratified by the compliment. To me the sight was painful, for I saw that this youthful tippler was on dangerous ground.

"Who is that young man in the bar?" I asked, a few minutes afterward, on being rejoined by the landlord.

Simon Slade stepped to the door and looked into the bar for a moment. Two or three men were there by this time; but he was at no loss in answering my question.

"Oh, that's a *son of Judge Hammond,* who lives in the large brick house just as you enter the village. Willy Hammond, as everybody familiarly calls him, is about the finest young man in our neighbourhood. There is nothing proud or put-on about him—nothing—even if his father is a judge, and rich into the bargain. Every one, gentle or simple, likes Willy Hammond. And then he is such good company. Always so cheerful, and always with a pleasant story on his tongue. And he's so high-spirited withal, and so honourable. Willy Hammond would lose his right hand rather than be guilty of a mean action."

"Landlord!" The voice came loud from the road in front of the house, and Simon Slade again left me to answer the demands of some new comer. I went into the bar-room, in order to take a closer observation of Willy Hammond, in whom an interest, not unmingled with concern, had already been awakened in my mind. I found him engaged in a pleasant conversation with a plain-looking farmer, whose homely, terse, common sense was quite as conspicuous as his fine play of words and lively fancy. The farmer was a substantial conservative, and young Hammond a warm admirer of new ideas and the quicker adaptation of means to ends. I soon saw that his mental powers were developed beyond his years, while his personal qualities were strongly attractive. I understood better, after being a silent listener and observer for ten minutes, why the landlord had spoken of him so warmly.

"Take a brand-toddy, Mr. H—?" said Hammond, after the discussion closed, good humouredly. "Frank, our junior bar-keeper here, beats his father, in that line."

"I don't care if I do," returned the farmer; and the two passed up to the bar.

"Now, Frank, my boy, don't belie my praises," said the young man; "do your handsomest."

"Two brandy-toddies, did you say?" Frank made the inquiry with quite a professional air.

"Just what I did say; and let them be equal to Jove's nectar."[3]

Pleased at this familiarity, the boy went briskly to his work of mixing the tempting compound, while Hammond looked on with an approving smile.

"There," said the latter, as Frank passed the glasses across the counter, "if you don't call that first-rate, you're no judge." And he handed one of them to the farmer, who tasted the agreeable draught, and praised its flavour. As before, I noticed that Hammond drank eagerly, like one athirst—emptying his glass without once taking it from his lips.

Soon after the bar-room was empty; and then I walked around the premises, in company with the landlord, and listened to his praise of everything and his plans and purposes for the future. The house, yard, garden, and out-buildings were in the most perfect order; presenting, in the whole, a model of a village tavern.

"Whatever I do, sir," said the talkative Simon Slade, "I like to do well. I wasn't just raised to tavern-keeping, you must know; but I'm one who can turn his hand to almost any thing."

"What was your business?" I inquired.

"I'm a miller, sir, by trade," he answered—"and a better miller, though I say it myself, is not to be found in Bolton county. I've followed milling these twenty years, and made some little money. But I got tired of hard work, and determined to lead an easier life. So I sold my mill, and built this house with the money. I always thought I'd like tavern-keeping. It's an easy life; and, if rightly seen after, one in which a man is sure to make money."

"You were still doing a fair business with your mill?"

"Oh yes. Whatever I do, I do right. Last year, I put by a thousand dollars above all expenses, which is not bad, I can assure you, for a mere grist mill. If the present owner comes out even, he'll do well!"

"How is that?"

"Oh, he's no miller. Give him the best wheat that is grown, and he'll ruin it in grinding. He takes the life out of every grain. I don't believe he'll keep half the custom that I transferred with the mill."

"A thousand dollars, clear profit, in so useful a business, ought to have satisfied you," said I.

"There you and I differ," answered the landlord. "Every man desires to make as much money as possible, and with the least labour. I hope to make two or three thousand dollars a year, over and above all expenses, at tavern-keeping. My bar alone ought to yield me that sum. A man with a wife and children very naturally tries to do as well by them as possible."

"Very true; but," I ventured to suggest, "will this be doing as well by them as if you had kept on at the mill?"

"Two or three thousand dollars a year against one thousand! Where are your figures, man?"

"There may be something beyond the money to take into the account," said I.

"What?" inquired Slade, with a kind of half credulity.

---

[3]The chief drink of the ancient Roman gods.

"Consider the different influences of the two callings in life—that of a miller and a tavern-keeper."

"Well! say on."

"Will your children be as safe from temptation here as in their former home?"

"Just as safe," was the unhesitating answer. "Why not?"

I was about to speak of the alluring glass in the case of Frank, but remembering that I had already expressed a fear in that direction, felt that to do so again would be useless, and so kept silent.

"A tavern-keeper," said Slade, "is just as respectable as a miller—in fact, the very people who used to call me 'Simon,' or 'Neighbour Dustycoat,' now say 'Landlord,' or Mr. Slade, and treat me in every way more as if I were an equal than ever they did before."

"The change," said I, "may be due to the fact of your giving evidence of possessing some means. Men are very apt to be courteous to those who have property. The building of the tavern has, without doubt, contributed to the new estimation in which you are held."

"That isn't all," replied the landlord. "It is because I am keeping a good tavern, and thus materially advancing the interests of Cedarville, that some of our best people look at me with different eyes."

"Advancing the interests of Cedarville! In what way?" I did not apprehend his meaning.

"A good tavern always draws people to a place, while a miserable old tumbledown of an affair, badly kept, such as we have had for years, as surely repels them. You can generally tell something about the condition of a town by looking at its taverns. If they are well kept, and doing a good business, you will hardly be wrong in the conclusion that the place is thriving. Why, already, since I built and opened the 'Sickle and Sheaf,' property has advanced over twenty per cent. along the whole street, and not less than five new houses have been commenced."

"Other causes, besides the simple opening of a new tavern, may have contributed to this result," said I.

"None of which I am aware. I was talking with Judge Hammond only yesterday—he owns a great deal of ground on the street—and he did not hesitate to say, that the building and opening of a good tavern here had increased the value of his property at least five thousand dollars. He said, moreover, that he thought the people of Cedarville ought to present me with a silver pitcher; and that, for one, he would contribute ten dollars for the purpose."

The ringing of the supper bell here interrupted further conversation; and with the best of appetites, I took my way to the room, where a plentiful meal was spread. As I entered, I met the wife of Simon Slade, just passing out, after seeing that everything was in order. I had not observed her before; and now could not help remarking that she had a flushed, excited countenance, as if she had been over a hot fire, and was both worried and fatigued. And there was, moreover, a peculiar expression of the mouth, never observed in one whose mind is entirely at ease—an expression that once seen is never forgotten. The face stamped itself, instantly, on my memory; and I can even now recall it with almost the original distinctness. How strongly it contrasted with that of her smiling, self-satisfied husband, who took his place at the head of his table with an air of conscious importance. I was too hungry to talk much, and so found greater enjoyment in eating than in conversation. The landlord had a more chatty guest by his side, and I left them to entertain each other, while I did ample justice to the excellent food with which the table was liberally provided.

After supper I went to the sitting-room, and remained there until the lamps were lighted. A newspaper occupied my time for perhaps half an hour; then the buzz of voices from the adjoining bar-room, which had been increasing for some time, attracted my attention, and I went in there to see and hear what was passing. The first person upon whom my eyes rested was young Hammond, who sat talking with a man older than himself by several years. At a glance, I saw that this man could only associate himself with Willy Hammond as a tempter. Unscrupulous selfishness was written all over his sinister countenance; and I wondered that it did not strike every one, as it did me, with instant repulsion. There could not be, I felt certain, any common ground of association, for two such persons, but the dead level of a village bar-room. I afterward learned, during the evening, that this man's name was Harvey Green, and that he was an occasional visitor at Cedarville, remaining a few days, or a few weeks at a time, as appeared to suit his fancy, and having no ostensible business or special acquaintance with anybody in the village.

"There is one thing about him," remarked Simon Slade, in answering some question that I put in reference to the man, "that I don't object to; he has plenty of money, and is not at all niggardly in spending it. He used to come here, so he told me, about once in five or six months; but his stay at the miserably kept tavern, the only one then in Cedarville, was so uncomfortable, that he had pretty well made up his mind never to visit us again. Now, however, he has engaged one of my best rooms, for which he pays me by the year, and I am to charge him full board for the time he occupies it. He says that there is something about Cedarville that always attracts him; and that his health is better while here than it is anywhere, except South during the winter season. He'll not leave less than two or three hundred dollars a year in our village—there is one item, for you, of advantage to a place in having a good tavern."

"What is his business?" I asked. "Is he engaged in any trading operations?"

The landlord shrugged his shoulders, and looked slightly mysterious, as he answered—

"I never inquire about the business of a guest. My calling is to entertain strangers. If they are pleased with my house, and pay my bills on presentation, I have no right to seek further. As a miller, I never asked a customer whether he raised, bought, or stole his wheat. It was my business to grind it, and I took care to do it well. Beyond that, it was all his own affair. And so it will be in my new calling. I shall mind my own business and keep my own place."

Besides young Hammond and this Harvey Green, there were, in the bar-room, when I entered, four others besides the landlord. Among these was a Judge Lyman,—so he was addressed—a man between forty and fifty years of age, who had a few weeks before received the Democratic nomination for member of Congress. He was very talkative and very affable, and soon formed a kind of centre of attraction to the bar-room circle.

Among other topics of conversation that came up was the new tavern, introduced by the landlord, in whose mind it was, very naturally, the uppermost thought.

"The only wonder to me is," said Judge Lyman, "that nobody had wit enough to see the advantage of a good tavern in Cedarville ten years ago, or enterprise enough to start one. I give our friend Slade the credit of being a shrewd, far-seeing man; and, mark my word for it, in ten years from to-day he will be the richest man in the country."

"Nonsense—Ho! ho!" Simon Slade laughed outright. "The richest man! You forget Judge Hammond."

"No, not even Judge Hammond, with all deference for our clever friend Willy"— and Judge Lyman smiled pleasantly on the young man.

"If he gets richer, somebody will be poorer!" The individual who uttered these words had not spoken before; and I turned to look at him more closely. A glance showed him to be one of a class seen in all bar-rooms; a poor, broken-down inebriate, with the inward power of resistance gone—conscious of having no man's respect, and giving respect to none. There was a shrewd twinkle in his eyes, as he fixed them on Slade, that gave added force to the peculiar tone in which his brief, but telling sentence was uttered. I noticed a slight contraction on the landlord's ample forehead, the first evidence I had yet seen of ruffled feelings. The remark, thrown in so untimely, (or, timely, some will say,) and with a kind of prophetic malice, produced a temporary pause in the conversation. No one answered, or questioned the intruder, who, I could perceive, silently enjoyed the effect of his words. But soon the obstructed current ran on again.

"If our excellent friend, Mr. Slade," said Harvey Green, "is not the richest man in Cedarville at the end of ten years, he will at least enjoy the satisfaction of having made his town richer."

"A true word that," replied Judge Lyman—"as true a word as ever was spoken. What a dead-and-alive place this has been until within the last few months. All vigorous growth had stopped, and we were actually going to seed."

"And the graveyard too"—muttered the individual who had before disturbed the self-satisfied harmony of the company, remarking upon the closing sentence of Harvey Green. "Come, landlord," he added, as he strode across to the bar, speaking in a changed, reckless sort of a way, "fix me up a good hot whisky-punch, and do it right; and there's another sixpence toward the fortune you are bound to make. It's the last one left—not a copper more in my pockets"—and he turned them inside-out, with a half-solemn, half-ludicrous air. "I send it to keep company in your till with four others that have found their way into that snug place since morning, and which will be lonesome without their little friend."

I looked at Simon Slade, his eyes rested on mine for a moment or two, and then sunk beneath my earnest gaze. I saw that his countenance flushed, and that his motions were slightly confused. The incident, it was plain, did not awaken agreeable thoughts. Once I saw his hand move toward the sixpence, that lay upon the counter; but, whether to push it back, or draw it toward the till, I could not determine. The whisky-punch was in due time ready, and with it the man retired to a table across the room, and sat down to enjoy the tempting beverage. As he did so, the landlord quietly swept the poor unfortunate's last sixpence into his drawer. The influence of this strong potation[4] was to render the man a little more talkative. To the free conversation passing around him he lent an attentive ear, dropping in a word, now and then, that always told upon the company like a well-directed blow. At last, Slade lost all patience with him, and said, a little fretfully,—

"Look here, Joe Morgan, if you will be ill-natured, pray go somewhere else, and not interrupt good feeling among gentlemen."

"Got my last sixpence," retorted Joe, turning his pockets inside-out again. "No more use for me here tonight. That's the way of the world. How apt a scholar is our good friend Dustycoat, in this new school! Well, he was a good miller—no one ever disputed that—and it's plain to see that he is going to make a good landlord. I thought his heart was a little too soft; but the indurating process has begun; and, in less than ten years, if it isn't as hard as one of his old millstones, Joe Morgan is no prophet. Oh, you needn't knit your brows so, friend Simon, we're old friends; and friends are privileged to speak plain."

"I wish you'd go home. You're not yourself, tonight," said the landlord, a little coaxingly—for he saw that nothing was to be gained by quarrelling with Morgan. "Maybe my heart *is* growing harder," he added, with affected-good humour; "and it is time, perhaps. One of my weaknesses, I have heard even you say, was being too woman-hearted."

"No danger of that now," retorted Joe Morgan. "I've known a good many landlords in my time, but can't remember one that was troubled with the disease that once afflicted you."

Just at this moment the outer door was pushed open with a slow, hesitating motion; then a little pale face peered in, and a pair of soft blue eyes went searching about the room. Conversation was instantly hushed, and every face, excited with interest, turned toward the child, who had now stepped through the door. She was not over ten years of age; but it moved the heart to look upon the saddened expression of her young countenance, and the forced bravery therein, that scarcely overcame the native timidity so touchingly visible.

"Father!" I have never heard this word spoken in a voice that sent such a thrill along every nerve. It was full of sorrowful love—full of a tender concern that had its origin too deep for the heart of a child. As she spoke, the little one sprang across the room, and laying her hands upon the arm of Joe Morgan, lifted her eyes, that were ready to gush over with tears, to his face.

"Come, father! won't you come home?" I hear that low, pleading voice even now, and my heart gives a quicker throb. Poor child! Darkly shadowed was the sky that bent gloomily over thy young life.

Morgan arose, and suffered the child to lead him from the room. He seemed passive in her hands. I noticed that he thrust his fingers nervously into his pocket, and that a troubled look went over his face as they were withdrawn. His last sixpence was in the till of Simon Slade!

The first man who spoke was Harvey Green, and this not for a minute after the father and his child had vanished through the door.

"If I was in your place, landlord"—his voice was cold and unfeeling—"I'd pitch that fellow out of the bar-room the next time he stepped through the door. He's no busi-

---

[4]drink

ness here, in the first place; and, in the second, he doesn't know how to behave himself. There's no telling how much a vagabond like him injures a respectable house."

"I wish he would stay away," said Simon, with a perplexed air.

"I'd *make* him stay away," answered Green.

"That may be easier said than done," remarked Judge Lyman. "Our friend keeps a public-house, and can't just say who shall or who shall not come into it."

"But such a fellow has no business here. He's a good-for-nothing sot. If I kept a tavern, I'd refuse to sell him liquor."

"That you might do," said Judge Lyman—"and I presume your hint will not be lost on our friend Slade."

"He will have liquor, so long as he can get a cent to buy it with," remarked one of the company; "and I don't see why our landlord here, who has gone to so much expense to fit up a tavern, shouldn't have the sale of it as well as anybody else. Joe talks a little freely sometimes; but no one can say that he is quarrelsome. You've got to take him as he is, that's all."

"I'm one," retorted Harvey Green, with a slightly ruffled manner, "who is never disposed to take people as they are when they choose to render themselves disagreeable. If I was Mr. Slade, as I remarked in the beginning, I'd pitch that fellow into the road the next time he put his foot over my door-step."

"Not if I were present," remarked the other coolly.

Green was on his feet in a moment; and I saw, from the flash of his eyes, that he was a man of evil passions. Moving a pace or two in the direction of the other, he said sharply—

"What is that, sir?"

The individual against whom his anger was so suddenly aroused was dressed plainly, and had the appearance of a working-man. He was stout and muscular.

"I presume you heard my words. They were spoken distinctly," he replied, not moving from where he sat, nor seeming to be in the least disturbed. But there was cool defiance in the tones of his voice and in the steady look of his eyes.

"You're an impertinent fellow, and I'm half tempted to chastise you."

Green had scarcely finished the sentence, ere he was lying at full length upon the floor! The other had sprung upon him like a tiger, and with one blow from his heavy fist, struck him down as if he had been a child. For a moment or two, Green lay stunned and bewildered—then, starting up with a savage cry, that sounded more bestial than human, he drew a long knife from a concealed sheath, and attempted to stab his assailant; but the murderous purpose was not accomplished, for the other man, who had superior strength and coolness, saw the design, and with a well-directed blow almost broke the arm of Green, causing the knife to leave his hand and glide far across the room.

"I'm half tempted to wring your neck off," exclaimed the man, whose name was Lyon, now much excited; and seizing Green by the throat, he strangled him until his face grew black. "Draw a knife on me, ha! You murdering villain!" And he gripped him tighter.

Judge Lyman and the landlord now interfered, and rescued Green from the hands of his fully aroused antagonist. For some time they stood growling at each other, like two parted dogs, struggling to get free, in order to renew the conflict, but gradually cooled

off. In a little while Judge Lyman drew Green aside, and the two men left the bar-room
together. In the door, as they were retiring, the former slightly nodded to Willy Hammond, who soon followed them, going into the sitting-room; and from thence, as I could
perceive, upstairs, to an apartment above.

"Not after much good," I heard Lyon mutter to himself. "If Judge Hammond don't
look a little closer after that boy of his, he'll be sorry for it, that's all."

"Who is this Green?" I asked of Lyon, finding myself alone with him in the bar-
room, soon after.

"A black-leg,[5] I take it," was his unhesitating answer.

"Does Judge Lyman suspect his real character?"

"I don't know any thing about that; but, I wouldn't be afraid to bet ten dollars, that
if you could look in upon them now, you would find cards in their hands."

"What a school, and what teachers for the youth who just went with them!" I could
not helping remarking.

"Willy Hammond?"

"Yes."

"You may well say that. What can his father be thinking about to leave him exposed
to such influences!"

"He's one of the few who are in raptures about this tavern, because its erection has
slightly increased the value of his property about here; but, if he is not the loser of fifty
per cent. for every one gained, before ten years go by, I'm very much in error."

"How so?"

"It will prove, I fear, the open door to ruin for his son."

"That's bad," said I.

"Bad! It is awful to think of. There is not a finer young man in the country; nor one
with better mind and heart than Willy Hammond. So much the sadder will be his destruction. Ah, sir! this tavern-keeping is a curse to any place."

"But I thought, just now, that you spoke in favour of letting even the poor drunkard's
money go into our landlord's till, in order to encourage his commendable enterprise in
opening so good a tavern."

"We all speak with covert irony sometimes," answered the man, "as I did then. Poor
Joe Morgan! He is an old and early friend of Simon Slade. They were boys together, and
worked as millers under the same roof for many years. In fact, Joe's father owned the
mill, and the two learned their trade with him. When old Morgan died, the mill came into
Joe's hands. It was in rather a worn-out condition, and Joe went in debt for some pretty
thorough repairs and additions of machinery. By and by, Simon Slade, who was hired by
Joe to run the mill, received a couple of thousand dollars at the death of an aunt. This
sum enabled him to buy a share in the mill, which Morgan was very glad to sell in order
to get clear of his debt. Time passed on, and Joe left his milling interest almost entirely
in the care of Slade, who, it must be said in his favour, did not neglect the business. But
it somehow happened—I will not say unfairly—that, at the end of ten years, Joe Morgan
no longer owned a share in the mill. The whole property was in the hands of Slade. Peo-

<hr>
[5]swindler

ple did not much wonder at this; for while Slade was always to be found at the mill, industrious, active, and attentive to customers, Morgan was rarely seen on the premises. You would oftener find him in the woods, with a gun over his shoulder, or sitting by a trout brook, or lounging at the tavern. And yet everybody liked Joe; for he was companionable, quick-witted, and very kind-hearted. He would say sharp things, sometimes, when people manifested little meannesses; but there was so much honey in his gall, that bitterness rarely predominated.

"A year or two before his ownership in the mill ceased, Morgan married one of the sweetest girls in our town—Fanny Ellis, that was her name, and she could have had her pick of the young men. Everybody affected to wonder at her choice; and yet nobody really did wonder, for Joe was an attractive young man, take him as you would, and just the one to win the heart of a girl like Fanny. What if he had been seen, now and then, a little the worse for drink! What if he showed more fondness for pleasure than for business! Fanny did not look into the future with doubt or fear. She believed that her love was strong enough to win him from all evil allurements; and, as for this world's goods, they were matters in which her maiden fancies rarely busied themselves.

"Well. Dark days came for her, poor soul! And yet, in all the darkness of her earthly lot, she has never, it is said, been any thing but a loving, forbearing, self-denying wife to Morgan. And he—fallen as he is, and powerless in the grasp of the monster intemperance—has never, I am sure, hurt her with a cruel word. Had he added these, her heart would, long ere this, have broken. Poor Joe Morgan! Poor Fanny! Oh, what a curse is this drink!"

The man, warming with his theme, had spoken with an eloquence I had not expected from his lips. Slightly overmastered by his feelings, he paused for a moment or two, and then added.

"It was unfortunate for Joe, at least, that Slade sold his mill, and became a tavern-keeper; for Joe had a sure berth, and wages regularly paid. He didn't always stick to his work, but would go off on a spree every now and then; but Slade bore with all this, and worked harder himself to make up for his hand's shortcoming. And no matter what deficiency the little store-room at home might show, Fanny Morgan never found her meal barrel empty without knowing where to get it replenished.

"But, after Slade sold the mill, a sad change took place. The new owner was little disposed to pay wages to a hand who would not give him all his time during working hours; and in less than two weeks from the day he took possession, Morgan was discharged. Since then, he has been working about at one odd job and another, earning scarcely enough to buy the liquor it requires to feed the inordinate thirst that is consuming him. I am not disposed to blame Simon Slade for the wrong-doing of Morgan; but here is a simple fact in the case—if he had kept on at the useful calling of a miller, he would have saved this man's family from want, suffering, and a lower deep of misery than that into which they have already fallen. I merely state it, and you can draw your own conclusion. It is one of the many facts, on the other side of this tavern question, which it will do no harm to mention. I have noted a good many facts besides, and one is, that before Slade opened the "Sickle and Sheaf," he did all in his power to save his early friend from the curse of intemperance; now he has become his tempter. Heretofore, it was his hand that provided the means for his family to live in some small degree of comfort; now he takes the poor pittance the wretched man earns, and dropping it in his till, forgets the wife and children at home who are hungry for the bread this money should have purchased.

"Joe Morgan, fallen as he is, sir, is no fool. His mind sees quickly yet; and he rarely utters a sentiment that is not full of meaning. When he spoke of Slade's heart growing as hard in ten years as one of his old millstones, he was not uttering words at random, nor merely indulging in a harsh sentiment, little caring whether it were closely applicable or not. That the indurating process had begun, he, alas! was too sadly conscious."

The landlord had been absent from the room for some time. He left soon after Judge Lyman, Harvey Green, and Willy Hammond withdrew, and I did not see him again during the evening. His son Frank was left to attend at the bar; no very hard task, for not more than half a dozen called in to drink from the time Morgan left until the bar was closed.

While Mr. Lyon was giving me the brief history just recorded, I noticed a little incident that caused a troubled feeling to pervade my mind. After a man, for whom the landlord's son had prepared a fancy drink, had nearly emptied his glass, he sat it down upon the counter and went out. A tablespoonful or two remained in the glass, and I noticed Frank, after smelling at it two or three times, put the glass to his lips and sip the sweetened liquor. The flavour proved agreeable; for after tasting it, he raised the glass again and drained every drop.

"Frank!" I heard a low voice, in a warning tone, pronounce the name, and glancing toward a door partly opened, that led from the inside of the bar to the yard, I saw the face of Mrs. Slade. It had the same troubled expression I had noticed before, but now blended with more of anxiety.

The boy went out at the call of his mother; and when a new customer entered, I noticed that Flora, the daughter, came in to wait upon him. I noticed, too, that while she poured out the liquor, there was a heightened colour on her face, in which I fancied that I saw a tinge of shame. It is certain that she was not in the least gracious to the person on whom she was waiting; and that there was little heart in her manner of performing the task.

Ten o'clock found me alone and musing in the bar-room over the occurrences of the evening. Of all the incidents, that of the entrance of Joe Morgan's child kept the most prominent place in my thoughts. The picture of that mournful little face was ever before me; and I seemed all the while to hear the word "Father," uttered so touchingly, and yet with such a world of childish tenderness. And the man, who would have opposed the most stubborn resistance to his fellow men, had they sought to force him from the room, going passively, almost meekly out, led by that little child—I could not, for a time, turn my thoughts from the image thereof! And then thought bore me to the wretched home, back to which the gentle, loving child had taken her father, and my heart grew faint in me as imagination busied itself with all the misery there.

And Willy Hammond. The little that I had heard and seen of him greatly interested me in his favour. Ah! upon what dangerous ground was he treading. How many pitfalls awaited his feet—how near they were to the brink of a fearful precipice, down which to fall was certain destruction. How beautiful had been his life-promise! How fair the opening day of his existence! Alas! the clouds were gathering already, and the low rumble of the distant thunder presaged the coming of a fearful tempest. Was there none to warn him of the danger? Alas! all might now come too late, for so few who enter the path in which his steps were treading will hearken to friendly counsel, or heed the solemn warning. Where was he now? This question recurred over and over again. He had left the bar-room with Judge Lyman and Green early in the evening, and had not made his appearance since. Who and what was Green? And Judge Lyman, was he a man of principle? One with whom it was safe to trust a youth like Willy Hammond?

While I mused thus, the bar-room door opened, and a man past the prime of life, with a somewhat florid face, which gave a strong relief to the gray, almost white hair that, suffered to grow freely, was pushed back, and lay in heavy masses on his coat collar, entered with a hasty step. He was almost venerable in appearance; yet, there was in his dark, quick eyes the brightness of unquenched loves, the fires of which were kindled at the altars of selfishness and sensuality. This I saw at a glance. There was a look of concern on his face, as he threw his eyes around the bar-room; and he seemed disappointed, I thought, at finding it empty.

"Is Simon Slade here?"

As I answered in the negative, Mrs. Slade entered through the door that opened from the yard, and stood behind the counter.

"Ah, Mrs. Slade! Good evening, madam!" he said.

"Good evening, Judge Hammond."

"Is your husband at home?"

"I believe he is," answered Mrs. Slade. "I think he's somewhere about the house."

"Ask him to step here, will you?"

Mrs. Slade went out. Nearly five minutes went by, during which time Judge Hammond paced the floor of the bar-room uneasily. Then the landlord made his appearance. The free, open, manly, self-satisfied expression of his countenance, which I had remarked on alighting from the stage in the afternoon, was gone. I noticed at once the change, for it was striking. He did not look steadily into the face of Judge Hammond, who asked him in a low voice, if his son had been there during the evening.

"He was here," said Slade.

"When?"

"He came in some time after dark and stayed, maybe, an hour."

"And hasn't been here since?"

"It's nearly two hours since he left the bar-room," replied the landlord.

Judge Hammond seemed perplexed. There was a degree of evasion in Slade's manner that he could hardly help noticing. To me it was all apparent, for I had lively suspicions that made my observation acute.

Judge Hammond crossed his arms behind him, and took three or four strides about the floor.

"Was Judge Lyman here to-night?" he then asked.

"He was," answered Slade.

"Did he and Willy go out together?"

The question seemed an unexpected one for the landlord. Slade appeared slightly confused, and did not answer promptly.

"I—I rather think they did," he said, after a brief hesitation.

"Ah, well! Perhaps he is at Judge Lyman's. I will call over there."

And Judge Hammond left the bar-room.

"Would you like to retire, sir?" said the landlord, now turning to me, with a forced smile—I saw that it was forced.

"If you please," I answered.

He lit a candle and conducted me to my room, where, overwearied with the day's exertion, I soon fell asleep, and did not awake until the sun was shining brightly into my windows.

I remained at the village a portion of the day, but saw nothing of the parties in whom the incidents of the previous evening had awakened a lively interest. At four o'clock I left in the stage, and did not visit Cedarville again for a year.

❧ Night the Second

THE CHANGES OF A YEAR

A cordial grasp of the hand and a few words of hearty welcome greeted me as I alighted from the stage at the "Sickle and Sheaf," on my next visit to Cedarville. At the first glance, I saw no change in the countenance, manner, or general bearing of Simon Slade, the landlord. With him, the year seemed to have passed like a pleasant summer day. His face was round, and full, and rosy, and his eyes sparkled with that good-humour which flows from intense self-satisfaction. Everything about him seemed to say—"All right with myself and the world."

I had scarcely expected this. From what I saw during my last brief sojourn at the "Sickle and Sheaf," the inference was natural, that elements had been called into activity, which must produce changes adverse to those pleasant states of mind that threw an almost perpetual sunshine over the landlord's countenance. How many hundreds of times had I thought of Joe Morgan and Willy Hammond—of Frank, and the temptations to which a bar-room exposed him. The heart of Slade must, indeed, be as hard as one of his old mill-stones, if he could remain an unmoved witness of the corruption and degradation of these.

"My fears have outrun the actual progress of things," said I to myself, with a sense of relief, as I mused alone in the still neatly arranged sitting-room, after the landlord, who sat and chatted for a few minutes, had left me. "There is, I am willing to believe, a basis of good in this man's character, which has led him to remove, as far as possible, the more palpable evils that ever attach themselves to a house of public entertainment. He had but entered on the business last year. There was much to be learned, pondered, and corrected. Experience, I doubt not, has led to many important changes in the manner of conducting the establishment, and especially in what pertains to the bar."

As I thought thus, my eyes glanced through the half open door, and rested on the face of Simon Slade. He was standing behind his bar—evidently alone in the room—with his head bent in a musing attitude. At first I was in some doubt as to the identity of the singularly changed countenance. Two deep perpendicular seams lay sharply defined on his forehead—the arch of his eyebrows was gone, and from each corner of his compressed lips, lines were seen reaching halfway to the chin. Blending with a slightly troubled expression, was a strongly marked selfishness, evidently brooding over the consummation of its purpose. For some moments I sat gazing on this face, half doubting at times if it were really that of Simon Slade. Suddenly, a gleam flashed over it—an ejaculation was uttered, and one clenched hand brought down, with a sharp stroke, into the open palm of the other. The landlord's mind had reached a conclusion, and was resolved upon action. There were no warm rays in the gleam of light that irradiated his countenance—at least none for my heart, which felt under them an almost icy coldness.

"Just the man I was thinking about," I heard the landlord say, as some one entered the bar, while his whole manner underwent a sudden change.

"The old saying is true," was answered in a voice, the tones of which were familiar to my ears.

"Thinking of the old Harry?" said Slade.

"Yes."

"True, literally, in the present case," I heard the landlord remark, though in a much lower tone; "for, if you are not the devil himself, you can't be farther removed than a second cousin."

A low, gurgling laugh met this little sally. There was something in it so unlike a human laugh, that it caused my blood to trickle, for a moment, coldly along my veins.

I heard nothing more except the murmur of voices in the bar, for a hand shut the partly opened door that led from the sitting-room.

Whose was that voice? I recalled its tones, and tried to fix in my thought the person to whom it belonged, but was unable to do so. I was not very long in doubt, for on stepping out upon the porch in front of the tavern, the well-remembered face of Harvey Green presented itself. He stood in the bar-room door, and was talking earnestly to Slade, whose back was toward me. I saw that he recognised me, although I had not passed a word with him on the occasion of my former visit; and there was a lighting up of his countenance as if about to speak—but I withdrew my eyes from his face to avoid the unwelcome greeting. When I looked at him again, I saw that he was regarding me with a sinister glance, which was instantly withdrawn. In what broad, black characters was the word TEMPTER written on his face! How was it possible for any one to look thereon, and not read the warning inscription!

Soon after, he withdrew into the bar-room, and the landlord came and took a seat near me on the porch.

"How is the Sickle and Sheaf coming on?" I inquired.

"First-rate," was the answer—"First-rate."

"As well as you expected?"

"Better."

"Satisfied with your experiment."

"Perfectly. Couldn't get me back to the rumbling old mill again, if you were to make me a present of it."

"What of the mill?" I asked. "How does the new owner come on?"

"About as I thought it would be."

"Not doing very well?"

"How could it be expected, when he didn't know enough of the milling business to grind a bushel of wheat right. He lost half of the custom I transferred to him in less than three months. Then he broke his main shaft, and it took over three weeks to get in a new one. Half of his remaining customers discovered by this time, that they could get far better meal from their grain at Harwood's mill near Lynwood, and so did not care to trouble him any more. The upshot of the whole matter is, he broke down next, and had to sell the mill at a heavy loss."

"Who has it now?"

"Judge Hammond is the purchaser."

"He is going to rent it, I suppose?"

"No; I believe he means to turn it into some kind of a factory—and, I rather think, will connect therewith a distillery. This is a fine grain-growing country, as you know. If he does set up a distillery, he'll make a fine thing of it. Grain has been too low in this section for some years: this all the farmers have felt, and they are very much pleased at the idea. It will help them wonderfully. I always thought my mill a great thing for the farmers; but what I did for them was a mere song compared to the advantage of an extensive distillery."

"Judge Hammond is one of your richest men?"

"Yes—the richest in the county. And what is more, he's a shrewd, far-seeing man, and knows how to multiply his riches."

"How is his son Willy coming on?"

"Oh! first-rate."

The landlord's eyes fell under the searching look I bent upon him.

"How old is he now?"

"Just twenty."

"A critical age," I remarked.

"So people say; but I didn't find it so," answered Slade, a little distantly.

"The impulses within and the temptations without, are the measure of its dangers. At his age, you were, no doubt, daily employed at hard work."

"I was, and no mistake."

"Thousands and hundred of thousands are indebted to useful work, occupying many hours through each day, and leaving them with wearied bodies at night, for their safe passage from yielding youth to firm, resisting manhood. It might not be with you as it is now, had leisure and freedom to go in and out when you pleased, been offered at the age of nineteen."

"I can't tell as to that," said the landlord, shrugging his shoulders. "But I don't see that Willy Hammond is in any especial danger. He is a young man with many admirable qualities—is social—liberal—generous almost to a fault—but has good common sense, and wit enough, I take it, to keep out of harm's way."

A man passing the house at the moment, gave Simon Slade an opportunity to break off a conversation, that was not, I could see, altogether agreeable. As he left me, I arose and stepped into the bar-room. Frank, the landlord's son, was behind the bar. He had grown considerably in the year—and from a rather delicate, innocent-looking boy, to a stout, bold lad. His face was rounder, and had a gross, sensual expression, that showed itself particularly about the mouth. The man Green was standing beside the bar talking to him, and I noticed that Frank laughed heartily, at some low, half obscene remarks that he was making. In the midst of these, Flora, the sister of Frank, a really beautiful girl, came in to get something from the bar. Green spoke to her familiarly, and Flora answered him with a perceptibly heightening colour.

I glanced toward Frank, half expecting to see an indignant flush on his young face. But no—he looked on with a smile! "Ah!" thought I, "have the boy's pure impulses so soon died out in this fatal atmosphere? Can he bear to see those evil eyes—he knows they are evil—rest upon the face of his sister? or to hear those lips, only a moment since polluted with vile words, address her with the familarity of friend?"

"Fine girl, that sister of yours, Frank! Fine girl!" said Green, after Flora had withdrawn—speaking of her with about as much respect in his voice as if he were praising a fleet racer or favourite hound.

The boy smiled, with a pleased air.

"I must try and find her a good husband, Frank. I wonder if she wouldn't have me?"

"You'd better ask her," said the boy, laughing.

"I would, if I thought there was any chance for me."

"Nothing like trying. Faint heart never won fair lady," returned Frank, more with the air of a man than a boy. How fast he was growing old!

"A banter, by George!" exclaimed Green, slapping his hands together. "You're a great boy, Frank! a great boy! I shall have to talk to your father about you. Coming on too fast. Have to be put back in your lessons—hey!"

And Green winked at the boy, and shook his finger at him. Frank laughed in a pleased way, as he replied—

"I guess I'll do."

"I guess you will," said Green, as, satisfied with his colloquy, he turned off and left the bar-room.

"Have something to drink, sir?" inquired Frank, addressing me in a bold, free way.

I shook my head.

"Here's a newspaper," he added.

I took the paper and sat down—not to read, but to observe. Two or three men soon came in, and spoke in a very familiar way to Frank, who was presently busy setting out the liquors they had called for. Their conversation, interlarded with much that was profane and vulgar, was of horses, horse-racing, gunning, and the like, to all of which the young bar-keeper lent an attentive ear, putting in a word now and then, and showing an intelligence in such matters quite beyond his age. In the midst thereof, Mr. Slade made his appearance. His presence caused a marked change in Frank, who retired from his place among the men, a step or two outside of the bar, and did not make a remark while his father remained. It was plain from this, that Mr. Slade was not only aware of Frank's dangerous precocity, but had already marked his forwardness by rebuke.

So far, all that I had seen and heard impressed me unfavorably, notwithstanding the declaration of Simon Slade, that everything about the "Sickle and Sheaf" was coming on "first-rate," and that he was "perfectly satisfied" with his experiment. Why, even if the man had gained, in money, fifty thousand dollars by tavern-keeping in a year, he had lost a jewel in the innocence of his boy that was beyond all valuation. "Perfectly satisfied?" Impossible! He was not perfectly satisfied. How could he be? The look thrown upon Frank when he entered the bar-room, and saw him "hale fellow, well met," with three or four idle, profane, drinking customers, contradicted that assertion.

After supper, I took a seat in the bar-room, to see how life moved on in that place of rendezvous for the surface-population of Cedarville. Interest enough in the characters I had met there a year before remained, for me to choose this way of spending the time, instead of visiting at the house of a gentleman who had kindly invited me to pass an evening with his family.

The bar-room custom, I soon found, had largely increased in a year. It now required, for a good part of the time, the active services of both the landlord and his son to meet the calls for liquor. What pained me most, was to see the large number of lads and young men who came in to lounge and drink; and there was scarcely one of them whose face did not show marks of sensuality, or whose language was not marred by obscenity, profanity, or vulgar slang. The subjects of conversation were varied enough, though politics was the most prominent. In regard to politics, I heard nothing in the least instructive; but only abuse of individuals and dogmatism on public measures. They were all exceedingly confident in assertion; but I listened in vain for exposition, or even for demonstrative facts. He who asseverated in the most positive manner, and swore the hardest, carried the day in the petty contests.

I noticed, early in the evening, and at a time when all the inmates of the room were in the best possible humour with themselves, the entrance of an elderly man, on whose face I instantly read a deep concern. It was one of those mild, yet strongly marked faces, that strike you at a glance. The forehead was broad, the eyes large and far back in their sockets, the lips full but firm. You saw evidences of a strong, but well balanced character. As he came in, I noticed a look of intelligence pass from one to another; and then the eyes of two or three were fixed upon a young man who was seated not far from me, with his back to the entrance, playing at dominos. He had a glass of ale by his side. The old man searched about the room for some moments, before his glance rested upon the individual I have mentioned. My eyes were full upon his face, as he advanced toward him, yet unseen. Upon it was not a sign of angry excitement, but a most touching sorrow.

"Edward!" he said, as he laid his hand gently on the young man's shoulder. The latter started at the voice, and crimsoned deeply. A few moments he sat irresolute.

"Edward, my son!" It would have been a cold, hard heart indeed that softened not under the melting tenderness of these tones. The call was irresistible, and obedience a necessity. The powers of evil had, yet, too feeble a grasp on the young man's heart to hold him in thrall. Rising with a half-reluctant manner, and with a shamefacedness that it was impossible to conceal, he retired as quietly as possible. The notice of only a few in the bar-room was attracted by the incident.

"I can tell you what," I heard the individual, with whom the young man had been playing at dominos, remark—himself not twenty years of age—"if my old man were to make a fool of himself in this way—sneaking around after me in bar-rooms—he'd get only his trouble for his pains. I'd like to see him try it, though! There'd be a nice time of it, I guess. Wouldn't I creep off with him, as meek as a lamb! Ho! ho!"

"Who is that old gentleman who came in just now?" I inquired of the person who thus commented on the incident which had just occurred.

"Mr. Hargrove is his name."

"And that was his son?"

"Yes; and I'm only sorry he doesn't possess a little more spirit."

"How old is he?"

"About twenty."

"Not of legal age, then?"

"He's old enough to be his own master."

"The law says differently," I suggested.

In answer, the young man cursed the law, snapping his fingers in its imaginary face as he did so.

"At least you will admit," said I, "that Edward Hargrove, in the use of a liberty to go where he pleases, and do what he pleases, exhibits but small discretion."

"I will admit no such thing. What harm is there, I would like to know, in a social little game such as we were playing? There were no stakes—we were not gambling."

I pointed to the half-emptied glass of ale left by young Hargrove.

"Oh! oh!" half sneered, half laughed a man, twice the age of the one I had addressed, who sat near by, listening to our conversation. I looked at him for a moment, and then said—

"The great danger lies there, without doubt. If it were only a glass of ale and a game of dominos—but it doesn't stop there, and well the young man's father knows it."

"Perhaps he does," was answered. "I remember him in his younger days; and a pretty high boy he was. He didn't stop at a glass of ale and a game at dominos; not he! I've seen him as drunk as a lord many a time; and many a time at a horse-race, or cock-fight, betting with the bravest. I was only a boy, though a pretty old boy; but I can tell you, Hargrove was no saint."

"I wonder not, then, that he is anxious for his son," was my remark. "He knows well the lurking dangers in the path he seems inclined to enter."

"I don't see that they have done him much harm. He sowed his wild oats—then got married, and settled down into a good, substantial citizen. A little too religious and pharisaical, I always thought; but upright in his dealings. He had his pleasures in early life, as was befitting the season of youth—why not let his son taste of the same agreeable fruit? He's wrong, sir—wrong! And I've said as much to Ned. I only wish the boy had showed the right spunk this evening, and told the old man to go home about his business."

"So do I," chimed in the young disciple in this bad school. "It's what I'd say to my old man, in double-quick time, if he was to come hunting after me."

"He knows better than to do that," said the other, in a way that let me deeper into the young man's character.

"Indeed he does. He's tried his hand on me once or twice during the last year, but found it wouldn't do, no how; Tom Peters is out of his leading-strings."

"And can drink his glass with any one, and not be a grain the worse for it."

"Exactly, old boy!" said Peters, slapping his preceptor on the knee. "Exactly! I'm not one of your weak-headed ones. Oh no!"

"Look here, Joe Morgan!"—the half angry voice of Simon Slade now rung through the bar-room,—"just take yourself off home!"

I had not observed the entrance of this person. He was standing at the bar, with an emptied glass in his hand. A year had made no improvement in his appearance. On the contrary, his clothes were more worn and tattered; his countenance more sadly marred.

What he had said to irritate the landlord, I know not; but Slade's face was fiery with passion, and his eyes glared threateningly at the poor besotted one, who showed not the least inclination to obey.

"Off with you, I say! And never show your face here again. I won't have such low vagabonds as you are about my house. If you can't keep decent and stay decent, don't intrude yourself here."

"A rum-seller talk of decency!" retorted Morgan. "Pah! You were a decent man once, and a good miller into the bargain. But that time's past and gone. Decency died out when you exchanged the pick and facing-hammer for the glass and muddler. Decency! Pah! How you talk! As if it were any more decent to sell rum than to drink it."

There was so much of biting contempt in the tones, as well as the words of the half intoxicated man, that Slade, who had himself been drinking rather more freely than usual, was angered beyond self-control. Catching up an empty glass from the counter, he hurled it with all his strength at the head of Joe Morgan. The missive just grazed one of his temples, and flew by on its dangerous course. The quick sharp cry of a child startled the air, followed by exclamations of alarm and horror from many voices.

"It's Joe Morgan's child!" "He's killed her!" "Good heavens!" Such were the exclamations that rang through the room. I was among the first to reach the spot where a little girl, just gliding in through the door, had been struck on the forehead by the glass, which had cut a deep gash, and stunned her into insensibility. The blood flowed instantly from the wound, and covered her face, which presented a shocking appearance. As I lifted her from the floor, upon which she had fallen, Morgan, into whose very soul the piercing cry of his child had penetrated, stood by my side, and grappled his arms around her insensible form, uttering as he did so heart-touching moans and lamentations.

"What's the matter? Oh, what's the matter?" It was a woman's voice, speaking in frightened tones.

"It's nothing! Just go out, will you, Ann!" I heard the landlord say.

But his wife—it was Mrs. Slade—having heard the shrieks of pain and terror uttered by Morgan's child, had come running into the bar-room-heeded not his words, but pressed forward into the little group that stood around the bleeding girl.

"Run for Doctor Green, Frank," she cried in an imperative voice, the moment her eyes rested on the little one's bloody face.

Frank came around from behind the bar, in obedience to the word; but his father gave a partial countermand, and he stood still. Upon observing which, his mother repeated the order, even more emphatically.

"Why don't you jump, you young rascal!" exclaimed Harvey Green. "The child may be dead before the doctor can get here."

Frank hesitated no longer, but disappeared instantly through the door.

"Poor, poor child!" Almost sobbed Mrs. Slade, as she lifted the insensible form from my arms. "How did it happen? Who struck her?"

"Who? Curse him! Who but Simon Slade?" answered Joe Morgan, through his clenched teeth.

The look of anguish, mingled with bitter reproach, instantly thrown upon the landlord by his wife, can hardly be forgotten by any who saw it that night.

"Oh, Simon! Simon! And has it come to this already?" What a world of bitter memories, and sad forebodings of evil, did that little sentence express. "To this already"—Ah! In the downward way, how rapidly the steps do tread—how fast the progress!

"Bring me a basin of water, and a towel, quickly!" she now exclaimed.

The water was brought, and in a little while the face of the child lay pure and white as snow against her bosom. The wound from which the blood had flowed so freely was found on the upper part of the forehead, a little to the side, and extending several inches back, along the top of the head. As soon as the blood stains were wiped away, and the effusion partially stopped, Mrs. Slade carried the still insensible body into the next room, whither the distressed, and now completely sobered father, accompanied her. I went with them, but Slade remained behind.

The arrival of the doctor was soon followed by the restoration of life to the inanimate body. He happened to be at home, and came instantly. He had just taken the last stitch in the wound, which required to be drawn together, and was applying strips of adhesive plaster, when the hurried entrance of some one caused me to look up. What an apparition met my eyes! A woman stood in the door, with a face in which maternal anxiety and terror blended fearfully. Her countenance was like ashes—her eyes straining wildly—her lips aparts, while the panting breath almost hissed through them.

"Joe! Joe! What is it? Where is Mary? Is she dead?" were her eager inquiries.

"No, Fanny," answered Joe Morgan, starting up from where he was actually kneeling by the side of the reviving little one, and going quickly to his wife. "She's better now. It's a bad hurt, but the doctor says it's nothing dangerous. Poor, dear child!"

The pale face of the mother grew paler—she gasped—caught for breath two or three times—a low shudder ran through her frame—and then she lay white and pulseless in the arms of her husband. As the doctor applied restoratives, I had opportunity to note more particularly the appearance of Mrs. Morgan. Her person was very slender, and her face so attenuated that it might almost be called shadowy. Her hair, which was a rich chestnut brown, with a slight golden lustre, had fallen from her comb, and now lay all over her neck and bosom in beautiful luxuriance. Back from her full temples it had been smoothed away by the hand of Morgan, that all the while moved over her brow and temples with a caressing motion that I saw was unconscious, and which revealed the tenderness of feeling with which, debased as he was, he regarded the wife of his youth, and the long suffering companion of his later and evil days. Her dress was plain and coarse, but clean and well fitting; and about her whole person was an air of neatness and taste. She could not now be called beautiful; yet in her marred features—marred by suffering and grief—were many lineaments of beauty; and much that told of a pure, true woman's heart beating in her bosom. Life came slowly back to the stilled heart, and it was nearly half an hour before the circle of motion was fully restored.

Then, the twain, with their child, tenderly borne in the arms of her father, went sadly homeward, leaving more than one heart heavier for their visit.

I saw more of the landlord's wife on this occasion than before. She had acted with a promptness and humanity that impressed me very favourably. It was plain, from her exclamations on learning that her husband's hand inflicted the blow that came so near destroying the child's life, that her faith for good in the tavern-keeping experiment had never been strong. I had already inferred as much. Her face, the few times I had seen her, wore a troubled look; and I could never forget its expression, nor her anxious, warning voice, when she discovered Frank sipping the dregs from a glass in the bar-room.

It is rarely, I believe, that wives consent freely to the opening of taverns by their husbands; and the determination on the part of the latter to do so, is not infrequently attended with a breach of confidence and good feeling, never afterward fully healed. Men look close to the money result; women to the moral consequences. I doubt if there be one dram-seller in ten, between whom and his wife there exists a good understanding—to say nothing of genuine affection. And, in the exceptional cases, it will generally be found that the wife is as mercenary, or careless of the public good, as her husband. I have known some women to set up grog-shops; but they were women of bad principles and worse hearts. I remember one case, where a woman, with a sober, church-going husband, opened a dram-shop. The husband opposed, remonstrated, begged, threatened—but all to no purpose. The wife, by working for the clothing stores, had earned and saved about three hundred dollars. The love of money, in the slow process of accumulation, had been awakened; and, in ministering to the depraved appetites of men who loved drink and neglected their families, she saw a quicker mode of acquiring the gold she coveted. And so the dram-shop was opened. And what was the result? The husband quit going to church. He had no heart for that; for, even on the Sabbath-day, the fiery stream was stayed not in his house. Next he began to tipple. Soon, alas! the subtle poison so pervaded his system that morbid desire came; and then he moved along quick-footed in the way to ruin. In less than three years, I think, from the time the grog-shop was opened by his wife, he was in a drunkard's grave. A year or two more, and the pit that was digged for others by the hand of the wife, she fell into herself. Ever breathing an atmosphere, poisoned by the fumes of liquor, the love of tasting it was gradually formed, and she too, in the end, became a slave to the Demon of Drink. She died, at last, poor as a beggar in the street. Ah! this liquor-selling is the way to ruin; and they who open the gates, as well as those who enter the downward path, alike go to destruction. But this is digressing.

After Joe Morgan and his wife left the "Sickle and Sheaf," with that gentle child, who, as I afterward learned, had not, for a year or more, laid her little head to sleep until her father returned home—and who, if he stayed out beyond a certain hour, would go for him, and lead him back, a very angel of love and patience—I re-entered the bar-room, to see how life was passing there. Not one of all I had left in the room remained. The incident which had occurred was of so painful a nature, that no further unalloyed pleasure was to be had there during the evening, and so each had retired. In his little kingdom the landlord sat alone, his head resting on his hand, and his face shaded from the light. The whole aspect of the man was that of one in self-humiliation. As I entered he raised his head, and turned his face toward me. Its expression was painful.

"Rather an unfortunate affair," said he. "I'm angry with myself, and sorry for the poor child. But she'd no business here. As for Joe Morgan, it would take a saint to bear his tongue when once set a going by liquor. I wish he'd stay away from the house. Nobody wants his company. Oh dear!

The ejaculation, or rather groan, that closed the sentence, showed how little Slade was satisfied with himself, notwithstanding this feeble effort at self-justification.

"His thirst for liquor draws him hither," I remarked. "The attraction of your bar to his appetite is like that of the magnet to the needle. He cannot stay away."

"He *must* stay away!" exclaimed the landlord, with some vehemence of tone, striking his fist upon the table by which he sat. "He *must* stay away! There is scarcely an evening that he does not ruffle my temper, and mar good feelings in all the company. Just see what he provoked me to do this evening. I might have killed the child. It makes my blood run cold to think of it! Yes, sir—he must stay away. If no better can be done, I'll hire a man to stand at the door and keep him out."

"He never troubled you at the mill," said I. "No man was required at the mill door?"

"No!" And the landlord gave emphasis to the word by an oath, ejaculated with a heartiness that almost startled me. I had not heard him swear before. "No! the great trouble was to get him and keep him there, the good-for-nothing, idle fellow!"

"I'm afraid," I ventured to suggest, "that things don't go on quite so smoothly here as they did at the mill. Your customers are of a different class."

"I don't know about that; why not?" He did not just relish my remark.

"Between quiet, thrifty, substantial farmers, and drinking bar-room loungers, are many degrees of comparison."

"Excuse me, sir!" Simon Slade elevated his person. "The men who visit my barroom, as a general thing, are quite as respectable, moral, and substantial as any who came to the mill—and I believe more so. The first people in the place, sir, are to be found here. Judge Lyman and Judge Hammond; Lawyer Wilks and Doctor Maynard; Mr. Grand and Mr. Lee; and dozens of others—all our first people. No, sir; you mustn't judge all by vagabonds like Joe Morgan."

There was a testy spirit manifested that I did not care to provoke. I could have met his assertion with facts and inferences of a character to startle any one occupying his position, who was in a calm, reflective state; but to argue with him then would have been worse than idle: and so I let him talk on until the excitement occasioned by my words died out for want of new fuel.

⤷ Night the Third

JOE MORGAN'S CHILD

"I don't see any thing of your very particular friend, Joe Morgan, this evening," said Harvey Green, leaning on the bar and speaking to Slade. It was the night succeeding that on which the painful and exciting scene with the child had occurred.

"No," was answered—and to the word was added a profane imprecation. "No; and if he'll just keep away from here, he may go to—on a hard trotting horse and a porcupine saddle as fast as he pleases. He's tried my patience beyond endurance, and my mind is made up, that he gets no more drams at this bar. I've borne his vile tongue and seen my company annoyed by him just as long as I mean to stand it. Last night decided me. Suppose I'd killed that child?"

"You'd have had trouble then, and no mistake."

"Wouldn't I? Blast her little picture! What business has she creeping in here every night?"

"She must have a nice kind of a mother," remarked Green, with a cold sneer.

"I don't know what she is now," said Slade, a slight touch of feeling in his voice—"heart-broken, I suppose. I couldn't look at her last night; it made me sick. But, there was a time when Fanny Morgan was the loveliest and best woman in Cedarville. I'll say that for her. Oh dear! What a life her miserable husband has caused her to lead."

"Better that he were dead and out of the way."

"Better a thousand times," answered Slade. "If he'd only fall down some night and break his neck, it would be a blessing to his family."

"And to you in particular," laughed Green.

"You may be sure it wouldn't cost me a large sum for mourning," was the unfeeling response.

Let us leave the bar-room of the "Sickle and Sheaf," and its cold-hearted inmates, and look in upon the family of Joe Morgan, and see how it is in the home of the poor inebriate. We will pass by a quick transition.

"Joe!" The thin white hand of Mrs. Morgan clasps the arm of her husband, who has arisen up suddenly, and now stands by the partly opened door. "Don't go out to-night, Joe. Please, don't go out."

"Father!" A feeble voice calls from the corner of an old settee, where little Mary lies with her head bandaged.

"Well, I won't then!" is replied—not angrily, nor even fretfully—but in a kind voice.

"Come and sit by me, father." How tenderly, yet how full of concern is that low, sweet voice. "Come, won't you?"

"Yes, dear."

"Now hold my hand, father."

Joe takes the hand of little Mary, that instantly tightens upon his.

"You won't go away and leave me to-night, will you, father? Say you won't."

"How very hot your hand is, dear. Does your head ache?"

"A little; but it will soon feel better."

Up into the swollen and disfigured face of the fallen father, the large, earnest blue eyes of the child are raised. She does not see the marred lineaments; but, only the beloved countenance of her parent.

"Dear father!"

"What, love?"

"I wish you'd promise me something."

"What, dear?"

"Will you promise?"

"I can't say until I hear your request. If I can promise, I will."

"Oh! you can promise—you can, father!"

"How very hot your hand is, dear. Does your head ache?"

"What is it, love?"

"That you'll never go into Simon Slade's bar any more."

The child raises herself, evidently with a painful effort; and leans nearer to her father.

Joe shakes his head, and poor Mary drops back upon her pillow with a sigh. Her lids fall, and the long lashes lie strongly relieved on her colourless cheeks.

"I won't go there to-night, dear. So let your heart be at rest."

Mary's lids unclose, and two round drops, released from their clasp, glide slowly over her face.

"Thank you, father—thank you. Mother will be so glad."

The eyes closed again; and the father moved uneasily. His heart is touched. There is a struggle within him. It is on his lips to say that he will never drink at the "Sickle and Sheaf" again; but resolution just lacks the force of utterance.

"Father!"

"Well, dear!"

"I don't think I'll be well enough to go out in two or three days. You know the doctor said that I would have to keep very still, for I had a great deal of fever."

"Yes, poor child."

"Now, won't you promise me one thing?"

"What is it, dear?"

"Not to go out in the evening until I get well."

Joe Morgan hesitated.

"Just promise me that, father. It won't be long. I shall be up again in a little while."

How well the father knows what is in the heart of his child. Her fears are all for him. Who is to go after her poor father, and lead him home when the darkness of inebriety is on his spirit, and external perception so dulled that not skill enough remains to shun the harm that lies in his path.

"Do promise just that, father, dear."

He cannot resist the pleading voice and look.

"I promise it, Mary; so shut your eyes now and go to sleep. I'm afraid this fever will increase."

"Oh! I'm so glad—so glad!"

Mary does not clasp her hands, nor show strong external signs of pleasure; but how full of a pure, unselfish joy is that low murmured ejaculation, spoken in the depths of her spirit, as well as syllabled by her tongue!

Mrs. Morgan has been no unconcerned witness of all this; but knowing the child's influence over her father, she has not ventured a word. More was to be gained, she was sure, by silence on her part; and so she has kept silent. Now she comes nearer to them, and says, as she lets a hand rest on the shoulder of her husband—

"You feel better for that promise, already; I know you do."

He looks up to her, and smiles faintly. He does feel better, but is hardly willing to acknowledge it.

Soon after Mary is sleeping. It does not escape the observation of Mrs. Morgan that her husband grows restless; for he gets up suddenly, every now and then, and walks quickly across the room, as if in search of something. Then sits down, listlessly—sighs—stretches himself, and says—"Oh dear!" What shall she do for him? How is the want of his accustomed evening stimulus to be met? She thinks, and questions, and grieves inwardly. Poor Joe Morgan! His wife understands his case, and pities him from her heart. But, what can she do? Go out and get him something to drink? "Oh, no! no! no! Never!" She answered the thought audibly almost, in the excitement of her feelings. An hour has passed—Joe's restlessness has increased instead of diminishing. What is to be done? Now Mrs. Morgan has left the room. She has resolved upon something, for the case must be met. Ah! here she comes, after an absence of five minutes, bearing in her hand a cup of strong coffee.

"It was kind and thoughtful in you, Fanny," says Morgan, as with a gratified look he takes the cup. But his hand trembles, and he spills a portion of the contents as he tries to raise it to his lips. How dreadfully his nerves are shattered! Unnatural stimulants have been applied so long, that all true vitality seems lost.

And now the hand of his wife is holding the cup to his lips, and he drinks eagerly.

"This is dreadful—dreadful! Where will it end? What is to be done?"

Fanny suppresses a sob, as she thus gives vent to her troubled feelings. Twice, already, has her husband been seized with the drunkard's madness; and, in the nervous prostration consequent upon even a brief withdrawal of his usual strong stimulants, she sees the fearful precursor of another attack of this dreadful and dangerous malady. In the hope of supplying the needed tone she has given him strong coffee; and this, for the time, produces the effect desired. The restlessness is allayed, and a quiet state of body and mind succeeds. It needs but a suggestion to induce him to retire for the night. After being a few minutes in bed, sleep steals over him, and his heavy breathing tells that he is in the world of dreams.

And now there comes a tap at the door.

"Come in," is answered.

The latch is lifted, the door swings open, and a woman enters.

"Mrs. Slade!" The name is uttered in a tone of surprise.

"Fanny, how are you this evening?" Kindly, yet half sadly, the words are said.

"Tolerable, I thank you."

The hands of the two women are clasped, and for a few moments they gaze into each other's face. What a world of tender commiseration is in that of Mrs. Slade!

"How is little Mary to-night?"

"Not so well, I'm afraid. She has a good deal of fever."

"Indeed! Oh, I'm sorry! Poor child! what a dreadful thing it was. Oh, Fanny! you don't know how it has troubled me. I've been intending to come around all day to see how she was, but couldn't get off until now."

"It came near killing her," said Mrs. Morgan.

"It's in God's mercy she escaped. The thought of it curdles the very blood in my veins. Poor child! is this her on the settee?"

"Yes."

Mrs. Slade takes a chair, and sitting by the sleeping child, gazes long upon her pale, sweet face. Now the lips of Mary part—words are murmured—what is she saying?

"No, no, mother; I can't go to bed yet. Father isn't home. And it's so dark. There's no one to lead him over the bridge. I'm not afraid. Don't—don't cry so, mother—I'm not afraid! Nothing will hurt me."

The child's face flushes. She moans, and throws her arms about uneasily. Hark again.

"I wish Mr. Slade wouldn't look so cross at me. He never did when I went to the mill. He doesn't take me on his knee now, and stroke my hair. Oh dear! I wish father wouldn't go there any more. Don't! don't, Mr. Slade. Oh! oh!"—the ejaculation pro-longed into a frightened cry, "My head! my head!"

A few choking sobs are followed by low moans; and then the child breathes easily again. But the flush does not leave her cheek; and when Mrs. Slade, from whose eyes the tears come forth drop by drop, and roll down her face, touches it lightly, she finds it hot with fever.

"Has the doctor seen her to-day, Fanny?"

"No, ma'am."

"He should see her at once. I will go for him;" and Mrs. Slade starts up and goes quickly from the room. In a little while she returns with Doctor Green, who sits down and looks at the child for some moments with a sober, thoughtful face. Then he lays his fingers on her pulse and times its beat by his watch—shakes his head, and looks graver still.

"How long has she had fever?" he asks.

"All day."

"You should have sent for me earlier."

"Oh doctor! She is not dangerous, I hope?" Mrs. Morgan looks frightened.

"She's a sick child, madam."

"You've promised, father."—The dreamer is speaking again.—"I'm not well enough yet. Oh, don't go, father; don't! There! He's gone! Well, well! I'll try and walk there—I can sit down and rest by the way. Oh dear! How tired I am! Father! Father!"

The child starts up and looks about her wildly.

"Oh, mother, is it you?" And she sinks back upon her pillow, looking now inquiringly from face to face.

"Father—where is father?" she asks.

"Asleep, dear."

"Oh! Is he? I'm glad."

Her eyes close wearily.

"Do you feel any pain, Mary?" inquired the doctor.

"Yes, sir—in my head. It aches and beats so."

The cry of "Father" has reached the ears of Morgan, who is sleeping in the next room, and roused him into consciousness. He knows the doctor's voice. Why is he here at this late hour? "Do you feel any pain, Mary?" The question he hears distinctly, and the faintly uttered reply also. He is sober enough to have all his fears instantly excited. There is nothing in the world that he loves as he loves that child. And so he gets up and dresses himself as quickly as possible; the stimulus of anxiety giving tension to his relaxed nerves.

"Oh father!" The quick ears of Mary detect his entrance first, and a pleasant smile welcomes him.

"Is she very sick, doctor?" he asks, in a voice full of anxiety.

"She's a sick child, sir; you should have sent for me earlier." The doctor speaks rather sternly, and with a purpose to rebuke.

The reply stirs Morgan, and he seems to cower half-timidly under the words, as if they were blows. Mary has already grasped her father's hand, and holds on to it tightly.

After examining the case a little more closely, the doctor prepares some medicine, and, promising to call early in the morning, goes away. Mrs. Slade follows soon after; but, in parting with Mrs. Morgan, leaves something in her hand, which, to the surprise of the latter, proves to be a ten-dollar bill. The tears start to her eyes; and she conceals the money in her bosom—murmuring a fervent "God bless her!"

A simple act of restitution is this on the part of Mrs. Slade, prompted as well by humanity as a sense of justice. With one hand her husband has taken the bread from the family of his old friend, and thus with the other she restores it.

And now Morgan and his wife are alone with their sick child. Higher the fever rises, and partial delirium seizes upon her over-excited brain. She talks for a time almost incessantly. All her trouble is about her father; and she is constantly referring to his promise not to go out in the evening until she gets well. How tenderly and touchingly she appeals to him; now looking up into his face in recognition; and now calling anxiously after him, as if he had left her and was going away.

"You'll not forget your promise, will you, father?" she says, speaking so calmly, that he thinks her mind has ceased to wander.

"No, dear; I will not forget it," he answers, smoothing her hair gently with his hand.

"You'll not go out in the evening again, until I get well?"

"No, dear."

"Father!"

"What, love?"

"Stoop down closer; I don't want mother to hear; it will make her feel so bad."

The father bends his ear close to the lips of Mary. How he starts and shudders! What has she said?—only these brief words—

"I shall not get well, father; I'm going to die."

The groans, impossible to repress, that issued through the lips of Joe Morgan, startled the ears of his wife, and she came quickly to the bed-side.

"What is it? What is the matter, Joe?" she inquired with a look of anxiety.

"Hush, father. Don't tell her. I only said it to you." And Mary put a finger on her lips, and looked mysterious. "There, mother—you go away; you've got trouble enough, anyhow. Don't tell her, father."

But the words, which came to him like a prophecy, awoke such pangs of fear and remorse in the heart of Joe Morgan, that it was impossible for him to repress the signs of pain. For some moments he gazed at his wife—then stooping forward, suddenly, he buried his face in the bed-clothes, and sobbed bitterly.

A suggestion of the truth now flashed through the mind of Mrs. Morgan, sending a thrill of pain along every nerve. Ere she had time to recover herself, the low, sweet voice of Mary broke upon the hushed air of the room, and she sung—

> Jesus can make a dying bed
>   Feel soft as downy pillows are,
> While on his breast I lean my head,
>   And breathe my life out, sweetly, there.

It was impossible for Mrs. Morgan longer to repress her feelings. As the softly breathed strain died away, her sobs broke forth, and for a time she wept violently.

"There," said the child,—"I didn't mean to tell you. I only told father, because—because he promised not to go to the tavern any more until I got well; and I'm not going to get well. So, you see, mother, he'll never go again—never—never—never. Oh dear! how my head pains. Mr. Slade threw it so hard. But it didn't strike father; and I'm so glad. How it would have hurt him—poor father! But he'll never go there any more; and that will be so good, won't it, mother?"

A light broke over her face; but seeing that her mother still wept, she said—

"Don't cry. Maybe I'll be better."

And then her eyes closed heavily, and she slept again.

"Joe," said Mrs. Morgan, after she had in a measure recovered herself—she spoke firmly. "Joe, did you hear what she said?"

Morgan only answered with a groan.

"Her mind wanders; and yet she may have spoken only the truth."

He groaned again.

"If she should die, Joe—"

"Don't; oh, don't talk so, Fanny. She's not going to die. It's only because she's a little light-headed."

"Why is she light-headed, Joe?"

"It's the fever—only the fever, Fanny."

"It was the blow, and the wound on her head, that caused the fever. How do we know the extent of injury on the brain? Doctor Green looked very serious. I'm afraid, husband, that the worst is before us. I've borne and suffered a great deal—only God knows how much,—I pray that I may have strength to bear this trial also. Dear child! She is better fitted for heaven than for earth; and it may be that God is about to take her to himself. She's been a great comfort to me—and to you, Joe, more like a guardian angel than a child."

Mrs. Morgan had tried to speak very firmly; but as sentence followed sentence, her voice lost more and more of its even tone. With the closing words all self-control vanished; and she wept bitterly. What could her feeble erring husband do, but weep with her?

"Joe,"—Mrs. Morgan aroused herself as quickly as possible, for she had that to say which she feared she might not have the heart to utter—"Joe, if Mary dies, you cannot forget the cause of her death."

"Oh, Fanny! Fanny!"

"Nor the hand that struck the cruel blow."

"Forget it? Never! And if I forgive Simon Slade—"

"Nor the place where the blow was dealt," said Mrs. Morgan, interrupting him.

"Poor—poor child!" moaned the conscience-stricken man.

"Nor your promise, Joe—nor your promise given to our dying child."

"Father! Father! Dear father!" Mary's eyes suddenly unclosed, as she called her father eagerly.

"Here I am, love. What is it?" And Joe Morgan pressed up to the bed-side.

"Oh! it's you, father! I dreamed that you had gone out, and—and—but you won't, will you, dear father?"

"No, love—no."

"Never any more until I get well."

"I must go out to work, you know, Mary."

"At night, father. That's what I mean. You won't, will you?"

"No, dear, no."

A soft smile trembled over the child's face; her eyelids drooped wearily, and she fell off into slumber again. She seemed not so restless as before—did not moan, nor throw herself about in her sleep.

"She's better, I think," said Morgan, as he bent over her, and listened to her softer breathing.

"It seems so," replied his wife. "And now, Joe, you must go to bed again. I will lie down here with Mary, and be ready to do any thing for her that she may want."

"I don't feel sleepy. I'm sure I couldn't close my eyes. So let me sit up with Mary. You are tired and worn out."

Mrs. Morgan looked earnestly into her husband's face. His eyes were unusually bright, and she noticed a slight nervous restlessness about his lips. She laid one of her hands on his, and perceived a slight tremor.

"You must go to bed," she spoke firmly. "I shall not let you sit up with Mary. So go at once." And she drew him almost by force into the next room.

"It's no use, Fanny. There's not a wink of sleep in my eyes. I shall lie awake anyhow. So do you get a little rest."

Even as he spoke there were nervous twitchings of his arms and shoulders; and as he entered the chamber, impelled by his wife, he stopped suddenly and said—

"What is that?"

"Where?" asked Mrs. Morgan.

"Oh, it's nothing—I see. Only one of my old boots. I thought it a great black cat."

Oh! what a shudder of despair seized upon the heart of the wretched wife. Too well she knew the fearful signs of that terrible madness from which, twice before, he had suffered. She could have looked on calmly and seen him die—but, "Not this—not this! Oh, Father in heaven!" she murmured, with such a heart-sinking that it seemed as if life itself would go out.

"Get into bed, Joe; get into bed as quickly as possible."

Morgan was now passive in the hands of his wife, and obeyed her almost like a child. He had turned down the bedclothes, and was about getting in, when he started back, with a look of disgust and alarm.

"There's nothing there, Joe. What's the matter with you?"

"I'm sure I don't know, Fanny," and his teeth rattled together, as he spoke. "I thought there was a great toad under the clothes."

"How foolish you are!"—yet tears were blinding her eyes as she said this. "It's only fancy. Get into bed and shut your eyes. I'll make you another cup of strong coffee. Perhaps that will do you good. You're only a little nervous. Mary's sickness has disturbed you."

Joe looked cautiously under the bedclothes, as he lifted them up still farther, and peered beneath.

"You know there's nothing in your bed; see!"

And Mrs. Morgan threw, with a single jerk, all the clothes upon the floor.

"There now! look for yourself. Now shut your eyes," she continued, as she spread the sheet and quilt over him, after his head was on the pillow. "Shut them tight and keep them so until I boil the water and make a cup of coffee. You know as well as I do that it's nothing but fancy."

Morgan closed his eyes firmly, and drew the clothes over his head.

"I'll be back in a very few minutes," said his wife, going hurriedly to the door. Ere leaving, however, she partly turned her head and glanced back. There sat her husband, upright and staring fearfully.

"Don't, Fanny! don't go away!" he cried, in a frightened voice.

"Joe! Joe! why will you be so foolish? It's nothing but imagination. Now do lie down and shut your eyes. Keep them shut. There now."

And she laid a hand over his eyes, and pressed it down tightly.

"I wish Doctor Green was here," said the wretched man. "He could give me something."

"Shall I go for him?"

"Go, Fanny! Run over right quickly."

"But you won't keep in bed."

"Yes, I will. There now." And he drew the clothes over his face. "There; I'll lie just so until you come back. Now run, Fanny, and don't stay a minute."

Scarcely stopping to think, Mrs. Morgan went hurriedly from the room, and drawing an old shawl over her head, started with swift feet for the residence of Doctor Green, which was not very far away. The kind doctor understood, at a word, the sad condition of her husband, and promised to attend him immediately. Back she flew at even a wilder speed, her heart throbbing with vague apprehension. Oh! what a fearful cry was that which smote her ears as she came within a few paces of home. She knew the voice, changed as it was by terror, and a shudder almost palsied her heart. At a single bound she cleared the intervening space, and in the next moment was in the room where she had left her husband. But he was not there! With suspended breath, and feet that scarcely obeyed her will, she passed into the chamber where little Mary lay. Not here!

"Joe! husband!" she called in a faint voice.

"Here he is, mother." And now she saw that Joe had crept into the bed behind the sick child, and that her arm was drawn tightly around his neck.

"You won't let them hurt me, will you, dear?" said the poor, frightened victim of a terrible mania.

"Nothing will hurt you, father," answered Mary, in a voice that showed her mind to be clear, and fully conscious of her parent's true condition.

She had seen him thus before. Ah! what an experience for a child!

"You're an angel—my good angel, Mary," he murmured, in a voice yet trembling with fear. "Pray for me, my child. Oh, ask your Father in heaven to save me from these dreadful creatures. There now!" he cried, rising up suddenly, and looking toward the door. "Keep out! Go away! You can't come in here. This is Mary's room; and she's an angel. Ah, ha! I knew you wouldn't dare come in here—

A single saint can put to flight,
Ten thousand blustering sons of night."

He added in a half wandering way, yet with an assured voice, as he laid himself back upon his pillow, and drew the clothes over his head.

"Poor father!" sighed the child, as she gathered both arms about his neck. "I will be your good angel. Nothing shall hurt you here."

"I knew I would be safe where you were," he whispered back—"I knew it, and so I came. Kiss me, love."

How pure and fervent was the kiss laid instantly upon his lips! There was a power in it to remand the evil influences that were surrounding and pressing in upon him like a flood. All was quiet now, and Mrs. Morgan neither by word nor movement disturbed the solemn stillness that reigned in the apartment. In a few minutes the deepened breathing of her husband gave a blessed intimation that he was sinking into sleep. Oh, sleep! sleep! How tearfully, in times past, had she prayed that he might sleep; and yet no sleep came for hours and days—even though powerful opiates were given—until exhausted nature yielded, and then sleep had a long, long struggle with death. Now the sphere of his loving, innocent child seemed to have overcome, at least for the time, the evil influences that were getting possession even of his external senses. Yes, yes, he was sleeping! Oh, what a fervent "Thank God!" went up from the heart of his stricken wife.

Soon the quick ears of Mrs. Morgan detected the doctor's approaching footsteps, and she met him at the door with a finger on her lips. A whispered word or two explained the better aspect of affairs, and the doctor said, encouragingly,

"That's good, if he will only sleep on."

"Do you think he will, doctor?" was asked anxiously.

"He may. But we cannot hope too strongly. It would be something very unusual."

Both passed noiselessly into the chamber. Morgan still slept, and by his deep breathing it was plain that he slept soundly. And Mary, too, was sleeping, her face now laid against her father's, and her arms still about his neck. The sight touched even the doctor's heart and moistened his eyes. For nearly half an hour he remained; and then, as Morgan continued to sleep, he left medicine to be given immediately, and went home, promising to call early in the morning.

It is now past midnight, and we leave the lonely, sad-hearted watcher with her sick ones.

I was sitting, with a newspaper in my hand—not reading, but musing—at the "Sickle and Sheaf," late in the evening marked by the incidents just detailed.

"Where's your mother?" I heard Simon Slade inquire. He had just entered an adjoining room.

"She's gone out somewhere," was answered by his daughter Flora.

"Where?"

"I don't know."

"How long has she been away?"

"More than an hour."

"And you don't know where she went to?"

"No, sir."

Nothing more was said, but I heard the landlord's heavy feet moving backward and forward across the room for some minutes.

"Why, Ann! where have you been?" The door of the next room had opened and shut.

"Where I wish you had been with me," was answered in a very firm voice.

"Where?"

"To Joe Morgan's."

"Humph!" Only this ejaculation met my ears. But something was said in a low voice, to which Mrs. Slade replied with some warmth,

"If you don't have his child's blood clinging for life to your garments, you may be thankful."

"What do you mean?" he asked, quickly.

"All that my words indicate. Little Mary is very ill!"

"Well, what of it."

"Much. The doctor thinks her in great danger. The cut on her head has thrown her into a violent fever, and she is delirious. Oh, Simon! if you had heard what I heard tonight."

"What?" was asked in a growling tone.

"She is out of her mind, as I said, and talks a great deal. She talked about you."

"Of me! Well, what had she to say?"

"She said—so pitifully—'I wish Mr. Slade wouldn't look so cross at me. He never did when I went to the mill. He doesn't take me on his knee now, and stroke my hair. Oh dear!' Poor child! She was always so good."

"Did she say that?" Slade seemed touched.

"Yes, and a great deal more. Once she screamed out, 'Oh don't! don't, Mr. Slade! don't! My head! my head!' It made my very heart ache. I can never forget her pale, frightened face, nor her cry of fear. Simon—if she should die!"

There was a long silence.

"If we were only back to the mill." It was Mrs. Slade's voice.

"There, now! I don't want to hear that again," quickly spoke out the landlord. "I made a slave of myself long enough."

"You had at least a clear conscience," his wife answered.

"Do hush, will you!" Slade was now angry. "One would think, by the way you talk sometimes, that I had broken every command of the Decalogue."

"You will break hearts as well as commandments, if you keep on for a few years as you have begun—and ruin souls as well as fortunes."

Mrs. Slade spoke calmly, but with marked severity of tone. Her husband answered with an oath, and then left the room, banging the door after him. In the hush that followed I retired to my chamber, and lay for an hour awake, pondering on all I had just heard. What a revelation was in that brief passage of words between the landlord and his excited companion!

❧ Night the Fourth

DEATH OF LITTLE MARY MORGAN

"Where are you going, Ann?" It was the landlord's voice. Time—a little after dark.

"I'm going over to see Mrs. Morgan," answered his wife.

"What for?"

"I wish to go," was replied.

"Well, *I* don't wish you to go," said Slade, in a very decided way.

"I can't help that, Simon. Mary, I'm told, is dying, and Joe is in a dreadful way. I'm needed there—and so are you, as to that matter. There was a time when, if word came to you that Morgan or his family were in trouble—"

"Do hush, will you!" exclaimed the landlord, angrily. "I won't be preached to in this way any longer."

"Oh, well; then don't interfere with my movements, Simon; that's all I have to say. I'm needed over there, as I just said, and I'm going."

There were considerable odds against him, and Slade, perceiving this, turned off, muttering something that his wife did not hear, and she went on her way. A hurried walk brought her to the wretched home of the poor drunkard, whose wife met her at the door.

"How is Mary?" was the visitor's earnest inquiry.

Mrs. Morgan tried to answer the question; but, though her lips moved, no sounds issued therefrom.

Mrs. Slade pressed her hands tightly in both of hers; and then passed in with her to the room where the child lay. A glance sufficed to tell Mrs. Slade that death had already laid his icy fingers upon her brow.

"How are you, dear?" she asked, as she bent over and kissed her.

"Better, I thank you," replied Mary, in a low whisper.

Then she fixed her eyes upon her mother's face, with a look of inquiry.

"What is it, love?"

"Hasn't father waked up yet?"

"No, dear."

"Won't he wake up soon?"

"He's sleeping very soundly. I wouldn't like to disturb him."

"Oh, no; don't disturb him. I thought, maybe, he was awake."

And the child's lids dropped languidly, until the long lashes lay close against her cheeks.

There was silence for a little while, and then Mrs. Morgan said, in a half-whisper to Mrs. Slade,

"Oh, we've had such a dreadful time with poor Joe. He got in that terrible way again last night. I had to go for Doctor Green and leave him all alone. When I came back, he was in bed with Mary; and she, dear child! had her arms around his neck, and was trying to comfort him; and would you believe it, he went off to sleep and slept in that way for a long time. The doctor came, and when he saw how it was, left some medicine for him, and went away. I was in such hopes that he would sleep it all off. But about twelve o'clock he started up, and sprung out of bed with an awful scream. Poor Mary! she too had fallen asleep. The cry wakened her, and frightened her dreadfully. She's been getting worse ever since, Mrs. Slade.

"Just as he was rushing out of the room, I caught him by the arm, and it took all my strength to hold him.

"'Father! father!' Mary called after him, as soon as she was awake enough to understand what was the matter—'Don't go out, father; there's nothing here.'

"He looked back toward the bed, in a frightful way.

"'See, father!' and the dear child turned down the quilt and sheet, in order to convince him that nothing was in the bed. 'I'm here,' she added. 'I'm not afraid. Come, father. If there's nothing here to hurt me, there's nothing to hurt you.'

"There was something so assuring in this, that Joe took a step or two toward the bed, looking sharply into it as he did so. From the bed his eyes wandered up to the ceiling, and the old look of terror came into his face.

"'There it is now! Jump out of bed, quick! Jump out, Mary!' he cried. 'See! it's right over your head.'

"Mary showed no sign of fear as she lifted her eyes to the ceiling, and gazed steadily, for a few moments, in that direction.

"'There's nothing there, father,' said she, in a confident voice.

"'It's gone now,' Joe spoke in a tone of relief. 'Your angel-look drove it away. Aha! There it is now, creeping along the floor!' he suddenly exclaimed, fearfully; starting away from where he stood.

"'Here, father! Here!' Mary called to him, and he sprung into the bed again; while she gathered her arms about him tightly, saying, in a low, soothing voice,—'Nothing can harm you here, father.'

"Without a moment's delay, I gave him the morphine left by Doctor Green. He took it eagerly, and then crouched down in the bed, while Mary continued to assure him of perfect safety. So long as he was clearly conscious as to where he was, he remained perfectly still. But, as soon as partial slumber came, he would scream out, and spring from the bed in terror, and then it would take us several minutes to quiet him again. Six times during the night did this occur; and as often, Mary coaxed him back. The morphine I continued to give, as the doctor had directed. By morning, the opiates had done their work, and he was sleeping soundly. When the doctor came, we removed him to his own bed. He is still asleep; and I begin to feel uneasy, lest he should never awake again. I have heard of this happening."

"See if father isn't awake," said Mary, raising her head from the pillow. She had not heard what passed between her mother and Mrs. Slade, for the conversation was carried on in low voices.

Mrs. Morgan stepped to the door, and looked into the room where her husband lay.

"He is still asleep, dear," she remarked, coming back to the bed.

"Oh! I wish he was awake. I want to see him so much. Won't you call him, mother?"

"I have called him a good many times. But you know the doctor gave him opium. He can't wake up yet."

"He's been sleeping a very long time; don't you think so, mother?"

"Yes, dear, it does seem a long time. But it's best for him. He'll be better when he wakes."

Mary closed her eyes, wearily. How deathly white was her face—how sunken her eyes—how sharply contracted her features!

"I've given her up, Mrs. Slade," said Mrs. Morgan, in a low, rough, choking whisper, as she leaned nearer to her friend. "I've given her up! The worst is over; but, oh! it seemed as though my heart would break in the struggle. Dear child! In all the darkness of my way, she has helped and comforted me. Without her, it would have been the blackness of darkness."

"Father! father!" The voice of Mary broke out with a startling quickness.

Mrs. Morgan turned to the bed, and laying her hand on Mary's arm said—

"He's still sound asleep, dear."

"No, he isn't, mother. I heard him move. Won't you go in and see if he is awake?"

In order to satisfy the child, her mother left the room. To her surprise, she met the eyes of her husband as she entered the chamber where he lay. He looked at her calmly.

"What does Mary want with me?" he asked.

"She wishes to see you. She's called you so many, many times. Shall I bring her in here?"

"No. I'll get up and dress myself."

"I wouldn't do that. You've been sick."

"Oh, no. I don't feel sick."

"Father! father!" The clear, earnest voice of Mary was heard calling.

"I'm coming, dear," answered Morgan.

"Come quick, father, won't you?"

"Yes, love." And Morgan got up and dressed himself—but with unsteady hands, and every sign of nervous prostration. In a little while, with the assistance of his wife, he was ready, and, supported by her, came tottering into the room where Mary was lying.

"Oh, father!"—What a light broke over her countenance.—"I've been waiting for you so long. I thought you were never going to wake up. Kiss me, father."

"What can I do for you, Mary?" asked Morgan, tenderly, as he laid his face down upon the pillow beside her.

"Nothing, father. I don't wish for any thing. I only wanted to see you."

"I'm here, now, love."

"Dear father!" How earnestly, yet tenderly she spoke, laying her small hand upon his face. "You've always been good to me, father."

"Oh, no. I've never been good to anybody," sobbed the weak, broken-spirited man, as he raised himself from the pillow.

How deeply touched was Mrs. Slade, as she sat, the silent witness of this scene!

"You haven't been good to yourself, father—but you've always been good to us."

"Don't, Mary! don't say anything about that," interposed Morgan. "Say that I've been very bad—very wicked. Oh, Mary, dear! I only wish that I was as good as you are; I'd like to die, then, and go right away from this evil world. I wish there was no liquor to drink—no taverns—no bar-rooms. Oh dear! Oh dear! I wish I was dead."

And the weak, trembling, half-palsied man laid his face again upon the pillow beside his child, and sobbed aloud.

What an oppressive silence reigned for a time through the room!

"Father." The stillness was broken by Mary. Her voice was clear and even. "Father, I want to tell you something?"

"What is it, Mary?"

"There'll be nobody to go for you, father." The child's lips now quivered, and tears filled into her eyes.

"Don't talk about that, Mary. I'm not going out in the evening any more until you get well. Don't you remember I promised?"

"But, father"—She hesitated.

"What, dear?"

"I'm going away to leave you and mother."

"Oh, no—no—no, Mary! Don't say that."—The poor man's voice was broken.—"Don't say that! We can't let you go, dear."

"God has called me." The child's voice had a solemn tone, and her eyes turned reverently upward.

"I wish he would call me! Oh, I wish he would call me!" groaned Morgan, hiding his face in his hands. "What shall I do when you are gone? Oh dear! Oh dear!"

"Father!" Mary spoke calmly again. "You are not ready to go yet. God will let you live here longer, that you may get ready."

"How can I get ready without you to help me, Mary? My angel child!"

"Haven't I tried to help you, father, oh, so many times?" said Mary.

"Yes—yes—you've always tried."

"But it wasn't any use. You would go out—you would go to the tavern. It seemed almost as if you couldn't help it."

Morgan groaned in spirit.

"Maybe I can help you better, father, after I die. I love you so much, that I am sure God will let me come to you, and stay with you always, and be your angel. Don't you think he will, mother?"

But Mrs. Morgan's heart was too full. She did not even try to answer, but sat, with streaming eyes, gazing upon her child's face.

"Father, I dreamed something about you, while I slept to-day." Mary again turned to her father.

"What was it, dear?"

"I thought it was night, and that I was still sick. You promised not to go out again until I was well. But you did go out; and I thought you went over to Mr. Slade's tavern. When I knew this, I felt as strong as when I was well, and I got up and dressed myself, and started out after you. But I hadn't gone far, before I met Mr. Slade's great bull-dog Nero, and he growled at me so dreadfully that I was frightened and ran back home. Then I started again, and went away round by Mr. Mason's. But there was Nero in the road, and this time he caught my dress in his mouth and tore a great piece out of the skirt. I ran back again, and he chased me all the way home. Just as I got to the door, I looked around, and there was Mr. Slade, setting Nero on me. As soon as I saw Mr. Slade, though he looked at me very wicked, I lost all my fear, and turning around, I walked past Nero, who showed his teeth, and growled as fiercely as ever, but didn't touch me. Then Mr. Slade tried to stop me. But I didn't mind him, and kept right on, until I came to the tavern, and there you stood in the door. And you were dressed so nice. You had on a new hat and a new coat; and your boots were new, and polished just like Judge Hammond's. I said—'O father! is this you?' And then you took me up in your arms and kissed me, and said—'Yes, Mary, I am your real father. Not old Joe Morgan—but Mr. Morgan now.' It seemed all so strange, that I looked into the bar-room to see who was there. But it wasn't a bar-room any longer; but a store full of goods. The sign of the 'Sickle and Sheaf' was taken down; and over the door I now read your name, father. Oh! I was so glad, that I awoke—and then I cried all to myself, for it was only a dream."

The last words were said very mournfully, and with a drooping of Mary's lids, until the tear-gemmed lashes lay close upon her cheeks. Another period of deep silence followed—for the oppressed listeners gave no utterance to what was in their hearts. Feeling was too strong for speech. Nearly five minutes glided away, and then Mary whispered the name of her father, but without opening her eyes.

Morgan answered, and bent down his ear.

"You will only have mother left," she said—"only mother. And she cries so much when you are away."

"I won't leave her, Mary, only when I go to work," said Morgan, whispering back to the child. "And I'll never go out at night any more."

"Yes; you promised me that."

"And I'll promise more."

"What, father?"

"Never to go into a tavern again."

"Never!"

"No, never. And I'll promise still more."

"Father?"

"Never to drink a liquor as long as I live."

"Oh, father! dear, dear father!" And with a cry of joy Mary started up and flung herself upon his breast. Morgan drew his arms tightly around her, and sat for a long time, with his lips pressed to her cheek—while she lay against his bosom as still as death. As death? Yes; for, when the father unclasped his arms, the spirit of his child was with the angels of the resurrection!

It was my fourth evening in the bar-room of the "Sickle and Sheaf." The company was not large, nor in very gay spirits. All had heard of little Mary's illness; which followed so quickly on the blow from the tumbler, that none hesitated about connecting the one with the other. So regular had been the child's visits, and so gently exerted, yet powerful, her influence over her father, that most of the frequenters at the "Sickle and Sheaf" had felt for her a more than common interest; which the cruel treatment she received, and the subsequent illness, materially heightened.

"Joe Morgan hasn't turned up this evening," remarked some one.

"And isn't likely to for a while," was answered.

"Why not?" inquired the first speaker.

"They say, the man with the poker[6] is after him."

"Oh, dear! that's dreadful. It's the second or third chase, isn't it?"

"Yes."

"He'll be likely to catch him this time."

"I shouldn't wonder."

"Poor devil! It won't be much matter. His family will be a great deal better without him."

"It will be a blessing to them if he dies."

"Miserable, drunken wretch!" muttered Harvey Green, who was present. "He's only in the way of everybody. The sooner he's off, the better."

---

[6]The devil with his pitchfork.

The landlord said nothing. He stood leaning across the bar, looking more sober than usual.

"That was rather an unlucky affair of yours, Simon. They say the child is going to die."

"Who says so?" Slade started, scowled, and threw a quick glance upon the speaker.

"Doctor Green."

"Nonsense! Doctor Green never said any such thing."

"Yes, he did, though."

"Who heard him?"

"I did."

"You did?"

"Yes."

"He wasn't in earnest?" A slight paleness overspread the countenance of the land-lord.

"He was, though. They had an awful time there last night."

"Where?"

"At Joe Morgan's. Joe has the mania, and Mrs. Morgan was alone with him and her sick girl all night."

"He deserves to have it; that's all I've got to say." Slade tried to speak with a kind of rough indifference.

"That's pretty hard talk," said one of the company.

"I don't care if it is. It's the truth. What else could he expect?"

"A man like Joe is to be pitied," remarked the other.

"I pity his family," said Slade.

"Especially little Mary." The words were uttered tauntingly, and produced murmurs of satisfaction throughout the room.

Slade started back from where he stood, in an impatient manner, saying something that I did not hear.

"Look here, Simon, I heard some strong suggestions over at Lawyer Phillip's office to-day."

Slade turned his eyes upon the speaker.

"If that child should die, you'll probably have to stand a trial for manslaughter."

"No—girl-slaughter," said Harvey Green, with a cold, inhuman chuckle.

"But, I'm in earnest," said the other. "Mr. Phillips said that a case could be made out of it."

"It was only an accident, and all the lawyers in Christendom can't make anything more of it," remarked Green, taking the side of the landlord, and speaking with more gravity than before.

"Hardly an accident," was replied.

"He didn't throw at the girl."

"No matter. He threw a heavy tumbler at her father's head. The intention was to do an injury; and the law will not stop to make any nice discriminations in regard to the individual upon whom the injury was wrought. Moreover, who is prepared to say, that he didn't aim at the girl?"

"Any man who intimates such a thing is a cursed liar!" exclaimed the landlord, half maddened by the suggestion.

"I won't throw a tumbler at your head," coolly remarked the individual whose plain speaking had so irriated Simon Slade. "Throwing tumblers I never thought a very creditable kind of argument—though, with some men, when cornered, it is a favourite mode of settling a question. Now, as for our friend the landlord, I am sorry to say, that his new business doesn't seem to have improved either his manners or his temper a great deal. As a miller, he was one of the best-tempered men in the world, and wouldn't have harmed a kitten. But, now, he can swear, and bluster, and throw glasses at people's heads, and all that sort of thing, with the best of brawling rowdies. I'm afraid he's taking lessons in a bad school—I am."

"I don't think you have any right to insult a man in his own house," answered Slade, in a voice dropped to a lower key than the one in which he had before spoken.

"I had no intention to insult you," said the other. "I was only speaking suppositiously, and in view of your position on a trial for manslaughter, when I suggested, that no one could prove, or say, that you didn't mean to strike little Mary, when you threw the tumbler."

"Well, I didn't mean to strike her; and I don't believe there is a man in this bar-room who thinks that I did—not one."

"I'm sure I do not," said the individual with whom he was in controversy. "Nor I"— "Nor I"—went round the room.

"But, as I wished to set forth," was continued, "the case will not be so plain a one when it finds its way into court, and twelve men, to each of whom you may be a stranger, come to sit in judgment upon the act. The slightest twist in the evidence, the prepossessions of a witness, or the bad tact of the prosecution, may cause things to look so dark on your side as to leave you but little chance. For my part, if the child should die, I think your chances for a term in the state's prison are as eight to ten; and I should call that pretty close cutting."

I looked attentively at the man who said this, all the while he was speaking, but could not clearly make out whether he were altogether in earnest, or merely trying to worry the mind of Slade. That he was successful in accomplishing the latter, was very plain; for the landlord's countenance steadily lost colour, and became overcast with alarm. With that evil delight which some men take in giving pain, others, seeing Slade's anxious looks, joined in the persecution, and soon made the landlord's case look black enough; and the landlord himself almost as frightened as a criminal just under arrest.

"It's bad business, and no mistake," said one.

"Yes, bad enough. I wouldn't be in his shoes for his coat," remarked another.

"For his coat? No, not for his whole wardrobe," said a third.

"Nor for the 'Sickle and Sheaf' thrown into the bargain," added a fourth.

"It will be a clear case of manslaughter, and no mistake. What is the penalty?"

"From two to ten years in the penitentiary," was readily answered.

"They'll give him five, I reckon."

"No—not more than two. It will be hard to prove malicious intention."

"I don't know that. I've heard him curse the girl and threaten her many a time. Haven't you?"

"Yes"—"Yes"—"I have, often," ran around the bar-room.

"You'd better hang me at once,"said Slade, affecting to laugh.

At this moment, the door behind Slade opened, and I saw his wife's anxious face thrust in for a moment. She said something to her husband, who uttered a low ejaculation of surprise, and went out quickly.

"What's the matter now?" asked one of another.

"I shouldn't wonder if little Mary Morgan was dead," was suggested.

"I heard her say dead," remarked one who was standing near the bar.

"What's the matter, Frank?" inquired several voices, as the landlord's son came in through the door out of which his father had passed.

"Mary Morgan is dead," answered the boy.

"Poor child! Poor child!" sighed one, in genuine regret at the not unlooked for intelligence. "Her trouble is over."

And there was not one present, but Harvey Green, who did not utter some word of pity or sympathy. He shrugged his shoulders, and looked as much of contempt and indifference as he thought it prudent to express.

"See here, boys," spoke out one of the company, "can't we do something for poor Mrs. Morgan? Can't we make up a purse for her?"

"That's it," was quickly responded; "I'm good for three dollars; and there they are," drawing out the money and laying it upon the counter.

"And here are five to go with them," said I, quickly stepping forward, and placing a five-dollar bill along side of the first contribution.

"Here are five more," added a third individual. And so it went on, until thirty dollars were paid down for the benefit of Mrs. Morgan.

"Into whose hands shall this be placed?" was next asked.

"Let me suggest Mrs. Slade," said I. "To my certain knowledge, she has been with Mrs. Morgan to-night. I know that she feels in her a true woman's interest."

"Just the person," was answered. "Frank, tell your mother we would like to see her. Ask her to step into the sitting-room."

In a few moments the boy came back, and said that his mother would see us in the next room, into which we all passed. Mrs. Slade stood near the table, on which burned a lamp. I noticed that her eyes were red, and that there was on her countenance a troubled and sorrowful expression.

"We have just heard," said one of the company, "that little Mary Morgan is dead."

"Yes—it is too true," answered Mrs. Slade, mournfully. "I have just left there. Poor child! she has passed from an evil world."

"Evil it has indeed been to her," was remarked.

"You may well say that. And yet, amid all the evil, she has been an angel of mercy. Her last thought in dying was of her miserable father. For him, at any time, she would have laid down her life willingly."

"Her mother must be nearly broken-hearted. Mary is the last of her children."

"And yet the child's death may prove a blessing to her."

"How so?"

"Her father promised Mary, just at the last moment—solemnly promised her—that, henceforth, he would never taste liquor. That was all her trouble. That was the thorn in her dying pillow. But he plucked it out, and she went to sleep, lying against his heart. Oh, gentlemen! it was the most touching sight I ever saw."

All present seemed deeply moved.

"They are very poor and wretched," was said.

"Poor and miserable enough," answered Mrs. Slade.

"We have just been taking up a collection for Mrs. Morgan. Here is the money, Mrs. Slade—thirty dollars—we place it in your hands for her benefit. Do with it, for her, as you may see best."

"Oh, gentlemen!" What a quick gleam went over the face of Mrs. Slade. "I thank you, from my heart, in the name of that unhappy one, for this act of true benevolence. To you the sacrifice has been small; to her the benefit will be great indeed. A new life will, I trust, be commenced by her husband, and this timely aid will be something to rest upon, until he can get into better employment than he now has. Oh, gentlemen! let me urge on you, one and all, to make common cause in favour of Joe Morgan. His purposes are good now; he means to keep his promise to his dying child—means to reform his life. Let the good impulses that led to this act of relief, further prompt you to watch over him, and, if you see him about going astray, to lead him kindly back into the right path. Never—oh! never encourage him to drink; but rather take the glass from his hand, if his own appetite lead him aside, and by all the persuasive influence you possess, induce him to go out from the place of temptation.

"Pardon my boldness in saying so much," added Mrs. Slade, recollecting herself, and colouring deeply as she did so. "My feelings have led me away."

And she took the money from the table where it had been placed, and retired toward the door.

"You have spoken well, madam," was answered. "And we thank you for reminding us of our duty."

"One word more—and forgive the earnest heart from which it comes"—said Mrs. Slade, in a voice that trembled on the words she uttered. "I cannot help speaking, gentlemen! Think if some of you be not entering the road wherein Joe Morgan has so long been walking. Save him, in heaven's name!—but see that ye do not yourselves become cast-aways!"

As she said this, she glided through the door, and it closed after her.

"I don't know what her husband would say to that," was remarked after a few moments of surprised silence.

"I don't care what *he* would say; but I'll tell you what *I* will say," spoke out a man whom I had several times noticed as rather a free tippler. "The old lady has given us capital advice, and I mean to take it, for one. I'm going to try to save Joe Morgan, and—myself too. I've already entered the road she referred to; but I'm going to turn back. So good-night to you all; and if Simon Slade gets no more of my six-pences, he may thank his wife for it—God bless her!"

And the man drew his hat with a jerk over his forehead, and left immediately.

This seemed the signal for dispersion, and all retired—not by way of the bar-room, but out into the hall, and through the door leading upon the porch that ran along in front of the house. Soon after the bar was closed, and a dead silence reigned throughout the house. I saw no more of Slade that night. Early in the morning, I left Cedarville; the landlord looked very sober when he bade me good-by through the stage-door, and wished me a pleasant journey.

❧ Night the Fifth

SOME OF THE CONSEQUENCES OF TAVERN-KEEPING

Nearly five years glided away before business again called me to Cedarville. I knew little of what passed there in the interval, except that Simon Slade had actually been indicted for manslaughter, in causing the death of Morgan's child. He did not stand a trial, however, Judge Lyman having used his influence, successfully, in getting the indictment quashed. The judge, some people said, interested himself in Slade more than was just seemly—especially, as he had, on several occasions, in the discharge of his official duties, displayed what seemed an over-righteous indignation against individuals arraigned for petty offences. The impression made upon me by Judge Lyman had not been favourable. He seemed a cold, selfish, scheming man of the world. That he was an unscrupulous politician, was plain to me, in a single evening's observation of his sayings and doings among the common herd of a village bar-room.

As the stage rolled, with a gay flourish of our driver's bugle, into the village, I noted here and there familiar objects, and marked the varied evidences of change. Our way was past the elegant residence and grounds of Judge Hammond, the most beautiful and highly cultivated in Cedarville. At least, such it was regarded at the time of my previous visit. But, the moment my eyes rested upon the dwelling and its varied surroundings, I perceived an altered aspect. Was it the simple work of time? or, had familiarity with other and more elegantly arranged suburban homes, marred this in my eyes by involuntary contrast? Or had the hand of cultivation really been stayed, and then marring fingers of neglect suffered undisturbed to trace on every thing disfiguring characters?

Such questions were in my thoughts, when I saw a man in the large portico of the dwelling, the ample columns of which, capped in rich Corinthian, gave the edifice the aspect of a Grecian temple. He stood leaning against one of the columns—his hat off, and his long gray hair thrown back and resting lightly on his neck and shoulders. His head was bent down upon his breast, and he seemed in deep abstraction. Just as the coach swept by, he looked up, and in the changed features I recognised Judge Hammond. His complexion was still florid, but his face had grown thin, and his eyes were sunken. Trouble was written in every lineament. Trouble? How inadequately does the word express my meaning! Ah! at a single glance, what a volume of suffering was opened to the gazer's eye. Not lightly had the foot of time rested there, as if treading on odorous flowers, but heavily, and with iron-shod heel. This I saw at a glance; and then, only the image of the man was present to my inner vision, for the swiftly rolling stage-coach had borne me onward past the altered home of the wealthier denizen of Cedarville. In a few minutes our driver reined up before the "Sickle and Sheaf," and as I stepped to the ground, a rotund, coarse, red-faced man, whom I failed to recognise as Simon Slade until he spoke, grasped my hand, and pronounced my name. I could not but contrast, in thought, his appearance with what it was when I first saw him, some six years previously; nor help saying to myself—

"So much for tavern-keeping!"

As marked a change was visible everywhere in and around the "Sickle and Sheaf." It, too, had grown larger by additions of wings and rooms; but it had also grown coarser in growing larger. When built, all the doors were painted white, and the shutters green, giving to the house a neat, even tasteful appearance. But the white and green had given place to a dark, dirty brown, that to my eyes was particularly unattractive. The bar-room had been extended, and now a polished brass rod, or railing, embellished the counter, and sundry ornamental attractions had been given to the shelving behind the bar—such as mirrors, gilding, etc. Pictures, too, were hung upon the walls, or more accurately speaking, coarse coloured lithographs, the subjects of which, if not really obscene, were flashing or vulgar. In the sitting-room, next to the bar, I noticed little change of objects, but much in their condition. The carpet, chairs, and tables were the same in fact, but far from being the same in appearance. The room had a close, greasy odour, and looked as if it had not been thoroughly swept and dusted for a week.

A smart young Irishman was in the bar, and handed me the book in which passenger's names were registered. After I had recorded mine, he directed my trunk to be carried to the room designated as the one I was to occupy. I followed the porter, who conducted me to the chamber which had been mine at previous visits. Here, too, were evidences of change; but not for the better. Then the room was as sweet and clean as it could be; the sheets and pillow-cases as white as snow, and the furniture shining with polish. Now all was dusty and dingy, the air foul, and the bed linen scarcely whiter than tow.[7] No curtain made softer the light as it came through the window; nor would the shutters entirely keep out the glare, for several of the slats were broken. A feeling of disgust came over me, at the close smell and foul appearance of everything; so, after washing my hands and face, and brushing the dust from my clothes, I went down-stairs. The sitting-room was scarcely more attractive than my chamber; so I went out upon the porch and took a chair. Several loungers were here; hearty, strong-looking, but lazy fellows, who, if they had any thing to do, liked idling better than working. One of them had leaned his chair back against the wall of the house, and was swinging his legs with a half circular motion, and humming "Old Folks at Home." Another sat astride of his chair, with his face turned toward, and his chin resting upon, the back. He was in too lazy a condition of body and mind for motion or singing. A third had slidden down in his chair, until he sat on his back, while his feet were elevated above his head, and resting against one of the pillars that supported the porch; while a fourth lay stretched out on a bench, sleeping, his hat over his face to protect him from buzzing and biting flies.

Though all but the sleeping man eyed me, inquisitively, as I took my place among them, not one changed his position. The rolling of eyeballs cost but little exertion; and with that effort they were contented.

"Hallo! who's that?" one of these loungers suddenly exclaimed, as a man went swiftly by in a light sulky; and he started up, and gazed down the road, seeking to penetrate the cloud of dust which the fleet rider had swept up with hoofs and wheels.

"I didn't see." The sleeping man aroused himself, rubbed his eyes, and gazed along the road.

"Who was it, Matthew?" The Irish bar-keeper now stood in the door.

"Willy Hammond," was answered by Matthew.

"Indeed! Is that his new three hundred dollar horse?"

"Yes."

---

[7]Light brown.

"My! but he's a screamer!"

"Isn't he! Most as fast as his young master."

"Hardly," said one of the men, laughing. "I don't think anything in creation can beat Hammond. He goes it, with a perfect rush."

"Doesn't he! Well; you may say what you please of him, he's as good-hearted a fellow as ever walked; and generous to a fault."

"His old dad will agree with you in the last remark," said Matthew.

"No doubt of that, for he has to stand the bills," was answered.

"Yes, whether he will or no, for I rather think Willy has, somehow or other, got the upper hand of him."

"In what way?"

"It's Hammond and Son, over at the mill and distillery."

"I know; but what of that?"

"Willy was made the business man—ostensibly—in order, as the old man thought, to get him to feel the responsibility of the new position, and thus tame him down."

"Tame *him* down! Oh, dear! It will take more than business to do that. The curb was applied too late."

"As the old gentleman has already discovered, I'm thinking, to his sorrow."

"He never comes here any more; does he, Matthew?"

"Who?"

"Judge Hammond."

"Oh, dear, no. He and Slade had all sorts of a quarrel about a year ago, and he's never darkened our doors since."

"It was something about Willy and——." The speaker did not mention any name, but winked knowingly and tossed his head toward the entrance of the house, to indicate some member of Slade's family.

"I believe so."

"D'ye think Willy really likes her?"

Matthew shrugged his shoulders, but made no answer.

"She's a nice girl," was remarked in an under tone, "and good enough for Hammond's son any day; though, if she were my daughter, I'd rather see her in Jericho[8] than fond of his company."

"He'll have plenty of money to give her. She can live like a queen."

"For how long?"

"Hush!" came from the lips of Matthew. "There she is now."

I looked up and saw, at a short distance from the house, and approaching a young lady, in whose sweet, modest face, I at once recognised Flora Slade. Five years had developed her into a beautiful woman. In her alone, of all that appertained to Simon Slade, there was no deterioration. Her eyes were as mild and pure as when first I met her at gentle sixteen, and her father said "My daughter," with such a mingling of pride and affection in his tone. She passed near where I was sitting, and entered the house. A closer view showed me some marks of thought and suffering; but they only heightened the

---

[8]Famous doomed city of the Old Testament (Joshua 5–6).

attractions of her face. I failed not to observe the air of respect with which all returned her slight nod and smile of recognition.

"She's a nice girl, and no mistake—the flower of this flock," was said, as soon as she passed into the house.

"Too good for Willy Hammond, in my opinion," said Matthew. "Clever and generous as people call him."

"Just my opinion," was responded. "She's as pure and good, almost, as an angel; and he?—I can tell you what—he's not the clear thing. He knows a little too much of the world—on its bad side, I mean."

The appearance of Slade put an end to this conversation. A second observation of his person and countenance did not remove the first unfavourable impression. His face had grown decidedly bad in expression, as well as gross and sensual. The odour of his breath, as he took a chair close to where I was sitting, was that of one who drank habitually and freely; and the red, swimming eyes evidenced, too surely, a rapid progress toward the sad condition of a confirmed inebriate. There was, too, a certain thickness of speech, that gave another corroborating sign of evil progress.

"Have you seen any thing of Frank this afternoon?" he inquired of Matthew, after we had passed a few words.

"Nothing," was the bar-keeper's answer.

"I saw him with Tom Wilkins as I came over," said one of the men who was sitting in the porch.

"What was he doing with Tom Wilkins?" said Slade, in a fretted tone of voice. "He doesn't seem very choice of his company."

"They were gunning."

"Gunning!"

"Yes. They both had fowling-pieces. I wasn't near enough to ask where they were going."

This information disturbed Slade a good deal. After muttering to himself for a little while, he started up and went into the house.

"And I could have told him a little more, had I been so inclined," said the individual who mentioned the fact that Frank was with Tom Wilkins.

"What more?" inquired Matthew.

"There was a buggy in the case; and a champagne basket. What the latter contained you can easily guess."

"Whose buggy?"

"I don't know any thing about the buggy; but if 'Lightfoot' doesn't sink in value a hundred dollars or so before sundown, call me a false prophet."

"Oh, no," said Matthew, incredulously. "Frank wouldn't do an outrageous thing like that. Lightfoot won't be in a condition to drive for a month to come."

"I don't care. She's out now; and the way she was putting it down when I saw her, would have made a locomotive look cloudy."

"Where did he get her?" was inquired.

"She's been in the six-acre field, over by Mason's Bridge, for the last week or so," Matthew answered. "Well; all I have to say," he added, "is that Frank ought to be slung up and well horsewhipped. I never saw such a young rascal. He cares for no good, and fears no evil. He's the worst boy I ever saw."

"It would hardly do for you to call him a boy to his face," said one of the men, laughing.

"I don't have much to say to him in any way," replied Matthew, "for I know very well, that if we ever do get into a regular quarrel, there'll be a hard time of it. The same house will not hold us afterward—that's certain. So I steer clear of the young reprobate."

"I wonder his father don't put him to some business," was remarked. "The idle life he now leads will be his ruin."

"He was behind the bar for a year or two."

"Yes; and was smart at mixing a glass—but——"

"Was himself becoming too good a customer?"

"Precisely. He got drunk as a fool before reaching his fifteenth year."

"Good gracious!" I exclaimed, involuntarily.

"It's true, sir," said the last speaker, turning to me. "I never saw any thing like it. And this wasn't all. Bar-room talk, as you maybe know, isn't the most refined and virtuous in the world. I wouldn't like my son to hear much of it. Frank was always an eager listener to everything that was said, and in a very short time became an adept in slang and profanity. I'm no saint myself; but it's often made my blood run cold to hear him swear."

"I pity his mother," said I; for my thought turned naturally to Mrs. Slade.

"You may well do that," was answered. "I doubt if Cedarville holds a sadder heart. It was a dark day for her, let me tell you, when Simon Slade sold his mill and built this tavern. She was opposed to it in the beginning."

"I have inferred as much."

"I know it," said the man. "My wife has been intimate with her for years. Indeed, they have always been like sisters. I remember very well her coming to our house, about the time the mill was sold, and crying about it as if her heart would break. She saw nothing but trouble and sorrow ahead. Tavern-keeping she had always regarded as a low business; and the change from a respectable miller to a lazy tavern-keeper, as she expressed it, was presented to her mind as something disgraceful. I remember, very well, trying to argue the point with her—assuming that it was quite as respectable to keep tavern as to do any thing else; but I might as well have talked to the wind. She was always a pleasant, hopeful, cheerful woman before that time; but, really, I don't think I've seen a true smile on her face since."

"That was a great deal for a man to lose," said I.

"What?" he inquired, not clearly understanding me.

"The cheerful face of his wife."

"The face was but an index of her heart," said he.

"So much the worse."

"True enough for that. Yes, it was a great deal to lose."

"What has he gained that will make up for this?"

The man shrugged his shoulders.

"What has he gained?" I repeated. "Can you figure it up?"

"He's a richer man, for one thing."

"Happier?"

There was another shrug of the shoulders. "I wouldn't like to say that."

"How much richer?"

"Oh, a great deal. Somebody was saying, only yesterday, that he couldn't be worth less than thirty thousand dollars."

"Indeed? So much."

"Yes."

"How has he managed to accumulate so rapidly?"

"His bar has a large run of custom. And, you know, that pays wonderfully."

"He must have sold a great deal of liquor in six years."

"And he has. I don't think I'm wrong in saying, that in the six years which have gone by since the 'Sickle and Sheaf' was opened, more liquor has been drank than in the previous twenty years."

"Say forty," remarked a man who had been a listener to what we said.

"Let it be forty then," was the according answer.

"How come this?" I inquired. "You had a tavern here before the 'Sickle and Sheaf' was opened."

"I know we had, and several places besides where liquor was sold. But, everybody far and near knew Simon Slade the miller, and everybody liked him. He was a good miller, and a cheerful, social, chatty sort of a man, putting everybody in a good humour who came near him. So it became the talk everywhere, when he built this house, which he fitted up nicer than anything that had been seen in these parts. Judge Hammond, Judge Lyman, Lawyer Wilson, and all the big-bugs of the place at once patronised the new tavern; and, of course, everybody else did the same. So, you can easily see how he got such a run."

"It was thought in the beginning," said I, "that the new tavern was going to do wonders for Cedarville."

"Yes," answered the man laughing, "and so it has."

"In what respect?"

"Oh, in many. It has made some men richer, and some poorer."

"Who has it made poorer?"

"Dozens of people. You may always take it for granted, when you see a tavern-keeper, who has a good run at his bar, getting rich, that a great many people are getting poor."

"How so?" I wished to hear in what way the man, who was himself, as was plain to see, a good customer at somebody's bar, reasoned on the subject.

"He does not add to the general wealth. He produces nothing. He takes money from his customers, but gives them no article of value in return—nothing that can be called property, personal or real. He is just so much richer and they just so much poorer for the exchange. Is it not so?"

I readily assented to the position as true, and than said—

"Who, in particular, is poorer?"

"Judge Hammond, for one."

"Indeed! I thought the advance in his property, in consequence of the building of this tavern, was so great, that he was reaping a rich pecuniary harvest."

"There was a slight advance in property along the street after the 'Sickle and Sheaf' was opened, and Judge Hammond was benefited thereby. Interested parties made a good deal of noise about it; but it didn't amount to much, I believe."

"What has caused the judge to grow poorer?"

"The opening of this tavern, as I just said."

"In what way did it affect him?"

"He was among Slade's warmest supporters, as soon as he felt the advance in the price of building lots; called him one of the most enterprising men in Cedarville—a real benefactor to the place—and all that stuff. To set a good example of patronage, he came over every day and took his glass of brandy, and encouraged everybody else that he could influence to do the same. Among those who followed his example was his son Willy. There was not, let me tell you, in all the country for twenty miles around, a finer young man than Willy, nor one of so much promise, when this man-trap"—he let his voice fall, and glanced around, as he thus designated Slade's tavern—"was opened; and now, there is not one dashing more recklessly along the road to ruin. When too late, his father saw that his son was corrupted, and that the company he kept was of a dangerous character. Two reasons led him to purchase Slade's old mill, and turn it into a factory and a distillery. Of course, he had to make a heavy outlay for additional buildings, machinery, and distilling apparatus. The reasons influencing him were the prospect of realizing a large amount of money, especially in distilling, and the hope of saving Willy, by getting him closely engaged and interested in business. To accomplish, more certainly, the latter end, he unwisely transferred to his son, as his own capital, twenty thousand dollars, and then formed with him a regular copartnership—giving Willy an active business control.

"But the experiment, sir," added the man, emphatically, "has proved a failure. I heard yesterday, that both mill and distillery were to be shut up, and offered for sale."

"They did not prove as money-making as was anticipated?"

"No, not under Willy Hammond's management. He had made too many bad acquaintances—men who clung to him because he had plenty of money at his command, and spent it as freely as water. One half of his time he was away from the mill, and while there, didn't half attend to business. I've heard it said—and I don't much doubt its truth—that he's squandered his twenty thousand dollars, and a great deal more besides."

"How is that possible?"

"Well; people talk, and not always at random. There's been a man staying here, most of his time, for the last four or five years, named Green. He does not do anything, and don't seem to have any friends in the neighbourhood. Nobody knows where he came from, and he is not at all communicative on that head himself. Well, this man became acquainted with young Hammond after Willy got to visiting the bar here, and attached himself to him at once. They have, to all appearance, been fast friends every since; riding about, or going off on gunning or fishing excursions almost every day, and secluding themselves somewhere nearly every evening. That man, Green, sir, it is whispered, is a gambler; and I believe it. Granted, and there is no longer a mystery as to what Willy does with his own and his father's money."

I readily assented to this view of the case.

"And so assuming that Green is a gambler," said I, "He has grown richer, in consequence of the opening of a new and more attractive tavern in Cedarville."

"Yes, and Cedarville is so much the poorer for all his gains; for I've never heard of his buying a foot of ground, or in any way encouraging productive industry. He's only a blood-sucker."

"It is worse than the mere abstraction of money," I remarked; "he corrupts his victims, at the same time that he robs them."

"True."

"Willy Hammond may not be his only victim," I suggested.

"Nor is he, in my opinion. I've been coming to this bar, nightly, for a good many years—a sorry confession for a man to make, I must own," he added, with a slight tinge of shame; "but so it is. Well, as I was saying, I've been coming to this bar, nightly, for a good many years, and I generally see all that is going on around me. Among the regular visitors are at least half a dozen young men, belonging to our best families—who have been raised with care, and well educated. That their presence here is unknown to their friends, I am quite certain—or, at least, unknown and unsuspected by some of them. They do not drink a great deal yet; but all try a glass or two. Toward nine o'clock, often at an earlier hour, you will see one and another of them go quietly out of the bar, through the sitting-room, preceded, or soon followed, by Green and Slade. At any hour of the night, up to one or two, and sometimes three o'clock, you can see light streaming through the rent in a curtain drawn before a particular window, which I know to be in the room of Harvey Green. These are facts, sir; and you can draw your own conclusion. I think it a very serious matter."

"Why does Slade go out with these young men?" I inquired. "Do you think he gambles, also?"

"If he isn't a kind of a stool-pigeon for Harvey Green, then I'm mistaken again."

"Hardly. He cannot, already, have become so utterly unprincipled."

"It's a bad school, sir, this tavern-keeping," said the man.

"I readily grant you that."

"And it's nearly seven years since he commenced to take lessons. A great deal may be learned, sir, of good or evil, in seven years, especially if any interest be taken in the studies."

"True."

"And it's true in this case, you may depend upon it. Simon Slade is not the man he was, seven years ago. Anybody with half an eye can see that. He's grown selfish, grasping, unscrupulous, and passionate. There could hardly be a greater difference between men than exists between Simon Slade the tavern-keeper, and Simon Slade the miller."

"And intemperate, also?" I suggested.

"He's beginning to take a little too much," was answered.

"In that case, he'll scarcely be as well off five years hence as he is now."

"He's at the top of the wheel, some of us think."

"What has led to this opinion?"

"He's beginning to neglect his house, for one thing."

"A bad sign."

"And there is another sign. Heretofore, he has always been on hand, with the cash, when desirable property went off, under forced sale, at a bargain. In the last three or four months, several great sacrifices have been made, but Simon Slade showed no inclination to buy. Put this fact against another,—week before last, he sold a house and lot in the town for five hundred dollars less than he paid for them, a year ago—and for just that sum less than their true value."

"How came that?" I inquired.

"Ah! there's the question! He wanted money; though for what purpose, he has not intimated to anyone, as far as I can learn."

"What do you think of it?"

"Just this. He and Green have been hunting together in times past; but the professed gambler's instincts are too strong to let him spare even his friend in evil. They have commenced playing one against the other."

"Ah! you think so?"

"I do; and if I conjecture rightly, Simon Slade will be a poorer man, in a year from this time, than he is now."

Here our conversation was interrupted. Some one asked my talkative friend to go and take a drink, and he, nothing loath, left me without ceremony.

Very differently served was the supper I partook of on that evening, from the one set before me on the occasion of my first visit to the "Sickle and Sheaf." The table-cloth was not merely soiled, but offensively dirty; the plates, cups, and saucers, dingy and sticky; the knives and forks unpolished; and the food of a character to satisfy the appetite with a very few mouthfuls. Two greasy-looking Irish girls waited on the table, at which neither landlord nor landlady presided. I was really hungry when the supper-bell rang; but the craving of my stomach soon ceased in the atmosphere of the dining-room, and I was the first to leave the table.

Soon after the lamps were lighted, company began to assembly in the spacious bar-room, where were comfortable seats, with tables, newspapers, backgammon boards, dominos, etc. The first act of nearly every one who came in, was to call for a glass of liquor; and sometimes the same individual drank two or three times in the course of half an hour, on the invitation of newcomers who were convivially inclined.

Most of those who came in were strangers to me. I was looking from face to face to see if any of the old company were present, when one countenance struck me as familiar. I was studying it, in order, if possible, to identify the person, when some one addressed him as "Judge."

Changed as the face was, I now recognised it as that of Judge Lyman. Five years had marred that face terribly. It seemed twice the former size; and all its bright expression was gone. The thickened and protruding eyelids half closed the leaden eyes, and the swollen lips and cheeks gave to his countenance a look of all-predominating sensuality. True manliness had bowed itself in debashing submission to the bestial. He talked loudly, and with a pompous dogmatism—mainly on political subjects—but talked only from memory; for any one could see, that thought came into but feeble activity. And yet, derationalized, so to speak, as he was, through drink, he had been chosen a representative in Congress, at the previous election, on the antitemperance ticket, and by a very handsome majority. He was the rum candidate; and the rum interest, aided by the easily swayed "indifferents," swept aside the claims of law, order, temperance, and good morals; and the district from which he was chosen as a National Legislator sent him up to the National Councils, and said in the act—"Look upon him we have chosen as our representative, and see in him a type of our principles, our quality, and our condition as a community."

Judge Lyman, around whom a little circle soon gathered, was very severe on the temperance party, which, for two years, had opposed his election, and which, at the last struggle, showed itself to be a rapidly growing organization. During the canvass, a paper was published by this party, in which his personal habits, character, and moral principles were discussed in the freest manner, and certainly not in a way to elevate him in the estimation of men whose opinion was of any value.

It was not much to be wondered at, that he assumed to think temperance issues at the polls were false issues; and that when temperance men sought to tamper with elections, the liberties of the people were in danger; nor that he pronounced the whole body of temperance men as selfish schemers and canting hypocrites.

"The next thing we will have," he exclaimed, warming with his theme, and speaking so loud that his voice sounded throughout the room, and arrested every one's attention, "will be laws to fine any man who takes a chew of tobacco or lights a cigar. Touch the liberties of the people in the smallest particular, and all guarantees are gone. The Stamp Act, against which our noble forefathers rebelled, was a light measure of oppression to that contemplated by these worse than fanatics."

"You are right there, judge; right for once in your life, if you (hic) were never right before!" exclaimed a battered looking specimen of humanity, who stood near the speaker, slapping Judge Lyman on the shoulder familiarly as he spoke. "There's no telling what they will do. There's (hic) my old uncle Josh Wilson, who's been keeper of the Poor-house these ten years. Well, they're going to turn him out, if ever they get the upper hand in Bolton county."

"If? That word involves a great deal, Harry?" said Lyman. "We mus'n't let them get the upper hand. Every man has a duty to perform to his country in this matter, and every one must do his duty. But what have they got against your Uncle Joshua? What has he been doing to offend this righteous party?"

"They've nothing against him, (hic) I believe. Only, they say, they're not going to have a Poor-house in the county at all."

"What! Going to turn the poor wretches out to starve?" said one.

"Oh no! (hic)," and the fellow grinned, half shrewdly and half maliciously, as he answered—"no, not that. But, when they carry the day, there'll be no need of Poor-houses. At least, that's their talk—and I guess maybe there's something in it, for I never knew a man to go to the Poor-house, who hadn't (hic) rum to blame for his poverty. But, you see, I'm interested in this matter. I go for keeping up the Poor-house (hic); for I guess I'm travelling that road, and I should'nt like to get to the last milestone (hic) and find no snug quarters—no Uncle Josh. You're safe for one vote, anyhow, old chap, on next election day!" And the man's broad hand slapped the member's shoulder again. "Huzza for the rummies! That's (hic) the ticket! Harry Grimes never deserts his friends. True as steel."

"You're a trump!" returned Judge Lyman, with low familiarity. "Never fear about the Poor-house and Uncle Josh. They're all safe."

"But look here, judge," resumed the man. "It isn't only the Poor-house, the jail is to go next."

"Indeed!"

"Yes, that's their talk; and I guess they ain't far out of the way neither. What takes men to jail? You can tell us something about that, judge, for you've jugged a good many in your time. Didn't pretty much all of 'em drink rum? (hic.)"

But the judge answered nothing.

"Silence (hic) gives consent," resumed Grimes. "And they say more; once give 'em the upper hand—and they're confident of beating us—and the Courthouse will be to let. As for judges and lawyers, they'll starve, or go into some better business. So you see, (hic) judge, your liberties are in danger. But fight hard, old fellow; and if you must die, (hic) die game!"

How well Judge Lyman relished this mode of presenting the case, was not very apparent; he was too good a politician and office-seeker, to show any feeling on the subject, and thus endanger a vote. Harry Grimes's vote counted one, and a single vote, sometimes, gained or lost an election.

"One of their gags," he said, laughing. "But I'm too old a stager not to see the flimsiness of such pretensions. Poverty and crime have their origin in the corrupt heart, and their foundations are laid long and long before the first step is taken on the road to inebriety. It is easy to promise results; for only the few look at causes, and trace them to their effects."

"Rum and ruin, (hic). Are they not cause and effect?" asked Grimes.

"Sometimes they are," was the half extorted answer.

"Oh, Green! is that you?" exclaimed the judge, as Harvey Green came in with a soft cat-like step. He was, evidently, glad of a chance to get rid of his familiar friend and elector.

I turned my eyes upon the man, and read his face closely. It was unchanged. The same cold, sinister eye; the same chiselled mouth, so firm now, and now yielding so elastically; the same smile "from the teeth outward"—the same lines that revealed his heart's deep, dark selfishness. If he had indulged in drink during the five intervening years, it had not corrupted his blood, nor added thereto a single degree of heat.

"Have you seen any thing of Hammond this evening?" asked Judge Lyman.

"I saw him an hour or two ago," answered Green.

"How does he like his new horse?"

"He's delighted with him."

"What was the price?"

"Three hundred dollars."

"Indeed!"

The judge had already arisen, and he and Green were now walking side by side across the bar-room floor.

"I want to speak a word with you," I heard Lyman say.

And then the two went out together. I saw no more of them during the evening.

Not long afterward, Willy Hammond came in. Ah! there was a sad change here; a change that in no way belied the words of Matthew the bar-keeper. He went up to the bar, and I heard him ask for Judge Lyman. The answer was in so low a voice, that it did not reach my ear.

With a quick, nervous motion, Hammond threw his hand toward a row of decanters on the shelf behind the bar-keeper, who immediately set one of them containing brandy before him. From this he poured a tumbler half full, and drank it off at a single draught, unmixed with water.

He then asked some further question, which I could not hear, manifesting, as it appeared, considerable excitement of mind. In answering him, Matthew glanced his eyes upward, as if indicating some room in the house. The young man then retired, hurriedly, through the sitting-room.

"What's the matter with Willy Hammond to-night?" asked some one of the bar-keeper. "Who's he after in such a hurry?"

"He wants to see Judge Lyman," replied Matthew.

"Oh!"

"I guess they're after no good," was remarked.

"Not much, I'm afraid."

Two young men, well dressed, and with faces marked by intelligence, came in at the moment, drank at the bar, chatted a little while familiarly with the bar-keeper, and then quietly disappeared through the door leading into the sitting-room. I met the eyes of the man with whom I had talked during the afternoon, and his knowing wink brought to mind his suggestion, that in one of the upper rooms gambling went on nightly, and that some of the most promising young men of the town had been drawn, through the bar attraction, into this vortex of ruin. I felt a shudder creeping along my nerves.

The converstion that now went on among the company was of such an obscene and profane character, that, in disgust, I went out. The night was clear, the air soft, and the moon shining down brightly. I walked for some time in the porch, musing on what I had seen and heard; while a constant stream of visiters came pouring into the bar-room. Only a few of these remained. The larger portion went in quickly, took their glass, and then left, as if to avoid observation as much as possible.

Soon after I commenced walking in the porch I noticed an elderly lady go slowly by, who, in passing, slightly paused, and evidently tried to look through the bar-room door. The pause was but for an instant. In less than ten minutes she came back, again stopped—this time longer—and again moved off slowly, until she passed out of sight. I was yet thinking about her, when, on lifting my eyes from the ground, she was advancing along the road, but a few rods distant. I almost started at seeing her, for there no longer remained a doubt on my mind, that she was some trembling, heart-sick mother, in search of an erring son whose feet were in dangerous paths. Seeing me, she kept on, though lingeringly. She went but a short distance before returning; and this time, she moved in closer to the house, and reached a position that enabled her eyes to range through a large portion of the bar-room. A nearer inspection appeared to satisfy her. She retired with quicker steps; and did not again return during the evening.

Ah! what a commentary upon the uses of an attractive tavern was here! My heart ached, as I thought of all that unknown mother had suffered; and was doomed to suffer. I could not shut out the image of her drooping form as I lay upon my pillow that night; she even haunted me in my dreams.

❧ Night the Sixth

More Consequences

The landlord did not make his appearance on the next morning until nearly ten o'clock; and then he looked like a man who had been on a debauch. It was eleven before Harvey Green came down. Nothing about him indicated the smallest deviation from the most orderly habit. Clean shaved, with fresh linen, and a face every line of which was smoothed into calmness, he looked as if he had slept soundly on a quiet conscience, and now hailed the new day with a tranquil spirit.

The first act of Slade was to go behind the bar and take a stiff glass of brandy and water; the first act of Green, to order beefsteak and coffee for his breakfast. I noticed the meeting between the two men, on the appearance of Green. There was a slight reserve on the part of Green, and an uneasy embarrassment on the part of Slade. Not even the ghost of a smile was visible in either countenance. They spoke a few words together, and then separated as if from a sphere of mutual repulsion. I did not observe them again in company during the day.

"There's trouble over at the mill," was remarked by a gentleman with whom I had some business transactions in the afternoon. He spoke to a person who sat in his office.

"Ah! what's the matter?" said the other.

"All the hands were discharged at noon, and the mill shut down."

"How comes that?"

"They've been losing money from the start."

"Rather bad practice, I should say."

"It involves some bad practices, no doubt."

"On Willy's part?"

"Yes. He is reported to have squandered the means placed in his hands, after a shameless fashion."

"Is the loss heavy?"

"So it is said."

"How much?"

"Reaching to thirty or forty thousand dollars. But this is rumour, and, of course, an exaggeration."

"Of course. No such loss as that could have been made. But what was done with the money? How could Willy have spent it. He dashes about a great deal; buys fast horses, drinks rather freely, and all that; but thirty or forty thousand dollars couldn't escape in this way."

At the moment a swift trotting horse, bearing a light sulky and a man, went by.

"There goes young Hammond's three hundred dollar animal," said the last speaker.

"It was Willy Hammond's yesterday. But there has been a change of ownership since then; I happen to know."

"Indeed."

"Yes. The man Green, who has been loafing about Cedarville for the last few years—after no good, I can well believe—came into possession to-day."

"Ah? Willy must be very fickle-minded. Does the possession of a coveted object so soon bring satiety?"

"There is something not clearly understood about the transaction. I saw Mr. Hammond during the forenoon, and he looked terribly distressed."

"The embarrassed condition of things at the mill readily accounts for this."

"True; but I think there are causes of trouble beyond the mere embarrassments."

"The dissolute, spendthrift habits of his son," was suggested. "These are sufficient to weigh down the father's spirits,—to bow him to the very dust."

"To speak out plainly," said the other, "I am afraid that the young man adds another vice to that of drinking and idleness."

"What?"

"Gaming."

"No!"

"There is little doubt of it in my mind. And it is further my opinion, that his fine horse, for which he paid three hundred dollars only a few days ago, has passed into the hands of this man Green, in payment of a debt contracted at the gaming table."

"You shock me. Surely, there can be no grounds for such a belief."

"I have, I am sorry to say, the gravest reasons for what I allege. That Green is a professional gambler, who was attracted here by the excellent company that assembled at the 'Sickle and Sheaf' in the beginning of the lazy miller's pauper-making experiment, I do not in the least question. Grant this, and take into account the fact that young Hammond has been much in his company, and you have sufficient cause for the most disastrous effects."

"If this be really so," observed the gentleman, over whose face a shadow of concern darkened, "then Willy Hammond may not be his only victim."

"And is not, you may rest assured. If rumour be true, other of our promising young men are being drawn into the whirling circles that narrow toward a vortex of ruin."

In corroboration of this, I mentioned the conversation I had held with one of the frequenters of Slade's bar-room, on this very subject; and also what I had myself observed on the previous evening.

The man, who had until now been sitting quietly in a chair, started up, exclaiming as he did so—

"Merciful heaven! I never dreamed of this! Whose sons are safe?"

"No man's," was the answer of the gentleman in whose office we were sitting—"No man's—while there are such open doors to ruin as you may find at the 'Sickle and Sheaf.' Did not you vote the anti-temperance ticket at the last election?"

"I did," was the answer; "and from principle."

"On what were your principles based?" was inquired.

"On the broad foundations of civil liberty."

"The liberty to do good or evil, just as the individual, may choose?"

"I would not like to say that. There are certain evils against which there can be no legislation that would not do harm. No civil power in this country has the right to say what a citizen shall eat or drink."

"But may not the people, in any community, pass laws, through their delegated lawmakers, restraining evil-minded persons from injuring the common good?"

"Oh, certainly—certainly."

"And are you prepared to affirm, that a drinking shop, where young men are corrupted—ay, destroyed, body and soul—does not work an injury to the common good?"

"Ah! but there must be houses of public entertainment."

"No one denies this. But can that be a really Christian community which provides for the moral debasement of strangers, at the same time that it entertains them? Is it necessary that, in giving rest and entertainment to the traveller, we also lead him into temptation?"

"Yes—But—but—it is going too far to legislate on what we are to eat and drink. It is opening too wide a door for fanatical oppression. We must inculcate temperance as a right principal. We must teach our children the evils of intemperance, and send them out into the world as practical teachers of order, virtue, and sobriety. If we do this, the reform becomes radical, and in a few years there will be no bar-rooms, for none will crave the fiery poison."

"Of little value, my friend, will be, in far too many cases, your precepts, if temptation invites our sons at almost every step of their way through life. Thousands have fallen, and thousands are now tottering, soon to fall. Your sons are not safe; nor are mine. We cannot tell the day nor the hour when they may weakly yield to the solicitation of some companion, and enter the wide open door of ruin. And are we wise and good citizens to commission men to do the evil·work of enticement? To encourage them to get gain in corrupting and destroying our children? To hesitate over some vague ideal of human liberty, when the sword is among us, slaying our best and dearest? Sir! while you hold back from the work of staying the flood that is desolating our fairest homes, the black waters are approaching your own doors."

There was a startling emphasis in the tones with which this last sentence was uttered; and I did not wonder at the look of anxious alarm that it called to the face of him whose fears it was meant to excite.

"What do you mean, sir?" was inquired.

"Simply, that your sons are in equal danger with others."

"And is that all?"

"They have been seen, of late, in the bar-room of the 'Sickle and Sheaf.' "

"Who says so?"

"Twice within a week I have seen them going in there," was answered.

"Good heavens! No!"

"It is true, my friend. But who is safe? If we dig pits, and conceal them from view, what marvel if our own children fall therein?"

"My sons going to a tavern!" The man seemed utterly confounded. "How *can* I believe it? You must be in error, sir."

"No. What I tell you is the simple truth. And if they go there—"

The man paused not to hear the conclusion of the sentence, but went hastily from the office.

"We are beginning to reap as we have sown," remarked the gentleman, turning to me as his agitated friend left the office. "As I told them in the commencement it would be, so it is happening. The want of a good tavern in Cedarville was over and over again alleged as one of the chief causes of our want of thrift, and when Slade opened the 'Sickle and Sheaf,' the man was almost glorified. The gentleman who has just left us failed not in laudation of the enterprising landlord; the more particularly, as the building of the new tavern advanced the price of ground on the street, and made him a few hundred dollars richer. Really, for a time, one might have thought, from the way people went on, that Simon Slade was going to make every man's fortune in Cedarville. But all that has been gained by a small advance in property, is as a grain of sand to a mountain, compared with the fearful demoralization that has followed."

I readily assented to this, for I had myself seen enough to justify the conclusion.

As I sat in the bar-room of the "Sickle and Sheaf" that evening, I noticed, soon after the lamps were lighted, the gentleman referred to in the above conversation, whose sons were represented as visitors to the bar, come in quietly, and look anxiously about the room. He spoke to no one, and, after satisfying himself that those he sought were not there, went out.

"What sent him here, I wonder?" muttered Slade, speaking partly to himself, and partly aside to Matthew, the bar-keeper.

"After the boys, I suppose," was answered.

"I guess the boys are old enough to take care of themselves."

"They ought to be," returned Matthew.

"And are," said Slade. "Have they been here this evening?"

"No, not yet."

While they yet talked together, two young men whom I had seen on the night before, and noticed particularly as showing signs of intelligence and respectability beyond the ordinary visiters at a bar-room, came in.

"John," I heard Slade say, in a low, confidential voice, to one of them, "your old man was here just now."

"No!" The young man looked startled—almost confounded.

"It's a fact. So you'd better keep shady."

"What did he want?"

"I don't know."

"What did he say?"

"Nothing. He just came in, looked around, and then went out."

"His face was dark as a thunder-cloud," remarked Matthew.

"Is No. 4 vacant?" inquired one of the young men.

"Yes."

"Send us up a bottle of wine and some cigars. And when Bill Harding and Harry Lee come in, tell them where they can find us."

"All right," said Matthew. "And now take a friend's advice and make yourselves scarce."

The young men left the room hastily. Scarcely had they departed, ere I saw the same gentleman come in, whose anxious face had, a little while before, thrown its shadow over the apartment. He was the father in search of his sons. Again he glanced around, nervously; and this time appeared to be disappointed. As he entered, Slade went out.

"Have John and Wilson been here this evening?" he asked, coming up to the bar and addressing Matthew.

"They are not here," replied Matthew, evasively.

"But haven't they been here?"

"They *may* have been here; I only came in from my supper a little while ago."

"I thought I saw them entering, only a moment or two ago."

"They're not here, sir." Matthew shook his head and spoke firmly.

"Where is Mr. Slade?"

"In the house, somewhere."

"I wish you would ask him to step here."

Matthew went out, but in a little while came back with word that the landlord was not to be found.

"You are sure the boys are not here," said the man, with a doubting, dissatisfied manner.

"See for yourself, Mr. Harrison!"

"Perhaps they are in the parlour?"

"Step in, sir," coolly returned Matthew. The man went through the door into the sitting-room, but came back immediately.

"Not there?" said Matthew. The man shook his head. "I don't think you will find them about here," added the bar-keeper.

Mr. Harrison—this was the name by which Matthew had addressed him—stood musing and irresolute for some minutes. He could not be mistaken about the entrance of his sons, and yet they were not there. His manner was much perplexed. At length he took a seat, in a far corner of the bar-room, somewhat beyond the line of observation, evidently with the purpose of waiting to see if those he sought would come in. He had not been there long, before two young men entered, whose appearance at once excited his interest. They went up to the bar and called for liquor. As Matthew set the decanter before them, he leaned over the counter, and said something in a whisper.

"Where?" was instantly ejaculated, in surprise, and both of the young men glanced uneasily about the room. They met the eyes of Mr. Harrison, fixed intently upon them. I do not think, from the way they swallowed their brandy and water, that it was enjoyed very much.

"What the deuce is he doing here?" I heard one of them say, in a low voice.

"After the boys, of course."

"Have they come yet?"

Matthew winked as he answered, "All safe."

"In No. 4!"

"Yes. And the wine and cigars all waiting for you."

"Good."

"You'd better not go through the parlour. Their old man's not at all satisfied. He half suspects they're in the house. Better go off down the street, and come back and enter through the passage."

The young men, acting on this hint, at once retired, the eyes of Harrison following them out.

For nearly an hour Mr. Harrison kept his position, a close observer of all that transpired. I am very much in error, if, before leaving that sink of iniquity, he was not fully satisfied as to the propriety of legislating on the liquor question. Nay, I incline to the opinion, that, if the power of suppression had rested in his hands, there would not have been, in the whole State, at the expiration of an hour, a single dram-selling establishment. The goring of his ox had opened his eyes to the true merits of the question. While he was yet in the barroom, young Hammond made his appearance. His look was wild and excited. First he called for brandy, and drank with the eagerness of a man long athirst.

"Where is Green?" I heard him inquire, as he set his glass upon the counter.

"Haven't seen any thing since supper," was answered by Matthew.

"Is he in his room?"

"I think it probable."

"Has Judge Lyman been about here to-night?"

"Yes. He spouted here for half an hour against the temperance party, as usual, and then"—Matthew tossed his head toward the door leading to the sitting-room.

Hammond was moving toward this door, when, in glancing around the room, he encountered the fixed gaze of Mr. Harrison—a gaze that instantly checked his progress. Returning to the bar, and leaning over the counter, he said to Matthew,

"What has sent him here?"

Matthew winked knowingly.

"After the boys?" inquired Hammond.

"Yes."

"Where are they?"

"Up-stairs."

"Does he suspect this?"

"I can't tell. If he doesn't think them here now, he is looking for them to come in."

"Do they know he is after them?"

"O yes."

"All safe then?"

"As an iron chest. If you want to see them, just tap at No. 4."

Hammond stood for some minutes leaning on the bar, and then, not once again looking toward that part of the room where Mr. Harrison was seated, passed out through the door leading to the street. Soon afterward Mr. Harrison departed.

Disgusted, as on the night before, with the unceasing flow of vile, obscene, and profane language, I left my place of observation in the bar-room and sought the open air. The sky was unobscured by a single cloud, and the moon, almost at the full, shone abroad with more than common brightness. I had not been sitting long in the porch, when the same lady, whose movements had attracted my attention, came in sight, walking very slowly—the deliberate pace assumed, evidently, for the purpose of better observation. On coming opposite the tavern, she slightly paused, as on the evening before, and then kept on, passing down the street, until she was beyond observation.

"Poor mother!" I was still repeating to myself, when her form again met my eyes. Slowly she advanced, and now came in nearer to the house. The interest excited in my mind was so strong, that I could not repress the desire I felt to address her, and so stepped from the shadow of the porch. She seemed startled, and retreated backward several paces.

"Are you in search of any one?" I inquired, respectfully.

The woman now stood in a position that let the moon shine full upon her face, revealing every feature. She was far past the meridian of life; and there were lines of suffering and sorrow on her fine countenance. I saw that her lips moved, but it was time before I distinguished the words.

"Have you seen my son to-night? They say he comes here."

The manner in which this was said caused a cold thrill to run over me. I perceived that the woman's mind wandered. I answered—

"No, ma'am; I haven't seen any thing of him."

My tone of voice seemed to inspire her with confidence, for she came up close to me, and bent her face toward mine.

"It's a dreadful place," she whispered, huskily. "And they say he comes here. Poor boy! He isn't what he used to be."

"It is a very bad place," said I. "Come"—and I moved a step or two in the direction from which I had seen her approaching—"come, you'd better go away as quickly as possible."

"But if he's here," she answered, not moving from where she stood, "I might save him, you know."

"I am sure you won't find him, ma'am," I urged. "Perhaps he is home, now."

"Oh, no! no!" and she shook her head mournfully. "He never comes home until long after midnight. I wish I could see inside of the bar-room. I'm sure he must be there."

"If you will tell me his name, I will go in and search for him."

After a moment of hesitation, she answered,

"His name is Willy Hammond."

How the name, uttered so sadly, and yet with such moving tenderness by the mother's lips, caused me to start—almost to tremble.

"If he is in the house, ma'am," said I, firmly, "I will see him for you." And I left her and went into the bar.

"In what room do you think I will find young Hammond?" I asked of the bar-keeper.

He looked at me curiously, but did not answer. The question had come upon him unanticipated.

"In Harvey Green's room?" I pursued.

"I don't know, I am sure. He isn't in the house to my knowledge. I saw him go out about half an hour since."

"Green's room is No.—?"

"Eleven," he answered.

"In the front part of the house?"

"Yes."

I asked no further question, but went to No. 11, and tapped on the door. But no one answered the summons. I listened, but could not distinguish the slightest sound within. Again I knocked; but louder. If my ears did not deceive me, the clink of coin was heard. Still there was neither voice nor movement.

I was disappointed. That the room had inmates, I felt sure. Remembering, now, what I had heard about light being seen in this room through a rent in the curtain, I went down-stairs, and out into the street. A short distance beyond the house, I saw, dimly, the woman's form. She had only just passed in her movement to and fro. Glancing up at the window, which I now knew to be the one in Green's room, light through the torn curtain was plainly visible. Back into the house I went, and up to No. 11. This time I knocked imperatively; and this time made myself heard.

"What's wanted?" came from within. I knew the voice to be that of Harvey Green.

I only knocked louder. A hurried movement and the low murmur of voices was heard for some moments; then the door was unlocked and held partly open by Green, whose body so filled the narrow aperture that I could not look into the room. Seeing me, a dark scowl fell upon his countenance.

"What d'ye want?" he inquired, sharply.

"Is Mr. Hammond here? If so, he is wanted down-stairs."

"No, he's not," was the quick answer. "What sent you here for him, hey?"

"The fact that I expected to find him in your room," was my firm answer.

Green was about shutting the door in my face, when some one placed a hand on his shoulder, and said something to him that I could not hear.

"Who wants to see him?" he inquired of me.

Satisfied, now, that Hammond was in the room, I said, slightly elevating my voice.

"His mother."

The words were an "open sesame" to the room. The door was suddenly jerked open, and with a blanching face, the young man confronted me.

"Who says my mother is down-stairs?" he demanded.

"I come from her in search of you," said I. "You will find her in the road, walking up and down in front of the tavern."

Almost with a bound he swept by me, and descended the stairway at two or three long strides. As the door swung open, I saw, besides Green and Hammond, the landlord and Judge Lyman. It needed not the loose cards on a table near which the latter were sitting to tell me of their business in that room.

As quickly as seemed decorous, I followed Hammond. On the porch I met him, coming in from the road.

"You have deceived me, sir," said he, sternly—almost menacingly.

"No, sir!" I replied. "What I told you was but too true. Look! There she is now."

The young man sprung around, and stood before the woman, a few paces distant.

"Mother! oh, mother! what *has* brought you here?" he exclaimed, in an under tone, as he caught her arm, and moved away. He spoke—not roughly, nor angrily—but with respect—half reproachfulness—and an unmistakable tenderness.

"Oh, Willy! Willy!" I heard her answer. "Somebody said you came here at night, and I couldn't rest. Oh, dear! They'll murder you! I know they will. Don't, oh!—"

My ears took in the sense no further, though her pleading voice still reached my ears. A few moments, and they were out of sight.

Nearly two hours afterward, as I was ascending to my chamber, a man brushed quickly by me. I glanced after him, and recognised the person of young Hammond. He was going to the room of Harvey Green!

❧ Night the Seventh

Sowing the Wind

The state of affairs in Cedarville, it was plain, from the partial glimpses I had received, was rather desperate. Desperate, I mean, as regarded the various parties brought before my observation. An eating cancer was on the community, and so far as the eye could mark its destructive progress, the ravages were fearful. That its roots were striking deep, and penetrating, concealed from view, in many unsuspected directions, there could be no doubt. What appeared on the surface was but a milder form of the disease, compared with its hidden, more vital, and more dangerous advances.

I could not but feel a strong interest in some of these parties. The case of young Hammond, had from the first, awakened concern; and now a new element was added in the unlooked-for appearance of his mother on the stage, in a state that seemed one of partial derangement. The gentleman at whose office I met Mr. Harrison on the day before—the reader will remember Mr. H. as having come to the "Sickle and Sheaf" in search of his sons—was thoroughly conversant with the affairs of the village, and I called upon him early in the day in order to make some inquiries about Mrs. Hammond. My first question, as to whether he knew the lady, was answered by the remark—

"Oh, yes. She is one of my earliest friends."

The allusion to her did not seem to awaken agreeable states of mind. A slight shade obscured his face, and I noticed that he sighed involuntarily.

"Is Willy her only child?"

"Her only living child. She had four; another son, and two daughters; but she lost all but Willy when they were quite young. And," he added, after a pause—"it would have been better for her, and for Willy too, if he had gone to a better land with them."

"His course of life must be to her a terrible affliction," said I.

"It is destroying her reason," he replied, with emphasis. "He was her idol. No mother ever loved a son with more self-devotion than Mrs. Hammond loved her beautiful, fine-spirited, intelligent, affectionate boy. To say that she was proud of him, is but a tame expression. Intense love—almost idolatry—was the strong passion of her heart. How tender, how watchful was her love! Except when at school, he was scarcely ever separated from her. In order to keep him by her side, she gave up her thoughts to the suggestion and maturing of plans for keeping his mind active and interested in her society— and her success was perfect. Up to the age of sixteen or seventeen, I do not think he had a desire for other companionship than that of his mother. But this, you know, could not last. The boy's maturing thoughts must go beyond the home and social circle. The great world, that he was soon to enter, was before him; and through loopholes that opened here and there, he obtained partial glimpses of what was beyond. To step forth into this world, where he was soon to be a busy actor and worker, and to step forth alone, next came in the natural order of progress. How his mother trembled with anxiety, as she saw him leave her side. Of the danger that would surround his path, she knew too well; and these were magnified by her fears—at least so I often said to her. Alas! how far the sad reality has outrun her most fearful anticipations.

"When Willy was eighteen—he was then reading law—I think I never saw a young man of fairer promise. As I have often heard it remarked of him, he did not appear to have a single fault. But he had a dangerous gift—rare conversational powers, united with great urbanity of manner. Every one who made his acquaintance became charmed with his society; and he soon found himself surrounded by a circle of young men, some of whom were not the best companions he might have chosen. Still, his own pure instincts and honourable principles were his safeguard; and I never have believed that any social allurements would have drawn him away from the right path, if this accursed tavern had not been opened by Slade."

"There was a tavern here before the 'Sickle and Sheaf' was opened," said I.

"Oh, yes. But it was badly kept, and the bar-room visitors were of the lowest class. No respectable young man in Cedarville would have been seen there. It offered no temptations to one moving in Willy's circle. But the opening of the 'Sickle and Sheaf' formed a new era. Judge Hammond—himself not the purest man in the world, I'm afraid—gave his countenance to the establishment, and talked of Simon Slade as an enterprising man who ought to be encouraged. Judge Lyman and other men of position in Cedarville followed his bad example; and the bar-room of the 'Sickle and Sheaf' was at once voted respectable. At all times of the day and evening you could see the flower of our young men going in and out, sitting in front of the bar-room, or talking hand and glove with the landlord, who, from a worthy miller, regarded as well enough in his place, was suddenly elevated into a man of importance, whom the best in the village were delighted to honour.

"In the beginning, Willy went with the tide, and, in an incredibly short period, was acquiring a fondness for drink that startled and alarmed his friends. In going in through Slade's open door, he entered the downward way, and has been moving onward with fleet footsteps ever since. The fiery poison inflamed his mind, at the same time that it dimmed his noble perceptions. Fondness for mere pleasure followed, and this led him into various sensual indulgences, and exciting modes of passing the time. Every one liked him—he was so free, so companionable, and so generous—and almost every one encouraged, rather than repressed, his dangerous proclivities. Even his father, for a time, treated the matter lightly, as only the first flush of young life. 'I commenced sowing my wild oats at quite as early an age,' I have heard him say. 'He'll cool off, and do well enough. Never fear.' But his mother was in a state of painful alarm from the beginning. Her truer instincts, made doubly acute by her yearning love, perceived the imminent danger, and in all possible ways did she seek to lure him from the path in which he was moving at so rapid a pace. Willy was always very much attached to his mother, and her influence over him was strong; but in this case he regarded her fears as chimerical. The way in which he walked was, to him, so pleasant, and the companions of his journey so delightful, that he could not believe in the prophesied evil; and when his mother talked to him in her warning voice, and with a sad countenance, he smiled at her concern, and made light of her fears.

"And so it went on, month after month, and year after year, until the young man's sad declensions were the town talk. In order to throw his mind into a new channel—to awaken, if possible, a new and better interest in life—his father ventured upon the doubtful experiment we spoke of yesterday: that of placing capital in his hands, and making him an equal partner in the business of distilling and cotton-spinning. The disastrous—I might say disgraceful result—you know. The young man squandered his own capital, and heavily embarrassed his father.

"The effect of all this upon Mrs. Hammond has been painful in the extreme. We can only dimly imagine the terrible suffering through which she has passed. Her present aberration was first visible after a long period of sleeplessness, occasioned by distress of mind. During the whole of two weeks, I am told, she did not close her eyes; the most of that time walking the floor of her chamber, and weeping. Powerful anodynes, frequently repeated, at length brought relief. But, when she awoke from a prolonged period of unconsciousness, the brightness of her reason was gone. Since then, she has never been clearly conscious of what was passing around her, and well for her, I have sometimes thought it was, for even obscurity of intellect is a blessing in her case. Ah, me! I always get the heart-ache, when I think of her."

"Did not this event startle the young man from his fatal dream, if I may so call his mad infatuation?" I asked.

"No. He loved his mother, and was deeply afflicted by the calamity; but it seemed as if he could not stop. Some terrible necessity appeared to be impelling him onward. If he formed good resolutions—and I doubt not that he did,—they were blown away like threads of gossamer, the moment he came within the sphere of old associations. His way to the mill was by the 'Sickle and Sheaf;' and it was not easy for him to pass there without being drawn into the bar, either by his own desire for drink or through the invitation of some pleasant companion, who was lounging in front of the tavern."

"There may have been something even more impelling than his love of drink," said I.

"What?"

I related, briefly, the occurrences of the preceding night.

"I feared—nay, I was certain—that he was in the toils of this man! And yet your confirmation of the fact startles and confounds me," said he, moving about his office in a disturbed manner. "If my mind has questioned and doubted in regard to young Hammond, it questions and doubts no longer. The word 'mystery' is not now written over the door of his habitation. Great Father! and is it thus that our young men are led into temptation? Thus that their ruin is premeditated, secured? Thus that the fowler is permitted to spread his net in the open day, and the destroyer licensed to work ruin in darkness? It is awful to contemplate!"

The man was strongly excited.

"Thus it is," he continued; "and we who see the whole extent, origin, and downward rushing force of a widely sweeping desolation, lift our voices of warning almost in vain. Men who have everything at stake—sons to be corrupted, and daughters to become the wives of young men exposed to corrupting influences—stand aloof, questioning and doubting as to the expediency of protecting the innocent from the wolfish designs of bad men, who, to compass their own selfish ends, would destroy them body and soul. We are called fanatics, ultraists, designing, and all that, because we ask our law-makers to stay the fiery ruin. Oh, no! we must not touch the traffic. All the dearest and best interests of society may suffer; but the rum-seller must be protected. He must be allowed to get gain, if the jails and poor-houses are filled, and the graveyards made fat with the bodies of young men stricken down in the flower of their years, and of wives and mothers who have died of broken hearts. Reform, we are told, must commence at home. We must rear temperate children, and then we shall have temperate men. That when there are none to desire liquor, the rumseller's traffic will cease. And all the while society's true benefactors are engaged in doing this, the weak, the unsuspecting, and the erring must be left an easy prey, even if the work requires for its accomplishment a hundred years. Sir! a human soul destroyed through the rum-seller's infernal agency, is a sacrifice priceless in value. No considerations of worldy gain can, for an instant, be placed in comparison therewith. And yet souls are destroyed by thousands every year; and they will fall by tens of thousands ere society awakens from its fatal indifference, and lays its strong hand of power on the corrupt men who are scattering disease, ruin, and death, broadcast over the land!

"I always get warm on this subject," he added, repressing his enthusiasm. "And who that observes and reflects can help growing excited? The evil is appalling; and the indifference of the community one of the strangest facts of the day."

While he was yet speaking, the elder Mr. Hammond came in. He looked wretched. The redness and humidity of his eyes showed want of sleep, and the relaxed muscles of his face exhaustion from weariness and suffering. He drew the person with whom I had been talking aside, and continued in earnest conversation with him for many minutes—often gesticulating violently. I could see his face, though I heard nothing of what he said.

The play of his features was painful to look upon, for every changing muscle showed a new phase of mental suffering.

"Try and see him, will you not?" he said, as he turned, at length, to leave the office.

"I will go there immediately," was answered.

"Bring him home, if possible."

"My very best efforts shall be made."

Judge Hammond bowed, and went out hurriedly.

"Do you know the number of the room occupied by the man Green?" asked the gentleman, as soon as his visitor had retired.

"Yes. It is No. 11."

"Willy has not been home since last night. His father, at this late day, suspects Green to be a gambler! The truth flashed upon him only yesterday; and this, added to his other sources of trouble, is driving him, so he says, almost mad. As a friend, he wishes me to go to the 'Sickle and Sheaf,' and try and find Willy. Have you seen any thing of him this morning?"

I answered in the negative.

"Nor of Green?"

"No."

"Was Slade about when you left the tavern?"

"I saw nothing of him."

"What Judge Hammond fears may be all too true—that, in the present condition of Willy's affairs, which have reached the point of disaster, his tempter means to secure the largest possible share of property yet in his power to pledge or transfer,—to squeeze from his victim the last drop of blood that remains, and then fling him, ruthlessly, from his hands."

"The young man must have been rendered almost desperate, or he would never have returned, as he did, last night. Did you mention this to his father?"

"No. It would have distressed him the more, without effecting any good. He is wretched enough. But time passes, and none is to be lost now. Will you go with me?"

I walked to the tavern with him; and we went into the bar together. Two or three men were at the counter, drinking.

"Is Mr. Green about this morning?" was asked by the person who had come in search of young Hammond.

"Haven't seen any thing of him."

"Is he in his room?"

"I don't know."

"Will you ascertain for me?"

"Certainly. Frank,"—and he spoke to the landlord's son, who was lounging on a settee,—"I wish you would see if Mr. Green is in his room."

"Go and see yourself. I'm not your waiter," was growled back, in an ill-natured voice.

"In a moment I'll ascertain for you," said Matthew, politely.

After waiting on some new customers, who were just entering, Matthew went upstairs to obtain the desired information. As he left the bar-room, Frank got up and went behind the counter, where he mixed himself a glass of liquor, and drank it off, evidently with real enjoyment.

"Rather a dangerous business for one so young as you are," remarked the gentleman with whom I had come, as Frank stepped out of the bar, and passed near where we were standing. The only answer to this was an ill-natured frown, and an expression of face which said, almost as plainly as words, "It's none of your business."

"Not there," said Matthew, now coming in.

"Are you certain?"

"Yes, sir."

But there was a certain involuntary hesitation in the bar-keeper's manner, which led to a suspicion that his answer was not in accordance with the truth. We walked out together, conferring on the subject, and both concluded that his word was not to be relied upon.

"What is to be done?" was asked.

"Go to Green's room," I replied, "and knock at the door. If he is there, he may answer, not suspecting your errand."

"Show me the room."

I went up with him, and pointed out No. 11. He knocked lightly, but there came no sound from within. He repeated the knock; all was silent. Again and again he knocked, but there came back only a hollow reverberation.

"There's no one there," said he, returning to where I stood, and we walked downstairs together. On the landing, as we reached the lower passage, we met Mrs. Slade. I had not, during this visit at Cedarville, stood face to face with her before. Oh! what a wreck she presented, with her pale, shrunken countenance, hollow, lustreless eyes, and bent, feeble body. I almost shuddered as I looked at her. What a haunting and sternly rebuking spectre she must have moved, daily, before the eyes of her husband.

"Have you noticed Mr. Green about this morning?" I asked.

"He hasn't come down from his room yet," she replied.

"Are you certain?" said my companion. "I knocked several times at the door just now, but received no answer."

"What do you want with him?" asked Mrs. Slade, fixing her eyes upon us.

"We are in search of Willy Hammond; and it has been suggested that he is with Green."

"Knock twice lightly, and then three times more firmly," said Mrs. Slade; and as she spoke, she glided past us with noiseless tread.

"Shall we go up together?"

I did not object, for, although I had no delegated right of intrusion, my feelings were so much excited in the case, that I went forward, scarcely reflecting on the propriety of so doing.

The signal knock found instant answer. The door was softly opened, and the unshaven face of Simon Slade presented itself.

"Mr. Jacobs!" he said, with surprise in his tones. "Do you wish to see me?"

"No, sir; I wish to see Mr. Green," and with a quick, firm pressure against the door, he pushed it wide open. The same party was there that I had seen on the night before,—Green, young Hammond, Judge Lyman, and Slade. On the table at which the three formerly were sitting, were cards, slips of paper, an inkstand and pens, and a pile of banknotes. On a side table, or, rather, butler's tray, were bottles, decanters, and glasses.

"Judge Lyman! Is it possible?" exclaimed Mr. Jacobs, the name of my companion: "I did not expect to find you here."

Green instantly swept his hands over the table to secure the money and bills it contained; but, ere he had accomplished his purpose, young Hammond grappled three or four narrow strips of paper, and hastily tore them into shreds.

"You're a cheating scoundrel!" cried Green, fiercely, thrusting his hand into his bosom as if to draw from thence a weapon; but, the words were scarcely uttered, ere Hammond sprung upon him with the fierceness of a tiger, bearing him down upon the floor. Both hands were already about the gambler's neck, and, ere the bewildered spectators could interfere, and drag him off, Green was purple in the face, and nearly strangled.

"Call me a cheating scoundrel!" said Hammond, foaming at the mouth, as he spoke,—"Me! whom you have followed like a thirsty bloodhound. Me! whom you have robbed, and cheated, and debased from the beginning! Oh! for a pistol to rid the earth of the blackest-hearted villain that walks its surface. Let me go, gentlemen! I have nothing left in the world to care for,—there is no consequence I fear. Let me do society one good service before I die!"

And, with one vigorous effort, he swept himself clear of the hands that were pinioning him, and sprung again upon the gambler with the fierce energy of a savage beast. By this time, Green had got his knife free from its sheath, and, as Hammond was closing upon him in his blind rage, plunged it into his side. Quick almost as lightning, the knife was withdrawn, and two more stabs inflicted ere we could seize and disarm the murderer. As we did so, Willy Hammond fell over with a deep groan, the blood flowing from his side.

In the terror and excitement that followed, Green rushed from the room. The doctor, who was instantly summoned, after carefully examining the wound, and the condition of the unhappy young man, gave it as his opinion that he was fatally injured.

Oh! the anguish of the father, who had quickly heard of the dreadful occurrence, when this announcement was made. I never saw such fearful agony in any human countenance. The calmest of all the anxious group was Willy himself. On his father's face his eyes were fixed as if by a kind of fascination.

"Are you in much pain, my poor boy!" sobbed the old man, stooping over him, until his long white hair mingled with the damp locks of the sufferer

"Not much, father," was the whispered reply. "Don't speak of this to mother, yet. I'm afraid it will kill her."

What could the father answer? Nothing! And he was silent.

"Does she know of it?" A shadow went over his face.

Mr. Hammond shook his head.

Yet, even as he spoke, a wild cry of distress was heard below. Some indiscreet person had borne to the ears of the mother the fearful news about her son, and she had come wildly flying toward the tavern, and was just entering.

"It is my poor mother," said Willy, a flush coming into his pale face. "Who could have told her of this?"

Mr. Hammond started for the door, but ere he had reached it, the distracted mother entered.

"Oh! Willy, my boy! my boy!" she exclaimed, in tones of anguish that made the heart shudder. And she crouched down on the floor, the moment she reached the bed whereon he lay, and pressed her lips—oh, so tenderly and lovingly!—to his.

"Dear mother! Sweet mother! Best of mothers!" He even smiled as he said this; and, into the face that now bent over him, looked up with glances of unutterable fondness.

"Oh, Willy! Willy! Willy! my son, my son!" And again her lips were laid closely to his.

Mr. Hammond now interfered, and endeavoured to remove his wife, fearing for the consequence upon his son.

"Don't, father!" said Willy; "let her remain. I am not excited nor disturbed. I am glad that she is here, now. It will be best for us both."

"You must not excite him, dear," said Mr. Hammond—"he is very weak."

"I'll not excite him," answered the mother. "I'll not speak a word. There, love"— and she laid her fingers softly upon the lips of her son—"don't speak a single word."

For only a few moments did she sit with the quiet formality of a nurse, who feels how much depends on the repose of her patient. Then she began, weeping, moaning, and wringing her hands.

"Mother!" The feeble voice of Willy stilled, instantly, the tempest of feeling. "Mother, kiss me!"

She bent down and kissed him.

"Are you there, mother?" His eyes moved about, with a straining motion.

"Yes, love, here I am."

"I don't see you, mother. It's getting so dark. Oh, mother! mother!" he shouted suddenly, starting up and throwing himself forward upon her bosom—"save me! save me!"

How quickly did the mother clasp her arms around him—how eagerly did she strain him to her bosom! The doctor, fearing the worst consequences, now came forward, and endeavoured to release the arms of Mrs. Hammond, but she resisted every attempt to do so.

"I will save you, my son," she murmured in the ears of the young man. "Your mother will protect you. Oh! if you had never left her side, nothing on earth could have done you harm."

"He is dead!" I heard the doctor whisper; and, a thrill of horror went through me. The words reached the ears of Mr. Hammond, and his groan was one of almost mortal agony.

"Who says he is dead?" came sharply from the lips of the mother, as she pressed the form of her child back upon the bed from which he had sprung to her arms, and looked wildly upon his face. One long scream of horror told of her convictions, and she fell, lifeless, across the body of her dead son!

All in the room believed that Mrs. Hammond had only fainted. But the doctor's perplexed, troubled countenance, as he ordered her carried into another apartment, and the ghastliness of her face when it was upturned to the light, suggested to every one what proved to be true. Even to her obscured perceptions, the consciousness that her son was dead came with a terrible vividness—so terrible, that it extinguished her life.

Like fire among dry stubble ran the news of this fearful event through Cedarville. The whole town was wild with excitement. The prominent fact, that Willy Hammond had been murdered by Green, whose real profession was known by many, and now declared to all, was on every tongue; but a hundred different and exaggerated stories as to the cause and the particulars of the event were in circulation. By the time preparations to remove the dead bodies of mother and son from the "Sickle and Sheaf," to the residence of Mr. Hammond, were completed, hundreds of people, men, women, and children, were assembled around the tavern; and many voices were clamorous for Green; while some called out for Judge Lyman, whose name, it thus appeared, had become associated in the minds of the people with the murderous affair. The appearance, in the midst of this excitement, of the two dead bodies, borne forth on settees, did not tend to allay the feverish state of indignation that prevailed. From more than one voice, I heard the words, "Lynch the scoundrel!"

A part of the crowd followed the sad procession, while the greater portion, consisting of men, remained about the tavern. All bodies, no matter for what purpose assembled, quickly finding leading spirits who, feeling the great moving impulse, give it voice and direction. It was so in this case. Intense indignition against Green was firing every bosom; and when a man elevated himself a few feet above the agitated mass of humanity, and cried out—

"The murderer must not escape!"

A wild responding shout, terrible in its fierceness, made the air quiver.

"Let ten men be chosen to search the house and premises," said the leading spirit.

"Ay! ay! Choose them! Name them!" was quickly answered.

Ten men were called by name, who instantly stepped in front of the crowd.

"Search everywhere; from garret to cellar; from hayloft to dog-kennel. Everywhere! everywhere!" cried the man.

And instantly the ten men entered the house. For nearly a quarter of an hour, the crowd waited with increasing signs of impatience. These delegates at length appeared, with the announcement that Green was nowhere about the premises. It was received with a groan.

"Let no man in Cedarville do a stroke of work until the murderer is found," now shouted the individual who still occupied his elevated position.

"Agreed! agreed! No work in Cedarville until the murderer is found," rang out fiercely.

"Let all who have horses, saddle and bridle them as quickly as possible, and assemble, mounted, at the Court House."

About fifty men left the crowd hastily.

"Let the crowd part in the centre, up and down the road, starting from a line in front of me."

This order was obeyed.

"Separate again, taking the centre of the road for a line."

Four distinct bodies of men stood now in front of the tavern.

"Now search for the murderer in every nook and corner, for a distance of three miles from this spot; each party keeping to its own section; the road being one dividing line, and a line through the centre of this tavern the other. The horsemen will pursue the wretch to a greater distance."

More than a hundred acquiescing voices responded to this, as the man sprung down from his elevation and mingled with the crowd, which began instantly to move away on its appointed mission.

As the hours went by, one, and another, and another, of the searching party returned to the village, wearied with their efforts, or confident that the murderer had made good his escape. The horsemen, too, began to come in, during the afternoon, and by sundown, the last of them, worn out and disappointed, made their appearace.

For hours after the exciting events of the forenoon, there were but few visitors at the "Sickle and Sheaf." Slade, who did not show himself among the crowd, came down soon after its dispersion. He had shaved and put on clean linen; but still bore many evidences of a night spent without sleep. His eyes were red and heavy and the eyelids swollen; while his skin was relaxed and colourless. As he descended the stairs, I was walking in the passage. He looked shy at me, and merely nodded. Guilt was written plainly on his countenance; and with it was blended anxiety and alarm. That he might be involved in trouble, he had reason to fear; for, he was one of the party engaged in gambling in Green's room, as both Mr. Jacobs and I had witnessed.

"This is dreadful business," said he, as we met, face to face, half an hour afterward. He did not look me steadily in the eyes.

"It is horrible!" I answered. "To corrupt and ruin a young man, and then murder him! There are few deeds in the catalogue of crime blacker than this."

"It was done in the heat of passion," said the landlord, with something of apology in his manner. "Green never meant to kill him."

"In peaceful intercourse with his fellow men, why did he carry a deadly weapon? There was murder in his heart, sir."

"That is speaking very strongly."

"Not stronger than facts will warrant," I replied. "That Green is a murderer in heart, it needed not this awful consummation to show. With a cool, deliberate purpose, he has sought, from the beginning, to destroy young Hammond."

"It is hardly fair," answered Slade, "in the present feverish excitement against Green, to assume such a questionable position. It may do him a great wrong."

"Did Willy Hammond speak only idle words, when he accused Green of having followed him like a thirsty bloodhound?—of having robbed, and cheated, and debased him from the beginning?"

"He was terribly excited at the moment."

"Yet," said I, "no ear that heard his words could for an instant doubt that they were truthful utterances, wrung from a maddened heart."

My earnest, positive manner had its effect upon Slade. He knew that what I asserted, the whole history of Green's intercourse with young Hammond would prove; and he had, moreover, the guilty consciousness of being a party to the young man's ruin. His eyes cowered beneath the steady gaze I fixed upon him. I thought of him as one implicated in the murder, and my thought must have been visible in my face.

"One murder will not justify another," said he.

"There is no justification for murder on any plea," was my response.

"And yet, if these infuriated men find Green, they will murder him."

"I hope not. Indignation at a horrible crime has fearfully excited the people. But I think their sense of justice is strong enough to prevent the consequences you apprehend."

"I would not like to be in Green's shoes," said the landlord, with an uneasy movement.

I looked him closely in the face. It was the punishment of the man's crime that seemed so fearful in his eyes; not the crime itself. Alas! how the corrupting traffic had debased him.

My words were so little relished by Slade, that he found some ready excuse to leave me. I saw but little more of him during the day.

As evening began to fall, the gambler's unsuccessful pursuers, one after another, found their way to the tavern, and by the time night had fairly closed in, the bar-room was crowded with excited and angry men, chafing over their disappointment, and loud in their threats of vengeance. That Green had made good his escape, was now the general belief; and the stronger this conviction became, the more steadily did the current of passion begin to set in a new direction. It had become known to every one, that, besides Green and young Hammond, Judge Lyman and Slade were in the room engaged in playing cards. The merest suggestion as to the complicity of these two men with Green in ruining Hammond, and thus driving him mad, was enough to excite strong feeling against them; and now that the mob had been cheated of its victim, its pent up indignation sought eagerly some new channel.

"Where's Slade?" some one asked, in a loud voice, from the centre of the crowded bar-room. "Why does he keep himself out of sight?"

"Yes; where's the landlord?" half a dozen voices responded.

"Did he go on the hunt?" some one inquired.

"No!" "No!" "No!" ran round the room. "Not he."

"And yet, the murder was committed in his own house, and before his own eyes!"

"Yes, before his own eyes!" repeated one and another, indignantly.

"Where's Slade? Where's the landlord? Has anybody seen him tonight? Matthew, where's Simon Slade?"

From lip to lip passed these interrogations; while the crowd of men became agitated, and swayed to and fro.

"I don't think he's home," answered the bar-keeper, in a hesitating manner, and with visible alarm.

"How long since he was here?"

"I haven't seen him for a couple of hours."

"That's a lie!" was sharply said.

"Who says it's a lie?" Matthew affected to be strongly indignant.

"I do!" And a rough, fierce-looking man confronted him.

"What right have you to say so?" asked Matthew, cooling off considerably.

"Because you lie!" said the man, boldly. "You've seen him within a less time than half an hour, and well you know it. Now, if you wish to keep yourself out of this trouble, answer truly. We are in no mood to deal with liars or equivocators. Where is Simon Slade?"

"I do not know," replied Matthew, firmly.

"Is he in the house?"

"He may be, or he may not be. I am just as ignorant of his exact whereabouts as you are."

"Will you look for him?"

Matthew stepped to the door, opening from behind the bar, and called the name of Frank.

"What's wanted?" growled the boy.

"Is your father in the house?"

"I don't know, nor don't care," was responded in the same ungracious manner.

"Some one bring him into the bar-room, and we'll see if we can't make him care a little."

The suggestion was no sooner made, than two men glided behind the bar, and passed into the room from which the voice of Frank had issued. A moment after they reappeared, each grasping an arm of the boy, and bearing him like a weak child between them. He looked thoroughly frightened at this unlooked for invasion of his liberty.

"See here, young man." One of the leading spirits of the crowd addressed him, as soon as he was brought in front of the counter. "If you wish to keep out of trouble, answer our questions at once, and to the point. We are in no mood for trifling. Where's your father?"

"Somewhere about the house, I believe," Frank replied, in an humbled tone. He was no little scared at the summary manner with which he had been treated.

"How long since you saw him?"

"Not long ago."

"Ten minutes?"

"No: nearly half an hour."

"Where was he then?"

"He was going up-stairs."

"Very well, we want him. See him, and tell him so."

Frank went into the house, but came back into the bar-room after an absence of nearly five minutes, and said that he could not find his father anywhere.

"Where is he then?" was angrily demanded.

"Indeed, gentlemen, I don't know." Frank's anxious look and frightened manner showed that he spoke truly.

"There's something wrong about this—something wrong—wrong," said one of the men. "Why should he be absent now? Why has he taken no steps to secure the man who committed a murder in his own house, and before his own eyes?"

"I shouldn't wonder if he aided him to escape," said another, making this serious charge with a restlessness and want of evidence that illustrated the reckless and unjust spirit by which a mob is ever governed.

"No doubt of it in the least!" was the quick and positive response. And at once this erroneous conviction seized upon every one. Not a single fact was presented. The simple, bold assertion, that no doubt existed in the mind of one man as to Slade's having aided Green to escape, was sufficient for the unreflecting mob.

"Where is he? Where is he? Let us find him. He knows where Green is, and he shall reveal the secret."

This was enough. The passions of the crowd were at fever heat again. Two or three men were chosen to search the house and premises, while others dispersed to take a wider range. One of the men who volunteered to go over the house was a person named Lyon, with whom I had formed some acquaintance, and several times conversed with on the state of affairs in Cedarville. He still remained too good a customer at the bar. I left the bar at the same time that he did, and went up to my room. We walked side by side, and parted at my door, I going in, and he continuing on to make his searches. I felt, of course, anxious and much excited, as well in consequence of the events of the day, as the present aspect of things. My head was aching violently, and in the hope of getting relief, I laid myself down. I had already lighted a candle, and turned the key in my door to prevent intrusion. Only for a short time did I lie, listening to the hum of voices that came with a hoarse murmur from below, to the sound of feet moving along the passages, and to the continual opening and shutting of doors, when something like suppressed breathing reached my ears. I started up instantly, and listened; but my quickened pulses were now audible to my own sense, and obscured what was external.

"It is only imagination," I said to myself. Still, I sat upright, listening.

Satisfied, at length, that all was mere fancy, I laid myself back on the pillow, and tried to turn my thoughts away from the suggested idea that some one was in the room. Scarcely had I succeeded in this, when my heart gave a new impulse, as a sound like a movement fell upon my ears.

"Mere fancy!" I said to myself, as some one went past the door at the moment. "My mind is over excited."

Still I raised my head, supporting it with my hand, and listened, directing my attention inside, and not outside of the room. I was about letting my head fall back upon the pillow, when a slight cough, so distinct as not to be mistaken, caused me to spring to the floor, and look under the bed. The mystery was explained. A pair of eyes glittered in the candlelight. The fugitive, Green, was under my bed. For some moments I stood looking at him, so astonished that I had neither utterance nor decision; while he glared at me with a fierce defiance. I saw that he was clutching a revolver.

"Understand!" he said, in a grating whisper, "that I am not to be taken alive."

I let the blanket, which had concealed him from view, fall from my hand, and then tried to collect my thoughts.

"Escape is impossible," said I, again lifting the temporary curtain by which he was hid. "The whole town is armed, and on the search; and should you fall into the hands of the mob, in its present state of exasperation, your life would not be safe an instant. Remain, then, quiet, where you are, until I can see the sheriff, to whom you had better resign yourself, for there's little chance for you except under his protection."

After a brief parley, he consented that things should take this course, and I went out, locking the room door after me, and started in search of the sheriff. On the information I gave, the sheriff acted promptly. With five officers, fully armed for defence, in case an effort were made to get the prisoner out of their hands, he repaired immediately to the "Sickle and Sheaf," I had given the key of my room into his possession.

The appearance of the sheriff, with his posse, was sufficient to start the suggestion that Green was somewhere concealed in the house; and a suggestion was only needed to cause the fact to be assumed, and unhesitatingly declared. Intelligence went through the reassembling crowd like an electric current, and ere the sheriff could manacle and lead forth his prisoner, the stairway down which he had to come was packed with bodies, and echoing with oaths and maledictions.

"Gentlemen, clear the way!" cried the sheriff, as he appeared with the white and trembling culprit at the head of the stairs. "The murderer is now in the hands of the law, and will meet the sure consequences of his crime."

A shout of execration rent the air; but not a single individual stirred.

"Give way, there! Give way!" And the sheriff took a step or two forward, but the prisoner held back.

"Oh, the murdering villain! The cursed blackleg! Where's Willy Hammond!" was heard distinctly above the confused mingling of voices.

"Gentlemen! the law must have its course; and no good citizen will oppose the law. It is made for your protection—for mine—and for that of the prisoner."

"Lynch law is good enough for him," shouted a savage voice. "Hand him over to us, sheriff, and we'll save you the trouble of hanging him, and the county the cost of a gallows. We'll do the business right."

Five men, each armed with a revolver, now ranged themselves around the sheriff, and the latter said firmly,

"It is my duty to see this man safely conveyed to prison; and I'm going to do my duty. If there is any more blood shed here, the blame will rest with you." And the body of officers pressed forward, the mob slowly retreating before them.

Green, overwhelmed with terror, held back. I was standing where I could see his face. It was ghastly with mortal fear. Grasping his pinioned arms, the sheriff forced him onward. After contending with the crowd for nearly ten minutes, the officers gained the passage below; but the mob was denser here, and blocking up the door, resolutely maintained their position.

Again and again the sheriff appealed to the good sense and justice of the people.

"The prisoner will have to stand a trial; and the law will execute sure vengeance."

"No, it won't!" was sternly responded.

"Who'll be judge in the case?" was asked.

"Why, Judge Lyman!" was contemptuously answered.

"A blackleg himself!" was shouted by two or three voices.

"Blackleg judge, and blackleg lawyers! Oh, yes! The law will execute sure vengeance! Who was in the room gambling with Green and Hammond?"

"Judge Lyman!" "Judge Lyman!" was answered back.

"It won't do, sheriff! There's no law in the country to reach the case but Lynch law; and that the scoundrel must have. Give him to us!"

"Never! On, men, with the prisoner!" cried the sheriff resolutely, and the *posse* made a rush toward the door, bearing back the resisting and now infuriated crowd. Shouts, cries, oaths, and savage imprecations blended in wild discord; in the midst of which my blood was chilled by the sharp crack of a pistol. Another and another shot followed; and then, as a cry of pain thrilled the air, the fierce storm hushed its fury in an instant.

"Who's shot? Is he killed?"

There was a breathless eagerness for the answer.

"It's the gambler!" was replied. "Somebody has shot Green."

A low muttered invective against the victim was heard here and there; but the announcement was not received with a shout of exultation, though there was scarcely a heart that did not feel pleasure at the sacrifice of Harvey Green's life.

It was true as had been declared. Whether the shots were aimed deliberately, or guided by an unseen hand to the heart of the gambler, was never known; nor did the most careful examination, instituted afterward by the county, elicit any information that even directed suspicion toward the individual who became the agent of his death.

At the coroner's inquest, held over the dead body of Harvey Green, Simon Slade was present. Where he had concealed himself while the mob were in search of him, was not known. He looked haggard; and his eyes were anxious and restless. Two murders in his house, occurring in a single day, were quite enough to darken his spirits; and the more so, as his relations with both the victims were not of a character to awaken any thing but self-accusation.

As for the mob, in the death of Green its eager thirst for vengeance was satisfied. Nothing more was said against Slade, as a participator in the ruin and death of young Hammond. The popular feeling was one of pity rather than indignation toward the land-lord; for it was seen that he was deeply troubled.

One thing I noticed, and it was that the drinking at the bar was not suspended for a moment. A large proportion of those who made up the crowd of Green's angry pursuers, were excited by drink as well as indignation, and I am very sure that, but for the mad-dening effects of liquor, the fatal shot would never have been fired. After the fearful catastrophe, and when every mind was sobered, or ought to have been sobered, the crowd returned to the bar-room, where the drinking was renewed. So rapid were the calls for liquor, that both Matthew, and Frank, the landlord's son, were kept busy mixing the various compounds demanded by the thirsty customers.

From the constant stream of human beings that flowed toward the "Sickle and Sheaf," after the news of Green's discovery and death went forth, it seemed as if every man and boy within a distance of two or three miles had received intelligence of the event. Few, very few of those who came, but went first into the bar-room; and nearly all who entered the bar-room called for liquor. In an hour after the death of Green, the fact that his dead body was laid out in the room immediately adjoining, seemed utterly to pass from the consciousness of every one in the bar. The calls for liquor were incessant; and, as the excitement of drink increased, voices grew louder, and oaths more plentiful, while the sounds of laughter ceased not for an instant.

"They're giving him a regular Irish wake," I heard remarked, with a brutal laugh.

I turned to the speaker, and to my great surprise, saw that it was Judge Lyman, more under the influence of drink than I remembered to have seen him. He was about the last man I expected to find here. If he knew of the strong indignation expressed toward him a little while before, by some of the very men now excited with liquor, his own free drinking had extinguished fear.

"Yes, curse him!" was the answer. "If they have a particularly hot corner 'away down below,' I hope he's made its acquaintance before this."

"Most likely he's smelled brimstone," chuckled the judge.

"Smelled it! If old Clubfoot[9] hasn't treated him with a brimstone-bath long before this, he hasn't done his duty. If I thought as much, I'd vote for sending his majesty a remonstrance forthwith."

"Ha! ha!" laughed the judge. "You're warm on the subject."

---

[9]The devil.

"Ain't I? The blackleg scoundrel! Hell's too good for him."

"H-u-s-h! Don't let your indignation run into profanity," said Judge Lyman, trying to assume a serious air; but the muscles of his face but feebly obeyed his will's feeble effort.

"Profanity! Poh! I don't call that profanity. It's only speaking out in meeting, as they say,—it's only calling black, black—and white, white. You believe in a hell, don't you, judge?"

"I suppose there is one; though I don't know very certain."

"You'd better be certain!" said the other, meaningly.

"Why so?"

"Oh! because if there is one, and you don't cut your cards a little differently, you'll be apt to find it at the end of your journey."

"What do you mean by that?" asked the judge, retreating somewhat into himself, and trying to look dignified.

"Just what I say," was unhesitatingly answered.

"Do you mean to insinuate any thing?" asked the judge, whose brows were beginning to knit themselves.

"Nobody thinks you are a saint," replied the man, roughly.

"I never professed to be."

"And it is said,"—the man fixed his gaze almost insultingly upon Judge Lyman's face—"that you'll get about as hot a corner in the lower regions as is to be found there, whenever you make the journey in that direction."

"You are insolent!" exclaimed the judge, his face becoming inflamed.

"Take care what you say, sir!" The man spoke threateningly.

"You'd better take care what *you* say."

"So I will," replied the other. "But—"

"What's to pay here?" inquired a third party, coming up at the moment, and interrupting the speaker.

"The devil will be to pay," said Judge Lyman, "if somebody don't look out sharp."

"Do you mean that for me, ha?" The man, between whom and himself this slight contention had so quickly sprung up, began stripping back his coat sleeves, like one about to commence boxing.

"I mean it for anybody who presumes to offer me an insult."

The raised voices of the two men now drew toward them the attention of every one in the bar-room.

"The devil! There's Judge Lyman!" I heard some one exclaim, in a tone of surprise.

"Wasn't he in the room with Green when Willy Hammond was murdered?" asked another.

"Yes, he was; and what's more, it is said he had been playing against him all night, he and Green sharing the plunder."

This last remark came distinctly to the ears of Lyman, who started to his feet instantly, exclaiming fiercely—

"Whoever says that is a cursed liar!"

The words were scarcely out of his mouth, before a blow staggered him against the wall, near which he was standing. Another blow felled him, and then his assailant sprang over his prostrate body, kicking him, and stamping upon his face and breast in the most brutal, shocking manner.

"Kill him! He's worse than Green!" somebody cried out, in a voice so full of cruelty and murder that it made my blood curdle. "Remember Willy Hammond!"

The terrible scene that followed, in which were heard a confused mingling of blows, cries, yells, and horrible oaths, continued for several minutes, and ceased only when the words—"Don't, don't strike him any more! He's dead!" were repeated several times. Then the wild strife subsided. As the crowd parted from around the body of Judge Lyman, and gave way, I caught a single glance at his face. It was covered with blood, and every feature seemed to have been literally trampled down, until all was a level surface! Sickened at the sight, I passed hastily from the room into the open air, and caught my breath several times, before respiration again went on freely. As I stood in front of the tavern, the body of Judge Lyman was borne out by three or four men, and carried off in the direction of his dwelling.

"Is he dead?" I inquired of those who had him in charge.

"No," was the answer. "He's not dead, but terribly beaten," and they passed on.

Again the loud voices of men in angry strife arose in the bar-room. I did not return there to learn the cause, or to witness the fiend-like conduct of men, all whose worst passions were stimulated by drink into the wildest fervour. As I was entering my room, the thought flashed through my mind that, as Green was found there, it needed only the bare suggestion that I had aided in his concealment, to direct toward me the insane fury of the drunken mob.

"It is not safe to remain here." I said this to myself, with the emphasis of a strong internal conviction.

Against this, my mind opposed a few feeble arguments; but, the more I thought of the matter, the more clearly did I become satisfied, that to attempt to pass the night in that room was to me a risk it was not prudent to assume.

So I went in search of Mrs. Slade, to ask her to have another room prepared for me. But she was not in the house; and I learned, upon inquiry, that since the murder of young Hammond, she had been suffering from repeated hysterical and fainting fits, and was now, with her daughter, at the house of a relative, whither she had been carried early in the afternoon.

It was on my lips to request the chambermaid to give me another room; but this I felt to be scarcely prudent, for if the popular indignation should happen to turn toward me, the servant would be the one questioned, most likely, as to where I had removed my quarters.

"It isn't safe to stay in the house," said I, speaking to myself. "Two, perhaps three, murders, have been committed already. The tiger's thirst for blood has been stimulated, and who can tell how quickly he may spring again, or in what direction?"

Even while I said this, there came up from the bar-room louder and madder shouts. Then blows were heard, mingled with cries and oaths. A shuddering sense of danger oppressed me, and I went hastily downstairs, and out into the street. As I gained the passage, I looked into the sitting-room, where the body of Green was laid out. Just then, the bar-room door was burst open by a fighting party, who had been thrown, in their fierce contention, against it. I paused only for a moment or two; and even in that brief period of time, saw blows exchanged over the dead body of the gambler!

"This is no place for me," I said, almost aloud, and hurried from the house, and took my way to the residence of a gentleman who had shown me many kindnesses during my visits at Cedarville. There was needed scarcely a word of representation on my part, to secure the cordial tender of a bed.

What a change! It seemed almost like a passage from Pandemonium[10] to a heavenly region, as I seated myself alone in the quiet chamber a cheerful hospitality had assigned me, and mused on the exciting and terrible incidents of the day. They that sow the wind shall reap the whirlwind.[11] How marked had been the realization of this prophecy, couched in such strong but beautiful imagery!

On the next day I was to leave Cedarville. Early in the morning I repaired to the "Sickle and Sheaf." The storm was over, and all was calm and silent as desolation. Hours before, the tempest had subsided; but the evidences left behind of its ravaging fury were fearful to look upon. Doors, chairs, windows, and tables were broken, and even the strong brass rod that ornamented the bar had been partially wrenched from its fastenings by strong hands, under an impulse of murder, that only lacked a weapon to execute its fiendish purpose. Stains of blood, in drops, marks, and even dried-up pools, were to be seen all over the bar-room and passage floors, and in many places on the porch.

In the sitting-room still lay the body of Green. Here, too, were many signs to indicate a fierce struggle. The looking-glass was smashed to a hundred pieces, and the shivered fragments lay yet untouched upon the floor. A chair, which it was plain had been used as a weapon of assault, had two of its legs broken short off, and was thrown into a corner. And even the bearers, on which the dead man lay, were pushed from their true position, showing that even in its mortal sleep, the body of Green had felt the jarring strife of elements he had himself helped to awaken into mad activity. From his face, the sheet had been drawn aside; but no hand ventured to replace it; and there it lay, in its ghastly paleness, exposed to the light, and covered with restless flies, attracted by the first faint odours of putridity. With gaze averted, I approached the body, and drew the covering decently over it.

No person was in the bar. I went out into the stable yard, where I met the hostler with his head bound up. There was a dark blue circle around one of his eyes, and an ugly-looking red scar on his cheek.

"Where is Mr. Slade?" I inquired.

"In bed, and likely to keep it for a week," was answered.

"How comes that?"

"Naturally enough. There was fighting all around last night, and he had to come in for a share. The fool! If he'd just held his tongue, he might have come out of it with a whole skin. But, when the rum is in, the wit is out, with him. It's cost me a black eye and a broken head; for how could I stand by and see him murdered outright?"

"Is he very badly injured?"

"I rather think he is. One eye is clean gone."

---

[10]Pandemonium was the name of Satan's palace in John Milton's (1608–1674) *Paradise Lost* (1667).

[11]Hos. 8:7.

"Oh, shocking!"

"It's shocking enough, and no mistake."

"Lost an eye!"

"Too true, sir. The doctor saw him this morning, and says the eye was fairly gouged out, and broken up. In fact, when we carried him up-stairs for dead last night, his eye was lying upon his cheek. I pushed it back with my own hand!"

"Oh, horrible!" The relation made me sick. "Is he otherwise much injured?"

"The doctor thinks there are some bad hurts inside. Why, they kicked and trampled upon him, as if he had been a wild beast! I never saw such a pack of blood thirsty devils in my life."

"So much for rum," said I.

"Yes, sir; so much for rum," was the emphatic response. "It was the rum, and nothing else. Why, some of the very men who acted the most like tigers and devils, are as harmless persons as you will find in Cedarville when sober. Yes, sir; it was the rum, and nothing else. Rum gave me this broken head and black eye."

"So you had been drinking also?"

"Oh, yes. There's no use in denying that."

"Liquor does you harm."

"Nobody knows that better than I do."

"Why do you drink, then?"

"Oh, just because it comes in the way. Liquor is under my eyes and nose all the time, and it's as natural as breathing to take a little now and then. And when I don't think of it myself, somebody will think of it for me, and say—'Come, Sam, let's take something.' So you see, for a body such as I am, there isn't much help for it."

"But ain't you afraid to go on in this way? Don't you know where it will all end?"

"Just as well as anybody. It will make an end of me—or of all that is good in me. Rum and ruin, you know, sir. They go together like twin brothers."

"Why don't you get out of the way of temptation?" said I.

"It's easy enough to ask that question, sir; but how am I to get out of the way of temptation? Where shall I go, and not find a bar in my road, and somebody to say— 'Come, Sam, let's take a drink? It can't be done, sir, nohow. I'm a hostler, and don't know how to be anything else."

"Can't you work on a farm?"

"Yes; I can do something in that way. But, when there are taverns and bar-rooms, as many as three or four in every mile all over the country, how are you to keep clear of them? Figure me out that."

"I think you'd better vote on the Maine Law[12] side at next election," said I.

"Faith, and I did it last time!" replied the man, with a brightening face—"and if I'm spared, I'll go the same ticket next year."

"What do you think of the Law?" I asked.

"Think of it! Bless your heart! if I was a praying man, which I'm sorry to say I ain't—my mother was a pious woman, sir"—his voice fell and slightly trembled—"if I

---

[12]In 1851, Neal Dow (1804–1897) helped pass an alcohol prohibition law in the state of Maine.

was a praying man, sir, I'd pray, night and morning, and twenty times every day of my life, for God to put it into the hearts of the people to give us that Law. I'd have some hope then. But I haven't much as it is. There's no use in trying to let liquor alone."

"Do many drinking men think as you do?"

"I can count up a dozen or two myself. It isn't the drinking men who are so much opposed to the Maine Law, as your politicians. They throw dust in the people's eyes about it, and make a great many who know nothing at all of the evils of drinking in themselves, believe some bugbear story about trampling on the rights of I don't know who, nor they either. As for rum-seller's rights, I never could see any right they had to get rich by ruining poor devils such as I am. I think, though, that we have some right to be protected against them."

The ringing of a bell here announced the arrival of some traveller, and the hostler left me.

I learned, during the morning, that Matthew the bar-keeper, and also the son of Mr. Slade, were both considerably hurt during the affrays in the bar-room, and were confined, temporarily, to their beds. Mrs. Slade still continued in a distressing and dangerous state. Judge Lyman, though shockingly injured, was not thought to be in a critical condition.

A busy day the sheriff had of it, making arrests of various parties engaged in the last night's affairs. Even Slade, unable as he was to lift his head from his pillow, was required to give heavy bail for his appearance at court. Happily, I escaped the inconvenience of being held to appear as a witness, and early in the afternoon had the satisfaction of finding myself rapidly borne away in the stage-coach. It was two years before I entered the pleasant village of Cedarville again.

❧ Night the Eighth

Reaping the Whirlwind

I was in Washington City during the succeeding month. It was the short or closing session of a regular Congressional term. The implication of Judge Lyman in the affair of Green and young Hammond had brought him into such bad odour in Cedarville, and the whole district from which he had been chosen, that his party deemed it wise to set him aside, and take up a candidate less likely to meet with so strong, and, it might be, successful an opposition. By so doing, they were able to secure the election, once more, against the growing temperance party, which succeeded, however, in getting a Maine Law man into the State legislature. It was, therefore, Judge Lyman's last winter at the Federal Capital.

While seated in the reading-room at Fuller's Hotel, about noon, on the day after my arrival in Washington, I noticed an individual, whose face looked familiar, come in and glance about, as if in search of some one. While yet questioning in my mind who he could be, I heard a man remark to a person with whom he had been conversing—

"There's that vagabond member away from his place in the House, again."

"Who?" inquired the other.

"Why, Judge Lyman," was answered.

"Oh!" said the other, indifferently; "it isn't of much consequence. Precious little wisdom does he add to that intelligent body."

"His vote is worth something at least, when important questions are at stake."

"What does he charge for it?" was coolly inquired.

There was a shrug of the shoulders, and an arching of the eyebrows, but no answer.

"I'm in earnest, though, in the question," said the last speaker.

"Not in saying that Lyman will sell his vote to the highest bidders?"

"That will depend altogether upon whom the bidders may be. They must be men who have something to lose as well as gain—men, not at all likely to bruit[13] the matter, and in serving whose personal interests no abandonment of party is required. Judge Lyman is always on good terms with the lobby members, and may be found in company with some of them daily. Doubtless, his absence from the House, now, is for the purpose of a special meeting with gentlemen who are ready to pay well for votes in favour of some bill making appropriations of public money for private or corporate benefit."

"You certainly cannot mean all you say to be taken in its broadest sense," was replied to this.

"Yes; in its very broadest. Into just this deep of moral and political degradation has this man fallen, disgracing his constituents, and dishonouring his country."

"His presence at Washington doesn't speak very highly in favour of the community he represents."

"No; still, as things are now, we cannot judge of the moral worth of a community by the men sent from it to Congress. Representatives show merely the strength of parties. The candidate chosen in party primary meetings is not selected because he is the best man they have, and the one fittest to legislate wisely in national affairs; but he who happens to have the strongest personal friends among those who nominate, or who is most likely to poll the highest vote. This is why we find, in Congress, such a large preponderance of tenth-rate men."

"Men, such as you represent Judge Lyman to be, would sell his country like another Arnold."[14]

"Yes, if the bid were high enough."

"Does he gamble?"

"Gambling, I might say, is a part of his profession. Very few nights pass, I am told, without finding him at the gaming table."

I heard no more. At all this, I was not in the least surprised; for my knowledge of the man's antecedents had prepared me for allegations quite as bad as these.

During the week I spent at the Federal Capital, I had several opportunities of seeing Judge Lyman, in the House and out of it,—in the House only when the yeas and nays were called on some important measure, or a vote taken on a bill granting special privileges. In the latter case, his vote, as I noticed, was generally cast on the affirmative side.

---

[13]report

[14]Benedict Arnold (1741–1801) was a brilliant American general who shifted his allegiance to the British in the middle of the American Revolution.

Several times I saw him staggering on the Avenue, and once brought into the House for the purpose of voting, in so drunken a state, that he had to be supported to his seat. And even worse than this—when his name was called, he was asleep, and had to be shaken several times before he was sufficiently aroused to give his vote!

Happily, for the good of his country, it was his last winter in Washington. At the next session, a better man took his place.

Two years from the period of my last visit to Cedarville, I found myself approaching that quiet village again. As the church-spire came in view, and house after house became visible, here and there, standing out in pleasant relief against the green background of woods and fields, all the exciting events which rendered my last visit so memorable came up so fresh in my mind. I was yet thinking of Willy Hammond's dreadful death, and of his broken-hearted mother, whose life went out with his, when the stage rolled by their old homestead. Oh, what a change was here! Neglect, decay, and dilapidation were visible, let the eye fall where it would. The fences were down, here and there; the hedges, once so green and nicely trimmed, had grown rankly in some places, but were stunted and dying in others; all the beautiful walks were weedy and grass-grown, and the box-borders dead; the garden, rainbow-hued in its wealth of choice and beautiful flowers when I first saw it, was lying waste,—a rooting-ground for hogs. A glance at the house showed a broken chimney, the bricks unremoved from the spot where they struck the ground; a moss-grown roof, with a large limb from a lightning-rent tree lying almost balanced over the eaves, and threatening to fall at the touch of the first wind-storm that swept over. Half of the vines that clambered about the portico were dead, and the rest, untrained, twined themselves in wild disorder, or fell grovelling to the earth. One of the pillars of the portico was broken, as were, also, two of the steps that went up to it. The windows of the house were closed, but the door stood open, and, as the stage went past, my eyes rested, for a moment, upon an old man seated in the hall. He was not near enough to the door for me to get a view of his face; but the white flowing hair left me in no doubt as to his identity. It was Judge Hammond.

The "Sickle and Sheaf" was yet the stage-house of Cedarville, and there, a few minutes afterward, I found myself. The hand of change had been here also. The first object that attracted my attention was the sign-post, which, at my earlier arrival, some eight or nine years before, stood up in its new white garment of paint, as straight as a plummet line, bearing proudly aloft the golden sheaf and gleaming sickle. Now, the post, dingy and shattered, and worn from the frequent contact of wheels, and gnawing of restless horses, leaned from its trim perpendicular at an angle of many degrees, as if ashamed of the faded, weather-worn, lying symbol it bore aloft in the sunshine. Around the post was a filthy mud-pool, in which a hog lay grunting out its sense of enjoyment. Two or three old empty whisky barrels lumbered up the dirty porch, on which a coarse, bloated, vulgar-looking man sat leaning against the wall—his chair tipped back on its hind legs—squinting at me from one eye, as I left the stage and came forward toward the house.

"Ah! is this you?" said he, as I came near to him, speaking thickly, and getting up with a heavy motion. I now recognised the altered person of Simon Slade. On looking at him closer, I saw that the eye which I had thought only shut was in fact destroyed. How vividly, now, uprose in imagination the scenes I had witnessed during my last night in his bar-room; the night, when a brutal mob, whom he had inebriated with liquor, came near murdering him.

"Glad to see you once more, my boy! Glad to see you! I—I—I'm not just—you see. How are you? How are you?"

And he shook my hand with a drunken show of cordiality.

I felt shocked and disgusted. Wretched man! down the crumbling sides of the pit he had digged for other feet, he was himself sliding, while not enough strength remained even to struggle with his fate.

I tried for a few minutes to talk with him; but his mind was altogether beclouded, and his questions and answers incoherent; so I left him, and entered the bar-room.

"Can I get accommodations here for a couple of days?" I inquired of a stupid, sleepy-looking man, who was sitting in a chair behind the bar.

"I reckon so," he answered, but did not rise.

I turned, and walked a few paces toward the door, and then walked back again.

"I'd like to get a room," said I.

The man got up slowly, and going to a desk, fumbled about in it for a while. At length he brought out an old, dilapidated blank-book, and throwing it open on the counter, asked me, with an indifferent manner, to write down my name.

"I'll take a pen, if you please."

"Oh, yes!" And he hunted about again in the desk, from which, after a while, he brought forth the blackened stump of a quill, and pushed it toward me across the counter.

"Ink," said I—fixing my eyes upon him with a look of displeasure.

"I don't believe there is any," he muttered. "Frank," and he called the landlord's son, going to the door behind the bar as he did so.

"What d'ye want?" a rough, ill-natured voice answered.

"Where's the ink?"

"Don't know any thing about it."

"You had it last. What did you do with it?"

"Nothing!" was growled back.

"Well, I wish you'd find it."

"Find it yourself, and——" I cannot repeat the profane language he used.

"Never mind," said I. "A pencil will do just as well." And I drew one from my pocket. The attempt to write with this, on the begrimed and greasy page of the register, was only partially successful. It would have puzzled almost any one to make out the name. From the date of the last entry, it appeared that mine was the first arrival, for over a week, of any person desiring a room.

As I finished writing my name, Frank came stalking in, with a cigar in his mouth, and a cloud of smoke around his head. He had grown into a stout man—though his face presented little that was manly, in the true sense of the word. It was disgustingly sensual. On seeing me, a slight flush tinged his cheeks.

"How do you do?" he said, offering me his hand. "Peter,"—he turned to the lazy-looking bar-keeper—"tell Jane to have No. 11 put in order for a gentleman immediately, and tell her to be sure and change the bed-linen."

"Things look rather dull here," I remarked, as the bar-keeper went out to do as he had been directed.

"Rather; it's a dull place, anyhow."

"How is your mother?" I inquired.

A slight, troubled look came into his face, as he answered—

"No better."

"She's sick, then?"

"Yes; she's been sick a good while; and I'm afraid will never be much better." His manner was not altogether cold and indifferent, but there was a want of feeling in his voice.

"Is she at home?"

"No, sir."

As he showed no inclination to say more on the subject, I asked no further questions, and he soon found occasion to leave me.

The bar-room had undergone no material change, so far as its furniture and arrangements were concerned; but a very great change was apparent in the condition of these. The brass rod around the bar, which, at my last visit, was brightly polished, was now a greenish-black, and there came from it an unpleasant odour of verdigris.[15] The walls were fairly coated with dust, smoke, and fly-specks, and the windows let in the light but feebly, through the dirt-obscured glass. The floor was filthy. Behind the bar, on the shelves designed for a display of liquors, was a confused mingling of empty or half-filled decanters, cigar-boxes, lemons and lemon-peel, old newspapers, glasses, a broken pitcher, a hat, a soiled vest, and a pair of blacking brushes, with other incongruous things, not now remembered. The air of the room was loaded with offensive vapours.

Disgusted with everything about the bar, I went into the sitting-room. Here, there was some order in the arrangement of the dingy furniture; but you might have written your name in dust on the looking-glass and table. The smell of the torpid atmosphere was even worse than that of the bar-room. So I did not linger here, but passed through the hall, and out upon the porch, to get a draught of pure air.

Slade still sat leaning against the wall.

"Fine day this," said he, speaking in a mumbling kind of voice.

"Very fine," I answered.

"Yes, very fine."

"Not doing so well as you were few years ago," said I.

"No—you see—these—these 'ere blamed temperance people are ruining every thing."

"Ah! Is that so?"

"Yes. Cedarville isn't what it was when you first came to the 'Sickle and Sheaf.' I—I—you see. Curse the temperance people! They've ruined everything, you see. Every-thing! Ruined——"

And he muttered, and mouthed his words in such a way, that I could understand but little he said; and, in that little, there was scarcely any coherency. So I left him, with a feeling of pity in my heart for the wreck he had become, and went into the town to call upon one or two gentlemen with whom I had business.

In the course of the afternoon, I learned that Mrs. Slade was in an insane asylum, about five miles from Cedarville. The terrible events of the day on which young Ham-

---

[15] A greenish poisonous pigment that collects on corroding copper.

mond was murdered completed the work of mental ruin, begun at the time her husband abandoned the quiet, honourable calling of a miller, and became a tavern-keeper. Reason could hold its position no longer. When word came to her that Willy and his mother were both dead, she uttered a wild shriek and fell down in a fainting fit. From that period the balance of her mind was destroyed. Long before this, her friends saw that reason wavered. Frank had been her idol. A pure, bright, affectionate boy he was, when she removed with him from their pleasant cottage-home, where all the surrounding influences were good, into a tavern, where an angel could scarcely remain without corruption. From the moment this change was decided on by her husband, a shadow fell upon her heart. She saw, before her husband, her children, and herself, a yawning pit, and felt that, in a very few years, all of them must plunge down into its fearful darkness.

Alas! how quickly began the realization of her worst fears in the corruption of her worshipped boy! And how vain proved all effort and remonstrance, looking to his safety, whether made with himself or his father! From the day the tavern was opened, and Frank drew into his lungs full draughts of the changed atmosphere by which he was now surrounded, the work of moral deterioration commenced. The very smell of the liquor exhilarated him unnaturally; while the subjects of conversation, so new to him, that found discussion in the bar-room, soon came to occupy a prominent place in his imagination, to the exclusion of those humane, childlike, tender, and heavenly thoughts and impressions it had been the mother's care to impart and awaken.

Ah! with what an eager zest does the heart drink in of evil. And how almost hopeless is the case of a boy, surrounded, as Frank was, by the corrupting, debasing associations of a bar-room! Had his father meditated his ruin, he could not have more surely laid his plans for the fearful consummation; and he reaped as he had sown. With a selfish desire to get gain, he embarked in the trade of corruption, ruin, and death, weakly believing that he and his could pass through the fire harmless. How sadly a few years demonstrated his error, we have seen.

Flora, I learned, was with her mother, devoting her life to her. The dreadful death of Willy Hammond, for whom she had conceived a strong attachment, came near depriving her of reason also. Since the day on which that awful tragedy occurred, she had never even looked upon her old home. She went away with her unconscious mother, and ever since had remained with her—devoting her life to her comfort. Long before this, all her own and mother's influence over her brother had come to an end. It mattered not how she sought to stay his feet, so swiftly moving along the downward way, whether by gentle entreaty, earnest remonstrance, or tears; in either case, wounds for her own heart were the sure consequences, while his steps never lingered a moment. A swift destiny seemed hurrying him on to ruin. The change in her father—once so tender, so cheerful in his tone, so proud of and loving toward his daughter—was another source of deep grief to her pure young spirit. Over him, as well as over her brother, all her power was lost; and he even avoided her, as though her presence were an offence to him. And so, when she went out from her unhappy home, she took with her no desire to return. Even when imagination bore her back to the "Sickle and Sheaf," she felt an intense, heart-sickening repulsion toward the place where she had first felt the poisoned arrows of life; and in the depths of her spirit she prayed that her eyes might never look upon it again. In her almost cloister-like seclusion, she sought to gather the mantle of oblivion about her heart.

Had not her mother's condition made Flora's duty a plain one, the true, unselfish instincts of her heart would have doubtless led her back to the polluted home she had left, there, in a kind of living death, to minister as best she could to the comfort of a debased father and brother. But she was spared that trial—that fruitless sacrifice.

Evening found me once more in the bar-room of the "Sickle and Sheaf." The sleepy, indifferent bar-keeper, was now more in his element—looked brighter, and had quicker motions. Slade, who had partially recovered from the stupefying effects of the heavy draughts of ale with which he washed down his dinner, was also in a better condition, though not inclined to talk. He was sitting at a table, alone, with his eyes wandering about the room. Whether his thoughts were agreeable or disagreeable, it was not easy to determine. Frank was there, the centre of a noisy group of coarse fellows, whose vulgar sayings and profane expletives continually rung through the room. The noisiest, coarsest, and most profane was Frank Slade; yet did not the incessant volume of bad language that flowed from his tongue appear in the least to disturb his father.

Outraged, at length, by this disgusting exhibition, that had not even the excuse of an exciting cause, I was leaving the bar-room, when I heard some one remark to a young man who had just come in—

"What! you here again, Ned? Ain't you afraid your old man will be after you, as usual?"

"No," answered the person addressed, chuckling inwardly, "he's gone to a prayer-meeting."

"You'll at least have the benefit of his prayers," was lightly remarked.

I turned to observe the young man more closely. His face I remembered, though I could not identify him at first. But, when I heard him addressed soon after as Ned Hargrove, I had a vivid recollection of a little incident that occurred some years before, and which then made a strong impression. The reader has hardly forgotten the visit of Mr. Hargrove to the bar-room of the "Sickle and Sheaf," and the conversation among some of its inmates, which his withdrawal, in company with his son, then occasioned. The father's watchfulness over his boy, and his efforts to save him from the allurements and temptations of a bar-room, had proved, as now appeared, unavailing. The son was several years older; but it was sadly evident, from the expression of his face, that he had been growing older in evil faster than in years.

The few words that I have mentioned as passing between this young man and another inmate of the bar-room, caused me to turn back from the door, through which I was about passing, and take a chair near to where Hargrove had seated himself. As I did so, the eyes of Simon Slade rested on the last-named individual.

"Ned Hargrove!" he said, speaking roughly—"if you want a drink, you'd better get it, and make yourself scarce."

"Don't trouble yourself," retorted the young man, "you'll get your money for the drink in good time."

This irritated the landlord, who swore at Hargrove violently, and said something about not wanting boys about his place who couldn't stir from home without having "daddy or mammy running after them."

"Never fear!" cried out the person who had first addressed Hargrove—"his old man's gone to a prayer meeting. We shan't have the light of his pious countenance here to-night."

I fixed my eyes upon the young man to see what effect this coarse and irreverent allusion to his father would have. A slight tinge of shame was in his face; but I saw that he had not sufficient moral courage to resent the shameful desecration of a parent's name. How should he, when he was himself the first to desecrate that name?

"If he were forty fathoms deep in the infernal regions," answered Slade, "he'd find out that Ned was here, and get half an hour's leave of absence to come after him. The fact is, I'm tired of seeing his solemn, sanctimonious face here every night. If the boy hasn't spirit enough to tell him to mind his own business, as I have done more than fifty times, why, let the boy stay away himself."

"Why don't you send him off with a flea in his ear, Ned?" said one of the company, a young man scarcely his own age. "My old man tried that game with me, but he soon found that I could hold the winning cards."

"Just what I'm going to do the very next time he comes after me."

"Oh, yes! So you've said twenty times," remarked Frank Slade, in a sneering, insolent manner.

Edward Hargrove had not the spirit to resent this; he only answered,

"Just let him show himself here to-night, and you will see."

"No, we won't see," sneered Frank.

"Wouldn't it be fun!" was exclaimed. "I hope to be on hand, should it ever come off."

"He's as 'fraid as death of the old chap," laughed a sottish looking man, whose age ought to have inspired him with some respect for the relation between father and son, and doubtless would, had not a long course of drinking and familiarity with debasing associates blunted his moral sense.

"Now for it!" I heard uttered, in a quick, delighted voice. "Now for fun! Spunk up to him, Ned! Never say die!"

I turned toward the door, and there stood the father of Edward Hargrove. How well I remembered the broad, fine forehead, the steady, yet mild eyes, the firm lips, the elevated superior bearing of the man I had once before seen in that place, and on a like errand. His form was slightly bent now; his hair was whiter; his eyes farther back in his head; his face thinner and marked with deeper lines; and there was in the whole expression of his face a touching sadness. Yet, superior to the marks of time and suffering, an unflinching resolution was visible in his countenance, that gave to it a dignity, and extorted involuntary respect. He stood still, after advancing a few paces, and then, his searching eyes having discovered his son, he said mildly, yet firmly, and with such a strength of parental love in his voice that resistance was scarcely possible.

"Edward! Edward! Come, my son."

"Don't go." The words were spoken in an under tone, and he who uttered them turned his face away from Mr. Hargrove, so that the old man could not see the motion of his lips. A little while before, he had spoken bravely against the father of Edward; now, he could not stand up in his presence.

I looked at Edward. He did not move from where he was sitting, and yet I saw that to resist his father cost him no light struggle.

"Edward." There was nothing imperative—nothing stern—nothing commanding in the father's voice; but its great, its almost irresistible power, lay in its expression of the father's belief that his son would instantly leave the place. And it was this power that prevailed. Edward arose, and, with eyes cast upon the floor, was moving away from his companions, when Frank Slade exclaimed,

"Poor, weak fool!"

It was a lightning flash of indignation, rather than a mere glance from the human eye, that Mr. Hargrove threw instantly upon Frank; while his fine form sprung up erect. He did not speak, but merely transfixed him with a look. Frank curled his lip impotently, as he tried to return the old man's withering glances.

"Now look here!" said Simon Slade, in some wrath, "there's been just about enough of this. I'm getting tired of it. Why don't you keep Ned at home? Nobody wants him here."

"Refuse to sell him liquor," returned Mr. Hargrove.

"It's my trade to sell liquor," answered Slade, boldly.

"I wish you had a more honourable calling," said Hargrove, almost mournfully.

"If you insult my father, I'll strike you down!" exclaimed Frank Slade, starting up and assuming a threatening aspect.

"I respect filial devotion, meet it where I will," calmly replied Mr. Hargrove,—"I only wish it had a better foundation in this case. I only wish the father had merited—"

I will not stain my page with the fearful oath that Frank Slade yelled, rather than uttered, as, with clenched fist, he sprung toward Mr. Hargrove. But ere he had reached the unruffled old man—who stood looking at him as one would look into the eyes of a wild beast, confident that he could not stand the gaze—a firm hand grasped his arm, and a rough voice said—

"Avast there, young man! Touch a hair of that white head, and I'll wring your neck off."

"Lyon!" As Frank uttered the man's name, he raised his fist to strike him. A moment the clenched hand remained poised in the air; then it fell slowly to his side, and he contented himself with an oath and a vile epithet.

"You can swear to your heart's content. It will do nobody any harm but yourself," cooly replied Mr. Lyon, whom I now recognised as the person with whom I had held several conversations during previous visits.

"Thank you, Mr. Lyon," said Mr. Hargrove, "for this manly interference. It is no more than I should have expected from you."

"I never suffer a young man to strike an old man," said Lyon, firmly. "Apart from that, Mr. Hargrove, there are other reasons why your person must be free from violence where I am."

"This is a bad place for you, Lyon," said Mr. Hargrove; "and I've said so to you a good many times." He spoke in rather an under tone. "Why *will* you come here?"

"It's a bad place, I know," replied Lyon, speaking out boldly, "and we all know it. But habit, Mr. Hargrove—habit. That's the cursed thing! If the bar-rooms were all shut up, there would be another story to tell. Get us the Maine law, and there will be some chance for us."

"Why don't you vote the temperance ticket?" asked Mr. Hargrove.

"Why did I? you'd better ask," said Lyon.

"I thought you voted against us."

"Not I. Ain't quite so blind to my own interests as that. And, if the truth were known, I should not at all wonder if every man in this room, except Slade and his son, voted on your side of the house."

"It's a little strange, then," said Mr. Hargrove, "that with the drinking men on our side, we failed to secure the election."

"You must blame that on your moderate men, who see no danger and go blind with their party," answered Lyon. "We have looked the evil in the face, and know its direful quality."

"Come! I would like to talk with you, Mr. Lyon."

Mr. Hargrove, his son, and Mr. Lyon went out together. As they left the room, Frank Slade said—

"What a cursed liar and hypocrite he is!"

"Who?" was asked.

"Why, Lyon," answered Frank, boldly.

"You'd better say that to his face."

"It wouldn't be good for him," remarked one of the company.

At this Frank started to his feet, stalked about the room, and put on all the disgusting airs of a drunken braggart. Even his father saw the ridiculous figure he cut, and growled out—

"There, Frank, that'll do. Don't make a miserable fool of yourself!"

At which Frank retorted, with so much of insolence that his father flew into a towering passion, and ordered him to leave the bar-room.

"You can go out yourself if you don't like the company. I'm very well satisfied," answered Frank.

"Leave this room, you impudent young scoundrel!"

"Can't go, my amiable friend," said Frank, with a cool self-possession that maddened his father, who got up hastily, and moved across the bar-room to the place where he was standing.

"Go out, I tell you!" Slade spoke resolutely.

"Would be happy to oblige you," Frank said, in a taunting voice; "but, 'pon my word, it isn't at all convenient."

Half intoxicated as he was, and already nearly blind with passion, Slade lifted his hand to strike his son. And the blow would have fallen had not some one caught his arm, and held him back from the meditated violence. Even the debased visiters of this bar-room could not stand by and see nature outraged in a bloody strife between father and son; for it was plain from the face and quickly assumed attitude of Frank, that if his father had laid his hand upon him, he would have struck him in return.

I could not remain to hear the awful imprecations that father and son, in their impotent rage, called down from heaven upon each other's heads. It was the most shocking exhibition of depraved human nature that I had ever seen. And so I left the bar-room, glad to escape from its stifling atmosphere and revolting scenes.

❧ Night the Ninth

A FEARFUL CONSUMMATION

Neither Slade nor his son was present at the breakfast table on the next morning. As for myself, I did not eat with much appetite. Whether this defect arose from the state of my mind, or the state of the food set before me, I did not stop to inquire; but left the stifling, offensive atmosphere of the dining-room in a very few moments after entering that usually attractive place for a hungry man.

A few early drinkers were already in the bar-room—men with shattered nerves and cadaverous faces, who could not begin the day's work without the stimulus of brandy or whisky. They came in, with gliding foot-steps, asked for what they wanted in low voices, drank in silence, and departed. It was a melancholy sight to look upon.

About nine o'clock the landlord made his appearance. He, too, came gliding into the bar-room, and his first act was to seize upon a brandy decanter, pour out nearly half a pint of the fiery liquid, and drink it off. How badly his hand shook—so badly that he spilled the brandy both in pouring it out, and in lifting the glass to his lips! What a shattered wreck he was! He looked really worse now than he did on the day before when drink gave an artificial vitality to his system, a tension to his muscles, and light to his countenance. The miller of ten years ago, and the tavern-keeper of to-day! Who could have identified them as one?

Slade was turning from the bar, when a man came in. I noticed an instant change in the landlord's countenance. He looked startled; almost frightened. The man drew a small package from his pocket, and after selecting a paper therefrom, presented it to Slade, who received it with a nervous reluctance, opened, and let his eye fall upon the writing within. I was observing him closely at the time, and saw his countenance flush deeply. In a moment or two it became pale again—paler even than before.

"Very well—all right. I'll attend to it," said the landlord, trying to recover himself, yet swallowing with every sentence.

The man, who was no other than a sheriff's deputy, and who gave him a sober, professional look, then went out with a firm step, and an air of importance. As he passed through the outer door, Slade retired from the bar-room.

"Trouble coming," I heard the bar-keeper remark, speaking partly to himself, and partly with the view, as was evident from his manner, of leading me to question him. But this I did not feel that it was right to do.

"Got the sheriff on him at last," added the bar-keeper.

"What's the matter, Bill?" inquired a man who now came in with a bustling, important air, and leaned familiarly over the bar. "Who was Jenkins after?"

"The old man," replied the bar-keeper, in a voice that showed pleasure rather than regret.

"No!"

"It's a fact." Bill, the bar-keeper, actually smiled.

"What's to pay?" said the man.

"Don't know, and don't care much."

"Did he serve a summons or an execution?"[16]

"Can't tell."

"Judge Lyman's suit went against him."

"Did it?"

"Yes; and I heard Judge Lyman swear, that if he got him on the hip, he'd sell him out, bag and basket. And he's the man to keep his word."

---

[16]Enforcing a legal judgment.

"I never could just make out," said the bar-keeper, "how he ever came to owe Judge Lyman so much. I've never known of any business transactions between them."

"It's been dog eat dog, I rather guess," said the man.

"What do you mean by that?" inquired the bar-keeper.

"You've heard of dogs hunting in pairs?"

"Oh, yes."

"Well, since Harvey Green got his deserts, the business of fleecing our silly young fellows, who happened to have more money than wit or discretion, has been in the hands of Judge Lyman and Slade. They hunted together, Slade holding the game, while the Judge acted as blood-sucker. But that business was interrupted about a year ago; and game got so scarce, that, as I suggested, dog began to eat dog. And here comes the end of the matter, if I'm not mistaken. So mix us a stiff toddy. I want one more good drink at the 'Sickle and Sheaf,' before the colours are struck."

And the man chuckled at his witty effort.

During the day, I learned that affairs stood pretty much as this man had conjectured. Lyman's suits had been on sundry notes, payable on demand; but nobody knew of any property transactions between him and Slade. On the part of Slade, no defence had been made—the suit going by default. The visit of the sheriff's officer was for the purpose of serving an execution.

As I walked through Cedarville on that day, the whole aspect of the place seemed changed. I questioned with myself, often, whether this were really so, or only the effect of imagination. The change was from cheerfulness and thrift, to gloom and neglect. There was, to me, a brooding silence in the air; a pause in the life-movement; a folding of the hands, so to speak, because hope had failed from the heart. The residence of Mr. Harrison, who, some two years before, had suddenly awakened to a lively sense of the evil of rum-selling, because his own sons were discovered to be in danger, had been one of the most tasteful in Cedarville. I had often stopped to admire the beautiful shrubbery and flowers with which it was surrounded; the walks so clear—the borders so fresh and even—the arbours so cool and inviting. There was not a spot upon which the eye could rest, that did not show the hand of taste. When I now came opposite to this house, I was no longer in doubt as to the actuality of a change. There were no marked evidences of neglect; but the high cultivation and nice regard for the small details were lacking. The walks were cleanly swept; but the box borders were not so carefully trimmed. The vines and bushes that in former times were cut and tied so evenly, could hardly have felt the keen touch of the pruning-knife for months.

As I paused to note the change, a lady, somewhat beyond the middle age, came from the house. I was struck by the deep gloom that overshadowed her countenance. Ah! said I to myself, as I passed on, how many dear hopes, that once lived in that heart, must have been scattered to the winds. As I conjectured, this was Mrs. Harrison, and I was not unprepared to hear, as I did a few hours afterward, that her two sons had fallen into drinking habits; and, not only this, had been enticed to the gaming table. Unhappy mother! What a lifetime of wretchedness was compressed for thee into a few short years!

I walked on, noting, here and there, changes even more marked than appeared about the residence of Mr. Harrison. Judge Lyman's beautiful place showed utter neglect; and so did one or two others that, on my first visit to Cedarville, charmed me with their order, neatness, and cultivation. In every instance, I learned, on inquiring that the owners of these, or some members of their families, were, or had been, visitors at the "Sickle and Sheaf;" and that the ruin, in progress or completed, began after the establishment of that point of attraction in the village.

Something of a morbid curiosity, excited by what I saw, led me on to take a closer view of the residence of Judge Hammond than I had obtained on the day before. The first thing that I noticed, on approaching the old, decaying mansion, were handbills, posted on the gate, the front door, and on one of the windows. A nearer inspection revealed their import. The property had been seized, and was now offered at sheriff's sale!

Ten years before, Judge Hammond was known as the richest man in Cedarville: and now, the homestead he had once so loved to beautify—where all that was dearest to him in life once gathered—worn, disfigured, and in ruins, was about being wrested from him. I paused at the gate, and leaning over it, looked in with saddened feelings upon the dreary waste within. No sign of life was visible. The door was shut—the windows closed—not the faintest wreath of smoke was seen above the blackened chimney-tops. How vividly did imagination restore the life, and beauty, and happiness, that made their home there only a few years before,—the mother and her noble boy, one looking with trembling hope, the other with joyous confidence, into the future—the father, proud of his household treasures, but not their wise and jealous guardian.

Ah! that his hands should have unbarred the door, and thrown it wide, for the wolf to enter that precious fold! I saw them all in their sunny life before me; yet, even as I looked upon them, their sky began to darken. I heard the distant mutterings of the storm, and soon the desolating tempest swept down fearfully upon them. I shuddered as it passed away, to look upon the wrecks left scattered around. What a change!

"And all this," said I, "that one man, tired of being useful, and eager to get gain, might gather in accursed gold!"

Pushing open the gate, I entered the yard, and walked around the dwelling, my footsteps echoing in the hushed solitude of the deserted place. Hark! was that a human voice?

I paused to listen.

The sound came, once more, distinctly to my ears. I looked around, above, everywhere, but perceived no living sign. For nearly a minute I stood still, listening. Yes: there it was again—a low, moaning voice, as of one in pain or grief. I stepped onward a few paces; and now saw one of the doors standing ajar. As I pushed this door wide open, the moan was repeated. Following the direction from which the sound came, I entered one of the large drawing-rooms. The atmosphere was stifling, and all as dark as if it were midnight. Groping my way to a window, I drew back the bolt and threw open a shutter. Broadly the light fell across the dusty, uncarpeted floor, and on the dingy furniture of the room. As it did so, the moaning voice which had drawn me thither swelled on the air again; and now I saw, lying upon an old sofa, the form of a man. It needed no second glance to tell me that this was Judge Hammond. I put my hand upon him, and uttered his name: but he answered not. I spoke more firmly, and slightly shook him; but only a piteous moan was returned.

"Judge Hammond!" I now called aloud, and somewhat imperatively.

But it availed nothing. The poor old man aroused not from the stupor in which mind and body were enshrouded.

"He is dying!" thought I; and instantly left the house in search of some friends to take charge of him in his last, sad extremity. The first person to whom I made known the fact shrugged his shoulders, and said it was no affair of his, and that I must find somebody whose business it was to attend to him. My next application was met in the same spirit; and no better success attended my reference of the matter to a third party. No one to whom I spoke seemed to have any sympathy for the broken-down old man. Shocked by this indifference, I went to one of the county officers, who on learning the condition of Judge Hammond, took immediate steps to have him removed to the Alms-house, some miles distant.

"But why to the Alms-house?" I inquired, on learning his purpose. "He has property."

"Everything has been seized for debt," was the reply.

"Will there be nothing left after his creditors are satisfied?"

"Very few, if any, will be satisfied," he answered. "There will not be enough to pay half the judgments against him."

"And is there no friend to take him in—no one, of all who moved by his side in the days of prosperity, to give a few hours' shelter, and soothe the last moments of his unhappy life?"

"Why did you make application here?" was the officer's significant question.

I was silent.

"Your earnest appeals for the poor old man met with no words of sympathy?"

"None."

"He has, indeed, fallen low. In the days of his prosperity, he had many friends, so called. Adversity has shaken them all like dead leaves from sapless branches."

"But why? This is not always so."

"Judge Hammond was a selfish, worldly man. People never liked him much. His favouring, so strongly, the tavern of Slade, and his distillery operations, turned from him some of his best friends. The corruption and terrible fate of his son—and the insanity and death of his wife—all were charged upon him in people's minds; and every one seemed to turn from him instinctively after the fearful tragedy was completed. He never held up his head afterward. Neighbours shunned him as they would a criminal. And here has come the end at last. He will be taken to the Poor-house, to die there—a pauper!"

"And all," said I, partly speaking to myself, "because a man, too lazy to work at an honest calling, must needs go to rum-selling."

"The truth, the whole truth, and nothing but the truth," remarked the officer with emphasis, as he turned from me to see that his directions touching the removal of Mr. Hammond to the Poor-house were promptly executed.

In my wanderings about Cedarville during that day, I noticed a small, but very neat cottage, a little way from the centre of the village. There was not around it a great profusion of flowers and shrubbery; but the few vines, flowers, and bushes that grew green and flourishing about the door, and along the clean walks, added to the air of taste and comfort that so peculiarly marked the dwelling.

"Who lives in that pleasant little spot?" I asked of a man whom I had frequently seen in Slade's bar-room. He happened to be passing the house at the same time that I was.

"Joe Morgan," was answered.

"Indeed!" I spoke in some surprise. "And what of Morgan? How is he doing?"

"Very well."

"Doesn't he drink?"

"No. Since the death of his child, he has never taken a drop. That event sobered him, and he has remained sober ever since."

"What is he doing?"

"Working at his old trade."

"That of a miller?"

"Yes. After Judge Hammond broke down, the distillery apparatus and cotton spinning machinery were all sold and removed from Cedarville. The purchaser of what remained, having something of the fear of God, as well as regard for man, in his heart, set himself to the restoration of the old order of things, and in due time the revolving mill-wheel was at its old and better work of grinding corn and wheat for bread. The only two men in Cedarville competent to take charge of the mill were Simon Slade and Joe Morgan. The first could not be had, and the second came in as a matter of course.

"And he remains sober and industrious?"

"As any man in the village," was the answer.

I saw but little of Slade or his son during the day. But both were in the bar-room at night, and both in a condition sorrowful to look upon. Their presence, together, in the bar-room, half intoxicated as they were, seemed to revive the unhappy temper of the previous evening, as freshly as if the sun had not risen and set upon their anger.

During the early part of the evening, considerable company was present, though not of a very select class. A large proportion were young men. To most of them the fact that Slade had fallen into the sheriff's hands was known; and I gathered from some aside conversation which reached my ears, that Frank's idle, spendthrift habits had hastened the present crisis in his father's affairs. He, too, was in debt to Judge Lyman—on what account, it was not hard to infer.

It was after nine o'clock, and there was not half a dozen persons in the room, when I noticed Frank Slade go behind the bar for the third or fourth time. He was just lifting a decanter of brandy, when his father, who was considerably under the influence of drink, started forward, and laid his hand upon that of his son. Instantly a fierce light gleamed from the eyes of the young man.

"Let go of my hand," he exclaimed.

"No, I won't. Put up that brandy bottle,—you're drunk now."

"Don't meddle with me, old man!" angrily retorted Frank. "I'm not in the mood to bear any thing more from *you*."

"You're drunk as a fool now," returned Slade, who had seized the decanter. "Let go the bottle."

For only an instant did the young man hesitate. Then he drove his half-clenched hand against the breast of his father, who went staggering away several paces from the counter. Recovering himself, and now almost furious, the landlord rushed forward upon his son, his hand raised to strike him.

"Keep off!" cried Frank. "Keep off! If you touch me, I'll strike you down!" At the same time raising the half-filled bottle threateningly.

But his father was in too maddened a state to fear any consequences, and so pressed forward upon his son, striking him in the face the moment he came near enough to do so.

Instantly, the young man, infuriated by drink and evil passions, threw the bottle at his father's head. The dangerous missile fell, crashing upon one of his temples, shivering it into a hundred pieces. A heavy, jarring fall too surely marked the fearful consequences of the blow. When we gathered around the fallen man, and made an effort to lift him from the floor, a thrill of horror went through every heart. A mortal paleness was already on his marred face, and the death-gurgle in his throat! In three minutes from the time the blow was struck, his spirit had gone upward to give an account of the deeds done in the body.

"Frank Slade! you have murdered your father!"

Sternly were these terrible words uttered. It was some time before the young man seemed to comprehend their meaning. But the moment he realized the awful truth, he uttered an exclamation of horror. Almost at the same instant, a pistol-shot came sharply on the ear. But the meditated self-destruction was not accomplished. The aim was not surely taken; and the ball struck harmlessly against the ceiling.

Half an hour afterward, and Frank Slade was a lonely prisoner in the county jail!

Does the reader need a word of comment on this fearful consummation? No: and we will offer none.

❧ Night the Tenth

THE CLOSING SCENE AT THE "SICKLE AND SHEAF"

On the day that succeeded the evening of this fearful tragedy, placards were to be seen all over the village, announcing a mass meeting at the "Sickle and Sheaf" that night.

By early twilight, the people commenced assembling. The bar, which had been closed all day, was now thrown open, and lighted; and in this room, where so much of evil had been originated, encouraged, and consummated, a crowd of earnest-looking men were soon gathered. Among them I saw the fine person of Mr. Hargrove. Joe Morgan—or rather Mr. Morgan—was also of the number. The latter I would scarcely have recognised, had not some one near me called him by name. He was well dressed, stood erect, and, though there were many deep lines on his thoughtful countenance, all traces of his former habits were gone. While I was observing him, he arose, and addressing a few words to the assemblage, nominated Mr. Hargrove as chairman of the meeting. To this a unanimous assent was given.

On taking the chair, Mr. Hargrove made a brief address, something to this effect.

"Ten years ago," said he, his voice evincing a light unsteadiness as he began, but growing firmer as he proceeded, "there was not a happier spot in Bolton county than Cedarville. Now, the marks of ruin are everywhere. Ten years ago, there was a kind-hearted, industrious miller in Cedarville, liked by every one, and as harmless as a little child. Now, his bloated, disfigured body lies in that room. His death was violent, and by the hand of his own son!"

Mr. Hargrove's words fell slowly, distinctly, and marked by the most forcible emphasis. There was scarcely one present who did not feel a low shudder run along his nerves, as the last words were spoken in a husky whisper.

"Ten years ago," he proceeded, "the miller had a happy wife, and two innocent, glad-hearted children. Now, his wife, bereft of reason, is in a mad-house, and his son the occupant of a felon's cell, charged with the awful crime of parricide!"

Briefly he paused, while his audience stood gazing upon him with half suspended respiration.

"Ten years ago," he went on, "Judge Hammond was accounted the richest man in Cedarville. Yesterday he was carried, a friendless pauper, to the Almshouse; and to-day he is the unmourned occupant of a pauper's grave! Ten years ago, his wife was the proud, hopeful, loving mother of a most promising son. I need not describe what Willy Hammond was. All here knew him well. Ah! what shattered the fine intellect of that noble-minded woman? Why did her heart break? Where is she? Where is Willy Hammond?"

A low, half repressed groan answered the speaker,

"Ten years ago, you, sir," pointing to a sad-looking old man, and calling him by name, "had two sons—generous, promising, manly-hearted boys. What are they now? You need not answer the question. Too well is their history and your sorrow known. Ten years ago, I had a son—amiable, kind, loving, but weak. Heaven knows how I sought to guard and protect him! But he fell also. The arrows of destruction darkened the very air of our once secure and happy village. And who was safe? Not mine, nor yours!

"Shall I go on? Shall I call up and pass in review before you, one after another, all the wretched victims who have fallen in Cedarville during the last ten years? Time does not permit. It would take hours for the enumeration! No: I will not throw additional darkness into the picture. Heaven knows it is black enough already! But what is the root of this great evil? Where lies the fearful secret? Who understands the disease? A direful pestilence is in the air—it walketh in darkness, and wasteth at noonday. It is slaying the first-born in our houses, and the cry of anguish is swelling on every gale. Is there no remedy?

"Yes! yes! There is a remedy!" was the spontaneous answer from many voices.

"Be it our task, then, to find and apply it this night," answered the chairman, as he took his seat.

"And there is but one remedy," said Morgan, as Mr. Hargrove sat down. "The accursed traffic must cease among us. You must cut off the fountain, if you would dry up the stream. If you would save the young, the weak, and the innocent—on you God has laid the solemn duty of their protection—you must cover them from the tempter. Evil is strong, wily, fierce, and active in the pursuit of its ends. The young, the weak, and the innocent can no more resist its assaults, than the lamb can resist the wolf. They are help-less, if you abandon them to the powerers of evil. Men and brethren! as one who has him-self been wellnigh lost—as one who, daily, feels and trembles at the dangers that beset his path—I do conjure you to stay the fiery stream that is bearing every thing good and beautiful among you to destruction. Fathers! for the sake of your young children, be up now and doing. Think of Willy Hammond, Frank Slade, and a dozen more whose names I could repeat, and hesitate no longer! Let us resolve, this night, that from henceforth, the traffic shall cease in Cedarville. Is there not a large majority of citizens in favour of such a measure? And whose rights or interest can be affected by such a restriction? Who, in

fact, has any right to sow disease and death in our community? The liberty, under suf-
ferance, to do so, wrongs the individual who uses it, as well as those who become his victims. Do you want proof of this. Look at Simon Slade, the happy, kind-hearted miller;
and at Simon Slade, the tavern-keeper. Was he benefited by the liberty to work harm to
his neighbour? No! no! In heaven's name, then, let the traffic cease! To this end, I offer
these resolutions:—

"Be it resolved by the inhabitants of Cedarville, That from this day henceforth, no
more intoxicating drink shall be sold within the limits of the corporation.

"Resolved, further, That all the liquors in the 'Sickle and Sheaf' be forthwith
destroyed, and that a fund be raised to pay the creditors of Simon Slade therefor, should
they demand compensation.

"Resolved, That in closing up all other places where liquor is sold, regard shall be
had to the right of property which the law secures to every man.

"Resolved, That with the consent of the legal authorities, all the liquor for sale in
Cedarville be destroyed; provided the owners thereof be paid its full value out of a fund
specially raised for that purpose."

But for the calm, yet resolute opposition of one or two men, these resolutions would
have passed by acclamation. A little sober argument showed the excited company that no
good end is ever secured by the adoption of wrong means.

There were, in Cedarville, regularly constituted authorities, which alone had the
power to determine public measures; or to say what business might or might not be pursued by individuals. And through these authorities they must act in an orderly way.

There was some little chafing at this view of the case. But good sense and reason
prevailed. Somewhat modified, the resolution passed, and the more ultra-inclined contended themselves with carrying out the second resolution, to destroy forthwith all the
liquor to be found on the premises; which was immediately done. After which the people dispersed to their home, each with a lighter heart, and better hopes for the future of
their village.

On the next day, as I entered the stage that was to bear me from Cedarville, I saw a
man strike his sharp axe into the worn, faded, and leaning post that had, for so many
years, borne aloft the "Sickle and Sheaf;" and just as the driver gave word to his horses,
the false emblem which had invited so many to enter the way of destruction, fell crashing to the earth.

13

Antiabolition Tracts

TRACTS WERE EVERYWHERE in nineteenth-century American print culture. While the American Tract Society (founded in 1825) might have been the largest producer of such pieces, other organizations and causes also promoted their beliefs through tracts. Thus, tracts on such diverse topics as peace, frontier settlement, vegetarianism, temperance, slavery, phrenology, political candidates, and various religious traditions all mixed in the increasingly diverse American print marketplace.

Slavery was a topic that created a vast amount of tract literature both before and after the Civil War. One manifestation of this literature was a series of antiabolition tracts published and circulated in the North, which reached Southern audiences as well. Among its several titles, this series included *The Six Species of Men*. Although nothing is known of its author, *The Six Species* is interesting not only because of its content, but also because its place and date of publication show that not all Northerners were against slavery and the issue of slavery did not die out immediately after the end of the Civil War.

The tract is also worthy of note because it captures one of the principal scientific trajectories of the age. Even though its bent is antievolutionary, the tract's strong argument for the existence of different species would be one of many sources that helped lay the groundwork for the growing acceptance of Darwin's views on natural selection and evolution. In the latter part of the nineteenth century, natural and social Darwinists would provide a range of arguments on how different species had evolved to different levels. Such arguments contained a pronounced component of the strong having a natural right to rule over, if not destroy, the weak. In turn, various American politicians, scientists, educators, religious leaders, and laypeople would use these arguments to help frame discussions on a wide array of issues including slavery, class inequality, Native American policy, gender relations, and the problems brought on by massive immigration into the United States in the latter part of the century.

THE SIX SPECIES OF MEN

❧ The World

How singular and how wonderful, when we think of it, is this *World* which we inhabit! A great ball swinging in the air, eight thousand miles in diameter, and twenty-five thousand in circumference! For thousands of years the wisest and greatest men that lived thought the world was as flat as a griddle. Cicero, Demosthenes, Socrates, Plato, even Aristotle,[1] all thought so, and died in the belief. The old Romans thought so. Great historians, like Herodotus, Livy, Tacitus, and Cæsar,[2] died in ignorance of the simple truth which is now known by every child ten years old. Down to the time of Christopher Columbus,[3] the map of the world looked no more like the world itself, than it did like the moon. A man was imprisoned for declaring that the world was round like a ball, and when Columbus talked of sailing *around* it, people thought him *mad*. However, the real *shape* of our world and its motion, and its relation to other planets, has now been fully determined, and can be calculated with mathematical precision. But when we come to look at the vast number of animals of all *kinds,* and men of all *kinds* that inhabit it, we see a field of investigation before us which astounds us, and oppresses us with the conviction that after we learn all we can, we shall then have learned but little of the wonders of the Great Creator.

We see some animals made to live in the frozen North, which would die if taken to a hot climate, and we know there are many in warm climates, that if taken to the arctic zone would perish at once. We see also great differences in men. Some love to live among icebergs, because they are created and adapted to the climate. Others are made for warm climates, and bask in the hottest sun with impunity. It is supposed there are at least eight hundred millions of men on the face of the globe, of all *kinds,* but there a good many races or Species of which we still know but very little. Now, if it took thousands of years to find out the shape and motions of the earth, it is no wonder that the real character and proper relations of different races is not yet fully understood. In the following

---

The Six Species of Men, with Cuts Representing the Types of the Caucasian, Mongol, Malay, Indian, Esquimaux and Negro. With Their General Physical and Mental Qualities, Laws of Organization, Relations to Civilization, &c. Anti-Abolition Tracts. No. 5. New York: Van Evrie, Horton & Company, 1866.

[1]These figures all had a pronounced influence on Western civilization. Marcus Tullius Cicero (106–43 B.C.) and Demosthenes (384–322 B.C.) were great politicians and orators; Socrates (470–399 B.C.), Plato (427?–348? B.C.), and Aristotle (384–322 B.C.) all stand as eminent Greek philosophers.

[2]Among their other many accomplishments, Herodotus (484?–430? B.C.), Livy (59? B.C.–A.D. 17), Gaius Cornelius Tacitus (A.D. 56–120), and Julius Caesar (100?–44 B.C.) all made lasting contributions to the areas of Greek and Roman history writing.

[3]Christopher Columbus (1451–1506) was an Italian master mariner and navigator who did much to discover and map regions touching upon North and South America.

pages it is proposed to give a few fundamental facts upon the *races* or *Species* of men, which will guide every person who wishes to understand this subject. For after all, though nature presents a boundless field for investigation, yet her fundamental laws are so simple and easily comprehended when explained, that not even the most ignorant can go astray.

❧ Laws of Organization

The material universe is divided by naturalists into *organic* and *inorganic,* or into that governed by vital forces, or the principle we call *life,* and that subject to mere mechanical and chemical laws. The former, or *organic* world, is again divided into *animate* and *inanimate,* or what has been called the animal and vegetable kingdoms, in fact into beings that have a nervous system, and are therefore capable of sensation, and those that have no organs or agencies to connect them with the outer world. Naturalists have also divided the animal world into Classes, Orders, Genera, Species, and Varieties, which, for the purposes of teaching was necessary, perhaps, but they are so arbitrary in most publications on this subject, that they nearly as often lead astray as otherwise. The essential and wonderful feature that pervades the whole animated world is their *sameness* and their *difference*—thus the function of digestion, of reproduction, of even the nourishment of offspring by mamary glands, is absolutely the same in human beings as it is in pigs and dogs, but yet what a world of difference between them in the mode or manifestation of this function!

It is this seeming anomaly that has originated so many false classifications, and that has led Linnæus[4] and his followers to place human creatures in the Class Mammalia, and therefore nearer pigs and dogs than these are to birds, &c. The simple truth is, that the animal creation is composed of innumerable creations, each rising above the other, and resembling it, but absolutely distinct and independent, *a perfect world in itself.* Thus the popular notion of a connecting link or a chain of creation, is a mistake, for while it is a perpetual series of gradations from the worm at our feet to ourselves, there are no necessary connections between these countless families or forms of being. True, it is not probable that any of the beings created by the Almighty master of life, have perished from the earth, but it might, or indeed any number might, and yet the universe would be perfect. If, for example, creation were confined to the vegetable world, it would be perfect, and if added to this there was only a single family, lowest in the series of animal being, it would still be the same perfection, and if with the animal world as it is now, there were no human creation, the wisdom and beneficence of the Creator would be perfect. This would be as absolutely true if there was only the lowest and simplest human Species, that of the negro, and it is only when the ascending limit is finally reached in the white or Caucasian man, the most elevated *Species* of the human creation, that *comple-*

---

[4]Carolus Linnaeus (1707–1778) was a Swedish botanist and explorer who first framed principles for dividing the natural world into certain categories more conducive for naming and comparative study, such as "species."

tion as well as *perfection* is impressed on the mind. From the simplest insect under our feet to ourselves, then, there is creation after creation, and world piled upon world, each ascending series embodying all below it, but each absolutely independent and perfect in itself. It is not like building a house with a perfect basement, for such basement, however perfect would be useless if the other stories were not added, but rather as a family with a single child would be perfect in their domestic life, and when a second and third, &c., are finally added to the household, we may suppose completion of the domestic circle, but no more *perfection* than that realized in the birth of the first.

Leaving out of view the division of Classes, Orders, &c., usually found in text-books, on this subject, if we start with the simplest Genus in animated existence, it will be found to consist of a certain number of Species, *for in the whole range of creation there is no such thing as a single Species.* The lowest or most elementary of those has a certain physical structure with faculties or qualities corresponding. The next above it embodies all that made the first, but in addition has something more, and this something, being peculiar to itself as compared with the other, constitutes its specific character, and is termed a *Species.* There may be half a dozen or score of these Species belonging to the Genus or family, each embodying all that are below it, and constantly ascending until the final limit is reached, and then creation is complete. Thus a family or Genus composed of a certain number of Species, have a certain *unity* as well as *diversity,* that is, they are *generally* alike, but *specifically* unlike each each other. A Genus, or family, is, we repeat, a perfect creation or world in itself, and instead of any connecting link with other families or forms of being, the chasm that separates them is forever impassible. Thus dogs and cats domesticated together are never attracted sexually, and even if it were true, as held by some naturalists, that in a few of the lower forms of life this chasm has been traversed, no product has ever followed. All the several Species that compose a Genus or family, on the contrary, *may* mate and mix together, though it is doubted if this ever occurs save in domestication, and in all cases the hybrid and mongrel progeny have a limited power of reproduction, and utterly perish within a certain fixed limit.

A Genus, family, or form of being, is therefore a perfect creation, entirely independent of all the creations or worlds below it, though actually embodying all of these lower worlds. Each of these creations, families, or forms of being, comprises a given number of *Species;* each also an original and independent creation, and each embodying within itself all the qualities of those below it, but with its own higher nature added, and which constitutes its *specific* character.

The human creation composed, therefore, of say half a dozen Species, begins with the negro, the lowest and simplest in its organism. He is separated, of course, by an impassible chasm from the animal world or worlds, but embodies all of these lower creations, and thus the Esquimaux, Indian, Malay, &c., rising above him, and above each other, recede further and further from animal being, until the highest and most complete of all God's wonderful works, the Caucasian, completes the whole.

Thus, the most elevated *Species* is no more absolutely human than the lowest, and the negro is no more absolutely connected with the lower animals than we are, save in degree. That is, the qualities or functions peculiar to the Mammalia are more strongly marked in the lower Species, and especially in the negro, but the master race, or lordly Caucasian, in degree, is also of the earth, earthy.

European naturalists and ethnologists seem utterly incapable of comprehending this very simple subject, and while all, or nearly all, of any reputation assent to the great American doctrine of the diverse origin of the human races, they really have no truthful conception of *different* human Species. Agreeing, for example, with Agassiz,[5] that the human races, like all other beings, were created in certain zones or centres of life, they fancy them, nevertheless, the same Species, as if the Creator had done His work so bunglingly as not only to duplicate it, but to endow them with ample powers of migration never to be used, a matter of supererogation quite as absurd as to have given us four eyes or a double set of senses throughout.

The several human Species, just as all other Species in the animal world, are adapted to, and therefore were created in, certain great centres of existence, and they differ from each other in their physical structure, and their qualities or nature, and therefore in the purposes assigned them by the Creator, just as clearly and absolutely as do the several Species of animals that belong to a creation or form of being. The physical structure, the faculties, in a word, the nature of the negro, is *specifically* as absolutely different from the nature of the Caucasian as the body and the nature of the crow are different from the eagle, or as the body and nature of a garden snake are specifically different from those of a rattle-snake. The crow and eagle are both birds, as the garden and rattle-snake are both serpents, that is, they have certain general qualities as birds or as snakes, but what a mighty space between the specific nature of those beings! So, too, the Felines, the lion, tiger, panther, down to our domestic cat, have all a general, or generic resemblance, but what a mighty difference in the specific character of these beings, or between the cat lying at our kitchen fires and the lordly lion of the desert! The human creation is just as plainly marked by the hand of God, and the Negro, Malay, Mongol, Caucasian, &c., are as absolutely original and independent creations as the panther, tiger, lion, &c.

Such, in conclusion, are the general laws of the organic world, fixed and immutable by the hand of the Infinite, and however wilfully or blindly we may butt our heads against them, we of course can only destroy ourselves. If we sought to force the lion and panther, or eagle and crow, to live the same life because we had a theory that they had the same nature, of course we would destroy them, just as we may destroy a certain number of whites and negroes in our blind and sinful assumption that they have the same nature; but that is all. The works of God are everlasting and immovable, and no human power, accident, time or circumstance, can change or modify them the millionth part of an elementary atom.

➤ The Species of Men

Man belongs in the human creation to what is called by naturalists the *Genus Homo.* This *genus* is made up, like all other forms of being, of several *Species.* Some have called the differences in men *varieties,* for *Species,* it is universally acknowledged, are the cre-

---

[5]Louis Agassiz (1807–1873) was a naturalist, geologist, and university professor who revolutionized the teaching and practice of natural science in the United States.

ation of God, and cannot be permanently changed. The latest investigations in the science of ethnology, however, have proved beyond a doubt that there are at least six distinct *Species* of men, viz.:

1. THE CAUCASIAN.
2. THE MONGOLIAN.
3. THE MALAY.
4. THE AMERICAN INDIAN.
5. THE ESQUIMAUX.
6. THE NEGRO.

We propose to give a cut representing a typical man of each species, and a brief description of the prominent characteristics of each.

[Caucasian] is derived from Mt. Caucasus, as in its neighborhood is found the supposed typical white man. This Species includes the following nations, ancient and modern: the Assyrians, Medes, Persians, Jews, Egyptians, Chaldeans, Georgians, Circassians, Armenians, Arabs, Syrians, Affghans, Greeks, Persians, and the nations of all modern Europe, and their descendants in America. The Caucasian can be confounded with no other Species, for though in some localities climate and other causes darken the skin sometimes with a dark olive tint, extending, as with the Bedouins, and the Jews of the Malabar coast, to almost black, yet the flowing beard, more constant than even color, projecting forehead, oval features, erect position, and lordly presence, stamp him as the *master race,* wherever found. A peculiar feature of this Species is the advancement of the forehead to the line of the face. As we descend in the scale of creation, we find the face increasing at the expense of the cranium. In the Caucasian Species the facial angle is from 80 to 85 degrees, but it decreases in the other Species, until, in the case of the negro it is as low as 65 degrees. As we descend to reptiles and fishes, the jaws seem to consti-

The Caucasian Species

tute almost all the head, and these are the most voracious of animals. Animals with the longest snouts are always considered the most stupid and gluttonous, and on the contrary, as the facial angle increases, the Species approach a higher type.

All the *Species* of men are divided into families, which are the effect of habits of life, intermarriage, &c., &c. There are three great divisions of this kind in the Caucasian species: 1st. *The Celtic* division, comprising the inhabitants of Western Europe, (except the English,) and the ancient Britons, Welsh, Irish, and Scotch. The *Germanic* division, comprising Germans, Danes, Swedes, Norwegians, Saxons, and English. The *Sclavonic* division, comprising the Russians, Poles, Bohemians, Cossacks, and the inhabitants of a part of Western Asia and Northern Africa.

The Caucasian is the only historical race, and is the only one capable of those mental manifestations which have a permanent impression behind. It is the only race that can be said to leave a history. Blot out from the world the record of Caucasian genius and attainments, and it would be a blank. The white man has never been a barbarian, as some people suppose. Some few of the race have been more learned, more civilized, (if we may call certain phases of society in which wealth abounds civilization,) than other portions, but no such nondescript as a *white savage* was ever discovered. The men of Abraham's time[6] were just such men as exist today, lacking only the accumulated knowledge which has since been stored up. The Greeks and Persians were not one whit behind our own age in intellectual power. Such is the Caucasian man, the highest in the scale of creation. It has its specific character, its own capacities for acquiring and retaining knowledge, its own habits and modes of thought, and it cannot impose these upon another being specifically different. If any superior power were to take it and compel it to live out a life to which the Creator had not adapted it, it would unquestionably result in the destruction of the Species. We shall see, as we follow up the subject, how definite and distinct are the characteristics of each Species. The following cut represents [the Mongolian Species].

This race appears to have originated from the central plains of Africa, whence it is inferred they have wandered in all directions. It comprises the Chinese, Japanese, the

The Mongolian Species

---

[6]Early second millennium B.C.

inhabitants of Thibet, Tonquin, Siam, Cochin China, Hindostan, Ceylon, &c., &c. The color of the Mongolian is olive yellow, the eyes dark, the hair black and straight; face beardless; features indistinct; the face between the eyes is very broad and flat; the cheeks high and prominent; the eyes almond-shaped, and the head pyramidal. In stature he is inferior to the white man.

This race is the one nearest to the Caucasian, and has shown a limited intellectual development, but its powers and attainments have been much exaggerated. The Chinese pretend to trace their history back to a period long anterior to our own, but this claim is itself sufficient proof of its own worthlessness. No one will suppose that the individual Chinaman has a larger brain or greater breadth of intellect than the individual Caucasian, and if not, what folly to suppose that the aggregate Chinese mind was capable of doing that which the aggregate Caucasian mind could not do! The truth is, what is supposed to be Chinese history is a mere collection of fables and impossibilities, and it may be doubted if they can trace back their annals even five hundred years with any degree of certainty. At a remote period, a considerable portion of the Chinese population was Caucasian, indeed a considerable portion is still Caucasian. There is little doubt that Confucius[7] was a white man; indeed it is known that the leaders of those Mongol hordes which swept over Europe, shortly after the Christian era, were of Caucasian blood. Attilla was a full-blooded white man; so was Tamerlane. Genghis Khan[8] was a cross of Mongol and Caucasian. So wide and so diversified have been the affiliations and intermixtures of the Caucasian and Mongol in the East, that it is difficult, in the present state of our knowledge of human races, to state with confidence the exact boundaries they occupy. The early Caucasian invaders of India amalgamated with the Indian and negro there. The pure Caucasians again intermarrying, there have grown up these numerous *castes* in India which even learned men are often puzzled to account for. One point seems to be settled in relation to the Mongol race. It cannot advance beyond a given point. It has been stationary for years and years. It can never become an element of modern civilization, and the trade carried on with China is not likely to vary to any considerable extent from what it is now. Its intellectual and moral grasp is limited, and in no exalted sense can the race reach the ideas or virtues of Caucasian civilization.

[The Malay species] inhabits the Asiatic and Polynesian Islands. The color of the skin in the true Malay is light brown or tawny; the hair is black, lank, coarse, and abundant; the eyes moderately separated; the nose prominent but broad and thickest at the end; the mouth is large and the lips thick; the face broad; the jaws prominent; the forehead low and slanting. In many of the islands it appears to be extensively mixed with the negro, and in others, as in New Zealand, there is evidently a considerable infusion of Caucasian blood, as is shown by the tall, erect forms, fair complexion, and manly presence of its inhabitants.

The Malays are inferior to the Mongols. Their character is treacherous, and their disposition ferocious and implacable, while their nervous system is almost insensible to bodily pain. In a fit of passion they commit the most indiscriminate murders. These

---

[7]Confucius (551–479 B.C.) is China's most famous ancient philosopher and political theorist.

[8]Genghis Khan (1155?–1227) was a Mongolian warrior who was one of the most successful conquerors in history. He ruled one of the largest empires the world has ever known.

The Malay Species

occur so frequently among them, that in European settlements, where this race congregates, particular police regulations and precautions are taken to obviate the mischief. It will not do to apply to them "Equal Civil Rights Bills," and if any "philanthropic" Sumner or Stevens[9] should try it, he might find himself transfixed with a spear before he had completed his designs. The race has really no history.

This race or *Species* of men [the American Indian] is more or less familiar to all Americans. No one can mistake an Indian for a white man, however much he may fancy a negro to be one. No doubt the entire aboriginal inhabitants of this continent, with the exception of the Esquimaux, belong to this race. The color of the skin is brown or cinnamon-hued; the iris dark; the hair long, black and straight; no beard; the eyes are deeply seated; the nose flat, but prominent; the lips full and rounded. The face is broad,

The American Indian

[9]Charles Sumner (1811–1874) and Thaddeus Stevens (1792–1868) were both American politicians widely known for their antislavery views.

especially the cheeks, which are prominent and high. The general shape of the head is square; the forehead low and broad; the orbital and nasal cavities large, indicating a corresponding acuteness of sight and smell, in which they greatly excel the Caucasian race. The character of the Indian is well known. His disposition is revengeful and stealthy; he never forgets an injury, and in his wars knows neither age nor sex, but slaughters all indiscriminately. Many people have supposed the time was when the Indians of this continent were more civilized than when Columbus found them, and have ascribed the ruins of Central America, Mexico, and South America to them. But there is no reasonable grounds for any such conclusions. It is almost certain, however, that Caucasians found their way to this continent even before the date of authentic history. No one who has visited the ruins of Mexico can doubt for a moment that they are the remains of extinct Caucasians, who came here centuries ago and perished in the gulf of mongrelism! The Indian mind is capable of a certain development, but that is fixed and determinate, beyond which it cannot go, any more than it can alter the color of its skin. Powhatan's[10] empire in Virginia undoubtedly called out the utmost resources, and reached the utmost limit of the Indian mind. The Indian does manifest, to a certain extent, a capacity of mental action, but this is too feeble to make a permanent impression on the physical agents that surround him, and therefore he can have no history, for there are no materials— nothing to record. Our real duties to this race have never yet been understood. The attempt to "civilize" him after the Caucasian idea, has killed him, but it does not follow that a true understanding of the laws of races may not evolve a mode of treatment of our Indian population which shall insure its own as well as our happiness. The idea that the Creator has made anything in vain, or brought races of men into the world "to die out," as the phrase is, impeaches His wisdom and beneficence, and is little better than downright Atheism.

The Esquimaux, or Polar *Species* of men, is least known of all, and prior to the explorations of that true hero and gallant son of science, the late Dr. Kane,[11] was scarcely

The Esquimaux

---

[10]Great Algonkin chief who is most famous as the father of Pocahontas.

[11]Elisha Kent Kane (1820–1857) was an early explorer of Greenland and the Arctic region.

known at all. It is of but little importance either in a general or anthropological point of view, but it is superior to the negro in the scale of creation, for the necessities of its existence, the terrible struggle for life in those bleak and desolate regions, infer the possession of powers superior to those of a race whose centre of existence is in the fertile and luxuriant tropics, where nature produces spontaneously, and where the idle and sensual negro only needs to gather those products to exist and multiply his kind.

The Esquimaux inhabit the shores of all the seas, bays, inlets, and islands of America north of latitude 60 degrees from the east coast of Greenland to Behrings Straits. They are a small, broad-shouldered race, usually less than five feet high, with high cheek bones, flat faces, small, lustreless eyes, round cheeks, small, round mouths, long, straight, coal-black hair. Their bodies are of a *dark gray color,* and their faces brown or *blue.* Polygamy is universal among them. Their dwellings are made of wood, stone, and sometimes snow. They dress in furs, and show a good deal of ingenuity in preparing them. They live almost exclusively upon fish and animal food, which they *eat raw!* Fish oil is considered a great delicacy! They are great thieves. Their constitution is so adapted to their place and condition of existence, that they would probably perish at once by any application of "equal rights" to them. To compel them to live out the life of the Caucasian would kill them even sooner than the polar bear pines away and dies when transferred to this climate. The Creator has evidently fixed upon them the indelible marks of a distinct Species of the *Genus Homo.*

We now come to the sixth and lowest *Species* in the human family; and it may here he mentioned as not a little remarkable that while the lines of demarkation between the Caucasian and other races are generally acknowledged to be distinct—so distinct, in fact, that no one has ever yet announced himself so fanatical as to demand that the Chinese, the Malays, the Indian, or the Esquimaux should have "equal rights" with white men, and become a part and parcel of their political and social system—yet, strange to say, this demand has been made for the negro, the very lowest in the scale of the human

The Negro

creation! We do not propose to do more in this place than to call attention to this singular fact. Tract No. 1[12] of this series points out the reason for it.

The negro race, or Species of men, is scattered over the entire continent of Africa, except its more northern parts. There are many different tribes or varieties, many of them, doubtless, hybrid populations, the expiring remains of the admixture with Caucasians in northern Africa. Vast numbers of white men in Egypt, Carthage, and all along the southern coast of the Mediterranean, have perished by the foul sin of amalgamation. The negro race has no history, no learning, no literature, no laws. For six thousand years he has been a *savage.* The researches of Champolian and Rawlinson reveal the fact that he was precisely the same being in the time of the ancient Egyptians that he now is. He has never invented anything, or advanced a single step in civilization when left to himself. He is sunk in the grossest superstitions, and is guilty of the most revolting practices. The only ones that have ever shown any advancement are those who have been brought to this country and placed under the control of Christian masters. The humane Las Cases,[13] seeing some three centuries ago that there was absolutely no one to till the ground in the tropical regions of America, bethought him of the philanthropic idea of bringing this savage *Species* of men to this continent, and thus it was that they were first introduced into this hemisphere. No one ever suggested that these people ought to have the rights of Caucasians until after our Revolution of 1776. Then it was declared by the monarchists, whom we had whipped, that we held this negro *Species of men* in slavery, because we did not give them the same *status* as that occupied by the Caucasian *Species.* It will ever be regarded as very strange and unaccountable, but it is nevertheless true, that we assented to this charge, and acknowledged that because this negro *Species* of men did not occupy the same position in political and social affairs as the Caucasian *Species* did, that it was therefore in bondage, in slavery! It is strange that people who knew *practically* that the negro was a different Species of man, could have assented to the palpable absurdity that it was slavery to recognize distinctions which the Creator had so plainly marked. But as there are many people who believe, or affect to believe, that there are no organic distinctions, except color, between negroes and Caucasians, we propose to notice them with a little particularity, and shall show that color is only one, and in fact not the greatest distinction between the races or Species of men. We will take them up in their order.

COLOR

The color of the negro is black. A great many reasons have been given for the cause of the negro's color, but after all, we only know that it is black, because the Creator so made it. If it be the *pigmenlum nigrum,* a substance lying immediately beneath the outward

---

[12]Advertised as: *Abolition and Secession: or, Cause and Effect, Together with the Remedy for Our Sectional Troubles,* by a Unionist.

[13]Bartolemé de Las Casas (1474–1566) was a Spanish historian and Dominican missionary in the Americas. Although Las Casas did recruit farmers for colonizing the New World, he was not responsible for introducing to the region what would later become the institution of African American slavery.

skin or cuticle, as is generally supposed, then it is evident that that substance is a specific difference between the races, implanted by the Maker of all, for the Caucasian race does not have it. It is common to call negroes "colored men," and yet it would be just as proper to speak of "colored horses," "colored birds," or "colored cattle." There is no such monstrosity in the world as a "colored man," that is, a being like ourselves in all except color. It is just as absurd as a white body with a negro head on its shoulders, or as a dog with the head of a hog. The negro face cannot express those higher emotions which give such beauty to the Caucasian countenance, and as nature has denied them the outward manifestation, it is no more than reasonable to suppose they do not have the emotions themselves. Color, however, is no more a difference between white men and negroes, than any other fact out of a countless million of facts that separate them. It is more palpable to the senses, but no more universal or invariable than the difference in the hair, voice, features, the form of the limbs, the single globules of blood, or the myriad of specific qualities that constitute the negro's being.

THE FIGURE

The negro is incapable of an erect or direct perpendicular position. The general structure of his limbs, the form of the pelvis, the spine, the way the head is set on the shoulders, in short, the entire anatomical formation, forbids an erect position. But while the whole structure is thus adapted to a slightly stooping posture, the head would seem to be the most important agency, for with any other head, or the head of any other race, it would be impossible to retain an upright position at all! The negro's head is narrow and longitudinal, projecting posteriorly, thus placing his eyes at an angle with the horizon; and if he had the broad forehead and small cerebellum, or posterior brain, of the white man, on the same body, he would no longer possess a centre of gravity. It is obvious, therefore, if Gen. Howard[14] and the Yankee school marms could "educate" Sambo into intellectual equality with the white man, their *protege* would be as incapable of standing on his feet as he would if they had cut his head entirely off! The negro does not walk flat on his feet, but on the outer sides, in consequence of the sole of his foot having a direction inwards, from the legs and thighs being arched outwards, and the knees bent. While it is not assumed that he is not entirely human, yet he approximates the lower animals in all respects more closely than the Caucasian man. Indeed, take the most advanced species of the ape *Genus,* and compare them with the negro, the lowest in the human *Genus,* and an anatomist would say that Nature had apparently been puzzled where to place them, and had finally compromised the matter by giving an exactly equal inclination to the form and attitude of each other.

THE HAIR

Next to the color of the negro, there is no one of his specific differences so palpable as the hair. The hair of the Caucasian is a graceful ornament, and varies in color from black to

---

[14]Oliver Howard (1830–1909) was a Union officer who headed the Freedmen's Bureau after the Civil War (1865–1872), tirelessly working to better the situation of former slaves.

auburn, giving variety and beauty to that species. In the negro it is always black, and is matted in the head as a protection from tropical heats. Such a being as a light-haired, or flaxen-haired negro was never known. Microscopic observations have shown that its elementary structure differs from ordinary hair as widely as its appearance. The popular notion that it is "wool" that covers the head of the negro, instead of hair, is fallacious. It is *hair.* Specific to the negro race alone, and however widely it may differ from the Caucasian's, it is really no more different than any other quality or feature of the negro being. The negro's hair is so matted together as to be wholly impenetrable to the rays of a tropical sun, and it furnishes a vastly better protection to the brain than the thickest felt hat does to that of the white man. A hat is really a "fashionable folly" in the South for a negro. It does not add to his happiness, for Nature has made ample provision for him in this respect.

Another peculiarity of the negro is absence of beard. The Caucasian is really the only bearded race, and this is the most striking mark of its supremacy over all others. All other races approximate to it in this respect, but the typical, woolly-headed negro, except a little tuft on the chin, and sometimes on the upper lip, has nothing that can be confounded with a beard. Negroes are sometimes seen with considerable beard on their faces, but it should be remembered that it is common to call all who are not pure Caucasians, negroes. Bearded negroes have a large infusion of white blood. A negro with the flowing, dignified, and majestic beard of the Caucasian, would indeed be a curiosity, and about as amusing a specimen of humanity as it is possible to conceive of. If Sumner & Co. expect to make anything of Sambo, they must strike for "equal beard" for him as well as for "equal education," or "equal voting." When they have endowed the negro with the full and flowing beard of the Caucasian, there will be some prospect of the success of their efforts in "reconstructing" the races.

THE FEATURES

The features reflect the inner nature, and they are more or less distinctly developed as we ascend or descend in the scale of being. The features of the white reflect all the higher and nobler as well as baser qualities of the mind. The negro has more or less of a dead conformity. On visiting a plantation of them at the South, it is difficult to tell one from another. The flat nose, enormous lips, and protuberent jaws, together with his flat, indistinct and shapeless features, strikingly approximate to the lower animals, and they are as utterly incapable of reflecting certain emotions as so much flesh and blood in any other part of the body. If the Creator, therefore, gave the negro the higher capacities that the Abolitionists claim, it is very evident that He denied him all opportunity to reflect them in his countenance.

LANGUAGE

Every *Species* of created beings has its own specific language. The hiss of the snake, the growl of the tiger, the roar of the lion, are all peculiar, and one cannot exchange with the other. Space does not allow to go into details, but suffice it to say the vocal organs of the negro differ widely from those of the white man, and no typical negro can speak the language of the white man, no matter how much effort may be made to "educate" him. Indeed, any one accustomed to negroes can distinguish the negro voice at night among any number of those of white men, by its tones alone. It is thus seen that in every peculiarity he differs from the white man.

THE SENSES

The senses of the negro are more powerful, but less delicate and discriminating than in the white man. He approximates the lower animals in the sense of smell, and can detect snakes by that sense alone. The sense of sight is seldom impaired. The sense of touch is feeble in the hand, the coarse, blunt, webbed fingers of the negress, for example, could never produce those delicate fabrics and exquisite embroideries which are the handiwork of the Caucasian. The sense of touch in the negro seems to be developed over the whole body, giving him a greater fear of a whipping than any other punishment it is possible to inflict upon him. The sensibility of negroes in this respect is very similar to that of children, and when we consider the obtuse sensibility of the brain, it is probable that a good sound whipping is a greater punishment to the negro than hanging.

THE BRAIN

The brain of the negro is ten to fifteen per cent smaller than that of the white man, the former averaging seventy-five to eighty-five cubic inches. When we consider, however, that the posterior or animal portion is much larger in proportion than the same in the Caucasian, the inferiority of mental powers is still more marked. If no other evidence existed, the brain of the negro would prove his specific distinctions from the white race, and establish the impossibility of his reaching the standard of the Caucasian without a re-creation. Those "smart" people who expect to "educate" the negro to be the equal of the white man, had better set to work and see if they can contrive to get fifteen or twenty per cent, more brain in his cranium, and then "reconstruct" such as he has, so that the animal portion shall not preponderate over the intellectual.

We have now gone through with some few of the more palpable and *specific* differences which distinguish the negro from the Caucasian and other races. They might be multiplied to an indefinite extent, but they are sufficient to show that these differences are not artificial, nor the result of time, climate, or circumstances, but organic, indestructable, and unchangable. That the negro is in fact a distinct species of the *Genus Homo,* and that it ought to be, and must be, thus recognised legally and socially, or the most disastrous consequences will follow.

THE BIBLICAL OBJECTIONS

The Naturalist, reasoning alone on *basis of fact,* says, that which has been uniform and undeviating for three hundred years, in all kinds of climate and under all kinds of circumstances, in a state of "freedom" or condition of "slavery," under the burning Equator and amid the snows of Canada, without change, or symptom of change, must have been thus three thousand years ago. And he reasons truly, for the excavations of Champolion[15] and others demonstrate the specific character of the negro race four thousand years ago, with as absolute and unmistakable certainty as it is now actually demonstrated to the external sense of the present generation. And the Naturalist, reasoning on this basis of fact, says, "that which has existed four thousand years, without the slightest change or modification, which in all kinds of climate, and under every condition of circumstances preserves its integrity, and transmits, in the regular and normal order, to each succeeding generation the exact and complete type of itself, must have been thus at the beginning, and when the existing order was first called into being by the Almighty Creator." And contemplating the subject from this stand-point, and reasoning from analogy, or exactly as we do in respect to other and all other forms of existence, the conclusion is irresistible and unavoidable that the several human races or species originally came into being exactly as they now exist, as we know they have existed through all human experience, and without a recreation, must continue to exist so long as the world itself lasts, or the existing order remains.

But a large portion of the "world" believe that the Bible teaches the descent of all mankind from a single pair, and consequently that there must have been a supernatural interposition at some subsequent period, which changed the human creation into its actual and existing form of being. And if there has been at any time a special revelation made to man, and supernatural interposition in regard to other things, then this alteration or re-creation of separate species is no more irrational or improbable than other things pertaining to that revelation, and which are universally assented to by the religious world.

A revelation is necessarily supernatural; that is, in direct contradiction to the normal order; but it may be said that the Creator is not the slave of His own laws, and in His immaculate wisdom and boundless power might see fit to change the order of the human creation; and certainly the same Almighty power which took the Hebrews over the Red Sea on dry land,[16] that saved a pair of all living things in the ark of Noah,[17] or dispersed the builders of Babel,[18] could, with equal case, reform, or recreate human life, and in future ordain that instead of one there should be several species of men. This is a matter, however, in regard to which we do not assume to decide, to question, to venture an opinion, or even to hazard a conjecture. It is clearly and absolutely beyond the reach of human intelligence, and therefore not within the province of legitimate inquiry. The Almighty has, in His infinite wisdom and boundless beneficence, hidden from us many things, a knowledge of which would doubtless injure us, and the origin of the human races belongs to this catalogue. Men may labor to investigate it, to tear aside the veil the Creator has drawn about it, to unlock the mystery in which He has shrouded it, and after

---

[15]Jean-François Champollion (1790–1832) was a French Egyptologist and linguist who played a major role in deciphering Egyptian hieroglyphics.

[16]Exod. 14.

[17]Gen. 7–8.

[18]Gen. 11.

millions of years thus appropriated, come back to the starting-point, the simple, palpable, unavoidable truth. *They exist.* But why or wherefore, whither they came, or whence they go, is beyond the range of human intelligence. We only know, and are only permitted to know, that the several species now known to exist have been exactly as at present in their physical natures and intellectual capacities, through all human experience, and without a supernatural interposition or re-creation, must continue thus through countless ages, and as long as the existing order of nature itself continues. This we *know* is beyond doubt or possible mistake, while, whether it was thus at the beginning, or changed by a supernatural interposition at some subsequent period, is now, and always must be, left to conjecture.

Those who interpret the Book of Genesis, or who believe that the Book of Genesis teaches the origin of the human family from a single pair, will, of course, believe that the Creator subsequently changed them into their present form, while those who do not thus interpret the Bible will believe, with equal confidence, perhaps, that they were created thus at the beginning. It is not, nor could it be of the slightest benefit to us to really and truly know the truth of this matter. All that is essential to our welfare we already know, or may know, if we properly apply the faculties with which the Creator has so beneficently endowed us. We only need to apply these faculties—to investigate the question— to study the differences existing among the several species of men, and compare their natures and capabilities with our own, to understand our true relations with them, and thus to secure our own happiness as well as their well-being, when placed in juxtaposition with them.

All this is so obvious, and the remote and abstract question of origin so hypothetical and entirely non-essential, that it seems impossible that intelligent and conscientious men would ever seek to raise an issue on it, or that they would overlook the great practical duties involved in the question, and engage in a visionary and unprofitable discussion about that of which they neither do nor can know anything whatever.

Nevertheless, some few persons seem to be especially desirous to provoke an issue on this matter, not only with science but with common sense, and a certain reverend and rather distinguished gentleman has publicly and repeatedly declared "that the doctrine of a single human race underlies the whole fabric of religious belief, and if it is rejected, Christianity will be lost to mankind!" What miserable folly, if nothing worse, is this! It is a virtual declaration that we must believe, or pretend to believe, what we *know* to be a *lie,* in order to preserve what we *believe* to be a truth. The existence of different species of men belongs to the category of *physical fact*—a thing subject to the decision of the senses, and belief neither has nor can have anything to do with the matter. It is true the reverend gentleman in question may shut *his* eyes and remain in utter ignorance of the fact, or rather of the laws governing the fact, and while thus ignorant, may believe, or pretend to believe, that widely different things constitute the same thing—that white and black are identical—that white parents had at some remote time, and in some strange and unaccountable manner, given birth to negro offspring; but what right has he to say to those who are conscious of the fact of different species, and who *know,* moreover, that negroes could no more originate from white parentage than they could from dogs or cats, that they shall stultify themselves and dishonestly pretend to believe otherwise, on pain of eternal reprobation! It is not the desire of the writer to either reconcile the merits of science with those peculiar interpretations of the Bible, or to exhibit any contradictions with those interpretations. An undoubting believer himself in the great doctrines of Christianity, he finds no difficulty whatever in this respect, and would desire to simply state the *facts, or what he knows to be truth,* and leave the reader to form his own conclusions.

The assumption, however, that belief in the dogma of a single human race or species is vital to the preservation of Christianity, needs to be exposed, as it is in reality as monstrous in morals as stupid and absurd in fact. We cannot *believe* that which we *know* to be untrue, and to affect such belief, however good the motive may seem, must necessarily debauch and demoralize the whole moral structure. There are many things, such as the belief in the doctrine of election, original sin, or justification by faith, that admit of belief, honest, earnest, undoubting belief, for they are abstractions, and purely matters of faith that can never be brought to the test of physical demonstration, or to the standard of material fact, but the question of race, the fact of distinct races, or rather the existence of Species of Caucasians, Mongols, Negroes, &c., are physical facts, subject to the senses, and it is beyond the control of the will to refuse assent to their actual presence. Can a man, by taking thought, add a cubit to his stature? Can he believe himself something else—a woman, a dog, or that he does not exist—that black is white, or that red is yellow, or that the negro is a white man? It is possible to deceive and delude ourselves, and believe, or think that we believe many things which our interest, our prejudices, and our caprices prompt us to believe, but they must be things of an abstract nature, where there are no physical tests to embarrass us, or to compel the will to bow to that fixed and immutable standard of truth which the Eternal has planted in the very heart of things, and which otherwise the laws of the mental organism absolutely force us to recognize. But the existence of distinct Species of men does not belong to this category. It is fact, palpable, immediate, demonstrable and unescapable fact. We know, and we cannot avoid knowing, that the negro is a negro, and is not a white man, and therefore we cannot believe, however much we may strive to do so, that he is the same being that we are, or in other words, that all mankind constitute a single race or Species. All that is possible or permissible is to make liars and hypocrites of ourselves—to pretend to believe in a thing that we do not and cannot believe in—to force this hypocrisy and pretended belief on others who may happen to have confidence in our honesty and respect for our ability; and finally, as a salve for our outraged conscience, to deceive ourselves with the notion that our motives are good, and the end justifies the means.

But why should these men deem this absurd doctrine essential to *their* interpretation of the Bible? That the Almighty Creator subsequently changed the order of the human creation is in entire harmony with the universally received history of the Christian Revelation. All the Christian sects of the day admit the doctrine of miracles, or supernatural interposition, down to the time of the Apostles, and the largest of all (the Roman Catholics) credit this interpretation at the present day, and therefore those ready to recognize it in such numerous instances, many, too, of relatively trifling importance, but, determined to reject it in this matter of races, are only imitating their brethren of old, and straining at gnats while swallowing camels with the greatest case. To many persons the great doctrines of the Christian faith carry with them innate and irresistible proof of their divine origin, but the professional teachers of theology depend mainly upon supernatural interposition to convince the world of its truth, and yet by a strange and unaccountable perversity, some of them would reject it in the most important, or at all events, one of the most important instances in which it ever did or ever could occur. But will the sensible and really conscientious Christian priest or layman venture to persist in forcing this assumption, this palpable, demonstrable, unmistakable falsehood, that the single-race dogma is essential to the preservation of Christianity upon the public? If he does, and if it is accepted by those who look upon him as a teacher, then it is certain that he will inflict infinite mischief on the cause of Christianity.

To assume that all mankind have white skins, or straight hair, or any other specific feature of our own race, involves no greater absurdity, indeed, involves the exact absurdity, that the assumption of a single human Species does. If it were assumed that we must stultify ourselves, and believe, or pretend to believe, that all mankind have white skins, or Christianity would be lost to the world, there is not a single man in this Republic that would not reject such an assumption with scorn and contempt. White and black are specialties, but no more so than all the other things that constitute the negro being, and therefore the assumption put forward substantially and indeed exactly, is thus: We must believe that Whites, Indians, Negroes, &c., have the same color, or the whole fabric of Christianity will be overthrown and lost to mankind!

But enough. All Americans know—for they cannot avoid knowing—that negroes are negroes, and specifically different from themselves; they know, moreover, that they differed just as widely when first brought to this continent, and all who understand the simplest laws of organization, know that they must always remain thus different from ourselves, and therefore they know that they were made so by the act and will of the Almighty Creator, while when, or how, or why they are thus, is beyond the province of human enquiry, and of no manner of importance whatever.

❧ Consequences of Violating Organic Laws

In the foregoing pages it has been briefly shown, 1st, what are the general laws of *organization;* 2nd, the natural history of the several human *Species,* as actually revealed to our senses as well as reason, has been presented, and in conclusion, it is proposed to show the consequences of violating, or rather of ignoring these laws, fixed and fashioned by the hand of the Infinite.

There are two fundamental principles that cover the whole mighty subject, and which constantly kept in mind, will enable the reader to grasp the details with absolute certainty.

1. The more extended and multiplied are the interminglings or intermarriages of *Varieties* of the same *Species,* the more vigorous and prolific will be the progeny; or in other words, that nation whose people are most extensively mixed with the people of other nations will be—other things equal—the most vigorous, progressive, and prosperous.

2. But that nation or people who intermingle most extensively with people of a *different Species,* will be—other things equal—the most feeble, sterile, and contemptible. Or in other words, the nation that most extensively intermingles with different *Species* of human kind will most rapidly lose its vitality and perish or disappear as a nationality.

These two fundamental laws that pervade the entire organic world, and permit no possible departure from them, have, as observed, only to be constantly remembered to grasp all the secondary consequences with absolute certainty. Starting with marriage or mating of a brother and sister, there might be offspring, but it would be impotent or idiotic, and incapable of reproduction. This is the extreme violation, and of course a nation or community where brothers and sisters mated together would be so deteriorated in its organization that it would rapidly perish and disappear. And if, instead of the mating of brothers and sisters, cousins were to mate together, then there would be the same final result, differing only in degree or in the time necessary to extinction. If, for example, we can suppose a nation, community, or people, where it was the custom of mating cousins, the progeny, though capable of reproduction in the first generation, would be feeble, effete and imbecile, with such direct tendencies to impotency, idiotcy, or other disorganization, that it would only be a question of time when such nation or community would die out as absolutely as that where brothers and sisters mated together. It may therefore be assumed as absolutely true that a nation could no more increase or live where such custom prevailed than could a nation spring from or originate from brother and sister.

A nation is dead when it no longer propagates or increases its population. If, for example, there was peace, order, industry, morality, but as we sometimes see in these isolated populations in the Alps, &c., there was no annual increase of the population, that nation or community, in a social sense, is *dead,* for it is only a question of time when the individuals die out, and the nation totally disappears. The utmost vitality, and therefore the greatest energy, progress and prosperity, will always be of necessity manifested by those nations or communities that are the furthest removed from this intermarriage of cousins, &c. Or in other words, the feeblest and most miserable people are those who are least mixed with other nations, and that people who most extensively amalgamate with different varieties of their own race or Species, will, as observed—other things being equal—be more vigorous, prosperous, and powerful.

Nature is perpetually striving to restore health, whether of the individual or the community, and in cases where both husband and wife have certain tendencies to diseases, the offspring *may* be healthy. If they were of the same nation or community that was isolated from the rest of the world, and though no actual blood relationship were traceable, their diseased tendencies would unite and be exaggerated in their offspring. But if of widely different countries, and both parents with certain diseased tendencies, these, to a very great extent, are neutralized in the progeny. The popular, and indeed medical notion of the transmission of disease is, to a great extent, erroneous, for beyond the mere tendency to scrofula,[19] &c., it may be doubted if disease is ever transmitted from parent to child, and it is only in those cases where families or neighborhoods, or communities, rarely mate with strangers, that the offspring inherits the disease of its parents. There are so many things entering into and modifying the sexual relations, and the reproduction of offspring, that the subject can only be glanced at here, but it is certain that marriage, as a general rule, is desirable with strangers rather than with those of the same neighborhood, for this is in accord with the great fundamental law pervading the organic world,

---

[19]tuberculosis

and that renders that nation most potent and prosperous that is most extensively inter-mixed with other varieties. The unequal distribution of wealth, the vices and moral dis-eases of the elder nations of the world, have rendered marriage a convenience rather than a sacred and imperative *duty,* as designed by nature, and the progeny suffers accordingly.

That the sins of the fathers are visited on the offspring is a physiological truth as well as declaration of Holy Writ, and the diseased offspring in time transmit their ten-dencies, so that the stationary communities of the old world are getting feebler and more imbecile in each succeeding generation.

If a man marries a woman of a distant community or variety of his kind, both phys-ically healthy, and impelled by actual love for each other, the offspring will be still more vigorous and free of diseased tendencies; but if he mates with a female of his neighbor-hood from mean or mercenary impulses, without love to purity and exalt the function of reproduction, the offspring suffers, and if the parents have diseased tendencies, these are multiplied and exaggerated in the progeny. But in the stationary or slowly advancing populations of the old world, there are few, save the aristocracy, that knowingly inter-marry with blood relations, or that grossly and wilfully violate the laws of consanguin-ity. To preserve their prestige of assumed superiority, aristocrats intermarry within their "order," and thus the very means they use to perpetuate a wrong become the instruments of their punishment.

The medieval soldiers and adventurers that in France seized on Provinces, and while feudalism prevailed, ruled by the sword, in more modern times were forced to continue their ascendancy by fraud, by laws of primogeniture and special legislation, &c., through the contrivance called the government, and intermarrying with cousins, &c., of course vitiated the organism of their progeny. And when the masses discovered this, and saw how effete and contemptible were those who ruled them, they rose up and demol-ished them.

In a contest with the healthy and vigorous "commons," the nobility, with their defective organization, were utterly contemptible, and had not the "nobles" of all Europe come to their aid against the French Democracy, the "reign of terror"[20] would never have existed.

The English aristocracy, though of quite modern origin, have also reached this stage of imbecility, and when the "commons" discover the fact, they will doubtless make short work of their present rulers. It is thus that nature defends her rights and punishes those who violate, or rather disregard her laws, and renders a permanent aristocracy a *physical impossibility.*

But the most marked result of the physiological law which forbids intermarriage with relatives, is seen in the European "royalties" of the present day. True, they are of different countries, often widely separated, and these climatic and local causes modify to some extent the results, but intermarriage with cousins and blood relations render

---

[20]During the French Revolution, there was a period between September 1793 and July 1794 that came to be known as the "Reign of Terror." During this period, the French government enacted extremely harsh measures (including countless executions) against any suspected enemies of the revolution.

these "royalists" idiotic, impotent, or disorganized in some way, and, save the parvenue Bonapartes and Bernadottes,[21] there is not a "royal" family in Europe that is not, physiologically considered, inferior to the general average of their people.

Nature, perpetually striving to recover from the outrages inflicted on her, dooms these "royalties" to impotency or idiotcy, and final extinction.

All European history confirms these physiological laws: the more extended the admixture of populations, the more vigorous, progressive, and prosperous the people, and the more isolated, stationary, and less amalgamated people, the feebler, less progressive and powerless.

All the European nations are Caucasian, Pelasquin, Hellenic, Teuton, like the more modern Celt, Germanic, and Sclavonian, as the nations of our own time. French, English, Russian, Spanish, &c, are simply *Varieties* of the great bearded and master Species of human kind. These *Varieties* are simply the result of *chance,* of time, climate, religion, and political institutions; in a word, of external circumstances, in contradiction to Species, as Mongols, Malays, Negroes, &c.—*the work of God.*

Chance, time, climate, human power, affect the individual man, or a generation, perhaps; but stops here and goes no further. The English noble and peasant of this day, though living in the same generation, and on the same estate, differ as widely, no doubt, as we do from the antique Greeks, or from those imaginary "barbarians" who overran Rome, or indeed from those suppositious "Ancient Britons" who are said to have been savages; but this British noble and peasant changed in their cradles, would have shown us the exact reverse. The peasant would be the elegant and gracious duke, and the latter the miserable, stolid, clod-hopping hind, fit for nothing save to toil for his lord's luxury, in company with the four-footed beasts he labored with. God made them alike, and sent them into the world equal, to enjoy the same happiness and suffer the same miseries, but human agencies, the vile contrivance called a government, took possession of them at the moment of their birth, and marching them in precisely opposite directions, we see the result. But it stops with the individual or the generation, and the offspring of this noble and peasant again come into the world externally equal, and again the government takes possession of them, and moulds one into a lord and the other into a beast of burden. But, as observed, the laws of nature cannot be violated with impunity, and this aristocracy mating within its "order," becomes effete and imbecile, and when the "commons" feel this, they rise up and slough off the rotten encumbrance, and the nation, as we now witness in France, becomes more potent and prosperous than ever, until another aristocracy or monarchy again gets possession of it, to go through the same circle of rottenness and renovation, of disease and health. Sometimes a nation is too feeble to slough off this rottenness, or in other words, to get up a rebellion against its rulers, and then it becomes a conquest of some outside power. And this violation of the laws of consanguinity in our own race or Species, punished with rottenness and final extinction, has its exact parallel in the penalties involved in the admixtures of different Species, though the latter, no doubt, presents much more that is repulsive and loathsome in its phenomena. It is

---

[21]Napoléon Bonaparte (1769–1821) and Jean-Baptiste Bernadotte (1763–1844) established their families as new European royal houses in the early nineteenth century.

strange, indeed, but none the less a physiological truth, that a hereditary prince and a mulatto have a certain resemblance in mental qualities, if not in physical appearance. There is, it is true, a mighty difference in their matings, for "royal" cousins may be impelled by love, but no such instinct, passion or sentiment was ever possible between the sexes of different *Species* of mankind. Nothing but lust, and the most monstrous and unnatural lust at that, ever attracted whites and negroes, and the sins of the progenitors are visited on the mongrel offspring. A white man and negress cohabiting together, she will have fewer children than if mated with a negro. These children mated with other hybrids of the same remove, will have fewer still. The third generation, mating with similar removes, will have still fewer, and the fourth generation are absolutely as incapable of reproduction as mules. Each form of being has its phenomena in this respect, the horse and ass beget the mule; it has great endurance, but no powers of reproduction, and ends with a single generation.

The progeny of whites and negroes, with constantly diminishing vitality, exist through four generations, and this different phenomena of hybridity is in keeping with the difference of being or form of life—one being human and the other animal. But writers on hybridism, not truly comprehending the subject, have supposed that the same laws were applicable to men and animals, and thus furnished the advocates of the single human Species theory with the only seeming scientific argument they have been able to make in defense of their doctrine. It is a recognized principle among naturalists that hybrids do not propagate, and therefore, when there is a doubt in regard to the specific character of the progenitors, it is settled at once by this test of the fecundity or sterility of the offspring. Thus horses and asses beget mules, who are sterile, *therefore* horses and asses are different Species. Pritchard[22] and others applied this test to the progeny of whites and negroes, and as the mulatto had offspring, *therefore* the former, they said, were of the same Species. There was here a false statement of fact, and then a perverted application of the laws of hybridism, so plain that they should not be mistaken, and yet this absurd argument has been extensively accepted by scientific men. The offspring of whites and negroes are as absolutely, fixedly, and everlastingly sterile as mules, but in a different and higher form of being this sterility is embodied in four generations instead of a single one, as in the case of animals. But save in the general law, applicable alike to men and animals, that renders hybrids sterile, the mule and mulatto have no resemblance, for while the former has great powers of endurance, the latter is remarkable for his feebleness of constitution. The resemblance, however, between hereditary "royalty" and mulattoes is almost perfect. There is the same feebleness, tendency to imbecility, to idiotcy and impotency. Nature abhors them both, for both are the results of her violated laws, and though the mulatto is most repulsive to us, if the people everywhere really knew what a poor creature a royal king is in fact, they would regard him with an equal contempt. If, for example, a thousand believers in the single Species theory, or of those who profess to believe that all mankind originate from the same source, were to practically live out their belief, and were isolated in some island with an equal number of negroes, the following consequences would result: 1st. In the second generation whites

---

[22]Possibly Andrew Pritchard (1804–1882), renowned naturalist and author.

and negroes would be extinct, there would only be hybrids or mulattoes. 2nd. These hybrids, with their feeble constitutions and limited virility, would beget offspring still more viscious, and the constantly diminishing vitality and virility within four generations, and most likely within one hundred years, would doom them to total extinction. And if all the "royal" houses of Europe were isolated in some island, without any chance of intermarriage with the "commons," it is probable that they would also become totally extinct within a hundred years. Of course this would depend to some extent on the degree of disease among them, and therefore the period of extinction would be uncertain, but if they were all the progeny of first cousins, the case would be parallel with that of the mulatto, and their absolute extinction unavoidable. It is thus that nature vindicates herself, and punishes with unrelenting hand all who ignore or violate her laws; and we see the wisdom as well as justice of the Creator in this. Were it otherwise, could human power, time, climate, or chance, dominate the work of God, the whole material creation would soon collapse into general confusion. If chance could transform the white man or negro into mulattoes, into beings so radically unlike either that God made, where would be the limit of this chance short of universal disorganization of His creation? Or if European aristocrats could have modified the *nature* as well as the *habits* of peasants, &c., and transmit their artificial impurities to their descendants, long before this the working classes of the old world would have been turned into dogs, or things harmless while useful to their rulers.

But all the results of chance, of time, climate, or human interference, end with the life of the individual, or the generation. The white man and negro, all the several species of human kind, and of the animal world, remain at this moment just as they came from the hand of the Creator, and though we are permitted to destroy ourselves, as nations as well as individuals, in our blind and impotent attempts to "reform" the work of the Creator, we cannot change or modify an elementary atom either in our own or the organism of other beings. The negroes in this country have made wonderful progress from their African condition. They came from different tribes, and their transition here from New England to the Central, and finally to the Gulf States, has no doubt increased their physical development, and as a whole, they were the healthiest, and therefore, in a sense, the happiest four millions of human creatures that ever lived upon the earth. Save in sex and age, they all looked alike; there were no giants nor pigmies, no deformities nor perversions of the natural order; indeed they alone had reached that perfect physical development which God designed for all His creatures—that equality of condition which corresponds with nature, and which it may need many centuries of struggling and suffering before we reach it for our own Species. There were only two considerable exceptions to the well-being of these negroes—there were too many of them retained in localities unsuited to their industrial adaptations, and the vices of that portion of the whites that *forced* on them a sexual commingling was still more unwholesome to them. The first, however, was always neutralized by the extension of territory, and as the nation grew in power, the industrial adaptation and well-being of the negro followed; but the last, the viscious and degrading sexual intercourse of white and negro, though limited in extent, was a serious injury to the latter.

There is a class—it is hoped a small one—that is so ignorant as well as sinful as to descend, not to a level, but vastly below the brutes, and pervert the holy function of reproduction into a beastial gratification of the senses. In the North this class go to houses of prostitution, but in the South they seek the negress, both hideous outrages on nature, but the former vastly more so of course, for no progeny follows, but mulattoism is a disease, and the sole disturbance to the perfect physical health of the negro. This admixture of different Species has prevailed far more extensively with the whites and aboriginals of this continent, and assumed a radically different form among the Spanish, French, and Portuguese conquerors of the continent. They brought few females with them, and sought the native women for wives, and the result has been those vast mongrel hordes whom we dignify by the name of Spanish American Republics, but in fact have no elements of nationality, or indeed of social life, let alone republicanism. A hybrid or meztizo[23] has two natures or tendencies in his own person, white and Indian, and there-fore necessarily in conflict with himself. Another, perhaps, is only a quarter Indian, and yet another only a quarter white, and in a whole population of fifty thousand, there is sometimes not a single human being of pure or unmixed blood. So long as Spain ruled over these people, there was a certain degree of order, prosperity, and even progress, though she withheld all their natural rights from the Creole, or native born white people. This was resented, of course, and when Spain was embarrassed by the French invasion under Napoleon, the Creoles took advantage of it, and calling the Indians and mongrels to their aid, finally overthrew the Spanish dominion, and set up the Spanish American Republics.

If they had cast off the Spanish dominion without disturbing the old relations of the whites to the mongrels and natives, and preserved their natural supremacy over them, republicanism would have been practicable and successful. But instead of this they "emancipated" even the negroes, and thus the half million of white Creoles abandoning their natural superiority, and voluntarily degrading themselves to a common "liberty" with Indians, negroes, &c., have utterly lost themselves, and not merely republicanism but society itself is impossible. In the South American "Republics" it was even worse than in Mexico, for the latter has but a handful of negroes, while in some of the former the negroes and negro mongrels make up a third of the population. Chili is, to some extent, an exception, the white Creolean element being much larger than elsewhere, and it is barely possible that it may slough off mongrelism without collapsing into original Indianism, the unavoidable fate of the other "Republics."

The admixture of Caucasian and Indian has more vitality than the mulatto or negro mongrel, nevertheless they rapidly die out.

Mexico, with a population of two hundred thousand under the Spanish dominion, has now a little over one hundred thousand; Peubla has dwindled down from one hun-dred and twenty thousand to some fifty thousand, and Jalappa, Perote, Vera Cruz, and all the great cities on the national road are diminished in similar proportions. Society does not exist and cannot exist under such conditions, for though such elements may be arranged or socially organized as to secure a certain degree of prosperity, it is forever impossible for these to exist on the terms now recognized. The only approach to social order is the Church, which, composed of white men, had a system that was practicable,

---

[23]Variation of *mestizo,* person of mixed blood.

and around this there was gathered all that had life or progress in it. The hybrid, of course, is in natural antagonism to both white and Indian, and equally so with the quadroon, and the latter with all shades and degrees of mongrelism, as in the republics of South America, there were the negro and negro mongrel added, and finally the same individual often presented these antagonisms in his own person, and thus was naturally at war with himself, as well as with all these abnormal specimens of human kind. Of course no mere outside system or formulas of government could preserve or secure prosperity with such material, and therefore though the "United States of Mexico" were modelled after the United States of America, and their Constitution was a counterpart of our own, it is repeated there never was any republicanism in Mexico, nor indeed social order, after the overthrow of the Spanish dominion.

Thus all the revolutions or pronunciamentos,[24] are blind, irregular, and accidental, without any guiding principle or object, as irrelevant and disconnected as the diseased symptoms of some incurable disease in the individual, and while they diminish the powers of life, they do not in any instance tend to improve the condition of the country.

The rural, or unmixed population, is stationary, though in some districts it increases slowly, but the mongrel element of the cities, as observed, is rapidly dying out. If it were possible for the white people to restore the natural order, and reduce the Indian and mongrel elements to their normal condition and natural relations, social order would be practicable, for it is not the mere fact of their existence that renders society impracticable, but it is the abnormal, social adaptation that is attempted in Mexico, &c., that naturally forbids it. The whites have abdicated their natural rule, and if there were no mongrels, social order would be as impossible as order in a family where parents abandon their duties and equalize with their children. And when to this is added the vast horde of mongrels who partake of the sins of their origin, then it may be easily seen how utterly hopeless is the future of these countries. But if the whites, either through the humbug[25] of monarchy, or any other way, could recover their natural position, and rule the native element, as nature ordains, however viscious and disorganizing the mongrel element, it might be restrained and society restored. But this is hardly possible, for even the tomfooleries of monarchism complicate the matter.

Monarchy consists in artificial distinctions in our own race, and therefore is itself in necessary conflict with the natural order, or with what is called slavery on this continent, and the great "anti-slavery enterprise" of the last half century is merely a struggle of European monarchists to break down republican institutions. There is then no future for the Spanish-American Republics; the same bloody and absurd anarchy must go on until the mongrel element dies out and the native element collapses into the condition in which Cortez[26] found it in the fifteenth century. It may be that our people will become so enlightened by their trials on this subject of race, that they will fit out expeditions and conquer these effete and diseased populations, and saving the white element still among

---

[24]proclamations

[25]deception

[26]Hernán Cortés (1485–1547) was a Spanish military leader who was responsible for the overthrow of the Aztec empire and winning Mexico for Spain.

them, organize social order on a natural basis, and restore industry and prosperity to those beautiful countries. But if the present ignorance, folly and madness of our own people continue, we are more likely to lose ourselves, as the Spaniards have, than restore civilization to Mexico, &c. The same general laws govern the negro and mongrel of the islands. They were all in a state of great prosperity a hundred years ago, though there is no doubt that the "slave trade," which brought over adult males mainly, was greatly abused, and as in later days in Cuba, great outrages were practiced on these people.

All human creatures have a natural right to multiply their kind, to marry, to beget offspring, to enjoy affection, to love their children, and to deny them this right, to bring over negroes from Africa, and doom them to a life of toil, without wife or child, was a stupendous crime against the natural order, but otherwise the negroes of the island were probably as well cared for as the white laboring populations of the old world.

Soon after the successful American Revolution of 1776, which established the great natural and fundamental principle of equality as the basis of the political system, the monarchists of the old world sought to neutralize and destroy it by applying it to the subordinate races of this continent, and calling the condition of the negro by the term slavery, they deluded their own people with the greatest ease. Furthermore, the aristocrats of England desired to direct the attention of the masses from their own oppressions and miseries, and what so available or easy as this imaginary slavery in America.

Thus, when Democracy in France[27] had overturned the Bourbon Monarchy, Pitt and Wilberforce pointed them to San Domingo, and demanded an application of their principles to the negroes of that island, and the French leaders, utterly ignorant of the nature of negroes, and supposing them men like themselves, save in color, fell into the trap laid for them, and issued a decree declaring the negroes "free," or in other words, that the natural supremacy of the whites of the island should be *abolished.* An outside power thus striking down the foundations of social order, of course society could no longer exist in that island, and the mulattoes leading on the negroes, the handfull of white people were exterminated or driven from the island. Then came a conflict between mulattoes and negroes, and after some years of bloody and beastial struggle, the mulattoes were exterminated, or driven into the Spanish part of the island.

Since then the negro is every day getting nearer to his African condition. In the interior he has lost the Christian religion, even the French language, and gone back to snake worship and his African dialects, and here unencumbered by mongrelism, he again multiplies himself.

Forty years later the British Parliament did the same thing in Jamaica, &c., but keeping up numerous garrisons, prevented a conflict, as in Hayti. The whites resented this monstrous crime as long as possible, but instead of abandoning the island, finally consented to remain on terms of legal equality. The result is that they are rotting out at the rate of seven per cent., and fifty years hence there will probably not be a white person left

---

[27]"Democracy in France" here refers to the period of the French Revolution. During this period, the British statesmen William Pitt (1759–1806) and William Wilberforce (1759–1833) told the French they should set up egalitarian political structures in their colony of San Domingo to mirror the principles they were enacting on their home soil.

in all Jamaica. The negro, encumbered with this degraded white element, also diminishes, though slowly, in number, but even if the British garrisons are kept up, the whites must soon disappear, and Jamaica, like Hayti, must become a simple, unadulterated, nonadvancing African heathenism, and the great tropical centre of the continent as utterly lost to American civilization as if Africa itself had been physically removed to America, and set down right in the heart of our great continent.

Assuming, then, that the ignorance and folly, and madness of the American mind continues as at present, it is only a question of time when the entire continent south of our present limits collapses into simple Indianism, just as the Spaniards found it in the fifteenth century, and all the great tropical islands that nestle in the bosom of the continent are the home of a huge African heathenism, differing in no degree or form whatever from what Africa is now and always has been, and always must be, when isolated from the control or guidance of the white man. It is a frightful prospect to contemplate, but as certain, inevitable, and unavoidable—*should the present "ideas" prevail*—as a law of gravitation, or that men must die, and all the combined powers of human kind, acting through millions of years, cannot prevent it, or even protract it one single hour.

Of course only two things are possible when different Species are *forced* to a legal equality, or when so-called slavery is abolished by external power—extermination as in Hayti, or amalgamation as in Jamaica, &c. If the natural order is not restored in the southern States, and the negroes are not exterminated, then of course amalgamation must follow, and involve the whole American people in this hideous disease of mongrelism. There being, however, nearly thirty millions of whites, and only four millions of negroes, a time would come when it would be sloughed off, and the nation, relieved from this horrible burden, would again recover its vitality, and become capable of progress and self-government. It would involve, of necessity, as great a physical death of the whites, and therefore an equal number of them would rot out and perish through this monstrous crime against the natural order, and morally immeasurably greater suffering than that inflicted on their hapless victims, the four millions of negroes. But as the Indian in Mexico sloughs off the mongrel, and tends to the restoration of simple, undiluted Indianism, and the negro of the islands under the same law tends to his original Africanism, and both of them would work out the process in less than a century, so, too, the white men of these States would slough off the negro element, and though it would require centuries, nevertheless a time would come when the nation would recover its health, and the negro blood as absolutely disappear as if there had never been a negro in our midst. Here then would be the end of the monstrous crusade of our time against the order of nature—the Indian and Negro, and Caucasian, would be again just what God made them at the beginning, and after all the boundless suffering, disease and death inflicted on them by "impartial freedom," each would finally recover his specific nature. The Indian or native would again be a simple savage as the Spanish found him; the negro of the islands would be a non-producing and non-advancing, snake-worshipping African, and the white people of these States, in the shadow of these huge savageisms, would again be capable of self-government and a progressive civilization.

It must always be remembered by the reader that when discussing amalgamation of Species, this term does not apply to the mulattoism of the South, but on the contrary, to that monstrous condition common to Mexico, Jamaica, &c., where the different Species are amalgamated together under the same laws, and intermixture necessarily involves both races.

Mulattoism at the South is one-sided, confined alone to the negro element, and though a disease and burden to it, the purity and integrity of the white race is untouched and untainted. As observed, it corresponds somewhat with northern prostitution, though infinitely less horrible and less damaging even to the negro, but it never approaches the white female, and therefore the health and purity of society proper is untouched. And even in the negro element it is limited, and in a sense innoxious, for its sterility and low grade of vitality prevent its expansion, and it disappears perhaps as fast as it is generated. Thus, though a disease and a burden to the negro element, mulattoism in the South could never become a social danger, or disturb the white population. It is only where amalgamation exists, where "impartial freedom" is attempted, where whites and negroes are forced to live under the same laws, and the white woman mates with the negro or the mongrel, in a word, where these widely different Species are amalgamated together in the same "freedom," or condition, as in Mexico, Jamaica, &c., that both rot out and utterly perish from the earth they pollute with their sins.

Finally, there is another phase or form of disease that follows from admixture of Species, so hideous and loathsome, that even the "friend of impartial freedom," if he understood it, would revolt from with horror.

The indiscriminate intercourse of the sexes in our own race or Species is punished by a local disease that medical men term gonorhæ. Nature always punishes the violation of her laws, and this disease is as old as the history of the race. But however painful, disgusting, and troublesome, it never involved the constitution or life of the subject. But with the discovery of America, a new and frightful disease was brought to the attention of medical men.

The soldiers and sailors of Columbus and other early conquerors, indulged in indiscriminate sexual commerce with the native females, and there resulted from this a disease so fatal as well as disgusting, that the writers of the period represent it as really destroying millions of people. It could only originate with soldiers, or under such circumstances.

A white man might mate with or have children by a native woman, and the offspring would be doomed to the general penalty that nature exacts for the violation of her laws, but when to this was added the hideous and loathsome sin of a score of men having indiscriminate intercourse with that woman, then nature exacts a corresponding penalty, and a disease is evolved so horrible, and indeed so fatal, that it has been said millions have perished from it. It was carried to Europe, and has made the circuit of the world, under the name of syphilis, and inflicted more suffering on mankind than any other disease ever known to human experince. Vast numbers of the hapless Indians perished from it, indeed the Spanish writers represent that millions died from it. When first brought to Europe, it was regarded as fatal, even if the patient did not die at once, but in the course of centuries, and acting through white constitutions, it became so mild that in our times it is rarely fatal, save in those extreme cases where intemperance, filth and poverty, rather than the disease itself, destroy the patient. But we are now to witness a more horrible and more fatal form of this disease than even that which three centuries ago decimated the natives of this continent, and spread such death and suffering throughout Christendom.

The northern troops that invaded and overrun the South, by their indiscriminate intercourse with the hapless negresses, have developed this disease with more than its original virulence, and vast multitudes of these hapless people have already, no doubt, perished from it. The negro is further removed from us than the Indian or aboriginal, and therefore this disease must be more virulent and fatal.

As observed, indiscriminate intercourse with a female of our own Species is punished by gonorhæ, a local disease as old as the history of the race. The same monstrous sin with the Indian female originated syphilis three centuries ago that has had its millions of victims, and now this fatal and terrible poison, originating from commerce with negroes still further removed from us, will, no doubt, demand a still greater number of victims. Again, as three centuries ago, it will make the circuit of Christendom, and the disease that had become so modified and mild that no one died of it, will now involve an amount of human misery and actual mortality, that, if they could grasp or realize it in all its horrors, every Christian Abolitionist would go mad with remorse, and become a raving lunatic the rest of his days. In the course of years, or at all events of centuries, and the poison acting through white constitutions, it will become modified and quite controllable no doubt, but in the meantime, when we are told of the terrible mortality of those negro camps on the Mississippi, the sea islands and elsewhere, we may be certain that with the other wrongs and outrages so blindly inflicted on these hapless people by the madmen of the North, this hideous and loathsome disease, thus originated, is an essential part. Nature always vindicates her outraged laws, and though the negro is now, no doubt, the greater sufferer, the final punishment falls upon the criminal, and centuries hence the descendants of this generation will have to bear the penalties of their fathers' sins in this respect, as well as others.

In conclusion, then, the solemn, indeed the awful question presented to every American, is just this—shall we exercise the reason and respond to the instincts God has given us, and accept the *facts* that confront us, or shall this ignorance, blindness, impiety and crime that strive to carry out an "idea" of a single race, go on until the extermination of four millions of our own Species as well as that of our victims, the negroes, shall teach posterity the truth of this matter?

14

Bret Harte

(1836–1902)

BRET HARTE BEGAN his literary career early, publishing some short verses when he was eleven. In 1854, he left Brooklyn, New York, for the mining country of California. Once there, he became a newspaper writer, gaining a modest reputation as a satirist who wrote parodies of such popular and famous authors as James Fenimore Cooper, Charles Dickens, Victor Hugo, and Timothy Shay Arthur in a series of "condensed novels." In 1868, he published "The Luck of Roaring Camp," a short story that moved his reputation beyond its local confines for the first time. Immediately following this success, he published "Plain Language from Truthful James," better known as "The Heathen Chinee," a poem that earned him a national reputation.

Harte's early writings gained immense popularity because they offered Americans a glimpse of Western life. Beginning with the gold rush of 1849, hundreds of thousands of Americans began a westward movement that would colonize both the mid- and far-west regions of the country. Harte's Western writings with their folksy morals, realism, quirky humor, and pathos found an admiring audience all across the country.

His Western writings are studies on civilization and what it means to be civilized. His own activities with social causes—such as protesting an Indian massacre, which cost him a newspaper job in Northern California, and his work with various abolitionist groups—made him keenly aware of issues of race, class, and regionalism in America. His work serves as a vivid reminder that Americans lived in a country made up of humorous contrasts and violent contradictions, where different races, dreams, and regions all tested the boundaries of what it meant to be part of something possibly misnamed the United States.

JOHN JENKINS

Or, The Smoker Reformed

BY T. S. A–TH–R[1]

CHAPTER I

"One cigar a day!" said Judge Boompointer.

"One cigar a day!" repeated John Jenkins, as with trepidation he dropped his half-consumed cigar under his work-bench.

"One cigar a day is three cents a day," remarked Judge Boompointer gravely; "and do you know, sir, what one cigar a day, or three cents a day, amounts to in the course of four years?"

John Jenkins, in his boyhood, had attended the village school, and possessed considerable arithmetical ability. Taking up a shingle which lay upon his work-bench, and producing a piece of chalk, with a feeling of conscious pride he made an exhaustive calculation.

"Exactly forty-three dollars and eighty cents," he replied, wiping the perspiration from his heated brow, while his face flushed with honest enthusiasm.

"Well, sir, if you saved three cents a day, instead of wasting it, you would now be the possessor of a new suit of clothes, an illustrated Family Bible, a pew in the church, a complete set of Patent Office Reports, a hymn-book, and a paid subscription to 'Arthur's Home Magazine,'[2] which could be purchased for exactly forty-three dollars and eighty cents; and," added the Judge, with increasing sternness, "if you calculate leap-year, which you seem to have strangely omitted, you have three cents more, sir—*three cents more!* What would that buy you, sir?"

"A cigar," suggested John Jenkins; but, coloring again deeply, he hid his face.

"No, sir," said the Judge, with a sweet smile of benevolence stealing over his stern features; "properly invested, it would buy you that which passeth all price. Dropped into the missionary-box, who can tell what heathen, now idly and joyously wantoning in nakedness and sin, might be brought to a sense of his miserable condition, and made, through that three cents, to feel the torments of the wicked?"

The following selections follow the text as published in the Houghton, Mifflin 1896 multivolume set: *The Writings of Bret Harte*. Boston: Houghton, Mifflin and Co., 1896. Volumes 1 and 12.

[1]Timothy Shay Arthur (1809–1885) was one of the most prolific writers of the antebellum period, producing more than 150 novels and collections of short stories. He also edited several influential periodicals. Among his many works, he wrote countless reform tales. The best known of these was his immensely popular temperance story, *Ten Nights in a Bar-Room* (1854), reprinted in this volume (pp. 651–750).

[2]Timothy Shay Arthur was the editor of a popular Philadelphia-based magazine named *Arthur's Home Magazine*.

With these words the Judge retired, leaving John Jenkins buried in profound thought. "Three cents a day," he muttered. "In forty years I might be worth four hundred and thirty-eight dollars and ten cents,—and then I might marry Mary. Ah, Mary!" The young carpenter sighed, and drawing a twenty-five cent daguerreotype[3] from his vest-pocket, gazed long and fervidly upon the features of a young girl in book muslin and a coral necklace. Then, with a resolute expression, he carefully locked the door of his work-shop, and departed.

Alas! his good resolutions were too late. We trifle with the tide of fortune, which too often nips us in the bud and casts the dark shadow of misfortune over the bright lexicon of youth! That night the half-consumed fragment of John Jenkins's cigar set fire to his work-shop and burned it up, together with all his tools and materials. There was no insurance.

CHAPTER II

❧ The Downward Path

"Then you still persist in marrying John Jenkins?" queried Judge Boompointer, as he playfully, with paternal familiarity, lifted the golden curls of the village belle, Mary Jones.

"I do," replied the fair young girl, in a low voice that resembled rock candy in its saccharine firmness,—"I do. He has promised to reform. Since he lost all his property by fire"—

"The result of his pernicious habit, though he illogically persists in charging it to me," interrupted the Judge.

"Since then," continued the young girl, "he has endeavored to break himself of the habit. He tells me that he has substituted the stalks of the Indian rattan,[4] the outer part of a leguminous plant called the smoking-bean, and the fragmentary and unconsumed remainder of cigars, which occur at rare and uncertain intervals along the road, which, as he informs me, though deficient in quality and strength, are comparatively inexpensive." And blushing at her own eloquence, the young girl hid her curls on the Judge's arm.

"Poor thing!" muttered Judge Boompointer. "Dare I tell her all? Yet I must."

"I shall cling to him," continued the young girl, rising with her theme, "as the young vine clings to some hoary ruin. Nay, nay, chide me not, Judge Boompointer. I will marry John Jenkins!"

The Judge was evidently affected. Seating himself at the table, he wrote a few lines hurriedly upon a piece of paper, which he folded and placed in the fingers of the destined bride of John Jenkins.

"Mary Jones," said the Judge, with impressive earnestness, "take this trifle as a wedding gift from one who respects your fidelity and truthfulness. At the altar let it be a

---

[3]A daguerreotype was a picture produced by an early photographic process developed in France in the 1830s.

[4]Palm plant with long, tough stems.

reminder of me." And covering his face hastily with a handkerchief, the stern and iron-willed man left the room. As the door closed, Mary unfolded the paper. It was an order on the corner grocery for three yards of flannel, a paper of needles, four pounds of soap, one pound of starch, and two boxes of matches!

"Noble and thoughtful man!" was all Mary Jones could exclaim, as she hid her face in her hands and burst into a flood of tears.

The bells of Cloverdale are ringing merrily. It is a wedding. "How beautiful they look!" is the exclamation that passes from lip to lip, as Mary Jones, leaning timidly on the arm of John Jenkins, enters the church. But the bride is agitated, and the bridegroom betrays a feverish nervousness. As they stand in the vestibule, John Jenkins fumbles earnestly in his vest-pocket. Can it be the ring he is anxious about? No. He draws a small brown substance from his pocket, and biting off a piece, hastily replaces the fragment and gazes furtively around. Surely no one saw him? Alas! the eyes of two of that wedding party saw the fatal act. Judge Boompointer shook his head sternly. Mary Jones sighed and breathed a silent prayer. Her husband chewed!

CHAPTER III AND LAST

"What! more bread?" said John Jenkins gruffly. "You're always asking for money for bread. D—nation! Do you want to ruin me by your extravagance?" and as he uttered these words he drew from his pocket a bottle of whiskey, a pipe, and a paper of tobacco. Emptying the first at a draught, he threw the empty bottle at the head of his eldest boy, a youth of twelve summers. The missile struck the child full in the temple, and stretched him a lifeless corpse. Mrs. Jenkins, whom the reader will hardly recognize as the once gay and beautiful Mary Jones, raised the dead body of her son in her arms, and carefully placing the unfortunate youth beside the pump in the back yard, returned with saddened step to the house. At another time, and in brighter days, she might have wept at the occurrence. She was past tears now.

"Father, your conduct is reprehensible!" said little Harrison Jenkins, the youngest boy. "Where do you expect to go when you die?"

"Ah!" said John Jenkins fiercely; "this comes of giving children a liberal education; this is the result of Sabbath-schools. Down, viper!"

A tumbler thrown from the same parental fist laid out the youthful Harrison cold. The four other children had, in the mean time, gathered around the table with anxious expectancy. With a chuckle, the now changed and brutal John Jenkins produced four pipes, and filling them with tobacco, handed one to each of his offspring and bade them smoke. "It's better than bread!" laughed the wretch hoarsely.

Mary Jenkins, though of a patient nature, felt it her duty now to speak. "I have borne much, John Jenkins," she said. "But I prefer that the children should not smoke. It is an unclean habit, and soils their clothes. I ask this as a special favor!"

John Jenkins hesitated,—the pangs of remorse began to seize him.

"Promise me this, John!" urged Mary upon her knees.

"I promise!" reluctantly answered John.

"And you will put the money in a savings-bank?"

"I will," repeated her husband; "and *I*'ll give up smoking, too."

"'Tis well, John Jenkins!" said Judge Boompointer, appearing suddenly from behind the door, where he had been concealed during this interview. "Nobly said! my man. Cheer up! I will see that the children are decently buried." The husband and wife fell into each other's arms. And Judge Boompointer, gazing upon the affecting spectacle, burst into tears.

From that day John Jenkins was an altered man.

MUCK-A-MUCK

A Modern Indian Novel
After Cooper [1]

CHAPTER I

It was toward the close of a bright October day. The last rays of the setting sun were reflected from one of those sylvan lakes peculiar to the Sierras of California. On the right the curling smoke of an Indian village rose between the columns of the lofty pines, while to the left the log cottage of Judge Tompkins, embowered in buckeyes, completed the enchanting picture.

Although the exterior of the cottage was humble and unpretentious, and in keeping with the wildness of the landscape, its interior gave evidence of the cultivation and refinement of its inmates. An aquarium, containing goldfishes, stood on a marble centre-table at one end of the apartment, while a magnificent grand piano occupied the other. The floor was covered with a yielding tapestry carpet, and the walls were adorned with paintings from the pencils of Van Dyke, Rubens, Tintoretto, Michael Angelo, and the productions of the more modern Turner, Kensett, Church, and Bierstadt. Although Judge Tompkins had chosen the frontiers of civilization as his home, it was impossible for him to entirely forego the habits and tastes of his former life. He was seated in a luxurious armchair, writing at a mahogany escritoire,[2] while his daughter, a lovely young girl of seventeen summers, plied her crotchet-needle on an ottoman beside him. A bright fire of pine logs flickered and flamed on the ample hearth.

Genevra Octavia Tompkins was Judge Tompkins's only child. Her mother had long

---

[1] James Fenimore Cooper (1789–1851) was one of the most popular American writers of the early nineteenth century. He is best known for his books on the early American frontier, and he is credited with giving the American Western genre many of its best-known characteristics. His complex literary style and Latinate vocabulary did not always seem the best fit for his books' crude frontier settings and characters.

[2] Writing desk.

since died on the Plains. Reared in affluence, no pains had been spared with the daughter's education. She was a graduate of one of the principal seminaries, and spoke French with a perfect Benicia accent. Peerlessly beautiful, she was dressed in a white moiré[3] antique robe trimmed with tulle.[4] That simple rosebud, with which most heroines exclusively decorate their hair, was all she wore in her raven locks.

The Judge was the first to break the silence.

"Genevra, the logs which compose yonder fire seem to have been incautiously chosen. The sibilation produced by the sap, which exudes copiously therefrom, is not conducive to composition."

"True, father, but I thought it would be preferable to the constant crepitation which is apt to attend the combustion of more seasoned ligneous fragments."

The Judge looked admiringly at the intellectual features of the graceful girl, and half forgot the slight annoyances of the green wood in the musical accents of his daughter. He was smoothing her hair tenderly, when the shadow of a tall figure, which suddenly darkened the doorway, caused him to look up.

CHAPTER II

It needed but a glance at the new-comer to detect at once the form and features of the haughty aborigine,—the untaught and untrammeled son of the forest. Over one shoulder a blanket, negligently but gracefully thrown, disclosed a bare and powerful breast, decorated with a quantity of three-cent postage-stamps which he had despoiled from an Overland Mail stage a few weeks previous. A cast-off beaver of Judge Tompkins's, adorned by a simple feather, covered his erect head, from beneath which his straight locks descended. His right hand hung lightly by his side, while his left was engaged in holding on a pair of pantaloons, which the lawless grace and freedom of his lower limbs evidently could not brook.

"Why," said the Indian, in a low sweet tone,—"why does the Pale Face still follow the track of the Red Man? Why does he pursue him, even as O-kee chow, the wild cat, chases Ka-ka, the skunk? Why are the feet of Sorrel-top, the white chief, among the acorns of Muck-a-Muck, the mountain forest? Why," he repeated, quietly but firmly abstracting a silver spoon from the table,—"why do you seek to drive him from the wigwams of his fathers? His brothers are already gone to the happy hunting-grounds. Will the Pale Face seek him there?" And, averting his face from the Judge, he hastily slipped a silver cake-basket beneath his blanket, to conceal his emotion.

"Muck-a-Muck has spoken," said Genevra softly. "Let him now listen. Are the acorns of the mountain sweeter than the esculent and nutritious bean of the Pale Face miner? Does my brother prize the edible qualities of the snail above that of the crisp and oleaginous bacon? Delicious are the grasshoppers that sport on the hillside,—are they

---

[3]silk

[4]Silk netlike fabric.

better than the dried apples of the Pale Faces? Pleasant is the gurgle of the torrent, Kish-Kish, but is it better than the cluck-cluck of old Bourbon from the old stone bottle?"

"Ugh!" said the Indian,—"ugh! good. The White Rabbit is wise. Her words fall as the snow on Tootoonolo, and the rocky heart of Muck-a-Muck is hidden. What says my brother the Gray Gopher of Dutch Flat?"

"She has spoken, Muck-a-Muck," said the Judge, gazing fondly on his daughter. "It is well. Our treaty is concluded. No, thank you,—you need *not* dance the Dance of Snow-shoes, or the Moccasin Dance, the Dance of Green Corn, or the Treaty Dance. I would be alone. A strange sadness overpowers me."

"I go," said the Indian. "Tell your great chief in Washington, the Sachem Andy,[5] that the Red Man is retiring before the footsteps of the adventurous pioneer. Inform him, if you please, that westward the star of empire takes its way, that the chiefs of the Pi-Ute nation are for Reconstruction to a man, and that Klamath will poll a heavy Republican vote in the fall."[6]

And folding his blanket more tightly around him, Muck-a-Muck withdrew.

CHAPTER III

Genevra Tompkins stood at the door of the log-cabin, looking after the retreating Overland Mail stage which conveyed her father to Virginia City. "He may never return again," sighed the young girl, as she glanced at the frightfully rolling vehicle and wildly careering horses,—"at least, with unbroken bones. Should he meet with an accident! I mind me now a fearful legend, familiar to my childhood. Can it be that the drivers on this line are privately instructed to dispatch all passengers maimed by accident, to prevent tedious litigation? No, no. But why this weight upon my heart?"

She seated herself at the piano and lightly passed her hand over the keys. Then, in a clear mezzo-soprano voice, she sang the first verse of one of the most popular Irish ballads:—

> "O *Arrah ma dheelish,* the distant *dudheen*
> Lies soft in the moonlight, *ma bouchal vourneen:*
> The springing *gossoons* on the heather are still,
> And the *caubeens* and *colleens* are heard on the hill."

But as the ravishing notes of her sweet voice died upon the air, her hands sank listlessly to her side. Music could not chase away the mysterious shadow from her heart. Again she rose. Putting on a white crape bonnet, and carefully drawing a pair of lemon-colored gloves over her taper fingers, she seized her parasol and plunged into the depths of the pine forest.

---

[5]Andrew Jackson (1767–1845) was president for two terms (1829–1837).

[6]Harte is mixing time periods in this paragraph. Andrew Jackson's presidency was years before the founding of the Republican party, and the issues of Reconstruction came after the Civil War.

CHAPTER IV

Genevra had not proceeded many miles before a weariness seized upon her fragile limbs, and she would fain seat herself upon the trunk of a prostrate pine, which she previously dusted with her handkerchief. The sun was just sinking below the horizon, and the scene was one of gorgeous and sylvan beauty. "How beautiful is nature!" murmured the innocent girl, as, reclining gracefully against the root of the tree, she gathered up her skirts and tied a handkerchief around her throat. But a low growl interrupted her meditation. Starting to her feet, her eyes met a sight which froze her blood with terror.

The only outlet to the forest was the narrow path, barely wide enough for a single person, hemmed in by trees and rocks, which she had just traversed. Down this path, in Indian file, came a monstrous grizzly, closely followed by a California lion, a wild cat, and a buffalo, the rear being brought up by a wild Spanish bull. The mouths of the three first animals were distended with frightful significance, the horns of the last were lowered as ominously. As Genevra was preparing to faint, she heard a low voice behind her.

"Eternally dog-gone my skin ef this ain't the puttiest chance yet!"

At the same moment, a long, shining barrel dropped lightly from behind her, and rested over her shoulder.

Genevra shuddered.

"Dern ye—don't move!"

Genevra became motionless.

The crack of a rifle rang through the woods. Three frightful yells were heard, and two sullen roars. Five animals bounded into the air and five lifeless bodies lay upon the plain. The well-aimed bullet had done its work. Entering the open throat of the grizzly it had traversed his body only to enter the throat of the California lion, and in like manner the catamount, until it passed through into the respective foreheads of the bull and the buffalo, and finally fell flattened from the rocky hillside.

Genevra turned quickly. "My preserver!" she shrieked, and fell into the arms of Natty Bumpo,[7] the celebrated Pike Ranger of Donner Lake.

CHAPTER V

The moon rose cheerfully above Donner Lake. On its placid bosom a dug-out canoe glided rapidly, containing Natty Bumpo and Genevra Tompkins.

Both were silent. The same thought possessed each, and perhaps there was sweet companionship even in the unbroken quiet. Genevra bit the handle of her parasol, and blushed. Natty Bumpo took a fresh chew of tobacco. At length Genevra said, as if in half-spoken reverie:—

"The soft shining of the moon and the peaceful ripple of the waves seem to say to us various things of an instructive and moral tendency."

"You may bet yer pile on that, miss," said her companion gravely. "It's all the preachin' and psalm-singin' I've heern since I was a boy."

---

[7]Perhaps Cooper's most famous character, Natty Bumpo (Hawkeye) appears in several of his novels as the archetype of the noble, self-sufficient frontiersman.

"Noble being!" said Miss Tompkins to herself, glancing at the stately Pike as he bent over his paddle to conceal his emotion. "Reared in this wild seclusion, yet he has become penetrated with visible consciousness of a Great First Cause." Then, collecting herself, she said aloud: "Methinks 't were pleasant to glide ever thus down the stream of life, hand in hand with the one being whom the soul claims as its affinity. But what am I saying?"—and the delicate-minded girl hid her face in her hands.

A long silence ensued, which was at length broken by her companion.

"Ef you mean you're on the marry," he said thoughtfully, "I ain't in no wise partikler."

"My husband!" faltered the blushing girl; and she fell into his arms.

In ten minutes more the loving couple had landed at Judge Tompkins's.

CHAPTER VI

A year has passed away. Natty Bumpo was returning from Gold Hill, where he had been to purchase provisions. On his way to Donner Lake, rumors of an Indian uprising met his ears. "Dern their pesky skins, ef they dare to touch my Jenny," he muttered between his clenched teeth.

It was dark when he reached the borders of the lake. Around a glittering fire he dimly discerned dusky figures dancing. They were in war paint. Conspicuous among them was the renowned Muck-a-Muck. But why did the fingers of Natty Bumpo tighten convulsively around his rifle?

The chief held in his hand long tufts of raven hair. The heart of the pioneer sickened as he recognized the clustering curls of Genevra. In a moment his rifle was at his shoulder, and with a sharp "ping" Muck-a-Muck leaped into the air a corpse. To knock out the brains of the remaining savages, tear the tresses from the stiffening hand of Muck-a-Muck, and dash rapidly forward to the cottage of Judge Tompkins, was the work of a moment.

He burst open the door. Why did he stand transfixed with open mouth and distended eyeballs? Was the sight too horrible to be borne? On the contrary, before him, in her peerless beauty, stood Genevra Tompkins, leaning on her father's arm.

"Ye 'r not scalped, then!" gasped her lover.

"No. I have no hesitation in saying that I am not; but why this abruptness?" responded Genevra.

Bumpo could not speak, but frantically produced the silken tresses. Genevra turned her face aside.

"Why, that's her waterfall!"[8] said the Judge.

Bumpo sank fainting to the floor.

The famous Pike chieftain[9] never recovered from the deceit, and refused to marry Genevra, who died, twenty years afterwards, of a broken heart. Judge Tompkins lost his fortune in Wild Cat. The stage passes twice a week the deserted cottage at Donner Lake. Thus was the death of Muck-a-Muck avenged.

---

[8] wig

[9] An expert marksman, Natty Bumpo was so well known for the long-barreled gun he carried that he was nicknamed "La Longue Carabine."

THE LUCK OF ROARING CAMP

There was commotion in Roaring Camp. It could not have been a fight, for in 1850 that was not novel enough to have called together the entire settlement. The ditches and claims were not only deserted, but "Tuttle's grocery" had contributed its gamblers, who, it will be remembered, calmly continued their game the day that French Pete and Kanaka Joe shot each other to death over the bar in the front room. The whole camp was collected before a rude cabin on the outer edge of the clearing. Conversation was carried on in a low tone, but the name of a woman was frequently repeated. It was a name familiar enough in the camp,—"Cherokee Sal."

Perhaps the less said of her the better. She was a coarse and, it is to be feared, a very sinful woman. But at that time she was the only woman in Roaring Camp, and was just then lying in sore extremity, when she most needed the ministration of her own sex. Dissolute, abandoned, and irreclaimable, she was yet suffering a martyrdom hard enough to bear even when veiled by sympathizing womanhood, but now terrible in her loneliness. The primal curse had come to her in that original isolation which must have made the punishment of the first transgression so dreadful. It was, perhaps, part of the expiation of her sin that, at a moment when she most lacked her sex's intuitive tenderness and care, she met only the half-contemptuous faces of her masculine associates. Yet a few of the spectators were, I think, touched by her sufferings. Sandy Tipton thought it was "rough on Sal," and, in the contemplation of her condition, for a moment rose superior to the fact that he had an ace and two bowers[1] in his sleeve.

It will be seen also that the situation was novel. Deaths were by no means uncommon in Roaring Camp, but a birth was a new thing. People had been dismissed the camp effectively, finally, and with no possibility of return; but this was the first time that anybody had been introduced *ab initio*.[2] Hence the excitement.

"You go in there, Stumpy," said a prominent citizen known as "Kentuck," addressing one of the loungers. "Go in there, and see what you kin do. You've had experience in them things."

Perhaps there was a fitness in the selection. Stumpy, in other climes, had been the putative head of two families; in fact, it was owing to some legal informality in these proceedings that Roaring Camp—a city of refuge—was indebted to his company. The crowd approved the choice, and Stumpy was wise enough to bow to the majority. The door closed on the extempore surgeon and midwife, and Roaring Camp sat down outside, smoked its pipe, and awaited the issue.

The assemblage numbered about a hundred men. One or two of these were actual fugitives from justice, some were criminal, and all were reckless. Physically they exhibited no indication of their past lives and character. The greatest scamp had a Raphael face,[3] with a profusion of blonde hair; Oakhurst, a gambler, had the melancholy air and

---

[1]Trump, or winning, cards.

[2]From the beginning.

[3]A face of an angel.

intellectual abstraction of a Hamlet; the coolest and most courageous man was scarcely over five feet in height, with a soft voice and an embarrassed, timid manner. The term "roughs" applied to them was a distinction rather than a definition. Perhaps in the minor details of fingers, toes, ears, etc., the camp may have been deficient, but these slight omissions did not detract from their aggregate force. The strongest man had but three fingers on his right hand; the best shot had but one eye.

Such was the physical aspect of the men that were dispersed around the cabin. The camp lay in a triangular valley between two hills and a river. The only outlet was a steep trail over the summit of a hill that faced the cabin, now illuminated by the rising moon. The suffering woman might have seen it from the rude bunk whereon she lay,—seen it winding like a silver thread until it was lost in the stars above.

A fire of withered pine boughs added sociability to the gathering. By degrees the natural levity of Roaring Camp returned. Bets were freely offered and taken regarding the result. Three to five that "Sal would get through with it;" even that the child would survive; side bets as to the sex and complexion of the coming stranger. In the midst of an excited discussion an exclamation came from those nearest the door, and the camp stopped to listen. Above the swaying and moaning of the pines, the swift rush of the river, and the crackling of the fire rose a sharp, querulous cry,—a cry unlike anything heard before in the camp. The pines stopped moaning, the river ceased to rush, and the fire to crackle. It seemed as if Nature had stopped to listen too.

The camp rose to its feet as one man! It was proposed to explode a barrel of gunpowder; but in consideration of the situation of the mother, better counsels prevailed, and only a few revolvers were discharged; for whether owing to the rude surgery of the camp, or some other reason, Cherokee Sal was sinking fast. Within an hour she had climbed, as it were, that rugged road that led to the stars, and so passed out of Roaring Camp, its sin and shame, forever. I do not think that the announcement disturbed them much, except in speculation as to the fate of the child. "Can he live now?" was asked of Stumpy. The answer was doubtful. The only other being of Cherokee Sal's sex and maternal condition in the settlement was an ass. There was some conjecture as to fitness, but the experiment was tried. It was less problematical than the ancient treatment of Romulus and Remus,[4] and apparently as successful.

When these details were completed, which exhausted another hour, the door was opened, and the anxious crowd of men, who had already formed themselves into a queue, entered in single file. Beside the low bunk or shelf, on which the figure of the mother was starkly outlined below the blankets, stood a pine table. On this a candle-box was placed, and within it, swathed in staring red flannel, lay the last arrival at Roaring Camp. Beside the candle-box was placed a hat. Its use was soon indicated. "Gentlemen," said Stumpy, with a singular mixture of authority and *ex officio* complacency,—"gentlemen will please pass in at the front door, round the table, and out at the back door. Them as wishes to contribute anything toward the orphan will find a hat handy." The first man entered with his hat on; he uncovered, however, as he looked about him, and so unconsciously set an example to the next. In such communities good and bad actions are catch-

---

[4]Romulus and Remus were the legendary founders of Rome who, as infants, were nursed by a wolf.

ing. As the procession filed in comments were audible,—criticisms addressed perhaps rather to Stumpy in the character of showman: "Is that him?" "Mighty small specimen;" "Hasn't more'n got the color;" "Ain't bigger nor a derringer."[5] The contributions were as characteristic: A silver tobacco box; a doubloon; a navy revolver, silver mounted; a gold specimen; a very beautifully embroidered lady's handkerchief (from Oakhurst the gambler); a diamond breastpin; a diamond ring (suggested by the pin, with the remark from the giver that he "saw that pin and went two diamonds better"); a slung-shot; a Bible (contributor not detected); a golden spur; a silver teaspoon (the initials, I regret to say, were not the giver's); a pair of surgeon's shears; a lancet; a Bank of England note for £5; and about $200 in loose gold and silver coin. During these proceedings Stumpy maintained a silence as impassive as the dead on his left, a gravity as inscrutable as that of the newly born on his right. Only one incident occurred to break the monotony of the curious procession. As Kentuck bent over the candle-box half curiously, the child turned, and, in a spasm of pain, caught at his groping finger, and held it fast for a moment. Kentuck looked foolish and embarrassed. Something like a blush tried to assert itself in his weather-beaten cheek. "The d—d little cuss!" he said, as he extricated his finger, with perhaps more tenderness and care than he might have been deemed capable of showing. He held that finger a little apart from its fellows as he went out, and examined it curiously. The examination provoked the same original remark in regard to the child. In fact, he seemed to enjoy repeating it. "He rastled with my finger," he remarked to Tipton, holding up the member, "the d—d little cuss!"

It was four o'clock before the camp sought repose. A light burnt in the cabin where the watchers sat, for Stumpy did not go to bed that night. Nor did Kentuck. He drank quite freely, and related with great gusto his experience, invariably ending with his characteristic condemnation of the newcomer. It seemed to relieve him of any unjust implication of sentiment, and Kentuck had the weaknesses of the nobler sex. When everybody else had gone to bed, he walked down to the river and whistled reflectingly. Then he walked up the gulch past the cabin, still whistling with demonstrative unconcern. At a large redwood-tree he paused and retraced his steps, and again passed the cabin. Halfway down to the river's bank he again paused, and then returned and knocked at the door. It was opened by Stumpy. "How goes it?" said Kentuck, looking past Stumpy toward the candle-box. "All serene!" replied Stumpy. "Anything up?" "Nothing." There was a pause—an embarrassing one—Stumpy still holding the door. Then Kentuck had recourse to his finger, which he held up to Stumpy. "Rastled with it,—the d—d little cuss," he said, and retired.

The next day Cherokee Sal had such rude sepulture[6] as Roaring Camp afforded. After her body had been committed to the hillside, there was a formal meeting of the camp to discuss what should be done with her infant. A resolution to adopt it was unanimous and enthusiastic. But an animated discussion in regard to the manner and feasibility of providing for its wants at once sprang up. It was remarkable that the argument

---

[5]A small pistol, named for its inventor Hanery Deringer (1796–1868).
[6]burial

partook of none of those fierce personalities with which discussions were usually conducted at Roaring Camp. Tipton proposed that they should send the child to Red Dog,—
a distance of forty miles,—where female attention could be procured. But the unlucky
suggestion met with fierce and unanimous opposition. It was evident that no plan which
entailed parting from their new acquisition would for a moment be entertained.
"Besides," said Tom Ryder, "them fellows at Red Dog would swap it, and ring in somebody else on us." A disbelief in the honesty of other camps prevailed at Roaring Camp,
as in other places.

The introduction of a female nurse in the camp also met with objection. It was
argued that no decent woman could be prevailed to accept Roaring Camp as her home,
and the speaker urged that "they didn't want any more of the other kind." This unkind
allusion to the defunct mother, harsh as it may seem, was the first spasm of propriety,—
the first symptom of the camp's regeneration. Stumpy advanced nothing. Perhaps he felt
a certain delicacy in interfering with the selection of a possible successor in office. But
when questioned, he averred stoutly that he and "Jinny"—the mammal before alluded
to—could manage to rear the child. There was something original, independent, and
heroic about the plan that pleased the camp. Stumpy was retained. Certain articles were
sent for to Sacramento. "Mind," said the treasurer, as he pressed a bag of gold-dust into
the expressman's hand, "the best that can be got,—lace, you know, and filigree-work and
frills,—d—n the cost!"

Strange to say, the child thrived. Perhaps the invigorating climate of the mountain
camp was compensation for material deficiencies. Nature took the foundling to her
broader breast. In that rare atmosphere of the Sierra foothills,—that air pungent with
balsamic odor, that ethereal cordial at once bracing and exhilarating,—he may have
found food and nourishment, or a subtle chemistry that transmuted ass's milk to lime and
phosphorus. Stumpy inclined to the belief that it was the latter and good nursing. "Me
and that ass," he would say, "has been father and mother to him! Don't you," he would
add, apostrophizing the helpless bundle before him, "never go back on us."

By the time he was a month old the necessity of giving him a name became apparent. He had generally been known as "The Kid," "Stumpy's Boy," "The Coyote" (an
allusion to his vocal powers), and even by Kentuck's endearing diminutive of "The
d—d little cuss." But these were felt to be vague and unsatisfactory, and were at last dismissed under another influence. Gamblers and adventurers are generally superstitious,
and Oakhurst one day declared that the baby had brought "the luck" to Roaring Camp.
It was certain that of late they had been successful. "Luck" was the name agreed upon,
with the prefix of Tommy for greater convenience. No allusion was made to the mother,
and the father was unknown. "It's better," said the philosophical Oakhurst, "to take a
fresh deal all round. Call him Luck, and start him fair." A day was accordingly set apart
for the christening. What was meant by this ceremony the reader may imagine who has
already gathered some idea of the reckless irreverence of Roaring Camp. The master of
ceremonies was one "Boston," a noted wag, and the occasion seemed to promise the
greatest facetiousness. This ingenious satirist had spent two days in preparing a bur-
lesque of the Church service, with pointed local allusions. The choir was properly
trained, and Sandy Tipton was to stand godfather. But after the procession had marched
to the grove with music and banners, and the child had been deposited before a mock

altar, Stumpy stepped before the expectant crowd. "It ain't my style to spoil fun, boys," said the little man, stoutly eying the faces around him, "but it strikes me that this thing ain't exactly on the squar. It's playing it pretty low down on this yer baby to ring in fun on him that he ain't goin' to understand. And ef there's goin' to be any godfathers round, I'd like to see who's got any better rights than me." A silence followed Stumpy's speech. To the credit of all humorists be it said that the first man to acknowledge its justice was the satirist thus stopped of his fun. "But," said Stumpy, quickly following up his advantage, "we're here for a christening, and we'll have it. I proclaim you Thomas Luck, according to the laws of the United States and the State of California, so help me God." It was the first time that the name of the Deity had been otherwise uttered than profanely in the camp. The form of christening was perhaps even more ludicrous than the satirist had conceived; but strangely enough, nobody saw it and nobody laughed. "Tommy" was christened as seriously as he would have been under a Christian roof, and cried and was comforted in as orthodox fashion.

And so the work of regeneration began in Roaring Camp. Almost imperceptibly a change came over the settlement. The cabin assigned to "Tommy Luck"—or "The Luck," as he was more frequently called—first showed signs of improvement. It was kept scrupulously clean and whitewashed. Then it was boarded, clothed, and papered. The rosewood cradle, packed eighty miles by mule, had, in Stumpy's way of putting it, "sorter killed the rest of the furniture." So the rehabilitation of the cabin became a necessity. The men who were in the habit of lounging in at Stumpy's to see "how 'The Luck' got on" seemed to appreciate the change, and in self-defense the rival establishment of "Tuttle's grocery" bestirred itself and imported a carpet and mirrors. The reflections of the latter on the appearance of Roaring Camp tended to produce stricter habits of personal cleanliness. Again Stumpy imposed a kind of quarantine upon those who aspired to the honor and privilege of holding The Luck. It was a cruel mortification to Kentuck—who, in the carelessness of a large nature and the habits of frontier life, had begun to regard all garments as a second cuticle, which, like a snake's, only sloughed off through decay—to be debarred this privilege from certain prudential reasons. Yet such was the subtle influence of innovation that he thereafter appeared regularly every afternoon in a clean shirt and face still shining from his ablutions. Nor were moral and social sanitary laws neglected. "Tommy," who was supposed to spend his whole existence in a persistent attempt to repose, must not be disturbed by noise. The shouting and yelling, which had gained the camp its infelicitous title, were not permitted within hearing distance of Stumpy's. The men conversed in whispers or smoked with Indian gravity. Profanity was tacitly given up in these sacred precincts, and throughout the camp a popular form of expletive, known as "D—n the luck!" and "Curse the luck!" was abandoned, as having a new personal bearing. Vocal music was not interdicted, being supposed to have a soothing, tranquilizing quality; and one song, sung by "Man-o'-War Jack," an English sailor from her Majesty's Australian colonies, was quite popular as a lullaby. It was a lugubrious recital of the exploits of "the Arethusa, Seventy-four,"[7] in a muffled minor, ending with a prolonged dying fall at the burden of each verse, "On b-oo-o-ard of the Arethusa."

---

[7]A large British warship with seventy-four guns.

It was a fine sight to see Jack holding The Luck, rocking from side to side as if with the motion of a ship, and crooning forth this naval ditty. Either through the peculiar rocking of Jack or the length of his song,—it contained ninety stanzas, and was continued with conscientious deliberation to the bitter end,—the lullaby generally had the desired effect. At such times the men would lie at full length under the trees in the soft summer twilight, smoking their pipes and drinking in the melodious utterances. An indistinct idea that this was pastoral happiness pervaded the camp. "This 'ere kind o' think," said the Cockney Simmons, meditatively reclining on his elbow, "is 'evingly." It reminded him of Greenwich.

On the long summer days The Luck was usually carried to the gulch from whence the golden store of Roaring Camp was taken. There, on a blanket spread over pine boughs, he would lie while the men were working in the ditches below. Latterly there was a rude attempt to decorate this bower with flowers and sweet-smelling shrubs, and generally some one would bring him a cluster of wild honeysuckles, azaleas, or the painted blossoms of Las Mariposas. The men had suddenly awakened to the fact that there were beauty and significance in these trifles, which they had so long trodden carelessly beneath their feet. A flake of glittering mica, a fragment of variegated quartz, a bright pebble from the bed of the creek, became beautiful to eyes thus cleared and strengthened, and were invariably put aside for The Luck. It was wonderful how many treasures the woods and hillsides yielded that "would do for Tommy." Surrounded by playthings such as never child out of fairyland had before, it is to be hoped that Tommy was content. He appeared to be serenely happy, albeit there was an infantine gravity about him, a contemplative light in his round gray eyes, that sometimes worried Stumpy. He was always tractable and quiet, and it is recorded that once, having crept beyond his "corral,"—a hedge of tessellated pine boughs, which surrounded his bed,—he dropped over the bank on his head in the soft earth, and remained with his mottled legs in the air in that position for at least five minutes with unflinching gravity. He was extricated without a murmur. I hesitate to record the many other instances of his sagacity, which rest, unfortunately, upon the statements of prejudiced friends. Some of them were not without a tinge of superstition. "I crep' up the bank just now," said Kentuck one day, in a breathless state of excitement, "and dern my skin if he wasn't a-talking to a jaybird as was a-sittin' on his lap. There they was, just as free and sociable as anything you please, a-jawin' at each other just like two cherrybums." Howbeit, whether creeping over the pine boughs or lying lazily on his back blinking at the leaves above him, to him the birds sang, the squirrels chattered, and the flowers bloomed. Nature was his nurse and playfellow. For him she would let slip between the leaves golden shafts of sunlight that fell just within his grasp; she would send wandering breezes to visit him with the balm of bay and resinous gum; to him the tall redwoods nodded familiarly and sleepily, the bumblebees buzzed, and the rooks cawed a slumbrous accompaniment.

Such was the golden summer of Roaring Camp. They were "flush times," and the luck was with them. The claims had yielded enormously. The camp was jealous of its privileges and looked suspiciously on strangers. No encouragement was given to immigration, and, to make their seclusion more perfect, the land on either side of the mountain wall that surrounded the camp they duly preëmpted. This, and a reputation for singular proficiency with the revolver, kept the reserve of Roaring Camp inviolate. The expressman—their only connecting link with the surrounding world—sometimes told wonderful stories of the camp. He would say, "They've a street up there in 'Roaring' that would lay over any street in Red Dog. They've got vines and flowers round their houses, and they wash themselves twice a day. But they're mighty rough on strangers, and they worship an Ingin baby."

With the prosperity of the camp came a desire for further improvement. It was proposed to build a hotel in the following spring, and to invite one or two decent families to reside there for the sake of The Luck, who might perhaps profit by female companionship. The sacrifice that this concession to the sex cost these men, who were fiercely skeptical in regard to its general virtue and usefulness, can only be accounted for by their affection for Tommy. A few still held out. But the resolve could not be carried into effect for three months, and the minority meekly yielded in the hope that something might turn up to prevent it. And it did.

The winter of 1851 will long be remembered in the foothills. The snow lay deep on the Sierras, and every mountain creek became a river, and every river a lake. Each gorge and gulch was transformed into a tumultuous watercourse that descended the hillsides, tearing down giant trees and scattering its drift and débris along the plain. Red Dog had been twice under water, and Roaring Camp had been forewarned. "Water put the gold into them gulches," said Stumpy. "It's been here once and will be here again!" And that night the North Fork suddenly leaped over its banks and swept up the triangular valley of Roaring Camp.

In the confusion of rushing water, crashing trees, and crackling timber, and the darkness which seemed to flow with the water and blot out the fair valley, but little could be done to collect the scattered camp. When the morning broke, the cabin of Stumpy, nearest the river-bank, was gone. Higher up the gulch they found the body of its unlucky owner; but the pride, the hope, the joy, The Luck, of Roaring Camp had disappeared. They were returning with sad hearts when a shout from the bank recalled them.

It was a relief-boat from down the river. They had picked up, they said, a man and an infant, nearly exhausted, about two miles below. Did anybody know them, and did they belong here?

It needed but a glance to show them Kentuck lying there, cruelly crushed and bruised, but still holding The Luck of Roaring Camp in his arms. As they bent over the strangely assorted pair, they saw that the child was cold and pulseless. "He is dead," said one. Kentuck opened his eyes. "Dead?" he repeated feebly. "Yes, my man, and you are dying too." A smile lit the eyes of the expiring Kentuck. "Dying!" he repeated; "he's a-taking me with him. Tell the boys I've got The Luck with me now;" and the strong man, clinging to the frail babe as a drowning man is said to cling to a straw, drifted away into the shadowy river that flows forever to the unknown sea.

MIGGLES[1]

We were eight including the driver. We had not spoken during the passage of the last six miles, since the jolting of the heavy vehicle over the roughening road had spoiled the Judge's last poetical quotation. The tall man beside the Judge was asleep, his arm passed through the swaying strap and his head resting upon it,—altogether a limp, helpless looking object, as if he had hanged himself and been cut down too late. The French lady on the back seat was asleep too, yet in a half-conscious propriety of attitude, shown even in the disposition of the handkerchief which she held to her forehead and which partially veiled her face. The lady from Virginia City, traveling with her husband, had long since lost all individuality in a wild confusion of ribbons, veils, furs, and shawls. There was no sound but the rattling of wheels and the dash of rain upon the roof. Suddenly the stage stopped and we became dimly aware of voices. The driver was evidently in the midst of an exciting colloquy with some one in the road,—a colloquy of which such fragments as "bridge gone," "twenty feet of water," "can't pass," were occasionally distinguishable above the storm. Then came a lull, and a mysterious voice from the road shouted the parting adjuration—

"Try Miggles's."

We caught a glimpse of our leaders as the vehicle slowly turned, of a horseman vanishing through the rain, and we were evidently on our way to Miggles's.

Who and where was Miggles? The Judge, our authority, did not remember the name, and he knew the country thoroughly. The Washoe traveler thought Miggles must keep a hotel. We only knew that we were stopped by high water in front and rear, and that Miggles was our rock of refuge. A ten minutes' splashing through a tangled byroad, scarcely wide enough for the stage, and we drew up before a barred and boarded gate in a wide stone wall or fence about eight feet high. Evidently Miggles's, and evidently Miggles did not keep a hotel.

The driver got down and tried the gate. It was securely locked.

"Miggles! O Miggles!"

No answer.

"Migg-ells! You Miggles!" continued the driver, with rising wrath.

"Migglesy!" joined in the expressman persuasively. "O Miggy! Mig!"

But no reply came from the apparently insensate Miggles. The Judge, who had finally got the window down, put his head out and propounded a series of questions, which if answered categorically would have undoubtedly elucidated the whole mystery, but which the driver evaded by replying that "if we didn't want to sit in the coach all night we had better rise up and sing out for Miggles."

So we rose up and called on Miggles in chorus, then separately. And when we had

---

[1]In the wake of the success of "The Luck of Roaring Camp," Harte wrote several other short stories that were greeted with immediate popularity. One of these was "Miggles," which appeared in 1869. Harte later included "Miggles" in a collection of six stories that he released in 1870 under the title *The Luck of Roaring Camp and Other Sketches*.

finished, a Hibernian fellow passenger from the roof called for "Maygells!" whereat we all laughed. While we were laughing the driver cried, "Shoo!"

We listened. To our infinite amazement the chorus of "Miggles" was repeated from the other side of the wall, even to the final and supplemental "Maygells."

"Extraordinary echo!" said the Judge.

"Extraordinary d—d skunk!" roared the driver contemptuously. "Come out of that, Miggles, and show yourself! Be a man, Miggles! Don't hide in the dark; I wouldn't if I were you, Miggles," continued Yuba Bill, now dancing about in an excess of fury.

"Miggles!" continued the voice, "O Miggles!"

"My good man! Mr. Myghail!" said the Judge, softening the asperities of the name as much as possible. "Consider the inhospitality of refusing shelter from the inclemency of the weather to helpless females. Really, my dear sir"—But a succession of "Miggles," ending in a burst of laughter, drowned his voice.

Yuba Bill hesitated no longer. Taking a heavy stone from the road, he battered down the gate, and with the expressman entered the inclosure. We followed. Nobody was to be seen. In the gathering darkness all that we could distinguish was that we were in a garden—from the rose bushes that scattered over us a minute spray from their dripping leaves—and before a long, rambling wooden building.

"Do you know this Miggles?" asked the Judge of Yuba Bill.

"No, nor don't want to," said Bill shortly, who felt the Pioneer Stage Company insulted in his person by the contumacious Miggles.

"But, my dear sir," expostulated the Judge, as he thought of the barred gate.

"Lookee here," said Yuba Bill, with fine irony, "hadn't you better go back and sit in the coach till yer introduced? I'm going in," and he pushed open the door of the building.

A long room, lighted only by the embers of a fire that was dying on the large hearth at its farther extremity; the walls curiously papered, and the flickering firelight bringing out its grotesque pattern; somebody sitting in a large armchair by the fireplace. All this we saw as we crowded together into the room after the driver and expressman.

"Hello! be you Miggles?" said Yuba Bill to the solitary occupant.

The figure neither spoke nor stirred. Yuba Bill walked wrathfully toward it and turned the eye of his coach-lantern upon its face. It was a man's face, prematurely old and wrinkled, with very large eyes, in which there was that expression of perfectly gratuitous solemnity which I had sometimes seen in an owl's. The large eyes wandered from Bill's face to the lantern, and finally fixed their gaze on that luminous object without further recognition.

Bill restrained himself with an effort.

"Miggles! be you deaf? You ain't dumb anyhow, you know," and Yuba Bill shook the insensate figure by the shoulder.

To our great dismay, as Bill removed his hand, the venerable stranger apparently collapsed, sinking into half his size and an undistinguishable heap of clothing.

"Well, dern my skin," said Bill, looking appealingly at us, and hopelessly retiring from the contest.

The Judge now stepped forward, and we lifted the mysterious invertebrate back into his original position. Bill was dismissed with the lantern to reconnoitre outside, for it was evident that, from the helplessness of this solitary man, there must be attendants

near at hand, and we all drew around the fire. The Judge, who had regained his authority, and had never lost his conversational amiability,—standing before us with his back
to the hearth,—charged us, as an imaginary jury, as follows:—

"It is evident that either our distinguished friend here has reached that condition
described by Shakespeare as 'the sere and yellow leaf,'[2] or has suffered some premature
abatement of his mental and physical faculties. Whether he is really the Miggles"—

Here he was interrupted by "Miggles! O Miggles! Migglesy! Mig!" and, in fact, the
whole chorus of Miggles in very much the same key as it had once before been delivered
unto us.

We gazed at each other for a moment in some alarm. The Judge, in particular,
vacated his position quickly, as the voice seemed to come directly over his shoulder. The
cause, however, was soon discovered in a large magpie who was perched upon a shelf
over the fireplace, and who immediately relapsed into a sepulchral silence, which contrasted singularly with his previous volubility. It was, undoubtedly, his voice which we
had heard in the road, and our friend in the chair was not responsible for the discourtesy.
Yuba Bill, who reëntered the room after an unsuccessful search, was loth to accept the
explanation, and still eyed the helpless sitter with suspicion. He had found a shed in
which he had put up his horses, but he came back dripping and skeptical. "Thar ain't
nobody but him within ten mile of the shanty, and that ar d—d old skeesicks[3] knows it."

But the faith of the majority proved to be securely based. Bill had scarcely ceased
growling before we heard a quick step upon the porch, the trailing of a wet skirt, the door
was flung open, and with a flash of white teeth, a sparkle of dark eyes, and an utter
absence of ceremony or diffidence, a young woman entered, shut the door, and, panting,
leaned back against it.

"Oh, if you please, I'm Miggles!"

And this was Miggles! this bright-eyed, full-throated young woman, whose wet
gown of coarse blue stuff could not hide the beauty of the feminine curves to which it
clung; from the chestnut crown of whose head, topped by a man's oil-skin sou'wester, to
the little feet and ankles, hidden somewhere in the recesses of her boy's brogans, all was
grace,—this was Miggles, laughing at us, too, in the most airy, frank, off-hand manner
imaginable.

"You see, boys," said she, quite out of breath, and holding one little hand against her
side, quite unheeding the speechless discomfiture of our party or the complete demoralization of Yuba Bill, whose features had relaxed into an expression of gratuitous and
imbecile cheerfulness,—"you see, boys, I was mor'n two miles away when you passed
down the road. I thought you might pull up here, and so I ran the whole way, knowing
nobody was home but Jim,—and—and—I'm out of breath—and—that lets me out."
And here Miggles caught her dripping oilskin hat from her head, with a mischievous
swirl that scattered a shower of raindrops over us; attempted to put back her hair;
dropped two hairpins in the attempt; laughed, and sat down beside Yuba Bill, with her
hands crossed lightly on her lap.

The Judge recovered himself first and essayed an extravagant compliment.

---

[2]*Macbeth,* act 5, scene 3, line 23.

[3]scarecrow

"I'll trouble you for that ha'rpin," said Miggles gravely. Half a dozen hands were eagerly stretched forward; the missing hairpin was restored to its fair owner; and Miggles, crossing the room, looked keenly in the face of the invalid. The solemn eyes looked back at hers with an expression we had never seen before. Life and intelligence seemed to struggle back into the rugged face. Miggles laughed again,—it was a singularly eloquent laugh,—and turned her black eyes and white teeth once more towards us.

"This afflicted person is"—hesitated the Judge.

"Jim!" said Miggles.

"Your father?"

"No!"

"Brother?"

"No!"

"Husband?"

Miggles darted a quick, half-defiant glance at the two lady passengers, who I had noticed did not participate in the general masculine admiration of Miggles, and said gravely, "No; it's Jim!"

There was an awkward pause. The lady passengers moved closer to each other; the Washoe husband looked abstractedly at the fire, and the tall man apparently turned his eyes inward for self-support at this emergency. But Miggles's laugh, which was very infectious, broke the silence.

"Come," she said briskly, "you must be hungry. Who'll bear a hand to help me get tea?"

She had no lack of volunteers. In a few moments Yuba Bill was engaged like Caliban in bearing logs for this Miranda;[4] the expressman was grinding coffee on the veranda; to myself the arduous duty of slicing bacon was assigned; and the Judge lent each man his good-humored and voluble counsel. And when Miggles, assisted by the Judge and our Hibernian[5] "deck-passenger," set the table with all the available crockery, we had become quite joyous, in spite of the rain that beat against the windows, the wind that whirled down the chimney, the two ladies who whispered together in the corner, or the magpie, who uttered a satirical and croaking commentary on their conversation from his perch above. In the now bright, blazing fire we could see that the walls were papered with illustrated journals, arranged with feminine taste and discrimination. The furniture was extemporized and adapted from candle-boxes and packing-cases, and covered with gay calico or the skin of some animal. The armchair of the helpless Jim was an ingenious variation of a flour-barrel. There was neatness, and even a taste for the picturesque, to be seen in the few details of the long, low room.

The meal was a culinary success. But more, it was a social triumph,—chiefly, I think, owing to the rare tact of Miggles in guiding the conversation, asking all the questions herself, yet bearing throughout a frankness that rejected the idea of any concealment on her own part, so that we talked of ourselves, of our prospects, of the journey, of the weather, of each other,—of everything but our host and hostess. It must be confessed

---

[4]Caliban is the sole inhabitant of an island in Shakespeare's *The Tempest.* Miranda and her father, Prospero, land on the island, and Caliban becomes their servant.

[5]Irish

that Miggles's conversation was never elegant, rarely grammatical, and that at times she employed expletives the use of which had generally been yielded to our sex. But they were delivered with such a lighting up of teeth and eyes, and were usually followed by a laugh—a laugh peculiar to Miggles—so frank and honest that it seemed to clear the moral atmosphere.

Once during the meal we heard a noise like the rubbing of a heavy body against the outer walls of the house. This was shortly followed by a scratching and sniffling at the door. "That's Joaquin," said Miggles, in reply to our questioning glances; "would you like to see him?" Before we could answer she had opened the door, and disclosed a half-grown grizzly, who instantly raised himself on his haunches, with his fore paws hanging down in the popular attitude of mendicancy, and looked admiringly at Miggles, with a very singular resemblance in his manner to Yuba Bill. "That's my watch-dog," said Miggles, in explanation. "Oh, he don't bite," she added, as the two lady passengers fluttered into a corner. "Does he, old Toppy?" (the latter remark being addressed directly to the sagacious Joaquin). "I tell you what, boys," continued Miggles, after she had fed and closed the door on Ursa Minor, "you were in big luck that Joaquin wasn't hanging round when you dropped in to-night."

"Where was he?" asked the Judge.

"With me," said Miggles. "Lord love you! he trots round with me nights like as if he was a man."

We were silent for a few moments, and listened to the wind. Perhaps we all had the same picture before us,—of Miggles walking through the rainy woods with her savage guardian at her side. The Judge, I remember, said something about Una and her lion;[6] but Miggles received it, as she did other compliments, with quiet gravity. Whether she was altogether unconscious of the admiration she excited,—she could hardly have been oblivious of Yuba Bill's adoration,—I know not; but her very frankness suggested a perfect sexual equality that was cruelly humiliating to the younger members of our party.

The incident of the bear did not add anything in Miggles's favor to the opinions of those of her own sex who were present. In fact, the repast over, a chillness radiated from the two lady passengers that no pine boughs brought in by Yuba Bill and cast as a sacrifice upon the hearth could wholly overcome. Miggles felt it; and suddenly declaring that it was time to "turn in," offered to show the ladies to their bed in an adjoining room. "You, boys, will have to camp out here by the fire as well as you can," she added, "for thar ain't but the one room."

Our sex—by which, my dear sir, I allude of course to the stronger portion of humanity—has been generally relieved from the imputation of curiosity or a fondness for gossip. Yet I am constrained to say, that hardly had the door closed on Miggles than we crowded together, whispering, snickering, smiling, and exchanging suspicions, surmises, and a thousand speculations in regard to our pretty hostess and her singular companion. I fear that we even hustled that imbecile paralytic, who sat like a voiceless Mem-

---

[6]A character in Edmund Spenser's (1552?–1599) epic poem *The Faerie Queen* (1590), Una is the companion of the heroic St. George. In the course of her travels, she is befriended and protected by a lion. Una stands for "truth" because truth is "one."

non[7] in our midst, gazing with the serene indifference of the Past in his passionless eyes upon our wordy counsels. In the midst of an exciting discussion the door opened again and Miggles reëntered.

But not, apparently, the same Miggles who a few hours before had flashed upon us. Her eyes were downcast, and as she hesitated for a moment on the threshold, with a blanket on her arm, she seemed to have left behind her the frank fearlessness which had charmed us a moment before. Coming into the room, she drew a low stool beside the paralytic's chair, sat down, drew the blanket over her shoulders, and saying, "If it's all the same to you, boys, as we're rather crowded, I'll stop here to-night," took the invalid's withered hand in her own, and turned her eyes upon the dying fire. An instinctive feeling that this was only premonitory to more confidential relations, and perhaps some shame at our previous curiosity, kept us silent. The rain still beat upon the roof, wandering gusts of wind stirred the embers into momentary brightness, until, in a lull of the elements, Miggles suddenly lifted up her head, and, throwing her hair over her shoulder, turned her face upon the group and asked,—

"Is there any of you that knows me?"

There was no reply.

"Think again! I lived at Marysville in '53. Everybody knew me there, and everybody had the right to know me. I kept the Polka Saloon until I came to live with Jim. That's six years ago. Perhaps I've changed some."

The absence of recognition may have disconcerted her. She turned her head to the fire again, and it was some seconds before she again spoke, and then more rapidly—

"Well, you see I thought some of you must have known me. There's no great harm done anyway. What I was going to say was this: Jim here"—she took his hand in both of hers as she spoke—"used to know me, if you didn't, and spent a heap of money upon me. I reckon he spent all he had. And one day—it's six years ago this winter—Jim came into my back room, sat down on my sofy, like as you see him in that chair, and never moved again without help. He was struck all of a heap, and never seemed to know what ailed him. The doctors came and said as how it was caused all along of his way of life,—for Jim was mighty free and wild-like,—and that he would never get better, and couldn't last long anyway.[8] They advised me to send him to Frisco to the hospital, for he was no good to any one and would be a baby all his life. Perhaps it was something in Jim's eye, perhaps it was that I never had a baby, but I said 'No.' I was rich then, for I was popular with everybody,—gentlemen like yourself, sir, came to see me,—and I sold out my business and bought this yer place, because it was sort of out of the way of travel, you see, and I brought my baby here."

With a woman's intuitive tact and poetry, she had, as she spoke, slowly shifted her position so as to bring the mute figure of the ruined man between her and her audience, hiding in the shadow behind it, as if she offered it as a tacit apology for her actions. Silent and expressionless, it yet spoke for her; helpless, crushed, and smitten with the Divine thunderbolt, it still stretched an invisible arm around her.

---

[7]Gigantic stone statues in ancient Egypt.

[8]Jim's imbecility has all the marks of the advanced dementia caused by syphilis.

Hidden in the darkness, but still holding his hand, she went on:—

"It was a long time before I could get the hang of things about yer, for I was used to company and excitement. I couldn't get any woman to help me, and a man I dursn't trust; but what with the Indians hereabout, who'd do odd jobs for me, and having everything sent from the North Fork, Jim and I managed to worry through. The Doctor would run up from Sacramento once in a while. He'd ask to see 'Miggles's baby,' as he called Jim, and when he'd go away, he'd say, 'Miggles, you're a trump,—God bless you,' and it didn't seem so lonely after that. But the last time he was here he said, as he opened the door to go, 'Do you know, Miggles, your baby will grow up to be a man yet and an honor to his mother; but not here, Miggles, not here!' And I thought he went away sad,—and—and"— and here Miggles's voice and head were somehow both lost completely in the shadow.

"The folks about here are very kind," said Miggles, after a pause, coming a little into the light again. "The men from the Fork used to hang around here, until they found they wasn't wanted, and the women are kind, and don't call. I was pretty lonely until I picked up Joaquin in the woods yonder one day, when he wasn't so high, and taught him to beg for his dinner; and then thar's Polly—that's the magpie—she knows no end of tricks, and makes it quite sociable of evenings with her talk, and so I don't feel like as I was the only living being about the ranch. And Jim here," said Miggles, with her old laugh again, and coming out quite into the firelight,—"Jim—Why, boys, you would admire to see how much he knows for a man like him. Sometimes I bring him flowers, and he looks at 'em just as natural as if he knew 'em; and times, when we're sitting alone, I read him those things on the wall. Why, Lord!" said Miggles, with her frank laugh, "I've read him that whole side of the house this winter. There never was such a man for reading as Jim."

"Why," asked the Judge, "do you not marry this man to whom you have devoted your youthful life?"

"Well, you see," said Miggles, "it would be playing it rather low down on Jim to take advantage of his being so helpless. And then, too, if we were man and wife, now, we'd both know that I was *bound* to do what I do now of my own accord."

"But you are young yet and attractive"—

"It's getting late," said Miggles gravely, "and you'd better all turn in. Good-night, boys;" and throwing the blanket over her head, Miggles laid herself down beside Jim's chair, her head pillowed on the low stool that held his feet, and spoke no more. The fire slowly faded from the hearth; we each sought our blankets in silence; and presently there was no sound in the long room but the pattering of the rain upon the roof and the heavy breathing of the sleepers.

It was nearly morning when I awoke from a troubled dream. The storm had passed, the stars were shining, and through the shutterless window the full moon, lifting itself over the solemn pines without, looked into the room. It touched the lonely figure in the chair with an infinite compassion, and seemed to baptize with a shining flood the lowly head of the woman whose hair, as in the sweet old story, bathed the feet of him she loved. It even lent a kindly poetry to the rugged outline of Yuba Bill, half reclining on his elbow between them and his passengers, with savagely patient eyes keeping watch and ward. And then I fell asleep and only woke at broad day, with Yuba Bill standing over me, and "All aboard" ringing in my ears.

Coffee was waiting for us on the table, but Miggles was gone. We wandered about the house and lingered long after the horses were harnessed, but she did not return. It was evident that she wished to avoid a formal leave-taking, and had so left us to depart as we had come. After we had helped the ladies into the coach, we returned to the house and solemnly shook hands with the paralytic Jim, as solemnly setting him back into position after each handshake. Then we looked for the last time around the long low room, at the stool where Miggles had sat, and slowly took our seats in the waiting coach. The whip cracked, and we were off!

But as we reached the highroad, Bill's dexterous hand laid the six horses back on their haunches, and the stage stopped with a jerk. For there, on a little eminence beside the road, stood Miggles, her hair flying, her eyes sparkling, her white handkerchief waving, and her white teeth flashing a last "good-by." We waved our hats in return. And then Yuba Bill, as if fearful of further fascination, madly lashed his horses forward, and we sank back in our seats.

We exchanged not a word until we reached the North Fork and the stage drew up at the Independence House. Then, the Judge leading, we walked into the bar-room and took our places gravely at the bar.

"Are your glasses charged, gentlemen?" said the Judge, solemnly taking off his white hat.

They were.

"Well, then, here's to *Miggles*—God bless her!"

Perhaps He had. Who knows?

———

PLAIN LANGUAGE FROM TRUTHFUL JAMES

(TABLE MOUNTAIN, 1870)

Which I wish to remark,
    And my language is plain,
That for ways that are dark
    And for tricks that are vain,
The heathen Chinee is peculiar,
    Which the same I would rise to explain.

Ah Sin was his name;
    And I shall not deny,
In regard to the same,
    What that name might imply;
But his smile it was pensive and childlike,
    As I frequent remarked to Bill Nye.

It was August the third,
    And quite soft was the skies;
Which it might be inferred

That Ah Sin was likewise;
Yet he played it that day upon William
   And me in a way I despise.

Which we had a small game,
   And Ah Sin took a hand:
It was Euchre.[1] The same
   He did not understand;
But he smiled as he sat by the table,
   With the smile that was childlike and bland.

Yet the cards they were stocked
   In a way that I grieve,
And my feelings were shocked
   At the state of Nye's sleeve,
Which was stuffed full of aces and bowers,[2]
   And the same with intent to deceive.

But the hands that were played
   By that heathen Chinee,
And the points that he made,
   Were quite frightful to see,—
Till at last he put down a right bower,
   Which the same Nye had dealt unto me.

Then I looked up at Nye,
   And he gazed upon me;
And he rose with a sigh,
   And said, "Can this be?
We are ruined by Chinese cheap labor,"—
   And he went for that heathen Chinee.

In the scene that ensued
   I did not take a hand,
But the floor it was strewed
   Like the leaves on the strand
With the cards that Ah Sin had been hiding,
   In the game "he did not understand."

In his sleeves, which were long,
   He had twenty-four jacks,—
Which was coming it strong,
   Yet I state but the facts;
And we found on his nails, which were taper,
   What is frequent in tapers,—that's wax.

---

[1]A card game involving five cards where three tricks must be taken to win a hand.

[2]Trump, or winning, cards.

Which is why I remark,
   And my language is plain,
That for ways that are dark
   And for tricks that are vain,
The heathen Chinee is peculiar,—
   Which the same I am free to maintain.

———

FURTHER LANGUAGE FROM TRUTHFUL JAMES

(NYE'S FORD, STANISLAUS, 1870)

Do I sleep? do I dream?
Do I wonder and doubt?
Are things what they seem?
Or is visions about?
Is our civilization a failure?
Or is the Caucasian played out?

Which expressions are strong;
Yet would feebly imply
Some account of a wrong—
Not to call it a lie—
As was worked off on William, my pardner,
And the same being W. Nye.

He came down to the Ford
On the very same day
Of that lottery drawed
By those sharps at the Bay;
And he says to me, "Truthful, how goes it?"
I replied, "It is far, far from gay;

"For the camp has gone wild
On this lottery game,
And has even beguiled
'Injin Dick' by the same."
Then said Nye to me, "Injins is pizen:[1]
But what is his number, eh, James?"

I replied, "7, 2,
9, 8, 4, is his hand;"

[1]worthless

When he started, and drew
Out a list, which he scanned;
Then he softly went for his revolver
With language I cannot command.

Then I said, "William Nye!"
But he turned upon me,
And the look in his eye
Was quite painful to see;
And he says, "You mistake; this poor Injin
I protects from such sharps as *you* be!"

I was shocked and withdrew;
But I grieve to relate,
When he next met my view
Injin Dick was his mate;
And the two around town was a-lying
In a frightfully dissolute state.

Which the war dance they had
Round a tree at the Bend
Was a sight that was sad;
And it seemed that the end
Would not justify the proceedings,
As I quiet remarked to a friend.

For that Injin he fled
The next day to his band;
And we found William spread
Very loose on the strand,
With a peaceful-like smile on his features,
And a dollar greenback in his hand;

Which the same, when rolled out,
We observed, with surprise,
Was what he, no doubt,
Thought the number and prize—
Them figures in red in the corner,
Which the number of notes specifies.

Was it guile, or a dream?
Is it Nye that I doubt?
Are things what they seem?
Or is visions about?
Is our civilization a failure?
Or is the Caucasian played out?

THE LATEST CHINESE OUTRAGE

It was noon by the sun; we had finished our game,
And was passin' remarks goin' back to our claim;
Jones was countin' his chips, Smith relievin' his mind
Of ideas that a "straight" should beat "three of a kind,"
When Johnson of Elko came gallopin' down,
With a look on his face 'twixt a grin and a frown,
And he calls, "Drop your shovels and face right about,
For them Chinees from Murphy's are cleanin' us out—
    With their ching-a-ring-chow
    And their chic-colorow
    They're bent upon making
    No slouch of a row."

Then Jones—my own pardner—looks up with a sigh;
"It's your wash-bill," sez he, and I answers, "You lie!"
But afore he could draw or the others could arm,
Up tumbles the Bates boys, who heard the alarm.
And a yell from the hill-top and roar of a gong,
Mixed up with remarks like "Hi! yi! Chang-a-wong,"
And bombs, shells, and crackers, that crashed through the trees,
Revealed in their war-togs four hundred Chinees!
    Four hundred Chinee;
    We are eight, don't ye see!
    That made a square fifty
    To just one o' we.

They were dressed in their best, but I grieve that that same
Was largely made up of our own, to their shame;
And my pardner's best shirt and his trousers were hung
On a spear, and above him were tauntingly swung;
While that beggar, Chey Lee, like a conjurer sat
Pullin' out eggs and chickens from Johnson's best hat;
And Bates's game rooster was part of their "loot,"
And all of Smith's pigs were skyugled to boot;
But the climax was reached and I like to have died
When my demijohn,[1] empty, came down the hillside,—
    Down the hillside—
    What once held the pride
    Of Robertson County
    Pitched down the hillside!

---

[1]Large liquor bottle.

Then we axed for a parley. When out of the din
To the front comes a-rockin' that heathen, Ah Sin!
"You owe flowty dollee—me washee you camp,
You catchee my washee—me catchee no stamp;
One dollar hap dozen, me no catchee yet,
Now that flowty dollee—no hab?—how can get?
Me catchee you piggee—me sellee for cash,
It catchee me licee—you catchee no 'hash;'
Me belly good Sheliff—me lebbee when can,
Me allee same halp pin as Melican man!
        But Melican man
        He washee him pan
        On *bottom* side hillee
        And catchee—how can?"

"Are we men?" says Joe Johnson, "and list to this jaw,
Without process of warrant or color of law?
Are we men or—a-chew!"—here he gasped in his speech,
For a stink-pot had fallen just out of his reach.
"Shall we stand here as idle, and let Asia pour
Her barbaric hordes on this civilized shore?
Has the White Man no country? Are we left in the lurch?
And likewise what's gone of the Established Church?
One man to four hundred is great odds, I own,
But this 'yer's a White Man—I plays it alone!"
And he sprang up the hillside—to stop him none dare—
Till a yell from the top told a "White Man was there!"
        A White Man was there!
        We prayed he might spare
        Those misguided heathens
        The few clothes they wear.

They fled, and he followed, but no matter where;
They fled to escape him,—the "White Man was there,"—
Till we missed first his voice on the pine-wooded slope,
And we knew for the heathen henceforth was no hope;
And the yells they grew fainter, when Petersen said,
"It simply was human to bury his dead."
        And then, with slow tread,
        We crept up, in dread,
        But found nary mortal there,
        Living or dead.

But there was his trail, and the way that they came,
And yonder, no doubt, he was bagging his game.
When Jones drops his pickaxe, and Thompson says "Shoo!"

And both of 'em points to a cage of bamboo
Hanging down from a tree, with a label that swung
Conspicuous, with letters in some foreign tongue,
Which, when freely translated, the same did appear
Was the Chinese for saying, "A White Man is here!"
     And as we drew near,
     In anger and fear,
     Bound hand and foot, Johnson
     Looked down with a leer!

In his mouth was an opium pipe—which was why
He leered at us so with a drunken-like eye!
They had shaved off his eyebrows, and tacked on a cue,[2]
They had painted his face of a coppery hue,
And rigged him all up in a heathenish suit,
Then softly departed, each man with his "loot."
     Yes, every galoot,
     And Ah Sin, to boot,
     Had left him there hanging
     Like ripening fruit.

At a mass meeting held up at Murphy's next day
There were seventeen speakers and each had his say;
There were twelve resolutions that instantly passed,
And each resolution was worse than the last;
There were fourteen petitions, which, granting the same,
Will determine what Governor Murphy's shall name;
And the man from our district that goes up next year
Goes up on one issue—that's patent and clear:
     "Can the work of a mean,
     Degraded, unclean
     Believer in Buddha
     Be held as a lien?"

---

[2] A hairstyle of a single braided strand proceeding from the back of the head.

15

Elizabeth Stuart Phelps

(1844–1911)

ELIZABETH STUART PHELPS was one of those fortunate few whose first novel, *The Gates Ajar* (1868), became an international best-seller and catapulted her to fame when she was just twenty-four years old. *The Gates Ajar* offered its readers a rather liberal Christian view of heaven, where loved ones were reunited with each other and Christ after death. It was an extremely comforting tale in the wake of the massive death and grief caused by the Civil War. The recognition Phelps received from the novel ushered her into Boston's literary circles. It also gave her a wide audience for her future works, which came to number fifty-six books along with hundreds of short stories, magazine articles, and poems. The breadth and popularity of her writings made her one of the most read female authors in the latter part of the nineteenth century.

Phelps's life and writing were marked by a deep interest in social issues. Principal among these was a deep and lasting concern with the rights of women. As early as 1867, she was advocating women's equality in matters of voting, roles within marriage, occupations, and education. Her stories are dominated by strong female characters, while her male characters range from weak to insignificant to dangerous.

Three years after the amazing success of *The Gates Ajar,* Phelps wrote *The Silent Partner.* Rather than speculating on heaven and focusing on the hope one enjoys waiting for the afterlife, in *The Silent Partner* Phelps turned her full attention to the problems of the current world. She wrote *The Silent Partner* with fierce conviction, having done a great deal of research on factory conditions in the Northeast. The book stands as an early example of female fiction that moved beyond the domestic ideals of the woman as subservient and maternal.

It is a compelling novel for several reasons. It uncovers, in often gruesome detail, the horrid life of the factory worker. It is a study in boundary crossing, whether those boundaries be based on gender, class, or social conventions. Finally, it is a story about male and female management, the destructive influence of the former, and the restorative influence of the latter.

THE SILENT PARTNER

Read not to contradict or confute, nor to believe and take for granted, nor to find talk and discourse, but to weigh and consider.

—BACON

❧ Note

In the compilation of the facts which go to form this fiction, it seems desirable to say that I believe I have neither overlooked nor libelled those intelligent manufacturers who have expended much Christian ingenuity, with much remarkable success, in ameliorating the condition of factory operatives, and in blunting the edge of those misapprehensions and disaffections which exist between capital and labor, between employer and employed, between ease and toil, between millions and mills, the world over.

Had Christian ingenuity been generally synonymous with the conduct of manufacturing corporations, I should have found no occasion for the writing of this book.

I believe that a wide-spread ignorance exists among us regarding the abuses of our factory system, more especially, but not exclusively, as exhibited in many of the country mills.

I desire it to be understood that every alarming sign and every painful statement which I have given in these pages concerning the condition of the manufacturing districts could be matched with far less cheerful reading, and with far more pungent perplexities, from the pages of the Reports of the Massachusetts Bureau of Statistics of Labor, to which, with other documents of a kindred nature, and to the personal assistance of friends who have "testified that they have seen," I am deeply in debt for the ribs of my story.

E. S. P.
Andover, December, 1870.

CHAPTER I

❧ Across the Gulf

The rainiest nights, like the rainiest lives, are by no means the saddest.

This occurred to Miss Kelso one January night, not many winters ago. Though, to be exact, it was rather the weather than the simile which occurred to her. The weather may happen to anybody, and so serves a purpose like photography and weddings. Reflections upon life you run your chance of at twenty-three.

Elizabeth Stuart Phelps, *The Silent Partner.* Boston: James R. Osgood and Company, 1871.

If, in addition to the circumstance of being twenty-three, you are the daughter of a gentleman manufacturer, and a resident of Boston, it would hardly appear that you require the ceremony of an introduction. A pansy-bed in the sun would be a difficult subject of classification. Undoubtedly, pages might with ease be occupied in treating of Miss Kelso's genealogy. Her descent from the Pilgrims[1] could be indisputably proved. It would be possible to ascertain whether or not she cried at her mother's funeral. Thrilling details of her life in the nursery are upon record. Her first composition is still legible. Indeed, three chapters, at the least, might be so profitably employed in conveying to the intelligence of the most far-sighted reader the remotest intimation of Miss Kelso's existence, that one feels compelled into an apology to high art for presenting her in three lines and a northeaster.[2]

Perhaps it should be added that this young lady was engaged to be married to her father's junior partner, and that she was sitting in her father's library, with her hands folded, at the time when the weather occurred to her; sitting, as she had been sitting all the opaque, gray afternoon, in a crimson chair by a crimson fire, a creamy profile and a creamy hand lifted and cut between the two foci of color. The profile had a level, generous chin. The hand had—rings.

There are people who never do anything that is not worth watching; they cannot eat an apple or button a shoe in an unnoticeable, unsuggestive manner. If they undertake to be awkward, they do it so symbolically that you feel in debt to them for it. Miss Kelso may have been one of these indexical persons; at any rate, there was something in her simple act of sitting before a fire, in her manner of shielding her eyes from the warmth to which her figure was languidly abandoned, which to a posture-fancier would have been very expressive.

She had noticed in an idle way, swathed to the brain in her folds of heat and color, that the chromatic run of drops upon a window, duly deadened by drawn damask, and adapted nicely to certain conditions of a cannel blaze, had a pleasant sound. Accurately, she had not found herself to be the possessor of another thought since dinner; she had dined at three.

It had been a long storm, but Miss Kelso had found no occasion to dampen the sole of her delicate sandals in the little puddles that dotted the freestone steps and drained pavement. It had been a cold storm, but the library held, as a library should, the tints and scents of June. It had been a dismal storm; but what of that? Miss Kelso was young, well, in love, and—Miss Kelso. Given the problem, Be miserable, she would have folded her hands there by her fire, like a puzzled snow-flake in a gorgeous poppy, and sighed, "But I do not understand!"

To be sure, her father was out of town, and she had mislaid the score of *La Grande Duchesse*,[3] undesirable circumstances, both, but not without their compensations. For the placid pleasantness of five o'clock paternal society, she had the rich, irregular

---

[1] The Pilgrims were among the founders of the first permanent colony in New England in 1620.

[2] A storm of unusual force with winds from the northeast.

[3] *La Grande-Duchesse de Gerolstein* (1867) is a three-act comic opera by Jacques Offenbach (1819–1880).

delights of solitude in a handsome house,—a dream, a doubt, a daring fancy that human society would snap, an odd hope pellmell upon the heels of an extraordinary fear, snatches of things, the mental chaos of a liberated prisoner. Isolation in elegance is not apt to be productive of thought, however, as I intimated.

Opposed to the loss of *La Duchesse* would be the pleasure of making Maverick look for it. Miss Kelso took a keen, appreciative enjoyment in having a lazy lover; he gave her something to do; he was an occupation in himself. She had indeed a weakness for an occupation; suffered passions of superfluous life; at the Cape she rebelled because Providence had not created her a bluefisher; in Paris she would make muslin flowers, and learn the *métier*[4] to-morrow.

This was piquant in her; her plighted husband found himself entertained by it always; he folded her two hands like sheets of rice-paper over his own, with an easy smile.

The weather occurred to the young lady about six o'clock in the form of a query: Was it worth while to go out to-night? She cultivated an objection to *Don Giovanni*[5] in the rain,—and it always rained on *Giovanni;* Maverick could talk Brignoli[6] to Mrs. Silver, and hold a fan for Fly, as well without her; she happened to find herself more interested in an arm-chair than in anything else in the world, and slippers were the solution of the problem of life. Was it worth while?

This was one of those vital questions which require immediate motives for a settlement, and of immediate motives Miss Kelso possessed very few. Indeed, it was as yet unanswered in her own mind, when the silver handle of her carriage-door had shut with a little shine like a smile upon her, and Fly's voice, like boiling candy, bubbled at her from the front seat.

Maverick had called; there had been a whiff of pleasant wet air in her face; and, after all, life and patent springs are much alike in doors or out.

Miss Kelso sank languidly back into the perfumed cushions; the close doors and windows shut in their thick sweetness; the broken lights of the street dropped in, and Maverick sat beside her.

"You have had your carriage re-scented, Perley, I'm sure," said Fly, who was just enough at home with Perley to say it.

"From Harris's,—yes."

"Santalina, unless I am quite mistaken?"

This, softly, from Mrs. Silver; Mrs. Silver was apt to speak very softly.

"I was tired to death of heliotrope," said Perley, with a weary motion of her well-shaped head; "it clings so. There was some trouble, I believe, to take it out; new stuffing and covering. But I think it pays."

---

[4]Vocation or trade.

[5]*Don Giovanni* (1787) is one of Wolfgang Amadeus Mozart's (1756–1791) most famous operas. It is a story of a licentious nobleman who pays with eternal damnation for his deeds of seduction and murder.

[6]Born in Naples, Italy, Pasquale Brignoli (1824–1884) came to the United States in 1855 and became one of the country's most popular opera singers.

"Indeed, yes, richly."

"It always pays to take trouble for *sachet*,[7] I think," said Fly, sententiously.

"Perley never makes a mistake in a perfume,"—that came, of course, from Maverick.

"Perley never did make a mistake in a perfume," observed Mrs. Silver, in the mild motherly manner which she had acquired from frequently matronizing Perley. "Never from the day Burt made the blunder of tuberoses for her poor mother. The child flung them out of the casket herself. She was six years old the day before. It was a gratification to me when Burt went out of fashion."

Perley, it may be presumed, feeling always some awkwardness at the mention of a dead parent for whom propriety required her to mourn, and in connection with whose faint memory she could not, do the best she might, acquire an unhappiness, made no reply, and *sachet* and Mrs. Silver dropped into silence together. Fly broke it, in her ready way: "So kind in you to send for us, Perley!"

"It was quite proper," said Perley.

She did not think of anything else to say, and fell, as her santalina and her chaperone had fallen, a little noticeably out of the conversation.

Fly and Maverick Hayle did the talking. Mrs. Silver dropped in now and then properly.

Perley listened lazily to the three voices; one sometimes hears very noticeable voices from very unnoticeable people; these were distinct of note as a triplet; idle, soft, and sweet—sweetly, softly idle. She played accompaniments with them to her amused fancy.

The triplet rounded into a chord presently, and made her a little sleepy. Sensitive only to an occasional flat or sharp of Brignoli or Kellogg,[8] she fell with half-closed eyes into the luxury of her own thoughts.

What were they? What does any young lady think about on her way to the opera? One would like to know. A young lady, for instance, who is used to her gloves, and indifferent to her stone cameos; who has the score by heart, and is tired of the *prima donna*;[9] who has had a season ticket every winter since she can remember, and will have one every winter till she dies?

The ride to the theatre was not a short one, and slow that night on account of the storm, which was thickening a little, half snow.

Perley, through the white curtains of her falling eyelids, looked out at it; she was fond of watching the streets when no one was watching her, especially on stormy nights, for no reason in particular that she knew of, except that she felt so dry and comfortable. So clean too! There were a great many muddy people out that night; the sleet did not wash them as fast as the mud spattered them; and the wind at the corners sprang on them sharply. From her carriage window she could look on and see it lying in wait for them,

---

[7]Small bag containing perfumed powder or potpourri to scent clothes and linens.

[8]Clara Louise Kellogg (1842–1916) was the first female American opera singer to gain wide fame in Europe, as well as in the United States.

[9]Principal female singer in an opera company.

and see it crouch and bound and set teeth on them. She really followed with some interest, having nothing better to do, the manful struggles of a girl in a plaid dress, who bat-
tled with the gusts about a carriage-length ahead of her, for perhaps half a dozen blocks.
This girl struck out with her hands as a boxer would; sometimes she pommelled with her
elbows and knees like a desperate prize-fighter; she was rather small, but she kept her
balance; when her straw hat blew off, she chased headlong after it, and Perley languidly
smiled. She was apt to be amused by the world outside of her carriage. It conceived such
original ways of holding its hands, and wearing its hats, and carrying its bundles. It had
such a taste in colors, such disregard of clean linen, and was always in such a hurry. This
last especially interested her; Miss Kelso had never been in a hurry in her life.

"There!" said Fly.

"Where?" said Perley, starting.

"I've broken my fan; made a perfect wreck of it! What shall I do? No, thank you. Mr.
Hayle, I am in blue to-night. You know you couldn't fail to get me a green one if you
tried. You must bring me out—but it's too wet to bring fans out. Mother, we must go in
ourselves."

So it came about that in the land of fans, or in the region roundabout, Maverick and
the Silvers disappeared in the flash of a fancy-store, and Perley, in the carriage, was left
alone.

"Dear me!" said Mrs. Silver, placidly, as the umbrella extinguished her, "we are
making our friends a great deal of trouble, Fly, for a little thing."

Now Perley did not find it a trouble. She was rather glad to be alone for a few minutes. In fact, she took it very kindly in Fly to break that fan, and, as she afterwards
thought, with reason.

The carriage door was left open, by her orders. She found something pleasant in the
wet wildness of the storm; it came near enough almost to dampen her cheek as she
leaned forward towards it; and the street came into the frame that was left, in a sharp
picture.

The sidewalk was very wet; in spots the struggling snow drifted grayish white, and
went out into black mud under a sudden foot; the eaves and awnings dripped steadily,
and there was a little puddle on the carriage step; the colored lights of a druggist's window shimmered and broke against the pavement and the carriage and the sleet, leaving
upon the fancy the surprise of a rainbow in a snow-storm; people's faces dipped through
it curiously; here, a fellow with a waxed mustache struck into murderous red, and
dripped so horridly that a policeman, in the confusion of the storm, eyed him for half a
block; there, a hale old man fell suddenly into the last stages of jaundice; beyond, a girl
straggling jealously behind a couple of very wet, but very happy lovers, turned deadly
green; a little this way, another stepped into a bar of lily white, and stood and shone in it
for an instant, "without spot or stain, or any such thing," but stepped out of it, quite out,
shaking herself a little as she went, as if the lighted touch had scorched her.

Still another girl (Miss Kelso expressed to herself some languid wonder that the
night should find so many young girls out, and alone, and noted how little difference the
weather appeared to make with that class of people)—the girl in plaid, whom the storm
had buffeted back for the last few moments—came up with the carriage, and stopped,
full against the druggist's window, for breath. She looked taller, standing in the light,

than she had done when boxing the wind at the corners, but still a little undersized; she had no gloves, and her straw hat hung around her neck by the strings; she must have been very cold, for her lips were blue, but she did not shiver.

Who has not noticed that fantastic fate of galleries, which will hang a saint and a Magdalene, a Lazarus and Dives,[10] face to face? And who has not felt, with those trans-fixed glances, doomed by sunlight, starlight, moonlight, twilight, in crowds and in hush, from year unto year, to struggle towards each other,—vain builders of a vain bridge across the fixed gulf of an irreparable lot,—a weariness of sympathy, which wellnigh extinguished the artistic fineness of the chance? Something of this feeling would have struck a keen observer of Miss Kelso and the little girl in plaid.

Their eyes had met, when the girl lifted her arms to tie on her hat. Against the burn-ing globes of the druggist's window, which quivered and swam through the sheen of the fall of sleet, and just where the perfect spectrum broke about her, she made a miserably meagre figure. Miss Kelso, from the soft dry gloom of her carriage door, leaned out resplendent.

The girl's lips moved angrily, and she said something in a sharp voice which the wind must have carried the other way, for the druggist heard it, and sent a clerk out to order her off. Miss Kelso, obeying one of her whimsical impulses,—who had a better right, indeed, to be whimsical?—beckoned to the girl, who, after swearing a little at the druggist's clerk, strode up rather roughly to the carriage.

"What do you want of me? and what were you staring at? Didn't you ever see any-body lose his hat in a sleet-storm before?"

"I beg your pardon," said Miss Kelso; "I did not mean to be rude."

She spoke on the instinct of a lady. She was nothing of a philanthropist, not much of a Christian. Let us be honest, even if inbred sin and courtesy, not justification by faith, and conscience, induced this rather remarkable reply. I call it remarkable, from the standpoint of girls in plaid. That particular girl, without doubt, found it so. She raised her eyes quickly and keenly to the young lady's face.

"I think I must have been sorry for you," observed Miss Kelso; "that was why I looked at you. You seemed cold and wet."

"*You*'re not cold and wet, at any rate."

This was raggedly said, and bitter. It made Miss Kelso feel singularly uncomfort-able; as if she were to blame for *not* being cold and wet. She felt a curious impulse towards self-defence, and curiously enough she followed it by saying, "I cannot help that!"

"No," said the girl, after a moment's thought. "N-no; but I hate to be pitied by car-riage-folks. I won't be pitied by carriage-folks!"

"Sit down on the steps," said Miss Kelso, "and let me look at you. I do not often see people just like you. What is your name?"

"What's yours?"

"I am called Miss Kelso."

---

[10]Mary Magdalene (Luke 8) and Lazarus (Luke 16) are biblical figures known for their destitute conditions, while a Dives (Luke 16) is a rich man.

"And *I* am called Sip Garth."

That ragged bitterness was in the girl's voice again, much refined, but distinct. Miss Kelso, to whom it seemed quite natural that the small minority of the world should feel at liberty to use, at first sight, the Christian name of the large remainder, took little or no notice of it.

But what could bring her out in such a storm, asked Miss Kelso of Sip Garth.

"The Blue Plum brings out better than me. Who cares for a little sleet? See how wet I am! *I* don't care." She wrung out her thin and dripping shawl, as she spoke, between her bare, wet hands.

"The Blue Plum?" Miss Kelso hesitated, taking the thing daintily upon her lips. What did she, or should she, know of the Blue Plum?

"But the theatre is no place for you, my poor girl." She felt sure of as much as that. She had dimly understood as much from her father and the newspapers. No theatre patronized by the lower classes could be a place for a poor girl.

"It's no place for you," she said again. "You had so much better go home."

Sip Garth laughed. She swung herself upon the highest step of Miss Kelso's carriage, and laughed almost in Miss Kelso's fine, shocked face.

"How do *you* know whether I had so much better go home? Wait till *you*'ve been working on your feet all day, and wait till *you* live where *I* live, before you know whether I had so much better go home! Besides"—she broke off with a quick change of tone and countenance—"I don't go for the Plum. The Plum doesn't make much odds to me. I go to see how much better I could do it."

"Could you?"

"*Couldn't* I!"

"I don't quite understand."

"I don't suppose you do. Give me the music, give me the lights, and the people, and the poetry, and *I*'d do it. I'd make 'em laugh, wouldn't I? I'd make 'em cry, you may make up your mind on that. That's what I go to the Plum for. I do it over. That's what you think of in the mills, don't you see? That's so much better than going home,—to do it over."

"You seem," said Miss Kelso, with some perplexed weariness in her expression,—perhaps she had carried her whim quite far enough,—"you seem to be a very singular girl."

Evidently Miss Kelso's coachman, whose hatbrim appeared and peered uneasily over the box at disgusted intervals, thought so too. Evidently the passers, such of them as had preserved their eyesight from the ravages of the sleet, thought so too. Evidently it was quite time for the girl in plaid to go.

"I wonder what *you* seem like," said Sip Garth, thoughtfully. She leaned, as she spoke, into the sweet dimness of the carriage, and gravely studied the sweet dimness of the young lady's face. Having done this, she nodded to herself once or twice with a shrewd smile, but said nothing. Her wet shawl now almost brushed Miss Kelso's dress; the girl was not filthy, but the cleanliest poverty in a Boston tenement-house fails to acquire the perfumes of Arabia, and Perley sickened and shrank. Yet it struck her as odd, for the moment, if you will believe it, that she should have santalina in her carriage cushions; not as ill-judged, not as undesirable, not as in any way the concern of girls from tenement-houses, not at all as something which she would not do again to-morrow, but only as odd.

She had thought no more than this, when the disgusted coachman, with an air of infinite personal relief, officially announced Mr. Hayle, and Fly came laughing sweetly back. It was quite time for Sip to go.

In the confusion she dripped away among the water-spouts like one of them, before Miss Kelso could speak to her again.

The street came into the frame that was left in a sharp picture. The sidewalk was once more very wet; in spots the struggling snow drifted, grayish white, and went out into black mud under sudden feet; the eaves and awnings dripped steadily, and there was a little puddle on the carriage steps.

Miss Kelso had a young, fresh imagination, a little highly colored, perhaps, by opera music, and it made of these things a vivid background for the girl in plaid, into which and out of which she stepped with a fanciful significance.

With the exception of her servants, her seamstresses, and the very little members of a very little Sabbath-school class, which demanded of her very little thought and excited in her very little interest, Miss Kelso had never in her life before—I think I speak without exaggeration—had never in her life before exchanged a dozen words with an example of what Maverick Hayle was pleased to term the οἱ πολλοί,[11] thereby evincing at once his keen appreciation of the finer distinctions both of life and letters, as well as the fact, that, though a successful manufacturer, he had received a collegiate education and had not yet forgotten it. And, indeed, as he was accustomed to observe, "Nothing gives a man such a *prestige* in society."

The girl in plaid then, to repeat, was a novelty to Perley Kelso. She fell back into her cushions again to think about her.

"Poor Perley! I hope she found herself amused while we were gone," sympathized Fly, fluttering in with her new fan. Perley thanked her, and had found herself amused, much amused.

Yet, in truth, she had found herself saddened, singularly saddened. She could scarcely have understood why. Nothing more definite than an uncomfortable consciousness that all the world had not an abundance of *sachet* and an appreciation of Brignoli struck her distinctly. But how it rained on that girl looking in at her from the carriage steps! It must rain on many girls while she sat in her sweet, warm, sheltered darkness. It must be a disagreeable thing, this being out in the rain. She did not fancy the thud of drops on her carriage-roof as much as usual; the wind waiting at corners to crouch and spring on people ceased to amuse her; it looked cruel and cold. She shivered and looked so chilly that Maverick folded her ermines like a wonderful warm snow-cloud tenderly about her, and drowned the storm from her hearing with his tender, lazy voice.

In the decorous rustle of the crowd winding down through the corridors, like a glittering snake, after *Giovanni* that night, Fly started with a little faint scream, and touched Perley on the arm.

"My *dear* Perley!—Mr. Hayle, there is a girl annoying Perley."

---

[11]"Hoi polloi," common people, in Greek.

At Perley's elbow, trying quietly but persistently to attract her attention, Perley was startled and not well pleased to see the girl in plaid. In the heat and light and scent and soft babble of the place, she cut a jagged outline. The crowd broke in beautiful billows about her and away from her. It seemed not unlike a radiant sea out of which she had risen, black and warning as a hidden reef. She might have been thought to be not so much a foreign horror as a sunken danger in the shining place. She seemed, indeed, rather to have bounded native from its glitter, than to have forced herself upon it. Her eyes were very large and bright, and she drew Perley's beautiful, disturbed face down to her own with one bare hand.

"Look here, young lady, I want to speak to you. I want to know why you tell *me* the Plum is no place for *me?* What kind of a place is this for you?—now say, what kind of a place? You don't know; but I do. I followed you here to see. I tell you it's the plating over that's the difference; the plating over.[12] At the Plum we say what we mean; and we mean bad enough, very like. We're rough, and we're out with it. Up at this place they're in with it. They plate over. The music plates over. The people plate over. It's different from us, and it ain't different from us. Don't you see? No, you don't. I do. But you'd ought to,— you'd ought to. You're old enough and wise enough. I don't mean to be saucy; but I put it to you honest, if I haven't seen and heard that in this grand place tonight—all plated over—that's no more fit for a lady like you seem to be to sit and see and hear, than it's fit for me and the like of me to sit and see and hear the Plum. I put it to you honest, and that's all, and I'm sorry to plague you with all your fine friends about, for I liked the looks of you right well when I sat on your carriage steps. But it ain't often you'll have the chance to hear truer words from a rough girl like me; and it ain't likely you hear no more words true nor false from me; so good by, young lady. I put it to you honest!"

"Hush!" said Miss Kelso, somewhat pale, as Maverick stepped up to drive the girl away. "Let her alone. It's only a girl I—amused myself with when you went with Fly for the fan. Let her be. It was only a whim of mine, and, as it has proved, a foolish one. I am not used to such people. She was coarse and hurt me. But let her go."

"I should advise you to choose your amusements more wisely another time," said Maverick Hayle, looking angrily after Sip, who was edging her way, with a sharp motion, through the radiant sea. She disappeared from view on the stairway suddenly, and the waves of scent and light and heat and babble met and closed over her as merrily as waves are wont to meet and close over sunken reefs.

The ripple of Miss Kelso's disturbed thoughts closed over her no less thoroughly, after the momentary annoyance was past. She had done a foolish thing, and been severely punished for it. That was all. As Maverick said, the lower classes could not bear any unusual attention from their betters, without injury. Maverick in his business connection had occasion to know. He must be right.

Maverick in his business connection had occasion to know another thing that night. Maverick in his business connection was met by a telegram, on returning with Miss Kelso to her father's house. The senior partner held the despatch in his hand. He was sitting in Miss Kelso's parlor. His face was grave and disturbed.

---

[12]Cover with a layer of a usually expensive metal.

"Losses, perhaps," thought Perley, and left father and son alone. They did not seem inclined to remain alone, however. She had not yet taken off her wraps in the hall, when she heard Maverick say in an agitated voice, "I can't! I cannot do it!" and Mr. Hayle the senior came out. The despatch was still in his hand.

"My dear Miss Perley," he said, with some hesitation.

"Yes, sir?" said Perley, unfastening her corded fur.

"Your father—"

"Wait a minute!" said Perley, speaking fast. She unfastened the fur, and folded the cape up into a white heap with much pains and precision.

She was struck with a childish dread of hearing a horrible thing. She felt singularly confused. Snatches of *Giovanni* danced through her brain. She thought that she saw the girl in plaid sitting on her front stairs, with a worldful of rain upon her head. Her own thought came curiously back to her, in words: "How disagreeable it must be to sit out in the rain!" Her youth and happiness shrank with a sudden faint sickness at being disturbed. It was with as much fright as grief that she took the paper from her father's old friend and read:—

"*Crushed at six o'clock this afternoon, in the freight depot at Five Falls. Instant death.*"

CHAPTER II

❧ The Slippery Path

Nothing is more conducive to one's sense of personal comfort than to live in a factory town and not be obliged to answer factory bells. This is especially to be said of those misty morning bells, which lay a cloudy finger upon one's last lingering dream, and dip it and dimple it into shreds; of those six-o'clock winter bells, whose very tongues seem to have stiffened with the cold, and to move thickly and numbly against their frosted cheeks. One listens and dozes, and would dream again but for listening again, and draws one's silk and eider shoulder-robe closer to one's warm throat with a shiver of rare enjoyment. Iron voices follow, and pierce the shoulder-robe. They are distinct in spite of the eider, though a little hoarse. One turns and wraps one's self again. They are dulled, but inexorable. One listens and dozes, and would dream again but for listening. The inexorable is the delightful. One has to take only the pleasure of listening. A dim consciousness of many steps of cold people cutting the biting, sunless air, gives a crispness to the blankets. The bells shiver in sympathy with the steps, and the steps shiver in response to the bells. The bells hurry, hurry, hurry on the steps. The steps hurry, hurry, hurry to the bells. The bells grow cross and snappish,—it is so cold. The steps grow pert and saucy,—it is so cold. Bells and steps, in a convulsion of ill-temper, go out from hearing together, and only a sense of pillows and two hours before breakfast fills the world.

Miss Kelso, waking to the six-o'clock bells of a winter morning, appreciates this with uncommon keenness; with the more uncommon keenness that she has never waked to the six-o'clock bells of a winter morning before. She has experienced the new sensation of spending, for the first time, a February night in her July house, and is so thoroughly convinced that she ought to be cold, and so perfectly assured that she isn't, that the dangerous consideration of the possible two hours before mentioned, and the undeniable fact that she has invited Maverick to breakfast at seven, incite between her delicate young flesh and her delicate young conscience one of those painful and prolonged struggles which it is impossible for any one who is obliged to get up in the morning to appreciate. Conscience conquering, after a protracted contest, the vanquished party slips reluctantly and slowly out of silk and eider[13] into *crépins*[14] and Persiana,[15] just as Mr. Maverick Hayle's self-possessed ring plays leisurely through the house.

The ghastly death of the managing partner has had its effect upon his business and his daughter, without doubt. Upon his business—as might be assumed from the fact that Maverick Hayle should breakfast at seven o'clock—a confusing effect, requiring care and time to adjust with wisdom. Upon his daughter,—what, for instance? If he slipped from her life, as he slips from her story, so heart slips away from heart, and love from love, with the slide of every hour. To cross the gap from life with a father to life without, very much as the February night descended upon the July house, were not unnatural. One must be warm, at all events. Her grief was wrapped in swaddling-clothes. It was such a young grief, and she so young a griever; and the sun shone, and the winter air was crisp.

Perley had been fond of her father,—of course; and mourned him,—of course: but fondness is not friendship, and mourning is not desolation. Add to this a certain obstinate vein in this young woman, which suggested it to her fancy as a point of loyalty to her father's memory not to strain her sorrow beyond its honest altitude, and what follows? To be at first very sadly shocked, to be next very truly lonely; to wish that she had never been cross to him (which she had), and to be sure that he had never been cross to her (which he had); to see, and love to see, the best of the departed life and the sweetest of the departed days; and then to wander musing away, by sheer force of contrast, upon her own unfinished life, and into the sweetness of her own coming days, and repent of it next moment; to forget one afternoon to notice the five-o'clock solitude because Maverick comes in; to take very much to her Prayer-Book the first fortnight, and entirely to Five Falls the second; and to be pouring out her lover's coffee this morning, very lovely, a little quiet, and less unhappy.

"But pale?" suggested Maverick, leaning back in his chair, with the raised eyebrow of a connoisseur, to pronounce upon the effect of her. The effect was good, very good. Her black dress, and the little silver *tête-à-tête* service[16] over which she leaned, set one another off quaintly; and a trifle more color in her face would have left the impression of a sketch finished by two artists who had failed of each other's idea.

Perley did not know that she was pale; did not feel pale; felt perhaps—and paused. How did she feel?

Apparently she did not feel like explaining to Maverick Hayle. Something in the

---

[13]A comforter filled with eider duck down.

[14]A delicate netlike fabric used to hold the hair of ladies.

[15]Fabric decorated with designs of roses.

[16]Tea service for two.

delicate motion with which he raised the delicate napkin in his well-shaped hand to his delicately trimmed mustache acted perhaps as a counter-irritant to some delicate shading of her thought. It would not have been the first time that such a thing had happened. He was as necessary to Perley Kelso as her Axminster carpets;[17] he suited her in the same way; in the same way he—sometimes—wearied her. But how did she feel?

"As nearly as I can make out," said Perley, "I feel like a large damask curtain taken down for the first time off its cornice," with a glance at the heavy walnut mouldings of her windows. "All in a heap, you know, and surprised. Or like a—what do you call it? that part of a plane that runs in a groove, when you stop the groove up. And I'm not used, you know, Maverick, to feeling at all; it's never been asked of me before."

She smiled and playfully shook her head; but her young eyes were perplexed and gently sad.

"It was coming to this cold house, under the circumstances," suggested Maverick.

No; Perley shook her head again; the house was not cold; never mind. Was his cup out? The milk was cold, at any rate; he must wait a minute; and so sat thoughtfully silent while she touched the bell, with the little silver service shining against her shoulder and the curve of her arm.

"What did you come down here for?" asked Maverick, over his second cup.

Perley didn't know.

"When shall you go back?"

Perley didn't know that.

"What are you going to do?"

Perley didn't know that, either. "Perhaps I shall not go back. I am tired of town. Perhaps I shall stay here and look after—things."

"Things? For instance?"

"The mills, for instance. My property, for instance."

Maverick lazily laughed; pushing back his chair, and raising the connoisseur's eyebrow again at the little shining service, and the black curve of the womanly, warm arm.

Perhaps she would take his place this morning; he was late, now; she could rake over a shoddy-heap, he was sure, or scold an overseer. He would agree to sit by the fire and order dinner, if she would just run over to father's for him and bring him his slippers.

"I'll run over to the counting-room with you, and bring you to repentance," said Perley; "the air must be like wine this morning, and the sun like heaven."

The air was so much like wine and the sun like heaven, that Perley, upon leaving the junior partner at the mill-gates, strolled on by a path on the river's brink through and beyond the town, finding herself loath to go back and sit by the fire and order dinner; the more so, possibly, because she was a bit annoyed that Maverick should have hit with such exactness her typical morning; it had, somehow, a useless, silly sound.

A useless, silly sound in this town of Five Falls was artistically out of place. She almost felt herself to be a superfluity in the cold, crisp air filled to the full with business noises; and took a pleasure in following the river almost out of hearing of the mill machinery, and quite into the frozen silence of the upper stream.

---

[17]Carpets woven by a machine into patterns involving pile tuft inserts.

Though the stream was large, the town was not; neither had the mills, from that distance, an imposing air. Perley, with a sudden remembrance of the size of her income, wondered at this for the first time. "The business" had been a standing mystery in the young lady's careless fancy, the existence of which she had dimly understood from her father, as she had dimly understood the existence of "The Blue Plum"; perhaps both had been about equally withheld from her comprehension. That there was some cotton in it she felt sure; that it was a responsible business and a profitable business she understood; that there were girls in little shawls, ragged men, and bad tobacco, an occasional strike, and a mission Sunday school connected with it, she remembered.

Upon the cool of her summer rest the hot whir of the thing had never breathed. Factory feet had trodden as lightly as dewdrops upon her early dreams.

She put on Five Falls for a few months every year as she put on a white dress,—a cool thing, which kept wash-people busy.

Five Falls in July agreed with her, and she fancied it. Five Falls in February entertained her, and she found it suggestive; and indeed Five Falls in February was not a barren sight.

She had wandered, it might be, half a mile up stream, and had turned to look behind her, just at the spot from which the five cascades, which named the town, broke into view; more accurately, there were four cascades—pretty, swift, slender things—and the dam. The stream was a deep one, with a powerful current, and Perley noticed the unusual strength of the bridge below the dam. It was a county bridge and well built; its stone piers, freckled and fringed with heavy frost, had the sombre, opulent air of time-worn frescos, behind which arches of light and sky drew breath like living things, and palpitated in time to the irregular pulse of the water.

The pulse of the water was sluggish, half choked by swathings of beautiful ice; the falls, caught in their tiny leap, hung, frozen to the heart, in mid-air; the open dam, swift, relentless, and free, mocked at them with peals of hollow laughter; and great puffs and palls of smoke, which overhung the distant hum of the little town, made mouths, one fancied, at the shining whiteness of the fields and river bank.

Miss Kelso, turning to retrace her steps with her face set thoughtfully towards this sight, was disturbed by a quick, loud tread behind her; it came abreast of her and passed her, and, in so doing, thrust the flutter of a dingy plaid dress against her in the narrow path.

Either some faded association with the faded dress or with the energetic tread, or both, puzzled Miss Kelso, and she stopped to consider it. Apparently the girl stopped to consider something, but without turning her head. Miss Kelso, after a moment's hesitation, stepped up and touched her on the shoulder.

"I knew you," said the girl abruptly, still without turning her head. "I didn't suppose you'd know me. You needn't unless you want to."

"I *had* forgotten you," said Perley, frankly. "But I remember now. I remember very well. I am surprised to see you in Five Falls."

"You needn't never be surprised to see factory folks anywhere," said Sip Garth. "We're a restless set. Wanderers on the face of the earth."

"Are you in my father's—in the mills?"

"Yes," more gently, and with a glance at Perley's mourning, "in your mills, I suppose; the brick ones,—yes. I supposed they were yours when I heard the names. But folks told me you only come down here in summer-time. I didn't expect to see you. I've been here three weeks."

"You like it here?" asked Miss Kelso, somewhat at a loss how to pursue the art of conversation under what she found to be such original circumstances,—she and Sip were walking towards the town now, in the widening path, side by side.

"I hope you like it here?" she repeated.

"Catty likes. It doesn't make much odds to me."

"Who is Catty?"

"That's my sister; we're the last of us, she and I. Father got smashed up three weeks ago last Friday; caught in the gearing by the arm. They wouldn't let Catty and me look at him, he was smashed so. But I looked when there wasn't anybody round. I wanted to see the last of him. I never thought much of father, but I wanted to see the last of him."

In her controlled, well-bred way, Perley sickened and shrunk again, as she had sickened and shrunk from this girl before, but said quickly, "O, I am sorry!"

"You needn't be," said Sip Garth. "Haven't I told you that I didn't think much of father? I never did neither."

"But that is dreadful!" exclaimed Miss Kelso. "Your own father! and now he is dead!"

Something in their kindred deprivation moved Perley; an emotion more like sympathy than recoil, and more like attraction than disgust, took possession of her as they walked slowly and more slowly, in the ever-widening path, side by side into the town.

"He beat Catty," said Sip, after a pause, in a low voice. "He beat me, but I didn't make so much of that. He used to take my wages. I had to hide 'em, but he used to find 'em. He spent it on drink. You never saw a man get drunker than my father could, Miss Kelso."

Miss Kelso presumed that she never had; thinking swiftly how amused Maverick would be at that, but said nothing.

"Drunk as a beast," continued Sip, in an interested tone, as if she were explaining a problem in science,—"drunk as a fool. Why, so drunk, he'd lie on a rummy's floor for twenty-four hours, dead as a door-nail. I've seen them kick him out, down the steps, into the ditch, you know, when they couldn't get rid of him no other way. Then"—lowering her voice again—"then he came home and beat Catty."

"You seem to be fond of your sister," observed Miss Kelso.

"Yes," said Sip, after some silence,—"yes, I love Catty."

"You have not been to work this morning?" asked Perley, for want of something better to say.

"No, I asked out to-day. Catty's sick. I've just been up river to Bijah's after some dock-weed for her; he had some dock-weed, and he told me to come; he's a well-meaning old chap, Bijah Mudge."

Not having the pleasure of the acquaintance of Mr. Mudge, Perley was perplexed how to follow the topic, and did not try.

"I suppose you think I was saucy to you," said Sip, suddenly, "in the Opera House, I mean. I didn't expect you'd ever notice me again."

"You 'put it to me honest,' certainly," said Miss Kelso, smiling. "But though, of course, you were quite mistaken, I did not think, as far as I thought at all about it, that you meant to be impertinent. The Opera question, Sip, is one which it takes a cultivated lover of music to understand."

"Oh!" said Sip with a puzzled face.

"Poetry, fiction, art, all are open to the same objections which you found to *Giovanni*. People are affected by these things very differently. Superior music is purity itself; it clears the air; and only—"

Miss Kelso remembered suddenly that she was talking to an ignorant factory-girl; a girl who went to the Blue Plum, and had never heard of Mozart; wondered how she could have made such a blunder; collected her scattered pearls into a hasty change of subject,—something about the cold weather and mill-hours and Catty.

"Catty's deaf," said Sip again in her sudden way, after they had walked in silence for a few moments down the shining, slippery, broadening way. She lifted her little brown face sidewise to Perley's abstracted one, to watch the effect of this; hesitating, it seemed, whether it were worth while to bestow some lingering confidence upon her.

"Ah!" said Perley; "poor thing!"

The little brown face fell, and with it fell another pause. It had been a thoughtful pause for Miss Kelso, and she broke it in a thoughtful voice.

"Can you stop with your dock-weed long enough to sit down here a minute? It is warm in the sun just here on these rocks, and we are so close to town; and I want you to talk to me."

"I haven't got anything to say to you," said Sip a little sullenly, sitting down, however, upon a broad, dry rock, and spreading her hands, which were bare and purple, out upon her lap in the sun.

"Don't you earn enough to buy you gloves?" asked Miss Kelso.

"Catty had my gloves," said Sip, evasively. "What do you want of me? I can't stay long."

"Why, I hardly know," said Perley, slowly. "I want you to talk without being questioned. I don't like to question you all the time. But I want to hear more about you, and—you didn't speak of your mother; and where you live, and how; and many other things. I am not used to people who live as you do. I presume I do not understand how to treat you. I do not think it is curiosity. I think it is—I do not know what it is. I suppose I am sorry."

"You needn't trouble yourself to be sorry, as I've said before," replied Sip, chafing her purple fingers. "Besides, I haven't much to tell. There's folks in your mills has enough to tell, that would make stories in newspapers, I bet you! Foreigners mostly. If you want stories to amuse you, you've come to the wrong place. I'm a Yankee, and my mother was a Yankee. Father wasn't; but I don't know what he was, and I don't believe he knew himself. There's been six of us, put together; the rest died, babies mostly, of drink and abuse. I wish Catty and me'd been two of 'em! Well, mother she died with one of 'em four years ago (it was born of a Tuesday, and Thursday morning she was to work, and Saturday noon she was dead), and father he died of the gearing, and Catty and me moved here where there was easy work for Catty. We was in a hoop-skirt factory before, at Waltham;[18] I used to come in nights to the Blue Plum, as you see me in your carriage. I guess that's all. I've worked to cotton-mills before the hoops; so they put me right to weaving. I told you we're a restless lot. But we're always at factory jobs someways, from father to son and mother to daughter. It's in the blood. But I guess that's all.

"You have good prompt pay," said Miss Kelso, properly. "I suppose that you could not have a better or healthier occupation. You get so much exercise and air."

She had heard her father say this, in times long past.

Sip shrugged her shoulders with a suppressed laugh; the unmistakable, incorrigible, suppressed laugh of "discontented labor," but said nothing.

"I should like to see your sister Catty," said Perley, obliged to reintroduce conversation.

"We're on the Company board. You can come when she gets well."

"How long has she been deaf?"

"It may not please you to hear," said Sip, reluctantly.

Miss Kelso was sure that it would not displease her to hear.

"Well, they were running extra time," said Sip, "in the town where we was at work before Catty was born. They were running fourteen hours a day. Mother she was at work, you know. There was no two ways to that. Father was on a spree, and we children were little shavers, earning next to nothing. She begged off from the extra; but it was all, or quit; it's always all or quit. Quit she couldn't. I'll say this for Jack Bench,—he was our boss,— Jack, he hadn't got it through his head what condition she was in. But she worked till a Saturday night, and Catty was born on a Monday morning. Father came off his drunk Sunday, and Jack Bench he always laid it on to that; but Catty was born deaf. Father did fly round pretty well that Sunday night, and maybe it helped. But he didn't strike mother. I was round all day to see to it that he shouldn't strike. But Catty was born deaf—and," half under her breath, "and—queer, and dumb, you know; but I've taught her a little talk. She talks on her fingers. Sometimes she makes sounds in her throat. But I can always understand Catty. Poor Catty! It's never her fault, but she's a world of care and wear."

"But such things," said Miss Kelso, rising with a shocked face from the sunny stone, "do not often happen in our New England factories!"

"I only know what I know," said Sip, shortly; "I didn't blame anybody. I never knew any other woman as it turned out so bad to. They're mostly particular about women in that state; fact is, they're mostly more particular than the women themselves. I've seen a boss threaten a woman with her notice to get her home, and she wouldn't stir. But it's all or quit, in general."

"But these people cannot be in such need of money as that!" said Perley.

"Folks don't do such things for fun," said Sip, shortly.

"But in our mills—"

"Your own mills are your own affairs," interrupted Sip. "You'd better find out for yourself. It ain't to complain to you that I talk to you."

They had come now quite into the town, and stopped, at the parting of their several

---

[18]Waltham is a city in eastern Massachusetts, located on the Charles River. Its abundant water supply attracted grist, textile, and paper mills.

ways. Miss Kelso held out her hand to the girl, with a troubled face. The mills were making a great noise and confused her, and she felt that it was of little use to say anything further than that she should try to come and see Catty, and that she thanked her for—but she was sure that she did not know for what, and so left the sentence unfinished, and bade her good morning instead.

Sip Garth stood still in a snow-drift, and rubbed her hands, which had grown pink and warm. Her brown little face was puzzled.

"It wasn't all the sun, nor yet the touch. It was the newness, I think," she said.

She said it again to Catty, when she got home with the dock-weed.

"Eh!" said Catty. She made a little harsh sound like a croak.

"O, no matter," said Sip, talking upon her fingers, "you couldn't understand! But I think it must have been the newness."

CHAPTER III

❧ A Game of Chess

"I beg your pardon?" said Maverick Hayle. He said it in simple bewilderment.

Perley repeated her remark.

"You wish—excuse me—*do* I understand you to wish—"

" 'Partner' was undoubtedly the word that she used, Maverick," said Mr. Hayle the senior, with an amused smile.

"I want to be a partner in the firm," reiterated Perley, with great distinctness; "you're very stupid this morning; Maverick, if you'll excuse *me*. I thought I had expressed myself clearly. I want to be a partner in Hayle and Kelso."

They were sitting—the two gentlemen and the young lady—around a table in Miss Kelso's parlor: a little table which Perley had cleared to its pretty inlaid surface, with some indefinite idea, which vastly entertained Maverick, of having room in which to "conduct business." Some loose papers, a new glazed blank-book, and a little gold pencil lay upon the table. The pattern of the table was a chess-board of unusual beauty: Miss Kelso's hand, slightly restless, traced the little marble squares, sometimes with the pencil, sometimes without, while she talked. The squares were of veined gray and green.

"I sent for you this morning," said Perley, turning to the elder gentleman, "because it seemed to me quite time that I should understand the state of my affairs as my father's death has left them. I am very ignorant, of course. He never talked to me about the business; but I suppose that I could learn. I should prefer to learn to understand my own affairs. This is not inconsistent, I am sure you will appreciate, with that confidence which it is my delight to feel in you and Maverick."

Maverick, at the sound of his own name, looked up with a faint effort to recall what had preceded it, having plunged suddenly and irretrievably into the depths of a decision that Story,[19] the next time he was in the country, should make a study of a hand upon squares of gray and green. In self-defence he said so.

---

[19]William Wetmore Story (1819–1895) was a Massachusetts-born, internationally recognized sculptor.

"Whatever responsibilities," said Perley, with a slight twitch of annoyance between her eyes, and speaking still to the elder gentleman,—"whatever responsibilities rest upon me, as sole heir to my father's property, I am anxious to fulfil in person. Whatever connection I have with the Hayle and Kelso Mills, I am anxious, I am exceedingly anxious, to meet in person. And I thought," added the young lady, innocently, "that the simplest way would be for me to become a partner."

"Now I don't know another woman," said Maverick, rousing, with an indulgent smile, "who could have originated that, father, if she had tried. Let us take her in. By all means take her in. As she says, what could be simpler?"

"Miss Perley will of course understand what would be in due time legally and suitably explained to her," observed Mr. Hayle, "that she has, and need have, no responsibilities as heir to her father's property; that she has, and can have, no such connection with the Hayle and Kelso Mills as requires the least exertion or anxiety upon her part."

"But I don't understand at all," said Perley.

"I thought I fell heir to all that, with the money. At least I thought I could if I wished to."

"But we're private, not corporate, don't you see?" explained Maverick, carelessly. "You don't fall heir to a partnership in a company as you would to stock in a corporation, Perley. You must see that."

Probably Perley did not see that in the least. The little gold pencil traced a row of greens and skipped a row of grays in a sadly puzzled, unbusiness-like way.

"You could not fall heir to the partnership even if you were a man," continued Maverick, in his patronizing fashion. "The choice of a new partner, or whether, indeed, there shall be a new partner, is a matter resting wholly with the Senior and myself to settle. Do I make it clear?"

"Quite clear," said Perley, brightening; "so clear, that I do not see anything in the world to prevent your choosing me."

Both gentlemen laughed; about as much as they seemed to think was expected of them: Maverick took up the pencil which Perley had laid down, and jotted green squares at his end of the table. Perley, at hers, slipped her empty fingers musingly along a soft gray vein. She was half vexed, and a little mortified. For the first time in her life, she was inclined to feel ashamed of being a woman. She was seriously interested,—perhaps, again, for the first time in her life, seriously interested—in this matter. A faint sense of degradation at being so ignorant that she could not command the respect of two men sufficiently to the bare discussion of it possessed her.

"One need not be a child because one is a woman!" she said, hotly.

"The case is just this, my dear," said the Senior, kindly observant of her face tone. "Your father dies"—this with a slight, decorous sadness in his voice, but mathematically withal, as he would propound a sum for Perley's solution: A man buys a bushel; or, A boy sold a yard—"your father dies. Maverick and I reorganize the firm in our own way: that is our affair. You fall heir to a certain share of interest in the business: that is your affair. It is for you to say what shall be done with your own property. You are even quite at liberty to withdraw it entire from the concern, or you can leave it in our hands, which, I am free to say, we should, in the existing state of affairs, prefer—"

"And expect," interrupted Maverick, pleasantly, making little faces on Perley's pink, shell-like nails with the pencil.

"Which we prefer, and very naturally, under the circumstances, expect," continued the Senior. "You then receive certain dividends, which will be duly agreed upon, and have thus the advantage of at once investing your property in a safe, profitable, and familiar quarter, and of feeling no possible obligation or responsibility—business obligation and responsibility are always so trying to a lady—about it. You thus become, in fact and in form, if you prefer, a silent partner. Indeed, my dear," finished the Senior, cheerfully, "I do not see but this would meet your fancy perfectly."

"Especially as you are going to marry into the firm," observed Maverick.

"Has a silent partner a voice and vote in—questions that come up?" asked Perley, hesitating, and rubbing off the little faces from her nails with a corner of her soft handkerchief.

"No," said Maverick; "none at all. An ordinary, unprivileged dummy, I mean. If you have your husband's, that's another matter. A woman's influence, you know; you've heard of it. What could be more suitable?"

"Then, if I understand," said Perley, "I invest my property in your mills. You call me a silent partner, to please me and to stop my asking questions. I have nothing to do with the mills or the people. I have nothing to do but to spend the money and let you manage it. That's all it amounts to."

"That's all," said Maverick.

Perley's light finger and the Junior's pencil skirmished across the chess-table for a few moments in silence; the finger from gray to gray; the pencil on green and green; the finger, by chance, it seemed, pursuing; the pencil, unconsciously, it seemed, retreating, as if pencil-mark and finger-touch had been in the first idle stages of a long game.

"Who will go into the firm if I can't?" asked Perley, suddenly.

"Father talks of our confidential clerk," said Maverick, languidly, "a fellow we've promoted from East Street, but smart. Smart as a trap. Garrick by name. You've seen him, perhaps,—Stephen Garrick. But nothing is settled; and this is submitted," bowing, "to the close confidence of our silent partner."

Perley did not seem to be in a mood for gallantry; did not smile, but only knitted her soft brows.

"Still, I do not see that there is anything to prevent my becoming an active partner. There is nothing the matter with the law, I suppose, which forbids a woman becoming an active partner in anything?"

Maverick assured her that there was nothing the matter with the law; that the matter was entirely with the existing firm. Excepting, indeed, some technicality, about which he could not, at the moment, be precise, which, he believed, would make formal partnerships impossible in the case of husband and wife.

"But that case we are not considering," said Perley, quickly. "That case it will be time enough to consider when it occurs. As long as I am unmarried and independent, Maverick, I am very much in earnest in my wish to manage my mills myself. I do not like to think that a great many people may be affected by the use of my property in ways over which I can have no possible control. Of course, I don't know what else to do with my money, and if it must be, it must be,"—Perley noticed with some wonder here an amused glance between father and son. "But I shall be very much disappointed; and I am much, I am very much, in earnest."

"I verily believe she is," said Maverick, with sudden conviction. "Now, I admire that! It is ingenuous and refreshing."

"Then why don't you take my part, Maverick, instead of laughing at me?" asked Perley, and was vexed at herself for asking immediately.

"O, that," said Maverick, "is another matter. I may find myself entertained to the last degree by the piquancy, originality, *esprit,*[20] of a lady, when I may be the last man upon earth to consent to going into business with my wife. Seriously, Perley," for Perley did not bear this well, "I don't see what has given you this kink, nor why you have become so suddenly reluctant to intrust the management of your property to me."

"It is not my property," said Perley, in a low voice, "which I am reluctant to intrust to you."

"What, then, may it be?"

"My people,—the people. Perhaps I have thought of them suddenly. But it may be better to remember a thing suddenly than never to remember it at all."

"People! O, the hands, the mill-people. A little Quixotic fancy there. Yes, I understand now; and very pretty and feminine it is too. My dear Perley, you may set your kind heart at rest about the mill-people,—a well-paid, well-cared-for, happy set of laboring people as you could ask to see. You can go down into our mission school and take a class, if that is what you are troubled about."

"Suppose I were to withdraw my share of the business," suggested Perley, abruptly. "Suppose, upon being refused this partnership for which I have asked this morning, I should prefer to withdraw my interest in the mills?"

"We should regret it," said Mr. Hayle, courteously; "but we should have nothing to do but to make the best of circumstances."

"I see, I see now!" Perley flushed as the eyes of the two gentlemen met again and again with suppressed amusement in them. "I ought to have said that before I told you that I didn't know what else to do with the money. Of course! I see, I've made a bad business blunder. I see that you think I should always make bad business blunders. Now, Maverick Hayle, I don't believe I should!"

"My dear Perley," said Maverick, wearily, "just listen to reason for reason's sake. A lady's patience and a gentleman's time are too valuable to throw away at this rate. Even if you possessed any other qualification, which you do not, or all other qualifications, which you cannot, for this ridiculous partnership, you lack an absolutely essential one,—the acquaintance of years with the business. Just reflect upon your acquaintance with the business!"

"I will acquire an acquaintance of years with the business," said Perley, firmly.

"Begin at the spools, for example?"

"I will begin at the spools."

"Or inspect the cotton?"

"Or inspect the cotton."

"Wear a calico dress, and keep the books in a dingy office?"

"Wear a dozen calico dresses, and keep books in the dingiest office you have. I repeat, I am in earnest. I ask for the vacant partnership, or a chance to fit myself for a

---

[20]spirit

partnership, in Hayle and Kelso. Whatever my disqualifications, I am ready to remove them, any and all. If you refuse it to me, while I suppose we shall all go on and be very good-natured about it, I shall feel that you refuse it to me because I *am* a young lady, not because I do not stand ready to remove a young lady's disqualifications."

"Really, Perley, this is becoming absurd, and the morning is half gone. If you won't take a gallant dismissal of a foolish subject, then I *do* refuse it to you because you *are* a young lady."

"We must refuse it to you certainly, on whatever grounds," remarked the Senior, with politeness, "however unpleasant it may be to refuse you even the gratification of an eccentric fancy."

Perley's pursuing finger on the little gray squares thoughtfully traced the course of Maverick's retreating pencil on the green. Pencil-mark and finger-touch played faster now, as if in the nervous stages of a shortening game.

"What do you do," asked the young lady, irrelevantly, and still with her light fingers thoughtfully tracking the chess-board, and still watching the little gold pencil, which still retreated before it, "in your mills, when you have occasion to run extra time?"

"Run it," said Maverick, laconically.

"But what do you do with the people,—the operatives, I mean?"

"Pay them extra."

"But they are not obliged, unless they desire, to work more than eleven hours a day?"

"No," said the Junior, nonchalantly; "they can leave if they prefer."

Perley's face, bent over the squares of gray and green, changed color slightly. She would have spoken, it seemed, but thought better of it, and only played with her thoughtful finger silently along the board.

"Your remark will leave an unfortunate impression upon the young lady, my son," observed the elder Mr. Hayle, "unless you explain to her that in times of pressure it would be no more possible for a mill to thin out its hands in extra hours than it would be for her to dismiss her cook when she has a houseful of company. The state of the market is an inexorable fact, an in-ex-or-able fact, Miss Perley, before which employer and *employé*,[21] whose interests, of course, are one, have little liberty of choice. The wants of the market must be met. In fast times, we are all compelled to work pretty hard. In dull times, we rest and make up for it. I can assure you that we have almost universally found our hands willing and anxious to run an extra hour or so for the sake of extra pay."

"How long a day's work has the state of the market ever required of your mills?" asked Perley, still with her head bent and her finger moving.

"Perhaps thirteen hours and a half. We ran thirteen hours and a half for a week last July, wasn't it, Maverick?"

"What is the use of talking business to a woman?" said Maverick, with such unusual animation that he said it almost impatiently.

"I understand then," said Perley, with the same abruptness which had characterized her words so often that morning, "that my application to look after my mills in an official capacity is refused?"

---

[21]employee

"Is refused."

"In any official capacity?"

"In any official capacity."

"But that," with a faint smile, "of silent partner."

"But that," with a bow, "of silent partner."

"It is quite impossible to gratify me in this respect?" pursued Perley, with her bent head inclined a little to the Senior.

"Quite impossible," replied the Junior.

"So, out of the question."

"And so, out of the question."

The finger-touch brought the pencil-mark abruptly to a stop upon a helpless square of green.

"Checkmate?" asked the young man, smiling.

"Checkmate," said the young lady, smiling too.

She closed the pencil-case with a snap, tossed the little glazed blank-book into the fire, and rang for luncheon, which the three ate upon the chess-table,—smiling.

CHAPTER IV

❧ The Stone House

If you are one of "the hands" in the Hayle and Kelso Mills, you go to your work, as is well known, from the hour of half past six to seven, according to the turn of the season. Time has been when you went at half past four. The Senior forgot this the other day in a little talk which he had with his silent partner,—very naturally, the time having been so long past; but the time has been, is now, indeed, yet in places. Mr. Hayle can tell you of mills he saw in New Hampshire last vacation, where they ring them up, if you'll believe it, winter and summer, in and out, at half past four in the morning. O no, never let out before six, of course. Mr. Hayle disapproves of this. Mr. Hayle thinks it not humane. Mr. Hayle is confident that you would find no mission Sunday school connected with that concern.

If you are one of "the hands" in the Hayle and Kelso Mills—and again, in Hayle and Kelso,—you are so dully used to this classification, "the hands," that you were never known to cultivate an objection to it, are scarcely found to notice its use or disuse. Being surely neither head nor heart, what else remains? Conscious scarcely, from bell to bell, from sleep to sleep, from day to dark, of either head or heart, there seems even a singular appropriateness in the chance of the word with which you are dimly struck. Hayle and Kelso label you. There you are. The world thinks, aspires, creates, enjoys. There you are. You are the fingers of the world. You take your patient place. The world may have need of you, but only that it may think, aspire, create, enjoy. It needs your patience as well as your place. You take both, and you are used to both, and the world is used to both, and so, having put the label on for safety's sake, lest you be mistaken for a thinking, aspiring, creating, enjoying compound, and so some one be poisoned, shoves you into your place upon its shelf, and shuts its cupboard door upon you.

If you are one of "the hands," then, in Hayle and Kelso, you have a breakfast of bread and molasses probably; you are apt to eat it while you dress; somebody is heating the kettle, but you cannot wait for it; somebody tells you that you have forgotten your shawl, you throw it over one shoulder, and step out, before it is fastened, into the sudden raw air; you left lamp-light in-doors; you find moonlight without; the night seems to have overslept itself; you have a fancy for trying to wake it, would like to shout at it or cry through it, but feel very cold, and leave that for the bells to do by and by. You and the bells are the only waking things in life. The great brain of the world is in serene repose. The great heart of the world lies warm to the core with dreams. The great hands of the world, the patient, perplexed, one almost fancies at times, just for the fancy, seeing you here by the morning moons, the dangerous hands, alone are stirring in the dark.

You hang up your shawl and your crinoline, and understand, as you go shivering by gaslight to your looms, that you are chilled to the heart, and that you were careless about your shawl, but do not consider carefulness worth your while by nature or by habit; a little less shawl means a few less winters in which to require shawling. You are a godless little creature, but you cherish a stolid leaning, in these morning moons, towards making an experiment of death and a wadded coffin.

By the time that gas is out, you cease, perhaps, though you cannot depend upon that, to shiver, and incline less and less to the wadded coffin, and more to a chat with your neighbor in the alley. Your neighbor is of either sex and any description, as the case may be. In any event, warming a little with the warming day, you incline more and more to chat. If you chance to be a cotton-weaver, you are presently warm enough. It is quite warm enough in the weaving-room. The engines respire into the weaving-room; with every throb of their huge lungs you swallow their breath. The weaving-room stifles with steam. The window-sills of this room are guttered to prevent the condensed steam from running in streams along the floor; sometimes they overflow, and water stands under the looms; the walls perspire profusely; on a damp day, drops will fall from the roof.

The windows of the weaving-room are closed; the windows must be closed; a stir in the air will break your threads. There is no air to stir. You inhale for a substitute motionless, hot moisture. If you chance to be a cotton-weaver, it is not in March that you think most about your coffin.

Being "a hand" in Hayle and Kelso, you are used to eating cold luncheon in the cold at noon, or you walk, for the sake of a cup of soup or coffee, half a mile, three quarters, a mile and a half, and back. You are allowed three quarters of an hour in which to do this. You come and go upon the jog-trot.

You grow moody, being "a hand" at Hayle and Kelso's, with the growing day; are inclined to quarrel or to confidence with your neighbor in the alley; find the overseer out of temper, and the cotton full of flaws; find pains in your feet, your back, your eyes, your arms; feel damp and sticky lint in your hair, your neck, your ears, your throat, your lungs; discover a monotony in the process of breathing hot moisture, lower your window at your risk; are bidden by somebody whose threads you have broken at the other end of the room to put it up, and put it up; are conscious that your head swims, your eyeballs burn, your breath quickens; yield your preference for a wadded coffin, and consider whether the river would not be the comfortable thing; cough a little, cough a great deal, lose your balance in a coughing fit, snap a thread, and take to swearing roundly.

From swearing you take to singing; both perhaps are equal relief, active and diverting. There is something curious about that singing of yours. The time, the place, the singers, characterize it sharply,—the waning light, the rival din, the girls with tired faces. You start some little thing with a refrain and a ring to it; a hymn, it is not unlikely; something of a River and of Waiting, and of Toil and Rest, or Sleep, or Crowns, or Harps, or Home, or Green Fields, or Flowers, or Sorrow, or Repose, or a dozen things, but always, it will be noticed, of simple, spotless things, such as will surprise the listener who caught you at your oath of five minutes past. You have other songs, neither simple nor spotless, it may be; but you never sing them at your work, when the waning day is crawling out from spots between your looms, and the girls lift up their tired faces to catch and keep the chorus in the rival din.

You like to watch the contest between the chorus and the din; to see—you seem almost to see—the struggle of the melody from alley to alley, from loom to loom, from darkening wall to darkening wall, from lifted face to lifted face; to see—for you are very sure you see—the machinery fall into a fit of rage. That is a sight! You would never guess, unless you had watched it just as many times as you have, how that machinery will rage. How it throws its arms about, what fists it can clench, how it shakes at the elbows and knees, what teeth it knows how to gnash, how it writhes and roars, how it clutches at the leaky, strangling gas-lights, and how it bends its impotent black head, always, at last, without fail, and your song sweeps triumphant, like an angel, over it! With this you are very much pleased, though only "a hand," to be sure, in Hayle and Kelso.

You are singing when the bell strikes, and singing still when you clatter down the stairs. Something of the simple spotlessness of the little song is on your face, when you dip into the wind and dusk. Perhaps you have only pinned your shawl, or pulled your hat over your face, or knocked against a stranger on the walk; but it passes; it passes and is gone. It is cold and you tremble, direct from the morbid heat in which you have stood all day; or you have been cold all day, and it is colder, and you shrink; or you are from the weaving-room, and the wind strikes you faint, or you stop to cough and the girls go on without you. The town is lighted, and people are out in their best clothes. You pull your dingy veil about your eyes. You are weak and heart-sick all at once. You don't care to go home to supper. The pretty song creeps, wounded, back for the engines in the deserted dark to crunch. You are a miserable little factory-girl with a dirty face.

A broken chatter falls in pieces about you; all the melody of the voices that you hear has vanished with the vanquished song; they are hoarse and rough.

"Goin' to the dance to-night, Bet?"

"Nynee Mell! yer alway speerin' awa' after some young mon. Can't yer keep yer een at home like a decint lassie?"

"An' who gave *you* lave to hoult a body's hand onasked an' onrequested, Pathrick Donnavon?"

"Sip Garth, give us 'Champagne Charley'; can't you?"

"Do you think the mules will strike?"

"More mules they, if they do. Did ye never see a mouse strike a cat?"

"There's Bub beggin' tobacco yet! How old is that little devil?"

"The Lord knows!"

"Pity the Lord don't know a few more things as one would suppose might fall in his line."

"A tract?"

"A tract. Bless you, four pages long. Says I, What in ——'s this? for I was just going in to the meetin' to see the fun. So he stuffs it into my hand, and I clears out."

"Sip, I say! Priscilla! Sip Garth—"

But Sip Garth breaks out of sight as the chatter breaks out of hearing; turns a corner; turns another; walks wearily fast, and wearily faster; pushes her stout way through a dirty street and a dirtier street; stops at shadowy corners to look for something which she does not find; stops at lighted doors to call for something that does not answer; hesitates a moment at the dismal gate of a dismal little stone house by the water, and, hesitating still and with a heavy sigh, goes in.

It is a damp house, and she rents the dampest room in it; a tenement boasting of the width of the house, and a closet bedroom with a little cupboard window in it; a low room with cellar smells and river smells about it, and with gutter smells and drain smells and with unclassified smells of years settled and settling in its walls and ceiling. Never a cheerful room; never by any means a cheerful room, when she and Catty—or she without Catty—come home from work at night.

Something has happened to the forlorn little room to-night. Sip stops with the door-latch in her hand. A fire has happened, and the kerosene lamp has happened, and drawn curtains have happened; and Miss Kelso has happened,—down on her knees on the bare floor, with her kid gloves off, and a poker in her hands.

So original in Perley! Maverick would say; Maverick not being there to say it, Perley spoke for herself, with the poker in her hand, and still upon her knees.

"I beg your pardon, Sip, but they told me, the other side of the house, that you would be in in five minutes, and the room was dark and so I took the liberty. If you wouldn't mind me, and would go right on as if I hadn't come, I should take it very kindly."

"All right," said Sip.

"The fact is," said Miss Kelso, meditatively twirling her poker, "that that is the first fire I ever made in my life. Would you believe it, to look at it?"

"I certainly shouldn't," said Sip.

"And you're quite sure that you wouldn't mind me?"

"No, not quite sure. But if you'll stay awhile, I'll find out and tell you."

"Very well," said Miss Kelso.

"See how dirty I am," said Sip, stopping in the full light on her way to the closet bedroom.

"I hadn't seen," said Miss Kelso to the poker.

"O, well. No matter. I didn't know but *you*'d mind."

There was dust about Sip, and oil about her, and a consciousness of both about her, that gave her a more miserable aspect than either. In the full light she looked like some half-cleared Pompeian statue[22] just dug against the face of day.

---

[22]Pompeii was an ancient Roman city that was buried suddenly after the eruption of a volcano in A.D. 79. The ashes encased and preserved the town, so that artifacts excavated from the ruins are always initially covered in ash.

"We can't help it, you see," said poor Sip; "mill-folks can't. Dust we are and to dust do we return. I've got a dreadful sore-throat to-night."

"Have you taken cold?"

"O no. I have it generally. It comes from sucking filling through the shuttle. But I don't think much of it. There's girls I know, weavers, can't even talk beyond a whisper; lost their voices some time ago."

Sip washed and dressed herself after this in silence. She washed herself in the sink; there was no pump to the sink; she went out bare-headed, and brought water in from a well in the yard; the pail was heavy, and she walked wearily, with her head and body bent to balance it, over the slippery path. She coughed while she walked and when she came in,—a peculiar, dry, rasping cough, which Perley learned afterwards to recognize as the "cotton-cough." She washed herself in a tin basin, which she rinsed carefully and hung up against the wall. While she was dressing in the closet bedroom, Perley still knelt, thoughtfully playing with the poker beside the fire.

"I don't suppose," said Sip, coming out presently in her plaid dress, with her hair in a net, and speaking as if she had not been interrupted,—"I don't suppose you'd ever guess how much difference the dirt makes. I don't suppose you ever *could*. Cotton ain't so bad, though. Once I worked to a flax-mill. *That* was dirt."

"What difference?"

"Hush!" said Sip, abruptly, "I thought I heard—" She went to the window and looked out, raising her hands against her eyes, but came back with a disappointed face.

"Catty hasn't come in," she said, nervously. "There's times she slips away from me; she works in the Old Stone, and I can't catch her. There's times she doesn't come till late. Will you stay to tea?" with a quick change of voice.

"Thank you. I don't understand about Catty," with another.

Sip set her table before she spoke again; bustled about, growing restless; put the kettle on and off the hob; broke one of her stone-china plates; stopped to sweep the floor a little and to fill her coal-hod; the brown tints of her rugged little face turning white and pinched in spots about the mouth.

She came, presently, and stood by the fire by Miss Kelso's side, in the full sweep of the light. "Miss Kelso," her hands folding and unfolding restlessly, "there's many things you don't understand. There's things you *could*n't understand."

"Why?"

"I don't know why. I never did quite know why."

"You may be right; you may be wrong. How can you tell till you try me?"

"How can I tell whether I can skate on running water till I try it?—I wish Catty would come!"

Sip walked to the window again, and walked back again, and took a look at the teapot, and cut a slice or two of bread.

"So you've left the Company board," observed Miss Kelso, quite as if they had been talking about the Company board. "You didn't like it?"

"I liked well enough."

"You left suddenly?"

"I left sudden." Sip threw her bread-knife down, with an aimless, passionate gesture. "I suppose it's no good to shy off. I might as well tell o't first as last. They turned us off!"

"Turned you off?"

"On account of Catty."

Miss Kelso raised a confused face from the poker and the fire.

"You see," said Sip, "I *told* you there's things you couldn't understand. Now there ain't one of my own kind of folks, your age, wouldn't have understood half an hour ago, and saved me the trouble of telling. Catty's queer, don't you see? She runs away, don't you see? Sometimes she drinks, don't you understand? Drinks herself the dead kind. That ain't so often. Most times she just runs away about streets. There's sometimes she does—worse."

"Worse?" The young lady's pure, puzzled face dropped suddenly. "O, I was very dull! I am sorry. I am not used—" And so broke off, with a sick look about the lips,—a look which did not escape the notice of the little brown, pinched face in the firelight, for it was curving into a bitter smile when the door opened, banging back against the wall as if the opener had either little consciousness or little care of the noise it made.

"There's Catty," said Sip, doggedly. "Come and get warm, Catty." This in their silent language on her rapid, work-worn fingers.

"If you mind me now, I'll go," said Miss Kelso, in a low voice.

"That's for you to say, whether I shall mind you now."

"Poor Catty!" said Perley, still in a very low voice. "Poor, poor Catty!"

Sip flushed,—flushed very sweetly and suddenly all over her dogged face. "*Now* I don't mind you. Stay to supper. We'll have supper right away. Come here a minute, Catty dear."

Catty dear would not come. Catty dear stood scowling in the middle of the room, a sullen, ill-tempered, ill-controlled, uncontrollable Catty dear as one could ask to see.

"For love's sake," said Sip, on her patient fingers; "here a minute, for love's sake, Catty."

"For love's sake?" repeated Catty, in her pathetic language.

"Only for love's sake, dear," said Sip.

Catty came with this, and laid her head down with a singularly gentle motion on Sip's faded plaid lap. Miss Kelso could see her now, in the light in which they three were sitting. A girl possibly of fifteen years,—a girl with a low forehead, with wandering eyes, with a dull stoop to the head, with long, lithe, magnetic fingers, with a thick, dropping under lip,—a girl walled up and walled in from that labyrinth of sympathies, that difficult evolution of brain from beast, the gorgeous peril of that play at good and evil which we call life, except at the wandering eyes, and at the long, lithe, magnetic fingers. An ugly girl.

She lay, for an ugly girl, very still in her sister's lap. Sip softly stroked her face, talking now to the child and now to her visitor, wound about in a pretty net of soft sounds and softer emotions. A pleasant change had fallen upon her since the deaf-mute came in.

"See how pleasant it is to come home early, Catty," (She won't talk to-night, because you're here.) "For love's sake, dear, you know." (That's the way I get along with her. She likes that.) "For love's sake and my sake, and with the lamp and fire bright. So much better—" (It's never her fault, poor dear! God knows, I never, never laid it up against her as it was her fault.) "Better than the dark street-corners, Catty—"

"There's light in the shops," said Catty, on her long fingers, with a shrewd, unpleasant smile.

"And supper at home," said Sip, quickly, rising. "For love's sake, you know. And company to supper!"

"For love's sake?" asked Catty, rising too.

"*I* don't know for whose sake!" said Sip, all the pleasantness gone in a minute from her.

The young lady and Catty were standing now, between the lamp-glow and the fire-glow, side by side. They were a startling pair to be standing side by side. They stood quite still, except that Catty passed her fingers curiously over Miss Kelso's dress,—it seemed that she saw quite as much with her fingers as with her eyes,—and that she nodded once or twice, as if she were talking to herself, in a stupid way. Perley's fine, fair, finished smile seemed to blot out this miserable figure, and to fill the room with a kind of dazzle.

"Good God!" cried Sip, sharply. "You asked me for the difference. Look at that! You asked what difference the dirt makes. *That*'s the difference! To be born in it, breathe it, swallow it, grow on it, live it, die and go back to it—bah! If you want to go the devil, work in the dirt. Look at her!"

"I look at her," said Perley, with a solemn, frightened look upon her young face,— "I look at her, Sip. For love's sake. Believe me if you can. Make her understand. I look for love's sake."

Is it possible? Is Miss Kelso sure? Not for a whim's sake? Not for fancy's sake? Not for the sake of an idle moment's curiosity? Not to gratify an eccentric taste,—playing my Lady Bountiful for a pretty change in a pretty life? Look at her; it is a very loathsome under lip. Look well at her; they are not pleasant eyes. An ugly girl,—a very ugly girl. For love's sake, Miss Kelso?

Catty sat down to supper without washing her face. This troubled Sip more than it did her visitor. Her visitor, indeed, scarcely noticed it. Her face wore yet something of the solemn fright which had descended on it with Catty's coming in.

She noticed, however, that she had bread and butter for her supper, and that she was eating from a stone-china plate, and with a steel fork and with a pewter spoon. She noticed that the bread was toasted, it seemed in deference to the presence of a guest, and that the toasting had feverishly flushed Sip's haggard face. She noticed that Sip and Catty ate no butter, but dipped their bread into a little blue bowl of thick black molasses. She noticed that there was a kind of coarse black tea upon the table, and noticed that she found a single pewter spoonful of it quite sufficient for her wants. She noticed that Sip made rather a form than a fact of playing with her toasted bread in the thick black molasses, and that she drained her dreadful teacup thirstily, and that she then leaned, with a sudden sick look, back into her chair.

Everything tasted of oil, she said. She could not eat. There were times that she could not eat day nor night for a long time. How long? She was not sure. It had been often two days that nothing passed her lips. Sometimes, with the tea, it was longer. There were times that she came home and got right into bed, dirt and all. She couldn't undress, no, not if it was to save her soul, nor eat. But, generally, she managed to cook for Catty. Besides, there was the work.

"What work?" asked Miss Kelso, innocently.

"Washing. Ironing. Baking. Sweeping. Dusting. Sewing. Marketing. Pumping.

Scrubbing. Scouring," said Sip, drumming out her periods on a teaspoon with her hard, worn fingers.

"Oh!" said Miss Kelso.

"For two, you see," said Sip.

"But all this,—you cannot have all this to do after you have stood eleven hours and a half at your loom?"

"When should I have it to do! There's Sunday, to be sure; but I don't do so much now Sundays, except the washing and the brushing up. I like," with a gentle, quick look at the deaf and dumb girl, who still sat dipping bread crusts into black molasses, absorbed and still, "to make it a kind of a comfortable day for Catty, Sunday. I don't bother Catty so much to help me, you know," added Sip, cheerfully. "I like," with another very pleasant look, "to make it comfortable for Catty."

"I went into the mills to-day," said Miss Kelso, in reply. It was not very much to the point as a reply, and was said with an interrogatory accent, which lessened its aptness.

"Yes?" said Sip, in the same tone.

"I never was in a mill before."

"No?"

"No."

There was a pause, in which the young lady seemed to be waiting for a leading question, like a puzzled scholar. If she were, she had none. Sip sat with her dogged smile, and snapped little paper balls into the fire.

"I thought it rather close in the mills."

"Yes?"

"And—dirty. And—there was one very warm room; the overseer advised me not to go in."

"It was very good advice."

"I went into the Company boarding-house too."

"For the first time?"

"For the first time. I went to inquire after you. The landlady took me about. Now I think of it, she invited me to tea."

"Why didn't you stay?"

"Why, to tell the truth, the—tablecloth was—rather dirty."

"Oh!"

"And I saw her wipe her face on—the dish-towel. Do the girls often sleep six in a room? They had no wash-stands. I saw some basins set on trunks. They carried all the water up and down stairs themselves; there were two or three flights. There wasn't a ventilator in the house. I saw a girl there sick."

"Sick? O, Bert Bush. Yes. Pleurisy.[23] She's going to work her notice when she gets about again. Given out."

"She coughed while I was there. I thought her room was rather cold. I thought all the rooms were rather cold. I didn't seem to see any fire for anybody, except in the common sitting-room. But the bread was sweet."

---

[23]Dangerous inflammation of the lungs usually accompanied by difficulty breathing, fever, and a cough.

"Yes, the bread was sweet."

"And the gingerbread."

"Very sweet."

"And, I suppose, the board—

"The board is quarter of a dollar cheaper than in other places."

Sip stopped snapping paper balls into the fire, and snapped instead one of her shrewd, sidewise glances at her visitor's face.

The fine, fair, finished face! How puzzled it looked! Sip smiled.

Catty had crept around while they were talking, and sat upon the floor by Miss Kelso's chair. She was still amusing herself with the young lady's dress, passing her wise fingers to and fro across its elegant surface, and nodding to herself in her dull way. Miss Kelso's hand, the one with the rings, lay upon her lap, and Catty, attracted suddenly by the blaze of the jewels, took it up. She took it up as she would a novel toy, examined it for a few moments with much pleasure, then removed the rings and dropped them care-lessly, and laid her cheek down upon the soft flesh. It was such a dusty cheek, and such a beautiful, bare, clean hand, that Sip started anxiously to speak to Catty, but saw that Perley sat quite still, and that her earnest eyes were full of sudden tears.

"You will not let me say, you know, that I am sorry for you. I have been trying all the evening. I can't come any nearer than this." This she said smiling.

"Look here!" said Sip; her brown face worked and altered. She said, "Look here!" again, and stopped. "That's nigh enough. I'll take that. I like that. I like you. Look here! I never said that to one of your kind of folks before; I like you. Generally I hate your kind of folks."

"Now that," said Miss Kelso, musing, "perplexes me. We feel no such instinct of aversion to you. As far as I understand 'my kind of folks,' they have kindly hearts, and they have it in their hearts to feel very sorry for the poor."

"Who wants their pity? And who cares what's in their hearts?"

Sip had hardened again like a little growing prickly nut. The subject and her softer mood dropped away together.

"Sip," said Perley, fallen into another revery, "you see how little I know—"

Sip nodded.

"About—people who work and—have a hard time."

"They don't none of 'em know. That's why I hate your kind of folks. It ain't because they don't care, it's because they don't *know;* nor they don't care enough *to* know."

"Now I have always been brought up to believe," urged Miss Kelso, "that our fac-tory-people, for instance, had good wages."

"I never complained of the wages. Hayle and Kelso couldn't get a cotton-weaver for three dollars a week, like a paper-factory I know about in Cincinnati. I knew a girl as worked to Cincinnati. Three dollars a week, and board to come out of it! Cotton-weaving's no play, and cotton-weavers are no fools."

"And I always thought," continued Miss Kelso, "that such people were—why, happy and comfortable, you know. Of course, I knew they must economize, and that, but—"

She looked vaguely over at the supper-table; such uncertain conceptions as she might hitherto be said to have had of "economizing" acquiring suddenly the form of thick, black molasses, a little sticky, to be sure, but tangible.

Sip made no reply, and Perley, suddenly aware of the lateness of the hour, started in dismay to take her leave. It occurred to her that the sticky stone-china dishes were yet to be washed, and that she had done a thoughtless thing in imposing, for a novel evening's entertainment, upon the scanty leisure of a worn-out factory-girl.

She turned, however, neither an entertained nor a thoughtless face upon Sip when she tried to rise from her chair. Catty had fallen asleep, with her dirty cheek upon the shining hand, from which the rings were gone. Her ugly lower lip protruded, and all the repulsive lines about her eyes came out. Her long fingers moved a little, as is often the way with the deaf and dumb in sleep, framing broken words. Even in her dreams, this miserable creature bore about her a dull sense of denial and distress. Even in her dreams she listened for what she never heard, and spoke that which no man understood.

"Mother used to say," said Sip, under her breath, "that it was the noise."

"The noise?"

"The noise of the wheels. She said they beat about in her head. She come home o' nights, and says to herself, 'The baby'll never hear in this world unless she hears the wheels'; and sure enough" (Sip lifted her face to Perley's, with a look of awe), "it is true enough that Catty hears the wheels; but never anything besides."

CHAPTER V

❧ Bub Mell

It was a March night, and a gray night, and a wild night; Perley Kelso stepped out into it, from the damp little stone house, with something of the confusion of the time upon her. Her head and heart both ached. She felt like a stranger setting foot in a strange land. Old, home-like boundary lines of things to which her smooth young life had rounded, wavered before her. It even occurred to her that she should never be very happy again, for knowing that factory-girls ate black molasses and had the cotton-cough.

She meant to tell Maverick about it. She might have meant many other things, but for being so suddenly and violently jerked by the elbow that she preserved herself with difficulty from a smart fall into the slushy street. Striking out with one hand to preserve her balance, she found herself in the novel position of collaring either a very old young child or a very young old man, it was impossible at first sight to tell which. Whatever he was, it was easy at first sight to tell that he was filthy and ragged.

"Le' go!" yelled the old young creature, writhing. "Le' go, I say, dern yer! Le' me be!"

Perley concluded, as her eyes wonted to the dark street, that the old young creature was by right a child.

"If yer hadn't le' go I'd 'a' made yer, yer bet," said the boy, gallantly. "Pretty way to treat a cove as doin' yer a favor. You bet. Hi-igh!"

This, with a cross between a growl of defiance and a whine of injury.

"Guess what I've got o' yourn? You couldn't. You bet."

"But I don't bet," said Perley, with an amused face.

"Yer don't? *I* do. Hi-igh! Don't I though? *You* bet! Now what do you call that? Say!"

"I call that my glove. I did not miss it till this minute. Did you pick it up? Thank you."

"You needn't thank me till you've got it, *you* needn't," said the child. "*I*'m a cove as knows a thing or two. I want ten cents. You bet I do."

"Where do you live?" asked Perley.

He lived down to East Street. Fust Tenement. No. 6. What business was it of hern, he'd like to know.

"Have you a father and mother?"

Lor yes! Two of 'em. Why shouldn't he?

"I believe I will go home with you," said Perley, "it is so near by; and—I suppose you are poor?"

Lor, yes. She might bet.

"And I can make it right about the recovery of the glove when I get there?"

"N-n-oo you don't!" promptly, from the cove as knew a thing or two. "You'll sling over to the old folks, I'll bet. You don't come that!"

"But," suggested Perley, "I can, perhaps, give your father and mother a much larger sum of money than I should think it best to give you. If they are poor, I should think you would be glad that they should have it. And I can't walk in, you know, and give your father and mother money for nothing."

"You give *me* ten cents," said this young old man, stoutly, "or what do you s'pose I'll do with this 'ere glove? Guess now!"

Perley failed to guess now.

"I'll cut 'n' run with it. I'll cut 'n' run like mad. *You* bet. I'll snip it up with a pair of shears I know about. I'll jab holes in it with a jackknife I've got. No, I won't. I'll swop it off with my sister, for a yaller yaggate I've got my eye on in the 'pothecarry's winder. My sister's a mill-gal. She'll wear it on one hand to meetin', an' stick the t'other in her muff. That's what I'll do. How'll you like that? Hi-igh! You bet!"

"At least, I can go home with you," said Perley, absently effecting an exchange between her glove and a fresh piece of ten-cent scrip, which the boy held up in the light from a shop-window, and tested with the air of a middle-aged counterfeiter; "you ought to have been at home an hour ago."

"Lor now," said this promising youth, "I was just thinkin' so ought you."

"What is your name?" asked Perley, as they turned their two faces (one would have been struck, seeing them together, with thinking how much younger the woman looked than the child), toward East Street, the First Tenement, and No. 6.

"My name's Bub. Bub Mell. They used to call me Bubby, for short, till I got so large they give it up."

"How old are you?"

"Eight last Febiverry."

"What do you do?"

"Work to the Old Stone."

"But I thought no children under ten years of age were allowed to work in the mills."

"You must be green!" said Bub.

"But you go to school?"

"I went to school till I got so large they give it up."

"But you go a part of the time, of course?"

"No, I don't neither. Don't you s'pose I knows?"

"What is that you have in your mouth?" asked Perley, suddenly.

Bub relieved himself of a quid of fabulous size, making quite superfluous the concise reply, "Terbaccer."

"I never saw such a little boy as you chew tobacco before," said Perley, gasping.

"You must be green! I took my fust swag a year and a half ago. We all does. I'm just out, it happens," said Bub, with a candid smile. "That's what I wanted your ten cents for. I smokes too," added Bub, with an air of having tried not to mention it, for modesty's sake, but of being tempted overmuch. "You bet I do! Sometimes it's pipes, and sometimes it's ends. As a gener'l thing, give me a pipe."

"What else do you do?" demanded Perley, faintly.

"What else?" Bub reflected, with his old, old head on one side. He bet on marbles. He knew a tip-top gin-sling, when he see it, well as most folks. He could pitch pennies. He could ketch a rat ag'in any cove on East Street. Lor! couldn't he?

"But what else?" persisted Perley.

Bub was puzzled. He thought there warn't nothin' else. After that he had his supper. "And after that?"

Lor. After that he went to bed.

"And after that?"

After that he got up and went in.

"Went in where?"

She must be green. Into the Old Stone. Spoolin', you know.

Did he go to church?

She might bet he didn't! Why, when should he ketch the rats?

Nor Sunday school?

He went to the Mission once. Had a card with a green boy onto it. Got so old he give it up.

What did he expect, asked Perley, in a sudden, severe burst of religious enthusiasm, would become of him when he died?

Eh?

When he died, what would become of him?

Lor.

Could he read?

Fust Primer. Never tried nothin' else.

Could he write?

No.

Was he going to school again?

Couldn't say.

Why didn't his parents send him?

Couldn't say that. Thought they was too old; no, thought he was too old; well, he didn't know; thought somebody was too old, and give it up.

Was this where he lived?

She must be green! Of course he did. Comin' in?

Perley was coming in. With hesitation she came in.

She came into what struck her as a very unpleasant place; a narrow, crumbling place; a place with a peculiar odor; a very dark place. Bub cheerfully suggested that she'd better look out.

For what?

Holes.

Where?

Holes in the stairs. *He* used to step into 'em and sprain his ankles, you bet, till he got so old he give it up. She'd better look out for the plaster too. She'd bump her head. She never saw nothin' break like that plaster did; great cakes of it. Here, this way. Keerful now!

By this way and that way, by being careful now and patient then and quite persistent at all times, Perley contrived to follow Bub in safety up two flights of villanous stairs and into the sudden shine of a low, little room, into which he shot rather than introduced her, with the unembarrassing remark that he didn't know what she'd come for, but there she was.

There were six children, a cooking-stove, a bed, a table, and a man with stooped shoulders in the room. There was an odor in the room like that upon the stairs. The man, the children, the cooking-stove, the bed, the table, and the odor quite filled the room.

The room opened into another room, in which there seemed to be a bureau, a bed, and a sick woman.

Miss Kelso met with but a cool reception in these rooms. The man, the children, the cooking-stove, the bed, the odor, and the woman thrust her at once, she could not have said how, into the position of an intruder. The sick woman, upon hearing her errand, flung herself over to the wall with an impatient motion. The man sullenly invited her to sit down; gave her to understand—again she could hardly have told how—that he wanted no money of her; no doubt the boy had had more than he deserved; but that, if she felt inclined, she might sit down.

"To tell the truth," said Perley, in much confusion, "I did not come so much on account of the glove as on account of the boy."

What had the boy been up to now? The sullen man darted so fierce a look at the boy, who sat with his old, old smile, lighting an old pipe behind the cooking-stove, that Perley hastened to explain that she did not blame the boy. Who could blame the boy?

"But he was out so late about the streets, Mr. Mell. He uses tobacco as most children use candy. And a child of that age ought not to be in the mills, sir," said Perley, warming, "he ought to be at school!"

O, that was all, was it? Mr. Mell pushed back his stooped shoulders into his chair with an air of relief, and Bub lighted his pipe in peace. But he had a frowning face, this Mr. Mell, and he turned its frown upon his visitor. He would like to know what business it was of hers what he did with his boy, and made no scruple of saying so.

"It ought to be some of my business," said the young lady, growing bolder, "when a child of eight years works all the year round in these mills. I have no doubt that I seem very rude, sir; but I have in fact come out, and come out alone as you see me, to see with my own eyes and to hear with my own ears how people live who work in these mills."

Had she? Mr. Mell smiled grimly. Not a pleasant job for a lady he should think; and uncommon.

"It's a job I mean to finish," said Miss Kelso, firmly. "The stairs in this house are in a shocking condition. What is—excuse me—the very peculiar odor which I notice on these premises? It must be poisonous to the sick woman,—your wife?"

It was his wife. Yes; consumption; took it weaving; had been abed this four month; couldn't say how long she'd hold out. Doctor said, five month ago, as nothin' would save her but a change. So he sits and talks about Florida and the South sun, and the folks as had been saved down there. It was a sort of a fretful thing to hear him. Florida! Good God! How was the likes of him to get a dyin' wife to Florida?

She didn't like strangers overmuch; better not go nigh her; she was kind of fretful; the children was kind of fretful too; sometimes they cried like as his head would split; he kept the gell home to look after 'em; not the first gell; he couldn't keep her to home at all; she made seven; he didn't know's he blamed her; it was a kind of a fretful place, let alon' the stairs and the smell. It come from the flood, the smell did.

"The flood?"

Yes, the cellar flooded up every spring from the river; it might be drained, he should think; but it never was as he heard of. There was the offal from the mills floated in; it left a smell pretty much the year round; and a kind of chill. Then they hadn't any drain, you see. There was that hole in the wall where they threw out dishwater and such. So it fell into the yard under the old woman's window, and made her kind of fretful. It made her fretful to see the children ragged too. She greeted over it odd times. She had a clean way about her, when she was up and about, the old woman had.

"Who owns this house?" asked Miss Kelso, with burning eyes.

The man seemed unaccountably reluctant to reply; he fixed the fire, scolded Bub, scolded a few other children, and shook the baby, but was evidently unwilling to reply.

Upon Perley's repeating her question, the sick woman, with another impatient fling against the wall, cried out sharply, What was the odds? Do tell the girl. It couldn't harm her, could it? Her husband, very ill at ease, believed that young Mr. Hayle owned the house; though they dealt with his lessee; Mr. Hayle had never been down himself.

For a sullen man, with a stoop in the shoulders, a frown in the face, seven children, a sick wife, and no drain-spout, Mr. Mell did very well about this. He grew even communicative, when the blaze in Miss Kelso's eyes went out, paled by the sudden fire in her cheek.

He supposed he was the more riled up by this and that, he said, for being English; Scotch by breed, you know; they'd named the first gell after her grandma,—Nynee; quite Scotch, ye see; she was a Hielander, grandma,—but married to England, and used to their ways. Now there was ways and ways, and *one* way was a ten-hour bill. There was no mistaking that, one way was a ten-hour bill, and it was a way they did well by in England, and it was a way they'd have to walk in this side the water yet—*w-a-l-k in y-e-t!* He'd been turned out o' mills in this country twice for goin' into a ten-hour strike; once to Lawrence and once up to New Hampshire. He'd given it up. It didn't pay. Since the old woman was laid up, he must get steady work or starve.

He'd been a factory operative* thirty-three years; twenty-three years to home, and

---

*Mr. Mell's "testimony" may be found in the reports of the Massachusetts Bureau of Labor.

ten years to the United States, only one year as he was into the army; he was forty-three years old. Why didn't he send that boy to school? Why didn't he drive a span of grays! He couldn't send the boy to school, nor none of the other boys to school, except as may-hap they took their turn occasional. He made it a point to send them till they was eight if he could; he didn't like to put a young un to spoolin' before he was eight, if he could help it. The law? O yes, there was a law, and there was ways of getting round a law, bless you! Ways enough. There was parties as had it in their hands to make it none so easy, and again to make it none so hard.

"What parties?"

Parties as had an interest in spoolin in common with the parent.

"The child's employers?"

Mr. Mell suddenly upon his guard. Mr. Mell trusted to the good feelin' of a young lady as would have a heart for the necessities of poverty, and changed the subject.

"But you cannot mean," persisted Perley, "that a healthy man like you, with his grown children earning, finds it impossible to support his family without the help of a poor baby like Bub over there?"

Mr. Mell quite meant it. Didn't know what other folks could do; he couldn't; not since the rise in prices, and the old woman givin' out. Why, look at here. There was the gell, twenty year old; she worked to weaving; there was the boy as was seventeen, him reading the picture paper over to the table there, he draws and twists; there was another gell of fifteen, you might say, hander at the harnesses into the dressing-room; then there was Bub, and the babies.

Counting in the old woman and the losses, he must have Bub. The old woman ate a powerful sight of meat. He went without himself whensoever he could; but his work was hard; it made him kind of deathly to the stomach if he went without his meat.

What losses did he speak of? Losses enough. High water. Low water. Strikes. Machinery under repair. Besides the deathly feelin' to the stomach. He'd been out for sickness off and on, first and last, a deal; though he looked a healthy man, as she said, and you wouldn't think it. Fact was, he'd never worked but *one whole* month in six year; nor he'd never taken a week's vacation at a time, of his own will an' pleasure, for six year. Sometimes he lost two days and a half a week, right along, for lack of work.* Sometimes he give out just for the heat. He'd often seen it from 110° to 116° Fahrenheit in the dressing-room. He wished he was back to England. He wouldn't deny but there was advantages here, but he wished he was back.

(This man had worked in England from 6 A. M. to 8 o'clock P. M., with no time allowed for dinner; he paid threepence a week to an old woman who brought hot water into the mills at noon, with which she filled the tin pot in which he had brought tea and sugar from home. He had, besides, a piece of bread. He ate with one hand and worked with the other.)

He warn't complainin' of nobody in particular, *to* nobody in particular, but he thought he had a kind of a fretful life. He hadn't been able to lay by a penny, not by this way nor that, considerin' his family of nine and the old woman, and the feelin' to the

---

*"We may here add that our inquiries will authorize us to say that three out of every five laboring men were out of employ."—*Statistics of Labor.*

stomach. Now that made him fretful sometimes. He was a temperate man, he'd like to have it borne in mind. He was a member of a ten-hour society, of the Odd Fellows, Good Templars, and Orthodox Church.[24]

Anything for him? No; he didn't know of anything she could do for him. He'd never taken charity from nobody's hands yet. He might, mayhap, come to it some day. He supposed it was fretful of him, but he'd rather lay in his grave. The old woman she wouldn't never know nothing of that; it was a kind of a comfort, that was. He was obliged to her for wishing him kindly. Sorry the old woman was so fretful to-night; she was oncommon noisy; and the children. He'd ask her to call again, if the old woman wasn't so fretful about strangers. Hold the door open for the lady, Bub. Put down your pipe, sir! Haven't ye no more manners than to smoke in a lady's face? There. Now, hold the door open wide.

Wide, very wide, the door flung that Bub opened to Perley Kelso. As wide it seemed to her as the gray, wild, March night itself. At the bottom of the stairs, she stood still to take its touch upon her burning face.

Bub crept down after her, and knocked the ashes out of his pipe against the door.

"Ain't used to the dark, be ye?"

No; not much used to the dark.

"Afraid?"

Not at all afraid.

Lor. He was goin' to offer to see her home,—for ten cents. *He* used to be afraid. Got so old he give it up.

Half-way home, Miss Kelso was touched upon the arm again; this time gently, and with some timidity. Sip Garth, with a basket on her arm, spoke as she turned; she had been out marketing, she said; getting a little beef for to-morrow's dinner; had recognized and watched her half up the street; it was very late; Miss Kelso was not so used to being out late as mill-girls were; and if she cared for company—

"I do not know that there is any reason why I should not be out as late as mill-girls are," mused Miss Kelso, struck by the novelty of the idea. But she was glad of the company, certainly; fell into step with the mill-girl upon the now crowded walk.

"This is very new to me," she said in a low voice, as they turned a corner where a gust of oaths met her like an east-wind and took away her breath.

"You'll see strange sights," said Sip, with her dogged smile.

She saw strange sights, indeed; strange sights for delicate, guarded, fine young eyes; but so pitifully familiar to the little mill-girl with the dogged smile! As familiar, for instance, as Maverick and Axminster carpets to Miss Kelso? Miss Kelso wondered.

The lights of the little town were all ablaze; shops and lounging-places full. Five Falls was as restless as the restless night.

"Always is," said Sip, "in a wind. Take a good storm, or even take the moon, and it's different. When mill-folks have a man to hate, or a wife to beat, or a child to drown, or a

---

[24]Aside from not being a drunk, Mr. Mell is a member of several respectable organizations. Ten-hour societies helped organize workers to push for shorter, ten-hour work days. Odd Fellows and Good Templars were secret men's societies that served both social and benevolent purposes, and the Orthodox Church probably refers to the Greek Orthodox Church.

sin to think of, or any ugly thing to do, you may notice, ten to one, they'll take a windy night; a dark night like this, when you can't see what the gale is up to, when you're blown along, when you run against things, when you can't help yourself, when nothing seems to be anybody's fault, when there's noises in the world like the engines of ten thousand factories let loose. You can't keep still. You run about. You're in and out. You've got so used to a noise. You feel as if you were part and parcel of it. I do. Next morning, if you've lost your soul,—why, the wind's down, and you don't understand it."

Sip's dark face lighted fitfully, as if the gusty weather blew its meaning to and fro; she gesticulated with her hands like a little French woman. It struck Perley that the girl was not far wrong in fancying that she could "do it over" at the Blue Plum.

But Perley saw strange sights. Five Falls in the gusty weather was full of them. Full of knots of girls in bright ribbons singing unpleasantly; of knots of men at corners drinking heavily; of tangles where the two knots met with discordant laughter; of happy lovers that one sighed over; of haggard sinners that one despaired of praying over; of old young children with their pipes, like Bub; of fragments of murderous Irish threats; of shattered bits of sweet Scotch songs; of half-broken English brogue; of German gutturals thick with lager; only now and then the shrewd, dry Yankee twang.

It was to be noticed of these people that the girls swore, that the babies smoked, that the men, more especially the elder men, had frowns like Mr. Mell.

"One would think," said Miss Kelso, as she watched the growing crowd, "that they had no homes."

"They have houses," said Sip.

They passed a dark step where something lay curled up like a skulking dog.

"What's that?" said Miss Kelso, stopping and stooping. It was a little girl,—a very little girl. She had a heavy bundle or a pail upon her arm; had been sent upon an errand, it seemed, and had dropped upon the step asleep; had been trodden on once or twice, for her clothes bore the mark of muddy feet.

"That's Dib Docket," said Sip. "Go home, Dib!" Sip shook her, not ungently.

The little thing moved away uncertainly like a sleep-walker, jostled to and fro by people in the street. She seemed either too weak or too weary to sit or stand.

"That's Dib Docket," repeated Sip. "That child walks, at her work in the mills, between twenty and thirty miles a day. I counted it up once. She lives three quarters of a mile from the factory besides. She's not so bright as she might be. It's a wicked little devil; knows more wickedness than you've ever *thought* of, Miss Kelso. No, you'd better not go after her; you wouldn't understand."

Women with peculiar bleached yellow faces passed by. They had bright eyes. They looked like beautiful moving corpses; as if they might be the skeletons among the statues that were dug against the face of day. Miss Kelso had noticed them since she first came out.

"What are they?"

"Cotton-weavers. You can tell a weaver by the skin."

Threading her way through a blockade of loud-speaking young people by the railroad station (there was always plenty going on at the station, Sip said), Miss Kelso caught a bit of talk about "the Lord's day." Surprised at this evidence of religious feeling where she was not prepared to expect it, she expressed her surprise to Sip.

"O," said Sip, "we mean pay-day; that's all the Lord's day we know much about."

There was an old man in this crowd with very white hair. He had a group of young fellows about him, and gesticulated at them while he talked. The wind was blowing his hair about. He had a quavering voice, with a kind of mumble to it, like the voice of a man with a chronic toothache.

"Hear him!" said Sip.

Perley could hear nothing but a jargon of "Eight hour," "Ten hour," "Labor reform," "Union," "Slaves and masters," "Next session," and "Put it through." Some of the young fellows seemed to listen, more laughed.

"Poor old Bijah!" said Sip, walking on; "always in a row,—Bijah Mudge; can't outgrow it. He's been turned out of half the mills in New England, folks say. He'll be in hot water in Five Falls before long, if he don't look out. But he's a lonesome old fellow,—Bijah."

Just beyond the station Sip suddenly stopped. They were in the face of a gay little shop, with candy and dry goods in the windows.

"And rum enough in the back room there to damn an angel!" said Sip, passionately, "and he will have her in there in five minutes! Hold on, will you?" She broke away from Miss Kelso, who "held on" in bewilderment.

A pretty girl was strolling up and down the platform of this place, with her hand upon the arm of a young fellow with a black mustache. The girl had a tint like that of pale gold about her hair and face, and large, vain, unhappy eyes. She wore blue ribbons, and looked like a Scotch picture.

Sip stopped at the foot of the platform, and called her. The girl came crossly, and yet with a certain air of relief too.

"What do you want, Sip Garth?"

"I want you to go home, Nynee Mell."

"Home!" said Nynee, with weak bitterness.

"Yes, home; it's better than this."

"It frets me so, to go home!" said Nynee, impatiently. "I hate to go home."

"It is better than this," repeated Sip, earnestly. "Come. I don't set up to be a preacher, Nynee, but I *do* set up that Jim's no company fit for a decent girl."

"I'm a decent girl," said poor Nynee, trying to toss her silly head, but looking about her with an expression of alarm. "Who said I wasn't?"

Sip's reply Miss Kelso lost. The two girls talked together for a few moments in low tones. Presently Nynee walked slowly away.

"Jim'll be cross to-morrow, if I give him the slip," she said, pettishly, but still she walked away.

"There!" exclaimed Sip, stopping where she stood, "that will do. Dirk! Dirk, I say!"

Dirk I say stopped too. He had been walking rapidly down the street when Sip spoke. He was a young man of perhaps twenty-five, with a strong hand and a kindly eye. He looked very kindly at Sip.

"I want you to go home with Nynee Mell," said Sip.

"I'd a sight rather go home with some others than Nynee Mell," said the kindly young man.

"I know what I'm about," said Sip. "I know who'll keep Nynee Mell out of mischief. Go quick, can't you?"

The kindly young man kindly went; not so quickly as he might, but he went.

"Who was that young man?" asked Miss Kelso, as they climbed the hill.

"Jim? A miserable Irishman, Jim is; hasn't been in Five Falls a month, but long enough to show his colors, and a devilish black mustache, as you see. You see, they put him to work next to Nynee; he must go somewhere; they put him where the work was; they didn't bother their heads about the girl; they're never bothered with such things. And there ain't much room in the alley. So she spends the day with him, pushing in and out. So she gets used to him and all that. She's a good girl, Nynee Mell; wildish, and spends her money on her ribbons, but a good girl. She'll go to the devil, sure as death, at this rate. Who wouldn't? Leastways, being Nynee Mell."

"But I meant the other young man," observed Miss Kelso.

"Him? O, that's Dirk Burdock; watchman up at the Old Stone."

"A friend of yours?"

"I never thought of it," said Sip, gravely. "Perhaps that's what you'd call him. I like Dirk first-rate."

Sip pointed out one other young man to Miss Kelso before they were quite at home. They were passing a dingy hall where the mission, Sip said, held a weekly prayer meeting. The young man came out with the worshippers. It was Mr. Garrick (said Sip), the new partner. He'd been in the way of going since he was in the dressing-room himself; folks thought he'd give it up now; she guessed it was the first time you'd ever caught the firm into the mission meeting; meaning no offence, however.

He was a grave man, this Mr. Garrick; a man with premature wrinkles on the forehead; with a hard-worked, hard-working mouth; with a hard hand, with a hard step; a man, you would say, in a hard place, acquired by a hard process; a man, perhaps, who would find it hard to hope, and harder to despair. But a man with a very bright, sweet, sudden smile. A man of whom Perley Kelso had seen or heard half her life; who had been in and out of the house on business; who had run on her errands, or her father's,—it made little difference—in either case she had never troubled herself about the messenger; but a man whose face she could no more have defined than she could, for instance, that of her coachman. Her eyes followed him, therefore, with some curiosity, as he lifted his hat in grave surprise at passing her, and went his way.

Perley counted the people that came out from the mission meeting. There were six in all.

"There must be sixty folks within sight," observed Sip, running her quick eye up and down the gaudy little street, "as many as sixty loafin', I mean."

Miss Kelso made no answer, and they reached and entered her own still, clean, elegantly trimmed lawn in silence.

"Now I've seen you safe home," said the mill-girl, "I shall feel better. The fact was, I didn't know but the boys would bother you; they're a rough set; and you ain't used to 'em."

"I never thought of such a thing!" exclaimed the young lady. "They all know me, you know."

"Yes; they all know you."

"I supposed they would feel a kind of interest, or respect—"

"What reason have you ever given them," said Sip in a low tone, "to feel any special interest or respect for you?"

"You are right," said Miss Kelso, after a moment's thought. "They have no reason. I have given them none. I wish you would come in a minute."

"Have I been saucy?"

"No; you have been honest. Come in a minute; come, I want you."

The lofty, luxurious house was lighted and still. Sip held her breath when the heavy front door shut her into it. Her feet fell on a carpet like thick, wild moss, as she crossed the warm wide hall. Miss Kelso took her, scarcely aware, it seemed, that she did so, into the parlors, and shut their oaken doors upon their novel guest. She motioned the girl to a chair, and flung herself upon another.

Now, for a young lady who had had a season ticket to the Opera every winter since she could remember, it will be readily conjectured that she had passed an exciting evening. In her way, even the mill-girl felt this. But in her way, the mill-girl was embarrassed and alarmed by the condition in which she found Miss Kelso.

The young lady sat, white to the lips, and trembled violently; her hands covered and recovered each other, with a feeble motion, as they lay upon her lap; the eyes had burned to a still white heat; her breath came as if she were in pain.

Suddenly she rose with a little crouch like a beautiful leopardess and struck the gray and green chess-table with her soft hand; the blow snapped one of her rings.

"You do not understand," she cried, "you people who work and suffer, how it is with us! We are born in a dream, I tell you! Look at these rooms! Who would think—in such a room as this—except he dreamed it, that the mothers of very little children died for want of a few hundreds and a change of climate? Why, the curtains in this room cost six! See how it is! You touch us—in such a room—but we dream; we shake you off. If you cry out to us, we only dream that you cry. We are not cruel, we are only asleep. Sip Garth, when we have clear eyes and a kind heart, and perhaps a clear head, and are waked up, for instance, without much warning, it is *nature* to spring upon our wealth, to hate our wealth, to feel that we have no right to our wealth; no more moral right to it than the opium-eater has to his drug!

"Why, Sip," rising to pick up the chess-table, "I never knew until to-night what it was like to be poor. It wasn't that I didn't care, as you said. I didn't *know.* I thought it was a respectable thing, a comfortable thing; a thing that couldn't be helped; a clean thing, or a dirty thing, a lazy thing, or a drunken thing; a thing that must be, just as mud must be in April; a thing to put on overshoes for."

And now what did she think?

"Who knows what to think," said Perley Kelso, "that is just waked up?"

"Miss Kelso?" said Sip.

"Yes," said Miss Kelso.

"I never knew in all my life how grand a room could be till I come into this grand room to-night. Now, you see, if it was mine—"

"What would you do, if this grand room were yours?" asked Miss Kelso, curiously.

"Just supposing it, you know,—am I very saucy?"

"Not very, Sip."

"Why," said Sip, "the fact is, I'd bring Nynee Mell in to spend an evening!"

An engraving that lay against a rich easel in a corner of the room attracted the girl's attention presently. She went down on her knees to examine it. It chanced to be Lemude's dreaming Beethoven.[25] Sip was very still about it.

"What is that fellow doing?" she asked, after a while,—"him with the stick in his hand."

She pointed to the leader of the shadowy orchestra, touching the *baton* through the glass, with her brown finger.

"I have always supposed," said Perley, "that he was only floating with the rest; you see the orchestra behind him."

"Floating after those women with their arms up? No, he isn't!"

"What is he doing?"

"It's riding over him,—the orchestra. He can't master it. Don't you see? It sweeps him along. He can't help himself. They come and come. How fast they come! How he fights and falls! O, I know how they come. That's the way things come to me; things I could do, things I could say, things I could get rid of if I had the chance; they come in the mills mostly; they tumble over me just so; I never have the chance. How he fights! I didn't know there was any such picture as that in the world. I'd like to look at that picture day and night. See! O, I know how they come."

"Miss Kelso—" after another silence and still upon her knees before the driving Dream and the restless dreamer. "You see, that's it. That's like your pretty things. I'd keep your pretty things if I was you. It ain't that there shouldn't be music anywhere. It's only that the music shouldn't ride over the master. Seems to me it is like that."

CHAPTER VI

❧ Mouldings and Bricks

"Maverick!"

"At your service."

"But Maverick—"

"What then?"

"Last year, at Saratoga, I paid fifteen dollars apiece for having my dresses done up!"

"Thus supporting some pious and respectable widow for the winter, I have no doubt."

"Maverick! how much did *I* think about the widow?"

"I should say, from a cursory examination of the subject, that your thoughts would be of less consequence—excuse me—to a pious and respectable widow, than—how many times fifteen? Without doubt, a serious lack of taste on the part of a widow; but, I fear, a fatal fact."

"But, Maverick! I know a man on East Street whom I never could make up my mind to look in the face again, if he should see the bill for santalina in those carriage cushions!"

---

[25]Ludwig van Beethoven (1770–1827) was a German composer. He is widely considered to have been a musical genius and one of the greatest composers who ever lived.

The bill was on file, undoubtedly, suggested Maverick. Allow her friend an opportunity to see it, by all means.

"Maverick! do you see that shawl on the arm of the *tête-à-tête?*[26] It cost me three thousand dollars."

Why not? Since she did the thing the honor to become it, she must in candor admit, amazingly.

"And there's lace up stairs in my bureau drawer for which I paid fifty dollars a yard. And, Maverick! I believe the contents of any single jewel-case in that same drawer would found a free bed in a hospital. And my bill for Farina cologne and kid gloves last year would supply a sick woman with beefsteak for this. And Maverick!"

"And what?" very languidly from Maverick.

"Nothing, only—why, Maverick! I am a member of a Christian church. It has just occurred to me."

"Maverick!" again, after a pause, in which Maverick had languished quite out of the conversation, and had entertained himself by draping Perley in the shawl from the *tête-à-tête,* as if she had been a lay-figure for some crude and gorgeous design which he failed to grasp. Now he made a Sibyl[27] of her, now a Deborah,[28] now a Maid of Orleans,[29] a priestess, a princess, a Juno;[30] after some reflection, a Grace Darling;[31] after more, a prophetess at prayer.

"Maverick! we must have a library in our mills."

"Must we?" mused Maverick, extinguishing his prophetess in a gorgeous turban.

"There; how will that do? What a Nourmahal[32] you are!"

"And relief societies, and half-time schools, and lectures, and reading-rooms, and, I hope, a dozen better things. Those will only do to start with."

"A modest request—for Cophetua,[33] for instance," said Maverick, dropping the shawl in a blazing heap at her feet.

"Maverick! I've been a lay-figure in life long enough, if you please. Maverick, Maverick! I cannot play any longer. I think you will be sorry if you play with me any longer."

Cophetua said this with knitted brows. Maverick tossed the shawl away, and sat down beside her. The young man's face also had a wrinkle between the placid eyes.

"Those will only do to start with," repeated Perley, "but start with those we must.

---

[26]A sofa for two persons, designed so that they might be able to converse face-to-face.

[27]Sybil was an ancient Greek prophet reportedly endowed with great wisdom and powers of divination.

[28]Deborah was an Old Testament prophet (Judg. 4 and 5) who inspired the Israelites to successfully attack their enemies the Canaanites.

[29]Another name for Joan of Arc (1412–1431).

[30]Juno was the chief Roman goddess and counterpart of Jupiter.

[31]Grace Horsely Darling (1815–1842) became a national hero in England when she and her father (a lighthouse keeper) made a daring sea rescue, saving the lives of several people.

[32]Inhabitant of India.

[33]Cophetua was a legendary medieval king known for his compassion and high sense of honor.

And, Maverick," with rising color, "some tenement-houses, if you please, that are fit for human beings to inhabit; more particularly human beings who pay their rentals to Christian people."

"It seems to me, Perley," said her lover, pleasantly, "a great blunder in the political economy of Hayle and Kelso that you and I should quarrel over the business. Why *should* we quarrel over the business? It is the last subject in the world that collectively, and as comfortable and amiable engaged people, *can* concern us. If you must amuse yourself with these people, and must run athwart the business, go to father. Have you been to father?"

"I had a long talk with your father," said Perley, "yesterday."

"What did he say to you?"

"He said something about Political Economy; he said something else about Supply and Demand. He said something, too, about the State of the Market."

"He said, in short, that we cannot afford any more experiments in philanthropy on this town of Five Falls?"

"He said, in short, just that."

"He said, undoubtedly, the truth. It would be out of the question. Why, we ran the works at a dead loss half of last year; kept the hands employed, and paid their wages regularly, when the stock was a drug in the market and lay like lead on our hands. Small thanks we get for that from the hands, or—you."

"Your machinery, I suppose, would not have been improved by lying unused?" observed Perley, quietly.

"It would have been injured, I presume."

"And it *has* been found worth while, from a business point of view, to retain *employés* even at a loss, rather than to scatter them?"

"It has been, perhaps," admitted Maverick, uneasily. "One would think, however, Perley, that you thought me destitute of common humanity, just because you *cannot* understand the ins and outs of the thousand and one questions which perplex a business man. I own that I do not find these people as much of a diversion as you do, but I protest that I do not abuse them. They go about their business, and I go about mine. Master and man meet on business grounds, and business grounds alone. Bub Mell and a young lady with nothing else to do may meet, without doubt, upon religious grounds; upon the highest religious grounds."

"These improvements which I suggest," pursued Perley, waving Maverick's last words away with her left hand (it was without ornament and had a little bruise upon one finger), "have been successful experiments, all of them, in other mills; most of them in the great Pacific. Look at the great Pacific!"

"The great Pacific can afford them," said Maverick, shortly. "That's the way with our little country mills always. If we don't bankrupt ourselves by reflecting every risk that the great concerns choose to run, some soft-hearted and soft-headed philanthropist pokes his finger into our private affairs, and behold, there's a hue and cry over us directly."

"For a little country mill," observed Perley, making certain figures in the air with her bruised white finger, "I think, if I may judge from my own income, that a library and a reading-room would not bankrupt us, at least this year. However, if Hayle and Kelso cannot afford some few of these little alterations, I think their silent partner can."

"Very well," laughed Maverick; "we'll make the money and you may spend it."

"Maverick Hayle," said Perley, after a silence, "do you know that every law of this State which regulates the admission of children into factories is broken in your mills?"

"Ah?" said Maverick.

"I ask," insisted Perley, "if you know it?"

"Why, no," said Maverick, with a smile; "I cannot say that I know it exactly. I know that nobody not behind the scenes can conceive of the dodges these people invent to scrape and screw a few dollars, more or less, out of their children. As a rule, I believe the more they earn themselves the more they scrape and screw. I know how they can lie about a child's age. Turn a child out of one mill for his three months' schooling, and he's in another before night, half the time. Get him fairly to school, and I've known three months' certificates begged or bribed out of a school-mistress at the end of three weeks. Now, what can I do? You can't expect a mill-master to have the time, or devote it to running round the streets compelling a few Irish babies to avail themselves of the educational privileges of this great and glorious country!"

"That is a thing," observed Perley, "that I can look after in some measure, having, as you noticed, nothing else to do."

"That is a thing," said Maverick, sharply, "which I desire, Perley, that you will let alone. I must leave it to the overseers, or we shall be plunged into confusion worse confounded. That is a thing which I must insist upon it that you do not meddle with."

Perley flushed vividly. The little scar upon her finger flushed too. She raised it to her lips as if it pained her.

"There is reason," urged Maverick;—"there is reason in all things, even in a young lady's fancies. Just look at it! You run all over Five Falls alone on a dark night, very improperly, to hear mill-people complain of their drains, and—unrebuked by you—of their master. You come home and break your engagement ring and cut your finger. Forthwith you must needs turn my mill-hands into lap-dogs, and feed them on—what was it? roast beef?—out of your jewelry-box!"

"I do not think," said Perley, faintly smiling, "that you understand, Maverick."

"I do *not* think I understand," said Maverick.

"You do not understand," repeated Perley, firmly but faintly still. "Maverick! Maverick! if you cannot understand, I am afraid we shall both be very sorry!"

Perley got up and crossed the room two or three times. There was a beautiful restlessness about her which Maverick, leaning back upon the *tête-à-tête,* with his mustache between his fingers, noted and admired.

"I cannot tell you," pursued Perley in a low voice, "how the world has altered to me, nor how I have altered to myself, within the past few weeks. I have no words to say how these people seem to me to have been thrust upon my hands,—as empty, idle, foolish hands, God knows, as ever he filled with an unsought gift!"

"Now I thought," mentioned Maverick, gracefully, "that both the people and the hands did well enough as they were."

Perley spread out the shining hands, as if in appeal or pain, and cried out, as before, "Maverick! Maverick!" but hardly herself knowing, it seemed, why she cried.

"One would think," pursued Maverick, with a jerk at his mustache, "to hear and to see you, Perley, that there were no evils in the country but the evils of the factory system;

that there was no poverty but among weavers earning ten dollars a week. Questions which political economists spend life in disputing, you expect a mill-master—"

"Who doesn't care a fig about them," interrupted Perley.

"Who doesn't care a fig about them," admitted the mill-master, "you are right; between you and me, you are right; who doesn't care a fig about them—to settle. Now there's father; he is *au fait*[34] in all these matters; has a theory for every case of whooping-cough,—and a mission school. Once for all, I must beg to have it understood that I turn you and the State committees over to father. You should hear him talk to a State committee!"

"And yet," said Perley, sadly, "your father and you tie my hands to precisely the same extent by different methods."

"No?" said Maverick, "really?"

"He with Adam Smith,[35] and you with a *tête-à-tête*. He is too learned, and you are too lazy. I have not been educated to reason with him, and I suppose I am too fond of you to deal with you," said the young lady. "But, Maverick, there *is* something in this matter which neither of you touch. There is *something* about the relations of rich and poor, of master and man, with which the state of the market has nothing whatever to do. There is *something,*—a claim, a duty, a puzzle, it is all too new to me to know what to call it,—but I am convinced that there is *something* at which a man cannot lie and twirl his mustache forever."

Being a woman, and having no mustache to twirl, urged Maverick, nothing could well be more natural than that she should think so. An appropriate opinion, and very charmingly expressed. Should he order the horses at half past ten?

"Maverick!" cried Perley, thrusting out her hands as before, and as before hardly knowing, it seemed, why she cried,—"Maverick, Maverick!"

Possibly it was a week later that the new partner called one evening upon Miss Kelso.

He was there, he said, at the request of Mr. Hayle the junior; was sorry to introduce business into a lady's parlor; but there was a little matter about the plans—

"Ah, yes," said Miss Kelso, hastily, "plans of the new mill?"

"A plan for the new mill; yes. Mr. Hayle desired your opinion about some mouldings, I believe; and, as I go in town to-morrow to meet an appointment with the architect, it fell to my lot to confer with you. Mr. Hayle desired me to express to you our wish—I think he said our wish—that any preference you might have in the ornamentation of the building should be rigidly regarded."

"Very thoughtful in Mr. Hayle," said Perley, "and characteristic. Sit down, if you please, Mr. Garrick."

He was a grave man, this Mr. Garrick; if there were a biting breath in the young lady's even voice, if a curl as light as a feather fell across her unsmiling mouth, one would suppose that Stephen Garrick, sitting gravely down with mill plans in his hand, beside her, was the last man upon earth to detect either.

---

[34]Fully competent.

[35]Adam Smith (1723–1790) was a Scottish philosopher and economist who sought to explain the relationship between individual and institutional responsibility in economic and political affairs.

"Now," said Miss Kelso, pulling towards her across the table a marvellous green mill on a gray landscape, with full-grown umber shade-trees where a sand heap rightfully belonged, and the architect's name on a sign above the counting-room, "what is this vital question concerning which Mr. Hayle desires my valuable opinion?"

"The question is, whether you would prefer that the mouldings—here is a section; you can see the design better about this door—should be of Gloucester granite or not."

"Or what?" asked Perley.

"Or not," said Mr. Garrick, smiling.

"I never saw you smile before," said Miss Kelso, abruptly, tossing away the plans. "I did not know that you could. It is like—"

"What is it like?" asked Stephen Garrick, smiling again.

"It is like making a burning-glass out of a cast-iron stove. Excuse me. That mill has tumbled over the edge of the table, Mr. Garrick. Thank you. Is Gloucester granite of a violet tint?"

"Outside of an architect's privileged imagination, not exactly. What shall I tell Mr. Hayle?"

"You may tell Mr. Hayle that I do not care whether the mouldings are of Gloucester granite or of green glass. No; on the whole, I will tell him myself.

"You see, Mr. Garrick," said Miss Kelso after an awkward pause, "when you are a woman and a silent partner, it is only the mouldings of a matter that fall to you."

Mr. Garrick saw.

"And so," piling up the plans upon the table thoughtfully, "you become a little sensitive upon the subject of mouldings. You would so much rather be a brick-maker!"

"I suppose," said Stephen Garrick, "that I have been what you would call a brick-maker."

"I suppose you have," said Miss Kelso, still thoughtfully. "Mr. Garrick?"

Mr. Garrick lifted his grave face inquiringly.

"I suppose you know what it is to be very poor?"

"Very poor."

"And now you will be very rich. That must be a singular life!"

"It is in some respects a dangerous life, Miss Kelso."

"It is in other respects a privileged life, Mr. Garrick."

"It is proverbial of men with my history," said Garrick, slowly,—"men who have crawled on their hands and knees from the very quagmires of life,—men who know, as no other men can know, that the odds are twenty to one when a poor man makes a throw in the world's play—"

"Are they?" interrupted the lady.

"Twenty to one," said Stephen Garrick, in a dry statistical tone, "against poverty, always. It is proverbial, I say, that men who know as God knows that it is by 'him who hath no money' that the upright, downright, unmistakable miseries of life are drained to the dregs,—that such men prove to be the hardest of masters and the most conservative of social reformers. It has been the fancy of my life, I may say that it has been more like a passion than a fancy," said the *parvenu*[36] in Hayle and Kelso, laying his hard hand

---

[36]One who has suddenly risen to an unaccustomed position of wealth or power.

hardly clenched upon the colored plates that Perley had piled up beside him, "as fast and as far as I got out of the mud myself to bring other people with me. I cannot find any dainty words in which to put this, Miss Kelso, for it is a very muddy thing to be poor."

"I have thought it—but very lately—to be a hard thing," said Perley.

The hard lines about Stephen Garrick's mouth worked, but he said nothing. Perley, looking up suddenly, saw what hard lines they were; and when he met her look he smiled, and she thought what a pleasant smile it was.

"Mr. Garrick, do you think it is possible,—this thing of which you speak? Possible to be Hayle and Kelso, and yet to pick people out of the mud?"

"I believe it to be *possible.*"

"You are not in an easy position, it strikes me, Mr. Garrick."

"It strikes me—I beg your pardon—that you are not in another, Miss Kelso."

Stephen Garrick took his leave with this; wisely, perhaps; would have taken his leave with a gravely formal bow, but that Miss Kelso held out to him a sudden, warm, impulsive woman's hand.

Walking home with his pile of colored plans under his arm, Mr. Garrick fell in with two of the mill-people, the young watchman Burdock and a girl whom he did not recognize. He said, What a pleasant evening for a walk it was! as he went by them, cheerily.

"It's nothing to say 'A pleasant evening,' I know," said Dirk as he passed them; "but it's a way I like about Mr. Garrick. A man thinks better of himself for it; feels as if he was somebody—almost. I mean to be somebody yet, Sip."

"Do you?" said Sip, with a patient smile. He said it so often! She had so little faith that he would ever do any more than say it.

"It's a hard rut to wrench out of, Dirk,—the mills. How many folks I've seen try to get out of the mills! They always came back."

"But they don't always come back, Sip. Look at Stephen Garrick."

"Yes, yes," said Sip patiently, "I know they don't always come back, and I've looked at Stephen Garrick; but the folks as I knew came back. I'd go back. I know I should."

"It would be never you that would go back," urged Dirk, anxiously. "You're the last girl I know for that."

Sip shook her head. "It's in the blood, maybe. I know I should go back. What a kind of a pleasantness there *is* about the night, Dirk!"

There was somehow a great pleasantness to Sip about the nights when she had a walk with Dirk; she neither understood nor questioned how; not a passion, only a pleasantness; she noticed that the stars were out; she was apt to hear the tiny trail of music that the cascades made above the dam; she saw twice as many lighted windows with the curtains up as she did when she walked alone; if the ground were wet, it did did not trouble her; if the ground were dry, it had a cool touch upon her feet; if there were a geranium anywhere upon a window-sill, it pleased her; if a child laughed, she liked the sound; if Catty had been lost since supper, she felt sure that they should find her at the next corner; if she had her week's ironing to do when she got home, she forgot it; if a rough word sprang to her lips, it did not drop; if her head ached, she smiled; if a boy twanged a jew's-harp, she could have danced to it; if poor little Nynee Mell flitted jealously by with Jim, in her blue ribbons, she could sit down and cry softly over her,—such a gentleness there was about the night.

It was only pleasantness and gentleness that ever lay between her and Dirk. Sip never flushed or frowned, never pouted or coquetted at her sparse happiness; it might be said that she never hoped or dreamed about it; it might even be that the doggedness of her little brown face came over it or into it, and that it was not without a purpose that she neither dreamed nor hoped. Miss Kelso sometimes wondered. Dirk dully perplexed himself about her now and then.

"I wish," said Sip, as they came into the yard of the damp stone house, "that you'd look in at the window for me a minute, Dirk."

"What shall I look at?" said Dirk, stepping up softly to the low sill, *"her?"*

Catty was in view from the window; sitting on the floor with her feet crossed, stringing very large yellow beads; she did this slowly, and with some hesitation; now and then a kind of ill-tempered fright seemed to fall upon her repulsive face; once or twice she dropped the toys, and once she dashed them with a little snarl like an annoyed animal's upon her lap.

"I give them to her to try her," whispered Sip. "Do you see anything about her that is new? anything, Dirk, that you never took a notice of before?"

"Why, no," said Dirk, "I don't see nothin' uncommon. What's the matter?"

"Nothing! It's nothing only a fear I had. Never mind!"

Sip drew a sudden long breath, and turned away.

Now it was pleasant to Sip to share even a fear with Dirk.

"Look in again," she said, with a low laugh, "over on the wall beyond Catty. Look what is hanging on the wall."

"O, that big picture over to the left of the chiny-closet?" Dirk pointed to the Beethoven dreaming wildly in the dingy little room.

"A little to the left of the cupboard,—yes. One night I walked in and found it, Dirk! She hung it there for me to walk in and find. I laid awake till three o'clock next morning, I laid and looked at it. I don't know anybody but you, Dirk, as could guess what a strangeness and a forgetting it makes about the room."

Now it was very new to Sip to have a "forgetting" that she could share with even Dirk.

"It looks like the Judgment Day," said Dirk, looking over Catty's head at the plunging dream and the solitary dreamer.

There chanced that night two uncommon occurrences; for one, the watchman at the Old Stone was sleepy; for another, Miss Kelso was not.

The regulations in Hayle and Kelso were inexorable at night. Two fires and three drunken watchmen within the limits of a year had put it out of the question to temper justice with mercy. To insure the fidelity of the watch, he was required to strike the hour with the factory bell from nine at night till four o'clock in the morning.

Now upon the night in question Miss Kelso's little silver clock struck twelve, but the great tongue of the Old Stone did not. In perhaps twenty minutes, Old Stone woke up with a jerk, and rang in the midnight stoutly.

To be exact, I should have said that there chanced that night three uncommon occurrences. For that a young lady should get up on a chilly and very dark spring midnight, dress herself, steal down stairs, unlock the front door, and start off alone to walk a quarter of a mile, and save a sleepy young watchman from disgrace, is not, it must be allowed, so characteristic an event as naturally to escape note.

It happened, furthermore, that it did not escape the note of the new partner, coming out on precisely the same errand at the same time. They met at the lady's gate: she just passing through, he walking rapidly by; she with a smile, he with a start.

"Miss Kelso!"

"Mr. Garrick?"

"Is anything wrong?"

"With the watchman? Yes, or will be. I had hoped I was the only person who knew that midnight came in at twenty minutes past twelve."

"And I had hoped that I was."

"It was very thoughtful in you, Mr. Garrick," said Perley, heartily,

He did not say that it was thoughtful in her. He turned and looked at her as she stood shivering and smiling, with her hand upon the gate,—the bare hand on which the bruise had been. He would have liked to say what he thought it, but it struck him as a difficult thing to do. Graceful words came so hardly to him; he felt this hardly at the moment.

"I suppose I must leave the boy to you then," said Perley, slowly.

"You are taking cold," said the mill-master, in his hard way. It was very dark where they stood, yet not so dark but that he could see, in bowing stiffly, how Miss Kelso, with her bruised hand upon the gate, shot after him a warm, sweet, impulsive woman's smile.

Dirk was sitting ruefully upon an old boiler in the mill-yard. He rubbed his eyes when Mr. Garrick came up. When he saw who it was, the boy went white to the lips.

"Burdock, the bell was not struck to-night at twelve o'clock."

"Certainly, sir," said Dirk, desperately making his last throw.

"Not at twelve o'clock."

"Punctually, sir, you may be sure; I never missed a bell in Hayle and Kelso yet."

"The bell rang," observed Mr. Garrick, with quiet sternness, "at twenty-one minutes past midnight, exactly."

"Mr. Garrick—" begged the watchman, but stammered and stopped.

"Of course you know the consequences," said the master, more gently, sitting down upon the rusty boiler beside the man, "of a miss in the bell,—of a single miss in a bell."

"I should think I'd been in Hayle and Kelso long enough to know," said Dirk, with his head between his knees. "Mr. Garrick, upon my word and honor, I never slept on watch before. I was kind of beat out to-night." The truth was, that Dirk had been carrying in coal for Sip half the afternoon. "Hadn't so much sleep as common to-day; but that's no excuse for me, I know." He thought he would not say anything about the coal. "I wouldn't ha' cared so much about keepin' the place," broke forth the young man, passionately, "but for a reason I had,—I worked so hard for the place! and so long, sir! And, God knows, sir, I had such a reason for lookin' on to keep the place!"

"Infidelity on the part of a watchman, you see, Burdock," urged the master, "is not a matter that his employer can dally with."

"I'm no fool, sir," said the man; "I see that. Of course I look to lose the place."

"Suppose I were to offer to you, with a reprimand and warning, the trial of the place again?"

"Sir!" Dirk's head came up like a diver's from between his knees. "You're—your're good to me, sir! I—I didn't look for that, sir!"

Mr. Garrick made no reply, but got up and paced to and fro between the boiler and a little old, disused cotton-house that stood behind it, absorbed in thought.

"Mr. Garrick," said the watchman, suddenly, "did you get out of bed and come over here to save the place for me?"

"For some such reason, I believe."

"Mr. Garrick, I didn't look to be treated like that. I thank you, sir. Mr. Garrick—"

"Well?" said the master, stopping his walk between the boiler and the cotton-house.

"I told you the first lie, sir, that I've told any man since I lied sick to stay to home from the warping-room, when I wasn't much above that boiler there in highness. I think I'd not have been such a sneak, sir, but for the reason that I had."

It seemed that the master said "Well?" again, though in fact he said nothing, but only stood between the boiler and the cotton-house, gravely looking at the man.

"There's a—girl I know," said Dirk, wiping rust from his hands upon his blue overalls, "I don't think, sir, there's a many like her, I don't indeed."

"Ah!" said Stephen Garrick, restlessly pacing to and fro again, in the narrow limit that the boiler and the cotton-house shut in.

"I don't indeed, sir. And I've always looked to being somebody, and pushin' in the mills on account of her. And I should have took it very hard to lose the place, sir,—on account of her. There don't seem to be what you might call a fair chance for a man in the mills, Mr. Garrick."

"No, not what might be called a fair chance, I think," said Mr. Garrick.

"Not comparing with some other calls in life, it don't seem to me," urged Dirk, disconsolately. "The men to the top they stay to the top, and the men to the bottom they stay to the bottom. There isn't a many sifts up like yourself, sir. It's like a strawberry-box packed for market, the factory trade is. And when there's a reason,—and a girl comes into the account, it's none so easy."

"No, it's not easy, I grant you, Burdock. What a place this is to spend a night in!"

"A kind of a churchly place," said the young watchman, glancing over the cotton-house at the purple shadow that the mill made against the purple sky; and at purple shadows that the silent village made, and the river, and the bridge. "Takin' in the screech of the dam, it's a solemn place; a place where if a man knows a reason,—or a girl, he thinks o' 't. It's a place where, if a man has ever any longin's for things 't he can call hisn,—wife, and home, and children, and right and might to make 'em comfortable, you know,—he'll consider of 'em. It is a kind of a surprising thing, sir,—the feelin's that a man will have for a good woman."

"A surprising thing," said Stephen Garrick

CHAPTER VII

❧ Checkmate!

"I do not love you, Maverick Hayle."

May sweetness was in the breakfast-room; broken, warm airs from the river; a breath of yellow jonquils, and a shadow of a budding bough; on a level with the low window-sill a narcissus with a red eye winked steadily. The little silver service was in the breakfast-room, in sharp *rilievo*[37] against a mourning-dress and the curve of a womanly, warm arm. Maverick Hayle, struck dumb upon his feet, where he stood half pushing back his chair, was in the breakfast-room.

On either side of the tiny teapot the man's face and the woman's lay reflected; it was a smooth, octagonal little teapot, and the two faces struck upon it without distortion; hung, like delicate engraving, as if cut into the pretty toy. There was something very cosey and homelike about this senseless little teapot, and there was something very lonely and cold about the man's face and the woman's, fixed and separated by the wee width of the polished thing.

Both faces in the teapot were a trifle pale. Both faces out of the teapot were a trifle paler.

"It is not possible!" exclaimed the man, instinctively.

"It is quite possible," explained the woman, calmly.

His face in the teapot flushed now scorching red. Hers in the teapot only whitened visibly.

The young man flung himself back into his chair and ground his teeth. The young woman sat and looked at the teapot and trembled.

"I do not believe it, Perley!" said her plighted husband, fiercely.

"I do not love you, Maverick," repeated Perley, firmly. "I have been afraid of it for a long time. I am very certain of it now. Maverick, Maverick, I am very sorry! I told you we should both be very sorry! But you could not understand."

"If it was your foolish *furor*[38] over a parcel of factory-girls that I could not understand—" began Maverick.

But Perley sternly stopped him.

"Never mind about the poor little factory-girls, Maverick. It is *you* that I do not love."

This was a thrust which even Maverick Hayle could not lightly parry; he was fond of Perley and fond of himself, and he writhed in his chair as if it actually hurt him.

"I do not know how it is nor why it is," said Perley, sadly, "but I feel as if there had been a growing away between us for a great while. It may be that I went away and you stood still; or that we both went away and both in different ways; or that we had never, Maverick, been in the same way at all, and did not know it. You kissed me, and I did not know it!"

"And if I kiss you again, you will not know it," said Maverick, with an argument of smothered passion in his voice.

"I would rather," said the lady, evenly, "that you did not kiss me again."

Her face in the teapot shone as if a silver veil fell over it. His face in the teapot clouded and dropped.

"We have loved each other for a long time, Perley," said the young man in a husky voice.

"A long time," said Perley, sorrowfully.

"And were very happy."

---

[37]relief

[38]passion

"Very happy."

"And should have had—I had thought we should have had such a pleasant life!"

"A miserable life, Maverick; a most miserable life."

"What in Heaven's name has come over you, Perley!" expostulated the young man. "There is no other man—"

"No other man," said Perley, thoughtfully, "could come between you and me. I do not see, Maverick, how I could ever speak of love to any other man." This she said with her head bent, and with grave, far-reaching eyes. "A woman cannot do that thing. I mean there's nothing in me that understands how she can do it. I was very fond of you, Maverick."

"That is a comfort to me now," said Maverick, bitterly.

"I was fond of you, Maverick. I promised to be your wife. I do not think I could ever say that to another man. The power to say it has gone with the growing away. There was the love and the losing, and now there's only the sorrow. I gave you all I had to give. You used it up, I think. But the growing-away came just the same. I do not love you."

"You women do not understand yourselves any better than you do the rest of the world!" exclaimed the rejected lover with a bewildered face. "Why *should* we grow away? You haven't thought how you will miss me."

"I shall miss you," said Perley. "Of course I shall miss you, Maverick. So I should miss the piano, if it were taken out of the parlor."

Maverick made no reply to this. He felt more humiliated than pained, as was natural. When a man becomes only an elegant piece of furniture in a woman's life, to be dusted at times, and admired at others, and shoved up garret at last by remorseless clean fingers that wipe the cobwebs of him off, it will be generally found that he endures the annoyance of neglected furniture—little more. The level that we strike in the soul that touches us most nearly is almost sure to be the high-water mark of our own.

Now Maverick, it will be seen, struck no tide-mark in Perley. It had never been possible for him to say to the woman, "Thus far shalt thou go." Men say that to women, and women to men. The flood mistakes a nilometer[39] for a boundary line, placidly. It is one of the bittersweet blunders of love, that we can stunt ourselves irretrievably for the loved one's sake, and be only a little sadder, but never the wiser, for it.

Perley Kelso thus swept herself over and around her plighted husband; and in her very fulness lay his content. He would probably have loved her without a question, and rested in her, without a jar, to his dying day. A man often so loves and so rests in a superior woman. He thinks himself to be the beach against which she frets herself; he is the wreck which she has drowned.

Maverick Hayle, until this morning in the breakfast-room, had loved Perley in this unreasonable, unreasoning, and, I believe, irreclaimable masculine manner; had accepted her as serenely as a child would accept the Venus de Milo[40] for a ninepin.[41] One day the ninepin will not roll. There is speculation in the beautiful dead eyes of the marble. The game is stopped. He gathers up his balls and sits down breathless.

---

[39]A marked pillar used to measure water depth.

[40]Immensely valuable ancient statue of Aphrodite, carved around 150 B.C.

[41]A bowling pin.

"But you love me!" cries the player. "It *must* be that you love me at times. It must *be* that you will love me in moods and minutes, Perley. I cannot have gone forever out of all the moods and minutes of your life. I have filled it too long."

He filled it, forsooth! Perley slightly, slowly, sadly smiled.

"If there is any love in the world, Maverick, that ought to be independent of moods and master of all moods, it is the love that people marry on. Now I'm neither very old nor very wise, but I am old enough and wise enough to understand that it is only that part of me which gets tired, and has the blues, and minds an easterly storm, and has a toothache, and wants to be amused, and wants excitement, and—somebody the other side of a silver teapot—which loves you. *I* do not love you, Maverick Hayle!"

"In that case," said Maverick, after a pause, "it is rather awkward for me to be sitting here any longer."

"A little."

"And I might as well take your blessing—and my hat."

"Good by," said Perley, very sadly.

"Good by," said Maverick, very stiffly.

"You'll tell your father?" asked the young lady.

"We're in an awkward fix all around," said the young man, shortly. "I suppose we shall have to make up our minds to that."

"But you and I need not be on awkward terms,—need we?" asked Perley.

"Of course not. 'Mutual thing; and part excellent friends,' " bitingly from Maverick.

"But I shall always be—a little fond of you!" urged the woman, with a woman's last clutch at the pleasantness of an old passion.

"Perley," said Maverick, suddenly holding out his hand, "I won't be cross about it. I've never deserved that you should be any more than a little fond of me. You've done the honorable thing by me, and I suppose I ought to thank you."

He shut the door of the breakfast-room upon a breath of yellow jonquils, and a shadow of a budding bough, and the narcissus winking steadily; upon the little silver service, and the curving, womanly, warm arm, and the solitary face that hung engraved upon the senseless little teapot.

CHAPTER VIII

❧ A Troublesome Character

Old Bijah Mudge stepped painfully over a tub of yellow ochre and crossed the print-room at the overseer's beck. There had been an order of some kind, but he was growing deaf, and the heavy engines were on. The overseer repeated it.

"*Sir?*"

"I said your notice, didn't I? I say your notice, don't I? You'll work your notice, *you* will."

"A-a-ah!" said Bijah, drawing a long breath. He stood and knotted his lean fingers together, watching the yellow dye drop off.

"Is there a reason given, sir?"

"No reason."

"Folks my age ain't often ordered on notice without reason," said the old man, feebly.

"Folks your age should be more particular how they give satisfaction," said the overseer, significantly.

"I've known o' cases as where a boss has guessed at a reason, on his own hook, you know, Jim."

Irish Jim was in the print-rooms at Hayle and Kelso at that time. Some said the new partner had a finger in getting him out of the weaving-room. It was a sharp fellow, and belonged somewhere. Here he would be brutal to old men and little boys; but there were no girls in the print-room.

"On his own hook and at a guess," said the "boss," "a man might ask who testified to Boston on a recent little hour-bill as we know of."

"*I* testified," cried the old man, shrilly, "before a committee of the Legislature of the State of Massachusetts. I'd do it ag'in, Jim! In the face of my notice, I'd do it ag'in! At the risk o' the poor-us, I'd do it ag'in! I call Hayle and Kelso to witness as I'd do it ag'in! In the name of the State of Massachusetts, I'd do it ag'in!"

"Do it again!" said Jim, with a brutal oath. "Who hinders you?"

"But there were no reasons!" added the overseer, sharply. "You fail to give satisfaction, that's all; there's no reasons."

"I am an old man to be turned out o' work sudden, sir." The thin defiance in Bijah's voice broke. He made an obsequious little bow to the Irishman, wringing his dyed hands dry, and lifting them weakly by turns to his mouth. "It's not always easy for an old man to get work, sir."

But Jim was at the other end of the print-room, having some trouble with the crippled tender, who always spilled the violet dye. The boy had cut himself upon a "doctor,"[42] it seemed, to-day. Bijah saw blood about, and felt faint, and slunk away.

"Can I have work?"

"What can you do?"

"Anything."

"Where from?"

"Five Falls."

"Hayle and Kelso?"

"Yes, sir."

"You talk like a man with a toothache."

"Ay? Folks has told me that before. An old habit, sir."

"You have been printing?"

"Yes, sir."

"For three months?"

"Just about, sir."

---

[42]A thin metal blade used to remove extraneous material from a fabric-printing machine cylinder.

"There's yellow ochre[43] on your clothes, I see."

"I've none better, sir. I—I'd not have travelled in my working-close if I'd had better; I'd not have done it once. But I'm an old man, and out of work."

"Your name is Bijah Mudge?"

"I'd not told you my name, sir."

"No, you'd not told your name; but you're Bijah Mudge. We've got no work for you."

"I am an old man, sir."

"You're a troublesome character, sir."

"I'm quite out of work, sir."

"You'll stay quite out as far as we're concerned. We've got no place for you, I say, on this corporation."

"Very well, sir," bowing with grim courtesy. "Good evening, sir. I can try elsewhere."

"O yes," with a slight laugh, "you can try elsewhere."

"It's a free country, sir!" cried the troublesome character, in a little spirit of his shrill defiance.

"O yes; it's a free country, without doubt; quite right. You'll see the door at your left, there.—Patrick! the door. Show the man the door."

"And this is the end on 't."

The old man said that to Perley Kelso three weeks later. He said it in bed in the old men's ward of the almshouse at Five Falls. There was a chair beside the bed.

The room was full of beds with chairs beside them. These beds and chairs ran in a line along the wall, numbered nicely. In general, when you had taken possession of your bed, your chair, and your number, and sat or lay with folded, thin hands and gazed about with weak, bleared eyes, and so sat or lay gazing till you died; you commanded such variety and excitement as consist in being bounded on both sides by another bed, another chair, another pair of folded hands, and another set of gazing eyes. Old Bijah's bed and chair stood the last in the line. So he lay and looked at the wall, when he said, "This is the end on 't."

He liked to talk, they said; talked a great deal; talked to the doctor, the paupers, the cat; talked to the chair and the wall; talked to Miss Kelso now, because she came between the chair and the wall; had talked since he was brought struggling in and put to bed with nobody knew what exactly the matter with him. He was dead beat out, he said.

He must have talked a great deal upon his journey; especially in its later days, since the earnings of the last "Lord's day" were gone; since he had travelled afoot and gone without his dinner; since he had taken to sleeping in barns and under fences, and in meadow-places undisturbed and wet with ebbing floods; since he had traversed the State, and ventured into New Hampshire, and come back into the State, and lost heart and gained it, and lost it again and never gained it again, and so begged his way back to

---

[43]pigment

his old shanty up the river, and been found there by Stephen Garrick, in a driving storm, dozing on the floor in a little pool of water, and with the door blown down upon him by the gale.

He had talked to the fences, the sky, the Merrimack, the sea when he caught a glimpse of it, the dam at Lawrence, and the Lowell bells, and the wind that sprang up in an afternoon, and gray clouds, and red sunsets, and the cattle on the road, especially, he said, to trees; but always rather to these things than to a human hearer.

"They listened to me," he said, turning shrewd eyes and a foolish smile upon his visitor. "They always listen to me. It's a free country and I'm a troublesome character, but they listen—they listen. It's a free country and there's room for them and me. I'm an old man to be turned out o' work. One night I sat down on Lawrence Bridge and said so. It was coming dark, and all the little trees were green. No, marm, I'm not out o' my head. I'm only a troublesome character out of work in a free country. The mill-gals they went by, but I'd rather tell the little trees. I hadn't eat no dinner nor no supper. It was dark ag'in the water and ag'in the sky; all the lights in the mills was blazin', and the streets was full; if I'd been a younger man I'd not have took it quite so hard, mebbe. A younger man might set his hand to this and that; but I've worked to factories fifty-six years, and I was very old to get my notice unexpected. I'm sixty-six years old.

"'We know you,' says they to me, 'we don't want you!' says they. Here and there, up to New Hampshyre and back ag'in, this place and that and t'other, 'We know you,' says they.

"So I set on Lawrence Bridge; there was cars and ingines come screechin' by; 'We know you,' says they; and the little trees held up like as it was their hands to listen. 'They know me,' says I, 'I'm a troublesome character out o' work!' There was a little Irish gal come by that night and took me home to supper. She lived in one o' them new little houses adown the road.

"There, there, there! Well, well, it's oncommon strange how much more cheery-like it is a talkin' to women-folks than it is to trees. And clearin' to the head. But you'd never guess, unless you was a troublesome character and out o' work, how them trees would listen—

"I like the looks of you setting up ag'in the chair; it makes a variety about the wall. You'd never know, onless you'd come to the end on 't, how little of what you may call variety there is about that wall.

"Now I remember what I had to say; I remember clear. I think I've had a fever-turn about me, and a man gets muddled now and then from talking to so many trees and furrests. There's a sameness about it. They're good listeners, but there's a sameness about 'em; and a lonesomeness.

"Now this is what I had to say; in the name of the State of Massachusetts, this is what I've got to say: I've worked to factories fifty-six years. I haven't got drunk not since I was fifteen year old. I've been about as healthy, take it off and on, as most folks, and I guess about as smart. I'm a moral man, and I used to be a Methodist class-leader. I've worked to factories fifty-six years steady, and I'm sixty-six year old, and in the poor-us.

"I don't know what the boys would say if they see me in the poor-us.

"I've married a wife and buried her. I've brought up six children and buried 'em all. Me and the bed and the chair and the wall are the end on 't.

"It kind o' bothers me, off and on, wonderin' what the boys would say.

"There was three as had the scarlet fever, and two as I lost in the war (three and two is five; and one—) there's one other, but I don't rightly remember what she died on. It was a gal, and kinder dropped away.

"I've worked fifty-six years, and I've earned my bread and butter and my shoes and hats, and I give the boys a trade, and I give 'em harnsome coffins; and now I'm sixty-six year old and in the poor-us.

"Once when I broke my leg, and the gal was sick, and the boys was in the tin-shop, and their mother she lay abed with that baby that kep' her down so long, I struck for higher wages, and they turned me off. There was other times as I struck for wages, I forget what for, and they turned me off. But I was a young man then, and so I sawed wood and waited my chances, and got to work ag'in, and bided my time, in the name of the State of Massachusetts.

"Now I've testified afore the Legislature, and I've got my notice; and away up in New Hampshyre they knew the yellow ochre on my close, and I couldn't get the toothache out o' my voice, and I wouldn't disown my honest name,—in the name of the State of Massachusetts, I wouldn't beg for honest work, unless I got it in my honest name,—and so I am sixty-six year old, and in the poor-us.

"Tell Hayle and Kelso,—will you?—that I'm sixty-six year old, and an honest man, and dead beat out and in the poor-us! Curse 'em!

"All the leaves o' the trees o' the State of Massachusetts knows it. All the fields and the rivers and the little clouds and the winds o' dark nights and the grasses knows it. I told 'em, I told 'em! And you'd never know how they listened—See here, marm. I'm no fool, except for the fever on me. I knew when I set out what I'd got to say. I'm no fool, and I never asked no favors from the State of Massachusetts. See here! A workingman, as is only a workingman, and as lives and dies a workingman, he'll earn enough to get him vittels, and to get him close, and to get him a roof above his head, and he genrilly won't earn much more; and I never asked it of the State of Massachusetts as he should. But now, look here! When I was to Boston on my journey, I picked up a newspaper to the depot, and I read as how a man paid forty thousand dollars for the plate-glass winders in his house. Now, look here! I say there's something out o' kilter in that Commonwealth, and in that country, and in that lot of human creeturs, and in them ways of rulin', and in them ways of thinkin', and in God's world itself, when a man ken spend forty thousand dollars on the plate-glass winders of his house, and I ken work industrious and honest all my life and be beholden to the State of Massachusetts for my poor-us vittels when I'm sixty-six year old!

"Not but what I've had money in the bank in my day, a many times. I had forty-six dollars laid by to once. I went into the dye-rooms that year, and my rubber boots was wore out. We stand about in dye, and it's very sloppy work, you know. I'd been off work and out o' cash, and so I tried to get along without; so I wet my feet and wet my feet, standing round in the stuff. So there was lung fever and doctors' bills enough to eat that bank account out as close as famine.

"Why wasn't I far-seein' enough to get my boots to the first place and save my fever? Now that's jest sech a question as I'd look to get from them as is them of property. That's jest a specimen o' the kind of stoopidity as always seems to be a layin' atween property and poverty, atween capital and labor, atween you settin' thar with yer soft ways and yer soft dress ag'in you, and me, and the bed, and the chair, and the wall, and the end on 't.

"How was I a goin' to get into that thar bank account forty mile away in East Boston? Say! You'd never thought on 't, would you? No, nor none the rest of you as has yer thousands, and the trust as thousands brings, and as would make no more of buyin' a pair o' rubber boots than ye would o' the breath ye draws. I was a stranger to town then, and it's not for the likes of me to get a pair of rubber boots on trust. So I'd had my lung fever and lost my bank account afore I could lay finger on it.

"So with this and that and t'other, I've come into my old age without a dollar, and I'm a troublesome character, and my boys are dead, and I'm in the poor-us, and I'm sixty-six years old.

"I won't say but there's those of us that lays up more than I did; but I will say that there's not a man of us that ever I knew to spend his life in the mills, and lay by that as would begin to keep him in his old age. If there's any such man, I'd like to see him.

"I tell you, marm, there's a many men and women in Hayle and Kelso, and there's a many men and women in a many factories of this here free country, as don't dare to testify afore a Legislature. When their testimony tells ag'in the interest of their employers, they don't *dare*. There's them as won't do it not for nobody. There's them as does it on the sly, a holdin' back their names onto the confidence o' the committee, out o' dread and fear. We're poor folks. We can't help ourselves, ye see. We're jest clutched up into the claws o' capital tight, and capital knows it, jest as well as we do. Capital says to us, 'Hold your tongue, or take your notice.' It ain't a many poor men as can afford to say, 'I'll take my notice, thankee!' *I* done it! And I'd do it ag'in! I'd do it ag'in! In the name o' the State of Massachusetts, I'd do it ag'in!"

Old Bijah lies for a while, with this, blankly gazing at the wall and at the visitor with the "soft dress ag'in her," and at the paupers, and at the cat. Now and then he shrewdly nods, and now and then he smiles quite foolishly, and now the rows of beds and chairs file into hickory-trees, he says, and lift up their leaves in the name of the State of Massachusetts, and listen—And now he sees the visitor again, and turns sharply on her, and the hickory-trees file off and wring their hands in going.

"I heerd the t'other day of a man as give thirty thousand dollars for a fancy mare!"

All the trees of the State of Massachusetts are filing out of the old men's ward of the alms-house at Five Falls now, and all in going wring their hands and listen—

"Thirty thousand dollars for a mare! Jest fur the fancy of the fancy creetur. Thirty thousand dollars for a mare!"

He lies quite still once more, till the last hickory hands have passed, wringing, out of the almshouse, and some one has shut the door upon them, and the visitor softly stirs in going after them. He notices that the visitor does not wring her hands, but holds them folded closely down before her as she stirs.

He cries out that he wonders what the boys would say, and that he give 'em harnsome coffins, and that she is to tell Hayle and Kelso, curse'em, as he's sixty-six year old, and out o' work, and in the poor-us; and when she opens the door in passing out, half the forests of New England jostle over her and jostle in, and fill the room, and stand and listen—

The visitor unclasps her hands on stepping into the heart of the southern storm; it may be fancy, or it may be that she slightly wrings them, as if she had mistaken herself for a hickory-tree.

"They are cold!" exclaims Stephen Garrick, who waits for her with an umbrella and an enigmatical face. He takes one of the hands upon his arm, and folds the other for her in her cloak. Apparently, neither the man nor the umbrella nor the action attracts her attention pointedly, till the man says: "It is a furious storm, and you will get very wet. What have you been about?"

"Feeling my way."

"I am afraid that is all you will ever do."

"I suppose that is all I can ever do."

"But that is something."

"Something."

"You are not expected to cut and carve a quarry with tied hands. You have at least the advantage of not being responsible for the quarry."

"Who can hold you responsible for a case like this? You are one of three, and, as you say, tied by the hands."

"That old man will hold me responsible to his dying day. Half our operatives will hold me responsible. Miss Kelso, I am one of those people of whom you will always find a few in the world, adjusted by fate or nature to a position of unavoidable and intolerable mistake and pain."

His face, through the gray of the growing storm, wears a peculiar and a patient smile which Perley notes; there being always something noteworthy about Stephen Garrick's smile.

"A position," he repeats slowly, "in which a man must appear, from force of circumstances, to pass the—the wounded part of the world by upon the other side. And I believe, before God, that I would begin over again in East Street tomorrow, if I could help to bind it up, and set it healthily upon its way!"

Perley believes he would, and says so, solemnly. She says too, very earnestly, that she cannot think it to be true that a man who holds to such a purpose, and who holds it with—she falters—with such a smile, can permanently and inevitably be misunderstood and pained. She cannot think it.

Stephen Garrick shakes his head.

"I suspect there always are and always will be a few rich men, Miss Kelso, who just because they *are* rich men will be forever mistranslated by the suffering poor, and I suspect that I am one of them. I do not know that it matters. Let us talk of something else."

"Of something else than suffering and poverty? Mr. Garrick,"—Perley turns her young face against the west, where the sultry storm is crouching and springing,—"why, Mr. Garrick! sometimes I do not see—in God's name I do not see—what else there can *be* to talk about in such a world as this! I've stepped into it, as we have stepped out into this storm. It has wrapped me in,—it has wrapped me in!"

The sultry rain wraps them in, as they beat against it, heavily. It is not until a little lurid tongue of light eats its way through and over the hill, and strikes low and sidewise against the wet clovers that brush against their feet, that Perley breaks a silence into which they fall, to say, in a changed tone, "It is not an uncommon case, this old man's?"

and that Mr. Garrick tells her, "Not an uncommon case"; and that she leaves him, nodding, at the corner of the road, and climbs the hill alone; and that he stands in the breaking storm for a moment there to watch her, brushing gilded wet clovers down about her as she climbs.

CHAPTER IX

⚬ A Fancy Case

The oculist shut the door. For a popular oculist, with a specialty for fancy cases, he looked disturbed.

A patient in waiting—a mild, near-sighted case—asked what was the matter with the girl.

"Why, the creature's deaf and dumb!"

"Not growing blind, I hope?"

"Incurably blind. A factory-girl, a charity case of Miss Kelso's. You know of Miss Kelso, Mr. Blodgett?"

Mr. Blodgett knew, he thought. The young lady from whom Wiggins bought that new house on the Mill-Dam. An eccentric young lady, buried herself in Five Falls ever since the old gentleman's death, broke an engagement, and was interested in labor reform, or something of that description.

"The same. Enthusiastic, very; and odd. Would send the girl to me, for instance; naturally it would have been a hospital case, you see. I have to thank her for a hard morning's work. There was a sister in the matter. She would be told then and there; a sharp girl, and I couldn't put her off."

Ah! Mr. Blodgett weakly sighs. Very sad! Worn out at the looms perhaps? He seemed to have heard that the gaslight is trying in factories.

"This is wool-picking, sir; a clear case, but a little extraordinary. There's a disease of the hands those people acquire from wool-picking sometimes; an ugly thing. The girl rubbed her eyes, I suppose. The mischief has been a long time in progress, or she might have stood a chance, which gaslight-work has killed, to be sure; but there's none for her here, none!"

Sip and Catty, in the entry, sat down upon the office stairs. Sip was dizzy, she said. She drew up her knees and put her face into her hands. She could hear the doctor through the door saying, "None for her!" and the near-sighted patient babbling pity, and the rumble of the street, as if it had been miles away, and a newsboy shrieking a New York wedding through it. A singular, painful, intense interest in that wedding took hold of her. She wondered what the bride wore, and how much her veil cost. Long bridal parties filed before her eyes, and flowers fell, and sweet scents were in the air. It seemed imperative to think about the wedding. The solid earth would reel if she did not think about the wedding. She clung to the banisters with both hands, lest she should not think about the wedding.

The newsboy shrieked the wedding out of hearing, and Catty touched her on the arm.

"Good God!" cried Sip. A whirl of flowers and favors shot like a rocket by and beyond her, and a ragged newsboy chased them, and all the brides were blind, and she thrust out her hands; and she was sitting in the entry on the stairs, and the wind blew up, and she had frightened Catty.

So she said, "There, there!" as if Catty could hear her, and held by the banisters and stood up.

Catty wanted to know what had happened, very petulantly; the more so because she could not see Sip's face. She had been very cross since the blur came over Sip's face.

"Nothing has happened," said Sip,—"nothing but a—pain I had."

"*I've* got the pain," scowled Catty. She put her hand to her shrunken eyes and cowered on the stairs, whining a little, like a hurt brute.

"Well, well," said Sip, on her fingers, stiffly, "very well. Stop that noise and come away, Catty! I cannot bear that noise, not for love's sake, I can't bear it. Come!"

They crept slowly down the stairs and out into the street. It was a bright day, and everybody laughed. This seemed to Sip very strange.

She tried to tie Catty's face up in a thick veil she had; but Catty pulled it off; and she took her hand upon her arm, but did it weakly, and Catty jerked away. She was quite worn out when they got to the depot and the cars, and sat with her head back and shut her eyes.

"What's the matter with the girl? Blind, ain't she?"

A curious passenger somewhere behind her said this loudly, as the train swept out of the station dusk. Sip turned upon him like a tiger. She could not remember that Catty could not hear. The word was so horrible to her; she had not said it herself yet. She put her arm about Catty, and said, "Don't you talk!"

"Dear, dear!" said the curious passenger, blandly, "I wouldn't harm ye."

"I hadn't told her," said Sip, catching her breath; "I hadn't gone away—by ourselves with the doors locked—to tell her. Do you think I'd have it said out loud before a carful of folks?"

Miss Kelso met her when she got home; looked at her once; put a quick, strong arm about her, and got the two girls into the carriage with the scented cushions immediately. Catty was delighted with this, and talked rapidly about it on her fingers all the way to the stone house. Sip pulled her hat over her eyes like a man, and sat up straight.

The little stone house was lighted, and supper was ready. The windows were open, and the sweet spring night airs wandered in and out. The children in the streets were shouting. Sip shut the window hard. She stood uncertainly by the door, while Catty went to take off her things.

"If I can do anything for you—" said Perley, gently.

Sip held up her hands and her brown face.

"Do you suppose," she said, "that you could—kiss me?"

Perley sat down in the wooden rocking-chair and held out her beautiful arms.

Sip crept in like a baby, and there she began to cry. She cried and cried. Catty ate her supper, and nobody said anything, and she cried and cried.

"My *dear!*" said Perley, crying too.

"Let me be," sobbed Sip,—"let me be for a minute. I'll bear it in a minute. I only wanted some women-folks to cry to! I hadn't anybody."

She sat down on the edge of the bed with Catty as soon as they were alone. She had dried her eyes to bear it now. Catty must understand. She was quite determined to have it over. She set her lips together, and knotted her knuckles tightly.

The light was out, but a shaft of wan moonlight from the kitchen windows struck into the closet bedroom, and lay across the floor and across the patch counterpane. Catty sat in it. She was unusually quiet, and her face indicated some alarm or uneasiness, when Sip held up her trembling hand in the strip of light to command her close attention, and touched her eyes. Catty put out her supple fingers and groped, poor thing, after Sip's silent words. Walled up and walled in now from that long mystery which we call life, except at the groping, lithe, magnetic fingers, she was an ugly girl.

Sip looked at her for a minute fiercely.

"I should like to know what God means!" she said. But she did not say it to Catty. She would not speak to Catty till she had wiped her dry lips to wipe the words off. Whatever He meant, Catty should not hear the words.

She tried, instead, to tell her very gently, and quite as if He meant a gentle thing by Catty, how it was.

In the strip of unreal light, the two hands, the groping hand and the trembling hand, interchanging unreal, soundless words, seemed to hang with a pitiful significance. One might have thought, to see them, how the mystery of suffering and the mystery of love grope and tremble forever after one another, with no speech nor language but a sign.

"There's something I've got to tell you, dear," said the trembling hand.

"For love's sake?" asked the hand that groped.

"For love's sake," said the trembling hand.

"Yes," nodded Catty, with content.

"A long time ago," said Sip; "before we went to Waltham, Catty, when you picked the wool—"

"And hurt my hands," said Catty, scowling.

"Something went wrong," said the trembling hand, "with your poor eyes, Catty. O your poor, poor eyes, my dear! All that you had left,—the dear eyes that saw me and loved me, and that I taught to understand so much, and to be so happy for love's sake! The poor eyes that I tried to keep at home, and safe, and would have died for, if they need never, never have looked upon an evil thing! The dear eyes, Catty, that I would have hunted the world over, if I could, to find pretty things for, and pleasant things and good things, and that I never had anything for but such a miserable little room that they got so tired of! The poor dear eyes!"

The shrunken and disfigured eyes, that had been such wandering, wicked eyes, turned and strained painfully in the half-light. Sip had said some of this with her stiff lips, but the trembling hand had made it for the most part plain to the groping hand. Catty herself sat and trembled suddenly.

When should she see the supper-table plain again? the groping hand made out to ask. And the picture by the china-closet? And the flies upon the window-pane?

"Never!" said the trembling hand.

But when should she see Sip's face again without the blur?

"Never! O Catty, never again!"

The trembling hand caught the groping hand to sting it with quick kisses. Sip could not, would not, see what the poor hand might say. She held it up in the streak of light. God might see. She held it up, and pulled Catty down upon her knees, with her face in the patch counterpane.

When Catty was asleep that night, Sip went out and got down upon the floor in the kitchen.

She got down, with her hands around her knees, in the wan lightness that fell about the picture behind the china-closet door. The driving dream seemed to fill the room. The factory-girl on the kitchen floor felt herself swept into it. Her lips worked and she talked to it.

"I could ha' borne it if it had been me," she said. Did the pictured women, with their arms up, nod as they drove wailing by? Sip could have sworn to it.

"We could have borne, if it had been we," they said.

"What's the sense of it?" asked Sip, in her rough way, half aloud. She had such a foolish way about that picture, often talking to it by the hour, upon the kitchen floor.

But the women only waved their arms and nodded solemnly. That which they could not know nor consider nor understand was in the question. They drifted over it with the helplessness of hopeless human pain.

"You're good for nothing," said Sip, and turned the picture to the wall.

She stumbled over something in doing this, and stooped to see what it was. It was an abused old book that Catty had taken once from the Mission Sunday School, and had never returned,—a foolish thing, with rough prints. Catty had thrown it under the table in ten minutes. It opened in Sip's hands now, by chance, at a coarse plate of the Crucifixion.

Sip threw it down, but picked it up again, lost the place, and hunted for it; bent over it for a few minutes with a puzzled face.

Somehow the driving dream and the restless dreamer hushed away before the little woodcut. In some way the girl herself felt quieted by the common thing. For some reason—the old, the unexplained, the inexplicable reason—the Cross with the Man upon it put finger on the bitter lips of Sip's trouble. She could not ask a Man upon a Cross, "What was the sense of it?" So she only said, "O my poor Catty! my poor, poor Catty!" and softly shut the foolish little book and went to bed.

Beethoven did not stay with his face to the wall, however. Sip took a world of curious comfort out of that picture; quite perplexed Perley, who had only thought in sending it to do a pleasant thing, who had at that time never guessed—how should she?—that a line engraving after De Lemude could make a "forgetting" in the life of a factory-girl.

"Sometimes now, when Catty is so bad," said Sip one day, "there's music comes out of that picture all about the room. Sometimes in the night I hear 'em play. Sometimes when I sit and wait for her, they sit and play. Sometimes when the floor's all sloppy and I have to wash up after work, I hear 'em playing over all the dirt. It sounds so clean!" said Sip.

"Is Catty still so troublesome?" asked Perley.

Sip's face dropped.

"Off and on a little worse, I think. The blinder she grows the harder it is to please her and to keep her still. I come home all beat out; and she's gone. Or, I try so hard to make her happy after supper, and along by nine o'clock she's off. She's dreadful restless since she left off workin', and gets about the street a'most as easy, for aught I see, as ever. She's so used to the turns and all; and everybody knows her, and turns out for her. I've heard of blind folks that was like her; she wasn't stupid, Catty wasn't, if she'd been like other folks. There's nights I sit and look for her to be run over and brought in. There's nights she gets at liquor. There's nights I follow her round and round, and follow her home, and make as if I sat there and she'd just come in. That's the worst, you see. What was that you said? No; I'll not have Catty sent anywhere away from me. There's no kind folks in any good asylum that would make it comfortable for Catty away from me. You needn't think,"—Sip set her tough little lips together—"you needn't think that you nor anybody could separate me and Catty. She's never to blame, Catty isn't. *I* know that. *I* can work. *I*'ll make her comfortable. It's only God in heaven that will separate me and Catty."

It was about this time that Miss Kelso attempted, in view of Sip's increasing care, a long-cherished plan of experiment in taking the girl out of the mills.

"It is not a girl to spend life in weaving cotton," said the young lady to Stephen Garrick. "That would be such exorbitant waste."

"There's waste enough at those looms," said Mr. Garrick, pointing to his mills, "to enrich a Commonwealth perceptibly. We live fast down there among the engines. It is hot-house growth. There's the difference between a man brought up at machinery and a man brought up at a hoe, for instance, that there is between forced fruit and frozen fruit. Few countries understand what possibilities they possess in their factory population. We are a fever in the national blood that it will not pay to neglect; there's kill or cure in us."

"What's the use?" said Sip, with sullen, unresponsive eyes. "You'll have all your bother for nothing, Miss Kelso. If I get away from my loom, I shall come back to my loom. Look at the factory-folks in England! From father to child, from children to children's children,—a whole race of 'em at their looms. It's in the blood."

"Try it," urged Perley. "Try it for Catty's sake, at least. There are so many ways in which it would be better for Catty."

"I should like it," said Sip, slowly, "to get Catty among some other folks than mill-folks. It seems as if I could have done it once; but it's too late now."

Now Sip was barely twenty-one. She said this with the unconscious assurance of fifty.

"I'd try anything for Catty; and almost anything for you; and almost anything to get out of the mills; but I'm afraid it's too late."

But Perley was persistent in her fancy, and between them they managed to "try it" faithfully.

Sip went out as somebody's cook, and burned all the soup and made sour bread. She drew about a baby's carriage for a day and a half, and left because the baby cried and she was afraid that she should shake it. She undertook to be a hotel table-girl, and was saucy to the housekeeper before night. She took a specimen of her sewing to a dressmaker, and was told that the establishment did not find itself in need of another seamstress. She stood behind a dry-goods counter, but it worried her to measure off calico for the old ladies. Finally, Perley put her at the printer's trade, and Sip had a headache and got inky for a fortnight.

Then she walked back to her overseer, and "asked in" for the next morning.

"I told you it was no use," she said, shaking her head at Miss Kelso, half whimsically, half sadly too. "It's too late. What am I fit for? Nothing. What do I know? Nothing. I can weave; that's all. I'm used to that. I'm used to the noise and the running about. I'm used to the dirt and the roughness. I can't sit still on a high stool all day. I don't know how to spell, if I do. They're too fussy for me in the shops. I hate babies. It's too late. I'm spoiled. I knew I should come back. My father and mother came back before me. It's in the blood."

Perley would have liked even then, had it seemed practicable, to educate the girl; but Sip shook her dogged head.

"It's too late for that, too. Once I would have liked *that*. There's things I think I could ha' done." Sip's sullen eyes wandered slowly to the plunging dream and the solitary dreamer behind the china-closet door, and, resting there, flashed suddenly. "There's things I seem to think I might ha' done with *that;* but I've lost 'em now. Nor that ain't the worst. I've lost the caring for 'em,—that's the thing I've lost. If I was to sit still and study at a grammar, I should scream. I must go back to the noise and the dirt. Catty and me must stay there. Sometimes I seem to think that I might have been a little different someways; if maybe I'd been helped or shown. There was an evening school to one place where I worked. I was running four looms twelve hours and a half a day. You're so dull about the head, you see, when you get home from work; and you ache so; and you don't feel that interest in an education that you might."

"Sometimes," added Sip, with a working of the face, "it comes over me as if I was like a—a patchwork bed-quilt. I'd like to have been made out of one piece of cloth. It seems as if your kind of folks got made first, and we down here was put together out of what was left.

"Sometimes, though," continued the girl, "I wonder how there came to be so much of me as there is. I don't set up for much, but I wonder why I wasn't worse. I believe you would yourself, if you knew."

"Knew what?"

"Knew what!" echoed the factory-girl. "Knew that as you know no more of than you know of hell! Haven't I told you that you *can't* know? You can't *understand*. If I was to tell you, you couldn't understand. It ain't so much the bringing up I got, as the smooch of it. That's the wonder of it. You may be ever so clean, but you don't *feel* clean if you're born in the black. Why, look here; there was my mother, into the mills off and on between her babies. There's me, from the time I run alone, *running* alone. She comes home at night. I'm off about the street all day. I learned to swear when I learned to talk. Before I'd learned to talk I'd seen sights that *you*'ve never seen yet in all your fine life long. That's the crock of it. And the wonder. And the talk in the mills—for a little girl to hear! Only eight years old—such a little girl—and all sorts of women working round beside you. If ever I'd like to call curses down on anybody, it's on a woman that I used to know for the way she talked to little girls! Why did nobody stop it? Why, the boss was as bad himself, every whit and grain. The gentlemen who employed that boss were professors of religion, all of them.

"But I've tried to be good!" broke off Sip, with a little sudden tremor of her bitter lip. "I know I'm rough, but I've tried to be a good girl!"

CHAPTER X

❧ Economical

There is something very pleasant about the town of Five Falls early on a summer morning.

There was something *very* pleasant about the town of Five Falls on one summer morning when Bub Mell got up at five o'clock to catch a rat.

To pluck a Five Falls morning in the bud, one should be up and in it before the bells,—like Bub. Until the bells are awake, there is a stillness and a cleanliness about the place that are noticeable; about the dew-laid dusty streets and damp sidewalks bare of busy feet; about the massive muteness of the mills; about the very tenements on East Street, washed and made shining by the quiet little summer shower that fell perhaps last night, like old sins washed out by tears; about the smooth, round cheek of the sky before the chimneys begin to breathe upon it; about the little cascades at play like babies upon the bosom of the upper stream; about the arches of the stone bridge, great veins, one thinks, for the pulsing dam; about the slopes of buttercups and clover which kneel to the water's edge with a reverent look, as if they knelt for baptism; about some groups of pines that stretch their arms out like people gone wearily to sleep. The pines, the clover slopes, the dam, the streets and houses, the very sky, everything, in fact, in Five Falls, except those babies of cascades, wears, upon a summer morning, that air of having gone or of having been wearily to sleep,—an air of having been upon its feet eleven hours and a half yesterday, and of expecting to be upon its feet eleven hours and a half to-day.

Bub has been awake for some fifteen minutes—he sleeps upon a mat, like a puppy, behind the door,—before he shakes himself a little in his rags (the ceremony of a toilet is one of Bub's lost arts; he can, indeed, remember faintly having been forcibly induced to take certain jerks at the street pump on mild mornings, at some indefinite past period of juvenile slavery, till his mother was nicely laid up out of the way in the bedroom, and he "got so old he give it up"), and trots down the wretched stairs, and out with the other puppies into the clean stillness of the early time.

The sick woman is troublesome this morning; there is a great deal of coughing and confusion going on; and the husband up since midnight. Bub finds it annoying to be broken of his sleep; suffers from some chronic sensitiveness on the dangers of being at hand to be despatched for the doctor; and finds in the rat at once an inspiration and a relief.

There is indeed peculiar inspiration in the case of that rat. Bub chuckles over his shoulder at himself as he trots out into the peaceful time; there is a large three-cornered jagged rag among Bub's rags; the rat bit it yesterday; it hangs down from his little trousers behind and wags as he trots. He put the rat into a hogshead[44] to pay for it; and

---

[44]A cask to hold liquids.

shut it down with that piece of board fence with which he provided himself last week (from Mr. Hayle's garden) for such emergencies. There is a richness about going to sleep overnight with the game for your morning's hunt in a hogshead, which is not generally appreciated by gentlemen of the chase. There is a kind of security of happiness, a lingering on the lips of a sure delight, a consciousness of duty done and pleasure in waiting, which have quite an individual flavor.

None the other coves know about that rat. You *bet*. Not much. Hi-igh.

Bub's right shoulder chuckles at his left shoulder, and his left shoulder chuckles at his right shoulder, and the jagged rag behind wags with delight. Won't he jab him now! Hi-igh, there. Hi-igh! See him! He thinks he's a goin' to cut 'n' run, does he? He must be green.

Away goes Mr. Hayle's board fence into the bean patch, and down goes Bub into the hogshead. There's a contest for you! All Bub's poor little puzzling soul is in his eyes. All his old young face—the only old young thing in the dawning time—is filled and fired. Won't he have that rat? Five hundred cascades might play upon the pure bosom of the river, and all the buttercups in Five Falls kneel for baptism,—but he'll have that rat.

The smooth, round cheek of the sky seems to stoop to the very hogshead, and lay itself tenderly down to cover the child and the vermin from the sight of the restful time.

Presently it begins to be very doubtful who shall cut 'n' run. And by and by it begins to be more than doubtful who must be green.

At one fell swoop of anguish, Bub finds his dirty little finger bitten to the bone, and himself alone in the hogshead.

Hi-*igh!*

Bub sits down in the bottom of the hogshead and grits his teeth. He doesn't cry, you understand. Not he. Used to cry when he got bit. And holler. But got so old he give it up. Lor. Ain't he glad none the other coves knows now. You bet. Hi-igh.

All the foreheads of the buttercups and clovers seem dripping with sacred water, when Bub lifts his little aged yellow face with the dirt and blood and tobacco upon it, over—just over—the edge of the hogshead to see what became of the rat. The cheek of the sky blushes a sadder red for shame. The sleepy pine-trees stretch their arms out solemnly towards the little fellow. The cascades are at play with each other's hands and feet. The great pulse of the dam, as sad as life, as inexorable as death, as mysterious as both, beats confused meanings into the quiet time.

"Lor," says Bub in the hogshead, looking out, half pausing for the instant with his gashed finger at his sly mouth,—"Lor, it's goin' to be a boozier of a day. I'll bet."

But the bells have waked, with a cross cry, and Five Falls starts, to stand for eleven hours and a half upon its feet. The peaceful time has slipped and gone. The pine-trees rub their eyes and sigh. The pulse of the dam throbs feverishly fast. The sun dries the baptismal drops from the heads of the buttercups and clovers. The dew-laid streets fill and throng; the people have dirty clothes and hurried faces; the dust flies about; the East Street tenements darken to the sight in the creeping heat, like the habit of old sins returned to darken a sad and sorry life; you see that there are villanous stairs and no drains; you hear coughing and confusion from the woman's bedchamber overhead. You see, too, that the spotless cheek of the sky is blackened now by the chimneys all about, and how still and patiently it lies to take the breath of the toil-worn town.

Only those tiny cascades play—eternal children—upon a mother's bosom; as if the heart of a little child, just for being the heart of a little child, must somehow, somewhere, play forever in the smile of an undying morning.

By means of stopping to have his finger bound, and of a search in the bean-patch for the rat, and of another search in the cellar for the rat, and of the delay occasioned by a vindictive kick or two at the hogshead, and by forgetting his breakfast and remembering it, and going back for it to find that it is all eaten, if indeed there has ever been any, which the confusion in the sick-room renders a probable theory, Bub is late this morning. Nynee was cross about the finger, too; pulled the thread and hurt him; wanted her own breakfast probably. Bub's little old face wears an extra shade of age and evil as he trots away to work, and he swears roundly by the way; swears loud enough to be heard across the street, for Mr. Garrick, on his way to the station, turns his head to look after the child. Bub shies away; has been a little skittish about Mr. Garrick, since they tried to put him to school and his father swore him off for ten years old. It is generally understood now in Hayle and Kelso that the firm occasionally pull in different ways; Mr. Mell knows where to trace any unusual disturbance of his family government which is calculated to arrest a child's steady stride to ruined manhood; everybody knows; Mr. Garrick is unpopular accordingly. He has his friends among his work-people, chiefly of the kind that do not easily come to the surface. The young watchman at the Old Stone is one of them, you may be sure. But he is not a popular master so far.

Bub, with his sly eyes, and tobacco-yellowed skin, and his pipe in his mouth, and the blood and dirt upon his clothes, and the little rag behind, and his old, old smile, trots away to the mills, whose open door has, to Mr. Garrick's fancy, an air of gaping after the child.

"As a prison-door will do in the end," muses Mr. Garrick.

He takes a note-book from his pocket, jotting something in it; about the child, perhaps. He has been making an estimate this week of the suffering and profligate children in his mills. There is scarcely a vice on the statute-book which he has not found in existence among the little children in those mills.

The leaf of the note-book turns, in closing, to recent entries, which run like this:—

"Said the chaplain of an English prison, after showing the cost of ninety-eight juvenile criminals to the State, in six years, to have amounted, in various ways, to £6,063 ($30,315): '*They have cost a sum of money which would have kept them at a boarding-school the whole time.*'

"Said the Honorable, the late Clerk of the Police of Fall River, Mass., in answer to an inquiry as to the number of children in that town peculiarly exposed to a life of crime:. . . . 'I should say, after consulting the docket of our Police Court, and inquiring as to the subsequent expenses, that the cost of such juvenile offenders as ultimately reach the State Prison would average two hundred and fifty dollars. We have had some who have cost much more than this; one as much as five hundred dollars.'"

Mr. Garrick glances over them with his peculiar smile, just as Bub and the little wagging rag disappear in the yawn of the mill-door.

There is another noticeable entry, by the way, in Mr. Garrick's note-book. It lies against little Dib Docket's name:—

"In H—— the Chief of the Police estimates the number of openly abandoned women at not less than seventy-five, besides an equal number of a less notorious and degraded class. 'They are,' said he, 'brought before the Police Court again and again. Most of them are under twenty years of age. They come from the country *and the man-ufacturing towns.* They are the children of drunken and vicious parents.'"

Bub dips into the mouth of the door and crawls up the stairs on "all fours," so much, so very much like a little puppy! He is a little afraid of his overseer, being so late. At the top of the stairs he loiters and looks down. In the blue distance beyond the windows, the cascades are just to be seen at their eternal play.

The machinery is making a great noise this morning. The girls are trying to sing, but the engines have got hold of the song, and crunch it well. Bub, on the threshold of the spooling-room, stops with a queer little chuckle like a sigh.

He wishes he needn't go in. It looks kinder jolly out. Lor! don't it? Would a'most go to school fur the sake uv gettin' out. But guesses he must be too old.

Won't that boss jaw this mornin'! He'll bet. Hi-igh!

The strain from down stairs struggles and faints as Bub goes in to work; as if the engines had a mouthful of it, and were ready for more.

The "boss" does "jaw" this morning. Bub expects it, deserves it, bears it, hangs his head and holds his tongue, glad, on the whole, that it is no worse. A cuff or a kick would not surprise him. The overseer is a passionate man, of a race of passionate men; an overseer by birthright; comes from a family of them, modernized, in a measure, to be sure. He can remember when his father, being an overlooker in a Rhode Island mill, carried to work a leathern strap, with tacks inserted, for the flagellation of children. This man himself can tell you of children whom he has run, in some parts of the country, at night work, when the little creatures dropped asleep upon their feet, and he was obliged to throw water over them to keep them awake and at work.

The girls down stairs are singing something this morning about a "Happy Day." Bub, dimly hearing, dimly wonders what; having never had but one green boy at the Mission, does not know; thinks it has a pretty sound, wishes the wheels would let it alone, hopes the boss is out of the way now, wishes he had a chew, finds himself out of tobacco, and recovers sufficiently from the mortification of the "jawing" to lift his little, wrinkled face—it seems as if it never before had borne such wrinkles—to see what he can do about it.

Another little wrinkled face, old, yellow, sly, and sad, works close beside him. It has mouth and pockets full of quids.[45]

"Give us a chaw," says Bub.

"Not much," says the little face, with a wink.

"Seems as if I should choke!" says Bub. "I must have a chaw, Bill."

"You don't do none of *my* chawin'," says Bill, "less'n five cents down."

"Fact is," says Bub, ruefully, "I'm out o'cash just now. Never you mind, though."

Bub minds, however. He goes to work again with one eye on Bill. Bill's pocket is torn down. He must be green. You could a'most get a quid out and he'd never know it. Bub watches his chance. He must have tobacco at any chance. The child lives upon it,

---

[45]Pieces of chewing tobacco.

like an old toper on his dram. Every inch of his little body craves it. He is in a dry, fever-ish heat. He thinks he shall burn up, if he does not get it. To work till nooning without it is not to be thought of. He meant to have sold that rat to a chap he knew, and to have been supplied.

Think a cove of his size can work all day without it? You—bet—not—

There is a spring and a cry. Bub has pounced upon Bill's torn pocket. Bill has backed, and dragged him. The wagging rag on Bub's little trousers has caught in a belt.

All over the spooling-room there is a spring and a cry.

All up the stairs there seems to be a spring and a cry. They come from the song about the Happy, Happy Day. The engines close teeth on the song and the child together.

They stop the machinery; they run to and fro; they huddle together; they pick up something here, and wipe up something there, and cover up something yonder, closely; they look at one another with white faces; they sit down sickly; they ask what is to do next.

There is nothing to do. Bub has saved the State his two hundred and fifty dollars, and has Bill's quid of tobacco in his mangled hand. There is nothing to do. Life, like everything else, was quite too young for Bub. He has got so old, he has given it up.

There is nothing to do but to carry the news now; nobody likes to carry the news to the sick woman; nobody offers; the overseer, half wishing that there had been an oath or two less in the, "jawing," volunteers to help about the—the—*pieces,* if they'll find somebody to go on ahead. That's all he objects to; goin' on ahead.

Mr. Hayle the senior, who has been summoned from the counting-room, takes his hat to go in search of some one; would go himself, but the fact is, he has never seen the woman, nor the father to know him by name, and feels a delicacy about obtruding his services. He mentions the matter to his son, but Maverick succinctly refuses; remembers just now, for the first time since it happened, some long-past allusion of Miss Kelso's to a drain, and concludes that his personal sympathy can hardly be the most desirable to offer to Mr. Mell.

Just without the mill-yard, bent upon some early errand of her own, the two gentle-men chance upon Perley.

"Ask *her,*" says the younger man, in a low voice; "*she* would do to break ill news to the mother of the Maccabees."[46]

They pause to tell her what has happened; their shocked faces speak faster than their slow words; she understands quite what is needed of her; has turned the corner to East Street, while their unfinished explanation hangs upon their decorous lips.

The young man stands for a moment looking after her swift, strong, helpful figure, as it vanishes from view, with a sense of puzzled loss upon his handsome face, but shrugs his shoulders, and back in the counting-room shrugs them again.

Perley is none too soon at the First Tenement and No. 6.

The overlooker and his covered burden, and the little crowd that trails whispering after it, are just in sight, as she climbs the villanous stairs.

---

[46]The Maccabees were members of a priestly Jewish family whose bold, military spirit helped them lead a successful rebellion in the second century B.C.

The overlooker, and the covered burden, and the whispering crowd, are none too late at the First Tenement and No. 6.

Mr. Mell comes out from the sick-room on tiptoe; the children crouch and hide their faces behind the door; the doctor, who has been, has gone, and the coughing and confusion are quite over.

Mr. Mell stands still in the middle of the kitchen, with his hand at his ear. Whether he is listening to a thing which Perley says,—a gentle, awful thing, said in a gentle, awful voice,—or whether he is listening to certain sounds of feet upon the stairs, it were difficult to say.

He stands still in the middle of the kitchen, with his hand behind his ear.

The feet upon the stairs have climbed the stairs, have passed the stairs, have passed the door, have paused.

The overlooker, with his hat in his hand, has laid the covered burden softly down upon the mat behind the door, where the little burden, like a little puppy, slept last night.

Mr. Mell sits down then in the nearest chair. He points at the open bedroom door. He seems to be weak from watching, and the hand with which he points trembles badly.

"Do you see?" he says. "Look there. See, don't ye? I'm glad ye didn't come ten minute sooner. It would ha' ben such a fretful thing for *her*. She would ha' greeted sair, I'm feared. Keep the laddie well covered, will ye? I wald na' like so much as her dead een to seem to see it. It would ha' ben sae fretful for her; I wald na' likit to see her greetin' ower the laddie. I wald na' likit yon; keep him covered, will ye?"

It is very touching to hear the man mourn in the old long-disused Scotch words of his youth, and very touching to hear what a cry there is in the words themselves.

But it is not heart-breaking, like the thing which he says in broad English, next. It is after the overlooker has gone, and the covered burden is laid decently upon a bed, and Perley has been busied in and out of the bedroom, and the children have been washed a little, and the "second gell," crying bitterly over a cup of coffee which she is trying to make, has been comforted, and a cleanly silence has fallen upon the two rooms, and upon the two beds with their mute occupants. It is after he has sat stupidly still with his face in his hands. It is just as Perley, seeing nothing more that she can do for him, is softly shutting the door to go and find flowers for little Bub.

"Look a here. Say! What damages do you think the mills'll give me? I'd ought to have damages on the loss of the boy's wages. He was earnin' reglar, and growin' too."

At the foot of the stairs Perley finds a girl with large eyes, and soiled blue ribbons on her hair, sitting and sobbing in her mill-dress, rubbing the dust about her pretty face.

"I wouldn't sit here, Nynee," suggests Perley gently; "go up and help your sister, and do not cry."

"It seems as if everything fretful happened to me," sobs Nynee, pettishly. "The mills was bad enough. Then it was mother, and then it was somebody comin' in to tell me about Bub, and now it's both of 'em. I wish I'd tied up Bub's finger pleasant this morning. It'll be fretfuller than ever to home now. I wish I was dead like them two; yes, I do. I had other things that bothered me besides. I didn't want no more!"

"What other things?" asks Perley, very gently sitting down on the stairs, and very wisely taking no heed just now of the little miserable, selfish sobs.

"O, different things. Things about somebody that I—like, and somebody that I don't like, and some folks that like some folks better than me. I was bothered to death before!" cries Nynee.

"Some time," says Perley, "you shall tell me all about them. Run up to your sister, now."

Nynee runs up, and Perley, in going for Bub's flowers, thinks that she would rather gain the hearing of that little love-story, sitting on the dirty stairs, than to get the girl to church with her for a year to come.

CHAPTER XI

❧ Going into Society

"Delighted, Perley, I am sure, and shall be sure to come. Nothing could give us greater pleasure than a day with you in your lovely, Quixotic, queer venture of a home. Mamma begs me, with her love and acceptance, to assure you that she appreciates," etc., etc.

"As for my friends, the Van Doozles of New York, you know, (it is Kenna Van Doozle who is engaged to Mr. Blodgett,) they are charmed. It was just like you to remember them in your kind," etc.

"And actually to see for ourselves one of your dear, benevolent, democratic, strong-minded *réunions,* of which we have heard so much! What could be more?" etc.

"I promise you that I will be very good and considerate of your *protégés.*[47] I will wear nothing gayer than a walking-suit, and I will inform myself beforehand upon the ten-hour question, and I will be as charming as I know how, so that you shall not regret having honored me by," etc.

And now, my dear Perley, I cannot come to Five Falls without telling you myself what I should break my heart if you should hear from anybody but myself.

"I know that you must have guessed my little secret before now. But Maverick and I thought that we should like at least to *pretend* that it was a secret for a little while.

"Ah, Perley, I see your great wise eyes smile! Do you know, I suspect that you were *too* wise for him, dear boy! He seems to think a little, foolish, good-for-nothing girl like me would make him happy.

"And I know he wants me to say, dear Perley, how we have neither of us ever had any hardness in our hearts towards you, or ever can. How *can* we now? We are so very happy! And I know *how* wise he thinks you still, and how good. So very good! A great deal better than his ridiculous little Fly, I have no doubt; but then, you see, we don't either of us mind that," etc., etc., etc.

Fly's note preceded Fly by but a few hours, it so chanced. That evening Miss Kelso's parlors presented what Fly perhaps was justified in calling "such a dear, delightful, uncommon appearance."

Kenna Van Doozle called it *outré.*[48] She was sitting on a sofa by Nynee Mell when she said so.

---

[47]People who are protected and guided by a person of greater experience and influence.
[48]bizarre

It was a stifling July night, and closed a stifling day. Mrs. Silver, in the cars, on the Shore Line, and swept by sea breezes, had "suffered agonies," so she said. Even in the close green dark of Miss Kelso's lofty rooms, life had ceased to be desirable, and the grasshopper had been a burden, until dusk and dew-fall.

"In the houses from which my guests are coming to-night," she had said at supper, "the mercury has not been below 90°, day nor night, for a week."

Her guests seemed to appreciate the fact; shunned the hot lawn and garden, where a pretty show of Chinese lanterns and a Niobe[49] at a fountain (new upon the grounds, this year) usually attracted them, and grouped in the preserved coolness of the parlor.

Her guests, in those parlors, were worth a ride from town in the glare to meet.

There were some thirty, perhaps, in all; families, for the most part, just as they came. Mr. Mell, for instance, in decent clothes; the "second gell," with one of the children; Nynee, in light muslin and bright ribbons; old Bijah Mudge in a corner with little Dib Docket,—they sent Dib to the poorhouse by especial permit to bring him, always; Catty, closely following the soft rustle of the hostess's plain white dress (Sip was delayed, nobody knew just why); and Dirk Burdock, apart from the other young fellows, drifting restlessly in and out of the hot, bright lawn; little knots of young people chattering over picture-racks; a sound of elections and the evening news in other knots where their fathers stood with hands behind them; the elder women easily seated in easy-chairs; a tangle about the piano, where a young weaver was doing a young waltz very well.

Now there was one very remarkable thing about these thirty people. With the exception of a little plainness about their dress (plainness rather than roughness, since in America we will die of bad drainage, but we will manage to have a "best suit" when occasion requires) and an air of really enjoying themselves, they did not, after all, leave a very different impression upon the superficial spectator from that of any thirty people whom Fly Silver might collect at a *musicale*.[50]

The same faces at their looms to-morrow you could not identify.

"I suppose they're on their best behavior," suggested Fly, in an opportunity.

"What have you and I been on all our lives?" asked Perley, smiling. "One does not behave till one has a chance."

"And not in the least afraid of us," observed Fly, with some surprise. "I was afraid we should make it awkward for them."

"But how," asked Miss Van Doozle, with her pale eyes full of a pale perplexity,— "you are exceedingly original, I know,—but *how*, for instance, have you ever brought this about? I had some such people once, in a mission class; I could do nothing with them; they pulled the fur out of my muff, and got up and left in the middle of the second prayer."

"*I* have brought nothing about," said Perley, "They have brought themselves about. All that I do is to treat these people precisely as I treat you, Miss Van Doozle."

"Ah?" blankly from Miss Van Doozle.

---

[49]Niobe is a Greek mythological figure who weeps for her slain children. She is turned into stone, but her tears continue to flow. She is an archetype for the bereaved mother.

[50]Social gathering based around music.

"For instance," said the hostess in moving away, "I get up thirty or so of those every fortnight. I don't know how this came here. Put it in your pocket, please."

She tossed from the card-basket a delicate French envelope, of the latest mode of monogram and tint, enclosing a defective invitation in her own generous hand, running:—

"Miss Kelso requests the pleasure of Mr. Mell's company at half past seven o'clock on Friday evening next.
"July 15."

"Perley," observed Mrs. Silver, pensively, "*ought* to have been a literary character. I have always said so; haven't I, Fly?"

"Why, mamma?" asked Fly.

"That excuses so much always, my dear," softly said Mrs. Silver.

There seemed to be some stir and stop in Miss Kelso's "evening," that hot Friday. Dirk Burdock, restlessly diving in and out of the lawn, finally found his hat, and, apparently at the hostess's request, excused himself and disappeared. The young weaver played the young waltz out, and politics in corners lulled.

"It is a Victor Hugo[51] evening," explained Miss Kelso to her friends from town, "and our reader has not come. We always manage to accomplish something. I wish you could have heard an essay on Burns[52] from a Scotchman out of the printing-rooms, a fortnight ago. Or some of our Dickens[53] readings. Something of that or this kind takes better with the men than a musical night; though we have some fine voices, I assure you. I wish, Fly, you would play to us a little, while we are waiting."

Fly, not quite knowing what else to do, but feeling surprisingly ill at ease, accomplished a sweet little thin thing, and was prettily thanked by somebody somewhere; but still the reader had not come.

It has been said, upon authority, that the next thing which happened was the *Andante*[54] from the Seventh Symphony, Miss Kelso herself at the keys.

Mrs. Silver looked at Miss Van Doozle. Miss Van Doozle looked at Mrs. Silver.

"She has made a mistake," said Mrs. Silver's look.

---

[51]Victor Hugo (1802–1885) was a French author whose works were tremendously popular in the United States throughout the nineteenth century. One of his best-loved works was the novel *Les Misérables* (1862), which focused on the plight of the poor in Paris.

[52]Robert Burns (1759–1796) was the national poet of Scotland. Much of his life and work reflects a rebellious attitude toward orthodox notions of religion and morality.

[53]The novels of Charles Dickens (1812–1870) enjoyed tremendous popularity among nineteenth-century American readers. Among other characteristics, Dickens's works are known for their concern with the evils of poverty and class inequality.

[54]An andante is a moderately slow movement, which is usually part of a larger musical piece. It should be noted that the context here implies Beethoven's Seventh Symphony, but this symphony has no andante.

"The people can*not* appreciate Beethoven," was Miss Van Doozle's look.

Now, in truth, Beethoven could not have asked a stiller hearing than he and Miss Kelso commanded out of those thirty work-worn factory faces.

The blind-mute Catty stood beside Miss Kelso while she played. She passed the tips of her fingers like feathers over the motion of Perley's hands. It was a privilege she had. She bent her head forward, with her lip dropped and dull.

"When she plays," she often said to Sip, "there's wings of things goes by."

"What, wings?" asked Sip.

"I don't know—wings. When I catch, they fly."

Miss Kelso's elegant white, without flaw or pucker of trimming, presented a broad and shining background to the poor creature's puzzled figure. Catty seemed to borrow a glory from it, as a lean Byzantine Madonna[55] will, from her gilded sky. Mrs. Silver fairly wiped her eyes.

After Beethoven there was Nynee Mell, with a creature, with heavy sodden circles about her eyes and mouth.

She was sorry to be so late, Sip was saying, "But Maggie'd set her heart so on coming, you see; and there she lay and fainted, and I haven't been able to bring her round enough to get over here till this minute. Her folks was all away, and I couldn't seem to leave her; and she did so set her heart on coming! She has been carried in a faint out of the mill four times to-day—out into the air, and a dash of water—and back again; and down again. The thermometer has stood at 115° in our room to-day. It hasn't been below 110° not since last Saturday. It's 125° in the dressing-room. There's men in the dressing-room with the blood all gathered black about their faces, just from heat; they look like men in a fit; they're all purple. You'd ought to see the clothes we wear!—drenched like fine folks' bathing-clothes. I could wring mine out. We call it the lake of fire,[56]—our room. That's all I could think of since Sunday: the Last Day and the lake with all the folks in it. I haven't been in such a coolness not since I was here last time, Miss Kelso. It's most as bad as hell to be mill-folks in July!"

"A blowzy, red-faced girl," Miss Van Doozle thought, when the reader came in.

"My Lords!" began the red-faced reader, "I impart to you a novelty. The human race exists". . . .

"We have nothing so popular," whispered Miss Kelso, "as that girl's readings and recitations. They ring well."

"An unappreciated Siddons,[57] perhaps?" The pale Van Doozle eyes assumed the homœopathic attenuation of a sarcasm. The Van Doozle eyes were not used to Sip exactly.

---

[55]Probably refers to a Greek Orthodox icon of the Madonna. Such icons often depicted the Madonna against a gold background or with a golden halo above her head.

[56]The lake of fire is thought to be the location in hell where souls suffer eternal torment. When Jesus comes to judge humankind on Judgment Day, those who are damned will be sent to this place.

[57]Sarah Siddons (1755–1831) was a well-known and well-respected British tragic actress.

"I have thought that there might be greater than Siddons in Sip," replied Miss Kelso, musingly; "but not altogether of the Siddons sort, I admit."

Sip followed Miss Kelso, in the breaking up of the evening, after the books and the ices were out of the way. They had some plan about the little Irish girl already; a week's rest at least. There was that family on the Shore Line; and the hush of the sea; where they took such care of poor Bert Bush. If Catty were well, Sip would take her down.

"I know the girl. She must be got away till this drought's over. She'll work till the breath is out of her, but she'll work; has a brother in an insane asylum, and likes to pay his board. Maggie's obstinate as death about such things. You'd ought to see her pushing back her hair and laughing out, when she come out of those faints to-day, and at it again, for all anybody could say. You wouldn't think that she'd ever take to Jim, would you? But got over it, I guess. Had a hard time, though. Look here! I found a piece in a newspaper yesterday, and cut it out to show to you."

Sip handed to Miss Kelso, with a smile, a slip from one of the leading city dailies, reading thus:—

"What is generally written about Lorenzo factory-girls is sensational and pure nonsense. They are described as an overworked class, rung up, rung out, rung in; as going to their labors worn, dispirited, and jaded; as dreading to meet their task-masters in those stifling rooms, where they have cultivated breathing as a fine art; as coming home from their thraldom happy but for thoughts of the resumption of their toil on the morrow. The fact is, sympathy has been offered where it was not needed. The officers of the mills and the girls themselves will tell you the tasks are not exhaustive. No one gets so tired that she cannot enjoy the evening, every thought of work dismissed. Her employment is such that constant attention is not demanded. She may frequently sit thinking of the past or planning for the future. She earns nearly four dollars per week, beside her board. The pleasantest relations subsist between her and her overseer, who is frequently the depositary of her funds, who perhaps goes with her to buy her wedding or household outfit, who is her counsellor and protector. Her step is not inelastic, but firm. . . . The mills are high studded, well ventilated, and scrupulously clean. The girls are healthy and well looking, and men and women, who have worked daily for twenty or thirty years, are still in undiminished enjoyment of sound lungs and limbs."

"I never was in Lorenzo," said Sip, drily, as Perley folded the slip, "but mills are mills. I'd like to see the fellow that wrote that."

Fly and her friends had sifted into the library, while Miss Kelso's guests were thinning.

"This, I suppose," Mrs. Silver was sadly saying, "is but a specimen of our poor dear Perley's life."

"You speak as if she were dead and buried, mamma," said Fly, making a dazzling little heap of herself upon a cricketful of pansies.

"So she is," affirmed Mrs. Silver, plaintively,—"so she is, my dear, as far as Society is concerned. I have been struck this evening by the thought, what a loss to Society! Why, Miss Kenna, I am told that this superb house has been more like a hospital or a set of public soup-rooms for six months past, than it has like the retiring and secluded home of a young lady. Those people overrun it. They are made welcome to it at all hours and under all circumstances. She invites them to tea, my dear! They sit down at her very table with her. I have known her to bring out Mirabeau from town to furnish their music for them. Would you credit it? Mirabeau! In the spring she bought a Bierstadt.[58] I was with her at the time. 'I have friends in Five Falls who have never seen a Bierstadt,' she said. Now what do you call that? *I* call it morbid," nodded the lady, making soft gestures with her soft hands,—"morbid!"

"I don't suppose anybody knows the money that she has put into her libraries, and her model tenements, and all that, either," mused Fly, from her cricket.

"It does well enough in that Mr. Garrick," proceeded Mrs. Silver, in a gentle bubble of despair; "I don't object to fanatical benevolence in a man like him. It is natural, of course. He is self-made entirely; twenty years ago might have come to Miss Kelso's evenings himself, you know. It is excusable in him, though awkward in the firm, as I had reason to know, when he started to build that chapel. Now there is another of poor Perley's freaks. What does she do but leave Dr. Dremaine's, where she had at least the dearest of rectors and the best pew-list in Five Falls, on the ground that the mill-people do not frequent Dr. Dremaine's, and take a pew in the chapel herself! They have a young preacher there fresh from a seminary, and Perley and the mill-girls will sit in a row together and hear him! Now that *may* be Christianity," adds Mrs. Silver, in a burst of heroism, "but *I* call it morbidness, sheer morbidness!"

"But these people are very fond of Perley, mamma," urged Fly, lifting some honest trouble in her face out of the pretty shine that she made in the dim library.

"They ought to be!" said Mrs. Silver, with unwonted sharpness.

Now Fly, in her own mind, had meant to find out something about that; she went after the Hugo reader, it just occurring to her, and took her into a corner before everybody was gone.

She made a great glitter of herself here too; she could not help it, in her shirred lace and garnets. Sip looked her over, smiling as she would at a pretty kitten. Sip was more gentle in her judgments of "that kind of folks" than she used to be.

"What do we think of *her?*" Sip's fitful face flushed. "How can I tell you what we think of her? There's those of us here, young girls of us," Nynee Mell's blue ribbons, just before them, were fluttering through the door, "that she has saved from being what you wouldn't see in here to-night. There's little children here that would be little devils, unless it was for her. There's men of us with rum to fight, and boys in prison, and debts to pay, and hearts like hell, and never a friend in this world or the other but her. There's others of us, that—that—God bless her!" broke off Sip, bringing her clenched little hands together,—"God bless her, and the ground she treads on, and the air she breathes, and the sky that is over her, and the friends that love her, and the walls of her grand house, and every dollar of her money, and every wish she wishes, and all the prayers she prays—but I cannot tell you, young lady, what we think of *her!*"

---

[58] Albert Bierstadt (1830–1902) was a tremendously popular painter of panoramic American landscapes, particularly of the American West.

"But Society," sighed Mrs. Silver,—"Society has rights which every lady is bound to respect; poor Perley forgets her duties to Society. Where we used to meet her in our circle three times, we meet her once now."

"Once of Perley is equal to three times of most people," considered Fly, appearing with Maverick (who had slipped in as the "evening" slipped out) from some lovers' corner. "And she doesn't trust, you must own, mamma; and seems to enjoy herself so, besides."

"I have understood," observed the elder Miss Van Doozle, "that she has been heard to say that she could never spend an evening in an ordinary drawing-room party happily again."

This, in fact, was a report very common about Miss Kelso at one time. Those well acquainted with her and with her movements in Five Falls will remember it.

"Poor Perley" herself came in just in time to hear it then.

"I always forgave the falsity of that, for the suggestiveness of it," she said, laughing.

"A thoughtful set of guests you have here," said Fly. "We have been finding fault with you all the evening."

"That is what I expected."

"So we supposed. Perley!"

"Well, my dear?"

"Are you happy?"

"Quite happy, Fly."

"I should be so miserable!" said Fly, with a shade of the honest trouble still on her pretty face.

"I have been saying," began Mrs. Silver, "that Society is a great loser by your philanthropy, Perley."

Perley lighted there.

"Society!" she said, "I feel as if I had but just begun to go into society!"

"But, on your theories," said Kenna Van Doozle, with a clumsy smile of hers, "we shall have our cooks up stairs playing whist with us, by and by."

"And if we did?" quietly. "But Miss Van Doozle, I am not a reformer; I haven't come to the cooks yet; I am only a feeler. The world gets into the dark once in a while, you know; throws out a few of us for groping purposes."

"Kenna and I, for instance, being spots on the wings?" asked Fly.

"Naturalists insist that the butterfly will pause and study its own wings, wrapt in—"

"O Maverick!"

"Admiration," finished Maverick.

"But one must feel by something," persisted Fly, "guess or measure. It is all very beautiful in you, Perley. But it seems to me such a venture. I should be frightened out of it a dozen times over."

Perley took a little book out of a rack upon one of the tables, where Mr. Mell's ice-cream saucer yet lay unremoved,—Isaac Taylor[59] in bevelled board.

---

[59]Isaac Taylor (1787–1865) was a English artist, inventor, and author. He was deeply concerned in his writings with the corruption of the Christian church and how this corruption might be remedied.

"Here," she said, "is enough to feel by, even if I feel my way to your cook, Miss Kenna."

"*'To insure, therefore, its large purpose of goodwill to man, the law of Christ spreads out its claims very far beyond the circle of mere pity or natural kindness, and in absolute and peremptory terms demands for the use of the poor, the ignorant, the wretched, and demands from every one who names the name of Christ, the whole residue of talent, wealth, time, that may remain after primary claims have been satisfied.'*"

CHAPTER XII

❧ Maple Leaves

An incident connected with Miss Kelso's experiments in Five Falls, valuable chiefly as indicative of the experimenter, and rather as a hint than as history, occurred in the ripening autumn. It has been urged upon me to find place for it, although it is fragmentary and incomplete.

A distant sea-swell of a strike was faintly audible in Hayle and Kelso.

Hayle and Kelso were in trouble. Standfast Brothers, of Town, solid as rock and old as memory, had gone down; gone as suddenly and blackly as Smashem & Co. of yesterday, and gone with a clutch on Five Falls cotton, under which Five Falls shook dizzily.

The serene face of the senior partner took, for the first time since 1857, an anxious, or, it might rather be called, an annoyed groove. All the manufacturing panics of the war had fanned it placidly, but Standfast Brothers were down, and behold, the earth reeled and the foundations thereof.

Two things, therefore, resulted. The progress of the new mill was checked, and a notice of reduction of wages went to the hands.

The sea-swell murmured.

Hayle and Kelso heard nothing.

The sea-swell growled.

Hayle and Kelso never so much as turned the head.

The sea-swell splashed out a few delegates and a request, respectful enough, for consultation and compromise.

"We will shut down the mills first!" said young Mr. Hayle between his teeth.

So the swell broke with a roar the next "Lord's day."

The groove grew a little jagged across the Senior's face. A strike, it is well known, is by no means necessarily an undesirable thing. Stock accumulates. The market quickens. You keep your finger on its pulse. You repair your machinery and bide your time. A thousand people, living from hand to mouth, may be under your finger, empty-handed. What so easy as a little stir of the finger now and then? *You* are not hungry meanwhile; *your* daughter has her winter clothes. You sit and file handcuffs playfully, against that day when your "hands" shall have gone hungry long enough. No more striking presently! Meantime, you may amuse yourself.

There is something noteworthy about this term "strike." A head would think and outwit us. A heart shall beat and move us. The "hands" can only struggle and strike us,—

foolishly too, and madly, here and there, and desperately, being ill-trained hands, never at so much as a boxing-school, and gashing each other principally in the contest.

There had been strikes in Hayle and Kelso which had not caused a ruffle upon the Senior's gentlemanly, smooth brow or pleasant smile; but just now a strike was unfortunate.

"*Very* unfortunate," said Mr. Hayle in the counting-room on pay-day, in the noise of the breaking swell.

The Company were all upon the ground, silent and disturbed. There was a heavy crowd at the gates, and the sound of the overseers' voices in altercation with them, made its way in jerks to the counting-room.

By a chance Miss Kelso was in the counting-room; had been over to put Mill's "Liberty"[60] into the library, and had been detained by the gathering crowd.

She was uneasy like the rest; was in and out, taking her own measure of the danger.

"There is nothing to be done," said Mr. Garrick, anxiously, the last time that she came into the little gloomy room where they were sitting. It was beginning to rain, and the windows, through which growing spots of lowering faces could be seen darkening the streets, were spattered and dirty. "There is nothing to do about it. If they will, they will. Had you better stay here? We may have a noisy time of it."

"There is one thing to do," said the young lady, decidedly, "only one. I wish, Mr. Garrick, that you had never shut me out of this firm. I belonged here! You do not one of you know now what it is for your own interest to do!"

Mr. Hayle signified, smiling across his groove of anxiety, that she was at liberty, of course, to offer any valuable suggestion with which she might be prepared for such an emergency.

"And fold my hands for a romantic woman after it. However, that does not alter the fact; there is just one thing to do to prevent the most serious strike known in Five Falls yet. I know those men better than you do."

"We know them well enough," said Maverick, with a polite sneer. "This is a specimen of 'intelligent labor,' a fair one! These fellows are like a horse blind in one eye; they will run against a barn to get away from a barrel. Loose the rein, and there's mischief immediately. You may invite them to supper to the end of their days, Miss Kelso; but when you are in a genuine difficulty, they will turn against you just as they are doing now. There's neither gratitude nor common business sense among them. There's neither trust nor honor. They have no confidence in their employers, and no foresight for themselves. They would ruin us altogether for fifty cents a week. A parcel of children with the blessed addition of a few American citizens at their head!"

"I was about to propose," said Perley, quietly, "that their employers should exhibit some trust or confidence in *them*. I want Mr. Garrick to go out and tell them *why* we must reduce their wages."

"Truly a young lady's suggestion," said the Senior.

---

[60]John Stuart Mill (1806–1873) was an English philosopher and economist, who was a strong advocate of utilitarianism. His essay "On Liberty" (1859) is a complex treatment of the need for active morality and the importance of freedom for the prosperity of both individual and society.

"It is none of their business," said Maverick, "why we reduce their wages."

Stephen Garrick said nothing.

"Such a course was never taken in the company," said the Senior.

"And never ought to be," said the Junior. "It is an unsuitable position for an employer to take,—unsuitable! And disastrous as a precedent. Next thing we know, we should have them regulating the salary of our clerks and the size of our invoices. Outside of the fancy of a cooperative economist, such a principle would be im—— What a noise they're making!"

"Every minute is precious," exclaimed Perley, rising nervously. "I tell you I know those men! They will trust Mr. Stephen Garrick, if he treats them like reasonable beings before it is too late!"

The counting-room door slammed there, behind a messenger from the clerk. Things looked badly, he said; the Spinners' Union had evidently been at work; there were a few brickbats about, and rum enough to float a schooner; and an ugly kind of *setness* all around; we were in for it, he thought, now. Were there any orders?

No, no orders.

The counting-room door slammed again, and the noise outside dashed against the sound with a little spurt of defiance.

"It would be a most uncommon course to take," said the Senior, uneasily; "but the emergency is great, and perhaps if Mr. Garrick felt inclined to undertake such an extraordinary—"

Miss Kelso overrated his chances of success, Mr. Garrick said, but she did not overrate the importance of somebody's doing something. He was willing to make the attempt.

The counting-room door slammed once more; the spurt died down; the swell reared its head, writhing a little to see what would happen.

Mr. Garrick took his hat off, and stood in the door.

It was an ugly crowd, with a disheartening "setness" about it. He wished, when he looked it over, that he had not come; but stood with his hat off, smiling.

He was smiling still when he came back to the counting-room.

"Well?" asked Perley.

"For an unpopular master—"

"O hush!" said Perley.

"For an unpopular master," repeated Mr. Garrick, "I did as well as I expected. In fact, just what I expected all the time has happened. Listen!"

He held the door open. A cry came in from outside,—

"*Ask the young leddy!*"

"You see, you should have gone in the first place," said the unpopular master, patiently. "The rest of us are good for little, without your indorsement."

"*Call the young leddy! Let's hear what the young leddy says to 't! The young leddy! The young leddy!*"

The demand came in at the counting-room door just as the "young leddy" went out.

The people parted for her right and left. She stood in the mud, in the rain, among them. They made room for her, just as the dark day would have made room for a sunbeam. The drunkest fellows, some of them, slunk to the circumference of the circle that had closed about her. Oaths and brickbats seemed to have been sucked out to sea by a sudden tide of respectability. It has been said by those who witnessed it that it was a scene worth seeing.

"She just stood in the mud and the rain," said Sip Garth, in telling the story. "If we'd all been in her fine parlors, we wouldn't have been stiller. There was a kind of a shame and a sense came to us, to see her standing so quiet in the rain. The fellow that opened his lips for a roughness before her would ha' been kicked into the gutter, I can tell you. It was just like her. There's never mud nor rain amongst us, but you look, and there she is! That day there seemed to be a shining to her. We were all worked up and angered; and she stood so white and still. There was a minute that she looked at us, and she looked— why, she looked as if she'd be poor folks herself, if only she could say how sorry she was for us. Then she blazed out at us! 'Did Mr. Garrick ever tell any man of us a word but honest truth?' she wanted to know. 'And hasn't he proved himself a friend to every soul of you that needed friendliness?' says she. 'And when he told you that he must reduce your wages, you shouldn't have sent for me!' says she. But then she talks to us about the trouble that the Company was in, and a foolishness creeps round amongst us, as if we wished we were at home. It's not that they so much disbelieved Mr. Garrick," said Sip, "but when *she* said she couldn't afford to pay 'em, they believed *that*."

"I don't understand about these things," said Reuben Mell, slowly stepping out from the crowd. "It's very perplexing to me. It doesn't mean a dollar's worth less of horses and carriages, and grand parties to the Company, such a trouble as this don't seem to. And it means as *we* go without our breakfast so's the children sha'n't be hungry; and it means as when our shoes are wore out, we know no more than a babby in its cradle where the next pair is to come from. That's what reduction o' wages means to *us*. I don't understand the matter myself, but I'm free to say that we'll not doubt as the young leddy does. I'll take the young leddy's word for it, this time, for one."

Mr. Mell, with this, peaceably stepped up and took the reduction from the counter, and peaceably went home with it.

There was a little writhing of the flood-tide at this, and then an ebb.

Miss Kelso came out of it, and left it to bubble by itself for a while.

Within half an hour it had ebbed away, leaving only a few weeds of small boys and a fellow too drunk to float in sight of the mill-gate.

Until at least next "Lord's day," there would be no strike in Hayle and Kelso.

By that time Mr. Garrick hoped that we should be upon our feet again.

Mr. Garrick walked home with Miss Kelso in the autumn rain.

Unfortunately for the weed of a fellow stranded in the mill-yard, they passed and recognized him. It was the overseer, Irish Jim. Next morning he received his notice. They had borne with him too long, and warned him too often, Mr. Garrick insisted. Go he should, and go he did.

But Mr. Garrick walked home with Miss Kelso in the autumn rain.

They passed between the cotton-house and the old boiler, in going out. Dirk Burdock had stepped through just before them, trying to overtake Sip in the distance, hurrying home. Either this circumstance or a mood of the mill-master's own recalled to his mind his midnight talk with the young watchman on that spot, and what Dirk had said of its being a "churchly place." It was a dreary, dingy place now, in the gray storm-light, prosaic and extremely rusty. He held the lady's cloak back from the boiler in passing by.

His hand had but brushed the hem of her garment, but it trembled visibly. He touched a priestess in a water-proof. Fire from heaven fell before his eyes upon the yellow boiler. Such a "churchliness" struck the mill-yard, that the man would have lifted his hat, but considered that he would take cold, and so kept it on like a sensible fellow.

Of course he loved her. How should he help it? Anybody but Perley would have thought of it, long ago.

Yet, oddly enough, nobody had thought of it. Occasionally one meets people, though they are rather apt to be men than women, who seem to go mailed through life in a gossip-proof armor. Perley Kelso is one of them. Rumor winks and blinks and shuts its eyes upon her. Your unpleasant stories, "had upon authority," pass her by unscathed. This young lady's life had been a peculiar, rather a public one, for now nearly two years, and in its most vital interests Stephen Garrick had stood heart and soul and hand in hand with her. Yet her calm eyes turned upon him that autumn afternoon as placidly as they did upon the old boiler. When she saw that tremble of the hand, she said: "You are cold? It is growing chilly. The counting-room was close."

How could man help it? Of course he loved her. He had seen the shining of her rare, fine face in such strange places! In sick-rooms and in the house of mourning he had learned to listen for the stealing, strong sweetness of her young voice. They had met by death-beds and over graves. They had burrowed into mysteries of misery and sin, in God's name, together. Wherever people were cold, hungry, friendless, desolate, in danger, in despair, she struck across his path. Wherever there was a soul for which no man cared, he found her footprints. Wherever there was a life to be lifted from miasmas to heights, he saw the waving of her confident white hand. If ever there were earnest work, solemn work, solitary work, mistrusted work, work misunderstood, neglected, discouraging, hopeless, thankless,—Christ's work, to be done, he faced her.

Now, among several hundred factory-operatives, it naturally happened that he had thus faced her not infrequently.

The woman's life had become a service in a temple, and he had lighted the candles for her. One would miss it, perhaps, to worship in the dark? The man asked himself the question, turning his face stiffly against the autumn storm.

There had been no sun since yesterday. The sky was locked with a surcharged cloud. A fine, swift rain blurred the outlines of the river-banks and hills.

"And yet," he said, "the day seems to be full of sun. Do you notice? There is light about us everywhere."

"It is from the hickories and maples," said Perley.

Ripened leaves streaked and dotted their path, wreathed blazing arms about the pine groves, smouldered over the fields, flung themselves scorched into the water, flared across the dam, and lighted the little cascades luridly. The singular effect of dying trees on a dead day was at its richest. One could not believe that the sun did not shine.

"An unreal light," said Stephen Garrick, hardly, "and ugly. We should find it cold to live by."

"I had not thought of that," said Perley, smiling; "I rather like it."

Her face, as she lifted it to his, seemed to warm itself at its own calm eyes; slowly, perhaps, as if the truant day had tried to leave a chill upon it, but thoroughly and brightly.

Garrick turned, and looked it over and over and through and through,—the lifted haunting face!

What a face it was! His own turned sharply gray.

"I see no room for me there!" he said, and stopped short where he stood.

No; he was right. There was no room. The womanly, calm face leaped with quick color, then drifted pale as his own.

"Let us walk on," said Garrick, with a twang in his voice.

They walked on nervously. Neither spoke just then. They walked on, under and through a solid arch of the unreal sunshine, which a phalanx of maples made in meeting over their heads.

"I had hoped," said Stephen Garrick then, between his breath, "that I had—a chance. I have been—stupid, perhaps. A man is so slow to feel that he has—no chance. I have not played at love like—many men. There has been such an awfulness," said Stephen Garrick, passing his hand confusedly over his eyes,—"such an awfulness about the ground I have seen you tread upon. Most men love women in parlors and on play-days; they can sing them little songs, they can tie up flowers for them, they can dance and touch their hands. I—I have had no way in which to love you. We have done such awful work together. In it, through it, by it, because of it, I loved you. I think there's something—in the love—that is like the work. It has struck me under a ledge of granite, I believe. Miss Kelso, it would come up—hard."

His hand dropped against his side, very slowly, but the blue nails clenched the flesh from its palm.

What did the woman mean? What should he do with the sight, sound, touch of her; the rustle of her dress, the ripple of her sweet breath, the impenetrable calm of her grieving eyes?

He felt himself suddenly lifted and swung from the centre of his controlled, common, regulated, and regulating days. Five Falls operatives ceased to appear absorbing as objects of life. How go dribbling ideal Christian culture through highways and hedges, if a man sat and starved on husks himself, before the loaded board? The salvation of the world troubled him yesterday. To-day there was only this woman in it.

They two, in the mock light of dying leaves, they two only and together, stood, the Alpha and Omega, in the name of nature and in the sight of God.

"I have loved you," said the man, trembling heavily, "so long! My life has not been like that of—many people. I have taken it—hard and slowly. I have loved you slowly, and—hard. You ought to love me. Before God, I say you ought to love me!"

"The fact is—" said Perley, in her sensible, every-day voice.

Stephen Garrick drew breath and straightened himself. His blanched face quivered and set into its accustomed angles. His shut fingers opened, and he cleared his throat. He struck to his orbit. Ah! Where had he been? Most too old a man for that! See how he had let the rain drip on her. He grasped his umbrella. He could go to a Mission meeting now. All the women in the world might shake their beautiful heads at him under yellow maple-trees in an autumn rain!

"The fact is?" he gravely asked.

"The fact is," repeated Perley, "that I have no time to think of love and marriage, Mr. Garrick. That is a business, a trade, by itself to women. I have too much else to do. As nearly as I can understand myself, that is the state of the case. I cannot spare the time for it."

And yet, as nearly as she understood herself, she might have loved this man. The dial of her young love and loss cast a little shadow in her sun to-day. She felt old before her time. All the glamour that draws men and women together had escaped her somehow. Possible wifehood was no longer an alluring dream. Only its prosaic and undesirable aspects presented themselves to her mind. No bounding impulse cried within her: That is happiness! There is rest! But only: It were unreasonable; it is unwise.

And yet she might have loved the man. In all the world, she felt as if he only came within calling distance of her life. Out of all the world, she would have named him as the knightly soul that hers delighted to honor.

Might have loved him? *Did* she love him? Garrick's hungry eyes pierced the lifted face again over and over, through and through. If not in this world, in another, perhaps? In any? Somewhere? Somehow?

"I cannot tell," said the woman, as if she had been called; "I do not need you now. Women talk of loneliness. I am not lonely. They are sick and homeless. I am neither. They are miserable. I am happy. They grow old. I am not afraid of growing old. They have nothing to do. If I had ten lives, I could fill them! No, I do not need you, Stephen Garrick."

"Besides," she added, half smiling, half sighing, "I believe that I have been a silent partner long enough. If I married you, sir, I should invest in life, and you would conduct it. I suspect that I have a preference for a business of my own. Perhaps that is a part of the trouble."

They had reached the house, and turned, faces against the scattering rain, to look down at the darkening river, and the nestling that the town made against the hill. The streets were full; and the people, through the distance and the rain, had a lean look, passing to and fro before the dark, locked mills.

Perley Kelso, with a curious, slow gesture, stretched her arms out toward them, with a face which a man would remember to his dying day.

"Shall they call," she said, "and I not answer? If they cried, should not I hear?"

"Mr. Garrick!" She faced him suddenly on the dripping lawn. "If a man who loves a woman can take the right hand of fellowship from her, I wish you would take it from me!"

She held out her full strong hand. The rain dripped on it from an elm-tree overhead. Stephen Garrick gently brushed the few drops, as if they had been tears, away, and, after a moment's hesitation, took it.

If not in this world in another, perhaps? In any? Somewhere? Somehow?

"I shall wait for you," said the man. Perhaps he will. A few souls can.

CHAPTER XIII

❧ A Feverish Patient

The Pompeian statues in Hayle and Kelso were on exhibition in a cleared and burnished condition for nearly a week last spring.

That is to say, Hayle and Kelso were off work, for high water. It will be well remembered how serious the season's freshets[61] were, and that Five Falls had her full share of drenching.

The river had been but two days on the gallop before the operatives, wandering through their holidays in their best clothes, began to knot into little skeins about the banks, watching the leap that the current made over the dam.

By the third day the new mill was considered in danger, and diked a little.

By the fourth day heavy wagons were forbidden the county bridge.

The skeins upon the banks interwound and thickened. Five Falls became a gallery. Sunbreak had flung back the curtain from a picture which hundreds crept up on tiptoe to see.

Between the silent, thronged banks and the mute, unclouded sky, the river writhed like a thing that was tombed alive. The spatter of the cascades had become smooth humps, like a camel's. The great pulse of the dam beat horribly. The river ran after it, plunged at it, would run full and forever. It looked as hopeless as sin, and as long as eternity. You gazed and despaired. There was always more, more, more. There was no chain for its bounding. There was no peace to its cries. No sepulchre could stifle it, no death still it. You held out your hands and cried for mercy to it.

Beautiful whirlpools of green light licked the base of the stone river-walls. Flecks of foam were picked up in the fields. People stood for hours in the spray, clinging to the iron railings by the dam, deafened and drenched, to watch the sinuous trail of the under-tints of malachite and gold and umber that swung through. As one looked, the awful oncoming of the upper waters ceased to be a terror, ceased, or seemed to cease, to be a fact. Mightiness of motion became repose. The dam lay like a mass of veined agate before the eyes, as solid as the gates of the city whose builder and maker is God; of the city in which sad things shall become joy, dark things light, stained things pure, old things new.

The evening and the morning were the fifth day. Between their solemn passing, Sip and Catty sat alone in the little damp, stone house.

The air was full of the booming of the flood, and Catty laid her head upon Sip's knee, listening, as if she heard it. The wind was high and blew a kind of froth of noise in gusts against the closed windows and doors; but never laid finger's weight upon the steady, deadly underflow of sound that filled the night. A dark night. Sip, going to the window, from whence she could dimly see the sparks of alarm-lights and the shadows of watchmen on the endangered bridge, felt a little displeasure with the night. It was noisy and confused her. It was wild and disturbed her. The crowds still lingered on the banks, where the green whirlpools had grown black, and where the tints of malachite and gold and umber, swinging on their bright arms through the dam, had become purple and gray and ghastliness, and wrapped the stone piers in dark files, as if they had been mourners at a mighty funeral. Cries of excitement or fear cut the regular thud of the water, now and then, and there was unwonted light about the dikes of the new mill, and on the railway crossing, which had been loaded with the heaviest freight at command, in anticipation of the possible ruin and attack of the upper bridge.

The water was still rising, and the wind. An undefined report had risen with them, through the day, of runaway lumber up the stream. Five Falls was awake and uneasy.

---

[61]Streams that have overflowed because of heavy rains.

"I don't wonder," thought Sip, coming back from the window. "It's a kind of night that I can't make out. Can you, Catty?"

It was a night that Catty could hear, or thought she could, and this pleased her.

"It is like wheels," she said, having never heard but those two things, the machinery in the mills and this thunder. It carried her round and round, she signified, making circles with her fingers in the air.

She got up presently and walked with the fancy in circles about the little kitchen. It seemed to perplex her that she always came back to her starting-point.

"I thought I was going to get out," she said, stretching out her arms.

"Don't!" said Sip, uneasily, covering her eyes. Catty looked so ugly when she took fancies! She never could bear them; begged her to come back again and put her head upon her knee.

"But where shall I stop?" persisted Catty. "I can't go round and go round. Who will stop me, Sip?"

"Never mind," said Sip. "There, there!" All the stone house was full of the boom of the river. The two girls sat down again, it seemed, in the heart of it. Sip took Catty's hands. She was glad to have her at home to-night. She kissed her finger-tips and her cropped, coarse hair.

"Last night," said Catty, suddenly, "I stayed at home."

"So you did, dear."

"And another night, besides."

"Many other nights," said Sip, encouragingly.

Did that make Sip happy? Catty asked.

Very, very happy.

For love's sake?

For love's sake, dear.

"I'll stay at home to-morrow night," Catty nodded sharply,—"I'll stay at home to-morrow night, for love's sake."

In the middle of the night, Sip, with a sense of disturbance or alarm, waked suddenly. The little closet bedroom was dark and close. A great shadow in the kitchen wrapped her pictured dreamer, and his long, unresting dream. It was so dark, that she could fairly touch, she thought, the solemn sound that filled the house. It took waves like the very flood itself. If she put her hand out over the edge of the bed, she felt an actual chill from it. There seemed to be nothing but that noise in all the world.

Except Catty, sitting up straight in bed, awake and talkative.

"What is it?" asked Sip, sitting up too.

In the dead dark, Catty put out her hands. In the dead dark Sip answered them.

"Sip," said Catty, "who was it?"

"Who was what, dear?"

"Who was it that made this?" touching her ears.

"Him that made this awful noise," said Sip.

"And this?" brushing her eyes.

"Him that made this awful dark," said Sip.

"And this?" She put her fingers to her mute, rough lips.

"Him that learned the wind to cry at nights," said Sip.

"Did he do it for love's sake?" asked Catty. "I can't find out. Did he do it for love's sake, Sip?"

"For—love's—sake?" said Sip, slowly. "I suppose he did. I pray to Heaven that he did. When I'm on my knees, I know he did."

"If it was for love's sake," said Catty, "I'll go to sleep again."

So the evening and the morning were the fifth day of the great freshets at Five Falls.

Catty woke early and helped Sip to get breakfast. She was very happy, though the coffee burned, and laughed discordantly when Sip made griddle-cakes for her of the Indian meal. Sip could not eat her own griddle-cakes for pleasure at this. She walked up and down the room with her hands behind her, kissing Catty's finger-tips and her ragged hair.

The Pompeian statues came to the face of the day; the crowds upon the river-brinks formed again, thickened, doubled; the bright-armed malachite and umber leaped again dizzily down the dams.

Still the pulse of the river rose. The county bridge shrunk and shivered in fits to it. The river had the appearance of having an attack of fever and ague.

The timber alarm, in the wearing on of the day, waxed and grew.

Five thousand feet of timber, in the upper floods, had broken loose, and were on their way down stream.

Ten thousand feet.

Twenty.

Five hundred thousand.

A million feet of logs, in the upper floods, had broken their chains, and would be at Five Falls before night.

Catty was sitting alone in the stone house, in the slope of the afternoon. She had been out with Sip, half the day, "to see the flood"; lifting her listening face against the spray, with pathetic pleasure; holding out her hands sometimes, they said, as if to measure the sweep of the sounding water; nodding to herself about it, with her dull laugh.

Sip would be back at dusk. Catty had promised, coming home a little tired, to sit still and wait for her; would not venture out again among the crowd; would go to sleep perhaps; would be a good girl, at any rate; stroked Sip's face a little as she went away. Sip kissed her, and, when she had shut the door, came back and kissed her again. A little shopping up town, and an errand at Miss Kelso's, and perhaps another look at the flood, would not delay her very long; and Catty had kept her promises lately. Sip bade her good by with a light heart, and shut the door again.

Catty sat still for a while after the door was shut. Then she slept awhile. Afterwards she sat still for a while again. She got up and walked about the kitchen. She sat down on the kitchen floor. She nodded and talked to herself. Sip might have been gone an hour; she might have been gone a week; Catty did not feel sure which; she lost her hold of time when she sat alone; she put her fingers down on the floor and counted them, guessing at how long Sip had been away.

Her fingers, when she put them on the floor, splashed into something cold.

Had the water-pail tipped over? If it had, it must have been very full. Catty discovered that she was sitting in a puddle of water; that water gurgled over her feet; that water rippled about the legs of the stove; that a gentle bubble of water filled the room.

She crawled, dripping, up, and made her way to the door. As she opened it, she let in a swash about her ankles.

She spattered across the entry to find the Irish woman who rented the other tene-ment; she had gone, like the rest of the world, to see the flood, it seemed; Catty received no answer to her uncouth calls; she was alone in the house.

This disturbed her. She felt puzzled about the water; alarmed, because she could neither see nor hear the reason of it; annoyed at the cold crawling that it made about her ankles, and anxious for Sip to come and explain it.

She went to the front door and opened that. A rush, like a tiny tide, met her. She stooped and put her hand out, over the step. It dipped into a pool of rising water.

Catty shrank back and shut the door. The noise like wheels was plain to her. It waited for her outside of that door. It struck like claws upon her locked ears. It frightened her. She would not for the world open the door to it. She drew the bolt hard, in a childish fright, and sat down again in the slow gurgle on the kitchen floor.

Suddenly it occurred to her that she might go and find Sip. But Sip would not be in the noise. Where would she be?

Catty pushed herself along on the floor, pushing out of the way of the water as she reflected. That was how another thing occurred to her.

The farther that she pushed herself the thinner the gurgle grew. In the closet bed-room it was scarcely wet.

At this side of the house she lost, or thought she lost, the noise. It must be at this side of the house that she should find Sip. Sip had often lost *her* out of the closet bedroom. She remembered, with a laugh, how many times she had climbed out of that little cup-board window after Sip was asleep. She felt her way to it eagerly. It was shut and but-toned. She pushed it, slamming, back, climbed to the high sill, and let herself drop.

Catty might have remained in the closet bedroom, had she but known it, high and dry. The stone house received a thorough soaking, but not a dangerous one. The water sucked in for a while at the locked front door, played drearily about the empty kitchen, mopped the entry floor, set the Irish woman's bread-pan and coal-hod afloat, and daw-dled away again down the steps; the result, it seemed, of a savage and transient shiver on the part of that fitful invalid, the river.

The county bridge, in fact, was as good as gone. The transient shiver in the lower floods had been caused by the sinking of a pier.

It had been a fine sight. Masses of men, women, and children hung, chained like galley-slaves, to either bank, intent and expectant on it. Foot and horse forsook the bridge. Police guarded it.

A red sunset sprang up and stared at it. An avalanche of dead-white spray chewed the malachite and umber. Curious, lurid colors bounded up where they sank, and bruised and beat themselves against the fallen and the falling piers.

The gorgeous peril of the tinted water, and the gorgeous safety of the tinted sky, struck against each other fancifully. There seemed a rescue in the one for the ruin of the other. One was sure that the drowned colors held up their arms again, secure, inviolate, kindled, living, in the great resurrection of the watching heavens.

It must have been not far from the moment when Catty dropped from the cupboard window, that, on the beautiful madness of the river, up where the baby souls of the cas-cades had transmigrated into camels, a long, low, brown streak appeared.

It appeared at first sight to lie quite still. At second sight, it undulated heavily, like a huge boa. At the third, it coiled and plunged.

"The logs! The logs! The logs are here!"

The cry ran round the banks. Maverick Hayle sat down on a stone and looked at his new mill stupidly. Passers cleared the railway crossing. People ran about and shouted. They climbed rocks and trees to look. The guards on the bridge disappeared. The smooth outlines of the boa grew jagged. The timber leaped and tangled in sweeping down. All through its wounded arches, the heavy bridge creaked and cried.

The people on the banks cried too, from sheer excitement.

"The logs, the logs, the logs! The bridge!" "Look on the bridge! Look *there!* Good God! How did she get there? *On the bridge! Woman on the bridge!*"

Past the frightened guards, past the occupied eyes of a thousand people, on the bridge, over the bridge, not twelve feet from the sunken piers, stood a girl with low forehead, and dropping lip, and long, outstretching hands.

"Catty! Catty! O Catty, Catty, Catty!"

The uncouth name rang with a terrible cry. It cleft the crowd like a knife. They parted before it, here and there and everywhere, letting a ghastly girl plunge through.

"O Catty, Catty, Catty! For love's sake, stop! For dear love's sake!"

It was too late for dear love to touch her. Its piteous call she could not hear. Its wrung face she could not see. Her poor, puzzled lips moved as if to argue with it, but made no sound.

Type of the world from which she sprang,—the world of exhausted and corrupted body, of exhausted and corrupted brain, of exhausted and corrupted soul, the world of the laboring poor as man has made it, and as Christ has died for it, of a world deaf, dumb, blind, doomed, stepping confidently to its own destruction before our eyes,—Catty stood for a moment still, a little perplexed, it seemed, feeling about her patiently in the spray-sown, lighted air.

One beck of a human hand would save her; but she could not see it. One cry would turn her; but her ears were sealed.

Still, in the great dream of dying, as in the long dream of life, this miserable creature listened for what she never heard, and spoke that which no man understood.

"She's making signs to me," groaned Sip; "she's making signs to call my name!"

Then Perley Kelso put both arms about her. Then the solid shore staggered suddenly. Then a ragged shadow loomed across the dam. Then there was a shock, and thunder.

Then some one covered her eyes, close.

When she opened them, timber was tearing by. Spray was in her face. Dirk was beside her on his knees, and men had their hats off.

On the empty ruin of the sliced bridge, two logs had caught and hung, black against the color of the water and the color of the sky. They had caught transversely, and hung like a cross.

CHAPTER XIV

❧ Swept and Garnished

It was Dirk who had covered Sip's eyes when the timber struck the bridge.

She did not think of it at the time, but remembered it afterwards.

She remembered it when he came that evening to the door of the lonely, sodden house, after Miss Kelso had gone, asking how she was, but refusing to enter lest, he said, he should be "one too many." She liked that. They did not want him—she and Catty—that night. This thing, in the solitude of the dripping house, had surprised her. God in heaven did not seem to have separated her and Catty, after all. The *silence* of death was spared her. Catty's living love had made no sound; her dead love made none either. A singular comfort came to Sip, almost with the striking of her sorrow. She and Catty could not be parted like two speaking people. Passed into the great world of signs, the deaf-mute, dead, grew grandly eloquent. The ring of the flood was her solemn kiss. The sunshine on the kitchen floor to-morrow would be her dear good-morning. Clouds and shadows and springing green gave her speech forever. The winds of long nights were language for her. Ah, the ways, the ways which Catty could find to speak to her!

Sip walked about the room with dry, burning eyes. She could not cry. She felt exultant, excited. The thing which she greatly feared had come upon her. The worst that ever could hurt her and Catty was over. And now how privileged and rich she was! What ways! How many ways! Only she and Catty knew. How glad she was now that Catty had never talked like other people!

This curious mood—if it should be called a mood—lasted, evenly, till the poor, disfigured heap found one day in the ebbing of the flood flung upright against a rock, a mile below the dam, with its long hands outstretched, spelling awful dumb words, had been brought to the stone house and carried away again, and left until the day when the lips of the dumb shall be unsealed, to spell its untranslated message through a tangle of myrtle into the smoky factory air.

After that she shrank suddenly, like a waked somnambulist, and went sick to bed.

One day she got up and went to work again.

That was the day that Dirk Burdock had watched for, had grown impatient about, seized impetuously when it came.

It had been a pleasant day, with a grave sunlight and a quiet sky. Sip took a grave and pleasant face out into it. She wore a grave and pleasant smile when the young watchman's eager step overtook her, where the rusty boiler (made rustier than ever by the flood, and since removed) had stood beside the cotton-house.

"I'm glad to see you out again, Sip," said the young man, awkwardly, striding out of step with her, and falling back with a jerk.

"Yes," said Sip, "it is quite time I should be at work again."

"It's a pleasant day," said Dirk.

"A very pleasant day," said Sip.

"Been to see the new mill since the repairs?" asked Dirk, as if struck by a bright thought. Now Dirk had vowed within himself, that, whatever else he said to Sip, he would say nothing about the flood. He had an idea that it might make her cry. He had another, that it was about time for her to forget it. He had another still, somewhat to the effect that he was the man to make her forget. In the face of these three ideas, Dirk could have bitten his tongue out for his question. However, Sip did not cry, neither did she seem to have forgotten the flood, neither did she seem anxious to forget it or avoid it.

She said, Yes, smiling, that she had walked by on her way to work this morning. There must have been a good deal of damage done?

"A sight," said Dirk, with a sigh of relief. "They say the young man lost the most out o' that affair."

"Young Hayle?"

"Yes; though they was all involved, I suppose, for that matter,—her among 'em. But she never bothered her head about it at the time o' 't. She was all taken up with—"

"I know," Sip ran on, gently, when poor Dirk stuck in despair. "I do not think she *thought* of anything else but Catty and me. It was like her,—like her."

"She must have lost," said Dirk, reviving again; "I thought the fall lectures would be broke off, but it seems they ain't."

Sip said nothing; did not seem inclined to talk, and the two young people turned a couple of corners on the way to the stone house in thoughtful silence. They were almost too young to be so thoughtful and so silent; more especially the young man, growing nervous, and taking furtive, anxious glances at the girl's face.

It was an inscrutable face.

Sip had shut her lips close; she looked straight ahead; the brown, dull tints of her cheeks and temples came out like a curtain, and folded all young colors and flushes and tremors, all hope and fear, all longing or purpose, need or fulness in her, out of sight. She only looked straight on and waited for Dirk to speak.

She quite knew that and what he would speak. When he began, presently, with a quivering face, "Well, Sip, I don't see that I'm getting on any in the mills, after all," she was neither surprised nor off her guard. She was not yet twenty-three, but she was too old to be put off her guard by a young man with a quivering face. If she had a thing to do, she meant to do it; put her hands together in that way she had, bent at the knuckles, resolutely.

"No," she said, "no; you'll never get any farther, Dirk."

"But I meant to," said Dirk, hotly. "I thought I should! Mebbe you think it's me that's the trouble, not the getting on!"

"Perhaps there *is* a trouble about you," said Sip, honestly; "I don't know; and I don't much care whether there is or not. But I think most of the trouble is in the getting on. Mills ain't made to get on in. It ain't easy, I know, Dirk. It ain't. It's the *staying put* of 'em, that's the worst of 'em. *Don't* I know? It's the staying put that's the matter with most o' folks in the world, it seems to me. For we *are* the most o' folks,—us that stay put, you know."

"Are we?" said Dirk, a little puzzled by Sip's social speculations. "But I'm getting steady pay now, Sip, at any rate; and I've a steady chance. Garrick's a friend o' mine, I believe, and has showed himself friendly. He'll keep me the watch, at least,—Mr. Garrick. I might be worse off than on watch, Sip."

"O yes," said Sip; "you've got a good place, Dirk."

"With a chance," repeated Dirk.

"With a chance? Maybe," answered Sip.

"And now," said Dirk, trembling suddenly, "what with the place and the chance— maybe, and the pay and the steadiness, sure, I've been thinking, Sip, as the time had come to ask you—"

"Don't!" said Sip.

All young colors and flushes and tremors, hopes and fears, longing and need, broke now out of the brown curtain of Sip's face. In the instant she was a very lonely, very miserable little girl, not by any means over twenty-three, and the young man had eyes so cruelly kind! But she said: "Don't, Dirk! O please, don't!"

"Well!" said Dirk. He stopped and drew breath as if she had shot him.

They had come to the stone house now, and Sip began walking back and forth in front of it.

"But I was going to ask you to be my wife!" said Dirk. "It's so long that I haven't dared to ask you, and now you say don't! Don't? But I will; I'll ask at any rate. Sip, will you marry me? There! I should choke if I didn't ask. You may say what you please."

"I *can't* say what I please," said Sip, in a low voice, walking faster.

"I don't know what's to hinder," said Dirk, in an injured tone; "I always knew I wasn't half fit for you, and I always knew you'd ought to have a man that could get on. But considering the steadiness and the chance, and that I—I set such a sight by you, Sip, and sometimes I've thought you—liked me well enough," concluded Dirk, candidly.

"I like you, Dirk," said Sip, slowly, "well enough."

"Well enough to be my wife?"

"Well enough to be your wife."

"Then I shouldn't think," observed Dirk, simply, and with a brightening face, "that you'd find it very hard saying what you please."

"Maybe I shouldn't," said Sip, "if I could be your wife; but I can't."

Her bent hands fell apart weakly; she did not look at Dirk; she fixed her eyes on a little clump of dock-weed at her feet, beside the fence; she looked sick and faint.

"I'll not marry you," said the girl feebly; "I'll not marry anybody. Maybe it isn't the way a girl had ought to feel when she likes a young fellow," added Sip, with a kind of patient aged bitterness crawling into her eyes. "But we don't live down here so's to make girls grow up like girls should, it seems to me. Things as wouldn't trouble rich folks troubles us. There's things that troubles me. I'll never marry anybody, Dirk. I'll never bring a child into the world to work in the mills; and if I'd ought not to say it, I can't help it, for it's the truth, and the reason, and I've said it to God on my knees a many and a many times. I've said it before Catty died, and I've said it more than ever since, and I'll say it till I die. I'll never bring children into this world to be factory children, and to be factory boys and girls, and to be factory men and women, and to see the sights I've seen, and to bear the things I've borne, and to run the risks I've run, and to grow up as I've grown up, and to stop where I've stopped,—never. I've heard tell of slaves before the war that wouldn't be fathers and mothers of children to be slaves like them. That's the way I feel, and that's the way I mean to feel. I won't be the mother of a child to go and live my life over again. I'll never marry anybody."

"But they needn't be factory people," urged Dirk, with a mystified face. "There's trades and—other things."

"I know, I know," Sip shook her head,—"I know all about that. They'd never get out of the mills. It's from generation to generation. It couldn't be helped. I know. It's in the blood."

"But other folks don't take it so," urged Dirk, after a disconsolate pause. "Other folks marry, and have their homes and the comfort of 'em. Other folks, if they love a man, 'll be his wife someways or nuther."

"Sometimes," said Sip, "I seem to think that that I'm not other folks. Things come to me someways that other folks don't understand nor care for." She crushed the dock-weed to a wounded mass, and dug her foot into the ground, and stamped upon it.

"I've made up my mind, Dirk. It's no use talking. It—it hurts me," with a tender motion of the restless foot against the bruised, rough leaves of the weed which she was covering up with sand. "I'd rather not talk any more, Dirk. There's other girls. Some other girl will do."

"I'll have no other girl if I can't have you!" said poor Dirk, turning away. "I never could set such a sight by another girl as I've set by you. If you don't marry, Sip, no more 'll I."

Sip smiled, but did not speak.

"Upon my word, I won't!" cried Dirk. "You think I'm one of other folks, I guess. You wait and see. I've loved you true. If ever man loved a girl, I've loved you true. If I can't have you, I'll have nobody!"

But Sip only smiled.

She went into the house after Dirk had gone, weakly. The flushing tremors in her face had set into a dead color, and her hands came together again at the knuckles.

The Irish woman was away, and the house was lonely and still. The kitchen fire was out. She went out into the little shed for kindlings, thinking that she would make a cup of tea directly, she felt so weak.

When she got there, she sat down on the chopping-block, and covered her face, her feet hanging listlessly against the axe. She wished that she need never lift her head nor look about again. She wished that when the Irish woman came home she should just step into the little shed and find her dead. What a close little warm sheltered shed it was! All the world outside of it seemed emptied, swept, and garnished. She felt as if her life had just been through a "house-cleaning." It was clean and washed, and proper and right, and as it should be, and drearily in order forever. Now it was time to sit down in it.

Sip had what Mr. Mill calls a "large share of human nature," and she loved Dirk, and she led a lonely life. She was neither a heroine, nor a saint, nor a fanatic, sitting out there in the little wood-shed on the chopping-block.

"I don't see why I couldn't have had *that,* leastways," she cried between her hands. "I haven't ever had much else. I don't see why *that* should go too."

But she did see. In about ten minutes she saw clearly enough to get up from the chopping-block, and go in and make her cup of tea.

CHAPTER XV

❧ A Preacher and a Sermon

She saw clearly enough in time to be a very happy woman.

Perley Kelso, at least, was thinking so, when she went the other day with young Mrs. Hayle to hear one of her street sermons.

Sip had "set up for a preacher," after all; she hardly knew how; nobody knew exactly how; it had come about, happened; taken rather the form of a destiny than a plan.

The change had fallen upon her since Catty's passing "out of sight." She was apt to speak of Catty so. She was not dead nor lost. She listened still and spoke. She only could not see her.

"But she talks," said Sip under her breath,—"she talks to me. There's things she'd have me say. That was how I first went to the meetings. I'd never cared about meetings. I'd never been religious nor good. But Catty had such things to say! and when I saw the people's faces, lifted up and listening, and when I talked and talked, it all came to me one night like this. Do you see? Like this. I was up to the Mission reading a little hymn I know, and the lights were on the people's faces, and in a minute it was like this. *God had things to say.* I'd been talking Catty's words. *God had words.* I cannot tell you how it was; but I stood right up and said them; and ever since there's been more than I could say."

"What is there about the girl that can attract so many people?" asked Mrs. Maverick Hayle, standing on tiptoe beside Perley on the outer edge of Sip's audience, and turning her wide eyes on it, like a child at a menagerie. "There are old men here, and old women. There's everybody here. The girl looks too young to instruct them."

She must judge for herself what there was about her, Miss Kelso said; it had been always so; since she started her first neighborhood meeting in the Irish woman's kitchen at the stone house, she had found listeners enough; they were too many for tenement accommodations after a while, and so the thing grew.

Sometimes she used the chapel. Sometimes she preferred a doorstep like this, and the open air.

"I undertook to help her at the first," said Miss Kelso, smiling, "but I was only *among* them at best; Sip is *of* them; she understands them and they understand her; so I left her to her work, and I keep to my own. Hush! Here she is; can you see? Just over there on the upper step."

They were in a little court, a miserable place, breaking out like a wart from one of the foulest alleys in Five Falls; a place such as Sip was more apt than not to choose for her "sermons." The little court was sheltered, however, and comparatively quiet. There may have been fifty people in it.

"Everybody," as Mrs. Hayle said,—old Bijah, with heavy crutches, sitting on a barrel, and offering his services as prompter now and then, out of a petition to the Legislature of the State of Massachusetts; Dib Docket, grown into long curls and a brass necklace; pretty little Irish Maggie, with her thin cheek upon her hand; Mr. Mell, frowningly attentive; the young watchman, and his young wife in blue ribbons, making a Scotch picture of herself up against the old court pump; all Sip's friends, and strangers who drifted in, from curiosity, or idleness, or that sheer misery which has an instinct always for such crowds.

Sip was used now to the Scotch picture, quite. She had expected it, was ready for it. Dirk was one of "other folks," in spite of himself. She had understood that from the first. She did not mind it very much. She framed the picture in with "God's words," with a kind of solemn joy. Dirk was happy. She liked to see it, know it, while she talked. She was glad that Nynee inclined to come with him so often to hear her.

Sip came out on the doorstep and stood for a moment with her hands folded down before her, and her keen eyes taking the measure of every face, it seemed, in the little court.

There was nothing saintly about Sip. No halo struck through the little court upon her doorstep. Florence Nightingale[62] or the Quaker Dinah would not have liked her. She was just a little rough, brown girl, bringing her hands together at the knuckles and talking fast.

"But such a curious preacher!" said Mrs. Maverick Hayle.

The little preacher had a wandering style, as most such preachers have. Such a style can no more be caught on the point of a pen than the rustle of crisp leaves or the aroma of dropping nuts. There was a syntax in Sip's brown face and bent hands and poor dress and awkward motions. There were correctness and perspicuity about that old doorstep. The muddy little court was an appeal, the square of sky above her head a peroration. In that little court Sip was eloquent. Here on the parlor sofa, in clean cuffs and your slippers, she harangues you.

"Look here," she was saying, "you men and women, and you boys and girls, that have come to hear me! You say that you are poor and miserable. I've heard you. You say you're worked and drove and slaved, and up early and down late, and hurried and worried and fretted, and too hot and too cold, and too cross and too poor, to care about religion. I know. I'm worked and drove, and up and down, and hurried and worried and fretted, and hot and cold, and cross and poor myself. I know about that. Religion will do for rich folks. That's what you say,—I know. I've said it a many times myself. Curse the rich folks and their religion!—that's what you say. I know. Haven't I said it a many times myself?

"Now see here! O you men and women, and you boys and girls, can't you *see?* It ain't a rich folks' religion that I've brought to talk to you. Rich religion ain't for you and ain't for me. We're poor folks, and we want a poor folks' religion. We must have a poor folks' religion or none at all. We know that.

"Now listen to me! O you men and women, and you girls and boys, listen to what I've got to tell you. The religion of Jesus Christ the Son of God Almighty is the only poor folks' religion in all the world. Folks have tried it many times. They've got up pious names and pious fights. There have been wars and rumors of wars, and living and dying, and books written, and money spent, and blood shed for other religions, but there's never been any poor folks' religion but that of Jesus Christ the Son of God Almighty. . . .

"O listen to me! You go on your wicked ways, and you drink, and fight, and swear, and you live in sinful shames, and you bring your little children up to shameful sins, and when Jesus Christ the Son of God Almighty does you the favor to ask you for your wicked hearts, you hold up your faces before him, and you say, 'We're poor folks, Lord. We're up early, and we're down late, and we're droved and slaved, and rich folks are hard on us. The mill-masters drive their fine horses, Lord, and we walk and work till we're worn out. There's a man with a million dollars, Lord, and we haven't laid by fifty yet against a rainy day!' Then you grow learned and wise, and you shake your heads, and you say, 'Capital has all the ease, Lord, and labor has all the rubs; and things ain't as they should be; and it can't be expected of us to be religious in such a state of affairs.' And you

---

[62]Florence Nightingale (1820–1910) was an English nurse who founded the profession of trained nursing for women.

say, 'I'm at work all day and nights, I'm tired'; or, 'I'm at work all the week, and of a Sunday I must sleep; I can't be praying'; and so you say, 'I pray thee, Lord, have me excused!' and so you go your wicked ways.

"O listen to me! This is what he says, '*I* was up, and down, and drove, and slaved, and hurried, myself,' he says, 'I was too hot, and too cold, and worried, and anxious, and *I* saw rich folks take their ease, and *I* was poor like you,' he says.

"O you men and women, and you boys and girls, listen to him! Never you mind about me any longer, listen to HIM!

"He won't be hard on you. Don't you suppose he knows how the lives you live are hard enough without that heaped against them? Don't you suppose he *knows* how the world is all a tangle, and how the great and the small, and the wise and the foolish, and the fine and the miserable, and the good and the bad, are all snarled in and out about it? And doesn't he know how long it is unwinding, and how the small and the foolish and the bad and the miserable places stick in his hands? And don't you suppose he *knows* what places they are to be born in and to die in, and to inherit unto the third and fourth generations of us, like the color of our hair, or the look about our mouths?

"I tell you, he knows, he knows! I tell you, he knows where the fault is, and where the knot is, and who's to blame, and who's to suffer. And I tell you he knows there'll never be any way but his way to unsnarl us all.

"Folks may make laws, but laws won't do it. Kings and congresses may put their heads together, but they'll have their trouble for nothing. Governments and churches may finger us over, but we'll only snarl the more.

"Rich and poor, big or little, there's no way under heaven for us to get out of our twist, but Christ's way.

"O you men and women, and you girls and boys, look in your own hearts and see what way that is. That way is in the heart. I can't see it. I can't touch it. I can't mark it and line it for you. Look. Mind that you don't look at the rich folks' ways! Mind that you don't stop to say, It's their way to do this, and that, and the other, that they'd never do nor think on. Perhaps it is. But that's none of your business, when the Lord Jesus Christ the Son of God Almighty does you the favor to ask for *you,* and *your* heart, and *your* ways, to gather 'em up into his poor cut hands and hold them, and to bow his poor hurt face down over them and bless them!

"O you men and women, and you boys and girls, Christ's way is a patient way, it is a pure way, it is a way that cares more for another world than for this one, and more to be holy than to be happy, and more for other folks than for itself. It's a long way and a winding way, but it's a good way and a true way, and there's comfort in it, and there's joy at the end of it, and there's *Christ all over it,* and I pray God to lead you in it, every one, forever.

"Christ in heaven! said Sip then, bending her lighted, dark face, "thou hast been Christ on earth. That helps us. That makes us brave to hunt for thee. We are poor folks, Christ, and we've got a load of poor folks' sorrows, and of poor folks' foolishness, and of poor folks' fears, and of poor folks' wickedness, and we've got nowheres else to take it. Here it is. Lord Christ, we seem to feel as if it belonged to thee. We seem to feel as if we was thy folks. We seem to know that thou dost understand us, someways, better than the most of people. Be our Saviour, Lord Christ, for thine own name's sake."

Miss Kelso and Mrs. Hayle left the little preacher still speaking God's words—and Catty's, and stole away before the breaking up of her audience. They walked in silence for a few minutes up the street.

"They listened to her," said Fly then, musingly. "On the whole, I don't know that I wonder. They looked as if they needed it."

"There are few things that they do not need," said Perley, quietly. "We do not quite understand that, I think,—we who never need. It is a hungry world, Fly."

"Yes?" said Fly, placidly perplexed; "I don't know much about the world, Perley."

Perley was silent. She was wondering what good it would do—either the world or Fly—if she did.

"Kenna Van Doozle was asking the other day," said Fly, suddenly, "whether you still went about among these people at all hours of the day and evening, as you used, alone. I should be so timid, Perley! And then, do you always find it quite proper?"

"I have no reason to feel afraid of my friends in Five Falls at any hour," said Miss Kelso, reservedly. There seemed such a gulf between her and this pretty, good-natured little lady. Proper! Why try to pass the impassable? Fly might stay where she was.

"And yet," sighed Mrs. Maverick Hayle, "this dreary work seems to suit you through and through. That is what troubles me about it."

Perley Kelso's healthy, happy face took the quiver of a smile. The fine, rare face! The womanly, wonderful face! Fly was right. It was a "suited" face. It begged for nothing. It was opulent and warm. Life brimmed over at it.

Stephen Garrick, on the opposite side of the road, climbed the hill alone. It was a late November day; a day of cleared heavens and bared trees. Yet he looked about for bright maples, and felt as if he walked under a sealed sky, and in an unreal light of dying leaves.

THE END

16

William Holmes McGuffey
(1800–1873)

RAISED ON A rugged farm in Ohio, William McGuffey enjoyed a strong work ethic and pioneer spirit his entire life. He began his teaching career at the age of fourteen, when he started teaching students six days a week, eleven hours a day. In 1826, he received his bachelor's degree and soon took a position on the faculty of Miami University in Oxford, Ohio. He would spend the rest of his life in various college and university positions in both Ohio and Virginia.

Approached by the Cincinnati publishing firm of Truman and Smith, McGuffey agreed to produce a series of school readers, which first appeared in 1836. Over the next several years, McGuffey produced a series of six graduated readers, along with primers, spellers, and rhetorical guides. All of these books were deeply concerned with the pupil's moral character, offering a clearly Christian social ethic and view of the world.

The McGuffey series would pass through the hands of a number of publishers during the nineteenth century, as the books were constantly revised to meet the competition of rival publishers and the changing educational needs of the country. After the initial versions of these readers, McGuffey had little to do with these revisions. Over the years, changes to the series maintained, yet softened, the moral content of the readers. In 1879, the firm of Van Antwerp, Bragg & Co. completely overhauled the readers, forsaking almost all of the earlier readers' theistic underpinnings in favor of a more secular view of morality. Virtue became motivated largely by earthly, not divine, rewards.

The popularity of the McGuffey reading series was staggering. More than 120 million copies of these books circulated in the United States before 1920. The *First Eclectic Reader* reproduced below represents the 1879 revision, when the McGuffey series was at the apex of its popularity. It is interesting to note that while the greatest volume of McGuffey readers were sold between 1870 and 1890, issues such as urbanization, industrialization, Southern Reconstruction, and immigration are largely ignored, while the sentimental, agrarian ideal of the early McGuffey readers continue to set the tone for much of the series' content.

McGUFFEY'S FIRST ECLECTIC READER
Revised Edition

Cover of *McGuffey's First Eclectic Reader: Revised Edition*
(Cincinnati: Van Antwerp, Bragg & Co., 1879).

William H. McGuffey, *McGuffey's First Eclectic Reader: Revised Edition*. Cincinnati: Van Antwerp, Bragg & Co., 1879.

ECLECTIC EDUCATIONAL SERIES.

M^CGUFFEY'S

FIRST

ECLECTIC READER.

REVISED EDITION.

VAN ANTWERP, BRAGG & CO.
CINCINNATI.   NEW YORK.

Title page from *McGuffey's First Eclectic Reader: Revised Edition*
(Cincinnati: Van Antwerp, Bragg & Co., 1879).

PREFACE.

In presenting McGuffey's Revised First Reader to the public, attention is invited to the following features:

1. Words of only two or three letters are used in the first lessons. Longer and more difficult ones are gradually introduced as the pupil gains aptness in the mastery of words.

2. A proper gradation has been carefully preserved. All new words are placed at the head of each lesson, to be learned before the lesson is read. Their number in the early lessons is very small, thus making the first steps easy. All words in these vocabularies are used in the text immediately following.

3. Carefully engraved script exercises are introduced for a double purpose. These should be used to teach the reading of script; and may also serve as copies in slate work.

4. The illustrations have been designed and engraved specially for the lessons in which they occur. Many of these engravings will serve admirably as the basis for oral lessons in language.

5. The type is large, strong, and distinct.

The credit for this revision is almost wholly due to the many friends of McGuffey's Readers,—eminent teachers and scholars, who have contributed suggestions and criticisms gained from their daily work in the school-room.

Cincinnati, June, 1879.

(iii)

SUGGESTIONS TO TEACHERS.

This First Reader may be used in teaching reading by any of the methods in common use; but it is especially adapted to the Phonic Method, the Word Method, or a combination of the two.

I. Phonic Method.—First teach the elementary sounds and their representatives, the letters marked with diacriticals, as they occur in the lessons; then, the formation of words by the combination of these sounds. For instance, teach the pupil to identify the characters ă, ŏ, n, d, ĕ, r, and th, in Lesson I, as the representatives of certain elementary sounds; then, teach him to form words by their combination, and to identify them at sight. Use first the words at the head of the lesson, then other words, as, *nag, on, and,* etc. Pursue a similar course in teaching the succeeding lessons. Having read a few lessons in this manner, begin to teach the names of the letters and the spelling of words. Do not teach the names of the letters and the spelling of words, and require the groups, "a man," "the man," "a pen," "the pen," to be read as a good reader would pronounce single words.

II. When one of the letters in the combinations *ou* or *ow,* is marked in the words at the head of the reading exercises, the other is silent. If neither is marked, the two letters represent a diphthong. All other unmarked vowels in the vocabularies, when *in combination,* are silent letters. In slate or blackboard work, the silent letters may be canceled.

III. Word Method.—Teach the pupil to identify at sight the words placed at the head of the reading exercises, and to read these exercises without hesitation. Having read a few lessons, begin to teach the names of the letters and the spelling of words.

IV. Word Method and Phonic Method Combined.—Teach the pupil to identify words and read sentences, as above. Having read a few lessons in this manner, begin to use the Phonic Method, combining it with the Word Method, by first teaching the words in each lesson *as words;* then, the elementary sounds, the names of the letters, and spelling.

V. Teach the pupil to use script letters in writing, when teaching the names of the letters and the spelling of words.

THE ALPHABET.

A a
B b
C c
D d
E e
F f
G g
H h
I i
J j
K k
L l
M m

N n
O o
P p
Q q
R r
S s
T t
U u
V v
W w
X x
Y y
Z z

(iv)

SCRIPT ALPHABET.

SCRIPT FIGURES.

1 2 3 4 5 6 7 8 9 0

(v)

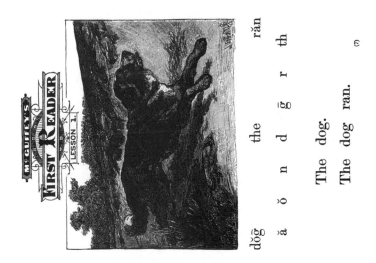

dŏḡ   the   răn

ă ŏ n d ḡ r th

The dog.

The dog ran. (3)

LESSON II.

căt   măt   ŏn

e   t   ĭ   m   ş   ĭş

The cat.   The mat.

Is the cat on the mat?

The cat is on the mat.

LESSON III.

ĭt   hĭş   pĕn   hănd

a   ĭn   hăş   măn

p   h   ĕ

The man.   A pen.

The man has a pen.

Is the pen in his hand?

It is in his hand.

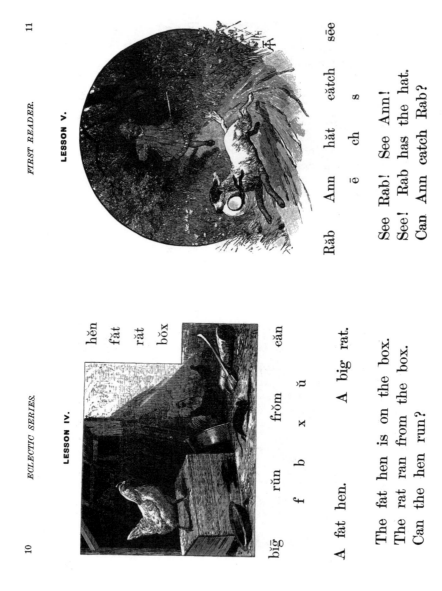

ECLECTIC SERIES.

10

LESSON IV.

bĭg	hĕn
rŭn	făt
frŏm	răt
eăn	bŏx

f   b   x   ŭ

A fat hen.   A big rat.

The fat hen is on the box.
The rat ran from the box.
Can the hen run?

FIRST READER.

11

LESSON V.

Răb	hăt
Ann	eătch
	sēe

ē   ch   s

See Rab! See Ann!
See! Rab has the hat.
Can Ann catch Rab?

12   *ECLECTIC SERIES.*

LESSON VI.

shē   păt   tōo   now
lĕt   mē

sh   ōo   ow   l

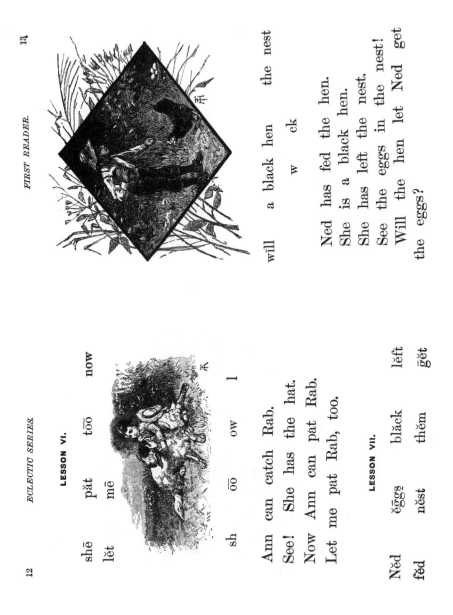

Ann can catch Rab.
See! She has the hat.
Now Ann can pat Rab.
Let me pat Rab, too.

LESSON VII.

Nĕd   ĕġġs   blăck   lĕft
fĕd   nĕst   thĕm   ġĕt

FIRST READER.   13

will   a black hen   the nest
w   ck

Ned has fed the hen.
She is a black hen.
She has left the nest.
See the eggs in the nest!
Will the hen let Ned get the eggs?

14   *ECLECTIC SERIES.*

LESSON VIII.

head	hē	Năt
come	wĭth	ănd
	ȯ	

Let me get the black hat.

Now Ned has it on his head, and he is a big man.

Come, Nat, see the big man with his black hat.

FIRST READER.   15

LESSON IX. REVIEW.

pat	catch	has	left
hat	can	black	eggs
Rab	Ann	fed	get

Ned is on the box. He has a pen in his hand. A big rat is in the box. Can the dog catch the rat?

Come with me, Ann, and see the man with a black hat on his head.

The fat hen has left the nest. Run, Nat, and get the eggs.

SLATE WORK.

The cat ran. Ann ran.

The man has a hat.

LESSON X.

Nĕll	sŏme
păn	hĭm
yĕs	dọ
yọu	hăve
I	tọ

ī   y   v   ọ

Do you see Nell?

Yes; she has a pan with some eggs in it.

Let me have the pan and the eggs, will you, Nell?

Has the black hen left the nest?

I will now run to catch Rab.

Will you run, too?

LESSON XI.

O	whip	Bĕn
ŭp	still	sĭt
ĭf	stănd	Jĭp

ō   wh   j

O Ben! let me get in, will you?

Yes, if you will sit still.

Stand still, Jip, and let Ann get in.

Now, Ben, hand me the whip.

Get up, Jip!

1,2

LESSON XII.

Kĭt'ty̆
nīçe
swēet
sĭng
jŭst
hăng
eāge
thĕn
sŏng

pĕt   pu̇t   nŏt

k   ġ   ç   ā   y̆   ng   u̇

Kitty has a nice pet. It can sing a sweet song.

She has just fed it.

She will now put it in the cage, and hang the cage up. Then the cat can not catch it.

LESSON XIII.

Tŏm   tŏp   Kĭt'ty̆s
ăt

băck
lŏŏk
ḡŏŏd   dŏll   thĭnk   spŏt

th   n   ŏŏ

Look at Tom and his dog. The dog has a black spot on his back. Do you think he is a good dog?

Tom has a big top, too. It is on the box with Kitty's doll.

FIRST READER.   21

Let us not stop at the pond now, for it is hot.

See how still it is! We will go to see Tom and his top.

LESSON XV.

Jŏhn	rŏck	sĕt	jŭmp
fŭn	mŭst	māy	ŭn′der
skĭp	băṉk	bŭt	tŏŭch

O John! the sun has just set. It is not hot, now.

Let us run and jump. I think it is fun to run, and skip, and jump.

See the duck on the pond! Her nest is up on the bank, under the rock.

We must not touch the nest, but we may look at it.

ECLECTIC SERIES.   20

LESSON XIV.

sŭn	wē	how	pŏnd
stŏp	fôr	ḡō	swĭm
hẽr	ŭs	hŏt	dŭck
	ẽ	ô	

The sun is up. The man has fed the black hen and the fat duck.

Now the duck will swim in the pond. The hen has run to her nest.

LESSON XVI. REVIEW.

The sun has set, and the pond is still.

John, Ned, Ben, Tom, and Nell stand on the bank, and look at the duck.

The dog with a black spot on his back, is with Tom. See! Tom has his hat in his hand. He has left his big top on the box.

Kitty's doll is on the rock.
Nell has put her pet in the cage. It will sing a sweet song. The duck has her nest under the rock.

It is not hot, now. Let us run, and skip, and jump on the bank. Do you not think it is fun?

LESSON XVII.

äre ĭnk mŏss thĭs tŭb upsĕt'
ä

SLATE WORK.

The pen and the ink are on the stand. Is this a good pen? The moss is on the rock. This duck can swim. Ben upset the tub.

LESSON XVIII.

nŭt dĭd shŭt shăll lŏst fŏx
mĕn mĕt stĕp ĭn'tọ hŭnt mŭd

SLATE WORK.

Will the dog hunt a fox? Ben lost his hat. Shall I shut the box? I met him on the step. Did you jump into the mud? I have a nut. I met the men.

LESSON XIX.

Kāte	ōld	nō	ḡràss
dēar	likes	bē	drink
mĭlk	cow	out	ḡĭveṣ

à

O Kate! the old cow is in the pond: see her drink! Will she not come out to get some grass?

No, John, she likes to be in the pond. See how still she stands!

The dear, old cow gives us sweet milk to drink.

LESSON XX.

mam mä′	lärġe	ăṣ	pa pä′
ärmṣ	rīde	fär	bärn
bōth	Prĭnçe	trŏt	yọur

Papa, will you let me ride with you on Prince? I will sit still in your arms.

See, mamma! We are both on Prince. How large he is!

Get up, Prince! You are not too fat to trot as far as the barn.

LESSON XXI.

ŏf (ŏv)   thăt   tŏss   fall
wĕll   Făn'nў   ball   wạll
wạṣ   pret'tў (prĭt')   dòne   whạt

ạ   ȧ

O Fanny, what a pretty ball!
Yes; can you catch it, Ann? I will
Toss it to me, and see. I will
not let it fall.
That was well done.

Now, Fanny, toss it to the
top of the wall, if you can.

LESSON XXII.

hăd   wĕnt   eạll   mĭght
flăḡ   nēar   swăm   swĭng

Did you call us, mamma?

I went with Tom to the pond. I had my doll, and Tom had his flag.

The fat duck swam to the bank, and we fed her. Did you think we might fall into the pond?

We did not go too near, did we, Tom?

May we go to the swing, now, mamma?

hēre	bănd	hēar	hôrse
plāy	they	pàss	whêre
frŏnt	fine	hōpe	cómeş
	ê	e̱	

Here comes the band! Shall we call mamma and Fanny to see it?

Let us stand still, and hear the men play as they pass.

I hope they will stop here and play for us.

See the large man in front of the band, with his big hat. What has he in his hand? How fine he looks!

Look, too, at the man on that fine horse.

If the men do not stop, let us go with them and see where they go.

LESSON XXIV.

Bĕss	hăp'py̆	māke	eärt
tĕnt	wŏodş	lĭt'tle	vĕr'y̆
bĕd	Rŏb'ert	gŏne	draw

Bess and Robert are very happy; papa and mamma have gone to the woods with them.

Robert has a big tent and a

flag, and Bess has a little bed for her doll.

Jip is with them. Robert will make him draw Bess and her doll in the cart.

LESSON XXV.

Jāmeş	Mā'ry̆
māde	săng
my̆	lāy
spōrt	spāde
lăp	dĭg
dŏll'ş	sănd
said (sĕd)	y̆

"Kate, will you play with me?"

said James. "We will dig in the sand with this little spade. That will be fine sport."

"Not now, James," said Kate; "for I must make my doll's bed. Get Mary to play with you."

James went to get Mary to play with him. Then Kate made the doll's bed.

She sang a song to her doll, and the doll lay very still in her lap.

Did the doll hear Kate sing?

LESSON XXVI.

ĭts	shāde	brŏŏk	pĭcks	all
bȳ	hĕlp	stōneṣ	ḡlăd	sŏft

Kate has left her doll in its little bed, and has gone to play

with Mary and James. They are all in the shade, now, by the brook.

James digs in the soft sand with his spade, and Mary picks up little stones and puts them in her lap.

James and Mary are glad to see Kate. She will help them pick up stones and dig, by the little brook.

34

LESSON XXVII. REVIEW.

"What shall we do?" said Fanny to John. "I do not like to sit still. Shall we hunt for eggs in the barn?"

"No," said John; "I like to play on the grass. Will not papa let us catch Prince, and go to the big woods?

"We can put the tent in the cart, and go to some nice spot where the grass is soft and sweet."

"That will be fine," said Fanny. "I will get my doll, and give her a ride with us."

"Yes," said John, "and we will get mamma to go, too. She will hang up a swing for us in the shade."

35

LESSON XXVIII.

pēep	while	tŭck	sāfe	ōh	wĕt	fēet
tāke	slēep	chĭck	căn't	fēelş		wĭng

Peep, peep! Where have you gone, little chick? Are you lost? Can't you get back to the hen?

Oh, here you are! I will take you back. Here, hen, take this little chick under your wing.

Now, chick, tuck your little,

This is a fine day. The sun shines bright. There is a good wind, and my kite flies high. I can just see it.

The sun shines in my eyes; I will stand in the shade of this high fence.

Why, here comes my dog! He was under the cart. Did you see him there?

What a good time we have had! Are you not glad that we did not go to the woods with John?

SLATE WORK.

The pond is still. How it shines in the hot sun! Let us go into the woods where we can sit in the shade.

wet feet under you, and go to sleep for a while.

Peep, peep! How safe the little chick feels now!

LESSON XXIX.

wind	time	thêre	fênçe
kite	high	eȳeş	bright
flieş	whȳ	dāy	shineş

LESSON XXX.

wĭsh	flōat	tie	knōw
rōpe	bōat	trȳ	shōre
ġive	pōle	dōn't	push
drăg	wŏn't	ōar	fŭn'ny

"Kate, I wish we had a boat to put the dolls in. Don't you?"

"I know what we can do. We can get the little tub, and tie a

rope to it, and drag it to the pond. This will float with the dolls in it, and we can get a pole to push it from the shore."

"What a funny boat, Kate! A tub for a boat, and a pole for an oar! Won't it upset?"

"We can try it, Nell, and see."

"Well, you get the tub, and I will get a pole and a rope. We will put both dolls in the tub, and give them a ride."

SLATE WORK.

The dolls had a nice ride to the pond. A soft wind made the tub float out. Nell let the pole fall on the tub, and upset it.

Rose went under, but she did not drown. Bess was still on the top of the water.

Ponto came with a bound, and jumped into the pond. He swam around, and got Bess in his mouth, and brought her to the shore.

Ponto then found Rose, and brought her out, too.

Kate said, "Good, old Ponto! Brave, old dog!"

What do you think of Ponto?

LESSON XXXII.

Jūne	Lū'çy's	âir	kīnd
trēeş	sĭng'ing	blūe	whĕn
pūre	sayş (sĕz)	skȳ	pĭe'nĭe
	ū	â	

LESSON XXXI.

bound	Rōşe
eạlled	ḡŏt
drown	found
brȧve	eāme

| Pŏn'tō | jŭmped | mouth |
| a round' | brôught | wạ'ter |

"Here, Ponto! Here, Ponto!" Kate called to her dog. "Come, and get the dolls out of the pond."

What a bright June day! The sky is pure. The air is as blue as it can be.

Lucy and her mamma are in the woods. They have found a nice spot, where there is some grass.

They sit in the shade of the trees, and Lucy is singing.

The trees are not large, but they make a good shade.

Lucy's kind mamma says that they will have a picnic when her papa can get a tent.

LESSON XXXIII. REVIEW.

James and Robert have gone into the shade of a high wall to play ball.

Mary and Lucy have come up from the pond near by, with brave, old Ponto, to see them play.

When they toss the ball up in the air, and try to catch it, Ponto runs to get it in his mouth.

Now the ball is lost. They all look for it under the trees

and in the grass; but they can not see it. Where can it be? Here he comes with it. He will lay it at little Lucy's feet, or put it in her hand.

LESSON XXXIV.

boy	our	spoil	hur răh'
ōwn	eoil	noiṣe	fourth
sŭch	join	thăṇk	a bout'
hoist	pāy	Ju lȳ'	plāy'ing

ŭ

"Papa, may we have the big flag?", said James.

"What can my little boy do with such a big flag?"

"Hoist it on our tent, papa. We are playing Fourth of July."

"Is that what all this noise

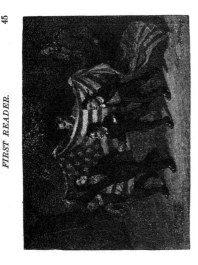

is about? Why not hoist your own flags?"

"Oh! they are too little."

"You might spoil my flag."

"Then we will all join to pay for it. But we will not spoil it, papa."

"Take it, then, and take the coil of rope with it."

"Oh! thank you. Hurrah for the flag, boys!"

LESSON XXXV.

fĭn′ished   ăm   wŏrk   bŏn′net

seăm′per   gär′den

sāved   I′ve

a wāy′   white

rĕad′ÿ   lĕs′son

THE WHITE KITTEN.

Kitty, my pretty, white kitty,
Why do you scamper away?
I've finished my work and my lesson,
And now I am ready for play.

Come kitty, my own little kitty,
I've saved you some milk, come and see;
Now drink it while I put on my bonnet,
And play in the garden with me.

LESSON XXXVI.

eâre   al′wāys   line   Frănk

rōw   been(bĭn)   kēeps   hōme

Frank has a pretty boat. It is white, with a black line near the water.

He keeps it in the pond, near his home. He always takes good care of it.

Frank has been at work in the garden, and will now row a while.

FIRST READER.   49

ECLECTIC SERIES.   48

LESSON XXXVII.

| mŭch | one (wŭn) | yĕt | 'hŭṉ'grȳ |
| sēen | grănd'mä | côrn | wọuld |

"What is that?" said Lucy, as she came out on the steps.

"Oh, it is a little boat! What a pretty one it is!"

"I will give it to you when it is finished," said John, kindly.

"Would you like to have it?"

"Yes, very much, thank you, John. Has grandma seen it?"

"Not yet; we will take it to her by and by. What have you in your pan, Lucy?"

"Some corn for my hens, John; they must be very hungry by this time."

LESSON XXXVIII.

mär′ket	brĕad
bȧs′ket	bôught
	mēat
	tēa
	trȳ′ing
	tĕll
	whĭch

James has been to market with his mamma.

She has bought some bread, some meat, and some tea, which are in the basket on her arm.

James is trying to tell his mamma what he has seen in the market.

LESSON XXXIX.

rēads	sō	weârṣ	plēaṣe
cọuld	hâir		
fȧst	lȯve		
ēaṣ′ẏ	grāy		
châir	whọ		
	glȧss′eṣ		

See my dear, old grandma in her easy-chair! How gray her hair is! She wears glasses when she reads.

She is always kind, and takes such good care of me that I like to do what she tells me.

When she says, "Robert, will you get me a drink?" I run as fast as I can to get it for her. Then she says, "Thank you, my boy."

Would you not love a dear, good grandma, who is so kind? And would you not do all you could to please her?

LESSON XL.

dŏeş   wŏn′der   mŏth′er   ŏth′er
bēe   hŏn′eỹ   lĭst′en   flŏw′er

"Come here, Lucy, and listen! What is in this flower?"

"O mother! it is a bee. I wonder how it came to be shut up in the flower!"

"It went into the flower for some honey, and it may be it went to sleep. Then the flower shut it in.

"The bee likes honey as well as we do, but it does not like to be shut up in the flower.

"Shall we let it out, Lucy?"

"Yes; then it can go to other flowers, and get honey."

ECLECTIC SERIES.

54

LESSON XLI.

bĕst	hĭtched	thêir	should
ôr	rīd'ing	live	hōlds
hāy	driv'ing	tight	ẽar'lỹ

Here come Frank and James White. Do you know where they live?

Frank is riding a horse, and James is driving one hitched to

FIRST READER.

55

a cart. They are out very early in the day. How happy they are!

See how well Frank rides, and how tight James holds the lines!

The boys should be kind to their horses. It is not best to whip them.

When they have done riding, they will give the horses some hay or corn.

SLATE WORK.

Some horses can trot very fast. Would you like to ride fast? One day, I saw a dog hitched to a little cart. The cart had some corn in it.

LESSON XLII.

lŏok′ing	thôught	pĭck′ing
hẽard		chĭrp
wẽre		tōld
sẽarch		dēar′lў
yŏung		g̃ĭrl
loved		bĭrdş
chĭl′dren	be·sideş′	

A little girl went in search of flowers for her mother. It was early in the day, and the grass was wet. Sweet little birds were singing all around her.

And what do you think she found besides flowers? A nest with young birds in it.

While she was looking at

them, she heard the mother-bird chirp, as if she said, "Do not touch my children, little girl, for I love them dearly."

The little girl now thought how dearly her own mother loved her.

So she left the birds. Then, picking some flowers, she went home, and told her mother what she had seen and heard.

LESSON XLIII.

ēight	àsk	äft′er	town
pàst	äh	tĭck′et	rīght
hälf	twọ	trāin	dĭng
		lïght′ning	

"Mamma, will you go to town?"
"What do you ask for a ticket on your train?"

"Oh! we will give you a ticket, mamma."

"About what time will you get back?"

"At half past eight."

"Ah! that is after bed-time. Is this the fast train?"

"Yes, this is the lightning train."

"Oh! that is too fast for me."

"What shall we get for you in town, mamma?"

"A big basket, with two good little children in it."

"All right! Time is up! Ding, ding!"

LESSON XLIV.

ē'ven (ē'vn)   thrēe
schōol   smạll
rōom

bŏŏk   tēach'er   nōon
rude   rēad'ing   pōor

It is noon, and the school is out. Do you see the children

FIRST READER. 61

LESSON XLV.

ĕCLECTIC SERIES 60

at play? Some run and jump, some play ball, and three little girls play school under a tree. What a big room for such a small school!

Mary is the teacher. They all have books in their hands, and Fanny is reading.

They are all good girls, and would not be rude even in playing school.

Kate and Mary listen to Fanny as she reads from her book.

What do you think she is reading about? I will tell you. It is about a poor little boy who was lost in the woods.

When Fanny has finished, the three girls will go home.

In a little while, too, the boys will give up their playing.

ăp′ple	mew	tēaṣe	crăck′er
down	new	sil′lȳ	aslēep′
waṇts	calls	knew	friĕndṣ
up ŏn′	flew	Pŏll	Pŏl′lȳ

Lucy has a new pet. Do you know what kind of bird it is? Lucy calls her Polly.

Polly can say, "Poor Poll! Poor

Poll! Polly wants a cracker;" and she can mew like a cat.

But Polly and the cat are not good friends. One day Polly flew down, and lit upon the cat's back when she was asleep.

I think she knew the cat would not like that, and she did it to tease her.

When Lucy pets the cat, Polly flies up into the old apple-tree, and will not come when she calls her. Then Lucy says, "What a silly bird!"

LESSON XLVI. REVIEW.

"Well, children, did you have a nice time in the woods?"

"Oh yes, mother, such a good time! See what sweet flowers

we found, and what soft moss. The best flowers are for grandma. Won't they please her?"

"Yes; and it will please grandma to know that you thought of her."

"Rab was such a good dog, mother.

We left him under the big tree by the brook, to take care of the dolls and the basket.

"When we came back, they were all safe. No one could get them while Rab was there.

64

ECLECTIC SERIES.

We gave him some of the crack-ers from the basket.

"O mother, how the birds did sing in the woods!

"Fanny said she would like to be a bird, and have a nest in a tree. But I think she would want to come home to sleep."

"If she were a bird, her nest would be her home. But what would mother do, I wonder, with-out her little Fanny?"

LESSON XLVII.

bēach	shĕllṣ	thēṣe	sēat
wāveṣ	ḡō'ing	ĕv'er	sēa
wạtch	é'ven ing	lā'zẙ	sīde

These boys and girls live near the sea. They have been to the

65

FIRST READER.

beach. It is now evening, and they are going home.

John, who sits on the front seat, found some pretty shells. They are in the basket by his side.

Ben White is driving. He holds the lines in one hand, and his whip in the other.

Robert has his hat in his hand, and is looking at the horses. He thinks they are very lazy; they do not trot fast.

The children are not far from home. In a little while the sun will set, and it will be bed-time.

Have you ever been at the sea-side? Is it not good sport to watch the big waves, and to play on the wet sand?

LESSON XLVIII.

lŏg	quī′et	proud	pulled
fish	stŭmp	rĭv′er	fä′ther

One evening Frank's father said to him, "Frank, would you like to go with me to catch some fish?

"Yes; can I go? and with you, father?"

"Yes, Frank, with me."

"Oh, how glad I am!"

Here they are, on the bank of a river. Frank has just pulled a fine fish out of the water. How proud he feels!

See what a nice, quiet spot they have found. Frank has the stump of a big tree for his seat, and his father sits on a log near by. They like the sport.

LESSON XLIX.

rain	out'side	ŏft'en	pĭt'ter
sāy	wĭn'dōw	sound	păt'ter
drŏps	sōme'timeş	ōn'lў	mū'şie

SLATE WORK.

I wish, Mamma, you would tell me where the rain comes from. Does it come from the sky? And when the little drops (pitter-patter) on the window, do you think they are playing with me? I can not work or read, for I love to listen to them. I often think their sound is like pretty music. But the rain keeps children at home, and sometimes I do not like that; then,

The little rain-drops only stay.
"Pit, pitter, patter, pat;"
While we play on the out-side,
Why can't you play on that?

LESSON L.

slĕd	thrōw	wĭn'ter	hûrt
īçe	eŏv'er	Hĕn'rў	nĕxt
skāte	ğround	mĕr'rў	snōw
sĭs'ter	lăugh'ing (lȧf'ing)		pâir

I like winter, when snow and ice cover the ground. What fun 'it is to throw snow-balls, and to skate on the ice!

See the boys and girls! How merry they are! Henry has his sled, and draws his little sister. There they go!

ECLECTIC SERIES.

I think Henry is kind, for his sister is too small to skate.

Look! Did you see that boy fall down? But I see he is not hurt, for he is laughing.

Some other boys have just come to join in the sport. See them put on their skates.

Henry says, that he hopes his father will get a pair of skates for his sister next winter.

FIRST READER.

LESSON LI.

pạw	po lite´
mēanṣ	iṣn't
spēak	sĭr
shāke	Fĭ'dō
trĭcks	tēach
dĭn'ner	
El'len	
bow-wow	

Ellen, do look at Fido! He sits up in a chair, with my hat on. He looks like a little boy; but it is only Fido.

Now see him shake hands.

Give me your paw, Fido. How do you do, sir? Will you take dinner with us, Fido? Speak!

FIRST READER. 73

rat in the shed; and old Nero tried to catch it."

"Did he catch it, Frank?"

"No, Nero did not; but the old cat did."

"My cat?"

"No, it was the other one."

"Do tell me how she got it, Frank. Did she run after it?"

"No, that was not the way. Puss was hid on a big box. The rat stole out, and she jumped at it and caught it."

"Poor rat! It must have been very hungry; it came out to get something to eat."

"Why, Hattie, you are not sorry puss got the rat, are you?"

"No, I can not say I am sorry she got it; but I do not like to see even a rat suffer pain."

ECLECTIC SERIES. 72

Fido says, "Bow-wow," which means, "Thank you, I will."

Isn't Fido a good dog, Ellen? He is always so polite.

When school is out, I will try to teach him some other tricks.

LESSON LII.

puss   shĕd
pāin   wāy
stōle   sąw
hĭd   ēat

Hăt′tie
sŭf′fer
sŏr′rў

sóme′thing   eaught   trĭed   Nē′rō

"O Hattie! I just saw a large

LESSON LIII.

rōll	buïld	g̅rănd′pä	härd
fōam	shĭps	hous̶′es̶	lŏng
sāil	breāk	wŏŏd′en	blōw

Mary and Lucy have come down to the beach with their grandpa. They live in a town near the sea.

Their grandpa likes to sit on the large rock, and watch the big ships as they sail far away on the blue sea. Sometimes he sits there all day long.

The little girls like to dig in the sand, and pick up pretty shells. They watch the waves as they roll up on the beach, and break into white foam.

They sometimes make little

houses of sand, and build walls around them; and they dig wells with their small wooden spades.

They have been picking up shells for their little sister. She is too young to come to the beach.

I think all children like to play by the sea-side when the sun is bright, and the wind does not blow too hard.

LESSON LIV.

wạnt'ed
Wĭll'ie's
răb'bits
eär'ried
tĕll'ing
mȧs'ter

àsked
fōur
nīght
lăd
çĕnts
fĭf'tỹ

One day, Willie's father saw a boy at the market with four little white rabbits in a basket.

He thought these would be nice pets for Willie; so he asked the lad how much he wanted for his rabbits.

The boy said, "Only fifty cents, sir."

Willie's father bought them, and carried them home.

Here you see the rabbits and their little master. He has a pen for them, and always shuts them in it at night to keep them safe.

He gives them bread and grass to eat. They like grass, and will take it from his hand. He has called in a little friend to see them.

Willie is telling him about their funny ways.

SLATE WORK.

Some rabbits are as white as snow; some are black, and others have white and black spots.

What soft, kind eyes they have!

78

LESSON LV.

bush eŭn'ning plāçe shōw

find brō'ken ō'ver brĭng

a ḡain' (a ḡĕn') fȧst'en (fȧs'n)

"Come here, Rose. Look down into this bush."

"O Willie! a bird's nest! What

---

cunning, little eggs! May we take it, and show it to mother?"

"What would the old bird do, Rose, if she should come back and not find her nest?"

"Oh, we would bring it right back, Willie!"

"Yes; but we could not fasten it in its place again. If the wind should blow it over, the eggs would get broken."

LESSON LVI.

strŏng round drȳ bĭll wõrked

sĕndṣ çlaẉṣ flĭt Gŏd sprĭng

"How does the bird make the nest so strong, Willie?"

"The mother-bird has her bill and her claws to work with, but

80 ECLECTIC SERIES.

she would not know how to make the nest if God did not teach her. Do you see what it is made of?"

"Yes, Willie, I see some horse-hairs and some dry grass. The old bird must have worked hard to find all the hairs, and make them into such a pretty, round nest."

"Shall we take the nest, Rose?"

"Oh no, Willie! We must not take it; but we will come and look at it again, some time."

SLATE WORK.

God made the little birds to sing,
And flit from tree to tree;
'Tis He who sends them in the spring
To sing for you and me.

FIRST READER. 81

LESSON LVII.

feath'erş a gō' flȳ wŏrm erŭmb
fēed'ing ŭg'lȳ ŏff fēed brown
ḡuĕss thĭngş

"Willie, when I was feeding the birds just now, a little brown bird flew away with a crumb in its bill."
1, 6.

ECLECTIC SERIES.

"Where did it go, Rose?"

"I don't know; away off, somewhere."

"I can guess where, Rose. Don't you know the nest we saw some days ago? What do you think is in it now?"

"O Willie, I know! Some little brown birds. Let us go and see them."

"All right; but we must not go too near. There! I just saw the old bird fly out of the bush. Stand here, Rose. Can you see?"

"Why, Willie, what ugly little things! What big mouths they have, and no feathers!"

"Keep still, Rose. Here comes the old bird with a worm in her bill. How hard she must work to feed them all!"

LESSON LVIII.

fall'ing	counts	wōeş	nigh
be ḡŭn'	ḡriĕfş	stärş	tēar
môrn'ing	Lôrd	ēach	joyş

When the stars at set of sun
Watch you from on high,
When the morning has begun,
Think the Lord is nigh.

All you do and all you say,
He can see and hear;
When you work and when you play,
Think the Lord is near.

All your joys and griefs He knows,
Counts each falling tear;
When to Him you tell your woes,
Know the Lord will hear.

LESSON LIX.

whĭs'tle (whĭs'l)

pŏck'et   wĭl'lōw

nōte	filled	dĕad	sĭck
wạlk	ĕv'er ў	blew	lāne
lāme	tāk'ing	cāne	tŏŏk

One day, when Mary was taking a walk down the lane, trying to sing her doll to sleep,

she met Frank, with his basket and cane.

Frank was a poor, little, lame boy. His father and mother were dead. His dear, old grandma took care of him, and tried to make him happy.

Every day, Mary's mother filled Frank's basket with bread and meat, and a little tea for his grandma.

"How do you do, Frank?" said Mary. "Don't make a noise; my doll is going to sleep. It is just a little sick to-day."

"Well, then, let us whistle it to sleep." And Frank, taking a willow whistle out of his pocket, blew a long note.

"Oh, how sweet!" cried Mary. "Do let me try."

LESSON LX.

tûrned	fãçe	crïed	lōw
al'mōst	sōon	mōre	erȳ
onçe(wŭns)	be çauşe'		

"Yes, Mary, I will give it to you, because you are so good to my grandma."

"Oh! thank you very much."

Mary blew and blew a long time.

"I can't make it whistle," said she, almost ready to cry.

"Sometimes they will whistle, and sometimes they won't," said Frank. "Try again, Mary."

She tried once more, and the whistle made a low, sweet sound.

"It whistles!" she cried.

In her joy, she had turned the doll's face down, and its eyes

shut tight, as if it had gone to sleep.

"There!" cried Frank, "I told you the way to put a doll to sleep, is to whistle to it."

"So it is," said Mary. "Dear, little thing; it must be put in its bed now."

So they went into the house. Frank's basket was soon filled, and he went home happy.

88

89

LESSON LXI.

stŏŏd	hĭm sĕlf′	flăp′ping	fĭrst
twĕlve	flăpped	walked	flăp
o bĕy′	bĕt′ter	Chĭp′pў̌	fōŏd
stōne	be fōre′	chĭck′ens̩	kĕpt

There was once a big, white hen that had twelve little chickens. They were very small, and

the old hen took good care of them. She found food for them in the day-time, and at night kept them under her wings.

One day, this old hen took her chickens down to a small brook. She thought the air from the water would do them good.

When they got to the brook, they walked on the bank a little while. It was very pretty on the other side of the brook, and the old hen thought she would take her children over there.

There was a large stone in the brook: she thought it would be easy for them to jump to that stone, and from it to the other side.

LESSON LXII.

chirped   nĕv'er   in dēed'
slōw'ly   rē'ally   be găn'
brōod
dĭdn't
ūse
dōor
bite
pieçe

"I never saw such children," said the old hen. "You don't try at all."

"We can't jump so far, mother. Indeed we can't, we can't!" chirped the little chickens.

"Well," said the old hen, "I must give it up." So she jumped back to the bank, and walked slowly home with her brood.

So she jumped to the stone, and told the children to come after her. For the first time, she found that they would not obey her.

She flapped her wings, and cried, "Come here, all of you! Jump upon this stone, as I did. We can then jump to the other side. Come, now!"

"O mother! we can't, we can't, we can't!" said all the little chickens.

"Yes you can, if you try," said the old hen. "Just flap your wings, as I did, and you can jump over."

"I am flapping my wings," said Chippy, who stood by himself; "but I can't jump any better than I could before."

"I think mother asked too much of us," said one little chicken to the others.

"Well, I tried," said Chippy.

"We didn't," said the others; "it was of no use to try."

When they got home, the old hen began to look about for something to eat. She soon found, near the back door, a piece of bread.

So she called the chickens, and they all ran up to her, each one trying to get a bite at the piece of bread.

"No, no!" said the old hen. "This bread is for Chippy. He is the only one of my children that really tried to jump to the stone."

LESSON LXIII.

lȧst   slātes   write   wāste
nēat   tāk'en   elēan   lēarn
rēad'er   pâr'ents   sĕe'ond

We have come to the last lesson in this book. We have finished the First Reader.

PHONIC CHART.

LONG VOCALS.

ā, as in āte. ē, as in ēve.
â, " câre. ē̇, " ẽrr.
ä, " ärm. ī, " īçe.
à, " làst. ō, " ōde.
a̤, " a̤ll. ū, " tūne.
  o͞o, as in fo͞ol.

SHORT VOCALS.

ă, as in ăm. ŏ, as in ŏdd.
ĕ, " ĕnd. ŭ, " ŭp.
ĭ, " ĭn. o͝o, " lo͝ok.

DIPHTHONGS.

oi, oy, as in oil, boy. | ou, ow, as in out, now.

ASPIRATES.

f, as in fīfe. t, as in tăt.
h, " hĭm. sh, " shē.
k, " kīte. ch, " chăt.
p, " pīpe. th, " thĭck.
s, " sāme. wh, " whȳ.

You can now read all the lessons in it, and can write them on your slates.

Have you taken good care of your book? Children should always keep their books neat and clean.

Are you not glad to be ready for a new book?

Your parents are very kind to send you to school. If you are good, and if you try to learn, your teacher will love you, and you will please your parents.

Be kind to all, and do not waste your time in school.

When you go home, you may ask your parents to get you a Second Reader.

96

FIRST READER.

SUBVOCALS.

b,	as in	bĭb.	v,	as in vălve.
d,	" "	dĭd.	th,	" " thĭs.
g,	" "	găg̃.	z,	" " zīne.
j,	" "	jŭg̃.	z,	" " āzure.
n,	" "	nīne.	r,	" " râre.
m,	" "	māim.	w,	" " wē.
ng,	" "	hăng.	y,	" " yĕt.

l, as in lŭll.

SUBSTITUTES.

ạ,	for ŏ,	as in whạt.	ȳ,	for ĭ, as in mȳth.
ê,	" ä,	" " thêre.	e,	" k, " " eăn.
ẹ,	" ā,	" " fẹint.	ç,	" s, " " çīte.
ï,	" ē,	" " polïçe.	çh,	" sh, " " çhâiṣe.
ï,	" ē,	" " sïr.	eh,	" k, " " ehăos.
ŏ,	" ŭ,	" " sŏn.	g̣,	" j, " " g̣ĕm.
ọ,	" ōō,	" " tọ.	ṇ,	" ng, " " ĭṇk.
ọ,	" ōō,	" " wọlf.	ṣ,	" z, " " ăṣ.
ô,	" ä:	" " fôrk.	s,	" sh, " " sụre.
ô,	" ōō,	" " wôrk.	x̣,	" g̣z, " " ex̣ăet.
ụ,	" ē,	" " fụll.	gh,	" f, " " läugh.
û,	" ōō,	" " bûrn.	ph,	" f, " " phlŏx.
ụ,	" ōō,	" " rụde.	qu,	" k, " " pïque.
ȳ,	" ȳ,	" " flȳ.	qu,	" kw, " " quit.

17

*T*homas *C*halmers *H*arbaugh

(1849–1924)

ONE OF THE most popular literary genres in nineteenth-century America was the dime novel. Dime novels were short, affordable literary pieces produced for mass circulation and renowned as vehicles of sensational adventure fiction. The most successful and well-known publishers of such fiction were the Beadle brothers, Irwin and Erastus. Beginning to publish works in the early 1850s, the Beadle brothers would later join forces with Robert Adams in 1856 to establish the publishing house of Beadle and Adams. Over the next forty years, millions of Beadle's dime and half-dime library volumes flooded the country.

One of the Beadle and Adams most successful genres focused on the American frontier. Their stories did much to contribute to the mythic status of characters such as Buffalo Bill, Kit Carson, Daniel Boone, Davy Crockett, Sitting Bull, and Calamity Jane. A host of authors would write these stories, including Thomas Chalmers Harbaugh. Writing his first piece for the Beadles in 1873, Harbaugh would go on to write dozens of stories for the Beadle libraries unders such pen names as Captain Howard Holmes, Howard Lincoln, Charles Howard, and Major S. S. Scott. The varied names often masked the not-so-varied plots.

In *Plucky Phil, of the Mountain Trail,* Harbaugh capitalizes on a Western formula that had worked time and again for the Beadles. Harbaugh fills his tale with adventure based on violence and deceit, while he also populates his story with provocative characters including Sitting Bull, the great Sioux chief. Appearing just five years after Sitting Bull's massacre of Lt. Col. George Armstrong Custer's Seventh Cavalry at Little Bighorn, Harbaugh's *Plucky Phil* gives its readers a tale that echoed the treacherous revenge the United States visited upon the Sioux nation in the wake of Custer's defeat. Harbaugh's tale is instructive because it gives insight into the American love affair with the ever-resourceful and virtuous frontiersman, as well as into the some of the attitudes that propelled the United States in its largely genocidal engagement with its Native American population.

PLUCKY PHIL, OF THE MOUNTAIN TRAIL

Or, Rosa, the Red Jezebel
A Tale of Siouxdom

CHAPTER I

❧ Deserted

"Thar's no use talkin', pards. We've got to the end ov the string. Pluck ar' a good dog sometimes, but Go-back shows more sagacity. We've got one-half ov Sittin' Bull's[1] tribe between us an' the fort now, the other half hover over us like the angels ov death. Look at Phil yonder, standin' with his back to us. I don't like to leave the young cap'n in this part ov the kentry, but we must go back er die whar we ar'."

These words fell from the lips of a burly fellow who addressed a group of rough-looking men from the top of a huge bowlder among the Big Horn Mountains not far from Custer's ill-fated battle-ground.[2]

Apart from the speaker and his little audience, with his back toward them, stood a youth who had scarcely completed his seventeenth year. He was handsome, athletic, and of course determined, for he had turned his back on men whose bravery had never been questioned.

"That settles it: they are going to desert me, and I can't blame them," he said to himself when the man on the bowlder paused. "Their term of enlistment has expired, and I have no right to attempt to detain them. Besides, they believe my hunt in these mountains a useless one, but I shall persevere as long as the mountain trail can be found. Let them go back. I don't want to face them, for I might plead again. I came hither to learn the fate of the wagon train or die. I am going to stay."

"Phil?" at this juncture called a rough voice. "We ar' goin' to vote on yer last propersition."

The youth bit his lip, but did not stir.

"Wal, you kin hear, anyhow. Now, pards, all who ar' in favor ov acceptin' the cap'n's tarms an' goin' on *till the end comes,* say I."

Thomas C. Harbaugh, *Plucky Phil, of the Mountain Trail; or, Rosa, the Red Jezebel, A Tale of Siouxdom.* New York: Beadle and Adams, 1881.

[1]Sitting Bull (1831–1890) was a Teton Dakota Indian chief who united the Sioux tribes in their struggle against the U.S. federal government in the 1870s.

[2]In 1876, Lt. Col. George Armstrong Custer (1839–1876) led every man under his command (more than two hundred) to his death when Custer attacked a large Sioux encampment at the Little Bighorn River in the Montana territory. This battle came to have the nickname "Custer's Last Stand." Custer's defeat so stunned and outraged the nation that the American government moved swiftly and brutally against the Sioux to bring them into submission.

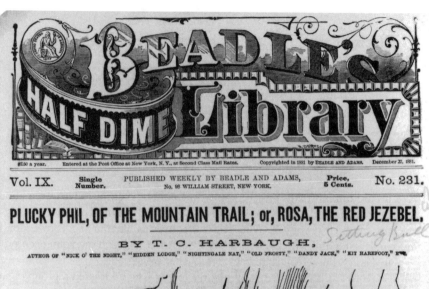

$2.50 a year.   Entered at the Post Office at New York, N. Y., at Second Class Mail Rates.   Copyrighted in 1881 by BEADLE AND ADAMS.   December 27, 1881.

Vol. IX.   Single Number.   PUBLISHED WEEKLY BY BEADLE AND ADAMS,   Price, 5 Cents.   No. 231.
No. 98 WILLIAM STREET, NEW YORK.

PLUCKY PHIL, OF THE MOUNTAIN TRAIL; or, ROSA, THE RED JEZEBEL.

BY T. C. HARBAUGH,

AUTHOR OF "NICK O' THE NIGHT," "HIDDEN LODGE," "NIGHTINGALE NAT," "OLD FROSTY," "DANDY JACK," "KIT HAREFOOT," ETC.

"NOW, VIPER, I WANT THE TRUTH," EXCLAIMED PLUCKY PHIL, SPRINGING TO COYOTE'S SIDE.

Cover of Beadle's Half Dime Library's *Plucky Phil, of the Mountain Trail,* 1881.

Not a voice responded.

"Contrary, no."

Six negatives spoken at once but in different tones replied.

"We go back, pards!" said the man on the stone with a glance at the boy. "Mebbe the cap'n will let us say good-by, but I hope he will go back with us."

"I stay!" suddenly cried the youth, whirling upon the six.[3] "Do not think that I blame you. Life is dear to every one. My place is here, yours, perhaps, behind the walls of some Government fort. Yes, I will say good-by."

He halted before the bronze men and held out his hand.

"There! don't argue the case over again," he said to them, thus putting a stop to their remonstrances. "Until I shall have ascertained the fate of every person in the train I will not turn my back on Sitting Bull's dominions. You have voted to go back. Be men. Keep your determination."

The parting scene was soon over, and Phil Steele, or Plucky Phil as the men had named him, saw the veterans withdraw.

The sun had already descended below the top of the mountain at whose base the decision had been reached, and the cool shadows of evening lay around the boy.

At the last moment some of the men showed signs of hesitation, but Plucky Phil had given them no encouragement; on the contrary, he had said: "Keep your decision. Go back."

At last he was alone; the men whom he had hired at the nearest fort many miles away were going back, leaving him on the mountain trail in the midst of the death-lands of the Sioux.

"Deserted but free!" cried the young trailer, springing upon the rock lately occupied by the leader of the six. "I can follow my own counsels from this time. Advice will no longer be driven into my ears, and my camp will not be cursed by the voice of the grumbler. They were brave fellows, but I believe I can get along without them. I must!" he added, with a smile as he jumped from his perch and packed up the rifle that leaned against the rock.

"I can explore the pass now," he said, starting off. "It will be a further advance into Sitting Bull's country, but what do I care? I am here to find or to die!"

These were brave words from one so young, but Plucky Phil had a right to use them.

After an hour's walk from the place of separation the young trailer reached the mouth of a kind of natural canyon. Dark shadows were creeping down the lofty walls, and if night had been an hour nearer, the center of the pass would have looked gloomy indeed.

"Forward!" cried Plucky Phil, as if addressing the men who had deserted him, and the next moment with his rifle at full cock he entered the pass.

Far above him towered the bush-covered sides of the canyon, but as he advanced objects became more distinct until he had no difficulty in picking his way.

"Here is where the red fiends might have attacked the train," he exclaimed, for all

---

[3]Making a 180-degree turn.

could have been butchered in this canyon. I am getting close to the fatal spot. Something tells me this. Great heavens! I am here now."

The last sentence dropped from the boy's lips as he suddenly recoiled from an object which his foot was about to strike, and standing aloof while a shiver of horror crept over his frame, he stared at a human skull whose grin was as grotesque as it was horrible.

Other objects speedily confirmed Plucky Phil's exclamation. He had reached the scene of some massacre, for half-burned parts of wagons and bones of horses mingled with those of unfortunate human beings told the dreadful tale.

Not long after his first discovery the mountain trailer stood in the very midst of the scene.

"I pray heaven that I may find some hopeful sign," fell from his lips. "I wonder if they fought hard. Ah! can I doubt them when they were led by such men as Overland Dick and Old Policy. Here they were attacked by a thousand Sioux, no doubt, and here among the wagons they died one by one. All? I will not believe it without proof!"

He fell to work and overturned or examined every bone and piece of wagon that encountered his gaze.

"I shall bury them when I get through," he said. "Perhaps, in giving all these bones a grave, I may be paying the last tribute to Nora. Then vengeance!"

Half an hour later he leaned against the wall of the canyon and gazed sorrowfully upon the heap of ghastly relics he had collected.

"Ah!" he suddenly exclaimed as his look wandered from the pile. "One poor fellow at least crept from the awful butcher-pen," and the next moment he was stooping over the skeleton of a man which lay thirty feet or more from the spot.

After a brief examination of the bones, Plucky Phil was on the point of turning away when the glitter of something beneath the skeleton hand attracted his attention, and he unearthed a few inches of a soldier's bayonet.

The point was much worn as though it had been used on stone, and the youth mechanically glanced at the canyon wall at the foot of which the steel had been found.

A lot of mountain creepers met his eye, but putting out his hand he brushed them aside to utter a cry of discovery.

On the stone thus brought to view were numerous scratches which soon began to assume the shapes of rough letters, and oblivious of his dangerous surroundings, he dropped his rifle and leaned eagerly forward. He seemed to hold his breath while he deciphered the last work of the dead man's hand. If the mountain vines had hidden the writing on the stone, fate or fortune was revealing it to him.

Letter by letter and word by word the boy trailer mastered the inscription, until at last he reached the end having read these brief sentences:

"We were attacked yesterday by five hundred Sioux. Not one of our party escaped. I am the only one alive at this moment, and I am dying. Nobody may ever see this, therefore, we may never be avenged. We fought to the last.

                                                                            Campbell."

The signature told Plucky Phil that the "last man" had fallen back from his task exhausted and really dying.

He knew Campbell the leader of the ill-fated train, and a man who deserved a better fate; but notwithstanding the assertion that no one had escaped, a look of doubt remained in the boy's eyes.

"I will not believe it! I cannot!" he cried. "The trail of a thousand hunters would end here, but mine does not. It only begins. I admit that Captain Campbell ought to have known all, for he lived till the day after the massacre, but I am going to doubt his dying words. I will avenge you, captain. Those five hundred Sioux are my bitterest enemies. Woe to their great chiefs if an Indian hatchet touched Nora Dalton's head that day. They have named me Plucky Phil, and the time for me to honor that name has come. First, sepulture[4] then, the long hunt and revenge."

Under a huge rock which at one place jutted from the canyon wall at its foot, the collected bones of the people of the train were placed, and the hands of the youthful trailer heaped earth and stones upon them.

Then he went back to his rifle.

For a moment he looked toward the end of the pass at which he had entered, then he turned to the west—toward the unknown lands of the Sioux.

"The mountain trail is not yet ended!" he exclaimed springing forward. "The bones I have found would have kept the boys at my back. They deserted me a little too soon. But never mind. I am willing to hunt alone."

At that moment the sound of a human voice struck his ear, and he stopped and turned toward the eastern mouth of the canyon.

"The boys have followed me," he said in a low tone. "I ought to exhibit nerve and send them back again."

No, the six bronze men were not coming back.

"I've seen it forty times since, 'Tana," said the unknown voice; "but I can't make out a letter 'cause I'm no scholar. Mebbe you kin."

Plucky Phil heard these words, and then saw two figures approach the rock bearing Captain Campbell's inscription.

One tore the vines aside and turned a face of triumph to his companion.

"Thar, 'Tana! make it out yerself ef you kin!" he exclaimed.

Plucky Phil crouched in the shadows and stared at the pair.

CHAPTER II

❧ Phil Shows His Pluck

The light in the mountain pass was fading fast, and the man called 'Tana was mastering the inscription on the rock with no little difficulty. He was closely watched by the long-haired athlete whose bronze hand held the vines aside.

"Can't you make it out?" asked this latter personage in a tone of impatience.

"I might if the light was stronger, but it's going too fast to help me any. See here,

---

[4]burial

Coyote, you know more about their fate than any one in these parts. There! don't start and say no. The telling of your story will not make us foes. If you did not take any part in the fight, you were there. I know it."

The mountain climbers having dropped from Coyote's hand, once more covered the lettering on the stone, and Coyote himself had started back and was regarding his companion with a look of indecision.

The men stood erect and faced each other.

"I am waiting for your story," said 'Tana. "Go on."

At the same time Plucky Phil caught a threatful gleam in his eye as he glanced at the butt of the revolver that protruded from his belt.

"I war thar, 'Tana, thet's a fact," said Coyote in a forced tone; "but I didn't lift a hand ag'in' 'em except to try and save, an' thar I failed. You see we knowed all along thet the train war comin'. Sitting Bull's scouts kept us posted, an' long afore the attack took place we knowed all about the party. Hyar the battle took place—not much ov a battle either, fur the Injuns killed nearly everybody at the first fire. Then they charged down the pass, but a small number of men led by a lank fellar called Policy Pete gave a volley thet emptied a dozen saddles. But the next charge the red niggers got to the wagons, an' then the usual work began. I rode up then to save a young gal what had handled a rifle durin' the hull fight like an old trapper, but I couldn't do it, 'Tana. The young bucks seein' what I war at turned on me, an' ef I hadn't pulled out, my bones would be yonder with them what they left behind in the fire."

To this narrative 'Tana and the unseen boy had listened with breathless interest. It was intended to give the death-blow to long cherished hopes. Coyote's positiveness told this, but his nearest auditor seemed to doubt.

"Are you sure, Coyote, that the girl was massacred after you left her?" he asked.

"She warn't with us when we went back," was the significant rejoinder. "Sittin' Bull took no prisoners thet time. I ought to know, 'Tana, for I war thar."

For a moment 'Tana did not reply, and when he for a second removed his gaze from Coyote's face, Plucky Phil, who had been watching it incessantly, uttered an ejaculation of discovery.

"Coyote is lying!" he cried. "'Tana, who ever he is, does not know how to deal with the rascal. The secret of Nora's fate has not been told. Those squaw-men[5] like Coyote are not all fools. They'd sooner sell a lie on credit than tell the honest truth for cash. There! 'Tana is going at him again. He doubts still. I wonder why he is so interested in the girl who wielded the rifle in this bloody pass that day?"

'Tana did return to the charge, but Coyote could not or would not tell more about the attack on the train.

"I thought the writing on the rock thar might be of some value to you," he said to 'Tana; "thet's why I brought you hyar."

"It amounts to nothing so far as I can make it out."

"I'm sorry."

"Another lie!" said Plucky Phil to himself. "Coyote seems to be well supplied with the useful, but he'll sing another song when I get at him."

---

[5] Male Native Americans.

'Tana lost hope at last. Coyote was baffling him.

"I can't think of my plans as lost ones," the former said, dejectedly.

"I'm afraid you'll hev to, cap'n. Wouldn't I hev seen the gal ef she hed been carried off?"

"It looks that way."

"Ov course! The Government doesn't know fur sartin what ever became of the train. Yonder it lies, 'Tana, men, hosses an' wagons all mixed together, an' thar hezn't been an avenger in these parts—none thet I've heard ov."

"There is one here now!" fell in determined tones from Plucky Phil's lips, as he stepped from the shadow of his rock into the light that lingered in the middle of the pass.

Coyote and 'Tana looked up, caught sight of his figure and sprung to their rifles.

"Lift a weapon and drop dead behind it!" shot over the shining barrel of his own rifle. "I am not here to kill if I can discover, but my fingers are itching to touch the trigger of the rifle that covers the heart of one who rode with Sitting Bull to the butchery of Campbell and his people. Stand where you are, mountain pards. You have lied, Coyote. I want the truth!"

The eyes of the bronzed squaw-man burned with a tigerish glare.

The rifle of the young trailer covered his heart.—

"Quick—the truth!" continued the boy, impatiently. "You know that Nora Dalton did not die that day. You have been lying to Tana, your companion, for a purpose. You sell me the same goods and I will pay you in bullets!"

'Tana was regarding Plucky Phil with eyes filled with astonishment. They had met for the first time, and as enemies at that. Their hunt for Nora Dalton could not make them friends.

From the boy he glanced at Coyote, who was in a predicament which he did not relish.

"Tell him the truth if you have lied to me," he said, in a low tone, to the squaw-man.

"Yes, out with it," cried Plucky Phil, who had caught a portion of the sentence.

"I've told the solid truth," was the surly answer. "Why should I lie?"

The next moment the crack of a rifle resounded throughout the mountain pass and Coyote, with a yell of pain, staggered back and dropped on the spot where Campbell's skeleton had bleached for two years.

"Winged, 'Tana!" he grated fiercely, looking up at his companion. "Give the young wolf a bullet. He'll bite you one ov these days ef you don't."

Spurred on by the idea of self-preservation, 'Tana turned and raised his rifle, but he found Plucky Phil standing not twenty feet away with a cocked revolver in his hand.

"Go back!" he said sternly to 'Tana. "Go back beyond where that yellow viper lies. I don't want your blood, although I may demand an explanation one of these days. You see I have not killed Coyote. A shot through the shoulder isn't a deadly one. He may live to serve you yet. Go back fifty paces, but first cast your weapons on the ground, the rifle and your revolvers. They shall not be lost if you behave yourself."

'Tana bit his lips and flung his weapons on the ground; then he moved backward past the helpless Coyote, but shot all the while flashes of vengeful eye-fire at the boy.

"Now, viper, I want the truth," exclaimed Plucky Phil springing to Coyote's side.

The eyes of the crippled squaw-man surveyed him from head to foot before he spoke.

"What do want to know?"

"The fate of the girl who fought that day with the rifle. She was not killed. Your lies deceived 'Tana, but not me."

"You war listenin', then?"

"Yes."

"Wal, pard, the gal arn't dead."

Plucky Phil's eyes dilated with joy.

"Where is she?"

"You've got to find her."

"What! Beware, Coyote, your last trail will end here if you prevaricate."

"I'm lookin' fur her myself. Honest Injun, pard."

"She's been taken from you, then?"

"That's jes' it."

"By whom?"

"I don't know exactly, but I've got an idea."

"Let me have it."

"Sittin' Bull wanted the gal arter the massacre, not fur his wife, mind you, pard, but to help 'im in some kind ov a plot ag'in' the whites. His red warriors tracked me fur months afore they found the gal. She's gone now; thet's all I know. Ef I war you an' wanted 'er I'd foller the old Sioux chief himself. I fancy you haven't made much by wingin' Coyote, though you've l'arned some news. The chap behind me ar' huntin' Nora, too."

"'Tana?"

"Cap'n Montana, er 'Tana fer short. You two might pool yer issues ef it warn't fur one thing."

"What's that?" asked Plucky Phil with burning eagerness.

"You couldn't be friends ef you wanted to be," answered Coyote with a smile. "Ever hear ov Cap'n 'Tana?"

"Never."

"That warn't his name ten year ago."

"What was it?"

"Goldboots."

Plucky Phil sprung up with an exclamation that fixed Coyote's gaze upon him.

"What!" he cried. "My mother's enemy here fighting me?"

A great bound carried him clear over Coyote's prostrate body, and, revolver in hand, he rushed toward the spot to which Captain 'Tana had retreated.

But all at once he stopped and uttered a cry of disappointment.

'Tana or Goldboots had disappeared.

"Discoveries are made too late," he said. "The greatest villain on earth has escaped me. I may be compelled to form an alliance with Coyote," and he turned toward that worthy.

At that moment a series of Indian yells broke the stillness that reigned at the westernmost mouth of the canyon.

A bound carried Plucky Phil to Coyote's side.

"What does that mean?" he cried.

"Injuns, ov course. They are mounted, too."

"I'm in for it now, but I'll stand my ground."

Coyote shot the boy a look of admiration.

"Clean grit, by hokey! he exclaimed. "Pick up my revolver, boy; then you'll hev two; but be careful who you shoot ef they ar' Injuns. Thar's sartin to be a tall red-skin in the gang who may turn out the best friend a boy in yer fix ever had. Don't kill him ef you want to win in this mountain game."

Even if Coyote had not concluded, the youth could have listened no longer, for a score of mounted Sioux had dashed into view.

With two revolvers thrust forward, Plucky Phil awaited the onset. He could not escape discovery, and he might as well open the ball.

A minute later the first red rank saw him braced and defiant in the canyon path, and as the whole band discovered him, the two deadly revolvers began the conflict.

"I never ran! I never will!" grated the boy as his fingers set the triggers in motion.

CHAPTER III

❧ Policy Pete

Stunned and confused by the deadly work of Plucky Phil's revolvers, the Sioux fell back.

"The tall, slim red-skin—don't drop him!" admonished Coyote from the ground, "You'll need him afore the mountain trail ends er I'm a saint."

"I don't see him," said Phil.

"Mebbe you've dropped 'im already. Ef you hev, boy—"

Phil broke the sentence with an exclamation of surprise, for out from the Indian ranks had dashed a single horseman who was about to run him down.

Instantly the two revolvers went upward again and the days of the reckless rider might have ended there and then if Coyote's voice had not checked the boy.

"Don't, youngster; let 'im come on. He is the tall Injun I refarred to. Lower your bulldogs and stand aside."

Phil obeyed.

A moment later the superb horse ridden by the slim red skin was at his side, and the hand that closed on his shoulder lifted him from the ground.

"I told ye so!" cried Coyote witnessing the feat. "I'll see you later, boy. I like your grit, boy I owe you a blood-debt which I'll hev to pay!"

Plucky Phil did not hear the squaw-man's last sentence, for the Indian's horse was bearing him eastward down the canyon, and the vise-like gripe of the Sioux he still felt at his shoulder.

Out from the mountain gulch dashed the horse, into the grayish twilight that had succeeded the day. The mountain trailer still clung to the two revolvers, his only weapons, for his sudden journey had caused him to leave his rifle behind.

How could his fate be in the hands of his painted captor? In what manner were their lives to be united?

Once beyond the canyon, Plucky Phil began to scrutinize his captor's face. The painting of it was ludicrous in the extreme, and not of that kind so frequently seen among the warriors of the Sioux nation. The Indian's dress was nearly half "civilized," and, altogether, after an inspection of several minutes while he was carried on, Plucky Phil concluded that he had been studying a puzzle—a human enigma.

"Whoa! Rocket," suddenly cried the Indian in a tone which dilated Phil's gray eyes. "It ain't my policy to travel all night, an' no piece ov horseflesh in the Big Horn hills knows that better nor you. By hookey! baby pard, what confounded policy brought you out hyar?"

Phil could not stammer a reply. His look was an impertinent stare, seeing which a smile became visible at the corners of the Sioux's mouth.

"What yer lookin' at?" he asked. "Ef you war a photograph machine my picture'd hev been taken afore this."

"You are Policy Pete!" cried the boy.

"By hookey! you wouldn't starve ef you hed to guess fur a livin'," was the answer. "The anatomy now before you b'longs to Policy Pete. Policy is policy at all times. I'm an Injun now an' hev been fur nigh two years, er ever since I crawled from the train nigher dead than alive."

Plucky Phil could not repress an exclamation of delight.

"I know now why Coyote told me to spare the tall, slim Indian," he said. "You are my friend, because I am hunting for Nora Dalton."

"You hyar alone lookin' fur thet gal?" cried old Policy. "Mebbe she's dead."

"No, she is not!" quickly cried the youth. "I forced the truth from Coyote after having given him a bullet in the shoulder. Ah! we shall hunt Nora together; we will stand by each other, and from what I've heard of you, I am not afraid to trust you in anything."

Policy Pete's eyes seemed to sparkle with satisfaction.

"One ov yer bullets clipped a lock ov my ha'r back yonder," he said. "I could hev finished you, but thet wouldn't hev been good policy. Afore we talk let us go down this little pass. I know a place, an' then I want to git some o' this Injun paint off my carkiss. Allus hev a policy; thet's my doctrine."

Guided by the old guide's hand the horse turned into a gloomy trail which led the strange pair to the foot of a mountain where Plucky Phil slid to the ground to be followed by Policy Pete.

A full moon creeping over the tops of some trees on the mountain side bathed the halting place in a weird silvery beauty, and the young trailer watched his companion bathe his face in a spring that bubbled near by.

"Fortune smiles at last," he murmured, to himself. "She has brought me face to face with Policy Pete, the guide of Campbell's train. With him for an ally I shall succeed. I cannot fail!"

When the lank guide turned from the spring and revealed his face Phil was inclined to smile. It still looked like an Indian's so far as coloring was concerned; mountain air and mountain suns had more than bronzed it. In the moonlight it looked almost black.

"Not ez purty ez a chromo,"[6] remarked Policy, noticing the boy's look. "Don't keep in the shade to save yer complexion. Thet's my policy. I war three weeks among the Sioux an' nigh Sittm' Bull's head-quarters afore their keenest eyes thought I war somebody besides a squaw-man, an' consequently a white-hater. Sittin' Bull himself would hev hed a fit ef he hed dreamed thet one ov the guides ov Campbell's train hed escaped an' war within smellin' distance ov his flesh-pots. I war carryin' out a policy, keepin' still an' playin' squaw-man, but at last I j'ined the tribe ez a half-breed from the Mussel Shell region, an' they took me in, policy an' all, an' never asked fur my pedigree."

Policy Pete paused to laugh over the recollections of his successful ruse.

"But Captain Campbell wrote on the rock that all were killed," said the youth, as the laugh subsided.

"Did, eh? Mebbe he thought so, but when I crawled out from the burnin' wagons hacked and shot, I looked like a fellar whose policy hed about expired. It war a time—a time, boy, but I won't tell about it hyar. You must tell me all about yerself. Ef you hev a policy, I want to know it."

Plucky Phil did not hesitate, but told the old guide how he had led or rather followed six men into the mountains on a hunt for the missing train, but especially for Nora Dalton, a young friend of his who had accompanied it. He narrated their adventures from the day of departure from the nearest Government fort to the desertion of the six, and continued his own up to the battle in the canyon.

"Now, yer policy?" said the guide, when Phil paused.

The youth blushed and smiled.

"I need hardly mention that I love Nora," he said. "Love has brought me to this place. My policy is to hunt for her till I find her—now that I know she lives—and then to rescue her if she is in danger."

"In danger?" echoed Policy Pete; "she is in danger. I know thet much. Thar's but one livin' person in this kentry who knows exactly whar Nora is, an' he won't tell."

"He shall tell!" cried Phil. "You an' I will force the secret from him, Policy!"

"Now ye'r' gittin off," was the reply, "Wait till I talk about thet fellar with the secret. In the first place, he runs the machine in these parts; he kin call ten thousand warriors into the field; he lifts his hand an' an army like Custer's is wiped out. He's a wolf an' a snake combined. He kin crush er tear, jest ez he likes."

"You mean Sitting Bull himself?" cried the boy.

"The clothes fit 'im, don't they?" was the reply. "I mean Sittin' Bull, an Injun who knows the value ov a policy, fur he hesn't been without one fur forty years. He's workin' up one now what will prove a big bonanza fur him, an' Nora is to help him."

"No!"

"Fact! I 'lowed you'd be surprised. Sittin' Bull knows whar Nora Dalton is. Coyote saved her from the train an kept her a long time, but Sittin' Bull's red detectives ferreted her out, an' Coyote found the nest empty one mornin'. Yes, pard, ef you want Nora you must ask the Sioux wolf fur her; but do you think he'll give 'er up!"

---

[6]Chromolithography (which produced chromolithographs or "chromos") was a popular nineteenth-century multicolored printing process.

Plucky Phil's eyes flashed.

"Time shall tell!" he exclaimed. "I say that Sitting Bull shall tell me the truth. I forced it from Coyote in the canyon. I will wring it from the Indian king."

"Complete yer policy first," said the guide looking calmly at him.

"Where is Sitting Bull now?"

"On the Big Horn."

"Come, then! We have rested long enough. You are going to stand by me. So I must wrest a secret from the great Indian chief of the West before I can find Nora? I accept the task! I didn't think it would come to this when I started on my mission; but the ten thousand braves led by Sitting Bull do not daunt me."

These sentences fell calmly from Plucky Phil's lips. His eyes sparkled while he spoke, that was all.

"We'll make a policy on the journey," said Pete. "We can't get along without one."

"I've formed mine."

"Wal?"

"We will go to Sitting Bull's camp, and at the muzzle of the revolver I'll force the secret from the killer of Custer and his men!"

Policy Pete uttered an exclamation of astonishment.

"Thet means death!" he said.

"Then death it shall be! I shall go alone—"

"Not while Policy Pete ar' in the neighborhood," was the interruption, and the bronze hand of the old guide fell assuringly upon Plucky Phil's shoulder.

If the friends at that moment had glanced up the slope of the mountain they might have caught sight of a pair of eyes and a triumphant face destined to seriously interfere with their plans.

But they saw it not, and when they turned their faces toward Sitting Bull's camp, a human figure crept panther-like in their wake.

It was Goldboots.

CHAPTER IV

❧ In Sitting Bull's Camp

"Wal, hyar we ar' Plucky. Down yonder is the lion's den. Look a minute, an' tell me ef you feel like enterin'."

The speaker was Policy Pete, and, while he looked at the boy who stood at his side in the mountain trail, his long arm pointed downward toward a scene not unfrequently witnessed in the Big Horn country.

The sun was setting behind the trees at their backs, but light enough remained to enable the young trailer's eyes to note the beautiful valley below dotted with the grotesque tepees of the red-men. Groups of horses were visible at the edge of the great camp, and here and there moved the stately forms of their lawless masters.

Sitting Bull's camp was before Plucky Phil.

"Don't go off half cocked," continued Old Policy, watching his young friend, who was regarding the scene in silence. "Take a good look at the lair ov the red lion. A man what goes down that fur bizness must hev a clean-cut policy. Look to yer heart's content, Plucky, an' don't answer me till ye'r' ready."

"The sight is enough to daunt some, Pete," the boy said, facing his companion; "but the secret is yonder. That decides me."

"Jest ez I expected. Now let me strike a policy. I'll go down an' reconnoiter; you stay hyar. I'll bring back su'thin' about Sittin' Bull, never fear! He war hyar four days ago."

"Go, Pete!" cried the youth. "I want to get to work. I will wait for you here."

Five minutes later, in the deepening shadows of the mountain side, Plucky Phil was alone, but the Indian camp was still visible. Policy Pete had vanished.

The old guide was not unknown in the Sioux camp. A hundred times since his escape from the massacre of the canyon, he had ridden across its boundaries, now in the ranks of the Indians, and now with the bronze squaw-men who came and went whenever they pleased. He knew that the band, faced and shot into by Plucky Phil in the canyon had not returned to the camp, therefore his strange rescue of the boy had not been made known to Sitting Bull.

He did not attempt to steal into the great village. On the contrary, he entered boldly, greeting in a rough voice several old acquaintances who lounged in the cooling shadows of evening.

"Ef I could find out suthin'," he ejaculated in a wishful tone. "The young cub up on the mountain's got more grit than his years kin handle, 'specially when he doesn't take arter policies. Ef I could ketch Sittin' Bull in a dream about the gal an' find 'im at the same time in a talkin' humor, I might git up a tarnal[7] good policy—one what would settle this hunt at short notice. But I won't be that lucky tonight."

Darkness found Policy Pete in the center of the camp. More than one Sioux dog had snuffed at his heels and eyed him suspiciously, but he kept on like a man with a mission.

Once or twice he glanced at the mountain and thought of the bold boy keeping vigils and counting the minutes on its lonely slope.

All at once his well known name was spoken on his left, in a low voice to be sure, but to Pete it sounded like the hoarse boom of a cannon.

He thought a second before he turned, and said to himself:

"Don't furgit yer policy, Pete."

Then he faced the speaker whose figure, not quite as tall as his, did not look much like a Sioux's.

"I might have called you Aggawam, yer Injun name," said the same voice as a hasty stride brought its owner to Policy's side. "We've all got red-skin handles, you know. Ov course you know me now."

"Coyote!" cried Old Policy.

For a moment the two men confronted each other in the faint light of the thousands of stars that glittered above the Sioux camp. The meeting seemed to delight Coyote; it annoyed Policy.

"Whar's the youngster, Pete?" suddenly asked the squaw-man.

---

[7] eternal

"Oh, the boy I jerked from the ground in the canyon? I wish you'd go an' find 'im, Coyote. You've heard ov eels in yer time, hevn't you? Wal, he's one."

Did not the searching eyes of Coyote call Policy Pete a liar while he spoke? They seemed to contain anything but a look of credulity.

"He got away, then?" he said, feigning belief.

"Slipped through my hands like a weasel, an' afore I could find out who he war an' what brought 'im hyar. He winged you, eh?"

"In the shoulder. Thet's why I'm hyar, Policy. The plagued thing doesn't heal ez briskly ez I like to hev it do. I knowed you when I saw yer shadder. I've kept yer secret fur two years, but Sittin' Bull doesn't dream about *you*."

Policy Pete started at the emphasis, and the eyes of the two men met.

"You've been lookin' fur the gal ever since the massacre," said Coyote. "I've knowed it all along, an' while I kept her hid from Sittin' Bull, I watched you like a hawk, fur you wasn't playin' Sioux an' squaw-man fur nothin'. The old chief's outwitted both of us, Policy. How does thet strike you?"

Coyote stepped back a pace and watched Policy Pete with an amused expression of countenance.

"He must hev the best policy," was the old guide's answer. "But we needn't discuss such matters hyar. I'm back to stay awhile. I'll see you in the mornin' Coyote; thet is, ef you ar' goin' to play fair. You want the chief's secret. Without me you kin never git it. Never!"

Old Policy was moving away, when Coyote bounded forward.

"We kin git it to-night—you and me." he exclaimed.

Pete shot him a searching look, not unmixed with astonishment.

"Sittin' Bull is alone in the big white tepee. A hand at his throat an' a revolver at his head will tear the secret from him."

"That's a poor policy," said Pete, quickly. "I kin do better than thet."

"Wal?"

"I'll go down an' tell him kinder mysteriously thet the gal hez disappeared. He will go an' see fur himself ef he swallows the bait. He kin be follered."

"I like the plan. Shel' we work together, Policy?"

Coyote was extending his hand to the gaunt guide.

"We'll shake arter the work, not afore it. Thet's never been my policy," said Pete, refusing the proffered hand. "I'll go an' tell the lie," he added, with a smile. "Kin you hev two hosses ready, Coyote?"

"I'll hev them ready."

"At the old rock."

"I'll be thar."

The two worthies separated, and Policy Pete, walking away, glanced over his shoulder at Coyote, but he had already disappeared.

"Arter all, I'm doin' suthin'," he murmured, "but who ever thought thet Coyote an' me would be pards in a thing like this? The fellow knowed me all the time an' kept his tongue! I owe him suthin' fur thet, an' I'm payin' 'im by makin' 'im help Plucky find the gal."

The "big white tepee" of Sitting Bull was known to every visitor to, and tenant of the camp on the Big Horn. From it the red king of the great red nation of the North-west had ridden to Custer's last battle-ground, and back again to its secret interior he had carried trophies of that memorable engagement.

A short walk brought Policy Pete in sight of the structure, which occupied the middle of a rough square, and was sixty yards from the nearest wigwam.

During his walk he had coined his story to the smallest particular, and confident that he would succeed, he stepped up to the tent and grasped the curtain that formed the door.

The next instant a figure darted from the dark ground just around the curve of the tepee and with the force of a tiger dashed against the old guide who went back under the assault.

At the same time a yell loud enough to penetrate to the confines of the Sioux camp cut the air, and fifty human figures sprung into the square from each of its four sides.

"Stan' off! I kin hold 'im!" exclaimed the voice of Policy's assailant, whose left hand held the guide's throat with a gripe that threatened to sever his wind-pipe. "You ar' a purty set ov Injuns! When the fox is caught you're allus ready to fight fur the hide. No, sir-ee! I hold my fox till Sittin' Bull comes."

"Sitting Bull is here!"

Sure enough the imposing figure of the warchief of the Sioux stood before Old Policy's captor, and the next moment the lank guide was hustled toward the chief. The merciless hand at his throat was paralyzing every nerve.

"Hyar's a snake fur you to kill," said the captor to the chief. "Look at 'im. You've see'd 'im afore, Bull. He's playin' Injun an' squaw-man jist ez it suited 'im ever since we struck Campbell an' his train in the deep gulch. He's the tall scout what helped Stanley along through the Yellowstone kentry—Policy Pete! I found 'im sneakin' into yer tent. He war goin' to find the white gal an' thet ef he hed to hold his revolver at yer heart. Take 'im, chief."

Policy Pete, suddenly released, had not recovered from his surprise when the red hand of Sitting Bull clutched his arm.

"White scout speak," commanded the chief.

"In one minute," said Pete, clearing his throat. "Honesty is the best policy when it wins. But I want a word with Coyote first."

He broke from Sitting Bull's gripe and started towards Coyote whose eyes danced triumphantly above his bronze cheeks.

"I war a fool to trust you," he said. "I might hev knowed thet a lone hunt war the best policy. You made the net when you first saw me. Wal, laugh while you kin, Coyote. I'm goin' to laugh last!"

"You, one ov Custer's scouts, laugh when Sittin' Bull is through with you?" cried Coyote. "I wouldn't give a fox pelt fur yer chances to see the sun rise in the mornin'. You war goin' to kill Sitting Bull fur the white gal."

The last sentence was intended for ears other than Policy's. It brought the Indian king forward with a cry of vengeance, but the old guide held him off with his left hand.

"Policy is policy," fell from his lips as his revolver leaped from his belt, and before Coyote could divine his intention he was staggering from the deadly flash that lit up the savage square.

"Thar! I've done you a sarvice, chief," said Pete turning to Sitting Bull. "Sparin' vipers like Coyote is tarnal poor policy."

CHAPTER V

❧ Striking a Trail

The faint echoes' of Old Policy's revolver reached the ears of the boy keeping watch on the dusky mountain slope that overlooked the Indian camp.

They seemed to tell him that some misfortune had befallen the lank guide, and, as the hours wore away without bringing him back, Plucky Phil became convinced that something had gone wrong.

"Policy would not have deserted me," he said aloud. "I will stand by him," and looking to his revolvers, one of which he held in his right hand, he left his post, and began to go down the mountain.

He discovered as he neared the Sioux village or camp, that it was far from being quiet, and while he slipped from shadow to shadow in the vain hope of finding Policy Pete he noticed fitting figures that commanded more than casual attention.

All at once he came suddenly upon a group of men whose dress as he saw it in the starlight told him at once that they were the treacherous Squaw-men of the West. It was well for Plucky Phil that he crouched and hugged the ground when he did, for the eyes of the bronze fellows might have caught sight of him.

"Sittin' Bull ar' goin' to turn 'im loose," said one. "He's convinced the old chief thet if he hedn't shot Coyote when he did, he'd hev found the gal, an' then thet big bonanza would hev disappeared like smoke.

"Coyote's over yonder tussling with death. I couldn't sarve 'im any longer—nobody kin. The bullet went crashin' through his face. Thet's what a feller gits fur doin' the chief a sarvice."

Plucky Phil heard all this and knew that some one—Old Policy, in all probability—had finished Coyote's career. The person whom Sitting Bull was about to "turn loose" according to the squaw-man must be the guide.

He waited to hear no more, but left the angry group and glided away hoping to find Sitting Bull whose presence he thought would not be far from Policy Pete.

He came abruptly upon the square, and at the same time a form appeared leading a horse by the bridle.

"Sitting Bull!" ejaculated Plucky Phil recognizing at once the peculiar garments that distinguished the Sioux chief from the rest of his people.

The Indian did not look about him to see whether or not he was followed, but hurried away closely trailed by the youth who kept the figures of horse and man in sight.

If Sitting Bull was going to quit the camp, why did he not mount? His action puzzled Phil, and he was further nonplused on seeing the old Sioux meet a figure at the foot of a hill. This figure looked more like a toad than a human being, for at a queer call from Sitting Bull's lips it hopped from beneath a huge bowlder, and sprung monkey-like upon the back of the horse which the chief had led to the spot.

"The Ape will go and guard the white girl!" Phil heard Sitting Bull say to the apish figure whose eyes glittered like two mad stars. "He will watch her closely for thieves are on the trail. Does the Ape hear?"

A nod and a laugh replied, and before Phil could interfere away went the horse with the red dwarf on his back.

The boy sprung up with a cry of dismay. The deformed was riding to Nora Dalton's hiding-place, and he had no horse with which to follow. To this hideous object, hunchback like Caliban,[8] Sitting Bull had given at least one of his secrets; he had sent him away to guard Nora, and perhaps to kill her, although death had not been mentioned.

With such thoughts clashing in his brain Plucky Phil heard the sounds of the horses' hoofs die away among the somber mountains. He saw only the figure of Sitting Bull erect in the starlight, and apparently listening with joy to the sounds rapidly leaving his keenest of ears.

Suddenly the chief turned toward the camp, and with a low cry the young mountain trailer rose and confronted him.

"Halt!" fell from his lips as he straightened himself in Sitting Bull's path, and thrust two revolvers into his red face. "One cry, one movement and the Sioux nation will be chiefless at dawn. I am not one of Custer's avengers. Uncle Sam will pay you for that massacre if you obey me to-night. I am a boy hunting for the dearest friend one ever had. Shall I introduce myself, chief? My name is Phil Steele, or Plucky Phil since my life-hunt began."

The old Sioux allowed an expression of contempt to mingle with the look of rage that sat enthroned on his swarthy face.

"A white boy!" he cried. "Where from?"

"Fort McKinney latterly, but that is immaterial. Where will the Ape stop? That is what I want to know."

Sitting Bull started.

"The secret is in danger, eh? To be sure it is! I am hunting the girl you keep concealed. My revolvers are at your heart. Do you want your brains on the ground where you now stand?"

"White boy would never get the girl if him shoot Sitting Bull."

"I'd feel somewhat satisfied anyway," said Phil. "If I leave you dead behind me I'd have only the Ape to overcome. Don't you see? Besides, Nora can bring no ransom to you—force no treaty from the Government."

"White boy lie!" said the Indian. "Girl big white chief's child."

"That is just where you're fooling yourself. Nora Dalton's father was with the train. Some of your hatchets killed him. She has told you so a hundred times, no doubt. Her beauty makes you think that she is the child of some great personage high in power and authorized to treat with you on your own terms. She is fatherless Nora Dalton, that is all!"

"White girl big soldier's child!" persisted the chief, in front of the cocked revolver. "Her worth much to Sitting Bull and his people. White boy no make the chief of the Sioux give her up by a lie."

---

[8]Caliban was the sole inhabitant of an island in Shakespeare's *The Tempest.* Prospero and his daughter are stranded on Caliban's island, and Caliban—who is misshapen and apelike—becomes their servant.

"That's plain talk," said Plucky Phil; "but let's proceed to business. Tell me where Nora is or by the stars above us I'll shoot you where you stand. Your rank shall not preserve you."

Did the Sioux chief suddenly discover that the boy of the mountain trail was in stern earnest? He might have seen the white fingers tighten behind the triggers of the revolvers.

At any rate, he turned half way round and pointed in the direction taken by the mounted dwarf.

Plucky Phil held his breath.

"White boy may have Nora if she not big chief's child," he said. "Him go straight on to the first trail on his right. Ground soft there, and the feet of the Ape's horse will guide him to him. Him must fight the Ape, though."

"I will do that!" cried Phil; "but I will spare the hunchback for your future use."

"Sitting Bull care not 'bout that," in a careless tone. "The Ape can see in the dark like an owl. White boy have to look out for his claws and teeth."

The revolvers crept slowly down.

"One word more, chief," the young trailer said. "Who shot Coyote?"

"Aggawam."

"Where is he?"

A singular light lit up Sitting Bull's eyes, as he answered:

"Aggawam go away; never come back to Sioux again."

Plucky Phil drew a breath of relief and joy.

Policy Pete was free!

"Go find white girl now," continued Sitting Bull. "Take her back to the white soldiers."

"I will, chief."

A moment later the boy was traversing the trail along which the Ape's horse had left fresh footprints.

Where was Sitting Bull?

An Indian was bounding toward the Sioux camp. It was the wily head of the red nation.

Five minutes afterward he came back mounted on a fresh horse, across whose neck lay an elegant rifle.

The fire of rage and pursuit blazed in his evil orbs as the cavalry spurs strapped to his heels drew streams of blood from his horse's bowels.

At the rate he was traveling he would soon overtake Plucky Phil, but a human figure leaped suddenly into his path at the foot of the mountain, and while one hand clutched the bridle-rein, the other pulled the old chief from his perch before he could lift an arm to defend himself.

Sitting Bull fell heavily upon the ground, and his assailant leaped upon the horse's back with a coarse ejaculation of triumph.

"A man without a policy ar' no man at all!" said the victor. "Me an' Plucky Phil hev pooled our issues in this gal-hunt. If you want to eucher[9] us, you'd better call out yer hull

---

[9]Trump, beat.

red tribe. Thet would be a 'tarnal good stroke ov policy. A most affectionate adieu, Sittin' Bull."

A laugh followed Old Policy's sarcastic goodby.

The Sioux chieftain sprung up and grasped the rifle which had fallen at his side, but the old guide had already disappeared.

"Sitting Bull has ten thousand warriors!" he hissed. "They shall all hunt Aggawam, the squaw-man, and the young white wolf."

It was a formidable threat, but the next few days were to witness that it was by no means an idle one.

CHAPTER VI

ᵔ The Red Jezebel[10]

The man who was riding away on Sitting Bull's horse seemed to know that Plucky was ahead of him. Policy Pete had already congratulated himself on his sudden release by the Sioux king when he expected death for shooting Coyote in the presence of his master.

He had asked himself the meaning of Sitting Bull's unexpected clemency, but had been unable to give his mind a satisfactory answer. It meant something which Policy Pete could not fathom.

Back in the Indian camp, held down to a rude pallet by four dark-skinned squaw-men writhed the man who had betrayed Policy into the hands of the great Sioux. The pistol bullet had made a horrible hole in his face, and it was evident that his end was near. The wound received at Plucky Phil's hands had not yet healed, but it gave him no concern. The last shot had rendered him delirious, and he was accordingly fastened to the cot by means of cords attached to posts hastily driven into the ground by his friends, and left to writhe in pain alone.

"To pay Policy and the boy back, that's all I want to live for," he groaned. "I'm willin' to give the gal over to Sittin' Bull. I could never make her fall in love with sech a lookin' man like me anyhow, but I could strike the boy through her ef I war on my pins, couldn't I? By hokey! thet's an idea, but hyar I am, a reg'lar livin' sieve tied to a b'ar-skin an' expected to be planted by my pards afore to-morrow night."

He ground his teeth at the thought of his helpless condition.

He was still bewailing his fate when the curtain of the lodge was lifted almost noiselessly, and the light footstep that advanced did not escape his ear.

"You never went back on Coyote yet, Rosa," he said to the slender girlish figure that bent over him. "After all I guess you're the best pard a man ever had. Can't you cut me loose? They tied me because they thought I war goin' mad, jest because I've got a bullet somewhar in my head."

The hands of the young Sioux girl were already at work on the ropes that kept the

---

[10]Queen to King Ahab in the Old Testament (1 Kings 17–21), Jezebel has become synonymous with the wicked, treacherous woman who stops at nothing to get her way.

stalwart squaw-man down, but she suddenly uttered a cry of vexation and seizing a knife severed the lines at a blow.

Coyote with an exclamation of joy attempted to rise but fell back against his will, exhausted. Rosa put her arm under his head and helped him in the second trial which proved partially successful. Coyote succeeded in sitting up.

"Listen to me, Rosa," he said to the devoted girl. "I'm goin' to tell you the truth at last. You've allus suspected thet I hed a gal somewhar thet I rated over you. Wal you warn't mistaken, an' ef it warn't for thet same gal I wouldn't be in this fix now."

The eyes of Rosa the Sioux fairly flashed.

"I want to git even with Aggawam and his young pard!" Coyote continued, "an' ef you'll help me—ef you prove ez true to me in the future ez you hev in the past—I'll let you do as you please with yer rival, the white girl."

"The white girl?" echoed Rosa. "Then Coyote did save the girl of the train and keep her hid from Sitting Bull?"

"Thet's jes' what I did, Rosa. You've suspected it all along? I thought so. Help me an' I'll turn the gal over to you."

The Indian girl sprung up.

"What must Rosa do for Coyote?" she asked eagerly.

"Bring two horses hyar; no! help me to the big rock at the edge of the camp, an' fetch the animiles to it. We will make a trail between us, Rosa, you fur the white gal, yer rival, Coyote fur Policy Pete an' his boy pard."

The wounded man was helped to his feet with difficulty and a few moments later he was tottering toward the westernmost side of the Sioux village. The arms of the Indian maid prevented him from falling, and he more than once looked thanks from his blood-shot wolfish eyes.

"I feel thet I'm worth ten dead men, Rosa." he murmured more than once. "Hyar we ar' at the rock, the place to which I war to hev brought the hosses fur Policy—in a horn! Now go an' git the critters. Don't let any grass grow under yer moccasins, fur the sooner we git started the sooner you'll see the white gal what hes robbed you of Coyote."

Rosa the Sioux did not hear the ending of the sentence, for she was hurrying toward the corral not very far away and the squaw-man sunk upon the rock grating his teeth as though by that means he could kill the pain which had suddenly darted through his head.

"I wonder what's become ov Montana?" he said half aloud to himself while he waited for the girl. "I left 'im in the canyon jis' afore the red-skins charged down on the boy. He's huntin' the gal, too. I never thought Goldboots would spend so much time on a hunt like thet."

If Coyote had glanced over his shoulder he might have seen the figure of the man about whose whereabouts he had just questioned himself. Standing slightly behind a tree was Captain 'Tana whose eyes were fixed on the wounded man on the rock.

"This is luck!" he had already ejaculated. "I don't have to thrust my precious figure into the Indian camp in order to recover the girl's trail, but Coyote the liar falls into my presence, and if I do not disturb him I'll be likely to hear the truth."

So the handsome figure of Captain 'Tana continued to remain motionless beside the tree. He might have touched Coyote by putting forth his hand, and certain it is that he heard every groan of pain that welled from the squaw-man's heart.

All at once Coyote uttered a terrible oath and almost fell from the rock upon which he had partially drawn his figure.

"Where is Rosa?" he exclaimed. "If she doesn't come soon I'll pass in my chips afore I kin mount my hoss. The gal's most infernal slow; an while she's foolin' among the animiles, the bullet in my head tries to git the best ov me."

Montana saw that the man on the rock was wrestling with death.

"I allus 'lowed thet death would never give me a fair deal," he grated, looking at the dark stain now on the starlit rock—his own blood. "If Rosa did come back now she couldn't help me. I'm at the end ov my string; in other words, Coyote, death rakes in the biggest pot ov the game ov life."

The man rolled from the stone and lay on his back with his face upturned to the stars. His hands clutched the ground in his agony.

Montana sprung forward, and as he bent over Coyote the eyes of the two men met.

"You?" cried the squaw-man attempting to shrink away. "You want to know whar the gal is? You wouldn't try to be my avenger."

"By heaven, I will, Coyote!" said Captain 'Tana. "First, tell me the truth about Nora Dalton, and I'll hunt your slayers down."

"No! arter you hed found the gal you'd go back an' be Goldboots the Pacific Nabob ag'in," said Coyote turning his head away.

"I wouldn't—I swear—"

"I'll tell Rosa, not you!" was the interruption. "I'll put her on Nora's trail an' leave you to find it. The person what will not avenge me must hunt fur the gal on his own hook. Besides, you'll be hunted like a mad-dog afore many days."

"By whom?"

"By one who found only a few hours ago thet you war Goldboots, an' ef thet person hesn't got a big account ag'in' you, then Sittin' Bull doesn't like rum!"

"You betrayed me, then?"

The rapidly glazing eyes of Coyote shot Montana a look of defiance.

"I told him thet your old name war Goldboots."

A curse fell from Captain 'Tana's lips and his hands darted like the talons of a vulture at the squaw-man's throat.

"You'll hev to tighten your grip ef you beat the bullet!" grated Coyote grimly.

"Gods! I will!"

A gurgle and a gasp followed the exclamation, and the mad eyes of Montana saw death put an end to Coyote's career.

His hands were still at the throat of the man beneath him when he heard the neigh of a horse, and looking up he saw Rosa the Sioux girl leading two steeds.

He had time to leap up when the red maiden saw him and drew back.

"She mustn't escape me. She may already know the secret!" fell from his lips and the next instant he darted forward, clutched the girl's arm, and continued. "Go yonder and look at Coyote. I tried to keep life in him till you came back, but death wouldn't let me."

With a cry that seemed to fill her eyes with flashes of fire, Rosa dropped the leathern bridles of the horses and sprung to Coyote's side.

There he lay, staring at the stars, dead!

She knelt over him with woman's tenderness and seemed about to imprint a kiss on his bloody face when she was seen to start as though a serpent had hissed under the squaw-man's head.

Had she seen the finger prints on the throat?

She wheeled upon Captain 'Tana, and with finger pointing to Coyote asked in a strange voice:

"White brother here when Coyote die! What he say about Rosa—what word him leave?"

"He said that we should hunt the white girl together," said Montana through whose brain a certain idea had flashed like a beam of light. "We shall be friends and help one another, Rosa."

"Coyote say so?"

"Yes. I am going to hunt the man who sent the bullet into his face."

"And the boy, too?"

"May I die if I forget one whom I have cause to hate!" was the answer.

"Who are you, white man? " Rosa asked.

"I am Captain Montana, but you shall know more of me by and by. Are you ready for the trail now?"

Rosa sent a look toward the silent man on the ground, then went toward the horses.

"Rosa is ready to hunt for the white girl who stole Coyote's heart!" she flashed.

Montana started at the look that filled her eyes as she spoke the sentence.

"I must watch her," he murmured. "She hunts Nora Dalton to kill her. I have linked my fortunes for the present to those of an Indian Jezebel; but I shall prove able to thwart her when I have used her awhile. Now," to Rosa, "let us be off."

He was already in the rather comfortable Indian saddle which the Sioux girl had placed on one of the horses for Coyote, and Rosa was at his side.

But the hand of the red princess, instead of taking up the rein, fell on his arm, and their eyes met.

"Just before Coyote died a snake crawled across his throat!" she said slowly.

Montana recoiled with an exclamation of terror. He almost lost his balance.

"Rosa will forget the crawl of the snake," she continued, without abating her fiery look; "she will not slay the serpent if he hereafter crawls for her."

"Now, more than ever, must I watch this scarlet viper," thought Goldboots.

The next moment they were off.

CHAPTER VII

❧ Rosa Wields a Tomahawk

"I must confess that one cannot get along well in this Indian land without help," said Plucky Phil, who stood in the earliest light of the next day on the summit of a mountain spur which he had ascended for the purpose of obtaining a view of the country by which he was surrounded. "Perhaps I had better have remained at my post on the mountain side, but the sight of that red-skinned dwarf riding toward Nora fired me with eagerness to follow him, and here I am. The red Caliban is far away; his horse has carried him to Nora, and I am here, as far from the fruition of my hopes as ever. I have made hundreds of new enemies since I invaded Sioux-land, and gained but one friend, but his fate, alas! is unknown to me!"

While the youth's words might indicate despair, he was far from giving up, although he was horseless on the spur.

He had followed Sitting Bull's directions only to discover that the Sioux king had purposely deceived him—that he stood far from Nora Dalton, and in the center of a country which might prove a death-trap.

"I cannot stand here and look and think!" he exclaimed. "I shall retrace my steps until I find the hoof-prints of the dwarf's horse. Rain has fallen lately, thank Heaven! and the mountain passes will betray the Ape."

He went down the mountain and turned his face once more toward Sitting Bull's village.

He still had a right to be called Plucky Phil.

The sun came up over the jagged spurs of the Big Horn range and revealed the passes which the boy was compelled to thread. His eyes were constantly examining the ground.

All at once he started and dropped on his knees.

Before him were the unmistakable prints of hoofs.

Plucky Phil's eyes dilated as he gazed, but a puzzled expression crept into them as he gradually discovered that two horses instead or one had lately passed down the trail.

"I see!" he exclaimed rising. "Some person is following the red Caliban. The Sioux chief himself may have taken a notion to carry out the commands he gave the Ape."

The next moment Plucky Phil was hurrying down the newly discovered trail. His long journey during the night had not exhausted him. A devouring flame seemed to flit through his veins.

"Somebody has got to die on this trail," he said to himself. "One thing I know, I shall never turn back."

On, on he went, guided by the hoof-prints plainly visible in the yielding earth of the mountain trail.

"Halt!"

Loud and clear the command rung out on the keen air, and Phil, who at the time was examining the trail, started up and drew his revolver as he sprung back.

In the path before him he saw the person whose lips had parted to utter the brigand's orders.

"It is mother's foe, Goldboots!" ejaculated the young trailer. "I would know him among a thousand."

Then he attempted to move forward, but the man in the saddle before him sent his voice again over the leveled rifle which covered Phil's breast.

"Stand where you are for the present!" he said. "We can settle accounts at this distance. I didn't expect to be followed by you in these parts, and when the echoes of Echo Gulch told me that somebody was behind, I never dreamed that it was you. That gulch, Rosa says, has doomed many a would-be avenger. So you know me as Goldboots?"

"I know you as the man who challenged my father because you were mother's foe, and slew him villainously by firing before the command. Is it strange that I should hate you? But I did not come into this country for the purpose of hunting you."

"Perhaps not, but you would not hesitate to send a bullet through my brain if you got the opportunity."

The flashing of Plucky Phil's eyes answered Montana.

"You are hunting lost Nora Dalton. So am I. It would hardly do for us to hunt her together. I have a partner already. I want you to see her. Rosa?"

A moment later Plucky Phil saw the Sioux girl ride into sight and halt in the narrow mountain path at Montana's side.

"Here she is, boy. What do you think of her?"

Phil did not reply. He was near enough to see the shapely figure of the Indian girl as well as to note the expression of her deep dark eyes. The latter were fixed upon him in a manner that rendered him uneasy.

"Rosa and I are full pards," continued Goldboots. "She was Coyote's sweetheart yesterday, and she knows that you're the boy who gave him a bullet. Therefore she holds you in high reverence," and the speaker laughed. "These Indian girls are regular Jazebels when you stir them up," he went on, " and Rosa seems to be taking a fancy to you."

Plucky Phil saw that while Goldboots spoke he had lowered his rifle and that Rosa the Sioux was advancing upon him.

Her horse came forward slowly, and the dark eyes of its rider were riveted upon him.

"I shall stand my ground and see what this red queen wants," said the boy to himself as he clutched his pistols with new resoluteness. "Fortune may be favoring me. She plays queer games in Indian land."

Rosa had almost reached Plucky Phil by this time; their eyes had met some time before and were still returning flash for flash.

Goldboots, seated like a statue in his saddle, looked eagerly on.

"White boy b'longs to Rosa the Sioux!" suddenly said the Indian girl, as her horse stepped beside the trailer. "Him hunts the pale flower that bloomed for Coyote somewhere among the mountains, and him shoot Coyote."

"Yes, I shot Coyote!" flashed the youth, looking fearlessly up into the dark yet beautiful face before him. "I shot him because he attempted to deceive me with a lie. I did not kill the worm, however."

"Coyote dead, though."

"Good! There is one viper less in Sioux-dom!"

For a moment Plucky Phil expected to be brained by the hatchet which Rosa held above her saddle, and raised his left arm for the purpose of arresting, if possible, the mad stroke, but it was not given.

On the contrary, the weapon was lowered, and the Sioux girl leaned forward and said in a low tone:

"White trailer find favor in Rosa's eyes. She come here to kill him, but she will make him a chief by and by if him go back with her to the great village of the Sioux."

Plucky Phil smiled.

"A proposition of marriage instead of the hatchet!" he exclaimed. "This is what I'd call a case of love at first sight. Fortune always had a singular way of befriending me. She hasn't forgotten it."

"What young trailer say?" asked the Sioux maiden, whose look now expressed the eagerness with which she waited for his reply. "Rosa stand between him and the red warriors. Him be big chief pretty soon."

"I must follow my trail to the end first," said Phil. "Until I have done this I cannot listen to your words."

The Indian girl looked dismayed.

"Boy go with Rosa, then?"

"May be so."

"Good! Him makes the heart of Rosa glad. She will have a chief to take Coyote's place."

"Was that yellow snake a chief?"

"Him never a chief for Sioux never trust him far enough."

"That's what I thought, but go back to your company. When I have reached the end of this mountain trail, I'll consider your proposition."

"Trailer go with Rosa now."

Plucky Phil started.

"Not while you stick to Gold-boots," he exclaimed darting a quick look at the man a few yards away. "We would be shooting at each other before we had traveled half a mile. He killed my father."

"Will trailer go with Rosa if she sends Cap'n 'Tana away?"

"For the present, yes," said Phil.

The Indian girl without replying turned her horse's head and rode toward Goldboots.

"What kind of bargain will the two make?" thought Phil who eagerly watched the red princess. "Goldboots will probably consent to disappear for a while, but at the first opportunity he will send a bullet after me. I shot the wrong man in the canyon; instead of Coyote in the shoulder, it should have been Goldboots through the head!"

Rosa had reached her companion by this time.

"You didn't touch him," said the Pacific Nabob derisively. "I expected to see you find his brain with that hatchet of yours; but his good looks unnerved your arm."

"Cap'n 'Tana knows nothing 'bout it!" resented Rosa the Sioux. "Let him look behind him and see a new enemy."

Instinctively Goldboots turned, and at the same moment the Sioux girl's hatchet ascended into the air. The next instant and while Plucky Phil held his breath, the weapon descended with crashing force on the adventurer's head, and he dropped from the saddle to the ground followed by the rifle which his nerveless hands could not retain.

Goldboots had hardly touched the earth when Rosa turned a triumphant face upon the boy trailer.

"Cap'n 'Tana dismissed now," she exclaimed. "See! there is an empty saddle for the young white trailer."

"Great heavens! must I become the companion of such a creature?" fell from Phil's lips. "Yet I am in her power. I have no choice. She had no right to kill Goldboots. He belonged to me."

He said no more but went forward for the expression of Rosa's countenance was changing.

"Ah! young trailer now knows that Rosa the Sioux is his friend. By and by him become a chief among the red people."

Phil, who had reached the scene of the red girl's brutal blow did not reply, but vaulted into the saddle vacated by Goldboots.

"I will end this terrible acquaintance now," fell suddenly from his lips, and the next instant he whirled upon Rosa and caught her vengefully by the shoulder.

"What white boy do?" she exclaimed, alarmed at his compressed lips and flashing eyes.

"I propose to continue my journey alone!" he said. "I thank you for this horse, but you must stay behind."

The next instant Rosa uttered a wild shriek as she found herself wrenched suddenly from the saddle, and unable to retain her hold, she was hurled to the ground.

As she struck, Plucky Phil gave her a parting look and dashed away.

Not a moment too soon, for the pass behind him resounded with wild savage yells, and a glance over his shoulder showed him twenty Sioux in swift pursuit.

"Better this than the companionship of that red girl!" he said to himself, as he clutched his revolvers more firmly, and leaned forward on his horse's neck.

CHAPTER VIII

❧ The Compliments of Sitting Bull

Yells and arrows admonished Plucky Phil that to escape from the scarlet fiends now in swift pursuit, he must needs have a fleet horse. He soon discovered that fortune had sent him a steed on whose mettle he could rely, and before long the yells of the red warriors died away, and their best arrows fell far short of their intended mark.

But he did not check his speed.

What was occurring on the spot where he had left Rosa and Goldboots he did not know, for a bend in the mountain trail hid it from his sight; but while he galloped on he could not but imagine the surprise of the Sioux on discovering Goldboots in that part of the country.

Miles away in a most lonely spot Plucky Phil ventured to stop his horse. The animal had faithfully carried him from the jaws of death and was not reluctant to obey his command.

"So far good!" ejaculated the trailer. "A horse like my new prize is worth having, and he and I must become friends. Ah! if I had but possessed him when I started after the Ape, I might be nearer Nora than I am now. However, I must put up with fortune as it comes."

He had scarcely ceased when a heavy object whizzed past his head and struck the ground with a thud that made his horse recoil.

"A foe above me!" cried Phil, as he looked up.

He had halted at the foot of an almost perpendicular ascent. The top was high overhead and fringed with bushes.

"From some point far up the sides of the mountainous wall or perhaps from the edge of the cliff had been hurled the quartz bowlder which had been intended for his head. Not a bush quivered to tell the lurking-place of his would-be slayer; the rock had not even disturbed a rock swallow on its downward flight.

A puzzled expression came into Plucky Phil's eyes as he gazed upward.

"That rock was thrown at me," he said. "It did not leave the wall of its own accord. Had it done so it would have dropped straight down to the foot of the cliff. On the contrary it was thrown by some enemy, some lurking Indian caught out without his rifle."

He might have continued if he had not caught sight of a horrible human head which crept into view like the head of a snake from its den of rocks.

"Ah!" thought Phil. "The quartz bowlder did not come from the top of the wall. I have found the den of a monster."

The head was all out now, and although it was many feet above him he could see the snaky eyes that peeped from beneath the hair that framed the face like the matted mane of a lion.

"Heavens! it is Sitting Bull's Caliban!" cried the boy.

The discovery almost took his breath.

"Who would have looked for the ape in such a place as this?" he murmured when the ogreish head was withdrawn. "Where the deformed is I will find Nora! Sitting Bull sent him to her last night. I do not wonder that Coyote failed to find Nora in her prison between Heaven and earth."

The boy trailer was not long in vacating the place. He feared that another attempt on his life by the cliff Caliban might prove successful.

He continued on down the road until he found a place at which he resolved to attempt to ascend to the cave in the wall.

The day was moving on, but the boy was undaunted. He left his horse at the foot of the ascent and began to climb upward.

His eyes beamed with eagerness and triumph. The mountain trail was nearing its end. He had found the hiding-place of Nora Dalton, and that was enough to cause his heart to beat fast.

He did not pause till he reached the top of the rock. Far below him lay one of the beautiful valleys of the Sioux-land. Down there Sitting Bull was plotting to run to earth the daring spirits who had dared to invade his domain, and dispute with him the possession of his fairest captive.

To find that part of the wall's edge directly above the mouth of the cavern was now Plucky Phil's object. Once or twice he leaned over the precipice, but saw only a perpendicular wall with swallows flying in and out like mountain bats.

The third time he uttered an exclamation of horror and almost sprung back from the edge of the cliff, for that hideous red face was upturned to his searching gaze and the eyes of the Sioux Caliban were scowling at him.

Plucky Phil drew back and reflected.

The mouth of the cavern was about five-and-twenty feet below the top of the wall, and the young trailer's eyes saw no contrivance for reaching it. How, then, could one reach and return from it?

"Ah!" he suddenly exclaimed, as his keen eyes fell upon a stout stake among the grass near his feet. "The Ape fastens his rope to this post and lets himself down over the cliff. I care not how he gets back: I will learn that after awhile."

He searched the vicinity of the stake for a rope, but in vain. He pried under bowlders and hunted the bushes, but fortune did not favor him.

"The means for getting up are where Nora is," he said. "I must descend at all hazards!"

Resolved to reach the cave below, the boy doffed his stout buckskin hunting jacket, and his knife was soon cutting it into strips. Each one was tested when cut to the proper length, and before long a series of knots had converted the strips into a rope, which was tried as a whole and pronounced satisfactory.

"I came to Siouxdom to find Nora Dalton!" he exclaimed, proudly. "Sitting Bull, you must hide your captives in places which a jacket cannot reach."

Once more he leaned over the fringe of the precipice, this time with a revolver clutched in his right hand.

It was his intention to drive a bullet between the eyes of Sitting Bull's dwarf if the hideous face should again present itself.

But nothing save the dull wall appeared, and Plucky Phil drew back and fastened one end of his buckskin rope to the stake in the ground.

"Here goes for Nora or death!" he said, clutching the blade of a bowie with his teeth, and the next moment he was hanging alongside the wall between earth and sky, with a frail buckskin cord between him and eternity.

He held his breath and harbored his strength as knot after knot was successfully passed. What if the red Caliban would swing himself from the mouth of the cave and wait for him, knife in hand?

Of one thing Plucky Phil was now assured: The rock hurled at his head told him that the Ape possessed no firearms, and to this circumstance he probably owed his life.

All at once a cry that made his heart stand still pierced his ear.

It came from the cavern in the rock below and was a long loud cry for help.

Plucky Phil seemed to descend several feet at once.

"Vengeance is not far away!" he murmured. "Hold out a minute longer against the apish monster, Nora, and he will quiver on the rocks beneath the cave."

If the young trailer had glanced over his shoulder at that moment, and down into the glen from which he had discovered the cave he would have witnessed a sight terrible enough to pale the cheek of the bravest.

Seated on a blanket-saddle fastened to the back of a magnificent steed was an Indian whose garments were more than half civilized.

He wore the traditional feather crest of the red chieftains of the bloody West, and the rifle which he held against his shoulder threatened Plucky Phil with immediate death.

"White boy brave as a bear!" crept from between the Indian's lips. "But him mustn't reach Sitting Bull's captive!"

The Indian, then, was the Sioux Napoleon[11] himself, not at the head of the ten thou-

---

[11]Napoléon Bonaparte (1769–1821) became ruler of France soon after the French Revolution. He kept Europe in an almost constant state of war for more than a decade and is widely considered one of the greatest military strategists of the last three centuries.

sand warriors whom a few hours before he had threatened to turn loose on the boy, but all alone.

Plucky Phil saw not the red chief, nor did he learn of an enemy's presence in the glen below until the Sioux's rifle sent a messenger of death at his swaying figure!

A sharp cry parted the boy's lips as one hand left the rope, and he swung madly around like a person mortally shot.

The knife clutched by his teeth fell glenward and landed on the rocks under Sitting Bull's horse with a musical jingle.

The eyes of the Indian blazed with fierce triumph, and a sardonic expression became fixed on his face as he watched the swirling figure on the buckskin cord.

"Him trail white girl no more!" he said. "Sitting Bull wonders how his eyes found the lodge hidden in the wall."

Suddenly the young trailer's hand slipped and his body dropped to a level with the gaping mouth of the cave.

Sitting Bull saw the movement and instinctively looked at the ground as if to see where the body would strike.

The next moment, however, he uttered a cry of astonishment.

A hand had darted from the cavern and seized Plucky Phil's shoulder.

It was not the copper-colored hand of his Caliban, but one small and white like a woman's.

"Girl find 'im!" cried the amazed chief. "Her try to pull him into the cave. Where is the Ape?"

The question was still unanswered when the body of Plucky Phil was drawn into the opening, and Sitting Bull, gazing from his saddle, saw only the rope swinging to and fro above the cave.

For a moment he did not stir.

His eyes were still staring upward, and he had not recovered his self possession.

Suddenly a cry of warning came down from above, and the chief of the Sioux nation recoiled as a human-like body shot toward him from the opening above.

A second later, so swiftly it descended, it struck him a resistless blow, hurling him to the ground before he could lift an arm to turn the horrible missile aside.

Although bruised and nearly senseless, Sitting Bull managed to gain his feet.

His first glance was at the cavern's mouth, his second at the object writhing on the ground scarcely ten feet away.

Yes, the bomb from the cave in the wall possessed life, and a fierce look flashed in the Sioux chief's eyes as he recognized the misshapen body of his red messenger—the mountain Caliban.

"The white trailer has found his grave!" he hissed. "The child of the big white soldier will yet help Sitting Bull make the kind of peace he wants!"

The chief walked to where the dwarf lay, and as their eyes met, the little fellow gave a whine, and, clasping his master's feet, fell dead.

"Not now," said Sitting Bull, glancing at the cave. "The warriors must be kept back. They shall not discover where Sitting Bull hid the white flower."

He sprung to his horse, and the next moment was riding away as though sounds of an approaching force had reached his ears.

At the mouth of the glen he leaped suddenly erect, and, with a loud cry and uplifted hand, halted what appeared to be an army of mounted red-skins.

CHAPTER IX

❧ Brave Nora Dalton

While Plucky Phil was preparing for the hazardous descent to the cave in the wall, scenes that should not be overlooked were transpiring there.

Sitting Bull had chosen a secure hiding-place for the prisoner whom his red detectives had wrested from Coyote's power.

Nora Dalton hoped, when she found herself in the hands of the Sioux chief's agents that the day of liberation was not far distant; but when she was conveyed to the wall cavern despair took new possession of her heart. Instead of liberty she was immured in a new prison guarded at times by the Indian dwarf whose eyes ever possessed the baleful glare of the serpent's.

A hundred times she had tried to convince Sitting Bull that she was simply Nora Dalton, the only child of a man killed in the attack on the wagon train in the canyon. But her beauty rendered her assertions valueless in the eyes of the chief who maintained that she was the daughter of an officer high in command. The old chief believed that the Government was about to inaugurate a campaign of vengeance for the Custer massacre, and hoped that by holding Nora he could secure terms which otherwise would not be accorded.

For months the rock cave had been the lost girl's abode. Since her recapture from Coyote, her sole visitors had been the dwarf and his master, the latter to see for himself that she still remained in his power, the former to watch her with his evil eye.

"You may come here once too often!" Nora had said to herself scores of times as she watched the misshapen guard whose body was revealed by the light that constantly burned on the floor of the prison. "One of these nights I will try to lasso the stake on the top of the cliff and leave you to your dreams."

She made the attempt when she thought the mountain Caliban asleep, but she found the rope too short for her purpose, and as she was jerked from the opening a wild laugh of triumph rung in his ears.

She had to desist, feeling that the deformed guard never slept.

Nora was the sole occupant of the cavern on the day of Plucky Phil's arrival. She had almost ceased to look down into the glen, for nobody ever entered it, no one with a white skin, at least.

The body of the dwarf swung suddenly into the mouth of the cave, and Nora started at sight of his face. It was all excitement.

"Ah!" she thought, "Sitting Bull considers me in danger. The Ape shares his master's fears," and her heart beat faster than it had beat for many a day.

But as the hours wore on without bringing a rescuer to her rocky abode, the soldier's daughter feared that after all her hopes had been raised in vain. The guard never left the mouth of the cave. Squatted like a toad at the entrance, he kept watch on the glen below.

All at once Nora saw him spring back and pick up a heavy bowlder which he bore to the opening. The next moment he launched it at some object and leaned forward to note the effect of his throw.

A cry of bitter disappointment parted his lips as he drew back. The stone had missed its intended victim.

"Thank Heaven!" ejaculated Nora, who could not but think that the person below must be her friend. "I trust that you have revealed my hiding-place, hideous atom!"

The Ape turned quickly upon her and advanced with an animal-like bound.

"The Ape kill the hunter who looks for the white girl!" he cried.

"That is not true!" was the fearless response. "I heard your expression of disappointment. You cannot deceive me. Your missile missed your enemy and my friend."

A threatening display of sharp teeth was the dwarf's reply.

"If your foe was crushed by your bowlder, you will let me look," she said, advancing toward the opening.

"White girl stay back!" and the dwarf threw himself in front of Nora Dalton and menacingly lifted his long arms.

If his body was small and misshapen at that, in those ape like arms lay the strength of a giant, and as Nora persisted in looking into the glen he sprung at her with a cry and threw her rudely back beyond the fire.

The poor girl lay stunned where she struck until consciousness gradually returned, and her first glance at her persecutor was a flash of resentment.

"I have endured too long already!" she exclaimed. "I am convinced that the quartz rock was not hurled at an Indian. If I want to escape I must assist the friends below. I must vanquish the ogre who watches me."

The dwarf was at the cavern's mouth gazing into the glen. For once his eyes were turned from Sitting Bull's prisoner, and Nora mechanically threw a searching glance around the cavern.

As she was searching for a weapon of attack none rewarded her gaze.

"Why did I not think of it before!" she exclaimed, as her eyes returned to the fire.

The next moment she had sprung to the blaze and drawn therefrom a burning stick. What if the end she held seemed to blister her hands? She believed that she must strike now or remain the Sioux chief's prisoner still.

The dwarf-guard heard the noise made by the stick as it left the fire, and sprung up and faced the determined girl.

Nora braced herself with the novel weapon drawn back for the blow.

A moment the little ogre faced her, then he jumped forward with his apish arms extended to ward off the stroke. Nora retreated almost to the wall of the cavern, and struck madly at the outstretched arms.

At the same time there rose from her throat the piercing cry which reached the ears of the boy descending the rope against the outside wall.

Down went the arms as thousands of sparks flew in every direction, and Nora followed up the stroke with another which sent the red Caliban reeling across the fire-lit and spark strewn floor. As he sunk like one dead at the foot of the wall, the scorching weapon fell from the girl's hands and she gazed at her work.

Suddenly the report of a rifle roused her, and as she looked toward the opening she saw a dark object appear in front of it and remain there.

"More foes?" fell from her lips as she went forward. "Merciful Heaven! am I never to see the face of a friend again?"

But the next instant a cry of another kind followed her question, for the figure swirling before the mouth of the cavern showed her a pale white face.

Clutching a rock above her head, she leaned far over the giddy edge and seized the youth, whose hand seemed about to relinquish the buckskin cord.

It took all Nora's strength to draw the young adventurer into the cave, but she succeeded, and the rope swung out again as Plucky Phil sunk with a groan on the ground.

The heart of Nora Dalton seemed to stand still when she knelt over the figure before her. The weird light of the fire fell athwart the boy trailer's face, to which sun and adventure had given a hue which she had never known it to possess.

All at once she seemed to recognize the boy.

"It is Phil!" she exclaimed, and the cry opened a pair of eyes that at once became riveted on her face.

"Nora?" asked the mountain hunter, in a half-uncertain manner, and then he touched the face whose eyes, sparkling with joy, seemed to burn his cheeks.

"We have met at last!" she exclaimed. "I often dreamed that you would come, but how could I look for you here?"

"I started out to find you. I had an oath to keep," was the reply, and the speaker's eyes glowed with enthusiasm as he continued: "The whole Sioux nation could not have kept me from you, Nora. I was bound to find you, although everything at first proclaimed you dead. I have Sitting Bull and his warriors against me. There is but one person save yourself in Sioux land who is my friend, and Heaven alone knows where he is."

"Who is he?"

"Policy Pete."

"What! does he live?" exclaimed Nora.

"I saw him last fighting like a tiger among the wagons, and I have always thought that I was the sole survivor of that dark day's butchery. But where is he?"

"I do not know, but I am confident that he will turn up all safe some time. How glad I am to see you!" and the boy's eyes danced with pride and joy while they regarded the happy face before him.

"We are not free yet. Do not forget that," Nora said.

"That is true!" he said, springing up. "Where is my wound, Nora? Do you see any?"

The girl looked curiously at the straight boyish figure that stood before her.

"I see no wound."

"It is strange," Phil said. "I heard a shot; then my hands seemed to leave my rope and darkness came. My head hurts yet here," and he put his hand against the left side of his face.

"I see!" cried Nora. "There is a streak there. You may thank fortune, Phil, that the bullet came no nearer."

"Fortune still befriends me!" he said, smiling. "But one of these days she will entirely desert me. I cannot be always her favorite. We are not out of Sioux-land Nora.

The finding of you is but the beginning of peril. The men who followed me into this country got discouraged and went back. We must stem the tide of Indian cunning and deviltry alone, unless Policy Pete turns up to help us."

"There is Coyote."

"I am convinced that he is dead."

"Dead? He used to say that one of these days he would give me liberty."

"Instead of liberty he has given you the bitterest enemy a girl ever had."

Nora started and threw a questioning look into Plucky Phil's eyes.

"Your foe is an Indian girl," he said. "Did you ever hear Coyote speak of Rosa?"

"Many times," cried Nora. "She is the Indian girl whom he discarded when he found me. One day I was sitting at the mouth of this cave when I saw an Indian girl in the glen below. She was searching the wall as though she thought my prison was not far away. Such mad eyes I never saw before, and their vengeful gleam made me draw back with a shudder. I am convinced that girl was Rosa, the Sioux."

"It must have been. May you never fall into her clutches, Nora, nor into the power of her late companion, if her tomahawk did not put an end to his career. I mean—"

A wild cry from the girl's lips made Plucky Phil turn, and just in time, too, for the dwarf was in the act of dealing him a blow from behind with the stick with which Nora Dalton had beat him off a few moments before.

Phil's first thought carried him forward, and he met the descending cudgel half-way, arrested its progress, and dealt the Ape a blow that sent him staggering away.

"I'll transform you into a rocket," he cried seizing the deformed as he struck the ground, and the next moment he was bearing him toward the mouth of the cavern.

Nora held her breath.

At the edge of the opening Plucky Phil looked down and saw the Indian on the horse.

"You have just sent me your compliments, Sitting Bull; now take mine!" he exclaimed, and downward shot the ogre to knock the chief of the Sioux nation from his horse, as we have seen.

"I think I have deprived Uncle Sam of one red pest," laughed the young trailer as he turned to the breathless girl who had witnessed his feat. "A dwarf doesn't make a bad bomb shell. We must now think of escape, Nora."

A joyous cry burst from the girl's heart.

Escape the word had never sounded so sweetly before.

Plucky Phil hastened back to the mouth of the cave and seized the buckskin rope which still dangled there.

As he jerked it, it parted somewhere, and a piece remained in his hands!

He turned and presented a white face to the girl.

"Do not let the accident frighten you," she said encouragingly. "We have the dwarf's rope to aid us."

As she finished, she bounded across the cave and put her hand into a dark niche in the wall above her head.

But the next moment she withdrew it with a shuddering cry.

The Caliban's rope was not there!

CHAPTER X

❧ Old Policy Trusts a Snake

"I kinder feel like a feller what had a policy an' lost it. Hyar I am astraddle ov Sittin' Bull's hoss in the middle ov nowhar an' alone. The boy didn't stay long on the mountain when I left him to smell round the Injun camp, for afore I struck Bull, I whistled for the youngster but he never answered. He's got too much grit fur these parts, an' it's the kind what euchers a chap out o' his h'ar."

The speaker was the redoubtable Policy Pete and a strange expression looked out from under his bunchy eyelashes while he gave vent to his thoughts from the back of the horse from which he had lately jerked no less a personage than the Sioux chief.

Many a mile of Narrow mountain pass the old guide had traversed, and it was not strange that calm reflection should make him feel like a man who had "no policy."

It was high noon of the day that witnessed the events of the foregoing chapter, and Policy Pete was not a great way from the spot where Rosa the Sioux girl dashed Gold-boots to the ground with a blow of her hatchet.

The guide felt that he had left his young companion to a fate which might remorse-lessly put an end to his career, and he had about concluded to go back when the sound of hoof-beats assailed his ear and he turned his face to the West.

"Thar come the fellars what never want a policy!" he exclaimed casting his eyes upon the army of Indians already in sight. "Git one yerself, Policy, er the little h'ar thet you want to keep may cause a sculp-dance in the Sioux town."

He instantly slid from the horse lest his position in the saddle might subject him to discovery by the braves, and led the animal into a dense thicket where he fastened his cap over the moist nostrils.

"I kin git a policy when I'm out quicker nor any man west ov the Missouri," he said with a grin as he moved back toward the spot from whence he had discovered the red cavalry.

It was a sight sufficient to make old Policy's eyes flash, for the whole plain below seemed covered with Indian horsemen. Straight as arrows the Sioux sat their well-limbed steeds.

"What would Uncle Sam give to hev a good battery planted hyar?" fell from his lips as he gazed and then as his eyes caught sight of a certain figure he exclaimed: "I thought the king bee would be somewhar among the swarm. Thar's Sittin' Bull himself, big ez life an' ez savage ez ever. What did he mean when he told me I could go arter boring Coyote through the face with my brain-opener? He had a policy in view when he dis-missed me, not exactly with his blessin'—he never gave thet to anybody—but without a blow on the head with his hatchet."

The guide continued to survey the stalwart figure of the Sioux chief as the cavalcade advanced at a smart gallop which soon caused it to strike the trail near which Policy stood.

With his finger at the trigger of a revolver, he saw the red army file past.

Suddenly his eyes dilated.

"Goldboots, by hokey!" he ejaculated. "I wonder whar the reddies made his acquaintance?"

Captain Montana was among the Indians, not exactly guarded although, but closely watched as Policy Pete could see.

"Thet's a part ov the policy, Sittin' Bull referred to when he told me thet he would make thet boy's trail the hottest one ov his life. Now he's huntin' the youngster with the wolves what chawed up Custer. It's bad enough to be hunted by Sittin' Bull alone, but when he's backed by the hull Sioux nation a man's sculp becomes mighty onsartin property."

The last look given by Policy Pete to the Indian band rested upon Goldboots whose presence among them puzzled the guide, but if he had witnessed the Nabob's overthrow by Rosa and his capture a short time afterward by the mounted Indians, the mystery would have been solved.

"I must foller thet band. They ar' on the boy's trail now."

He went back to his horse but did not immediately untie him. He quickly transformed himself into a passable looking Indian by means of some pigments which he took from a deep pocket on the inner side of his half-civilized frock. He next threw the horse's trappings upon the ground, lest they should cause Sitting Bull to recognize his property, and with a buffalo cord which he produced, he speedily made a bridle and a bit, and a moment later was flying down the mountain trail not exactly in the wake of the Indian army, but parallel with its line of march.

"It's risky," he said, "but I never go back on a policy when I've once formed it."

Half an hour later he slipped from a crevice among the hills and joined the cavalcade without exciting any undue attention.

By and by he nudged his way forward until he rode shoulder to shoulder with Goldboots.

The late Nabob of the Pacific coast did not notice his new comrade until their eyes suddenly met.

Goldboots started at the mute questioning of Policy Pete's orbs.

"Whar ar' this brigade goin'?" asked the guide in a low tone.

"You'd better ask Sitting Bull," was the rejoinder, for Montana evidently saw no friendship in Policy's look.

From beneath the lank guide's eyebrows came the retort, which said:

"If you can't be civil, I'll leave you to your fate."

It brought the Nabob to terms.

"You are not a squaw-man," he said, looking at Pete.

"I hev been fur the last two years, that is I've been playin' the *role* fur policy's sake."

The guide's expression—his favorite one of "for policy's sake"—seemed to let a flood of light into Captain 'Tana's mind.

"I know you now," he said. "But can't we be friends?"

"We might."

"On what terms?"

"In ther first place, tell me why ye'r' hyar," said Policy, not noticing 'Tana's eager question.

A grim smile was visible under the Nabob's mustache.

"A red wild-cat knocked me from my horse, and these Indians came across me before I could avoid them. You know Rosa, the girl who loved Coyote?"

"Wal, I ought to. It war her tomahawk thet did the tappin' I presume?"

"Yes, curse her!" grated Montana. "But thanks to a steel-lining which I wear in my cap, my skull was not broken and I live to throttle her one of these days."

"If she doesn't get the first call on you. What war the difficulty between you?"

Goldboots hesitated. Should he tell Policy Pete that he had seen Plucky Phil the boy whom the old guide was probably hunting? No; he would not do that, and with this resolve, a story carried to the minutest finish flashed through his brain, and it was launched at the man with a policy.

Policy Pete apparently swallowed the narrative without choking, and Montana was congratulating himself on the success of his ruse when Peter's stained hand touched his arm, and his lips scarcely parted to say.

"I see you hev a policy, too, Montana."

The Nabob's eyes suddenly dilated.

"Never mind. Let us pool our issues, er, in other words, j'ine our policies. I kin git you out ov this red pack."

"Do it, and by Jove! you will find Captain Montana at your back through thick and thin!"

Policy Pete said no more for a moment, during which time he had singled out Sitting Bull at the head of the cavalcade.

"I'll leave you now," he whispered, to Goldboots. "Keep eyes and ears open. In a few minutes you'll hear a shot an a yell. When they come leave the gang and dash down the first trail to yer right. Keep on fur a mile whether ye're hunted er not. You've been in tight places afore, cap'n. I saw you tried once. At the end ov a mile down the right-hand trail is a big tree with a rock fast in the first fork. Ef you ain't chased to thet point wait thar fur me. You see thar's nuthin' like hevin' a policy."

"I'll be there!" said Goldboots determinedly.

The withdrawal of Policy Pete from the band occasioned no comment. Indians were constantly leaving the trail.

Goldboots smiled when the figures of the old guide and himself disappeared. Might not Policy Pete be deceiving him?

Suddenly a shrill rifle-shot stopped the foremost braves and a horse fell dead in his tracks. Instantly the whole band was thrown into confusion; the warriors leaped erect upon their horses' backs and cocked their rifles. The shot and the falling horse had checked the army in the narrow pass.

"The old fellow is as good as his word," ejaculated Goldboots seeing his opportunity for a withdrawal, and a moment later his horse was bearing him down a mountain trail whose opening he had reached the moment of the shot.

"Let the white coyote go!" cried Sitting Bull, as a dash was made after Goldboots by a few warriors. "There is a snake in front of us whose sting is death."

The Pacific Nabob was therefore not pursued, and he kept on to the tree designated by Policy Pete.

He drew rein under the wide spreading branches for a moment and then dashed on again.

He had scarcely disappeared before the lank guide made his appearance.

"I sartinly heard a hoss," he said, looking around, "but Goldboots is not hyar."

Something on the trail under the tree attracted his attention, and after a brief inspection he rose with a prolonged whistle.

"I'm not the only man in these parts what hez a policy!" he exclaimed. "Goldboots didn't keep the app'intment, an' I ought to be kicked fur helpin' him out of his predicament. He'll hunt Plucky Phil with a vengeance now, an' never thank me fur my assistance. He won't forget the gal, Nora Dalton, either. It's a pity he hedn't lost thet steel-lined cap ov his jes' afore Rosa, the red wench, struck him with her hatchet!" and Policy Pete grated his teeth again as he looked down the trail whose sinuosities and distance hid the flying figure of the viper whose scalp he had in all probability preserved.

"We'll meet ag'in, cap'n," he said. "An' mebbe I'll take yer photygraph with the six-shootin' camera I carry about my anatomy."

They were to meet again.

CHAPTER XI

⋙ Before a Knife

"What shall we do?" gasped Nora Dalton, when she found her voice after discovering that the niche in which the dwarf had been in the habit of depositing the rope was empty. "The deformed always placed it there after reaching me from the cliff above, and I confidently expected to delight your eyes with it, Phil; but, as you see my hands do not clutch the prize."

The beautiful face of the girl was pale and a look of fear filled her eyes.

"The Caliban changed the hiding-place of the rope at the last moment, that is all," the young trailer said. "We must search the cave for it; it cannot be far away."

He pulled a burning brand from the fire as he finished and turned to Nora, ready to commence the search.

"You know something about this cavern, Nora? It has been your home a long time. You had better take the torch and I will follow you."

The girl complied by taking the flambeau from his hand. She led the way to the niche, and showed him that it was empty; then they went on deeper into the earth until Plucky Phil stopped and touched Nora's arm.

"How deep is this cave?" he asked.

"Heaven knows!" the girl said. "I have explored it until my limbs grew weary."

"Then there is no telling where the red dwarf hid the rope. Let us go back. We must trust to fortune and invention for escape."

They had taken up more than an hour in the search already completed, and, while Nora was reluctant to turn back without the rope, she did not oppose Plucky Phil's proposition, and back they went.

"Halt!" suddenly whispered the boy, and Nora stood still. "Our fire is out entirely. The main chamber has been invaded in our absence."

Invaded? The thought was enough to still the girl's heart, especially when she recalled the shot fired at Phil from the glen below.

The young pair listened in the darkness, but heard nothing. The light that entered at the mouth of the cavern did not extend far inward; it showed them nothing, because it possessed no revealing powers.

Silently Plucky Phil drew his revolvers and stood resolutely before the girl for whom he had hunted so long. Not a spark of the fire remained; it had been smothered as though by a buffalo-robe.

"The invader possesses more patience than I do," suddenly murmured the boy. "I'm going to put an end to this suspense."

He moved cautiously forward.

Nora, with a knife which had belonged to the dwarf, trod at his heels.

All at once, out of the gloom which seemed palpable, leaped an Indian, who fell upon Plucky Phil like an avalanche.

The boy staggered back under the assault, and, forced to drop his weapons, which were almost literally wrenched from his hands, he had no other alternative than to grapple with his assailant, which he did.

If the mountain trailer was a youth in limb, the human panther was not long in discovering that he possessed a man's strength.

Nora heard the tussle in the dark, but could see nothing. The combatants writhed like serpents at her very feet, and it was evident that each was depending on the arms and strength nature had given him.

When the desperate struggle reached its hight, the girl suddenly saw a human body swing into the light at the mouth of the cavern.

Another enemy.

Quick as thought, but without a cry that could alarm Plucky Phil or his antagonist, Nora sprung forward and reached the opening just as the new-comer set his foot on the edge of the stone.

"Back!" she cried as she pushed him out into mid air. "Go and join your brother the dwarf. We don't want you here."

A curse—a white man's oath—followed her action and made Nora look more closely at the invader. Then she saw that despite his half civilized garments he was a white man, although his face was a bronze one, and a great quantity of dark hair covered his broad shoulders.

As he swung back revealing his face, and a pair of eyes which were scintillating like twin stars, Nora Dalton instinctively shrunk away.

He regained his footing and spoke to the girl.

"I'm a friend!" he said. "You don't want to destroy me, do you?"

The girl could not speak.

It could not be possible that that handsome bronzed face belonged to a foe, and yet Nora did not feel like trusting him.

He released the rope while she hesitated, and stood before her in the uncertain light that surrounded them.

"Ah!" he suddenly exclaimed catching the sounds of the struggle going on between Plucky Phil and his red enemy.

"The boy and the Indian are at it like two bears."

"Yes, yes!" cried Nora. "If you are my friend prove it by helping the helpless."

She pointed toward the combatants as she spoke and the man sprung forward.

A bound brought him to the spot, and his hands easily distinguished the two grapplers. He possessed the strength of a Hercules for he tore the enemies apart, and Plucky Phil rose from the ground some distance away and wondered who had leaped to his rescue.

"You see I am your friend!" said the bronze-faced man appearing a moment later at Nora's side. "The boy is panting over yonder in the dark, and the chief I have choked into insensibility."

"The chief?" echoed Nora.

"Sitting Bull!"

"Now who are you?" she asked, but at that moment she seemed to recognize her helper. "You are Goldboots," she said.

The man's eyes answered her.

"Then you are not my friend," she continued. "Phil and you are mortal enemies."

He seemed to laugh.

"This is what a man gets for helping you. If I had not caught Sitting Bull descending the rope out there he would have finished the boy and kept you his captive. His red army is not far off. I have hunted you ever since Campbell's train left Fort McKinney. You are the only girl who could get me to run into the jaws of death. I am Goldboots to that boy yonder, but the wild West and the gold slope knows me as Captain Montana the Pacific Nabob."

"I have heard of you," said Nora, returning his triumphant look with one which told him that the prize was not yet won. "We cannot be friends now."

She stepped back.

"Hold on, my beauty!" he exclaimed following her. "I've never lost a game when black eyes were the pot. You don't know Captain 'Tana. Why, I have hunted you too long to lose you at this time."

His hand shot forward to seize Nora, when between her uplifted knife and his eager fingers sprung a form from the gloom and a blow dashed him back.

"You win when you have conquered me, villain!" cried the boy, for it was Plucky Phil himself who had come to the rescue. "I am here to dispute with you the possession of the prize we both seek."

"Agreed, boy! To you I am Goldboots."

"The coward who slew my father because his manliness took Ellen Danton, my mother, from your power. I know all! Fate—fortune—has brought us together on the mountain trail!"

Straight as an arrow, although weaponless, Plucky Phil faced Captain Montana.

His weapons lay somewhere on the floor of the cave, and he had pushed back the knife which Nora had extended.

"Keep it. You may need it yourself," he whispered.

They stood face to face for a moment, then the fearless boy leaped at Goldboots, and bore him back before he could draw the revolver that rested on his thigh.

"There's a good deal of the tiger in you!" hissed the Nabob. "But you're no match for me."

This boast seemed true, for he tore Phil loose and struck him a blow that sent him reeling against the wall behind the breathless girl.

"I might as well finish my work now," he said, drawing his revolver. "While the boy lives I cannot hope to make the girl the queen of the Pacific slope."

But he found an obstacle in the shape of Nora Dalton in his way. The girl had stationed herself before Plucky Phil, and she stood erect with a warning look, and with the naked knife menacingly uplifted.

"Stand where you are, Goldboots," she said sternly. "The knife I hold has probably hunted hearts before to-day. If you advance upon Phil Steele it shall hunt for yours."

"She's a fit companion for the young tiger," thought Goldboots. "I must deal the cards over and get a better hand. Knife is trumps now. I cannot afford to let it take the only heart I possess."

He did not shrink from Nora, but with his eyes fastened upon her, he began to plan another movement that would insure success.

CHAPTER XII

❧ Rosa Severs a Rope

Sitting Bull had left his band, hastened to the prison cliff, and lowered himself to the cave after his almost fatal shot at Plucky Phil.

Goldboots whom we left hurrying from the spot where Policy Pete rescued him from his red captors had returned to the trail, for he believed that by watching the Sioux chief he would the sooner find Nora Dalton and his young enemy Phil.

In this respect he had not reckoned wildly, for by following Sitting Bull when that worthy withdrew from his band, he was enabled to discover the cavern. He left his horse when he saw the red chief lower himself over the cliff, and did not hesitate to follow him down the same rope to the white girl's abode.

These actions account for the presence of Goldboots the Nabob on the spot in time to interfere in the fierce scuffle going on between Sitting Bull and Plucky Phil. He was surprised to find himself confronted by the young trailer, although he knew that the boy still lived, for Rosa the Sioux Jezebel had preserved him from his (Montana's) aim.

The Pacific Nabob found himself in an unpleasant predicament when he stood before the menacing knife of the girl whose beauty had brought him into the territory of the Sioux. The loss of Campbell's train was known everywhere, and the sad fate of pretty Nora Dalton, the Pride of Fort McKinnley, was mourned in the rich parlors of 'Frisco.

The words of a half-drunken Indian had caused Goldboots to leap up from a Denver gambling table. Could it be that Nora Dalton was not dead? From that day he possessed a new aim in life. He would find this beautiful girl and take her to 'Frisco as his wife; he would set coast society wild, and he would keep her, too, at the muzzle of the revolver and the point of his bowie.

He had found her at last, but in the heart of Sitting Bull's domain, and she stood between him and his boy rival with a knife raised against his heart.

Such an outcome of his hunt he had not expected.

Plucky Phil had evidently been knocked senseless by coming in contact with the dark wall of the cave. At least he made no noise, and this encouraged Goldboots.

"Well," he said to Nora, "I will let the boy go. He cannot baffle me, for did you not hear him strike the wall? I doubt whether his head would hold water just now."

The girl unconsciously uttered an exclamation of horror and lowered the knife. Phil might be dead, killed by being hurled against the wall by the Pacific Nabob.

She turned to find the boy, when a hand encircled her waist and a low voice assailed her ears.

"White girl never b'long to Goldboots!" said the voice, which caused Nora to stagger back as far as the hand would permit. "Sitting Bull make the peace he wants with her."

Nora could not speak.

The chief of the Sioux held her fast.

"Can't you find the boy?" called out the Nabob, impatiently.

"Sitting Bull got the White Flower!" was the answer, and the figure that stepped across the line of shadow thrust a revolver into Captain 'Tana's face.

"You're on deck again, eh?" ejaculated the Nabob, involuntarily shrinking from the shining barrel, behind which the dark eyes of Sitting Bull danced like twin dervishes. "It will not do to half-kill an Indian, and I'm a fool for trying the experiment. I had you by the throat awhile ago, chief, and I might have sent you to kingdom come, but we were friends once, you know."

"An' that is why Sitting Bull would not let his braves hurt Goldboots when they found him wandering about after Rosa hit him with her hatchet," was the reply. "Then, again, Sitting Bull kept his warriors from followin' Goldboots when he rode away 'while ago. Goldboots forgets this."

"It would do me no good to remember your kindness, as I am to be shot down here," the Nabob said, sarcastically. "Blaze away, chief, an' lose one of the best white friends a Sioux chief ever had. Yes, shoot and forget that some of my money purchased the powder that helped to wipe Custer out."

"Sitting Bull no kill Goldboots, but him must go."

Montana glanced at the mouth of the cave. The rope was still dangling in front of it.

"He must go and keep from Sitting Bull's trail forever!" reiterated the Sioux.

Goldboots glanced at the shadowy form held firmly by the Indian's left hand, and hesitated. The cocked revolver looked him squarely in the face.

"Go!" thundered the impatient Indian. "The finger of Sitting Bull is at the trigger!"

The Pacific Nabob stepped toward the opening with an oath. Under his mustache he was savagely biting his lips.

"Never mind! we'll meet again!" he hissed over his shoulder. "When I next reach the eagle's nest I will take care to attend to the old bird first. Your days are nearly numbered, killer of Custer!"

There was no reply, save a defiant glitter in the eyes that still looked over the steely barrel.

Goldboots reached the edge of the corridor and caught the rope which now hung motionless above the abyss.

It had lowered him to the cave and it would certainly again bear his weight.

Driven to despair by the menace of the deadly revolver, the Nabob grasped the cord firmly and swung himself from the cave.

The next moment he was drawing himself up.

"All this risk for a girl who as yet doesn't care a whit for me!" he said to himself. "But she's worth the powder! Great Heavens! she's prettier than romance made her. How she *would* shine on the slope! What a belle of 'Frisco she would make. I'm not by any means struck, but I'd try to cross a gulch on a bridge of spider-webs if Nora was on the further side, a prize for me! The old chief thought I couldn't watch the cave! I can watch, and, by Jove! I can kill! I am going to do both!"

Goldboots, encouraged by his communings with self, was making good progress up the rope, but all at once all color left his face and his hands seemed to shrink from the cord.

He had cast his eyes upward to note his progress, and they had encountered a pair of orbs that possessed the glare of the panther's. They were full of malice and revenge.

Nor was that all.

Just below the red face that leaned over the edge of the cliff was a naked arm that held a knife against the rope!

"Rosa the Sioux!" gasped Goldboots.

"Rosa find the snake that crawled 'cross Coyote's throat before he died!" came down from the Jezebel's lips. "She hit him hard with her hatchet, but him must have an iron head. Now she cut his cord, an' him never crawl across throats any more."

"Cut it an' never know where the white girl is!" flashed Goldboots. "I have found and hid her. Cut the cord, you red viper!"

The knife instead of severing the rope shrunk away, and a new curiosity beamed in Rosa's eyes. But a moment afterward she ventured:

"Girl Hunter make a lie to keep Rosa from sendin' him down the rocks. She know where White Flower is."

"Then cut the rope and find her!" said Goldboots.

"She in the cave in the wall," was the Indian girl's response. "Rosa see Sittin' Bull go down rope; by an' by Girl Hunter come along an' go down, too. Now him come up alone. Sittin' Bull drive 'im out, eh?"

"Girl-Hunter try to lie to Rosa, but him fail. She wait for Sittin' Bull. Him got another rope in the cave, an' by an' by him come up with the white girl whose pretty face took Coyote from Rosa long ago."

There was but one part of the Indian's last sentence that impressed the man completely at her mercy. The words "another rope" told him that the keen knife still clutched in her hand was going back to the work from which his manner had taken it.

He was not kept in suspense a great while.

"Rosa hunt white girl without Cap'n 'Tana to bother her!" suddenly grated the red Jezebel, and the knife was drawn across the cord with a vengeance that told the Pacific Nabob how terribly woman can hate!

A wild cry—a shriek—rose to his lips as the rope parted, and the next instant he was falling along the wall with his hands clutching madly at every minute projection.

From above the glittering eyes of Rosa the Sioux vixen were following him on his terrible descent, but suddenly a cry of horror dropped from her tongue.

Goldboots had, a second after the severing of the rope, reached the mouth of the cavern, and his bloodless hands had clutched the edge of the stone floor, to which they clung with the energy of despair.

He hung between life and death by the frail hold of a pair of almost nerveless hands. If Sitting Bull caught sight of him a bullet or a hatchet would terminate his career, if the chief did not merely loosen his hands and let him continue his descent!

A glance upward showed him the revengeful face of his red persecutor.

"Oh, for a hand at that viper's throat!" grated Goldboots. "She dare not let me hang here in peace one minute. I am getting stronger and I shall soon be able to draw myself into the cave. Then a thousand Sitting Bulls cannot make me recoil an inch. She is going to finish her devilish work!"

It was time.

Rosa was leaning over the cliff with uplifted hatchet.

"Girl-Hunter wear no cap now to save his head!" he heard her hiss. "Rosa make his hands leave the step of the White Flower's lodge."

The next moment down came the hatchet!

As it left Rosa's hand Goldboots dodged at random, and the weapon missed him by the breath of a hair, hissed past his cheek to strike the stones in the bottom of the glen far beneath him!

CHAPTER XIII

❧ Policy against Policy

Fortune evidently still smiled on Goldboots, for his escape from the hatchet of the revengeful Indian girl was a narrow one.

A look of chagrin became visible in Rosa's eyes as she watched the bloodless weapon's descent to the bottom of the glen.

The Nabob's joy over his escape cannot be described.

By a masterly effort he raised himself above the edge of the cavern's mouth and stood once more on the stony ground over which Sitting Bull had lately driven him at the pistol's muzzle.

"Here I stay until I am ready to depart!" fell in defiant tones from his lips.

He looked around. In the shadows which deepened into actual gloom a few feet in front of him, he saw no one, and silence reigned supreme. Goldboots was puzzled, to say the least.

He drew his revolvers and held his breath while he attempted to fathom the mystery shrouded in silence and shadows.

A few short moments since he had confronted Plucky Phil, Sitting Bull and Nora Dalton on the spot now occupied by him. Ten minutes had not passed, but they were not to be seen.

Through the darkness came the glimmer of a coal as a burned stick stirred in the fire which the Sioux chief had almost entirely extinguished when he entered the cave.

Goldboots sprung to the spot and unearthed a few crimson embers which he fanned into a flame. He was convinced that he was the only living tenant of the cavern.

"I must find the red wolf's trail," he said as he worked with the coals. "And to do that successfully I must have a torch."

When he had produced sufficient fire his first steps carried him to the spot where he supposed Plucky Phil to be lying unconscious.

His eyes dilated with wonder when he searched the place and found no traces of the young trailer.

"All gone!" he said. "If Sitting Bull carried Nora off he already has a foe on his track I should have finished the youngster when I had my hand on his throat. Delays are dangerous. I was a fool to let the girl and her knife deter me."

He ceased and began to examine the floor of the cave with his torch. It revealed nothing, but all at once Goldboots sprung up and hurried away. A dark corridor had been revealed by his search, and as a thought that there might be another outlet flashed through his brain, he leaped into the gloomy aisle.

"To play this game to the last card; that's my intention!" he said. "Who wouldn't risk his existence for such a girl as Nora Dalton?"

The corridor narrowed as he advanced with a cocked revolver on a level with his heart and the torch over his head.

"Halt!" he said suddenly to himself. "This is the end of the trail."

His words appeared true, for the passageway had terminated abruptly, and Goldboots the Nabob stood nonplused before a dark wall.

"Hello! what is this?" fell from his lips as a shower of sparks fell over him, for the torch which he had waved around his head had come in contact with some object. "By Jove! it is a rope!"

He could scarcely contain the joy born of this singular discovery.

A rope, not unlike the one by which he had followed Sitting Bull to the cave, dangled over his head like a hangman's noose, and it was this object which had been struck by his torch.

He seized the cord and tested it cautiously as though he feared it might be some enemy's trap, but at length he put out his torch and with a naked bowie between his teeth, began to climb upward, hand over hand.

A few moments' work enabled him to rest on a narrow platform a few feet above the floor of the cave proper, and he felt the rope slip from the rocky projection over which some hand had noosed it, and heard it fall upon the extinguished torch below.

The loss of the friendly cord occasioned no alarm in the Nabob's heart, for he had already caught a glimpse of natural light overhead. Five minutes later he crept into the evening shadows from beneath a huge mountain rock, and felt a cool breeze fan his cheeks.

For some time Captain Montana stood in the gathering shadows with the look of a detective who finds himself baffled by some shrewd criminal.

He could not think that Nora Dalton remained in the cave, for the rope told that Sitting Bull had escaped with the prize he had snatched from Coyote's hands. He stopped and examined the ground around the new opening, but he did not possess the eye of the lifelong trailer and it told him nothing.

At one time he thought of going back into the cave, but the loss of the rope deterred him, and he was forced to remain above-ground.

"I will find my horse first," he said. "One needs such an animal in this country every hour."

Having taken his bearings, he went over the ground and gradually descended into the valley where he had concealed his horse after having seen Sitting Bull descend to Nora's hiding-place.

The sun had gone down, but the brief twilight that peoples the Big Horn Mountains with shadows remained.

The Nabob of the coast reached his horse tethered where he had left him. The animal received him with a joyous whinny, and Goldboots had laid his hand on the rein when he saw a piece of dirty paper protruding from beneath the girth-strap.

He threw a startled look around as his hand shot toward the paper which he jerked from its strange envelope and began to unfold.

There was a scrawl of some kind on the dingy sheet, and Goldboots could not make out a word until he had subjected the ill-shaped letters to a close inspection.

Then this queer message was read:

"My policy ag'in' yourn, Goldboots! I'm a fool, an' ye'r' a dog."

No signature. None was needed to tell Captain 'Tana by whose bronzed fingers the scrawl had been traced.

He tore the paper into pieces which he crammed into the muzzle of the revolver his right hand clutched.

"I'm going to shoot his message into his head!" he grated. "I accept his challenge. My policy against his. I didn't expect to find him here, but such a devil as Policy Pete always turns up when one doesn't want him. However, I am prepared for him. He has given himself away by the letter. He is the fool he calls himself. His eagerness to talk about his hobby has got the upper hand of him again. That policy of his will kill him yet. My opinion is that he signed his death-warrant when he stuck that paper under my girth."

He mounted his horse as he concluded and rode toward the place where he had emerged from the cavern. It was half a mile away.

As he entered a shadowy pass—the ground over which he was riding was very broken—he saw a dark figure glide from the right-hand side of the trail and before he could cover the person he was looking into the muzzle of a revolver that touched his steed's mane.

"You got the letter, eh?" exclaimed the well known voice of Policy Pete. "I kin tell thet by the way you look. My policy ag'in' yours, cap'n, thet's fair, ain't it?"

"It is fair when we both have an equal chance," growled Goldboots. "But you've got the drop on me now."

"Jes' ez if you wouldn't git it on Policy Pete ef you hed a chance!" was the cutting rejoinder. "Ar' you in a hurry?"

Goldboots said "No" out of curiosity to see what would follow such a reply.

"Thet suits me because I want to show you a sight," continued the guide.

The Nabob started. Had Policy Pete discovered Nora?

"Jes' loan yerself to me fur five minutes," Pete said, taking hold of Montana's bridle, and as the girl-hunter did not object the guide led the horse away.

A few yards from the scene of the meeting they left the path and approached the cliff from which Rosa, the Sioux girl, had hurled the hatchet at the venturesome sport.

"We're going back to the cave," said Goldboots to himself.

"Git down," Policy Pete said in a low tone, and the Nabob immediately slid from his horse. "Ef that ar' a genuine Injun hoss he'll lie down an' keep still. Let me try 'im."

The long guide approached the animal, which obeyed his words and strokes, and was soon lying sidewise on the ground.

"He is too much the master of my horse," said the flashes that lit up Montana's eyes when he saw this display of authority. "He knows the animal too well for my own good."

The twain now went forward to the edge of the precipice.

Beneath them was the glen over which more than one of our characters had already hung suspended.

Goldboots glanced downward and started back with an exclamation of surprise.

A smile crossed Policy Pete's face.

"They're waitin' fur Sittin' Bull, the boss Injun ov this kentry," said the guide whose finger was pointing down into the glen. "There must be more than six hundred ov 'em. The old chief guv 'em orders in the afternoon to wait fur 'im back yonder in the valley, an' they did so till they got fidgety an' moved up hyar. They ar' wonderin' now what's become ov Bull. Whar is he, cap'n?"

The question and the look that accompanied it sent Goldboots back with his hand on his half drawn revolver.

The glen below was filled with mounted Indians. They were the red-skins who had annihilated Custer and his heroic riders. Their fierce looks and impatient movements had already told the Pacific Nabob that they would soon transgress Sitting Bull's commands and wait no longer for him.

"War my question too pers'nal?" continued Policy Pete whose eyes had followed the Nabob's hand to the silvered butt of his revolver. "I asked you whar Sittin' Bull is. You ought to know."

"You know as much about the whereabouts of that red wolf as I do!" flashed Goldboots.

"Mebbe I do—not," was the answer. "The reddies down thar hev mentioned yer name in loud tones fifty times durin' the half-hour. I laid hyar an' heard 'em. They cuss Sittin' Bull fur not lettin' 'em follow you when I hed given you an opportunity to escape. They'd like to ask you a few questions right now, cap'n, an' I'm goin' to send you down fur thet purpose."

Out flew the Nabob's revolver, but Policy Pete's left hand clutched his right arm and the old guide's weapon looked again into his face.

"Policy is policy!" came over the death-freighted barrel. "A man without a policy ar' no man at all. Ef you h'evn't got one jes' now you'll need one within the next five minutes. You want the boy Plucky Phil, but the gal's the apple ov yer eye. What a queen ov 'Frisco society she'd make, cap'n! I'm doin' you a favor when I send you down to the Injuns, fur I'll be keepin' you out ov Rosa's road. Don't you hear the wolves growlin' down yonder? They'll go an' hunt Sittin' Bull pretty soon; won't stand it much longer. So go down an' quiet 'em, ef you kin!"

With the last word the bronze hand of the speaker gave Goldboots's wrist a wrench which caused him to utter an oath and to drop the revolver, which went off as it struck the ground.

The next moment Policy Pete pushed him to the very edge of the cliff.

"Jump, cap'n!" cried the guide. "You kin study out a policy ez you go down."

Mechanically Goldboots glanced downward over his shoulder. Six hundred pairs of Indian eyes seemed to be fixed upon him.

"Jump! There's one chance in a million fur you!" resumed Policy Pete, coolly. "I'll send you empty-headed down thar in a minute. It's policy fur you, cap'n, to make the leap."

Montana's teeth fairly cracked as he grated them.

"Your infernal policy will suffer if I escape!" he hissed.

"Let 'er suffer!" was the tantalizing response.

The Nabob turned once more to the scene below, and then, with a half smothered curse and an appeal to fortune for aid, leaped far from the edge of the cliff and shot downward toward the sea of upturned Indian faces!

CHAPTER XIV

❧ The Jezebel Finds Her Prey

A mile or more from the spot upon which Goldboots emerged from the cavern, and at the time of his escape, the figure of an Indian girl threw a faint shadow against the white stones of a mountain pass as she crept forward with the stealthiness of the red race.

It was Rosa the Red Jezebel.

Until dusk she had watched for Sitting Bull to leave the cave with his captive and her white rival, but her eyes had not been gladdened by such a sight.

Afraid to descend to the cavern, even if she had possessed a rope, for the Pacific Sport was there, she had left her post, and, with a faint hope of finding another outlet somewhere among the mountains, had searched the uneven ground behind the precipice.

Rosa's eyes were keen ones, and revenge seemed to have helped her observation.

The shadows of approaching night could not prevent her from seeing the trail that led from the hidden outlet, and the dark eyes of Coyote's love fairly flashed when they fell on the figure of Sitting Bull seated on his horse. The Sioux chief had recovered his prize, for on the strong neck of the horse he held despairing Nora Dalton.

Rosa's horse had been left behind. She was afraid to go back for it, lest the white girl should be borne out of sight and beyond the possibility of her vengeance. She noted the character of the ground over which the chief's steed was picking his way, and resolving to keep the pair in sight, she continued after the game she had discovered.

"Rosa has found the White Flower at last!" fell from her lips. "She will not lose sight of her until she has paid her for stealing Coyote's heart. When Rosa has paid her she will go back and kill the golden snake whose scales bore down on Coyote's throat so that he died!"

Looking with triumph into the half-shut eyes of Nora as he rode along, going further from his warriors every minute, Sitting Bull seemed satisfied with the result of his present mission. He had selected another hiding-place for his captive. There were a thousand places in his wild domain where he could conceal the girl through whom he expected to force a treaty with the vindictive whites. If he had believed that Nora was but the humble child of an unknown man, he might not have been found riding down the mountain trail that day.

But no! her beauty made her the daughter of some one high in authority. She could not be of humble origin. Thus the head of the Sioux nation had reasoned a thousand times.

Where was Plucky Phil?

If he had recovered and was on the trail of his great enemy no one seemed aware of it. Certain it was, though, that the mountain trailer was not in the cavern, for Goldboots after his forced return to it had failed to find a single trace of him.

Rosa the jealous girl appeared to be the only person who had found the chief's trail, and it was certain that she would follow it to the bitter end.

Down among the deeper shadows she went with her eyes riveted upon the horse and his double burden. More than once she was within rifle shot and her fingers played nervously in the trigger-guard as her eyes flashed, but the weapon did not touch her shoulder.

It was not until Sitting Bull stopped and looked back that she paused. Crouching beside a bowlder, the Sioux girl eyed the chief as though he was about to disappear.

"White Flower near the new lodge," said Sitting Bull in response to a questioning glance from his captive.

"Always captivity!" sighed Nora, and a moment later an indignant light lit up the depths of her eyes.

"You dare not give me a gun—a pistol?" she said.

"What White Flower do?"

"If you did not then release me your nation would have to elect another chief."

"White Flower shoot Sitting Bull?"

"Need you ask? A thousand times I have told you that I am not a general's child. My father fell in the canyon massacre. I believe you know this, but yet you affect to believe otherwise."

"Girl stick to story well," said the Sioux. "Her never born in common soldier's lodge. By and by her father come to Sitting Bull and say, 'Let the Sioux make their own terms. Give up my child and the Great Father at Washington will put his name to the strong paper.' By and by all this be done, White-Flower."

"Never!" exclaimed Nora. "Were I the person you call me, I would never purchase my liberty on such terms!"

"We see!" was the sententious rejoinder, as Sitting Bull slid from the blanket and assisted his captive to alight.

Holding to the bridle and carrying Nora at the same time, the chief of the Sioux turned into a narrow trail which soon brought him to a place strewn with bowlders of every size. Many were piled in heaps as though the hands of a race of giants had thus deposited them.

Stepping past one heap as he dropped his steed's bridle, the chief raised a net-work of mountain creepers and displayed the mouth of another cave to the gaze of the wondering girl.

"Another prison!" she thought; "but thank Heaven one does not look from its door into an abyss."

She was led into the place thus revealed with the red hand of the killer of Custer at her wrist. She could not take note of the corridor, for it was dark, yet the Indian knew whither he was taking her.

"I must inspect my new home," she said, with a smile, taking up a torch after Sitting Bull had departed. "He has in some manner prevented me from escaping. I am satisfied that the opening behind the vines has been walled up with bowlders. Separated again, Phil! Fortune never smiles on us. Go back if you live, and leave Nora Dalton to her fate."

The young mountain trailer was not near enough to reply; but Nora knew that if he could have heard her, a ringing "Never!" would have fallen from his lips.

Her torch threw out a vivid light as she commenced her explorations.

The cave was a wonderful one, possessing numerous small chambers connected by narrow corridors, not unlike the caverns in certain portions of the Union east of the Mississippi.

"The Sioux king knows his dungeons well," ejaculated Nora, pausing at last. "I might as well go back to the fire and await the arrival of my new jailer. It will not be the dwarf this time."

"No! White Flower, the Ape is dead!"

The voice as much as the works made Nora Dalton recoil with a cry of terror.

As she sprung back, her torch revealed the speaker, not twenty feet away.

"I know you!" said Nora, recovering in a measure, although the glistening eyes of the Indian girl kept color from her cheeks. "I know why you came, too."

"Rosa help young trailer find White Flower!" exclaimed the artful girl, gliding forward. "Boy not far off, and she come to take White Flower to him."

But the chief's prisoner did not believe.

She recalled Plucky Phil's words.

He had told her that she possessed a bitter enemy in the person of Rosa, the Sioux. She knew, too, why red Jezebel hated her.

"You must stop where you are!" said Nora, tightening her gripe on her torch. "You follow me because jealousy has lied to you. I was Coyote's prisoner, that was all. You were welcome to the brute."

She talked to a rock.

"White Flower no believe that Rosa come to take her to young trailer," she said with a grin that disclosed her intentions. "Then she must know that Rosa come to pay her back for stealing Coyote's heart!"

Nora had not time for answer, for, with a cry and a panther-like leap, the scarlet Jezebel darted forward.

Madly the white girl struck with the flaming torch, but Rosa's arm warded off the blow, and before Nora could deal the second stroke she was in the hands of the jealous Sioux.

"What White Flower think now?" she hissed glaring at her with the eyes of an enraged tigress. "White boy not far off, mebbe. We go see. Sitting Bull going back to his braves now, thinking that him hide his pale flower from all eyes save the Great Spirit's. Ah! Rosa followed him when he knew it not. She wanted the dove whose pretty eyes stole the eagle's heart from his mate."

A moment later Nora was being dragged over the hard floor of the cavern. Torch and fire were left behind, and at length they stood beyond the vines, and in the light of the full round moon that looked down over a broken mountain spur.

Rosa's eyes still flashed triumphantly, and the fingers that encircled Nora's wrist seemed to burn their way to the bone.

"Look and listen, White Flower!" suddenly exclaimed the Sioux girl pointing down the trail.

"You see nothing," said Nora. "You hear the wind, and the moonlight makes shadows in the path. You should shade your eyes with your hands if you want to see anything."

Nora's heart seemed to stand still when her enemy's hand quitted her wrist. The Sioux girl was holding her shapely red hands above her eyes, and gazing down the path.

All at once Nora pushed the red Jezebel madly away and before she could recover, sprung off with a fervent ejaculation to fortune for aid.

Her situation seemed to lend speed to her hopes, and she was flying down the narrow shadow flecked path when Rosa recovered and darted in swift pursuit.

"White Flower must wither on the mountain trail!" she hissed, as knife in hand she followed the fleeting figure of the girl she hated.

It was, indeed, a race for life with Nora Dalton.

CHAPTER XV

❧ The Man in the Moon

"Help! help!" burst involuntarily from the throat of the beauty of Campbell's train when she heard the footsteps of her mad pursuer.

To look back might be to lose a step, so she cast no glance behind.

The trail was straight, and the mellow moon light revealed the mountain leaves that littered it.

Down upon her came the red Jezebel with the certainty of a doom which cannot be averted.

Still Nora kept on.

She did not possess a single weapon, else she would have wheeled and met Rosa face to face.

She kept on until the triumphant laugh of the scarlet vixen rung in her ears, until she appeared to feel the avenging knife in her back.

"I can go no further!" she exclaimed. "Fate has ever been against me, but it is better to perish in the light of the stars than in the gloom of an Indian cave."

Nora's heart had sunk within her, and all at once she fell exhausted at the edge of the trail.

Wild was the cry that pealed from Rosa's throat when she saw her long-sought victim in her meshes.

"Coyote's heart was the last one the White Flower stole. She will never steal another!" was the cry.

Nora saw the knife and its mad owner, heard the words just written as they fell hissing from her enemy's tongue, and shut her eyes for the blow. Entirely exhausted, she could do no more.

She did not see the figure that leaped suddenly into the path between her and the Indian girl, but Rosa recognized the new-comer with a startling cry and drew back with the look of a baffled tigress.

"In time to baffle you, demoness!" said the rescuer, whose build and garments proclaimed his identity, and without pity he dashed Rosa's uplifted knife arm down with the rifle he carried and sent her stunned to the bushes that fringed the trail.

It was Plucky Phil.

"I couldn't kill the tigress," he said, casting a look upon the Sioux girl before he turned to Nora. "She abandoned her horse for some reason or other, and fortune threw the animal in my way, and therefore I reached this spot in time to keep her knife from Nora's heart. Poor Nora! She does not think me near."

A moment later joy beamed in Nora Dalton's eyes, for they were looking into Plucky Phil's face, and he was carrying her toward a horse a few yards away.

The boy did not speak until he had taken a seat behind her on the animal's back.

"Thank fortune for this meeting," he said, joyfully. "We are not out of the woods yet, Nora, but the mid-air cave has been left behind, and I trust we have seen Sitting Bull for the last time."

"And Rosa, too," said Nora, with a shudder.

"Ah! you found her out," replied Phil. "She's more than fancy painted her, I suppose?"

"She must have loved Coyote."

"In her mad Indian way," the boy smiled. "It is the love which continually carries a knife in its hand."

The reunited pair were carried through the moonlight by Rosa's steed. Leaving the trail on the high land, they descended into a valley, through which the horse was carrying them at a brisk gallop, when Plucky Phil suddenly drew rein and cocked the rifle.

"Look ahead, Nora. There is a man in the moon," he said.

They were ascending a gentle rise, over whose summit the full-orbed moon was peeping, and photographed on the silver disk was the figure of a man and the head of a horse.

Nora could scarcely repress a cry when she saw the startling spectacle.

"White or red?" she asked, in low tones.

"That is what I cannot determine," said Phil, never taking his eyes from the apparition a minute. "I am going to find out, however."

He slid to the ground and left the reins in Nora's hands; then he crept forward and noiselessly up the little hill.

"I might have turned back," he murmured, "but turning back always puts a trailer on one's track in this country. Pete has taught me the value of a definite policy, but mine has always been 'advance! Never retire.' "

The man in the moon assumed almost gigantic proportions as Plucky Phil neared the summit of the hill. The boy now saw the strange skin cap that covered the head, but whether the person was red or white he could not determine.

He was now on all fours, creeping on inch by inch. A panther never approached its prey with less noise.

"I'll try the knife. I used to know how to use it," fell from Plucky Phil's lips as he laid the rifle down and drew the bowie. "The man in the moon is a squaw-man, therefore, a Sioux by nature. He is in my road, and the knife must remove him. I am throwing for Nora's safety. I care not for myself."

As the young trailer rose for the throw on which he had decided, he glanced over his shoulder and saw the dark figure of Nora's horse, then he caught the bowie at its point and hurled it straight at the apparition between him and the moon!

"Jehu! thar's another fellar with a policy!" exclaimed the stranger as the polished blade, turned from its path by fate, went flying past his face. "I'll jes' turn an' pit my policy ag'in' the one down the hill."

Plucky Phil started back amazed.

"I thank fortune for my bad aim!" he said. "I threw my bowie at my best friend. It is I, Policy—Plucky Phil!"

"Ther boy, by hookey!"

A moment afterward the gaunt guide was squeezing Phil's hand, and exhibiting a pair of dilated eyes beneath his bushy brows.

"Thet blade ov yourn, boy, nearly ended my policy," he said. "But whar's the gal?"

"Down yonder."

"You've got 'er at last, eh? Thet's the outcome ov some good policy. I choked off one fellar's policy back yonder."

Plucky Phil's eyes threw a question into Policy Pete's face.

"It war Goldboots."

The boy started and looked displeased.

"I was going to turn on him by and by," he said. "He killed my father—forced him into a duel because he hated mother, and then shot him. But you have killed him, Policy; you have baffled me."

"He may live," said the old guide "but—I—doubt it, Phil."

"What did you do to him?"

"Oh, nothin' much. I jes' made 'im jump off a cliff down among six hundred redskins," was the answer. "If he hed a cast-iron neck an' a good policy he may be livin' fur you, but it's almighty unsart'in, Plucky."

The young trailer did not reply, but turned his face upon the foot of the hill and the two went down.

"Whar's Nora?" asked Policy Pete stopping suddenly and looking into the boy's face. "Thar's the hoss; but—"

A cry of horror from Phil's lips had broken the sentence, and a bound carried him to the horse's side.

The animal stood where he had left him, but Nora had disappeared!

For a moment he stood bewildered where he had halted, and then wheeled upon Policy Pete.

"Where can Nora be?" he exclaimed.

"Thet's a tough question, but a good policy will find her," Pete said. "Let me tell you suthin' I've been achin' to talk about ever since I met you. This kentry is alive with red-skins. I war watchin' a sneakin' party while I war up thar on the hill. Goldboots must hev been in a condition to tell 'em who made 'im jump among 'em arter he landed. We may be in the midst ov the hull six hundred. Didn't I hear Sittin' Bull say thet he would hunt you with the entire tribe one o' these days? Plucky, ef you ever take Nora from Siouxdom it will be with the hull durned tribe at yer heels."

The boy's eyes flashed, and his lips met firmly as he clutched his revolver tighter and looked into Policy Pete's face.

"I always keep that threat before me," he said. "I came hither for Nora, and I will take her from this deathland if Sitting Bull and all his red allies oppose!"

CHAPTER XVI

ᔕ The Twin Mazeppas[12]

It was true that Nora Dalton had mysteriously disappeared. It was strange that she had been taken and the horse left.

Plucky Phil could not think that Rosa had followed them and recovered possession of her prey, nor did he believe that Nora had fallen back into Sitting Bull's hands.

"There is no trail here!" he said, as he rose from an examination of the path and fixed his eyes on Policy Pete.

"Wait till I pass jedgment," was the response.

The boy watched the lank guide with bated breath while the old fellow paid his attention to the ground. Policy Pete took his own time, and was scrutinizing the trail when the boy bounded forward and touched his shoulder.

"Wal?" ejaculated Pete, looking up at the boy trailer.

"There are Indians in the moon. Look!"

"Policy Pete obeyed.

"I told you the kentry war full ov the red niggers!" he said, after a glance at the silver world that peeped over the summit of the hill. "They're ridin' across the moon, as it war—gittin' round on our flank kinder like."

"Do you think so?"

Policy Pete sprung up.

"Look yonder!" he said, pointing down the narrow mountain trail. "Them ar'n't shadders, but Injuns!"

Plucky Phil instinctively lifted his weapon.

"We've got to take the bull by the horns, Plucky. We've got to ride through 'em. Thar's no gittin' round thet."

"I'm ready," was the boy's reply.

"Thet's the best policy. The wolves ar' behind us, too. Git up on the horse."

An agile bound seated Phil on the Indian blanket.

---

[12]Mazeppa was a historical figure (later made famous in a poem by Lord Byron) who was strapped to a wild horse and set adrift to die.

"If this be deserting Nora I do not move a foot." he said, looking down into Policy's face.

"It will be helpin' her in the end. We hev to hev strange policies sometimes, an' this ar' one ov 'em. Now go!"

"But you, Pete?"

"I'll tend to myself. It's a part ov my present policy. Ride straight ahead, ez if you heven't seen an Injun, an' when I whistle go off like an arrer."

Phil turned from Policy Pete and drew his second revolver, so that he had one in each hand.

Obeying a whispered word, the horse moved away while the boy's ears were waiting to catch old Policy's signal.

All at once it came, a cry between a hoot and a trill, and the next moment he went down the trail like an arrow.

A dozen shadowy figures rose suddenly before him, but fear of being trampled under the horse's feet made them hug the trees that bordered the path, and Plucky Phil's revolvers spoke on either hand as he dashed along.

Policy Pete had not been mistaken; the shadows of the mountain trail were living Indians.

Further on the daring boy rode into a pack of human wolves. They filled the little glen; they sprung at his bridle with the yells of demons and tried to drag him from his perch. He shot at point blank range into the devilish faces that appeared on both sides, emptied his revolvers among the infuriated Sioux and almost liberated himself. But at that moment fresh reinforcements came up; the whole Indian army surrounded him. His horse was knocked down with a club and he was torn from the blanket and held firmly by at least twenty hands.

"Five hundred against one are odds too great," said Phil, as he turned a defiant face to his captors. "You dare not let me reload my revolvers and give me a show."

"White boy talk to Sitting Bull presently," was the reply. "Him big chief, and mebbe him give young trailer his fast-shootin' guns ag'in."

"Show me your chief, the cause of my misfortunes," Phil said. "Where is this valiant chief of yours—the wolf that devoured Custer?"

At the name of Custer the whole party set up a yell and went through certain motions which told the mountain trailer that he had been captured by the red heroes of the Little Big Horn massacre.

Suddenly the ranks divided and Plucky Phil found himself in the presence of Sitting Bull. The boy started back amazed, for he had not thought that the Sioux chief had rejoined his command.

"White boy caught at last!" fell from the Indian's lips. "But him kill some braves before him yield."

"Who can avoid killing when he fights for life and liberty with a revolver in each hand?" was the quick response.

Sitting Bull nodded.

"Young white come into Sitting Bull's land from the forts of the white soldiers," continued the Sioux.

"Him hunt pale-face girl who came with the train across the great rivers. He would like to be safe in the forts now."

"Not without Nora!" said Phil. "I shall not go back alone."

"White boy brave. Him never go back, mebbe."

"That is true! It all lies in your hands, Sitting Bull. I admit that. If you had not hidden Nora Dalton, the six dead warriors lying back yonder would be alive to help you in your next campaign. Give me liberty and Nora, and my back shall be forever turned on your land."

For a moment the Sioux chief did not speak.

Plucky Phil watched him with deep interest.

"Put boy on Sudden Fire's horse," he said suddenly turning to some Indians at his left.

A moment later Phil was lifted to the back of a fiery young steed which had been reluctantly yielded by a young Sioux.

"Tie 'im now!" said Sitting Bull.

The tying operation did not last long when twenty Indians took part in it. The haughty head of the Sioux nation looked on with a gleam of grim satisfaction in his eyes.

"White boy take a long ride," fell from his lips. "Young horse full ov fire, but him go like the wind with his mate."

"What does the red tiger mean?" ejaculated Phil and then he thought: "He is going to make a Mazeppa of me."

Indian hands at the horse's head led the animal away, and the whole red army followed.

Plucky Phil's doubts were soon dispelled, for the band halted a few hundred yards from the scene of his capture. The mellow moonlight fell uninterrupted over the little dale.

"Ah! here comes the girl white boy been huntin'," said Sitting Bull, and the young trailer uttered a cry of surprise as his eyes fell on Nora Dalton whose horse was led forward by two braves.

The recognition was mutual.

"Phil!"

"Nora!"

The horses were brought together, and the eyes of the young couple became fixed upon each other.

"You would not go back after you escaped from the mid air cave," the girl said.

"Not without you. Nora!"

"We are going to leave Siouxdom together! Sitting Bull has determined to get rid of us."

"In what manner?"

"Heaven knows but he has come to the conclusion that I am not an important person."

Before Plucky Phil could reply Indians fell to fastening the two horses together at their heads, and he saw that Nora had already been lashed to her steed.

"Listen, white boy!" said Sitting Bull. "You came here for white Flower whom Sitting Bull long believed to be a great white war-chief's child. Him know better now: therefore, him willin' to send you both out of his country. The horses know the way mebbe, but if they git lost the white trailer will see his flower wither in the mountains. While him ride away, Sitting Bull go back and hunt for the guide's scalp, an' the hearts of all his pale foes. Good-by, young trailer."

"Your good-by, means death!" Plucky Phil said. "You would not send us away lashed thus to half-broken horses if you did not expect us to starve among the mountains of your accursed country. Cut me loose and meet me face to face. You can surround a body of United States troops and cut them to pieces, but you cannot fight a boy fairly. Sitting Bull, you are worse than the dog that gnaws the bones in your lodge, meaner and more merciless than the wolves of your mountains!"

The eyes of the stalwart chief flashed while the boy talked, but he did not reply.

His hand went up as a sign to the Indian who held the horses, and the next instant a hundred yells broke forth and twenty sticks descended upon the animals' backs.

Away they went like arrows shot from Indian bows, and scores of Sioux dashed after them with demoniac cries.

"This is leaving Sioux-land with a vengeance, Nora!" said Phil.

"It is better than captivity!" was the reply. "We are together once more! The hand of the red-man shall never separate us. When Sitting Bull slipped upon me and jerked me silently from my horse while you were gliding upon the man in the moon, his eyes emitted a devilish gleam I had never seen them possess before."

Plucky Phil did not hear more than one-half of these words. They were going away from Sitting Bull at a speed that deprived them of breath, and their followers were still making the air ring with their wild shouts.

On, on, until at last the pursuing Indians fell off like exhausted wolves. They had followed the twin Mazeppas for the purpose of urging the two horses forward as rapidly as possible, and they had returned to their leader.

Plucky Phil spoke to the steeds, but his strange voice had an ill effect, and he desisted.

Nora was exhausted. The cutting ropes had tightened, and she was constantly biting her lips to keep back shrieks of pain.

At last the animals stopped from sheer exhaustion.

The moon was approaching the horizon, and the shadows of the mountain trees looked like ghosts on stilts.

Phil turned and spoke words of cheer to the girl; but the face which she turned to him almost drew a cry of horror from his heart.

"This is the beginning of the end, Phil," she said. "We are lost, and our horses do not know where they are."

Then the girl sunk forward with a groan. She had fainted.

The young trailer grated his teeth and tugged at his bonds. He exerted all his strength, but the ropes were sinews and his limbs but flesh.

"Oh! for the strength of a Samson!" cried Phil. "Not for my sake, but Nora's!" and, having rested for a moment, he went to work again.

But he toiled in vain. The sinews seemed made of steel.

When he gave up he succeeded in getting the two horses close together, and leaning forward he gazed intently into the white face and half-closed eyes of his despairing companion.

Had he bravely entered the death-traps of Sioux-land to perish thus, reunited with Nora Dalton, but powerless to rescue her from a horrible death?

The horses stood like statues in the night; they refused to move at Phil's voice, and at last, exhausted and almost despairing, the mountain trailer dropped asleep beside the prize he had won at last.

CHAPTER XVII

❧ The Policy That Won

It was a tableau which the first gray streaks of dawn did not disturb.

Side by side in one of the most picturesque parts of the land of Sioux and bear, slept the brave young couple whose lives had been devoted to each other's love.

Plucky Phil was at last awakened by a neigh from his steed. Nora slept on, her pale face pressed against her dun steed's mane. The neigh had not roused her.

The boy trailer saw the fox-like ears of his horse standing stiffly erect. The animal must have heard the advance of one of his kind.

Presently from behind a deep copse came the answering whinny of an unseen horse, but it was suddenly checked, as though a cap had been thrust over the animal's mouth.

"Weaponless and tied to a horse, I suppose I am about to furnish some Indian marksman with a target," said the boy, bitterly. "A thousand curses on the red-skin who doomed Nora and I to a fate like this."

Although he did not shrink, he fixed his eyes on the spot where he expected to catch sight of the new foe. He was glad that Nora still slept.

All at once a horse and his rider came into full view.

A startling cry rung from Plucky Phil's throat.

"I was too merciful last night!" he murmured. "She will not refuse to profit by my leniency."

Well might the invader of Sitting Bull's territory glance from his confronter to the fair young girl at his side.

Rosa, the red Jezebel, had not left the trail of vengeance. She was before him with mad eyes, and grinning countenance, and her fingers rested within the boundary of her rifle guard.

Her astonishment was no less than the boy's, but in an instant she seemed to comprehend the scene before her.

"She has discovered that we are helpless!" thought Phil. "She will not keep off!"

Their cords had been discerned by the girl's keen eyes.

"White boy and his love fall tied into Rosa's hands!" she hissed as she moved forward. "Sitting Bull often send pale-faces from his huntin'-grounds tied to their horses. But he did not think he was sendin' the young whites to Rosa's rifle."

"All of which means that you are going to make the best of your opportunity for murder!" flashed Plucky Phil.

There was no reply as the rifle crept up until it touched the mane of Rosa's horse and covered the boy's breast.

Plucky Phil glanced at Nora. At that moment the girl opened her eyes.

"Alive yet, thank Heaven!" she exclaimed. "I was dreaming, Phil, that—"

She paused and started back, for Phil's quick glance at Rosa had revealed their peril.

"White Flower look how quick young trailer fall!" cried the red Jezebel. "Her become Rosa's captive for sure then!"

The cheeks of the speaker sunk once more to the rifle, and her eager finger touched the trigger when the clear report of a rifle on the right awoke the echoes of the mountain glen, and Rosa's horse staggered back shot through the head!

Down went the scarlet princess with her steed, and a moment later a lank individual appeared carrying a smoking rifle.

"I want to leave the kentry whar everybody hez a killin' policy!" he said as he came forward. "I ran you squar' into the red hornets last night when I thought I war gittin' you out ov a, diffikilty. But a policy doesn't always work, Phil. Some of the best ones turnout bad. Look at thet copper colored wildcat! The hoss ar' holdin' her down, an' she's shown' all her front fangs. Came jes' in time, didn't I? Got into a scrape myself with Sittin' Bull's beauties, but I came out right side up, an' hev been huntin' you two ever since. Didn't expect to find you together? Wal I jes't did, fur a lucky stroke ov policy made me acquainted with yer ride, an' I expected to find one whar I found the other! An Injun told me all."

Rosa meanwhile was trying to separate herself from her dead horse and reach her rifle which lay undischarged on the ground a few inches beyond her hands.

Policy Pete had already severed the bonds that held the young folks captive, and he turned with a revengeful ejaculation upon the jealous girl.

Madness distended the old guide's eyes.

"Wounded er captured wildcats ought ter be killed; thet's always been my policy!" he hissed, vindictively.

A moment later the career of Rosa the Sioux girl would have ended, but Plucky Phil caught the arm of the guide that held his rifle aloft.

"What kind ov a policy hev you got now, Phil?" asked Policy Pete turning an astonished face upon the young trailer.

"She's helpless!"

"Helpless? Leave 'er five minutes, an' thar'll be a bullet in Nora's heart."

"But you sha'n't kill her as she is." And Plucky Phil stepped resolutely between the guide and his victim. "Take the rifle up, and let her creep from beneath her horse the best way she can. No! I'll help her out."

He offered Rosa his hand, but she refused it with scorn.

"Rosa never touch white boy's hand, but to kill!" she flashed.

"What did I tell you?" laughed Policy Pete. "She sticks like a leech to the old policy."

But Phil seized Rosa's wrist and despite her looks, liberated her from her situation, only to see her slink away with eyes that threatened future vengeance.

"You kin go back an' hunt Goldboots!" Policy Pete said to her.

The Indian girl started at the name.

"What? is he still alive?" exclaimed Phil.

"Alive, but not ez handsome ez he used to be, boy. He lit squar'ly among the Injuns, and a hatchet sp'iled his beauty, but he's creepin' 'round somewhar. From what Sittin' Bull told me last night his photygraph wouldn't sell well in the music stores ov 'Frisco."

"Then you saw the chief himself?"

"Caught 'im nappin', ez it war. He's the Injun I referred to awhile ago. We used to be friends, you know, and the old fellar let me go arter I shot Coyote in the camp on account of a deed I did while I war playin' squaw-man an' huntin' fur Nora. I made Sittin' Bull tell me what he had done to you young folks, an' thet's partly how I came to be around in the nick ov time. Now don't talk about goin' back to deathdom fur Goldboots. Thet's not the kind ov policy we want jes' now. The Injun gal will 'tend to him, fur she owes him a grudge fur helpin' Coyote out ov the world a few minutes afore his time. We must git away. The old Injun made me a promise last night so we'll not hev the hull tribe at our heels arter all, ef we stir ourselves. Whar's Rosa?"

The Indian girl—Coyote's love—had already disappeared, and a few minutes later her stiffening steed was the only tenant of the little glen.

Need I say that not long afterward three persons rode up to the gates of Fort McKinney, and that one of the trio, a youth, turned to the west ere he entered the fort, and waved Sioux-land a long farewell.

The mountain trail was ended, and the stars and stripes once more waved over Plucky Phil and Nora Dalton.

Back in Siouxdom, in a certain wild pass almost at the same hour when McKinney opened its gates to the trio, a rifle broke the silence of the scene, and a man fell forward on his scarred face.

Another mad hunt was over.

Captain Montana, the Pacific Nabob, would never more frequent the gambling dens of Denver; he would no more boast how he slew Plucky Phil's father in a duel, nor would he exhibit lovely Nora Dalton as the wife of Goldboots, the gambler sport.

Vengeance plays queer tricks in Indian-land.

Goldboots had fallen before the red Jezebel's rifle because his hand was at Coyote's throat when the death gurgle was announcing the approach of that desperado's end.

Rosa went back to her people, to take up with another squaw-man, but not to love him as she had loved Coyote.

Of Sitting Bull we need not speak.

Not long after the arrival at Fort McKinney, the young couple journeyed eastward as Mr. and Mrs. Steele, and the old hunter who accompanied them was constantly talking about this policy and that.

"Your policy was to tie to the gal in the end, Phil," he remarked to the young trailer. "An' it war the boss policy, fur it surmounted every obsticle. I wouldn't giv' a red fur a man without a policy ov some kind!"

THE END

18

ℒaura 𝒥ean ℒibbey

(1862–1925)

LAURA JEAN LIBBEY spent much of her life in Brooklyn, New York, and many of her stories centered on the fortunes of young working girls attempting to make their way, often alone, in the modern American city. In the course of her career, Libbey edited a magazine, was a playwright, and wrote dozens of novels. At the height of her popularity, she was making more than $60,000 annually from her writing and editing activities, a truly astounding figure for the time.

As a novelist, Libbey reached the height of her popularity during the last two decades of the nineteenth century. She wrote serialized stories for such periodicals as the *New York Ledger,* the *Fireside Companion,* and the *Family Story Paper.* Many of these stories would then be collected and sold as cheap paperback books. As her popularity grew, her books were also produced in more durable library edition formats.

Although Libbey's novels are not all about the travails of urban working girls, her stories are best remembered for the following formula: independent working girl falls in love with a worthy young man but is accosted by an evil suitor against whom she must maintain her virtue, finally marrying her true love. The stories were so repetitious that many critics called them the same tale with the titles changed and the characters renamed. While critics howled at her work (her books became a byword for low-class, popular literature), the public loved it. So popular and ubiquitous were her stories, that working-girl romance novels became known as "Laura Jean Libbeys" by the early twentieth century.

The Master Workman's Oath is a classic Libbey tale drawn in her trademark working-girl mode. While it may not overtly challenge more traditional notions of class and gender stratification, the book does move the woman outside the domestic space and into the working world. Thus messages of female limitation and liberation are complexly woven into the fabric of the tale.

THE MASTER WORKMAN'S OATH

Or, Coralie, the Unfortunate
A Love Story, Portraying the Life, Romance, and Strange Fate of a
Beautiful New York Working-Girl

CHAPTER I

◦❧ Love at First Sight

No one is so accursed by fate,
No one so utterly desolate,
But some heart, though unknown,
Responds unto its own.
—LONGFELLOW[1]

Six o'clock!

The shrill steam whistles and factory bells throughout the metropolis proclaim the hour when work for the day is over.

From the Drexel Silk Mills throngs of young girls are hurrying out, laughing and chatting as they mingle with the surging mass of humanity that crowds the thoroughfare.

In the foremost of the group are two young and pretty girls; one of perhaps some twenty years, the other not more than seventeen.

The younger, Coralie Harding, despite the plainnesss of her attire—a neat-fitting navy-blue dress, with jacket and blue velvet turban to match—was so exceedingly beautiful that she would have attracted attention anywhere.

As pretty Coralie—the little beauty of the silk mills, as she was called—is destined to meet the strangest, ay, the most wonderful fate that ever came to the life of a lovely working-girl, beset, as that life is, with pitfalls and dangers, we will take more than a passing glance at her.

Coralie is small and *petite,* bright, joyous, with an airiness that is decidedly bewitching. Her blue veil was tossed carelessly back, revealing a lovely face, from which hard work in the mill had not as yet chased the wild-rose bloom and dimples.

A wealth of flaxen hair fell to her waist in heavy curls, and the wind blew some short rings of bright love-locks back from a pair of intensely blue, sparkling eyes, fringed with the longest and most curling of golden lashes.

Laura Jean Libbey, *The Master Workman's Oath: or, Coralie, the Unfortunate. A Love Story, Portraying the Life, Romance, and Strange Fate of a Beautiful New York Working-Girl.* New York: J. S. Ogilvie Publishing Company, 1892.

[1] Henry Wadsworth Longfellow (1807–1882) is considered by many to have been the most widely read American poet of the nineteenth century. Before his death, he had gained an international reputation.

Her companion, Fedora Burnham, is a decided brunette, piquant, pretty, but not one half so popular with the mill hands, from the handsome young overseer, down to the bobbin-boys, as mischievous, fun-loving Coralie was.

In every mill or workshop, or where there are a number of young girls, there is always one whose word is law among the other girls, who generally takes the lead of her companions. And in the Drexel Silk Mills Coralie Harding was the moving spirit.

Coralie and Fedora, judging from their talk and simultaneous bursts of laughter, are one in spirit and feeling; yet there is a vast difference between them, a difference that will fill a volume, though it can be told in a single word—a heart is the difference, and the girl with the yellow hair and baby-roses in her cheeks has it.

"I say, Coralie," cries Fedora, as the two girls pause for a moment on the pavement, "*do* go on the moonlight excursion up the Hudson with us girls to-night. Oh, it will be grand—a brass band, and dancing by moonlight on the deck, and a rousing supper and all that sort of thing; and by the way, our new overseer will be sure to be there, and if he follows in the footsteps of his predecessor, Coralie, he will fall deeply in love with you at first sight."

A scornful laugh ripples from Coralie's lips.

"I cannot endure the sight of him," she declared. "I saw him as he passed through the weaving-room to-day—he's too much of a dandy, and his eyes look too bold. Besides, I'm going to aspire higher," she went on with a saucy laugh. "I'm going to set my cap for old Mr. Drexel's handsome nephew, who, they say, is to return from Europe soon—Why, Fedora, how you clutch my arm! What's the matter?"

"It would be better for you, Coralie Harding, never to know Mr. Drexel's handsome nephew," she said, hoarsely. "He could want nothing of one of his uncle's mill-girls, though she were as beautiful as a houri.[2] Remember you are only a working-girl, Coralie, and he will be heir to three millions of money. Eagles never mate with sparrows. Keep out of the young heir's way, Coralie."

"You have awakened my curiosity about him. What is he like?" cried Coralie. "Is he short or tall, wicked or good, gay or quiet, clever or stupid?" she went on breathlessly, with all a young girl's curiosity.

"Do not think me rude if I change the subject," said Fedora Burnham, nervously. "We will talk of the moonlight excursion; anything save him."

And again a peal of laughter, sweet and clear as a silver bell, issued from Coralie's lips. And that merry laughter, and the gay, girlish voice attracted the attention of a handsome, slender young man who was passing hurriedly by. He paused abruptly and glanced back quite unnoticed by the two girls.

"I do hope you can come to the moonlight excursion to-night," said Fedora, earnestly. "If you can't, will you come down to the wharf and let us know?"

"Perhaps," answered Coralie; "but I cannot promise, though. You know how ill mamma is."

And at the thought, all the light laughter died out of the beautiful blue eyes, and the red mouth quivered grievously.

---

[2]The voluptuously beautiful women that in Muslim belief live with the blessed in paradise.

"You know how particular she is about allowing me to go out alone," she went on. "You must not expect me; still, I'll come down to see you off if I can. It doesn't look much like a moonlight night, I'm afraid. When the sun sets in a lurid, blood-red glow like that, it means a storm."

At the corner of Canal Street the two girls parted, Fedora to walk slowly on to her lodgings, and Coralie to hurry rapidly on in the direction of the lonely tenement rooms where her sick widowed mother, whose only support she was, awaited her with more than usual anxiety on this eventful, fatal night.

The handsome young man who had paused to take a glance at Coralie's pretty face, gazed admiringly after the slender, graceful, vanishing figure.

"What a lovely young girl!" he mused. "She must be employed in my uncle's silk mill. Such blue eyes, such an exquisite face; but, pshaw, why should I give the little fairy a thought? I'm done for as far as the fair sex is concerned, confound the fate!"

On the impulse of the moment Allan Drexel wheels about and retraces his steps, with no particular object in view; and very soon he found himself walking almost abreast of the little beauty who had attracted his attention a few moments before.

It seemed that others in that vast throng that flowed to and fro were not oblivious to the girl's beauty.

"By Jove!" cried one young man to his friend, as he caught sight of Coralie. "How's that for loveliness, eh? Isn't she a stunner? and only a shop-girl, too, I'll bet my life. Just wait here and see me pick up her acquaintance."

"Don't, Sinclair. Any one can see you've been taking a drop too much, and 'when the wine's in the wit is out,' as the old saying goes," warned his companion, "and, besides, the street is crowded."

Robert Sinclair shook himself free from his friend's detaining grasp with a rude laugh.

"Pshaw! I've only been celebrating my appointment as the new overseer of the Drexel Silk Mills, which goes into effect to-morrow!" he cried. "I'm not under the weather; only feeling devilishly like having a lark at somebody's expense. Stay here, I say, and watch me."

In an instant he had darted to Coralie's side.

"Lovely afternoon, isn't it?" he said, in a low voice, walking close beside her, an insolent smile on his mustached lips, a leering light in his pale blue eyes.

"Are you speaking to me, sir?" asked Coralie, drawing back indignantly.

"I am indeed so brave," he answered, with an impudent laugh.

Coralie wheeled about, the angry blood mounting her dimpled face, and crossed the walk to the opposite pavement.

In a trice[3] Robert Sinclair followed her.

"A wise thought," he hiccoughed, attempting to take her arm; "not half so many people on this side of the street."

"Step back and allow me to pass!" cried Coralie, fairly trembling with anger. "I know you, sir. You are the new overseer of the Drexel Silk Mills. But for all that, I shall

---

[3]Literally, a single pluck; hence, in an instant.

report this insult to the proprietor himself to-morrow, that he may see what kind of a fellow he has installed in a gentleman's place."

He stepped back as though he had been shot.

"By Jove! one of the Drexel mill-girls," he gasped.

In an instant the insolent smile had died from his face, and he grew fairly livid as he glowered down into the girl's brave young face.

"Repeat one word of this at your peril," he threatened, "and in a twinkling out of the mill you go. And I'll make it my business to see that you don't get into another place in New York."

"I do not fear you," retorted Coralie, scornfully. "I shall warn all the girls against you, be sure of that, besides reporting this to Mr. Drexel himself."

"You should have made a friend instead of an enemy of me," he hissed. "I will make you sue for pardon to me for that threat."

"Never!" cried Coralie. "I would die first!"

"Then hear the revenge I will take upon you for this," he cried fiercely, as he clutched her arm. "Come to the mill to-morrow if you dare! We will see who comes out ahead, you or I. I'll be on the lookout for you to-morrow morning, my defiant little beauty, and discharged you shall be, as sure as fate. I can find plenty of excuses, never fear."

He saw her recoil from him, and noted with gloating glee the awful terror that dilated the beautiful blue eyes, and blanched the lovely young face.

Only those who know the horror, the blank, pitiful despair compressed in that dread word "discharged," can realize the dull chill that swept over the girl's heart, and seemed to turn the blood in her veins to ice.

All in an instant poor Coralie thought of the mother lying so very ill in those dreary tenement rooms, whose only support she was.

Merciful Heaven! what should she do if she was thrown out of work now, just at this season of the year, when all work was so slack in great, big, desolate New York? Her mother and she might starve before she secured another place, and——

Her persecutor's voice broke in rudely upon her chaotic thoughts.

"I'll tell you how you can regain my good will, my dear," he said, leaning toward her, his voice dropping to a whisper.

Coralie Harding never heard the sentence through—she recoiled from him as though a serpent had stung her. A gasp fell from the white lips; the sunlit streets, the face of her persecutor, the whole world seemed to grow dark and whirl madly around her; she threw up her hands, and without a moan, without a cry, fell in a deep swoon at Robert Sinclair's feet.

"Great Scott!" he ejaculated, glancing nervously around. "What a predicament, to be sure. I did not reckon on this; here's a pretty go."

Suddenly a daring thought occurred to him as he looked down in dismay into the lovely, girlish face; a thought that, villain though he was, almost took his breath away. Then a horrible laugh broke from his lips.

"I'll see that you don't get back to the mill to-morrow, nor for many a to-morrow, my beauty," he said.

In an instant he had raised Coralie in his arms, and signaled a passing cab.

CHAPTER II

∾ The Master-Workman's Oath

"Hold!"

The word was rung out in a voice of thunder; a heavy hand fell upon Robert Sinclair's shoulder, and in a twinkling the girl's inanimate form was snatched from his grasp.

"It seems that I am just in time to foil a most daring abduction," cried the young man, white with rage. "Such scoundrels as you ought to be shot down; the world would be well rid of you. Take yourself off before I repent of my leniency and give you the thrashing you so richly deserve by daring to insult an unprotected girl."

A sudden change had come over Robert Sinclair's sinister face that was laughable to see. His face had grown ghastly as he muttered the stranger's name—"Allan Drexel." He needed no second bidding to take himself off, but there was a look on his white face terrible to behold.

"Its all up with me now," he muttered. "This little affair will cost me my situation as sure as fate, and it's all on account of that little prude, too. By Heaven! if I am discharged, I will take such a revenge upon that girl as will follow her to the end of her life; and upon young Drexel, too, curse him!"

Meanwhile Coralie had been taken to the nearest drug store, and a few moments after a restorative had been administered she opened her blue, dazed eyes; they fell upon a handsome, manly face—a face such as might have belonged to an Apollo,[4] the eyes were so dark and mesmeric,[5] the brow so high and white, and the lips, which the dark, curling mustache did not quite conceal, so smiling.

That face was to be photographed on Coralie's heart and brain to the last day of her life.

She struggled to her feet with a little cry, gazing apprehensively about her.

"You need not fear; you are safe," said Allan Drexel, reading her thoughts intuitively. "I rescued you from the dastardly scoundrel; he will not trouble you again."

"Oh, sir, how can I thank you?" said Coralie, triumphantly, great, pearly tears filling her pretty blue eyes as she looked up into the young man's handsome face.

"By not attempting it," he responded promptly. "Come, if you are sufficiently recovered, I will see you safely to your home. You may safely trust me," he added, noting how she shrunk from his proffered escort because he was a stranger. "I am the nephew of Mr. Drexel, the mill owner," and as he spoke he handed her his card with as much deferential courtesy as though she had been some great heiress instead of a poor little working-girl in his uncle's employ, adding hastily, "I judged you were one of the employees there, as I saw you leaving the mill a few minutes since."

He did not wait for Coralie's reply, but quietly drew her arm within his own with gentle authority, starting off with her toward the nearest cab stand.

---

[4]Strikingly handsome, Apollo was one of the most influential of the Greek and Roman gods. He was the god of sunlight and was guardian of religious and civic laws.

[5]irresistible

"Oh, Mr. Drexel, I—I should much prefer walking," stammered Coralie, confusedly. "I live only a few blocks from here on East Thirteenth Street, No.—."

"That is quite a long distance," he declared, smiling gravely down into the beautiful face framed in the babyish flaxen curls. "Kindly oblige me by getting into the cab, and you shall find yourself at your own door in a very few minutes, Miss——"

"My name is Coralie Harding," she said simply.

"A pretty name, but not half so pretty as the girl who bears it," he thought to himself, as he glanced at the shy, sweet, averted face, he dark eyes full of admiration.

Coralie never knew how it happened, but during that never-to-be forgotten drive homeward, she had told him the simple story of her young life—how up to two short years ago she and her widowed mother had lived in a small interior village, dependent upon a small pension that came to her mother regularly twice a year. Suddenly it ceased, and they were thrown upon their own resources.

"Mamma wrote to Master-workman Marshall, and he secured her a place in the Drexel Silk Mill," continued Coralie, "and that is how we happened to come to New York.

"But from the hour we came here mamma's health commenced to fail rapidly," pursued the girl, "and it was not long before she was unable to leave her bed.

" 'I do not care for myself, Coralie,' she moaned, 'but for you, child, for, God help us, we are both penniless—penniless.' "

Allan Drexel was greatly touched by this pitiful, touching recital, but he did not interrupt her.

" 'Do not fear, mamma, I can take, your place,' I cried; 'I am young and strong—we shall not starve.' I had begged to do this from the very first, and now the very worst that could happen—will happen to-morrow—that man declares he will discharge me to-morrow—and he, being the new overseer of your uncle's mill, will have full power to do so," said Coralie, in a faltering voice, choking down her sobs.

This was indeed news for the young man to hear.

"It remains to be seen whether you will be discharged to-morrow or not" he said slowly. "You need have no hesitation in coming to the mill to-morrow as usual, I can promise that much."

"Oh, I thank you so much, sir," responded Coralie, gratefully. "You have taken such a weight off my heart."

The cab stopped before the lonely tenement-house that Coralie called "home," she bade Mr. Drexel good-night, and fairly flew up the rickety stairs to the two meager rooms they occupied on the top floor.

Should she tell her mother of her thrilling adventure, and how a noble young man had come to her rescue—saving her from a villain's toils and promising she should not be discharged on the morrow?

"No, I had best not tell her," she mused, pausing a moment before the door, "her nerves are too weak to bear any shock of excitement. And then, too, mamma might be quite angry to think I came home with Mr. Drexel in a cab, despite the great service he rendered me. Poor mamma seems to be always seized with frantic horror if I even speak of a young man. I wish she could have seen how kind and agreeable and—and handsome he was," Coralie thought, with a blush like the heart of a June rose mantling her dimpled cheek.

A low moan from the interior of the room startled her, and her mother's voice wailed out sharply:

"Oh, my God, what keeps Coralie! will she *never* come?"

In an instant Coralie had flung open the door, crossed the room with a bound, and was kneeling by her mother's bedside.

"I am here, mamma," she cried; "did you miss me so much, dear?"

"I counted the minutes, Coralie," murmured her mother, faintly. "You are over half an hour late. I—I—was afraid I should die alone—all alone—Coralie."

Coralie choked back the scream that sprung to her lips; she had raised her eyes to her mother's face and saw an awful pallor there—a pallor that terrified her, made the blood turn to ice round her heart.

"You are not going to die, mamma, darling," she cried, with a forced, cheery laugh. "Why, I couldn't possibly spare you."

"The end is near—I feel that it is so," said Mrs. Harding, in a low, hushed gasp. "And, oh, Coralie, my darling—listen—there is something on my heart—a horrible secret that your young ears must not hear; I could not rest in my grave with this secret weighing down my soul—yet it is more bitter than death to reveal it. Oh, Coralie, poor, beautiful child."

"Mamma," sobbed the girl, flinging her arms around her, "tell me what this dread secret is. You can trust me—your own daughter."

Mrs. Harding shrunk back with a low cry.

"Not you—I cannot tell you, Coralie," she muttered.

"Then whom could you tell, mamma?" sobbed Coralie, piteously.

"There is but one whom I could trust, and that is Richard Marshall, the master-work-man. Surely he will not fail me in this dread hour. Send for him, Coralie, tell him he must come. I am dying, my darling, my moments are fleeting—oh, send for him quickly."

White with terror, Coralie obeyed. And in half an hour's time, despite the fierce storm that had set in, Richard Marshall, the master-workman, the cheery, genial friend of the bread-winners, stood beside Mrs. Harding's couch.

One glance showed him that in a very few moments all would be over with the poor lady.

"Leave the room, my child," murmured Mrs. Harding, "you will not be banished for long," and, choking back her bitter sobs, Coralie left the apartment.

"Now, my dear Mrs. Harding, tell me what I shall do for you," said Richard Marshall, pityingly, as the great, hollow eyes met his with such a burning intensity in their gaze.

"Are we quite alone?" she whispered. "Make sure that door is tightly closed between Coralie and me, then come nearer."

A half-hour passed. Oh, how the storm moaned and wailed outside! It made Coralie shudder as she listened.

As she paced the narrow little room back and forth, was it only her fancy, or over the fierce battling of the storm outside, did she hear Richard Marshall, the master-workman, cry out excitedly:

"Ask anything else of me, and I will gladly do it; but this that you ask of me I dare not do. I——"

The rest of the sentence—that is, if it were not an hallucination of Coralie's morbid fancy, was drowned in the wild howling of the warring elements outside.

Ten, fifteen, twenty minutes passed. No one save themselves will ever know what persuasion, prayers, entreaties the dying woman used to wring at last the fateful promise she desired from the master-workman's lips. We can but know that he did promise.

"Swear it!" cried the dying woman. "You must take a solemn oath that this thing shall be done!—an oath strong as life and your hopes of heaven and a hereafter, and deep as eternity."

With a face white as death, his hands trembling like aspen leaves, and great beads of perspiration standing out on his vein-knotted forehead, Richard Marshall, the master-workman, took the solemn oath that was the price of a soul, but he did it all for the best.

"Poor Coralie!" he muttered. "Poor, beautiful Coralie! how can I ever tell her that which I must say?"

"Never forget your oath!" murmured Mrs. Harding, huskily. "Now call Coralie to me."

He did as he was requested, and in another instant Coralie had sprung across the room to her mother's side.

"Are you no better, mamma?" she cried, anxiously bending down to kiss the white face lying back against the pillow. "Speak to your little Coralie, mamma."

Mrs. Harding's voice would answer her never again.

The thin, patient face was not turned toward Coralie as it was wont to do. No gentle hand was laid caressingly on the bowed, curly head.

Coralie stoops and gazes for one breathless moment into the pallid face—into the glazed eyes that flash back no look of recognition into her own. Then a wild, piercing shriek rings through the lonely tenement room:

"Oh, my God! my God! Mother is dead!"

Yes, she was dead, leaving Coralie, her darling, her idol, alone to fight out the bitter destiny that fate had mapped out for her, surely the cruelest a young girl ever faced.

CHAPTER III

❧ A Mad Marriage in Haste—To Repent at Leisure

Coralie Harding did not know for days afterward what happened after that fatal hour.

For a fortnight she hovered between life and death, and when, at last, she returned to consciousness she found that her mother had already been laid at rest, and she had been removed to the house of a kindly neighbor.

"I am all alone in the world, now," sobbed Coralie, laying her curly head back upon the pillow. "Oh, mamma, why did you leave me here to battle alone with the pitiless world? I wish that I had died, too."

Poor Coralie, so young, so lovely, so utterly friendless, and with a beauty which was destined to prove so cruel a curse; it would, indeed, have been better if she had died then and there, than lived to face the fate that was so soon to overtake her.

Mrs. Melville, the kind neighbor who had taken charge of Coralie, was delighted when she was able to sit up in the big arm-chair by the window.

"Here is a letter that came for you, my dear, the next day after you were taken ill," she said, placing an envelope in her hand; "I hope it will bring you good news."

"It is from Mr. Marshall," she murmured, as she glanced at the name signed to it. There were but a few lines, which read as follows:

"My dear Miss Harding,—

"Business calls me from the city to-day, and I shall probably be absent a fortnight, returning on the 19th inst. Can you find it convenient to call at my home the following day, any time after ten in the forenoon? I have something of the gravest importance to say to you.

"Yours in haste,
Richard Marshall."

"Why, to-day is the twentieth," cried Coralie, "I must go at once, Mrs. Melville, and from there I will go to the mill. Oh, I pray so earnestly that they have not got any one to take my place."

A cold chill crept through her heart at the thought of meeting the insolent overseer again, then the beautiful pink tint in her dimpled cheeks deepened as she remembered how nobly handsome Allan Drexel had rescued her from his insult, and how kind and considerate he had been during that homeward ride.

Meanwhile, at that very moment Coralie was thinking of him, Allan Drexel emerged from his carriage and ran lightly up the steps of the house where he had left Coralie Harding on the evening he had taken her home, and, after consulting a card to make sure that he was at the right number, hastily touched the bell.

"Can I see Miss Coralie Harding?" he asked, touching his hat courteously to the woman who answered the summons.

"No such person lives here now," she answered, wonderingly eying the handsome, stylish young man, who had driven up to that shabby tenement-house in such an elegant equipage, with footman and driver; "a family by that name had the two top rooms, but they moved away before I came in."

"Could you tell me where they went?" he asked eagerly.

"That I couldn't, sir," she answered, anxious to close the door and get back to her crying baby. "I think, though, they left the city for good."

His handsome face fell, the eager look died out of his bonny dark eyes.

He turned and walked slowly down the steps.

"Gone!" he murmured, "and perhaps I shall never see her again."

For the last two weeks he had been expecting her to put in an appearance at the mill, and at last his anxiety reached that point that he determined to see for himself why she did not.

The new overseer had been most earnest in his declaration that he had not seen the girl since that night.

All that week in the midst of his business, in crowded thoroughfares, in his dreams, a sweet, girlish, dimpled face framed in a mass of curling flaxen hair, had been constantly before Allan Drexel—the beautiful, pleading face of Coralie Harding.

"If there is such a thing as love at first sight, the fever is upon me," he told himself. "I have seen a sweet, girlish face and a pair of blue eyes, and they haunt me as no woman's eyes ever haunted me before."

He had barely gained the pavement ere a young girl, who was passing, ran directly into his arms in her eager attempt to hurry by.

She recoiled with a low cry.

"Why, is it possible, Coralie, Miss Coralie!" he cried, with tremulous emotion.

Looking up, Coralie found herself face to face with Allan Drexel.

If she had not dropped her blue eyes in sudden confusion, she would have noticed the keen delight in his face.

"Pray forgive me, if I have startled you," he said. "I saw you were not going to recognize me, and I could not let you pass without speaking. You did not come to the mill again. I feared we had lost you."

"I couldn't come," replied Coralie, with a husky sob. "A terrible sorrow has fallen upon me since that night I met you—a sorrow that has blighted my life and left me all alone in the cruel world."

"All alone," echoed Allan; "surely your mother is not——"

"Yes, she is dead," sobbed Coralie, her eyes filling with tears, and the lovely red mouth quivering piteously.

"I am sorry—so sorry for you," he answered, and his sympathetic voice touched her to the heart. "Get into my carriage and ride with me through Central Park. I would like to talk to you," he said earnestly.

And quietly leading her to the coupe, he assisted her into the vehicle, and took a seat beside her.

"We attracted too much attention talking on the street," he said quietly, as he gazed tenderly on the lovely, girlish, grief-stricken face. "Now then," he said, taking her hand in his strong, firm clasp, "consider me your friend, and tell me if there is any way that I can help you. I would give my life to be of service to you," he added, with all the impulsiveness of a youth of two-and-twenty.

Ah, how he longed to kiss away the tears from those lovely blue eyes and comfort her. She was so beautiful, so friendless.

"My mother, the only relative I had in all the world, was laid to rest two weeks ago," she sobbed. "I thought of coming to you and telling you about it, but I was too wretched! Mr. Drexel."

"You really thought of me?" he cried.

His eager voice broke through all restraint of will, and thrilled in a fervor of intense passion on the girl's ears.

"And I have done nothing but think of you, Coralie, since we first met. Forgive me, but the position in which I find you gives me courage to speak, makes me long for the right to protect you. Coralie, listen to me—I love you."

"Oh, Mr. Drexel," she stammered, shrinking back in affright, quite believing she must be in a dream. "Surely you could not care for me; you must be very rich, and I am only a poor little working-girl, and you have known me only such a little while."

"I am 'very rich,' as you quaintly phrase it, my dear little girl, but what has that to do with love?" he inquired loftily; "love levels all barriers. If you were a little queen I could not think more of you; and as for knowing you only a little while, don't you know what the poets tell us, 'that young hearts learn the lesson of love easily, and many a time at first sight'? It is quite true, Coralie. My heart went out to you the first time we met."

He held out his arms to her, pouring out such passionate words, such prayers and pleadings of his love and devotion, all mingled in one torrent of eloquence, that simply alarmed her.

Poor Coralie, she was so young, so friendless, so forlorn.

Had Heaven sent this love to her to shield her in this, the darkest hour of her life?

"Do not turn from me, Coralie; say you love me and will be my wife," he urged. "There will be no need for you to go on your errand to the master-workman's house. No doubt he simply wants to tell you he has secured another position for you; but you shall never work another day, Coralie. Be my wife, and these little hands shall be covered with shining jewels."

She looked so pretty, so bewildered between joy and sorrow, so dazzled by happiness, and yet so piteously uncertain, that Allan was more charmed than ever with her.

"My darling Coralie," he said with a low, happy laugh, "you do love me. I can read it in your eyes, even if your lips will not speak."

"Do you see that little church standing back there among the trees? Consent to be mine, and we will be married there at once, Coralie. It will take some little time to drive around by the main road, and while we are riding slowly there, I will tell you why you must consent to marry me at once if we are to be married at all. Is it yes or—or no, Coralie?" he whispered.

The answer was certainly a timid, faltering "yes," for the impetuous young lover caught her in his arms and covered her pretty face with passionate kisses, declaring she had made him the happiest fellow in the wide world, and that she should never rue her trust—never. And at that moment he believed what he said.

"They meant to make a married man of me, darling, whether I would or no," he went on laughingly. "By the word 'they' I mean my uncle and aunt. They are childless, and it was their intention three years ago to divide their fortune between my brother and me; but Alf, my brother, did that which gained him my uncle's enmity for life. I may as well tell you what he did. He is wild and reckless, and ended up a series of follies by forging my uncle's name, and fleeing to Europe to escape the consequences of it.

"I refused to turn my back on Alf, and that so enraged my uncle that he vowed neither of us should inherit a penny of his; he would make a bonfire of it first. I followed Alf to Europe, and after the lapse of nearly three years, I received a letter from my uncle calling me here without delay.

"'My boy,' he said, on the first night of my return, 'I have reconsidered my determination of disinheriting you—on one condition. You can become my heir—heir to the Drexel Mills and my millions—and on that one condition only.'

"'Name it, uncle,' I said, 'and if it is anything in reason, I will comply.'

"'It is certainly in reason, or I should not ask it,' he answered grimly. 'It can be stated in a few, brief words. To become my heir, you must marry my ward, Irene Hazleton; she loves you. Refuse, and you step from my presence a beggar. Consent, and you shall have a handsome little fortune down, and the remainder when I am through with it.'

"I confess the proposition stunned, bewildered me. I will not deceive you; I will conceal nothing from you, Coralie; after a long struggle with myself I consented."

A low cry broke from her lips.

"Then if you are to marry her, how could you ask me to be your wife?" asked Coralie, reproachfully. "Oh, Mr. Drexel, how could you?"

"Because Irene has not been informed of that decision yet, and as soon as the ceremony which binds you to me is over, Coralie, I will go to my uncle and tell him my marriage to Irene cannot take place now, for I am already married. Don't you see, little girl?"

"Would you lose all that great fortune for my sake, Mr. Drexel?" asked Coralie, in wonder.

"Yes; a thousand fortunes," he responded ardently. "That proves the depth of my love for you, Coralie, does it not? Besides, I am not quite as penniless as my uncle believes.

"Ah! here we are, Coralie, at the church door. Do not be frightened; in half an hour's time you will be my darling little bride. How you tremble, how cold your hands are! Is it so very terrible marrying a lover who adores you, darling?

"I sent a messenger on ahead while we drove so slowly," he said, "and all is in readiness. Come, Coralie, love, the maid is holding the door open for us."

There was sudden, eager entreaty in his voice, for there had come into the girl's face a swift, terrified look, as if she had suddenly realized the awful solemnity of the position in which she was about to place herself.

Her blue eyes looked entreatingly into Allan Drexel's face, as if searching for advice or relief there.

He took her trembling, chilled hands in his own, and led her into the little parlor of the parsonage, where the rector awaited them.

And still the strange, awful panic held Coralie's fluttering heart in its grasp.

She felt that she must fly from the place.

Her guardian angel was urging her to retreat before it was too late.

Yet she did not fly.

She did not retreat—she looked wistfully, eagerly into her lover's face—to read there only love and devotion.

And then, as if in a dream, she stood there by his side while the fatal marriage went on.

As if in a trance, she heard the questions and prompt responses of her lover.

Almost without knowledge or volition of her own, she answered suitably, and then Allan Drexel turned to her with a smile and a kiss.

"My little bride," he murmured, "mine until death do us part!"

It was done.

Whatever had prompted her—folly, loneliness, over-persuasion, thoughtlessness—it was done.

In a moment she had sown the seeds from which was to spring up such a harvest of woe so terrible that even her wildest imagination could not have pictured it—whose shadow already cast its gray gloom of vague presentiment over her.

It was a mad, rash marriage, but the die was cast—for weal or for woe, Coralie was Allan Drexel's wife.

CHAPTER IV

☙ "Stop, Good Minister! Stop, for the Love of Heaven! I Forbid This Marriage!"

They drove immediately to a fashionable up-town boarding-house, where Allan decided they should remain for at least a fortnight.

A beautiful suit of rooms was assigned to them overlooking a vast flower-bedded lawn—rooms such as Coralie, in all her simple life, had never seen before—all flowers, lace, plush, and gilding.

The moment she entered it her young husband smiled to himself, because she looked at the white carpet as though she were afraid to tread upon it.

Looking at her, the idea did not strike Allan how utterly out of place the pretty wild flower he had transplanted from a tenement-house to a mansion seemed amid all this luxury; he was too much in love with her to give a thought to Coralie's faults or imperfections, if she had any.

To Coralie the events of the last hour seemed like a dream.

She had read wonderful old German legends, she had heard of miracles, but nothing that she could remember was half so strange to her as her own story.

Only yesterday she had been thinking of her future and had cried herself to sleep over it—everything looked so dark.

She had decided that her life would have to be one of very hard work and very little pleasure; now how changed it was.

She was dazed and bewildered, as one who, after being long in utter darkness, comes suddenly into brilliant light.

Coralie was amazed at the vast grandeur; she was even more surprised at the nonchalance and dignified ease of her young husband; he did not stand the least in awe of the imposing-looking waiters, or the smart-looking chambermaid, while she felt very uncomfortable amid such unaccustomed surroundings.

She was inclined to call a solemn-looking waiter "sir," and to arise when he addressed her, and be very profuse in her thanks for any little service rendered; but she noticed that Allan did not do this, and she imitated his example.

After the wedding-dinner was over, and they found themselves quite alone, Allan crossed over to the divan on which his little bride sat, and seated himself beside her.

"You shall never regret marrying me, dear," he said, clasping his arms fondly around her slender waist. "We will show my uncle that we can get along famously without his gold. There is nothing like having a little wife dependent upon a man to sharpen his engeries and to make him ambitious," laughed Allan.

"I have sent to the hotel for my luggage; after it arrives——"

The sentence never was finished; there was an imperative tap at the door, and upon opening it, Allan found a messenger-boy there with a telegram.

"This has been sent up from the proprietor of the Astor House," said the boy. "It has been awaiting you since noon at the hotel, I am requested to say, sir."

"All right, my lad," replied Allan, taking the message and tossing the boy a silver dollar; he was in a most liberal mood.

"Did you deliver the telegram in person?" asked a man who stood impatiently awaiting the boy around the corner.

"That I did, sir," replied the boy. "I gave it into Mr. Allan Drexel's own hands; that was your order."

"Right—quite right, my lad," said Robert Sinclair, paying the boy. "We shall see which of us will win in this interesting game of hearts, my fine Allan Drexel!" he muttered savagely, as he turned on his heel. "It was lucky I happened to be passing that little church and learned of your secret marriage to-day with the lovely Coralie. Bask in the smiles of your pretty bride to-day, but, so help me Heaven! before the sun sets on the morrow your sunshine will set in the blackest gloom. You have succeeded in getting me discharged from the mill at last, and I will take a terrible revenge upon you for it.

"I will strike you through your love for fair Coralie, who might have been mine but for you," he muttered. "I will take a revenge upon you both so terrible that you shall curse each other, and that, too, ere the first day of your honeymoon shall pass."

Five, ten minutes passed by; he stood patiently at the street corner as though watching for some one. Suddenly a bright gleam shot into his eyes as he caught sight of Allan Drexel hurrying down the street.

"Ha! the leaven works well," he cried, with a diabolical laugh. "Hurry on to your doom, Allan Drexel."

Left by herself, Coralie nestled down into the easy-chair her handsome young husband had so lately occupied, and resting her dimpled chin in her little white hand, gave herself up to rosy, girlish day-dreams—this was her wedding-day; she was somebody's wife now; she was alone in the world no longer. How strange and unreal it all seemed to Coralie.

"I wonder what was in that telegram that made Allan look so white and nervous?" she mused. "How evasively he answered my question when I asked him what it was about. 'It would be better for you never to know, Coralie,' he said.

"How well Allan must love me to give up such a splendid fortune for me? I cannot love him too well to repay him for it. And that other girl loved him, too—the proud heiress—that's what he said, as we were driving on to the church. But she can never, never love Allan as well as I do. I—I would die for Allan's sake! Oh! here is the pocket-book Allan left with me to pay the expressman when he brought the luggage from the hotel. How full of money it is!"

She smiled as she opened it.

The pocket-book contained something else besides bank-notes—there was a photograph in it. With eager curiosity Coralie seized upon it.

One glance, and a pain keen and sharp as death shot through her heart: It was the portrait of a young and lovely girl, with a haughty face, dark, curling hair, and dark, dreamy eyes—a very queen of love.

"Can it be this is the proud heiress who cares for Allan," she sobbed, "and whom Allan gave up for me? After having seen this girl, how could he ever have married me?"

she cried, still gazing at the haughty, scornful, beautiful face, with her heart in her dilated eyes. "Will he ever regret that he did not wed her instead of me?" she sobbed. "Oh, I shall ask him just the minute he comes back. He said he would not be gone over half an hour at most, and it is almost that time now."

The sound of the maid's voice startled her.

"I knocked, but I guess you did not hear me—a visitor to see you, ma'am," and without waiting to be invited to enter, a tall woman, heavily veiled, pushed into the room.

"There must be some mistake," said Coralie, politely; "are you sure it is I whom you wish to see, madam?"

"There is no mistake," replied the woman; "you are Coralie Harding."

"I was Coralie Harding this morning. I am Coralie Drexel now, the wife of Mr. Allan Drexel," said the little bride, blushing furiously to the very roots of her fluffy, flaxen curls.

"Poor child," said the woman, softly, "is it really so bad as that? Did he tell you so, and did you believe him? Poor innocent child."

"Madam!" cried Coralie, turning from red to white; "what do you mean? Your words are uncommonly strange; of course I am Mr. Drexel's wife; would I be here if I were not?"

"I have a very painful duty to perform—alarming news to break to you, poor child," said the woman; "may Heaven give you strength to bear it. I may as well tell you the truth at once—*You are no more Allan Drexel's wife than I am,* child. You have been saved by a miracle in the shape of a telegram which called him from the city—from an awful fate. As I said, he has left the city. You will never look upon his face again. Learn to forget him.

"I will tell you the errand which takes him away—he is to be married to-morrow night to a wealthy heiress whom he loves; the wedding will take place at the Drexel Villa in the Orange Mountains."

Without another word she turned, and still heavily veiled, glided from the room, leaving Coralie stunned, speechless, horrified. One instant more and she lay with a stark, white face buried in the lilies of the velvet carpet. The pulse of life had momentarily stopped.

Oh, the pity of it, that God did not let poor Coralie die then and there. She was so young, and life held for her the bitterest woe that ever darkened a young girl's life—that life which was to have such a thrilling sequel.

The bright stars and the soft, pitying moonbeams were stealing into the room ere Coralie recovered from her death-like swoon.

For a single instant the terrible past seemed like a hideous, confused dream.

"Allan, my love, where are you?" she cried tremulously. "I have had such horrid dreams, and I am so frightened."

No young husband clasped his arms about her and caressed and soothed her. Then, like a meteoric flash all that had transpired swept across her dazed, bewildered brain.

She struggled to her feet with a little hushed cry.

"Oh, God! is it true, that horrible story?" she moaned, pressing her hands over her heart. "Dear Heaven, what have I done that I should be so sorely tried?"

Long hours had passed, yet he had not returned. Here was proof positive.

She walks with unsteady step to the window and gazes out. The moon is smiling in its grandeur overhead.

Below, the world is white with its glory. It is past midnight, and the stars begin to pale. Already the "world's heart" begins to throb. Yes—yes, it is horribly late. He does not intend to return; yet the poor little child-bride utters no curse against him. She loved him too well for that.

"Yes, I loved him so well I could have died for him," she murmurs. "When he clasped me in his arms and kissed my face, calling me his beautiful little wife, I wonder I did not die of joy, for I thought I had gained all Heaven in his love."

In the gray light of the early morning Coralie fled from the house.

The hour was early, yet throngs of people hurried along the streets, jostling against the beautiful, forlorn little creature with the death-white face half hidden by the sweeping flaxen hair, and the intense blue eyes that looked straight ahead, yet saw nothing; borne along by the crowd as a leaflet is carried along by a swift current without will-power of its own to choose its course.

Without a thought of where she was going, Coralie threaded one street after another; anywhere—anywhere out of the strange noise and bustle to find some quiet place to die.

After a time she found herself at the railroad depot. She had sunk down pale and exhausted, when suddenly a placard met her eye, bearing the following inscription:

"The train on the left to Orange."

All in an instant a sudden thought came to Coralie; she would go to Orange and confront Allan Drexel and learn from his own lips whether this story were true or false; surely she herself was his bride. Then how dare he wed another; there must be some horrible mistake.

It was dusk when she reached her destination, and a heavy rain had commenced to fall, gathering in force and volume with each passing moment.

By inquiry Coralie had learned that the Drexel Villa was situated on one of the highest peaks of the mountain fully three miles distant, and that one must take a serpentine road to reach it, which was extremely dangerous to traverse after nightfall.

"Is there no conveyance, no stage I could take?" asked Coralie, piteously.

"No," was the reply. "Every sort of a conveyance hereabouts has been engaged to take guests up the mountain to the grand wedding that is to take place at the old Drexel Castle to-night at eight o'clock; we call it a castle, it is such a grand old place.

"What! you're not going to start out on foot and on such a night as this?" said the man, as Coralie drew her cloak closer about her and started toward the door.

"I must!" she cried, "I must!"

The next instant she was out alone, braving the wild fury of the storm.

"That girl is stark mad," said the man, suspiciously, to his companion. "I shouldn't wonder a bit now if she is an escaped lunatic from Utica or Rome. Her eyes fairly burned, and her face is as white as the dead. What can be taking her up the mountain, I wonder; she don't look like one of the wedding guests."

Meanwhile Coralie dashed madly onward and upward through the wildness and darkness of that never-to-be-forgotten night.

"If I find the story is true—that I am not his wife, I will fall down dead at his feet," she sobbed.

Up the jagged, steep serpentine road step by step Coralie toiled on toward the red lights that had been pointed out to her from the foot of the mountain.

As she neared the gates, strains of bewildering music fell upon her ears, then suddenly ceased.

"My God! my God! I am too late!" she gasped, "too late!"

She sped across the broad porch, through the wide hallway which was gayly festooned with wreaths and pillars of roses, past the groups of servants that were too astounded to stay her footsteps, toward the grand parlors in which a magnificent bridal party were assembled beneath a floral bell.

Yes, there he stood—it was no horrible dream, no frightful delusion. Yes, there stood Allan Drexel with a proud-faced girl arrayed in bridal robes at his side, orange blossoms in her hands and crowning her bridal-veil. She was the original of the portrait.

With a desperate effort, Coralie, pallid with anguish keener than death itself, reached the doorway just as the minister uttered the solemn, impressive words:

"If any one has aught to say why these two should not be joined together in holy wedlock, let them speak now or else forever hold their peace."

"He is mine! In the sight of God and man I am his wife," muttered Coralie.

For an instant a death-like silence ensues, then a voice from the doorway, quivering with anguish, cries out:

"Hold!—the marriage must not go on!"

"Stop, good minister—stop for the love of Heaven! I forbid the bans!" and Coralie staggered blindly through the amazed and horror-stricken throng toward the group beneath the floral bell, and threw herself with a bitter cry at the handsome bridegroom's feet.

CHAPTER V

❧ My Answer Is, "No, I Will Never Be Your Wife!"

Those who witnessed that awful scene never forgot it while their lives lasted.

There was horror too great for words on the faces of the lovely young bride and pale, handsome bridegroom standing beneath the floral bell, as the beautiful stranger forced her way among the amazed guests, crying out piteously:

"Stop, good minister! stop for the love of Heaven! This marriage must not go on. I forbid it!"

In an instant the greatest confusion prevailed. Every one pressed forward curiously, eager to catch a glimpse of the lovely young girl, with a face white as death, who had interrupted the wedding ceremony.

The shocked and amazed minister was the first to regain anything like composure.

He turned his face full of wonder and consternation to Coralie, and solemnly asked:

"What have you to say why this marriage should not go on?"

Every one waited in breathless suspense for the answer.

Coralie turned and faced him with the bitterest sob that ever broke from girlish lips, as she answered drearily:

"Because, Heaven help me, he is my husband. Mine before God and man!"

There was no exultation in either look or tone. Every word seemed to have cost her a pang more bitter than death itself.

A murmur of intense surprise ran from lip to lip among the assembled guests.

The minister turned to the white-faced bridegroom.

"Speak! is that girl's story true?" he asked, pointing one trembling hand toward Coralie. "Speak, that I may understand this terrible affair at once."

The handsome bridegroom faced the amazed throng, pale but collected, answering firmly:

"I deny this girl's accusation. So help me God! I have never seen her before. She is an entire stranger to me."

No cry—no moan broke from Coralie's lips; it seemed to her that if she heard another word she would go mad. The lights and faces of the people seemed to be whirling around her; the perfume of the flowers seemed to suffocate her.

"Let that decide which of us has spoken falsely," moaned Coralie, drawing a folded paper from her bosom, and casting it at his feet. "May Heaven forgive you for those horrible lies, I never can—never while I live!"

And with those words—before any one could put out a hand to stay her steps—Coralie had staggered from the room blinded by pain and anger—out into the fury of the storm.

In an instant the bridegroom had picked up the folded paper and torn it open.

It was a marriage certificate.

One glance at it, and a strange light broke over his face.

"I see it all now!" he cried excitedly. "How strange that the truth did not occur to me before. Hear, one and all! This is a marriage certificate, which states that on the 20th instant, Allan Drexel and Coralie Harding were joined together in the holy bonds of matrimony. Allan is my twin brother, as most of you know; and you know, too, how closely we resemble each other. This is a fatal case of mistaken identity. In Heaven's name let the girl be brought back at once and informed of this!" added Alfred Drexel, hoarsely.

But this was easier said than done. Servants were dispatched in all directions; but one by one they came back with the intelligence that she could not be found.

For the time being, as there was so much excitement and confusion, the wedding had been postponed, and the bride was led away by her bridemaids, suffering from an intensely nervous shock.

And, to the intense annoyance of the would-be bride-groom, when she recovered, she refused to allow the ceremony to proceed.

"It is a warning sent to me from Heaven that we should part, Alfred," she said shiveringly. "Our friends, gathered here without even a day's notice, never dreamed that ours is a case of elopement. I am going back to my guardian as I came—Irene Hazleton still!"

"Irene, are you mad?" cried her lover, hoarsely; "think of the guests assembled in those parlors, waiting for the ceremony to proceed—it must go on!"

The heiress drew back and looked at him haughtily.

"Pardon me—I am not used to coercion," she said icily. "The word 'must' was illy chosen. I will not be forced into this marriage! I told you all along I was hardly sure of my own heart. Sometimes I thought I liked you the best, then again my heart went out to Allan, your twin brother."

Alfred Drexel crushed back an oath from between his white teeth.

"Irene, be reasonable!" he cried; "gaining Allan's love is out of the question now, you see. What have I done that you should turn from me in this fashion? I believe you are glad—yes, positively glad!—this thing has occurred. You see for yourself not a shadow of blame can be attached to me. Why then will you seek to disgrace both me and yourself by this outrageous refusal to allow the ceremony to go on? By Heaven, Irene, you will make me the laughing-stock of the whole country at large! Think of the scandal such a step would create—for your own sake, Irene, as well as mine, let the ceremony go on. Come, dear, put on your bridal veil and wreath again."

"Give me a few minutes to think," she sobbed. "Go into the conservatory and wait for me. I will bring my answer to you there."

He kissed the little jeweled hand, turned and walked rapidly toward the conservatory.

When he found himself alone. Alfred Drexel gave full vent to the ungovernable fury that possessed him.

"Can it be I am to be foiled now, with the prize I have schemed and toiled for so patiently almost within my very grasp? It shall not—it must not be!" he cried hoarsely.

"A very demon of a fate seems to pursue me," he went on, "and has from my very birth. Allan was always praised, and I was accursed; Allan was an angel, and I was a fiend, they said; and, although his twin brother—alike in form and feature—we were as widely apart in heart and feeling as heaven from earth. I was the forger and rascal, and Allan was the noble gentleman. It was the last straw which broke the camel's back when old Drexel sent for Allan, proposing he should have his millions, and the heiress' millions into the bargain, if he would but marry Irene Hazleton.

"Although I did not know of Allan's other love-affair, I strove to outwit him, and carry off the golden prize by cunning and strategy, persuasion and entreaty.

"Hark! how the guests are clamoring for the ceremony to proceed; they can't understand the delay—how should they? When once Irene Hazleton is my wife, she shall suffer for this mortifying hour. By Heaven, I will bend her haughty pride; she will learn that it was gold I married her for—not for love, and she shall know that my will is law; let her defy me if she dare! I am not Allan—to give way to a woman's whims and caprices. She will soon learn that, curses on the little fool!"

Believing himself quite alone, his hoarse voice had grown louder and louder as he ground out the words, interspersing them with a fierce imprecation at every breath.

The conservatory was so dim, and he made so much noise tramping up and down that he did not hear a door open near at hand; and the tall, flowering shrubs completely concealed the slim, graceful figure that glided toward him—pausing so near him that she could have put aside the green branches and touched him with her white hand.

It was Irene. Woman-like, on the instant she had sent her lover away she had repented it, and on the impulse of the moment had followed him.

She had no intention of playing the mean part of eavesdropper when she heard him pacing up and down so furiously, talking so loudly and wildly, but the first sentence that fell upon her ears held her spellbound.

Like one turned to stone she stood quite still and heard all.

A horrible chill crept over her.

"How miraculously fate had saved her from this fortune-hunter's snare!" she told herself. "He did not love her; he was marrying her for her wealth. It was a blessing she had found all this out before it was too late."

Tossing aside the green blossoming boughs, with firm tread and head haughtily erect, she stepped out into the dim light and confronted him.

"Irene—my darling!" he cried, springing eagerly forward and attempting to clasp her hands with his own outstretched ones. "It seems to me I have been waiting here an age for you, dear."

Irene Hazelton drew back from him, a bitter laugh falling from her scornful lips.

"You play the part of an anxious lover capitally, Mr. Drexel," she said. "Allow me to compliment you upon your perfect dissembling."

"Irene!" he cried, "what can you mean?"

She held up her hand with a gesture of silence.

"I am here according to agreement," she said. "I have brought you your answer."

"And that answer, my darling," he cried breathlessly, "is——"

"No!" she answered coolly.

"Irene!" he cried hoarsely, "surely you are jesting—you cannot—you do not mean it."

"I can and do mean it," she answered. "Here is your betrothal ring"—flinging the glittering diamond at his feet. "Thank Heaven the marriage-ring was not yet placed upon my finger! You are free as air; I am the same. Farewell, Mr. Drexel."

"You shall not leave me like this!" he cried, fairly beside himself with rage. "That marriage ceremony was half performed. You are mine whether you will or no. Every law in the land will consider it binding, and I can claim you. Have a care, Irene, how you goad me on—you can go too far!"

"Even while he was speaking he knew quite well that he could not claim her."

Without deigning to reply, she turned like a young queen and walked away.

"It's all over between us," he muttered, with the bitterest oath that ever fell from a man's lips. "The game is up, and I have lost three millions; and I owe all this to that Coralie. There will be a terrible reckoning when she and I meet; the revenge that I will take upon her will be likely to last her through life."

CHAPTER VI

❧ "Oh, My Love, to Learn to Forget You Will Be More Bitter Than Death"

Believing the bride-elect quite ill from the severe shock she had sustained, none of the wedding guests assembled were much surprised at the announcement that the ceremony would have to be postponed for a few days, and, despite the inclemency of the weather, as each party had their own coaches, the guests took their departure early.

Through courtesy to Alfred Drexel, the affair was kept extremely quiet, and the sensation which would have been such a choice morsel for gossip, did not find its way into the newspapers.

Irene Hazleton returned to New York the next day, and her guardian did not find out for many a long day afterward what took Irene on that sudden trip to Orange.

But to return to Coralie and that fatal hour in which she fled so madly from that grand mansion thronged with wedding-guests.

Like one dazed she turned and looked back as she reached the arched entrance gate.

"Oh, I was mad to love him so," she wailed, slipping down on her knees in the long grass, all unmindful of the down-pouring rain. "Oh, my love—my cruel love, to learn to forget you will be more bitter than death."

She remembered the story of the violet she had read of in her childhood; the modest wood violet that had dared look up to the sun, and that same sun had scorched it until it withered from the stem. Its sweet life had paid the price of its presumptuous folly.

"I am like that wood violet," Coralie told herself; "I, who am but a simple working-girl, was mad to dream that one so gifted and so far above me could stoop to love me."

Poor Coralie had read but little, and knew as little of the world as an innocent, dreaming child. Now that the great care of the future was thrust so suddenly upon her, she was completely prostrated, and was pitifully unprepared to battle with it.

She had nowhere—nowhere in the great wide world to go, yet she must not stay there.

She raised her desperate, white face up to the night-sky, then, without a moan or a cry, hurried on through the darkness and storm of the terrible night.

"It does not matter what becomes of me," she whispered, huskily, "there is no one to care. If I should lie down and die in one of these dense thickets no one would ever know—no one would ever miss me—and the great heart of the world would throb on as before.

"How cruel that beautiful heiress was to rob me of my love," she sobbed, "She is so lovely and so wealthy she could have chosen where she would. Why did she take my love from me? She can never care for him as I do, oh, no, no, no!"

Every heart has known its own sunshine and its gloomy shadows, but there is no shadow so dark and so pitiful as that of a broken love-dream.

To all young girls their love is their very life; how Coralie shrunk from the dark future in which she was to see Allan Drexel no more.

With the most piteous cry that ever broke from human lips Coralie flung herself down in the long green grass praying that Heaven would let her die. The swaying branches of the trees above her, the splashing of the rain drops on the green leaves seemed to whisper brokenly the terrible truth—she was not Allan Drexel's wife.

A sensation of burning shame dyed her fair, dimpled face.

How was she in all her fair, girlish innocence to know that men dared make a farce of anything so sacred as a marriage ceremony?

"Let me try to realize it." she sobbed. "Let me say the words over again to myself, that I may understand them. It was only a mock marriage, and he meant to deceive me into believing it was a true one, and while I trusted him, he was paying court to the haughty belle whom he was one day to wed."

She remembered how Allan had clasped her in his arms, murmuring tender, loving words to her, calling her over and over again his pretty little bride, and all the time he knew that he was acting a lie—a lie that must one day stalk forth and confront him in his treachery.

His passionate kisses seemed to burn her face even now; she had been so blind, she had loved him so well, had trusted and believed him, never knowing there was such a thing in the world as deceit or fickleness in love.

For long hours poor Coralie lay face downward in the long grass, her burning tears scorching the pitying wild-flowers, fighting the bitterest battle with outraged love, humiliation, and trampled pride that was ever fought in a young girl's loving bosom.

"I will learn to forget him," she cried bitterly, "or teach myself to think of him with burning hatred that will far outweigh my love. Let me cast him out of my poor, shattered heart as he has cast me out of his—without one regret. Oh, the madness, the folly of trusting too blindly to love!"

Was it only fancy, or did some one call her name in a low, cautious whisper?

Coralie raised her head from the long, rain-soaked grass and listened. A man's rapid footsteps were surely approaching, and a voice that sounded familiar called eagerly in the same low, cautious voice:

"Coralie, Coralie, where are you?"

Coralie listened intently. It was not the wind sighing among the branches; some one was surely calling her name.

What could any one want with her? Nearer and nearer drew the footsteps.

"I am here," answered Coralie, pushing the damp, golden hair back from her white, lovely face. "What do you want?"

The dark figure approached with long, swinging strides, and in another moment he had reached Coralie's side.

Flinging back his dark rubber cloak, the rays of a lantern which he had carefully concealed up to the present moment were flashed into her wondering, tear-stained face, and it lit up the wicked, leering, triumphant face of the young man bending over her.

With a low cry Coralie recognized him at a glance as the new overseer of the silk mills, who had insulted her so cruelly one afternoon as she was returning home from work.

"I see you recognize me, my dear," he said, with a low, taunting laugh. "I said to myself we should meet again, on that day that Drexel outwitted me and took you from me, and it seems to me I have put in an appearance at a very opportune moment. I saw all that happened up at the house, and I followed you, Coralie, to offer you my protection. Come, now, what do you say?"

No cry broke from the girl's pallid lips as she gazed up in terror into the face of her relentless foe. He saw her cast furtive glances about her and knew that she was measuring her chances of darting away from him and escaping in the impenetrable darkness beyond.

His grasp upon her slender, white arm tightened.

"You cannot escape me this time, my fair Coralie," he said, with a taunting laugh. "You are wholly in my power; you must come with me."

"Leave me," cried Coralie; "how dare you speak to me so?"

"Do you see those rocks beside you?" he answered; "well, you might as well plead to them as to waste words upon me. I have vowed that you shall be mine, fair Coralie.

You are a fool to take Drexel's desertion of you to heart like this. When one lover throws you over—find another; you will find plenty of lovers, with features like yours. Why, the moment my eyes first fell upon your pretty face I was madly in love with you—I——"

"Stop!" cried Coralie, bitterly. "Do not add insult to injury. I wonder that Heaven does not strike you down dead at my feet for your cruelty to a helpless orphan girl who has never wronged you."

"Heaven strike me dead!" he repeated tauntingly. "What a most horrible idea."

The course affairs were taking angered him. He had assured himself, as he saw Coralie turn from the house and dash madly out into the storm, that she would be only too glad to accept his protection now.

Coralie forgot all her terrible sorrow—forgot the drizzling rain falling about her— the isolation of the place—the lateness of the hour. She remembered only the cutting, sarcastic insult conveyed in every word the man was uttering.

How dared he speak to her so—it was monstrous. Her eyes flashed fire, and the hot color surged across her face in a burning wave as she stood facing her pitiless persecutor with all the dignity of an angered queen.

"Go away and leave me to myself," she panted, struggling to free herself from his strong hold, "or Heaven's vengeance will surely fall upon you. If you had a heart that could be touched by my woe I would fall on my knees at your feet, and beg you to go away."

Her eyes filled with tears and her sweet voice quivered piteously.

For an instant the hard, mocking light died out of Robert Sinclair's wicked eyes; it was not in human nature to look upon that beautiful face unmoved.

A sudden impulse he could never wholly account for, stole into his sin-hardened heart and changed his purpose.

"Coralie," he said hoarsely, attempting to draw her into a close embrace, "if I were to ask you to marry me this very hour, would you do it and come away with me? I never offered marriage to any girl before, but you have made me love you, little Coralie, with such a love as I have never experienced before. I am in earnest; will you marry me at once and return to the city with me?"

"No," she answered faintly; "I would die before I would marry you!"

"Why?" he asked angrily, in a hoarse, sneering voice.

"You are not an honorable gentleman," she gasped, recoiling from him shudder-ingly, "and I do not love you—I loathe you."

Coralie was not wise to make a merciless foe of the villain.

"Honor!" he cried, with a loud laugh; "that is rather rich, sweet Coralie. "How dare you prate to me of honor—you whose pretty face Drexel was rather taken with, and who threw you over in a day's time. You were eager enough to go to that up-town boarding-house with him, yet you were not his wife."

Coralie held up her little white hands with a piteous cry that the angels up in heaven must have heard and wept over. He was taunting her to the verge of madness.

"I did not know—I believed I was his wife," she added incoherently. "I did not know that men's lips could utter falsehoods that were more cruel than death to the one who believed and trusted in their truth. I would have died sooner than go wrong, and perhaps in the years to come I may atone for that one action of going with Allan—I loved him

so—oh, I loved him so well—and, God help me—I have tried to hate him but I cannot—
I love him still."

CHAPTER VII

❧ The Abduction

Never did good and evil fight such a terrible battle for a heart, as the momentary struggle that went on in Robert Sinclair's breast. He was tempted to turn away and leave her,
notwithstanding the passionate love for Coralie which had seized him. Her very refusal
of him had fanned the mad flame a thousand-fold.

"Marry me and you will learn to love me," he urged, eagerly.

She shook her golden, curly head, murmuring:

"It could never be."

"Remember I have offered to make you my wife—you scornfully refuse me," he
cried, in exasperation; "you, who have one of the darkest of blots on your fair name, and
which, in the eyes of the world, can never be forgiven you. Yet, despite all this, I swear
that I love you—you shall be mine by fair means or foul. It might have been better had
you temporized with me, and taken up my offer of marriage. A worse fate than that may
be in store for you. Remember," he added, tauntingly, "you are at my mercy."

"That's false!" replied Coralie. "I am at God's mercy—not yours."

"I shall waste no more useless words upon you, my pretty Coralie," retorted Sinclair. "You shall be mine—it is your fate. You might as well try to beat back the waves of
the mighty ocean with your frail white hands as to resist your fate."

She turned to fly from him, but in a twinkling he had caught her in a firm grasp, and
despite her struggles and frantic cries for help, he succeeded in throwing a long dark
cloak about her.

All in vain Coralie struggled to free herself. Useless—useless the clasp of the strong
arms tightened around her, and she felt herself raised from her feet and carried down a
steep, precipitous path, and with an agonizing fear, too great to be portrayed by words,
Coralie cried out to herself that God had indeed forsaken her.

A sweet, subtile odor seemed to rise up from the folds of the cloak and infold her,
benumbing her senses and locking them in a rigid embrace. She ceased to struggle; it
seemed almost impossible to move hand or foot. It seemed to Coralie as though she were
floating through space.

"The narcotic has done its work well," muttered Sinclair, triumphantly, as he hurried
to a coach in waiting.

It may as well be stated here that the separation of Allan Drexel and his bride had
been Robert Sinclair's dastardly work from beginning to end. From his hand had come
the decoy message that had taken the young husband from the side of his bride so hurriedly on their wedding day.

After the lapse of long hours—long enough so that Coralie should grow frightened
and nervous over the continued absence of Allan—he had sent a friend to call on Coralie,

and tell her that she was never to see Allan again; that she was not his wife, and that on the morrow's eve he was to wed another.

By a strange fate he had learned of Alf Drexel's intended marriage, and the dastardly scheme had occurred to him to give Coralie the impression that Alf was Allan. He knew well that the fatal resemblance between them would mislead any one.

He had believed Coralie would go there—steal into the grounds, and watch the bridegroom through the window, and believing it to be Allan, turn and fly from the place with a bitter cry, or fall down by the window in a deep swoon.

He had followed, intending to be on hand at this particular moment.

He had come breathlessly up the path just in time to see Coralie hurrying sobbingly away, piteously calling on Heaven to let her die.

Then he knew that his scheme had been successful.

Coralie and Allan Drexel would be parted as completely as though the whole world lay between them, and Coralie, believing herself wronged, would hate Allan a thousand-fold more than she had loved him, and her heart, in the rebound, might turn to Sinclair.

Then indeed would the latter be doubly avenged upon Allan Drexel for being the means of having him discharged from the Drexel Silk Mills—ay, it would be a glorious revenge.

But in order to explain the terrible event which followed, we must leave Coralie for a short space and return to Allan Drexel and the cause which tore him from his lovely young bride's arms.

It was a very ordinary message apparently which he received, but it caused him no end of anxiety, and read as follows:

"Allan,—Come as soon as you receive this to the steamer Alaska, I must see you. She sails in just two hours' time. I am in a little trouble—you, and you alone can help me."

There was no name signed to it, but of course Allan Drexel believed it to be from his twin-brother Alf. As to hearing that Alf was in trouble, he was not much surprised—his handsome, dissolute, reckless brother was always getting into scrapes of a more or less serious nature. He was always dreading to hear of some fearful calamity in which Alf figured as principal, and more than once Allan had missed narrowly some very trying encounters in being mistaken for handsome, dissipated Alf.

For this reason Allan had not read aloud the contents of the telegram to Coralie.

Bidding Coralie an affectionate good-bye, and promis-to return shortly, Allan hurried away in the direction of the Alaska. Boarding the steamer, he could not find Alf on deck or in the cabin, and sat down to wait for him, telling himself Alf would probably be along soon—the steamer did not sail for two hours yet.

At that moment a small lad stepped up to him. "Are you Mr. Allan Drexel?" he asked.

"That is my name," returned Allan.

"You are to come this way, sir, to stateroom No. 21, and wait for a gentleman there."

Allan followed the lad all unmindful of foul play.

It seemed rather unlike Alf to ask him to wait in the close stateroom instead of the cabin or on deck, still Allan did not mind.

A bouquet of rare exotics in a glass on the marble washstand attracted his attention at once, as well as the numerous sachels and bundles.

"Probably sent from one of Alf's admirers," he thought taking up the bouquet, and inhaling its subtle fragrance.

Alas for poor Allan—the bouquet contained something far different from the innocent perfume of the roses. One deep breath, then he knew no more.

An hour passed. Then in the noise, confusion, and bustle, amid the ringing of bells, the huge vessel moved from her moorings—sailed majestically down the bay and out to sea, and soon New York with its smoke and towering steeples, and the great Statue of Liberty that seemed to rise from the very midst of the white-capped waves, were lost to sight in the distance.

Yes, the steamer was sailing steadily out to sea, bearing with her the hapless young husband, torn thus rudely from the arms of his pretty child-bride, who was dearer to him than life itself.

It was some time after the steamer had been under headway that the gentleman to whom No. 21 had been assigned left the deck to go to his stateroom.

He had scarcely opened the door of No. 21 ere he started back with a cry of amazement. There, lying face downward upon the floor, was a young and handsome man, and near him lay the flowers that had fallen from his grasp,

"I cannot understand it, sir," said the captain, who had been summoned. "The man is evidently unconscious. He is not one of our passengers, though I remember I did see him out on deck before we started; I cannot think him a stowaway, he has every indication of a gentleman of wealth; yet we often get taken in pretty badly by these fine appearing fellows."

Allan was removed at once from No. 21.

His condition slightly puzzled the doctor on board, who was called to attend him; but by the aid of strong restoratives he soon regained consciousness.

The overwhelming sorrow and despair that seized poor Allan when the truth of his surroundings burst upon him can better be imagined than described.

He was like one mad. He leaped to the deck like a man distracted, and would have flung himself into the cruel, pitiless waves that every moment were separating him further and further from Coralie, who must even at that moment be waiting in an agony of suspense for his return, had not strong hands held him back.

Even the captain, stern, sea-faring man though he was, as well as the sympathetic passengers, was moved to tears when the agonizing story of the young husband fell from his lips, as he turned his handsome, pale face toward them, begging them not to hold him back.

"If I give myself up to the waves, some returning vessel will pick me up!" he declared, pushing the dark, clinging curls back from his damp brow.

The captain would not listen to it. Of course the vessel could not return, even though it were a matter of life or death; but he did promise to stop the vessel and send the distracted young husband back on the first steamer bound for New York that they came across, and a steamer was liable to come within hailing distance at any moment.

With a bitter groan, such as is wrung from the heart by the deepest anguish, Allan flung himself down upon a seat on the deck, refusing to be comforted.

Ladies gathered around him and wept for the handsome, boyish, young fellow torn so cruelly from his bride through the agency of such a cruel practical joke, as they all declared the decoy letter and chloroformed flowers to be, and gentlemen pressed his hand in tokens of sympathy, which men understand so well, a sympathy too heart-felt and eloquent to be expressed by words.

There was no help for it but to watch and wait for the next incoming steamer, and with a heart as heavy as lead Allan Drexel waited and watched, with a white, set, despairing face as the sun sank low behind the waste of water, and the gloaming crept over those dashing waves that heralded the approach of night.

"My God! will no steamer come in sight!" he cried, as hour after hour dragged their slow lengths by; and he bowed his dark curls on his hands, murmuring brokenly: "Oh, Coralie, my precious love, my poor darling."

CHAPTER VIII

❧ The Master-Workman's Terrible Secret

And, while these thrilling events were transpiring, another equally as strange was taking place in the library of Richard Marshall, the master-workman.

On the morning he was expecting Coralie, for long hours beforehand he had paced the floor in a state of great nervousness.

The long-continued sound of the steady tramping up and down attracted his wife's attention at last.

"Richard," she said, coming softly into the room, and laying her hand on his arm, "what is the matter?—you look so pale! You are laboring under some great excitement. I am sure of it! Come, confide in me; whatever concerns you must concern me, Richard; tell me what this secret is."

He turned from her keen, searching eyes with a forced smile.

"It is all your fancy, Martha," he declared. "There is no secret I am concealing from you."

"There is a secret, Richard," she answered. "You have been a changed man ever since that terrible night when you went in all the storm to the bedside of that dying woman who worked in the Drexel Silk Mill."

She saw him turn ghastly white, but he recovered himself with a violent effort.

"All your fancy, Martha," he repeated huskily.

"It is no fancy," she replied firmly, "nor is *this* fancy, Richard. This secret has troubled you so much, it has haunted even your dreams. You have started many a time out of a deep sleep crying loudly:

"'So young—oh, so young and lovely! God help her!'"

In an instant, Richard Marshall, the master-workman, was standing before his wife with a face pale as death.

"Did I say any more, Martha?" he asked. "Tell me, is that all I said?"

"No, not quite all," she answered, a little hesitatingly, shrinking back in affright from the husband's wild, haggard face. "Don't hold my wrist so tight, and I will tell you the rest. You—you—hurt my arm. Oh, Richard, what is coming over you?"

"Why don't you tell me what was said? You torture me, Martha!" he cried. "Don't you see you do?"

"It was not very much, Richard," she faltered; "only this: many a time since that night you have muttered again and again in your sleep, 'She must never go back to the Drexel mill! Some day she might meet him!' "

"Is that all I said?" asked Richard Marshall, after a profound, painful silence.

"Yes, all," replied his wife; "but that was enough for me to suspect that there was some great secret on your mind, and that it concerns the woman's daughter, the girl whom you expect here to-day, and whom you are waiting for even now with such ill-concealed impatience."

"Forget that you heard that, Martha, and leave me by myself to recover my composure. Before she comes, I will confess this much—it will not be betraying my trust—I *have* something weighing on my mind which I would give my life to be free from. Do not allude to this again, for it is a secret which even you cannot share."

He kissed her, and she left the room with a white, wondering face.

"He will not tell me—but I will set my woman's wits at work to find out what it is. Surely, a wife should try to find out, by any means, that which seems to concern her own husband so vitally. No husband should keep a secret from his wife. No matter what it is, a wife should know it."

Meanwhile, the master-workman paced up and down his library, muttering:

"Poor Coralie—poor, beautiful Coralie!"

Every few minutes he glanced at his watch.

"I told her to come any time after ten in the forenoon; it is almost eleven, still she is not here."

Five, ten, fifteen minutes passed; the hands of his watch dragged slowly around to a quarter of twelve, still there was no Coralie.

"Why does she not come?" he asked himself wonderingly. "What could have detained her? Surely she must have received my letter. In all probability she will come to-morrow."

Two days passed. He could restrain his impatience no longer. Sitting down at his desk he wrote a hurried note to Coralie, requesting that she should come to him with as little delay as possible; or, in case she could not come, to answer to that effect by bearer, and he would come to her.

This he dispatched by a messenger-boy, and again paced the floor with slow, measured strides, awaiting Coralie's appearance.

It was quite half an hour before the messenger-boy returned. He brought a letter for Mr. Marshall.

With a strange foreboding of impending evil, the master-workman tore open the envelope.

He saw at a glance it was not Coralie's signature at the bottom of the page, but Mrs. Melville's, the kind neighbor who took Coralie in on the night her mother died.

There were but a few short lines, and read as follows:

"Mr. Marshall:

"Respected Sir,—I have a painful duty to perform; therefore, the sooner it is gotten through with the better, so I will briefly come to the point at once. The girl, Coralie Harding, is not with me now; she remained here up to a short while ago, leaving my house for the ostensible purpose of calling upon you, she said; but, looking from my window, I saw her meet a young and handsome man. A coach was in waiting, and they both entered the vehicle and were driven away like the wind. She never returned. I have since learned from others who saw them who the young man was who lured beautiful Coralie away—he was young Mr. Drexel, the handsome nephew of the owner of the Drexel Silk Mills.

"Yours very truly,
"Mrs. Melville."

A cry terrible to hear broke from the master-workman's lips.

"She has gone—gone—and with him!" he cried wildly. "God help me! I must keep my oath, ay, even at the cost of a broken heart. She has taken fate into her own hands; only Heaven's mercy can save her now. I must find her, but where—how? This happened two days ago."

Like one wild with awful excitement, he fled from the house and into the street.

"I must find Coralie," he muttered; "and Heaven help her when she hears what I have to tell her. But I must keep my oath, come what may. Poor Coralie—poor child, whom I am powerless now to save, it would have been better for you had you died than lived to face the horrible doom which is so near!"

CHAPTER IX

❧ "I Will Not Believe My Darling Is False to Me!"

The hours that followed Allan Drexel's strange adventure dragged slowly by.

It was midnight before a returning vessel was sighted, and the sun was an hour high in the heavens ere it reached the New York dock.

He hurried down the gang-plank and hailed the nearest cab. It almost seemed to the impatient young husband that the vehicle crept along.

Twice he called out to the cabman that he must drive faster, and he groaned aloud when it came to a standstill ere half a dozen blocks had been traversed.

"I am sorry, sir," said the man; "we are blockaded in a crush of coaches. I will move on as soon as I can. You will be at No. — West Thirty-sixth Street in less than half an hour's time."

There was nothing for it but to control his impatience as best he could.

In half an hour Coralie would be folded in his arms. He would kiss her face, her lovely blue eyes, her sweet, dimpled lips. In half an hour. Ah, every moment of that time seemed an age to live through.

At last the coach stopped.

"Here you are, sir," said the driver.

Allan bounded up the brown-stone stoop three steps at a time.

A maid admitted him; in an instant he had gained the corridor above.

How his heart throbbed as he opened the door of Coralie's room.

No slender form sprung to meet him; no lovely face was turned toward him with a glad cry of welcome.

"Coralie!" he called softly—"Coralie!"

There was no answer.

"Coralie, my darling!" he called again, louder and more eagerly.

Still there was no answer, and he walked hurriedly into an inner apartment.

As he swept back the crimson velvet *portieres*,[6] he caught sight of a fair head resting against the velvet cushions of a large arm-chair whose back was toward him.

"Coralie, my love, my darling!" he cried, springing across the room, "have you no welcome for me?"

The figure in the arm-chair gave a little, startled cry and sprung from her seat, and Allan saw that it was not Coralie, but one of the maids.

"Oh! it's you, at last, is it, Mr. Drexel?" she cried, in a tone of relief. "My missus will be so glad; she has been so awfully perplexed what to do about the rooms with all your belongings still in them."

"Did you think I had run away?" said Allan, with a happy laugh. "Well, I suppose affairs did look a little that way. Where is Cor—my wife?" he asked, glancing hurriedly about.

"Oh, don't you know, sir," replied the maid, "she, your young bride, has gone?"

"Gone—Coralie gone—where?"

He gasped out the words as though they were the last he should ever speak, and a cry that was hardly human in its anguish fell from his lips.

"I—I do not believe you!" he cried abruptly; and the girl pardoned the words when she saw how white and tortured was the handsome face looking down into her own.

"It is quite true, sir," she answered. "We did not miss either of you until this morning, when, as you did not come down to breakfast, I came in to see what was the matter. I found a note on the table addressed to you. I admit frankly we read it, and discovered your young bride had fled from you, sir, with another. We thought you must have received the note, flung it down on the table, and started out in search of her."

Allan Drexel turned on the girl with the rapidity of lightning.

"My wife gone, and with another, you say? It is false! If an angel cried it out trumpet-tongued from yonder heavens, I should not believe it. The note, quick; where is the note!"

The girl crossed to the mantel, picked it up, and handed it to him, and knowing he would be best alone when he read it, silently quitted the room.

Allan Drexel unfolded the note with hands trembling like aspen leaves, strong man though he was; and these were the words he read, words that burned themselves into his brain like brands of fire while his life lasted:

---

[6]Curtain hanging across a doorway.

"Allan,—Your absence has brought me to a realization that we were never intended for each other. I bitterly regret having listened to your pleadings. Gone to another; but these words must not break a human heart. No, no, do not follow me, and search for me, for you cannnot find me. All love for you is dead in my heart.

"Coralie."

It was a strangely disconnected note, evidently written by one laboring under intense excitement, and was scarcely legible, it was so blotted by tears.

The young bridegroom, pallid as death itself, crushed the note for one-half second in his nerveless fingers, then turned like one mad, and rushed frantically from the room where he had received the cruelest blow that ever shattered "love's young dream."

The note had indeed been written by Coralie ere she fled from the house.

She had an idea that some day Allan might come back there to inquire how she had received the fatal intelligence that he had gone to wed another; then they would put that note in his hands.

Alas, for the strange complications of cruel fate, knowing nothing of the thrilling scene through which Coralie had passed in that very room in which she had left the note, the terrible word, "Gone to another," held but one meaning to him.

It was all too horribly true; she whom he had trusted so blindly, on whose loyalty and love he would have staked his life, had fled with some former lover.

"I should have taken time to woo and win her," muttered Allan, pushing his dark, damp curls back from his pallid brow. "I was mad to persuade her into marrying me on the spur of the moment, before the child knew her own mind, for she was but a child—only sixteen—but I thought such a love as mine must surely win love in return."

The mad idea of searching for her, claiming her, and forcing her to return with him surged through his heart and brain; but the next instant all his pride rose fiercely to his relief.

Force her to return! Ah, never, never! the marriage chain should be golden links that joins two hearts and souls together; not fetters that gall, heavy chains that are an irksome burden.

"No, I will not search for her," he muttered, setting his white teeth hard together. "I will bear this bravely as a man should."

He went back to his rooms at the Astor House, and the next day a newspaper with a marked paragraph was mailed to him.

Thinking it might possibly be from Coralie, containing a personal, he opened it hurriedly.

The curved lines indicating the paragraph the sender intended him to read, attracted his attention at once.

One glance, and then his face grew pale as death. It was to the effect that Coralie Drexel, through her attorneys, Messrs. Lane & Richards, had filed a petition for a legal separation from her husband, Allan Drexel, which she prayed would be granted her.

The paper fell from Allan's nerveless fingers, and the groan that he uttered died away on his white, set lips.

"She shall have the separation she craves," he said bitterly, bowing his dark, handsome head. "I will not oppose it, though it tears my heart out by the roots.

"Oh, the inconstancy of woman!" he groaned. "There is nothing under the light of heaven so alluringly beautiful as Coralie, yet so cruelly false—yes, as false of heart as she is fair of face."

"From this hour I will have but one aim in life," he muttered, striding fiercely up and down the room.

"I will show her that other women will appreciate the man she has so wantonly cast aside. I will meet her face to face, but I shall not reproach her—haughtily pass her by as a stranger would."

His kingly beauty had been of little consequence to him until now; but now he would make it his strong weapon to win favor, and to show her that others cared for him.

Although he admitted to himself he would love her madly, recklessly, hopelessly, under all this mask of gayety he would assume, until the day that he died, every golden hair of that curly golden head would be precious to him beyond price, yet she should never, never know it.

He would build a wall of pride between them that should stand while they both lived.

He would school himself to gaze into her eyes if they met, or hear her voice, crushing back the mad torrent of love that would thrill his heart, and resist the impulse that would urge him to clasp her madly to his heart, praying her to come back to him—to love him, that life was unendurable without her.

A mad desire surged through his heart to look upon the rival who had lured Coralie from him.

"I will hunt him down!" he cried, "and when our paths cross, I shall not be answerable for what happens after that."

The exact situation of affairs can be told in a few words. A woman, heavily veiled, had called upon the lawyers in question, and had placed the divorce case in their hands.

During the interview she did not raise the thick, dark veil that concealed her face, and, to their surprise, declined to give her address, preferring to call occasionally at the office to see if her presence was required.

Suffice it to say, this was the same veiled woman who had called upon Coralie, divulging to her the supposed falsity of her young husband—the dupe of Robert Sinclair, who had laid his dastardly plans well.

Coralie, believing Allan Drexel had willfully deceived and deserted her, would learn to hate him, while Drexel, believing Coralie had fled and desired a separation from him, would tear all love for her from his breast though it spoiled his life, wrecked his soul. Alas, the dastardly plan had worked well. Those two who loved each other so well, were torn as completely asunder as though one of them lay in the grave.

CHAPTER X

❧ Fate Marks Out Beautiful Coralie's Destiny

But to return to Coralie. With rapid steps Robert Sinclair hurried down the steep path with Coralie in his arms, stopping before a coach in waiting.

"Open the door," he called impatiently; "don't keep me standing here in the rain. I have the girl. What is the matter?" he called, with an angry imprecation, as the driver fumbled awkwardly at the door of the vehicle.

"Something seems to be the matter with the knob, it's hard to open," returned the man. "If I had a wrench I could fix it in about two minutes; but as I can't get one, maybe you'll lend a hand, sir?"

For a moment Robert Sinclair hesitated; the slender figure in his arms had ceased to struggle, and he laid her down in the green grass and turned to the coachman's assistance.

A cool, gentle breeze lifted the folds of the cloak and swept across Coralie's face; the rain dashed upon it and revived her.

With wonderful energy she fought hard against the dull, dazed feeling that was fast steeping her senses in its dread embrace.

With the quick intuition that sometimes comes to us in moments of peril, Coralie realized that if she would escape from the terrible danger that was closing in around her, she must make the effort without an instant's delay. Her brain seemed whirling and her breath to almost leave her.

With a quick, spasmodic movement she freed herself from the folds of the heavy cloak, and noiselessly gained her feet. And like a hunted deer fairly flew over the long damp grass, trusting to the impenetrable darkness to screen her.

She heard the exclamation of surprise and the deep imprecation that fell from Sinclair's lips, as he started in pursuit of her—breathlessly following the sound of her flying footsteps.

"Mother!" she gasped, holding out her little white hands to the dark, starless sky; "save me—save me, mother; hear the prayers of your child—my enemy is tracking me down."

She saw the glimmer of the lanterns they carried as they searched for her, and with beating heart she heard the threats they uttered of the revenge that would be taken upon her when they should find her.

They were gaining upon her so rapidly that in sheer fright she sprung aside from the path, crouching down in terror in the midst of a thick growth of young pines.

A moment more and they were abreast of her in the path; Coralie was quite sure they must hear the loud, spasmodic beating of her heart.

They were so near that she could have put out her little hand and touched them. That was the most intensely thrilling moment of Coralie's life.

To her horror they both stopped short in the path. She heard them debate as to whether they should remain where they were until morning, or move on, and when daylight came, commence the search with renewed vigor.

"I shall take good care she does not escape me again," said Sinclare harshly; "it was most assuredly my own fault."

They decided at last to move on, and Coralie told herself that God had heard her prayer.

A golden, rosy dawn was born of this darksome night, and at last Coralie ventured out of her place of concealment looking fearfully around her, but as there was no signs of her persecutor, she moved on, but, oh, how fearfully cramped and stiff her limbs were.

"Where shall I go?" she murmured piteously, putting her hand to her forehead in a dazed sort of way. "Alone in the great wide, cruel world—homeless, friendless, penniless—with no place to go—was ever a young girl so cruelly situated before?" she asked herself, with a dry, hard sob.

Her whole soul turned sick with horror when her thoughts reverted to that scene through which she had so lately passed, in which her handsome lover had so cruelly denounced her, vowing that he had never seen her before.

"Oh, cruel lie—oh, false, false heart of man! would God ever forgive him for those cruel words?" she wondered.

Though she believed Allan false, she did not call upon God to bring curses down upon his head—she loved him too well for that. She only prayed that she might forget his dark, handsome face, the winning smile, and the voice that had been all Heaven to her.

She had but one confused idea, and that was to get back to New York.

She had just money enough left to pay her fare; and when once there, she must find something to do, or starve.

"I would die before I would go back to the Drexel Mills," she murmured, gazing abstractedly out of the window as the train flashed in and out of the dark tunnels; "but where shall I go—oh, where?"

Fate decided the question for her in a strange way—a way that changed the whole course of her after life.

Coralie had traversed but a few streets in her vain search for work ere, turning one of the near corners, she came suddenly upon a little crowd collected in front of quite a large red brick building.

The second glance showed Coralie it was a medical institute, and that they were carrying a woman through the carved, arched doors.

"I do not know what will become of the poor creature," remarked some one in the crowd. "The trained nurses vow they will not go near her, and she must have attention, or she will surely die. I do not suppose an attendant could be found—"

A sweet, girlish voice interrupted the—sentence, and the little group of doctors fell back as beautiful little Coralie timidly advanced, saying hesitatingly, yet eagerly:

"Do you think my services would be accepted? I—I should be so very glad of the place if they would but engage me."

The doctors looked at each other in consternation.

"Pause before thinking of offering your services in such a case as this, my dear child," said an elderly gentleman stepping forward. "The disease is contagious—it is small-pox. Your fair young beauty would pay the forfeit of your heroic desire to aid that poor creature."

He expected to see her shrink back in affright, but Coralie looked up eagerly into his face.

"That would not matter," she answered. "God knows I care little enough about beauty."

In vain they tried to persuade her that it would be madness to persist in that course of action.

"Better that you should let her die," one of the young doctors exclaimed, "than that *you* should nurse her."

But Coralie was not to be shaken from her resolve. She applied for the position, and her services were gladly enough accepted, though the old nurse who put her in as a substitute did feel a pang of remorse when she looked at Coralie's fair, beautiful face, framed in its sheen of golden hair.

Six weeks passed, when, owing to Coralie's unwearied patience and careful nursing, her patient, Miss Montstrossor, struggled back from the gates of death to life, and convalescence commenced rapidly; and the day and hour came in which the doctors told her she had been saved all by her beautiful little nurse's faithful care.

She held out her thin, white hand to Coralie, her emotion too great for words, but from that moment Miss Montstrossor was always murmuring under her breath:

"I can make it up to her; I can and I will!"

And, oh! how fervently she prayed that Coralie might not be stricken down with the dread disease from which she had saved her.

Heaven proved kind indeed to heroic, beautiful little Coralie; she passed through the fiery furnace unscathed.

Miss Montstrosser had drawn from Coralie's lips that she was an orphan—alone, friendless and penniless in the world, searching for work. Coralie could not confide to her the story of that cruel love-dream so pitifully shattered.

Ah, no! no one must ever know of that. Poor Coralie told herself she had no right to Allan Drexel's name; she was Coralie Harding still.

"You shall stay with me, child," said Miss Montstrossor, warmly. "You and I will have a home together; you shall never know want again.

"Listen, child," she said, drawing Coralie toward her. "I am not the object of charity that they thought me when they brought me here. I have plenty of gold, and when I die you shall have it all, little Coralie, for being so faithful to me.

"Let me tell you how it came about that I was brought here; a few words will tell it, for the niece whose memory I curse is to be put aside, and you shall inherit all my money."

"No, no!" cried Coralie, starting back in dismay. "I would not take what belongs to another. Oh, not for world!"

"It belongs to me at present," said Miss Montstrossor, grimly, "and I propose to leave the money where I choose. I'll have it carefully nailed up in my coffin with me, and have the whole thing cremated ere she—my niece—shall ever inherit a dollar of mine. When I tell you why, you will not wonder," and a shudder came over the thin, white face framed in the sparse locks of iron-gray hair.

"Before you you see a blighted, misspent life," she went on bitterly. "All my girlhood and womanhood I was kept so steadily at work that I scarcely saw the light of day. Love did not search me out in the toil of the weary workshop, and years rolled their slow length by, and I awoke to the fact one day that I was an old and a pitifully lonely woman. In the midst of my loneliness, a strange event happened; a few thousand dollars was left me by the death of an old friend, whom I had known since her girlhood.

"To make a long story short, I was induced to invest it in a gold mine. Fortune favored me; my small investment reaped a harvest beyond my wildest dreams.

"I sent for my niece, the only relative I have in the great wide world, and educated her, bringing her home after her boarding-school days were over.

"I promised her she should inherit all I had; but, mind you, I did not tell her how much that 'all' was, and that was the beginning of the bitter end."

How little poor Coralie thought as she listened, how cruelly that other young girl's path was to cross her own.

CHAPTER XI

❧ Allan and Coralie Meet

"My niece was a girl of the most designing ambition," went on Miss Montstrossor, wearily, "and by cunning devices—or pretended affection—she at last coaxed me into signing over all the amount she supposed me possessed of—some forty thousand dollars—to her.

"Listen to the sequel: The ink was scarcely dry on the paper, and the document in her possession, before, to my horror, I noticed the change in her. I could never tell you what I suffered for the next fortnight; but trouble never comes singly, I was stricken down with this terrible malady, and then, little Coralie, I was turned out into the street—old, feeble, sick unto death—to live or to die as God saw fit; I was found wandering homeless, friendless on the street, and delirous, so of course they brought me to the charity institute.

"How often in my hours of convalescence have I thanked God I did not give up all, but a meager part of my wealth. I am a rich woman still, Coralie, and you, who have endangered your own brave, young life and your sweet face to save mine, shall have your reward.

"I am old and lonely, my heart craves sympathy and love; come and gladden the few declining years that I shall linger here. I can trust you, child. Come to me and I will make a grand lady of you. Those patient little hands shall be covered with shining gems. You shall know want, privation and care no more. Take what the gods provide, child."

"I—I should be so unfitted for such a life," sobbed Coralie, quite overcome by her new-found friend's magnificent offer. "Heaven intended me for only a poor little working-girl—I am sure of it."

"An honest, honorable working-girl is by far better fitted to occupy a noble position than a white-handed idler."

All of Coralie's objections were one by one overruled, and she consented at last that everything should be just as Miss Montstrossor wished.

She was bewildered, dazed, almost incapable of thought or action.

Could it be possible that such great good fortune was in store for her? she wondered—she, who had been used to such a weary routine of toil through summer's heat and winter's snows—glad, oh, so glad when Saturday night came, bringing with it the little envelope that contained her week's slight earnings.

Could it be that she was to be raised so strangely by the hand of fate from want to wealth?

Coralie was quite fearful lest she should wake up the next morning and find all this but the idle coinage of a dream.

But no, it was all quite real enough.

Miss Montstrossor was soon able to leave the institute, and with Coralie, as her *protegee,* took rooms at the Windsor at once.

"For the first time in my life I will live as becomes a woman of my wealth," said Miss Montstrossor. "I need hide no longer from the eyes of the world what I am really worth."

Modistes[7] were sent for, and in a very short space of time Coralie was transformed as if by magic from the simple, modest, shy young girl in the plain, dark merino dress, to a very magnificent *petite* young society belle.

"Oh, Miss Montstrossor, how do you think I look?" cried Coralie, flying into the room when she had her first elegant new dress on. "Not much like poor little Coralie Harding, think you?"

Miss Montstrossor gazed at the beautiful vision of girlish loveliness with dim eyes.

"You look like an angel, my dear," she answered; "but you must not be vain; that was the beginning of my niece's folly; she grew vain."

"I will not, my dear kind friend!" exclaimed Coralie, throwing her white arms impulsively around Miss Montstrossor's neck. "I am so glad if I please you, that is all."

"You are so fair! I am afraid I shall not be able to keep you with me long," sighed the old lady. "I may find you only to loose you."

And a tear rolled down her cheek as she caressed the pretty, golden head—gazing down into that faultlessly fair face, and lovely eyes like purple amethysts.

"I want to be one with you, little Coralie," she said softly; "to enter fully into your interests and your pleasures. I want you to have thorough trust in me; let me be a friend to consult and advise you; trust me—make me your confidante above all in your love affairs. I have never spoken to you of love or lovers before. I am going to do so now."

Coralie's lovely face grew deadly pale, a swift, sudden faintness threatened to overcome her, but by a valiant effort she controlled her emotion.

"We are going into what will be a new life," continued Miss Montstrossor, thoughtfully. "You, who have seen nothing of the world, will be in its midst, and because you are young, and fresh, and fair—ah, very fair!—you will have many admirers.

"Ah! my child, take care—beware! I want to warn you—not frighten you. You will see men of all kinds—young, handsome, clever; they will surround you, flatter you; they will pay you all kinds of homage; they will whisper sweet words to you; but mind—be careful to allow your heart to go out to the right one, for you will love some day, and marry. Ah, yes, you will; do not shake your head. You are only human, and it is human to love and to marry, sweet Coralie. I need not say do not let gold tempt you; you are too noble for that. Marry for love; but mind whom you love. Do not be attracted by a handsome face, by a caressing manner, by outward accomplishments, by wealth, rank or position but by real goodness and excellence."

Coralie, trembling like a leaf, hid her head on Miss Montstrossor's shoulder.

Should she keep the dark secret that overshadowed her young life, or should she reveal it.

---

[7]Sellers of fashionable clothes to women.

While she hesitated Miss Montstrossor went on:

"The greatest mistakes made in this world are, I believe, in its marriages—it makes or mars a life. Before entering this world of men I want to warn you. Be on your guard, do not fall in love with the first man who admires you—the first who makes love to you.

"How closely you cling to my hand, Coralie! You hurt my hand, dear," she added.

"I have given you good advice, dear," she went on, "and it remains for you to follow it. Do not fall in love with the first comer. Let sense and reason, not fancy and romance, guide you. My second warning is this; do not keep your love-secrets from me; make me your confidante; tell me about your lovers. Half the miserable marriages in the world are caused by girls not trusting their truest friends. Remember my words; when the first lover comes wooing, do not give up your heart all at once. Think if he be worth it.

"Now I have finished my lecture, child. Why, how ill you look! What is the matter? You frighten me, Coralie, you are so pale!"

A strong impulse had come to Coralie to kneel at Miss Montstrossor's feet and tell her all, but, oh! how could she rake up the ashes of that smoldering love-dream!

No, no; she could not confess even to her kind benefactress that cruel, false marriage of which she had been the victim. She could not speak of the valiant struggle she had made to forget Allan Drexel, her first and only love; but, alas! it was useless, useless; hers was a deathless love.

Fight against it hard as she would, in her own heart she knew she loved Allan—handsome Allan—still, and would love him until the day she died.

A restless longing possessed Coralie to enter that social world to which Allan belonged.

Sooner or later she would meet Allan and his bride at some reception, she well knew, and she prayed that Heaven would give her strength to bear the shock, that she might not fall dead at his feet.

And yet hoping—yet dreading to meet Allan, there was a great fascination about going to places where he would be likely to go.

She told herself she must see him just once, then she would be willing to shut herself away from the world forever.

Coralie's wondrous beauty, and her sweet simplicity, made a great furore in the fashionable world, as Miss Montstrossor was sure that face would do. Coralie was a favorite at once. Cards were received for the most exclusive New York socials. Receptions, balls, parties followed each other in rapid succession, and pretty Coralie was queen of them all; but she always came home with the same piteous pain in her lovely, childish eyes. It had been another evening lost out of her life, for she had not seen Allan Drexel.

Probably he was still away on an extended wedding trip with his bride, she told herself.

One evening just as Coralie entered the ballroom at a fashionable Lexington Avenue residence with Miss Montstrossor, she felt her hand clutch tightly on her arm. Looking up in wonder, she saw that her face was dark and stormy with concentrated passion.

"Coralie, my niece and I are to meet again, at last," she whispered hoarsely. "Look—there she is—that superb-looking girl in the amber satin and passion-roses standing beneath those arching palms talking to that handsome man with the red rose in the lappel of his coat. Let us advance and sweep by her, Coralie; this is my hour of triumph. Your hand is like ice. What is the matter?"

No answer fell from Coralie's lips; the whiteness of death was in her face.

She never saw the throng of admirers pressing eagerly forward to welcome her. She was gazing straight toward the arching palms with her soul in her eyes.

The dreamy dance-music seemed far off, and the faces, the jewels, the gleam of satin, fair women and brave men seemed to whirl confusedly around her.

She saw but one scene, clear and distinct—the proud young beauty in the amber satin dress, over whose white, jeweled hand the tall, dark-eyed, handsome man bent. He turned his face slightly toward Coralie's direction—that dark, splendid, winning face so like the picture of Romeo[8]—or Sir Lancelot.[9]

At the first glance Coralie had recognized him; he was Allan Drexel; they were to meet face to face at last.

CHAPTER XII

❧ Coralie and Allan Meet at the Grand Ball

Like one stricken dumb—turned to stone—Coralie stood gazing at the beautiful young girl over whose slim white hand Allan Drexel was bowing.

"Is your niece—his—his—bride?" she faltered, turning a face pale as death to Miss Montstrossor.

"No, she in not married," replied that lady, "and some man is spared from having a virago[10] for a wife."

Coralie did not hear the rest of the sentence; she was wondering if Allan's bride were present; of course she must be, she told herself bitterly, else why is he here?

"I must meet her face to face before the evening is over, and even though she recognizes me, I must not fall dead at her feet. I must learn fortitude, though my heart is breaking."

"How you tremble, child," said Miss Montstrossor, looking down into the lovely young face in alarm. "Are you ill? If you are, we will leave the ballroom at once. It is only for your sake I am here. I have long since lived over the time that laughter, mirth, and music could charm me."

"No, no, we will not go," said Coralie, with a little hysterical laugh that was almost a sob. "Why should we?"

"Just as you say, my dear," answered her companion, complacently.

They moved on, quite unnoticed by the two standing beneath the waving palm, and at that instant a partner came up to claim Miss Montstrossor's hand for the next waltz, and Allan turned away with a low bow. Her dark eyes follow him, and she sees he is by far the handsomest man in the ballroom.

---

[8]Romeo is the dashing, tragic hero of Shakespeare's play *Romeo and Juliet.*

[9]Lancelot was considered the greatest knight to sit at King Arthur's legendary roundtable.

[10]Loud, overbearing woman.

"Why is he—the only man whom I have ever seen that I could love—so coolly indifferent to me?" she wondered vaguely. "Other men court my smiles and sigh at my frowns; he is serenely unconscious of either, but I will win him despite that; he shall yet kneel at my feet and sue for my love. Inez Montstrossor never courted anything yet but what she obtained by fair means or foul. I will have great patience. If it is true that love really wins love, I will win in the end."

She noticed once or twice as she passed Allan in the waltz how bored his handsome face looked; neither the lights, the flowers, nor the music, even the pretty maidens that passed him by, challenging him with their bright eyes, seemed to have any attraction for him whatever.

He had thrown himself into the vortex of the fashionable world to forget Coralie, but he had never been able to pass an hour without thinking of her; even in his dreams that fair, dimpled, girlish face, crowned in golden hair, was ever before him.

His pride had prevented him from putting in a defense in that action for an absolute divorce, and he noticed some few weeks later the petition had been granted—Coralie was free from him.

Ah, if his guardian angel had but warned him just how matters stood; that Coralie quite believed that marriage ceremony to be a pitiful mockery, and believing that, could never have sued to be free from him; the whole course of two lives might have been different.

He had come to this ball at the solicitation of his friend, Captain Stafford, and quite an irksome affair he was finding it.

Suddenly a hand was laid on his arm, and he found Stafford beside him.

"What! not dancing, old boy!" cried his friend cheerily. "This won't do at all, while so many beauties are sighing because they must be wallflowers if they do not find partners. I cannot imagine what's coming over you of late. I can remember the time, Drexel, when you couldn't get enough of this sort of thing. What's the matter with you?"

"Constitutional laziness, as one grows old," said Drexel, dryly.

"As one grows old," repeated Stafford, with a rolicking laugh; "pretty talk for a fellow of five-and-twenty. But come, I want to introduce you to the belle of the ball—the loveliest girl in creation."

Allan laughed good-humoredly.

"Pray excuse me," he said; "she will have enough dancing attendance upon her whims and caprices without—"

"Nonsense!" out in his friend; "come along without another word. I promise to show you a beauty quite out of the ordinary—a faultless little creature whose smile or glance is so bewildering she quite dazzles a fellow."

"She seems to have quite dazzled you," observed Allan, laconically.

"It is quite true," declared his friend. "I may tell you this in all confidence, because you and I are life-long friends—the little beauty has bewitched me; when I first looked into her eyes my heart gave a strange throb—for the first time in a young girl's presence I seemed stricken dumb—I could find nothing to say. Before I had been in her company half an hour, I said to myself—here is the one woman in all the world for you—you must win her."

"What are you so anxious to present me to this divinity for?" asked Allan, a little curiously. "What if I should fall a victim to her charms—what then?"

"You will not," laughed his friend, a little uneasily, though, it must be confessed, "for you are a decided woman-hater. I will be frank with you, Drexel, the ladies all take to you—to use a common phrase, and I want you to speak a few good words for me in that quarter."

"Ah, I see," laughed Allan; "a sort of 'Miles Standish'[11] affair, but do you remember the words of the pretty maiden to the man who had come to plead for his bashful friend?—turn the case around and let it apply to you—always speak for yourself. I'm afraid there's something a trifle cowardly about you, anyhow, my dear captain. You would not be afraid to face an army with drawn swords, yet you shrink from meeting a refusal from a pretty girl's lips."

"Don't laugh at me, Drexel," replied his friend, earnestly; "when you have seen this girl you will understand why it is easy for me to feel as I do—she is like no other young girl whom I have ever met; one cannot tell whether he has made the slightest impression or not. She is not one to whom you can pay idle compliments or make the light, conventional ballroom speeches; she has a way, too, of looking past a fellow very eagerly about the room, and you never feel sure whether your presence is agreeable to her or whether she is searching out—with those bright eyes—some more favored fellow; and yet—she treats all her admirers in the same way—I am sure of that, for I have watched every one who spoke with her with breathless eagerness to see. And to finish up with the list of difficulties that beset this peerless little fairy, she is watched over by a grim, stern-faced duenna,[12] who frowns down anything like an attempt at a *tete-a-tete*."[13]

Allan concluded it would be far easier to go with his friend than to stand there and listen to another half hour's description of her charms.

"I see her moving toward the conservatory now," cried his friend, taking Allan eagerly by the arm. "Come on at once and head off the rest; scores of admirers will miss her and follow her there in the space of a minute."

With a good-natured smile, little dreaming of what was in store for him, Allan allowed himself to be led toward the conservatory.

Pleading fatigue, Coralie had slipped away to the conservatory quite unobserved, as she supposed. Among all that sea of faces—handsome women and brave men—Coralie had seen but one, the dark, debonair face of the lover who had proven the falsest of men to her, and whom a merciful fate had prevented from wrecking her life just in time.

Eagerly and patiently Coralie had searched among that vast throng for the proud-faced girl she had seen standing by Allan Drexel's side beneath the floral-bell on that never-to-be-forgotten wedding-night.

Quite an hour or more she had watched Allan intently, but she did not see him approach any of the ladies.

"She is not here," Coralie told herself; then she remembered, although not generally the custom, that gentlemen did go out without their wives occasionally.

---

[11]Myles Standish (1584–1656) was a military leader among the early settlers of the Plymouth colony. In Henry Wadsworth Longfellow's poem, *The Courtship of Miles Standish* (1858), a shy Standish has a friend propose marriage to the woman he loves.

[12]An elderly woman chaperon.

[13]Private conversation between two people.

He did not appear to take part in the dancing, nor was he observing those on the floor.

His time seemed to be occupied entirely in talking with the different gentlemen who passed him, exchanging salutations.

There was no longer the gay, happy smile on his handsome, debonair face that Coralie remembered so well.

"I must not give one thought to him," she murmured, pressing her little hands tightly over her heart. "He is not worth it; he is worthy of only my deepest scorn and indignation. Whenever I think of him, it must always be as the husband of another. That will help me to harden my heart against him."

She heard footsteps approaching; she did not turn her head, but drew nearer to the fountain to afford them more room to pass on.

But the footsteps did not pass on, they stopped directly beside her; and Coralie lifted her eyes from the rippling water of the fountain with a slight start.

One quick, startled glance; then the green palms, the fairy lights, the fragrant blooms, seemed to whirl about her. Yet she did not faint nor cry out, although standing before her, with Captain Stafford's hand on his arm, she beheld Allan Drexel.

To Allan Drexel the shock of being brought face to face with Coralie was intense.

"But was it Coralie?" he asked himself, as he bent breathlessly forward and scanned that perfect face, cold, hard, proud; yes, cold as marble, framed in that halo of golden hair. "Was he mad or dreaming?" he asked himself. "Could this really be Coralie, this peerless creature, blazing with diamonds and robed in shimmering satin and rich old lace, his Coralie?"

Allan never remembered in what words that presentation was made; he caught but two words of that sentence, and those two words were—Miss Harding.

Yes, it was Coralie, then. Allan stood before her incapable of action. Like one rooted to the spot, his face pale as death, he had a dim consciousness that his friend was looking from the one to the other in the greatest consternation.

CHAPTER XIII

❧ Fair and False

Coralie, with a woman's keen wit, in a case of emergency, was the first to gain anything like composure.

Allan Drexel could only stand and stare at her like a man turned to marble

"Have you and Mr. Drexel met before?" asked the captain, gazing from one to the other in the greatest bewilderment.

"If so, our acquaintance was so slight I have quite forgotten," responded Coralie, promptly, drawing her slender form up to its fullest height, and completely ignoring Allan's intense gaze, adding lightly: "If you will kindly escort me back to the ballroom, I shall be very much obliged to you, Captain Stafford."

The captain offered her his arm in silence, and together they quitted the conservatory, leaving Allan Drexel, the unhappy husband, the victim of such a cruel tissue of mistakes, standing there like a man carved in stone.

Coralie was never quite certain how she reached the ballroom, what Captain Stafford said, or what she replied, or if she replied at all.

She was conscious at last that he was leaving her with a low bow, and, thank Heaven, for one moment, one blessed little moment, she might be quite alone, but she found herself too excited to think clearly. Her thoughts were in a wild chaos.

She was glad the dance music struck up and took those around her out on the floor, they would not be so apt to notice her agitation.

She felt too dizzy to walk. When she could sufficiently control her emotion, she would cross the room to where Miss Montstrossor sat, and beg her to take her home, for she felt ill—ill unto death.

Suddenly, before she could put her thoughts into execution, she saw some one stop directly before her, and even before she glanced up, she knew by the wild throbbing of her heart that it was Allan.

"Coralie!" he cried, stooping down so near her that his hot breath scorched her cheek, "for God's sake come into the conservatory again if but for a moment. I must see you!—you *must* come."

In an instant all the girl's pride rose to her rescue.

"Let me remember that he tried to wreck my life with a false marriage. Yes, wreck my life before man and my soul before God, and let that thought harden my heart against him," was the thought that flashed across her mind as she drew back from him with scorn so haughty it must have fairly paralyzed any other man.

"Must," she repeated in a cold, proud voice, every vibration of which cut through his heart like a dagger's thrust. "Pardon me, I do not see how you *dare* address that word to me. What right have you to dictate to me?"

"Coralie!" he cried huskily, "do not torture me. I know I have lost all right. You are quick enough to fling that in my face, that you are free, yet for all that I do ask you to come to the conservatory with me. Hear what I have to say. For the love you bore me once, or pretended to bear me, when I clasped you in my arms and called you my darling little bride, I beseech you to come and listen to me."

"How dare you recall that miserable scene?" cried Coralie, white to the lips with outraged pride and bitter indignation. "Leave me, I will not listen to one word you have to say. Go, leave me—leave me with the memory of how I have learned to despise you— ay, abhor you. Never speak to me again. If we meet in future, let it be as strangers. No, do not touch my hand. I would rather cut it off than that it should lie one moment in your clasp."

"You must, indeed, hate me to say that, Coralie," he said, drawing back, and looking at her intently.

"I do, indeed," she said brusquely.

"In that case, nothing more remains to be said," he returned, with pride equal to her own. "It shall be as you wish, Coralie," he went on bitterly; "from this moment we meet as strangers."

And, turning on his heel, he left her quite as suddenly as he had appeared before her.

Half way across the ballroom he met Captain Stafford, who was making his way toward him.

"I have been looking everywhere for you," said the captain. "What, in Heaven's name, did that scene in the conservatory mean?" he asked quickly. "Do you know Miss Harding."

"A case of mistaken identity," replied Allan, and he was surprised at the hoarseness and strangeness of his own voice. "She is not the young girl I once knew. No, no!"

"I tried to apologize to her in your name," replied the captain, "but the look of anger in her face almost struck me dumb. I should never have suspected you, of all the people in the world, to have made a blunder of that kind; to say that I was dumfounded, is a weak way of putting it. What must she have thought of you? I'm afraid she will never forgive me for bringing such a stupid *contretemps*[14] about, by Jove!"

"If I were not so unfortunate as to be Inez Montstrossor's escort here to-night, I would leave at once!" said Allan, hoarsely, more to himself than to his friend.

"That would not mend matters," returned the captain. "You'd better face the affair out. You'll be sure to meet Miss Harding wherever you go. She is quite the rage of the season, you know."

"You are right, my dear friend; it will be better to stay and face this affair out. Excuse me; I must go in search of Miss Montstrossor. She will believe that I have deserted her; then I shall have made two enemies tonight instead of one."

Inez Montstrossor was bitterly angry at his neglect, but she forced a smile to her lips as she saw him approaching.

"Truant," she cried, tapping his arm with her pearl-and-silver fan, "where have you been?"

"I have been watching the waltzers," he said, forcing a gayety of tone that certainly was at variance with his pale, disturbed face. "Your admirers crowded about you so constantly, I saw there was little chance or opportunity for me."

"You should make your opportunities," she answered, in a low voice. "Faint heart never won, etc., etc.," she added, shyly.

"I shall remember those words in future," he replied. "Am I to have an opportunity of another waltz with you, Miss Inez, or are your tablets filled?"

"I saved a few waltzes for you," she replied, "despite your remark, when you asked me to go to the ball, that you did not dance much———"

"You are very kind," he said, filling his name in the blank spaces; "kinder than I deserve, Miss Inez."

"I had something so strange to tell you," said Inez, hurriedly, "I was hoping you would come half an hour ago."

He looked up quickly and inquiringly.

"I have made a strange discovery," she went on, hastily. "I have met my aunt here to-night."

"Your aunt?" he repeated, thoughtfully. "I was not aware that you had a living relative, Miss Montstrossor. I thought I had heard you express yourself to that effect."

"So I quite believed until to-night," she answered. "I lived with my aunt, who, several months ago, wandered away from the house in a fit of mental aberration. As I could find no trace of her, I always believed she had wandered to the river—she was fond of going there—and had fallen in.

---

[14]Embarrassing situation.

"Imagine my great amazement on meeting her here to-night—alive and well—and to hear from her lips that she had come into the possession of a great fortune!

"Now listen to the strangest and saddest part of the affair—she is under the complete control and influence of a young girl, whom my aunt believes to have rendered her some sort of service. She has adopted this girl, who is known as her ward, and I, her only living relative, am to be disinherited.

"Ah, well, I would not mind that if she had not estranged my aunt's love from me.

"Look—that is she, Mr. Drexel—as fair of face as an angel—but, oh, don't you think she must have a very wicked heart to do that?"

And, following the direction she pointed out, and the young girl indicated, he saw—Coralie.

"Surely you do not mean that *she* has been capable of estranging your aunt's affections from you, do you, Miss Montstrossor?" he asked, hoarsely.

Inez nodded—pleased to sow the seed of distrust in his heart of the beautiful girl, whom his eyes had been following about so constantly ever since he had been seated by her side.

It had been a terrible shock to the heartless niece to meet her angered aunt, and to learn of the vast fortune that had at one time been within her grasp, but which should now go to the lovely young stranger.

In vain Inez had endeavored to make friends with her aunt; the elder Miss Montstrossor repulsed every advance.

"I know you as you are, Inez Montstrossor," she said, grimly; "you cannot deceive me by your pretense of affection."

In vain—all in vain Inez pleaded and protested—nothing could change her aunt's fixed resolve.

"The time will come when you will be glad to turn to me, aunt," she said; "when you find out the falsity of the girl who has plotted and planned so cleverly to come between us."

"Do not think her as false as yourself," replied Miss Montstrossor, hotly. "Sweet Coralie is little less than an angel; she saved my life at the risk of her own. God bless her, and handsome shall be her reward."

Inez Montstrossor had turned away with something very like murder in her heart at these words.

"The girl may enjoy your wealth a little while, Aunt Montstrossor," she muttered, "but if she should die very suddenly, and you should as suddenly follow, who is there to inherit your money, I should like to know? The man nor woman never yet lived who could win that upon which I had set my heart, and I have set my heart upon two things—your money, Aunt Montstrossor, and handsome Allan Drexel's love."

CHAPTER XIV

❧ The Pangs of Jealousy Are More Cruel Than Death

To Allan Drexel, the story of Miss Montstrossor's ward and her expectations had been wonderful indeed.

The idea came to him suddenly that, if Coralie prized sordid gold so much, she must have wedded him for his wealth; but finding that he would lose the vast inheritance—the Drexel Mills—she had been only too eager to leave him.

"Ah, who can understand the faithlessness of woman," he groaned to himself, as he bowed his dark head on his hands.

Would Coralie care for him he wondered, if she knew that he was now in truth his uncle's heir?—that Miss Hazleton had married an old lover, thus putting it completely out of Allan's power to make her his bride, and that this so enraged old Mr. Drexel that he drew up the will at once which made Allan his heir? He had since died, and Allan was now in truth the owner of the Drexel Silk Mills.

Would Coralie care for him if she knew this? he wondered.

Then he clinched his hands fiercely together, muttering bitterly between his white teeth:

"The woman who would care for me for my wealth, must be nothing to me. I will tear her image from my heart, though it kills me."

On the week following, Allan was invited to spend a few weeks at Rathstone Villa on the banks of the Hudson.

"We are to have a very jolly party," his friend, Hubert Rathstone, wrote. "The party includes the pretty Miss Harding, whom you seemed to admire so much this past season, besides Captain Stafford and a host of others. Do come, old fellow. I promise you a glorious time."

Allan was on the point of refusing; but when he learned Coralie was to be there, it seemed quite beyond his power to remain away.

He would even brave her bitter anger for the poor privilege of being near her.

A thrill of intensely jealous pain shot through his heart to know that Captain Stafford would be among the guests, remembering how deeply in love he was with Coralie. The gallant captain had great expectations, too, and was considered a golden prize by many a maneuvering mamma.

As for Coralie, she had no interest whatever in the handsome young soldier who followed her about like a shadow.

The captain had quite won the good will of Miss Montstrossor. He had had the clever diplomacy to win the elder lady's favor first, and Miss Montstrossor was loud in her praises of the gallant captain to Coralie.

"When you marry, my dear," she said to Coralie one day, "I should like your husband to be like the captain."

Coralie had turned away with a gesture of entreaty.

"I shall never marry, Miss Montstrossor," she declared earnestly. "Oh, never, never!"

"Nonsense, my dear," returned the elder lady, complacently. "That's what every young girl declares until the right one comes along."

The captain was the first person whom Coralie met as the coach drew up in front of the wide, vine-covered veranda of Rathstone Villa.

"Miss Harding!" he exclaimed, delightedly, "this is, indeed, an unlooked-for pleasure," and his fair, flushed, Saxon face certainly looked the delight he expressed.

Then Hubert Rathstone approached and took charge of Coralie, and the Captain followed with Miss Montstrossor.

The meeting between Coralie and Inez Montstrossor was certainly a little constrained, but certainly among such a gay party of young ladies and gentlemen, it was not noticed.

Coralie was just turning away when she beheld the dark, handsome face of Allan Drexel among a group of gentlemen.

She caught her breath with a sharp gasp.

"*He* here!" she breathed piteously; "then surely his bride must be here with him. I must meet her face to face at last. Ah, Heaven, why did I ever come here? how can I live three weeks under the same roof with them? How can I witness his gaze resting upon her face, with the light of love in those dark eyes—and live?"

And Coralie strove to keep back the bitter tears that welled up to her blue eyes.

But at dinner, the ordeal Coralie had nerved herself to endure, did not take place. Allan's bride was not there; he came in to dinner with Inez Montstrossor leaning on his arm.

Coralie affected not to see him, but once or twice during the meal she felt the force of the steady gaze of Allan's dark, magnetic eyes fixed searchingly upon her.

Allan was amazed at Coralie's ready wit and sparkling repartee. Could it be that this brilliant girl was the sweet little Coralie who had nestled in his arms—her white arms twined around his neck, whispering piteously:

"Oh, Allan, I hope you will never regret having married me; because you are so far above me, and I am only a poor little working-girl; if you should, Allan, I should surely die."

That Coralie seemed to have vanished as completely as his broken dream of love, and in her place reigned this fair, young, imperious beauty over whom men raved.

As for Coralie, she glanced past him with indignant eyes.

"How dare he flirt so openly and outrageously with Inez Montstrossor?" she wondered. "Some one ought to warn Inez against wasting her time upon him. Some one should warn her that he was not free to woo and wed," she thought.

That afternoon the matter was settled in Coralie's hearing in quite an unexpected manner.

One of the young ladies on the lawn-tennis ground had asked Allan why he wore that crape band around his hat, and his answer, as he raised his voice slightly, fell with startling distinctness upon Coralie's ear:

"For the death of my uncle, and because I have lost—my—wife," he answered simply.

Coralie turned away abruptly. So that poor young bride was dead then, and Coralie felt more indignant than ever with Allan Drexel for respecting her memory so little as to flirt with Inez Montstrossor so soon.

"He who is false to one, will hardly prove true to another," she thought, her beautiful red lips curling in bitter scorn.

There was one who watched Allan Drexel with a smoldering light in the depths of her black eyes as she saw how constantly his gaze followed Coralie, and that was Inez Montstrossor.

"May Heaven have mercy on the girl if I find that my suspicions are true—that he is indeed in love with her," she muttered. "I would take a double vengeance upon her. I shall not only lay my plans deep to turn my aunt against her, but she shall rue the hour in which she captivated Allan Drexel's fancy. I will spoil her pretty face if I find that it is true—that he is attracted by her. I will make her an object so horrible women shall turn from her in terror, and men with a shudder. No one must come between me and Allan Drexel's love.

"I wonder if he will ask to be my escort with the riding-party?" she muttered, as she fastened a crimson rose in her bodice, and throwing the train of her riding-habit over her gauntleted arm, sauntered out to meet the group on the lawn.

Coralie was already there, surrounded as usual by a group of admirers, and Allan Drexel stood a little apart from the rest, intently watching that sweet, flushed, dimpled face framed in golden curls. How gayly she could talk to others! how sweetly those lovely lips could smile! while for him she had nothing but the haughtiest contempt, aversion and scorn.

What had he done to merit that? he asked himself bitterly. He had done nothing but love her—love her truly and dearly, given her the most devoted, faithful, earnest love that ever throbbed in a man's breast.

How dainty she looked, and peerless, as she stood there in her neat-fitting blue velvet riding-habit, and the blue velvet cap with its waving white plume that sat so jauntily on her golden curls. Allan could hardly repress the mad desire to turn and clasp her in his arms and kiss her as he passed her by, facing all the consequence, but reason prevailed.

Captain Stafford rode up, holding the pony Coralie was to ride by the bridle—a shining, glossy creature, prancing restlessly beneath the weight of the light saddle, with head thrown back, and a vicious, lurking mischief gleaming in its eye.

In a moment Allan Drexel forgot the barrier between them in the consternation of seeing Coralie about to mount the dangerous pony.

"I beg of you," he cried, springing eagerly forward and grasping the reins determinedly—"you must not ride this pony; she is not to be trusted. Your life might pay the penalty if you attempt it. You must not!"

Coralie drew back, all the bright color receding from her beautiful, dimpled face, an angry, scornful light in her blue eyes.

"I am not a schoolgirl to be dictated to, Mr.—Mr. Drexel," she said. "You have no right to do it."

He fell back as though she had struck him a blow, his handsome face paling to the lips.

"I know that I have no right," he admitted proudly. "You must not look at my words in that light. I feared only for your safety; I had no thought of dictating to you."

"Feared for my safety!" she cried, with a bitter laugh. "It is false—all false. Spare yourself all further uneasiness on my account, for I shall ride this black pony—Witch Hazel."

Allan forgot the stifled, angry words in his great anxiety for her safety.

"Do not, I beseech you!" he cried earnestly.

Her pretty, childish eyes flashed defiantly, and with a touch of all her old willfulness, she answered, spiritedly.

"If Captain Stafford, my escort, thinks the pony safe to ride, I do not understand why you interfere."

All the manly spirit in Allan Drexel's nature rose to his aid at once. He bowed his dark, handsome head stiffly, and turned away with a deathly sickness at his heart, which his set, white face did not reveal.

"How interested you seemed, Mr. Drexel," said Inez Montstrossor, spitefully.

He knew Coralie was listening, even though she had turned her golden head away, and he answered carelessly, and with a voice not quite steady:

"I am sure I did no more than any other gentleman would have done, upon seeing a young girl so willfully rash as to attempt to ride a horse like that."

"I would ride Witch Hazel now," thought Coralie, bitterly, "if I knew it would be sure death!" and gathering up the reins with a firm hand; and cresting her curly, golden head, she gave the pony a cut with her silver-mounted whip, and away she shot down the serpentine road like an arrow.

A hoarse cry rose from every throat of the group on the lawn.

"Heaven save Coralie! My God, the horse is running away!"

CHAPTER XV

❧ I Must Be Your Lover—Or Nothing

Captain Stafford had sprung into his saddle, and was tearing, like one mad, down the avenue in pursuit of the runaway pony to which poor Coralie was clinging in such terror; and Allan Drexel, and all the riding party, with faces white with fear, were scarcely a rod behind him.

A curve of the road brought them within sight of Coralie, and, with a deadly sinking of the heart, Allan saw her swaying to and fro in the saddle like a reed in the wind.

Despite the captain's endeavor, his own horse had become unmanageable and had shot down a side-path, and Coralie was left to her fate.

In an agony of fear, Allan urged his horse onward leaving his companions far behind.

Suddenly a terrible cry broke from his lips.

Witch Hazel was galloping riderless down the road, and he espied a little limp, blue figure lying, with white, upturned face, in the green grass by the roadside.

In an instant, Allan had leaped from the saddle, and was bending over her.

With a groan, wrung from the very depths of his heart, he raised her in his strong arms.

The rest of the party were far behind; there was no one to witness the surging wave of passionate grief that welled up from his heart, as he clasped once more to his bosom in a mad embrace the pretty, young bride whom he had so ardently worshiped and cruelly lost.

He could not resist the impulse of covering her white still face with passionate kisses, while the wild cry broke from his lips:

"Oh, my God! my darling is dead—dead!"

One instant more and the party was in sight—Captain Stafford following up the rear.

"Oh, Mr. Drexel, is Coralie hurt?" cried the young ladies, breathlessly, as they rode up.

"Is she hurt?" echoed the captain, as he dashed up, and sprung from the saddle, holding out his arms for the precious burden lying so still and white against Allan Drexel's throbbing breast, adding: "I will relieve you of your care now, if you please."

Insensibly Allan's arms tightened around her.

"I will relieve you of your burden," repeated Captain Stafford, flushing redly. "As her escort, I claim, of course, the right to protect her," he said haughtily, advancing closer with extended arms.

Slowly Allan Drexel unwound his strong arms from about her, but the pang that it cost him was more bitter than death.

"Yet what right had he to hold her?" he asked himself, sorrowfully.

At that instant Coralie's blue eyes fluttered wide open, and fell upon Allan Drexel's face with a smile of unutterable, childlike content; a glance which cut poor Allan's heart like a knife.

"Are you hurt, Coralie—Miss Harding?" cried the captain, anxiously, as he stood beside her, looking eagerly down into the lovely face.

Coralie shook back her golden curls with an impatient, forced laugh.

"Hurt? No!" she answered. "The fall only stunned me. I was determined to ride Witch Hazel. You shall help me mount again, and I shall ride back to Rathstone Villa none the worse for the Witch's naughty prank."

Against this Captain Stafford protested most vehemently, but Allan Drexel never opened his lips.

"He does not interfere. I was mad to think for a moment that he cares. My life or my safety is less to him than the roadside daisies he crushes so ruthlessly beneath his heel."

Allan and Inez Montstrossor had cantered rapidly on, and the captain could not help noticing how Coralie's wistful glance followed them with such a brooding, shadowy pain in their blue depths.

He bit his mustached lip savagely; all the jealousy of his nature was aroused.

"How desperately Miss Montstrossor is flirting with our handsome friend, Allan Drexel!" he remarked. "She should be careful, lest she finds her match there, for Drexel ought to be labeled the greatest of flirts."

And after he had uttered this rude, malicious speech, the captain had the grace left to feel just a little bit ashamed of himself for speaking so.

Old Miss Montstrossor was greatly worried when she heard of Coralie's perilous adventure, and that the girl had actually ridden the pony home again.

"It might have cost you your life," she declared, earnestly.

"It would not have mattered much," returned Coralie, wearily; and she added bitterly, under her breath: "I wish the pony had killed me—anyhow *he* would not have cared."

"It would have mattered very much to me, child," said Miss Montstrossor, laying her hand on the bowed, curly head.

All that night Coralie tossed restlessly on her pillow. Oh, what a cruel blighting of love's young dream hers had been.

Now she and her false lover—the man who had attempted to dupe her with a false marriage—had met again as strangers under one roof.

Of all the pitiful stories she had ever read—of all the sad poems—none were so sad as the story of her own life.

And yet she realized that she could not tear the deep-rooted love for him out of her heart. False, cruel though he had been, she loved him still.

Allan's attention to Inez Montstrossor, too, filled her with the keenest pain. They seemed to be always together—he was always Inez's escort during their rides and rambles. He wore her flowers, and hung enraptured over the piano while she sung tender, sentimental songs. All this was bitter indeed for Coralie to witness.

She never imagined all this was enacted for her benefit.

Inez' sharp eyes had long since discovered that handsome Allan Drexel smiled upon her only when Coralie was near.

"Can it be that he likes her?" she mused; "if so, why does he hold aloof from her so strangely? There is certainly a mystery here, and I will solve it," she muttered. "I have reason to hate the girl, now, if it is true that Allan Drexel cares for her—he, the only man I could ever love. I—I would almost be tempted to—murder her. I will settle the matter this very night."

On the afternoon that Inez Monstrossor made this resolve—ay, in that very hour—quite a little incident was transpiring in the rose-garden that lay back of the villa.

This was Coralie's favorite spot when she wished to spend a quiet half hour by herself, and thither she had gone this afternoon; and Captain Stafford, who had been patiently on the watch to find her alone for a week or more, eagerly followed.

Coralie had brought a book of poems with her, but she could not read—a dark, handsome face was between her and the printed page, and she laid down the book in despair.

She was looking out dreamily and thoughtfully over the roses, when she became suddenly conscious that some one was standing by her side; and, glancing up with a start, she saw—Captain Stafford.

She rose abruptly, not caring to have a *tete-a-tete* with the captain.

"Do not go just because I have come," he entreated. "I beg of you to sit down again. I have followed you here purposely, because I have something to say to you. I feel that I must speak to you or die."

She starts back and looks at him with a white face, her little hands trembling nervously.

She knows intuitively what is coming, for there was just such a look on Allan Drexel's face when he had proposed marriage to her.

But before she could utter one word of excuse to leave him, he had sprung forward, clasping her hand, pouring forth such a torrent of love that simply bewildered her.

"Don't, Captain Stafford!" gasped Coralie, piteously; "don't speak to me so. You must not love me, indeed, you must not."

"It is beyond the power of mortals to control the love that fills our hearts, Coralie," he replied eagerly. "Love is fate, and I would not help loving you were it even in my power to do so."

"I have no heart to give you, Captain Stafford," she replied, in a low voice.

"Tell me this much!" he cried, pale to the very lips. "Do you love any one else, Coralie? Have you a lover?"

She turned her face away as she answered:

"No."

How could she tell him that she was a forlorn creature, cast adrift on the world, cruelly deceived by the man she loved and trusted so blindly?

"Then why can you not love me?" asked the ardent, impetuous lover. "I love you—be my queen—my bride, sweet Coralie. Do not turn away from me; let me know my sentence; is it to be life or death? Your silence gives me hope. I am mad to love you so," he continued. "I love you with the whole strength of my soul, the whole fire of my heart," he went on eloquently. "From the first instantaneous glance I had of your sweet face I knew that I had met my fate, and I vowed to myself I would woo and win you if I could, or go down unwedded to the grave."

"Oh, Captain Stafford!" cried Coralie, earnestly, "I am sorry, but it can never be. I—I would love you if I could, but I cannot. I can realize what unreturned love is like, and believe me, I pity you——"

"You need not pity me," he answered. "I want no pity. Death from your hands would be sweeter than life from another's. Do not play with my heart, Coralie; I cannot bear it. Be patient with me if I have startled you so suddenly that you have not had time to measure your own heart's love."

"I am sorry, but we can never be anything more than friends," she answered gently.

He drew back, his face paling as he looked at her.

"I must be your lover or nothing, Coralie!" he cried, his voice husky with bitter disappointment. "There can be no such thing as falling back on 'friendship' when love has once entered the heart. Could I look into your eyes, feel the thrilling touch of your little hands, and be satisfied with simply your friendship? No, a thousand times no!

"If you favored a rival, Coralie, think you there could be any such thing as friendship between that rival and me? No, again! I should be his bitterest foe, were he my own brother. Such a deep, passionate love as mine is utterly selfish.

"No matter what the poets say, no man who has loved can ever be satisfied with friendship. Give me some hope, Coralie; tell me my love has not been given in vain."

"Oh, it can never be, Captain Stafford," she faltered. "Hate me—pity me—learn to forget me. I—I cannot deceive you, I do love another, and as deeply and hopelessly as you love me."

CHAPTER XVI

❧ I Will Show Him My Heart Is Not Broken

"You—love—another?" repeated Captain Stafford, white to the lips, and staggering back as though he had been struck a heavy blow.

"Yes," answered Coralie, gently; "and it has been the one aim of my life to tear that love from my heart—to learn to forget."

"But you have not succeded?" he asked, in a husky voice.

"I trust so," returned Coralie; "for he whom I loved can be nothing to me"—and those words brought great comfort to the captain.

He drew nearer to her, bending his fair, Saxon face over her little white hand.

"I cannot give up so readily the one bright dream that has brightened my existence—the hope of winning you at last," he said. "Take time to think this matter over, Coralie, remember how well I love you. I would give my life for you."

There was a sound of coming footsteps—he had no time to say more. Looking through the branches, he saw Inez Montstrossor and Alice Lee—one of the young lady guests—approaching.

"I cannot stay here and listen to their gay chatter," he said huskily; and bowing once more over Coralie's little white hand, he turned and hurried abruptly away in an opposite direction.

Coralie sat quite still on the garden bench where he had left her.

"How strange that love should be so unequally distributed," she mused. "Those whom we could love, fate destines we are not to get, and those who love us, we do not appreciate."

Like the captain, she did not care to listen to gay Alice Lee's merry speeches, particularly as Inez Montstrossor was with her. She drew back among the foliage until they should pass—quite unobserved, as she thought, but Inez' quick eyes had discerned the slim figure, and she had recognized Coralie, and it occurred to her to put into immediate execution a plan she had long since cleverly concocted in her scheming brain.

She stopped short—so near Coralie that she could have reached across the rose-bushes and touched her where she sat.

"It is to be kept quite secret for the present—that is Allan's wish," Coralie heard Inez say, "but I cannot help telling you, Allie—you and I have been such good friends always. Isn't it a beautiful ring?" she added, drawing a flashing diamond from her finger; "see, here is Allan's name and mine, intwined in a true-lover's knot. You shall be my chief bridemaid, Allie," and as Inez spoke she threw her arm lightly around her companion's waist and drew her down the path and out of Coralie's sight and hearing.

When Alice Lee could recover her breath—through astonishment at Inez changing the conversation so abruptly from what they were talking about as they came down the path—she turned to Inez in wonder:

"What in the world are you talking about, Inez?" she demanded blankly; "are you hinting to me that you and handsome Allan Drexel are engaged to be married, and that you want me to be a bridemaid?"

A fit of laughter broke from Inez' red lips.

"You goose, you—didn't you see through it when I pinched your arm so slyly?" she asked, still laughing immoderately. "Why, just as we reached the tallest rosebush," she went on, "I espied one of those old busybodies sitting on a bench on the opposite side; the spirit of mischief prompted me to say that—just to see if it wouldn't be known by everybody at the villa within the space of an hour."

"Then you are not engaged to Allan Drexel, Inez?"

"Didn't I say I wasn't?" replied Inez, impatiently.

"But what if it gets to Allan's ears?—that you said that—what will he think?" pursued Alice Lee.

"He would laugh at my mischievous joke, of course," said Inez.

Alice Lee thought no more of the matter then, but there came a day when she looked back to that time, and remembered the occurrence but too well.

For some minutes after the sound of the two girls' footsteps had died away, Coralie lay upon the green grass where she had fallen when those fatal, false words smote her ear.

There was no one near; no one heard the bitter cries that welled up from her heart to her white lips, and startled even the birds in the green branches above her head.

"He is going to marry Inez," she moaned. "I thought I would not care, but, oh, I do— I do! Oh, Heaven, how I wish I could die and end this wild, gnawing pain at my heart! But I must not sink under the weight of this pitiful blow!" she moaned. "Allan must never know that my heart slowly broke in my bosom when I head he was to be married. No, no! I must be brave! I must trample down my grief though it kills me? Other young girls should do that, why shouldn't I? I will with Heaven's help—yes, I will! Why should I care for one whose heart is another's, and who never wastes one poor thought on me?"

In her desperation a sudden thought occurred to Coralie.

She sprung from the ground and dashed the tears from her blue eyes with a very trembling little white hand, her face half shaded by the golden curls, whiter still.

A mad, reckless resolve had shaped itself in her mind, which she would rue to the end of her life, but she was too excited to count the cost now.

With swift-winged feet she flew across the lawn to the archery grounds where she knew she was pretty sure of finding Captain Stafford.

She sees him leaning carelessly against the trunk of a tree, and crosses over to where he stands, places one little white, fluttering hand on his arm, and whispers hurriedly while she has the strength to do it:

"I—I—have changed my mind, Captain Stafford. Take me—save me from myself! I am yours—if you—still want me!"

"Want you!" echoed the captain, so overjoyed that he really wondered whether or not his ears were deceiving him. "Oh, Coralie, my darling, can you really mean it? You will never realize how madly I love you. If each heart-throb could speak, it would tell its own eloquent story—that I would live for you, or I would die for you! My whole life will be spent in trying to make you happy!"

He raised her little white hands and kissed them, murmuring that "no being was as happy as he."

A shrill little laugh that sounded somehow like a sobbing cry broke from Coralie's red lips, but the impetuous lover never thought of this, so great was his joy.

The very strength of the passionate love she had evoked frightened and dismayed her.

It was well for the captain that he did not dream of the truth—that Coralie had sought his protecting love only through pique.

In less than an hour every one at Rathstone Villa knew of Coralie's engagement to Captain Stafford.

The intelligence was a horrible shock to Allan Drexel. He was with Inez Montstrossor when he heard of it, and his handsome face paled to the hue of death.

He could scarcely restrain the impulse of striding forward, facing Coralie, and crying out:

"Coralie, my little bride, you are mine. No other man must clasp your hands, or talk to you of love."

Then like a cold, chill wave came the remembrance that she was free from him—

freed by her own will—free as air to love whom she chose. He had no right to interfere, he was less to her than a stranger.

He forgot that Inez Montstrossor was clinging tenderly to his arm, smiling archly up into his eyes, and rallying him upon the whiteness of his face, and the sighs that broke unconsciously from his lips.

He neither saw nor heard her.

"Why did fate bring me here?" he was asking himself, bitterly, "face to face with her. If it were not cowardly I would leave at once. It would torture me to madness to remain under the same roof with her a fortnight and witness their love-making. It would end in a tragedy, I am sure."

Congratulations were in order, of course, and as Coralie entered the drawing-room that evening, each one of the young gentlemen present came gracefully forward with some pretty compliment.

Allan felt that he must not hold aloof, it would excite comment, he advanced mechanically and held out his hand.

"I have come to say good-bye, Cor——"

He stopped abruptly, extending his hand.

"I have heard the report that you are to marry Captain Stafford. Is it true?" he asked.

"Yes," answered Coralie, striving desperately for composure.

"I hope you may be happy," he responded, huskily.

For one brief instant their eyes meet as their hands clasp; her chill little, unresponsive fingers are cold as snow as they fall away from his clasp.

For one wild moment the thought flashes across her mind to fall down at his feet and cry out:

"I am to marry him, but, oh, Allan, my first love—my only love—my heart is yours!"

But she dashes the spell from her with a superhuman effort.

"Let me remember the foul wrong he has done me!" she cried out to her tortured heart. "Let me remember how he duped and deceived me, lured me on to destruction by his dark, cruel beauty, and tender, winning voice. And let me remember, too, how he cast me off to go and wed the heiress. What did he care for my agony when he sent his messenger to tell me the truth that I, who believed myself a bride, was no wife? Let me show him that the heart he trampled upon, with a smile upon his handsome, false lips, is not utterly broken."

In a moment all the pride of her nature was aroused.

With a proud, haughty gesture that was wholly foreign to the pretty, fond little Coralie whom he had loved so well, she turned from him to join the gay group standing around the piano; even in that moment the lines of an old poem come back to him:

> "Sparkles the dew and shines the river,
>   Glitters the tear in the lily's bell,
> Two are walking apart forever,
>   And wave their hands in a mute farewell."

"Yes, I may as well leave at once," Allan mutters, huskily, stepping out onto the moonlit porch. "I love Coralie so well I cannot see her smile on another and endure it."

He had muttered the words aloud, and they reached the ears of some one standing in the shadow of the heavy silken curtains.

That some one was Inez Montstrossor. She clutched her hand tightly over her heart.

"I thought so before, now I know it," she hissed. "It is well that the girl is going to marry Captain Stafford. If she had come between me and Allan Drexel, her life would have paid the price of it—even now, I think she loves Allan Drexel best."

CHAPTER XVII

❧ "I Would Kill You and Myself before I Would Give You Up"

"He could not see Coralie smile on another and live," muttered Inez Montstrossor to herself furiously. "Those were his words, and every time I look into the girl's pink-and-white baby face I shall remember them and hate her for it."

"Although Allan Drexel had made up his mind to leave the villa at once, his host would not hear of his taking his departure until after the fancy-dress garden-party which was to take place two days later, and though much against his will, Allan allowed himself to be persuaded into remaining.

"It will not matter much. Two days more of suffering," he told himself grimly.

A marked coolness had sprung up between Allan and the handsome, debonair captain.

With the quick eyes of a lover, Captain Stafford had discerned Allan's love for Coralie; but it never once occurred to him that Allan was the lover to whom Coralie had so touchingly referred.

"You shall have a handsome dowry, my dear," said old Miss Montstrossor, laying her jeweled hand on the curly golden head. "The captain will not gain a penniless bride by any means. Have you settled yet where the cememony is to take place, and when?"

Coralie shuddered, and her face grew as white as the white rose-buds she wore on her breast.

"Do not speak of it until the last moment," she faltered, piteously. "I beg of you do not—I cannot bear it."

Miss Montstrossor turned and looked at Coralie sharply—steadily.

"One would think to hear you talk, my dear, that you were not in love with the young man you have promised to marry."

Alas! how true those words were. Since Coralie had spoken those rash words she was beginning to fairly detest the captain.

"You must always remember it requires deep, true love between a husband and wife to make a happy marriage," Miss Montstrossor went on.

There was no answer, and looking around to see why Coralie didn't reply, she saw that she had quitted the room abruptly.

"She is a strange girl," she thought, smiling. "Other young girls would have been pleased to talk of their lover, she seems to dread it. I do not understand her—that is certain."

Coralie fled precipitately down to the drawing-room, a desperate thought in her brain.

Looking hastily around she espied Captain Stafford on the porch, smoking a cigar in the moonlight.

He had strolled out on the porch scarcely five minutes after Allan Drexel had left it, and Inez Montstrossor still stood in the shadow of the heavy-draped curtains, making up her mind as to whether she should join the captain or steal noislessly away unseen.

When she saw Coralie enter the drawing-room and cross the floor toward the porch, she concluded to remain where she was. Inez was not above playing the part of eavesdropper.

"Now I will see for myself if my suspicions were correct," she muttered, straining her ears to catch every sound.

Very swiftly Coralie crosses the room and stands by the open French window, so near the hidden listener that Inez fancies she must hear her heart beating, it is beating so loudly, but Coralie does not hear. Her thoughts are by far too confused for that.

"Captain Stafford," she faltered, stepping timidly out into the moonlight.

He turned in a flash, flung away his cigar, springing eagerly forward with outstretched hands.

"Coralie!" he exclaimed delightedly.

She drew back timidly, and in the white, bright light, he could see how pale her pretty, dimpled face was. Even Inez from her screen behind the heavy folds of lace curtains noticed it.

"Captain Stafford," faltered Coralie, timidly, "I have something to say to you, that is why I am here."

"Why, you are shivering, my darling!" cried the captain, bending low and kissing one of the pretty, death cold hands that lay on the heavy railing. "Come into the drawing-room or the library beyond."

"No, let us stay here," said Coralie. "I like the moonlight best."

"But you are still shivering," he declared. "Allow me to fetch you a wrap, a scarf——"

"No, no! I won't stay here long. I—I—could not take cold on such a warm evening as this if I tried. I cannot rest until I have told you, Captain Stafford, that which is in my heart. Oh, Captain Stafford, I—I—am so sorry that I promised this morning to marry you!"

He drew back as suddenly as though she had struck him a blow with that little white hand.

"The promise was given on the impulse of the moment, and——Oh, I—cannot tell you how I regret it! I have come to you to ask you to give me back my freedom."

"Coralie, I cannot believe you mean what you say," he cried. "Dear, why say those cruel things to me? They are but to test my love; my faithful love needs no test—none."

"You must believe me," said Coralie, piteously. "I mean it, indeed. I cannot marry you—it would be an irksome tie to me."

His face grew paler than her own, his eyes grew dim as though the very light of his soul had died out.

"Marriage is not an irksome tie when love goes with it," he said.

"There lies the whole matter," responded Coralie. "I have the greatest respect, the greatest regard for you, Captain Stafford, but I do not love you."

He looked at her with darkening face.

"You say you do not love me! Then why, in Heaven's name, did you not think of that before promising to marry me?" he asked sternly.

She had no answer for him; she was silent.

"Answer me, Coralie; if it was not love that prompted you to promise to be my wife, what was it?"

She could not answer him by saying it was pique.

"I—I—do not know," she replied with some hesitation. "I imagine it was because I liked you, and promised to please you."

He raised his handsome head.

"You like me!" he cried with infinite scorn. "What words are those to give me? I asked for bread and you gave me a stone. I asked for your love, not your liking. Sun and moon, heat and cold, night and day, are not more opposite than 'love and liking;' one is strong, the other weak. But I will not believe you only like me—you love me. Yes, you do!"

"I am sorry—but I—do not," she said, catching her breath with a little sob, her lover looked so angry, so desperate.

"Then you have deceived me," he cried. "You have encouraged me with false hopes, false words. It cannot be; you are the soul of truth and loyalty—you could not have done this."

"You frighten me," cried Coralie, drawing back from the white face and fierce words.

"You cannot be that most accursed of women, a coquette—fair of face and false of heart—who draw men on to propose, and after all his friends congratulate him on his happiness, fling his love back in his face. Ah, no! you cannot be that!"

And looking, she saw the swollen veins stand out like whip-cords on his forehead, and his strong hands tremble like leaves in the wind.

A great fear came over her; not pity for him, but fear for herself.

"I cannot believe you have done this vile thing—accepted me only to throw me over. Falsehood could not have so fair an outside. Have you won my heart from me to cast it at your feet to walk over it? If you have done such a cruel wrong as that, you have killed me!"

He stood looking at her, the great drops falling from his brow, his hands trembling, his face full of passion, such as in her whole life she had never seen there before.

"You have no right to speak to me in that fashion," murmured Coralie, faintly.

"I ask you a plain question," he cried; "have you purposely fooled me?"

She never forgot the face that looked into hers; the scorn and bitter anger mingled with passionate love.

"I have heard of beautiful young girls," he added, "who have used every gift that Heaven gave them, every charm, to wile the heart from a man's breast, to amuse themselves with it, and then, when the game has lasted long enough to suit their convenience, return it broken and bleeding. Did you think to do so with mine? Did you think I would submit to it tamely?

"If you had never misled me, I would not reproach you," he continued, in a hoarse, tremulous voice. "You must understand me rightly. I do not complain that you cannot love me; a lady has a perfect right to accept or reject the love offered to her.

"If this was an ordinary case, I would scorn to utter one word of complaint; but I resent it because you have led me on for this; because you have deceived and trifled with me; you have accepted me merely for the pleasure of rejecting me; to throw my love back in my face.

"What to you are the jeers of those who know of our betrothal only this morning? You have killed me in order to gratify your own vanity. You might have spared me. I feel that I am too good a man to have been the victim of a coquette's wiles."

He affected not to see how Coralie trembled, or to see the tears falling thick and fast from those lovely blue eyes raised so piteously to his face. His bitter anger and despair consumed him.

"You ask me to give you back your freedom. This is my answer: I cannot give you up; I cannot live without you. I hold you to your promise. A betrothal, in my eyes, is just as sacred and as binding as the marriage ceremony which follows. No, I will never give you up; you shall be mine in life and in death. You force me to say cruel words, but they have burned their way from my heart to my lips, and I must utter them. I would kill you and kill myself before I would ever give you up, Coralie—that is my answer."

CHAPTER XVIII

❧ "The Rival Lovers"

"Would you wed an unwilling bride?" asked Coralie, drawing back and gazing at him with dilated eyes, her face white as death.

"Yes!" he replied defiantly, flushing a little, for those eyes seemed to burn into his very heart. "I would hold you to your vow. I would marry you though you hated me. You see I am firm in my resolves, so why plead with me, Coralie?"

"I plead with you no more," she answered proudly; "but from this hour all the respect I have had for you is gone."

"Love will come after marriage," he said eagerly and confidently.

"Not when hatred and scorn precedes it," said Coralie, bitterly, cresting her golden head.

"It will be the one aim of my life to make you love me," he replied. "Surely a love so great and absorbing as mine must win love in return, though your heart is as cold as an icicle."

He had clasped her little slim, white hand, and had bent his fair, handsome head over it.

Coralie tried to withdraw her hand from his clasp; she tried to stem with one word the torrent that came from his lips; she might as well have attempted to beat back the waves of a mighty ocean.

"Even though your heart is as cold as an icicle, I will not despair of winning your love," he repeated; and the very vehemence of his passion startled her, a very flame of love seemed to glow in his face; his eyes were full of fire.

He was looking with wistful, longing gaze into her face.

"Oh, listen, my darling!" he cried. "Some men have had many loves, have worshiped many fair faces—I love only yours. I have known many beautiful women; many have smiled upon me, but your face is the only one that has ever haunted me. It is because of this, because my heart has never known another love, that I am so devoted to you."

When he paused for a moment, overcome by the vehemence of his own words, she had no answer.

Something of the responsibility attending a great love had struck her. She felt sorry for the handsome captain.

It was a strong, passionate soul, full of grand possibilities, that was laid at her feet.

"I am not asking you for the happiness of a few years," he went on; "the content of a few months. My whole life is at stake. I believe that in every heart good and evil are equally balanced. With you I should become a good man; if I gave you up it would make a fiend incarnate of me. I would go to the bad altogether, and I would not be the first man who has gone wrong for a lovely woman's sake. You would not like that laid at your door. Struggle no more against fate. You are bound to me by a solemn vow which you must not break—the marriage must go on!"

He released her hand, and without another word she turned from him and fled precipitately through the long French window into the drawing-room, and back to her own apartment.

"The marriage must go on," she moaned piteously. "Ah, well, it is part of the price I must pay for my folly in making that hurried engagement, and all through pique."

For an hour or more she paced up and down her room excitely, then her thoughts grew calmer.

"Why should I rebel against fate anyhow?" she mused. "I should be pleased to wed a man who loves me so well; but then I do not care for him. That is where the trouble lies."

There was no trace on Coralie's face of all she had gone through on the previous night, when she came down to breakfast the next morning.

Even Inez Montstrossor, as well as Captain Stafford himself, was surprised at the forced composure of the lovely face as she greeted them.

"You are just in time," chorused the young ladies, gathering around her. "Our host, Mr. Rathstone, has promised us a double pleasure for Tuesday next; as well as the garden-party, we are to have charades and tableaus.[15] It is to be a regular midsummer affair, without fuss or ceremony. Now the question we are debating over is, what shall we represent?"

"I have suggested a scene from some nice play," said Inez Montstrossor, joining the group. "Tableaus are so commonplace."

"She wants to give us that threadbare 'Romeo and Juliet' business," laughed Miss Lee. "Every one always suggests the balcony scene in that, and every one has seen it played on the stage, for it's as old as the hills. Now I think the 'Rival Lovers' would be perfectly charming."

"Suppose we represent both?" said Coralie; "both would be nice."

"I do not know as I have ever heard the 'Rival Lovers,' " said one of the girls, turning to Miss Lee. "Won't you skim over a few of the main incidents for us?"

"It is the story of a young and lovely girl who chose wealth instead of love," returned

[15]Depictions of scenes usually done by silent and motionless participants.

Miss Lee, "and who lived to rue it while her life lasted. It appears that the lover whom she first loved was not possessed of the fortune which she imagined was his, and she fled from him; and the next thing that he heard was that his fair, false love was soon to be wedded to another.

"This seemed to have driven the first lover to the verge of madness, and he brooded night and day over the terrible revenge he would take on the successful rival that had won his false love from him; he brooded over the matter until he became a monomaniac on the subject.

"At last the wedding evening rolled around, and surely a more perfect evening could not have been found to celebrate the great event. And as the story goes, when the bride was dressed for the ceremony, she stepped out on the balcony to enjoy the beauty of the night before joining her bridegroom.

"Suddenly something tall and dark loomed up between her and the silvery moonlight.

"She drew back with a wild cry—a man's white face was looking into her own—a man's hot breath was scorching her cheeks like a flame, and his horrible eyes were glaring into her soul.

"She saw it was her old lover at the first glance. Why was he here on her wedding-night, with that awful, death-like look on his face? she wondered, vaguely. She was to know all too soon.

"She was brave of heart, even as she was false.

"'Why are you here? what do you want?' she demanded.

"A laugh, horrible to hear, broke from his lips."

"'A kind greeting, surely,' he answered, 'but your question can be answered in three short words—I want you!'

"She turned from him haughtily, and he followed. Suddenly his eyes fell upon the bridal veil.

"He caught it in his hands. He tore it from her head and into shreds, trampling it under foot, stamping upon it in the violence of his rage.

"'So I would serve you, if I could!' he cried. 'So I would serve my rival—yet you deserve it more than he, for he is a victim to your wiles, as I have been.'

"She drew back as his anger increased, not frightened—she was physically too brave for that—but wondering where it would lead him to, what he would do or say next.

"You ought not to live!" he cried, 'you are a mortal enemy of man.'

"She should had cried out for help but she did not, though there were brave hearts near who would have shed their last drop of blood in her defense.

"'You are a madman!' she cried in contemptuous scorn, attempting to pass him by; but, divining her intention, he sprung between her and the entrance that led out onto the balcony.

"'If I am mad, you have driven me to it,' he answered harshly, and for a moment there was deep silence between them, broken only by the rush and roar of the dark, turbulent rapids that washed the western base of the castle—directly beneath the balcony on which they stood.

"'Let me pass!' she cried, but he reached out his hand and grasped her with a grasp of steel.

"'We stand here for the last time together,' he exclaimed, 'I, whom you call a madman, whom you have deserted and betrayed—you, the fair of face and false of heart, who have killed me. Yes, we stand here for the last time together—for you are going to die—I would far rather that you should die than wed my rival. I will give you one chance for your life: fly with me this very moment and I will spare you. Refuse, and as surely as yonder starlit sky bends above us, you die!' and as he spoke he drew her nearer to the edge of the balcony—nearer the water's brink.

"'Choose!' he cried. 'Is it to be life or death—you were mine before, you shall be mine again. If it is death, you shall not die alone, I will go with you.'

"It was too late to cry out for help then, her lips seemed frozen dumb.

"'Will you leave the lover who is waiting for you, and come with me?' he asked hoarsely.

"She shook her head.

"He dragged her nearer to the brink of the balcony, and looking down from that dizzy height they could see the sullen waters rushing past far down below with a silvery gleam.

"'Now,' he said, 'you can save your life if you will swear to go away with me. If you refuse I will fling you and myself into the river, and we shall be found there, when they come to search for the bride, drowned and dead. Take your choice.'

"She would not believe that he would carry out so horrible a threat, and again she shook her head.

"With strong arms he dragged her to the brink, and the next moment there was a terrible cry—a cry that rang over the river and through the woods, but which no one heard. There was a loud splash in the hurrying river, a hundred wide eddies that seemed to catch the light, then a deep, deathlike silence unbroken by sob or sigh. Once above the dark waters a woman's hand rose—a white, slender hand flashing with jewels; it disappeared, and the river ran swiftly on.

"The moon shone brightly all night on the river, and in the morning, when the sunlight flushed it with gold, they found her—dead, drowned—clasped close in her slayer's arms, and this was the rival lover's terrible revenge."

CHAPTER XIX

❧ Sweethearts

"A pathetic story, but the ending is horrible," declared the young ladies. "I never cared much about translations from the German, there's so much tragedy in them. Don't you think so, Mr. Drexel?" said Inez Montstrossor, turning to Allan.

His face was strangely white. No one noticed it, but the story had made a deep impression upon him.

All that night the words "he would rather die with the girl he loved than see her wedded to another," haunted him strangely, he could not forget them.

It was decided that the "Rival Lovers" would do very nicely. It was thrilling and intensely exciting to an audience.

"Mr. Drexel!" called Miss Lee, "as you are to be the master of ceremonies, you had better select who is to be the fair bride."

"Miss Harding has just the face for it," declared one of the girls.

Coralie turned away, her face flushing and paling, her heart beating.

No one must think of choosing me to play such an important *role*," she cried. "I could not do it. I should surely fail——"

"Well, then you must be cast for the principal *role* in "Sweethearts," chorused the girls, and despite Coralie's protests, she was cast for the part.

"Now then," cried Miss Lee, "who is to be Coralie's lover?"

"Captain Stafford, of course," laughed the young ladies.

All of that afternoon was spent in arranging and rehearsing the tableaus. They were very effective.

Coralie made a charming Dora, and the captain made a gallant wooer, more especially because his heart was in it.

It was certainly a pretty picture—Coralie in the bower in the stolen interview with her lover.

She sat in the most bewitching of attitudes at his feet looking up into his face.

"That will do excellently," declared Miss Lee, who had a perfect mania for tableaus. "There is just one fault, Miss Harding. Your pose is magnificent, but you do not give the right expression. Dora worshiped her lover, and you must contrive to look as if you worshiped the captain."

"Will it be so difficult, Coralie?" he whispered. "Oh, my darling, think as you look at me how dearly I love you."

"I have not the capability of worshiping," said Coralie to Miss Lee, "and I—I— really object to the kissing scene."

"You must learn," she said briefly. "Here, Mr. Drexel, you are master of ceremonies, while I drill the captain, please give Miss Harding a lesson. As to objecting to the kissing scene, what nonsense, and you engaged to the captain, too."

He came straight across the room to her; but Coralie would have nothing to say to Allan Drexel.

The evening of the lawn-party was bright and clear. The moon was at its full, lighting the merry scene with its white, bright radiance, fairy-colored globes of light swung from the trees, and gay ribbons of bunting floated on the breeze.

The guests began to arrive early, and the spacious grounds were soon crowded.

A large platform had been built, amid a leafy bower of trees for the tableaus, a heavy pair of velvet *portieres* suspended from two trees, serving admirably as a drop-curtain.

A shower of applause greeted the charades, then a murmur of expectation ran from lip to lip; the next was to be the tableau from the famous "Sweethearts," and all held their breath in expectancy.

But at almost the last moment a very extraordinary thing happened; Captain Stafford had fallen over some of the stage fixtures and had sprained his arm—or rather, wrenched it badly, and that, too, within almost a moment of ringing up the curtain.

"What shall we do?" cried Miss Lee. "There never was anything more unfortunate. 'Sweethearts' would have been the hit of the evening, and now we must give it up, I suppose."

"There is no need," replied Allan Drexel, flushing eagerly. "If you will allow me to be a substitute, I will do my very best to present the picture true to life. I—I hope Miss—Miss Harding will not object."

"It is too late to consult her now—she has no choice, I am sure, and it is more than kind of you to help us out of this dilemma, but do you know the positions?"

He knew but too well, he had watched the captain stand with his arm around Coralie—with a bitter, jealous fire in his heart that nearly consumed him.

It was not quite right, but a savage delight throbbed through his heart when he found the captain would not be able to play that part with Coralie.

"I shall be spared the pain of witnessing that," he told himself, dropping his handsome head down on his white hand, then a sudden idea seized him.

If he could but take the captain's place—ah, why not? He would barter his soul for the supreme happiness of holding Coralie for one moment in his arms—yes, he would make the attempt.

Miss Lee led him up to Coralie, and hurriedly explained the situation; and at that moment some one called her aside.

"I—I cannot go through that scene with *you*," gasped Coralie, shrinking back pale and trembling.

"You would have gone through that scene with Captain Stafford," he said hoarsely and reproachfully.

"That is different," she answered hurriedly, but before she could utter another word of protest the silver bell tinkled for the velvet curtain to be drawn aside.

Allan sprung forward and caught her in his arms, and at that instant the curtain was drawn back.

She could not struggle out of his arms—she could only stand there quite still.

To Coralie it seemed the cruelest irony of fate—by far more bitter than death.

As she stood there—clasped in his arms in a close embrace, the memory of other days came to her—and of caresses that had seemed all heaven to her. She could almost have moaned aloud at the pain those thoughts brought her.

There was a hush as the velvet curtains were drawn aside on this realistic picture—a murmur of admiration and surprise ran through the audience.

The tableau was the parting of the lover from his sweetheart in the rose-arbor close to the sea. The white waves seemed to dimple and sparkle in the moonlight, which fell upon the faces of the two lovers clasped for the last time in each other's arms.

It was little wonder people held their breath as they gazed upon the handsome, impassioned face of the lover. There was something almost sublime in the adoring love that lighted up his dark, kingly face as he bent over her.

If this was acting, what could the reality be they asked themselves in wonder too great for words.

But as they gazed upon the face of the fair young girl their wonder grew. Her fair hair fell around her like a veil, and her face seemed to whiten under their gaze, and her lips to grow ashen pale. Was it love or horror that shone in her upraised eyes? The scene seemed to hold the vast audience spell-bound, and frightened them almost as they gazed in bewildered fascination.

The velvet curtain fell amid soft strains of music.

It had been a terrible strain upon Coralie's nerves. The golden head fell backward, and her clinging arms fell from her lover. A cry of dismay broke from Allan Drexel's lips as he loosened the clasp of his strong arms, she reeled forward, and without a moan, without a cry, dropped in a dead faint at his feet.

"Oh, my God," gasped Allan, "she has swooned!" and he fell upon his knees beside her, calling loudly for water.

He was glad this was the last tableau; he could never have gone through another.

The gay waltz music struck up in another part of the grounds, and the joyous guests were soon whirling away in the merry measures of the dance, little knowing what had transpired behind the scenes.

When Coralie recovered from that deathlike swoon, she found Miss Lee bending over her, laving her white brow with cooling water.

"What caused you to faint?" Miss Harding, she asked in wonder, eying the lovely rosebud face that was now as white as it would ever be in death.

"I suppose it was the heat," murmured Coralie, "or perhaps the strange, stage-struck sensation you were telling about yesterday—feeling myself the cynosure of all eyes."

As for Allan Drexel, he was pacing up and down in a lonely part of the grounds, his heart on fire, his pulses throbbing.

All the old love had sprung up into his life again, a thousand times more passionate than before.

"And I am to lose her!" he cried fiercely. "She is the captain's betrothed bride; but like the rival lover of the story, I feel within my heart that I would rather see her dead than belong to another. It cannot—it must not—by Heaven, it shall not be! Once mine, forever mine!"

> "Oh, night! did you say
>   My love had grown false to me?
> That her vows like a breath passed away,
>   As the blossoms fall from a tree?
> Was it the wind said: 'Thy love is gone?'
>   False wind, thou wert never true!
> The whip-poor-will plaints for the dawn—
>   Poor soul! was your love false, too?"

CHAPTER XX

❧ A Cry in the Night

The garden-party was a brilliant success, but Allan Drexel scarcely remembered how it passed.

Coralie had recovered from her slight indisposition, and had returned to the grounds gayer than ever, even Captain Stafford looked at the flushed cheeks and feverishly bright eyes in wonder.

There was no more dancing for Allan; even the sweet strains of music sounded harsh and discordant to him. He left the merry revelers, and wandered down to the river that flowed through the lower portion of the grounds, dimpling and sparkling under the golden light of the stars.

When the fire had died from his veins, and the hot fever from his brain; when his heart beat calmly, and that terrible leaping was gone from his pulse, then he would think.

When Coralie was clasped close to his heart for one blissful moment, all the old pent-up love that he believed crushed and dead thrilled like an electric shock through his being, and he realized the truth—he loved her still—

"Loved her with a bitter yearning that would never pass away;
Loved her with a bitter yearning that would never know decay."

Standing there, with the echoes of the dance-music floating out to him, the story of the "Rival Lovers" recurred to him and seemed to haunt him.

Perhaps he, above all others, knew what the man suffered who had preferred that the woman he loved should go down to her death rather than to his rival's arms. Was he not suffering from the same cause? And would not the same tortures possess him on Coralie's wedding-day?

He dared not think of it; it drove him mad. And he wished again, for the twentieth time, that he had not been induced to remain for the garden party; it had but reawakened the old love in his heart—reopened the old wound.

He left the villa the next morning before any of the guests were astir, leaving his adieus to be made by his host.

He could not endure another day beneath the same roof with Coralie and Captain Stafford.

"Gone!" muttered Inez Montstrossor, when she heard of his departure. "Then Rathstone Villa holds little enough attraction for me from this time forth."

On the following day the little party broke up, Coralie and Miss Montstrossor returning to New York, accompanied by the devoted captain.

It had been settled that the wedding was to take place on the tenth of September, and it wanted but a fortnight to that time now.

The decorators were busy preparing Miss Montstrossor's elegant Fifth Avenue mansion for the all-important occasion, and the modistes were busy with that portion of Coralie's wardrobe which had not been ordered from abroad.

Already the elegant *trousseau*[16] had been received from Worth, and it was such a marvel of beauty it would have made any other young girl's heart flutter with delight.

But Coralie turned suddenly away, her eyes dim with tears.

"Oh, what a mockery this marriage will be!" she cried bitterly to herself, with a bitter sob.

"I do not believe my young mistress cares much for the gallant captain, though she is to marry him," declared Annie, Coralie's maid, down in the servant's hall one day. "When he sends bouquets, no matter how costly they are, she lays them down on the table, and there they lie until they wilt and die. If she cared for the captain she would care

[16]The personal possessions (clothes, accessories, linens, etc.) of a bride.

for his flowers. And then," went on Annie, thoughtlessly, "I am afraid she won't be any too happy with him."

"Why should you prophesy anything like that, I should like to know!" retorted the housekeeper, sharply.

"Because," declared Annie, "the almanac says there is to be rain on the tenth, and that is Miss Coralie's wedding-day, and you know yourself about the old adage which says, 'unhappy is the bride the rain falls on.' "

"Although I am not so superstitious as to put any faith in signs, still I should be better pleased if the sun shone on Miss Coralie's wedding-day," responded the housekeeper, slowly.

"And then there is another bad omen about Miss Coralie losing her betrothal-ring on the very day the captain placed it on her finger," continued Annie. "They say that those who lose their engagement-ring, never marry their lover, or if they do, some awful tragedy follows close on the heels of the marriage ceremony."

"I will not believe such things!" cried the housekeeper, angrily. "You make me nervous—make my blood run cold with hearing such uncanny things."

"Anyhow—believe it or not—the truth is the truth. Just watch and see how it turns out for yourself!" retorted Annie, as she quitted the room.

The fortnight rolled quickly around, and brought with it the tenth of September at last.

It was late when Coralie opened her eyes.

No one would have guessed that the bride-elect had spent half of the night in bitter, passionate tears.

Annie stood close by the lace-draped couch with a cup of fragrant chocolate in her hand.

"You looked so tired, Miss Coralie, I—I hated to wake you, although this is your wedding-day," said Annie, apologetically. "You moaned in your sleep the whole night through."

Coralie turned her face to the wall with a dreary sob! Her wedding-day! How strange it was that this should be her wedding-day.

Other girls always looked forward to such an event as the greatest epoch in their lives.

They would have been up with the break of day, their cheeks flushed, their eyes bright as stars, eagerly watching for their lover's coming, listening for his footsteps and the sound of his voice.

She only wanted to turn her face to the wall and forget that this was her wedding-day; but she must not give way to her gloomy fancy.

Annie was looking at her with curious eyes. She must not awaken her suspicion that she was not a happy bride.

There was to be a large gathering of guests, and although the ceremony was not to take place until nine in the evening, considerably before that hour the guests began to arrive.

Such an odor of orange blossoms, such fluttering of white dresses and rustling of silken robes; such sweet, silvery laughter and pleasant voices as floated through the mansion.

One heart was cold and heavy enough; on one heart the gay laughter fell like drops of hail, and that was Coralie, the beautiful bride-elect. As the hour for dressing drew near at hand, she grew faint even unto death.

"Heaven help me to go through the ceremony," was the prayer that rose to her heart.

Those who attired her wondered at the bride's white face; even the sight of the magnificent wedding-dress brought no smile to it. When the veil was thrown over her head, and the orange blossoms on her brow, she shuddered as though they had been robing her in a shroud.

"Is that rain tapping against the window-pane, Annie?" she asked suddenly.

"No, ma'am," answered the girl; "but it has been threatening rain all day. I don't think the storm will set in, though, much before midnight, when the wind changes. Won't you let me put a little rouge on, Miss Coralie.—you look so frightfully pale."

There was a tight clinching of the white hand, and a flush that died away, leaving still greater pallor on the lovely face.

"No, no!" she answered, waving Annie aside. "I will step out on the terrace; the cool wind will bring back the lost roses—and—and—revive me," she muttered.

"Do let me go with you, Miss Coralie," the maid pleaded anxiously. "You—you—look too ill to go by yourself—indeed you do!"

"I shall go by myself," said Coralie. "Call me when the clock strikes the half hour. I shall be sitting on the bench beneath the oleander-tree."

Oh, if Annie had but followed and saved her.

Ah, if the night-wind or sighing trees could but have warned the fair, young bride of the fatal tragedy which was to follow! but it did not.

With swift steps Coralie fled down the spiral stairway at the back of the house, through the conservatory to the garden beyond, and threw herself, sobbing wildly in the abandonment of her grief, upon the garden bench, beneath the drooping pink blossoms of the oleander-tree.

Hark! was it the night wind that rustled the leaves of the branches close at hand?

No; it was a face—a man's face; white and wild and haggard—that was thrust through them, and a pair of burning eyes that might have scorched her very soul, rested on her countenance.

She might have heard the wild, horrible laugh, such as a madman might have uttered, that was instantly hushed on his lips.

With swift tread he moved toward her.

Another moment a wild, terrible cry rang out on the night air.

"Help! Help! For Heaven's sweet mercy, spare me!"

Then the cry was instantly stifled, but no one heard or heeded.

Five minutes later, Annie came hurrying down the path.

"Miss Coralie, Miss Coralie," she cried, "you have forgotten your wrap! The dew is falling—you will ruin your white slippers as well as your dress and wedding-veil—"

She had reached the rustic seat beneath the oleander-tree.

No Coralie was there.

Again she called loudly, but there was no answer.

Then her quick eyes discerned something lying in a white heap on the grass close by the path.

In an instant it was in her hands—one glance—then a wild, horrified cry burst from her lips; it was Coralie's wedding veil, and the wreath of orange-blossoms crushed and torn in a shapeless mass.

Beautiful Coralie, who was to have been a bride within the hour, was gone!

CHAPTER XXI

❧ "Where Is the Bride?"

It was a moment of intense suspense; the girl's heart beat loud and fast—the cry that she uttered seemed to die in her throat.

Within, all was laughter, mirth and music—without, a tragedy had been enacted, and that within sound too of the assembled wedding guests.

Beneath the blossoming oleander, ground deep into the pebbled path, was the bridal-veil—torn into shreds; the wreath of orange-blossoms lay a little further on, trampled into a shapeless mass.

What could it mean? where was the bride?—only the nodding roses, the waving branches, and the startled birds who had witnessed what had transpired, could have answered that question.

"Miss Coralie!" she called again, in a weak, unsteady voice, waiting breathlessly for an answer. None came.

She turned and fled precipitately into the house—rushing almost into the arms of Captain Stafford, in her headlong haste.

He had a bouquet of rare white rosebuds in his hand, and was hurrying swiftly toward Coralie's boudoir.

"Captain Stafford," she whispered, timidly laying a detaining hand on his arm, "I was just coming in search or you, and—oh, Captain Stafford, I have something to tell you, and I scarcely know how to begin."

He wheeled around and looked at her, but as he caught sight of the white, terrified face, the frown of impatience deepened on his handsome countenance.

"Well, be quick about it, my good girl," he answered; "I haven't but a moment to spare, Coralie will be waiting for me."

"It is of her I wish to speak," she replied, sobbing out afresh. "Oh, Captain Stafford, there is something dreadfully wrong, and I—I—am afraid to tell you what it is."

"Something wrong! For Heaven's sake what can you mean, girl?" he cried hoarsely, springing forward and clutching her shoulder in a vise-like grasp. "Is it anything about your young mistress? Why don't you speak?"

She nodded, and in a few broken gasps had told him the whole story.

He drew back, pale as death itself—in a flash that scene that had happened on the porch at Rathstone Villa recurred to him—he remembered how Coralie had pleaded with him to give her back her freedom.

Had she destroyed herself?—thrown herself into the river to avoid this marriage? he wondered.

The greatest consternation prevailed when the announcement was made to the guests that the lovely bride-elect had disappeared.

And grave fears were entertained for her safety. It might be that she had wandered away under temporary mental excitement; if not, it was certainly a case of foul play.

A few moments later Annie went up to Miss Montstrossor's room to break the awful news to her.

She found the old lady walking up and down the floor in great excitement.

Like one turned to marble she listened to the maid's story of Coralie's mysterious disappearance.

When she had quite finished, a horrible laugh broke from Miss Montstrossor's lips.

"Gone! is she?" she cried shrilly; "well, well, this is gratitude for you—and I trusted the girl so, and she has abused my confidence at last.

"Look!" she cried, sweeping back the velvet curtains from an alcove between the long French windows, which disclosed an open safe. "That has been rifled—the money I kept in it is gone—every dollar—and all my jewels!"

The maid looked from the safe back to Miss Montstrossor's angry face in horror.

"Surely you don't think—you don't think——"

"I think that Coralie has stolen my money and jewels and fled—yes, I do!" she cried shrilly. "No one but she knew that I had just received a large sum of ready money and had it by me—or knew the combination which opens the lock of the safe.

"She could not stand the temptation of seeing money about without appropriating it, it seems. I had intended that princely sum to give the girl as her dowry; but then, it pays one, once in a while, to stand a little loss to find a person out. I had so much confidence in her," she went on, dropping into the nearest seat, and covering her face with her hands, "and this is the end of it all! Ah, who shall one trust in this world?"

The sound of subdued voices down below recalled her to a sense of her duty—she must go and disperse the guests, and seek Captain Stafford and tell him all.

He listened in wonder and dismay as Miss Montstrossor repeated to him all she had told the maid.

"I can scarcely believe this, madam," he answered, huskily. "She has treated me shamefully, deceived me outrageously, but I cannot think she would take that money."

"Generous, deluded lover!" sneered Miss Montstrossor. "No doubt if an angel shrieked it out trumpet-tongued from heaven, you would not believe it."

"No, that I should not," he admitted, frankly. "I can believe that she fled from me rather than marry me, but that she took one cent belonging to another—never! So fair a face could not hide a heart so treacherous—no, no!"

Inez Montstrossor heard of Coralie's flight and her aunt's bitter accusation with a strange, slow smile which would have been rather hard to define, and she could scarcely conceal her triumph when Miss Montstrossor sent for her the next day, and vowed to her that now *she* should be her heir, and *not* Coralie, who should be found and punished for what she had done, as surely as the sun shone.

"You have found out that strangers can be much more treacherous and cruel than relatives by bitter experience, aunt," declared Inez.

In the heat of Miss Montstrossor's passion, she stumbled over the same rocks she had stumbled over once before.

She made a new will, cutting Coralie off without a cent, and leaving everything to her niece, Inez.

She was old and near-sighted; she did not observe the gleam in the girl's black, restless eyes.

On that very night Inez herself superintended the making of her aunt's coffee.

"It is very bitter," said Miss Montstrossor, fretfully. "You must learn to make it as Coralie used to make it. I—I miss her so!" she muttered, not so low but what Inez' startled ear caught it. "If Coralie would but come back to me, I would forgive her, money or no money."

"She mourns for that girl so much that it would be just like her to advertise for her among the personals to come back, and she would be forgiven gladly; and, worse still, she is quite liable to make a new will again in favor of Coralie, but that must never be—never!" muttered Inez.

That night the cup of coffee Miss Montstrossor was so fond of taking just as she retired seemed more bitter than ever, and again she bemoaned Coralie's loss.

The next morning Miss Montstrossor was unable to leave her couch, and despite the efforts of the young and inexperienced doctor whom Inez called in, she failed rapidly, and a fortnight later she breathed her last, and the will was read, which bequeathed to Inez Montstrossor every dollar of her entire fortune.

But where, during all this time, was Coralie? If the earth had opened and swallowed her she could not have been more completely lost to the world.

Every effort human mind could suggest had been put forth by Captain Stafford and his friends to find her, but it was all useless.

And while this search was going on Allan Drexel—happy, laughing, handsome Allan—grew to be almost the shadow of his former self—white, nervous, morose, and haggard, shunning the world, startled at every footstep. What had come over him? his friends asked themselves in wonder.

No one thought of connecting him in any way with the disappearance of beautiful, hapless Coralie on her bridal eve—for no one knew of that past in which they had been all in all to each other—before "love's young dream" had been so cruelly blighted. Captain Stafford from that moment never looked kindly on a woman's face. He lived but for one aim now, but one thought—of finding Coralie and forcing her to keep her solemn pledge.

He grew morose and hard of heart. There was a complete and terrible transformation in the handsome captain.

The words Coralie had uttered—"I will not deceive you; I loved another, but fate parted us"—came back to him now with startling clearness.

He had not the least doubt but what she had eloped with her old lover, of whom she had once briefly spoken, and the thought tortured him to madness.

"I would follow them to the ends of the earth and separate them, if that were the case!" he muttered grimly. "No other man shall have Coralie's love and live; I swear it!"

It was a reckless, desperate oath, and it led to cruel results.

At the end of the third day of Coralie's disappearance, a new idea occurred to him—why had he not engaged a private detective to ferret out Coralie's whereabouts? Strange that he had not thought of that before.

He engaged the most skillful expert the bureau boasted of, and at the end of a fortnight the man confessed that, for the first time in his life, he was completely baffled; one by one each carefully concocted theory and trail was given up.

For the first time in a life of thrilling and varied experience, the detective could find no tangible clew by which to discover the whereabouts of beautiful, hapless Coralie.

CHAPTER XXII

❧ "I Want Something to Fill Up My Life"

"Was there any one who would be likely to be benefited by Coralie's death?" the detective had asked, and then he heard the story of Coralie's position with the late Miss Montstrossor, and how beautiful Coralie had stood in the way of the niece possessing the fortune of which old Miss Montstrossor was possessed.

The detective, Mr. Dent, listened patiently to all this, making no comments, but asking presently of the captain:

"Has there ever been any love-making between Miss Inez Montstrossor and yourself?—did she ever show any preference for your society?"

"No," replied the captain, wonderingly, "none in the least. On the contrary, the lady is, as far as I can see, quite desperately in love with a Mr. Allan Drexel.

Mr. Dent made a note of the name.

From that moment every movement of Allan Drexel's was carefully shadowed, and no one was better cognizant of this fact than Allan himself.

Six weeks of patient watching by night and by day, and then Mr. Dent came to the conclusion that the trail was a false one.

During the long surveillance Allan kept up bravely, but when he found he was no longer an object of careful scrutiny, his habits of life changed strangely.

He would absent himself from his usual haunts for days at a time. Where he spent those days no one knew—no one could find out. When he returned he was pale as death, worn out body and soul.

One day he met his old physician. "Allan, my boy," he said, looking in wonder too great for words, at the handsome, haggard face, "you are working too hard with the business of the mill. You must rest, I tell you."

"Rest!" the very word was a mockery to him. His heart beat with great, painful throbs, every pulse seemed to have the force and strength of a steam-hammer, the blood ran like fire through his veins. Rest! Why, every nerve shook. It was with difficulty he controlled himself. A fever of something very like madness was upon him.

He heard his friends discuss the most mysterious disappearance of beautiful Coralie, who within the hour was to have been Captain Stafford's bride, and he made no comment, vouchsafed no opinion, he was strangely silent.

No one accused Coralie of taking Miss Montstrossor's money, for the fact of the money and jewels being missing was known to but three persons, Captain Stafford, the maid, and the detective.

The great strain of mental excitement which Allan Drexel was laboring under began to tell at last.

One morning he was unable to leave his bed, and when the old family doctor was called he found him suffering from a severe attack of brain fever.

"It is a dangerous case," said the old experienced nurse, who had been called in to attend him, to her pretty young daughter.

"It would be a sad pity if he should die," replied her daughter Jenny, "he is so young, so rich, and so handsome."

"The rich have to die when God calls 'em, as well as the poor," retorted her mother sharply.

His handsome face appealed to young Jenny's heart, and she pleaded earnestly with her mother to be allowed to help nurse him back to health and strength.

"You might be falling in love with him," said her mother, mistrustfully; "and the rich young owner of the Drexel Silk Mills is not for a poor girl like you."

"Indeed, I should not be falling in love with him," replied Jenny, turning away her head, a guilty blush mantling her cheek, which might have warned her mother that the mischief was already done.

So, on the strength of that, Jenny was allowed to rerelieve her mother at intervals in watching beside Allan Drexel's couch.

One morning a note was handed into the detective bureau from Jenny—who had been a constant reader of the newspapers—declaring that the fate of beautiful Coralie, whose mysterious disappearance had been the theme of so much comment, could be revealed at last!

The detective lost no time in repairing to the house where Jenny lived.

He was met at the door by the grim-faced old nurse, whose face deepened into a deep and terrible frown when she learned his errand and his request to see her daughter.

"You may see her," she replied grimly; "but not one word concerning this matter shall pass her lips."

"Surely," cried Mr. Dent, "you would not have her remain silent on a vital subject like this, over which the whole country is agitated?"

"I, being Jenny's lawful guardian, refuse to allow her to speak," declared the old nurse.

"The ends of justice must not be foiled in this manner!" cried the detective, furiously. "Woman, your daughter can be forced to disclose the whereabouts of Coralie Harding, if she knows it, and whether the girl be living or dead; the law can compel her to speak!"

"I never yet heard of a law which can compel a woman to speak against her will," replied Jenny's mother. "As my daughter's guardian, I speak for her when it comes to that. You may make me talk, but I have yet to hear of a law which compels one to remember."

Coaxing, pleading, arguing even in the name of justice was fruitless.

The detective left her in a towering rage, muttering to himself:

> "When a woman will, she will, you may depend on't;
> And when a woman won't she won't so there's an end on't."

No inducement could make the woman speak, as she had emphatically declared, against her will.

Even trembling Jenny's lips were sealed, and that same afternoon the old nurse informed the detective that her daughter Jenny had left the city for good.

Of course he knew that the girl had been spirited away, but that knowledge availed him but little.

From that day the old nurse never allowed any one to remain long alone beside Allan Drexel's couch, and the bitter ravings he uttered during the ravages of delirum fall upon her ears alone.

It was long weeks before he was up and about. He had refused to take medicine, declaring, as he turned his face to the wall, that he wanted to die. But the death he longed for so ardently would not come to him.

The time came when he was able to be up and out, but life had lost all charm for Allan Drexel.

Once more he took his place among the world of men, but he was a ghost of his former self. A beautiful face haunted him; before his vision shone ever the gleam of golden hair, and a pair of soft, appealing eyes, like wood-violets steeped in dew, until the picture almost drove him mad.

One morning a note was brought to him from Inez Montstrossor, inviting him to call and expressing the warmest sympathy for his long and serious illness.

When she saw him she cried out in wonder, he was so changed.

Very adroitly she brought the subject around to Coralie's mysterious disappearance. She saw him start suddenly and turn deadly pale; by a great effort he regained his self-control.

It was maddening to him to sit calmly by and listen to Inez Montstrossor's theories regarding the missing bride-elect's whereabouts, and how Captain Stafford mourned for her.

And as Allan Drexel listened, something very like triumph shot through his heart at the thought: The captain would find her to claim her never again; she was lost to him forever.

Inez Montstrossor watched him narrowly as she spoke about Coralie; only the whiteness of his face betrayed his intense interest in the subject.

"How well he, too, loved that girl!" she muttered with passionate hate. "And I would give my life, almost, for half the love wasted so uselessly upon her. I will win him if I can; if I fail, I will take a terrible vengeance upon him," the beauty muttered in a cold, hard voice after he had gone.

"I know how I can bring him to my feet. Yes, I know how," she added with a strange laugh.

Despite all her efforts, Allan Drexel seemed hard to win.

"I will be patient and not despair," she told herself. "Surely my beauty must win him sooner or later."

One morning, in looking over the personals, she read among other paragraphs that Allan Drexel was soon to sail for England, intending to take an extended tour abroad.

The paper fell from her hand, and a low cry broke from her lips.

"If he goes, I must go with him as his bride," she cried out excitedly. "I cannot—I will not lose him!"

Inez was just about to send for him, when Allan put in an unexpected appearance to bid her good-bye.

"How long shall you be gone, Allan," she asked with pitiful eagerness and something like a sob in her voice.

"I don't know," he replied; "for years in all probability. Inez, I want something to fill up my life."

There was profound silence for some minutes, and when she spoke again, Allan would scarcely have recognized her voice. Tears sprung to her eyes and her face paled.

"Are you sorry, Inez?" he asked in wonder.

She turned away, burying her face in her hands.

"Why should I withhold the truth?" she sobbed. "Yes, I am sorry you are going, Allan. The sunshine of my life will have set in deepest gloom when I see your face no more."

CHAPTER XXIII

❧ "Will You Learn to Love Me"

It suddenly burst upon Allan's astonished senses that Inez Montstrossor loved him.

How she must love him—this proud, beautiful, imperious girl—to be sobbing over his going.

What horrible impulse was it that prompted him to take a seat on the velvet divan beside her, trying to draw the little jeweled hands away from the tear wet face.

"Is parting with me so hard to bear, Inez?" he asked kindly, his heart moved to the tenderest pity.

She clung to him sobbing:

"Death would be easier to contemplate."

He looked quite distressed, and his looks certainly did not belie his feelings.

"I did not know that my coming or going mattered in the least to any one," he answered distressedly, continuing impulsively: "If you care so much for me, Inez, my life is yours. I cannot deceive you by making any false pretenses. I admit candidly I have no heart to offer you, but if you are willing to trust your happiness to me without love, my wasted life is yours. I will try to make you a good and true husband."

To the day of his death Allan Drexel never forgot the look of startled happiness on the lovely face.

"Will you ever learn to love me, Allan?" she whispered, clinging closer to him.

"I will do my best," he answered honestly. "No man can promise more."

"I accept you, Allan," she murmured, "for I love you to."

He did not clasp her in his arms, raining passionate kisses on her face, trembling with delight at those sweet words, as he had done when little Coralie uttered them.

"Will you tell me about her whom you have loved, Allan?" she asked. "Tell me about your past life."

"I would rather not speak of it, Inez," he answered hoarsely. "Heaven knows I am doing my best to forget it. The torture of remembering is driving me mad."

"At last! at last!" murmured Inez, when he had left her; "he is mine. I will make him far happier than any one else could have done.

"He loves Coralie," she added; "for the second time that girl crossed my path, but he will behold her face never again."

And the very thought of Coralie's beautiful, pathetic face roused a very demon of jealousy in her heart, for she loved handsome, debonair Allen Drexel, with all the love her southern heart was capable of.

A love that would not hesitate at a crime to sweep a rival from her path.

Allan walked back through the starlight to his hotel thoughtfully enough.

He had asked Inez Montstrosser to marry him on the impulse of the moment, and now he was regretting it with all his heart; but he was a gentleman; he must marry her, he told himself.

Then he thought of the warning the old nurse had whispered in his ear, when he rose from the couch on which he had tossed for so many days in the ravages of brain fever.

"It was well that no one save myself and Jenny were at your bedside, sir," she said, "for you muttered strange things in your sleep."

His face had paled to the hue of death itself.

The thought occurred to him now—would Inez ever discover the dark, awful secret that was buried in his heart—making life but a living curse to him?

For hours after he reached his room he paced up and down his room, crying out.

"Coralie, oh, Coralie, my darling! Heaven have mercy upon me—I am going mad— and yet," he cried, incoherently, "I would rather you lay dead in your bridal robes than see you married to Captain Stafford, Coralie."

He looked at his haggard face, which the long French mirror reflected, and was startled at its wildness.

"I am haunted by my horrible secret, even in my dreams,"·he murmured with a shudder; and again he bowed his handsome head on his white hands, crying out that the dark secret buried in his breast was eating his life away.

Then he grew recklessly desperate again—what mattered it what his future was like—whether he lived or died—whether life went on in the same groove, or if he went to the bad altogether?—it was of little consequence to him.

What had come over handsome Allan Drexel, his friends asked themselves; but no one could answer that question. Not one of them dreamed that a secret sorrow was eating his life out.

Night and day a beautiful dimpled face rose before his mental vision; and he would rush madly from solitude into the crowded thoroughfares—amidst mirth and revelry— crying out:

"Heaven help me to forget you, Coralie—I am going mad!"

While the detectives were searching for her—while Captain Stafford was mourning for the bride so cruelly lost to him in the very hour he was to claim her—and her mysterious disappearance was being discussed in every paper—there was one who could have solved the deep mystery and revealed her whereabouts—*that one was Allan Drexel!*

The arrangements for Inez Montstrossor's marriage to Allan Drexel went steadily on—it was to be a quiet affair and a very hurried one, owing to Allan's prior arrangements to go abroad.

Yet this quite suited Inez—who seemed to have a decided objection to its becoming known.

Yet the news of it did leak out, careful as she was to conceal it.

It was chatted about among the servants, and it came to the ears of a dark-browed man who had managed to secure for himself a situation to look after the furnace, but who always managed to keep well out of Inez Montstrossor's way.

"So your mistress is really to be married?" he said to her maid one day; "and soon, I suppose."

"It's to be early next week," replied the maid, with a toss of her yellow curls, "and a handsome young man she's to get, too."

The man's brow darkened.

"Where do they go on the wedding-trip?" he asked sharply; "do you know?"

"Of course I do," the girl answered, with a laugh, "for I go with them—my lady wouldn't leave he maid behind. We go to Paris direct."

"Do you know how long you stay abroad?" he asked.

"Miss Inez says we may never come back."

A fierce oath broke from his lips.

"I—I beg your pardon, miss," he said hurriedly. "I was thinking of something else—something of great importance. I hope you won't mention this to your mistress, it might cost me my place, you know."

"Oh, I sha'n't mention it, if you promise not to so offend again," retorted the maid, with a toss of her yellow braids.

The promise was readily given.

"So my beautiful Miss Montstrossor thinks to outwit me, does she?" he muttered, under his breath; "but she will have to look pretty sharp to beat Robert Sinclair. I should like to see Drexel duped by the beautiful fiend, curse him; but before she leaves this country I have a little account to settle with her.

"She told me to come here on the twentieth—cunning plotter—when she expected to be wedded and away by the tenth. I have always thought she needed watching. There is nothing like getting into the house and into the servants' hall to find out what is transpiring in my lady's boudoir."

That night a note came for Miss Montstrossor by the evening mail.

One glance at the envelope which the maid handed her, and a suppressed cry fell from her lips.

She opened it with hands trembling with excitement. It contained but a few words, which were as follows:

"Inez,—Come to Central Park to-morrow afternoon at three. I shall be standing at the main entrance watching for you. If you are wise you will not fail me.

"*Yours in great haste,*
"*Robert Sinclair.*"

Dismissing the maid from her presence, Inez Montstrossor gave vent to the wildest passion of ungovernable fury.

"But a few days more and I should have been safe—safe," muttered the beauty, tearing the letter into a thousand fragments and grinding it into the lilies of the velvet carpet with the heel of her bronze satin slipper.

"I suppose I shall have to go. I can imagine what he wants and what he will have to say. My God! how I tremble when I think how completely that wretch has me in his power. If he should reveal all to Allan Drexel, I would be ruined for life."

It was three o'clock to the minute on the following afternoon when a close cab drove up to the main entrance of the park and a slim figure, heavily veiled, emerged from it.

Robert Sinclair stepped forward.

"You are here promptly, my dear Inez," he said with a leer; "you know better than to disappoint me."

As he leaned forward Inez Montstrossor detected the odor of strong brandy in his breath.

"I am here," she answered, drawing haughtily back; "now the question is—what do you want of me?"

"Come and let's sit down on the bench by the lake and I will tell you," he answered.

"What if I refuse?" she answered imperiously.

"If you would marry Allan Drexel—knowing what you do—you dare not refuse what I ask. Come, no airs with me, Inez!"

CHAPTER XXIV

∼ "Nothing Shall Stand between Me and His Love"

When Coralie had reached the rose-garden on that fatal wedding night, she flung herself on the rustic bench beneath the drooping branches of the magnolia-tree, sobbing as if her heart would break.

It was so cool, so bright, so still around her; the dew was gleaming on the grass, the moon and stars were shining in the sky; there was a rich odor of rare flowers; the night wind seemed to cool her heated brain; the burning sensation left her hands.

"I can remain here but a few minutes more," she murmured, "for Captain Stafford will be coming in search of his bride; within the hour I shall be his wedded wife; my lips must smile while the bitterness of death is in my heart. No one must know that the prayer of my very soul is: Oh, Heaven! be merciful—let me die here and now, and end it all."

A step sounded on the long grass, a shadow fell between her and the moonlight, a man emerged suddenly into the path and stopped before her—a man with a face wild and pale, and eyes shining like burning stars.

In the first quick, startled glance she recognized him.

"Allan Drexel," she exclaimed, starting to her feet, her heart throbbing, her eyes dilating, her face paling.

"Yes, it is I—Allan Drexel," he answered, with a horrible laugh; "the man you have so cruelly deceived—whose life you have wrecked and blasted most infamously. I am come to see the last act of this farce played—I am here, an uninvited guest at the wedding banquet. I could not stay away—the desire to look upon your fatally fair, false face once more was greater than my will power to resist." And again a horrible laugh fell from his lips.

Coralie sprung to her feet trembling with emotion. This, and from *him!* How dare he add insult to injury thus?

She created her beautiful golden head and turned haughtily away.

"Allow me to go," she cried, drawing her silken skirts away and attempting to pass him by.

"Not until you have heard all that I have to say, and answered a few questions that I have been longing to put to you. Yes, I will have the truth at last. You must answer me. I am a desperate man. You shall tell me why you fled from me, or this wedding does not go on."

"You are mad," she said coldly.

"If I am mad, it is you who have driven me to it," he cried. "No, you shall not go— you shall not leave me until you have answered me," he declared, catching at the thin bridal veil.

She stepped backward—the thin veil tearing in twain, and falling with the wreath of orange-blossoms at his feet.

They had been standing at the very brink of an old well, which no one thereabouts knew the existence of, even, it was so overgrown with shrubs and tangled creepers.

With that one fatal step backward, the earth seemed to open and swallow her.

One cry came from her lips as she fell—a low, smothered cry; and he, standing there, paralyzed with horror, heard after what seemed to him an endless interval, the sound of a heavy body falling into the waters of the old well—a dull, heavy splash, then all was still.

Only one minute before she was standing before him full of youth, strength, beauty, and life; the next, she had been hurled to an untimely death, and the fault was all his— all his.

"Help! oh, my God, help!" he cried.

But his voice did not penetrate to the interior of the grand mansion where mirth and merriment was at its height.

He tried to reach the house, but his limbs failed him, and he fell on the ground utterly unable to move.

He was paralyzed with dread, with anguish that had no words.

The horror of that awful splash had almost driven him mad.

"She is dead!" he said to himself. It was too fearful to realize, too dreadful even to understand.

Lying prone on the ground, powerless to move or stir, he cried out to himself that he was the cause of her death—he who would have given his life to have saved her.

It was terrible to see how he crept to the brink, looking over it, calling upon her name,

"Oh, Coralie, darling!" he cried, "I cannot live without you! I will not!"

In another instant he would have followed his love down into the dark shadows of death, but Heaven interfered; for at that moment the maid came in search of Coralie with her wrap.

He drew back into the shadow of a beech-tree until she should go in, but instead, she raised a great cry that brought all the guests about her.

They had missed her; he knew they would soon begin to search for her, and he realized that they must not find him prowling like a poacher about the grounds.

He gave one hurried glance around the scene which he was never to forget, then hurried away.

Before the light of another day dawned, Allan Drexel was tossing in the delirium of brain fever.

It was pitiful to hear his moaning cries for Coralie as he lay tossing on his bed of pain, and then the heart-rending cry:

"Oh, God, I have murdered my darling!" would burst from his foam-flecked lips.

This was the startling story the nurse's daughter Jenny would have revealed to the detective had not her mother spirited her away.

She had nursed handsome Allan in his infancy; she had seen him grow up to noble manhood; she could not, she would not, believe that his hands were stained with blood.

She would not believe he had anything to do with spiriting away the beautiful young girl of whom the papers said so much.

When Allan awoke to consciousness and found that long weeks had elapsed since Coralie's disappearance, bitter, heart-rending groans broke from his lips.

Should he reveal her resting-place after this late date? he asked himself, brooding over the matter by night and by day.

Only Heaven knew the agony the thought cost him.

He knew that the wells in that locality were supposed to be bottomless; the body in all probability would never be found. Why, then, not keep the secret of his darling's fate locked up in his own bosom?

What wonder, then, with this horrible secret weighing him down, making life a living curse to him, that handsome Allan Drexel should grow taciturn and morose, and so haggard and dispirited his friends feared for him.

It was quite a surprise to them when his engagement to Inez Montstrosser was announced in the society journals.

"A beautiful girl, that I grant you," said one of Allan's friends to a companion, "but as heartless—if report be true—as woman well can be. She has been so much worshiped for her mavelous beauty that she considers the life of every man she meets her lawful prey."

"She has very little trouble in winning them. A gleam from her splendid black eyes, a touch of her white, jeweled hand, a whisper from her musical voice, and the hearts of men go out to her. All that her victims win in return are a few smiles, a few *tete-a-tetes,* a week's fidelity, and then they have to make room for another. I am heartily sorry she has drawn Allan Drexel into her net. He is too good a man to marry a coquette."

"Allan would not thank you for your advice; better leave affairs of the heart of other people quite alone," advised his friend.

"I predict that it will be a most unhappy union," declared the other, stopping short on the street to light his cigar, and taking little notice of the tall, slim, graceful figure of a woman, heavily veiled, who halted also, as if waiting at the cross-walk for an up-town car, but in reality catching eagerly at every word that fell from their lips.

"Allan Drexel does not love Miss Montstrossor," the gentleman went on; "any one can see that. And, with the absence of that very essential element—love—what he is marrying her for will always be one of the unrevealed mysteries to me."

The slim figure moved on, her face ghastly white beneath her veil.

It was Inez Montstrossor.

She clinched her jeweled hand until the rings made great indentures in the tender flesh.

"Even strangers notice that he does not love me," she muttered, with a bitter laugh;

"still, I would rather be his wife—though he hated me—than any other man's wife, even though I were idolized. It is such love as mine that ends in tragedies."

The time was coming all to soon when those words would return to her with startling vividness.

When Allan called that evening, she observed his actions keenly; he did not meet her with a smile; he did not part from her with a kiss, and she his betrothed bride.

"It is quite true he does not love me," she decided. "Still he shall be mine; other women have won their husbands' love after marriage. I shall not despair of winning Allan Drexel's; that shall be the one hope, the one aim of my life."

CHAPTER XXV

❧ Coralie's Fate

It was on the following day Inez Montstrossor kept her appointment with Robert Sinclair at Central Park.

It was galling to her pride to be obliged to obey, when he proposed they should stroll through one of the by-paths and sit down on one of the benches to talk matters over.

"I should be pleased if you would tell me what you want?" she cried angrily. "You must understand the time has long since passed when I will come at your beck and call."

"What do I want?" he repeated, with a shrill laugh that was not pleasant to hear. "What do you suppose I want, my dear?"

To torture me, were the words that rose to her lips; but she was too wise to utter them, and she answereed evasively:

"I cannot imagine."

"Then I will inform you!" he answered harshly. "I am here to find out what you mean by putting off seeing me until the twentieth, when on the tenth you expected to leave here. A cunning little plot it was, I agree; but you should have learned by this time, it is not so easy to make a dupe of Robert Sinclair.

"If you had given me the slip, the world is not so wide but I should find you, and when I found you, I should take a terrible vengeance upon you!" he cried furiously, a terrible fire leaping into his eyes.

"You are mistaken if you think I fear you," replied Inez Montstrossor.

"I have you in my power, my beautiful Inez. You cannot play fast and loose with me. I am not a man to stand that sort of thing. Remember, I hold too many secrets of yours for you to think of throwing me over. If it came to that, I would go to Allan Drexel and confess all."

A stifled cry fell from her lips.

"I would say to him," he continued. "Beware of this woman you are about to wed. She has no more the right to the name Inez Montstrossor than I have. The story I could tell would sound more thrilling than a novel."

"Hush! in Heaven's name, hush!" she cried. "Some one may be within ear-shot. Some one may hear."

"It is well to refresh one's memory by going over the main points of your story once in awhile!" he cried, with a laugh.

She saw it was madness to attempt to reason with him.

There was but little use of trying to argue with a man maddened by wine.

"I could tell him of the clever scheme laid by you and me to answer the advertisement of old Miss Montstrossor for her niece—whom she believed still lived, and whom she had not seen since her infancy—and how you—a poor sewing-girl—carried out the plot successfully of foisting yourself upon her as her niece.

"I would tell him how fate laid out the work of check mating you by sending Coralie across the old lady's path to inherit her fortune.

"And last, but by no means least, how you came to me one day with the daring proposition to break into the house on the night of the wedding, and steal the bag of gold that was to be given the bride as her dowry."

"And the fact that you carried out that little affair prevents you forever from divulging it," returned Inez, triumphantly.

"But there was another which followed on the heels of it which I took no part in, and that was old Miss Montstrossor's death, on the day following the making of the new will in your favor. Ah, now you turn pale, my dear. No wonder!"

"Surely you do not suspect——"

"I really suspect she was put out of the way, my dear, and by you!"

"It is false!" she cried furiously. "How dare you intimate anything of the kind!"

"There is no limit as to what I may dare do," he answered. "It would be better to temporize with me, my dear."

"What do you want—what do you expect," she cried in a frenzy of rage, "for keeping silence?"

"The time was when I would have answered: your love, my girl. Now I answer, money. You have all of old Miss Montstrossor's money; you must either marry me or divide your fortune with me. That's fair, isn't it?"

She grew deathly white, the fire in her eyes amazed even him, it was of such a tigerish, greenish glare.

"You know I cannot share my fortune with you, why ask it? Be reasonable; say a few hundred dollars, and you shall have it," she said, speaking calmly with a great effort.

"Either half of Miss Montstrossor's fortune or nothing," he replied roughly. "By 'nothing' I mean, if you refuse me, the whole of it will go to its proper owner, for you shall never keep one dollar of it."

She gave a great gasp, and sat down on the nearest bench, trembling like a leaf.

"You cannot possibly be such a madman!" she gasped.

"We shall see," he responded. "I will give you until this day next week to raise the money. Bring it to this same spot where we are now standing. I will be waiting here."

"It is of no use telling you I cannot raise the money?" she said in despair.

"None in the least," he answered. "You can if you will."

"Give me time to think," she cried. "Yes, I—I will be here a week from to-day, and answer you then."

Robert Sinclair stood motionless in the park for an hour or more after she had left him.

"She will bring me the money; she will not dare refuse," he thought. "Then I will let the marriage between her and Allan Drexel go on, and in the midst of the honeymoon Allan Drexel shall hear from me. It will be a glorious revenge!

"I will tell him boldly to his face of the oath I made to wreck his life when he came between me and lovely little Coralie, the working-girl. And I will glory in telling him that it was I who parted them, and by the cunningest lie that ever came to a man's brain.

"I meant to hunt the girl down, but I lost trace of her," he mused. "And who can picture my amazement on entering the house to find in the bride whose wedding dowry I had planned with Inez to steal, the girl who had supplanted Inez in old Miss Montstrossor's affections, and who was to inherit her wealth—Coralie. Ah, it was a most thrilling surprise.

"Now I see a way to cap the climax of my revenge which I swore I should take upon Allan Drexel when he turned me from the silk mills—his marriage with Inez shall go on. Then he shall learn that Coralie, his lawfully wedded wife, from whom no divorce has ever been obtained—*still lives!* and that he is by this second marriage—a bigamist.

"When the prison-doors close upon him, then my revenge will be complete.

"I will go to him there and taunt him with the maddening knowledge that Coralie, whom they are searching for and all in vain—is in my power—that she is not buried in the depths of the old well, as he supposes, but still lives.

"I will tell him how I gained an entrance into the house and took from the safe the bag of gold which had been intended for the bride's dowry, and how, in hurrying through the grounds, I discovered the old well by being almost precipitated into it. I was saved from a horrible fate by catching at the wide ledge that runs around it, two feet below the surface, and drawing myself up into safety.

"It seems there was a fate in it," he muttered, "for I was just in time to witness the meeting between Coralie and Allan Drexel.

"That backward step she took would have plunged her into eternity, had I not stretched out my arm and caught her just in the nick of time. Ugh! what a horrible sound those stones made, that crumbled beneath my feet and went crashing down—down—into the depths of the dark water.

"And then to crown matters—the little fury wishes she had died—rather than have been saved by me.

"Despite her hatred of me, I like the girl; she would be free in an hour's time if she would but consent to be mine."

Hailing a passing cab at the park entrance, he was soon whirling rapidly up-town.

The cab turned into a narrow side street at length, and before a rather dingy, red-brick house which bore in gilt lettering upon a small sign outside the name—Dr. Ballon.

Robert Sinclair ran slightly up the steps and rang the bell.

It was the doctor himself—a small, dark, wiry Frenchman—who opened the door.

"Ah, good-morning, doctor," he said blandly, "how is your patient to-day. Is there no hope of an improvement?"

The doctor shook his head.

"Obstinate as ever," he said, with a laugh. "I'm afraid, sir, she means to kill herself; she openly declares she will, and we watch her constantly."

"That's right," cried Sinclair, hastily. "She must be watched carefully to prevent anything of that sort—she is just one of those high-strung creatures who would kill her-self rather than encourage the addresses of a man she hated—even to save her from cap-tivity for years—perhaps forever."

"She declares she will certainly kill herself. If there is no other way, she will starve herself," affirmed the doctor. "Really I am sorry you brought the girl here, I am indeed."

CHAPTER XXVI

❧ A Daring Game

Robert Sinclair frowned.

"You are well paid for it," he said, impatiently.

"True," returned the wiry little doctor; "but of all the women I have ever beheld, I can truly say I have seen none like Miss Harding. I am sure if we do not release her the girl will commit suicide."

Without replying, Robert Sinclair strode past him down the corridor and up the broad stairway to a sort of study and reception-room on the upper floor.

"Shall I send Miss Harding here to you?" asked the doctor, following him to the door.

"Yes," responded Sinclair.

A few moments later there was the sound of rustling skirts, and glancing up, Sinclair saw Coralie standing in the doorway.

He sprung to meet her with outstretched hands, but she drew haughtily back, with the pride of a young queen.

"Do not come near me—if you touch my hand I shall cut it off," she cried.

"So this is my reward for saving your life, my dear girl," said Sinclair, reproachfully.

"I might have thanked you gratefully for that act if you had not blotted out all feel-ings of gratitude by abducting me," she answered, bitterly. "I wish you had let me die."

"You have gone on in that way ever since you were brought here, yet I do not regret bringing you," returned Sinclair. "I have vowed no other man shall sun himself in your smiles, and I will keep my vow. You are lost to the world as completely as though you lay dead in your grave. You have sought every means of escape, but they have proven futile.

"On the day you were brought here, you succeeded in getting to the window, throw-ing up the sash, and shrieking aloud for help. What did it avail you, when you knew—for I had told you—the reputation of this place, which is well known as a retreat for ine-briates, brought under the doctor's special care? There are places in the great city of New York of which thrilling things might be written up, if the world but knew of them. But enough, Coralie—I am come to ask you for the last time if you will be mine?"

"For the twentieth time I refuse!" cried Coralie! "I abhor you—words are weak to tell how much. You may threaten to keep me here long years—you may even carry out that most inhuman threat—but my answer for all time is the same—I would *die* sooner than marry you!"

"Take care!" he replied. "You can turn, by constant demonstrations of hate, the deepest love."

"Your love or your hate is a matter of equal indifference to me," she answered, scornfully.

"I have been patient in trying to win your favor, but I shall be patient no longer!" he cried. "I will take other means——"

No answer fell from Coralie's white lips; she sat with her hands clasped in her lap, gazing dejectedly from the window.

"I leave the city to-night, and you go with me. I shall not stay here a day longer to humor a woman's whims and caprices."

"When I get into the street I shall scream for help," she was unwise enough to declare.

"Forewarned is forearmed," he replied. "I shall take good care to place that sort of thing beyond your power.

"I may as well tell you. I shall take you on board a steamer bound for London. Go willingly or not, it will be quite the same to me, my fair Coralie."

She sprung from her seat flinging herself on her knees before him.

"What have I ever done to you that you should persecute me like this from the first moment you ever saw me? See, I am kneeling to you—praying to you to spare me. Let me go my way, I can be nothing to you—nothing."

"Get up from your knees. You might as well attempt to plead and pray to that marble statue in the alcove as attempt to change my decision. You might as well realize that first as last. Neither Allan Drexel nor the charming Captain Stafford can save you from your fate."

"I will plead no more, your heart is marble," sobbed Coralie.

"When we are on the ocean I shall tell you a wonderfully interesting little story that may serve to awaken you from your dull apathy, particularly as handsome Allan Drexel is the hero of it. You were about to wed the gallant captain, but if I mistake not, your heart is Allan Drexel's still. It is not so easy to forget one's first love."

"I will hear no more," she cried, turning and abruptly quitting the room.

"I shall come for you at eight to-night. Be ready, my dear Coralie," Sinclair called out after her.

Like one driven mad, Coralie flew back to her own apartment.

"Why am I persecuted by this fiend!" she cried out, wringing her little hands piteously together. "I wonder, too, what I was ever born for; I seem to have nothing but trouble, trouble, trouble. Everything I have anything to do with comes out wrong. Everything turns to Dead Sea fruit on my lips. I would have been rightly named had they called me Coralie the Unfortunate. When love goes wrong life goes all wrong, for with love the trouble of life begins. Sometimes I cannot help thinking I must have been born under an unlucky star.

"But will he keep his promise of coming for me to-night?" she mused, pacing up and down the room, excitedly. "Once out of these walls where the shrieks of its inmates never reach the outer world with their tales of woe, and I shall breathe freer. I must think of some plan to outwit him. How Miss Montstrossor must be grieving for me, poor lady, and Captain Stafford, too."

Would Allan Drexel grieve for her too, she wondered, believing she slept beneath the waters of the old well.

Long and earnestly Coralie laid her plans to outwit Robert Sinclair when he should come for her. "I should not have forewarned him as to my intention," she murmured; "as he said, being forewarned is being forearmed."

This, indeed, proved to be the case, for, despite her desperate resistance, Coralie was taken from the dingy, red-brick house, her face so completely bound in the folds of the heavy shawl which was thrown about her as to make an outcry an impossibility.

And the hopeful plan of appealing for help to the first person she came across died in her heart.

Robert Sinclair clutched her arm in a tight grasp, as he forced her into an elevated car with the aid of Dr. Ballon who accompanied them.

Coralie tried to tear away the folds of the thick shawl, that nearly stifled her, and cry out.

"Don't attempt that or it will be worse for you," hissed Sinclair.

The car was not crowded; two or three vacant seats near the door had been chosen, and into one of these Coralie had been placed, her captors seating themselves on either side of her.

Even in New York where startling sensations are of hourly occurrence, a closely muffled young girl half lifted, half carried into a railway car by two gentlemen attracts general curiosity and comment, and Sinclair saw at once that something must be instantly done to divert suspicion from their daring game.

He could hear the conversation carried on in a low key by two strangers sitting opposite, who were regarding Coralie intently.

"I do not believe it is all right," one of them was saying. "Don't you see the appealing look of horror in her blue eyes? I cannot shake off the notion that they are saying as plainly as eyes can speak. 'Help me!'"

"Pshaw!" laughed his companion, adding in a subdued whisper: "If there was anything wrong about that affair, do you think the two men opposite would have boarded a train crowded like this? She's probably the sister or wife of one or the other.

The words suggested a bold idea to Sinclair.

"That was a long, tedious operation my sister has just gone through," he said, turning to his companion, and speaking in a voice loud enough for half of the persons in the car to hear, "but she stood it capitally; I told mother she was plucky."

As he spoke he patted Coralie on the cheek.

She shrunk from his touch as though a viper had stung her, but the villain was equal to the emergency.

"There, that's just like me, clumsy fellow that I am. I've hurt her. I'll not pat those rosy cheeks again until you get well and strong."

"Oh, the villain—the villain," thought Coralie, comprehending in an instant the bold game her captors were playing, but the wild cries would not penetrate the thick folds of the shawl; she was powerless to move hand or foot.

A strange drowsiness, caused by the sweet, unmistakable odor of chloroform which permeated the thick folds of the cloak, was overcoming her.

In vain her agonized gaze appealed to the strangers sitting opposite. She saw that the bold ruse of Sinclair had completely misled them. Would no one help her?

At the next station she saw, with the despair of death, that they were preparing to leave the car, and with them would depart her last hope of rescue from the fate that awaited her.

CHAPTER XXVII

❧ A Terrible Accident

This was perhaps the most thrilling moment of Coralie's life—the wild cry that sprung to her lips died away in a low moan that did not penetrate the thick folds of the shawl.

She realized, too, with horror words are weak to describe, that she was fast becoming powerless to move hand or foot.

A strange drowsiness was stealing over her, benumbing every sense.

In vain her agonized gaze appealed to the strangers sitting opposite. She saw that her captors' daring ruse had misled them, and her heart grew cold as death when they left the car, for, as we have said, with them departed Coralie's last hope of rescue.

With a violent effort she loosened her hands from the thick shawl, crying out:

"Help! oh, for the love of Heaven, will nobody help me? My enemy is abducting me. Help! help!"

The noise and confusion occasioned by the moving train, and the puffing of the engine, completely drowned that appeal for help.

Sinclair turned to her, white to the very lips.

"It will not be well for you to repeat this scene," he said harshly.

"I shall repeat it!" she panted defiantly. "I shall cry for help every time the train stops! I shall cry out until some one comes to my rescue."

"We shall see!" declared Sinclair, with a low, taunting laugh. "I have something here that will quiet you, I imagine."

As he spoke the suddenly pressed the shawl which he had wrapped about her still closer to her face. The strange, sweet, subtile odor grew stronger, and in spite of her valiant effort to throw off the terrible spell that was locking her senses in a horrible vise, the white lids drooped heavily over the blue eyes, the golden head sunk on her breast, and at last, pitifully unconscious, she was at Robert Sinclair's mercy.

"Well," said Dr. Ballon, "what is the programme now?"

"I shall take her to my boarding-place," answered Sinclair. "My landlady—who would sell her very soul for gold—can be induced to take care of the girl until the Servia sails. In the meantime I shall do my utmost to induce the girl to marry me. If I fail, why, she shall go with me all the same. I offer her marriage—if she accepts, so much the better."

"She is high-spirited. You will find that out," returned Dr. Ballon.

"Otherwise she would never have attracted my fickle fancy," laughed Sinclair. "She is difficult to win—therein her charm lies."

Robert Sinclair parted from the doctor at the next station, and hailing a passing coupe, was soon whirling away toward the lower part of the city.

"Now, my beautiful Coralie, you are mine—mine," he muttered triumphantly. "By this time three days hence we will be on the blue ocean, and I shall have completely separated you from Allan Drexel—it is a glorious revenge.

But his triumph was premature. No one will ever know how it happened. Whether through carelessness, or whether the driver had been drinking too heavily, there was a heavy, jolting motion, the vehicle rocked to and fro for an instant, then was whirled with lightning-like rapidity down the street.

"Great God! The horses are running away, I believe," muttered Sinclair, springing excitedly to his feet, tearing open the coupe door and thrusting his head out.

It was a fatal movement, for, before he could balance himself, the coach turned a sharp corner, and like a flash Robert Sinclair was precipitated from the vehicle, striking the curbstone with an awful thud, and on tore the coupe, dragged by the runaway horses with the velocity of the wind.

It was quite an hour before the night-watch, going his rounds, discovered the senseless form of a man lying prone upon his face against the curbstone.

He was carried to the nearest drug-store.

"It is a fatal case," declared the doctor who was summoned. "The man has sustained terrible injuries—in my opinion it will be a miracle if he recovers."

They carried him to Bellevue Hospital—where for two days he lay in a heavy stupor between life and death.

On the morning of the third day Robert Sinclair opened his eyes to consciousness, and to excruciating pain, and the first words that fell upon his ears, as some one bent over him, were:

"In my opinion he will not last the day out—do all you can, certainly, but it will be of little avail."

Robert Sinclair's eyes flashed open wide, falling upon the face of the doctor who bent over him.

"Where am I?" he muttered feebly.

"In the hospital," answered the nurse, gently. "You were picked up bruised and insensible on the pavement; when you are a little stronger you shall tell us how it happened, and who you are."

As she spoke, the nurse held a cooling draught to the parched lips.

"I shall never get any stronger," muttered Sinciair, with feverish eyes. "I heard what he said. Tell me, is it true that I am dying?—dying! Great God! I dare not die."

The nurse looked pityingly into the handsome, dissipated face—handsome still, even though cruelly bruised.

"I will have the truth!" he cried out shudderingly, in an awful voice—"the truth!"

"I am afraid—you cannot live," replied the nurse, wiping away her fast-falling tears as she spoke.

He looked up into her face with dim eyes.

"Is my time marked by days or hours?" he asked.

"I am afraid it will be but a few hours," she answered. "Is there anything you would like done for you?"

A spasm of pain shot over his face, which he turned to the wall.

"Yes," he whispered huskily, "there is. If I am really to die—there is some good I can do before the fatal end. I want some one sent for."

"It shall be done," said the nurse.

For the first time since consciousness returned he thought of Coralie—was she living—or dead?

Before he had time to ask, a cordial was held to his lips.

"Drink this," said the nurse, who was frightened at the look that had come over his face. "Then you shall tell me who it is that you wish sent for, and it shall be done at once."

He drank the cordial, and almost immediately fell into a deep, troubled sleep.

"When he awakes, I shall listen to what he has to say," thought the nurse.

It was heart-rending to stand by his narrow bed, and listen to his wild cries for pardon for some sin committed all for vengeance sake, and some atonement he must make to some one.

Perhaps, in her nervousness, the nurse might have made the fatal mistake of giving an overdose; or, perhaps the potion was too strong; for, instead of waking, as the hours rolled by, he sunk into a stupor, starting up every now and then, and crying that some one must be sent for, or two lives would be forever severed this side of the grave, which, by a few words, he could reunite.

The doctor looked down at his patient with a troubled face.

"I am almost certain he will not regain consciousness again up to the end," he said. "You should have heard what he had to say, and who it was that he wished sent for, before administering the cordial."

"I am so sorry," faltered the nurse. "I would give worlds to undo what I have done! Oh, doctor, could you not give him something to awaken him? There is some terrible secret on his conscience, I fear, and his spirit cannot go free until it is uttered!"

"I can give him nothing more," returned the doctor. "I have done everything that can be done; we must patiently watch results now."

The doctor was called away, and the nurse sat down by Robert Sinclair's bedside, white and troubled.

Slowly the minutes dragged themselves by.

There was the pallor of death on the ghastly face lying against the pillow—the breath came in short, labored gasps.

"Heaven help me!" sobbed the frightened nurse; "he is going to die with the terrible secret, that troubles him so, unspoken, and it is all my fault—all my fault!"

She bent over him trembling; the cold death-dew was gathering on his forehead, but his lips were moving.

She bent her ear to catch the sound.

He muttered a woman's name, but she could not quite catch what it was; it sounded like Cora, or Corinne.

"Heaven help me!" she cried again; "the end is drawing near."

She bent her face still closer over him.

"Listen!" she cried out, in sharp agony of remorse; "you are dying—yes, dying! Tell me, if you can, who it is you would have sent for! Use all your will-power to understand and answer me!"

A strange quiver passed over the white face over which the death-dew was gathering.

"Surely the words and meaning must penetrate that benumbed brain," she told herself.

Those were moments of great suspense.

He would not live the hour out; she could readily see that.

Slowly but surely the conviction came to her.

Even as she looked at him, he was dying with his terrible secret unrevealed.

CHAPTER XXVIII

❧ "Even Though He Hated Me, I Should Hold Him to This Marriage!"

The day set for Inez Montstrossor to meet Robert Sinclair and give him her answer as to whether she would divide half her fortune with him, or dare him to do his worst, had come and gone.

Inez had been prompt at the place appointed for the interview, but to her intense surprise, her enemy had not put in an appearance. She could not understand why. She had determined to put him off with excuses from time to time. It was not necessary now. Robert Sinclair, much to her amazement and wonder, did not seek her, did not write.

What could it mean?

She was in great fear lest he had been to Allan, telling him all; yet if that were the case Allan would come to her at once and ask that the engagement be broken; she was sure of that.

"How I love him, and how foolish I am!" she thought nervously. "I am in constant dread lest anything should happen to take him from me. It anything should," she muttered, "I love him so well that I—yes, I believe I could kill him rather than be parted from him forever, then kill myself. I do not see," see ruminated thoughtfully, "why people laugh at love, and think it weakness, or a girl's sentimental folly. It is the strongest of human passions."

She heard people speak of her marriage as "a grand match," he was so wealthy. Inez Montstrossor laughed a proud, happy laugh. She was marrying Allan Drexel for love, not for money.

The wedding was to take place at the Montstrossor Villa, a charming suburban place, just beyond Morningside Park.

As the news of the approaching marriage had leaked out, all hopes of having it a quiet one were abandoned. Invitations were sent out, and very soon the villa was crowded with young folks, who were to remain until after the ceremony, and the days flew by on rapid wings in a whirl of gayety.

Dinner parties were followed by *fetes*[17] on the green lawn, by charades and balls in the evening. The villa had never echoed with such frolicsome mirth before.

Allan Drexel plunged into the excitement with strange zest, but the bitterness of death was in his heart; waking or sleeping the beautiful face of Coralie, his lost love, haunted him.

It was the day before the wedding, and it had dawned bright and clear. Inez was expecting Allan Drexel up from the city by noon, but up to dusk he had not arrived.

---

[17]festivals

Ah! what could detain him?

Any one who saw Inez Montstrossor when she entered the drawing-room among the merry-hearted guests, would have said that she had never shed a tear or known a sigh.

No one would have believed that beneath her brilliant manner was an agony of fear.

She made appropriate answers to the young girls grouped around her, but their voices seemed afar off. Her heart and her thoughts were with Allan.

What if Robert Sinclair had sought him out and told him all! A terrible premonition seemed to weigh down her spirits; she could not shake it off.

"If anything happened now to break off the marriage, I—I should die," she told herself; she should never breathe freely until she was Allan's bride.

No one noticed Inez Montatrossor's anxiety. One moment flushed and excited, the queen of mirth and revelry, then pale and silent; with shadowed eyes furtively glancing down the broad, pebbled drive that led to the entrance gate. "A guilty conscience needs no accuser"—most truly the words were exemplified in her case.

Her face turned white when she heard the confusion of her lover's arrival.

Had he seen Robert Sinclair? Had he learned who and what she was, and had he come to denounce her for her treachery in his proud, clear voice, and declare the marriage broken off?

She dared not step forward to greet him, lest the piercing glance from his eyes would cause her to fall fainting at his feet.

She stood near the door when Allan entered, but he did not see her.

She was waiting in terrible suspense for him to call upon her name, or ask where she was, or speak some word in which she could read her sentence of happiness or despair in the tone of his voice.

She could not even catch the expression of his face; it was turned from her.

She watched him so eagerly she hardly dare draw her breath.

Allan walked hurriedly through the room, stopping to chat with this one or that one a moment; still his face was not turned for a single instant toward the spot where she stood.

Was he looking for her? She could not tell.

Presently he walked toward the conservatory, and a few moments later a servant came in search of her, saying that Mr. Drexel desired to see her immediately.

How Inez Montstrossor longed to ask if his face was smiling or stern, but she dared not.

"Where did you say he was?" she asked, simply, to gain a few moments of time to recover her composure.

"In the conservatory, ma'am," replied the man.

She walked slowly through the long drawing-room toward the conservatory.

Her heart almost stopped beating as she caught sight of Allan. He was pacing up and down impatiently.

She went forward hesitatingly—a world of anxiety and suspense on her face—to know her fate.

The color surged over her brow, then receded again as she looked at him with a smile—a smile that was more pitiful than a sigh.

"Allan," she said, holding out her hands to him with a fluttering, uncertain movement that stirred the perfumed laces of the exquisite robe she wore, "I am here."

He turned to her with a smile.

"I am a little late, Inez," he said pleasantly "but you must promise not to scold me, as you were the prime cause of my tardiness. I was waiting for the diamonds which I took to have reset for you; they were not quite completed at the time agreed upon. I had no other course left than to wait or leave them to be sent. Here they are."

As he spoke he produced two leather cases from his pocket and placed them in her hands.

"Kind fate has spared me," Inez whispered to herself. *"He has not seen Robert Sinclair!"*

The color came back to her cheeks, the light to her eyes; she drew a long breath of intense relief.

"You frightened me by staying away so long, Allan," she whispered.

She saw she had made a mistake the moment the words were uttered; he was looking at her in surprise.

"Frightened!" he repeated in wonder; "why do you say that, Inez?"

She was covered with confusion, but she looked up at him with a smile.

"Because I love you so well. When you do not come when I expect you, a terrible fear creeps into my heart that something has happened which might part us."

"What could happen?" he asked, touched at the depths of her great love for himself, and feeling profoundly sorry that there was not more love in his heart toward this beautiful girl who, on the morrow, was to become his bride.

"I—I—do not know," she sobbed.

Then she took a step nearer to him, laying a trembling hand on his arm.

"If anything should ever come between us to part us, I tell you solemnly here and now, Allan, that I should die. I would not live without you—I could not."

He laughed uneasily.

"A truce to such conversation, Inez," he said. "I must take you back among your guests—you seem strangely downcast—low-spirited. Come."

He took her hand, leading her hurriedly back to the drawing-room.

They had been standing alone together among the roses, yet he had not offered her one caress such as girlish hearts long for from their lovers; and they were to be married on the morrow.

She had hoped against hope that he was beginning to love her, but she knew at last, beyond a doubt, that it would be a loveless marriage.

"Even though he hated me I should hold him to it," she cried out bitterly, when she found herself alone that night; "even though he should see Robert Sinclair, and he should tell him the truth that I am not what I seem, and that it was my hand that sent old Miss Montstrossor to her grave, and my cunning brain that plotted the theft that was thrown on Coralie's shoulders.

"Hark! what is that?" she muttered. "Is it some one tapping on my window?"

The clock in an adjacent belfry tolled the hour of midnight, yet Inez knew no fear. She walked to the window and boldly threw up the sash; a gust of rain blew into her face.

"Only rain-drops tapping against the panes," she murmured, in great relief.

Then she anxiously scanned the night sky.

"I am not superstitious," she thought; "still, I hope it will not rain to-morrow—on my wedding-day; yet I could not believe that a few rain-drops could make or mar my future."

She sought her couch, but a fever of unrest was upon her.

"I must sleep," she muttered, "or I shall be a pale bride on the morrow."

But slumber would not come to those burning, restless eyes.

In desperation she rose at last, and, going to her writing desk, took from it a bottle filled with light, flaky crystals.

"It has long since come to this," she said with a reckless laugh. "I must be drugged to sleep."

With nervous hands she raised the vial to her lips and swallowed a small portion of its contents.

CHAPTER XXIX

❧ "I Parted You from Coralie—That Was My Revenge"

As Inez Montstrossor had feared, her wedding-day set in in gloom and a heavy fall of rain.

This quite checked the ardor of the young folks who were stopping at the villa.

"It is a cruel shame!" they cried, looking out at the terrible storm. "Inez must feel so terribly about this! I hope the old adage will not prove true in her case—'Unhappy is the bride the rain falls on.' "

All that day Inez was invisible to her guests, and as dusk commenced to gather, their curiosity to behold the marvelous *trousseau* they had heard so much about became intense.

It wanted now but a quarter to seven, and the ceremony was to take place at eight. And as the eventful hour drew near, the fury of the storm abated instead of increased.

And in the storm and the darkness, a horseman came hurriedly up to the entrance-gate of the villa, dismounted, and made his way breathlessly through the crush of vehicles to where the footman stood.

"My good man," he whispered, "I must see Mr. Drexel—Mr. Allan Drexel—at once. I hope to Heaven I am not too late—the ceremony has not taken place yet."

"It's impossible," declared the footman. "You can't see Mr. Drexel—it's an impossibility."

"I *must* see him," repeated the stranger. "It is a case of life and death. Here, take this note to Mr. Drexel. I will await his answer here."

A silver dollar slipped into the footman's hand removed the impossibility of Allan's receiving the note; and just as Allan glanced up at the ormolu clock on the mantel, noting that within half an hour's time the ceremony would begin, there was a quick, sharp rap at the door.

"A letter for you, sir," said the footman, thrusting in his head in answer to Allan's: "Come in."

Allan tore open the envelope with a perceptible frown. The folded paper within contained but these few brief words:

"Mr. Allan Drexel,—Come to me at once. I am dying. I have a startling revelation to make—and an atonement. Your marriage to Inez Montstrossor must not go on. I pray you to come to me, and without loss of time."

It was signed, "Robert Sinclair."

Allan read the crumpled note over a second and a third time.

"If it is a matter of life and death, I suppose I must go," he thought.

He gave the bell-rope an impatient jerk.

The footman was standing outside the door awaiting his order.

"Give this note to Miss Montstrossor, and say that I have gone to investigate the matter, and will have returned within an hour, and before I have been missed. And also take these roses to her," he said, handing the man a superb bouquet.

Half an hour later Allan Drexel was ushered into the room where Robert Sinclair lay dying; but as Allan entered, a wan smile stole over the ghastly face lying against the pillow, and he looked at him with dim, wistful eyes.

"You wish to see me?" said Allan, kindly, "and I am here; what can I do for you?"

The dim eyes looked more keenly at Allan.

"You have suffered," he muttered. "I see lines on your face, white threads in your bonny curls. I see signs of anguish and woe that have known no rest, no cessation. I should not tell you my secret now, but that I am dying, and the telling of it cannot hurt me. I have done many bad actions, and few good ones. I have cheated the scaffold and the law, and I will offset all this by one good deed, reuniting you—on the eve you were to wed another—to Coralie."

Allan Drexel reeled back as though he had been struck a fatal blow.

Was the man mad?

Coralie, his lost love, was lying beneath the waters of the old well.

"If you will hear all, it must be told quickly," gasped Sinclair, "my time is short. Listen: Coralie is *not* dead—she lives."

The words were magical in their effect upon Allan Drexel—he was about to speak, but Sinclair added, huskily:

"I saved her from the old well. I repeat—she is alive."

A great cry fell from Allan's lips that those who heard it never forgot.

"Let me tell my story in my own words," muttered Sinclair "I have had enough of my revenge—I am willing to forego it. I must go back to the time, Allan Drexel, when you came between me and fair Coralie. You remember the time and place—for it was on that day you first looked upon the fatally beautiful face of the woman we have both loved.

"Yes, I loved her, Allan Drexel, and as madly as man ever loved woman; and when I saw that you had won her—for quite by accident I learned of that secret marriage—I vowed that I would part you two just as sure as fate, and I kept my vow—I parted you in the very hour that you were wed.

"It is the truth, Allan Drexel, dying men never lie."

"Send for a magistrate and what other witnesses you desire. I will tell my story at once, and all may hear it."

His wishes were complied with, and when they were grouped about his bedside, he told the startling story of the past, which is already familiar to our readers.

Of the cruel plot he had conceived to get the bride-groom of an hour on board the steamer bound for Europe—leaving the beautiful, hapless little bride at his (Sinclair's) mercy—and of how the arch-fiend himself must have aided him in his plot by the secret marriage of Allan's twin-brother—whom he represented to Coralie to be Allan himself—telling her that her marriage to Allan had been but a farce—she was no wife. And that Allan was to be married to another that very night, and if she doubted it she might go and witness the marriage herself, and thus become convinced.

"She was young and artless, she believed all that I—who called upon her in disguise—told her. She fell at my feet, like one dead," pursued Sinclair, speaking with difficulty, "crying out that my words had killed her."

Allan Drexel sprung to his feet in the most intense excitement—his wonderful self-control was beginning to give way.

"Listen to me," said Robert Sinclair, "my time is short—the end is near."

"Yes, his time is short," whispered the doctor to Allan, and Allan did his best to control his emotion.

He listened like a man turned to stone, as Robert Sinclair told the story of how Coralie had gone to his brother's wedding—openly accusing him of treachery before all the guests—and had fled without discovering her mistake—fled, crying out that death itself would have been easier to bear than the knowledge of the falsity of him whom she had trusted and loved better than her own life.

"I shall not spare myself," continued Sinclair; and with husky voice he described how he had followed Coralie, laughing in triumph at the wonderful success of the dastardly plot, and how he had urged Coralie to come to his arms now that Allan had thrown her over.

If the man had not been dying, Allan Drexel would have throttled the villain on the spot—his blood boiled with indignation in his veins as he listened, and his face grew white as death.

He sat immovable as a rock as Sinclair told of pursuing Coralie, and how she escaped from him, and how he had lost track of her—discovering her whereabouts long months after, when he entered old Miss Montstrossor's house—to take from her safe a bag of gold—which was to be given as dowry to a young lady who was to wed Captain Stafford.

The daring robbery of the gold had been planned by Inez Montstrossor—whom Coralie had supplanted in the affections of old Miss Montstrossor.

He related, too, how with his booty he had fled into the garden, but, hearing footsteps, had taken refuge in the old well—how he had witnessed the meeting of Coralie and Allan Drexel, hearing all that passed, and explaining how he had caught Coralie and thereby saved her life when she took that fatal step backward, and would have been precipitated into the depths of the old well if he had not put out his arm and caught her.

And while in a deep swoon how he had removed her to the asylum of Dr. Ballon—and while there renewed his pleadings for her to become his wife.

He knew it could never have been legal—but she would never find out that she was still, as she had been from the very first—Allan Drexel's wife.

It had been a rascally lawyer engaged by himself who had instituted that proceeding for a divorce from Allan, and that she knew nothing of it—absolutely nothing.

And how Coralie had declared she would rather die than pay the debt of gratitude she owed him for saving her life, by marrying him—and how he was taking her off by force when the fatal accident happened that was to cost him his life.

"I will tell you where Coralie is," he concluded, gasping the words out with the greatest difficulty, for already the death-dew was gathering on his face, and the stamp of eternity was glazing the dim eyes.

"The driver of the cab came to see me yesterday—he says she is safe—unharmed—you could never find her unless I told you where to look for her—she is——"

Surely it was the very cruelty of fate that sealed his lips in that very moment, for with the secret of Coralie's whereabouts still unrevealed, Robert Sinclair dropped back on his pillow—dead.

CHAPTER XXX

✎ "I Will Force You to Disclose My Darling's Fate"

Allan Drexel's emotion, as he listened to this thrilling death-bed confession, words can but illy describe.

The veins stood out like whip-cords upon his forehead, great beads of prespiration rolled down his face, and his hands were clinched together like one enduring mortal pain.

"Tell me where I shall find my poor darling—my beautiful Coralie—who has suffered so foul a wrong, that it may be righted instantly, and I will forgive you all!" he cried.

But before Robert Sinclair could frame the reply that might have saved a world of woe to two loving hearts, he had fallen back dead.

Then commenced a search for Coralie that those who participated in never forgot; a week was spent in attempting to discover her whereabouts, but it seemed all in vain; every devise and project failed.

Allan Drexel was nearly wild with grief and pain.

"If I lose my darling now, when we are so near to happiness, I shall kill myself!" he declared, with reckless desperation.

On the night of Robert Sinclair's death Allan Drexel had honorably returned to Montstrossor Villa and told Inez all.

"That girl has wrecked my life a second time," she cried, "and I hate her with the bitterness of death. I hope you may never find her—never. If I should come across her first I—I should be tempted to slay her."

"Inez," he cried in horror, "your words pierce my heart like a sharp sword; I will not believe you mean such terrible words!"

"What am I to do with my ruined life?" she asked. "I am ruined—disgraced!"

"Disgraced!" cried Allan. "Oh, Heaven! that any living woman should use that word to me. I am sorry, Inez, so sorry; would that I could atone for it. You see, for yourself, I could not marry you now. I have a living wife."

She drew herself up with the *hauteur*[18] of a young queen. She raised her white bare arm as though appealing to the highest tribunal.

"Listen!" she cried. "That girl has outwitted me. She has triumphed over me. I curse her—I curse the fair beauty of her face, I would fain trample it out. She shall not triumph in the end, remember—I warn you. Sleeping, waking, eating, laughing, weeping I shall curse her, for I hate her—this girl who has come between us—with the hate of a demon."

He shuddered as he listened.

"There is one request I should like to make of you," she said, "and that is, to spare me as much as possible from curiosity and gossip. Let it be said I broke this marriage off, not you. No one need know the reason why. When you find her you can take her away and not return for long months—until after this has blown over."

"It shall be as you wish, Inez," he said, and so it was given out that at the very altar, almost, the capricious heiress and beauty changed her mind, refusing to marry handsome Allan Drexel.

There was wonder and comment at first, then people forgot it.

Inez Montstrossor plunged desperately into society—always the gayest of the gay.

No one dreamed her smiles covered a heart in which deadly vengeance was fostered.

Meanwhile the search for Coralie went steadily on—ten days had elapsed and Allan was growing desperate.

To avoid giving the affair publicity, he had refrained from putting advertisements and personals in the daily papers—it was resorted to at last.

On the evening of that day in which the advertisement appeared, a young girl called at the Fifth Avenue Hotel, requesting to see Mr. Drexel.

She was shown into the main parlor; and as she had no card, her name was carried up on a slip of paper to Allan.

"Fedora Burnhan—one of the girls in the silk mill—what can she want?" Allan mused, as he descended to the parlor.

The first words she uttered, affected him like an electric shock.

"I am here to tell you all I know concerning Coralie, Mr. Drexel," she said, and she was startled at the eager light that came over his face, for she did not know what Coralie was to him.

"Is she safe—is she well?" he gasped.

"I hope so—but I cannot tell," replied Fedora, thoughtfully. She saw him draw back, pale as death—but she went on quietly:

"Perhaps you do not know, sir, that Coralie and I were great friends—boon companions, I may say—when we were in the silk mills together. After her mother's death she suddenly left the mill—going none knew whither—and for a year and more I had lost sight of her.

"One night, some two weeks ago, as I was sitting out on the veranda of the place where I board—I was startled at seeing a coupe drawn by two coal-black horses coming down the street with lightning-like rapidity. I saw at once that the horses were running

---

[18]haughtiness

away. The carriage collided with a lamp-post directly in front of our door—and a lady was hurled violently from the vehicle to the sidewalk.

"She was carried into our parlor, where we all crowded around her to see if she was hurt.

"One glance at that face and I cried aloud, 'It is Coralie—Coralie Harding!'

"She was in a swoon, but we found she had had a miraculous escape from a serious injury. Ah, how glad she was to see me, sir, when consciousness returned. 'I will tell you all my history since last we parted to-morrow, Fedora,' she said, but before the morrow dawned a strange event happened.

"I remembered how anxious our master-workman, Mr. Richard Marshall, had been to find Coralie just after she left the mill. I sent him a note to tell him she was here. Despite the lateness of the hour, he called that evening and had a long talk with Coralie. She was not the same after that. All that night she paced the floor with bitter sobs, wringing her little hands, and crying out that Heaven was cruel to her.

"'You will make yourself ill, Coralie!' I exclaimed in alarm, 'if you take on like this. What in mercy's name is the matter, dear?'

"'To-morrow I will tell you, Fedora,' she sobbed, 'or at least the greater part of it. But first I must go early in the morning to Miss Montstrossor's; I will send for you.'

"Eagerly I awaited her return; Coralie never came back, Mr. Drexel. That has been nearly a fortnight ago. That is my story, Mr. Drexel. I saw the advertisement in this morning's paper, asking for any information concerning Coralie, and I came to tell what I knew."

Allan Drexel's emotion was intense. The last that was seen of her she went to Miss Montstrossor's. Great Heaven! could that beautiful fiend, who had uttered such fearful vows of vengeance against the poor child, have dealt foully with Coralie?

He dared not think—it would drive him mad. The terrible curse Inez had uttered came back to him with awful force.

He ordered a carriage, and drove like a frenzied being to Inez Montstrossor's residence.

The pretty maid admitted Inez' old lover with wonder, mentally concluding he had come to make up his quarrel with the heiress, and that they might have a wedding there after all.

"Is your mistress in?" he asked impatiently.

"She is out to most all callers to-day," replied the maid, "but"—with a roguish twinkle in her eye—"I think she might see you, sir."

He handed her his card.

"Say that I wish to see her particularly,' he said, his lips trembling in such agitation he could hardly speak.

It seemed to him the girl was gone an age. She came back with the reply, Miss Montstrossor would be down in the parlor directly.

A very few minutes later Inez entered the room. He sprung to meet her with a death-white face.

"Inez," he cried out, "for the love of Heaven, tell me if you know where Coralie, my wife, is!"

She drew back with a mocking laugh.

"What a dramatic scene, Allan!" she replied. "What causes you to imagine I can unravel such a mystery?"

His face grew dark and stormy.

"She was traced here, Inez!" he said hoarsely. "She was last seen alive within these doors. The butler tells me he admitted her. No one saw her depart. I ask you again, where is my wife? What have you done with my poor, beautiful, hapless Coralie? Do you deny she came here?"

The tone of his voice might have warned her not to anger him too far.

"Of what use for me to deny it, if you say she was traced here?" she answered with mocking defiance.

"Tell me her fate," he cried hoarsely; "I will know!"

"What if I refuse to answer?" she said.

"I will compel you to!" he cried. "I will force you to speak."

"No man can make me utter a word as to whether I know what became of her or not," she declared. "If I do know—and mind I have not admitted that such is a fact—I will carry the secret down to my grave with me. That will be Inez Montstrossor's vengeance against you. You shall not be happy while my heart is broken. I repeat no power on earth can make me speak. You shall never know Coralie's fate."

CHAPTER XXXI

❧ "No Oath Is Strong Enough to Part Coralie and Me"

"My God!" cried Allan Drexel, springing forward, "you cannot mean what you say, Inez! you cannot be so inhuman! Do not torture me!"

"That is what I cried out to you on the night you came to me telling me that our marriage could not be," she answered, pitilessly. "I am glad to know it tortures you; revenge is sweet, Allan Drexel."

"I will wring the truth from you," he cried. "There are ways and means!"

"Not of making a woman speak against her will," she answered, triumphantly; "and I repeat—I will take the secret down to the grave with me! You may throw me in prison, put me on the rack, but I will still be firm. I would suffer the tortures of death—do you hear me?—I would suffer the tortures of death rather than restore Coralie to you."

She turned haughtily and left him—left him standing there like a man turned to marble.

He hurried in haste to a prominent lawyer, and laid the case before him.

The lawyer shook his head sorrowfully.

"It is as she says," he answered. "We might arrest her, charge her with spiriting your young wife away, but, on such slight evidence, I doubt if we could hold her. Even if we did, we could not wring the secret from her by force."

"What am I to do, then?" groaned Allan, aloud. "My God! this suspense is killing me."

"You can do no more than continue your search with renewed vigor, keeping an eye on Miss Montstrossor. You say the young lady who called upon you at the hotel spoke of her having an interview with Mr. Marshall, the master-workman, after which she seemed greatly depressed; my advice is to see Mr. Marshall concerning the matter; possibly he may throw some light on the subject."

"How strange I did not think of that before!" cried Allan. "I will go there at once."

An hour later he was ushered into the master-workman's study.

Richard Marshall arose, pale and disturbed, to meet the young man, placing a chair for him; but Allan declined the proffered seat.

He stood by the mantel-piece, leaning with a careless grace against it.

"It is not the thing to smoke in a gentleman's study," he said, "but I must ask permission to do so. I shall derive some sort of comfort from it."

The master-workman bowed, and Allan Drexel applied himself to selecting and lighting a cigar.

Briefly he stated his errand, and begged Mr. Marshall to tell him if he knew some clew by which Coralie could be traced; for, after her conversation with himself, she had been greatly depressed.

Richard Marshall paced up and down the floor with a strangely white face.

"The hour has come when I must speak," he said. "Would to Heaven I need not, but I must!"

Allan Drexel bent breathlessly forward.

What mystery was this?

"I must go back some months," said the master-workman, slowly, "and explain what led to my seeking this interview with your young wife; and before I can fully explain, too, that which may have resulted from it.

"Over a year ago, on a terrible stormy night, as I was sitting in this very room, looking over some papers which had been sent me by the Labor League, I heard a timid, nervous ring at the door-bell.

"I answered it myself, and saw, standing out in the storm, a lovely young girl, with terrified face, and hands clasped beseechingly.

"At the first glance I recognized her as Coralie Harding, daughter of a widow who had been a weaver in your silk mills, sir, until illness laid her low; then her daughter took her place.

"I invited Coralie to come into my study, but she declined.

"'I am come to see if you will go with me to see my mother, Mr. Marshall,' she sobbed. 'I fear she is dying. She has sent for you; oh, *please* come.'"

"I did not wait for words; I accompanied her back to the lonely tenement rooms, where, as she had said, her mother lay dying.

"As I approached the couch, I saw it would be all over with the poor lady ere the morning dawned.

"'Send my child from the room,' she whispered, 'Coralie must not hear what I have to say—she must not know—at least not yet—why I have sent for you.

"'Listen, Mr. Marshall,' she cried. 'I have the strangest story to tell you that ever fell from mortal lips—so cruel, so bitter, that it will shock you when you hear it. Would to Heaven, for Coralie's sake——But come nearer—listen while I have strength to tell. Lay you hand upon that Bible, and swear to me—take the strongest oath man ever uttered—to reveal this to no one save my beautiful, hapless child after I am gone, and that, too, after I have been laid at rest.'

"I did as she requested, like a man moving about in a dazed dream.

"'And take an oath, too, that you will force my poor darling to carry out my solemn prayer, as far as it lies in her power.'

"I—I must have been mad to take that oath!" cried the master-workman, in great emotion, the perspiration trickling in beads down his cheeks, "but the fact remains—*I took the oath!*

"After the funeral, when I sought Coralie to tell her all, I could not find her. They said she had fled—and with *you,* Allan Drexel.

"I searched for her and you by day and by night. It was indeed a fate most strange that prevented me from finding you.

"I cannot tell you what an electric shock the news of her marriage with you, Allan Drexel, was to me. It almost seemed to me that God had taken fate into His own hands. I cried aloud in horror."

"Why?" asked Allan terribly moved. "In Heaven's name, I pray you, Mr. Marshall, tell me why?" he cried, laying his hand heavily on the master-workman's shoulder.

"I cannot tell you, sir," responded Richard Marshall, slowly and falteringly. "But let me add—this brings me to the present incident: some two weeks ago I was amazed to receive a letter from one of the girls in your mill, stating that Coralie was at her boarding-place—she had remembered how eagerly I was searching for her a few months ago.

"It was surely the irony of fate that made me seek Coralie—now that she was your wife—and tell her all, but my oath had to be kept.

"I can never forget the poor girl's horror as she listened, as I repeated to her, word for word, the message from the grave.

"'Oh, God, Allan, my love,' she cried; 'would that I had died before I met you and learned to love you—better death for me than the fulfillment of that oath;' and I left the poor child, weeping the bitterest tears of anguish that ever fell from mortal eyes."

"You say you dare not reveal the nature of that oath," crid Allan, pale as death. "Tell me this much—was it anything that could part Coralie and me?"

The master-workman bowed his head in assent.

Allan reeled heavily back—then he started eagerly forward, in a fever of excitement.

"Do you think my darling has made away with herself?" he asked, in a voice hardly human.

"No," responded Richard Marshall; "she is not one to take her life in her own hands."

"Then," said Allan, hoarsely, "I will devote my life to finding my darling. She is not bound by any oath to keep this horrible secret, and I will learn from her own lips whether our hearts are to be torn asunder or not."

"Yon have my warmest sympathy, sir," said Richard Marshall, "but I warn you it is best for you both to allow matters to remain as they are—to never seek her—rather to put the whole world between yon and poor, beautiful, hapless Coralie."

Allan Drexel returned to his hotel like one mad—driven to frenzy by repeated blows.

"I will devote my life to finding my darling," he cried, raising his right hand to the blue heavens, "and this mystery shall be cleared.

"I will not believe she fled voluntarily—no, her visit to Inez Montstrossor precludes such a possibility. No doubt she lies ill—dying somewhere—made ill by this horrible oath—whatever it may be, and—Inez Montstrossor knows where she is—I feel sure of it."

Another week dragged by, and he was as far from finding Coralie as ever.

He was beginning to despair, when one day he suddenly received news of her in a very unexpected manner.

CHAPTER XXXII

❧ A Deed of Vengeance

When Coralie left the boarding-house, she had, as Fedora Burnham had explained, gone directly to Miss Montstrossor's.

It had been several weeks since that fatal wedding-night on which she had been so boldly spirited away.

"Dear old lady," murmured Coralie, with tears in her eyes, "how frightened she must be, as well as poor Captain Stafford, but I will tell them the truth from beginning to end, and that I was abducted by that villain Sinclair. I suppose they thought I—ran—away."

She ran lightly up the brown stone steps and rang the bell.

The footman who answered the summons started back with a gasp as he saw her.

"Miss Coralie," he cried, "is it indeed you?"

"Yes, it is I, John," she answered. "Is Miss Montstrossor in her room?"

"You don't mean the old missis, do you, ma'am?" he gasped.

"Yes," she answered wonderingly, "who else should I mean?"

"Then you don't know?" he said huskily.

"What is there to know, John?" asked Coralie in alarm. "Is dear old Miss Montstrossor ill?"

"She is dead," he replied, "and buried long weeks ago."

A low cry broke from Coralie's white lips. She would have fallen to the floor if he had not put out his hand and caught her.

"Dead!" she cried hollowly, "oh, my God, it cannot be true!"

At that moment there was a rustle of silken skirts in the corridor above. Some one was leaning over the carved baluster.

It was Inez Montstrossor. One glance at the slender figure below, leaning so heavily against the marble Flora, and she recoiled with a tigerish cry.

Coralie, the girl whom Allan Drexel was wearing his life out searching for, who had come between her and his love, in her house, what could it mean?"

She fairly flew down the broad stairway to the corridor below, and confronted her.

"Leave us," she cried imperiously to the footman, motioning him away.

"Now," she cried bitterly, as she confronted Coralie, "will you tell me what you want here?"

Although for the moment stunned and bewildered, Coralie drew herself up proudly and answered with dignified sorrow:

"I came because I believed Miss Montstrossor was here—I did not know that she was dead—and to tell her I did not leave of my own accord that night, that I was taken away forcibly."

"A likely story," sneered Inez Montstrossor. "Every one knows better. No one doubts the story that you fled with some old lover. Now that he has tired of you—for of course such is the case—you come back here."

"Miss Montstrossor," gasped Coralie, "how dare you speak so."

"I would have you know, too," Inez went on mercilessly, "that this house is no longer a shelter for you. You are not my aunt's heir. Before she died she changed her will, leaving everything to me. Do you hear? everything that you planned and plotted to cheat me of is now mine. Go back from whence you came, I do not think any one has missed you much. Captain Stafford raged for a week, then, through pique, engaged himself to a gay Newport belle, that the world might see you had not succeeded in breaking his heart, and my lover, Allan Drexel said, 'What else could be expected of a person of that stamp?' "

Coralie's fair young face had turned from red to white as she listened.

As the last words fell from Inez' lips, she threw up her hands with a piteous cry, and fell at her feet in a deep, swoon.

Inez Montstrossor spurned the slight, inanimate figure from her with her slippered foot.

"Would to Heaven I could stamp out the fair beauty of her pink-and-white baby face," she muttered.

Suddenly an awful thought flashed across her brain—a thought that made her grow faint and dizzy because it led to a terrible crime.

In the horrible stillness a voice seemed to whisper to her:

"The girl is in your power; if you were brave enough to do it, she might be out of your way—separated forever from Allan Drexel."

The fair, delicate beauty of the upturned face seemed to madden her.

"I will do it!" she cried. "She shall not stand between me and my love."

She stepped to the door and threw it open, peering excitedly up and down the avenue.

A coupe was passing leisurely. She beckoned to the driver.

"A young lady has fainted in here," she said. "I wish her taken away; put her into your carriage as quickly as you can—I will join you at the corner and tell you the destination."

The man hesitated. Inez hurriedly drew her purse from her pocket.

"Let this be an inducement for you to act quickly," she said.

He took the bill—it was too great a temptation to resist—and lifted the slim figure in his arms, bearing her hastily to the vehicle outside.

Flying up to her room, Inez quickly donned a long circular cloak, dark hat and thick veil; stole out of the house by a rear entrance, meeting the coupe at the corner.

"I shall want to stop at the first drug-store we pass," she said carelessly, as she told him her destination.

In recalling that event in all its horror in the after days, the driver remembered that he stopped at the nearest drug store as requested, and the veiled lady alighted. When she re-entered the vehicle she carried a small package in her hand, and she was trembling as if with excitement.

Late that night Inez returned home. She succeeded in divesting herself of her wraps, and donning her wrapper ere her maid entered.

The girl drew back with a suppressed cry.

"What is the matter, Miss Inez?" she exclaimed. "You are as pale as death itself; and look, there is a stain of *blood* on your right hand."

Inez looked at the girl with frightened eyes.

"That was only your fancy," she declared, huskily. "I was putting a little red *rouge* on my cheeks. I—I—thought I looked pale—I am not skillful—I spilled it on my hand."

The maid readily accepted this explanation.

"It is on two of your lovely rings; Miss Monstrossor," she said. "If you will take them off I will clean them."

"I will attend to them myself," replied Inez, carelessly, as she turned away.

Becky must not see how her face was flushing and paling.

She went to a grand ball that night. She laughed and danced; she was the gayest of the gay. "Feverishly gay," her friends said of her. They little knew the impulse was strong upon her to cry out, the secret burdening of conscience, if she was by herself for a moment.

When she reached home, she sharply said to her maid:

"You are to sit by my couch, Becky, until I fall asleep. Pour me out a strong cordial with a sleeping powder in it—ay, double the dose to-night; I shall take two. My brain must have a little rest, or—or I shall go mad!" she cried out under her breath.

"Two, Miss Montstrossor!" exclaimed the maid, her eyes expanded in wonder. "Please forgive me for saying anything, of course you know best, but I'm afraid two powders are a little dangerous. You have been taking them ever since old missis died, and——Oh, I'm afraid they hurt you, I am, indeed."

"Do as I bid you," retorted Inez, imperatively.

The maid reluctantly obeyed, and Inez drained the silver goblet at a single draught.

The maid sat down patiently by her bedside. It had come to this; every night the proud beauty drugged herself to sleep.

With feverish restlessness the dark head tossed to and fro on the pillow for quite an hour. Then suddenly she starts up with a blood-curdling cry that makes the heart of poor Becky almost stop beating. She clutches at the maid's hand as she half springs from her couch, then cowers down among the pillows, shrieking out:

"There they are at the window, old Miss Montstrossor and Coralie. Do you hear them? They are crying out for vengeance. For the love of Heaven, do not let them in! See! they are pressing up the sash steadily, the bolt snaps, they are coming into the room."

With a gasp Inez Montstrossor sunk back on her pillow.

"There is no one outside; it is the branches of the trees swaying to and fro, which strike the window-pane; that is what you hear," said the maid soothingly.

"They are standing outside," whispered Inez Montstrossor, in an awful voice.

"I am afraid the cordial has gone to her head," thought Becky, in affright. "I will draw the curtain. The strange fancies she has makes me shiver."

She crossed to the other side of the room, stretching out her hand toward the silken drapery; and then a wild cry broke from her lips.

It had been no delusion of Inez Montstrossor's brain. There was a face at the window pressed close against the pane.

CHAPTER XXXIII

❧ "I Have Parted Them Forever— That Is My Revenge for a Broken Heart"

In an instant the room is full of servants, and in a strangled, sobbing voice the maid tells them what has happened, for Inez Montstrossor has fallen back in a dead swoon.

"A face at the window!" they all cry in a chorus.

"That's impossible. There is no balcony outside—no place for a person to gain a foothold, for the stone sill is sloping."

"It is true!" declared the girl, solemnly. "Miss Montstrossor saw it, and I saw it—a white, ghastly face, with streaks of blood across it. It vanished when I screamed."

They went out and searched the grounds, but no one was within sight.

There was no one there.

It was hours before Inez came out of her deathlike swoon—and then the gray dawn was just peeping over the eastern hills.

"Has it gone, Becky?" she cried, grasping the maid's hand, and clinging to it like a frightened child; "the face at the window?"

"There was no face!" Becky declared, wisely refraining from telling her she had seen it herself; "that must have been only your fancy, or some wild dream. The grounds were searched—there was no one there."

Inez turned away with a shudder.

"What is life worth, if I am to live in constant terror like this"—she muttered—"frightened at shadows?

"You and I are going away to-day, Becky," she added; "pack a few things quietly; let no one know."

"Is it to be a long or a short journey, miss?" asked the girl, well pleased at the thought of a trip.

"I do not know," answered Inez, vaguely. "I have not made up my mind yet as to where we shall go."

The girl looked at her in wonder.

Surely Miss Montstrossor was getting very uncanny—starting out on a journey without thinking or knowing her destination.

Who ever heard of such a thing?

"I asked because I shall know better what to pack—what you might need," said the maid. "I am going to give you notice that I intend to leave your service, Miss Montstrossor," she added suddenly; for the conviction had come upon her like a shock that Inez Montstrossor was out of her head—as crazy as a woman could well be.

"So you are turning traitor to me, too?" cried Inez, turning fiercely upon the girl. "Well, go, then! I can get along without you—you are only a bill of expense, anyhow. I got along once without a maid, I can again—at least for a few days. Here's your money. Go!"

Inez Montstrossor packed a few needful articles into her satchel, and, telling the servants that she was called hurriedly away, took a cab, and was driven quickly to the depot.

"A ticket for Boston," she said to the agent. "When does the next express start?"

It would be nearly an hour, he told her.

There was nothing for it but to wait.

The passengers in the waiting-room noticed how ghastly the beautiful face turned as she sunk down upon one of the benches.

"By this time they will have found a trace of Coralie," she muttered. "I—I—have a presentiment that it is so. I must fly from this accursed place. The memory of that girl's face, as I saw it last, is driving me mad!"

The Boston express steamed into the depot, and Inez was just about to step on board, when a hand fell heavily on her shoulder.

Starting back, she beheld a blue-coated officer of the law standing beside her.

"You are Miss Inez Montstrossor," he said. "I have a warrant for your arrest."

She drew back, white as a corpse, but she did not tremble, her voice did not falter as she asked, with the *hautuer* of a young queen:

"Upon what charge?"

"Upon the charge of abducting Coralie Drexel, better known, perhaps, as Coralie Harding."

A defiant laugh fell from her lips, a yellow fire seemed to pass over her face and scorch out all its beauty, her black eyes burned like gleaming stars.

She measured the distance between her and the slowly moving outgoing train.

If she sprung up the steps, he, being quite as fleet of foot, would follow her, or would telegraph on to the next station to hold her. That hope perished as soon as it was born.

She could not escape him; he was watching her narrowly.

"You are young," he said; "there is one thing that will save you from a prison cell, and that is to disclose here and now where Allan Drexel's young wife can be found. I would advise you to make a clean breast of it."

She looked at him defiantly.

"I would not tell you—that is, supposing I knew—if I could save my life by doing so."

"I have daughters, young like you, and quite as fair of face—for their sakes I would be lenient with you."

"I ask no mercy, no clemency at your hands or those of any one else," she answered proudly. "I am quite willing to go with you; but from this moment I refuse to utter one word, though you should put me on the rack."

"I would not believe you could be so hardened," replied the officer, as he placed her in a carriage and took a seat by her side.

She was taken to the chief's private room, but all attempts to coax or frighten the truth from her proved of little avail; she was firm in her purpose of not opening her lips to speak one word.

Allan Drexel was there, with a stern, white face. He came up to her, praying, pleading with her to speak and save herself the trouble ahead of her; but the black, burning eyes looked calmly over his head. The stony, set look never left her beautiful face—words were thrown away upon her.

"A night in a cell will bring her to her senses, I think," said the chief, thoughtfully. "We must forget her beauty and her refinement, treating her as a common criminal. With her rests the knowledge of the whereabouts of a fair young girl. She must speak and tell whether she be living or dead."

So, Inez Montstrossor, the beauty, who had broken more hearts than any other woman, whom men had worshiped and women had envied, was led to a cell, and the key of a grated door turned upon her.

All night long they heard the patter of her restless feet pacing up and down the stone floor.

When morning broke they sent for a clergyman. He pleaded hard with Inez to make a full confession as to what she had done with poor, hapless Coralie, picturing to her Allan Drexel's agony of mind, and the great sorrow of her friends.

She laughed aloud—such a terrible laugh, so full of mockery and defiance, that the minister was startled; but no word fell from her white lips. She looked over his head as she paced up and down, ignoring him completely.

He took his leave at last very sorrowfully. A heart of adamant would have been quite as impressible as Inez Montstrossor's.

That was the message they took to Allan Drexel.

It took time for a trial; days must elapse before the case would be called, and in the meantime where was his darling? Was she dying?—dead? Only Heaven knew.

No wonder he was almost driven to the verge of madness.

Experts in solving deep mysteries were detailed to search for her, but it was all useless; Coralie's whereabouts baffled them.

As the days passed, indignation against Inez Montstrossor grew to fever heat.

But there was nothing—nothing which would induce her to speak.

They might threaten her with prison for long years—they might carry out that threat, still they should never know the whereabouts of Coralie; the torture of death on the rack would not wring it from her lips.

"I have parted them forever," she would murmur to herself, as she paced up and down. "That is my revenge for a broken heart. No matter what I suffer, I know she is not with him; that he will clasp her in his arms, smile upon her, caress her never again."

On the day before her trial, her maid, Becky, came to see her. Although closely watched, she managed to whisper to the girl:

"There is a ring—an onyx ring—in my writing-desk. Bring me that—slip it to me without observation, and you shall have half my fortune."

Little dreaming what it would lead to, the girl promised faithfully to obey.

CHAPTER XXXIV

❧ "Let Me Know the Result of the Trial at the Earliest Moment"

But to return to that fatal hour in which Inez had entered that coach with Coralie.

She looked down on the lovely white face—a very fury of rage and hate stirring her soul to its depths.

When they reached the city limit Inez called out to the coachman to stop.

"This is our destination," she said curtly.

The man looked at her in utter bewilderment.

"Here!" he echoed, in amazement. "Why, miss——"

She raised her hand with an imperative gesture.

"We go to that little cottage among the trees; there is no carriage-road nearer than this—wait here for me."

By this time Coralie was beginning to revive. She opened her eyes and gazed in dismay at the dark face bending over her, and finding herself in a coach bowling rapidly along.

"Hush!" commanded Inez; "do not speak. I am taking you to your friends."

"Miss—Montstrossor——" gasped Coralie, wonderingly.

"Here we are," said Inez, as the coach stopped. "Come."

She assisted her to alight, keeping a close hold on her hand.

Coralie's senses seemed dazed—an awful blank was falling on her mind—she realized but dimly what Inez Montstrossor was saying, but followed where she was led, like a little child.

They passed down a narrow path, on and on through a dense woodland, losing the path at length, and picking their way through the trees.

No word had been spoken by Inez Montstrossor, and Coralie walked along in a stupor, seeing vaguely—yet realizing nothing of what was passing about her.

"It must be somewhere near here," she muttered below her breath. "Ah, yes, there it is."

Suddenly through the trees she had espied an old mill; toward this she hurried Coralie with little ceremony.

There had been a time when the old mill echoed with cheery voices, when the old wheel tossed the water of the spring about with mirth and glee the livelong day—now the spring was dry, the wheel was still, and the old structure had long since fallen into decay.

Inez, in riding, had lost her way in the wood, and came upon it by chance. A fiend must have put it in her head to bring Coralie thither.

"It looks like a storm; suppose we rest here for a few minutes," said Inez, drawing her companion inside the old mill.

The fatal drug which Inez had purchased and had held to Coralie's nostrils while they were in the coach had done its work well—a numbness had gradually stolen over her brain, locking her senses in a terrible vise—she went with Inez passively—she realized nothing of what was transpiring about her.

"It is stifling here—we will go to the floor above," said Inez, leading the way.

It was reached only by a rude ladder, up which she managed by great perseverance to get Coralie, who was fast becoming powerless to move even.

Once on the floor above a gleam of malignant triumph blazed from Inez' black eyes.

"Sit there and rest—wait here for me until I return," she said. "I am afraid we have lost our way, I——"

There was no need of inventing further falsehoods; while she was speaking Coralie's eyes had slowly closed, and she sunk back on the bench in a deep stupor, fell on her face with eyes distended and lips purple, as one in mortal pain.

"Lie there—die there!" cried Inez Montstrossor, fiercely. "The old ruined mill will be your tomb. If the whole world turned out to search for you, they would never think of looking for and finding you here. You will never know that your marriage with Allan Drexel was no sham, that you are his wedded wife, parted from him by Sinclair's treacherous thirst for revenge, and that it was the marriage of Allan's twin brother which you tried to stop, believing him to be Allan because of their fatal resemblance to each other. Ha, ha! you will never know this, for you will never leave this place alive. When Allan told me the whole story of the past, which Sinclair had told him on his death-bed, and which parted him from me—while he was telling me of his love for you—I vowed that I would part you two just as sure as the sun shone and the moon gave light, and I have kept my vow.

"While the man I love is searching for you—you will be dying here. You should never have crossed my path if you expected to live. Why, I would not let a hundred lives stand between me and Allan Drexel's love. Desperate situations demand desperate means.

"These hands are not stainless—one crime more or less will not matter to me. I leave you to your fate, my beautiful rival. Farewell, fair Coralie."

With a bitter laugh she turned on her heel, and sprung hastily down the ladder again, taking the precaution to remove the rickety old ladder after her, so that if Coralie should come to, she would find every means of escape cut off.

It took her almost half an hour to find her way back through the wood to where the coach stood in waiting. She would have lost her way if the far-off neighing of the impatient horses had not guided her toward them.

"Is the other young lady not coming with you?" asked the driver, looking suspiciously at her flushed face, and noting her excited appearance.

Inez Montstrossor raised her eyebrows haughtily.

"I took her to her home," she answered sharply.

Then she gave a violent start; he was gazing intently at her dress; it was torn by the brambles; she did not see that the brambles had torn the dainty white skin from her hands, and that they were covered with drops of blood.

From that hour, although her wicked plot triumphed even beyond her wildest expectation, she never knew one moment's peace.

The white face of Coralie, as she saw it last, was ever before her.

Inez' arrest for abduction was the beginning of the fatal end.

"It had been two weeks since that day, nothing had been heard from Coralie, she must have perished long since," Inez told herself as she paced restlessly up and down her narrow cell.

And again she renewed the vow to herself that, come what would, Coralie's fate should never be revealed.

Let Allan Drexel's heart break with suspense. If he could not love her, no one else should have him.

She had listened with breathless interest when Allan had spoken of Sinclair's confession. She thought Allan knew all. When Inez found Sinclair had died ere he reached that part of the story that concerned herself, she knew that she was safe. No one would ever know, to reveal now, that she was an impostor, inheriting old Miss Montstrossor's wealth by fraud.

If they had found out that they might have searched deeper, and might have found out how Miss Montstrossor died, and her prison cell might have been exchanged for a far worse fate.

The day of her trial rolled around at last, and Inez paced her cell from early morning in a state of great excitement.

Her maid had not come with the onyx ring which Inez had wanted so much. Would she come before the hour of the trial? Inez hoped so with all her heart.

As the hour drew near for her trial Allan Drexel's emotion was great.

Would Inez Montstrossor at the last moment relent, or would she keep her lips sealed and stand the consequeuce?

Captain Stafford, who had heard all, came to Allan and did his best to comfort him—to say something to cheer him—extending to him the hope that in a very few hours Coralie would be found.

"Inez Montstrossor is a fiend incarnate," he declared, "I firmly believe she will do as she says—refuse to utter a word. Go to the trial, Stafford, and let me know the result at the earliest moment. Come here and tell me, I am too prostrated to go myself."

And Captain Stafford took his leave. It seemed an age to Allan until his return—yet not more than half an hour had passed.

He heard the clatter of horses' hoofs outside, and a moment later the captain sprung into the room with a face white as death itself.

CHAPTER XXXV

❧ Madness from Thirst and Lack of Food

When Coralie followed Miss Montstrossor through the dim wood to the old mill, her senses were in a whirling, confused state, and when she sunk down on the decayed bench—although apparently unconscious—she was perfectly cognizant of all that was transpiring around her.

The powerful drug which Inez had held to her nostrils while in the coach, had thrown her into a deep trance.

With horror too terrible to be described, she heard every word that Inez had uttered, and realized, too, that Inez was about to abandon her, leave her there alone to die.

Oh, how wildly she tried to call out to her, tried to break the bonds of the horrible spell that bound her in a deadly vise, but it was useless, the white lips never moved, the closed eyelids never quivered.

She heard Inez descend the ladder, and in pitiful agony heard her draw it away from its place, thus cutting off all escape.

Then Heaven was, indeed, merciful to beautiful, hapless Coralie—unconsciousness came to her relief.

Darkness came, the night waned, and daylight broke cold and gray over the sleeping world again, before her locked senses began to relax and life took up its sway in the feeble, fluttering heart and cramped limbs.

Pitifully weak, Coralie staggered to her feet and crept to the window. The pure air from the broken panes seemed to revive her.

She drew a long, deep breath, and with it a sobbing cry fell from her lips as she realized her position.

When she gained strength she made an examination of the room for a means of exit; alas, there was none, save by the ladder, and that Inez had removed.

To think of jumping the distance to the floor below, or from the window, was sheer madness.

"God in Heaven, teach me what to do!" sobbed Coralie, wildly, as she sunk on her knees, wringing her little hands in an agony of despair.

In that moment she remembered all Inez had said in regard to Allan Drexel, and Robert Sinclair's cruel plot which had so successfully parted them.

He had been true to her after all—her handsome, noble Allan, whom she had believed to have been the most heartless of triflers—the most cruel of deceivers. But, God help her, the knowledge had come to her too late, for that most cruel of all cruel oaths—*if she carried it out*—would part him as effectually from her as though one of them lay in the grave.

Perhaps God had intended that she should die here—to avoid the conditions of that oath. She wished to Heaven that the master-workman had never revealed it to her.

If her mother could have known what was in store for her beautiful, hapless Coralie, she would never have asked her to do it—never, oh, never. Death would be easier to bear than to fulfill it.

Yet it was horrible to contemplate death in a place so horrible as that in which she found herself, with no human being near.

A gnawing hunger and a burning thirst for water seized her; she began to realize what was the horrible death that awaited her—death by starvation.

Who shall picture the hours that followed? They waned and the night stars came out again, and with ghastly face Coralie clung to the window sill, her face upturned to the soft white light, praying Heaven to send her death to take her out of her misery.

Her brain reeled, strange fancies came to her. She believed herself reveling in the midst of banks of roses, regaling herself with costly wines that flowed like water through golden urns, and she laughed aloud as she cooled her burning lips in the delightful draught.

It was the dreaded flightiness which precedes madness brought on by craving hunger and thirst.

"Allan!" she wailed, "Allan, shall I tell you what that awful curse is, which separates you and me forever?"

She must have heard a responsive answer in the night winds that rustled amongst the trees outside, for she went on gaspingly:

"Let me tell you all, Allan, while I have strength, then you will know why Heaven never smiled upon our love, though you and I were not to blame, dear. Ah, it seems such a cruel mockery of fate, that, out of the whole world of women, you cared for only me, and I should have been your bitterest foe, Allan; but fate has, alas, decreed that I should love you instead of hating you. Listen, Allan, while I read you the story of that oath my dying mother made the master-workman repeat to me, and see that I carried out. It is all in this letter in my pocket, Allan."

She drew a letter from her pocket, but it fluttered from her nerveless hands to the floor, where it lay in the dust all unheeded.

We will glance at its contents, dear reader, as it lies there, and in its pages discover the shadow that blighted Coralie's life.

The letter had been written by Mrs. Harding during her long illness, little by little, and had been sealed and addressed to the master-workman, to be delivered by Coralie in case she should pass away suddenly, before he could be sent for.

It was evidently written under great stress of excitement from beginning to end, and read as follows:

"To Richard Marshall:

"My Kind, Good Friend,—When you read what I have written here, I shall be no more. I have a strange confession to make, and I—a dying woman—charge you to reveal it to Coralie, only after I am laid at rest.

"Sooner or later Coralie must know the startling truth—that *she is not my child!*

"Her mother was my younger sister—as blithe and pretty a picture as the sun ever shone on, with her yellow, flying curls and deep blue eyes. We were a country doctor's daughters, who were orphaned when Matty was only sixteen and I two years her senior.

"The income which was left us barely sufficed to keep us. Still, the idea had entered my head to make a lady of pretty Matty. So I sent her off to boarding-school—it would have been better if I had put her in her coffin.

"Ere she had been gone six months, her letters to me suddenly ceased. In great anxiety I went on to the little town in which the boarding-school was situated, and there I learned the horrible story that three weeks before my darling had eloped with a handsome, smooth-voiced stranger, who had been loitering in the neighborhood. All search for her proved futile.

"A year later, as I was sitting by my lonely hearth-stone one terrible stormy night, thinking of Matty, I heard a low, faint tap at the window close beside me, and saw a woman's face pressed close to the pane. I sprung to my feet and flung open the door.

"There, all dripping with rain, stood Matty, with a tiny bundle in her arm.

"'Matty,' I cried aghast—'in Heaven's name, Matty, is this you?'

"She staggered into the room, falling in sheer exhaustion at my feet; the bundle rolled from her arms, and the wail of a tiny infant issued from it.

"'A baby, Matty!' I gasped. 'Oh! child, is it yours?'

"'Yes, Lida,' she whispered. 'Do not scold me, dear; I have come here to die and bring my baby home to you.'

"'But your—your—husband, Matty!' I cried—'where is he?'

"'He has left me, Lida,' she answered. 'Never speak of him again; I cannot bear it. You will know why soon enough.'

"I looked and thanked God that I saw a wedding-ring on her hand.

"Those were the last words Matty uttered for many a day.

"One afternoon she called for pen and paper.

"'If I should die, Lida, keep this letter until my child is sixteen years of age before you open it and read it,' she said, placing a sealed letter in my hand a little later; 'and, oh, Lida, if I should die, keep my little Coralie—my poor, pretty, hapless babe—and care for her as if she were your own.'

"Poor Matty died, and I put away the letter safe, and kept Matty's babe.

"A few months later I married John Harding, to whom I told all. We adopted little Coralie, and moved far away, and no one knew but what she was our own.

"Not long after, my husband died; then, by a strange fate that has often seemed almost incomprehensible to me since, I came to New York with Coralie, and, through the master-workman's—Richard Marshall's—influence, I secured work in the Drexel Silk Mills.

"But if I had known what I knew later, I would have seen the mill, along with its master, burned to the ground ere I would have set my foot across its thrice-accursed door-sill.

"I shall never forget the day I first met the owner of the mill; nor shall I ever forget the great aversion I felt for him. God help me, I was to know why all too soon.

"It was a fair June day. I was walking through the park holding little Coralie by the hand, when suddenly my attention was attracted to a gentleman walking slowly through the park, regarding the child intently.

"Suddenly the child broke from me and ran toward the gentleman. I saw he was holding out a cluster of roses to her.

" 'Coralie,' I said with a courtesy, 'you must thank the kind gentlaman.'

" 'What was the name you called her, madam?' he asked, springing excitedly to his feet, his face turning from red to white.

" 'Coralie, sir,' I answered.

" 'Is she your child?' he asked in a hoarse, constrained voice.

"I replied she was, and he turned suddenly on his heel with what sounded like a muttered imprecation, and walked away.

"The next day, the same gentleman was walking through the mills, and he was pointed out to me as the owner of the Drexel Silk Mills.

"Steadily time rolled on, the day came on which Coralie was sixteen years of age, and on that fatal day I broke the seal of poor Matty's letter, and the shock of it has placed me on my death-bed."

CHAPTER XXXVI

❧ The Curse of the Drexels

The letter of Coralie's mother to the master-workman continued as follows:

"It was a sad and cruel story of poor Matty's life. Of her marriage, and the pitiful fate that followed on the heels of it.

"The young husband took Matty to his home, and that was the beginning of the bitter end, for her husband's brother hated her at first sight, as did also his wife. Matty's husband was Theodore Drexel, the owner of the Drexel Silk Mills.

"His marriage was a bitter blow to Gordon Drexel, the brother, who had himself married a widow some few years before, who had two handsome boys—twins—by a former marriage. These boys, Theodore Drexel had often declared, should be his heirs in case he never married.

"And Matty had stepped in between the twin-boys and a fortune. No wonder they hated her.

"But their bitterness did not end there. They concocted a plot as cruel as death to part them.

"And at last the young husband was led to believe poor, innocent Matty false to him.

"In vain she knelt to him, and prayed to him to listen to her. He was hot-headed and would not listen, and in a moment of passion he drove her from his door out into the coldness and darkness of the night, vowing he would make his brother's child, Allan, his heir, or, perhaps, divide his money equally between his two boys.

"Fighting the battle of life against the world—ah, how poor Matty suffered in the terrible days that followed. Three months later, one stormy night, ill almost unto death, with her little babe in her arms, she made her way to Gordon Drexel's home and prayed him to refute the false charges he had made against her, and which he knew to be false, for her baby's sake.

"How he laughed in her face, and derided her, coolly avowing that he had taken too much pains to part them for her to imagine he would be apt to play the part of mediator to effect a reconcilation.

"He was a man of marble; neither tears, prayers or entreaties would move him, and in agony which could never be painted by words, Matty turned from him, laying her bitter curse on him for wrecking her life for so heartless and cruel a purpose, that one of his wife's sons might inherit her husband's possessions.

" 'May my curse be ever upon you and yours if you influence my husband to take it from his own child and leave it to strangers!' she cried. 'May blight follow him remorselessly who dares succeed to the ownership of the Drexel Mills, which should be left to my poor child. I shall work out that curse against you and yours in my own way sooner or later!' Matty cried out wildly; 'and if I die, I shall leave this curse to be worked out by my child as my dying legacy.'

"Clasping her child, poor little infant Coralie, close to her heart, Matty staggered out into the darkness of the night, to live or to die in the terrible storm, as God saw fit.

"Matty took passage on the steamer that came up the river that night for home. Every one remembers the wreck of the Gladiola. She went down that night in the storm with all on board. Many were saved; among them Matty and her child; but her name was among the missing.

"No one changed the report, for, indeed, no one but Matty knew that bitter past. In her own heart she said, 'Let the report stand as it is—it will soon be the truth, I shall be no more.'

"Thus it was that Theodore Drexel never knew that he had ever had an heir. Believing Matty dead, he married again; but to Gordon Drexel's great relief, no children blessed their union, and at last one of the twin brothers, Allan Drexel, was made heir to the Drexel Mills.

"Now, hark you, Richard Marshall," the letter continued, "now you know Matty's story. Her voice cries out from the grave for vengeance against this young heir—that his life may be blasted as was hers. She is dead, and Coralie must work out that curse. I charge you, by all you hold dear, to see that it is done."

This was the contents of the letter which lay by Coralie's side on the floor of the old mill.

Whether it was ever to be read by human eye the future alone would reveal.

During that long, never-to-be-forgotten night, consciousness came to Coralie at intervals, and there were moments too when her feverish brain was clear, but almost immediately she fell into a dull stupor again.

The day had closed in sultry, and night had set in with dark clouds, which now and then obscured the whole face of the Heavens, presaging a coming tempest.

By midnight the storm set in with all its fury. Thunder rolled and lightning flashed, lighting up the dark world now and then with a blinding sheet of white light—horrible in its awful grandeur to behold—then instantly dying out, leaving the world to darkness and the terrible storm.

The rain, which beat in through the open window, partially revived Coralie, and, struggling to her feet, she crept to the nearest one and leaned out—far out.

The cooling rain on her burning face seemed like an answered prayer from Heaven.

What was it that suddenly hurled her from her feet? There was a stunning bolt, a vivid white flash, and the old mill quivered like a leaf on its foundation.

The next instant a volume of smoke filled the air, a bright jet of flame springing from it.

And through the girl's brain flashed the horrible truth—the lightning had set the old mill on fire.

Coralie shrieked aloud—her piteous cries rent the night air—but only the mocking voice of the raging tempest answered her.

"Allan, my love!" she wailed piteously. "Oh, Allan, Allan, save me! I am so young to die! So young to die!"

All of her life she had had a horror of fire; now she was to meet her doom in the terrible flames.

She tried to pray, but the words died away on her lips, making no sound.

Nearer and nearer crept the fire-fiend; the building was but a miserable wooden shell; it was but a question of a few short moments ere it would be wrapped in a winding-sheet of flame.

"Allan!" she cried, sinking on her knees and clasping her little white hands; "you will never know how, in my last moments, I met death with your name on my lips; I cannot hate you for your father's sin, dear; I could easier die than blight your life more than I have blighted it already; we have been parted cruelly on earth, Allan, but there—up there we will be heart to heart."

The heat was becoming intense, and the smoke stifling.

Coralie leaned further out of the window, and shrieked again with the wildness of despair for help.

Would no aid reach her? Where was Allan in that hour of peril?

Heaven had granted her prayer; it seemed by the special directing of fate that he should be near at hand.

A few words will suffice to explain how it came about.

When Captain Stafford had hurriedly sought Allan, with a white, scared face to report the result of Inez Montstrossor's trial, he had rushed up to his room at the hotel, exclaiming excitedly:

"Something terrible has happened, Allan; the trial will never come off; Inez Montstrossor has poisoned herself, and she is dying, but even on the verge of the other world she will not reveal Coralie's fate, although she admits she knows where to find her."

It came about in this way: she had sent for one of her maids, she requested the girl to bring her an onyx ring which was to be found in her writing-desk.

It was to be slipped to her very cautiously, and without attracting the attention of the officials.

Thinking it was some treasured keepsake, the girl complied with her request.

She wore it on her finger into Inez' cell, and although closely watched during the interview—he was not clever enough to notice the girl came away without it—an hour later Inez Montstrossor was writhing in the agony of the poison which was in a receptacle in the ring.

It was an intense shock to Allan Drexel.

He went to Inez, praying her to find pardon in the other world for what she had done, by revealing where Coralie was to be found.

"I give you the same answer now that I have given you from the very first," gasped Inez, defiant still. "You will never know where Coralie is, and here on my dying bed, I confess that I led her on to her fate—out—of—revenge."

Allan turned away with the bitterness of death in his heart.

CHAPTER XXXVII

∾ A Terrible Fire at Midnight

In anguish of mind, pitiful to contemplate, Allan Drexel left Inez' presence. The very air he breathed seemed to burn his lips, his heart seemed bursting.

Would he never know the fate that had overtaken his darling? whether she was living or dead?

One of the grooms about the hotel stable was exercising Allan's favorite horse; he sprung into the saddle, grasped the reins, drove his spurs into the animal's side, and rode like the whirlwind away.

A feverish desire seemed to possess him to leave the city limits far behind. He wanted time to think what could be done, but no way presented itself to his mind as he rode along.

He was so much engrossed in his own thoughts, he let the horse pick his path where he would, heedless of which way he went.

Hours passed, but to Allan they seemed like so many moments. He was startled to find the sun going down, night coming on, and himself in a locality he never remembered having traversed before.

"It looks like rain, too, Prince," he exclaimed, stroking the animal's glossy neck. "We must turn homeward."

It seemed strange to him to find such a wild, weird locality of dense wood so near the throbbing heart of the great metropolis, and yet so isolated. It was not so easy to find the path that led to the main road.

Night came on all too quickly; the finding his way back seemed an utter impossibility; besides, his horse was tired. There seemed no other way for it than to picket his horse and wait patiently for morning, despite the threatened storm.

Thus it happened when the bolt of lightning struck the old mill and set it on fire, fate had decreed that Allan Drexel should be near at hand; he was scarcely a hundred yards away.

All in a moment the sky was lit up by a red glare of light, and over the terrific force of the storm he heard a woman's cry for help.

Leaving his horse securely tied, he made his way toward the scene of the conflagration at once.

"Help! help!" cried the voice again fainter than before, and there was something in the tone which sent a strange tremor to Allan's heart.

At the first glance as he approached, he recognized the old deserted mill which he had passed often before.

What would any one be doing there, especially a woman, and at such an hour? No doubt it was some belated pedestrian taking refuge from the storm.

"Courage!" he called like a bugle blast. "Help is near!"

Springing through the door, he rushed toward the ladder; it was not in its place. Ah, there it was standing against the opposite side of the wall. In an instant he had adjusted the ladder in its place and sprung up to the floor above.

He saw, through the dense volume of smoke, a slight girlish form outlined against the casement. One instant more, and the flames would reach her.

Tearing off his rain-soaked coat, he rushed forward and threw it about her, raising her in his strong arms as easily as though she were a little child; something white lay on the floor—a letter. He had presence of mind to seize that too.

Then, with his burden, he commenced the most heroic struggle for life that ever went unrecorded in the annals of bravery.

Step by step he fought the fierce fire-fiend and the blinding smoke.

Once a wild agony of despair seized him, a column of flame burst out between him and the ladder; death stared him in the face; but even in this trying moment he did not drop his burden, though the poor creature had sunk in a deep swoon in his arms.

He never remembered afterward how, through the raging fire, the intense heat, and the belching smoke and falling timbers, he ever reached the ladder and clambered down it, and staggered with his burden out into the pure air of heaven, and to a safe spot under the trees; safe alike from the scorching heat of the doomed building and the downpouring rain.

As yet he did not know who it was whom he had saved. Kneeling down in the long rush-grass, he unwound his coat from the inanimate figure.

The bright light from the burning building fell upon her white face, crowned in its sheen of shimmering, golden curls.

One glance, then the mightiest cry that ever was heard fell from Allan Drexel's lips. "Am I mad, or do I dream? Great God! it is Coralie!" he cried.

Only the waving trees saw how madly he snatched her in his arms, covering her face with passionate kisses, begging her to open her eyes and speak to him.

He laved her face with cooling water for long hours, terrified beyond words at the length of this deep swoon, from which he seemed unable to rouse her.

When morning broke, cold and gray, in the eastern sky, by its first faint streaks he beheld some little distance off the welcome sight of smoke curling up from a farmhouse.

He conveyed Coralie thither at once; by a curious fate he found that it was the home of a brother of Richard Marshall—the master-workman.

The farmer knew Allan well, and knew of his marriage and the strange loss of his bride; also of the trial pending and Miss Montstrossor's persistent refusal to divulge what had become of Coralie.

A few words sufficed to explain the condition of affairs to the farmer and his overjoyed wife, who received poor helpless Coralie from Allan's arms at once, and quickly proceeded in her own way to restore her.

Ten minutes later she entered the room where Allan was pacing up and down with a white, scared face.

"All my roots and herbs have failed, Mr. Drexel," she said. "I am afraid we shall have to send for a doctor."

One of the farmer's boys was quickly dispatched, but it was quite an hour before he returned with the doctor.

In the meantime Allan insisted upon sitting beside his darling's couch.

Suddenly the thought of the letter he had found on the floor beside Coralie, occurred to him.

Searching in his coat pocket he found it where he had thrust it.

He opened it and ran his eye down the front page.

In an instant he comprehended its import. Great Heavens! it was the revelation of the oath which the master-workman refused to reveal to Allan, and which he had said would part him from Coralie for life.

The letter shook in his trembling hand. Should he read it or not? If not he should never know what secret foe he had to fight against, or why Coralie, the bride he had wedded and loved so well—whom he worshiped with all the love of his heart—was not destined for him.

Yes, he must read to the very end.

Clasping one of Coralie's death-cold hands which lay on the coverlet in one of his, slowly, word by word, he read Mrs. Harding's letter through.

It was a wonderful revelation to him. His face turned white as death, his breath came in hot gasps.

Coralie, Theodore Drexel's child! Was there ever anything so wonderful? She was his child—the rightful heir to all the Drexel estate, and he himself was now penniless.

But even in this moment he thanked God that he should be able to give his darling back her inheritance.

He would give her all, and go out into the world beginning life anew with his two hands, a clear head and a willing heart. Coralie should not think that he was wooing and winning her again for her wealth.

There should be no contest, no going to law over the matter. Coralie should have her own, and he thanked God that since the business had been put into his hands he had nearly doubled the revenue of the estate.

This put quite a different face on the matter. He must go away, earn a name for himself in the great world of men, commence life without a dollar, and when he had achieved something, then, yes, then, he would come to Coralie, lay his heart and hand at her feet, and pray her to love him, to be his in truth as well as in name.

It was a bitter decision, but he felt that it was the only way under the circumstances, for he was not Allan Drexel, the millionaire owner of the Drexel silk mills now, but a penniless fellow, without name or position. What a strange turn in the wheel of fate!

CHAPTER XXXVIII

❧ "Will It Be Life or Death?"

Allan looked at the beautiful face lying so still and white against the pillow, tears coming to his handsome dark eyes.

She believed him false, a willful deceiver, every word of Robert Sinclair's horrible story came back to him now with a painful clearness.

Many another would have openly claimed her fortune in the very hour she heard all from the master-workman; Coralie did not. She allowed him to retain still the possessions which she knew were hers.

Did she do this because she loved him?

His musings were brought to an end suddenly by the entrance of the doctor.

After the usual greeting and a few casual remarks, the doctor advised Allan to take a turn or two out in the orchard, he was looking so white he was certainly afraid of having two patients on his hands instead of one, and promising to join him and report how his young wife was at the earliest moment.

Allan took the doctor's advice. Strolling out into the peach orchard, he lit a cigar, pacing patiently up and down awaiting the doctor's coming, trying to bring his chaotic thoughts meanwhile into subjection.

How earnestly he thanked Heaven, as he bared his handsome head to the glorious sunshine, that Coralie, his darling, had been found at last.

How slowly the moments dragged by; why had the doctor not come to him? He would go in presently and see what detained him.

Was it only his fancy or did he hear the farmer's wife cry out with a sharp, agonized cry.

Allan grew restless. He threw away his cigar and turned to go toward the house.

Some few minutes before, the doctor had hurriedly left the house, making his way quickly through the cornfields and across the orchard toward where Allan stood, his back toward him, his footfalls making no sound on the green grass.

But now as he approached his face paled. He scarcely knew how to tell the handsome young husband that which he had come there to say.

As Allan wheeled about he found himself standing face to face with the doctor.

"How is she, sir?" cried Allan, gazing apprehensively into the troubled face before him. "I—I hope she is not going to have a long spell of sickness. Why do you not speak, doctor? You look so grave—you—terrify me."

Dr. Burroughs stepped nearer, and laid one hand gently on the young man's arm.

"Can you bear a shock, Mr. Drexel?" he asked gently.

Allan staggered back as though he had dealt him a powerful blow, his face turning white as marble.

"Is she dead, doctor?" he cried. "Great God, man, do not keep me in suspense. Is my darling dead?"

"She is not dead nor dying, sir," responded the doctor, gravely, shaking his head, "but that has happened which is a thousand times worse. I have every reason to fear, sir, that your young wife has lost her reason. She has been through some terrible shock which has unhinged her mind completely."

A groan, so terrible in its anguish that it brought tears even to the doctor's eyes to hear it, used as he was to suffering and woe, fell from Allan's lips.

"Great God! what have I done to deserve such persecution from Heaven?" he cried. "Has my darling been restored to me for this? Do you give me no hope, doctor?" he groaned; "with careful nursing may she not recover?"

"I have found a severe scalp-wound," continued the doctor, "which seems to have resulted from a heavy fall. If a surgical operation was performed upon this wound, it would in all possibility restore reason; but, hark you, sir, nine cases out of ten of such delicate surgical operations result in death. In plain language, her reason is lost for life without the operation, but it may cause her death. You are to say whether or not it shall be done. Come to the house and see her."

Shaking like a leaf in the storm with his great emotion, the veins standing out like whip-cords on his forehead, the perspiration rolling down his white, haggard face in beads, Allan followed the doctor to the house, and into the room where Coralie lay.

The sunlight from the half-closed blind fell upon her face and on the golden curls tossed back on the pillow. She looked like one of the beautiful pictures of angels which Raphael used to paint.

The lovely blue eyes, fringed by their long, golden lashes, were wide open, but there was no gleam of reason in their depths.

Allan cried aloud in anguish as he sunk down by the couch and buried his white face in the counterpane. Few can realize what he suffered in that awful moment. The heart of the old farmer's good wife bled for him.

"I will leave you by yourself while you decide," said the doctor, turning away. "I would say, however, if you decide upon the operation, it had best be done quickly."

Allan heard the door open and close after him; then he raised his haggard face and looked at Coralie.

My darling—my beautiful love!" he cried, bending over her, "how can I consent to this horrible thing? it might mean death for you, dear, and yet—oh, God in heaven!— how can I see her like this while her young life lasts?"

He paced the floor like one driven mad. An hour passed, then came a slight tap at the door. It was Dr. Burroughs.

"I need hardly ask if you have come to some conclusion," said the doctor; "your face tells me you have."

"Yes," said Allan, huskily, "you are right—I have."

"The operation is to be performed?" queried the doctor.

Allan could not speak, his emotion was so great. He nodded his head in the affirmative.

"Would you like any of her relatives or friends sent for?" asked the doctor.

"She has no relatives. No one in the world save myself," replied Allan, with a groan.

"I charge you, doctor, to do your best," he added hoarsely. "If my darling dies, I shall die too, and by my own hand."

Oh, how he clasped the lovely form in his arms, straining her close to her heart in the wildest of despair and grief.

Then he turned abruptly away and fled from the room while he had strength.

"In an hour's time come, and you shall know if all is well," called the doctor, as he closed the door.

An hour's time—how should he live through the suspense of it without going mad.

He passed the old farmer in the clover field without seeing him. The sunshine seemed blotted out and the whole world dark.

He took out his watch, counting the minutes as he paced up and down the path beneath the blossoming apple-trees.

How could the birds sing and the sun shine, and all nature seem to smile while his darling lay in such peril.

He raised his face to the blue heavens, crying out that if Coralie died, one grave should be made for both. They had been cruelly parted in life, if death came to her, he would go also.

How slowly the moments dragged themselves by. Only half an hour had passed, but it seemed to Allan in his terrible anxiety the length of years.

How could he stand there beneath the trees while his darling faced death?

For the first time in long years his heart went out in a fervent prayer to Heaven to save his darling. The torture he endured was so great he was sorry he had consented to the surgical operation; he would have given his life almost if he had said "No."

Many a white hair found their way among Allan Drexels' dark curls on that sunlit morning. The half hour passed—ten minutes more, and still another ten, but still another ten remained.

He could stand it no longer—he must know if it was life or—or death.

What a hush seemed to fall over the summer air; a dark, ominous shadow crossed the sun; a bird flew away with a few wailing notes; Allan would not accept these as omens.

He entered the house. The farmer met him in the doorway.

"You must not go in there," he said; "the critical moment has come."

Allan stood transfixed on the threshold in awful agony. Then, piercing like a knife through his heart, he heard Coralie's voice break out in a mortal cry, and the doctor's in an awful groan.

Breaking from the farmer's restraining grasp, Allan burst open the door and dashed into the room, and up to the couch.

CHAPTER XXXIX

❧ "Virtue and Vice"

When Allan Drexel heard that pitiful cry, he burst open the door and dashed like one mad into the room.

The doctor advanced hurriedly to meet him.

"All is well, Mr. Drexel," he said, "the operation has proved successful. There was a time—scarcely a moment since—when I thought death would result from it."

Words could never express what Allan felt.

He grasped the doctor's hand, and the sound of the words he would have uttered died away on his lips.

"You must not speak to her now," continued the doctor, "she is not strong enough to bear any excitement.

"I have given her a sleeping potion and nourishing stimulant; to-morrow you shall see her, that must suffice; she will awaken with an unclouded intellect."

Allan's joy was indescribable; he drew his check-book from his breast-pocket to fill out a check for a magnificent sum for the doctor; then the thought came to him with a shock, that he was not worth a dollar.

He replaced it with a white, disturbed face, handing out instead a bill of large denomination, which he happened to have by him.

The morning dawned bright and clear, and with the first peep of early dawn Coralie opened her blue eyes.

A strange, but kindly, motherly face was bending over her, gentle hands were smoothing back the long, tangled golden curls.

" Where am I?" murmured Coralie, struggling up to a sitting posture. "How came I here? Oh, my God! I remember the terrible day and night in the old mill—the horrible lightning, and the fire that was creeping nearer and nearer. Who saved me?"

"Now, dearie, don't excite yourself," replied the farmer's wife; "take this broth, and lay quietly back on the pillow and I will tell you all about it."

Very obediently Coralie did as she was requested.

"There is some one waiting outside to speak to you, the young man who saved you; perhaps he had better come in and tell you in his own words, You owe your life to him, dearie, he saved you at the risk of being consumed in the flames himself."

She left the room hurriedly to call Allan, and Coralie closed her eyes with a weary sigh.

"I ought to thank God that my life has been spared," she murmured, "but somehow I am wicked enough to wish I had perished. Life is so hard to live without Allan."

And she turned her face to the wall with a sobbing cry.

A step sounded outside, some one gently pushed the door open and entered.

What was there in the sound of that step that sent the blood coursing so madly to her heart?

"Coralie—my love—my life," whispered a deep, tremulous voice. And she turned her startled eyes to behold Allan.

"It is a dream?" she gasped.

"It is no dream, love," he responded, kissing the lovely face with all a lover's rapture, clasping her in his arms, and calling her by every endearing name that affection could suggest as he caressed her.

"It I who saved you, love," he whispered. "I would have died with you if I could not have saved you."

Then he laid her gently back on the pillow, turning from her with a face white as death, for he remembered his resolve, he must go away.

She saw the motion, and caught timidly at his hand.

"You are going, Allan?" she whispered. "Even in this happy hour some shadow has fallen between us—I see it in your face."

He bowed his dark, handsome head until the bonny curls that clustered round his brow touched her little white hands.

"I will tell you what has come between us, Coralie," he whispered. "I am no longer the millionaire with a fortune to lay proudly at your feet. I know all, Coralie; I found this letter beside you on the floor of the old mill when I saved you. I have read it."

He produced the letter and laid it in her hand.

"Allan!" she gasped, piteously, "I would never do what you think, I would never take the possessions from you that you have learned to look upon as your own; I never meant to——I—I intended to go quietly away and believed you would never know."

He caught her in his arms with a low cry.

"You would have made that sacrifice for me?" he whispered, tremulously, and with intense emotion.

She nodded her beautiful, curly, golden head humbly.

"Then it is because you love me, my darling!" he cried. "Oh, Coralie, do you?"

Eagerly watching her face, he saw the color come and go in the lovely, dimpled cheeks, and a flush like that of the heart of a sea-shell surged from throat to dainty brow.

Where one would make such a great sacrifice for another, it must be prompted by love.

A light, almost divine, came over Coralie's lovely face and he was answered.

"I cannot claim you now, dear," he said hoarsely, "because I am going away. I shall deliver up to you all your possessions, and go out into the world to seek my fortune. When I have achieved something, I will come back and ask this same question of you, and pray you, plead with you to be mine. I have not forgotten that cruel oath that was put upon you to blast my fortune and my life. Fate caused you to carry out that part of it long since; and, my darling, now that the oath has been in truth carried out, I shall ask you, when I come back, to atone for it all by loving me and being my own true wife. Will you wait for me, Coralie? Give me something to hope and work for."

The lovely face grew white, the little hands crept up to his and nestled in their clasp.

"Going away!"

The words struck her with a chill as cold as death.

The light of the sun seemed to grow suddenly dark.

They had drifted apart once—could she be separated from him again?

Could she see him pass out of her life without making a great effort to keep him with her? Would he think her bold, forward and unmaidenly, if she knelt at his feet and cried out: "Do not go away, Allan, it would break my heart."

"You are weak now, dear," he said; "in a very few days the doctor promises you shall be up and about. I will remain until then."

In the days that followed Coralie's convalescence, Allan told her how it was that he happened to be so near to save her; of Robert Sinclair's death, and his death-bed confession which had been corroborated since by his twin brother—now traveling in Europe; and lastly of Inez Montstrossor lying in the Tombs,[19] ill unto death from the effects of poison administered by her own hand.

Very reluctantly Coralie admitted that it was Inez who took her to the old mill—and left her there—to die, and that the ladder had been willfully removed; but like the good little soul she was, Coralie insisted upon having Inez discharged at once.

"But such a crime, even though it failed signally of its purpose, should be punished," declared Allan. "What if you had died, my darling? Inez Montstrossor's hardness of heart is without parallel; she deserves no clemency."

He took Coralie, by her earnest request, to see Inez the next day. Miss Montstrossor was better—much better; she had taken an overdose—it was owing to this fact that her life was saved.

When she saw Coralie enter, leaning upon Allan's arm, she thought at first it was Coralie's ghost, come back from that land of mysteries, to haunt her.

Coralie came forward and stood before her with clasped hands.

"Inez," she said gently, "I forgive you for what you have done."

"So you have escaped, have you?" cried Inez Montstrossor, fiercely, turning to her with a laugh horrible to hear.

"It is like the close of a melodrama—Virtue, that is you, Coralie, triumphs; Fate brings you and your love together, and you are to be happy ever afterward. Vice, which I personify, is to be punished for her sin. Let me ask one question: I freely confess having tried to lead you to your death, Coralie, now I would like to know what you intend doing with me? I confess my crime, and I know a great punishment will be meted out; but I say this, I am sorry I have failed to part you and Allan Drexel."

"Inez—Miss Montstrossor!" cried Allan, in horror.

"If I had the same thing to do over again I would pursue exactly the same course—making sure of your death," panted Inez, hoarsely.

CHAPTER XL

❧ "What Is My Fate to Be?"

"Miss Montstrossor!" cried Allan, hotly, "are you a woman, or are you a fiend?"

"Whichever you like," she replied mockingly.

"It is too horrible. Come away, Coralie, do not waste words upon her; she is a

---

[19]Nickname for the New York City prison.

traitress, a would-be murderess! Ah, false, wicked girl that you are, what excuse can you offer for what you have done? I ought to denounce you before the whole world!" cried Allan. "What motive could you have had for such a crime?"

Slowly, gracefully, proudly, Inez Montstrossor turned to him—surely one of the most beautiful women ever seen; her magnificent wealth of hair falling over her white shoulders, her lovely face flushing, her dark eyes burning like purple fires.

"You ask me that question!" she said; "you taunt and upbraid me, you would denounce and upbraid me before the world. You would lay my crime bare before the eyes of men. You, for whose sake I have suffered and sinned! I will tell you why I took her to the old mill to die—it was because I loved you so well, Allan Drexel, that I would have committed any crime to have put her out of your way.

"I admit, I never thought it could be traced to me. I thought she would be found dead, and then when the horror of it had passed, your heart would turn to me for consolation and sympathy, Allan, knowing how well I love you.

"Ah, how I have planned to win you, and you would be the first one to denounce me!"

He grew pale as he listened to her. Even Coralie was struck dumb with pity at the vast depths of this girl's mad love for Allan.

"If you had loved me, my life would never have gone wrong," Inez went on in her high, clear voice. "The loss of it has made me what you called me just now—a fiend. I am utterly careless of what becomes of me. I do not care if you denounce me before the whole world, if you publish my sin from the housetops—you can do just as you please. I would like to know what you intend to do, what my fate is to be."

"You are to go free, Inez," said Coralie, gently. "The case shall be dismissed; and all I ask in return is that you may repent what you have done, and that in the future your life shall never know a fortnight like that which you have just passed."

"If it is your will to drop the matter, so be it," said Inez, proudly. "At the best, it galls me to accept my freedom from you, my hated rival."

She turned to the window without another word, and Coralie passed out of her presence, little dreaming under what circumstances she would look at Inez Montstrossor's face again.

"And now, my darling, where shall I take you?" said Allan, as he assisted Coralie into the coupe. "In an hour's time I shall leave New York for the West. You must give me my answer before I go, Coralie, darling. Have I the hope of winning you at last?"

"Why do you go at all, Allan?" she asked faintly.

"Because I am not a man to live on my wife's bounty," he declared. "No, no, Coralie—I could not do it."

Pride must not keep them asunder any more—she would make the great effort of her life to keep him with her.

She turned to him as shyly and shrinkingly as a school-girl.

"Do you remember what Ruth, in the Scripture, said to him whom she loved? 'Where thou goest, I will go.'[20] Oh, Allan, do not go!" she cried impulsively, throwing her white

---

[20]Ruth 1:16.

arms around his neck; "or if you go, take me with you. I—I am all alone in the world but for you, and—and——Oh, Allan, do not go and break my heart if you love me."

"If I love you! I *worship* you, my darling!" cried Allan. "Do not tempt me to stay."

"*Do* be tempted," she whispered. "You must not leave me; you *must* stay. We need never remember to whom the wealth belongs—what is the wife's should be the husband's, too."

There was one half moment of silence and hesitation on his part; there was an awful struggle in his heart between duty and love—the love conquered. He clasped her to his heart, murmuring that he could not leave her—love was stronger than pride.

"This shall be our real wedding-day, Coralie," he declared. "We will take up our lives from that sunny morning when we were wed and parted so cruelly; we will forget the past, and be happy in an unclouded future. Every life has its trials, its sorrows; some live their life and die without having known one gleam of brightness; we must thank God, Coralie, we are to be happy together at last."

"I have but one request to make, Allan," said Coralie, "and that is, that we go to Mr. Marshall, and ask him to sanction our being thus reunited. Surely he will not counsel me to keep longer that cruel oath."

They found Mr. Marshall in the garden amongst his flowers. How gladly he welcomed them!

Who shall describe the scene that followed, as Coralie knelt in the long grass at his feet, begging him to sanction her being reunited to Allan—her love?

"If my poor young mother or my aunt could have foreseen the future—how we were to meet and love each other—surely they would never have attempted to bind me to such an oath. You must absolve me from it."

"I think, with Allan, surely he has been blighted enough in the past—the oath has been kept but too well. Yes, yes, child, I believe if your mother could speak to you just now from the blue heavens, she would say:

"'Make your young husband happy, and may peace and joy be with you!'"

As if in eloquent approval of his words, the white clouds overhead suddenly parted, and a flood of golden sunlight shone down upon his earnest face, and upon the golden head of the lovely girl kneeling at his feet.

Of course Allan did his best to keep their romantic story from being noised about, but it was quite useless. The romance crept into the papers, and every one read it with wonder and delight.

It was read by the burning eyes of a beautiful woman, who had but just arrived in a Southern city.

Inez Montstrossor, for it was she, flung the paper from her with a cry of rage.

"Am I never to be able to forget him!" she cried, pacing up and down the floor. "Am I always to be reminded how happy he is with my rival? I will not endure it! Sooner or later I shall kill her! That is the vow I make to Heaven. Yes, if ever her path crosses mine again, one of us shall die."

From that hour Inez Montstrossor threw herself, soul and body, into the vortex of dissipation.

It was not long before she gained for herself in New Orleans the name of the "Bohemian Queen."

The doors of society were closed against her, but the world of men bowed at her feet—worshiping her dark, wondrous beauty.

She loved to win hearts and toss them away, laughing in derision at a young lover's anguish.

Her grand equipage, her matched, mettlesome ponies and liveried footmen, were the grandest on the boulevard; her silks and flashing diamonds were matchless; yet women averted their faces as they passed by her, but that mattered little enough to Inez Montstrossor.

One day she met Captain Stafford on the street. He was both pained and shocked to meet her. He gravely told her that her beauty had been her curse.

"Nay," she replied, sobered into thoughtfulness for one brief moment. "It was disappointment in love that has made me what I am.

"But what of them, captain—you know whom I mean—are they still happy together?"

"Happy as the day is long," replied the captain, in a low voice. "He worships her, and she idolizes him. It was hard for me to get over my love for sweet Coralie," he murmured; "but I conquered my heart. I can now look on and see her happy with him, and thank God that she is happy. I am married now, you know; my wife knows the past; but, strange to say, she is not jealous of the love I once gave to Coralie. 'It makes a man better, nobler to have loved such a woman,' she simply said, when I told her all.

"I must tell you a piece of news, Inez: Allan Drexel and Coralie are in the city; they came here for the same purpose that I did; to attend the Mardi Gras festival.[21] I hope to Heaven you will not meet them!"

Inez Montstrossor had grown as white as death.

CHAPTER XLI

ᴥ The Cloud with the Silver Lining

"Coralie, her hated rival, with Allan in New Orleans!"

The thought almost maddened Inez Montstrossor.

All that day she brooded over it, and her heart was on fire with bitter jealousy.

She soon found out what hotel they were stopping at. A cry of exultation escaped her lips:

"I will see her to-night," she muttered. "There will be a masked ball at that hotel—no mask, no domino could conceal her identity from me."

Night set in in the gay Southern city, odorous with the perfume of dew-sprinkled flowers and bright with the light of the stars.

The streets were thronged with people, gorgeous with flying bunting and ablaze with torches, for the great Mardi Gras carnival comes only once a year.

In her room Coralie was putting the finishing touches to her toilet, smiling half quizzically at the wistful, pretty dimpled face the mirror reflected.

---

[21]A costume festival celebrated on the Tuesday preceding Ash Wednesday and the season of Lent.

It had been Allan's wish that they should attend this masked ball, and he lived to rue it while his life lasted.

"How strange it is that I feel such a presentiment of coming evil," thought Coralie, pushing back the heavy golden curls from her face. "If Allan had not insisted I should not go down among the gay maskers.

"It is quite amusing, and rather romantic too, that I have succeeded in keeping it quite a secret from Allan, what my costume is to be. It would be the height of absurdity to try to inveigle Allan into a flirtation."

She had told Allan, as he started down to the smoking-room, to come to her in an hour, and she would be ready, with a mischievous smile that was more like the Coralie of old.

She hastily penned a note to him saying that she had gone to join the maskers, and inviting him to find her, and then slipped from the room.

The gorgeous ballroom below was crowded when Coralie entered—rather timidly, and took up her position beneath a group of palms.

A pair of dark, burning eyes that had been patiently watching the entrance, lit up with a savage glare as they beheld her.

"It is she," muttered Inez Montstrossor, advancing slowly. "I am sure of it."

With a gliding motion she reached Coralie's side, touching her on the arm.

Coralie turned with a start, and saw a tall, slim girl dressed in the garb of a gypsy-queen standing beside her.

"Wouldn't you like your fortune told, fair domino?"[22] she asked, disguising her voice carefully.

Coralie laughed a little, light, happy laugh that made the hot blood in Inez Montstrossor's veins fairly seethe with rage.

"You are very kind," she said; "but I know what my fortune is to be. I have met, and loved, and wed my bonny hero already. Find some one else my pretty gypsy girl, who would know what the future holds in store for her—pass me by."

"Nay," said Inez Montstrossor; "there is much that you do not know. Come to the balcony yonder; I would like to tell you something; people are observing you."

"Is there anything the matter with my domino—with my costume?" asked Coralie, quickly.

Inez Montstrossor caught at the idea quickly.

"Yes," she answered; "come out on the balcony or into the conservatory, and I will soon fix it for you."

Little dreaming of a hidden motive, Coralie followed her.

Each of the little balconies were crowded; her companion led her down the long porch, out into the grounds.

It never occurred to Coralie that this was a strange procedure.

Once beyond the glare of the lights, beyond the sound of the hum of voices, and the crash of the music, Inez Montstrossor tore off her mask and faced Coralie.

---

[22]A person wearing a loose-hooded cloak, usually also wearing a half-mask as a masquerade costume.

"You may well cry out with terror," she said hoarsely.

"Yes, it is, I—Inez Montstrossor, the girl whose life you have wrecked, and who has vowed a deadly vengeance on you, and the hour has now come for the execution of that vow. You have claimed to be a saint; now say your prayers, if you know any, for your last hour has come."

"Inez!" cried Coralie, in terror, "what would you do? Are you mad?"

A terrible laugh fell from Inez Montstrossor's lips that froze the blood in Coralie's veins, and in that very instant the blade of a long, thin steel knife flashed in the moonlight, but it never fell on Coralie's white breast, the mark Inez had aimed at.

There was a hoarse, startling cry, a man's dark form sprung from the shadows of the trees, a hand, strong as steel caught the white, upraised arm, grasped the steel blade, and tore it from Inez Montstrossor's white hand.

Coralie knew no more; she had fallen in a dead swoon at her rescuer's feet.

When she opened her eyes she found Allan bending anxiously over her; she was in her own room.

"My darling!" he cried in a trembling voice, as he clasped her in his arms.

"Was it a dream, Allan," she whispered fearfully, "or—or—a—reality?"

"It was a reality. It would have ended in a horrible tragedy if I had not been close at hand," he added. "I had gone out under the trees to smoke a cigar, thinking you would not be ready for the ball for some little time yet. I heard steps soon after, and, glancing toward the pebbled walk from the bench where I sat, saw two persons advancing. You both stopped so near me I could have reached out my hand and touched her or you.

"I heard and saw all, and sprung to your rescue. The shock of being discovered, and by me, proved too much for Inez Monstrossor. She fell back in my arms—dead. I threw away the knife, that the story of the attempted crime might not be found out, for Inez is beyond all punishment now—poor Inez, your rival, who loved with such a fatal love, is no more."

Coralie and Allan were glad to leave the beautiful Southern city at the earliest possible moment, but before they left they saw to it that all that was mortal of Inez Montstrossor received a decent burial.

They placed a white shaft over her resting-place, and planted crimson passion roses over her grave.

The magnificent possessions Inez had come into, through intrigue and fraud, were found to be entirely squandered.

A year has passed since that memorable day which neither Allan nor Coralie can recall without a shudder—and certain wonderful changes have taken place.

Allan and his pretty young wife occupy the old Drexel mansion, on the slope of the Orange Mountains[23] that overlooks the valley, not far from Eagle Rock.

Here their old friends delight to visit them, for it is a charming home—just far enough removed from the turmoil of the great metropolis to be delightful.

---

[23]The Orange Mountains are located in northwest New Jersey. Amid these mountains is an elevated position called Eagle Rock, which was used as an observation post by Gen. George Washington during the American Revolution.

There is one room in particular in her pretty home that Coralie loves to linger in, here she will sit for hours—beside a willow basket lined with pale blue silk and the dantiest of lace.

> "It is long, and deep, and wide,
> And has rockers at its side."

Within this willow shell—half smothered by dainty lace, is the future heir of the Drexel wealth—a sturdy, curly-haired little fellow—the pride of his handsome papa, and the delight of his mamma—pretty little Allan.

No one is more welcome at the Drexel mansion than the master-workman—Richard Marshall—and his good wife; and Fedora Burnham, the pretty, dark-eyed girl who was once Coralie's sole companion in the silk-mill when they ran their looms side by side together and counted their little envelopes when Saturday night came to see if they dared take just a little from their mite to buy some longed-for furbelow that struck their girlish fancy.

Fedora has, a little while since, given up her place in the mill; she will be Fedora Burnham but a few weeks more, then she will be led to the altar by a young lawyer—wealthy, good-looking—and, what is best of all, who loves her with all his heart.

There is little more to add, now that Coralie and Allan are happy together at last, despite all the trials through which they have passed.

Coralie is only twenty now, and her devoted, handsome young husband declares she is more beautiful than ever in his eyes, as he pushes back the heavy golden curls from her face and kisses the rosy, dimpled cheeks.

And Coralie never ceases thanking the fate that led her to the Drexel silk mill to seek employment—for, if she had never been, a working girl in his uncle's mill, the chances are that she would never have met Allan—and that he never would have won for his bride, Coralie, the pride of the mill.

THE END

19

Charles Monroe Sheldon
(1857–1946)

CHARLES SHELDON WAS born the son of a Congregational pastor and farmer. He followed his father's footsteps into the Congregational ministry in 1886, and eventually took a church in Topeka, Kansas, where he lived the rest of his life. He was an early crusader for race relations and class equality. In 1891, he spent three weeks living in Topeka's black ghetto. In the years to follow, he would tirelessly work to preach, educate, and see that material assistance reached the poorer elements of Topeka's population. He personified the Social Gospel claim that devout, hardworking Christians could indeed establish the kingdom of God on earth. Along with his concern for the poor, Sheldon also worked hard for various temperance, peace, and ecumenical causes.

In 1891, Sheldon began telling what he called "sermon stories" to his congregation during his Sunday evening services. He read thirty such stories before he retired from the pulpit in 1919. He published some of these stories in the Congregational periodical, *The Advance*. Little notice, however, was taken of Sheldon's writing ability until the appearance of *In His Steps* (1897). Like many of Sheldon's stories, *In His Steps* was part of a larger Social Gospel literary genre popular in the late nineteenth century, in which Christian values were focused on meeting specific social needs.

In His Steps is built around a simple narrative concerning a group of citizens who decide to guide their lives for a year by framing their decisions with the question: "What would Jesus do?" Once published, the book became an overnight sensation. Hundreds of thousands of copies were sold by its official publisher, but because of a problem with the copyright, no less than sixteen other publishers began to print their own editions soon after its initial appearance. By 1900, millions of copies were in print, and by 1930, Sheldon proclaimed that more than twenty million copies of the book were circulating in dozens of languages. From its humble beginnings as a sermon series, *In His Steps* became one of the best-known stories of the late nineteenth and early twentieth centuries.

IN HIS STEPS

"What Would Jesus Do?"

CHAPTER I

For hereunto were ye called; because Christ also suffered for
you, leaving you an example, that ye should follow his steps.[1]

It was Friday morning and the Rev. Henry Maxwell was trying to finish his Sunday morning sermon. He had been interrupted several times and was growing nervous as the morning wore away and the sermon grew very slowly towards a satisfactory finish.

"Mary," he called to his wife, as he went up stairs after the last interruption, "if any one comes after this, I wish you would say that I am very busy and cannot come down unless it is something very important."

"Yes, Henry. But I am going over to visit the Kindergarten and you will have the house all to yourself."

The minister went up into his study and shut the door. In a few minutes he heard his wife go out.

He settled himself at his desk with a sigh of relief and began to write. His text was from First Peter, ii: 21.

"For hereunto were ye called; because Christ also suffered for you, leaving you an example, that ye should follow his steps."

He had emphasized in the first part of his sermon the Atonement as a personal sacrifice, calling attention to the fact of Jesus' suffering in various ways, in his life as well as in his death. He had gone on to emphasize the Atonement from the side of example, giving illustrations from the life and teaching of Jesus, to show how faith in the Christ helped to save men because of the pattern or character he displayed for their imitation. He was now on the third and last point, the necessity of following Jesus in his sacrifice and example.

He had just put down, "3: Steps; What are they?" And was about to enumerate them in logical order when the bell rang sharply, It was one of those clock-work bells and always went off as a clock might go if it tried to strike twelve all at once.

Henry Maxwell sat at his desk and frowned a little. He made no movement to answer the bell. Very soon it rang again. Then he rose and walked over to one of his windows which commanded a view of the front door.

A man was standing on the steps. He was a young man very shabbily dressed.

Charles Sheldon, *In His Steps: "What Would Jesus Do?"* Chicago: Advance Publishing Co., 1898.
[1] 1 Pet. 2:21.

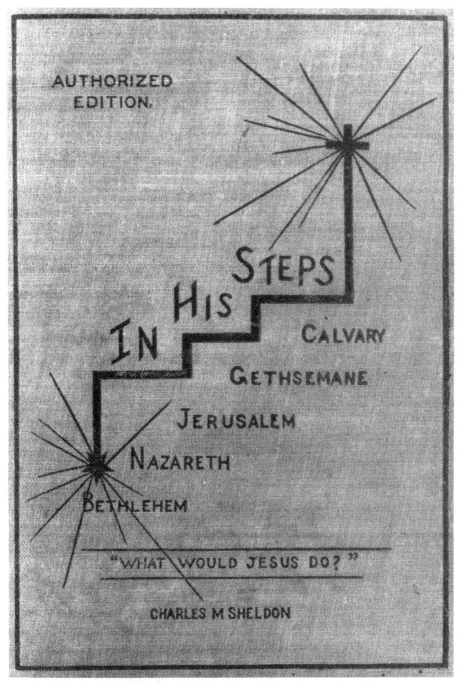

Cover of a copy of the first cloth edition of Charles Sheldon's *In His Steps*
(Chicago: Advance Publishing Co., 1898).

"Looks like a tramp," said the minister. "I suppose I'll have to go down, and—"

He did not finish the sentence, but he went down stairs and opened the front door.

There was a moment's pause as the two men stood facing each other; then the shabby-looking young man said,

"I'm out of a job, sir, and thought maybe you might put me in the way of getting something."

"I don't know of anything. Jobs are scarce," replied the minister beginning to shut the door slowly.

"I didn't know but you might perhaps be able to give me a line to the city railway or superintendent of the shops or something," continued the young man, shifting his faded hat from one hand to the other nervously.

"It would be of no use. You will have to excuse me. I am very busy this morning. I hope you will find something. Sorry I can't give you something to do here. But I keep only a horse and a cow and do the work myself."

The Rev. Henry Maxwell closed the door and heard the man walk down the steps. As he went up into his study he saw from his hall window that the man was going slowly down the street, still holding his hat between his hands. There was something in the figure so dejected, homeless and forsaken, that the minister hesitated a moment as he stood looking at it. Then he turned to his desk, and with a sigh began the writing where he had left off.

He had no more interruptions and when his wife came in two hours later, the sermon was finished, the loose leaves gathered up and neatly tied together and laid on his Bible, all ready for the Sunday morning service.

"A queer thing happened at the Kindergarten this morning, Henry," said his wife while they were eating dinner. "You know I went over with Mrs. Brown to visit the school, and just after the games, while the children were at the tables, the door opened and a young man came in, holding a dirty hat in both hands. He sat down near the door and never said a word. Only looked at the children. He was evidently a tramp, and Miss Wren and her assistant, Miss Kyle, were a little frightened at first, but he sat there very quietly and after a few minutes he went out."

"Perhaps he was tired and wanted to rest somewhere. The same man called here, I think. Did you say he looked like a tramp?"

"Yes, very dusty, shabby and generally tramp-like. Not more than thirty or thirty-three years old, I should say."

"The same man," said the Rev. Henry Maxwell thoughtfully.

"Did you finish your sermon, Henry?" his wife asked after a pause.

"Yes, all done. It has been a very busy week with me. The two sermons cost me a good deal of labor."

"They will be appreciated by a large audience to-morrow, I hope," replied his wife smilling. "What are you going to preach about in the morning?"

"Following Christ. I take up the Atonement under the heads of Sacrifice and Example, and then show the steps needed to follow his sacrifice and example.

"I am sure it is a good sermon. I hope it won't rain Sunday. We have had so many rainy days lately."

"Yes, the audiences have been quite small for some time. People will not come out to church in a storm." The Rev. Henry Maxwell sighed as he said it. He was thinking of the careful, laborious efforts he had made in preparing sermons for large audiences that failed to appear.

But Sunday morning dawned on the town of Raymond one of those perfect days that sometimes come after long periods of wind and rain and mud. The air was clear and bracing, the sky was free from all threatening signs, and every one in Henry Maxwell's parish prepared to go to church. When the service opened at eleven o'clock, the large building was filled with an audience of the best-dressed, most comfortable looking people in Raymond.

The First Church of Raymond believed in having the best music that money could buy and its quartette choir this morning was a great source of pleasure to the congregation. The anthem was inspiring. All the music was in keeping with the subject of the sermon. And the anthem was an elaborate adaptation to the most modern music, of the hymn,

> "Jesus, I my cross have taken,
> All to leave and follow thee."

Just before the sermon, the soprano sang a solo, the well known hymn,

> "Where He leads me I will follow,
> I'll go with Him, with Him all the way."

Rachel Winslow looked very beautiful that morning as she stood up behind the screen of carved oak which was significantly marked with the emblems of the cross and the crown. Her voice was even more beautiful than her face, and that meant a great deal. There was a general rustle of expectation over the audience as she rose. Henry Maxwell settled himself contentedly behind the pulpit. Rachel Winslow's singing always helped him. He generally arranged for a song before the sermon. It made possible a certain inspiration of feeling that he knew made his delivery more impressive.

People said to themselves they had never heard such singing even in the First Church. It is certain that if it had not been a church service, her solo would have been vigorously applauded. It even seemed to Henry Maxwell when she sat down that something like an attempted clapping of hands or a striking of feet on the floor swept through the church. He was startled by it. As he rose, however, and laid his sermon on the open Bible, he said to himself he had been deceived. Of course it could not occur. In a few moments he was absorbed in his sermon and everything else was forgotten in the pleasure of the delivery.

No one had ever accused Henry Maxwell of being a dull preacher. On the contrary he had often been charged with being sensational. Not in what he said so much as in his way of saying it. But the First Church people liked that. It gave their preacher and their parish a pleasant distinction that was agreeable.

It was also true that the pastor of the First Church loved to preach. He seldom exchanged.[2] He was eager to be in his own pulpit when Sunday came. There was an exhilerating half-hour for him as he stood facing a church full of people and knew that he had a hearing. He was peculiarly sensitive to variations in the attendance. He never preached well before a small audience. The weather also affected him decidedly. He was at his best before just such an audience as faced him now, on just such a morning. He felt a glow of satisfaction as he went on. The church was the first in the city. It had the best choir. It had a membership composed of the leading people, representatives of the wealth, society and intelligence of Raymond. He was going abroad on a three months' vacation in the summer, and the circumstances of his pastorate, his influence and his position as pastor of the first church in the city—

It is not certain that the Rev. Henry Maxwell knew just how he could carry on all that thought in connection with his sermon, but as he drew near the end of it he knew that he had at some point in his delivery had all these feelings. They had entered into the very substance of his thought, it might have been all in a few seconds of time; but he had been conscious of defining his position and his emotions as well as if he had held a soliloquy, and his delivery partook of the thrill of deep personal satisfaction.

The sermon was interesting. It was full of striking sentences. They would have commanded attention printed. Spoken with the passion of a dramatic utterance that had the good taste never to offend with a suspicion of ranting or declamation, they were very effective. If the Rev. Henry Maxwell that morning felt satisfied with the conditions of his pastorate, the parish of First Church also had a similar feeling as it congratulated itself on the presence in the pulpit of this scholarly, refined, somewhat striking face and figure, preaching with such animation and freedom from all vulgar, noisy, or disagreeable mannerism.

Suddenly, into the midst of this perfect accord and concord between preacher and audience, there came a very remarkable interruption. It would be difficult to indicate the extent of the shock which this interruption measured. It was so unexpected, so entirely contrary to any thought of any person present that it offered no room for argument, or, for the time being, of resistance.

The sermon had come to a close. The Rev. Henry Maxwell had turned the half of the big Bible over upon his manuscript and was about to sit down, as the quartette prepared to rise and sing the closing selection,

"All for Jesus, All for Jesus,
All my being's ransomed powers,"

when the entire congregation was startled by the sound of a man's voice. It came from the rear of the church, from one of the seats under the gallery. The next moment the figure of a man came out of the shadow there and walked down the middle aisle.

Before the startled congregation realized what was being done, the man had reached the open space in front of the pulpit and had turned about, facing the people.

"I've been wondering since I came in here—" they were the words he used under the

_____

[2]Let others preach in his pulpit through an arrangement made with fellow pastors.

gallery, and he repeated them, "if it would be just the thing to say a word at the close of this service. I'm not drunk and I'm not crazy, and I'm perfectly harmless; but if I die, as there is every likelihood I shall in a few days, I want the satisfaction of thinking that I said my say in a place like this, before just this sort of a crowd."

Henry Maxwell had not taken his seat and he now remained standing, leaning on his pulpit, looking down at the stranger. It was the man who had come to his house Friday morning, the same dusty, worn, shabby-looking young man. He held his faded hat in his two hands. It seemed to be a favorite gesture. He had not been shaved and his hair was rough and tangled. It was doubtful if any one like this had ever confronted the First Church within the sanctuary. It was tolerably familiar with this sort of humanity out on the street, around the Railroad shops, wandering up and down the avenue, but it had never dreamed of such an incident as this so near.

There was nothing offensive in the man's manner or tone. He was not excited and he spoke in a low but distinct voice. Henry Maxwell was conscious, even as he stood there smitten into dumb astonishment at the event, that somehow the man's action reminded him of a person he had once seen walking and talking in his sleep.

No one in the church made any motion to stop the stranger or in any way interrupt him. Perhaps the first shock of his sudden appearance deepened into genuine perplexity concerning what was best to do. However that may be, he went on as if he had no thought of interruption and no thought of the unusual element he had introduced into the decorum of the First Church service. And all the while he was speaking, Henry Maxwell leaned over the pulpit, his face growing more white and sad every moment. But he made no movement to stop him and the people sat smitten into breathless silence. One other face, that of Rachel Winslow, from the choir seats, stared white and intent down at the shabby figure with the faded hat. Her face was striking at any time. Under the pressure of the present unheard-of incident, it was as personally distinct as if it had been framed in fire.

"I'm not an ordinary tramp, though I don't know of any teaching of Jesus that makes one kind of a tramp less worth saving than another. Do you?" He put the question as naturally as if the whole congregation had been a small private Bible class. He paused just a moment and coughed painfully. Then he went on.

"I lost my job ten months ago. I am a printer by trade. The new linotype machines are beautiful specimens of invention, but I know six men who have killed themselves inside of the year just on account of those machines. Of course I don't blame the newspapers for getting the machines. Meanwhile, what can a man do? I know I never learned but the one trade and that's all I can do. I've tramped all over the country trying to find something. There are a good many others like me. I'm not complaining, am I? Just stating facts. But I was wondering, as I sat there under the gallery, if what you call following Jesus is the same thing as what he taught. What did he mean when he said, 'Follow me?' The minister said," here the man turned about and looked up at the pulpit, "that it was necessary for the disciple of Jesus to follow his steps, and he said the steps were, obedience, faith, love, and imitation. But I did not hear him tell just what he meant that to mean, especially the last step. What do Christians mean by following the steps of Jesus? I've tramped through this city for three days trying to find a job and in all that time I've not had a word of sympathy or comfort except from your minister here, who said he was sorry for me and hoped I would find a job somewhere. I suppose it is because you get so imposed on by the professional tramp that you have lost your interest in the other sort. I'm not blaming anybody, am I? Just stating facts? Of course I understand you can't all go out of your way to hunt up jobs for people like me. I'm not asking you to, but what I feel puzzled about is, what is meant by following Jesus? Do you mean that you are suffering and denying yourselves and trying to save lost suffering humanity just as I understand Jesus did? What do you mean by it? I see the ragged edge of things a good deal. I understand there are more than five hundred men in this city in my case. Most of them have families. My wife died four months ago. I'm glad she is out of trouble. My little girl is staying with a printer's family until I find a job. Somehow I get puzzled when I see so many Christians living in luxury and singing, 'Jesus, I my cross have taken, all to leave and follow thee,' and remember how my wife died in a tenement in New York city, gasping for air and asking God to take the little girl too. Of course I don't expect you people can prevent every one from dying of starvation, lack of proper nourishment and tenement air, but what does following Jesus mean? I understand that Christian people own a good many of the tenements. A member of a church was the owner of the one where my wife died, and I have wondered if following Jesus all the way was true in his case. I heard some people singing at a church prayer meeting the other night,

> 'All for Jesus, all for Jesus;
> All my being's ransomed powers;
> All my thoughts and all my doings,
> All my days and all my hours;'

and I kept wondering as I sat on the steps outside just what they meant by it. It seems to me there's an awful lot of trouble in the world that somehow wouldn't exist if all the people who sing such songs went and lived them out. I suppose I don't understand. But what would Jesus do? Is that what you mean by following his steps? It seems to me sometimes as if the people in the city churches had good clothes and nice houses to live in, and money to spend for luxuries, and could go away on summer vacations and all that, while the people outside of the churches, thousands of them, I mean, die in tenements and walk the streets for jobs, and never have a piano or a picture in the house, and grow up in misery and drunkenness and sin—" the man gave a queer lurch over in the direction of the communion table and laid one grimy hand on it. His hat fell upon the carpet at his feet. A stir went through the congregation. Dr. West half rose from his feet, but as yet the silence was unbroken by any voice or movement worth mentioning in the audience. The man passed his other hand across his eyes, and then, without any warning, fell heavily forward on his face, full length, up the aisle.

Henry Maxwell spoke, "We will consider the service dismissed." He was down the pulpit stairs and kneeling by the prostrate form before any one else. The audience instantly rose and the aisle was crowded. Dr. West pronounced the man alive. He had fainted away. "Some heart trouble," the doctor also muttered as he helped carry him into the pastor's study.

Henry Maxwell and a group of his church members remained some time in the study. The man lay on the couch there and breathed heavily. When the question of what to do with him came up, the minister insisted upon taking him to his house. He lived near by and had an extra room. Rachel Winslow said, "Mother has no company at present I am sure we would be glad to give him a place with us." She looked strangely agitated. No one noticed it particularly. They were all excited over the strange event, the strangest that First Church people could remember. But the minister insisted on taking charge of the man and when a carriage came, the unconscious but living form was carried to his house and with the entrance of that humanity into the minister's spare room a new chapter in Henry of Maxwell's life began, and yet no one, himself least of all, dreamed of the remarkable change it was destined to make in all his after definition of Christian discipleship.

The event created a great sensation in the First Church parish. People talked of nothing else for a week. It was the general impression that the man had wandered into the church in a condition of mental disturbance caused by his troubles, and that all the time he was talking he was in a strange delirium of fever and really ignorant of his surroundings. That was the most charitable construction to put upon his action; it was the general agreement also that there was a singular absence of anything bitter or complaining in what the man had said. He had throughout spoken in a mild apologetic tone, almost as if he were one of the congregation seeking for light on a very difficult subject.

The third day after his removal to the minister's house there was a marked change in his condition. The doctor spoke of it and offered no hope. Saturday morning he still lingered, although he had rapidly failed as the week drew near to its close. Sunday morning just before the clock struck one, he rallied and asked if his child had come. The minister had sent for her at once as soon as he had been able to secure her address from some letters found in the man's pocket. He had been conscious and able to talk coherently only a few moments since his attack. "The child is coming. She will be here," Henry Maxwell said as he sat there, his face showing marks of the strain of the week's vigil. For he had insisted on sitting up nearly every night.

"I shall never see her in this world," the man whispered. Then he uttered with great difficulty the words, "You have been good to me. Somehow I feel as if it was what Jesus would do." After a few moments he turned his head slightly, and before Henry Maxwell could realize the fact, the doctor said, "He is gone."

The Sunday morning that dawned on the city of Raymond was exactly like the Sunday of the week before. Henry Maxwell entered his pulpit to face one of the largest congregations that had ever crowded First Church. He was haggard and looked as if he had just risen from a long illness. His wife was at home with the little girl who had come on the morning train an hour after her father died. He lay in that spare room, his troubles over, and Henry Maxwell could see the face as he opened the Bible and arranged his different notices on the side of the desk as he had been in the habit of doing for ten years.

The service that morning contained a new element. No one could remember when the minister had preached in the morning without notes. As a matter of fact he had done so occasionally when he first entered the ministry, but for a long time he had carefully written out every word of his morning sermon, and nearly always his evening discourse as well. It cannot be said that his sermon this morning was very striking or impressive. He talked with considerable hesitation. It was evident that some great idea struggled in his thought for utterance but it was not expressed in the theme he had chosen for his preaching. It was near the close of his sermon that he began to gather a certain strength that had been painfully lacking at the beginning. He closed the Bible and stepping out at the side of the desk, he faced his people, and began to talk to them about the remarkable scene of the week before.

"Our brother," somehow the words sounded a little strange coming from Henry Maxwell's lips, "passed away this morning. I have not yet had time to learn all his history. He had one sister living in Chicago. I have written her and have not yet received an answer. His little girl is with us and will remain for the time."

He paused and looked over the house. He thought he had never seen so many earnest faces during the entire pastorate. He was not able yet to tell his people his experiences, the crisis through which he was even now moving. But something of his feeling passed from him to them, and it did not seem to him that he was acting under a careless impulse at all to go on and break to them, this morning, something of the message he bore in his heart. So he went on.

"The appearance and words of this stranger in the church last Sunday made a very powerful impression on me. I am not able to conceal from you or myself the fact that what he said, followed as it has been by his death in my house, has compelled me to ask as I never asked before, 'What does following Jesus mean?' I am not in a position yet to utter any condemnation of this people, or, to a certain extent, of myself, either in our Christlike relations to this man or the number he represents in the world. But all that does not prevent me from feeling that much that the man said was so vitally true that we must face it in an attempt to answer it or else stand condemned as Christian disciples. A good deal that was said here last Sunday was in the nature of a challenge to Christianity as it is seen and felt in our churches. I have felt this with increasing emphasis every day since. And I do not know that any time is more appropriate than the present for me to propose a plan or a purpose which has been forming in my mind as a satisfactory reply to much that was said here last Sunday."

Again Henry Maxwell paused and looked into the faces of his people. There were some strong, earnest men and women in the First Church. The minister could see Edward Norman, Editor of the Raymond "Daily News." He had been a member of First Church for ten years. No man was more honored in the community. There was Alexander Powers, Superintendent of the Railroad shops. There was Donald Marsh, President of Lincoln College, situated in the suburbs of Raymond. There was Milton Wright, one of the great merchants of Raymond, having in his employ at least one hundred men in various shops. There was Dr. West who, although still comparatively young, was quoted as authority in special surgical cases. There was young Jasper Chase, the author, who had written one successful book and was said to be at work on a new novel. There was Miss Virginia Page, the heiress, who through the recent death of her father had inherited a million at least, and was gifted with unusual attractions of person and intellect. And not least of all, Rachel Winslow from her seat in the choir glowed with her peculiar beauty of light this morning because she was so intensely interested in the whole scene.

There was some reason perhaps, in view of such material in the First Church, for Henry Maxwell's feeling of satisfaction whenever he considered his parish as he had the previous Sunday. There was a large number of strong individual characters who claimed membership there. But as he noted their faces this morning, Henry Maxwell was simply wondering how many of them would respond to the strange proposition he was about to make. He continued slowly, taking time to choose his words carefully and giving the people an impression they had never felt before, even when he was at his best, with his most dramatic delivery.

"What I am going to propose now is something which ought not to appear unusual or at all impossible of execution. Yet I am aware that it will be so regarded by a large number, perhaps, of the members of the church. But in order that we may have a thorough understanding of what we are considering, I will put my proposition very plainly, perhaps bluntly. I want volunteers from the First Church who will pledge themselves earnestly and honestly for an entire year not to do anything without first asking the question, 'What would Jesus do?' And after asking that question, each one will follow Jesus as exactly as he knows how, no matter what the results may be. I will of course include myself in this company of volunteers, and shall take for granted that my church here will not be surprised at my future conduct as based upon this standard of action, and will not oppose whatever is done if they think Christ would do it. Have I made my meaning clear? At the close of the service here I want all those members of the church who are willing to join such a company to remain, and we will talk over the details of the plan. Our motto will be, 'What would Jesus do?' Our aim will be to act just as he would if he were in our places, regardless of immediate results. In other words, we propose to follow Jesus' steps as closely and as literally as we believe he taught his disciples to do. And those who volunteer to do this will pledge themselves for an entire year, beginning with to-day, so to act."

Henry Maxwell paused again and looked over his church. It is not easy to describe the sensation that such a simple proposition apparently made. Men glanced at one another in astonishment. It was not like Henry Maxwell to define Christian discipleship in this way. There was evident confusion of thought over his proposition. It was understood well enough, but there was apparently a great difference of opinion as to the application of Jesus' teaching and example.

Henry Maxwell calmly closed the service with a brief prayer. The organist began his postlude immediately after the benediction and the people began to go out. There was a great deal of conversation. Animated groups stood all over the church discussing the minister's proposition. It was evidently provoking great discussion. After several minutes Henry Maxwell asked all who expected to remain, to pass into the lecture room on the side. He himself was detained at the front of the church talking with several persons there, and when he finally turned around, the church was empty. He walked over to the lecture room entrance and went in. He was almost startled to see the people who were there. He had not made up his mind about any of his members, but he had hardly expected that so many were ready to enter into such a literal testing of their discipleship as now awaited them. There were perhaps fifty members present. Among them were Rachel Winslow and Virginia Page, Mr. Norman, President Marsh, Alexander Powers the Railroad Superintendent, Milton Wright, Dr. West, and Jasper Chase.

The pastor closed the door of the lecture room and stood before the little group. His face was pale and his lips trembled with emotion. It was to him a genuine crisis in his own life and that of his parish. No man can tell until he is moved by the Divine Spirit what he may do, or how he may change the current of a lifetime of fixed habits of thought and speech and action. Henry Maxwell did not, as we have said, yet know himself all that he was passing through, but he was conscious of a great upheaval in his definitions of Christian discipleship and he was moved with a depth of feeling he could not measure, as he looked into the faces of these men and women on this occasion.

It seemed to him that the most fitting word to be spoken first was that of prayer. He asked them all to pray with him. And almost with the first syllable he uttered there was a distinct presence of the Spirit felt by them all. As the prayer went on, this presence grew in power. They all felt it. The room was filled with it as plainly as if it had been visible. When the prayer closed there was a silence that lasted several moments. All the heads were bowed. Henry Maxwell's face was wet with tears. If an audible voice from heaven had sanctioned their pledge to follow the Master's steps, not one person present could have felt more certain of the divine blessing. And so the most serious movement ever started in the First Church of Raymond was begun.

"We all understand," said Henry Maxwell, speaking very quietly, "what we have undertaken to do. We pledge ourselves to do everything in our daily lives after asking the question, 'What would Jesus do?' regardless of what may be the result to us. Some time I shall be able to tell you what a marvelous change has come over my life within a week's time. I cannot now. But the experience I have been through since last Sunday has left me so dissatisfied with my previous definition of discipleship that I have been compelled to take this action. I did not dare begin it alone. I know that I am being led by the hand of divine love in all this. The same divine impulse must have led you also. Do we understand fully what we have undertaken?"

"I want to ask a question," said Rachel Winslow.

Every one turned towards her. Her faced glowed with a beauty that no loveliness could ever create.

"I am a little in doubt as to the source of our knowledge concerning what Jesus would do. Who is to decide for me just what he would do in my case? It is a different age. There are many perplexing questions in our civilization that are not mentioned in the teaching of Jesus. How am I going to tell what he would do?"

"There is no way that I know of," replied Mr. Maxwell, "except as we study Jesus through the medium of the Holy Spirit. You remember what Christ said speaking to his disciples about the Holy Spirit:

"'Howbeit, when He, the Spirit of Truth is come, He shall guide you into all the truth: for He shall not speak from Himself; but what things soever He shall hear, these shall He speak: and He shall declare unto you the things that are to come. He shall glorify me: for He shall take of mine and shall declare it unto you. All things whatsoever the Father hath are mine: therefore said I that He taketh of mine and shall declare it unto you.'[3]

"There is no other test that I know of. We shall all have to decide what Jesus would do after going to that source of knowledge."

"What if others say of us when we do certain things, that Jesus would not do so?" asked the Superintendent of railroads.

---

[3]John 16:13–15.

"We cannot prevent that. But we must be absolutely honest with ourselves. The standard of Christian action cannot vary in most of our acts."

"And yet what one church member thinks Jesus would do, another refuses to accept as his possible course of action. What is to render our conduct uniformly Christlike? Will it be possible to reach the same conclusions always in all cases?" asked President Marsh.

Henry Maxwell was silent some time. Then he answered:

"No. I don't know that we can expect that. But when it comes to a genuine, honest, enlightened following of Jesus' steps, I cannot believe there will be any confusion either in our own minds or in the judgment of others. We must be free from fanaticism on one hand and too much caution on the other. If Jesus' example is the example for the world, it certainly must be feasible to follow it. But we need to remember this great fact. After we have asked the Spirit to tell us what Jesus would do and have received an answer to it, we are to act regardless of the results to ourselves. Is that understood?"

All the faces in the room were raised toward the minister in solemn assent. There was no misunderstanding the proposition. Henry Maxwell's face quivered again as he noted the President of the Endeavor Society,[4] with several members, seated back of the older men and women.

They remained a little longer talking over details and asking questions, and agreed to report to one another every week at a regular meeting the result of their experiences in following Jesus in this way. Henry Maxwell prayed again. And again, as before, the Spirit made Himself manifest. Every head remained bowed a long time. They went away finally in silence. There was a feeling that prevented speech. Henry Maxwell shook hands with them all as they went out. Then he went to his own study room back of the pulpit and kneeled down. He remained there alone nearly half an hour. When he went home, he went into the room where the dead body lay. As he looked at the face, he cried in his heart again for strength and wisdom. But not even yet did he realize that a movement had been begun which would lead to the most remarkable series of events that the city of Raymond had ever known.

CHAPTER II

He that saith he abideth in Him ought himself also to walk even as He walked.[5]

Edward Norman, editor of the Raymond "Daily News," sat in his office room Monday morning and faced a new world of action. He had made his pledge in good faith to do everything after asking, "What would Jesus do?" and as he supposed with his eyes open to all the possible results. But as the regular life of the paper started on another week's

---

[4]Christian Endeavor Societies were organized youth groups that functioned on both a local and a national level.

[5]1 John 2:6.

rush and whirl of activity he confronted it with a degree of hesitation and a feeling nearly akin to fear. He had come down to the office very early and for a few minutes was by himself. He sat at his desk in a growing thoughtfulness that finally became a desire which he knew was as great as it was unusual. He had yet to learn, with all the others in that little company pledged to do the Christlike thing, that the Spirit of Life was moving in power through his own life as never before. He rose and shut his door and then did what he had not done for years. He kneeled down by his desk and prayed for the divine presence and wisdom to direct him.

He rose with the day before him and his promise distinct and clear in his mind. "Now for action," he seemed to say. But he would be led by events as fast as they came on.

He opened his door and began the routine of the office work. The managing editor had just come in and was at his desk in the adjoining room. One of the reporters there was pounding out something on a type writer.

Edward Norman began an editorial. The "Daily News" was an evening paper and Norman usually completed his leading editorial before eight o'clock.

He had been writing about fifteen minutes when the managing editor called out, "Here's this press report of yesterday's prize fight at the Resort. It will make up three columns and a half. I suppose it all goes in?"

Edward Norman was one of those newspaper men who keep an eye on every detail of the paper. The managing editor always consulted his chief in matters of both small and large importance. Sometimes as in this case it was merely a nominal inquiry.

"Yes—No. Let me see it."

He took the type-written matter just as it came from the telegraph editor, and ran over it carefully. Then he laid the sheets down on his desk and did some very hard thinking.

"We won't run this in to-day," he said finally.

The managing editor was standing in the doorway between the two rooms. He was astonished at the editor's remark and thought he had perhaps misunderstood him.

"What did you say?"

"Leave it out. We won't use it."

"But—" The managing editor was simply dumfounded. He stared at Norman as if the editor were out of his mind.

"I think, Clark, that it ought not to be printed, and that's the end of it," said Edward Norman, looking up from his desk.

Clark seldom had any words with the chief. Norman's word had always been law in the office and he had seldom been known to change his mind. The circumstances now, however, seemed to be so extraordinary that Clark could not help expressing himself.

"Do you mean that the paper is to go to press without a word of the prize fight in it?"

"Yes, that's just what I mean."

"But it's unheard of. All the other papers will print it. What will our subscribers say? Why, it's simply—" Clark paused, unable to find words to say what he thought.

Edward Norman looked at Clark thoughtfully. The managing editor was a member of a church of a different denomination from that of Norman's. The two men had never talked together on religious matters although they had been associated on the paper for several years.

"Come in here a minute, Clark, and shut the door," said Norman.

Clark came in and the two men faced each other alone. Norman did not speak for a minute. Then he said abruptly,

"Clark, if Christ were editing a daily paper do you honestly think he would print three columns and a half of prize fight in it?"

Clark gasped in astonishment. Finally he replied—"No, I don't suppose he would."

"Well, that's my only reason for shutting this account out of the "News." I have decided not to do a thing in connection with the paper for a whole year that I honestly believe Jesus would not do."

Clark could not have looked more amazed if the chief had suddenly gone crazy. In fact, he did think something was wrong, though Mr. Norman was one of the last men in the world, in his judgment, to lose his mind.

"What effect will that have on the paper?" he finally managed to ask in a faint voice.

"What do you think?" asked Edward Norman, with a keen glance.

"I think it will simply ruin the paper," replied Clark promptly. He was gathering up his bewildered senses and began to remonstrate. "Why, it isn't feasible to run a paper now-a-days on any such basis. It's too ideal. The world isn't ready for it. You can't make it pay. Just as sure as you live, if you shut out this prize fight report you will lose hundreds of subscribers. It doesn't take a prophet to say that. The very best people in town are eager to read it. They know it has taken place and when they get the paper this evening they will expect half a page at least. Surely, you can't afford to disregard the wishes of the public to such an extent. It will be a great mistake if you do, in my opinion."

Edward Norman sat silent a minute. Then he spoke gently, but firmly.

"Clark, what in your honest opinion is the right standard for determining conduct? Is the only right standard for every one the probable action of Jesus? Would you say that the highest best law for a man to live by was contained in asking the question, 'What would Jesus do?' and then doing it regardless of results? In other words do you think men everywhere ought to follow Jesus' example as close as they can in their daily lives?"

Clark turned red, and moved uneasily in his chair before he answered the editor's question.

"Why,—yes,—. I suppose if you put it on the ground of what they ought to do there is no other standard of conduct. But the question is, what is feasible? Is it possible to make it pay? To succeed in the newspaper business we have got to conform to the customs and the recognized methods of society. We can't do as we would do in an ideal world."

"Do you mean that we can't run the paper strictly on Christian principles and make it succeed?"

"Yes, that's just what I mean. It can't be done. We'll go bankrupt in thirty days."

Edward Norman did not reply at once. He was very thoughtful.

"We shall have occasion to talk this over again, Clark. Meanwhile, I think we ought to understand each other frankly. I have pledged myself for a year to do everything connected with the paper after answering the question, 'What would Jesus do?' as honestly as possible. I shall continue to do this in the belief that not only can we succeed but that we can succeed better than we ever did."

Clark rose. "Then the report does not go in?"

"It does not. There is plenty of good material to take its place, and you know what it is."

Clark hesitated.

"Are you going to say anything about the absence of the report?"

"No, let the paper go to press as if there had been no such thing as a prize fight yesterday."

Clark walked out of the room to his own desk feeling as if the bottom had dropped out of everything. He was astonished, bewildered, excited and considerably enraged. His great respect for Norman checked his rising indignation and disgust, but with it all was a feeling of growing wonder at the sudden change of motive which had entered the office of the "Daily News" and threatened as he firmly believed, to destroy it.

Before noon every reporter, pressman and employee on the "Daily News" was informed of the remarkable fact that the paper was going to press without a word in it about the famous prize fight of Sunday. The reporters were simply astonished beyond measure at the announcement of the fact. Every one in the stereotyping and composing rooms had something to say about the unheard of omission. Two or three times during the day when Mr. Norman had occasion to visit the composing rooms, the men stopped their work or glanced around their cases looking at him curiously. He knew that he was being observed strangely and said nothing, and did not appear to note it.

There had been several changes in the paper suggested by the editor, but nothing marked. He was waiting, and thinking deeply. He felt as if he needed time and considerable opportunity for the exercise of his best judgment in several matters before he answered his ever present question in the right way. It was not because there were not a great many things in the life of the paper that were contrary to the spirit of Christ that he did not act at once, but because he was yet greatly in doubt concerning what action Jesus would take.

When the "Daily News" came out that evening it carried to its subscribers a distinct sensation. The presence of the report of the prize fight could not have produced anything equal to the effect of its omission. Hundreds of men in the hotels and stores down town, as well as regular subscribers, eagerly opened the paper and searched it through for the account of the great fight. Not finding it, they rushed to the news stand and bought other papers. Even the newsboys had not all understood the fact of the omission. One of them was calling out, "Daily News! Full 'count great prize fight 't Resort. News, Sir!"

A man on the corner of the Avenue close by the "News" office bought the paper, looked over its front page hurriedly and then angrily called the boy back.

"Here boy! What's the matter with your paper! There is no prize fight here! What do you mean by selling old papers?"

"Old papers, nuthin!" replied the boy indignantly. "Dat's to-day's paper. What's de matter wid you?"

"But there's no account of any prize fight here! Look!"

The man handed back the paper and the boy glanced at it hurriedly. Then he whistled, while a bewildering look crept over his face. Seeing another boy running by with papers he called out, "Say, Sam, lemme see your pile!" A hasty examination revealed the remarkable fact that all the copies of the "News" were silent on the prize fight.

"Here, give me another paper! One with the prize fight account!" shouted the customer. He received it and walked off, while the two boys remained comparing notes and lost in wonder at the event. "Somp'n slipped a cog in the Newsy sure," said first boy. But he couldn't tell why and rushed over to the "News" office to find out.

There were several other boys at the delivery room and they were all excited and disgusted. The amount of slangy remonstrances hurled at the clerk back of the long counter would have driven any one else to despair. He was used to more or less of it all the time and consequently hardened to it.

Mr. Norman was just coming down stairs on his way home and he paused as he went by the door of the delivery room and looked in.

"What's the matter here, George?" he asked the clerk as he noted the unusual confusion.

"The boys say they can't sell any copies of the 'News' to-night because the prize fight is not in it," replied George looking curiously at the editor as so many of the employees had done during the day.

Mr. Norman hesitated a moment, then walked into the room and confronted the boys.

"How many papers are there here, boys? Count them out and I'll buy them to-night."

There was a wild stare and a wild counting of papers on the part of the boys.

"Give them their money, George, and if any of the other boys come in with the same complaint buy their unsold copies. Is that fair?" he asked the boys who were smitten into unusual silence by the unheard-of action on the part of the editor.

"Fair! Well, I should—But will you keep dis up? Will dis be a continual performance for de benefit of de fraternity?"

Mr. Norman smiled slightly but he did not think it was necessary to answer the question. He walked out of the office and went home. On the way he could not avoid that constant query, "Would Jesus have done it?" It was not so much with reference to this last transaction as to the entire motive that had urged him on since he had made the promise. The news boys were necessarily sufferers through the action he had taken. Why should they lose money by it? They were not to blame. He was a rich man and could afford to put a little brightness into their lives if he chose to do it. He believed as he went on his way home that Jesus would have done either what he did or something similar in order to be free from any possible feeling of injustice. He was not deciding these questions for any one else but for his own conduct. He was not in a position to dogmatize and he felt that he could answer only with his own judgment and conscience as to his interpretation of Jesus' probable action. The falling off in sales of the paper he had in a certain measure foreseen. But he was yet to realize the full extent of the loss to the paper if such a policy should be continued.

During the week he was in receipt of numerous letters commenting on the absence from the "News" of the account of the prize fight. Two or three of these letters may be of interest.

Editor of the "News."
Dear Sir:

I have been deciding for some time to change my paper. I want a journal that is up to the times, progressive and enterprising, supplying the public demand at all points.

The recent freak of your paper in refusing to print the account of the famous contest at the Resort has decided me finally to change my paper. Please discontinue it.

Very truly yours,

———. ———.

(Here followed the name of a business man who had been a subscriber for many years.)

Edward Norman.
Editor of the "Daily News": Raymond.
Dear Ed.

What is this sensation you have given the people of your burg? Hope you don't intend to try the "Reform Business," through the avenue of the Press. It's dangerous to experiment much along that line. Take my advice and stick to the enterprising modern methods you have made so successful for the "News." The public wants prize fights and such. Give it what it wants and let some one else do the Reforming business.

Yours,

———. ———.

(Here followed the name of one of Norman's old friends, the editor of a daily in an adjoining town.)

My dear Mr. Norman:

I hasten to write you a note of appreciation for the evident carrying out of your promise. It is a splendid beginning and no one feels the value of it better than I do. I know something of what it will cost you, but not all.

Your Pastor,
Henry Maxwell.

One letter which he opened immediately after reading this from Maxwell revealed to him something of the loss to his business that possibly awaited him.

Mr. Edward Norman;
Editor of the "Daily News":
Dear Sir.

At the expiration of my advertising limit you will do me the favor not to continue as you have done heretofore. I enclose check for payment in full and shall consider my account with your paper closed after date.

Very truly yours,

———. ———.

(Here followed the name of one of the largest dealers in Tobacco in the city. He had been in the habit of inserting a column of conspicuous advertising and paying for it a very large price.)

Edward Norman laid this letter down very thoughtfully, and then after a moment he took up a copy of his paper and looked through the advertising columns. There was no connection implied in the tobacco merchant's letter between the omission of the prize fight and the withdrawal of the advertisement. But he could not avoid putting the two together. In point of fact, he afterwards learned that the tobacco dealer withdrew his advertisement because he had heard that the editor of the "News" was about to enter upon some queer reform policy that would be certain to reduce its subscription list.

But the letter directed Norman's attention to the advertising phase of his paper. He had not considered this before. As he glanced over the columns he could not escape the conviction that Jesus could not permit some of them in his paper. What would Jesus do with that other long advertisement of liquor? Raymond enjoyed a system of high license, and the saloon and the billiard hall and the beer garden were a part of the city's Christian civilization. He was simply doing what every other business man in Raymond did. And it was one of the best paying sources of revenue. What would the paper do if it cut these out? Could it live? That was the question. But—was that the question after all? "What would Jesus do?" That was the question he was answering, or trying to answer, this week. Would Jesus advertise whisky and tobacco in his paper?

Edward Norman asked it honestly, and after a prayer for help and wisdom he asked Clark to come into the office.

Clark came in feeling that the paper was at a crisis and prepared for almost anything after his Monday morning experience. This was Thursday.

"Clark," said Norman, speaking slowly and carefully, "I have been looking at our advertising columns and have decided to dispense with some of the matter as soon as the contracts run out. I wish you would notify the advertising agent not to solicit or renew the ads. I have marked here."

He handed the paper with the marked places over to Clark, who took it and looked over the columns with a very serious air.

"This will mean a great loss to the 'News.' How long do you think you can keep this sort of thing up?" Clark was astonished at the editor's action and could not understand it.

"Clark, do you think if Jesus were the editor and proprietor of a daily paper in Raymond he would print advertisements of whisky and tobacco in it?"

Clark looked at his chief with that same look of astonishment which had greeted the question before.

"Well—no—I don't suppose he would. But what has that to do with us? We can't do as he would. Newspapers can't be run on any such basis."

"Why not?" asked Edward Norman quietly.

"Why not! Because they will lose more money than they make, that's all." Clark spoke out with an irritation that he really felt. "We shall certainly bankrupt the paper with this sort of business policy."

"Do you think so?" Norman asked the question not as if he expected an answer but simply as if he were talking with himself. After a pause he said,

"You may direct Marks to do as I said. I believe it is what Jesus would do, and as I told you, Clark, that is what I have promised to try to do for a year, regardless of what the results may be to me. I cannot believe that by any kind of reasoning we could reach a conclusion justifying Jesus in the advertisement, in this age, of whisky and tobacco in a newspaper. There are some other advertisements of a doubtful character I shall study into. Meanwhile I feel a conviction in regard to these that cannot be silenced."

Clark went back to his desk feeling as if he had been in the presence of a very peculiar person. He could not grasp the meaning of it all. He felt enraged and alarmed. He was sure any such policy would ruin the paper as soon as it became generally known that the editor was trying to do everything by such an absurd moral standard. What would become of business if this standard were adopted? It would upset every custom and introduce endless confusion. It was simply foolishness. It was downright idiocy. So Clark said to himself, and when Marks was informed of the action, he seconded the managing editor with some very forcible ejaculations. What was the matter with the chief? Was he insane? Was he going to bankrupt the whole business?

But Edward Norman had not faced his most serious problem.

When he came down to the office Friday morning he was confronted with the usual program for the Sunday morning edition. The "News" was one of the few evening papers to issue a Sunday edition, and it had always been remarkably successful financially. There was an average of one page of literary and religious items to thirty or forty pages of sport, theater, gossip, fashion, society and political material. This made a very interesting magazine of all sorts of reading matter and had always been welcomed by all the subscribers, church members and all, as a Sunday necessity.

Edward Norman now faced this fact and put to himself the question, "What would Jesus do?" If he were editor of a paper would he deliberately plan to put into the homes of all the church people and Christians of Raymond such a collection of reading matter on the one day of the week which ought to be given up to something better and holier? He was of course familiar with the regular argument for the Sunday paper that the public needed something of the sort and the working man, especially, who would not go to church any way, ought to have something entertaining and instructive on Sunday, his only day of rest. But suppose the Sunday morning paper did not pay? Suppose there was no money in it? How eager would the editor or the proprietor be then to supply this crying need of the working man? Edward Norman communed honestly with himself over the subject. Taking everything into account, would Jesus probably edit a Sunday morning paper? No matter whether it paid. That was not the question. As a matter of fact the Sunday "News" paid so well that it would be a direct loss of thousands of dollars to discontinue it. Besides, the regular subscribers had paid for a seven-day paper. Had he any right now to give them anything less than they had supposed they had paid for?

He was honestly perplexed by the question. So much was involved in the discontinuance of the Sunday edition that for the first time he almost declined to be guided by the standard of Jesus' probable action. He was sole proprietor of the paper. It was his to shape as he chose. He had no board of directors to consult as to policy. But as he sat there surrounded by the usual quantity of material for the Sunday edition, he reached some definite conclusions. And among them was the determination to call in the force of the paper and frankly state his motive and purpose.

He sent word for Clark and the other men in the office, including the few reporters who were in the building and the foreman, with what men were in the composing room. (It was early in the morning and they were not all in) to come into the mailing room. This was a large room, and the men came in, wondering, and perched around on the tables and counters. It was a very unusual proceeding, but they all agreed that the paper was being run on new principles any how, and they all watched Mr. Norman curiously as he spoke.

"I called you in here to let you know my plans for the future of the "News." I propose certain changes which I believe are necessary. I understand that some things I have already done are regarded by the men as very strange. I wish to state my motive in doing what I have done." Here he told the men what he had already told Clark and they stared, as he had done, and looked as painfully conscious.

"Now in acting on this standard of conduct I have reached a conclusion which will, no doubt, cause some surprise. I have decided that the Sunday morning edition of the "News" shall be discontinued after next Sunday's issue. I shall state in that issue my reasons for discontinuing. In order to make up to the subscribers the amount of reading matter they may suppose themselves entitled to, we can issue a double number on Saturday, as is done by very many evening papers that make no attempt at a Sunday edition. I am convinced that, from a Christian point of view, more harm than good has been done by our Sunday morning paper. I do not believe that Jesus would be responsible for it if He were in my place to-day. It will occasion some trouble to arrange the details caused by this change with the advertisers and subscribers. That is for me to look after. The change itself is one that will take place. So far as I can see, the loss will fall on myself. Neither the reporters nor the press men need make any particular changes in their plans."

Edward Norman looked around the room and no one spoke. He was struck for the first time in his life with the fact that in all the years of his newspaper life he had never had the force of the paper together in this way. "Would Jesus do that? That is, would He probably run a newspaper on some loving family plan where editors, reporters, pressmen and all, met to discuss and devise and plan for the making of a paper that should have in view—"

He caught himself drawing almost away from the facts of typographical unions and office rules and reporters' enterprise, and all the cold business-like methods that make a great daily successful. But still, the vague picture that came up in the mailing room would not fade away, even when he had gone into his office and the men had gone back to their places with wonder in their looks and questions of all sorts on their tongues as they talked over the editor's remarkable actions.

Clark came in and had a long serious talk with the chief. He was thoroughly roused and his protest almost reached the point of resigning his place. Norman guarded himself carefully. Every minute of the interview was painful to him but he felt more than ever the necessity of doing the Christlike thing. Clark was a very valuable man. It would be difficult to fill his place. But he was not able to give any reasons for continuing the Sunday paper that answered the question, "What would Jesus do?" by letting Jesus print that edition.

"It comes to this, then," said Clark finally. "You will bankrupt the paper in thirty days. We might as well face that future fact."

"I don't think we shall. Will you stay by the "News" until it is bankrupt?" asked Edward Norman with a strange smile.

"Mr. Norman, I don't understand you. You are not the same man this week that I ever knew."

"I don't know myself, either, Clark. Something remarkable has caught me up and borne me on. But I was never more convinced of final success and power for the paper. You have not answered my question. Will you stay with me?"

Clark hesitated a moment and finally said, yes. Norman shook hands with him and turned to his desk. Clark went back into his room stirred by a number of conflicting emotions. He had never before known such an exciting and mentally disturbing week, and he felt now as if he were connected with an enterprise that might at any moment collapse and ruin him and all connected with it.

Sunday morning dawned again on Raymond, and Henry Maxwell's church was again crowded. Before the service began, Edward Norman attracted general attention. He sat quietly in his usual place about three seats from the pulpit. The Sunday morning issue of the "News" containing the statement of its discontinuance had been read by nearly every man in the house. The announcement had been expressed in such remarkable language that every reader was struck by it. No such series of distinct sensations had ever disturbed the usual business custom of Raymond. The events connected with the "News" were not all. People were eagerly talking about the strange things done during the week by Alexander Powers at the Railroad shops, and by Milton Wright in his stores on the avenue. The service progressed upon a distinct wave of excitement in the pews, Henry Maxwell faced it all with a calmness which indicated a strength and purpose more than usual. His prayers were very helpful. His sermon was not so easy to describe. How would a minister be apt to preach to his people if he came before them after an entire week of eager asking, "How would Jesus preach? What would He probably say?" It is very certain that Henry Maxwell did not preach as he had done two Sundays before. Tuesday of the past week he had stood by the grave of the dead stranger and said the words, "Earth to earth, ashes to ashes, dust to dust," and still he was moved by the spirit of a deeper impulse than he could measure as he thought of his people and yearned for the Christ message when he should be in his pulpit again.

Now that Sunday had come and the people were there to hear, what would the Master tell them? He agonized over his preparation for them and yet he knew he had not been able to fit his message into his ideal of the Christ. Nevertheless no one in the First Church could remember hearing such a sermon before. There was in it rebuke for sin, especially hypocrisy. There was definite rebuke of the greed of wealth and the selfishness of fashion, two things that First Church never heard rebuked this way before, and there was a love of his people that gathered new force as the sermon went on. When it was finished there were those who were saying in their hearts, "The Spirit moved that sermon." And they were right.

Then Rachel Winslow rose to sing. This time, after the sermon, by Henry Maxwell's request. Rachel's singing did not provoke applause this time. What deeper feeling carried people's hearts into a reverent silence and tenderness of thought? Rachel was beautiful. But the consciousness of her remarkable loveliness had always marred her singing with those who had the deepest spiritual feeling, It had also marred her rendering of certain kinds of music with herself. To-day this was all gone. There was no lack of power in her grand voice. But there was an actual added element of humility and purity which the audience strictly felt and bowed to.

Before the service closed, Henry Maxwell asked those who had remained the week before to stay again for a few moments for consultation, and any others who were willing to make the pledge taken at that time. When he was at liberty he went into the lecture room. To his astonishment it was almost filled. This time a large proportion of young people had come. But among them were a few business men and officers of the church.

As before, Henry Maxwell asked them to pray with him. And as before a distinct answer came in the presence of the Divine Spirit. There was no doubt in the minds of any one present that what they proposed to do was so clearly in line with the divine will, that a blessing rested on it in a very special manner.

They remained some time to ask questions and consult together. There was a feeling of fellowship such as they had never known in their church membership. Edward Norman's action was well understood by them all, and he answered several questions.

"What will be the probable result of your discontinuance of the Sunday paper?" asked Alexander Powers who sat next to him.

"I don't know yet. I presume it will result in a falling off of subscriptions and advertisements. I anticipate that."

"Do you have any doubts about your action? I mean do you regret it or fear it is not what Jesus would do?" asked Henry Maxwell.

"Not in the least. But I would like to ask for my own satisfaction, if any one of you here thinks Jesus would issue a Sunday morning paper?"

No one spoke for a minute. Then Jasper Chase said, "We seem to think alike on that, but I have been puzzled several times during the week to know just what He would do. It is not always an easy question to answer."

"I find that trouble," said Virginia Page. She sat by Rachel Winslow. Every one who knew Virginia Page was wondering how she would succeed in keeping her promise.

"I think perhaps I find it specially difficult to answer the question on account of my money. Jesus never owned any property, and there is nothing in his example to guide me in the use of mine. I am studying and praying. I think I see clearly a part of what He would do, but not all. 'What would Jesus do with a million dollars?' is my question really. I confess that I am not yet able to answer it to my satisfaction."

"I could tell you what to do with a part of it," said Rachel, turning her face towards Virginia.

"That does not trouble me," replied Virginia with a slight smile. "What I am trying to discover is a principle of Jesus that will enable me to come the nearest possible to His action as it ought to influence the entire course of my life so far as my wealth and its use are concerned."

"That will take time," said Henry Maxwell slowly. All the rest in the room were thinking hard of the same thing. Milton Wright told something of his experience. He was gradually working out a plan for his business relations with his employees and it was opening up a new world to him and them. A few of the younger men told of special attempts to answer the question. There was almost general consent over the fact that the application of the Jesus spirit and practice to every day life was the serious thing. It required a knowledge of Him and an insight into His motives that most of them did not yet possess.

When they finally adjourned after a silent prayer that marked with growing power the Divine Presence, they went away discussing earnestly their difficulties and seeking light from one another.

Rachel Winslow and Virginia Page went out together. Edward Norman and Milton Wright became so interested in their mutual conference that they walked on past Norman's home and came back together. Jasper Chase and the President of the Endeavor Society stood talking earnestly in one corner of the room. Alexander Powers and Henry Maxwell remained even after all the others had gone.

"I want you to come down to the shops to-morrow and see my plan and talk to the men. Somehow I feel as if you could get nearer to them than any one else just now."

"I don't know about that, but I will come," replied Henry Maxwell a little sadly. How was he fitted to stand before two or three hundred working men and give them a message? Yet in the moment of his weakness, as he asked the question, he rebuked himself for it. What would Jesus do? That was an end to the discussion.

He went down the next day and found Alexander Powers in his office. It lacked a few minutes of twelve and the Superintendent said, "Come up stairs, and I'll show you what I've been trying to do."

They went through the machine shops, climbed a long flight of stairs and entered a very large empty room. It had once been used by the company for a store room.

"Since making that promise a week ago I have had a good many things to think of," said the Superintendent, "and among them is this: Our company gives me the use of this room and I am going to fit it up with tables and a coffee plant in the corner there where those steam pipes are. My plan is to provide a good place where the men can come up and eat their noon lunch and give them, two or three times a week, the privilege of a fifteen minutes' talk on some subject that will be a real help to them in their lives."

Maxwell looked surprised and asked if the men would come for any such purpose.

"Yes, they'll come. After all, I know the men pretty well. They are among the most intelligent working men in the country to-day. But they are as a whole, entirely removed from all church influence. I asked, 'What would Jesus do?' And among other things it seemed to me He would begin to act in some way to add to the lives of these men more physical and spiritual comfort. It is a very little thing, this room and what it represents, but I acted on the first impulse to do the first thing that appealed to my good sense and I want to work out this idea. I want you to speak to the men when they come up at noon. I have asked them to come up and see the place and I'll tell them something about it."

Henry Maxwell was ashamed to say how uneasy he felt at being asked to speak a few words to a company of working men. How could he speak without notes, or to such a crowd? He was honestly in a condition of genuine fright over the prospect. He actually felt afraid of facing these men. He shrank from the ordeal of confronting such a crowd, so different from the Sunday audiences he was familiar with.

There were half a dozen long rude tables and benches in the great room, and when the noon whistle sounded the men poured up stairs from the machine shop below and seating themselves at the tables began to eat their lunch. There were perhaps three hundred of them. They had read the Superintendent's notice which he had posted up in various places, and came largely out of curiosity.

They were favorably impressed. The room was large and airy, free from smoke and dust and well warmed from the steam pipes.

About twenty minutes of one, Alexander Powers told the men what he had in mind. He spoke very simply, like one who understands thoroughly the character of his audience, and then introduced the Rev. Henry Maxwell of the First Church, his pastor, who had consented to speak a few minutes.

Henry Maxwell will never forget the feelings with which for the first time he confronted that grimy-faced audience of working men. Like hundreds of other ministers he had never spoken to any gathering except those made up of people of his own class in the sense that they were familiar, in their dress and education and habits, to him. This was a new world to him, and nothing but his new rule of conduct could have made possible his message and its effect. He spoke on the subject of satisfaction with life; what caused it; what its real sources were. He had the great good sense on this first appearance not to recognize the men as a class distinct from himself. He did not use the term "working men," and did not say a word to suggest any difference between their lives and his own.

The men were pleased. A good many of them shook hands with him before going down to their work, and Henry Maxwell telling it all to his wife when he reached home, said that never in all his life had he known the delight he then felt in having a hand-shake from a man of physical labor. The day marked an important one in his Christian experience, more important than he knew. It was the beginning of a fellowship between him and the working world. It was the first plank laid down to help bridge the chasm between the church and labor in Raymond.

Alexander Powers went back to his desk that afternoon much pleased with his plan and seeing much help in it for the men. He knew where he could get some good tables from an abandoned eating house at one of the stations down the road, and he saw how the coffee arrangement could be made a very attractive feature. The men had responded even better than he anticipated and the whole thing could not help being a great benefit to them.

He took up the routine of his work with a glow of satisfaction. After all, he wanted to do as Jesus would, he said to himself.

It was nearly four o'clock when he opened one of the company's long envelopes which he supposed contained orders for the purchasing of stores. He ran over the first page of type-written matter in his usual quick, businesslike manner before he saw that he was reading what was not intended for his office but for the Superintendent of the Freight Department.

He turned over a page mechanically, not meaning to read what was not addressed to him, but, before he knew it, he was in possession of evidence which conclusively proved that the company was engaged in a systematic violation of the Interstate Commerce Laws of the United States. It was as distinct and unequivocal breaking of law as if a private citizen should enter a house and rob the inmates. The discrimination shown in rebates was in total contempt of all the statute. Under the laws of the state it was also a distinct violation of certain provisions recently passed by the legislature to prevent railroad trusts. There was no question that he held in his hand evidence sufficient to convict the company of willful, intelligent violation of the law of the Commission and the law of the state also.

He dropped the papers on his desk as if they were poison, and instantly the question flashed across his mind, "What would Jesus do?" He tried to shut the question out. He tried to reason with himself by saying it was none of his business. He had supposed in a more or less indefinite way as did nearly all of the officers of the Company, that this had been going on right along in nearly all the roads. He was not in a position, owing to his place in the shops, to prove anything direct, and he had regarded it all as a matter which did not concern him at all. The papers now before him revealed the entire affair. They had through some carelessness in the address come into his hands. What business of his was it? If he saw a man entering his neighbor's house to steal would it not be his duty to inform the officers of the law? Was a railroad company such a different thing, was it under a different rule of conduct so that it could rob the public and defy law and be undisturbed because it was such a great organization? What would Jesus do? Then there was his family. Of course if he took any steps to inform the Commission it would mean the loss of his position. His wife and daughters had always enjoyed luxury and a good place in society. If he came out against this lawlessness as a witness it would drag him into courts, his motives would be misunderstood and the whole thing would end in his disgrace and the loss of his position. Surely, it was none of his business. He could easily get the papers back to the Freight Department and no one be the wiser. Let the iniquity go on. Let the law be defied. What was it to him? He would work out his plans for bettering the conditions just about him. What more could a man do in this railroad business where there was so much going on any way that made it impossible to live by the Christian standard? But what would Jesus do if He knew the facts? That was the question that confronted Alexander Powers as the day wore into evening.

The lights in the office had been turned on. The whir of the great engine and the crash of the planer in the big shop continued until six o'clock.

Then the whistle blew, the engines slowed down, the men dropped their tools and ran for the block house.

Alexander Powers heard the familiar click, click, of the blocks as the men filed passed the window of the block house just outside. He said to his clerks, "I'm not going just yet. I have something extra to-night." He waited until he heard the last man deposit his block. The men behind the block case went out. The engineer and his assistants had work for half an hour, but they went out at another door.

At seven o'clock that evening any one who had looked into the Superintendent's office would have seen an unusual sight. He was kneeling down and his face was buried in his hands as he bowed his head upon the papers on his desk.

CHAPTER III

> If any man cometh unto me and hateth not his own father and
> mother and wife and children and brethren and sisters, yea, and
> his own life also, he cannot be my disciple. * * * And whosoever
> forsaketh not all that he hath, he cannot be my disciple.[6]

When Rachel Winslow and Virginia Page separated after the meeting at the First Church on Sunday, they agreed to continue their conversation the next day. Virginia asked

---

[6]Luke 14:26 and 33.

Rachel to come and lunch with her at noon, and Rachel accordingly rang the bell at the Page mansion about half past eleven, Virginia herself met her and the two were soon talking earnestly.

"The fact is," Rachel was saying, after they had been talking a few minutes, "I cannot reconcile it with my judgment of what He would do. I cannot tell another person what to do, but I feel that I ought not to accept this offer."

"What will you do, then?" asked Virginia with great interest.

"I don't know yet. But I have decided to refuse this offer."

Rachel picked up a letter that had been lying in her lap and ran over its contents again. It was a letter from the manager of a comic opera offering her a place with a large traveling company for the season. The salary was a very large figure, and the prospect held out by the manager was flattering. He had heard Rachel sing that Sunday morning when the stranger had interrupted the service. He had been much impressed. There was money in that voice and it ought to be used in comic opera, so said the letter, and the manager wanted a reply as soon as possible.

"There's no virtue in saying No to this offer when I have the other one," Rachel went on thoughtfully. "That's harder to decide. But I've about made up my mind. To tell the truth, Virginia, I'm completely convinced in the first case that Jesus would never use any talent like a good voice just to make money. But now take this concert offer. Here is a reputable company to travel with an impersonator and a violinist and a male quartette. All people of good reputation. I'm asked to go as one of the company and sing leading soprano. The salary—I mentioned it, didn't I?—is to be guaranteed two hundred dollars a month for the season. But I don't feel satisfied that Jesus would go. What do you think?"

"You mustn't ask me to decide for you," replied Virginia with a sad smile. "I believe Mr. Maxwell was right when he said we must each one of us decide according to the judgment we felt for ourselves to be Christlike. I am having a harder time than you are, dear, to decide what He would do."

"Are you?" Rachel asked. She rose and walked over to the window and looked out. Virginia came and stood by her. The street was crowded with life and the two young women looked at it silently for a moment. Suddenly Virginia broke out as Rachel had never heard her before.

"Rachel, what does all this contrast in conditions mean to you as you ask this question of what Jesus would do? It maddens me to think that the society in which I have been brought up, the same to which we are both said to belong, is satisfied year after year to go on dressing and eating and having a good time, giving and receiving entertainments, spending its money on houses and luxuries and, occasionally, to ease its conscience, donating, without any personal sacrifice, a little money to charity. I have been educated, as you have, in one of the most expensive schools of America. Launched into society as an heiress. Supposed to be in a very enviable position. I'm perfectly well, I can travel or stay at home. I can do as I please. I can gratify almost any want or desire and yet, when I honestly try to imagine Jesus living the life I have lived and am expected to live, and doing for the rest of my life what thousands of other rich people do, I am under condemnation for being one of the most wicked, selfish, useless creatures in the world. I have not looked out of this window for weeks without a feeling of horror towards myself as I see the humanity that pours by this house."

Virginia turned away and walked up and down the room. Rachel watched her and could not repress the rising tide of her own growing definition of discipleship. Of what Christian use was her own talent of song? Was the best she could do to sell her talent for so much a month, go on a concert company's tour, dress beautifully, enjoy the excitement of public applause and gain a reputation as a great singer? Was that what Jesus would do?

She was not morbid. She was in sound health, was conscious of great powers as a singer, and knew that if she went out into public life she could make a great deal of money and become well known. It is doubtful if she overestimated her ability to accomplish all she thought herself capable of. And Virginia—what she had just said smote Rachel with great force because of the similar position in which the two friends found themselves.

Lunch was announced and they went out and were joined by Virginia's grandmother, Madam Page, a handsome, stately woman of sixty-five, and Virginia's brother, Rollin, a young man who spent most of his time at one of the clubs and had no particular ambition for anything, but a growing admiration for Rachel Winslow, and whenever she dined or lunched at the Page mansion, if he knew of it, he always planned to be at home.

These three made up the Page family. Virginia's father had been a banker and grain speculator. Her mother had died ten years before. Her father within the past year. The grandmother, a Southern woman in birth and training, had all the traditions and feelings that accompany the possession of wealth and social standing that have never been disturbed. She was a shrewd, careful, business woman of more than average ability. The family property and wealth were invested, in large measure, under her personal care. Virginia's portion was, without any restriction, her own. She had been trained by her father to understand the ways of the business world, and even the grandmother had been compelled to acknowledge the girl's capacity for taking care of her own money.

Perhaps two persons could not be found anywhere less capable of understanding a girl like Virginia than Madam Page and Rollin. Rachel, who had known the family since she was a girl playmate of Virginia's could not help thinking of what confronted Virginia in her own home when she once decided on the course which she honestly believed Jesus would take. To-day at lunch, as she recalled Virginia's outbreak in the front room, she tried to picture the scene that would at some time occur between Madam Page and her granddaughter.

"I understand that you are going on the stage, Miss Winslow. We shall all be delighted, I'm sure," said Rollin, during one of the pauses in the conversation which had not been animated.

Rachel colored and felt annoyed.

"Who told you?" she asked, while Virginia, who had been very silent and reserved suddenly roused herself and appeared ready to join in the talk.

"Oh! we hear a thing or two on the street. Besides, every one saw Crandall the manager at church two weeks ago. He doesn't go to church to hear the preaching. In fact I know other people who don't either, not when there's something better to hear."

Rachel did not color this time, but she answered quietly,

"You're mistaken. I'm not going on the stage."

"It's a great pity. You'd make a hit. Everybody is talking about your singing."

This time Rachel flushed with genuine anger.

Before she could say anything, Virginia broke in.

"Whom do you mean by 'everybody?' "

"Whom? I mean all the people who hear Miss Winslow on Sunday. What other time do they hear her? It's a great pity, I say, that the general public outside of Raymond cannot hear her voice."

"Let us talk about something else," said Rachel a little sharply. Madam Page glanced at her and spoke with a gentle courtesy.

"My dear, Rollin never could pay an indirect compliment. He is like his father in that. But we are all curious to know something of your plans. We claim the right from old acquaintance, you know. And Virginia had already told us of your concert company offer."

"I supposed of course that was public property," said Virginia, smiling across the table. "It was in the "News" yesterday."

"Yes, yes," replied Rachel hastily. "I understand that, Madam Page. Well, Virginia and I have been talking about it. I have decided not to accept, and that is as far as I have gone yet."

Rachel was conscious of the fact that the conversation had, up to this point, been narrowing her hesitation concerning the company's offer down to a decision that would absolutely satisfy her own judgment of Jesus' probable action. It had been the last thing in the world, however, that she had desired to have her decision made in any way so public as this. Somehow what Rollin Page had said and his manner in saying it had hastened her judgment in the matter.

"Would you mind telling us, Rachel, your reasons for refusing the offer? It looks like a good opportunity for a young girl like you. Don't you think the general public ought to hear you? I feel like Rollin about that. A voice like yours belongs to a larger audience than Raymond and the First Church."

Rachel Winslow was naturally a girl of great reserve. She shrank from making her plans or her thoughts public. But with all her repression there was possible in her an occasional sudden breaking out that was simply an impulsive, thoughtful, frank, truthful expression of her most inner personal feeling. She spoke now in reply to Madam Page in one of those rare moments of unreserve that added to the attractiveness of her whole character.

"I have no other reason than a conviction that Jesus would do the same thing," she said looking in Madam Page's eyes with a clear earnest gaze.

Madam Page turned red and Rollin stared. Before her grandmother could say anything, Virginia spoke. Her rising color showed how she was stirred. Virginia's pale, clear complexion was that of health, but it was generally in marked contrast to Rachel's tropical type of beauty.

"Grandmother, you know we promised to make that the standard of our conduct for a year. Mr. Maxwell's proposition was plain to all who heard it. We have not been able to arrive at our decisions very rapidly. The difficulty in knowing what Jesus would do has perplexed Rachel and me a good deal."

Madam Page looked sharply at Virginia before she said anything.

"Of course, I understand Mr. Maxwell's statement. It is perfectly impracticable to put it into practice. I felt confident at the time that those who promised would find it out after a trial and abandon it as visionary and absurd. I have nothing to say about Miss Winslow's affairs, but—" (she paused and continued with a sharpness that was new to Rachel,) "I hope you have no foolish notions in this matter, Virginia."

"I have a great many notions," replied Virginia quietly. "Whether they are foolish or not depends upon my right understanding of what He would do. As soon as I find out, I shall do it."

"Excuse me, ladies," said Rollin rising from the table. "The conversation is getting beyond my depth. I shall retire to the library for a cigar."

He went out of the dining room and there was silence for a moment. Madam Page waited until the servant had brought in something and then asked her to go out. She was angry and her anger was formidable, although checked in some measure by the presence of Rachel.

"I am older by several years than you, young ladies," she said, and her traditional type of bearing seemed to Rachel to rise up like a great frozen wall between her and every conception of Jesus as a sacrifice. "What you have promised in a spirit of false emotion, I presume, is impossible of performance."

"Do you mean, grandmother, that we cannot possibly act as Jesus would, or do you mean that if we try to, we shall offend the customs and prejudices of society?" asked Virginia.

"It is not required! It is not necessary! Besides how can you act with any—"

Madam Page paused, broke off her sentence, and then turned to Rachel.

"What will your mother say to your decision? My dear, is it not foolish? What do you expect to do with your voice, any way?"

"I don't know what mother will say yet," Rachel answered, with a great shrinking from trying to give her mother's probable answer. If there was a woman in all Raymond with great ambitions for her daughter's success as a singer, Mrs. Winslow was that woman.

"O you will see it in a different light after wise thought of it. My dear," continued Madam Page rising from the table, "you will live to regret it if you do not accept the concert company's offer or something like it."

Rachel said something that contained a hint of the struggle she was still having. And after a little she went away, feeling that her departure was to be followed by a painful conversation between Virginia and her grandmother. As she afterward learned Virginia passed through a crisis of feeling during that scene with her grandmother that hastened her final decision as to the use of her money and her social position.

Rachel was glad to escape and be by herself. A plan was slowly forming in her mind and she wanted to be alone to think it out carefully. But before she had walked two blocks she was annoyed to find Rollin Page walking beside her.

"Sorry to disturb your thought, Miss Winslow, but I happened to be going your way and had an idea you might not object. In fact I've been walking here for a whole block and you haven't objected."

"I did not see you," replied Rachel.

"I wouldn't mind that if you only thought of me once in a while," said Rollin suddenly. He took one last nervous puff of his cigar, tossed it into the street and walked along with a pale face.

Rachel was surprised but not startled. She had known Rollin as a boy, and there had been a time when they had used each other's first names familiarly. Lately, however, something in Rachel's manner had put an end to that. She was used to his direct attempts at compliment and was sometimes amused by them. To-day she honestly wished him anywhere else.

"Do you ever think of me, Miss Winslow?" asked Rollin after a pause.

"Oh, yes, quite often!" said Rachel with a smile.

"Are you thinking of me now?"

"Yes, that is—yes, I am."

"What?"

"Do you want me to be absolutely truthful?"

"Of course."

"Then I was thinking that I wished you were not here."

Rollin bit his lip and looked gloomy. Rachel had not spoken anything as he wished.

"Now look here, Rachel—Oh, I know that's forbidden, but I've got to speak sometime; you know how I feel. What makes you treat me so hard? You used to like me a little, you know."

"Did I? Of course we used to get on very well as boy and girl. But we are older now."

Rachel still spoke in the light, easy way she had used since her first annoyance at seeing him. She was still somewhat preoccupied with her plan which had been disturbed by Rollin's appearance.

They walked along in silence a little way. The avenue was full of people. Among the persons passing was Jasper Chase. He saw Rachel and Rollin and bowed as he went by. Rollin was watching Rachel closely.

"I wish I were Jasper Chase; maybe I'd stand some show then,'" he said moodily.

Rachel colored in spite of herself. She did not say anything, and quickened her pace a little. Rollin seemed determined to say something and Rachel seemed helpless to prevent him. After all, she thought, he might as well know the truth one time as another.

"You know well enough, Rachel, how I feel towards you. Isn't there any hope? I could make you happy. I've loved you a good many years—"

"Why, how old do you think I am?" broke in Rachel with a nervous laugh. She was shaken out of her usual poise of manner.

"You know what I mean," went on Rollin doggedly. "And you have no right to laugh at me just because I want you to marry me."

"I'm not! But it is useless for you to speak,—Rollin," said Rachel after a little hesitation, and then using his name in such a frank, simple way that he could attach no meaning to it beyond the familiarity of the family acquaintance. "It is impossible." She was still a little agitated by the fact of receiving a proposal of marriage on the avenue. But the noise on the street and sidewalk made the conversation as private as if they were in the house.

"Would you—that is—do you think—if you gave me time I would—"

"No!" said Rachel. She spoke firmly; perhaps, she thought afterwards, although she did not mean to, she spoke harshly.

They walked on for some time without a word. They were nearing Rachel's home and she was anxious to end the scene.

As they turned off the avenue into one of the quiet streets, Rollin spoke suddenly and with more manliness than he had yet shown. There was a distinct note of dignity in his voice that was new to Rachel.

"Miss Winslow, I ask you to be my wife. Is there any hope for me that you will ever consent?"

"None in the least." Rachel spoke decidedly.

"Will you tell me why?" He asked the question as if he had a right to a truthful answer.

"I do not feel towards you as a woman ought to feel towards the man she ought to marry."

"In other words you do not love me?"

"I do not. And I cannot."

"Why?" That was another question and Rachel was a little surprised that he should ask it.

"Because—" she hesitated for fear she might say too much in an attempt to speak the exact truth.

"Tell me just why. You can't hurt me more than you have already."

"Well, I don't and can't love you because you have no purpose in life. What do you ever do to make the world better? You spend your time in club life, in amusements, in travel, in luxury. What is there in such a life to attract a woman?"

"Not much, I guess," said Rollin with a little laugh. "Still, I don't know as I am any worse than the rest of the men around me. I'm not so bad as some. Glad to know your reason."

He suddenly stopped, took off his hat, bowed gravely and turned back. Rachel went on home and hurried into her room, disturbed in many ways by the event which had so unexpectedly thrust itself into her experience.

When she had time to think it all over, she found herself condemned by the very judgment she had passed on Rollin Page. What purpose had she in life? She had been abroad and studied music with one of the famous teachers of Europe. She had come home to Raymond and had been singing in the First Church choir now for a year. She was well paid. Up to that Sunday two weeks ago, she had been quite satisfied with herself and her position. She had shared her mother's ambition, and anticipated growing triumphs in the musical world. What possible career was before her except the regular career of every singer?

She asked the question again and, in the light of her recent reply to Rollin, asked again if she had any very great purpose in life herself? What would Jesus do? There was a fortune in her voice. She knew it, not necessarily as a matter of personal pride or professional egotism but simply as a fact. And she was obliged to acknowledge that until two weeks ago she had purposed to use her voice to make money and win admiration and applause. Was that a much higher purpose after all, than Rollin Page lived for?

She sat in her room a long time and finally went down stairs, resolved to have a frank talk with her mother about the concert company's offer and her new plan which was gradually shaping in her mind. She had already had one talk with her mother and knew that she expected Rachel to accept the offer and enter on a successful career as a public singer.

"Mother," Rachel said, coming at once to the point, as much as she dreaded the interview, "I have decided not to go out with the company. I have a good reason for it."

Mrs. Winslow was a large, handsome woman, fond of much company, ambitious for a distinct place in society, and devoted, according to her definitions of success, to the success of her children. Her youngest boy, Lewis, ten years younger than Rachel, was ready to graduate from a military academy in the summer. Meanwhile she and Rachel were at home together. Rachel's father, like Virginia's had died while the family were abroad. Like Virginia she found herself, under her present rule of conduct, in complete antagonism with her own immediate home circle.

Mrs. Winslow waited for Rachel to go on.

"You know the promise I made two weeks ago, mother?"

"Mr. Maxwell's promise?"

"No, mine. You know what it was, mother?"

"I suppose I do. Of course all the church members mean to imitate Christ and follow him as far as is consistent with our present day surroundings. But what has that to do with your decision in the concert company's matter?"

"It has everything to do with it. After asking, 'What would Jesus do?' and going to the source of authority for wisdom, I have been obliged to say that I do not believe He would, in my case, make that use of any voice."

"Why? Is there anything wrong about such a career?"

"No, I don't know that I can say there is."

"Do you presume to sit in judgment on other people who go out to sing in this way? Do you presume to say that they are doing what Christ would not do?"

"Mother, I wish you to understand me. I judge no one else. I condemn no other professional singers. I simply decide my own course. As I look at it, I have a conviction that Jesus would do something else."

"What else?" Mrs. Winslow had not yet lost her temper. She did not understand the situation, nor Rachel in the midst of it, but she was anxious that her daughter's career should be as distinguished as her natural gifts promised. And she felt confident that, when the present unusual religious excitement in the First Church had passed away, Rachel would go on with her public life according to the wishes of the family. She was totally unprepared for Rachel's next remark.

"What? Something that will serve mankind where it most needs the service of song. Mother, I have made up my mind to use my voice in some way so as to satisfy my own soul that I am doing something better than please fashionable audiences or make money, or even gratify my own love of singing. I am going to do something that will satisfy me when I ask, 'What would Jesus do?' And I am not satisfied, and cannot be, when I think of myself as singing myself into the career of a concert company performer."

Rachel spoke with a vigor and earnestness that surprised her mother. Mrs. Winslow was angry now. And she never tried to conceal her feelings.

"It is simply absurd! Rachel, you are a fanatic. What can you do?"

"The world has been served by men and women who have given it other things that were gifts. Why should I, because I am blessed with a natural gift at once proceed to put a market price on it and make all the money I can out of it? You know, mother, that you have taught me to think of a musical career always in the light of a financial and social success. I have been unable, since I made my promise, two weeks ago, to imagine Jesus joining a concert company to do what I would do and live the life I would have to live if I joined it."

Mrs. Winslow rose and then sat down again. With a great effort she composed herself.

"What do you intend to do then? You have not answered my question."

"I shall continue to sing for the time being in the church. I am pledged to sing there through spring. During the week, I am going to sing at the White Cross meetings down in the Rectangle."

"What! Rachel Winslow! Do you know what you are saying? Do you know what sort of people those are down there?"

Rachel almost quailed before her mother. For a moment she shrank back and was silent.

"I know very well. That is the reason I am going. Mr. and Mrs. Gray have been working there several weeks. I learned only this morning that they wanted singers from the churches to help them in their meetings. They use a tent. It is in a part of the city where Christian work is most needed. I shall offer them my help. Mother!" Rachel cried out with the first passionate utterance she had yet used, "I want to do something that will cost me something in the way of sacrifice. I know you will not understand me. But I am hungry to suffer something. What have we done all our lives for the suffering, sinning side of Raymond? How much have we denied ourselves or given of our personal ease and pleasure to bless the place in which we live or imitate the life of the Savior of the world? Are we always to go on doing as society selfishly dictates, moving on its narrow little round of pleasures and entertainments and never knowing the pain of things that cost?"

"Are you preaching at me?" asked Mrs. Winslow slowly. Rachel understood her mother's words.

"No, I am preaching at myself," she replied gently. She paused a moment as if she thought her mother would say something more and then went out of the room. When she reached her own room she felt that, so far as her mother was concerned, she could expect no sympathy or even a fair understanding from her.

She kneeled down. It is safe to say that within the two weeks since Henry Maxwell's church had faced that shabby figure with the faded hat, more members of his parish had been driven to their knees in prayer than during all the previous term of his pastorate.

When she rose, her beautiful face was wet with tears. She sat thoughtfully a little while and then wrote a note to Virginia Page. She sent it to her by a messenger, and then went down stairs again and told her mother that she and Virginia were going down to the Rectangle that evening to see Mr. and Mrs. Gray, the evangelists.

"Virginia's uncle, Dr. West, will go with us if she goes. I have asked her to call him up by telephone and go with us. The Doctor is a friend of the Grays, and attended some of the meetings last winter."

Mrs. Winslow did not say anything. Her manner showed her complete disapproval of Rachel's course and Rachel felt her unspoken bitterness.

About seven o'clock the Doctor and Virginia appeared, and together the three started for the scene of the White Cross meetings.

The Rectangle was the most notorious district in all Raymond. It was in the territory close by the great Railroad Shops and the packing houses. The slum and tenement district of Raymond congested its most wretched elements about the Rectangle. This was a barren field used in the summer by circus companies and wandering showmen. It was shut in by rows of saloons, gambling hells, and cheap, dirty boarding and lodging houses.

The First Church of Raymond had never touched the Rectangle problem. It was too dirty, too coarse, too sinful, too awful for close contact. Let us be honest. There had been an attempt to cleanse this sore spot by sending down an occasional committee of singers, of Sunday-school teachers, or gospel visitors from various churches. But the church of Raymond as an institution had never really done anything to make the Rectangle any less a stronghold of the devil as the years went by.

Into this heart of the coarse part of the sin of Raymond, the traveling evangelist and his brave little wife had pitched a good sized tent and begun meetings. It was the spring of the year and the evenings were beginning to be pleasant. The evangelists had asked for the help of Christian people and had received more than the usual amount of encouragement. But they felt a great need of more and better music. During the meetings on the Sunday just gone, the assistant at the organ had been taken ill. The volunteers from the city were few and the voices of ordinary quality.

"There will be a small meeting to-night, John," said his wife, as they entered the tent a little after seven o'clock and began to arrange the chairs and light up.

"Yes, I think so." Mr. Gray was a small energetic man with a pleasant voice and the courage of a high-born fighter. He had already made friends in the neighborhood and one of his converts, a heavy faced man who had just come in, began to help in the arrangement of the seats.

It was after eight o'clock when Alexander Powers opened the door of his office and started to go home. He was going to take a car at the corner of the Rectangle. But as he neared it he was roused by a voice coming from the tent.

It was the voice of Rachel Winslow. It struck through his consciousness of struggle over his own question that had sent him into the Divine presence for an answer. He had not yet reached a conclusion. He was troubled with uncertainty. His whole previous course of action as a railroad man was the poorest possible preparation for anything sacrificial. And he could not yet say what he would do in the matter.

Hark! What was she singing? How did Rachel Winslow happen to be down here? Several windows near by went up. Some men quarreling in a saloon stopped and listened. Other figures were walking rapidly in the direction of the Rectangle and the tent.

Surely Rachel Winslow never was happier in her life. She never had sung like that in the First Church. It was a marvelous voice. What was it she was singing? Again Alexander Powers, Superintendent of the Machine Shops, paused and listened.

> "Where He leads me I will follow,
> Where He leads me I will follow,
> Where He leads me I will follow,

I'll go with Him, with Him,
All the way."

The brutal, stolid, coarse, impure life of the Rectangle stirred itself into new life, as the song, as pure as the surroundings were vile, floated out into saloon and den and foul lodging. Some one stumbling hastily by Alexander Powers said in answer to a question,
"The tent's beginning to run over to-night. That's what the talent calls music, eh?"
The Superintendent turned towards the tent. Then he stopped. And after a moment of indecision he went on to the corner and took the car for his home. But before he was out of the sound of Rachel's voice he knew that he had settled for himself the question of what Jesus would do.

CHAPTER IV

If any man would come after me, let him deny himself and
take up his cross daily and follow me.[7]

Henry Maxwell paced his study back and forth. It was Wednesday and he had started to think out the subject of his evening service which fell upon that night.
Out of one of his study windows he could see the tall chimneys of the railroad shops. The top of the evangelist's tent just showed over the buildings around the Rectangle.
The pastor of the First Church looked out of this window every time he turned in his walk. After a while he sat down at his desk and drew a large piece of paper towards him.
After thinking several moments he wrote in large letters the following:

A NUMBER OF THINGS THAT JESUS WOULD PROBABLY DO IN THIS PARISH

1. Live in a simple, plain manner, without needless luxury on the one hand or undue asceticism on the other.
2. Preach fearlessly to the hypocrites in the church no matter what their social importance or wealth.
3. Show in some practical form sympathy and love for the common people as well as for the well to do, educated, refined people who make up the majority of the church and parish.
4. Identify himself with the great causes of Humanity in some personal way that would call for self denial and suffering.
5. Preach against the saloon in Raymond.
6. Become known as a friend and companion of the sinful people in the Rectangle.

---

[7]Luke 9:23.

7. Give up the summer trip to Europe this year. (I have been abroad twice and cannot claim any special need of rest. I am well, and could forego this pleasure, using the money for some one who needs a vacation more than I do. There are probably plenty of such people in the city.)

8. What else would Jesus do as Henry Maxwell?

He was conscious, with a humility that once was a stranger to him, that his outline of Jesus' probable action was painfully lacking in depth and power, but he was seeking carefully for concrete shapes into which he might cast his thought of Jesus' conduct. Nearly every point he had put down, meant, for him, a complete overturning of the custom and habit of years in the ministry. In spite of that, he still searched deeper for sources of the Christlike spirit. He did not attempt to write any more, but sat at his desk absorbed in his attempt to catch more and more of the spirit of Jesus in his own life. He had forgotten the particular subject for his prayer meeting with which he had begun his morning study.

He was so absorbed over his thought that he did not hear the bell ring and he was roused by the servant who announced a caller. He had sent up his name, Mr. Gray.

Maxwell stepped to the head of the stairs and asked Gray to come up.

"We can talk better up here."

So Gray came up and stated the reason for his call.

"I want you, Mr. Maxwell, to help me. Of course you have heard what a wonderful meeting we had Monday night and last night. Miss Winslow has done more with her voice than I could, and the tent won't hold the people."

"I've heard of that. It's the first time the people there have heard her. It's no wonder they are attracted."

"It has been a wonderful revelation to us, and a most encouraging event in our work. But I came to ask if you could not come down to-night and preach. I am suffering with a severe cold. I do not dare to trust my voice again. I know it is asking a good deal for such a busy man. But if you can't come, say so freely and I'll try somewhere else."

"I'm sorry, but it's my regular prayer meeting night," said Henry Maxwell. Then he flushed and added, "I shall be able to arrange it in some way so as to come down. You can count on me."

Gray thanked him earnestly and rose to go.

"Won't you stay a minute, Gray, and let us have a prayer together?"

"Yes," said Gray, simply.

So the two men kneeled together in the study. Mr. Maxwell prayed like a child. Gray was touched to tears as he kneeled there. There was something almost pitiful in the way this man who had lived his ministerial life in such a narrow limit of exercise now begged for wisdom and strength to speak a message to the people in the Rectangle.

Gray rose and held out his hand.

"God bless you, Mr. Maxwell. I'm sure the Spirit will give you power to-night."

Henry Maxwell made no answer. He did not even trust himself to say that he hoped so. But he thought of his promise and it brought a certain peace that was refreshing to his heart and mind alike.

So that is how it came about that when the First Church audience came into the lecture room that evening it was met with another surprise.

There was an unusually large number present. The prayer meetings ever since that remarkable Sunday morning, had been attended as never before in the history of the First Church.

Henry Maxwell came at once to the point. He spoke of Gray's work and of his request.

"I feel as if I were called to go down there to-night, and I will leave it with you to say whether you will go on with the meeting here. I think perhaps the best plan would be for a few volunteers to go down to the Rectangle with me prepared to help in the after-meeting, and the rest remain here and pray that the Spirit's power may go with us."

So half a dozen of the men went with Henry Maxwell, and the rest of the audience stayed in the lecture room. Maxwell could not escape the thought as he left the room that probably in his entire church membership there might not be found a score of disciples who were capable of doing work that would successfully lead needy, sinful men into the knowledge of Christ. The thought did not linger in his mind to vex him as he went on his way, but it was simply a part of his whole new conception of the meaning of Christian discipleship.

When he and his little company of volunteers reached the Rectangle, the tent was already crowded. They had difficulty in getting to the little platform. Rachel was there with Virginia and Jasper Chase who had come instead of the Doctor to-night.

When the meeting began with a song in which Rachel sang the solo and the people were asked to join in the chorus, not a foot of standing room was left in the tent. The night was mild and the sides of the tent were up and a great border of faces stretched around, looking in and forming part of the audience.

After the singing, and a prayer by one of the city pastors who was present, Gray stated the reasons for his inability to speak, and in his simple manner turned the service over to "Brother Maxwell of the First Church."

"Who's de bloke?" asked a hoarse voice near the outside of the tent.

"De Fust Church parson. We've got de whole high tone swell outfit to-night."

"Did you say Fust Church? I know him. My landlord has got a front pew up there," said another voice and there was a laugh, for the speaker was a saloon keeper.

"Trow out de life line 'cross de dark wave!" began a drunken man near by, singing in such an unconscious imitation of a local traveling singer's nasal tone that roars of laughter and jeers of approval rose around him. The people in the tent turned in the direction of the disturbance. There were shouts of "Put him out!" "Give the Fust Church a chance!" "Song! Song! Give us another song!"

Henry Maxwell stood up, and a great wave of actual terror went over him. This was not like preaching to the well-dressed, respectable, good-mannered people on the boulevard. He began to speak, but the confusion increased. Gray went down into the crowd but did not seem able to quiet it. Henry Maxwell raised his arm and his voice. The crowd in the tent began to pay some attention, but the noise on the outside increased. In a few minutes the audience was beyond Maxwell's control. He turned to Rachel with a sad smile.

"Sing something, Miss Winslow. They will listen to you," he said, and then sat down and put his face in his hands.

It was Rachel's opportunity and she was fully equal to it. Virginia was at the organ and Rachel asked her to play a few notes of the hymn,

> "Savior, I follow on,
> Guided by Thee,
> Seeing not yet the hand
> That leadeth me;
> Hushed be my heart and still,
> Fear I no farther ill,
> Only to meet thy will,
> My will shall be."

Rachel had not sung the first line before the people in the tent were all turned towards her, hushed and reverent. Before she had finished the verse the Rectangle was subdued and tamed. It lay like some wild beast at her feet and she sang it into harmlessness. Ah! What were the flippant, perfumed, critical audiences in concert halls compared with this dirty, drunken, impure, degraded, besotted humanity that trembled and wept and grew strangely, sadly thoughtful, under the touch of the divine ministry of this beautiful young woman. Henry Maxwell, as he raised his head and saw the transformed mob, had a glimpse of something that Jesus would probably do with a voice like Rachel Winslow's. Jasper Chase sat with his eyes on the singer, and his greatest longing as an ambitious author was swallowed up in the thought of what Rachel Winslow's love might sometime mean to him. And over in the shadow, outside, stood the last person any one might have expected to see at a gospel tent service—Rollin Page, who, jostled on every side by rough men and women who stared at the swell in the fine clothes, seemed careless of his surroundings and at the same time evidently swayed by the power that Rachel possessed. He had just come over from the club. Neither Rachel nor Virginia saw him that night.

The song was over. Henry Maxwell rose again. This time he felt calm. What would Jesus do? He spoke as he thought once he never could. Who were these people? They were immortal souls. What was Christianity? A calling of sinners, not the righteous, to repentance. How would Jesus speak? What would He say? He could not tell all that his message would include, but he felt sure of a part of it. And in that certainty he spoke on. Never before had he felt "compassion for the multitude." What had the multitude been to him during his ten years in the First Church, but a vague, dangerous, dirty, troublesome factor in society, outside of the church and his reach, an element that caused him, occasionally, an unpleasant feeling of conscience; a factor in Raymond that was talked about at associations as the "masses," in papers written by the brethren in attempts to show why the "masses" were not being reached. But to-night, as he faced the "masses," he asked himself whether, after all, this was not just about such a multitude as Jesus faced oftenest, and he felt the genuine emotion of love for a crowd which is one of the best indications a preacher ever has that he is living close to the heart of the world's eternal Life. It is easy to love an individual sinner, especially if he is personally picturesque, or interesting. To love a multitude of sinners, is distinctly a Christlike quality.

When the meeting closed, there was no special interest shown. The people rapidly melted away from the tent, and the saloons, which had been experiencing a dull season while the meetings progressed, again drove a thriving trade. The Rectangle, as if to make up for lost time, started in with vigor on its usual night-life of debauch. Henry Maxwell and his little party, including Virginia, Rachel, and Jasper Chase, walked down past the row of saloons and dens, until they reached the corner where the cars passed.

"This is a terrible spot," said Henry Maxwell, as they stood waiting for their car. "I never realized that Raymond had such a festering sore. It does not seem possible that this is a city full of Christian disciples."

He paused and then continued:

"Do you think any one can ever remove this great curse of the saloon? Why don't we all act together against the traffic? What would Jesus do? Would He keep silent? Would He vote to license these causes of crime and death?"

Henry Maxwell was talking to himself more than to the others. He remembered that he had always voted for license, and so had nearly all of his church members. What would Jesus do? Could he answer that question? Would Jesus preach and act against the saloon, if he lived to-day? How would he preach and act? Suppose it was not popular to preach against license? Suppose the Christian people thought it was all that could be done, to license the evil, and so get revenue from a necessary sin? Or suppose the church members owned property where the saloons stood—what then? He knew that these were the facts in Raymond. What would Jesus do?

He went up into his study, the next morning, with that question only partly answered. He thought of it all day. He was still thinking of it, and reaching certain real conclusions, when the evening "News" came. His wife brought it up, and sat down a few minutes while he read it to her.

The "Evening News" was at present the most sensational paper in Raymond. That is to say, it was being edited in such a remarkable fashion, that its subscribers had never been so excited over a newspaper before.

First, they had noticed the absence of the prize fight, and gradually it began to dawn upon them, that the "News" no longer printed accounts of crime with detailed descriptions, or scandals in private life. Then they noticed that the advertisements of liquor and tobacco were being dropped, together with certain other advertisements of a questionable character. The discontinuance of the Sunday paper caused the greatest comment of all, and now the character of the editorials was creating the greatest excitement. A quotation from the Monday paper of this week will show what Edward Norman was doing to keep his promise. The editorial was headed,

THE MORAL SIDE OF POLITICAL QUESTIONS.

The editor of the 'News' has always advocated the principles of the great political party at present in power, and has, therefore, discussed all political questions from a standpoint of expediency, or of belief in the party, as opposed to other organizations. Hereafter, to be perfectly honest with all our readers, the editor will present and discuss political questions from the standpoint of right and wrong. In other words, the first question will not be, 'Is it in the interest of our party?' or 'Is it according to the principles laid down by the party?' but the question first asked will be, 'Is this measure in accordance with the spirit and teachings of Jesus, as the author of the greatest standard of life known to men?' That is, to be perfectly plain, the moral side of every political question will be considered its most important side, and the ground will be distinctly taken, that nations, as well as individuals, are under the same law, to do all things to the glory of God, as the first rule of action.

The same principle will be observed in this office towards candidates for places of responsibility and trust in the Republic. Regardless of party politics, the editor of the 'News' will do all in his power to bring the best men into power, and will not, knowingly, help to support for office any candidate who is unworthy, however much he may be endorsed by the party. The first question asked about the man, as about the measure, will be, 'Is he the right man for the place? Is he a good man with ability?'

There had been more of this; but we have quoted enough to show the character of the editorials. Hundreds of men in Raymond had read it, and rubbed their eyes in amazement. A good many of them had promptly written to the "News," telling the editor to stop their paper. The paper still came out, however, and was eagerly read all over the city. At the end of the week, Edward Norman knew very well that he had actually lost already a large number of valuable subscribers. He faced the conditions calmly, although Clark, the managing editor, grimly anticipated ultimate bankruptcy, especially since Monday's editorial.

To-night, as Henry Maxwell read to his wife, he could see on almost every column evidences of Norman's conscientious obedience to his promise. There was an absence of slangy, sensational scare-heads. The reading matter under the head lines was in perfect keeping with them. He noticed in two columns that the reporters names appeared, signed, at the bottom. And there was a distinct advance in the dignity and style of their contributions.

"So Norman is beginning to get his reporters to sign their work. He has talked with me about that. It is a good thing. It fixes responsibility for items where it belongs, and raises the standard of work done. A good thing all around, for public and writers."

Henry Maxwell suddenly paused. His wife looked up from some work she was doing. He was reading something with the utmost interest.

"Listen to this, Mary," he said after a moment, while his voice trembled:

This morning Alexander Powers, Superintendent of the L. and T. R. R. shops in this city, handed his resignation to the road, and gave as the reason the fact that certain proof had fallen into his hands of the violation of the Interstate Commerce Law, and also of the State law which has recently been framed to prevent and punish railroad pooling for the benefit of certain favored shippers. Mr. Powers states in his resignation that he can no longer consistently withhold the information he possesses against the road. He has placed his evidence against the company in the hands of the Commission, and it is now for them to take action upon it.

The "News" wishes to express itself on this action of Mr. Powers. In the first place, he has nothing to gain by it. He has lost a valuable place, voluntarily, when, by keeping silent, he might have retained it. In the second place, we believe his action ought to receive the approval of all thoughtful, honest citizens, who believe in seeing law obeyed and law-breakers brought to justice. In a case like this, where evidence against a railroad company is generally understood to be almost impossible to obtain, it is the general belief that the officers of the road are often in possession of criminating facts, but do not consider it to be any of their business to inform the authorities that the law is being defied. The entire result of this evasion of responsibility on the part of those who are responsible, is demoralizing to every young man connected with the road. The editor of the "News" recalls the statement made by a prominent railroad official in this city a little while ago, that nearly every clerk in a certain department of the road who understood how large sums of money were made by shrewd violations of the Interstate Commerce Law, was ready to admire the shrewdness with which it was done, and declared that they would all do the same thing, if they were high enough in railroad circles to attempt it.*

It is not necessary to say that such a condition of business is destructive to all the nobler and higher standards of conduct; and no young man can live in such an atmosphere of unpunished dishonesty and lawlessness, without wrecking his character.

In our judgment, Mr. Powers did the only thing that a Christian man can do. He has rendered brave and useful service to the state and the general public. It is not always an easy matter to determine the relations that exist between the individual citizen and his fixed duty to the public. In this case, there is no doubt in our minds that the step which Mr. Powers has taken commends itself to every man who believes in law and its enforcement. There are times when the individual must act for the people, in ways that will mean sacrifice and loss to him of the gravest character. Mr. Powers will be misunderstood and misrepresented; but there is no question that his course will be approved by every citizen who wishes to see the greatest corporations, as well as the weakest individual, subject to the same law. Mr. Powers has done all that a loyal, patriotic citizen could do. It now remains for the Commission to act upon his evidence, which, we understand, is overwhelming proof of the lawlessness of the L. and T. Let the law be enforced, no matter who the persons may be who have been guilty.' "

Henry Maxwell finished reading and dropped the paper.

"I must go and see Powers. This is the result of his promise."

He rose, and as he was going out, his wife said,

"Do you think, Henry, that Jesus would have done that?"

Henry Maxwell paused a moment. Then he answered slowly,

"Yes, I think He would. At any rate, Powers has decided so, and each one of us who made the promise understands that he is not deciding Jesus' conduct for any one else, only for himself."

"How about his family? How will Mrs. Powers and Celia be likely to take it?"

"Very hard, I have no doubt. That will be Powers's cross in this matter. They will not understand his motive."

Henry Maxwell went out and walked over to the next block, where the Superintendent lived. To his relief, Powers himself came to the door.

The two men shook hands silently. They instantly understood each other, without words. There had never been such a bond of union between the minister and his parishioner.

"What are you going to do?" Henry Maxwell asked, after they had talked over the facts in the case.

"You mean another position? I have no plans yet. I can go back to my old work as a telegraph operator. My family will not suffer except in a social way."

Alexander Powers spoke calmly, if sadly. Henry Maxwell did not need to ask him how his wife and daughter felt. He knew well enough that the Superintendent had suffered deepest at that point.

"There is one matter I wish you would see to," said Powers after a while, "and that is the work begun at the Shops. So far as I know, the Company will not object to that

---

*This was actually said in one of the General Offices of a great western railroad, to the author's knowledge.

going right on. It is one of the contradictions of the railroad world that the Y. M. C. A.'s, and other Christian influences, are encouraged by the roads, while all the time the most un-Christian and lawless acts are being committed in the official management of the roads themselves. Of course it is understood that it pays a railroad to have in its employ men who are temperate, and honest, and Christian. So I have no doubt the Master Mechanic will have the same courtesy extended to him that I had, in the matter of the room and its uses. But what I want you to do. Mr. Maxwell, is to see that my plan is carried out. Will you? You understand what the idea was in general. You made a very favorable impression on the men. Go down there as often as you can. Get Milton Wright interested to provide something for the furnishing and expense of the coffee plant and reading tables. Will you do it?"

"Yes," replied Henry Maxwell. He stayed a little longer. Before he went away, he and the Superintendent had a prayer together, and they parted with that silent hand-grasp that seemed to them like a new token of their Christian discipleship and fellowship.

The pastor of the First Church went home stirred deeply by the events of the week. Gradually the truth was growing upon him that the pledge to do as Jesus would was working out a revolution in his parish and throughout the city. Every day added to the serious results of obedience to that pledge. Henry Maxwell did not pretend to see the end. He was, in fact, only now at the very beginning of events that were destined to change the history of hundreds of families, not only in Raymond but throughout the entire country. As he thought of Edward Norman and Rachel and Mr. Powers, and of the results that had already come from their actions, he could not help a feeling of intense interest in the probable effect, if all the persons in the First Church who had made the pledge, faithfully kept it. Would they all keep it, or would some of them turn back when the cross became too heavy?

He was asking this question the next morning, as he sat in his study, when the President of the Endeavor Society called to see him.

"I suppose I ought not to trouble you with my case," said young Morris, coming at once to his errand, "but I thought, Mr. Maxwell, that you might advise me a little."

"I'm glad you came. Go on, Fred." Henry Maxwell had known the young man ever since his first year in the pastorate, and loved and honored him for his consistent, faithful service in the church.

"Well, the fact is, I'm out of a job. You know I've been doing reporter work on the morning 'Sentinel' since I graduated last year. Well, last Saturday Mr. Burr asked me to go down the road Sunday morning and get the details of that train robbery at the Junction, and write the thing up for the extra edition that came out Monday morning, just to get the start of the 'News.' I refused to go, and Burr gave me my dismissal. He was in a bad temper, or I think perhaps he would not have done it. He has always treated me well before. Now, don't you think Jesus would have done as I did? I ask because the other fellows say I was a fool not to do the work. I want to feel that a Christian acts from motives that may seem strange to others, sometimes, but not foolish. What do you think?"

"I think you kept your promise, Fred. I cannot believe Jesus would do newspaper work on Sunday as you were asked to do it."

"Thank you, Mr. Maxwell. I felt a little troubled over it, but the longer I think it over the better I feel."

Morris rose to go, and Henry Maxwell rose and laid a loving hand on the young man's shoulder.

"What are you going to do, Fred?"

"I don't know yet. I have thought some of going to Chicago, or some large city."

"Why don't you try the 'News'?"

"They are all supplied. I have not thought of applying there."

Henry Maxwell thought a moment.

"Come down to the 'News' office with me, and let us see Norman about it."

So, a few minutes later, Edward Norman received into his room the minister and young Morris, and Henry Maxwell briefly told the cause of their errand.

"I can give you a place on the 'News'," said Edward Norman, with his keen look softened by a smile that made it winsome. "I want reporters who won't work Sundays. And what is more, I am making plans for a special kind of reporting which I believe young Morris here can develop because he is in sympathy with what Jesus would do."

He assigned Morris a definite task, and Henry Maxwell started back to his study, feeling that kind of satisfaction (and it is a very deep kind) which a man feels when he has been even partly instrumental in finding an unemployed person a situation.

He had intended to go back to his study, but on his way home he passed by one of Milton Wright's stores. He thought he would simply step in and shake hands with his parishioner and bid him God-speed in what he had heard he was doing to put Christ into his business. But when he went into the office, Milton Wright insisted on detaining him to talk over some of his new plans. Henry Maxwell asked himself if this was the Milton Wright he used to know, eminently practical, business-like, according to the regular code of the business world, and viewing everything first and foremost from the standpoint of "Will it pay?"

"There is no use to disguise the fact, Mr. Maxwell, that I have been compelled to revolutionize the whole method of business since I made that promise. I have been doing a great many things, during the last twenty years in this store, that I know Jesus would not do. But that is a small item compared with the number of things I begin to believe Jesus would do. My sins of commision have not been as many as those of omission in business relations."

"What was the first change you made?" asked Henry Maxwell. He felt as if his sermon could wait for him in his study. As the interview with Milton Wright continued, he was not so sure but that he had found material for a sermon without going back to his study.

"I think the first change I had to make was in my thought of my employees. I came down here Monday morning after that Sunday and asked myself, 'What would Jesus do in His relation to these clerks, book-keepers, office boys, draymen, salesmen? Would He try to establish some sort of personal relation to them different from that which I have sustained all these years?' I soon answered the question by saying, Yes. Then came the question of what it would lead me to do. I did not see how I could answer it to my satisfaction without getting all my employes together and having a talk with them. So I sent invitations to all of them, and we had a meeting out there in the warehouse Tuesday night.

"A good many things came out of that meeting. I can't tell you all. I tried to talk with the men as I imagined Jesus might. It was hard work, for I have not been in the habit of it, and I must have made mistakes. But I can hardly make you believe, Mr. Maxwell, the effect of that meeting on some of the men. Before it closed, I saw more than a dozen of them

with tears on their faces. I kept asking, 'What would Jesus do?' and the more I asked it, the
farther along it pushed me into the most intimate and loving relations with the men who
have worked for me all these years. Every day something new is coming up, and I am right
now in the midst of a reconstructing of the entire business, so far as its motive for being
conducted is concerned. I am so practically ignorant of all plans for co-operation and its
application to business that I am trying to get information from every possible source. I
have lately made a special study of the life of Titus Salt, the great mill owner of Bradford,
England, who afterwards built that model town on the banks of the Aire. There is a good
deal in his plans that will help. But I have not yet reached definite conclusions in regard to
all the details. I am not enough used to Jesus' methods. But see here."

Milton eagerly reached up into one of the pigeon holes of his desk and took out a
paper.

"l have sketched out what seems to me a program such as Jesus might go by in a
business like mine. I want you to tell me what you think about it."

WHAT JESUS WOULD PROBABLY DO IN MILTON WRIGHT'S PLACE AS A BUSINESS MAN

1. He would engage in business for the purpose of glorifying God, and not for the
   primary purpose of making money.
2. All money that might be made he would never regard as his own, but as trust
   funds to be used for the good of humanity.
3. His relations with all the persons in his employ would be the most loving and
   helpful. He could not help thinking of them all in the light of souls to be saved.
   This thought would always be greater than his thought of making money in
   business.
4. He would never do a single dishonest or questionable thing or try in any
   remotest way to get the advantage of any one else in the same business.
5. The principle of unselfishness and helpfulness in all the details of the business
   would direct its details.
6. Upon this principle he would shape the entire plan of his relations to his
   employes, to the people who were his customers, and to the general business
   world with which he was connected.

Henry Maxwell read this over slowly. It reminded him of his own attempts, the day
before, to put into a concrete form his thought of Jesus' probable action. He was very
thoughtful, as he looked up and met Milton Wright's eager gaze.

"Do you believe you can continue to make your business pay on those lines?"

"I do. Intelligent unselfishness ought to be wiser than intelligent selfishness, don't
you think? If the men who work as employes begin to feel a personal share in the profits
of the business and, more than that, a personal love for themselves on the part of the firm,
won't the result be more care, less waste, more diligence, more faithfulness?"

"Yes, I think so. A good many other business men don't, do they? I mean as a general thing. How about your relations to the selfish world that is not trying to make money
on Christian principles?"

"That complicates my action of course."

"Does your plan contemplate what is coming to be known as co-operation?"

"Yes, as far as I have gone, it does. As I told you, I am studying out my details care-fully. I am absolutely convinced that Jesus in my place would be absolutely unselfish. He would love all these men in his employ. He would consider the main purpose of all the business to be a mutual helpfulness, and would conduct it all so that God's kingdom would be evidently the first object sought. On those general principles, as I say, I am working. I must have time to complete the details."

When Henry Maxwell finally left Milton Wright, he was profoundly impressed with the revolution that was being wrought already in the business. As he passed out of the store he caught something of the new spirit of the place. There was no mistaking the fact that Milton Wright's new relations to his employes were beginning, even so soon, after less than two weeks, to transform the entire business. This was apparent in the conduct and faces of the clerks.

"If Milton Wright keeps on, he will be one of the most influential preachers in Ray-mond," said Henry Maxwell to himself, when he reached his study. The question rose as to his continuance in this course when he began to lose money by it, as was possible. Henry Maxwell prayed that the Holy Spirit, who had shown Himself with growing power in the company of the First Church disciples, might abide long with them all. And with that prayer on his lips and in his heart, he began the preparation of a sermon in which he was going to present to his people on Sunday the subject of the saloon in Ray-mond, as he now believed Jesus would do. He had never preached against the saloon in this way before. He knew that the things he should say would lead to serious results. Nevertheless he went on with his work, and every sentence he wrote or shaped was pre-ceded with the question, "Would Jesus say that?" Once in the course of his study, he went down on his knees. No one except himself could know what that meant to him. When had he done that in the preparation of sermons, before the change that had come into his thought of discipleship? As he viewed his ministry now, he did not dare to preach without praying for wisdom. He no longer thought of his dramatic delivery and its effect on his audience. The great question with him now was, "What would Jesus do?"

Saturday night at the Rectangle witnessed some of the most remarkable scenes that Mr. Gray and his wife had ever known. The meetings had intensified with each night of Rachel's singing. A stranger passing through the Rectangle in the daytime might have heard a good deal about the meetings, in one way and another. It cannot be said that, up to that Saturday night, there was any appreciable lack of oaths and impurity and heavy drinking. The Rectangle would not have acknowledged that it was growing any better, or that even the singing had softened its conversation, or its outward manner. It had too much local pride in being "tough." But in spite of itself, there was a yielding to a power it had never measured and did not know well enough to resist beforehand.

Gray had recovered his voice, so that Saturday he was able to speak. The fact that he was obliged to use his voice carefully made it necessary for the people to be very quiet if they wanted to hear. Gradually they had come to understand that this man was talking these many weeks, and using his time and strength, to give them a knowledge of a Sav-ior, all out of a perfectly unselfish love for them. To-night the great crowd was as quiet as Henry Maxwell's decorous audience ever was. The fringe around the tent was deeper, and the saloons were practically empty. The Holy Spirit had come at last, and Gray knew that one of the great prayers of his life was going to be answered.

And Rachel—her singing was the best, most wonderful, Virginia or Jasper Chase had ever known. They had come together again to-night with Dr. West, who had spent all his spare time that week in the Rectangle with some charity cases. Virginia was at the organ, Jasper sat on a front seat looking up at Rachel, and the Rectangle swayed as one man towards the platform as she sang:

> "Just as I am, without one plea,
> But that thy blood was shed for me,
> And that thou bidst me come to thee,
> O Lamb of God, I come, I come."

Gray hardly said a word. He stretched out his hand with a gesture of invitation. And down the two aisles of the tent, broken, sinful creatures, men and women, stumbled towards the platform. One woman out of the street was near the organ. Virginia caught the look of her face, and, for the first time in the life of the rich girl, the thought of what Jesus was to a sinful woman came with a suddenness and power that was like nothing but a new birth. Virginia left the organ, went to her, looked into her face and caught her hands in her own. The other girl trembled, then fell on her knees, sobbing, with her head down upon the back of the bench in front of her, still clinging to Virginia. And Virginia, after a moment's hesitation, kneeled down by her and the two heads were bowed close together.

But when the people had crowded in a double row all about the platform, most of them kneeling and crying, a man in evening dress, different from the others, pushed through the seats and came and kneeled down by the side of the drunken man who had disturbed the meeting when Henry Maxwell spoke. He kneeled within a few feet of Rachel Winslow, who was still singing softly. And as she turned for a moment and looked in his direction, she was amazed to see the face of Rollin Page! For a moment her voice faltered. Then she went on:

> "Just as I am, thou wilt receive,
> Wilt welcome, pardon, cleanse, relieve;
> Because thy promise I believe,
> O Lamb of God, I come, I come."

The voice was as the voice of divine longing, and the Rectangle, for the time being, was swept into the harbor of redemptive grace.

CHAPTER V

If any man serve me, let him follow me.[8]

It was nearly midnight before the service at the Rectangle closed. Gray stayed up long into Sunday morning, praying and talking with a little group of converts that, in the great experience of their new life, clung to the evangelist with a personal helplessness that

---

[8]John 12:26.

made it as impossible for him to leave them as if they had been depending upon him to save them from physical death. Among these converts was Rollin Page.

Virginia and her uncle had gone home about eleven o'clock, and Rachel and Jasper Chase had gone with them as far as the avenue where Virginia lived. Dr. West had walked on a little way with them to his own house, and Rachel and Jasper had then gone on together to her mother's.

That was a little after eleven. It was now striking midnight, and Jasper Chase sat in his room staring at the papers on his desk and going over the last half-hour with painful persistence.

He had told Rachel Winslow of his love for her, and she had not given her love in return.

It would be difficult to know what was most powerful in the impulse that had moved him to speak to her to-night. He had yielded to his feelings without any special thought of results to himself, because he had felt so certain that Rachel would respond to his love for her. He tried to recall, now, just the impression she made on him when he first spoke to her.

Never had her beauty and her strength influenced him as to-night. While she was singing he saw and heard no one else. The tent swarmed with a confused crowd of faces, and he knew he was sitting there hemmed in by a mob of people; but they had no meaning to him. He felt powerless to avoid speaking to her. He knew he should speak when they were once alone.

Now that he had spoken, he felt that he had misjudged either Rachel or the opportunity. He knew, or thought he did, that she had begun to care for him. It was no secret between them that the heroine of Jasper's first novel had been his own ideal of Rachel, and the hero of the story was himself, and they had loved each other in the book, and Rachel had not objected. No one else knew. The names and characters had been drawn with a subtle skill that revealed to Rachel, when she received a copy of the book from Jasper, the fact of his love for her, and she had not been offended. That was nearly a year ago.

To-night, Jasper Chase recalled the scene between them, with every inflection and movement unerased from his memory. He even recalled the fact that he began to speak just at that point on the avenue where, a few days before, he had met Rachel walking with Rollin Page. He had wondered at the time, what Rollin was saying.

"Rachel," Jasper had said, and it was the first time he had ever spoken her first name, "I never knew until to-night how much I love you. Why should I try to conceal any longer what you have seen me look? You know I love you as my life. I can no longer hide it from you if I would."

The first intimation he had of a refusal was the trembling of Rachel's arm in his own. She had allowed him to speak and had neither turned her face towards him nor away from him. She had looked straight on, and her voice was sad but firm and quiet when she spoke.

"Why do you speak to me now? I cannot bear it—after what we have seen to-night."

"Why—what—" he had stammered, and then was silent.

Rachel withdrew her arm from his, but still walked near him.

Then he cried out, with the anguish of one who begins to see a great loss facing him where he expected a great joy.

"Rachel! Do you not love me? Is not my love for you as sacred as anything in all of life itself?"

She had walked on silent for a few steps, after that. They had passed a street lamp. Her face was pale and beautiful. He had made a movement to clutch her arm. And she had moved a little farther from him.

"No," she had replied. "There was a time—I cannot answer for that—you should not have spoken to me to-night."

He had seen in these words his answer. He was extremely sensitive. Nothing short of a joyous response to his own love would have satisfied him. He could not think of pleading with her.

"Some time—when I am more worthy?" he had asked in a low voice; but she did not seem to hear, and they had parted at her home, and he recalled vividly the fact that no good-night had been said.

Now as he went over the brief but significant scene, he lashed himself for his foolish precipitancy. He had not reckoned on Rachel's tense, passionate absorption of all her feeling in the scenes at the tent which were so new in her mind. But he did not know her well enough, even yet, to understand the meaning of her refusal. When the clock in the First Church steeple struck one, he was still sitting at his desk, staring at the last page of manuscript of his unfinished novel.

Rachel Winslow went up to her room and faced her evening's experience with conflicting emotions. Had she ever loved Jasper Chase? Yes. No. One moment she felt that her life's happiness was at stake over the result of her action. Another, she had a strange feeling of relief that she had spoken as she did. There was one great overmastering feeling in her. The response of the wretched creatures in the tent to her singing, the swift, awesome presence of the Holy Spirit, had affected her as never in all her life before. The moment Jasper had spoken her name and she realized that he was telling her of his love, she had felt a sudden revulsion for him, as if he should have respected the supernatural events they had just witnessed. She felt as if it were not the time to be absorbed in anything less than the divine glory of those conversions. The thought that all the time she was singing with the one passion of her soul to touch the conscience of that tent full of sin, Jasper Chase had been moved by it simply to love her for himself, gave her a shock as of irreverence on her part as well as on his. She could not tell why she felt as she did, only she knew that if he had not told her to-night she would still have felt the same towards him as she always had. What was that feeling? What had he been to her? Had she made a mistake? She went to her book-case and took out the novel which Jasper had given her. Her face deepened in color as she turned to certain passages which she had read often and which she knew Jasper had written for her. She read them again. Somehow they failed to touch her strongly. She closed the book and let it lie on the table. She gradually felt that her thought was busy with the sight she had witnessed in that tent. Those faces, men and women, touched for the first time with the Spirit's glory—what a wonderful thing life was after all! The complete regeneration revealed in the sight of drunken, vile, debauched humanity kneeling down to give itself to a life of purity and Christlikeness—oh, it was surely a witness to the superhuman in the world! And the face of Rollin Page by the side of that miserable wreck out of the gutter—she could recall as if she now saw it, Virginia crying with her arms about her brother just before she left the tent, and Mr. Gray kneeling close by, and the girl Virginia had taken into her heart bending her head while Virginia whispered something to her. All these pictures drawn by the Holy Spirit in the human tragedies brought to a climax there in the most abandoned spot in all Raymond, stood out in Rachel's memory now, a memory so recent that her room seemed for the time being to contain all the actors and their movements.

"No! No!" She had said aloud. "He had no right to speak to me after all that! He should have respected the place where our thoughts should have been! I am sure I do not love him. Not enough to give him my life!"

And after she had thus spoken, the evening's experience at the tent came crowding in again, thrusting out all other things. It is perhaps the most striking evidence of the tremendous spiritual factor which had now entered the Rectangle that Rachel felt, even when the great love of a strong man had come very near to her, that the spiritual manifestation moved her with an agitation far greater than anything Jasper had felt for her personally, or she for him.

The people of Raymond awoke Sunday morning to a growing knowledge of events which were beginning to revolutionize many of the regular, customary habits of the town. Alexander Powers's action in the matter of the railroad frauds had created a sensation, not only in Raymond but throughout the country. Edward Norman's daily changes of policy in the conduct of his paper had startled the community and caused more comment than any recent political event. Rachel Winslow's singing at the Rectangle meetings had made a stir in society and excited the wonder of all her friends. Virginia Page's conduct, her presence every night with Rachel, her absence from the usual circle of her wealthy, fashionable acquaintances, had furnished a great deal of material for gossip and question. In addition to these events which centered about these persons who were so well known, there had been all through the city, in very many homes and in business and social circles, strange happenings. Nearly one hundred persons in Henry Maxwell's church had made the pledge to do everything after asking, "What would Jesus do?" and the result had been, in many cases, unheard-of actions. The city was stirred as it had never been. As a climax to the week's events had come the spiritual manifestation at the Rectangle, and the announcement which came to most people before church time of the actual conversion at the tent of nearly fifty of the worst characters in the neighborhood, together with the conversion of Rollin Page, the well-known society and club man.

It is no wonder that, under the pressure of all this, the First Church of Raymond came to the morning service in a condition that made it quickly sensitive to any large truth.

Perhaps nothing had astonished the people more than the great change that had come over the minister since he had proposed to them the imitation of Jesus in conduct. The dramatic delivery of his sermons no longer impressed them. The self-satisfied, contented, easy attitude of the fine figure and the refined face in the pulpit, had been displaced by a manner that could not be compared with the old style of his delivery. The sermon had become a message. It was no longer delivered. It was brought to them with a love, an earnestness, a passion, a desire, a humility, that poured its enthusiasm about the truth and made the speaker no more prominent than he had to be as the living voice of God. His prayers were unlike any the people had ever heard before. They were often broken, even once or twice they had been actually ungrammatical in a phrase or two. When had Henry Maxwell so far forgotten himself in a prayer as to make a mistake of that sort? He knew that he had often taken as much pride in the diction and the delivery of his prayers as of his sermons. Was it possible he now so abhorred the elegant refinement of a formal public petition that he purposely chose to rebuke himself for his previous precise manner of prayer? It is more likely that he had no thought of all that. His great longing to voice the needs and wants of his people made him unmindful of an occasional mistake. It is certain he had never prayed so effectively as he did now.

There are times when a sermon has a value and power due to conditions in the audience rather than to anything new or startling or eloquent in the words or the arguments presented. Such conditions faced Henry Maxwell this morning as he preached against the saloon, according to his purpose determined on the week before. He had no new statements to make about the evil influence of the saloon in Raymond. What new facts were there? He had no startling illustrations of the power of the saloon in business or politics. What could he say that had not been said by temperance orators a great many times? The effect of his message this morning owed its power to the unusual fact of his preaching about the saloon at all, together with the events that had stirred the people. He had never in the course of his ten years' pastorate mentioned the saloon as something to be regarded in the light of an enemy, not only to the poor and the tempted, but to the business life of the place and the church itself. He spoke now with a freedom that seemed to measure his complete sense of the conviction that Jesus would speak so. At the close he pleaded with the people to remember the new life that had begun at the Rectangle. The regular election of city officers was near at hand. The question of license would be an issue in that election. What of the poor creatures surrounded by the hell of drink while just beginning to feel the joy of deliverance from sin? Who could tell what depended on their environment? Was there one word to be said by the Christian disciple, business man, professional man, citizen, in favor of continuing to license these crime and shame-producing institutions? Was not the most Christian thing they could do to act as citizens in the matter, fight the saloon at the polls, elect good men to the city offices, and clean the municipality? How much had prayers helped to make Raymond better while votes and actions had really been on the side of the enemies of Jesus? Would not Jesus do this? What disciple could imagine Him refusing to suffer or take up His cross in the matter? How much had the members of the First Church ever suffered in an attempt to imitate Jesus? Was Christian discipleship a thing of convenience, of custom, of tradition? Where did the suffering come in? Was it necessary in order to follow Jesus' steps to go up Calvary as well as the Mount of Transfiguration?

His appeal was stronger at this point than he knew. It is not too much to say that the spiritual tension of the First Church reached its highest point right there. The imitation of Jesus which had begun with the volunteers in the church was working like leaven in the organization, and Henry Maxwell would, even this early in his new life, have been amazed if he could have measured the extent of desire on the part of his people to take up the cross. While he was speaking this morning, before he closed with a loving appeal to the discipleship of two thousand years' knowledge of the Master, many a man and woman in the church was saying, as Rachel had said so passionately to her mother, "I want to do something that will cost me something in the way of sacrifice;" "I am hungry to suffer something." Truly Mazzini[9] was right when he said, "No appeal is quite so powerful in the end as the call, 'Come and suffer.' "

The service was over, the great audience had gone, and Henry Maxwell again faced the company gathered in the lecture-room as on the two previous Sundays. He had asked all to remain who had made the pledge of discipleship, and any others who wished to be included. The after-service seemed now to be a necessity. As he went in and faced the people there, his heart trembled. There were at least two hundred present. The Holy Spirit was never so manifest. He missed Jasper Chase. But all the others were present. He asked Milton Wright to pray. The very air was charged with divine possibilities. What could resist such a baptism of power? How had they lived all these years without it?

They counseled together, and there were many prayers. Henry Maxwell dated from that meeting some of the serious events that afterwards became a part of the history of the First Church of Raymond. When finally they went home, all of them were impressed with the joy of the Spirit's power.

Donald Marsh, President of Lincoln College, walked home with Henry Maxwell.

"I have reached one conclusion, Maxwell," said Marsh speaking slowly. "I have found my cross, and it is a heavy one; but I shall never be satisfied until I take it up and carry it."

Maxwell was silent and the President went on.

"Your sermon to-day made clear to me what I have long been feeling I ought to do. What would Jesus do in my place? I have asked the question repeatedly since I made my promise. I have tried to satisfy myself that he would simply go on as I have done, tending to the duties of my college, teaching the classes in Ethics and Philosophy. But I have not been able to avoid the feeling that he would do something more. That something is what I do not want to do. It will cause me genuine suffering to do it. I dread it with all my soul. You may be able to guess what it is?"?

"Yes, I think I know," Henry Maxwell replied. "It is my cross, too, I would almost rather do any thing else."

Donald Marsh looked surprised, then relieved. Then he spoke sadly, but with great conviction.

"Maxwell, you and I belong to a class of professional men who have always avoided the duties of citizenship. We have lived in a little world of scholarly seclusion, doing work we have enjoyed, and shrinking from the disagreeable duties that belong to the life of the citizen. I confess with shame that I have purposely avoided the responsibility that I owe to this city personally. I understand that our city officials are a corrupt, unprincipled set of men, controlled in large part by the whisky element, and thoroughly selfish so far as the affairs of city government are concerned. Yet all these years I, with nearly every teacher in the college, have been satisfied to let other men run the municipality, and have lived in a little world of my own, out of touch and sympathy with the real world of the people. 'What would Jesus do?' I have tried even to avoid an honest answer. I can no longer do so. My plain duty is to take a personal part in this coming election, go to the primaries, throw the weight of my influence, whatever it is, towards the nomination and

---

[9]Giuseppe Mazzini (1805–1872) was an uncompromising Italian revolutionary who fought for a republican government that would represent the interests of all Italians.

election of good men, and plunge into the very depths of this entire horrible whirlpool of deceit, bribery, political trickery and saloonism as it exists in Raymond to-day. I would sooner walk up to the mouth of a cannon any time than do this. I dread it because I hate the touch of the whole matter. I would give almost anything to be able to say, 'I do not believe Jesus would do anything of the sort.' But I am more and more persuaded that He would. This is where the suffering comes to me. It would not hurt me half so much to lose my position or my home. I loathe the contact with this municipal problem. I would much prefer to remain quietly in my scholastic life with my classes in Ethics and Philosophy. But the call has come to me so plainly that I cannot escape: 'Donald Marsh, follow me. Do your duty as a citizen of Raymond at the point where your citizenship will cost you something. Help to cleanse this great municipal stable, even if you do have to soil your aristocratic feelings a little.' Maxwell, this is my cross. I must take it up or deny my Lord."

"You have spoken for me also," replied Maxwell, with a sad smile. "Why should I, simply because I am a clergyman, shelter myself behind my refined, sensitive feelings and, like a coward, refuse to touch, except in a sermon possibly, the duty of citizenship? I am unused to the ways of the political life of the city. I have never taken an active part in any nomination of good men. There are hundreds of ministers like me. As a class, we do not practice, in the municipal life, the duties and privileges we preach from the pulpit. What would Jesus do? I am now at a point where, like you, I am driven to answer the question one way. My duty is plain. I must suffer. All my parish work, all my little trials or self-sacrifices, are as nothing to me compared with the breaking into my scholarly, intellectual, self-contained habits of this open, coarse, public fight for a clean city life. I could go and live at the Rectangle the rest of my days and work in the slums for a bare living and I could enjoy it more than the thought of plunging into a fight for the reform of this whisky-ridden city. It would cost me less. But with you I have been unable to shake off my responsibility. The answer to the question, 'What would Jesus do?' in this case leaves me no peace, except when I say, 'Jesus would have me act the part of a Christian citizen.' Marsh, as you say, we professional men, ministers, professors, artists, literary men, scholars, have almost invariably been political cowards. We have avoided the sacred duties of citizenship, either ignorantly or selfishly. Certainly Jesus, in our age, would not do that. We can do no less than take up this cross and follow Him."

These two men walked on in silence for a while. Finally President Marsh said.

"We do not need to act alone in this matter. With all the men who have made the promise, we certainly can have companionship and strength, even of numbers. Let us organize the Christian forces of Raymond for the battle against rum and corruption. We certainly ought to enter the primaries with a force that will be able to do more than utter a protest. It is a fact that the saloon element is cowardly and easily frightened, in spite of its lawlessness and corruption. Let us plan a campaign that will mean something, because it is organized righteousness. Jesus would use great wisdom in this matter. He would employ means. He would make large plans. Let us do so. If we bear this cross, let us do it bravely, like men."

They talked over the matter a long time, and met again the next day in Henry Maxwell's study to develop plans. The city primaries were called for Friday. Rumors of strange and unheard-of events to the average citizen were current in political circles throughout Raymond. The Crawford system of balloting for nominations was not in use in the state, and the primary was called for a public meeting at the court-house.

The citizens of Raymond will never forget that meeting. It was so unlike any political meeting ever held in Raymond before, that there was no attempt at comparison. The special officers to be nominated were Mayor, City Council, Chief of Police, City Clerk, and City Treasurer.

The "Evening News," in its Saturday edition, gave a full account of the primaries, and in the editorial column Edward Norman spoke with a directness and conviction that the Christian people of Raymond were learning to respect deeply, because it was so evidently sincere and unselfish. A part of that editorial is also a part of this history:

> "It is safe to say that never before in the history of Raymond was there a primary like the one in the court-house last night. It was, first of all, a complete surprise to the city politicians, who have been in the habit of carrying on the affairs of the city as if they owned them and every one else was simply a tool or a cipher. The over-whelming surprise of the wire-puller last night consisted in the fact that a large number of the citizens of Raymond who have heretofore taken no part in the city affairs, entered the primary and controlled it, nominating some of the best men for all the offices to be filled at the coming election.
>
> "It was a tremendous lesson in good citizenship. President Marsh of Lincoln College, who never before entered a city primary, and whose face even was not known to many of the ward politicians, made one of the best speeches ever heard in Raymond. It was almost ludicrous to see the faces of the men who for years have done as they pleased, when President Marsh rose to speak. Many of them asked, 'Who is he?' The consternation deepened as the primary proceeded, and it became evident that the old-time ring of city rulers was outnumbered. Henry Maxwell, Pastor of the First Church, Milton Wright, Alexander Powers, Professors Brown, Willard and Park of Lincoln College, Rev. John West, Dr. George Maine of the Pilgrim Church, Dean Ward of the Holy Trinity, and scores of well-known business and professional men, most of them church members, were present, and it did not take long to see that they had all come with the direct and definite purpose of nominating the best men possible. Most of these men had never been seen in a primary. They were complete strangers to the politicians. But they had evidently profited by the politician's methods and were able, by organized and united effort, to nominate the entire ticket.
>
> "As soon as it became plain that the primary was out of their control, the regular ring withdrew in disgust and nominated another ticket. The 'News' simply calls the attention of all decent citizens to the fact that this last ticket contains the names of whisky men, and the line is distinctly and sharply drawn between the machine and corrupt city government, such as we have known for years, and a clean, honest, capable, business-like city administration, such as every good citizen ought to want. It is not necessary to remind the people of Raymond that the question of local option comes up at the election. That will be the most important question on the ticket. The crisis of our city affairs has been reached. The issue is squarely before us. Shall we continue the rule of rum and boodle and shameless incompetency, or shall we, as President Marsh said in his noble speech, rise as good citizens and begin a new order of things, cleansing our city of the worst enemy known to municipal honesty, and doing what lies in our power to do with the ballot, to purify our civic life?
>
> "The 'News' is, positively and without reservation, on the side of the new movement. We shall henceforth do all in our power to drive out the saloon and destroy its political

strength. We shall advocate the election of men nominated by the majority of citizens met in the first primary, and we call upon all Christians, church members and lovers of right, purity, temperance, and home, to stand by President Marsh and the rest of the citizens who have thus begun a long-needed reform in our city."

President Marsh read this editorial and thanked God for Edward Norman. At the same time he understood well enough that every other paper in Raymond was on the other side. He did not misunderstand the importance and seriousness of the fight which was only just begun. It was no secret that the "News" had lost enormously since it had been governed by the standard of, "What would Jesus do?" The question now was, "Would the Christian people of Raymond stand by it?" Would they make it possible for Norman to conduct a daily Christian paper? Or would their desire for what is called "news," in the way of crime, scandal, political partisanship of the regular sort, and a dislike to champion so remarkable a reform in journalism, influence them to drop the paper and refuse to give it their financial support? That was, in fact, the question Edward Norman was asking, even while he wrote the Saturday editorial. He knew well enough that his action expressed in that editorial would cost him very dearly from the hands of many business men of Raymond. And still, as he drove his pen over the paper, he asked another question, "What would Jesus do?" That question had become a part of his whole life now. It was greater than any other.

But, for the first time in its history, Raymond had seen the professional men, the teachers, the college professors, the doctors, the ministers, take political action and put themselves definitely and sharply in antagonism to the evil forces that had so long controlled the machine of the municipal government. The fact itself was astonishing. President Marsh acknowledged to himself with a feeling of humiliation, that never before had he known what civic righteousness could accomplish. From that Friday night's work he dated for himself and his college a new definition of the worn phrase, "the Scholar in Politics." Education for him and those who were under his influence, ever after meant some element of suffering. Sacrifice must now enter into the factor of development.

At the Rectangle that week, the tide of spiritual life rose high, and as yet showed no signs of flowing back. Rachel and Virginia went every night. Virginia was rapidly reaching a conclusion with respect to a large part of her money. She had talked it over with Rachel, and they had been able to agree that if Jesus had a vast amount of money at his disposal he might do with some of it as Virginia planned. At any rate, they felt that whatever Jesus might do in such a case would have as large an element of variety in it as the difference in persons and circumstances. There could be no one, fixed, Christian way of using money. The rule that regulated its use was unselfish utility.

But meanwhile the glory of the Spirit's power possessed all their best thought. Night after night that week witnessed miracles as great as walking on the sea, or feeding the multitude with a few loaves and fishes. For what greater miracle than a regenerated humanity? The transformation of these coarse, brutal, sottish lives, into praying rapturous lovers of Jesus, struck Rachel and Virginia every time with the feelings that people may have had when they saw Lazarus walk out of the tomb. It was an experience full of profound excitement to them.

Rollin Page came to all the meetings. There was no doubt of the change that had come over him. He was wonderfully quiet. It seemed as if he were thinking all the time.

Certainly he was not the same person. He talked more with Gray than with any one else.
He did not avoid Rachel, but he seemed to shrink from any appearance of seeming to
wish to renew the old acquaintance with her. Rachel found it even difficult to express to
him her pleasure at the new life he had begun to know. He seemed to be waiting to adjust
himself to his previous relations before this new life began. He had not forgotten those
relations. But he was not yet able to fit his consciousness into new ones.

The end of the week found the Rectangle struggling hard between two mighty
opposing forces. The Holy Spirit was battling with all his supernatural strength against
the saloon devil which had so long held a jealous grasp on its slaves. If the Christian people of Raymond once could realize what the contest meant to the souls newly awakened
to a new life, it did not seem possible that the election could result in the old system of
license. But that remained yet to be seen. The horror of the daily surroundings of many
of the converts was slowly burning its way into the knowledge of Virginia and Rachel,
and every night as they went up town to their luxurious homes they carried heavier
hearts.

"A good many of those poor creatures will go back again," Gray would say with a
sadness too deep for tears. "The environment does have a good deal to do with the character. It does not stand to reason that these people can always resist the sight and smell
of the devilish drink all about them. O Lord! how long shall Christian people continue to
support, by their silence and their ballots, the greatest form of slavery now known in
America?"

He asked the question, and did not have much hopes of an immediate answer. There
was a ray of hope in the action of Friday night's primary; but what the result would be,
he did not dare to anticipate. The whisky forces were organized, alert, aggressive, roused
into unusual hatred by the events of the last week at the tent and in the city. Would the
Christian force act as a unit against the saloon? Or would it be divided on account of its
business interests, or because it was not in the habit of acting altogether, as the whisky
powers always did? That remained to be seen. Meanwhile the saloon reared itself about
the Rectangle like some deadly viper, hissing and coiling, ready to strike its poison into
any unguarded part.

Saturday afternoon, as Virginia was just stepping out of her house to go and see
Rachel to talk over her new plans, a carriage drove up containing three of her fashionable friends. Virginia went out to the driveway and stood there talking with them. They
had not come to make a formal call, but wanted Virginia to go riding with them up on the
boulevard. There was a band concert in the Park. The day was too pleasant to be spent in
doors.

"Where have you been all this time, Virginia?" asked one of the girls, tapping her
playfully on the shoulder with a red silk parasol. "We hear that you have gone into the
show business. Tell us about it."

Virginia colored, but after a moment's hesitation she frankly told something of her
experience at the Rectangle. The girls in the carriage began to be really interested.

"Tell you what, girls, let's go slumming with Virginia this afternoon instead of
going to the band concert! I've never been down to the Rectangle. I've heard it's an awful
wicked place and lots to see. Virginia will act as a guide, and it would be real,"—"fun,"
she was going to say, but Virginia's look made her substitute the word, "interesting."

Virginia was angry. At first thought she said to herself she would never go under any such circumstances. The other girls seemed to be of the same mind as the speaker. They chimed in with earnestness and asked Virginia to take them down there.

Suddenly she saw in the idle curiosity of the girls an opportunity. They had never seen the sin and misery of Raymond. Why should they not see it, even if their motives in going down there were simply to pass away an afternoon.

"Very well, I'll go with you. You must obey my orders, and let me take you where you can see the most," she said, as she entered the carriage and took the seat beside the girl who had first suggested the trip to the Rectangle.

"Hadn't we better take a policeman along," said one of the girls with a nervous laugh. "It really isn't safe down there, you know."

"There's no danger," said Virginia briefly.

"Is it true that Rollin has been converted?" asked the first speaker looking at Virginia curiously. It impressed her during the drive to the Rectangle that all three of her friends were regarding her with close attention as if she were very peculiar.

"Yes, he certainly is. I saw him myself on the night of the first interest shown, a week ago Saturday," replied Virginia who did not know just how to tell that scene.

"I understand he is going around to the clubs talking with his old friends there, trying to preach to them. Doesn't that seem funny?" said the girl with the red silk parasol.

Virginia did not answer, and the other girls were beginning to feel sober as the carriage turned into the street leading to the Rectangle. As they neared the district, they grew more and more nervous. The sights and smells and sounds which had become familiar to Virginia, struck the senses of these refined, delicate, society girls as something horrible. As they entered farther into the district, the Rectangle seemed to stare as with one great, bleary, beer-soaked countenance at this fine carriage with its load of fashionably dressed young ladies. "Slumming" had never been a fad with Raymond society, and this was perhaps the first time that the two had come together in this way. The girls felt that, instead of seeing the Rectangle, they were being the objects of curiosity. They were frightened and disgusted.

"Let's go back. I've seen enough," said the girl who was sitting with Virginia.

They were at that moment just opposite a notorious saloon and gambling house. The street was narrow and the sidewalk crowded. Suddenly, out of the door of the saloon a young woman reeled. She was singing, in a broken, drunken sob that seemed to indicate that she partly realized her awful condition, "Just as I am, without one plea;" and as the carriage rolled past she leered at it, raising her face so that Virginia saw it very close to her own. It was the face of the girl who had kneeled sobbing that night, with Virginia kneeling beside her and praying for her.

"Stop!" cried Virginia motioning to the driver, who was looking around. The carriage stopped, and in a moment she was out and had gone up to the girl and taken her by the arm.

"Loreen," she said, and that was all. The girl looked into her face, and her own changed into a look of utter horror. The girls in the carriage were smitten into helpless astonishment. The saloon-keeper had come to the door of the saloon and was standing there looking on, with his hands on his hips. And the Rectangle from its windows, its saloon steps, its filthy sidewalk, gutter and roadway, paused, and with undisguised wonder stared at the two girls. Over the scene the warm sun of spring poured its mellow light. A faint breath of music from the band stand in the park floated into the Rectangle. The concert had begun, and the fashion and wealth of Raymond were displaying themselves up town on the boulevards.

CHAPTER VI

For I came to set a man at variance against his father, and
the daughter against her mother, and the daughter-in-law against
her mother-in-law; and a man's foes shall be they of his own household.

Be ye therefore imitators of God, as beloved children; and
walk in love even as Christ also loved you.[10]

When Virginia left the carriage and went to Loreen, she had no definite idea as to what she would do or what the result of her action would be. She simply saw a soul that had tasted of the joy of a better life slipping back again into its old hell of shame and death. And before she had touched the drunken girl's arm, she had asked only one question, "What would Jesus do?" That question was becoming with her, as with many others, a habit of life.

She looked around now, as she stood close by Loreen, and the whole scene was cruelly vivid to her. She thought first of the girls in the carriage.

"Drive on; don't wait for me! I am going to see my friend here home," she said, calmly enough.

The girl with the red parasol seemed to gasp at the word "friend" when Virginia spoke it. She did not say anything. The other girls seemed speechless.

"Go on! I cannot go back with you," said Virginia.

The driver started the horses slowly. One of the girls leaned a little out of the carriage.

"Can't we—that is—do you want our help? Couldn't we—"

"No, no!" exclaimed Virginia; "you cannot be of any use to me."

The carriage moved on, and Virginia was alone with her charge.

She looked up and around. Many faces in the crowd were sympathetic. They were not all cruel or brutal. The Holy Spirit had softened a good deal of the Rectangle.

"Where does she live?" asked Virginia.

No one answered. It occurred to Virginia afterwards, when she had time to think it over, that the Rectangle showed a delicacy in its sad silence that would have done credit to the boulevard.

For the first time it flashed upon her that the immortal being, who was flung like wreckage upon the shore of this earthly hell called the saloon, had no place that could be called home.

---

[10]Matt. 10:35–36 and Eph. 5:1–2.

The girl suddenly wrenched her arm from Virginia's grasp. In doing it she nearly threw Virginia down.

"You shall not touch me! Leave me! Let me go to hell! That's where I belong! The devil is waiting for me. See him!" she exclaimed hoarsely. She turned and pointed with a shaking finger at the saloon-keeper. The crowd laughed.

Virginia stepped up to her and put her arm about her.

"Loreen," she said firmly, "come with me. You do not belong to hell. You belong to Jesus, and He will save you. Come."

The girl suddenly burst into tears. She was only partly sobered by the shock of meeting Virginia.

Virginia looked around again. "Where does Mr. Gray live?" she asked. She knew the evangelist boarded somewhere near that tent.

A number of voices gave her the direction.

"Come, Loreen, I want you to go with me to Mrs. Gray's," she said, still keeping her hold of the swaying, trembling creature, who still moaned and sobbed, and now clung to Virginia as before she had repulsed her.

So, the two moved on through the Rectangle towards the evangelist's lodging place. The sight seemed to impress the Rectangle seriously. It never took itself seriously when it was drunk; but this was different. The fact that one of the most beautifully-dressed girls in Raymond was taking care of one of the Rectangle's most notorious characters, who reeled along under the influence of liquor, was a fact astonishing enough to throw more or less dignity and importance about Loreen herself. The event of Loreen stumbling through the gutter dead drunk always made the Rectangle laugh and jest. But Loreen staggering along with a young lady from the society circles up town supporting her, was another thing. The Rectangle viewed it with soberness and more or less wondering admiration.

When they reached Mr. Gray's boarding place, the woman who answered Virginia's knock said that both Mr. and Mrs. Gray were out somewhere, and would not be back until six o'clock.

Virginia had not planned anything farther than a possible appeal to the Grays, either to take charge of Loreen for awhile, or find some safe place for her until she was sober again. She stood now at the lodging after the woman had spoken, and she was really at a loss to know what to do. Loreen sank down stupidly on the steps and buried her face in her arms. Virginia eyed the miserable figure with a feeling that she was fearful would grow into disgust.

Finally a thought possessed Virginia that she could not resist. What was to hinder Loreen from going home with her? Why should not this homeless, wretched creature, reeking with the fumes of liquor, be cared for in Virginia's own home, instead of being consigned to strangers in some hospital or house of charity? Virginia really knew very little about any such places of refuge. As a matter of fact, there were two or three such institutions in Raymond; but it is doubtful if any of them would have taken a person like Loreen in her present condition. But that was not the question with Virginia just now. "What would Jesus do with Loreen?" was what Virginia faced, and she finally answered it by touching Loreen again.

"Loreen, come. You are going home with me. We will take the car here at the corner."

Loreen staggered to her feet, and to Virginia's relief, made no trouble. She had expected resistance, or a stubborn refusal to move. When they reached the corner and took the car, it was nearly full of people going up town. Virginia was painfully conscious of the stare that greeted her and her companion as they entered. But her thought was directed more and more to the approaching scene with her grandmother. What would Madam Page say when she saw Loreen?

Loreen was nearly sober now. But she was lapsing into a state of stupor. Virginia was obliged to hold fast to her arm. Several times she lurched heavily against Virginia, and as the two went up the avenue a curious crowd of people turned and gazed at them. When she mounted the steps of the handsome house, Virginia breathed a sigh of relief, even in the face of the interview with her grandmother; and when the door shut and she was in the wide hall with her homeless outcast, she felt equal to anything that might now come.

Madam Page was in the library. Hearing Virginia come in, she came into the hall. Virginia stood there supporting Loreen, who stared stupidly at the rich magnificence of the furnishings around her.

"Grandmother—" Virginia, spoke without hesitation and very clearly—"I have brought one of my friends from the Rectangle. She is in trouble and has no home. I am going to care for her a little while."

Madam Page glanced from her granddaughter to Loreen in astonishment.

"Did you say she was one of your friends?" She asked in a cold, sneering voice that hurt Virginia more than anything she had yet felt.

"Yes, I said so." Virginia's face flushed but she seemed to recall the verse that Mr. Gray had used for one of his recent sermons, "A friend of publicans and sinners." Surely Jesus would do this that she was doing.

"Do you know what this girl is?" asked Madam Page in an angry whisper, stepping near Virginia.

"I know very well. She is an outcast. You need not tell me, Grandmother. I know it even better than you do. She is drunk at this minute. But she is also a child of God. I have seen her on her knees repentant. And I have seen Hell reach out its horrible fingers after her again. And by the grace of Christ, I feel that the least I can do is to rescue her from such peril. Grandmother, we call ourselves Christians. Here is a poor, lost human creature, without a home slipping into a possible eternal loss, and we have more than enough. I have brought her here and shall keep her."

Madam Page glared at Virginia and clenched her hands. All this was contrary to her social code of conduct. How could society excuse such familiarity with the scum of the streets? What would Virginia's actions cost the family; in the way of criticism and the loss of standing, and all that long list of necessary relations which people of wealth and position must sustain to the leaders of society? To Madam Page, society represented more than the church or any other institution. It was a power to be feared and obeyed. The loss of its good will was a loss more to be dreaded than anything, except the loss of wealth itself.

She stood erect and stern, and confronted Virginia, fully roused and determined. Virginia placed her arm about Loreen and calmly looked her grandmother in the face.

"You shall not do this, Virginia. You can send her to the asylum for helpless women.

We can pay all the expenses. We cannot afford, for the sake of our reputations, to shelter such a person."

"Grandmother, I do not wish to do anything that is displeasing to you; but I am going to keep Loreen here to-night, and longer if I think it is best."

"Then you can answer for the consequences! I do not stay in the same house with a miserable—" Madam Page lost her self-control. Virginia stopped her before she could speak the next word.

"Grandmother, this house is mine. It is your home with me as long as you choose to remain. But in this matter I shall act as I fully believe Jesus would in my place. I am willing to bear all that society may say or do. Society is not my God. By the side of this poor, lost soul, I do not count the verdict of society as of any value."

"I shall not remain here, then," said Madam Page. She turned suddenly and walked to the end of the hall. She then came back, and said, with an emphasis that revealed her intense excitement and passion,

"You can always remember that you have driven your grandmother out of your house in favor of a drunken woman." Then, without waiting for Virginia to reply, she turned again and went up stairs.

Virginia called for a servant, and soon had Loreen cared for. She was fast lapsing into a wretched condition. During the brief scene in the hall, she had clung to Virginia so hard that Virginia's arm was sore from the clutch of the girl's fingers.

Virginia did not know whether her grandmother would leave the house or not. She had abundant means of her own; was perfectly well and vigorous, and capable of caring for herself. She had sisters and brothers living in the South, and was in the habit of spending several weeks in the year with them. Virginia was not anxious about her welfare, so far as that went; but the interview had been a painful one to her. Going over it, as she did in her room before she went down to tea, she found little cause for regret, however. "What would Jesus do?" There was no question in Virginia's mind that she had done the right thing. If she had made a mistake, it was one of the judgment and not of the heart. When the bell rang for tea, she went down, and her grandmother did not appear. She sent a servant to her room, and the servant brought back word that Madam Page was not there. A few minutes later Rollin came in. He brought word that his grandmother had taken the evening train for the South. He had been at the station to see some friends off, and had by chance met his grandmother as he was coming out. She told him her reason for going.

Virginia and Rollin confronted each other at the table with earnest, sad faces.

"Rollin," said Virginia, and, for the first time almost since his conversion, she realized what a wonderful thing her brother's change of life meant to her. "Do you blame me? Am I wrong?"

"No, dear, I cannot believe you are. This is very painful for us. But if you think this poor creature owes her safety and salvation to your personal care, it was the only thing for you to do. O Virginia! to think that we have all these years enjoyed our beautiful home and all these luxuries selfishly, forgetful of the multitude like this woman! Surely Jesus in our places would do what you have done."

And so Rollin comforted Virginia and counselled with her that evening. And of all the wonderful changes that Virginia was henceforth to know on account of her great pledge, nothing affected her so powerfully as the thought of Rollin's change in life. Truly, this man in Christ was a new creature. Old things were passed away. Behold, all things in him had become new.

Dr. West came that evening at Virginia's summons, and did everything necessary for the outcast. She had drunk herself almost into delirium. The best that could be done for her now was quiet nursing, and careful watching, and personal love. So in a beautiful room, with a picture of Christ walking by the sea hanging on the wall, where her bewildered eyes caught daily something more of its hidden meaning, Loreen lay, tossed she hardly knew how into this haven; and Virginia crept nearer the Master than she had ever been, as her heart went out towards this wreck which had thus been flung torn and beaten at her feet.

Meanwhile the Rectangle waited the issue of the election with more than usual interest. And Gray and his wife wept over the pitiable creatures who, after a struggle with surroundings that daily tempted them, too often wearied of the struggle and, like Loreen, threw up their arms and went whirling into the boiling abyss of their previous condition.

The after-meeting at the First Church was now regularly established. Henry Maxwell went into the lecture-room on the Sunday succeeding the week of the primary, and was greeted with an enthusiasm that made him tremble, at first, for its reality. He noted again the absence of Jasper Chase, but all the others were present and they seemed drawn very close together by a bond of common fellowship that demanded and enjoyed mutual confidences. It was the general feeling that the spirit of Jesus was a spirit of very open, frank confession of experience. It seemed the most natural thing in the world for Edward Norman to be telling all the rest of the company about the details of his newspaper.

"The fact is, I have lost a good deal of money during the last three weeks. I cannot tell how much. I am losing a great many subscribers every day."

"What do the subscribers give as their reason for dropping the paper?" asked Henry Maxwell. All the rest were listening eagerly.

"There are a good many different reasons. Some say they want a paper that prints all the news; meaning by that, the crime details, sensations like prize fights, scandals, and horrors of various kinds. Others object to the discontinuance of the Sunday edition. I have lost hundreds of subscribers by that action, although I have made satisfactory arrangements with many of the old subscribers by giving them even more in the extra Saturday edition than they formerly had in the Sunday issue. My greatest loss has come from a falling off in advertisements, and from the attitude I have felt obliged to take on political questions. This last action has really cost me more than any other. The bulk of my subscribers are intensely partisan. I may as well tell you all frankly that, if I continue to pursue the plan which I honestly believe Jesus would in the matter of political issues and their treatment from a non-partisan and moral standpoint, the 'News' will not be able to pay its operating expenses, unless one factor in Raymond can be depended on."

He paused a moment, and the room was very quiet. Virginia seemed specially interested. Her face glowed with interest. It was like the interest of a person who had been thinking hard of the same thing Norman went on now to mention.

"That one factor is the Christian element in Raymond. Say the 'News' has lost heavily from the dropping off of people who do not care for a Christian daily, and from others who simply look upon a newspaper as a purveyor of all sorts of material to amuse and interest them—are there enough genuine Christian people in Raymond who will rally to the support of a paper such as Jesus would probably edit, or are the habits of the people so firmly established in their demands for the regular type of journalism that they will not take a paper unless it is stripped largely of the Christian and moral purpose? I may also say, in this fellowship gathering, that owing to recent complications in my business affairs outside of my paper, I have been obliged to lose a large part of my fortune. I have had to apply the same rule of Jesus' probable conduct to certain transactions with other men who did not apply it to their conduct, and the result has been the loss of a great deal of money. As I understand the promise we made, we were not to ask any questions about, "Will it pay?" but all our action was to be based on the one question, 'What would Jesus do?' Acting on that rule of conduct, I have been obliged to lose nearly all the money I have accumulated in my paper. It is not necessary for me to go into details. There is no question with me now, after the three weeks' experience I have had, that a great many men would lose vast sums of money under the present system of business, if this rule of Jesus were honestly obeyed. I mention my loss here because I have the fullest faith in the final success of a daily paper conducted on the lines I have recently laid down, and I had planned to put into it my entire fortune in order to win final success. As it is now, unless, as I said, the Christian people of Raymond, the church members and professing disciples, will support the paper with subscriptions and advertisements, I cannot continue its publication on the present basis."

Virginia asked a question. She had followed Mr. Norman's confession with the most intense eagerness.

"Do you mean that a Christian daily ought to be endowed with a large sum like a Christian college in order to make it pay?"

"That is exactly what I mean. I have laid out plans for putting into the 'News' such a variety of material, in such a strong and truly interesting way, that it would more than make up for whatever was absent from its columns in the way of un-Christian matter. But my plans called for a very large outlay of money. I am very confident that a Christian daily such as Jesus would approve, containing only what He would print, can be made to succeed financially if it is planned on the right lines. But it will take a large sum of money to work out the plans."

"How much do you think?" asked Virginia quietly.

Edward Norman looked at her keenly, and his face flushed a moment, as an idea of Virginia's purpose crossed his mind. He had known her when she was a little girl in the Sunday-school, and he had been on intimate relations in business with her father.

"I should say a half million dollars, in a town like Raymond, could be well spent in the establishment of a paper such as we have in mind," he answered. And his voice trembled a little. The keen look on Edward Norman's grizzled face flashed out with a stern but thoroughly Christian anticipation of great achievements in the world of newspaper life, as it had opened up to him within the last few seconds.

"Then," said Virginia, speaking as if the thought were fully considered, "I am ready to put that amount of money into the paper on the one condition, of course, that it be carried on as it has been begun."

"Thank God!" exclaimed Henry Maxwell softly. Edward Norman was pale. The rest were looking at Virginia. She had more to say.

"Dear friends," she went on—and there was a sadness in her voice that made an impression on the rest that deepened when they thought it over afterwards—"I do not want any of you to credit me with an act of great generosity or philanthropy. I have come to know lately that the money which I have called my own is not my own, but God's. If I, as a steward of His, see some wise way to invest His money, it is not an occasion of vain glory or thanks from any one simply because I have proved honest in my administration of the funds He has asked me to use for His glory. I have been thinking of this very plan for some time. The fact is, dear friends, that in our coming fight with the whisky power in Raymond—and it has only just begun—we shall need the 'News' to champion the Christian side. You all know that all the other papers are for the saloon. As long as the saloon exists, the work of rescuing dying souls at the Rectangle is carried on at a terrible disadvantage. What can Mr. Gray do with his gospel meetings when half his converts are drinking people, daily tempted and enticed by the saloon on every corner? The Christian daily we must have. It would be giving up to the enemy to have the 'News' fail. I have great confidence in Mr. Norman's ability. I have not seen his plans; but I have the confidence that he has in making the paper succeed if it is carried forward on a large enough scale. I cannot believe that Christian intelligence in journalism will be inferior to un-Christian intelligence, even when it comes to making the paper pay financially. So that is my reason for putting this money—God's, not mine—into this powerful agent for doing as Jesus would. If we can keep such a paper going for one year, I shall be willing to see that amount of money used in the experiment. Do not thank me. Do not consider my promise a wonderful thing. What have I done with God's money all these years but gratify my own selfish, physical, personal desires? What can I do with the rest of it but try to make some reparation for what I have stolen from God? That is the way I look at it now. I believe it is what Jesus would do."

Over the lecture-room swept that unseen yet distinctly felt wave of divine presence. No one spoke for a while. Henry Maxwell standing there, where the faces lifted their intense gaze into his, felt what he had already felt before—a strange setting back out of the nineteenth century into the first, when the disciples had all things in common, and a spirit of fellowship must have flowed freely between them such as the First Church of Raymond had never known. How much had his church membership known of this fellowship in daily interests, before this little company had begun to do as Jesus would do? It was with difficulty that he thought of his present age and its surroundings. The same thought was present with all the rest also. There was an unspoken comradeship such as they had never known. It was present with them while Virginia was speaking, and during the silence that followed. If it had been defined by any one of them, it would, perhaps, have taken some such shape as this: "If I shall, in the course of my obedience to my promise, meet with loss or trouble in the world, I can depend upon the genuine, practical sympathy and fellowship of any other Christian in this room who has with me made the pledge to do all things by the rule, 'What would Jesus do?' "

All this the distinct wave of spiritual power expressed. It had the effect that a physical miracle may have had on the early disciples in giving them a feeling of confidence in their Lord that helped them to face loss and martyrdom with courage and even joy.

Before they went away this time, there were several confidences like those of Edward Norman. Some of the young men told of the loss of places owing to their honest obedience to their promise. Alexander Powers spoke briefly of the fact that the Commission had promised to take action at the earliest date possible. He was already at his old work of telegraphy. It was a significant fact that since his action in resigning his position, neither his wife nor daughter had appeared in public. No one but himself knew the bitterness of that family estrangement and misunderstanding of the higher motive. Yet many of the disciples present in the meeting carried similar burdens. These were things which they could not talk about. Henry Maxwell, from his knowledge of his church people, could almost certainly know that obedience to this pledge had produced in the heart of families separation of sympathy and even the introduction of enmity and hatred. Truly "a man's foes are they of his own household," when the rule of Jesus is obeyed by some and disobeyed by others. Jesus is a great divider of life. One must walk either parallel with Him or directly across His path.

But more than any other feeling at this meeting, rose the tide of fellowship for one another. Henry Maxwell watched it, trembling for its climax, which he knew was not yet reached. When it was, where would it lead them? He did not know, but he was not unduly alarmed about it. Only, he watched with growing wonder the results of that simple promise as it was being obeyed in these various lives. Those results were already being felt all over the city. Who could measure their influence at the end of the year?

One practical form of this fellowship showed itself in the assurances which Edward Norman received in support of his paper. There was a general flocking towards him when the meeting closed, and the response to his appeal for help from the Christian disciples in Raymond was fully understood by this little company. The value of such a paper in the homes and in behalf of good citizenship, especially at the present crisis in the city, could not be measured. It remained to be seen what could be done now that the paper was endowed so liberally. But it still was true, as Edward Norman insisted, that money alone could not make the paper a power. It must receive the support and sympathy of the Christians in Raymond, before it could be counted as one of the great Christian forces of the city.

The week that followed this Sunday meeting was one of great excitement in Raymond. It was the week of the election. Donald Marsh, true to his promise, took up his cross and bore it manfully, but with shuddering, with groans and even tears, for his deepest conviction was touched, and he tore himself out of the scholarly seclusion of years with a pain and anguish that cost him more than anything he had ever done as a follower of Christ. With him were a few of the college professors who had made the pledge in the First Church. Their experience and suffering were the same as the President's; for their isolation from all the duties of citizenship had been the same. The same was also true of Henry Maxwell, who plunged into the horror of this fight against whisky and its allies, with a sickening dread of each day's encounter with it. For never had he borne such a cross. He staggered under it, and in the brief intervals when he came in from the work and sought the quiet of his study for rest, the sweat broke out on his forehead, and he felt the actual terror of one who marches into unseen, unknown horrors. Looking back on it, afterwards, he was amazed at his experience. He was not a coward; but he felt a dread that any man of his habits feels, when confronted suddenly with a duty which carries with it the doing of certain things so unfamiliar that the actual details connected with it betray his ignorance and fill him with the shame of humiliation.

When Saturday, the election day, came, the excitement rose to its height. An attempt was made to close all the saloons. It was partly successful. But there was a great deal of drinking going on all day. The Rectangle boiled and heaved and cursed and turned its worst side out to the gaze of the city. Gray had continued his meetings during the week and the results had been even greater than he had dared to hope. When Saturday came, it seemed to him that the crisis in his work had been reached. The Holy Spirit and the Satan of rum seemed to rouse up to a desperate conflict. The more interest in the meetings, the more ferocity and vileness outside. The saloon men no longer concealed their feelings. Open threats of violence were made. Once during the week Gray and his little company of helpers were assailed with missiles of various kinds, as they left the tent late at night. The police sent down special protection, and Virginia and Rachel were always under the protection of Rollin or Dr. West. Rachel's power in song had not diminished. Rather, with each night it seemed to add to the intensity and reality of the Spirit's presence.

Gray had, at first, hesitated about having a meeting that night. But he had a simple rule of action, and was always guided by it. The Spirit seemed to lead them to continue the meeting, and so Saturday night he went on as usual.

The excitement all over the city had reached its climax when the polls closed at six o'clock. Never had there been such a contest in Raymond. The issue of license or no license had never been an issue under such circumstances. Never before had such elements in the city been arrayed against each other. It was an unheard-of thing that the president of Lincoln College, the pastor of the First Church, the dean of the Cathedral, the professional men living in the fine houses on the boulevard, should come personally into the wards and, by their presence and their example, represent the Christian conscience of the place. The ward politicians were astonished at the sight. However, their astonishment did not prevent their activity. The fight grew hotter every hour; and when six o'clock came neither side could have guessed at the result with any certainty. Every one agreed that never had there been such an election in Raymond, and both sides awaited the announcement of the result with the greatest interest.

It was after ten o'clock when the meeting at the tent was closed. It had been a strange and, in some respects, a remarkable meeting. Henry Maxwell had come down again, at Gray's request. He was completely worn out by the day's work, but the appeal from Gray came to him in such a form that he did not feel able to resist it. Donald Marsh was also present. He had never been to the Rectangle, and his curiosity was aroused from what he had noticed of the influence of the evangelist in the worst part of the city. Dr. West and Rollin had come with Rachel and Virginia; and Loreen, who had stayed with Virginia, was present near the organ, in her right mind, sober, with a humility and dread of herself that kept her as close to Virginia as a faithful dog. All through the service Loreen sat with bowed head, weeping a part of the time, sobbing when Rachel sang the song, "I was a wandering sheep," clinging with almost visible, tangible yearning to the one hope she had found, listening to prayer and appeal and confession all about her like one who was a part of a new creation, yet fearful of her right to share in it fully.

The tent had been crowded. As on some other occasions there was more or less disturbance on the outside of the tent. This had increased as the night advanced, and Gray thought it wise not to prolong the service. Once in a while a shout as from a large crowd swept into the tent. The returns from the election were beginning to come in, and the Rectangle had emptied every lodging house, den and hovel into the streets.

In spite of the distractions, Rachel's singing kept the crowd in the tent from dissolving. There were a dozen or more conversions. Finally the crowd became restless, and Gray closed the service, remaining a little while with the converts.

Rachel, Virginia, Loreen, Rollin and the Doctor, President Marsh and Henry Maxwell, went out together, intending to go down to their usual waiting place for their car. As they came out of the tent they at once were aware that the Rectangle was trembling on the edge of a drunken riot, and, as they pushed through the gathering mobs in the narrow streets, they began to realize that they themselves were objects of great attention.

"There he is, the bloke in the tall hat. He's the leader!" shouted a rough voice. President Marsh, with his erect, commanding figure, was conspicuous in the little company.

"How has the election gone? It is too early to know the result yet, isn't it?" He asked the question aloud, and a man answered, "They say second and third wards have gone almost solid for no license.[11] If that is so, the whisky men have been beaten."

"Thank God! I hope it is true," exclaimed Henry Maxwell. "Marsh, we are in danger here. Do you realize our situation? We ought to get the ladies to a place of safety."

"That is true," said Marsh gravely. At that moment a shower of stones and other missiles fell over them. The narrow street and sidewalk in front of them were completely choked with the worst elements of the Rectangle.

"This looks serious," said Maxwell. With Marsh and Rollin and Dr. West he started to go forward through the small opening, Virginia, Rachel and Loreen following close and sheltered by the men, who now realized something of their danger. The Rectangle was drunk and enraged. It saw in Daniel Marsh and Henry Maxwell two of the leaders in the election contest who had perhaps robbed them of their beloved saloon.

"Down with the aristocrats!" shouted a shrill voice more like a woman's than a man's.

A shower of mud and stones followed. Rachel remembered afterwards that Rollin jumped directly in front of her and received on his head and chest a number of blows that would probably have struck her if he had not shielded her from them.

And just then, before the police reached them, Loreen darted forward at the side of Virginia and pushed her aside, looking up and screaming. It was so sudden that no one had time to catch the face of the one who did it. But out of the upper window of a room over the very saloon where Loreen had come out a week before, some one had thrown a heavy bottle. It struck Loreen on the head and she fell to the ground. Virginia turned and instantly kneeled down by her. The police officers by that time had reached the little company.

Donald Marsh raised his arm and shouted over the howl that was beginning to rise from the wild beast in the mob,

---

[11]Later in the novel it is revealed that this report was false, and that the city voted for license by "a very meager majority."

"Stop! You've killed a woman!"

The announcement partly sobered the crowd.

"Is it true?" Henry Maxwell asked it, as Dr. West kneeled on the other side of Loreen, supporting her.

"She's dying!" said Dr. West briefly.

Loreen opened her eyes and smiled at Virginia. Virginia wiped the blood from her face, and then bent over and kissed her. Loreen smiled again, and the next moment her soul was in Paradise.

And yet, this is only one woman out of thousands killed by this drink devil. Crowd back, now, ye sinful men and women in this filthy street! Let this august, dead form be borne through your stupified, sobered ranks. She was one of your own children. The Rectangle had stamped the image of the beast on her. Thank Him who died for sinners, that the other image of a new soul now shines out of her pale clay! Crowd back! Give them room! Let her pass reverently, followed and surrounded by the weeping, awestruck company of Christians. Ye killed her, ye drunken murderers! And yet, and yet, O Christian America! who killed this woman? Stand back! Silence there! A woman has been killed. Who? Loreen. Child of the streets. Poor, drunken, vile sinner! O Lord God, how long? Yes. The saloon killed her. That is, the voters in Christian America who license the saloon. And the Judgment Day only shall declare who was the murderer of Loreen.